Nora Roberts

3 Complete Novels

ALSO BY NORA ROBERTS

Honest Illusions
Private Scandals
Hidden Riches
Born in Fire
Born in Ice
Born in Shame
Daring to Dream
Holding the Dream
Finding the Dream
Homeport
Sea Swept
Rising Tides
Inner Harbor
The Reef
River's End
Jewels of the Sun
Carolina Moon
Tears of the Moon
Heart of the Sea
The Villa
From the Heart

WRITING AS J. D. ROBB

Naked in Death
Glory in Death
Immortal in Death
Rapture in Death
Ceremony in Death
Vengeance in Death
Holiday in Death
Conspiracy in Death
Loyalty in Death
Witness in Death
Judgment in Death
Betrayal in Death

Nora Roberts

3 Complete Novels

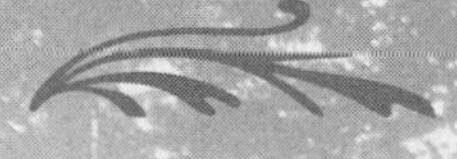

True Betrayals

Montana Sky

Sanctuary

G. P. Putnam's Sons New York

This book is a work of fiction. Names, characters, places, and incidents either are the product of the author's imagination or are used fictitiously, and any resemblance to actual persons, living or dead, events, or locales is entirely coincidental.

G. P. Putnam's Sons
Publishers Since 1838
a member of
Penguin Putnam Inc.
375 Hudson Street
New York, NY 10014

Published simultaneously in Canada

Library of Congress Cataloging-in-Publication Data

Roberts, Nora.
[Novels. Selections]
Three complete novels / Nora Roberts.
p. cm.
Contents: True betrayals—Montana sky—Sanctuary.
ISBN 0-399-14731-4
1. Virginia—Fiction. 2. Montana—Fiction. 3. Georgia—Fiction. I. Title.
PS3568.O243 A6 2001 00-067327
813'.54—dc21

Printed in the United States of America

1 3 5 7 9 10 8 6 4 2

This book is printed on acid-free paper. ♾

Book design by Patrice Sheridan

Table of Contents

True Betrayals

To Phyllis Grann and Leslie Gelbman

1

When she pulled the letter from her mailbox, Kelsey had no warning it was from a dead woman. The creamy stationery, the neatly handwritten name and address, and the Virginia postmark seemed ordinary enough. So ordinary, she had simply stacked it with her other mail on the old Belker table under her living room window while she slipped out of her shoes.

She went into the kitchen and poured herself a glass of wine. She would sip it slowly, she told herself, before she opened her mail. She didn't need the drink to face the slim letter, or the junk mail, the bills, the cheery postcard from a friend enjoying a quick trip to the Caribbean.

It was the packet from her attorney that had shaken her. The packet she knew contained her divorce decree. The legal paper that would change her from Kelsey Monroe back to Kelsey Byden, from married woman to single, from half of a couple to a divorcée.

It was foolish to think that way, and she knew it. She hadn't been married to Wade in anything but the most technical legal sense for two years, almost as long as they'd been husband and wife.

But the paper made it all so final, so much more so than the arguments and tears, the separation, the lawyers' fees and legal maneuvers.

Till death do us part, she thought grimly, and sipped some wine. What a crock. If that were true she'd be dead at twenty-six. And she was alive—alive and well and back in the murky dating pool of singles.

She shuddered at the thought.

She supposed Wade would be out celebrating with his bright and spiffy-looking associate in the advertising agency. The associate he had had an affair with, the liaison that he told his stunned and furious wife had nothing to do with her or with their marriage.

Funny, Kelsey hadn't thought of it that way. Maybe she didn't feel she'd had to die, or kill Wade, in order to part, but she'd taken the rest of her marriage vows seriously. And forsaking all others had been at the top of the list.

No, she felt the perky and petite Lari with the aerobically sculpted body and cheerleader smile had had everything to do with her.

No second chances had been given. His slip, as Wade had termed it, was never to be repeated. She had moved out of their lovely town house in Georgetown on the spot, leaving behind everything they had accumulated during the marriage.

It had been humiliating to run home to her father and stepmother, but there were degrees of pride. Just as there were degrees of love. And her love had snapped off like a light the instant she'd found Wade cozied up in the Atlanta hotel suite with Lari.

Surprise, she thought with a sneer. Well, there'd been three very surprised people when she'd walked into that suite with a garment bag and the foolishly romantic intention of spending the weekend leg of Wade's business trip with him.

Perhaps she was rigid, unforgiving, hard-hearted, all the things Wade had accused her of being when she'd refused to budge on her demand for a divorce. But, Kelsey assured herself, she was also right.

She topped off her wine and walked back into the living room of the immaculate Bethesda apartment. There was not a single chair or candle-stick in the sun-washed room that had stood in Georgetown. Clean break. That's what she had wanted, that's what she'd gotten. The cool colors and museum prints that surrounded her now were hers exclusively.

Stalling, she switched on the stereo, engaged the CD changer, and filled the room with Beethoven's *Pathétique*. Her taste for the classics had been passed down from her father. It was one of the many things they shared. Indeed, they shared a love of knowledge, and Kelsey knew she'd been in danger of becoming a professional student before she'd taken her first serious job with Monroe Associates.

Even then she'd been compelled to take classes, in subjects ranging from anthropology to zoology. Wade had laughed at her, apparently intrigued and amused by her restless shuffling from course to course and job to job.

She'd resigned from Monroe when she married him. Between her trust fund and Wade's income, she hadn't needed a job. She'd wanted to devote herself to the remodeling and redecorating of the town house they'd bought. She'd loved every hour of stripping paint, sanding floors, hunting in dusty antique shops for just the right piece for just the right spot. Laboring in the tiny courtyard, scrubbing brick, digging weeds, and designing the formal English garden had been pure pleasure. Within a year, the town house had been a showplace, a testament to her taste and her effort and her patience.

Now it was simply an asset that had been assessed and split between them.

She'd gone back to school, that academic haven where the real world could be pushed aside for a few hours every day. Now she worked part-time at the National Gallery, thanks to her art history courses.

She didn't have to work, not for money. The trust fund from her paternal grandfather could keep her comfortable enough so that she could drift from interest to interest as she chose.

So, she was an independent woman. Young, she thought, and, glancing over at the stack of mail, single. Qualified to do a little of everything and a lot of nothing. The one thing she'd thought she'd excelled at, marriage, had been a dismal failure.

She blew out a breath and approached the Belker table. She tapped her fingers against the legal packet, long narrow fingers that had received piano lessons, art lessons, fingers that had learned to type, to cook gourmet meals, to program a computer. A very competent hand that had once worn a wedding ring.

Kelsey passed over the thick envelope, ignoring the little voice that hissed the word *coward* inside her head. Instead she picked up another, one with handwriting oddly like her own. It had the same bold, looping style, neat but a little flashy. Only mildly curious, she tore it open.

Dear Kelsey: I realize you might be surprised to hear from me.

She read on, the vague interest in her eyes turning to shock, the shock to disbelief. Then the disbelief turned into something almost like fear.

It was an invitation from a dead woman. A dead woman who happened to be her mother.

In times of crisis, Kelsey had always, for as long as she could remember, turned to one person. Her love for and trust in her father had been the one constant in her restless nature. He was always there for her, not so much a port in a storm, but a hand to hold until the storm was over.

Her earliest memories were of him, his handsome, serious face, his gentle hands, his quiet, infinitely patient voice. She remembered him tying bows in her long straight hair, brushing the pale blond tresses while Bach or Mozart sang from the stereo. It was he who had kissed her childhood hurts better, who had taught her to read, to ride a bike, who had dried her tears.

She adored him, was almost violently proud of his accomplishments as the chairman of the English department at Georgetown University.

She hadn't been jealous when he'd married again. At eighteen she'd been delighted that he'd finally found someone to love and share his life with. Kelsey had made room in her heart and home for Candace, and had been secretly proud of her maturity and altruism in accepting a stepmother and teenage stepbrother.

Perhaps it had been easy because she knew deep in her heart that nothing and no one could alter the bond between herself and her father.

Nothing and no one, she thought now, but the mother she'd thought was dead.

The shock of betrayal was warring with a cold, stony rage as she fought her way through rush-hour traffic toward the lush, palatial estates in Potomac, Maryland. She'd rushed out of her apartment without her coat, and had neglected to switch on the heater in her Spitfire, but she didn't feel the chill of the February evening. Temper had whipped color into her face, adding a becoming rosy glow to the porcelain complexion, a snap to lake-gray eyes.

She drummed her fingers against the steering wheel as she waited for a light to change, as she willed it to change so she could hurry, hurry. Her mouth was clamped in a thin line that masked its lush generosity as she fought to keep her mind a blank.

It wouldn't do to think now. No, it wouldn't do to think that her mother was alive, alive and living hardly an hour away in Virginia. It wouldn't do to think about that or Kelsey might have started to scream.

But her hands were beginning to tremble as she cruised down the majestically tree-lined street where she'd spent her childhood, as she pulled into the drive of the three-story brick colonial where she'd grown up.

It looked as peaceful and tidy as a church, its windows gleaming, its white trim pure as an unblemished soul. Puffs of smoke from the evening fire curled from the chimney, and the first shy crocuses poked their delicate leaves up around the old elm in the front yard.

The perfect house in the perfect neighborhood, she'd always thought. Safe, secure, tasteful, only a short drive to the excitement and culture of D.C. and with the well-polished hue of quiet, respectable wealth.

She slammed out of the car, raced to the front door, and shoved it open. She'd never had to knock at this house. Even as she started down the Berber runner in the white-tiled foyer, Candace came out of the sitting room to the right.

She was, as usual, immaculately dressed. The perfect academic wife in conservative blue wool, her mink-colored hair swept back from her lovely, youthful face to reveal simple pearl earrings.

"Kelsey, what a nice surprise. I hope you can stay for dinner. We're entertaining some of the faculty and I can always use—"

"Where is he?" Kelsey interrupted.

Candace blinked, surprised by the tone. She could see now that Kelsey was in one of her snits. The last thing she needed an hour before her house filled up with people was one of her stepdaughter's explosions. Automatically she shifted her stance.

"Is something wrong?"

"Where's Dad?"

"You're upset. Is it Wade again?" Candace dismissed the problem with a wave of her hand. "Kelsey, divorce isn't pleasant, but it isn't the end of the world, either. Come in and sit down."

"I don't want to sit, Candace. I want to talk to my father." Her hands clenched at her sides. "Now, are you going to tell me where he is, or do I have to look for him?"

"Hey, sis." Channing strode down the stairs. He had his mother's strong good looks and a thirst for adventure that had, according to his mother, come from nowhere. Though he'd been fourteen when Candace married Philip Byden, Channing's innate good humor had made the transition seamless. "What's up?"

Kelsey deliberately took a deep breath to keep from shouting. "Where's Dad, Channing?"

"The Prof's in his study, buried in that paper he's been writing."

Channing's brows lifted. He, too, recognized the signs of a rage in the making—the spark in the eye, the flush on the cheeks. There were times he would put himself out to bank that fire. And times he would indulge himself and fan it.

"Hey, Kels, you're not going to hang around with these bookworms tonight, are you? Why don't you and I skip out, hit a few clubs?"

She shook her head and tore down the hall toward her father's study.

"Kelsey." Candace's voice, sharp, annoyed, trailed after her. "Must you be so volatile?"

Yes, Kelsey thought as she yanked open the door of her father's favorite sanctuary. *Yes.*

She slammed the door at her back, saying nothing for a moment as the words were boiling up much too hot and much too fast in her throat. Philip sat at his beloved oak desk, nearly hidden behind a stack of books and files. He held a pen in his bony hand. He'd always maintained that the best writing came from the intimacy of *writing,* and stubbornly refused to compose his papers on a word processor.

His eyes behind the silver-framed glasses had the owlish look they took on when he amputated himself from the reality of what was around him. They cleared slowly, and he smiled at his daughter. The desk light gleamed on his close-cropped pewter hair.

"There's my girl. Just in time to read over this draft of my thesis on Yeats. I'm afraid I might have gotten long-winded again."

He looked so normal, was all she could think. So perfectly normal sitting there in his tweed jacket and carefully knotted tie. Handsome, untroubled, surrounded by his books of poetry and genius.

And her world, of which he was the core, had just shattered.

"She's alive," Kelsey blurted out. "She's alive and you've lied to me all my life."

He went very pale, and his eyes shifted from hers. Only for an instant, barely a heartbeat, but she'd seen the fear and the shock in them.

"What are you talking about, Kelsey?" But he knew, he knew and had to use all of his self-control to keep the plea out of his voice.

"Don't lie to me now." She sprang toward his desk. "Don't lie to me! She's alive. My mother's alive, and you knew it. You knew it every time you told me she was dead."

Panic sliced through Philip, keen as a scalpel. "Where did you get an idea like that?"

"From her." She plunged her hand into her purse and dragged out the letter. "From my mother. Are you going to tell me the truth now?"

"May I see it?"

Kelsey tilted her head, stared down at him. It was a look that could pick clean down to the bone. "Is my mother dead?"

He wavered, holding the lie as close to his heart as he held his daughter. But he knew, as much as he wished it could be otherwise, if he kept one, he would lose the other.

"No. May I see the letter?"

"Just like that." The tears she'd been fighting swam dangerously close to the surface. "Just a no? After all this time, all the lies?"

Only one lie, he thought, and not nearly enough time. "I'll do my best to explain it all to you, Kelsey. But I'd like to see the letter."

Without a word she handed it to him. Then, because she couldn't bear to watch him, she turned away to face the tall, narrow window where she could see evening closing in on the last bloom of twilight.

The paper shook so in Philip's hand that he was forced to set the sheet on the desk in front of him. The handwriting was unmistakable. Dreaded. He read it carefully, word by word.

Dear Kelsey:

I realize you might be surprised to hear from me. It seemed unwise, or at least unfair, to contact you before. Though a phone call might have been more personal, I felt you would need time. And a letter gives you more of a choice on your options.

They will have told you I died when you were very young. In some ways, it was true, and I agreed with the decision to spare you. Over twenty years have passed, and you're no longer a child. You have, I believe, the right to know that your mother is alive. You will, perhaps, not welcome the news. However, I made the decision to contact you, and won't regret it.

If you want to see me, or simply have questions that demand answers, you'd be welcome. My home is Three Willows Farm, outside of Bluemont, Virginia. The invitation is an open one. If you decide to accept it, I would be pleased to have you stay as long as it suited you. If you don't contact me, I'll understand that you don't wish to pursue the relationship. I hope the curiosity that pushed you as a child will tempt you to at least speak with me.

Yours,
Naomi Chadwick

Naomi. Philip closed his eyes. Good God, Naomi.

Nearly twenty-three years had passed since he'd seen her, but he remembered everything about her with utter clarity. The scent she'd worn that reminded him of dark, mossy glades, the quick infectious laugh that never failed to turn heads, the silvery blond hair that flowed like rain down her back, the sooty eyes and willowy body.

So clear were his memories that when Philip opened his eyes again he thought he saw her. His heart took one hard, violent leap into his throat that was part fear, part long-suppressed desire.

But it was Kelsey, her back stiff, facing away from him.

How could he have ever forgotten Naomi, he asked himself, when he had only to look at their daughter to see her?

Philip rose and poured a scotch from a crystal decanter. It was kept there for visitors. He rarely touched anything stronger than a short snifter of blackberry brandy. But he needed something with bite now, something to still the trembling of his hands.

"What do you plan to do?" he asked Kelsey.

"I haven't decided." She kept her back to him. "A great deal of it depends on what you tell me."

Philip wished he could go to her, touch her shoulders. But she wouldn't welcome him now. He wished he could sit, bury his face in his hands. But that would be weak, and useless.

More, much more, he wished he could go back twenty-three years and do something, anything, to stop fate from running recklessly over his life.

But that was impossible.

"It isn't a simple matter, Kelsey."

"Lies are usually complicated."

She turned then, and his fingers clutched reflexively on the lead crystal. She looked so much like Naomi, the bright hair carelessly tumbled, the eyes dark, the skin over those long, delicate facial bones flushed luminously with passion. Some women looked their best when their emotions were at a dangerous peak.

So it had been with Naomi. So it was with her daughter.

"That's what you've done all these years, isn't it?" Kelsey continued. "You've lied to me. Grandmother lied. She lied." Kelsey gestured toward the desk where the letter lay. "If that letter hadn't come, you would've continued to lie to me."

"Yes, as long as I continued to think it was best for you."

"Best for me? How could it be best for me to believe my mother was dead? How can a lie ever be best for anyone?"

"You've always been so sure of right and wrong, Kelsey. It's an admirable quality." He paused, drank. "And a terrifying one. Even as a child, your ethics were unwavering. So difficult for mere mortals to measure up."

Her eyes kindled. It was close, much too close to what Wade had accused her of. "So, it's my fault."

"No. No." He closed his eyes and rubbed absently at a point in the center of his forehead. "None of it was your fault, and all of it was because of you."

"Philip." After a quick knock, Candace opened the study door. "The Dorsets are here."

He forced a weary smile onto his face. "Entertain them, dear. I need a few moments with Kelsey."

Candace flashed a look at her stepdaughter. Disapproval mixed with resignation. "All right, but don't be long. Dinner's set for seven. Kelsey, shall I set another place?"

"No, Candace, thank you. I'm not staying."

"All right, then, but don't keep your father long." She eased the door shut.

Kelsey drew a breath, stiffened her spine. "Does she know?"

"Yes. I had to tell her before we were married."

" 'Had to tell her,' " Kelsey repeated. "But not me."

"It wasn't a decision that I made lightly. That any of us made lightly. Naomi, your grandmother, and I all believed it was in your best interest. You were only three, Kelsey. Hardly more than a baby."

"I've been an adult for some time, Dad. I've been married, divorced."

"You have no idea how quickly the years go." He sat again, cradling the glass. He'd convinced himself that this moment would never come. That his life was too staid, too stable to ever take this spinning dip on the roller coaster again. But Naomi, he thought, had never settled for staid.

Neither had Kelsey. And now it was time for truth.

"I've explained to you that your mother was one of my students. She was beautiful, young, vibrant. I've never understood why she was attracted to me.

It happened quite quickly, really. We were married within six months after we met. Not nearly long enough for either of us to understand how truly opposite we were in nature. We lived in Georgetown. We'd both come from what we could call privileged backgrounds, but she had a freedom I could never emulate. A wildness, a lust for people, for things, for places. And, of course, her horses."

He drank again, to ease some of the pain of remembering. "I think it was the horses more than anything else that first came between us. After you were born, she wanted desperately to move back to the farm in Virginia. She wanted you to be raised there. My ambitions and hopes for the future were here. I was working on my doctorate, and even then I had my eye set on becoming the English department chairman at Georgetown. For a while we compromised, and I spent what weekends I could spare in Virginia. It wasn't enough. It's simplest to say we grew apart."

Safer to say it, he thought, staring into his scotch. And certainly less painful. "We decided to divorce. She wanted you in Virginia with her. I wanted you in Georgetown with me. I neither understood nor cared for the racing crowd she ran with, the gamblers, the jockeys. We fought, bitterly. Then we hired lawyers."

"A custody suit?" Stunned, Kelsey gaped at her father. "You fought over custody?"

"It was an ugly business, unbelievably vile. How two people who had loved each other, had created a child together, could become such mortal enemies is a pathetic commentary on human nature." He looked up again, finally, and faced her. "I'm not proud of it, Kelsey, but I believed in my heart that you belonged with me. She was already seeing other men. It was rumored that one of them had ties to organized crime. A woman like Naomi would always attract men. It was as though she was flaunting them, the parties, her lifestyle, daring me and the world to condemn her for doing as she pleased."

"So you won," Kelsey said quietly. "You won the suit, and me, then decided to tell me she'd died." She turned away again, facing the window that was dark now. In it she could see the ghost of herself. "People divorced in the seventies. Children coped. There should have been visitation. I should have been allowed to see her."

"She didn't want you to see her. Neither did I."

"Why? Because she ran off with one of her men?"

"No." Philip set the glass aside, carefully, on a thin silver coaster. "Because she killed one of them. Because she spent ten years in prison for murder."

Kelsey turned slowly, so slowly because the air was suddenly thick. "Murder. You're telling me that my mother is a murderess?"

"I'd hoped never to tell you." He rose then, sure he could hear his own bones creak in the absolute silence. "You were with me. I thank God you were with me rather than on the farm the night it happened. She shot her lover, a man named Alec Bradley. They were in her bedroom. There was an argument and she took a gun from the drawer of the bedside table and killed him. She was twenty-six, the same age as you are now. They found her guilty of murder in the second degree. The last time I saw her, she was in prison. She told me she would rather you believe her dead. If I agreed, she swore she wouldn't contact you. And she kept her word, until now."

"I can't understand any of this." Reeling, Kelsey pressed her hands over her eyes.

"I would have spared you." Gently Philip took her wrists, lowering her hands so he could see her face. "If protecting you was wrong, then I'll tell you. I was wrong, but without apology. I loved you, Kelsey. You were my entire life. Don't hate me for this."

"No, I don't hate you." In an old habit, she laid her head on his shoulder, resting it there while ideas and images spun in her brain. "I need to think. It all seems so impossible. I don't even remember her, Dad."

"You were too young," he murmured, rocked by relief. "I can tell you that you look like her. It's almost uncanny how much. And that she was a vibrant and fascinating woman, whatever her flaws."

A crime of violence being one of them, Kelsey thought. "There are so many questions, but I can't seem to latch on to one."

"Why don't you stay here tonight? As soon as I can get away, we'll talk again."

It was tempting to give in, to close herself into the safe familiarity of her old room, to let her father soothe away the hurts and the doubts, as he always did.

"No, I need to go home." She drew away before she could weaken. "I should be alone for a while. And Candace is already annoyed with me for keeping you from your guests."

"She'll understand."

"Of course she will. You'd better get along. I think I'll go out the back. I'd just as soon not run into anyone right now."

The passionate flush had died away, he noted, leaving her skin pale and fragile. "Kelsey, I wish you'd stay."

"I'm all right, really. All I need to do is absorb it. We'll talk later. Go see to your guests, and we'll talk more about this later." She kissed him, as much a sign of forgiveness as to hurry him along. Once she was alone, she walked behind the desk and stared at the letter.

After a moment, she folded it and slipped it back into her purse.

It had been a hell of a day, she decided. She'd lost a husband, and gained a mother.

2

Sometimes it was best to follow your impulses. Perhaps not best, Kelsey corrected as she drove west along Route 7 through the rolling Virginia hills. But it was certainly satisfying.

Speaking to her father again might have been wiser. Taking time to think things through. But it was much more satisfying to simply hop into the car and head to Three Willows Farm and confront the woman who'd played dead for two decades.

Her mother, Kelsey thought. The murderess.

To distract herself from that image, Kelsey turned up the radio so that Rachmaninoff soared through the half-open window. It was a beautiful day for a drive. That's what she'd told herself when she'd hurried out of her lonely apartment that morning. She hadn't admitted her destination then, even though she'd checked the map to find the best route to Bluemont.

No one knew she was coming. No one knew where she'd gone.

There was freedom in that. She pressed down on the gas and reveled in the speed, the whip of the chilly air through the windows, the power of the music. She could go anywhere, do anything. There was no one to answer to, no one to question. It was she who had all the questions now.

Maybe she'd dressed a bit more carefully than a casual drive in the country warranted. That was pride. The peach tone of the silk jacket and slacks was a good color for her, the breezy lines flattering to her slim frame.

After all, any woman who was about to meet her mother for the first time as an adult would want to look her best. She'd fixed her hair into a neat and intricate braid, and spent more time than usual on her makeup and accessories.

All the preparations had eased her nerves.

But she was beginning to feel them again as she approached Bluemont.

She could still change her mind, Kelsey told herself as she stopped the car in front of a small general store. Asking for directions to Three Willows didn't mean she had to follow them. She could, if she wanted, simply turn the car around and head back to Maryland.

Or she could just drive on. Through Virginia, into the Carolinas. She could turn west, or east toward the shore. One of her favorite indulgences was hopping in her car and driving wherever the whim took her. She'd spent an impulsive weekend at a lovely little bed-and-breakfast on the Eastern Shore after she'd left Wade.

She could go there again, she mused. A call in to work, a stop at a mall along the way for a change of clothes, and she'd be set.

It wasn't running away. It was simply leaving.

Why should it feel so much like running away?

The little store was so crammed with shelves and dairy cases and walls of tools that three customers made a crowd. The old man behind the counter had an ashtray full of butts at his elbow, a head as bald and shiny as a new dime, and a fresh cigarette dangling from the corner of his mouth. He squinted at Kelsey through a cloud of smoke.

"I wonder if you could tell me how to get to Three Willows Farm."

He stared at her another minute, his smoke-reddened eyes narrowing with speculation. "You'd be looking for Miss Naomi?"

Kelsey borrowed a look from her grandmother, one designed to put the questioner firmly in his place. "I'm looking for Three Willows Farm. I believe it's in this area."

"Oh yeah, it is." He grinned at her, and somehow the cigarette defied gravity and stuck in place. "Here's what you do. You go on down the road a piece. Say 'bout two miles. There's a fence there, a white one. You're gonna wanna make a left on Chadwick Road, and head on down another five miles or so. Go on past Longshot. Got a big wrought-iron fence with the name on it, so's you can't miss it. Next turn you come to's got two stone posts with rearing horses on 'em. That's Three Willows."

"Thank you."

He sucked in smoke, blew it out. "Your name wouldn't be Chadwick, would it?"

"No, it wouldn't." Kelsey went out, letting the door swing shut behind her. She felt the old man's eyes on her even as she pulled the car back onto the road.

Understandable, she supposed. It was a small town and she was a stranger. Still, she hadn't liked the way he'd stared.

She found the white fence and made the left out of town. The houses were farther apart now as the land took over, rolling and sweeping with the hills that were still caught between the haze of winter and the greening of spring. Horses grazed, manes ruffling in the breeze. Mares, their coats still thick with winter, cropped while their young gamboled nearby on spindly, toothpick legs. Here and there a field was plowed for spring planting, squares of rich brown bisecting the green.

She slowed the car at Longshot. It wasn't a road, as she'd assumed, but a farm. The curvy wrought-iron gate boasted the name, and through it she could see the long sweep of a macadam lane leading up to a cedar and stone house on the crest of a hill. Attractive, she mused. Commanding. Its many levels and terraces would afford breathtaking views from every inch.

The lane was lined with elms that looked much older and much more traditional than the house itself, which was almost arrogantly modern, yet it perched on the hill with a territorial pride.

Kelsey sat there for some time. Not that she was terribly interested in the architecture or the scenery, as compelling as it was. She knew if she continued down this road, she wouldn't turn back.

Longshot, she decided, was the point of no return. It seemed ironically appropriate. Closing her eyes, she willed her system to level. This was something she should do coolly, pragmatically. This wasn't a reunion where she would launch herself weeping into the arms of her long-lost mother.

They were strangers who needed to decide if they would remain so. No, she corrected. *She* would decide if they would remain so. She was here for answers, not love. Not even reasons.

And she wouldn't get them, Kelsey reminded herself, if she didn't continue on and ask the questions.

She'd never been a coward. She could add that to her list of vanities, Kelsey told herself as she put the car in gear again.

But her hands were cold as she gripped the wheel, as she turned between the two stone posts with their rearing horses, as she drove up the gravel lane toward her mother's house.

In the summer, the house would have been shielded by the three graceful willows for which it had been named. Now, the bowed branches were just touched with the tender green of approaching spring. Through their spindly fans she could see the white Doric columns rising up from a wide covered porch, the fluid curves of the three-story plantation-style house. Feminine, she thought, almost regal, and like the era it celebrated, gracious and stately.

There were gardens she imagined would explode with color in a matter of weeks. She could easily picture the scene heightened by the hum of bees and the chirp of birdsong, perhaps the dreamy scent of wisteria or lilac.

Instinctively her gaze lifted to the upper windows. Which room? she wondered. Which room had been the scene of murder?

A shiver walked down her spine as she stopped the car. Though her intention had been to go straight up to the front door and knock, she found herself wandering to the side of the house where a stone patio spilled out of tall French doors.

She could see some of the outbuildings from there. Tidy sheds, a barn that looked nearly as stately as the house itself. Farther out, where the hills curved up, she could see horses cropping and the faint glitter of sun striking water.

All at once another scene flipped over the vision. The bees were humming, the birds singing. The sun was hot and bright and she could smell roses, so strong and sweet. Someone was laughing and lifting her up, and up, until she felt the good strong security of a horse beneath her.

With a little cry of alarm, Kelsey pressed a hand to her lips. She didn't remember this place. She didn't. It was her imagination taking over, that was all. Imagination and nerves.

But she could swear she heard that laughter, the wild, free seduction of it.

She wrapped her arms around her body for warmth and took a step in retreat. She needed her coat, she told herself. She just needed to get her coat out of the car. Then the man and woman swung around the side of the house, arm in arm.

They were so beautiful, staggeringly so in that flash of sunlight, that for a moment Kelsey thought she was imagining them as well.

The man was tall, an inch or more over six feet with that fluid grace certain men are born with. His dark hair was windblown, curled carelessly over the collar of a faded chambray shirt. She saw his eyes, deeply, vividly blue in a face of angles and shadows, widen briefly in what might have been mild surprise.

"Naomi." His voice had the faintest of drawls, not slow so much as rich, like a fine, aged bourbon. "You have company."

Nothing her father had told her had prepared her. It was like looking in a mirror at some future time. A mirror polished to a high sheen so that it dazzled the eyes. Kelsey might have been looking at herself. For one mad moment, she was afraid she was.

"Well." Naomi's hand clamped hard on Gabe's arm. It was a reaction she wasn't aware of, and one she couldn't have prevented. "I didn't think I would hear from you so soon, much less see you." She'd learned years before that tears were useless, so her eyes remained dry as she studied her daughter. "We were about to have some tea. Why don't we go inside?"

"I'll take a rain check," Gabe began, but Naomi clung to his arm as if he were a shield, or a savior.

"That's not necessary." Kelsey heard her own voice, as from a distance. "I can't stay long."

"Come inside, then. We won't waste what time you have."

Naomi led the way through the terrace doors into a sitting room as lovely and polished as its mistress. There was a low, sedate fire in the hearth to ward off the late-winter chill.

"Please sit down, be comfortable. It'll only take me a moment to see about the tea." Naomi shot one quick glance at Gabe, and fled.

He was a man accustomed to difficult situations. He sat, drew out a cigar, and flashed Kelsey a smile fashioned to charm. "Naomi's a bit flustered."

Kelsey lifted a brow. The woman had seemed as composed as an ice sculpture. "Is she?"

"Understandable, I'd say. You gave her a shock. Took me back a step myself." He lighted the cigar and wondered if the raw nerves so readable in Kelsey's eyes would allow her to sit. "I'm Gabe Slater, a neighbor. And you're Kelsey."

"How would you know?"

Queen to peasant, he thought. It was a tone that would normally challenge a man, certainly a man like Gabriel Slater. But he let it pass.

"I know Naomi has a daughter named Kelsey whom she hasn't seen in some time. And you're a little young to be her twin sister." He stretched out his legs and crossed them at his booted ankles. They both knew he'd yet to take his eyes off her. And he knew he didn't intend to.

"You'd pull off the dignified act better if you sat down and pretended to relax."

"I'd rather stand." She moved to the fire and hoped it would warm her.

Gabe merely shrugged and settled back. It was nothing to him, after all. Unless she took a few potshots at Naomi. Not that Naomi couldn't handle herself. He'd never known a woman more capable or, in his mind, more resilient. Nonetheless, he was too fond of her to let anyone, even her daughter, hurt her.

Neither did it concern him that Kelsey had obviously decided to ignore him. He took a lazy drag on his cigar and enjoyed the view. Stiff shoulders and a rigid spine didn't spoil it, he mused. It was a nice contrast to the long, fluid limbs and fancy hair.

He wondered how easily she spooked, and if she'd be around long enough for him to test her himself.

"Tea will be right in." Steadier, Naomi came back into the room. Her gaze locked on her daughter, and her smile was practiced. "This must be horribly awkward for you, Kelsey."

"It isn't every day my mother comes back from the grave. Was it necessary for me to think you were dead?"

"It seemed so, at the time. I was in a position where my own survival was a priority." She sat, looking tailored and unruffled in her dun-colored riding habit. "I didn't want you visiting me in prison. And if I had, your father would never have agreed to it. So, I was to be out of your life for ten to fifteen years."

Her smile shifted a few degrees, going brittle. "How would the parents of your friends have reacted when you told them your mother was doing time for murder? I doubt you'd have been a popular little girl. Or a happy one."

Naomi broke off, looking toward the hallway as a middle-aged woman in a gray uniform and white apron wheeled in a tea tray. "Here's Gertie. You remember Kelsey, don't you, Gertie?"

"Yes, ma'am." The woman's eyes teared up. "You were just a baby last time. You'd come begging for cookies."

Kelsey said nothing, could say nothing to the damp-eyed stranger. Naomi put a hand over Gertie's and squeezed gently. "You'll have to bake some the next time Kelsey visits. Thank you, Gertie. I'll pour."

"Yes, ma'am." Sniffling, she started out, but turned when she came to the doorway. "She looks just like you, Miss Naomi. Just like you."

"Yes," Naomi said softly, looking at her daughter, "she does."

"I don't remember her." Kelsey's voice was defiant as she took two strides toward her mother. "I don't remember you."

"I didn't think you would. Would you like sugar, lemon?"

"Is this supposed to be civilized?" Kelsey demanded. "Mother and daughter reunite over high tea. Do you expect me to just sit here, sipping oolong?"

"Actually, I think it's Earl Grey, and to tell you the truth, Kelsey, I don't know what I expect. Anger certainly. You deserve to be angry. Accusations, demands, resentments." With hands that were surprisingly steady, Naomi passed Gabe a cup. "To be honest, I doubt there's anything you could say or do that wouldn't be justified."

"Why did you write me?"

Taking a moment to organize her thoughts, Naomi poured another cup. "A lot of reasons, some selfish, some not. I'd hoped you'd be curious enough to want to meet me. You were always a curious child, and I know that at this point in your life you're at loose ends."

"How do you know anything about my life?"

Naomi's gaze lifted, as unreadable as the smoke wafting up the flue. "You thought I was dead, Kelsey. I knew you were very much alive. I kept track of you. Even in prison I was able to do that."

Fury had Kelsey stepping forward, fighting the urge to hurl the tea tray and all the delicate china. It would be satisfying, oh so satisfying. But it would also make her look like a fool. Only that kept her from striking out.

Sipping tea, Gabe watched her struggle for control. High-strung, he decided. Impassioned. But smart enough to hold her ground. She might, he thought, be more like her mother than either of them knew.

"You spied on me." Kelsey bit off the words. "You hired, what, detectives?"

"Nothing quite so melodramatic as that. My father kept track of you while he could."

"Your father." Kelsey sat down. "My grandfather."

"Yes, he died five years ago. Your grandmother died the year after you were born, and I was an only child. You're spared a flood of aunts and uncles and cousins. Whatever questions you have, I'll answer, but I'd appreciate it if you'd give us both a little time before you make up your mind about me."

There was only one she could think of, one that had continued to hammer at the back of her mind. So she asked it, quickly, before she could draw away from it.

"Did you kill that man? Did you kill Alec Bradley?"

Naomi paused, then lifted her cup to her lips. Over the rim, her eyes stayed steady on Kelsey's. She set the cup down again without a rattle.

"Yes," she said simply. "I killed him."

"I'm sorry, Gabe." Naomi stood at the window, watching her daughter drive away. "It was really unforgivable of me to put you in that position."

"I met your daughter, that's all."

On a weak laugh, Naomi squeezed her eyes shut. "Always the master of understatement, Gabe." She turned then, standing in the strong light. It didn't bother her that the sun would highlight the fine lines around her eyes, show her age. She'd spent too long away from it. Too long away. "I was afraid. When I saw her, so much came flooding back. Some expected, some not expected. I couldn't deal with it alone."

He rose and went to her, laying his hands on her shoulders to soothe the strong, tensed muscles. "If a man isn't happy to help a beautiful woman, he might as well be dead."

"You're a good friend." She lifted a hand to his, squeezed. "One of the very few I can drop all pretenses with." Her lips curved again. "Maybe it's because we've both done time."

A quick smile lifted the corners of his mouth. "Nothing like prison life to pack down common ground."

"Nothing like prison life. Of course, a youthful run-in over a poker game doesn't quite come up to murder two, but—"

"There you go, one-upping me again."

She laughed. "We Chadwicks are so competitive." She moved away from him, shifting a vase of early daffodils an inch to the right on a table. "What did you think of her, Gabe?"

"She's beautiful. The image of you."

"I thought I was prepared for that. My father had told me. And the photographs. But to look at her and see myself, it still staggered me. I remember the child, remember the child so well. Now, seeing her grown up . . ." Impatient with herself, she shook her head. The years passed. She knew that better than anyone. "But beyond that." She glanced over her shoulder. "What did you think of her?"

He wasn't sure he could, or would, explain precisely what he'd thought. He, too, had been staggered, and he was a man rarely surprised. Beautiful women had walked in and out of his life, or he in and out of theirs. He appreciated them, admired them, desired them. But his first glimpse of Kelsey Byden had all but stopped his heart.

He would dissect that interesting little fact later, but for now Naomi was waiting. And he knew his answer mattered.

"She was running on nerves and temper. She doesn't quite have your control."

"I hope she never needs it," Naomi murmured.

"She was angry, but smart enough, and curious enough, to hold on to her temper until she gauges the lay of the land. If she were a horse, I'd have to say I need to see her paces before I could judge if she has heart, endurance, or grace. But blood tells, Naomi. Your daughter has style."

"She loved me." Her voice shook, but she didn't notice. Nor did she notice the first tear that spilled over and trailed down her cheek. "It's difficult to explain to someone who's had no children what it's like to be the recipient of that kind of total, uncompromising love. Kelsey felt that for me, and for her father. It was Philip and I who lacked. We didn't love enough to keep that unit whole. And so I lost her."

Naomi brushed at the tear, caught it on her fingertip. She studied it as if it were some exotic specimen just discovered. She hadn't cried since she buried her father. Hadn't seen the point.

"I'll never be loved that way again." She flicked the tear away and forgot it. "I don't think I understood that until today."

"You're rushing your fences, Naomi. That's not like you. You had all of fifteen minutes with her today."

"Did you see her face when I told her I killed Alec?" There was a smile on her lips as she turned back to Gabe, but it was hard, brittle as glass. "I've seen it in dozens of others. Civilized horror. Decent people don't kill."

"People, decent or otherwise, do what they need to do to survive." He had reason to know.

"She won't think so. She might have my looks, Gabe, but she'd have her father's mores. Christ, they don't come any more decent than Dr. Philip Byden."

"Or more foolish, since he let you go."

She laughed again, easier this time, and kissed him firmly on the mouth. "Where

were you twenty-five years ago?" She shook her head, nearly sighed. "Playi
your Crayolas."

"I don't recall ever playing with them. Betting with them, maybe. Speaking
bets, I've got a hundred that says my colt will outrun yours at the Derby in May

Her brow rose. "And the odds?"

"Even."

"You're on. Why don't you come down and take a look at my prize yearling before you leave? In a couple of years she'll leave anything you put against her in the dust."

"What did you name her?"

Her eyes glinted as she opened the terrace doors. "Naomi's Honor."

She'd been so cool, Kelsey thought as she unlocked her apartment door. So cold. Naomi had admitted to murder as casually as another woman might admit to dyeing her hair.

What kind of a woman was she?

How could she have served tea and made conversation? So polite, so controlled, so horribly detached. Leaning against the door, Kelsey rubbed at the headache storming behind her temples. It was all like some insane dream—the big, beautiful house, the placid setting, the woman with her face, the dynamic man.

Naomi's newest lover? Did they sleep in the same room where a man had died? He'd looked capable of it, she thought. He'd looked capable of anything.

With a shudder, Kelsey pushed away from the door and began to pace.

Why had Naomi written the letter? she wondered. There'd been no emotional storm, no fatted calf, no desperate apologies for the lost years. Only a polite invitation to tea.

And the calm, unhesitating admission of guilt.

So, Naomi Chadwick wasn't a hypocrite, Kelsey thought wryly. Just a criminal.

When the phone rang she glanced over and saw that her message machine was blinking. Kelsey turned away and ignored both. She had two hours before her shift at the museum, and no need, no desire, to speak with anyone before then.

All she had to do now was convince herself that her mother's reappearance didn't have to change her life. She could go on just as she had before—her job, her classes, her friends.

She dropped down on the sofa. Who was she trying to fool? Her job was no more than a hobby, her classes a habit, and her friends . . . Most of them had been shared with Wade, and therefore, in the odd by-product of divorce, they had divvied up sides or simply faded into the background so as not to be touched by the trauma.

Her life was a mess.

She ignored the knock at the door.

"Kelsey." Another quick, impatient rap. "Open the door or I'll have the apartment manager open it for me."

ose and obeyed. "Grandmother."

k for the expected kiss, Milicent Byden strode into the ways, flawlessly dressed and coiffed. Her hair was tinted swept back from a polished face that could, at a glance, pass than eighty. She kept her figure trim with unsentimental diet and er size-six Chanel suit was a pale blue. She tugged off matching kid and set them down on an occasional table, then laid her mink over a chair.

"You disappoint me. Sulking in your room like a child." Her almond-colored eyes scraped over her granddaughter as she sat, crossing her legs. "Your father's desperately worried about you. Both he and I have called you at least half a dozen times today."

"I've been out. And Dad has no reason to be worried."

"No?" Milicent tapped a lacquered fingernail against the arm of the chair. "You burst in on him last night with the news that that woman has contacted you, then you dash off and refuse to answer your phone."

"That woman is my mother, and you and he knew she was alive. It caused an emotional scene, Grandmother, which I'm aware you might consider to be in poor taste, but that I felt was very justified."

"Don't take that tone with me." Milicent leaned forward. "Your father has done everything to protect you, to give you a decent upbringing and a stable home. And you attack him for it."

"Attack him?" Kelsey threw up her hands, knowing such an outward display would count against her. "I confronted him. I demanded answers. I demanded the truth."

"And now that you have it, are you satisfied?" Milicent inclined her head. "You would have been better off, all of us would have been better off, if she had stayed dead to you. But she was always selfish, always more concerned with herself than anyone else."

For reasons Kelsey could never have explained, she picked up the spear of battle. "And did you always hate her?"

"I always recognized her for what she was. Philip was blinded by her looks, by what he saw as vivacity and verve. And he paid for his mistake."

"And I look like her," Kelsey said softly, "which explains why you've always looked at me as though I might commit some horrible crime at any moment—or at least an unforgivable breach of etiquette."

Milicent sighed and sat back. She wouldn't deny it, saw no reason why she should. "I was concerned, naturally, about how much of her was in you. You're a Byden, Kelsey, and for the most part you've been a credit to the family. Every mistake I've watched you make has her stamp on it."

"I prefer to think I've made my own mistakes."

"Such as this divorce," Milicent said wearily. "Wade comes from a good family. His maternal grandfather is a senator. His father owns one of the most prestigious and well-respected advertising agencies in the east."

"And Wade is an adulterer."

On a little sound of impatience, Milicent waved a hand. The diamond w ring on her widow's hand glinted like ice. "You would blame him, rather yourself or the woman who seduced him."

Almost amused, Kelsey smiled. "That's right. I would blame him. The divor is final, Grandmother, as of yesterday. You're wasting your time there."

"And you have the dubious honor of being the second Byden in family history to divorce. In your father's case, it was unavoidable. You, however, have done what you've made a habit of doing all your life: reacting impulsively. But that's another issue. I want to know what you intend to do about the letter."

"Don't you think that's between me and my mother?"

"This is a family matter, Kelsey. Your father and I are your family." She tapped her finger again, carefully selecting both words and tone. "Philip is my only child. His happiness and well-being have always been primary in my life. You are his only child." With genuine affection, she reached up and took Kelsey's hand. "I want only the best for you."

There was no arguing with that. However much her grandmother's code of behavior grated, Kelsey knew she was loved. "I know. I don't want to fight with you, Grandmother."

"Nor I with you." Pleased, she patted Kelsey's hand. "You've been a good daughter, Kelsey. No one who knows you and Philip would doubt your devotion. I know you'd do nothing to hurt him. I think it would be best if you gave me the letter, let me handle this business for you. You've no need to contact her, or put yourself through this turmoil."

"I've already contacted her. I went to see her this morning."

"You . . ." Milicent's hand jerked, then settled. "You saw her. You went to her without discussing it first?"

"I'm twenty-six years old, Grandmother. Naomi Chadwick is my mother, and I don't have to discuss meeting her with anyone. I'm sorry if it upsets you, but I did what I had to do."

"What you wanted to do," Milicent corrected. "Without thought for the consequences."

"As you like, but they're my consequences. I'd think you and Dad would have to agree it's a normal reaction on my part. It may be difficult for you, but I can't imagine why it would make you so angry."

"I'm not angry." Though she was. Furious. "I'm concerned. I don't want some foolish emotional reaction to influence you. You don't know her, Kelsey. You have no idea how clever or how vindictive she is."

"I know she wanted custody of me."

"She wanted to hurt your father because he'd begun to see through her. You were the tool. She drank, and she had men, and she flaunted her flaws because she was so sure she would always win. And she ended by killing a man." Milicent drew a deep breath. Even the thought of Naomi burned at her heart. "I suppose she tried to convince you it was self-defense. That she was protecting her honor. Her *honor*."

longer, Milicent rose. "Oh, she was clever, and she was against her hadn't been so damning she might have olve her. But when a woman entertains a man in her dle of the night in nothing more than a silk robe, it's difficult

Kelsey repeated, but the word was only a shocked whisper and Milicent hear.

"Some believed her, of course. Some will always believe that kind of woman." Eyes hard, she snatched her gloves from the table and began to tap them against her palm. "But in the end, they convicted her. She was out of Philip's life, and yours. Until now. Will you be so stubborn, so selfish as to let her back in? To cause your father this kind of grief?"

"This isn't a choice between him or her, Grandmother."

"That's exactly what it is."

"For you, not for me. Do you know, before you came here, I wasn't sure I would see her again. Now I know I will. Because she didn't defend herself to me. She didn't ask me to choose. I'm going to see her again and decide for myself."

"No matter whom it hurts?"

"As far as I can see, I'm the only one who's risking anything."

"You're wrong, Kelsey, and it's a dangerous mistake. She corrupts." Stiffly, Milicent smoothed on her gloves, finger by finger. "If you insist on pursuing this relationship, she'll do whatever she can to destroy the bond between you and your father."

"No one could do that."

Milicent lifted her gaze, and it was sharp as steel. "You don't know Naomi Chadwick."

3

No, Kelsey didn't know Naomi Chadwick. But she would.

Kelsey's years of higher education hadn't been wasted. If there was one thing she knew how to do well, it was how to research a subject. Any subject. Naomi was no exception.

For the next two weeks, she spent most of her free time poring over microfilm at the public library. Her first stop was the society page, where she read the announcement of the engagement of Naomi Anne Chadwick, twenty-one, daughter of Matthew and Louise Chadwick of Three Willows Farm, Bluemont, Virginia, to Professor Philip James Byden, thirty-four, son of Andrew and Milicent Byden, Georgetown.

A June wedding was planned.

Kelsey found the wedding announcement. It was a shock to see her father looking so young, so carelessly happy, his fingers entwined at his heart with

Naomi's. He'd worn a rosebud boutonniere. Kelsey wondered if it had been white, or perhaps a sunny yellow.

Beside him, Naomi glowed. The grainy newsprint couldn't diminish the luster. Her face was impossibly young, heartbreakingly beautiful, her lips curved, her eyes bright, as if on the verge of a laugh.

They looked as though they could face anything together.

It shouldn't hurt. Kelsey told herself it was foolish to be hurt by a divorce that had happened without her knowledge. But these two young, vital people had created her. Now they were no more to each other than painful memories.

She made hard copies of what she wanted, made notes on the rest, as she would for any report. With feelings of amusement and bafflement, she found her own birth announcement.

There was little after that, an occasional squid about attendance at a ball or charity function. It seemed her parents had lived a quiet life, out of the Washington glitter for the short term of their marriage.

Then there was the custody suit, a terse little article that had merited space in *The Washington Post,* she imagined, due to her paternal grandfather's position as undersecretary of the Treasury. She read the names—her own, Naomi's, her father's—with a sense of detachment. The *Post* hadn't wasted much of its dignity on a domestic squabble.

She found a few articles on Three Willows and racing. One mentioned the tragedy of a promising colt who had broken down at a race and was shot. It merited a single picture, of Naomi's beautiful, tear-streaked face.

Then there was murder.

Such matters rated more space, a few prominent headlines.

LOVERS' QUARREL ENDS IN TRAGEDY
PASTORAL VIRGINIA SCENE OF VIOLENT DEATH

Her mother was described as the estranged wife of a Georgetown English professor and the daughter of a prominent Thoroughbred breeder. The victim was somewhat flippantly referred to as a playboy with ties to the racing world.

The story was straightforward enough. Alec Bradley had been shot and killed in a bedroom at Three Willows Farm. The weapon belonged to Naomi Chadwick Byden, who had notified the police. She and Bradley had been alone in the house at the time of the shooting. Police were investigating.

The Virginia papers were a bit more informative. Naomi never denied firing the fatal shot. She claimed, through her attorney, that Bradley had attacked her and she had resorted to the weapon in self-defense.

The facts were reported that Naomi and Bradley had a friendly relationship, and had been seeing each other socially for weeks. And, of course, that Naomi was in the midst of a messy custody suit over her three-year-old daughter.

A week after the murder, there were more headlines:

VIRGINIA WOMAN ARRESTED FOR MURDER
NEW EVIDENCE DERAILS CLAIMS OF SELF-DEFENSE

And damning evidence it was. Kelsey's blood chilled as she read of the photograph taken by a detective hired by her father's lawyers to obtain ammunition for the custody battle. Rather than an illicit affair, the detective had recorded murder.

He'd testified at the trial as well. Stubbornly moving from page to page, she read on. About witnesses who agreed, under oath, that Naomi and Bradley behaved, in public, as intimate friends. That Naomi was an expert marksman. That she enjoyed parties, champagne, the attention of men. That she and Bradley had quarreled the evening of his death over his flirtation with another woman.

Then Charles Rooney had taken the stand and told his story. He'd taken dozens of photographs of Naomi, at the track, at the farm, at various social events. He was a licensed private investigator in the state of Virginia, and his surveillance reports were carefully documented.

They formed a picture of a reckless, beautiful woman who craved excitement, who was eager to break the bonds of an inhibiting marriage to an older man. And one who, on the night of the murder, invited the victim into her home, where she was alone and dressed only in a negligee.

Rooney was unable to swear to what was said between the two, but his photographs and his observations said a great deal. The couple had embraced, brandy was poured. Then, they appeared to argue and Naomi had stormed upstairs. Bradley had followed.

Eager to fulfill his duties, Rooney had climbed a handy tree and aimed his telephoto lens at the bedroom window. The argument had continued there, becoming more heated. Naomi had slapped Bradley's face, but when he'd turned to go, she'd pulled a gun out of the night-stand drawer. The camera had captured the shock on his face, and the fury on Naomi's as she fired.

Kelsey stared at the photo for a long time, and at the headline above it that shouted GUILTY! Carefully, she made more copies, then shut off the machine and gathered her files and notes. Before logic could interfere with emotion, she found a pay phone and dialed.

"Three Willows."

"Naomi Chadwick, please."

"May I ask who's calling?"

"This is Kelsey Byden."

There was a small, strangled sound quickly muffled. "Miss Naomi's down at the stables. I'll buzz her."

Moments later an extension was picked up. Kelsey heard Naomi's voice, cool as sherbet, over the line. "Hello, Kelsey. It's good to hear from you."

"I'd like to talk to you again."

"Of course. Whenever you like."

"Now. It'll take me an hour to get there. And I'd prefer that we be alone this time."

"Fine. I'll be here."

Naomi hung up and wiped her damp hands on her jeans. "My daughter's coming, Moses."

"So I gathered." Moses Whitetree, Naomi's trainer, trusted employee, and longtime lover, continued to study his breeding reports. He was half Jew, half Choctaw, and had never taken the mix for granted. He wore his hair in a long graying braid down his back. There was the glint of a silver Star of David around his neck.

Whatever there was to know about horses, he knew. And he preferred them, with few exceptions, to people.

"She'll have questions."

"Yes."

"How do I answer them?"

He didn't glance up, didn't need to. He knew every nuance of Naomi's face. "You could try the truth."

"A lot of good the truth's done me."

"She's your blood."

It was always so simple for Moses, Naomi thought impatiently. "She's a grown woman. I hope she's her own woman. She won't accept me simply because we share blood, Moses. I'd be disappointed if she did."

He set his paperwork aside and rose. He wasn't a big man, only a few pounds and a few inches over his onetime dream of being a jockey. In his worn-down boots he was eye level with Naomi. "You want her to love you, to accept you, but you want her to do it on your terms. You've always wanted too much, Naomi."

With tenderness she touched a hand to his wind-bitten cheek. It was impossible to stay irritated with him. He was the man who had waited for her, who never questioned her, who had always loved her.

"So you've always told me. I didn't know I would need her so much until I saw her again, Moses. I didn't know it would matter as much as it does."

"And you wish it didn't."

"Oh, I wish it didn't."

That he understood. He'd spent most of his life wishing he didn't love Naomi. "My people have a saying."

"Which people?"

He smiled. They both knew he made up half of his sayings and twisted the other half to suit his purposes. "Only the foolish waste their wishes. Let her see what you are. It'll be enough."

"Moses." A groom looked into the office, then tipped his hat toward Naomi. "Miss. I don't like the way Serenity's favoring her near foreleg. Got some swelling, too."

"She ran well this morning." Moses's brow puckered. He'd been up before dawn to watch the early workouts. "Let's take a look."

Moses kept his office in a small area at the front of the stables. It was cramped and often smelled of horse urine, but he preferred it to the airy space his predecessor had used in a whitewashed building near the west paddock.

Moses often said the earthy smell of horses was French perfume to him and he didn't want any fancy digs away from the action.

In truth, the stables were nearly as sparkling as any luxury hotel, and usually busier. The concrete slope between the lines of stalls was scrubbed and spotless. The individual stalls were marked with an enameled plaque with the name of each horse scrolled in gold. It was an affectation of Naomi's father's that she'd continued when she'd taken over running the farm.

There were scents of horses, of liniment, of hay and grain and leather—a potpourri Naomi had missed sorely during her years in prison and one she never failed to appreciate.

It was, to her, the scent of freedom.

As Moses passed, horses stuck their heads out of stalls. He, too, had a scent, one they recognized. His boots might have clattered quickly along the slope, but there was always time for a quick stroke, a murmured word.

Stable hands continued their work. Perhaps pitchforks or currycombs moved with more enthusiasm now that the man was in view.

"I was going to take her out to pasture when I saw how she favored the leg." The groom paused beside Serenity's box stall. "Noticed the swelling and thought you'd want to take a look for yourself."

Moses merely grunted, passing his hands over the glossy chestnut coat. He studied the filly's eyes, smelled her breath, murmuring to her as he worked his way down from cheek to chest to leg.

There was swelling just above the fetlock, and some heat. As he applied some slight pressure, the filly jerked back and blew a warning. "Looks like she's knocked into something."

"Reno was riding her this morning." Naomi remembered that the jockey had made a special trip to the farm for the workout. "See if he's still here."

"Yes'm." The groom scurried off.

"She had a beautiful run this morning." Eyes narrowed, Naomi crouched beside Moses and examined the lame leg herself, gently lifting it forward and back to check for shoulder strain. "Looks like an overreach," she muttered. There was discoloration, a sign of blood clotting under the skin. The bone was probably bruised, she thought. If they were lucky, there'd be no fracture. "She was due in Saratoga next week."

"She might still make it." But he didn't think so, not on that leg. "We can get the swelling down. Better call the vet, though. An X ray wouldn't hurt."

"I'll take care of it. And I'll talk to Reno." She straightened, hooking an arm around the mare's neck. They were an investment, a business, but that didn't negate her love for them. "She's got the heart of a champion, Moses. I don't want to hear that she can't race again."

. . .

Less than an hour later, Naomi watched grimly as the filly's injury was treated. Already a stream of cold water had been applied directly to the wound. Now Moses himself was massaging the bruise with a mixture of vinegar and cool water. Her vet stood in the stall and prepared a syringe.

"How long before she can start training again, Matt?"

"A month. Six weeks would be better." He glanced toward Naomi. Matt Gunner had a long, pleasant face, kind eyes. "The bone's bruised, Naomi, and there's some tissue damage, but there's no fracture. You keep her stabled, keep up the massage, some light exercise, and she'll do."

"We were going at a fast pace," Reno put in. The jockey stood just outside the box, watching the procedure. He'd changed from his morning workout into one of the smart tailored suits he preferred. But he was a racetracker. There was nothing of more concern to him, or the others, than a Thoroughbred's delicate legs. "I didn't notice any change of gait."

"Neither did I," Naomi added. "Reno says she didn't stumble. I was watching the run this morning and I would have noticed if she had. This filly has a quiet temperament. She's not one to kick in her stall."

"Well, she took a hard knock," Matt said. "If your groom hadn't been alert, it would have been a great deal worse. This'll ease the pain. There you go, girl. Easy now." He slid the needle under Serenity's flesh just above the wound. She rolled her eyes, snorted, but didn't struggle. "She's strong and she's healthy," Matt said. "She'll run again. Moses, there's nothing I can tell you about treating that leg that you don't already know. You give me a call if it heats up. Otherwise . . ." He trailed off, staring over Naomi's shoulder.

"Excuse me." Kelsey stood back, clutching her purse and her file. "I'm sorry to interrupt. I was told up at the house I'd find you here."

"Oh." Distracted, Naomi dragged a hand through her hair. "I lost track of time. We've had a small crisis here. Matt, this is my daughter, Kelsey. Kelsey Byden, Matt Gunner, my vet."

Matt reached out, the syringe still in his hand. He drew it back, flushed. "Sorry. Hello."

Nerves aside, she had to smile. "Nice to meet you."

"And Moses Whitetree," Naomi continued. "My trainer."

Moses continued to massage the mare's leg and merely nodded.

"Reno Sanchez, one of the best jockeys on the circuit."

"*The* best," he said with a wink. "Nice to meet you."

"And you," Kelsey said automatically. "You're busy here. I can wait."

"No, there's nothing more I can do. Thanks for coming so quickly, Matt. Sorry I interrupted your day, Reno."

"Hey, no problem. I've got plenty of time before the first post!" He looked at Kelsey again with undisguised admiration. "You'll have to come to the track, see me ride."

"I'm sure I'd enjoy it."

"Moses, I'll be back to check on her myself again later. Why don't we go up to the house?" Naomi gestured, careful, very careful not to make contact, then led the way out the rear of the building.

"You have a sick horse?"

"Injured, I'm afraid. We'll have to scratch her from her races for the next several weeks."

"That's a shame."

Kelsey glanced toward a paddock where a yearling was being put through his paces on a longe line. Another, with a rider up, was being led by a handler toward the walking ring. A groom was giving a glossy chestnut a bath, spraying streams of water over the gelding with a hose. Other horses were simply being walked in wide, repetitive circles.

"Busy place," Kelsey murmured, aware that eyes had turned her way.

"Oh, most of the work gets done in the morning, but it'll be busy again when the track closes this afternoon."

"You're racing today?"

"There's always a race," Naomi said absently. "But right now we've still got mares dropping foals, so what doesn't get done in the morning happens in the middle of the night." She smiled a little. "They always seem to have them in the middle of the night."

"I guess I didn't realize you had such a large operation."

"In the last ten years we've become one of the top Thoroughbred farms in the country. We've had a horse do no less than show in the last three Derbies. Won the St. Leger and Belmont. Took the Breeders' Cup two years running. One of our mares took a gold in the last Olympics." Naomi cut herself off with a laugh. "Don't get me started. I'm worse than a grandmother with a wallet full of snapshots."

"It's all right. I'm interested." More, Kelsey mused, than she'd realized. "Actually, I took riding lessons when I was a girl. I guess most of us go through a horse-crazy stage. Dad hated it, but . . ." She trailed off, suddenly understanding why he'd been so unhappy when she'd developed the traditional girlhood obsession with horses.

"Of course he did," Naomi said with a thin smile. "It's perfectly understandable. But you had your lessons anyway?"

"Yes, I hounded him for them." She stopped, and looked straight into her mother's eyes. She could see the small, subtle signs of aging that she'd been too nervous to notice at their first meeting. Fine lines fanning out from the eyes. Others, either from temper or worry, gently scoring the high, creamy forehead. "It must have hurt him to see me, simply to see me day after day."

"I don't think so. However Philip came to feel about me, he adored you." She looked away then because it was easier to stare at the hills. A horse whinnied, high and bright, a sound sweeter to Naomi than any aria. "I haven't asked you about him. How is he?"

"He's well. He's the chairman of the English department at Georgetown now. Has been for seven years."

"He's a brilliant man. And a good one."

"But not good enough for you."

Naomi lifted a brow. "Darling Kelsey, I was never good enough for him. Ask anyone." Naomi tossed her hair back and continued to walk.

"I'm told he married again."

"Yes, when I was eighteen. They're very happy together. I have a stepbrother, Channing."

"And you're fond of them, your family."

"Very."

Naomi crossed the same patio, used the same terrace doors as she had the first time. "What can I get you? Coffee, tea? Some wine, perhaps?"

"It isn't necessary."

"I hope you'll indulge Gertie. She made cookies when she heard you were coming. I know you don't remember, but you meant a great deal to her."

Trapped, Kelsey thought, by manners and compassion. "Tea and cookies then. Thanks."

"I'll tell her. Please sit down."

She didn't sit. It seemed only fair that she take a closer look at her mother's things. At first glance the room was quietly elegant, a world apart from the bustle and manure-coated boots of the stable area. The low fire burned sedately, rose-colored drapes were pulled back to welcome the sun. That sun shone on a dozen or so lovely crystal horses in clear and jewel hues. The Oriental rug on the polished chestnut floor picked up the colors of the drapes and the creamy tones of the sofa.

Nothing ostentatious, nothing jarring. Until you looked again. The walls were covered in watered silk, the same cool ivory as the upholstery. But the paintings, large and abstract, were explosions of bold and restless color. Violent works, Kelsey thought, sated with passion and anger. And signed, she saw with a jolt, with a bloodred N C.

Naomi's work? she wondered. No one had mentioned that her mother painted. No amateurish works these, Kelsey decided, but skilled and capable and disturbing.

They should have unbalanced the steady dignity of the room, she thought as she turned away. Yet they humanized it.

There were other telling touches throughout the room. A statue of a woman, her alabaster face carved in unfathomable grief, a glass heart in pale green with a jagged crack down the center, a small bowl filled with colored stones.

"Those were yours."

Guiltily, Kelsey dropped a pebble back into the bowl and turned. Gertie had wheeled in the tea tray and stood, beaming at her. "I'm sorry?"

"You always liked pretty rocks. I kept them for you when you . . ." Her smile wobbled. "When you went away."

"Oh." How was she supposed to answer that? "You've worked here a long time, then."

"I've been at Three Willows since I was a girl. My mother kept house for Mr.

Chadwick, then I took over when she retired. Moved to Florida. Chocolate chip was always your favorite."

The woman looked as though she could devour Kelsey whole. The desperate yearning in her eyes was difficult to face, the desperate joy beneath that, worse. "They still are," Kelsey managed.

"You come sit and help yourself. Miss Naomi got a phone call, but she'll be right along." All but humming with happiness, Gertie poured tea, arranged cookies on a plate. "I always knew you'd come back. Always knew it. Miss Naomi didn't think so. She fretted about it all the time. But I says to her, 'She's your girl, isn't she? She'll come back to see her mama all right.' And here you are."

"Yes." Kelsey made herself sit and accept the tea. "Here I am."

"And all grown up." Unable to help herself, Gertie stroked a hand over Kelsey's hair. "A grown-up woman now." Her lined face crumpled as she let her hand fall. Turning quickly, she hurried from the room.

"I'm sorry," Naomi said when she came in moments later. "This is an emotional time for Gertie. It must make you uncomfortable."

"It's all right." Kelsey sipped her tea. Oolong this time, she noted with a tiny smile. Understanding, Naomi laughed.

"Just my subtle sense of humor." She poured herself a cup, then sat. "I wasn't sure you'd come back."

"Neither was I. I'm not sure I would have, at least so soon, if Grand-mother hadn't all but forbade me to."

"Ah, Milicent." Trying to relax, Naomi stretched out her long legs. "She always detested me. Well," she said, and shrugged, "it was mutual. Tell me, have you been able to satisfy her high standards?"

"Not quite." Kelsey's smile came and went. It felt disloyal to discuss her grandmother.

"Family honor," Naomi said, nodding. "You're absolutely right. I shouldn't goad you into criticizing Milicent. Besides, I'm not the one who should be asking the questions."

"How can this be so easy for you?" Kelsey set down her cup with a snap of china against china. "How can you sit there so calmly?"

"I learned a great deal about taking what comes when I was in prison. You have the reins here, Kelsey. I've had a lot of time to think this through, and I had to promise myself before I contacted you that I would accept whatever happened."

"Why did you wait so long? You've been out of prison for..."

"Twelve years, eight months, ten days. Ex-cons are more obsessive than ex-smokers, and I'm both." She smiled again. "But that doesn't answer your question. I considered contacting you the day I got out. I even went to your school. Every day for a week I sat in my car across the street and watched you in the little playground. Watched you and the other girls watching the boys and pretending not to. Once I even got out of my car and started across the street. And I wondered if you'd smell prison on me. I could still smell it on myself."

Naomi moved her shoulders, chose a cookie. "So, I got back in my car and drove away. You were happy, you were secure, you didn't know I existed. Then my father became ill. The years passed, Kelsey. Every time I thought about picking up the phone or writing a letter or just walking back into your life, it seemed wrong."

"Why now?"

"Because it seemed right. You're not so happy, not so secure, and I thought it was time you knew I existed. Your marriage is over, you're at a crossroads. Perhaps you don't think I can understand how you feel, but I do."

"You know about Wade."

"Yes. And your job, your academic career. You're fortunate you inherited your father's brain. I was always a lousy student. If you don't want the cookies, stick a few in your purse, will you? Gertie will never know the difference."

With a sigh, Kelsey picked one up and took a bite. "I don't know how to feel about all of this. I don't know how to feel about you."

"Reality is rarely like those big, emotional reunions on *Oprah*," Naomi commented. "Long-lost mother reunited with daughter. All is forgiven. I'm not asking for all to be forgiven, Kelsey. I'm hoping you'll give me a chance."

Kelsey reached for the file she'd set beside her on the sofa. "I've done some research."

The hell, Naomi decided, and reached for another cookie. "I thought you might. Newspaper articles on the trial?"

"Among other things."

"I can arrange for you to have a transcript."

Kelsey's fingers faltered on the file. "A transcript?"

"I'd want one if I were in your place. It's public record, Kelsey. If I had something to hide, I couldn't."

"When I came here before, I asked if you were guilty and you said yes."

"You asked if I'd killed Alec, and I said yes."

"Why didn't you tell me you'd claimed self-defense?"

"What difference does it make? I was convicted. I paid my debt to society, and I am, according to the system, rehabilitated."

"Was it a lie, then? Was it a legal maneuver when you said you'd shot him to protect yourself from rape?"

"The jury thought so."

"I'm asking you," Kelsey shot back, firing up. "A simple yes or no."

"Taking a life isn't simple, whatever the circumstances."

"And what were they? You let him into your house, into your bedroom."

"I let him into my house," Naomi said evenly. "He came into my bedroom."

"He was your lover."

"No, he was not." Hands icily calm, Naomi poured more tea. "He might have been eventually. But I hadn't slept with him." Her gaze met her daughter's. "The jury didn't believe that, either. I was attracted to him. I thought he was a charming fool, harmless and amusing."

"You fought with him over another woman."

"I'm territorial," Naomi said blithely. "He was supposed to be madly in love with me—which meant I was allowed to flirt and he wasn't. And because he was beginning to bore and annoy me, I decided to break off the relationship. Alec didn't want it to be broken. So we had a scene, in public. Then another one later, in private. He was furious, called me a few names, tried to make his case with some rough handling. I didn't care for it and ordered him to leave."

Though she fought to keep it calm, her voice shook as the night flooded back. "Instead, he followed me upstairs and called me several more names, and got quite a bit rougher. Apparently he decided he would show me what I'd been missing by forcing me into bed. I was angry, and I was afraid. We struggled, and I realized he would do exactly what he'd threatened to do. I broke away, got my gun. And I shot him."

Without a word, Kelsey flipped open the file and took out the copy of the newspaper photo. When Naomi took it only a quick spasm at the side of her mouth betrayed any emotion.

"Not terribly flattering to either of us, is it? But then, we didn't know we had an audience."

"He isn't touching you. He has his hands up."

"Yes. I guess you had to be there." She handed the photo back. "I'm not asking you to believe me, Kelsey. Why should you? Whatever the circumstances, I'm not blameless. But I've paid. Society has given me another chance. That's all I'm asking you to do."

"Why did you let me think you were dead? Why did you allow that?"

"Because I felt I was. Part of me was. And whatever my crimes, I loved you. I didn't want you to grow up knowing I was in a cage. I couldn't have survived those ten years thinking of that. And I needed to survive."

There were other questions, dozens of them swirling around in Kelsey's head like bees. But she didn't think she could bear to hear the answers. "I don't know you," she said at last. "I don't know if I'll ever feel anything for you."

"Your father would have instilled a sense of duty in you. Certainly Milicent would have. I'm going to use it and ask you to come here, to stay here for a few weeks. A month."

Kelsey was completely taken aback for a few moments. "You want me to live here?" she finally managed to say.

"An extended visit. A few weeks of your life, Kelsey, for the lifetime I lost." She didn't want to beg. God, she didn't want to beg, but she would if there was no other choice. "It's selfish of me, and not terribly fair, but I want the chance."

"It's too much to ask."

"Yes, it is. But I'm asking anyway. I'm your mother. You can't avoid that. You can choose to avoid me if that's what you want, but I'll still be your mother. We'll have time to see if there's anything between us. If not, you'll walk away. I'm betting you won't walk away." Naomi leaned forward. "What are you made of, Kelsey? Is there enough Chadwick in there for you to accept a dare?"

Kelsey angled her chin. It was a risk. Perhaps she'd needed it to be put that way rather than as a request. "I won't promise a month. But I'll come." She was surprised to see Naomi's lips tremble once before they curved into that cool, steady smile.

"Good. If I can't enchant you, Three Willows should. We'll have to see how much you picked up in those riding lessons."

"I don't get thrown easily."

"Neither do I."

4

Dinner with the family was a civilized affair. Excellent food was served with dignity—like any last meal, Kelsey thought as she spooned up her leek soup. She didn't want to think of the evening in her father's house as an obligation, or worse, as a trial, but she knew it was both.

Philip made casual conversation, but his smile was strained. Since Kelsey had told him of her upcoming visit to Three Willows, he'd been able to think of little else but the past. It seemed disloyal somehow to Candace that his mind should be so full of his first wife, his nights restless and disturbed by memories of her. No matter how often he told himself it was illogical, foolish, even indulgent, he couldn't quite chase away the fear that he was losing the child he'd fought so hard to keep.

A woman now. He had only to look at her to be reminded of that. Yet he had only to close his eyes to remember the girl. And the guilt.

Milicent waited until the roast chicken was served. Normally, she disliked discussing unpleasant matters over a meal. But, as she saw it, she'd been given no choice.

"You leave tomorrow, I'm told."

"Yes." Kelsey took a sip from her water glass. Watched the thin lemon slice dip and float. "First thing in the morning."

"And your job?"

"I've resigned." Kelsey lifted a brow in challenge and acknowledgment. "It was little more than volunteer work. I may look for something at the Smithsonian when I get back."

"It may be difficult to get anything with your record of coming and going."

"It may."

"The Historical Society's always looking for an extra pair of hands," Candace put in. "I'm sure I could put in a word for you."

"Thank you, Candace." Always the peacemaker, Kelsey thought. "I'll think about it."

"Maybe you'll catch racing fever." Channing winked at Kelsey. "Buy yourself some stud and make the circuit."

"That would hardly be acceptable, or wise." Milicent dabbed a napkin at her lips. "Such things may seem romantic and exciting at your age, Channing, but Kelsey's old enough to know better."

"It sounds like a great deal to me, hanging out at the stables, placing a few bets at the track." He shrugged, making quick work of his dinner. "I wouldn't mind spending a few weeks playing in the country."

"You could visit me. It'd be fun."

"Is that all you can think of?" Incensed, Milicent set her fork down with a clatter. "Fun? Have you no idea what this is doing to your father?"

"Mother—"

But Milicent overrode Philip's objection with an impatient wave of her hand. "After all the pain and unhappiness we went through, to have that woman simply snap her fingers to make Kelsey come running. It's appalling."

"She didn't snap her fingers." Under the table, Kelsey balled her hands into fists. It would be much too easy to create a scene, she told herself. "She asked, I agreed. I'm sorry if this hurts you, Dad."

"My concern's for you, Kelsey."

"I wonder . . ." Candace spoke up, hoping to ward Milicent off and salvage some of the evening. "Is it really necessary for you to stay there? It's only an hour or so away, after all. You could move more slowly, go out on a weekend now and then." She glanced toward Philip to gauge his reaction, then smiled bolsteringly at Kelsey. "It seems more sensible."

"If she was sensible, she would never have gone out there."

Kelsey bit back a sigh at her grandmother's comment and sat back. "It's not as if I've signed a contract. I can leave at any time: I want to go." This she addressed to her father. "I want to find out who she is."

"Sounds natural to me," Channing said over a bite of chicken. "If I'd found out I had a long-lost mother who'd done time, that's what I'd do. Did you ask her what it was like inside? I'm a sucker for those women-in-prison movies."

"Channing." Candace's voice was a horrified whisper. "Must you be so crude?"

"Just curious." He speared a perfectly boiled new potato. "Bet the food sucked."

Delighted with him, Kelsey let out a laugh. "I'll be sure to ask her. God, are Channing and I the only ones around here who don't see this as some drawing-room melodrama? You should be relieved I'm not running traumatized to some therapist or washing my shock away with cheap wine. I'm the one who has to make the adjustments here, and I'm doing the best I can."

"You're thinking only of yourself," Milicent said between stiffened lips.

"Yes, I am. I'm thinking of myself." Enough was enough, Kelsey decided, and she pushed back from the table. "It might interest you to know that she had nothing but good things to say about you," she told her father. "There's no insidious plot to turn me against you. And nothing could." She walked to him, bending down to kiss his cheek. "Thanks for dinner, Candace. I really have to get home and finish packing. Channing, if you have a free weekend, give me a call. Good night, Grandmother."

She hurried out. The moment she shut the door behind her, she took a deep gulp of air. It tasted like freedom, she thought. She intended to enjoy it.

In the morning, Gertie met Kelsey at the door. "You're here." The woman snatched Kelsey's suitcases before Kelsey could object. "Miss Naomi's down to the stables. We didn't know what time you'd come, so she told me to call her when you got here."

"No, don't bother her. I'm sure she's busy. Let me take those. They're heavy."

"I'm strong as an ox." Gertie backed up, still beaming. "I'll show you up to your room. You just bring yourself, that's all."

She might have been small and thin, but Gertie strode effortlessly up the stairs, chattering. "We got everything ready. It's good to be busy again. Miss Naomi, she doesn't take any care at all. Hardly needs me around."

"I'm sure that's not true."

"Oh, for company, she does. But she eats like a bird and does for herself mostly before I can do for her." Gertie led the way down a wide hall, carpeted in faded cabbage roses. "Sometimes she has people over, but not like there once was. Used to be there was always people and parties."

She stepped across a threshold and set both cases on an elegant four poster bed.

The room streamed with light from a double window seat that faced the hills, the long slim windows overlooking the gardens. Deep colors and floral accents gave the room an elegant, European feel.

"It's lovely." Kelsey stepped to a cherry vanity table where tulips speared up out of fluted crystal. "Like sleeping in a garden."

"It was your room before. 'Course it was done up different then, all pink and white—like a candy cane." Gertie gnawed at her lip when she saw the surprise in Kelsey's eyes. "Miss Naomi said if you didn't like it, you could take the room across the hall."

"This is fine." She waited for a moment, wondering if she'd be bombarded with some sensory memory. But all she felt was curiosity.

"Your bathroom's through here." Anxious to please, Gertie opened a door. "You just ask if you need any more towels. Or anything, anything at all. I'll go call Miss Naomi."

"No, don't." On impulse Kelsey turned away from the suitcases. "I'll go on down. I can unpack later."

"I'll do that for you. Don't you worry about that. You go on down and have a nice visit, then you can have lunch. You want to button that jacket. The air's chilly."

Kelsey fought back a smile. "All right. I'll be back for lunch."

"Make your mama come. She needs to eat."

"I'll tell her." Kelsey left Gertie happily opening the suitcases.

It was tempting to do a quick turn around the house, to poke into rooms and explore hallways. But it could wait. The day might have held the chill of the dying winter, but it was gloriously sunny. And, Kelsey hoped as she went out, promising.

She wasn't going to start the visit by chasing at shadows. It would have to be done, of course. Still, it seemed harmless to enjoy one uncomplicated day in the country, with the smells of hardy spring blooms and new grass in the air, the panorama of hills and horses and sky. She could look on it, at least for now, as a short vacation. Until she'd literally packed her bags, she hadn't realized just how much she'd needed to get away from the confinement of her apartment, the fill-in job, the tedious routine of learning to be single again.

And here, she thought as she caught the first poignant smell of horse, was something else to be learned, after all. She knew nothing about the racing world, nothing of the people and little of the animals that composed it.

So, she would study and find out. It seemed to follow that the more she discovered, the better she would understand her mother.

As before, there was activity at the stables, horses being walked or washed, men and women carrying tack, hauling wheelbarrows. Kelsey tolerated the sidelong glances and outright stares and walked inside.

A groom was bandaging a mare's legs in the first box. Kelsey hesitated when he cut his eyes up to hers. His eyes were shadowed under the bill of his cap, and his face was incredibly old, cracked like neglected leather left in the sun.

"Excuse me, I'm looking for Ms. Chadwick."

"Grew up, did ya?" The man shifted a tobacco plug into the pocket of his cheek. "Heard you was coming. There now, sweet thing, hold your water."

It took Kelsey a moment to realize the last comment was addressed to the mare and not to her. "Is something wrong with her?" Kelsey asked. "The horse?"

"Just a little sprain. Old she is, but still likes to run. You remember the days, don't you, girl? Won her first race and her last, and a goodly number between. Twenty-five she is. Was a spry young filly when you last saw her." His grin, mostly toothless, flashed. "Don't remember, I expect, her nor me. I'm Boggs. Put you up on your first pony. Forget how to ride, have you?"

"No. I can ride." Kelsey reached out a hand to stroke the old mare's cheek. "What's her name?"

"Queen Vanity Fair. I just call her Queenie."

The mare whickered, her soft brown eyes looking deeply into Kelsey's. "She's too old to race now," Kelsey murmured.

"Or to breed. Queenie's in retirement, but she gets to thinking she's still a girl and kicks up her heels. If I was to bring a saddle in here, her ears would perk right up."

"She can still be ridden, then?"

"With the right rider. Your ma's in the breeding shed, out the back, to your left. Big doings today."

"Oh. Thank you . . ."

"Boggs. Welcome home." He turned back, running his gnarled, callused hands as gently as silk over the mare's legs. "Best to wear boots around here next time."

"Yes." Nonplussed, Kelsey looked down at her soft Italian flats. "You're right."

She walked through the stables, pausing with a quick look over her shoulder before stopping by Serenity's box. She was rewarded by a welcoming snort and nuzzle.

Outside, she didn't require Boggs's directions. There was enough activity around the outbuilding to the left to have drawn her in any case.

She recognized Gabe, and was torn for a moment as to who looked more magnificent, he or the rearing chestnut stallion he was fighting to control. He stood at the horse's head, boots planted, muscles straining, the reins shortened while the stallion quivered and called.

His own hair flying in the breeze, Gabe tossed back his head and laughed. "Anxious, are you? Don't blame you a bit. Nothing like having a beautiful female ready for sex to get the blood moving. Hello, Kelsey." He continued to control the stallion without looking around. He'd known she was there. He almost believed he'd smelled her, as the stallion scented the mare. "You're just in time for the main event. Aren't skittish, are you?"

"No, I'm not."

"Good. Naomi's inside with the mare. Longshot and Three Willows are about to breed a champion."

Kelsey skimmed her gaze over the horse. Handlers were positioned around him, helping Gabe to keep the stud from charging the shed. Magnificent he was, his coat already gleaming like flame from sweat, his eyes fierce, his muscles bunched.

"You're going to turn him loose on some poor, unsuspecting mare?"

Gabe grinned. "Believe me, she'll be grateful."

"She'll be terrified," Kelsey disagreed, and strode into the shed. She saw her mother and Moses calming the mare, who looked to be every bit as eager to get on with things as the stallion. She, too, was a chestnut, as regal as her intended mate. Even though she was hobbled, protected at the neck by a thick jacket of leather and canvas, she looked proud and valiant.

"Kelsey." Covered with grime and sweat, Naomi wiped a hand over her brow. "Gertie was supposed to let me know when you got here."

"I told her not to bother. I'm in the way?"

"No . . ." Naomi looked doubtfully at Moses. "But things are about to get a little frantic. And graphic."

"I know a little about sex," Kelsey said dryly.

"Stay here," Moses added, "and you'll learn more. She's ready," he said to one of the handlers.

"Keep back out of the way," Naomi warned her daughter. "This isn't as simple as an hour in the local motel."

She could smell the sex. Even as Gabe and his handlers brought the stallion in, the air in the shed thickened with it. Sharp, edgy, elemental. The mare called out, in protest or welcome, and the stallion answered with a sound that caused something to tighten in Kelsey's stomach.

Orders were given; movements were quick. In a powerful lunge, the stallion reared up and mounted the mare. Wide-eyed, Kelsey stared as Moses stepped in and assisted in the most technical aspect of the coupling. Then her breath caught as she saw why the mare wore the leather neck cover. Surely the stallion would have bitten through her flesh without it. He plunged wildly, his need frantic and somehow human.

He covered her, commanding, demanding. She accepted, her eyes rolling in what Kelsey thought must surely be pleasure.

Hardly realizing it, she moved closer, fascinated by the passionate frenzy of mating. Her own heart was pounding, her blood hot. The quick, sharp pang of arousal staggered her.

She found herself looking at Gabe. Sweat was running down his face. His muscles strained against his shirt. And his eyes were on hers. It was shocking to see her own primitive and unexpected reaction mirrored there. Staggering to have the vision flash through her mind of being taken as the mare was being taken, fiercely, violently, heedlessly.

He smiled, a slow movement of lips that was both arrogant and charming. Smiled, she thought, as if he knew exactly what she was thinking. As if he'd intended her to think it.

"Incredible, isn't it?" Naomi stepped back beside her. It was the third mare they'd bred that morning and her body was aching with the effort. "Hundreds of pounds lost in the most basic of needs."

"Does it—" Kelsey cleared her throat. "Does it hurt her?"

"I doubt she notices if it does." Out of her back pocket Naomi took a plain blue bandanna to mop her damp throat. "Some stallions breed very kind, like a shy or longtime lover." She grinned wryly at the panting horses. "There's not a shy bone in that one's body. He's a beast. And what woman doesn't want a beast now and again?" She glanced at Moses.

The intellect, Kelsey thought as her pulse danced. It would be better, or at least more comfortable, to explore the logistics. "How do you choose which stallion for what mare?"

"Bloodlines, dispositions, tendencies, even color. We make up genetic charts. Then you cross your fingers. Christ, I know it's a cliché, but I could use a cigarette. Let's get some air. They're nearly done here."

Naomi pulled a stick of gum out of her pocket as she stepped outside. "Want some?"

"No, thanks."

"It's a poor substitute for tobacco." She sighed a little as she folded the stick in her mouth. "But most substitutes are poor in any case." Tilting her head, she studied her daughter more thoroughly. "You look tired, Kelsey. Restless night?"

"Somewhat."

Naomi sighed again. Her daughter had once been so open with her, a chatterbox of news and questions. Those days, like so many others, were over. "You can tell me if you'd rather I leave it alone, but I'd like to ask if Philip is against this visit."

"I think it's more accurate to say he's hurt by my decision to accept your invitation."

"I see." Naomi looked down at the ground, and nodded once. "I'd tell you I'd talk to him myself, try to reassure him, but I think it would only make matters worse."

"It would."

"All right, then. He'll be uneasy for a few weeks." Her eyes were hard when she looked up again. Dammit, she deserved this—one short month out of so many years. "He'll survive. I can't be dead just because so many people would prefer it." She glanced over as Gabe led the sweaty stallion out of the shed. Her smile bloomed, softening her face again. "So, do you think we have a merger?"

"If not, it's not for lack of trying." He slapped the stallion's neck before giving the reins to a handler. "The first of many, I hope. Well, Kelsey, you've had an interesting initiation into life on a horse farm. If you stick around till after the first of next year, you'll see the results of today's tryst."

"That's a very understated description for what went on in there. She didn't appear to have much choice in the matter."

"Neither did he." Grinning, Gabe took out a cigar. "That kind of primitive attraction doesn't allow for choice. Moses will let me know if we need a repeat performance," he said to Naomi, "but I've got a hunch we won't."

"I'd ask for odds, but I prefer to go with your hunch on this one. Excuse me just a minute. I want to check on the mare."

Kelsey looked over to where the stallion was being cooled down. "Shouldn't you be over there, exchanging lies and letting him puff on that cigar?"

"I gave up lying about my sex life in high school. Do I make you nervous, Kelsey, or is it just the atmosphere?"

"Neither." He made her something, all right, she thought. But that was her problem. "So you own the neighboring farm, then? Longshot?"

"That's right."

"I admired your house from the road. It's quite a bit less traditional than the others in the area."

"So am I. The very dignified Cape Cod that stood on the hill when the farm passed into my hands didn't suit me. So I tore it down." He blew out a stream of smoke. "You'll have to come over, have a tour."

"I'd like that, but I think I'll concentrate on touring Three Willows first."

"You won't find a better operation on the East Coast. Unless it's mine." The snort from behind him made him turn, then grin at Moses. "Of course, I'd have the best in the country if I could lure Whitetree away. Double what she pays you, Moses."

"Keep your money, boy. Buy yourself another fancy suit." Moses handed the mare to a stableboy for a rubdown. "Owners like you—flash in the pan."

"That's what you said five years ago."

"That's what I say now. Give me a cigar."

"You're a hard man, Whitetree." Gabe obliged him.

"Yep." Moses stuck the cigar in his pocket for later. "Your groom with the broken nose? There was gin on his breath."

Gabe's easy smile faded, his eyes narrowed. "I'll take care of it."

"Tell your trainer to take care of it," Moses shot back. "It's his job."

"My horses." Gabe corrected. "Excuse me." He turned on his heel and headed for the trailer where the stallion was being loaded.

"He'll never learn, that one," Moses muttered.

"There's no chain of command as far as Gabe is concerned." Watching Gabe confront the groom, Naomi shook her head. "You should have told his trainer, Moses."

"And Jamison shouldn't need me to tell him what goes on under his nose."

"Ah." Kelsey held up a hand. "Would you mind telling me what's going on?"

"Gabe's firing one of his grooms," Naomi told her.

"Just like that?"

"You don't drink when you're working." Moses hissed a breath out of his teeth as the groom's enraged voice carried to them. "Owners should stay out of shedrow business."

"Why?" Kelsey asked.

"Because they're owners." With a shake of his head, Moses strode off toward the stables.

"Never a dull moment." Naomi touched Kelsey's arm. "Why don't we . . . shit."

"What?" Kelsey looked over in time to see the groom swing at Gabe. And to see Gabe evade, once, twice, fluid as a shadow.

Gabe didn't strike back, though the instinct was there, the back alley that always lurked under the civilized man he'd made himself. The groom was pitiful, he thought, and half his size. And the worst of it was that it had taken Moses to point out that he'd had a drunk handling his horse.

"Go back and get your gear, Lipsky," Gabe repeated, icily calm as the groom stood with cocked fists. "You're through at Longshot."

"Who are you to tell me I'm through?" Lipsky ran a hand over his mouth. He wasn't drunk, not yet. He'd had only enough of the gin in his flask to make him feel tall. And mean. "I know more about horses than you ever will. You lucked your way into the big time, Slater. Lucked and cheated and everybody knows it. Just like everybody knows your old man's a drunken loser."

The heat that flashed into Gabe's eyes had the handlers easing back. In tacit agreement they silently formed a ring. It was, they believed, nearly showtime.

"Know my father, do you, Lipsky? I'm not surprised. You're welcome to look him up, have a few drinks. But in the meantime, pick up your gear and the pay that's coming to you. You're fired."

"Jamison hired me. I've been at Cunningham Farm for ten years, and I'll be there after you've gone back to your roulette wheels and blackjack tables."

Over Lipsky's head Gabe saw two of the handlers exchange glances. So, he thought, those were the cards he was dealt. He'd play them out later, but now he had to finish this hand.

"There is no Cunningham Farm, and no place for you at Longshot. Jamison might have hired you, Lipsky, but I write your checks. I don't write checks for drunks. If I see you near any of my horses, I can promise you, it won't be Jamison who deals with you."

He turned, his gaze cutting straight to Kelsey. She stood, like the handlers, watching the show. She had a moment to think she'd prefer that the calm disdain in Gabe's eyes wasn't directed at her before she caught the glint of sun on steel.

The warning strangled in her throat, but Gabe was already whipping back to face the knife. The first lunge sliced almost delicately down his arm rather than plunging into his back. The sight and smell of blood had the handlers shifting quickly from their mildly interested attitudes.

"Keep back," Gabe ordered, ignoring the pain in his arm. His mistake, he thought, was in not judging correctly how far the drink would push. "You want to take me on, Lipsky?" His body was coiled now, ready. When you couldn't walk away from a fight, you dove in and played the odds. "Well, you'll need that knife. So come on."

The blade trembled in Lipsky's hand. For a moment, he couldn't remember how it had gotten there. The hilt had seemed to leap into his hand. But it was there now, and so was first blood. Pride stirred by gin wouldn't allow him to back off.

He crouched, feinted, and began to circle.

"We have to do something." The horror in Kelsey's throat tasted like rusted copper. "Call the police."

"No, not the police." Pale as wax, Naomi clenched her hands at her sides. "Not the police."

"Something. Good God." She watched the blade gleam and lunge, slipping by inches from Gabe's body. No one moved but the two in the center of the circle, then the stallion began to kick in his trailer, excited anew by the scent of blood and violence.

Before she could think, Kelsey grabbed a pitchfork leaning against the side of the shed. She didn't want to dwell on what the tines would do to flesh, so she hefted it and began running forward, only to stumble to a halt when the knife flashed again. It arched up, flying free, as Lipsky hit the ground.

She hadn't seen the blow. Gabe hadn't appeared to move at all. But now he was standing over the groom, his eyes cold, his face as calm as carved stone.

"Let Jamison know where you end up. He'll send your gear and your money." In an effortless move he hauled Lipsky up by the scruff of the neck. The stink of gin and blood curdled in his stomach, sour memories. "Don't let me catch you around here again or I might forget I'm a gentleman now, and break you in half."

He tossed the limp groom down again, and turned to his men. "Let him off on the road. He can ride his thumb out of here."

"Yes, sir, Mr. Slater." They scrambled, as impressed as boys at a schoolyard brawl, dragging Lipsky up and carrying him to the truck.

"Sorry, Naomi." In a careless gesture, Gabe raked the hair out of his eyes. "I should have waited to fire him until we were back at Longshot."

She was trembling, and hated it. "Then I would have missed the performance." Forcing a smile on her face, she moved closer. Blood was dripping down his arm. "Come on up to the house. We'll clean that arm."

"That's my cue to say it's just a scratch." He glanced down at it, grateful it wasn't much more than that, no matter how nastily it throbbed. "But I'd be a fool to turn down nursing by beautiful women." He looked at Kelsey then.

She still held the pitchfork, her knuckles white as bone on the handle. Valiant color rode high on her cheeks and shock glazed her eyes.

"I think you can put that down now." He took it from her, gently. "But I appreciate the thought."

Her knees began to shake, so she locked them stiff. "You're just going to let him go?"

"What else?"

"People are usually arrested for attempted murder." She looked back at her mother, saw the wry smile curve Naomi's lips. "Is this how things are handled around here?"

"You'll have to ask Moses," Naomi replied. "He does the firing at Three Willows." Taking the bandanna out of her pocket, she stanched the blood on Gabe's arm. "Sorry I don't have a petticoat to tear up for you."

"So am I."

"Hold it there, press hard," she instructed him. "Let's go up to the house and get it bandaged."

They started off, Gabe keeping his pace slow until Kelsey caught up. He turned his face to hers, and grinned. "Welcome home, Kelsey."

5

Kelsey left the first aid to her mother, and the bustling and clucking to Gertie. She would have voted for a trip to the emergency room, but no one seemed particularly interested in her opinion.

Knife wounds, it seemed, were to be taken philosophically and mopped up in the kitchen.

Once Gabe's arm was cleaned, medicated, and bandaged, bowls of chicken soup and hot biscuits were served. Talk was of horses, of blood-lines and races, of times and tracks. Since it wasn't a world Kelsey understood, she was free to observe and speculate.

She had yet to determine Naomi's relationship with Gabriel Slater. It appeared intimate, easy. It was he who rose to refill coffee cups, not his hostess. They touched each other often, casually. A hand over a hand, fingertips against an arm.

She told herself it didn't matter what they were to each other. After all, her mother and father had been divorced for more than twenty years. Naomi was free to pursue any relationship she chose.

And yet it bothered her on some elemental level.

Certainly they suited each other. Beyond the easy flow between them, over and above their interest in horses that consumed them both, there was a strain of violence in each. Controlled, on ice. But as she knew with her mother, and as she'd seen for herself with Gabe, deadly.

"Kelsey might enjoy a trip to the track for some morning workouts," Gabe put in. He was enjoying his coffee, enjoying watching Kelsey. He could almost see the thoughts circling around in her head.

"The track?" She was interested, despite having her private musing interrupted. "I thought you worked the horses out here."

"We do both," Naomi told her. "Using the track gives a horse a feel for it."

"And the handicappers a chance to gauge their bets," Gabe put in. "The track draws an interesting and eclectic group, particularly in those dawn hours long before post time."

"Dawn's no exaggeration." Naomi smiled at her daughter. "You might not like to start your day quite so early."

"Actually, I'd like to see how it's done."

"Tomorrow?" The lift of Gabe's brow was a subtle challenge.

"Fine."

"We'll meet you there." Naomi glanced at her watch. "I've got to get down to the stables. The farrier's due." As she rose she pressed a hand to Gabe's shoulder. "Finish your coffee. Kelsey, you'll keep Gabe company, won't you? He'll tell you what to expect in the morning." She grabbed a denim jacket and hurried out.

"She doesn't stay in one place very long," Kelsey murmured.

"First part of the year is the busiest in the business." Gabe leaned back, the coffee cup in his hand. "So, should I tell you what to expect?"

"I'd rather be surprised."

"Then tell me something. Would you have used that pitchfork?"

She considered, let the question hang. "I guess neither of us will know the answer to that."

"I'd lay odds you would have. A hell of a picture you made, darling. More than worth a prick on the arm to see it."

"You're going to have a scar, Slater. You're lucky it was your arm and not your pretty face."

"He was aiming for my back," Gabe reminded her. "I didn't thank you for the warning."

"I didn't give you one."

"Sure you did. Your face was as good as a shout." He slipped a hand into his pocket and pulled out a worn deck of cards. Casually he began a riffling shuffle. "Do you play poker?"

Confused, she scowled at him. "I don't as a rule, but I know the game."

"If you take it up, never bluff. You'd lose more than your shirt."

"Have you? Lost more than your shirt?"

"More times than I care to remember." Out of habit, he began to deal two hands of stud, faces up. "Would you bet on your queen?"

Kelsey moved her shoulders. "I suppose."

He flipped up the next cards. "After a while, if you're smart, you don't risk what you can't afford to lose. I've got plenty of shirts. Your queen's still high."

"So it is." For some absurd reason, she was enjoying the game. On the third card, her spade queen still reigned. And on the fourth. "Still mine. Is it the betting or the horses that interests you?"

"I've got more than one interest."

"Including Naomi?"

"Including Naomi." He turned over the last card, smiled easily. "A pair of fives," he mused. "Looks like they usurp your queen."

Her mouth moved into what was very close to a pout. "It's a shame to lose to such pathetic cards."

"No cards are pathetic if they win." He took her hand, amused when the fingers went rigid. "An old southern tradition. Ma'am." He brought her hand to his lips, watching her. "I owe you for Lipsky. Payment's your choice."

It had been a long time since she'd felt this quickening in the blood. Since it couldn't be ignored, it would have to be fought. "Don't you think it's in questionable taste for you to make a move on me in the kitchen?"

Christ, he loved the way she could come up with those prim little phrases and deliver them in that husky voice. "Darling, this isn't even close to a move." Keeping her hand firmly in his, he turned it palm up. "Lady hands," he murmured. "Teacup hands. I've always had a real weakness for long narrow hands with soft skin."

He pressed his lips to the center, lingering while her pulse bumped like a hammer under his thumb. "That," he said, curling her fingers closed as if to ensure she kept the imprint of his lips there, "was a move. As far as taste goes, yours suits me. You'll probably want to keep that in mind."

He released her hand, scooped up his cards, and rose. "I'll see you in the morning. Unless you're having second thoughts."

Dignity, she reminded herself, was as important as pride. "I'm not having any thoughts at all, Slater, that involve you."

"Sure you are." He leaned down until they were face-to-face. "I warned you not to bluff, Kelsey. You lose."

He left her steaming over cold coffee. It was a damn shame, he thought, that he couldn't indulge himself in a few afternoon fantasies. But he had work to do.

As soon as he returned to Longshot, Gabe sought out Jamison. The trainer had been Cunningham's man, but when Gabe took over the farm, it hadn't taken much to induce Jamison to stay.

His loyalties had always been more with the horses than with the owner.

He was a big-bellied man who liked his food and his beer. Though he'd trained generations of horses that had finished in the money, no one but his staunchest friends would have considered him in Moses Whitetree's league.

He'd come from the county of Kerry as a babe in his mother's arms. His earliest memories were of the shedrow, the smell of the horses his father had groomed.

Jamison had lived his entire life in the shadow of the Thoroughbred. Now, at sixty-two, he sometimes dreamed of owning his own small farm and one champion, just one to carry him comfortably into retirement.

"Well, Gabe." He set aside his condition book and rose as Gabe walked in. "I shipped Honest Abe to Santa Anita, and Reliance to Pimlico. Missed the first post." He smiled wanly. "But I heard you'd had a spot of trouble and thought you'd want to see me before I headed to the track."

"How many times have you caught Lipsky drinking on the job?"

No prevaricating or how was your day with the likes of Gabriel Slater, Jamison thought. He'd known the boy for some twenty years, and had yet to fully understand him. "Twice before. I gave him a warning and told him he'd be cut loose if it happened again. He's a good hand. A weakness for gin, it's true, but he's worked on this farm for a decade." He glanced at the bandage on Gabe's arm and sighed. "I swear on my mother's heart I'd no notion the man would try to stick you."

"Drunks are unreliable, Jamie. You know my feelings about that."

"I do indeed." Jamison folded his hands over his belly. He should be at the track, not here, smoothing feathers. "And maybe I understand why you've no tolerance for that particular weakness. Still, the lads are my province, aren't they? And I followed my own judgment."

"Your judgment was faulty."

"It was."

"A hand drinks on the job, from you down to the lowest stableboy, he's gone. No more warnings, Jamie. No exceptions."

Irritation might have flickered in his eyes, but Jamison nodded. "You're holding the bat, Gabe."

Satisfied, Gabe picked up the condition book himself, skimming pages. "I'll be spending more time around the barn and the backstretch," he said. "I don't want you to feel I'm breathing down your neck."

"It's your barn," Jamie returned, his voice stiffening. "Your backstretch."

"Yes, it is. And it was very clear to me today that the men don't consider me an integral part of this operation. That's my fault." He set the book down again. "The first couple of years after the farm changed hands I was involved with building the house and shoehorning my way into the tight little club of owners. Since then I've let most of the day-to-day business stay in your hands and played owner. Now I'm going to get down to work. You're my trainer, Jamie, and as far as the horses go, I'll accept what advice you give me. But I'm back in the game now. I don't intend to lose."

It would pass, Jamison decided. Owners rarely concerned themselves with the real work for long. All they wanted was their spot in the paddock and the purse. "You know your way around a shedrow as well as anyone."

"It's been a long time since I picked up a pitchfork." Gabe smiled as the image of Kelsey brandishing one like a spear flashed into his mind. He looked at the big-faced clock Jamison had nailed to the wall of his office. "We can make it to Pimlico by three. Who'd you send with the filly?"

"Carstairs. Torky's up on her, Lynette's groom."

"Let's go see what kind of team they make."

Since she was left to her own devices, Kelsey changed her shoes for boots and headed out. She didn't go toward the stables, aware that she would just be in the way, or stared at as if she were an oddity. Instead she walked toward the soft roll of hills where the horses were at grass.

The quiet, the undeniable peace were a welcome change from the frantic morning. Even so, she had to fight a restlessness that urged her to keep walking, keep moving, until she found what was over the next rise.

How could she have walked here as a child and remember nothing? It frustrated her to think that the first three years of her life were a virtual blank. It wouldn't matter in most cases, but her destiny had been skewed in those early years. She wanted them back, wanted to decide for herself what was right, what was wrong.

She stopped by a tidy white fence, leaning on it while a trio of mares began an impromptu race, their babies skipping after them. Another mother stood patiently, cropping grass while her foal suckled.

It was almost too perfect, Kelsey thought. A postcard that was just slightly too clear, too bright for reality. Yet she found herself smiling at the foal, admiring the impossibly delicate legs, the tilt of the somehow elegant head. What would he do, she wondered, if she climbed the fence and tried to pet him?

"Spectacular, aren't they?" Naomi joined her at the fence. The breeze ruffled the hair she'd cut to chin length for convenience more than fashion. "I never get tired of watching them. Spring after spring, year after year. It's soothing, the routine of it. And exciting, the possibility of it."

"They're beautiful. Sedate somehow. It's hard to imagine them streaking down a racetrack."

"They're athletes, bred for speed. You'll see that for yourself tomorrow." Naomi tossed back her hair, then impatient with it, pulled a soft cap out of her jacket pocket and put it on. "The one there, nursing? He's five days old."

"Five?" Surprised, Kelsey turned back, studying the mother and her baby more closely. The foal was sleek and healthy and appeared wise to the ways of the paddock. "That doesn't seem possible."

"They grow quickly. In three years he'll be prime. It starts here, or more accurately in the breeding shed, then goes to that final blur of color at the wire.

He'll be fifteen, sixteen hands, perhaps twelve hundred pounds, and he'll race the oval with a man on his back. It's a beautiful thing to watch."

"But not easy," Kelsey commented. "It can't be easy to take something so delicate and turn it into a competitor."

"No." Naomi smiled then. Her daughter already understood. That, she supposed, was in the blood. "It's work and dedication and quite often disappointment. But it's worth it. Every time." She angled her hat so the brim shaded her eyes. "I'm sorry I left you so long. The farrier likes to talk. He was a friend of my father's. He does the work for me here rather than at the track because of old ties."

"It's all right. I don't expect you to entertain me."

"What do you expect?"

"Nothing. Yet."

Naomi looked back at the nursing mare, wishing it could be that easy to bond with her own child. "Are you still angry about this morning?"

"Angry's the wrong word." Kelsey turned away from the fence so she could study her mother's profile. "Baffled is better. Everyone just stood there."

"You didn't." With a grin, Naomi shook her head. "I thought you were going to run that drunken fool through. I envy you that, Kelsey, that knee-jerk reaction that comes from a lack of fear, or a surplus of honor. I froze. I have too much fear and not nearly enough honor left. A lifetime ago, I wouldn't have hesitated either."

She braced herself and shifted to face her daughter. "You're wondering why the police weren't called. Gabe did that for me. He may or may not have handled it differently on his own place. But here . . . well, he would have known I'd be reluctant to talk to the police again. Ever again."

"It's none of my business."

Naomi closed her eyes. The simple fact they both had to face was that it was all Kelsey's business now. "I wasn't afraid when they came to arrest me. I was so arrogantly sure that they would end up looking like fools, and I a heroine. I wasn't afraid when I sat in the interrogation room with its long mirror, gray walls, the hard chair designed to make you squirm." She opened her eyes again. "I didn't squirm. Not at first. I was a Chadwick. But the fear creeps up on you, inch by crafty inch. You can beat it back. Not away, but back. Before I left that horrible room with the mirror and the gray walls, I was afraid."

She took a steadying breath, reminded herself she was free of that. Free of it, but for the memories. "Through the trial, the headlines, the stares, I was afraid. But I didn't want to show it. I hated the idea of everyone knowing I was terrified. Then they tell you to stand up, so the jury of your peers can deliver the verdict. Your verdict. You can't beat it back then. It has a choke hold on you and you can't breathe. You might stand there, pretending to be calm, pretending to be confident because you know they're watching you. Every eye is on you. But inside, you're jelly. When they say 'guilty,' it's almost anticlimactic."

She drew another deep breath. "So you see, I'm very reluctant to talk to the police again." She said nothing for a moment, expected no response. "Do you know, we used to come here when you were little? I'd sit you up on the fence. You always loved visiting the foals."

"I'm sorry." And she was, suddenly, deeply sorry. "I don't remember."

"It doesn't matter. See the one there sunning himself? The black? He's a champion. I knew it when he was born. He might prove himself to be one of the best to come out of Three Willows."

Kelsey studied the foal more closely. He was charming, certainly, but she didn't see anything to separate him from the other young in the pasture. "How can you tell?"

"It's in the eyes. Mine and his. We just know."

She leaned on the fence, looking out over the fields with her daughter. And was, for a moment, nearly content.

Late that night when the house was quiet and the wind tapped seductively at the windows, Naomi curled her body to Moses. She liked it best when he came to her bed. It had more of a sense of permanence than when she crept up to his rooms above the trainer's shed.

Not that she didn't enjoy the thrill of doing just that. The first time, their first time, she'd walked into his room, surprising him as he sat in his underwear nursing a beer and poring over paperwork.

He'd been a tough seduction, she recalled, stroking a hand along the firm skin of his chest. But his eyes had given him away. He'd wanted her, just as he'd always wanted her. It had just taken her sixteen years to realize she wanted him, too.

"I love you, Moses."

It always jolted him to hear her say it. He supposed it always would. He laid his hand over hers, over his heart. "I love you, Naomi. How else could you have talked me into coming up here with your daughter down the hall?"

She laughed, shifting her head so that she could nibble on his neck. "Kelsey's an adult. I doubt she'd be traumatized even if she knew I had you in bed." She rolled over, straddling him. "And I do have you, Moses."

"It's hard to argue with that since all the blood just drained from my head and into my lap." In an old habit he skimmed his hands up her slim torso to cup her breasts. "You get more beautiful every day, Naomi. Every year."

"That's because your eyes get older."

"Not when they look at you."

Her heart simply melted. "Christ, you destroy me when you get sentimental. I look at Kelsey and see how much I've changed. It's wonderful to see her, to have her close even for a little while." She laughed, shaking her hair back. "And I'm still vain enough to look away from her and into the mirror and see every goddamned line."

"I'm crazy about every goddamned line."

"Being beautiful used to be so important to me. It was like a mission—no, like a duty. Then for so many years it didn't mean anything. Until you." She smiled, bending down to brush his lips with hers. "And now you tell me you like wrinkles."

Moses cupped a hand behind her head, drawing her more firmly to him. As she flowed into the kiss, he shifted her, raising her hips, lowering them so that he slid deep into her. He watched her arch back, thrilling to her quick, throaty moan. He set the rhythm slow, holding her to his pace, drawing the pleasure out for both of them.

From the hallway outside her room, Kelsey heard the muffled sounds of lovemaking, the creak of the old mattress, the breathy moans and murmurs. She stood, the cup of tea she'd gone down to brew in one hand, a book in the other, flustered into immobility.

Not once had she ever heard her father and Candace in the night. She assumed they were both too restrained and polite to make noisy love. There was certainly nothing restrained or polite about the sounds only partially smothered by the closed door down the hall.

Nor, she reminded herself, was it polite to stand out here listening. She fumbled with the knob, spilling tea in her rush to get inside.

Her mother, she thought, barraged by dozens of conflicting emotions. And Gabe Slater, she assumed. The emotions his presence behind that door conjured up were best not explored.

The moment she had her own door safely closed, she leaned back against it. Part of her wanted to laugh at the absurdity of it. A grown woman shocked because another grown woman, who happened to be her mother, had an active sex life.

But she wasn't very amused at the moment, at the situation or her own reaction to it. No longer wanting either, she set the tea and book aside. The dark, still-sleeping garden beneath her window was silvered with moonlight. Romantic, she thought, laying her brow against the glass. Mysterious. As so much of Three Willows was.

She didn't want romance. She didn't want mystery. At least, she didn't want to want them. She was here because it was important to learn about the half of her parentage that had been taken away from her.

Turning from the window she went back to bed. But she didn't sleep until long after she heard the door down the hall open and close, and the sound of quiet footsteps moving past her room toward the stairs.

6

The track, at dawn. It was a different world from the one Kelsey had expected. Racing to her meant more than speed. It meant gambling and gamblers, fat cigars and bad suits, the smell of stale beer and losers' sweat.

The drunken groom Gabe had fired the day before fit her image of the world she'd imagined much more cozily than the tranquil, somehow mystical reality of the dawn horse.

The track was cloaked in mist when she arrived with Naomi. The horses had left even earlier, to be off-loaded, saddled, and prepped for their workouts. It was quiet, almost serene. Voices were muffled by the fog, and people moved in and out of the trailing mist like ghosts. Men leaned against the sagging rail around the oval, sipping from steaming paper cups.

"They're clockers," Naomi told her. "Speedboys. Some work for the track or *Daily Racing Form.* They'll be here for hours, timing the horses, handicapping them." She smiled. "Chasing speed. I guess that's what we all do. I thought you'd like to see it from this angle first."

"It's . . . well, it's beautiful, isn't it? The fog, the trees slipping through it, the all but empty grandstands. It's not what I pictured." She turned to the woman beside her, the slim, lovely blonde in denim jacket and jeans. "Nothing seems to be."

"Most people see only one aspect of racing. Two minutes around the oval, over and done in a flash. Thrilling, certainly. Sometimes terrifying. Triumphant or tragic. Often a man or woman is judged the same way. By one aspect, or one act." There was no bitterness in her voice now, but simple acceptance. "I'll take you around to the shedrow. That's where the real action is."

And the real characters, Kelsey discovered. Aging jockeys who'd failed at the post or put on weight hustled for the forty dollars they'd earn per ride as exercise boys. Others, hardly more than children, with an eager look in the eye, loitered, hoping for their chance. Horses were discussed, strategies outlined. A groom in a tweed hat gently walked a crippled horse, singing to it in a soothing monotone.

There was no particular excitement, or anticipation. Just routine, one she realized went on day after day while most people slept or nodded over their first cup of coffee.

She spotted a man in a pale blue suit and shiny boots in earnest conversation with a placid-eyed man in a tattered cardigan. Now and again the man in the suit would punctuate his words with a jab of a pudgy finger. A flashy diamond ring in the shape of a horseshoe winked with every move.

"Bill Cunningham," Naomi said, noting who had captured Kelsey's attention.

"Cunningham?" Kelsey frowned, and flipped through her memory. "Isn't that the name I heard that groom Gabe fired yesterday mention?"

"Longshot used to be Cunningham Farm. Bill inherited it, oh, about twenty-five years ago, I guess." The disdain in her voice leaked through. "He was doing a first-class job of running it into the ground when he lost it to Gabe. Now he has an interest in several horses, owns one or two mediocre ones outright. He lives in Maryland. The trainer's Carmine, works for Bill and several other owners. Right now Carmine's listening to Bill's instructions, his pontificating, and he's agreeing with everything. Then Carmine will do as he pleases because he knows Bill's an ass. Oops." She let out a sigh. "He spotted us. I'll apologize ahead of time."

"Naomi." In a strutting stride that showed off his boots, Cunningham closed in on them. His eyes glittered like polished marbles as he took Naomi's hands. "A beautiful sight on a gloomy morning."

"Bill." The years had given Naomi a high tolerance for fools, and she offered her cheek. "We don't often see you at workouts."

"Got me a new horse. Claiming race at Hialeah. She took the win as the rider pleased. I was just telling Carmine how she should be worked today. Don't want her rated."

"Of course not," Naomi said sweetly. "Bill, this is my daughter, Kelsey."

"Daughter?" He puffed out his cheeks in feigned surprise. Like everyone else in the area, he already knew about Kelsey. "You must mean sister. Glad to meet you, dearie." He slapped a hand to Kelsey's and pumped vigorously. "Going to follow in your ma's bootsteps, are you?"

"I'm just here to watch."

"Well, there's plenty to see. We'll have her hooked by dusk," he added with a wink to Naomi. "You check with me before you make any bets this afternoon, honey. I'll show you how it's done."

"Thank you."

"Nothing's too good for Naomi's little girl. You know, if I hadn't shied at the gate, I might be your papa. You take care now."

"In a pig's eye," Naomi muttered under her breath as Bill strutted away to harass his trainer. "He likes to think we were an item when the closest we came was me not quite avoiding one sloppy kiss."

"I appreciate your taste. What the hell was he saying about his horse?"

"Oh." Naomi set her hands on her hips and enjoyed a good laugh. "Bill likes to toss the lingo around, thinks it fools people into believing he knows something. Let's see . . . in plain English. He picked up the filly in a claiming race, meaning the owners had put it up for sale. The horse won easily, and Bill met the asking price. He feels the horse shouldn't be rated, or slowed, during the workout." She frowned at his back. "He's the type who pays a jockey extra for every hit of the stick. If a horse isn't whipped over the finish line, Bill feels cheated."

"I'm surprised you were so polite."

"It doesn't cost me anything." She shrugged. "And I know what it is to be an outcast. Come on, Moses should have a rider up by now."

They moved through the paddock area where exercise boys were being given a leg up onto their mounts. With little between them, Kelsey noted. The saddle was so tiny, hardly more than a slip of leather. The boys, as they were called regardless of sex, stood in the high stirrups while mounted trainers walked beside or behind them toward the track.

"That's one of ours." Naomi pointed to a trotting bay. "Virginia's Pride. If you can't resist betting today, you might want to put a couple of dollars on him. He's an amazing athlete, and he likes this particular track."

"Do you bet?"

"Mmmm." Naomi's eyes were on Moses, who rode a half-length behind the bay. "I've always hated to refuse a gamble. Let's watch him run."

There were other horses on the track. The mist was lifting now, and they cut through it like bullets through mesh, exploding through it, shredding it. Kelsey's breath caught at the sight of it, the sounds of it. Huge bodies on thin legs, spewing up dirt, necks straining forward with their tiny riders bent low. Her heartbeat picked up the pulse of the muffled thunder of hooves.

"There." Excitement lifted her voice as she pointed. "That's your horse."

"Yes, that's ours. The track's fast today, but I imagine Moses told the boy to keep him just under two minutes."

"How would the rider know?"

"He has a clock in his head." Gabe's voice came from behind her. Though Kelsey started, she didn't take her eyes off the horse rocketing around the track. "He looks good, Naomi."

"He'll look even better by Derby time." Her eyes narrowed. "That one's yours, isn't he?"

"Double or Nothing." Gabe leaned on the rail as his horse sped past. "He'll look better by May, too."

Kelsey didn't see how. Both horses looked magnificent now, eating up the track, tossing pieces of it toward the sky. They were airborne, those terrifyingly delicate legs lifting off the earth like wings.

She could have stayed there for hours, watching horse after horse, lap after lap. True, it took only a minute or two, and the clockers stood with their stopwatches, the trainers with theirs, but it was timeless to her. Like a lovely animated painting in a worn frame.

"Picked your favorite yet?" Gabe asked her.

"No." She didn't look at him, didn't want him or the memory of what she'd heard in the night to spoil the mood. "I'm not much of a gambler."

"Then I don't suppose you'd like to bet that you'll hit the windows before the afternoon's over."

She shrugged, then found she couldn't resist. "Bill Cunningham offered to give me some tips."

"Cunningham?" Gabe let out a roar of laughter. "Then I hope you've got deep pockets, darling." He leaned against the fence. He considered taking out a cigar, but decided it would spoil his enjoyment of Kelsey's scent. Soft and subtle it was, the kind that crept into a man's senses and lingered long after the woman had slipped away.

"Morning's the best time," Naomi murmured, shading her eyes as the sun broke through the thinning mist and dazzled. "Clean slate."

"Possibilities." Gabe looked down at Kelsey. "It's all about possibilities."

Later, they walked back to the shedrow. Horses steamed in the cool air as they were unsaddled and walked. Legs were checked for strains, sprains, and bruises. A roan's hooves were oiled. A groom posed another, crouching down, searching for injury. A farrier with leather apron and battered toolbox hammered a shoe.

"Like a painting, isn't it?" Gabe asked, as if he'd plucked the image from Kelsey's brain.

"Yes, it is."

"Everything you see here would have been true a hundred years ago, five hundred. Thoroughbreds' legs can go anytime, so we obsess about them. Look there. Where's the trainer looking?"

She turned to watch a horse being led in, the trainer behind. "At the horse's feet."

"And he'll keep his eyes there." He nodded in another direction. "They were probably around a thousand years ago."

A man in a racing cap dogged Moses at the heels. He was talking fast, puffing to keep up. "Who is he?"

"Jockey agent. They hustle from barn to barn trying to convince everyone they represent the next Willie Shoemaker." Casually, he tucked Naomi's hair behind her ear. "Can I get you some coffee?"

"I'd love some. Kelsey?"

"Sure. Thanks. Is it all right if I get a closer look at your horse while he's being walked?"

"Go ahead."

Naomi settled down on an upturned bucket. The morning's work was nearly done. And the waiting would start. She'd gotten very good at waiting. There was a pleasure in it now, watching her daughter circle with the hot walker. Asking questions, Naomi imagined. The child had always been full of questions. But never aloof, as she was now.

For a moment that morning, as they stood in the mist watching the first horses round the practice track, she'd felt something relax between them. Then the stiffness had come back. Subtle, but then there were so many subtleties to her daughter. So many contrasts.

Kelsey laughed. It was the first time Naomi had heard the sound, easy, without reservations.

"She's enjoying herself," Gabe commented as he passed Naomi a cup of coffee.

"I know. It's good to see it. I'm sitting here telling myself that it won't always be so awkward between us." She eased her dry throat with the hot, sweetened coffee. "I just want to touch her. To hold her, just once. And I can't. She might let me, out of pity. That would be worse than rejection."

"She's here." Gently he ran a hand down her hair, over her shoulder. "She doesn't strike me as the type to be here if she didn't want to be."

"I don't expect her to love me again. But I do want her to let me love her." She reached for the hand on her shoulder, covered it with her own.

Kelsey tried to ignore the intimacy of the pose when she walked back to them. It was their business, she reminded herself. She kept a smile on her face and reached out for the coffee Gabe offered. "Thanks. I've just been given the winner in every race today. I should leave here, I'm told, flush."

"Jimmy's always got a tip," Naomi said. "And they're right as often as they're wrong."

"Oh, but these are sure things." Kelsey grinned as she lifted her cup. "He swore he'd never give Miss Naomi's daughter anything but a cinch tip. I'm supposed to bet on Necromancer in the first because the field's slow and he's generous and should win laughing." She arched a brow. "Did I get that right?"

"No one would guess it's your first day," Gabe said soberly.

"Oh, I'm a quick study." She glanced around. The pace was definitely slowing down, she noted. "What happens now?"

"We wait." Naomi rose, stretched. "Come on. I'll buy us some doughnuts to go with this coffee."

Waiting, it seemed, was a way of life around the track. By ten the workday was over for the horses not scheduled to race. Trailers pulled in and pulled out. The track was groomed.

By noon, the grandstands began to fill. The glassed-in restaurant behind them served lunch, catering to those who preferred their racing experience away from the noise and smells of the masses.

In the shedrow, horses were prepped once again. Swollen legs were iced down in buckets. According to personal strategy, some were kept on edge, others soothed like babies. Jockeys donned their silks.

Now the anticipation was there. The excitement that had been missing from the mist-coated morning. Horses pranced, fidgeted, athletes eager to run. Some calmed when their jockeys were tossed onto their backs; others pawed and quivered.

From the paddock area they walked toward the track, single file, some led by grooms, some unaccompanied.

Now the grandstands buzzed, newcomers sprinkled among regulars. All of them hoping today would be their day. The post parade, the foundation of the dozens of racing rituals, began with the horses stepping onto the track. At the bugler's call they circled it, in order of post position. Those eager to bet studied racing forms, horses, jockeys, hoping to pick a winner.

If a horse was sweating, he might be nervous. Advantage or disadvantage? Each player had his own opinion. Bandaged forelegs. Could be trouble. Ah, that one hauling at his bit. Might be bad-tempered today. Or he might be fast.

That one *looks* like a winner.

At the finish line, barely five minutes after it had begun, the parade dissolved like colorful confetti tossed in the air.

It didn't matter to Kelsey. There was too much to see. Odd, the track wasn't really flat at all. It was wide, textured with furrows and air pockets, a circular mile of speed and dreams.

She could all but smell the dreams as she stood at the rail. From the jockeys, from the grandstands. Some were fresh and floral, others stale, powdered dry with dust. And she understood, standing there, what a powerful drug it was to want to win.

"I think I'll take that first tip."

Naomi laughed. She had been expecting it. "Take her up, will you, Gabe? Nobody should face their first window alone."

"I'm sure I can handle it," Kelsey said when Gabe took her hand.

"Everybody thinks that." He wound his way up, inside, where lines were already forming at the windows. "Let me give you a quick lesson on playing the horses. Have you figured out how much cash you'd play?"

She frowned, annoyed. "About a hundred."

"Double it. Whatever you figure you'll play, double it. Then consider it gone. Now, you've got your racing form."

"Yeah, I got it." She didn't understand it, but she had it.

"Normally, you'd need about four hours in a quiet place to study it, reviewing the races in order, eliminating horses, ranking others. Best to whittle it down to two or three. No binoculars, huh?"

"No, I didn't think—"

"Never mind, you can borrow mine." He eased her into a line, draped an arm companionably over her shoulder. He didn't smile. He wanted to, but he didn't. She was listening to him as a prized student would to a veteran teacher. "Now you want to forget betting the doubles or the exactas, any of the combinations. And you want to bet to win."

"Of course I do."

"That's right, aggressive betting—it's its own reward. Betting to show is for wimps." He had the satisfaction of seeing the man in the line beside him wince and curl his shoulders. "Did you check the odds board?"

"No," she said, feeling like a fool.

"Your horse is at four to one. That's fine. Betting favorites is for cowards. Too bad you told me you weren't much of a gambler or I wouldn't have let you eat or drink before betting."

"What?"

"Never eat or drink before you pick a winner, Kelsey."

Her eyes narrowed. "You're making this up."

"Nope. It's all gospel." Now he grinned. "And it's all bullshit. Bet to play because it's fun. Close your eyes and pick a number. Horses are athletes, not machines. You can't figure them."

"Thanks a lot." Amused now, she stepped up to the window. "Ten dollars on Necromancer." She shot a look at Gabe. "To win."

With his arm still around her shoulder, Gabe reached for his wallet. "Fifty on number three. To win."

Clutching her own ticket, she frowned. "Who's number three?"

"Couldn't say." He slipped the ticket into his pocket.

"You just bet a number, just a number?"

"A hunch. Want to make a side bet on who comes in first? Your tip or my hunch?"

"Another ten," she shot back.

"And you said you weren't much of a gambler."

He got her back to the rail just as the horses entered the starting gate. Foolish it might have been, but her heart was thudding, her palms damp. At the clang of the bell she strained forward, dazzled by the blur of color.

No misty workout now, but a crowd of muscled bodies fighting for position, their riders a burr on their backs. In seconds they reached full stride, with front-runners hugging the rail. The sound was overwhelming, thunder in front, roaring in back. Then they were at the turn.

"Number three's got it," Gabe said in her ear.

Kelsey shook him off. "They've barely started."

She could hear jockeys screaming, threats or encouragement, while their whips flashed. Down the stretch, the wire in sight, and Kelsey had forgotten the bet entirely. Every emotion was caught up in the race itself, the showmanship of it, the drama of speed. She saw a horse coming from behind, straining, digging in. Hardly aware of the decision, she began to root for him, thrilled by that flash of courage and heart.

He nipped the leader on the outside and took the wire by half a length.

"Oh, did you see him!" She threw her head back and laughed. "He was beautiful."

Gabe hadn't seen the finish, but he'd seen her. The polite mask had melted away with excitement, revealing the passion and energy of the woman beneath. He wanted that woman more than he'd ever wanted a winning hand.

Lips pursed, Naomi considered the look in Gabe's eyes. That was something she'd have to think about. "Your horse finished fifth," she told Kelsey.

"It doesn't matter." Kelsey drew a deep breath. She could still smell the glamour. "It was worth it. Did you see how he came up like that? It was almost out of nowhere."

"Number three," Gabe said, and waited until her eyes met his. "My hunch paid off."

"That was number three?" She turned toward the winner's circle, torn between annoyance at losing to him, and her enjoyment of watching the horse win. "This must be your lucky day."

"You could be right."

"So." She slid her eyes up to his and smiled. "Who do you like in the next race?"

Sometime during the afternoon she devoured a hot dog and washed it down with a watered-down soft drink. She felt a surprising stab of pride, very personal, when Virginia's Pride dominated his field. It was so obvious, she thought, even to her untrained eye, that there wasn't another horse in the race to compare with him.

Another less identifiable emotion pricked her when Gabe's horse crossed the wire first.

As dusk fell, the grandstands were littered with losing tickets, cigarette butts, and shattered hopes.

"Can I interest you two ladies in some dinner?"

"Oh." Distracted, Naomi buttoned up her jacket. She was already looking for Moses. "I'm going to be at least another hour here. Why don't you take Kelsey?"

Instinctively, Kelsey sidestepped. "I don't mind waiting for you."

"No, go ahead. Have fun. I'll see you at home in a couple of hours."

"Really, I—" But Naomi was already hurrying away. "I appreciate the offer, Gabe, but—"

"You're too well mannered to refuse." He took her arm.

"No, I'm not."

"Then you're too hungry. A single hot dog doesn't fuel all that energy. And I can help you count your winnings."

"I don't think that's going to strain anyone's math." In any case, she was hungry. She let him guide her through the parking lot to a bottle-green Jaguar. "Nice car."

"She's fast."

He was right. Kelsey leaned back and enjoyed the ride through the pearling twilight. She'd always liked to drive fast, top down, radio blasting. Wade had lectured her countless times as he'd stuck to the heart of the speed limit. Sensible, she thought now. Responsible.

But he'd never understood that now and again she had to cut loose, do something, anything, full out. He'd preached moderation, and she had agreed—except when she couldn't. An impulsive spending spree, a speeding ticket, a last-minute urge to fly to the Bahamas. Those quick-silver changes in her had been the cause of most of their domestic quarrels.

Small stuff, she'd always thought. Incorrectly, she realized now. What had her impulsive surprise visit to Atlanta gotten her?

Freedom, she reminded herself, and determinedly closed the book on it.

When she began to pay attention to the scenery again, she realized they were nearly at Bluemont. "I thought we were going to have dinner."

"We are. Do you like seafood?"

"Yes. Is there a restaurant out here?"

"One or two. But we're eating in. I called home earlier. How does grilled swordfish strike you?"

"That's fine." She straightened in her seat, listening to the alarm bells in her head. "How did you know I'd be coming to dinner?"

"I had a hunch." He cruised down the road, zipped through the iron gates and up the drive. "You can take a look at the house before we eat."

His gardener had been busy. Beds had been tidied for spring so perennials could flaunt their new growth. A few brave daffodils had already bloomed, their bright yellow heads nodding charmingly.

Funny, she'd never have picked Gabe as the daffodil type.

The front door was flanked by beveled glass panels etched in geometric designs. With the light inside glowing through them, they glinted like diamonds. She remembered now that his jockeys' silks had resembled diamonds as well. A dramatic red and white.

"How did you pick your colors, the silks?"

"A straight flush, diamonds, eight through king." He opened the door. "A hand of cards. I drew the ten and jack against the odds. People will tell you that's how I came into this place. Winning a hand of cards."

"Did you?"

"More or less."

She stepped inside into a tiled atrium, all open space, dizzying ceilings with arched skylights. The copper rail that circled the second floor followed a gently curving staircase. Huge terra-cotta pots hung suspended, spilling out greenery.

"Quite an entrance," she managed.

"I don't like to be closed in. I'll get you a drink."

"All right." She followed him through a wide arch into a living area. This too opened into another room through archways. Glass doors invited the night inside; lamps, already lit, softened it.

There was a fire crackling in a hearth of river stone. A table was set in front of it. For two, she noted. A white cloth, candles. Champagne chilled in a bucket beside it.

"Did you also have a hunch that Naomi wouldn't be joining us?"

"She usually goes into conference with Moses after a day at the track." He opened the bottle with a quick, celebrational *pop*. "Do you want to look around, or would you rather have dinner right away?"

"I'll look around, since I'm here." She accepted the glass, noting there was no matching flute by the second plate. "You're not celebrating?"

"Sure I am. I don't drink. Why don't we start upstairs and work down?"

He led her out, up the curving stairs. She counted four bedrooms before they climbed a short flight into the master suite. This was a split-level affair, the bedroom three tiled steps above the sitting area. A stone fireplace would warm the foot of the lake-sized platform bed, and the skylight would invite a restless sleeper to watch the moon.

Like the rest of the house, it was a mix of the classic and the modern. A

Chippendale table held an abstract bronze-and-copper sculpture. A Persian carpet glowed on the floor beneath a free-form coffee table of polished teak.

Meissen vases beside modern art. The art, the painting, drew her. Even from across the room, Kelsey recognized it as a work by the same artist who had done those in her mother's home.

So much passion, she thought, as she studied the frenetic brushstrokes, the violent juxtaposition of primary colors. "Not a very restful piece for a bedroom."

"It seemed to belong here."

"N.C.," she murmured. "Did Naomi paint this?"

"Yes. Didn't you know she painted?"

"No, no one mentioned it. She's very talented. I know several art dealers who would be begging at her door."

"She wouldn't thank you for it. Her art's personal."

"All art's personal." She turned away from it. "Has she always painted?"

"No. You should ask her about it sometime. She'll tell you whatever you want to know."

"I'll have to decide what that is first." Sipping her champagne, she wandered the room. "I don't know what that dignified Cape Cod looked like, but I doubt it could have measured up to this." More at ease, she turned back. "Did you horrify the neighborhood by having it razed?"

"Appalled everyone within twenty miles."

"And enjoyed every minute of it."

"Damn right. What's the use of having a reputation if you can't live up to it?"

"And what is your reputation?"

"Slippery, darling, very slippery. Anyone would tell you that being alone with me in my bedroom's the first step to perdition."

"It's a long way from the first step to the last fall."

"Not as far as you might think."

With a shrug, she tossed back the rest of her drink. "Tell me about the card game."

"Over dinner." He held out a hand. "I'm a sucker for atmosphere, and a lot closer to that last fall than most."

Intrigued, she put her hand in his. "That doesn't sound very slippery to me, Slater."

"I'm just getting started."

Downstairs he refilled her glass. Some invisible servant had already set two silver-domed plates on the table, lit the candles, and switched on music. They sat down to Gershwin.

"The card game?"

"All right. How much do you know about poker?"

"I know what beats what. I think." She took a bite of the delicately grilled fish and closed her eyes. "This definitely beats the track cooking all to hell."

"I'll tell the cook you said so. Anyway, about five years ago I was in a game, a marathon. Big stakes, heavy hitters."

"Around here?"

"Not around here, here. In the dignified Cape Cod."

She narrowed her eyes. "Isn't gambling illegal in this state?"

"Call a cop. Do you want to hear this or not?"

"I do. So you were in a big, illegal poker game. Then what?"

"Cunningham was having a run of bad luck. Not just during the game, but for several months. His horses were breaking down. He hadn't had any finish in the money for more than a year. He had a pile of outstanding debts. He figured, like most do when they're on a downswing, that all he needed was one big score."

"Hence the poker game."

"Exactly. I had interest in a horse, and he'd been running well. So I was"—he smiled devilishly—"flush. I wanted a farm like this, always had. I went into the game thinking that if I didn't lose my stake I might finesse enough for another horse. Work my way up."

"Sounds sensible, in a skewed sort of way." Reckless was how it sounded, she thought. Admirably reckless. "Obviously you won more than a horse."

"I couldn't lose. It was one of those sweet moments when everything falls in your lap. If he had three of a kind, I had a full house. He had a straight, I had a flush. His trouble really started when he couldn't let it go. He was down about sixty, sixty-five."

"Hundred?"

Charmed, he took her hand, kissed it lavishly. "Thousand, darling. And he didn't have it to lose. Not cash, anyway. So he upped the stakes, wouldn't take no for an answer."

"And, of course, you tried your best to bring him to his senses."

"I told him he was making a mistake. He said he wasn't." Gabe moved his shoulders. "Who am I to argue? There were only four of us left by then. We'd been at it for about fifteen hours. This was going to be the last hand. Five thousand to open, no limit on raises."

"That was twenty thousand before you even got started?"

"And over a hundred and fifty by the time it got down to me and Cunningham."

Her fork stopped halfway to her mouth. "A hundred and fifty thousand dollars on one hand?"

"He thought he had a winner, kept bumping the pot. I had the last raise, bumped it another fifty myself. I thought it might put him out of his misery. But he matched it."

She lifted her glass and sipped slowly to wet her dry throat. She felt she could almost be there, sweaty-palmed and dry-mouthed with a small fortune riding on the turn of a card.

"That's a quarter of a million dollars."

He grinned. "You are a quick study. I felt sorry for him, but I'm not going to say I didn't relish the moment when I laid down that straight flush to his three kings. He didn't have the cash." Gabe tipped more champagne into her glass. "He barely had the assets. So we made a deal. You could say Cunningham bet the farm and lost it."

"You just kicked him out?"

Gabe inclined his head, studied her. "What would you have done?"

"I don't know," she said after a moment. "But I don't think I could have thrown the man out of his own house."

"Even after he'd gambled with money he didn't have?"

"Even then."

"So, you're a soft touch. We made a deal," Gabe said again, "that satisfied both of us. And, because I played against the odds, I got something I'd wanted my whole life."

"That's quite a story. I guess you met the unlucky Bill Cunningham at the track."

"No, at least not initially. I used to work for him."

"Here?" She set down her fork. "You used to work here?"

"I walked hots, shoveled manure, polished tack. For three years I was one of Cunningham's boys. He had a fine line back then. Of course, he never gave a good goddamn about the horses. They were just money to him. He cared a lot less about the people who took care of them. Our rooms were like little cells, cramped, dingy. He didn't believe in putting any of his capital into unnecessary improvements."

"I don't think it bothered you at all to take his house."

"I didn't lose any sleep over it. When I left here, I did some time at Three Willows. Now, that's a farm. Chadwick had the touch. So does your mother. When I left—I was about seventeen then—I figured I'd come back one day, money dripping out of my pockets, and buy myself one place or the other."

"And you did."

"In a manner of speaking."

"What did you do while you were away?"

"That's another story."

"Fair enough." Relaxed with food and wine, she propped her chin on her fist. "I bet you hated that Cape Cod."

"Every fucking inch of it."

Laughing, she leaned back again and picked up her glass. "I think I'm starting to like you. I hope you didn't make all that up."

"I didn't have to. Want dessert?"

"I can't." With a little moan, she pushed away from the table to wander the room. "When I first saw this house, I thought it looked arrogant and territorial. I think I was right." She closed her eyes for a moment. "My point of no return."

"What?"

"Nothing." She shook her head and walked closer to the windows. "It must be quite a feeling to look out any window and see so much of your own."

"What do you see out of yours?"

"A restaurant, a small shopping center with a terrible little boutique and a wonderful bakery. It's practically next door to the Metro and I thought I wanted convenience."

He put his hands on her shoulders, then turned her so that they were face-to-face. "But you don't."

"No." The quick tremble caught her by surprise when he skimmed his hand up the side of her neck.

"What then?"

"I haven't decided."

He framed her face, letting his fingers dip into her hair. "I have."

His mouth lowered to hers, soft at first, testing, hardly more than a nibble that gave them both the choice to step back. But she didn't, not with his taste still vibrating on her lips and the low, drugging ache of unexpected need churning.

She didn't step back, but forward, her arms winding recklessly around his neck, her mouth melding hotly with his.

So much to feel. She'd forgotten there was so much to feel. Or perhaps she'd never known. There was nothing civilized or tentative about this embrace. It was groping and wild, an explosion of sensation that mocked the gentle candlelight and soft music.

She stripped his mind clean. There was nothing left for him but naked sensation, the smell of her, the taste, which mixed together like some exotic drug. The feel of her straining against him, the sound of his quickened breathing as she dragged him greedily closer. The need for her, sharp and edgy as a knife, peeled away the layers of manners, behavior, and ethics he'd carefully crafted, and bared the reckless man beneath.

He needed to touch her. His hands streaked down, over, in a desperate race to possess. She arched under them, eager for more. Hurry, she wanted to beg him to hurry, not to let her think, not to let her reason.

Then he ran a hand over her face, combing her hair behind her ear. The image of him performing that same careless gesture for her mother only hours before flashed into her mind.

The horror, and the shame, were like two vicious, heavy blows. She shoved away, fighting for air. "Don't." She stumbled back when he reached for her. "Don't touch me." She could still taste him. Still want him. "How could you do this? How could I do this?"

"I want you." He had to fight every instinct in his body to keep from lunging forward and taking what had nearly been his. "You want me."

Because it was true, urgently true, she had no choice but to strike back. "I'm not a mare to be hobbled and serviced. And I didn't come here tonight so you could find out if the daughter takes after the mother."

To restrain them, Gabe stuck his hands in his pockets. "Clarify."

"I'm not excusing myself, but at least I have the decency to stop this before it goes any further. You have no decency at all." She shoved her tumbled hair back. Fury, fueled by an acid guilt, turned her voice into a whip. "Is this all just another game to you, Slater? Lure the daughter, wine and dine her, charm her into bed and see if she's as good as the mother? Did you place bets, calculate the odds?"

He took a moment before he answered. When he did, neither his face nor his voice revealed any of the clawing anger. "You think I'm sleeping with Naomi?"

"I know you are."

"I'm flattered."

"You're—What kind of a man are you?"

"You have no idea, Kelsey. None at all. I doubt very much you've come across my kind in that nice, comfortable little world of yours." He stepped forward, curling his hand around the back of her neck. It was a small, nasty way of paying her back. But he was feeling small, and he was feeling nasty.

However stiff she held her spine, her body began to tremble. "Take your hands off me."

"You like my hands on you," he said softly. "Right now you're afraid, excited, but afraid, and wondering what you would do if I dragged you upstairs. Hell, why go to all that trouble when there's a floor right here?" His voice was smooth and cool as cream, but there was a light in his eyes, a dangerous burn. "What would you do, Kelsey, if I took you right here, right now?"

Fear clawed up her throat, shredding her voice. "I said take your hands off me."

He could read the terror on her face. It was clear as a scream even when he released her and stepped back. It didn't quite fade, nor did the feelings of disgust that simmered inside him.

"I'll apologize for that. Only for that." He studied her for a moment. The color he'd deliberately frightened out of her cheeks was coming back. "You're quick to judge, Kelsey. Since you've made up your mind, we won't waste time discussing fact or fantasy. I'll take you home."

7

Naomi was tying the belt of her robe when she heard the front door slam. Surprised by the angry sound, she hesitated before going out into the hall. Was it her place, she wondered, to question Kelsey after an evening out? She had no precedent. If she'd lived through those teenage years with Kelsey, through the late-night talks, the arguments and worries, through the triumphs and tragedies of adolescence, she'd know.

But she had no guideposts, only instincts. The sound of Kelsey's feet rushing up the stairs decided her.

She opened her own door, certain she could keep the whole experience very casual. No prying, just a quick how was your evening. One look at Kelsey's face erased all intentions.

"What happened?" Before either of them could think, she moved forward to take Kelsey's arms. "Are you all right?"

Still revving on temper, Kelsey went instantly on the attack. "How can you associate with him, much less . . . God, you all but asked me to spend the evening with him."

"Gabe?" Naomi's fingers tightened. She trusted Gabe implicitly, without question. But a small female dread curled in her gut. "What did he do?"

"He kissed me," Kelsey shot back. Her color flared at the ridiculously lame understatement of what had happened between them.

"Kissed you," Naomi repeated, while relief and amusement twined through her. "And that's it?"

"Don't you care?" Frustrated, Kelsey jerked back. "I'm telling you he kissed me. I kissed him back. We were groping at each other. And it wouldn't have stopped if I hadn't remembered."

Out of your depth, Naomi, she thought. If they couldn't deal as mother to daughter, perhaps they could begin as woman to woman. "Come in and sit down."

"I don't want to sit." But Kelsey followed Naomi into the bedroom.

"I do." Rearranging her thoughts, Naomi settled on the padded stool of her vanity table. "Kelsey, I know you might still be raw from your divorce. But you are divorced, and free to develop other relationships."

Kelsey stopped her restless pacing and gaped. "*I'm* free? This isn't about me. It's about you."

"Me?"

"What's wrong with you?" Now there was insult added to temper, insult that the woman who shared her blood could be so shallow. "Don't you have any pride?"

"Actually," Naomi said slowly, "I've often been told I have too much. But I don't see how that applies at the moment."

"I'm telling you that your lover wanted to sleep with me, and it doesn't apply?"

Naomi's mouth worked silently before she could get it around the words. "My lover?"

"God knows how you can let him touch you," Kelsey barreled on. "You've known him for years and you must see what he is. Oh, he's attractive, and he may be charming on the surface. But he has no scruples, no honor, no loyalties."

Naomi's eyes flashed, her jaw stiffened. "Who are you talking about?"

"Slater." On the edge, it was all Kelsey could do to keep from screaming. "Gabriel Slater. How many lovers do you have?"

"Just one." Naomi folded her hands and drew a deep breath. "And you think it's Gabe." After a moment's consideration, she began to smile. Then, to Kelsey's astonishment, she began to laugh. "I'm sorry. I'm sorry. I'm sure this isn't funny to you." Helpless, she pressed a hand to her stomach. "But it's wonderful, really. I'm so flattered."

Kelsey spoke through gritted teeth. "He said the same thing."

"Did he?" Chuckling, Naomi wiped a tear from her eye. "You mean you actually asked him if he was sleeping with me? God, Kelsey, he's in his thirties. I'm nearly fifty."

"What difference does that make?"

She couldn't stop it. Naomi's smile spread like a sunbeam. "Now I'm really flattered. Do you actually believe a gorgeous—God knows he's gorgeous—hot-blooded man like Gabe would be romantically interested in me?"

She studied Naomi as dispassionately as her mood allowed, taking in the classic features, the slim, elegant body in the simple white robe. "I didn't say anything about romance," Kelsey said flatly.

"Oh." Naomi nodded, struggling to compose herself. "Well, now. So you assume that Gabe and I are, what, engaged in a hot, sexual affair?" She pursed her lips. "I'm feeling younger all the time."

"Before you bother to deny it, I'll say two things." Head high, Kelsey looked down at her mother. "First, it's none of my business who you sleep with. You can have twenty lovers and it's none of my concern. Second, I heard you last night. In here, with him."

"Oh." Naomi blew out air. "That is awkward."

"Awkward?" The word all but exploded out of her mouth. "This is *awkward?*"

Realizing she was going to have to be very clear and precise, Naomi lifted a hand. "Let's handle your statements in order. First, despite what you think or have been told, I've never been promiscuous. You may not choose to believe me, but your father was my first lover. There was no one else until two years after I got out of prison. He's been my only lover since." She stood so they were eye to eye.

"If that's true, it's even worse. How can you not care that he would cheat on you this way?"

"No man would cheat on me more than once," Naomi said in a tone Kelsey not only believed, but understood. "It wasn't Gabe you heard in here with me last night, Kelsey. It was Moses."

She couldn't speak. It was impossible to ignore the truth when it was slapped so neatly across her face. Silently she sank to the bench herself. "Moses. Your trainer."

"Yes, Moses. My trainer. My friend, and my lover."

"But Gabe—he's always touching you."

"To risk a cliché, we're very good friends. Gabe is, excepting Moses, my closest friend. I'm sorry you misunderstood."

"Jesus." Kelsey squeezed her eyes shut as everything she'd said rushed back to humiliate her. "Oh, Jesus, no wonder he was so angry. The things I said."

Risking rejection, Naomi brushed a hand over Kelsey's hair. "I don't suppose you bothered to ask him?"

"No." Her own words came back to her, stinging like bullets. "No, I was so sure, and I was so ashamed that he'd made me forget myself, even for just a minute. I've never—With Wade it was always—It doesn't matter," she said quickly. "The point is, I jumped in with both feet and said some filthy things to him."

"You were in a difficult position. I'll call him and explain."

"No, I'll go over in the morning and apologize face-to-face."

"Hateful, isn't it? Apologizing?"

"Almost as bad as being wrong." It was always a chore to swallow pride. "I'm sorry."

"There's no need where I'm concerned. You've walked into a world filled with strangers, Kelsey. You trusted your instincts. Whatever you did tonight, you did because you have a strong moral code, a finely developed sense of right and wrong."

"You're making excuses for me."

"I'm your mother," Naomi said quietly. "Maybe we'll both get used to that in time. Go get some sleep. And if you don't want to face the lion in his den alone tomorrow, I'll go with you."

But she went alone. It was a matter of self-respect. At first she thought she'd drive over, but that would be so quick. Despite lying restless most of the night, she had yet to come up with the exact words or tone she wanted to use.

She decided to ask for a mount, and clear both head and nerves with a ride from farm to farm.

She found Moses rubbing liniment over the throat of a roan gelding. Foolishly she found herself hesitating. How did she approach him now that she knew he was Naomi's lover?

For the moment she just stood back and watched him. His hands were gentle, darkly tanned, wide at the palm. At his wrist he wore a bracelet of hammered copper. There was nearly as much gray as black in his braid. He had a distinctive face, though no one would have called it handsome, with its prominent nose and weather-scored skin. His body was tough and wiry, with little of the lithe muscular grace of Gabe's.

"Hard to figure, isn't it?" There was a touch of amusement in Moses's voice. He didn't have to turn for Kelsey to deduce it would be reflected in his eyes. "A beautiful woman like her. Rich. Classy. And a half-breed runt like me." He set the liniment aside and reached for a bowl of watery gruel. "Can't blame you for being surprised. Surprises me all the time."

"I'm sorry?"

"Naomi figured she should let me know she told you about us."

Wincing, Kelsey rubbed a hand over her face. How much more embarrassing could it possibly get? "Mr. Whitetree."

"Moses, let's make it Moses considering the situation. Come on, boy." Murmuring, he urged the gruel on the gelding. "Try a little now. Just a little at a time. I fell in love with her when I first came to work here as a groom. She'd have been about eighteen then. I'd never seen anything like her in all my life. Not that I expected her to look at me twice. Why should she?"

Kelsey watched him nurse the horse, saw the kindness, the strength, the simple sturdiness. "I think I can see why." Making the gesture, she stepped into the box until they were shoulder to shoulder. "What's wrong with him?"

"King Cole here's got laryngitis."

"Laryngitis? Horses get laryngitis? How can you tell?"

"See here?" Taking her hand, Moses guided it over the throat. "You can feel it's swollen."

"Yes, poor thing." She made soothing noises as she rubbed gently. "Is it serious?"

"Can be. If it's severe, the air passage gets blocked and he can choke."

"You mean die?" Alarmed, she pressed her cheek to the gelding's. "But it's just a sore throat."

"In you. In him it's different. But he's coming along, aren't you, fella? He can't take food yet, but gruel or some linseed tea."

Tea for a horse, Kelsey thought. "Shouldn't the vet see him?"

"Not unless it worsens. We keep him warm, use eucalyptus inhalations, smear camphor on his tongue three, four times a day. He's not coughing anymore, and that's a good sign."

"How much of the doctoring do you do yourself?"

"We only call Matt in when we can't handle it."

"I thought a trainer trained."

"A trainer does everything. Sometimes it seems the horses are the least of it. You spend a day with me sometime, you'll see."

"I'd like that."

It had been an offhand remark, nothing he'd expected her to pick up on. Thoughtful, he eyed her. "I start before dawn."

"I know. And you probably don't want me tagging along. But I was wondering if there was something I could do while I'm here. Muck out stables or clean tack. I wouldn't expect to be trusted with the horses, but I hate doing nothing."

Her mother's daughter, Moses mused. Well, they'd see. "There's always something to do around here. When do you want to start?"

"This afternoon, maybe tomorrow. There's something I have to do this morning." Her mood shifted downward at the thought. "I'd rather shovel manure than do it, but it can't be avoided."

"Come down when you're ready, then."

"I appreciate it. I wonder, is there a riding horse I could borrow this morning? I do know how to ride."

"You're Naomi's daughter. That means you know how to ride and you don't have to ask for permission to take a horse."

"I'd rather ask."

"We'll saddle up Justice, then," he decided. "He'd suit you."

The roan gelding liked to run. He'd been retired for three years, but he had never accepted his lowered status as a riding mount. He was often used to pony a contender onto the track for the post parade, and though he preferred to run, he performed his duties with dignity.

He'd never been a champion, as Moses explained to Kelsey. But neither had he been common, and he had finished steadily in the money throughout his career.

She didn't care if he'd lost every race, not when he took her flying over the hills, his body running like an oiled engine beneath hers.

He responded eagerly to the slightest pressure of her knees, moving from churning trot to fluid gallop, as happy as she to have the morning and the rising fields stretched out before them.

This was a pleasure she realized she'd denied herself for too long. And one she wouldn't deny herself again, no matter how her muscles might ache later. Even when she left Three Willows, she'd find a way to indulge herself in this one delight.

Maybe she'd give up her apartment entirely, move out of town. There was no reason she couldn't buy a small place of her own, and a horse. She might have to have it stabled, of course, but that could be arranged. If she absorbed enough from Moses, she could even work at a stable.

She gulped in the cool wine of early spring, the smell of grass and young growing things. Why in the world did she ever think she had to stay in an office or gallery hour after hour when she could be outside, doing something for the sheer joy of it?

She shook back her hair and laughed as they sailed over a narrow creek and thundered up a rise.

Then she reined in, spotting the spread of buildings below.

Longshot. Leaning forward, she patted Justice's neck and studied the scene. The ride had done her a great deal of good, but it hadn't solved the essential problem. She still hadn't a clue how to approach Gabe.

"So, we'll play it by ear," she muttered, and clucked Justice into a dignified trot.

Gabe saw her come down the rise. He stayed where he was, by the fence watching a yearling respond to the longe. He wasn't any more calm than he'd been the evening before. Nor, he realized as she rode closer, so slim and straight and golden on the majestic Thoroughbred, did he want her any less.

He took another drag on his cigar, expelled smoke lazily. And waited.

As she dismounted and walked the gelding toward Gabe, Kelsey supposed she had been more miserable. But past miseries never seem as huge as current ones.

"You ride well," he commented. "An old trooper like this takes a steady hand."

"I usually have one. If you have a few minutes, I'd like to talk to you."

"Go ahead."

Why should he make it easy? she asked herself, and swallowed another lump of pride. "Privately. Please."

"Fine." He took the reins and signaled a groom. "Cool him off, Kip."

"Yes, sir."

Kelsey lengthened her stride to keep up as Gabe turned away from the stables. "You have a nice operation here. It all looks very similar to Three Willows."

"Want to talk shop?"

"No." She let the attempt at small talk wither and die. "I realize you're busy. I'll try not to take up much of your time." Then she closed her mouth and said nothing more until he slid open a glass door at the rear of the house.

It opened into the tropics. Lushly blooming plants tumbled from pots and basked in the sunlight that streamed through the glass roof. A tiled pool glinted in the center, oval-shaped and invitingly blue.

"It's beautiful." She trailed a finger over a flashy red hibiscus. "I guess we didn't get this far last night."

"Continuing the tour didn't seem appropriate." He sat on a striped lounge chair and stretched out his legs. "This is private."

She watched the smoke curl from the tip of his cigar toward the gently rotating fans suspended from the ceiling. "I came to apologize." Nothing, absolutely nothing tasted less palatable.

He merely arched a brow. "For?"

"My behavior last evening."

As if considering, he tapped out his cigar in a silver bucket of sand. "You demonstrated varied behavior last evening. Can you be more specific?"

She rose, helplessly, to the bait. "You're hateful, Slater. Cold, arrogant, and hateful."

"That's quite an apology, Kelsey."

"I did apologize. I came over here choking on it, but I apologized. You don't even have the decency to accept it."

"As you pointed out last night, I'm lacking in decency." Lazily, he crossed his ankles. "I'm to assume from this sudden turnabout that you confronted Naomi and she set you straight."

Her only defense was to angle her chin. "You could have denied it."

"Would you have believed me?"

"No." Infuriated all over again, she whirled away from him. "But you could have denied it. You have to be able to see what it felt like to believe what I believed and to find myself..."

"What?"

"Crawling all over you." She all but spat the words as she spun around. "I won't deny it. I jumped right into your arms. I didn't think—couldn't think. I'm not proud of it, but I won't pretend it was one-sided. I have needs, too, and urges, and—dammit, I'm not cold!"

He wasn't sure which surprised him most, the sudden vehemence of her last statement or the tears glittering in her eyes. "I'm the last one you'd have to convince of that. Why in hell would you have to convince yourself?"

Appalled, she fought back the tears. "That's not the point," she said. "The point is I made an enormous mistake. I said things to you that you didn't deserve and that I regret." She dragged both hands through her hair, then let them fall. "God, Gabe, I thought you'd been in her room the night before. I'd heard..."

"Moses?" he finished.

She shut her eyes, sighed. "The fool's always the last to know. I thought it was you. And the idea that you'd go from her to me—that I'd let you..." She trailed off again. "I'm sorry."

She looked so lovely, the sun gilding her hair, regret darkening her eyes. He nearly sighed himself. "You know, I really wanted to stay pissed off at you. I figured it was going to be easy and, Christ knows, safer." He pushed out of the chair. "You look tired, Kelsey."

"I had a lousy night."

"Me too." He reached up to touch her cheek, but she stepped back.

"Don't. Okay? I feel like an idiot saying it. More than an idiot knowing it, but I'm in a vulnerable state right now. And you seem to set me off."

He bit back a groan. "I appreciate you sharing that with me, darling. It's sure to help me sleep at night. 'Don't touch me, Gabe, I might start crawling all over you again.'"

She had to smile. "Something like that. Why don't we start this whole business from the top?" She offered a hand. "Friends?"

He looked down at her hand, then back into her eyes. "I don't think so." Watching her, he edged closer.

"Listen..." She could already feel the heat, moving up from her toes. "I don't want to get involved. It's lousy timing for me." Cautious, she took a step back.

"Too bad. I'm real pleased with the timing myself."

"I'm telling you—" She stepped back again, met empty air. Kelsey caught the grin in his eyes seconds before she hit the water. It was pleasantly cool, but no less of a shock. She surfaced, dragging wet hair out of her eyes. "You bastard."

"I didn't push you. Thought about it, but didn't." Helpfully, he offered a hand to haul her out.

Her eyes lit. She grasped it, tugged. She might as well have pulled at a redwood.

"Don't bluff, Kelsey." He simply released her hand and sent her under again. This time she took it philosophically and dragged herself over the side. Sat.

"Nice pool."

"I like it." He sat cross-legged beside her. "Come back sometime, take a real swim."

"I might just do that."

"It's almost better in the winter. You can feel smug watching the snow fall outside."

"I bet." Idly, she wrung out her hair, then flicked water in his face. "Gotcha."

He merely took her hand, pressed the wet palm to his lips, and watched her eyes go smoky. "Gotcha," he echoed.

She scrambled up while her heart flailed around in her chest. "I've got to get back."

"You're wet."

"It's warm enough out." She resisted, barely, the urge to retreat again when he unfolded his legs and rose. "A textbook spring day."

He wondered if she had any idea how desirable she was, flustered with nerves. "I'll drive you back."

"No, really. I want to ride. I'd almost forgotten how much I enjoy it. I want to take advantage of it while I'm here, and—" She pressed a hand to her jittery stomach. "Oh, God, I've got to stay away from you."

"Not a chance." He hooked a finger in the waistband of her jeans and jerked her an inch closer. "I want you, Kelsey. Sooner or later I'm going to have you."

She forced a breath in and out. "Maybe."

He grinned. "Place your bets." And released her. "I'll get you a jacket down at the stables."

She got out fast. Ten minutes later she was galloping back toward Three Willows. Gabe waited until she'd disappeared over the first rise before he turned away.

"Fine-looking filly, that."

The voice was like a twisting knife in his side. A sneak attack, impossible to defend against. But he didn't startle easily. Gabe's face was a neutral mask as he looked at his father.

Not much change, he noted. Rich Slater still had style. Maybe it leaned toward snake-oil salesman, but it was style nonetheless. He was a big man, broad through the shoulders, long through the arms. His natty gabardine suit was just a little snug around the chest. His shoes shone like mirrors, and his hair, glossily black, was trimmed under a snappy gray fedora.

He'd always been striking, and had used his looks—the stunning blue eyes, the quick smile—to charm the unwary. Nearly six years had passed since Gabe had seen him, but he knew what signs to look for.

The lines etched deep that no amount of pampering or praying could smooth out. The broken capillaries, the overbright sparkle in the eye. Rich Slater was exactly as he'd been six years earlier and for most of his life. Drunk.

"What the fuck do you want?"

"Now, is that any way to greet your old man?" Rich laughed heartily and, as if Gabe had tossed out the red carpet, wrapped his arms around his son. There was the unmistakable scent of whiskey under the peppermint on his breath.

It was a combination that had always turned Gabe's stomach.

"I asked what you wanted."

"Just came by to see how you were doing, son." He slapped Gabe on the back before he leaned away. He didn't sway, didn't totter. Rich Slater could hold his drink, he liked to say.

Until the second bottle. And there was always a second bottle.

"You've done it this time, Gabe. Hit the jackpot. No more shooting craps in alleys for you, hey, son?"

Gabe took Rich by the arm and pulled him aside. "How much?"

Though his eyes flashed once, he feigned hurt. "Now, Gabe, can't a father come visit his own flesh and blood without you thinking I'm after a handout? I'm doing fine, I'll have you know. Built me up a stake out West. Been playing the horses, just like you." He laughed again, all the while judging and calculating the worth around him. "But I wouldn't like settling down your way. You know me, boy, got to keep footloose."

He took out a cigarette, snapped a gold-plated lighter he'd had monogrammed at the mall. "So, who was the sexy blonde? Always had an eye for the ladies." He winked. "And they always had an eye for you. Just like your old man."

Even the thought of it had Gabe's blood boiling. "How much do you want this time?"

"Now, I told you, not a dime." Not a dime, Rich thought as he looked toward the near paddock where the yearling was still being worked. A man could make a splash with a couple of horses like that. A real splash. No, he didn't want a dime. He wanted a great deal more.

"Fine horse, that I recollect how you used to pay more attention to the horses at the track than the game."

And whenever he had, Gabe remembered, he'd been treated to the back of his father's big hand. "I don't have time to discuss my horses with you. I have work to do."

"When a man makes a score like you've done here, he doesn't need to work." Or to sweat, Rich thought bitterly. Or to hustle for petty cash. "But I'm not going to hold you up, no indeed. Thing is, I'm planning on being in the area a while, looking up some old friends." He smiled as he blew out smoke. "Since I'm going to be in the neighborhood I wouldn't say no to spending a few days in that fancy house of yours. Have a nice visit."

"I don't want you in my house. I don't want you on my land."

Rich's easy smile dimmed. "Too good for me now, are you? Is that it? Got yourself all dolled up now and don't want to be reminded where you come from. You're an alley cat, Gabe." He jabbed a finger into his son's chest. "You always will be. Don't matter if you live in a fine house and fuck fancy women. You're still a stray. You forget who put a roof over your head, food in your belly."

"I haven't forgotten sleeping in doorways or going hungry because you'd gotten drunk and lost every penny my mother had slaved for." He didn't want to remember. He hated that the memories dogged him like his own shadow. "I haven't forgotten sneaking out of some stinking room in the middle of the night because we didn't have the rent money. There's a lot I haven't forgotten. She died in a charity ward, coughing up blood. I haven't forgotten that."

"I did my best by your mother."

"Your best sucked. Now, how much is it going to cost me to make you disappear?"

"I need a place to stay." His nerves were taking over, bringing a whine to his voice. Unable to help himself, he reached for the flask in his back pocket. "Just for a few days."

"Not here. Nothing about you is going to touch this place."

"Christ Almighty." He took a long drink, then another. "I'll tell you straight; I've got some trouble. A little misunderstanding about a game in Chicago. I was working it with this other guy, and he got sloppy."

"You got caught cheating and now somebody's looking to blow off your kneecaps."

"You're a cold-blooded son of a bitch." The flask was from the second bottle. Rich was working through it quickly. "You owe me, and don't you forget it. I just need to lay low for a few weeks, till it cools off."

"Not here."

"You're just going to kick me out, let them kill me?"

"Oh, yeah." Gabe studied his father with a humorless smile. "But I'll give you an even chance. Five thousand ought to help you go to ground and keep you there."

Rich looked around the farm, the well-tended buildings, the glossy horses. He was never too drunk not to calculate his take. "It isn't enough."

"It'll have to be. Keep away from the house, and my horses. I'll go write you a check."

Rich tipped up the flask again while Gabe strode away. It wasn't enough, he thought as the whiskey turned to bitterness in his blood. The boy had hit the big time and all he wanted was a piece of the action.

And he'd get it, Rich promised himself. He'd given the boy a chance. Now they'd play out the game another way.

8

It was foolish to be nervous. Yet Philip continued to check his watch between sips of white wine. Kelsey wasn't late. He was early.

It was even more foolish to think she might have changed in some way during the two weeks she'd been gone. That she might look at him differently somehow. Or find him lacking—as he'd found himself lacking when he'd watched the woman he'd once loved taken away to prison.

There was nothing he could have done. And no matter how many times he'd told himself that, the words rang hollow. The guilt had eaten at him for years, soothed only by the care and love he'd given his daughter.

Yet even now, two decades later, he could see Naomi's face as it had looked the last time he'd seen her.

It was a six-hour drive from Washington to Alderson, West Virginia. Six hours to travel from the tidy, civilized world of university life to the gray and bitter reality of a federal facility. Both were regimented, both cloistered for their own purposes. But one was fueled by hope and energy, the other by despair and anger.

No matter how he'd prepared himself, it had been a shock to see Naomi, vivid, arrogantly alive Naomi, behind the security screen. The months between her arrest and her sentencing had taken their toll. Her body had lost its subtle feminine roundness, so she'd appeared angular and bony in the shapeless prison uniform. Everything had been gray—her clothes, her eyes, her face. It had taken every ounce of will inside him to meet her silent, steady gaze.

"Naomi." He felt foolish in his suit and tie, his starched collar. "I was surprised you wanted to see me."

"Needed to. You learn quickly in here that what you want is rarely a consideration." She was three weeks into her sentence, and for the sake of her sanity had already stopped crossing off days on her mental calendar. "I appreciate your coming, Philip. I realize you must be dealing with a lot of backlash right now. I hope it won't affect your position at the university."

"No." He said it flatly. "I assume your attorneys will appeal."

"I'm not hopeful." She folded her hands, linking her fingers tight to keep them from moving. Hope was another weight on her sanity that she'd coldly dispatched. "I asked you to come here, Philip, because of Kelsey."

He said nothing, couldn't. One of his deepest fears was that she would ask him to arrange for Kelsey to visit, to bring his child into this place.

She had a right. He knew in his heart she had a right to see her child. And he knew in his heart he would fight her to the last breath to keep Kelsey away from the horror of it.

"How is she?"

"She's fine. She's spending a day or two at my mother's so I could . . . make the trip."

"I'm sure Milicent's delighted to have her." The sarcasm whipped back into her voice. The ache crept back into her heart. Determined to finish what she'd begun, Naomi banished both. "I assume you haven't explained to her, as yet, where I am."

"No. It seems . . . No. She believes you're visiting someone far away for a while."

"Well." A ghost of a smile flitted around her mouth. "I am far away, aren't I?"

"Naomi, she's only a child." However unfair, he would use her love for Kelsey. "I haven't found the right way to tell her. I hope, in time, to—"

"I'm not blaming you," Naomi interrupted. She leaned closer, the shadows under her eyes mocking him. "I'm not blaming you," she repeated. "For any of this. What happened to us, Philip? I can't see where it all started to go wrong. I've tried. I think if I could pinpoint one thing, one time, one event, it would be so much easier to accept everything that happened after. But I can't." She squeezed her eyes shut, waiting until she was sure she could speak without a tremor in her voice. "I can't see what went wrong, but I can see so many things that went right. Kelsey. Especially Kelsey. I think of her all the time."

Pity, the overwhelming weight of it, smothered him. "She asks about you."

Naomi looked away then, around the drab visiting room. Someone nearby was weeping. But tears were as much a part of this place as the air. She studied the walls, the guards, the locks. Especially the locks.

"I don't want her to know I'm here."

It wasn't what he'd expected from her. Off balance, he fumbled between gratitude and protest. "Naomi—"

"I've thought this through very carefully, Philip. I have plenty of time to think now. I don't want her to know they took away everything and put me in a cage." She drew a deep steadying breath. "It won't take long for the scandal to die down. I've been out of your circle for nearly a year as it is. Memories are short. By the time she goes to school, I doubt there'll be much more than a murmur, if that, about what happened in Virginia."

"That may be, but it hardly deals with now. I can't just tell her you've disappeared, Naomi, and expect her to accept it. She loves you."

"Tell her I'm dead."

"My God, Naomi, I can't do that!"

"You can." Suddenly intense, she pressed a hand to the security screen. "For her sake, you can. Listen to me. Do you want her to visualize her mother in a place like this? Locked up for murder?"

"Of course I don't want it. She can't be expected to understand, much less cope with it, at her age. But—"

"But," Naomi agreed. Her eyes were alive again, passionate, burning. "In a few years she'll understand, and she'll have to live with it. If I can do anything for her, Philip, I can spare her from that. Think," she insisted. "Think. She could be eighteen by the time I get out. All her life she'll have pictured me here. Would she feel obligated to come here herself to see me? I don't want her here." The tears came then, breaking through the dam of self-control. "I can't bear it, even the thought of her coming here, seeing me like this. What would it do to her? How would it damage her? I tell you, I won't take that chance. Let me protect her from this, Philip. Dear God, let me do this one last thing for her."

He reached out so that their fingertips met through the iron mesh. "I can't stand to see you in here."

"Could any of us bear to see her sit where you are?"

No, he couldn't. "But to tell her you're dead. We can't predict what that would do to her. Or how any of us would live with the lie."

"Not so big a lie." She drew her fingers back, stemmed the tears. "Part of me is dead. The rest wants to survive. Quite desperately wants to survive. I don't think I could if she knew. She'll be hurt, Philip. She'll grieve, but you'll be there for her. In a few years she'll barely remember me. Then she won't remember me at all."

"Can you live with that?"

"I'll have to. I won't contact her or interfere in any way. I won't ask you to visit me here again, nor will I see you if you come. I'll be dead to her, and to you." She braced herself. Their time was almost up. "I know how much you love her, and the kind of man you are. You'll give her a good life, a happy one. Don't scar it by making her face this. Please, promise me."

"And when you're released?"

"We'll deal with that when it happens. Ten to fifteen years, Philip. It's a long time."

"Yes." It made his stomach knot to imagine it. What, he thought, would it do to a child? "All right, Naomi. For Kelsey's sake."

"Thank you." She rose then, fighting nausea. "Good-bye, Philip."

"Naomi—"

But she walked straight to the guard, through the door that clanged shut behind her. She hadn't looked back.

"Dad?" Kelsey put her hand on Philip's shoulder and gave it a little shake. "What century are you in?"

Flustered, he rose. "Kelsey. I didn't see you come in."

"You wouldn't have seen a fleet of Mack trucks come in." She kissed him, drew back, then with a laugh kissed him again. "It's good to see you."

"Let me look at you." Did she seem happier? he wondered. More settled? The thought caused a quick, ungenerous tug-of-war inside him.

"I can't have changed that much in two weeks."

"Just tell me if you feel as good as you look."

"I feel great." She slipped into a chair and waited for him to settle across from her. "The country air, I suppose, someone else's cooking, and manual labor."

"Labor? You're working on the farm?"

"Only in the most menial of capacities." She smiled up at the waitress. "A glass of champagne."

"Nothing else for me, thank you." Philip looked back at his daughter. "Are you celebrating?"

"Pride took his race at Santa Anita today." Kelsey was still flushed with pleasure at the win. "I muck out his stall when he's at Three Willows, so I feel some part of responsibility for the victory. In May Virginia's Pride is going to take the Derby." She winked. "That's a sure thing."

Philip sipped his wine, hoping it would open his throat. "I didn't realize you'd become so involved . . . with the horses."

"They're wonderful." She took the glass the waitress set in front of her, lifted it in a toast. "To Pride, the most gorgeous male I've ever seen. On four legs, anyway." She let the bubbles explode on her tongue. "So, tell me, how is everyone? I thought Candace would be with you."

"I suppose she understood that I wanted you to myself for a couple of hours. She sends her love, of course. And Channing. He has a new girl."

"Of course he does. What happened to the philosophy major?"

"He claimed she talked him to death. He met this one at a party. She designs jewelry and wears black sweaters. She's a vegetarian."

"That ought to last about five minutes. Channing can't go much longer than that without a burger."

"Candace is certainly counting on that. She finds Victoria—that's her name—unsettling."

"Well." Kelsey opened her menu and skimmed. "She wouldn't find anyone settling right now where Channing's concerned. He's still her baby."

"The most difficult thing any parent ever does is to let go. That's why most of us just don't." He covered her hand with his. "I've missed you."

"I haven't really gone anywhere. I wish you wouldn't worry so much."

"Old habit. Kelsey"—he tightened his grip on her hand—"I asked you to have dinner with me for a couple of reasons. I'm not sure you won't find one of them unpleasant, but I felt you'd prefer to hear it from me."

She stiffened. "You said everyone was all right."

"Yes. It's about Wade, Kelsey. He's announced his engagement." He felt her hand go limp. "Apparently it's to be a small wedding, in a month or two."

"I see." Odd, she thought, that there should still be so much emotion to swirl and collide inside her. "Well, that was quick work." She hissed out a breath, annoyed by the edginess of her own tone. "Stupid of me to resent it, even for a minute."

"Human, I'd say. However long you were separated, the divorce is barely final."

"That was just a paper. I know that. The marriage ended in Atlanta, more than two years ago." She picked up her glass, considered the wine bubbling inside. "I was going to be civilized and wish him the best. Nope." She drank deeply. "I hope she makes his life hell. Now, I think I'll try the blackened redfish. I feel like something with a little bite to it."

"Are you going to be all right?"

"I'm going to be fine. I am fine." She closed her menu. After they'd given their order, she found herself smiling at her father. "Were you afraid I'd throw a tantrum?"

"I thought you might need a shoulder to cry on."

"I can always use your shoulder, Dad, but I'm finished crying over what's done. Maybe working, really working for a living's changing my outlook."

"You've been working for years, Kelsey, since you graduated from high school."

"I've been playing at jobs for years. None of them mattered to me."

"And this does? Mucking out stalls matters to you?"

The snap in his voice warned her. She chose her words carefully. "I suppose I feel a part of a system there. It's not simply one race or one horse. There's a continuity, and everyone has a part in it. Some of it's tedious, some of it's rushed, and it's all repetitive. But every morning it's new. I can't explain it."

And he would never understand it. All he knew at that moment was that she sounded so much like Naomi. "I'm sure it's exciting for you. Different."

"It is. But it's also soothing. And demanding." Might as well get it done, she told herself, and she continued quickly. "I'm thinking of giving up my apartment."

"Giving it up? And what? Moving permanently to Three Willows?"

"Not necessarily." Why did it have to hurt him? she wondered, then sighed. Why had it hurt her to hear Wade was about to remarry? "That hasn't been discussed. But I've been giving some thought to moving out to the country. I like seeing trees out of my window, Dad. Seeing land instead of the next building. And I enjoy very much what I'm doing now. I'd like to keep doing it, see if I'm good at it."

"Naomi's influencing you. Kelsey, you can't let these kinds of impulses seduce you into rushing from one way of life to another. You can't possibly understand the world you're toying with after so short a time."

"No, I can't claim to understand it fully. But I want to." She held back as their salads were served. "And I want to understand her. You can't expect me to walk away from her until I do."

"I'm not asking you to walk away, but I am asking you not to leap in without considering all the consequences. There's more than the romance of a horse at dawn, or that last gallop over the finish line. There's ruthlessness, cruelty, ugliness. Violence."

"And it's as much a part of who I am as the smell of books in the university library."

"Why, it's Kelsey, isn't it? Naomi's lovely daughter." Bill Cunningham sauntered over, a drink from the lounge in one hand, his diamond horseshoe winking on the other. "No mistaking that face."

Perfect timing, she thought, and forced a smile. "Hello, Bill. Dad, this is Bill Cunningham, an associate of Naomi's. Bill, my father, Philip Byden."

"Why, I'll be goddamned. It's been years." Bill stuck out a hand. "Don't believe I've seen you since the day you snatched Naomi out from under my nose. Teacher, aren't you?"

"Yes." With the coolness he reserved for careless students, Philip nodded. "I'm a professor at Georgetown University."

"Big time." Bill grinned, laying a hand on Kelsey's shoulder for a quick, intimate squeeze. "You got yourself a real beauty here, Phil. It's a pure pleasure seeing her around the track. Heard your mama's top three-year-old outdistanced the field at Santa Anita today."

"Yes, we're very pleased."

"Things are going to shake down different in Kentucky. Don't let her talk you into laying your paycheck on Three Willows' colt, Phil. I've got me the winner. You give your mama a kiss for me, honey. I've got to get back to the bar. Little meeting."

As he walked away, Kelsey picked up her salad fork and began to eat with every appearance of interest.

"That's the kind of person you want to associate with?"

"Dad, you sound like Grandmother. 'Standards, Kelsey. Never lower your standards.'" But Philip didn't smile. "Dad, the man's an idiot. Very similar to the pompous, blustering idiots I've run into at the university, in advertising, at galleries. You can't escape them."

"I remember him," Philip said stiffly. "There were rumors that he bribed jockeys to lose, or to deliberately force another horse into the rail."

She frowned, and shoved the salad aside. "So add sleazy to pompous and blustering. He's still an idiot, and not someone I intend to cultivate a friendship with."

"He runs in the same circle as your mother."

"Parallel lanes, perhaps. There's a great deal I don't know about her, or trust about her, at this point. But I do know that Three Willows is more than a farm to her, the horses more than business assets. It's her life."

"It always was."

"I'm sorry." Kelsey reached out helplessly to take his hands. "I'm sorry that she hurt you. I'm sorry that what I'm doing now has brought all that hurt back. I'm asking you to trust me to look at the whole, to make my own choices. I need a goal in my life, Dad. I may have found it."

He was afraid she had, and that when she reached it he would no longer recognize her. "Just promise me you'll take more time, Kelsey. Don't commit to anything, or to anyone, without more time."

"All right." She hesitated. "You haven't asked about her."

"I was working up to it," Philip admitted. "I wanted your impressions."

"She seems very young. She has this incredible well of energy. I've seen her start at dawn and keep going until after dark."

"Naomi loved to socialize."

"I'm speaking of work," Kelsey corrected. "She never socializes. At least she hasn't since I've been there. To tell you the truth, with all the work, I don't see how anyone would have the strength left to party. She's usually in bed before ten." No point, she thought, in mentioning that Naomi wasn't always sleeping alone. "She's very controlled, very contained."

"Naomi? Controlled? Contained?"

"Yes." She paused, waiting while their entrées were served. "I take it she wasn't always, but that's exactly how I'd describe her now."

"How do you feel about her?"

"I don't know. I'm grateful she isn't forcing the issue."

"You surprise me. Patience was never part of her makeup."

"I suppose people can change. I may not understand her, but I do admire her. She knows what she wants and she works for it."

"And what does she want?"

"I'm not sure," Kelsey murmured. "But *she* is."

From the shadows of the bar, Cunningham watched Kelsey and her father talk over their meal. A pretty picture, he thought. All dignity and class. He rattled the ice in his bourbon.

"Quite a looker," Rich Slater said from beside him. "Something familiar about her." He laughed, carefully pacing himself with his own drink. It wouldn't do to muddle his thinking just now. "I guess there's something familiar about all beautiful young women after a man passes a certain age."

"Naomi Chadwick's daughter. Spitting image of her."

"Naomi Chadwick." Rich's eyes gleamed, with pleasure and with bitter memory. He was here, after all, to dredge up memories. And to profit by them. "There's a filly a man doesn't forget. My son's neighbor now. Small world." He enjoyed another swallow of whiskey. Quality stuff—since Cunningham was buying. "You know, I think I saw her around the boy's place a couple of weeks ago. He'd have his eye on her if I know Gabe."

"He's been cozy with the mother. Guess it follows he'd be cozy with the daughter." And Gabe Slater wouldn't have had the chance to be cozy with either, Cunningham thought now, if it hadn't been for a hand of cards. Things would be different.

Things were going to be different.

"If he plays his cards right," Cunningham continued, picking at his own scab, "he could erase the border between the farms."

Rich eyed Kelsey with more interest. So, his son was making time with the ice bitch's daughter. That would be something he could use. "Now, wouldn't that be something? That kind of merger would make them the top outfit in the state, I'd say."

"It might." Cunningham lifted one finger, signaling another round. "Wouldn't care for it myself. I'd just as soon see that connection shaken a bit." He reached into the nut bowl, popped three into his mouth. Casual, he told himself. Keep it casual. It wouldn't do for Rich Slater to know just how much he was banking on the deal. "Now, this business we're talking about. It might just accomplish that in the long term."

Calculating, Rich admired the diamond ring on Cunningham's finger. "And would that extra benefit be worth an appropriate bonus?"

"It would."

"Well now, we'll just see what we can do about that." He shot Kelsey another look. "We'll just see what we can do. I'm going to need those traveling expenses, Billy boy."

Reaching inside his jacket, Cunningham took out an envelope. He slipped it into Rich's eager hands under the bar. The unsettling sense of déjà vu had him glancing over his shoulder. "Count it later."

"No need, no need at all. You and me go back a ways, Billy. I trust you." Once the envelope was safely tucked away, he lifted his glass again. "And may I say it's a pleasure doing business with you again. Here's to old times."

By noon the next day, Kelsey was concentrating on her lesson on the longe line. The five-year-old mare on the other end was patient, and knew a great deal more about the process than she did.

It wasn't the horse being trained, but Kelsey.

"Bring her to a trot, change her direction," Moses demanded. The girl had potential, he'd decided. She wanted to learn, therefore she would. "She'll do anything you want. You get a yearling in there, he won't be so accommodating."

"Then give me a yearling," she called back, and flipped her whip. "I can handle it."

"Keep dreaming." But perhaps in a few weeks he'd assign her one. If she was still around. She had good hands, he mused, a good voice, quick reflexes.

"How long has she been at it?" Naomi asked.

"About thirty minutes."

Naomi rested a boot on the lowest fence rail. "Both Kelsey and the mare still look fresh."

"They've both got stamina."

"I appreciate your taking the time to teach her, Moses."

"It's no hardship. Except I think she's got her eye on my job."

She laughed, then saw he wasn't quite joking. "Do you really think she's that interested in training?"

"Every time I spend an hour with her I feel like a sponge that's been wrung dry. The girl never quits asking questions. I made the mistake of giving her one of my breeding books a few days ago. When she came back with it she all but gave me a goddamned quiz. Pumped me about blood factors, dominant and co-dominant alleles."

"Did you pass?"

"Just. I used to watch you do this." Grinning, he tugged on his earlobe. "Ah, the fantasies. A man without fantasies is a man without a soul. I had a hell of a soul where you were concerned."

"You still do. I'll prove it to you later. Here comes Matt."

"I didn't know you'd sent for the vet."

"I didn't." Naomi ran her tongue around her teeth. "He said he was in the neighborhood and thought he'd stop in to check out that case of sore shins."

Moses glanced back at Kelsey. Ah, the fantasies, he thought again. "Yeah. Right."

Smothering a laugh, Naomi welcomed the vet. "Well, Matt, what's the verdict?"

"She's doing fine. A blister's not necessary."

"Nice of you to take the time to stop by," Moses commented.

"I was over at Longshot. One of his colts was injured."

"Serious?" Naomi asked.

"Could have been. A puncture. It was small, easily overlooked. There was a lot of infection." He kept his eyes on Kelsey as he spoke, admiring. "I had to lance it. Too bad. Jamison said the horse was supposed to ship off to Hialeah tomorrow."

"Three Aces?" Instantly sympathetic, Naomi laid a hand on Matt's arm. "Gabe was going down with him. That horse has been running like a dream."

"They'll both be staying home for now."

"I'll give Gabe a call later. Try to cheer him up."

"He could use it." Matt switched his attention back to Kelsey. "Everyone seems healthy around here." When Kelsey acknowledged him with a quick wave, he grinned. "She looks like she's been doing that all her life."

When Moses took pity on him and signaled Kelsey to stop, she walked the horse over to the fence. "She's so sweet-natured." She rubbed her cheek against the mare's. "I wish you'd give me a brat, Moses, so I could feel I was accomplishing something."

"All journeys begin with one step. We'll see how many more you take before you trip."

"He's always boosting my confidence." She tipped back the cotton cap she wore. "Well, Matt, is this a professional or a social visit?"

"A mix. I had to stop in at Longshot."

"Oh?" As casually as possible, Kelsey led the mare out of the paddock. "Problem?"

"An injury." He repeated his explanation.

"But Three Aces looked wonderful the last time I saw him run. When did it happen?"

"From the look of it, three or four days ago."

"He ran at Charles Town three days ago. Won by a full length." Frowning, she stroked the mare. "A puncture?"

"About the size of a sixpenny nail, just above the fetlock."

"How does that happen?"

"Could have happened in transport, some sharp edge. That's likely. Unlikely it was deliberate."

"You mean that someone might have injured the colt so he couldn't run, or worse."

"Unlikely," Matt repeated. "It wasn't that serious."

"How do you treat it?"

She listened carefully as he spoke of lancing and antiseptics, the difference between punctures and tears.

"See what I mean?" Moses muttered to Naomi. "She'll be cramming veterinary books next." His eyes narrowed as he looked toward the stables. "Expecting anyone?"

"No." Naomi pursed her lips and studied the young man approaching. Lean, narrow-shouldered, pretty face. Levi's and a sweatshirt. Ordinary enough, she mused. But the boots gave him away. They would have cost a cool three hundred.

"Anyone know the cowboy?"

"Hmm?" Curious, Kelsey turned, then let out a shout of pleasure. "Channing!" She raced forward, cracking Matt's heart when she threw her arms around the young man. "What are you doing here?"

"Thought I'd check the place out before I head down to Lauderdale. Spring break."

"Haven't you outgrown that yet?"

"Outgrown girls in bikinis? I don't think so. Man, look at you. You look like an ad for country living." He slung an arm around her shoulders and glanced at the trio by the fence. "Don't tell me that's your mother."

"That's Naomi. Come on, I'll introduce you." She kept her arm around his waist. "Channing, this is Naomi Chadwick, Moses Whitetree, and Matt Gunner. Channing Osborne, my stepbrother."

"Welcome to Three Willows." Naomi extended a hand, amused and charmed when Channing brought it to his lips. "Kelsey's told me about you."

"Only the good parts, I hope. You've got a great place here."

"Thanks. We'll give you a tour. I hope you can stay a while."

"I'm loose." Unable to resist, he reached over the fence to stroke a hand down the mare's nose. "Just heading down to Florida for a week or so."

"To ogle coeds," Kelsey put in. "Channing's in pre-med, so he calls it anatomy lessons."

He grinned and reached up to scratch the mare's ears. "Hey, youth is fleeting. Ask anyone. Am I breaking something up?"

"Not at all," Naomi assured him. "You're just in time for lunch. Matt, you'll join us, won't you?"

"Wish I could. I've got to get over to the Bartlett farm. One of their foals is colicky."

"Hey, you're a vet?" Channing perked up. "I always thought it would be cool to treat animals. They don't complain as much as people, right?" he added quickly when Kelsey shot him a surprised look.

"There's that. But people don't generally bite and kick. I'll take a rain check, Naomi, thanks. Kelsey, good to see you again. Nice to meet you."

"I'll walk you up. Kelsey, bring Channing along when you're ready."

"If I know you, you're ready now. Want to take that tour after you eat?"

"Sounds good to me."

"I didn't know you were interested in animal medicine."

He shrugged, embarrassed. "Just in passing. It's a kid thing."

They began to walk slowly. "I remember you wanting to save birds when they bashed into the picture window. And that old fleabag mutt you brought home one time, with the limp?"

"Yeah." He smiled, but the humor didn't reach his eyes. "Mom put the skids on that. Off to the pound. I guess he walked the last mile on three legs."

"I'd forgotten that." She laid her head against his shoulder. "She was afraid he'd turn. He must have been a hundred years old."

"He wasn't a pureblood," Channing corrected, then shrugged. "No big deal. She could never handle animals around the house with her allergies. Besides, like I said, it was a kid thing."

Why hadn't she ever heard that resigned tone in his voice before? she wondered. Maybe she hadn't listened to it. "Do you want to be a doctor, Channing?"

"Family tradition," he said easily. "I never thought about being anything else. Oh, except for an astronaut when I was six. Osborne men are surgeons, and that's that."

"Candace would never push you into doing something if she knew your heart wasn't in it."

With a half laugh Channing stopped and looked at her. "Kels, you were eighteen when they got married, and you had one foot out the door. Mom runs things. She does it subtly and she does it well. But me and the Prof, we pretty much do what we're told."

"You're angry with her over something. What is it?"

"Hell, she yanked the allowance from my trust fund because I balked at taking a full course load this summer. I wanted to work, you know. Get a taste of the real world. I had a construction gig lined up. You know, so I could wear a hard hat and make rude kissy noises at the secretaries who walked by at lunchtime. I just wanted a couple of months away from the books."

"That sounds reasonable enough. Maybe if I talk to her for you . . . ?"

"No, she's not too happy with you at the moment, either. This business," he said, gesturing to encompass the farm. "She sees it as a strain on the Prof. The Magnificent Milicent is feeding that little neurosis."

Kelsey blew out a breath. "So, we're in the same boat. Listen, are you really set on Lauderdale and bikinis?"

"If you're about to suggest that I go home, kiss and make up—"

"No. I was going to suggest that you spend spring break here. I don't think Naomi would object if you hung out with me and the horses."

"Playing big sister?"

"Yeah, got a problem with it?"

"No." He leaned down and kissed her forehead. "Thanks, Kels."

9

The groom's name was Mick. He'd been born and bred in Virginia and liked to boast that he'd forgotten more about horses than most people ever learned. It might have been true. Certainly throughout his fifty-odd years as a racetracker he'd tried every aspect of the game. In the early years he'd risen from stableboy to exercise boy. He often boasted of how he'd gotten up on horses for Mr. Cunningham during the man's heyday.

Before he'd hit twenty, he'd still been small and light enough to jockey. Though he'd never moved from apprentice to journeyman, he'd worn the silks. He didn't like people to forget it.

For a short unmemorable time, he'd bluffed his way into the trainer's position at a small farm in Florida. He'd even owned a gelding for a year—or at least fifteen percent of one. Maybe the horse had never lived up to his potential, proving himself to be nothing more than a Morning Glory who worked out fast and raced slow. But Mick had been an owner, and that was the important thing.

He'd come back to Cunningham's when he'd heard the farm had changed hands. His position as groom satisfied him, particularly since Gabriel Slater had the look of a winner. And always had, in Mick's memory.

He enjoyed the fact that the younger hands often deferred to him. They might have called him Peacock behind his back because he always sported a bright blue cap and tended to strut. But it was done with affection.

His thin, lined face was known at every track from Santa Anita to Pimlico. That was just the way Mick wanted it.

"Track's slow," Boggs commented, and meticulously rolled a cigarette.

Mick nodded. The hard morning rain had tapered off to an incessant drizzle, and that was fine. Slater's Double or Nothing shone on a muddy track.

It was the slow time between workout and post. Mick sat under an overhang watching the rain drip from the eaves and thinking about the ten dollars burning a hole in his pocket. He figured to put it on Double's nose and watch it grow.

He pulled out a crumpled pack of Marlboros to join Boggs in a smoke.

It was quiet. The jockeys would be in their quarters, or taking a steam to sweat off one more pound before post time. The trainers would be poring over the books, and the owners huddled inside, enjoying the dry warmth and coffee. There was little activity around the shedrow, but it would liven up again soon.

"Funny seeing Miss Naomi's girl around," Mick said conversationally. "She rode over to Longshot a couple of weeks ago, rode off again soaking wet."

Boggs nodded, blew out smoke. "Heard."

"She was up on that roan gelding of yours. Handled him fine."

"Rides like her mother. Makes a picture."

They sat, two lifelong bachelors, and smoked in silence.

A full five minutes passed before Mick spoke again. "Somebody else came by the barn that day."

"Yeah?" Boggs wouldn't ask who. It wasn't the way they communicated.

"Haven't seen him around for a while, but I recognized him, all right." He tossed the minute stub of his cigarette into a puddle and watched it sizzle out. "Forgot his connection with the man till I seen them together. Hit me then, all right. I remember when Mr. Slater was working as a stableboy for Mr. Cunningham."

"Yep. About fifteen years ago. Came over to Three Willows after. Stayed a time."

"Year or two. Hard worker, didn't chew your ear off. Still doesn't say nothing 'less it's supposed to be said. Always was a loner." He chuckled a bit. "Never did think I'd be working for him."

"Made something of himself."

"That he did. Lots wouldn't think he coulda done it, the way he used to hang around and hustle up card games. Just another track rat, they'd figure. But I knew different."

"Always liked the boy myself." Boggs rubbed at a bruise on his forearm where a yearling had nipped him. "Had a look about him. Still does."

"Yeah. I was there the day Lipsky tried to stick him. Didn't say no more than he had to then, either."

Boggs spat on the wet ground, more an assessment of Lipsky than out of necessity. "Man's got no business being drunk and handling a stud."

"That's the truth." Mick fell silent again, thought idly about lighting up another smoke. "Mr. Slater, he's got no use for drunks. I forgot how his father used to slide into the bottle till I saw him 'round the barn that day."

"Rich Slater?" Boggs's interest perked up. "He came around Longshot?"

"That's what I'm telling you. The day Miss Naomi's girl rode off wet. Had himself all polished up like a Bible salesman." To better enjoy the relay of information, Mick decided to indulge in that second smoke. "They talked for a little bit. Couldn't hear what Mr. Slater had to say. No reading that boy's face either. Gambler's eyes he's got." He chuffed out smoke, then inhaled deeply, secure in his old friend's interest. "You could hear the old man, though, a-laughing and a-jawing about how he was in the money and he'd just come by to see how his boy was doing."

"Come by to soak him, more likely."

"Gotta figure it. Didn't like the way he was looking 'round the place, like he was adding up figures on a computer. Polly had a yearling on the longe. Inside Straight, Mr. Slater named him. That Polly's got fine hands, she does."

"She does," Boggs agreed, seeing nothing odd about Mick's circuitous story. He nodded a greeting to one of the track grooms as the man passed. "A good yearling manager. Might be Moses is grooming Miss Kelsey for that at Three Willows. Old Chip's talking about retiring again."

"Always is. Just blowing smoke. So"—Mick rounded back to his point. "Mr. Slater, he goes on up to the house. Old Rich, he hangs around, sipping outta his flask. Silver one, shiny. He corners Jamison for a while. Pumping him, I figure. Then Mr. Slater, he comes back, gives the old man a check, and boots him out. Subtle-like, but he gave him the boot for all that."

"Never had much use for Rich Slater."

"Me neither. Some say the apple it don't fall far from the tree. But with these two I figure it took a long roll. He's got class, Mr. Slater does. And he listens when you tell him something. Asks me the other day what I might think about that puncture in Three Aces' foreleg."

"That's a good horse."

"He is that. So I tell Mr. Slater it don't look like no accident to me. He just looks, and he thanks me, real polite-like." He rose, bones creaking. "I'm gonna take me a look at Double."

"I think I'll get me some coffee."

They parted, Mick wandering into the gloom of the stables. The rain drummed on the roof, muffling the sounds of horses shifting in their boxes. Another groom was adjusting a blanket on a filly. Mick stopped a moment, studying the lines.

A little wide-fronted, he decided. The filly would probably paddle. No problem like that with Double. He was an even sixteen hands high, pure black with well-sloped shoulders and a short, strong body that had plenty of heart room.

Most of all, Double had courage.

Mick sauntered back toward the box. He liked to give Double a little pep talk before a race. And to look into the colt's eyes and see if it was a day to put a bet down.

"Well now, boy, we called out some rain just for you." Mick opened the box door, and scowled. "What the hell you doing in here, Lipsky? You got no business around Mr. Slater's horse."

Lipsky remained crouched, and eyed Mick as he ran a hand up and down Double's leg. "Just taking a look. Thought I might lay down a bet."

"You go ahead and do that, but you clear out."

"I'm going. I'm going." Lipsky angled his body away, but Mick's eyes were keen.

"What the hell you doing with that?" In one fierce move, Mick clamped a hand on Lipsky's arm. The knife glinted, thin-bladed and bright in the dim light. "You bastard. Going to cut him, were you?"

"I wasn't going to hurt him." Wary, Lipsky shifted his eyes over the door of the box. There wasn't much time. "I was just going to fix it so he wouldn't race today." Or ever, he thought, once he'd severed a tendon. "Slater's got it coming."

"You got what you had coming," Mick corrected. "And nobody messes with my horses. You lowlife, you did Three Aces, too."

"Don't know what you're talking about. Look, it was a bad idea. No harm done, though. You can see for yourself I never touched him."

"I'll take a look, all right. Now we'll go see what Mr. Slater wants done about this."

Lipsky jerked back, furious that the scrawny old man had such an iron grip. "You ain't turning me in."

"The hell I ain't. I'm turning you in, and you put a mark on this colt, I'll spit on your grave if Mr. Slater decides to kill you."

"I ain't touched his fucking horse." Desperate, Lipsky struck out. As the two men began to grapple, Double danced nervously to the side.

The knife sliced through the air, and deflected by Mick's forearm, the point nipped across the colt's flank. Shocked by the pain, Double reared. Mick cursed and drew in the breath to shout. Then there was no air at all as the blade plunged in, just above his belt.

"Jesus." As stunned as his opponent, Lipsky yanked the blade free and stared at the spreading blood. "Jesus Christ, Mick. I didn't mean to stick you."

"Bastard," Mick managed. He stumbled forward just as the colt, aroused and terrified by the scent of blood, reared. A hoof caught Mick at the base of the skull. After one bright flash of pain, he felt nothing, even when he fell face forward and the colt's thrashing hooves trampled him.

Panic nearly had Lipsky racing from the box, but he held on, cowering in the corner. It wasn't his fault, he told himself. Hell, he wasn't no murderer. He'd never have pulled a knife on Old Mick, especially seeing as he was stone-cold sober. If Mick had just listened, it wouldn't have happened. Wiping his fist across his sweaty mouth, he backed toward the door. He eased the bloody knife into his boot before slipping silently out of the box. Back hunched, he hurried out into the rain.

He needed a drink.

"This is great." Channing stood in the wet grandstands, eating a hot dog. "I mean," he said through a mouthful, "who'd have thought there was so much to it? It's been like watching rehearsals for some hot Broadway play."

Charmed by him, Naomi smiled. If she could have handpicked a sibling for her daughter, it would have been Channing Osborne. "I'm sorry we couldn't provide better weather."

"Hey, it just adds to the drama. Horses thundering through the rain, colors flying, mud spewing." He grinned and washed down the hot dog with Coke. "I can't wait."

"Well, it won't be long now," Kelsey assured him. "In fact, they must be about ready to prep the horses for the post parade. You want to go take a look?"

"Sure. It's really nice of you to let me hang out, Naomi."

"I'm just glad you chose us over sun, sand, and bikinis."

"This is better." In a gesture she found charming, he offered her his arm. "When I get back next week, I can brag to all my sunburned, hungover pals how I juggled two gorgeous women."

"What about the vegetarian?" Kelsey asked him.

"Who, Victoria?" His grin was quick and careless. "She dumped me when she realized I was an unconvertible carnivore."

"Very shortsighted of her," Naomi decided.

"That's what I said. I'm a prize, right, Kels?" He glanced down at his stepsister and saw that her attention was focused elsewhere. Well, well, he thought, studying Gabe. He hadn't seen that look in Kelsey's eyes for a long, long time. "Somebody you know?"

"Hmmm? Oh." Distracted, she reached up to adjust the brim of her cap. "Just a neighbor."

Gabe broke off his conversation with Jamison and turned to watch them approach. Damn, the woman looked good wet. He shifted his gaze from her to the man with his arm around her shoulder.

Too young to be competition, he decided. He doubted if the guy was old enough to buy beer. But there was a territorial sense in the drape of the arm and a look in the eyes that was a combination of curiosity and warning.

The stepbrother, Gabe concluded, and he stepped forward to meet them.

"Haven't you dried off yet?" he said to Kelsey, and watched the vague annoyance flit over her face.

"It's a new day, Slater. This is Channing Osborne, Gabriel Slater."

"It's nice you could pay your sister a visit."

"I thought so."

It amused Gabe that Channing increased his grip several unnecessary degrees for the handshake. "How's the mare, Naomi? I've been meaning to come by and take a look myself."

"She's definitely in foal. And healthy. I heard about Three Aces when Matt stopped by yesterday. Is he healing well?"

Gabe's thoughts darkened, but his eyes remained placid. "Yeah. He'll be back in top form in a few weeks."

"You've got Double or Nothing running today, don't you?"

Gabe looked back at Kelsey. Because he wanted to touch her, and to irritate her, he skimmed a knuckle down her cheek. "Keeping track of the competition, darling?"

"You could say that. Your colt's running head to head with ours."

"Want another side bet? You still owe me ten."

"Fine. In the spirit of things, we'll say... double or nothing."

"You're on. Want to take a look at the winner?"

"I've already seen Virginia's Pride, thanks."

He grinned, took her hand. "Come on."

As he tugged her away, Channing frowned. "Has that been going on long?"

"I'm beginning to think so." Looking after them, Naomi rubbed her wet nose. "Does it worry you?"

"She took the whole divorce thing hard. I don't want somebody taking advantage of that. How much do you know about him?"

"Quite a bit, really." Naomi sighed. "I'll fill you in later. Now I suppose we'll go with them so you can stop worrying."

"Good idea." He glanced down at her as they walked into the barn. "You're okay, Naomi."

Pleased, she took his hand. "So are you, Channing."

"You know I want to whip your butt out on the track, Slater, but I am sorry about Three Aces. I don't suppose there's anything I can do, but..."

"Fallen for them, haven't you?"

Kelsey tipped up her brim to get a better look at him. "For who?"

"The horses."

She shrugged and continued to walk toward the rear of the stables. "So what if I have?"

"It looks good on you, the way it softens you up." Deliberately he slowed her down. He wanted another moment before they reached the box. "When are you coming back?"

She didn't pretend to misunderstand him, but she did choose to evade. "I've been busy. Moses gives us a lot to do."

"Would you rather I came to you?"

"No." Edgy, she glanced over her shoulder. Naomi and Channing were only a few paces behind. "No," she repeated. "And this isn't the time to discuss it."

"Do you think your brother would go for my throat if I scooped you up and kissed you right here?"

"Certainly not." Dignity was failing her. "But I might."

"You're tempting me, Kelsey." Instead, he brought her hand to his lips. "Tonight," he murmured. "I want to see you tonight."

"I've got company, Gabe. Channing's visiting."

"Tonight," Gabe repeated. "You come to me, or I come to you. Your choice." He stopped at the box, keeping her hand in his. "Hello, boy. Ready to . . ." He trailed off as he spotted the line of blood, still red and fresh against the black coat. "Goddammit."

He yanked open the door and had hardly taken a step inside before he saw the body crumpled in the bedding.

"Stay back." Without looking, he flung out an arm to block Kelsey.

"What happened to him? The poor thing's bleeding." Focused on the colt, she pressed forward. When Gabe was forced to snatch at the halter to keep the horse from rearing, she saw the form sprawled in the bloody hay. "Oh, God. Oh, my God, Gabe."

"Hold him!" Snapping out the order, Gabe wrapped Kelsey's limp fingers around the halter.

"What is it?" Alarmed by the pallor of Kelsey's cheeks, Naomi surged forward. The breath hissed between her teeth. "I'll call an ambulance." She pressed her hand over Kelsey's. "Can you handle this?"

Kelsey blinked, nodded, then cleared her throat. "Yes, yes, I'm all right." But she was squeamish enough to keep her back to what lay in the corner of the box.

"Oh, man." Channing swallowed hard, then put himself between Kelsey and Gabe, who crouched over the body. "I'm only pre-med," he said quietly, and squatted down. "But maybe . . ."

It took only one close look to realize that he could have been as skilled and experienced a surgeon as his father had been, and he would still have been helpless.

There was blood everywhere, pools of it coagulating in the stained hay. The gouge in the back of the skull had welled with it. A bright blue cap, now streaked with red, lay partially under the bedding.

"That horse must have gone crazy," Channing said grimly. "Kelsey, get out of here. Get away from him."

"No, I've got him." Fighting to keep her breath even, she stroked the colt's neck. "He's shaking. He's terrified."

"Dammit. He just killed this guy!"

"No, he didn't." Gabe's voice was low and hard. He'd gently rolled Mick over. The groom's pulled-up shirt exposed a vicious stab wound in the abdomen. "But somebody did."

. . .

Later, Kelsey stood shivering in the drizzle trying to pretend she was drinking the coffee Channing had pressed on her.

"You should get away from here," he said again. "Let me take you home, or at least inside the clubhouse."

"No, I'm all right. I need to wait. That poor man." She looked away, out into the shedrow. It didn't seem energetic or glamorous now. It was simply muddy, dreary. People were gathered in tight little groups, eyeing the barn, waiting. "Gabe's been in there a long time with the police."

"He can handle himself." He glanced over to where Naomi sat on a barrel, under an overhang. "Maybe you should go over with your mother. She looks really spooked."

Kelsey stared at the entrance to the barn. She wanted to be in there, to hear what was being said, to know what was being done. "Gabe and I found him," she murmured. "I feel like I should help."

"Then go help Naomi."

Kelsey let out a long breath. "All right. You're right." But it was hard to walk over, to face that blank look in Naomi's eyes. "Here." She held out her untouched coffee. "Brandy'd be better, but I don't have any handy."

"Thanks." Naomi accepted the cup and forced herself to sip. It had nothing to do with her, she reminded herself again. The police wouldn't come, they wouldn't take her away this time. "Poor Mick."

"Did you know him very well?"

"He's been around a long time." She sipped again. No, it didn't have that slapping warmth of brandy, but it helped. "He and Boggs played gin rummy once a week, gossiping like little old ladies. I guess Mick knew as much about my horses as he knew about Gabe's. He was loyal." She drew in a shaky breath. "And he was harmless. I don't know who could have done this to him."

"The police will find out." After a moment's hesitation she laid a hand on Naomi's shoulder. "Do you want me to take you home?"

"No." Naomi reached up, covered her daughter's hand with hers. They both realized it was the first time they'd touched without reservation. "I'm sorry, Kelsey. This is a horrible experience for you."

"For all of us."

"I would have spared you from it." She looked up, her eyes meeting Kelsey's. "I'm not much good under these circumstances."

"Then I'll have to be." Kelsey turned her hand so that their fingers meshed. Naomi's were stiff with cold. "You're going home," she said firmly. "The police may want to talk to me, so Channing will take you."

"I don't want to leave you here alone."

"I'm not alone. Gabe's here, and Moses. Boggs." She glanced over to where the old man stood alone in the rain, grieving. "It's pointless for you to stay when you're so upset. You go home, take a hot bath, and lie down. I'll come up as soon as I get back." She softened her tone, leaned closer. "And I don't want Channing here. He'd feel as if he was doing some manly act if he took you away."

"That was a nice touch." Hating herself for the weakness, Naomi rose. "All right, I'll go. My being around a crime scene only causes more speculation in any case, but please, don't stay any longer than you have to."

"I won't. Don't worry."

Alone, Kelsey settled down on the barrel her mother had vacated and prepared to wait.

It didn't take long.

A uniformed officer stepped outside, scanned the groups of people, and focused in on her. "Miss Byden? Kelsey Byden?"

"Yes."

"The lieutenant would like to speak with you. Inside."

"All right." She ignored the speculative looks and slid off the barrel.

Inside, the routine of death was already under way. The last police photos had been taken, the yellow tape cordoning off the far end of the barn was in place.

Gabe's eyes blazed once when he spotted her. "I told you there was no need for her to be here."

"You both found the body, Mr. Slater." Lieutenant Rossi stepped over the tape and nodded to Kelsey. He was a twenty-year veteran of the force with a craggy, handsome face and sharp cop's eyes. His hair, dark and thick and streaked with dignified gray, was only one of his many vanities. His body was a temple, fueled with vitamins, health juices, and a stringent low-fat diet, and honed by exercise.

He might spend most of his time behind a desk with a phone at his ear, but it didn't mean he had to go to seed.

He loved his work, and thrived on procedure. And he hated murder.

"Ms. Byden, I appreciate your waiting."

"I want to cooperate."

"Good. You could start by telling me exactly what happened this morning. You were here since dawn."

"That's right." She told him everything, from unloading the horses through the morning workouts. "We stayed down at the track awhile. It was my stepbrother's first trip, and we decided that he might like to watch the horses being prepped for post time."

"And that would have been about what time?"

"Close to noon. Things are quiet between about ten and noon. We walked up here from the track and ran into Gabe. He was in the shedrow, talking to his trainer."

She glanced over Rossi's shoulder to look for him, and saw with dull horror the shiny plastic bag being carried out on a stretcher.

Cursing under his breath Gabe ducked beneath the tape and blocked her view. "This doesn't have to be done now. And certainly not here."

"No, it's all right." Gamely, Kelsey swallowed her nausea. "I'd rather get it over with."

"I appreciate that. So, you ran into Mr. Slater just outside here?"

"Yes. We talked for a few minutes, ragged each other because we had a horse running in the same race. I came in with Gabe to look at his colt. My mother and stepbrother were a little behind us."

"Your mother?"

"Yes. It was actually her horse that was to run against Gabe's. She owns Three Willows. Naomi Chadwick."

"Chadwick." It rang a distant bell. Rossi jotted it down. "So the four of you came in."

"Yes, but they were behind us a bit. They didn't get to the box until after—after we did. I guess Gabe and I saw the wound on the colt's left flank at the same time. He went in, and stopped, tried to block me. But I was worried about the colt, so I followed behind him. I saw the blood, and the body in the corner. I held the horse's head because he was starting to rear, and Channing and Naomi came up. She went right away to call an ambulance and Channing went into the box, thinking, I suppose, that he might be able to help. I thought—I suppose we *all* thought for a moment—that the horse had done it. Until Gabe turned the body over, and we saw . . ." She would never forget what she'd seen. "We saw he hadn't. Gabe told Channing to call the police."

"And there was no one around the stall when you and Mr. Slater came in."

"No. I didn't see anyone. Some of the grooms were inside, of course. But it was still a little early for prepping."

"Did you know the deceased, Ms. Byden?"

"No. But I've only been at Three Willows for a few weeks."

"You don't live there?"

"No, I live in Maryland. I'm just spending a month or so there."

"I'll need your permanent address for the record, then." When she gave it to him, he slipped his pad back into his pocket. "I appreciate your time, Ms. Byden. I'd like to talk to your mother and your step-brother now."

"I had Channing take her home. She was very upset." In an unconscious move, Kelsey shifted her stance, placing her feet a bit wider, straightening her shoulders. "In any case, they were both with me all morning. Neither of them could have seen anything I didn't."

"You'd be surprised what one person sees that another doesn't. Thank you." He dismissed her by turning back to Gabe. "My information is that a man named Boggs might have been the last person to see the victim alive. Does he also work for you?"

"He works for Three Willows."

"He's outside," Kelsey informed Rossi. "I'll tell him to come in." She hurried out, eager to be away from the flat-voiced questions and shrewd eyes. Boggs was where she'd seen him last, simply standing in the rain. "There's a Lieutenant Rossi who wants to speak to you." She took his hands, vainly trying to warm them between hers. "I'm so sorry, Boggs."

"We was just talking. Just sitting over there and talking. We had a card game on for tonight." Tears streamed down his face along with the rain. "Who'da done that to him, Miss Kelsey? Who'da done Old Mick that way?"

"I don't know, Boggs. Come on, I'll go in with you." She slipped her arm around him and guided him back toward the barn.

"He don't have no family, Miss Kelsey. A sister, but he hadn't seen her in more'n twenty years. I've got to take care of things for him, see that he gets buried proper."

"I'll take care of it, Boggs." Gabe stepped outside, intercepting them before they entered. "You tell me what you want him to have, and we'll arrange it."

Boggs nodded. It was only right. "He thought high of you, Mr. Slater."

"I thought high of him. Come and see me as soon as you're able. We'll set everything up."

"He'da appreciated it." Head bowed, Boggs walked inside.

"The lieutenant says you're free to go." Gabe took Kelsey's arm and steered her away. "I'll take you home."

"I should wait for Boggs. He shouldn't be alone now."

"Moses will see to him. I want you out of here, Kelsey. Away from it."

"I can't be. I'm as close to it as you are."

"You're wrong." He half dragged her across the muddy shedrow. "The box is mine. The colt is mine. And, dammit, Mick was mine."

"Slow down!" She dug in her heels and managed to grab him by the jacket. He might have shown little more than a flare or two of emotion inside the barn, but he was on slow burn now and ready for flash point. No cool gambler's eyes now, she thought. They were hot and lethal.

"You're getting out of here now. And you're staying out of it."

She could have argued. She certainly could have struggled against the grip he had on her arm. But she waited until they'd reached his car.

Then she simply turned and wrapped her arms around him. "Don't do this to yourself," she murmured.

He held himself rigid, prepared to jerk away and shove her into the car. "Do what?"

"Don't blame yourself, Gabe."

"Who else?" But his body relaxed, and curled itself to hers. He pressed his face into the cool, damp comfort of her hair. "Jesus, Kelsey, who else am I going to blame? He was trying to protect my horse."

"You can't know that."

"I feel it." He drew her away. His eyes were calmer now, but whatever was going on just behind that deep, cool blue had Kelsey trembling. "And I'm going to find whoever did this to him. Whatever it takes."

"The police—"

"Work their way. I work mine."

10

Death couldn't interfere with the routine of a thoroughbred farm. Not the death of a horse, or a man. Dawn still signaled workouts. There were races to be run, legs to be wrapped, coats to be quartered and strapped. Talk around the paddocks or shedrow at sunrise might have been of murder and Old Mick, but the pace didn't flag. It couldn't.

There was a foal with a case of eczema, a yearling filly who still refused a rider, and a colt competing in a maiden race. Grieving and gossip had to be accomplished while filling feed tubs and walking hots.

"Maybe you want to see to strapping Pride now that he's been cooled, Miss Kelsey." Though his eyes were shadowed, his face drawn, Boggs was up and about his duties. He offered Kelsey the reins. "He always seems happier when you do it."

"All right, Boggs." Her hand covered his gnarled one. "Is there anything I can do for you?"

His eyes drifted past her as they focused on something private. "Ain't nothing to do, Miss Kelsey. Just don't seem right, that's all. Don't seem right."

She simply couldn't turn away. "Would you mind coming with me? I'm still a little nervous about grooming the next Derby winner."

They both knew it was an excuse, but Boggs nodded and trudged along beside her. It was raining again, the same slow, incessant drizzle that had marred the previous afternoon. Though it was closing in on ten A.M., the mist hung stubbornly. Inside the barn, stableboys were busy mucking out, so the air was perfumed with the smells of manure, hay, and mud.

At Queenie's box, Kelsey paused and handed the colt's reins back to Boggs. "This'll only take a minute."

She took a carrot out of her back pocket, offering it to the mare while she nuzzled the soft ears. "There you go, old lady. You didn't think I'd forget, did you?" The mare nibbled the carrot, then Kelsey's shoulder, curving her neck in response to the caress. Though she was aware of Boggs's interest, Kelsey completed what had become a daily routine with a kiss on Queenie's cheek.

"I know, I've already taken plenty of ribbing about female equiphilia." After a last pat, Kelsey turned back to Boggs and the colt. "And maybe I'm hooked, but I've caught more than one male groom cozying up to a horse."

"Your granddaddy loved that mare." Boggs led Pride to his box where Kelsey had already cleaned out the soiled night bedding and replaced it with clean wheat straw for day. "He'd sneak her sugar cubes every afternoon. We all pretended not to notice."

"What was he like, Boggs?"

"He was a good man, fair. He had a quick temper in him and could crack like lightning." As he spoke, his eyes scanned the box, noting that Kelsey had seen to the colt's fresh water and hay net. His job usually, but he was sharing it with her, as he shared the colt. "Wouldn't tolerate laziness, no sir, but if you did your work you got paid well and on time. Known him to sit up all night with a sick horse and to fire a man on the spot for a shoddy grooming."

Kelsey crouched down, running her hands down Pride's legs to check for swellings or injuries. Boggs had already washed the leg wraps and hung them with the clothespins he kept clipped to his pant leg.

"Sounds as though he was a hard man to work for." Satisfied, she rubbed the light dampness of rain from the colt with straw.

"Not if you did what you was hired to do." He watched as she took the dandy brush from Pride's grooming kit. "You've got the touch, Miss Kelsey," he said after a moment.

"I feel as though I've been doing this all my life." She soothed the colt with murmurs and strokes as he shifted and shied. His temperament, like most aristocrats, was high-strung. "He's a little restless this morning."

"Sharp's what he is. His mind's already at the starting gate."

Kelsey continued to remove mud from the colt's saddle area, belly, and fetlocks. "I'm told he ran well yesterday." She set the dandy brush aside and took up a hoof pick. "I guess it seems cold, thinking about races and times after yesterday."

"Can't be no other way."

"You were friends with him a long time."

"About forty years." Boggs took out a tin of tobacco and helped himself to a pinch. "He was already an old hand when I come along."

"I've never lost anyone close to me." Kelsey thought of Naomi, but it was impossible to remember whatever grief she'd felt at three. "I don't want to say I can imagine what you must be feeling, but I know if you want some time off, Naomi would give it to you."

"No place else I'd rather be than here. That policeman, he had a look about him. He'll find who done that to Mick."

Kelsey dampened a sponge and wiped the colt's eyes, outward from the corners. She enjoyed the way he looked at her while she tended to him, the recognition and the trust they'd begun to build between them. "Lieutenant Rossi. I didn't like him. I don't know why."

"Well, there's cold blood in there. But cold blood means he'll think, and keep thinking step by step till it's done."

Kelsey set the sponge aside and picked up the body brush and currycomb. She remembered the light in Gabe's eyes. There had been a need for revenge there, she decided. And she understood the sentiment too well. "Will that be enough for you, Boggs?"

"It'll have to be."

"There you are." Channing leaned against the box door. He watched her a moment, the steady hands, the new muscles working in her shoulders. "You look just like you know what you're doing."

"I do know what I'm doing." And the fact never failed to delight her. "Missed you at breakfast."

"Overslept." His grin was more charming than sheepish. "My body clock's not used to eating at five A.M. Listen, Matt dropped by. I'm going to go hang out with him on a couple of house calls. Barn calls. Whatever."

"Have fun."

He hesitated. "You're okay, right?"

"Sure, I'm okay."

"I'll be back in a couple of hours. Oh, and Moses said if I found you, he wants you back on the longe line."

"Slave driver," she muttered. "As soon as I'm finished here."

She had no time to brood. A thorough strapping of a horse took an experienced groom an hour, and Kelsey about a quarter hour longer. Then it was time for the midday feeding, oats, bran, and nuts that needed to be mixed, measured, weighed. She added a tablespoon of salt, Pride's vitamin supplement, and electrolytes. Because he tended to be a finicky eater, she treated him to a helping of molasses to sweeten the feed.

Later, she would bring him an apple. Not just to spoil him, she thought. Moses had explained that horses required succulents added to their feed. Pride preferred apples to carrots. He had a taste for the tart Granny Smith variety.

"Now you're set," she murmured when he settled into his midday meal. "And you eat it all, hear?"

He munched, eyeing her.

"We've got a lot riding on you, sweetheart. And I think you'd like standing in the winner's circle with a blanket of red roses."

He snorted, what Kelsey took as the equine equivalent of a shrug. She chuckled, giving him one last caress. "You can't fool me, boy. You want it as much as we do."

Rolling her shoulders, she left the barn to face the rest of the day's work.

She doubted that Moses had anything sadistic in mind when he whipped her through the morning, but the result was the same. By three, her still developing muscles were sore, she was covered with mud, and her system was sending out urgent signals for fuel.

After thoroughly scraping her boots, she went into the house through the kitchen and headed straight for the refrigerator. With a little cry of pleasure, she pounced on a platter of fried chicken.

She had her mouth full of drumstick when Gertie came in. "Miss Kelsey!" Outraged by the sight of her little girl leaning against the counter in filthy jeans, Gertie bustled to a cupboard for a plate. "That's no way to eat."

"It's working for me," Kelsey said with her mouth full. "This is great, the best chicken I've had in my entire life." She swallowed. "This is my second piece."

"Sit down at the table. I'll fix you a proper lunch."

"No, really." Sometimes manners simply didn't apply. Kelsey bit in again. "I'm too dirty to sit anywhere, and too hungry to clean up first. Gertie, I've taken three cooking courses, one of them at the Cordon Bleu, and I could never make chicken like this."

Flushing delightedly, Gertie waved a hand. "Sure you could. It was my mama's recipe. I'll walk you through it sometime."

"Well, you outdo the Colonel all to hell." At Gertie's blank look, Kelsey laughed. "Kentucky Fried. Gertie, I could compose a sonnet to this drumstick."

"Go on. You're teasing me." Red as a beet now, Gertie poured Kelsey a glass of milk. "Just like that brother of yours. Why, you'd think the boy hadn't eaten a home-cooked meal in his life."

"He's been in here charming you out of house and home, hasn't he?"

"I like to see a boy with a healthy appetite."

"He's got that." And so, Kelsey thought, did she, as she debated whether or not to eat one more piece. "Is Naomi around?"

"Had to go out."

"Mmm." So, Kelsey thought, it was just the two of them. Perhaps it was time she took advantage of the opportunity and asked Gertie some questions. "I've wondered, Gertie, about that night. Alec Bradley."

Gertie's face sobered. "That's done and gone."

"You weren't home," Kelsey prodded gently.

"No." Gertie picked up a dishcloth and began polishing the already spotless range. "And I've cursed myself every day for it. There we were, my mama and me, at the movies and eating pizza pie while Miss Naomi was all alone with that man."

"You didn't like him."

"Hmmph." She sniffed and slapped her rag on the stove. "Slick he was. Slick like you'd slide right off if you was to put a hand on him. Miss Naomi had no business with the likes of him."

"Why do you suppose she . . . went around with him?"

"Had her reasons, I suppose. She's got a stubborn streak does Miss Naomi. And I expect she was feeling stubborn about your daddy. Then she was feeling low about losing a horse at the track. He went down and they had to shoot him. She took that hard. That'd be about the time she was seeing that man."

Gertie's derision was plain. She refused, had always refused, to call Alec Bradley by name.

"He was handsome. But handsome is as handsome does, I say. I tell you what the crime was, Miss Kelsey. The crime was putting that sweet girl in jail for doing what she had to do."

"She was protecting herself."

"She said she was, so she was," Gertie said flatly. "Miss Naomi wouldn't lie. If I'd been home that night, or her daddy, it wouldn't have happened. That man would never have laid a hand on her. And she wouldn't have needed the gun."

Gertie sighed, took the rag to the sink and rinsed it out thoroughly. "Used to make me nervous, knowing she had that gun in her drawer. But I'm glad she had it that night. A man's got no right to force a woman. No right."

"No," Kelsey agreed. "No right at all."

"She still keeps it there."

"What?" Uneasy, Kelsey set down the half-eaten chicken leg. "Naomi still has the gun upstairs?"

"Not the same one, I expect. But one like it. It was her daddy's. Law says she can't own a gun now, but she keeps it just the same. Says it reminds her. I say what does she need to be reminded of such a time for? But she says some things you don't want to ever forget."

"No, I suppose she's right," Kelsey said slowly. But she wasn't certain she would sleep more peacefully knowing it.

"Maybe it's not my place to say it, but I'll say it anyway." Gertie sniffled once, then snatched a tissue to blow her nose. "You were the sun and the moon to her, Miss Kelsey. You coming back here like this, it's made up for a lot. There's no getting back what was lost, no taking back what was done, but old wounds can still be healed. That's what you're doing."

Was it? Kelsey wondered. She was still far from sure of her own motivations, her own feelings. "She's lucky to have you, Gertie," she murmured. "Lucky to have someone who thinks of her first, and last." Wanting to clear the tears from Gertie's eyes, she lightened her voice. "And very lucky to have someone who can cook like you."

"Oh, go on." Gertie waved a hand, then dashed it over her eyes. "Plain food, that's what I do. And you haven't finished that last piece you took. You need more meat on your bones."

Kelsey shook her head just as the chimes sounded from the front door. "No, Gertie, I'll get the door. Otherwise I'll eat this, platter and all."

She took the milk with her, guzzling as she went. She passed a mirror and rolled her eyes. Dirt streaked her cheeks. The cap she'd tossed aside in the mudroom hadn't prevented her hair from becoming hopelessly tangled. She hoped, as she wiped at the mud with the sleeve of her manure-stained shirt, that the visitor was horse-related.

Far from it.

"Grandmother!" Kelsey's shock mixed with chagrin as Milicent winced at her appearance. "What a surprise."

"What, in the name of God, have you been doing?"

"Working." Kelsey saw the spotless Lincoln outside, the driver stoically behind the wheel. "Out for a drive?"

"I've come to speak with you." Head erect, Milicent crossed the threshold with the same unbending dignity that Kelsey imagined French aristocrats had possessed when approaching the guillotine. "I felt this was much too important to discuss over the phone. Believe me, I do not enter this house lightly, or with any pleasure."

"I believe you. Come in, please, and sit down." At least Naomi was out of the house on some errand. Kelsey could thank fate for that. "Can I offer you something? Coffee, tea?"

"I want nothing from this house." Milicent sat, her starched linen suit barely creasing with the movement. She refused to satisfy petty curiosity by studying the room and focused instead on her granddaughter. "Is this how you spend your time? You're as grimy as a field hand."

"I've just come in. You might have noticed, it's raining."

"Don't take that tone with me. This is inexcusable, Kelsey, that you would waste your talents and your upbringing. Worse still, that you would send this family into a tailspin while you play out this little drama."

"Grandmother, we've been through all this." Kelsey set the milk aside and moved over to stir up the fire. Whether it was the rain or the visit, the room was suddenly chilled. "I'm well aware of your feelings, and your opinions. I can't believe you came all this way just to reprise them for me."

"You and I have rarely been sympathetic to each other's wishes, Kelsey."

"No." Thoughtfully, Kelsey replaced the poker and turned back. "I suppose we haven't."

"But in this, I can't believe you would go against me. Your name was in the paper this morning. Your name, in connection with a murder at a racetrack."

News travels, Kelsey mused. She'd been up and at the barn before the first paper delivery. "I didn't realize that. If I had, I certainly would have called Dad to reassure him. I was there, Grandmother. The man who was killed was a groom at the neighboring farm. My part in the investigation is very incidental."

"That you were there at all is the entire point, Kelsey, at a racetrack, associating with the sort of people they attract."

Kelsey tilted her head. "They attract me."

"Now you're being childish." Milicent's lips compressed. "I expect more of you. I expect you to think of the family."

"What does that poor man being killed yesterday have to do with the family?"

"Your name was linked with Naomi's. And her name in connection with a murder brings up old scandals. I shouldn't have to spell all this out for a woman of your intelligence, Kelsey. Do you want your father to suffer for this?"

"Of course not! And why should he? Why would he? Grandmother, an old man was brutally murdered. By sheer coincidence I happened to find him. Naturally, I had to give a statement to the police, but it ends there. I didn't even know him. And as far as Dad goes, he's completely removed from this."

"Stains are never completely removed. This world, Kelsey, is not ours. You were warned what to expect, what kind of people you would mingle with. Now the worst has happened. And because your father is too softhearted to take a stand, it's up to me. I'm going to insist that you pack your things and come home with me today."

"How little things change." Naomi stood in the doorway, pale as marble. Her slate-gray suit only accented the delicate fragility of her frame. But fragility can be deceptive. When she stepped forward, she was as elegant and as powerful as one of her prized fillies. "I believe I overheard you say something quite similar to Philip once."

Milicent's face went still and hard. "I came to speak with my grandchild. I have no desire to speak to you."

"You're in my home now, Milicent." Naomi set her purse aside, and with seamless poise chose a chair. "You're certainly free to say whatever you like to Kelsey, but you won't run me off. Those days are over."

"Prison taught you little, I see."

"Oh, you can't begin to know all it taught me." Her blood was cold now, without sentiment. That pleased her. She'd never been sure how she would react if she confronted Milicent again.

"You're the same as you ever were. Calculating, sly, unprincipled. Now you'd use Philip's daughter to satisfy your own ends."

"Kelsey is her own woman. You don't know her well if you believe she can be used."

"No, I can't." Kelsey stepped between them, not to block the venom, but to speak her mind. "And don't talk around me, either of you. I'm not a pawn in anyone's game. I came here because I wanted to, and I'll stay until I decide to leave. You can't order me to pack, Grandmother, as though I were a child, or a servant."

Color leaped into Milicent's cheeks and rode high. "I can insist that you do what's right for the family."

"You can ask me to consider what's right. And I will."

"You've pushed yourself on her." Milicent rose, her eyes boring into Naomi. "Using sentiment and sympathy to draw her to you. Have you told her about the men, Naomi, the drinking, the total disregard for your marriage, your husband and child? Have you told her that you set out to ruin a man, to destroy my son, but only succeeded in ruining yourself?"

"That's enough." Kelsey stepped back, hardly realizing the gesture put her squarely in Naomi's corner. "Whatever questions I have, whatever answers I'm given, don't involve you. I'll make my own judgments, Grandmother."

Milicent fought to keep her breathing even. Her heart was thumping dangerously fast. She, too, would make her own judgments. "If you stay here, you'll force me to take steps. I'll have no choice but to alter my will, and to use the power I have to revoke your grandfather's trust."

It was sorrow rather than shock that settled in Kelsey's eyes. "Oh, Grandmother, do you think the money matters so much? Do you think so little of me?"

"Consider the consequences, Kelsey." She picked up her bag, certain the threat would bring the girl quickly to heel.

"Hey, Kels, you'll never guess what I . . ." Channing came to an almost comical halt two strides in front of Milicent. "Grandmother!"

Enraged, Milicent whirled on Naomi. "So, you'd have him as well? Philip's daughter, and now the son he considers his own."

"Grandmother, I'm just—"

"Quiet!" Milicent snapped at him. "You paid once, Naomi. And I swear to God you'll pay again."

After she swept out, Channing hunched his shoulders. "Ah, bad scene, huh?"

"And one of the more colorful ones." Drained, Kelsey rubbed her hands over her face. "Channing, you did call Candace and tell her you were here, didn't you?"

"I called her." He stuck his hands in his pockets, then drew them out again. "I just told her I was okay and settled in. I didn't mention where I was settled. I thought I'd avoid the complications." He blew out a breath as Kelsey continued to stare at him. "I guess I'd better let her know before it gets any stickier."

Kelsey shook her head as he clattered up the stairs. "Channing's prone to leaving out vital pieces of information." She glanced back at her mother. "Want a drink?"

Naomi managed a smile and eased her shoulders back against the cushion. "Why not? Two fingers of whiskey ought to take out some of the sting."

"We'll try it." Kelsey walked to the sideboard and poured. "I'm sorry for that."

"So am I. Kelsey, the money might not be important to you, but it's your heritage. I don't want to be responsible for your losing it."

Absently Kelsey ran a fingertip over one of Naomi's crystal horses, following the flow of glass from withers to tail. "I have no idea if she can block my trust fund. And if she can, well, I haven't exactly been squandering the interest to date." With a shrug, she handed Naomi a glass. "I don't particularly want to lose it, either, but I'll be damned if she'll rein me in with dollar signs. Cheers." She rapped her glass against Naomi's.

"Cheers?" With a shake of her head, Naomi began to laugh. Letting her eyes close, she ordered her body to relax. "Oh, Christ, what a day."

She'd spent the last two hours with her lawyers, working out the details on how to align her own wishes with the ones her father had outlined before his death. Now, she thought, if Milicent made good on her threats to cut Kelsey off, she'd have to make further adjustments.

She opened her eyes again and tossed back the first swallow. "I was awfully proud of you, the way you stood up for yourself."

"Same goes. When I saw you in the doorway, I thought, Jesus, she's like a lightning bolt, frozen. Cold, sharp, and deadly."

"She's always affected me that way. Not that everything she said was completely off the mark. I've made mistakes, Kelsey, very bad mistakes."

Kelsey turned the glass in her hand, around and around. "Did you love Dad when you married him?"

"Yes, oh yes." For a moment, Naomi's eyes softened. "He was so shy and smart. And sexy."

Kelsey choked on a laugh. "Dad? Sexy?"

"Those tweed jackets. That dreamy, poetic look in his eyes, that calm, patient voice reciting Byron. That unflagging kindness. I adored him."

"When did you stop?"

"It wasn't a matter of stopping." Naomi set her half-finished whiskey aside. "I wasn't so patient, or so kind. And the dreams we had were different ones. When things began to go wrong, I wasn't smart enough to compromise. To bend. It was one of my mistakes. I thought I could hold him by proving I didn't need him. I opened the distance, raced away from him. And I lost. I lost Philip, I lost you, I lost my freedom. A very high price for pride."

She grimaced as the doorbell rang again. "It looks like the day isn't over yet."

"I'll get it." For the second time that afternoon, the visitor was unwelcome. "Lieutenant Rossi."

"Ms. Byden, sorry to disturb you. I have a few follow-up questions for you and your mother."

"We're in the sitting room. Is there any progress, Lieutenant?" she asked, as she led the way.

"We're investigating."

Trained eyes took in the sedate comfort of the room, as well as the two glasses of whiskey, the half-full glass of milk. Naomi rose as he entered. As a man, he appreciated her grace. As a cop, he admired her control.

"Lieutenant Rossi." Though her skin had gone cold, she offered a hand. "Won't you sit down? Would you care for some coffee?"

"I appreciate the offer, Ms. Chadwick, but I've had my quota for the day. I just have a few more questions."

"Of course." They always had a few more questions. She sat again, keeping her spine erect. "What can I help you with?"

"You were fairly well acquainted with the victim."

"I knew Mick." Keep the answers short, Naomi reminded herself. Say nothing more than necessary.

"He was employed at Longshot for the last five years, approximately."

"I believe that's correct."

"He also worked for the previous owner, Cunningham?"

"On and off."

"Off," Rossi continued, "when he was fired, about seven years ago."

"Bill Cunningham let Mick go, as I recall, because he felt Mick was too old. At the time, my trainer offered Mick a position here, but he decided to leave the area."

"The information I have is that he worked the tracks in Florida during that two-year period."

"I believe so."

"Would you know if he had any enemies?"

"Mick?" She dropped her guard for a moment, the question was so absurd. "Everyone loved Old Mick. He was an institution, a kind of monument to the best in racing. Hardworking, tough-minded, big-hearted. No one disliked him."

"But someone killed him." Rossi waited a beat, fascinated by the way Naomi drew herself in. "The horse was injured. Mick Gordon was assigned to that horse as groom. My report is that there was a long, shallow slice on the left flank, approximately twelve inches in length." He took out his book as if checking facts.

"Preliminary reports indicate that this wound was caused by the same weapon used against the victim."

"Obviously someone was trying to hurt the colt, and Mick tried to stop him," Kelsey put in. "Moses told me that colt's very levelheaded. He'd never have trampled Mick if he hadn't been hurt or frightened."

"That may be." Rossi had to wait for the autopsy report before he could be sure if the knife had killed Mick Gordon, or the horse had. Murder or attempted murder, he intended to close the case. "Mr. Slater's colt was competing with yours that day, Ms. Chadwick."

"Yes, or he would have been if it hadn't been necessary to scratch him."

"And your horse won, didn't he?"

She kept her eyes level, steady. "By a neck, as we say. He paid three to five."

"You and Mr. Slater have a history of competition. Particularly in the last year between these two horses. He's edged you out of the top spot several times."

"Double or Nothing is an admirable colt. A champion. So is my Virginia's Pride. They're incredibly well matched."

"I don't know much about racing myself." He smiled placidly. "But, from an amateur's standpoint, it seems it would be to your benefit to"—he tipped his flattened hand back and forth—"shift the odds."

"That's an uncalled-for accusation, Lieutenant." In automatic support, Kelsey dropped a hand on her mother's shoulder. "Absolutely uncalled-for."

"It's not an accusation, Ms. Byden. It's an observation. Horses are sometimes deliberately injured, drugged, even killed to up another's chances, aren't they, Ms. Chadwick?"

"Unscrupulous and criminal behavior happens in all walks of life." She fought against trembling. Cops' eyes could detect even the slightest fear. "Those of us in racing prefer to say it happens much more often in the show ring than at the track."

"Three Willows doesn't need to resort to tactics like that," Kelsey said, furious. "And I've told you that my mother was with me all morning. Dozens of people saw us."

"They did," Rossi agreed. "As a veteran of the racing world, Ms. Chadwick, wouldn't you agree that an owner, or a trainer, interested in improving his chances would hire someone to do the job rather than risk harming a horse himself?"

"Yes, I would."

"You don't have to answer questions like this." The outrage of it seared Kelsey's throat.

"I'm sure your mother is well aware of her rights," Rossi said coolly. "And the procedure of a murder investigation."

"I'm perfectly aware of both, Lieutenant. And equally aware that those rights don't always protect the innocent." Her lips curved humorlessly. "Certainly not the half-innocent. I could remind you that my colt wasn't the only other contender in that race, and that not once in the fifty years that Three Willows has been in operation have we been cited for any infraction. But I'm sure you know that. Just as I know an exconvict always carries a cloud of suspicion. Is there anything else I can tell you?"

"Not for the moment." A hell of a woman, he thought, and tucked away his pad. He was going to have to schedule extra time to study her file a little more closely. "I appreciate the time. One thing, Ms. Byden. You did say you met Mr. Slater outside the barn yesterday, before the two of you went in to look over the horse."

"Yes, he was talking to his trainer."

"Thank you. I'll see myself out."

"That was outrageous!" Kelsey exploded the moment the door closed. "How could you just sit there and take it? He all but accused you of paying for murder."

"I expected it. And he won't be the only one to consider the possibility. After all, I'm once guilty."

"Don't be so calm, dammit!"

"I'm not. The pretense is all I've got." Weary, she rose. She needed a quiet room, a bottle of aspirin, and the coward's escape of sleep. But she paused, took a chance by framing Kelsey's face in her hands. "You're not even considering it a possibility, are you? That I might have had a hand in this."

"No." There was no hesitation.

"Then I'm wrong," Naomi murmured. "It seems I have a great deal more than pretense. Go for a ride, Kelsey. Work off some of that anger."

She went for a ride, but her temper continued to rage. She headed for Longshot with a dual purpose. Handing over Justice's reins to a willing groom, she strode from barn to house.

Too stirred up to think of the propriety of knocking on the front door, she went in through the pool house, moving from spring to high summer, then up a short flight of stairs into the steady warmth of a casually furnished great room.

She realized then, because she hadn't a clue which direction to take, that she was trespassing. Upbringing warred with instinct until she turned left and headed down a corridor. So, she thought, she'd work her way to the front door, go outside, and knock. Unless, of course, she found Gabe in the meantime.

It wasn't his voice she heard, not immediately. It was Boggs's, his grainy tones coming through an open door.

"He wouldn't want no fancy service, Mr. Slater. None of that flowers and organ music stuff. Once when we were sitting around, he told me how he thought he'd want to be cremated, and maybe his ashes could be spread over the practice track here. So's he'd always be a part of the place. Sounds kinda funny, I guess."

"If that's what he wanted, that's what we'll do."

"That's good, then. I've got some money set aside. I don't know what it costs to do things that way, but—"

"Let me do this for him, Boggs," Gabe interrupted. "I'm not sure I'd be sitting here today if it hadn't been for Mick. I'd appreciate it if you'd let me take care of him."

"I know it ain't the money, Mr. Slater. Maybe it's not my place to say, but he was real proud of you. Told me he knew the first time he saw you hustling to walk hots at the track that you'd amount to something. I sure am going to miss him."

"So am I."

"Well, I better get back." He stepped out of the doorway, flushed a bit when he saw Kelsey. "Miss," he muttered, tipping his cap and hurrying off.

Ashamed at having so blatantly eavesdropped on a private conversation, she stepped into the doorway to apologize.

He sat at a beautiful old desk, the arched window behind him letting in the watery sunlight. Wherever there wasn't glass welcoming the light, there were books. The two-level library was stunning, and unmistakably masculine.

The man who owned it had his head in his hands.

Embarrassment melted into compassion. She stepped forward, murmuring his name. Her arms were around him before he lifted his head. "I didn't know you were so close to him. I'm sorry. I'm so sorry."

He hadn't felt grief, not in years. Not since his mother. It surprised him how deep it could cut. "He was good to me. I must have been about fourteen the first time he grabbed me by the scruff of the neck. He took an interest in me—I don't know why—and talked Jamie into hiring me. And he made sure I learned. Goddammit, Kelsey, he was seventy. He should have died in bed."

"I know." She drew away. "Gabe, Rossi was just at the house."

"Busy man." Gabe dragged his hands through his disheveled hair. "He left here less than an hour ago."

"I think he's got some idea that Naomi's involved." When Gabe said nothing, she moistened her lips. "I need to know if you think so."

Composed again, he studied her. "No, I don't. And neither, I see, do you. Rossi has a couple of ideas. The other is that I arranged the business myself." He waited a beat. "Double or Nothing's heavily insured."

"You'd shoot yourself in the foot first." She let out a sigh. "That was the other reason I came over. I could tell when he was questioning me that he was toying with the idea. I guess I came over to warn you."

"I appreciate it." He rotated his shoulders once to ease the lingering tension. Kelsey, standing there in splattered work clothes, compassion in her eyes, took care of the rest. "You look good, darling."

"Yeah, mud's becoming."

"On you." He took her hand, played with her fingers. "Why don't you sit on my lap awhile?"

Amused, she tilted her head. "Is that the setup, or the punch line, Slater?"

In answer he tugged, cradling her when she tumbled. "Yeah." He inhaled deeply, nuzzling her hair. It smelled of rain, and of spring. "This is exactly what I needed. Sit still, Kelsey. You'll cause a lot more trouble by wriggling around. Believe me."

"I'm not a lap sitter."

"So learn." Testing, he grazed his teeth over her earlobe, pleased with her quick shudder. "You only came over to tell me about Rossi?"

"That's right."

This time he exhaled deeply. "Okay. But I'm going to have to find a way to make you pick up the pace here. I'm starting to suffer."

"I think you're tougher than that." She rested her head in the curve of his shoulder. It was entirely too comfortable, entirely too tempting. "I'm not playing games."

"That's too bad. I usually win."

11

"Sure you don't want a blindfold?" Kelsey tucked an arm around Channing's waist. "A last cigarette?"

He tipped down his red-framed Oakley sunglasses. "You're a riot, Kels."

"No, really, I feel like I'm sending you off to the firing squad alone."

"I can handle Mom." He unstrapped his helmet from the back of his Harley. "And the Prof's no problem."

"And Grandmother?"

With a grimace, he slipped on the helmet. "Hey, I've been dodging those bullets for years. As long as my brilliant mind keeps me in the top fifteen percent of my class, they can't hassle me much."

"The trusty shield of a four-point-oh." She'd used it herself. "What about this summer?"

"Mom's just going to have to accept that there's more to my life than hitting the books."

"My brother." Grinning, she tapped her fingers on the side of his helmet. "The hard hat."

"Actually, Naomi offered me a job here this summer."

"Here?"

"Channing Osborne, stableboy. I like it. I like her." In a lithe move, he straddled the bike. "You know, I stopped by here to be sure you were all right. I had this image planted of some hard-faced, hard-living bitch with a drink in one hand and a forty-five in the other."

"Sowed," Kelsey said dryly, "by the Magnificent Milicent."

"With a few seeds tossed out by Mom. They're as solidly aligned against you being here as they were *for* you marrying Wade the Weenie."

He glanced back toward the house. It made a lovely picture with the willows greening, the daffodils and hyacinths spearing up in their Easter-egg hues of yellow and blue and pink.

"She's not anything like she's painted, is she?"

"It doesn't seem so," Kelsey murmured. "I'm glad you came, Channing. I'm glad you got to meet her."

"Hey, it was the most interesting spring break I've ever had." He leaned forward to kiss her good-bye. "And I'll be back. See you in a couple of months."

"I—" She wanted to tell him she couldn't guarantee she'd be here, but he'd kicked the engine to life. With a final salute, he roared off down the drive.

Lost in her own thoughts, she walked back to the house. Had she decided to stay? Kelsey asked herself. The month Naomi had asked of her was almost up. Yet neither of them had mentioned plans to leave.

And what was waiting for her back in Maryland, in that tidy Bethesda apartment? Job hunting, solitary meals, and the occasional lunch with a friend who would sympathize over the divorce, then mention a cousin office pal old friend who just happened to be single.

The idea was more than depressing.

Here, she had work and a world she already loved, a lifestyle that suited her nature, people who accepted her for what she could do.

And there was Gabe.

She wasn't quite sure what was going on there, but it would be a great deal more difficult, and certainly inconvenient, to try to figure it out if she moved away.

It would be dishonest to say he didn't fascinate her. His moods, impossible to read one minute, bold as a banner headline the next. She appreciated his humor, the easy charm, the equally easy arrogance.

He'd moved her in so many ways. The way he'd grieved for Old Mick, standing solemnly in the soft dawn light while Boggs had ridden slowly around the practice track, spreading the old man's ashes. He'd held her hand, she remembered, trusting her to understand the ritual.

That kind of loyalty and love couldn't be learned.

Yet he could be hard, ruthless enough to gamble and win a small fortune. Even that intrigued, and the underlying recklessness that had pushed him to raze another man's house and build his own.

Then, of course, there was that basic animal attraction, the kind she'd never felt before for any man. Even her husband.

"Kelsey?" Naomi paused at the foot of the stairs. The girl looked so solemn, she thought. "Missing Channing already?"

"No, I was thinking of . . ." She trailed off, blew her breeze-tousled hair out of her eyes. "Nothing really." Realigning her thoughts, she studied Naomi. Slim, strong, self-contained. "It was nice of you to offer him a job this summer."

"Not that nice. He has a strong back, willing hands, and I enjoy having him around. The house has been empty a long time."

"I think he wants to be a vet."

"So he told me."

"He told you." With a baffled laugh, Kelsey shook her head. "He's never mentioned it to me. Not once. I've always thought he was revved to be a surgeon, like his father."

"Sometimes it's easier to tell those secret hopes to someone who isn't so close. He loves you. Admires you. Could be he's afraid you'd be disappointed in him."

"I couldn't be." Her breath came out in an impatient gush. "Candace has been talking for years about him carrying on the Osborne tradition. I just assumed he wanted it too. Why do people try to shoehorn their children into slots?"

"Family honor. A terrifying obligation."

She opened her mouth, closed it again. Family honor. Hadn't that been why she'd married Wade? How many times had she been told how perfect he was for her, until she'd believed it. Good family, good prospects, excellent social standing. It had been her duty, after all, to marry well, and to marry properly.

God, had she loved him at all?

"And when you can't hold up that obligation," Kelsey said slowly, "it's the worst kind of failure. I don't want that for Channing."

"He'll do what's right for himself. You did."

"Eventually."

"You can talk about eventually when you're my age. Kelsey . . ." She wasn't quite sure of her approach. Casual, she decided, was probably best. "I'm going down to Hialeah. I want to watch Virginia's Pride run. And I want to stick close to him after what happened at Charles Town."

"Oh." So, she wasn't to have the last week after all. "That makes sense. When are you leaving?"

"In the morning. I thought you might like to go with me."

"To Florida?"

"Well, it's not spring break, but it should be quite a spectacle."

As cautious as Naomi, she nodded. "I'd like to see it."

"Good. How would you feel about taking the rest of the day off?"

Kelsey's brows lifted. She hadn't seen Naomi take more than an hour off in over three weeks. "For?"

"What else?" Naomi's laugh was quick, bright, and young. "Shopping. What's the fun of taking a trip if you can't splurge on some new clothes first?"

Kelsey's grin flashed. "I'll get my purse."

In a dingy hotel room off Route 15, Lipsky gulped down warm Gilbey's gin. The ice machine a few feet outside his door was on the fritz. Not that he cared. Warm or chilled, the liquor went down the same.

"I tell you, sooner or later they're going to come looking for me."

"You're probably right. You got sloppy." Rich straightened his bolo tie. "Neatness counts, friend."

"I was just going to take care of the horse." With his free hand, Lipsky reached for the cigarette smoldering in a chipped glass ashtray crammed with butts. "Just enough so he couldn't race, that's all."

"But that wasn't your job," Rich reminded him with an affable grin. "Eyes and ears open, remember? Just eyes and ears until I told you different."

"You didn't bitch when I fixed his other colt." Resentment gleamed in Lipsky's red-rimmed eyes. "You gave me another hundred for it."

"You were tidy, Fred. I did tell you, I believe, not to take chances. But"—he spread his arms wide—"that's behind us now. And Gabe's favorite colt won't be wearing a saddle for another week or so." It fit nicely into the master plan, the damaged horses, even the murder. Such things stirred gossip and excited the press. Feeling generous, Rich reached into his pocket. He carried his lucky money clip, the oversize silver dollar sign he'd picked up in Houston. There was nothing he liked better than to have it straining with bills.

Normally, he would load it with singles, putting a fifty or, if he was lucky, a C-note on the outside. He was really in the groove now, he thought. The money clip was fat with hundreds. He peeled one off and laid it on the table.

Lipsky stared at it with a mixture of hunger and guilt. "I wouldn't have hurt the Peacock. Nobody coulda paid me to hurt Old Mick."

"An unfortunate accident." In sympathy, Rich patted a hand on his shoulder.

Lipsky gulped more gin. "I never killed nobody. Maybe I cut a few, when they deserved it. But I never killed nobody before." He could still see Mick's face, the shock, the pain, the way his eyes had rolled back right before the horse reared and felled him.

And he could see the blood pumping and pooling, Mick's trademark blue cap going red with it . . .

He snatched the bottle and poured another shot. "He shouldn't have poked his nose in."

"An excellent rationalization." Rich poured a glass for himself. He hated to see a man drinking alone, even a revolting specimen like Lipsky. But he kept his cigarettes and his monogrammed lighter tucked away. "Now it's time to consider the next move."

"The cops are going to come looking for me. Plenty of people saw me around the track that day, at the shedrow."

"You were hustling rides," Rich reminded him. "Perfectly permissible. You're a familiar face at the track, Fred. Otherwise, the guards would have blocked you from entering the barn."

"Yeah, and sooner or later somebody's going to remember that I did. Then they'll notice I ain't been back." He tamped out his cigarette, spilling ash and old butts over the rickety table. "Then they'll remember I carry a blade."

"Your deductive powers are admirable. My advice is to run, lose yourself in Florida, California, Kentucky. Maybe Mexico. They've got tracks south of the border."

"I ain't living in no foreign country. I'm an American."

"Ah, patriotism." Rich toasted with his glass of gin. "You're a resourceful man, Fred. Otherwise I wouldn't have put you on the payroll. But I'm afraid we'll have to sever our relationship, under the circumstances."

"It's going to take more than a hundred."

Rich's smile never wavered, but his eyes turned gelid. "Now, Fred, you wouldn't put the arm on me, would you?"

Desperation was leaking sweat down Lipsky's back. He could smell himself. "I can't take the rap for this alone. If I'm going to run, I need money. Fuck, Rich, I was working for you. You got a part in this."

"Is that the way you see it?"

"The way I see it, I need ten thousand. To hide, and to keep my mouth shut about you if I don't hide good enough. It ain't too much to ask, Rich."

Rich sighed. He'd been afraid it would come to this. "I understand your position, Fred. I truly do. Listen, let me make a phone call, see what I can come up with." He bolstered his smile with another pat on Lipsky's shoulder. "Give me a little privacy, huh?"

"Yeah, okay. I gotta piss anyhow." He rose and staggered into the bathroom.

Rich didn't pick up the phone. Instead, he took a small vial out of his inside coat pocket. It really was a shame, but he couldn't afford to call Lipsky's bluff. Even if he paid, odds were the man would sing like a bird the minute the cops nailed him. And they'd nail him, Rich thought, as he tapped the liquid into Lipsky's gin.

"Come on back, Fred. We got it all taken care of." He was beaming when Lipsky reeled back into the room. "I'll have the money for you tomorrow."

Relief and liquor had Lipsky tumbling into his chair. "No shit, Rich?"

"Hey, we go back a ways, don't we? Rollers like us, we take care of each other." He lifted his glass. "Here's to old friends."

"Yeah." Eyes tearing in gratitude, Lipsky brought his glass to his lips. "I knew I could count on you."

"Yeah." Rich's smile hardened as he watched Lipsky literally drink himself to death. "You can count on me, Fred."

Palm trees and striped awnings, brilliant sunshine and trailing bougainvillea. Men in white suits and women in sundresses. The ambience added to the glamour of the track. But Hialeah Park was still about racing.

At the Gulfstream receiving barn, horses arched their necks, pranced, sniffed the air, athletes psyching themselves up for competition. Many of the sights and sounds were the same as Charles Town; vendors still hawked *Daily Racing Form*, handicappers still hovered, working the odds. But the weather itself, the sheer glory of it, drew a different breed from the chilly spring in West Virginia.

Kelsey amused herself watching a woman teetering on ice-pick heels leading a filly around the walking ring. Her shoulder-length rhinestone earrings flashed.

"Nobody could call a horse a dumb animal looking at that."

Kelsey glanced up at Gabe. "Meaning?"

"What do you see when you look at her face?"

"The horse or the woman?"

"The horse."

Obliging, Kelsey looked back at the filly, plodding, head down behind the giggling woman. "Embarrassment."

"You got it. That's Cunningham's latest acquisition."

"The horse or the woman?"

"Both."

She let loose a laugh, and realized how glad she was she'd come. Maybe it was the quick peek at summer, or the simple pleasure of discovering herself a part of a close-knit group. But she was glad.

"I heard you'd be here, but I didn't see you at morning workout."

"I just got in an hour ago," he told her. "What do you think of Miami?"

"Well, some of the grooms were grumbling this morning about losing sleep—gunshots outside their quarters—and I cruised the beach yesterday and it hit me that I must be an adult: I had no desire to strap on Rollerblades. Other than that"—she drew in a deep breath—"I love it. It's a beautiful park."

"The bottom line. Racetrackers don't have much use for the outside world anyway."

"I wouldn't go that far."

"You're not a racetracker." He looked down at her. "At least not yet."

She frowned, unsure if she'd been complimented or insulted. Rather than pursue it, she watched the losers returning from the first race. The winners, she knew, would be taken to the "spit box" so that samples of urine and saliva could be tested for drugs.

But it was the losers she thought about now, her heart aching a little to see them limping in, their flanks sweaty, faces dirty. If a filly could feel embarrassed by being led around in public by a tarted-up Barbie doll, she wondered how deeply these suffered the pangs of failure.

"Sad, isn't it?" she murmured. "Like watching soldiers struggling back from the front. All that color and show, and in just a couple of minutes, it's done."

"It's a hell of a couple of minutes. Too bad you missed the Florida Derby. Now, that's a show. Acrobats, a camel race."

"Camels? Really?"

"Never bet on one."

They walked past the tack rooms around the backstretch. It was nearly time for the second race, and Pride was in the third. She wanted to see Reno before Moses gave him that leg up. It had become her personal superstition to add her last wish for good luck before he walked his horse from the paddock.

"Not going to head for the windows?" Gabe asked her.

"Nope. I've picked my horses. Pride in the third and Three Aces in the fifth." She stopped to buy a lukewarm Pepsi from an ancient black man. "I've got my own system now."

Gabe accepted the can, took a swallow, and handed it back to her. "And what is that?"

"Sentiment. I just bet my heart."

"It's a lot to lose."

She shrugged. "Gambling's no fun without the risk."

"Damn right. Come here." They were nearly at Pride's saddling stall and there was plenty of traffic.

"Cut it out, Slater." But he'd already caught the ponytail she'd looped through the back of her cap.

"I'm just going to kiss you. The risk's on both sides."

She thought she heard some of the grooms hooting with laughter before her mind went blank. She'd wondered if that first, that only, intellect-sapping kiss had been a fluke. A coincidence. A one-time trip.

Apparently not.

There was something about his mouth. She opened hers to it eagerly, swamped in the taste, the texture, the heat. It moved against hers, clever and tormentingly slow, as if there was all the time in the world to sample. On a moan of agreement, she plunged her hands into his hair, holding on until the sounds of the track were no more than misty white noise.

I want. It was all he could think. He'd spent so much of his life wanting—decent food, a clean bed, the simple peace of living without fear. As he'd grown, those wants had grown with him. He'd wanted women and power and the money that would ensure both.

But he'd never craved anything, certainly not anyone, as he craved now. One woman. One night. He'd have gambled everything he had for the chance of it.

"How much longer?" he murmured against her lips.

"I don't know." She struggled to catch her breath. "I don't know you."

"Sure you do."

"I didn't know you existed a couple of months ago." She drew away, surprised her legs didn't fold under her. "I'm not—" She straightened her cap with a shaky hand as applause rang out behind them. "We need to talk about this later. Without an audience."

"Well." He skimmed a fingertip over her jaw. "I accomplished something, anyway. The word's already going out that you're off limits."

"That I'm—" She set her teeth. "Is that what that was for? Some sort of macho claim staking?"

"No. It was for me, darling. But it worked. See you around."

She kicked the soda can she'd dropped when he'd kissed her. "Idiot," she muttered. Fighting for dignity, she turned and nearly ran into Naomi.

"It's odd," Naomi began while Kelsey struggled for words. "Watching that. If you'll pardon the analogy, I often have the same sensation when I see one of my horses led to the track. It's like watching your child get on the school bus, or recite in a class play. You suddenly realize that they're not just your child anymore, and that there's so much you don't know about them."

"He just did it to annoy me."

Though her heart was still swelling, Naomi smiled. "Oh, I don't think so." She took a chance and lifted a hand to Kelsey's cheek. "Confused?"

"Yes."

But not ready to talk about it. "Would you like me to speak with Gabe? He won't appreciate it, but he's fond enough of me to put up with the intrusion."

"No. I'll handle it." She glanced around. There were still a number of grinning faces pointed her way. "Don't we have a race coming up?" she snapped. "You're not being paid to gawk."

As Kelsey stalked over to the saddling stall, Naomi let out a grin of her own.

On the track, Pride ran like a dream, bursting through the gate with a fierce look in his eyes and Reno driving him on. At the first turn, he was fighting for position, but after that it was over. Down the back-stretch there were three lengths of daylight between him and the closest contender.

"Looks like a rich man's horse," she heard someone comment behind her.

Yes, she thought, he did. But money had nothing to do with it.

Gabe joined her at the fifth race, as cool and casual as if they'd recently shared a sandwich rather than a torrid, public embrace. "Reno ran a smart race."

"He and Pride make a good team." She shot Gabe a look. "The best team on the circuit."

"We'll see," he murmured. "Keep your eye on Cunningham's Big Sheba. Tell me what you see."

Frowning, Kelsey watched the horses being loaded in the gate. The big bay filly was fractious, nervous. She took a swipe, a bad-tempered kick, at a groom and sent him sprawling.

"She's wound up. That's not unusual." She shifted her gaze to Three Aces. He was giving his own handlers a fight. "Your colt's feeling frisky himself."

"Just watch."

The bell sounded. Horses charged. Cunningham's filly took the lead, her long legs extended, digging up dirt. Kelsey narrowed her eyes behind the binoculars. Big Sheba was sweating heavily by the first turn.

"She's fast. Why is he pushing her so hard?" She winced as the jockey used the bat, quick and often.

"He's doing what he's been told."

At the halfway mark she began to flag, just a fraction, but enough for the field to close. Kelsey felt her eyes begin to tear. Big Sheba had gallantry, but she didn't have wind. And they were hurting her.

On the backstretch she fell a half-length behind Gabe's colt, then a length. Sheer heart kept her in the place position by a nose when they crossed the wire.

"That's inexcusable." Furious, she whirled on Gabe. "There have to be rules."

"We've got plenty of them. None say you can't push a horse past its limits. Rumor is she's got lung trouble. So the idiot has his jockey run her full out at seven furlongs. He wants the fucking Derby so much he'll kill her to have a shot at it."

"I thought he was just a fool."

"He's a fool, all right. An ambitious one. He wants that first jewel."

"Don't we all?"

"Yeah. The difference is just how far we'll go to get it."

He left her to head down to the winner's circle. Kelsey turned her back on the track. Suddenly it had lost a great deal of its glamour.

12

Jack Moser ran a clean place. Maybe some of his clientele rented a room by the hour, but that was none of his nevermind. Jack figured what went on behind closed doors went on behind closed doors at the Ritz Hotel just as it did at his place.

Only they paid more for it.

He didn't have bugs, wouldn't tolerate carryings-on after the decent hour of midnight, and paid extra so his guests could have cable.

At twenty-nine dollars a pop for a single, it wasn't a bad deal.

Children under eighteen stayed for free.

He gave his guests the amenity of a sliver-sized bar of Ivory soap along with the bath-mat-size towels, and for their convenience, he had a deal going with the nearby diner to deliver meals after six A.M. and before ten P.M.

Maybe he slipped some of the cash under the table and didn't push for ID, but that was his business.

The sheets were laundered, the bathrooms disinfected, and there was a good sturdy lock on each and every door.

He liked the summers best, when vacationing families heading north or south spotted his blinking vacancy sign. Mostly they just tumbled out of their aging station wagons and into bed. Didn't have to worry about them spraying beer on the walls or tearing up the sheets.

He'd been watching people come and go for twelve years and figured he knew a thing or two about them. He knew when a couple rented a room to cheat on a spouse, when a woman was hiding out from the guy who was as likely to put his fist in her eye as look at her. He recognized the losers, the drifters, the runners.

He'd pegged room 22 as a runner.

None of my nevermind, Jack told himself as he hooked the passkey from the Peg-Board. The guy had paid cash for three nights in advance. So what if he'd had the smell of fear around him, or if he'd had a way of looking over his shoulder as if he was expecting somebody to shove a knife in his back?

He'd paid his eighty-seven bucks plus tax and hadn't made a peep since.

Which was the problem. Room 22's time was up, and according to skinny-butted Dottie, the housekeeper, his lock was still bolted and the DO NOT DISTURB sign was out. Just the way it had been for three days.

Well, he was going to have to be disturbed, Jack thought as he strode across the parking lot to the line of identical gray doors and shaded windows. Room 22 could come up with another day's rent, or get his butt moving.

Jack Moser didn't extend credit.

He knocked first, sharp, authoritative. Nobody but Jack knew the secret pleasure it gave him to hustle along a deadbeat. "Manager," he said crisply, and caught Dottie poking her head out of 27 where her cart was parked, to give him the eye.

"Probably dead drunk," she called out.

Jack sighed, and straightened his sloped shoulders. "Just do your job, Dottie. I'll handle this." He knocked again, missing the face she made at him. "Manager," he repeated, then slipped his key into the lock.

The smell hit him first, gagging him. His first thought was that 22 had ordered something from the diner that had disagreed with him, violently. His second was that it would take a frigging case of Lysol to cover the stench.

Then he had no thought at all. He saw what sat slumped at the tiny, scarred table, eyes staring, body bloated. Whoever had checked into 22 had metamorphosed in three days into a thing as horrible as anything Jack had ever seen on a late-night horror movie.

He staggered back, overwhelmed by the sight and the odor. A strangled cry caught in his throat, and he threw up on his shoes. It didn't stop him from running. He continued to run even after Dottie hurried into room 22 and began to scream.

The body had already been bagged by the time Rossi pulled up at the motel. It had been through sheer doggedness and a touch of luck that he was there at all. His ears didn't perk up at every suspicious or unattended death that came into Homicide. But the name Fred Lipsky had rung a bell. It was a name on his list, one he'd been unable to check out.

Now, it seemed, he had his chance.

The medical examiner, Dr. Agnes Lorenzo, was packing up. Rossi nodded to the small, athletic woman with graying hair and puppy-dog eyes. "Lorenzo."

"Rossi. I thought this was Newman's case."

"It ties into one of mine. What have we got?" He hooked his badge to his pocket and moved through the uniformed men stationed at the open door.

The body was already zipped, ready for transfer to the morgue. The air still smelled ripe, but it wasn't a smell that affected him much anymore. He scanned the room, taking in the unmade bed, the bag of clothes tossed in the corner, the dust left over from the forensics team. A bottle of gin, three-quarters empty, a single glass, and an ashtray full of Lucky Strike butts.

"Don't ask me for cause of death, Rossi," Dr. Lorenzo began. "I can tell you it occurred forty-eight to sixty hours ago. No wounds, no sign of a struggle."

"Cause of death?"

She'd known he would ask, and smiled thinly. "His heart stopped, Rossi. They all do."

He ignored the jibe and formed a picture. A man drinking alone. Angry? Guilty? Afraid? Why did a man rent a cheap room to drink in when he already had a cheap room thirty miles away?

And if Lipsky had been running, it meant he had something to hide.

Since he'd taken her sarcasm well, Dr. Lorenzo decided to give him a break. "He had about three hundred in his wallet, and an expired credit card. There was a copy of *Daily Racing Form* in his bag, four days old, and a knife in his left boot."

Rossi sprang to attention like a setter on point. "What kind of knife?"

"Six inches long, thin blade, smooth edge."

Rossi's cop's heart began to swell. Forensics would have the knife, and if there was any trace of blood, man or horse, they'd find it. "Who found him?"

"Manager. Name's Moser. He might still be in the office over there, with his head between his knees."

"Not everyone's as tough as you, Lorenzo."

"You're telling me." She stepped outside again, sorry the spring air was marred by the whoosh of traffic on Route 15. She'd left a body on the slab, and now she had another to add to her backlog. Every day, she thought, was a picnic.

"I'll need a copy of the autopsy report."

"Two days."

"Twenty-four hours, Lorenzo. Be a pal."

"We're nobody's pals, Rossi." She turned away and got into her car.

"Hey." He grabbed her door before she could close it. He'd known Agnes Lorenzo for three years. She didn't have many buttons that could be pushed, but he'd uncovered a few. "You know that stiff you did last week? Gordon. Mick Gordon. Old man, gut-knifed."

She pulled out a cigarette, a habit she no longer bothered to feel guilty about. "The one who got his skull cracked and most of his internal organs smashed for good measure? Yeah, I remember."

"I think this stiff's the one who did him."

She blew out smoke. She hadn't gotten a close look at the knife. There had been no need for her to examine it. But she remembered the wound. She had dozens of wounds filed in her head, never to be forgotten.

She nodded. "The weapon could be right. Okay, Rossi, I'll burn the midnight oil for you, but I can't promise all the tests will be done."

"Thanks." He closed her door, forgot her, and zeroed in on the office and Jack Moser.

Gabe learned about Lipsky ten minutes after he returned from Florida. The press had found a gold mine in Dottie, the housekeeper.

The news that Lipsky had died in a motel room spread from barn to track, from groom to exercise boy. Gabe's twice-weekly housekeeper brought him the news, and the paper, before he'd done more than tossed his bags on his bed.

Fury flared, like a gasoline-soaked match. He was working on banking it when Rossi tracked him down.

"Nice to see you again, Mr. Slater."

"Lieutenant." Gabe offered the paper he'd brought down with him, then sat in the sun-drenched living room. "Odds are you're here to tell me about this."

"You win." Rossi set the paper aside and made himself comfortable. "Fred Lipsky worked for you up until a few weeks ago."

"Up until I fired him, which I'm sure you know. He was drunk."

"And objected to the termination."

"That's right. He pulled a knife, I knocked him down, and I thought, mistakenly, that that was the end of it." His face still sternly controlled, he edged forward. "If I'd had any suspicion that he would have used that knife on one of my men, or one of my horses, he wouldn't have walked away."

"You don't want to make statements like that to a cop, Mr. Slater. It hasn't leaked to the press yet, but the knife in Lipsky's possession at the time of his death was the weapon that killed Mick Gordon. As yet, no one can definitely place Lipsky at the scene at the time of the murder. But we have a weapon and we have motive—revenge."

"Case closed?" Gabe finished.

"I like them neat before I close them. This one isn't neat. How well did you know Lipsky?"

"Not well. He came with the farm."

The statement made Rossi smile. "An interesting way of putting it."

"When I took over here, I kept on anyone who wanted to stay. It wasn't their fault Cunningham played lousy poker."

Intrigued, Rossi tapped his pencil against his pad. "That's a true story, then. Sounded made up. No point in mentioning a deal like that would be on the shady side of the law?"

"No point at all," Gabe agreed.

"I'll talk to your trainer again, and the men. I'm interested to know if anyone who did know him thinks he was suicidal."

"You want me to think Lipsky killed himself?" The rage began to work in him again, gnawing away. "Why? Out of guilt? Remorse? That's shit, Lieutenant. He was as likely to stick a gun in his mouth or put a rope around his neck as he was to dance on Broadway."

"You said you didn't know him well, Mr. Slater."

"Not him, but I know the type." He'd been raised by Lipsky's type. "They blame everyone else, never themselves. And they don't take that last dive because they're always figuring the angles. They drink and they cheat and they talk a big game. But they don't kill themselves."

"An interesting theory." And one Rossi subscribed to himself. "Lipsky didn't eat a gun or string himself up. He drank a nasty cocktail of gin and what I'm told is called acepromazine. Are you familiar with it?"

Gabe's voice was carefully blank. "It's used to relax horses. It's a tranquilizer."

"Yeah, so I'm told. Funny, I thought when a horse broke his leg, you put a gun behind his ear."

"The noise annoys the customers," Gabe said dryly. "And every break isn't terminal. There's a lot that can be done so that a horse doesn't have to be put down. Quite often he can race again, or breed. When there's nothing else to be done, a vet gives the horse an injection. There's not supposed to be any pain. I've always wondered how the hell anyone knows that."

"You won't be able to check with Lipsky. Do you keep any of that stuff around here?"

"It's administered by a vet, as I said. Nobody puts a horse down on a whim, Lieutenant."

"I'm sure you're right. It would be a hell of an investment to lose."

"Yeah." Gabe's voice was cool. "Have you ever seen it happen?"

"No."

"The horse stumbles on the track, falls. The jockey's off him like a flash, panicked, fighting it back. Everything gets quiet and grooms race out from everywhere. It doesn't have to be their horse. It's everybody's horse. Then you call the vet, and when there's no choice, when it can't be put off, the vet finishes him—behind a screen, for privacy."

"Have you ever lost one that way?"

"Once, about a year ago during a morning workout. That's a more dangerous time than a race. The rider's relaxed. Everybody is." He could still remember it, the helplessness, the impotent anger.

"This was a pretty filly. The Queen of Diamonds, I called her. The groom in charge of her cried like a baby when it was over. That was Mick." Gabe resisted the urge to ball his hands into fists. "So if you're telling me that somebody finished off Lipsky the way you finish off a terminal horse, I have to say they sent him off in better style than he deserved."

"Do you hold a grudge, Mr. Slater?"

"Yes, Lieutenant, I do." Gabe's eyes were steady and shielded. "You want to ask me if I killed Lipsky, I have to say no. I'm not sure what the answer would be if I'd known what you've told me today, and if I had found him first."

"You know something, Mr. Slater, I like you."

"Is that so?"

"It is." Rossi offered one of his rare smiles, an expression that never sat quite comfortably on his face. "Some people dance all around questions, some fumble, some sweat. But not you." Rossi picked a mote of lint from the leg of his trousers. "You hated the son of a bitch, and might have killed him if you'd had the chance. And you're not afraid to say so. Thing is, not only do I like you, I believe you." He rose. "Now, it could be you're bluffing me through this, and I'll find out if you paid a quick visit to that motel. But I always circle around, so that doesn't worry me." He took another long, careful study. "But I don't think so. Lipsky would've gotten one peep at you through the judas hole and barricaded himself in for the duration. Do you mind if I go down and talk to your men now?"

"No, I don't mind." Gabe stayed where he was; Rossi knew the way. He closed his eyes and concentrated on relaxing one vertebra at a time.

He gave Rossi an hour before he went down to the barn himself. The atmosphere was charged with the combination of excitement and dread that blooms around death. Men stopped their gossiping and instantly looked busy when Gabe appeared.

He found Jamison in conference with Matt over the injured colt.

"The inflammation's down," Matt was saying. "It's healing well. Go to changing the dressing once a day, using the same antiseptic."

"He's going to scar."

Matt nodded, eyeing the long healing slice along the flank. "More than likely."

"Goddamned shame." Jamison picked up the syringe to bathe the wound. "Prime-looking horse like this."

"It'll add to his prestige," Gabe commented, moving up to take the colt's halter himself. He ran his knuckles down Double's cheek, as a man might caress a woman. The colt responded by butting his hand, playful as a puppy. "Battle scars," he murmured. "It won't affect his time, or his ambition. How soon can we put a rider up on him?"

"Don't be in a hurry." Matt jerked aside as the colt swung his head and aimed for his shoulder, no longer a puppy but nine hundred pounds of temperament. The teeth missed by an inch or so. "This one's always testing me. Like to take a chunk out of me, would you, fella?" He gave the colt a good-natured slap on the neck when he was sure Gabe had tightened his grip. "He'll run in Kentucky for you, Gabe. If I was a betting man, I'd put money on him myself."

Gabe accepted Matt's diagnosis, then turned to his trainer. "Jamie?"

"I've been laying out a new training schedule for him. It'll either work, or it won't."

"That'll have to do, then. Did Rossi talk to you?"

Jamison's eyes turned grim as he completed the new dressing. "Yeah. He was down here, asking his questions. Got everybody all stirred up. Peterson figures it was a mob hit. Kip thinks it was a woman. Lynette didn't take to that and took some skin off his nose. They've been arguing over it, with the boys taking sides."

"Nobody thinks it was suicide?"

Jamison shot Gabe a look and stepped out of the box. "Nobody that knew him."

"He could have gotten his hands on some acepromazine," Matt reminded Jamison. "He'd have known what it would do. Surely he had to know the authorities would catch up with him eventually."

"A man like Lipsky could have lost himself at a hundred tracks." Jamison looked back at the colt. He was dressing the wound himself, as penance for his part in it. "I should have fired him months ago. Everything might've been different then." And Mick might have been alive.

"That part's done," Gabe said. "But it's not over. Whoever gave Lipsky that last drink is part of it."

"I'll tell you what I told Rossi." Matt scratched his chin as they headed outside. "It had to be someone who knows horses, and who had access to veterinary supplies." He smiled wanly. "Which doesn't narrow it down too much."

"It includes all of us." Gabe watched Matt's jaw go slack. "And several hundred others. Thanks for stopping by."

Matt swallowed nervously. "No problem. I'll check on the colt in a couple of days. I, um, think I'll drop by Three Willows."

"Oh." Eyeing Matt, Gabe took out a cigar and lit it casually. "Is there a problem over there?"

"No, no. I just . . . Well."

Gabe's smile came easily. Most of the tension drained away. "She's a pleasure to look at, isn't she?"

Matt flushed, a curse of pale skin. "It isn't a hardship. Channing told me he thinks she might stay around a while." He'd done his best to pump Channing for details, but the young man was either very discreet or very dense when it came to his stepsister.

"Oh, I think she'll stay a while." Gabe was going to make certain of that. "And you look all you want." He swung an arm over Matt's shoulder as he walked Matt to his truck. "A saint couldn't blame you for it. But watch where you touch, Doc."

As Matt fumbled for a response, Gabe opened the truck door for him. "Mine," he said simply.

"You—" He broke off, flushed crimson. "I didn't realize. Kelsey never . . . I never—"

"If I thought you had, I'd have to hurt you." Gabe's smile was friendly, even sympathetic, but the warning was clear. "Give Kelsey my best when you see her."

"Sure." Scurrying to leave, Matt scrambled into the truck. "But you know, maybe I should just get back. I've got a pile of paperwork."

"Then I'll let you get to it." Gabe stepped back, grinning as he watched the truck zip up the long lane.

"You scared the boy white." Jamison thumbed out one of his favored cherry Life Savers.

"Just saving him some trouble down the road."

"That may be." Studying the last of Matt's dust, Jamison let the cool, slick flavor dissolve on his tongue. "Does she know you've put your brand on her?"

Gabe chuffed out smoke, remembering, with fondness, her reaction to his very deliberate public kiss. "She's a bright woman."

"Bright women are the ones who give a man the most trouble."

"I haven't had any trouble in a long time." And he hadn't known just how much he'd wanted some. "I might just drive over myself, and see if I can stir some up." The distraction would do him good, he decided, and he turned to look at his trainer.

He'd been focused on the colt in the barn, and on Matt. Now he could see the lines of weariness, the shadowed eyes. "You look beat, Jamie."

He'd been sleeping poorly, and he'd found it harder yet to choke down a decent meal since Mick's murder.

"I've got a lot on my mind."

"One thing you can get off of it is any responsibility for what happened to Mick." When Jamison merely looked away, Gabe tossed down his cigar and ground it out. The expression in Jamison's eyes only churned up his own feelings of guilt. "Okay, you used poor judgment in keeping him on. I used it in firing him in front of the men. You want to consider that the trigger, fine. But it wasn't the finger that pulled it."

"I see him—Mick—every time I close my eyes." Jamison's voice was low, strained. "The way he must have looked when Lipsky and the colt got done with him. It should never have happened, Gabe." He let out a sigh. There was no answer for that. He knew there was none. "The Derby's in three and a half weeks. That colt's got to be ready, and it's my job to make him so. But I look at him, and I think how proud Mick was to be grooming him."

Saying nothing, Gabe looked out over the hills. His hills. The Derby was more than a race. More even than a goal. It was the Holy Grail he'd been chasing all of his life.

Now, after a lifetime of struggle, and five years of concentrated effort, it was nearly within reach. Maybe it would be empty when he finally grasped it, but he had to know.

"The colt's got to run, Jamie. If you can't work with him, I'll pass him to Duke." Duke Boyd, the assistant trainer, was competent. They both knew it. But he didn't have that extra flair Jamison had been born with. "One way or another, he'll be ready for Churchill Downs."

"I'll do my job," Jamison said, and rubbed his tired eyes.

"I need your heart in it."

Jamison dropped his hands. "You'll have it, goddammit. And my soul as well." He turned away and stalked back to the barn.

Kelsey knew she wasn't supposed to fall in love with the horse. But intellect had nothing to do with it. She was as fascinated with the new wobbly-legged foal as she was with the older colts—and had been kicked only once in return for her affection.

Perhaps because she'd taken that philosophically, and had hauled herself up and brushed herself off, Moses began to increase her training.

He liked her style, the way she responded to the horses. And what was more important, he liked the way they responded to her.

Still, he was pleased when he saw she was as much nerves as eagerness when he took her to the yearling stable. He'd consulted with the yearling manager, and between them, they'd culled out this particular filly, a bold little chestnut, weighing in at a trim seven hundred and fifty pounds.

The light was gold, almost liquid with dawn. It poured onto the filly's coat, inflamed it. Eyes dazzled, Kelsey stood just inside the box. She was sure she'd never seen anything quite so beautiful in her life.

"She's got spirit," Moses said as he worked with a handler to calm her as she was saddled. "And she's got heart. That's why Naomi called her Honor. Naomi's Honor."

As if responding to her name, the filly butted Moses, hard. The vibration sang up his shoulder. He gave a firm jerk on the shortened reins, and continued.

"You'll be the first weight she's had on her back. Now, don't go thinking she's sweet and eager to please. She's used to having her freedom. We can't know what to expect. She's a lot stronger than you." He glanced back at Kelsey, as if dismissing her slight frame in the padded jacket and hat. "So you have to be smarter." He stroked a hand over the yearling, neck to withers. "And kinder."

That was why he'd chosen Kelsey. No one could work successfully with yearlings without kindness.

The stall was quiet. Moses spoke so softly they might have been in church. He clucked to the yearling, then to Kelsey, signaling her to move in and make her connection.

Her heart was thudding, so loud and hard in her throat she was sure it would spook the yearling. But her hands were gentle, her movements slow. She spoke barely above a whisper, watching Honor's ears prick to the sound of her voice.

"You're so pretty. So pretty, Honor. I can't wait to ride you. We're going to be friends, you and I."

The yearling snorted, reserving judgment. Her ears laid back when Moses slipped the bridle over her head.

"Easy now," Kelsey murmured. "Nobody's going to hurt you. Before long, you'll be a queen around here. I bet that feels strange, doesn't it?" She continued to soothe while Moses tightened the saddle. "You should try panty hose. I'll lay odds they're more uncomfortable than this little saddle."

The light changed subtly, warmed.

"I'm going to give you a leg up," Moses told her. "Remember what I said to do?"

"Yes." She had to take a deep, clearing breath. "I don't sit in the saddle yet. The bellying comes first."

"That's right. Remember, it's an announcement. You're telling her this is what she's here for. Slow now. And remember where the door is if you need to get out quick."

The idea of that had Kelsey taking one more breath before she put her knee, and her welfare, in Moses's hands.

The yearling shied, surprised, annoyed as Kelsey draped herself over the saddle. Kelsey felt the agitated movement under her and refused to think about being sprawled over several hundred pounds of irritated horse. She followed Moses's instructions and her own instincts, easing herself up and around, shifting her weight to saddle and stirrups.

Honor danced, kicking out with a hind leg, trying to shift to get a good clean shot at Moses. Instinctively, Kelsey leaned forward, spoke softly, firmly in the yearling's ear.

"Stop that. You don't want everyone to think you're common."

It wasn't magic. The voice and the tone didn't immediately calm her. But after a few more arrogant maneuvers, the yearling settled.

"She likes me," Kelsey announced.

"She's thinking about how to shake you off her back."

"No." Kelsey grinned down at Moses. "She likes me."

"We'll see." He made Kelsey sit until he was satisfied. "All right. Let's get to work."

This, as Moses explained, was kindergarten. Kelsey would simply sit in the saddle while the handler walked Honor on the yearling track, the high walls preventing both of them from being distracted from the job at hand.

Once the yearling had become accustomed to a rider's weight, she would be turned loose by the handler. And Kelsey would guide her.

They'd learn together.

"How did she do?" Naomi asked when she joined him.

"Like you'd expect. She's got plenty of Chadwick in her." Moses put a hand over hers, squeezed briefly in one of his rare displays of public affection. "I thought you'd come down and watch for yourself."

"I was too nervous." She watched Kelsey control the yearling with a light tug on the reins. "She's been here a month, Moses. She hasn't said anything about leaving." Naomi hooked her thumbs in her front pockets. "With everything that's happened in the past couple of weeks, I keep waiting for her to pack up and go."

"You're not looking close enough, Naomi." He smiled a little when Kelsey forgot the training and leaned forward to press her face into the yearling's mane. "She's not going anywhere."

At Moses's signal, Kelsey straightened, then walked the yearling sedately over. "She's gorgeous, isn't she?"

"Yes." The pride that welled up in Naomi was almost frightening. She lifted a hand to stroke the yearling, and let her fingertips brush against Kelsey's. "You look wonderful together."

"I feel wonderful." After Moses had fed Honor a carrot as a reward, Kelsey held out a hand. "Don't I deserve one?"

"I guess you do, at that."

She accepted one and bit in. "Now that I've stopped being terrified, I can enjoy it." After patting Honor on the neck, she tried not to gloat. "Can I work her tomorrow, Moses?"

"And the day after," he said. "She's your responsibility now."

"Really?" She wanted to leap off and kiss him, but settled for beaming at him. "I won't let you down."

"You do, and I'll dock your pay."

Now she grinned. "I'm not getting paid."

"You've been on the payroll for two weeks." He had the satisfaction of seeing her jaw drop. "You get your first check on Friday."

"But it isn't necessary. I'm just—"

"You do the work, you get the pay." He said it firmly. He was, after all, in charge of this particular matter. "Of course, you're starting at the bottom. That's about where you started, isn't it, Naomi?"

"Rock bottom," she replied with a grimace. "My father insisted I earn every penny of my salary, paltry as it was. The idea was, when it all came to be mine, I'd appreciate it more. He was right."

Kelsey considered. It was probably best, more of a business arrangement. "How paltry?"

"You should probably clear about two hundred a week," Moses told her.

She lifted a brow. "When do I get a raise?"

With a laugh, Naomi stepped closer. "He'd have appreciated you." Gently, she skimmed her fingertips over the yearling's throat. "She likes you."

Kelsey sent Moses a smug smile. "That's what I said."

"I missed twenty-three birthdays." Naomi's tone shifted Kelsey's attention back. And now her eyes were wary. "Twenty-three Christmases. A lot to make up for." Steadying herself, she looked up and met her daughter's eyes. "I'd like to start, if you'll let me. Will you take her?"

"Take her?" Staggered, Kelsey stared. "Honor? You want to give her to me?"

"I'd like you to accept her. No strings. I realize it might be a bit awkward to keep a horse in an apartment"—she struggled to keep her voice light—"but she can stay here as long as you like. Moses can work with her, if that's what you want. But she'd be yours, if you'll talk her."

Swamped with emotion, Kelsey dismounted, slowly. Her palms grew damp on the reins, and she felt the warm breath of the yearling across the nape of her neck.

"I'd love to take her. Thank you."

"You're welcome. I have to get back. I have a lunch meeting."

Kelsey took a step forward, then stopped, suddenly pushing the reins into Moses's hand. She had to dash to catch up with Naomi's long strides. She laid a tentative hand on Naomi's shoulder, and did what came more simply, more naturally than she'd imagined. She kissed her.

"Thank you," she said again, but the rest of the words slid down her throat when Naomi embraced her, held her hard.

And where, Kelsey thought as she felt the urgency, the need pulse from her mother, had this passion come from? How could it have been there all along and never showed?

"I'm sorry," Naomi murmured, and stepped back quickly. "I'll have the ownership papers drawn up right away. I'm late," she managed, and hurried away.

Conflicting emotions battered her. Kelsey stood helplessly, wishing she understood herself, much less the woman who'd given birth to her.

"I don't know what to do."

"You're doing fine." Moses handed her back the reins. "Now go groom your horse."

13

Days passed quickly. Kelsey had a horse of her own, an intriguing romance with a fascinating and frustrating man, and a fresh curiosity about the mother she was beginning to love.

She hadn't expected to love Naomi. To wonder about her, certainly. Perhaps to come to respect her. But it was impossible to live in such close proximity with a woman of Naomi's breed and not have emotions become tangled.

There wasn't much time to dwell on it. As the Bluegrass Stakes approached, the gateway for the all-important Derby, both Three Willows and Longshot were hives of activity.

Kelsey wasn't ready to admit it, but she was already visualizing Honor covered in a blanket of red roses a couple of Derbies down the road.

Today, she was taking an important step toward that goal.

A starting gate was set up outside the practice oval at Three Willows. Though there was no longer any bite of winter, the air was still cool. Kelsey tugged nervously at her jacket, hoping she wasn't transmitting any of her tension to Honor.

A Thoroughbred was born to run, she reminded herself. This was just a lesson in format. No amount of champion blood could carry a horse over the finish line if it didn't learn how to go through a steel cage and come out running.

"Heard you think you've got a contender here." Gabe sauntered over and rubbed a hand over the yearling's nose. Honor laid her ears back and eyed Gabe, then, approving of scent and touch, perked them up again and sidled closer.

"I know I've got one." Kelsey put a proprietary hand on Honor's halter. "I haven't seen you around in a couple of days."

"Miss me?"

"Not particularly." Kelsey could be grateful she hadn't fallen into that humiliating habit of waiting by the phone. Yet. "We're all pretty busy these days."

"We've got Double back in full training."

She dropped all pretense and caught his hand. "Oh, that's wonderful! I'm so glad."

He pleased himself by taking a nip at her knuckles. "Remember you said that after he wins the Derby."

"My money's on Pride." And so was her heart. "Though I might set some aside for Double to place."

"We're sending him out to Keeneland for a race. Jamie wants him to have a solid test before the Bluegrass Stakes."

"Are you going?" she said casually.

"I'm going everywhere the colt goes, including the winner's circle at Churchill Downs." He stroked a hand down her hair, in much the same way he had caressed the horse. "Want to keep me company?"

She turned to check the cinches on Honor's saddle. "I'm planning on joining Naomi in the winner's circle."

He gave her hair a sharp tug. "To Keeneland, darling. A couple of days, more or less alone." He moved closer. She carried the scent of horses about her now, twined with her own fragrance of citrus and spring. "I wonder how many times I can make love with you on one quick out-of-town trip."

The muscles in her thighs turned to warm wax. "Is there a record?"

"There would be." Eyes on hers, he leaned down and caught her bottom lip between his teeth. "You have"—he nipped once, and watched her pupils widen—"the most incredible mouth."

"Leave the girl alone." Trying to look annoyed, Moses gave Gabe a hefty shove on the arm. "You going to fraternize with the competition, Kelsey, or are you going to do your job?"

She picked up her hat and lifted her chin. "I can do both." She turned toward her horse, and Moses obliged her with a leg up.

"Cocky," he muttered at her.

"Confident," she corrected. And anything but, she walked Honor toward the steel cage.

The gate doors were open, to ease the yearling into the notion of moving through the confining tunnel. Honor swung her head once and tried to veer off. Testing, Kelsey knew, the balance of power.

"Oh no, you don't," she muttered. "I'm still in charge here. You don't want to embarrass us both in front of company, do you?" A touch of the knees, a firm hold on the reins, and Kelsey pressed her on, bringing Honor to a full halt when they were closed in by the gate.

"It's not so bad, is it?" she murmured. "And you hardly have to spend any time in here at all. What really counts is once you're through." Slowly, they walked out the other side, circled, and repeated the process.

"She's got good hands," Moses commented.

"She looks more like Naomi than ever on the back of a horse." Gabe tucked his hands in his pockets. There might have been a better way to spend the morning than watching Kelsey guide the flashy yearling through the lesson. But he couldn't think of one. "How's it going between them?"

"Slow, steady. It's not a flashy sprint, but I'd say they passed the first turn when Naomi gave her that yearling."

"She has high hopes for that horse."

"She's got higher hopes for the girl." Gauging the timing, Moses angled himself to face Gabe. "I know she's got a father, but he isn't here. So I'm taking it on myself to tell you to mind your step. Kelsey isn't one of the disposable types, and it would upset Naomi if you hurt her girl."

Gabe's face closed up. When he spoke there was none of the resentment he felt, none of the temper, only mild curiosity in his voice. "And you're assuming I will."

Moses plucked a cigar from Gabe's pocket and stuck it in his own. "Don't pull that inscrutable shit on me. My tribe held the trophy for inscrutable while your ancestors were still huddled in caves eating their meat raw. And I'm not assuming anything. The two of you look good together." He shifted his eyes to check on Kelsey's progress. "Just make sure you think it through. You don't know if a roll in the hay's going to hurt anybody until you're picking the straw out of your hair."

Gabe's lips quivered into a smile. "Which tribe did that one come from? The inscrutable one or the lost one?"

"Just don't push her over the wire too fast. She's got heart." Irritated with himself, Moses trudged across the grass to fine-tune Kelsey's work.

Yes, she had heart, Gabe agreed, studying her as she listened intently to the trainer's advice. And blue blood.

There were plenty who knew him who would say he had no heart at all. And no one would mistake his blood for blue. It hadn't stopped him before. He didn't intend to let it stop him now.

There were any number of women who were willing to overlook those particular flaws in his breeding. Many who had. More, he thought coolly, who would shrug aside a drunk, abusive father, a short stint in a cell, and a lingering taste for playing against the odds.

But he didn't want any number of women, he decided, while Kelsey guided her mount into the gate and steadied her in the confining tunnel. He wanted this woman.

He waited, taking out a pair of sunglasses as the sun grew stronger. The morning was slipping away, and he needed to get back to his own operation. But he drew on his store of patience, staying on the sidelines until Kelsey dismounted.

"She did well," Kelsey said, pressing a kiss to the yearling's cheek before offering her a carrot. "She wasn't afraid at all."

"I want to see you tonight."

"What?" She turned her head, her cheek still brushing Honor's glossy hide.

"I'd like to take you out tonight. Dinner, a movie, a drive. Your choice. A date," he continued when she only studied him with eyes that grew more speculative. "I realize I've neglected that particular ritual with you."

"A date?" She rolled the idea around. "Such as you pick me up, we go somewhere and do some planned activity, then you bring me home and walk me to the door?"

"That's more or less what I had in mind."

"Well, it would be different." She cocked her head, considering. "I have to be up at five, so we'll need to make it an early evening. I wouldn't mind seeing a movie, say a seven o'clock show. Maybe a pizza after."

Now it was his turn to consider. It wasn't the sort of evening he'd expected her to choose. Maybe it was about time they learned about each other. "An early movie and a pizza. I'll pick you up around six." He tipped up her chin, kissed her almost absently.

"Hey, Slater," she called after him. "Do I get to pick the movie?"

He kept walking but glanced over his shoulder. "No subtitles."

"On a first date?" She laughed at him. "What kind of woman do you think I am?"

"Mine," he shot back, and she stopped laughing.

There was nothing romantic about a pizzeria crowded with teenagers. Which had been precisely Kelsey's point. Keep it casual, she'd decided. Avoid a situation where things could become too intense and try to find out what made Gabriel Slater tick.

"This is perfect." She settled into the booth with paper place mats of Italy printed in red and green. "I'd almost forgotten there was life beyond racing horses."

"It happens to all of us." Amused at finding himself dining with a woman in a place that sported pictures of grinning pizzas and calzones on the wall, he stretched out his legs. "You've taken to it quickly, and in a big way."

"A talent of mine. Or a flaw, depending on your point of view. Why do anything if you don't do it full out?" She relaxed and propped her feet on his bench. "That way you either reap the glory, or you crash and burn."

"Is that what you're after, Kelsey? Glory?"

She smiled. "I always get glory and satisfaction confused." She glanced up at the waitress, back at Gabe. "Your pick. I'll eat anything."

"I won't. Bring us a small—"

"*Large,*" Kelsey corrected him.

"Large," he said with a nod. "Pepperoni and mushrooms, a couple of Pepsis."

"Very conservative," Kelsey noted when the waitress walked off.

"I like to know what I'm eating." It came, he supposed, from a lifetime of scrambling for scraps. "Speaking of which, wasn't it you who ate about two gallons of popcorn less than an hour ago?"

Still smiling, she toyed with the simple gold chain around her neck. "Movie popcorn doesn't count. It's simply part of the experience, like the music score."

"Was there a music score? Hard to tell."

"So I'm shallow," she said with a shrug. "I like action films. I actually wrote a script once, for this course I was taking. Lots of good battling evil in car chases and gunfire."

"What did you do with it?"

Absently she tapped her foot in rhythm with the Guns N' Roses number blaring from the jukebox. "I got an *A*, then I put it away. I decided against sending it off because if anyone actually bought it, they'd start changing everything and it wouldn't be mine anymore." The waitress served their drinks in big red plastic cups. "Besides, I didn't want to be a writer."

"What, then?"

"Lots of different things." She moved her shoulders, then leaned forward for her cup. "It always depended on my mood. And the courses I was taking." Her smile was quick and slightly off center. "I'm very big on taking courses. If you want to know a little about anything, from computer science to interior design, I'm your girl."

"Makes sense. You grew up with a college professor." He lifted his cup. "Knowledge is sacred."

"That's part of it, I suppose. But mostly I figured if I tried enough things, sooner or later I'd hit on the right thing."

"And have you?"

"Yes." She sighed. "My family would be quick to point out that I've said that before. But this is different. I've said that before, too," she murmured. "But it is. Nothing I've done has ever felt as right as this, as natural. As real. God knows I've never worked as hard in my life."

To remind herself, she glanced down at her hands. They were toughening up, she thought. She liked to believe she was toughening up with them.

"What about you? Have you hit on the right thing?"

He kept his eyes on hers. For an instant she thought she saw secrets behind them, and hungers that had nothing to do with the scents of garlic and melted cheese.

"It's possible."

"Do you always look at a woman so that she thinks you could start nibbling away at her, from the toes up?"

His lips curved, slow, easy, but his eyes didn't change. "No one's ever asked." He laid a hand on her ankle, which rested on the seat beside him, and began to caress it. "But now that you mention it, it might be an interesting way to end the evening."

The waitress plopped down their pizza, along with a couple of white plastic plates. "Enjoy your meal," she said automatically, and hurried off to fill her next order.

"I love the atmosphere here." Cautious, Kelsey put her feet on the floor and sat up. "But I got off the track. I was asking about your farm. Have you found what you wanted there?"

He used a plastic knife to separate some slices, then slid one onto her plate, one onto his. "It suits me."

"Why?"

"You know, darling, you might have made a mistake giving up writing. At least journalism."

"You can't have the answers without asking the questions." She took her first bite, stinging with red-pepper flakes, stringy with cheese, and sighed with approval. "At least with some people. Don't you like questions, Slater?"

He avoided that one and skipped back to the one before. "It suits me because it's mine."

"It's that simple?"

"No, it's that complicated. You don't want to spoil the evening with a rundown of my life story, Kelsey. Bad for the appetite."

"I have a strong stomach." She licked sauce from her thumb. "You know mine, Gabe. At least several of the highs and lows. There's no moving to the next stage for me without some understanding of who I'm moving with." She continued to eat while he frowned at her. "That's not an ultimatum, or a guarantee. It's just a fact. I'm attracted to you, and I like being with you. But I don't know you."

If she did, he knew there was a good chance her other feelings would dim considerably. Long odds. Well, he'd played them before. When the prize was rich enough. "Let me tell you something about yourself first. The only child of a devoted daddy. Well connected, sheltered. Spoiled."

The last rankled a little, but she wouldn't deny it. "All right. It's true I got almost everything I wanted when I was growing up. Emotionally. Materialistically. I suppose a lot of it was to make up for the lack of having a mother. But I didn't notice the lack."

"A big house in the suburbs," he went on. "Good schools. Summer camp, three squares, and ballet lessons."

If he was trying to annoy her, he was succeeding. Coolly, she chose another slice. "You forgot piano, swimming, and equestrian."

"It's all part of the whole. Proms, the college of your choice, and a big splashy wedding to top it off."

"Don't forget the long, tedious divorce. What's your point, Slater?"

"You haven't got a clue where I came from, Kelsey. I'll tell you and you still won't understand it."

But he would tell her, he decided. And see how the cards fell.

"Maybe I'd go to bed at night not quite hungry. There might have been enough money for food that time, or I'd managed to steal or beg enough. Kids make good panhandlers, good thieves," he added, watching her eyes. "Adults feel sorry for them, or overlook them."

"A lot of people are put in the position where they have to ask for money," she said carefully. "It's nothing to be ashamed of."

"That's because you've never had to ask. Or take." He rattled the ice in his cup, then set it down. "At night I'd probably be listening, or trying not to listen, to the fighting going on in the next room. Or my mother crying. Or the neighbor earning an hour's pay with some faceless john. If I was lucky, I'd wake up in the same bed I went to sleep in. If I wasn't, my mother would come in in the middle of the night, and we'd sneak out before we were tossed out because my father had lost the rent money again."

She saw the picture he was painting for her, and it was dark with harsh edges. "Where did you grow up?"

"Nowhere. It might have been in Chicago, or Reno, or Miami. In the winter we stuck to the south, because the weather's better and the tracks run longer. It might have been anywhere. Places all look the same if you're broke and running. Of course, the old man would say we were just moving on. That he was working on a big score. My mother scrubbed toilets so we didn't starve, and he took most of her pay and blew it on the horses, or the cards, or how far a fucking grasshopper would jump. It didn't matter what the bet was as long as he could flash a few bills and play the big shot."

He spoke without passion, the bitterness barely a flicker in his eyes. "He liked to cheat. Mostly he was good at it, but if he wasn't, my mother scraped enough together to keep him from getting his arms broken. She loved him." And that was the most bitter of all the pills he had had to swallow. "Lots of women loved Rich Slater."

He continued to eat, as if to prove to himself it didn't matter anymore. "He liked to hurt them. Some women keep coming back for another fist in the face. They wear their black eyes and split lips like badges. My mother was one of those. If I tried to stop him, he'd just beat the hell out of both of us. She never thanked me for it, used to tell me I just didn't understand. She was right," he added. "I never understood it."

"There must have been somewhere you could have gone. A shelter. Social services. The police."

He simply looked at her, the flawless complexion, the breeding that went down to the bone. "Some people get swept into dirty corners, Kelsey. That's the way the system works."

"No, it doesn't have to. It shouldn't."

"You've got to look for help, expect it to be there, have the nerve to ask for it. My mother didn't do any of that. She kept her eyes down, expected nothing, asked for nothing."

It was Kelsey's eyes that held him now, the horror and the pity that darkened them.

"But you were only a child. Someone should have . . . done something."

"I wouldn't have thanked them for it. I grew up being taught to spit if I saw a cop, to think of social workers as interfering paper pushers whose job it was to keep you from doing what you wanted. So I avoided them. Sometimes I went to school, sometimes I didn't. Christ knows he didn't care, and my mother didn't have the energy left to reel me in. So I did pretty much as I pleased. The old man liked me to hang out with him, sometimes to shill, or to drum up a game of my own. And if I was there I could make sure some money was left once he got too drunk to care."

"You must have thought of running away, of getting away from him."

"Sure, I thought about it. But I figured if I stayed, I could keep him from beating her to death. And I did, for what good it did any of us. My mother died in a charity ward. Pneumonia. I gave it six months, squirreling away the money I made hustling games or jobs at the track. Then I took off. I was thirteen."

And tall for his age, he remembered. Canny. Already old.

"The old man caught up with me a few times. The problem was I had a taste for the horses, so I usually ended up at a track. So did he. He'd knock me around, shake me down. I could usually buy him off."

"Buy him off?"

"If I'd been having a run of luck, I'd have money. A couple of hundred would send him off to a game of his own, or the nearest bar." Of course, Gabe thought, the price had gone up since then. "Every time I cut loose, I'd start over—with one thing in mind. One day I'd have my own. He wouldn't touch me. Nobody would. You're not eating."

"I'm sorry." She reached out and caught his hand firmly in hers. "I'm really sorry, Gabe."

It wasn't pity he was looking for. He realized now that he'd wanted her to be horrified, wanted her to look at him and cringe back. He'd have an excuse then, wouldn't he, to step away from her and stop the headlong race to a future he couldn't see.

"I spent some time in jail over a poker game I wasn't quick enough to spot as a sting." He waited for her to comment on that, but she said nothing. "I was a small fish, but I got reeled in with the big ones. When I got out, I was smarter. I worked some short cons, but I was more into gambling than the grift. Working at stables was a good way to earn a stake. And I liked the horses. I stayed clean because I didn't like prison. I didn't drink because every time I started to I smelled my old man. And I got lucky."

Finished, he sat back and lit a cigar. "Understand better now?"

Did he really think she couldn't see the anger, the scarred-over hurt? People might pass by their table and see a man chatting over a meal, enjoying the company. But if they looked into his eyes, really looked, how could they miss that cold, steely rage? Determined, she put her hand back on his.

"Maybe I can't understand the way you mean. But I think I know it was a nightmare to live with an alcoholic who—"

"He's not an alcoholic," Gabe cut in, his tone frigid. "There's a difference between an alcoholic and a drunk, Kelsey. No twelve-step program is going to change the fact that he's a drunk, a mean one, who likes to beat up on women, or anyone weaker than he is. And it wasn't a nightmare. It was life. My life."

She withdrew her hand. "You'd rather I didn't understand."

He turned his cigar, stared at the tip. He hadn't realized that simple, unquestioning sympathy would bring so many memories, and the feelings that went with them, swirling to the surface. "You're right. I'd rather you look at me and take what you see. Or leave it."

"We're both a product of our upbringing, Gabe. One way or another. I'm not going to care about someone because of what they seem to be. Not again. And if you want me, you're going to have to accept that I care."

He tapped out his cigar. "That definitely sounds like an ultimatum."

"It is." She shoved her plate aside and picked up her jacket. "It's a long drive home. We'd better get started."

She would think a great deal about the little boy who had hustled and conned his way through childhood. A child who had gone to bed at night listening to whores and drunks instead of lullabies.

How much of the boy remained with the man, she didn't know. More, she thought, than Gabe believed. More, she was certain, than anyone would ever be allowed to see.

He had, quite simply, refashioned himself. The smooth, easy manners, the stunning house on the hill, his stable of champions. How many of the upper crust of the racing circle knew his back-alley upbringing? If they did, was it considered some amusing eccentricity?

Whatever Gabe wanted to the contrary, she was beginning to understand him. And whether he could see it or not, she already cared.

It was nearly one A.M. when Bill Cunningham hurried to answer the banging at his front door. Over his naked paunch he wrapped a Chinese red silk robe. A peek through the window made him glad Marla, his latest honey, was a sound sleeper. He liked to think it was great sex that had her snoring away in his big water bed. But more likely it was the 'ludes she ate like candy.

Whatever the reason, it relieved him that he was alone to greet his late and unwelcome visitor.

"I told you never to come here," Cunningham hissed while smoothing down what was left of his hair. Once the Derby was over, he was going to treat himself to a weave.

"Now, now, Billy boy, nobody saw me." Rich was past the midpoint of a solid drunk. He didn't wobble, didn't so much as slur a word. But it showed in the sun-bright glitter in his eyes. "And if they did, hell—no law against a man visiting an old poker buddy, is there?" He grinned, casting his gaze around the opulent foyer. Old Bill had bounced back pretty well, Rich noted, and figured he could squeeze his pal for a few more bills. "How about a drink?"

"Are you crazy?" Despite the fact that only Marla was in the house, and she was cruising on barbiturates, Cunningham whispered. "Do you know the cops have been here? *Here,*" he repeated, as if his overdone home were as sacrosanct as a church. "Asking questions because some big-mouthed groom told them I'd let Lipsky shovel shit for a couple of days."

"Told you that was a mistake. But a little one." He held up two fingers close together, squinted at them. "Where's the bar, Bill? I'm dry as the fucking Sahara."

"I don't want you drinking in my house."

Rich's grin only widened, but his eyes turned hard. "Now, you don't want to talk to a business partner like that, Bill. Especially since I have a new proposition for you."

Cunningham moistened his lips. "We've got our deal."

"Just what I want to talk about. Over a friendly drink."

"All right, all right. But make it quick." He shot a look up the stairs as he walked by them, going into a sunken living room done in golds and royal blue. "And quiet. I've got a woman upstairs."

"You dog." Rich gave him a friendly poke in the ribs. "Don't suppose she's got a friend. I've been dry there a while, too."

"No. And keep your distance. I don't want her to know about you, or any of this. She's built, but she's not bright."

"Best kind of woman." With an appreciative sigh, Rich dropped down into a wide-backed chair covered in gold velvet. "You sure know how to live, pal. I always said, that Billy boy, he knows how to live."

"Just make sure you don't go around saying it now." Cunningham poured two drinks, both twelve-year-old scotch. It seemed like a waste on Rich, but he needed to impress. Always. "You were supposed to handle Lipsky."

"I did." Pleased with himself, Rich swirled the scotch, sniffed it, then swallowed it. "Classy, don't you think, to put him down like you put down a horse?"

Cunningham's hand shook as he lifted his glass. "I don't want to hear about that. I'm talking about before. Jesus, Rich, nobody was supposed to get killed. Old Mick was like a saint around the track."

"An unforeseen complication," Rich said, getting up to refill his glass. "And Lipsky certainly paid for it. But seeing that he did adds to my overhead, Bill. It's going to cost you another ten thousand."

"Are you nuts?" Cunningham sprang up, spilling some scotch. "You did that on your own, Rich."

"To protect your investment. It would have taken the cops five minutes to have Lipsky pointing the finger at me. It points at me," he said affably, "it points at you. So, another ten, Billy. It's a fair price."

He swallowed hard. The money that had come into his hands for Big Sheba had been a miracle. But the miracle had a price. "You might as well ask for ten million. I'm leveraged to the hilt."

Rich had expected that and was ready to be reasonable. "I can wait until after May, no problem. What's a couple of weeks between friends? Now . . ." He crossed his legs. "I've come up with an idea, Billy. A little variation on our theme that will pay off for both of us. You want to collect at Churchill Downs, and so do I. But I also have a job to do, and a score to settle with that boy of mine."

"I don't give a good goddamn about your family problems, as long as the job gets done." But the idea of paying Gabe back began to creep through him, warming more thoroughly than the scotch. "This business with Lipsky damn near ruined things."

"Not to worry. Not to worry." Lazily, Rich waved his glass. "I've got it covered—with, as I said, a little alteration."

"What kind of alteration?"

"Well now," Rich sighed, sipped. "I'm going to tell you. And I think you're going to appreciate the irony of the deal, Billy boy. I really think you are."

Later, when Cunningham crawled back into bed, he was shivering. He wasn't a bloodthirsty man, he assured himself. It wasn't his fault two people were dead. Just the luck of the draw, as Rich had said.

Maybe he was crazy to have tied in with Rich Slater, but he was desperate. And the timing had fallen so perfectly in his lap, he'd considered it a sign. Rich's adjusted plan made a hideous kind of sense.

What choice did he have? Cunningham asked himself. If he lost at Churchill Downs there would be no more Marlas, no more big country house, no more strutting into the paddock.

Big Sheba was, he'd thought, his ace in the hole. He'd sunk his money, every spare dollar and all he could borrow, into that filly. And she had short lungs. He squeezed his eyes shut, cursing himself for gambling on the horse.

He needed the Derby, just the Derby, to recoup. Once that was done, he'd breed her. He could live well on the price of her foals.

It had been done before, he thought, going back over Rich's plan. And he'd slipped through that without much more than a ripple. One race, he thought, just one good race.

Needing warmth, he wrapped himself around Marla until her snoring lulled him to sleep.

14

It was a longer drive than Kelsey remembered from rural Virginia to suburban Maryland. A long time to think. She didn't doubt she would meet with resistance. And unless things had changed in the last few weeks, formidable resistance. Candace was sure to have contacted Milicent to tell her Kelsey was on her way.

Better to face them all at once, Kelsey decided. To shock them, disappoint them, outrage them. A perfect description, she thought with a wry smile. Candace would be shocked, her father disappointed, and her grandmother outraged.

And she, she hoped, would be happy.

When she pulled up in the drive, her father was working in the flower bed. He wore an old sweater, patched at the elbows, and grimy-kneed chinos to weed the just-budding azaleas.

The surge of love came first as she dashed from her car and across the neatly trimmed lawn to hug him. They stayed, knee to knee, admiring the flourishing shrubs.

"I love this house," she murmured, resting her head on his shoulder. "Just recently I realized how lucky I was to grow up here." She thought of Gabe and brushed a hand over salmon-colored blooms. "How lucky I was to have you, to have flowers in the yard." She smiled a little. "Ballet lessons."

"You hated ballet lessons after six months," he remembered.

"But I was lucky to have them."

He studied her face, brushed at the hair that tumbled over her shoulders. "Is everything all right, Kelsey?"

"Yes."

"We've been worried about you. This recent violence—"

"I know." She cut him off. "It's horrible, what happened to both of those men. I wish I could tell you it doesn't affect me, but of course it does. But I am all right."

"I like seeing that for myself. Phone calls aren't the same." He gathered his gardening tools in a wire basket. "Well, you're home now. That's what matters. Let's go around through the back or Candace will skin me alive for tracking the floors."

Kelsey slipped an arm around his waist as they walked. "I see Grandmother's car."

"Yes, Candace phoned her when you said you were driving in. They're inside, planning for the spring charity ball at the club." He shot her a sympathetic smile. "I believe finding you a suitable escort is at the top of their list."

She winced automatically, then remembered. "The spring ball. That's in May, isn't it?"

"Yes, the first Saturday."

That was the day when spring came to Kentucky, she thought. The same day every year. Derby day. She supposed missing the ball would be another sin on her part.

"Dad." She waited as he set down his tools in the little mudroom that was as spotless as the rest of the house. "I'm not going to be in town that weekend."

"Not in town?" He moved through to the kitchen to wash his hands. "Kelsey, you haven't missed a spring ball since you were sixteen."

"I realize that. I'm sorry, but I have plans." He said nothing, only dried his hands on a towel. The disappointment, she thought, had already begun. "I have plans," she repeated. "I'd better tell all of you about them at once."

"All right, then." Trying not to worry, he went with her to the sitting room.

Candace and Milicent were already there, chatting over tiny, crustless sandwiches and Dresden cups of tea. Jasmine, Kelsey deducted after a discreet sniff of the air. It occurred to her that if she'd been at the barn at this time of day, she might be wolfing down a sloppy cold-cut sub and strong black coffee.

Her tastes, among other things, had changed quickly.

"Kelsey." With a delighted laugh, Candace rose to kiss both of her stepdaughter's cheeks. Kelsey caught the subtle scent of L'Air du Temps that mixed with the tea and her grandmother's signature Chanel.

Drawing-room scents, Kelsey thought; she'd gotten entirely too used to barnyard ones. She embraced Candace with more enthusiasm, almost in apology.

"You look wonderful. New hairdo?"

Instinctively Candace patted her short sable locks. "You don't think it's too ingenue, do you? I swear Princeton can talk me into anything."

"It's perfect," Kelsey assured her, remembering suddenly that she hadn't visited Princeton, or any other hairdresser, for that matter, in weeks. "Hello, Grandmother." The greeting, like the kiss on the cheek, was stiff and dutiful. "You're looking well too."

"You've gained back some weight, I see." Milicent sipped her tea, appraising Kelsey over the rim. "It's flattering. Be careful you don't let it go too far, though. Small bones don't carry weight well."

"Most of it's muscle." Kelsey flexed her biceps just to irritate. "It comes from shoveling manure and hauling hay." Smiling, she turned to a dubious Candace. "I'd love some tea. Don't worry, I washed up after the morning workout."

"Of course, of course. Sit down, dear. Philip, you're not carrying that garden with you?"

"Not a speck." He accepted the tea and a tiny sandwich without complaint. When Channing returned home that evening, Philip knew he'd have company on a refrigerator raid. "The azaleas are early this year. I don't think they've ever looked better."

"You say that every spring." Affectionately, Candace patted his hand. "You know, we're the only house on this block without a gardener, and there isn't a yard that can compete with ours. Not when Philip gets done working his magic."

"A nice hobby," Milicent agreed. "I've always preferred tending my own roses."

She turned her attention to Kelsey. At least, she thought, the girl had had enough sense to dress suitably. She'd been nearly certain Kelsey would flaunt her prickly stubbornness by driving out in muddy boots. But the apricot-toned jacket and slacks were flattering, and tasteful.

"As it happens," she began. "Candace and I were just discussing the floral arrangements for the spring ball. We're on the committee. You have a good eye for such things, Kelsey. We'll delegate you to work with the florist."

"I appreciate the confidence, but I'll have to pass. I'm afraid I won't be here."

"For the ball?" Candace laughed again, poured more tea. "Of course you will, dear. It's expected. I realize you might feel a little awkward, with the divorce finalized, and Wade attending with his fiancée, but you mustn't let it bother you. In fact, Milicent and I were just working on a solution to that problem."

Kelsey started to explain, then stopped. "Oh, were you?"

"Yes, indeed." All enthusiasm, Candace added a lump of sugar to her tea. "It was certainly sweet of Channing to escort you last year, but we hardly want that to become a tradition. In any case, people will talk less if you have a more conventional date." The perfect hostess, she offered around the tray of cucumber sandwiches. "As it happens, June and Roger Miller's son has just moved back to the area. You must remember Parker, Kelsey. He's been practicing oral surgery in New York for the last few years, and has just taken a position with a prestigious practice in D.C." She add with a sly smile, "Parker's never married."

"Yes, I remember him." Excellent family, social status. The right schools, the right profession, the right everything. It wasn't his fault, Kelsey supposed, that she saw him as a Wade Monroe clone.

"I've already spoken with the Millers." Pleased with the maneuver, Milicent sipped the delicately fragrant tea. "Parker will escort you. It's all arranged."

Typical, Kelsey thought, fighting a rising anger. It was all so typical. "I'm sure Mr. and Mrs. Miller are delighted to have Parker back in the area, and you'll have to give him my best. But I won't be here. I'm leaving for Kentucky this week, and won't be back until after the first weekend in May."

"Kentucky?" Milicent snapped her cup down in its saucer. "Why on earth are you going to Kentucky?"

"The Derby. Even in your circles, Grandmother, it's an acceptable event. I imagine it'll be a very hot topic of conversation at the ball after Three Willows' colt wins it." She looked at her father, hoping he would understand. "I'm going to be there when he does."

"This is inexcusable," Milicent shot back. "The Bydens are founding members of that club, back to your great-grandfather. We have always attended the ball."

"Things change." Kelsey fought to keep her tone reasonable rather than hard. "I have a job, a responsibility, and a need. I'm not willing to overlook any of them for a dance at the country club. And, Candace, as much as I appreciate your concern, I don't want an arranged escort. I'm involved with someone."

"Oh." Candace blinked and struggled to look pleased. "Well, of course, dear, that's delightful. You must bring him."

"I don't think so." In sympathy, she squeezed Candace's hand. "I don't think he's the country club type."

"One of your stable hands, I suppose," Milicent said bitterly.

"No." Unable to help herself, Kelsey didn't leave it at that. "He's a gambler."

"You're just like your mother." Spine ramrod stiff, Milicent rose. "I warned you," she said to Philip. "You wouldn't listen to me about Naomi, and you wouldn't listen to me about her daughter. Now we all pay the price."

"Milicent." Standing quickly, Candace hurried out of the room after her mother-in-law.

Kelsey set her tea aside. She'd been sorry almost before the words were out. Not because of Milicent's feelings, but her father's.

"That wasn't very tactful of me," she began.

"Honesty was always more your forte than tact."

His voice was weary and stirred up more guilt.

"You're disappointed. I wish there was a way I could do what I need to do and not disappoint you."

"It's a situation that can't please everyone." He rose, turning his back to her as he walked to the windows. He could see his azaleas, the tight buds just freeing up the inner blossoms. The blossoms wouldn't stay trapped, but would burst through the well-meaning protection and spring defiantly to life.

"You've connected with her," he said softly. "I can't say I didn't expect it. So much about you is the same, so much than your looks. A part of me, a part I'm ashamed of, wants to tell you that you're making a mistake. That you don't belong there. That part of me doesn't want to see how happy it makes you that you do belong there."

"I feel as though I've found what I'm supposed to do. That I don't need to race around the next corner to see if there's something there more interesting, more important. That's all I was doing with my life. We both know it."

"You were searching, Kelsey. That's nothing to be ashamed of."

"I'm not ashamed of it. But I'm tired of it. I'm good with the horses, with the work, with the people. I can't go back to my apartment, to busywork jobs, to weekends at the club. I feel as if I'm . . ."

"Opening up?" Because it hurt him to look at them now, he turned away from the flowers. "Breaking free?"

"Yes. I didn't know how dissatisfied I was—especially with myself."

"That may be." Candace swept back in. Her jaw was set, her eyes angry. "But you had no reason to be rude. Your father and I, and your grandmother, are only trying to help you through a difficult time."

"I think," Kelsey said slowly, "the problem is that this isn't as difficult for me as you think."

"Then you might think of others. About how Philip feels. About how all of this looks to outsiders."

"Candace," Philip said, "this isn't necessary."

"Isn't it?"

"Maybe you're right, Candace. I'm very much concerned how Dad feels. I'm sorry, but I don't have your sensibility about what outsiders think. I don't want to embarrass you," she continued, "or cause problems between the two of you."

"Yet you encouraged Channing to deceive me and stay at that place."

Boggy ground, Kelsey thought, and cursed Channing for leading her onto it. "I encouraged him to stay, yes."

"Now he has some notion about going back there, working there this summer." Flushed with emotion, Candace gripped the back of a chair. "She might have lured you away, Kelsey, but I won't have her corrupting Channing."

"Good God." At wits' end, Kelsey dragged her hands through her hair. "Where does this come from? You haven't even met the woman, but you've cast her as some B-movie siren who seduces young boys and destroys all she touches. She didn't open her home to Channing to corrupt him or to spite any of you. She did it for me. And she offered him the job because he showed an interest in the farm."

"Well, I won't have it." Candace detested sounding shrewish, resented the fact that Kelsey's stubbornness made her so. "I won't have my son loitering around racetracks and associating with gamblers and a convicted murderer."

Kelsey dropped her hands. "That's certainly between you and Channing."

"Yes, it is. It's quite true I have no right to tell you what to do." Her lips quivered. She'd done her best by Kelsey, her very best to be a friend, a guiding force instead of the textbook stepmother. And now, it seemed, she'd failed. "Even if I did, you'd continue to do as you choose. As you've always done."

Philip stepped forward, as perplexed as he was hurt by the outburst. "Candace, we're losing the perspective here. It's only a club dance."

"I'm sorry, Philip." Her angry embarrassment over the scene with Milicent pushed her forward. Milicent was more than her mother-in-law. She was her friend, and her ally. "I feel I must have my say in this. It's much more than a dance. It's a matter of loyalty, and proper behavior. This situation cannot go on. You've hurt your father enough by choosing Naomi over him."

"Is that what you think I'm doing?" She whirled on her father. "Is that what you think? Can't you believe that I'm capable of caring for both of you? Of learning to accept, and forgive?"

"You've nothing to forgive Philip for." Candace put in staunchly. "He did everything that was right."

"I did what I thought best," he murmured. "This is difficult for me, Kelsey. I can't tell you it isn't. But I still want what's best for you."

"I'm trying to find out what that is. Or, if not what's best, at least what's right. I don't want to hurt you in the process."

"I'm sure you don't," Candace said wearily. She'd never really understood her stepdaughter. Why should that change now? "The problem here, Kelsey, is the same as it's always been. You look straight ahead toward a goal and don't notice the consequences of achieving it. And when you have it, you don't always want it."

The thumbnail analysis stung more than any whip of anger. "Which makes me cold and shallow." Her voice trembled no matter how she fought to control it. "It's not the first time that's been pointed out to me, so it's hard to argue."

"That's not true." Philip took her by the shoulders. "And certainly not what Candace meant. You're strong-minded. Kelsey, and you can be stubborn. Those are virtues as well as flaws."

Candace took a mental step in retreat. She knew from experience her preferences would never hold against a united front. "We're concerned about you, Kelsey. If I criticized too harshly, it's only because of that concern, and the fact that the situation is becoming difficult for everyone. The recent publicity has stirred up old memories. People are beginning to talk, and that puts your father in a delicate position."

"Two men were killed." Steadier, Kelsey stepped back. "I had no control over that, nor do I have any over the gossip it generates."

"Two men were killed," Philip repeated. "Can you expect us not to worry?"

"No. I can only tell you it had nothing to do with me, or Three Willows. Violence happens everywhere. The racing world isn't a hive of vice and debauchery. There's no time or energy for either when you're up at dawn every morning. It's work. Hard work. Some of it tedious, some of it exciting, and all of it, to me, rewarding. There's no partying every night with champagne and mobsters. Hell, most nights we're sound asleep before ten. I've watched foals being born and seen grown men sing a sick horse to sleep at night. It's not a Disney movie, but it's no orgy of sin, either."

Philip said nothing. He knew he'd lost. It might have been Naomi standing there, defending a world he had never understood, and could never belong to.

"I'm sure it has its merits." Candace tried for calm. "I've watched the Kentucky Derby myself on television, and there's no denying the horses are magnificent, the entire event exciting. Why, the Hanahans had an interest in a racehorse a few years ago. You remember, Philip. We're not condemning the entire . . . profession"—she supposed it was called—"we're concerned about your associations. You did say you were involved with a gambler."

Kelsey let out a huff of breath. "I said that to needle Grandmother. What I should have said was that I'm interested in a man who owns a neighboring farm. I'm sorry I caused trouble. Now I'll apologize in advance because I'm about to cause more. I'm not renewing the lease on my apartment. I'm going to stay on at Three Willows, at least for the time being. I may look for a house later in the year, but I'm going to keep working at the farm."

Candace put a hand on Philip's arm, a gesture of support and unity. "No matter what the consequences?"

"I'll do my best to minimize them. I realize you won't want to visit me there, so I'll come to you as often as I can. I'll be out of town for a while, but I'll call." She picked up her purse and twisted the strap in her hands. "I don't want to lose you, either of you."

"You can't. This will always be your home." As Philip gathered his daughter close, Candace said nothing.

It seemed to take longer to drive back. A sobering interlude where Kelsey wavered between tears and anger. Most of the anger died by the time she pulled up at Three Willows. It left too much room for hurt.

She turned from the front door. She didn't want to go inside just yet and face Naomi. Certainly it would be poor form to discuss with her what had been said about her and the world she lived in. Better, Kelsey decided, to get over it first. To just sit with the fading daffodils and blooming dogwoods until the inner storm passed.

She lost her chance for solitude when Gabe stepped onto the patio.

"I've been looking for you."

"Oh. I thought you'd gone."

He joined her on the narrow stone bench that looked out over early pinks and columbine. "I'm not leaving until tonight." He'd wanted to see her again. A simple-enough reason to juggle his plans. Taking her chin in his hand, he had a good look. She'd been crying. Both that and the fact that it unnerved him came as a surprise.

"What's wrong?"

She shook her head, shifted away. "Do you spend much time on self-reflection?"

"Not if I can avoid it."

"It's hard to do that when your faults are held up in front of you like a mirror. You look at them, and you see yourself."

He slipped an arm around her shoulders, and kept his voice light. "Who's been mean to you, baby? I'll go beat him up."

With a half laugh she nuzzled against him, then drew away. "I'm not a nice person, Gabe. And I hardly ever think about trying to be. It used to surprise me when someone would tell me I was spoiled or stubborn or single-minded. And I could say to myself, that's not true. I'm just doing what seems right to me."

Restless, she rose, leaving him on the bench while she took a few steps along the bricked path that wound through the infant flowers. "When Wade said I was cold and self-absorbed, rigid, unforgiving, all those things, I could rationalize that he'd said it to justify his own adultery. I wasn't hot enough in bed, so he found someone who was. I wasn't sympathetic enough, interested enough in his career; someone else was. I refused to overlook the fact that I'd found him cozied up with another woman. If I was too rigid to understand his physical needs, well, that was my problem. I've never had any trouble tossing the baby out with the bathwater. Break a marriage vow? The marriage is over, and that's that. Well, I am rigid."

She spun back, ready to dare him to disagree. "There's right and there's wrong. There's truth and there are lies. There's law and there's crime. Take seat belts."

Cautious, he nodded. "All right. Take seat belts."

"Maybe before it was passed into law I'd forget to use mine. You're busy, you're in a hurry, you're just going down the block. Why bother? But the minute the law was passed, Kelsey straps herself in. Every time, no question."

"And you figure that makes you rigid."

"Before they passed the law it was just as stupid not to use them. The law didn't change the basic common sense. But I could ignore common sense, never the law. Well, speed limits," she admitted. "But whenever I overlooked them, I rationalized it. If I went to Atlanta to try to fix my marriage, if I knew something was wrong with it and I was willing to make the effort to work on it, why wasn't I willing to forgive what I found there? Because he'd made a promise. He'd taken a vow, and he'd broken it. That was enough for me."

Gabe rubbed a hand over his chin. "Do you want me to tell you that you were wrong to dump the bastard, Kelsey? I can't, for two reasons. One, I agree with you, and two, I want you myself. I can say that if it had been you and me, and I'd walked in on you cozied up with another guy, he'd be dead and you'd be sorry. Does that help any?"

She closed her eyes, scrubbed both hands over her face. "How did I get into all of this?"

"My guess is you've had a rough morning. Where've you been?"

"I went to see my father." She wanted to cry again, ridiculously, and turned away until she had the tears fought back. "I wanted to tell him, face-to-face, that I was giving up my apartment and staying on here. At least for now."

"So, he gave you a hard time."

"No, not really. Not him. He's the kindest man in the world. I'm hurting him." She let the tears come now. The hell with them. "I don't want to. I don't want to make him unhappy, but I just can't bend enough, not enough to make it all right for everyone."

He didn't say anything, but simply rose and gathered her close. He never battled words against tears. It was best to let them flow until they ran clean.

"This is stupid." Sniffling, she searched her pocket for a tissue, then took the bandanna Gabe offered. "This whole thing started over a stupid dance, the Derby, and the dentist."

"Why don't we sit down again and you can decode that for me?"

"It's tradition," she said, and plopped down on the bench again. "And living up to family expectations. I'm not going to claim that my childhood was fraught with peril, but there's always been the Byden name to live up to, especially where my grandmother's concerned."

She balled the bandanna in her hand, wished she could ball her anger and resentments with it and heave it away. "She's still miffed at me for divorcing Wade, putting that blot on the family honor. Needless to say, she's furious about my being here." Struggling to lighten her own mood, she forced a smile. "I have been, in the best gothic tradition, cut out of her will."

"Well . . ." He picked up her hand and toyed with her fingers. "You can always move in with me. Be a kept woman. That ought to show her."

"Christ, I'd have my name expunged from the family Bible for that."

When he realized he'd been only half joking, he released her hand. "Can't have that, can we? So, what about the dance, the Derby, and the dentist?"

"Sounds like the title of a very bad play." Trying to relax, she lifted her hair off her neck and shoulders, then let it fall again. "When I went to see Dad, I had the bonus of Grandmother and Candace, my stepmother, eating cucumber sandwiches and planning the floral arrangements for the spring ball at the country club. Which they fully expected me to attend. They'd even arranged for my escort, since I've refused to date since I walked out on Wade. They'd—"

"Hold it." He held up a hand. "For my personal interest, run that last part by me again. About not dating."

"I haven't gone out with anyone in two years. Partly because until the divorce was final, it felt wrong, and partly, mostly because I didn't want to. Sex has never been a driving force in my life."

He picked up her hand again, kissed it. "We can fix that."

"I'm trying to explain." She tugged on her hand, found it firmly caught in his, and gave up. "The dentist, an oral surgeon, is the son of friends who's recently relocated to D.C. He meets all the Byden standards. You, by the way, don't."

"That's the nicest thing you've ever said to me. Let's go back to my place and celebrate."

"You're making me feel better. I wasn't ready to feel better." Smiling, she laid her head against his shoulder. "Anyway, I had to tell them not only that I wasn't interested in Doctor Acceptable, but that I wouldn't make it to the spring ball at all. It's the first Saturday in May."

"The Derby. Now all the pieces fall into place."

"Yes, the Derby. That started a row, a fairly civilized one initially, but Grandmother was getting under my skin. So"—she gazed slyly at him from under her lashes—"I told her I was involved with a gambler, just to piss her off."

"You've got a nasty streak." He caught her face in his hand and kissed her hard before she could decide to evade or not. "I like it."

"They didn't. Grandmother stormed out, my father looked devastated, and Candace was so angry. We've butted heads before, but this time she aimed low. And she hit the mark. The longer I stay here, the more it disturbs the family. And since I'm too rigid to bend, I won't look for a compromise."

"Sometimes there isn't any compromise."

"Nice people find them."

A delicate situation, he thought, studying the young geraniums in the patio pots. A family situation, and he had very little experience with family.

"Did it ever occur to you that your family isn't looking for a compromise either?" He watched as she turned her face slowly to his. "All or nothing. Isn't that basically how they've put it?"

"I . . . hadn't thought of it that way."

"No, because you're so cold, you're so rigid, you're so hard that you've automatically taken all the blame for it. They can toss out the guilt, threaten to disinherit you, tell you how selfish you are, but it's all your fault?"

To her knowledge no one had ever taken her side against the family. Certainly not Wade. It had always been she who'd caused the scenes, ruffled the feathers. Strange that it had never passed through her mind that their side of issues was as unyielding as her own.

"I'm doing what I want, regardless—"

"Regardless of what?" he demanded. Perhaps he'd never had a family to shelter him, but neither had he had one to lock him in with guilt and obligation. "Regardless of the fact that some people have to make adjustments? If you trotted off to your dance with the designated dentist, would it make any difference?"

"No," she said after a long moment. "It would just postpone the next scene."

"Are you staying here to spite them?"

"Of course not." Insulted, she snapped her head back. "Of course not," she said again, this time more subdued. "This must seem awfully foolish to you. All of this chaos over propriety and tradition."

"I just figure you've beaten yourself up long enough over who you are and what you want. Feeling better?"

"Much." She let out a big, cleansing sigh. "I'm glad you were still around, Slater."

"I wanted to see you again before I left." His fingers slid over the nape of her neck, teasing out chills. "You're screwing up my schedule, Kelsey."

"Oh?" She kept her eyes on the hands she'd folded in her lap.

"I'm starting to think about you before my eyes are open in the morning. I figure there are three times when a man's most vulnerable. When he's drunk, when he's lost himself in sex, and at that instant right before he wakes up. I don't drink and I haven't had any interest in sex with another woman since I saw you. But you've caught me in that one instant when the defenses are down."

She'd had men recite poetry to her who hadn't stirred her so deeply. Emotionally, romantically, sexually. She'd lifted her gaze to his as he'd spoken, drawn by that soft, alluring voice. Now she was caught. Now she was defenseless.

"I'm afraid of you." She'd had no idea she'd felt it, much less that she'd been about to say it.

"Good, that makes us even."

He framed her face, slowly combing her hair back with his fingers, drawing out the moment so that they would both remember. Birdsong, spring flowers, the slant of the afternoon sun. Then the jolt of mouth against mouth, the quick leap of a heart, the long, slow moan of mutual pleasure.

"What happens inside me when I do that scares the hell out of me." He rested his brow against hers while the new and almost familiar emotions worked through him. "The fact that as soon as I've done it I want to do it again scares me even more."

"Me too. It's probably best you're going away for a few days. There's so much to think about."

"I've about finished thinking, Kelsey."

She nearly had her breath back and nodded. "Me too." With some regret she eased away. "Good luck at Keeneland, and thanks for the shoulder. I needed it. I guess I needed you."

15

Naomi didn't question Kelsey's decision to accompany the team to Kentucky. She'd wanted her there, badly, but hadn't allowed herself to take it for granted. Naomi no longer took anything for granted.

The only disagreement between them occurred when Kelsey insisted on paying her own expenses. Naomi simmered over it privately during the packing and preparations, throughout the flight, and while they'd checked into their hotel. It wasn't until she'd asked Kelsey to join her in her suite that the simmering boiled over.

"This is absurd." Agitated. Naomi paced, ignoring the light meal and bottle of wine she'd ordered up to help keep the discussion amiable. "You're here with Three Willows Farm. You'll be helping Boggs with Pride. It's a simple business expense."

"I'm here," Kelsey corrected, "because I want to be here, because I wouldn't miss the Bluegrass Stakes or the Derby for anything in the world. And I'm extra baggage as far as Pride's concerned. Moses and his team don't need me."

"I do." Naomi shot back before she could stop herself. "Do you know what it means to me to have you here? To have you *want* to be here? To know after all this time and all the loss that you'll be standing with me, not just at post time, but through all the wonderful foolishness that goes on before that final two minutes? I'd rather have you here from now until the first Saturday in May than win a dozen Derbies. And you won't even let me settle your hotel bill."

More than a little taken aback, Kelsey stared as her mother stalked around the room. She'd never seen Naomi so overwrought, so brimful of emotion. Finally, here was the woman who had laughed for her wedding photo, who had flirted recklessly with men. Who had killed one.

"It just didn't seem right to me," Kelsey began, but stopped the moment Naomi whirled on her.

"Why isn't it right? Because I wasn't the conventional mother? Because I was in a cell when I should have been teaching you to tie your shoes?"

"That's not what I—"

"I don't expect you to forgive that," Naomi snapped back. "I don't expect you to forget it. You're not required to love me, or even to think of me as your mother. But I thought you were beginning to think of Three Willows as your home."

And how, Kelsey wondered, had she started this whirlwind by simply using her own charge card? "I do," she said carefully, ready to parry the next explosion. "That doesn't mean I want to take advantage of it, or you.

But the explosion didn't come. Naomi sat, deliberately fighting back her anger. "If you don't want to accept the trip from me, I'd like you to accept it from

Three Willows. Your association there might very well have cost you at least part of your inheritance. I regret that."

"So, this is a payment on guilt? All right." Kelsey threw up her hands when Naomi's eyes went to smoke. "This is silly. I didn't realize you were so worked up over it. Pay the bill if it's important to you." She tossed back her hair. "You know, I've always wondered where my temper came from. Dad is placid as a lake. And you, you're so cool, so controlled, so in charge. It's worth losing a fight to have seen that I come by my temperament honestly."

"I'm glad I could solve one of life's little mysteries for you." After a jerky shrug, Naomi plucked a strawberry from the fruit plate she'd ordered. "Win or lose, a fight makes me hungry. Want to eat?"

"Yeah." Kelsey chose a slice of apple. "I want to tell you something," she began in a tone that had Naomi's hand pausing as she poured wine. "I do think of you as my mother. I wouldn't still be here if I didn't."

Naomi leaned forward and kissed Kelsey's cheek; then, steadying her hand, she filled their glasses.

"To the women of Three Willows." She tapped her glass against Kelsey's. "I've waited a long time to drink to that."

The days before the Bluegrass Stakes passed in a blur. Kelsey met more people than she could ever remember. She rose each morning at dawn to watch the workouts, worrying, comparing Pride to every other colt and filly who soared through the mist. She haunted the shedrow, studying jockeys, judging trainers, and badgering Boggs for tidbits of news or speculation.

Whenever she could corner him, she harassed Reno, prodding him for his thoughts, grilling him over strategy. She worried over him, over the colt, over the track.

"Hey," he asked her, "who's going to ride that colt, you or me?"

She pouted a bit, rocking back on her heels as the two of them spent a private moment with Pride. "You are. But—"

"But you'd rather have your hands on the reins."

The pout turned into a small smile. "Maybe." She stroked Pride's nose, enjoying its warmth, its softness. "I guess I've got the fever."

"You're burning up with it." Reno hooked his thumbs in the pockets of his navy silk suit. He had a woman waiting for him, and a great deal on his mind.

"That's part of it, isn't it? The nerves, the ambition." She took the apple she'd been saving and held it out to Pride. "The love."

"It gets to you," Reno agreed. It would be of no use telling her that sooner or later other things would interfere with the innocence of it. The numbers, the angles, the odds. She'd find out for herself, he thought, and gave her a friendly pat on the back. "You keep our boy happy, kiddo. And remind him about that Kentucky colt. Keep him on edge."

With a wink, Reno sauntered out of the barn.

"You don't have to worry about that flash in the pan," Kelsey assured Pride. "He can't compare to you."

Pride crunched his apple, obviously in complete agreement.

Midnight Hour, a Kentucky-bred colt, was the local favorite. He'd been the surprise winner of the Florida Derby, outdistancing both Pride and Double by a neck. The small, easily spooked roan was getting a lot of national press.

And Kelsey had to admit, this one was a beauty. The classic lines, the unpredictable disposition, the fire in the eyes. The colt used a shadow roll on the track, to prevent him from shying at shadows and things that weren't there. But he could run. She'd seen that for herself.

Bill Cunningham's filly had her supporters as well. One didn't have to admire the man to admire his horse. Sheba had heart and courage and could break through the gate like a tornado. But the sound of her wheezing after a hard workout chilled Kelsey's blood.

There were others who showed heart and grit, not the least of which was Gabe's Double. But Kelsey's money was on Pride. She told herself it wasn't simply loyalty, not even simply love, but the eye she was beginning to develop under Moses's careful tutelage. The colt was one in a million. As she was sure her own Honor was.

The day of the Stakes, she stood beside her mother, eager to have her confidence justified.

"He looked so good this morning."

Kelsey took long, deep breaths. She wanted to enjoy the post parade, the pageantry, the anticipation. But she couldn't stop talking.

"Moses said he had Reno hold him back a little, because he wanted to keep him on edge. The field's hard and fast, just the way he likes it. I heard some of the clockers. The sentiment's riding with Midnight Hour, but the cool heads are split almost even between Pride and Double." She rubbed a hand over her mouth. "Still, Sudden Force might be the missing link. That's the chestnut colt in from Arkansas. He looked ready this morning. And we can't count out Cunningham's filly. She's got such heart."

Amused and impressed, Naomi ran a soothing hand up and down Kelsey's arm. "Just take a deep breath. It'll all be over in a few minutes."

"I just have time to wish my two favorite ladies good luck." Gabe slipped between them, kissed them both. "Looks like we're both seven to five," he commented, studying the odds board. "What do you say the winner buys dinner?"

"And the loser springs for the champagne." Naomi gave him a quick grin. "I've always preferred to have a man buy my drinks."

"Good one," Kelsey murmured. Then, rather than taking a breath, she held it. The horses were being led to the gate.

From the shelter of the stands. Rich watched his son. The boy had always had taste in females. And the devil's own luck with them. Just like his old man. Rich thought, and patted the derriere of the tipsy little blonde he'd picked up the night before.

"Keep your eye on number three," he told her. "I've got me an interest in that horse. A real close interest."

The bell sounded. The horses surged forward and the woman beside him squealed and began to cheer boozily for number three.

Rich narrowed eyes shielded behind mirrored lenses. The local favorite had the lead, with the colt from Arkansas pressing close to the rail. The pack was hardly more than a blur of color and pounding legs, but he never lost sight of number three. Cunningham's filly ran valiantly, clipping the lead down to a neck by the first turn. But already Virginia's Pride was bursting out of the pack, eating up the light, spewing up turf.

Rich nodded slowly, a smile beginning to curve his mouth. Double won the rail and streaked up the inside on the backstretch. Even the thunder of hooves was lost in the wild cheers of the crowd. For an instant, one of those gorgeous photographic moments, three horses were neck and neck, strides almost in unison, silks blazing.

Then Pride drove forward, a nose, a neck, a half-length. They crossed the wire within fractions of a second, Virginia's Pride, Double or Nothing, Big Sheba. Win, place, show.

Rich tossed back his head and laughed. "Honey, I've hit the big time."

She pouted, swirled her beer. "Number three didn't win."

Rich laughed again, fingering the ticket for the thousand dollars he'd put on Pride's nose. "That's what you think, darling. Old Richie's hunches always pay off."

"Oh, God." Kelsey still had her hands covering her mouth. Toward the end she'd nearly given in to the urge to place them over her eyes. "He did it! He won!" On a whoop of laughter she tossed her arms around Naomi. "Congratulations! It's just the prelude to the Derby. I can feel it."

"So can I." Naomi squeezed back hard, ignoring the sudden intrusion of cameras and press. "Come with me to the winner's circle. I want you with me."

"You couldn't keep me away." She swung back to Gabe. For someone who'd just lost by half a length, he looked awfully pleased with himself. "Your colt ran a good race."

"He did. Yours ran better." He tugged the braid that rained down her back. "This time. See you at dinner."

The victory glow wasn't allowed to distract anyone from the job at hand. They'd stay in Kentucky until after the Derby, moving from Keeneland to Churchill Downs.

Dawn still meant workouts, clockers, black coffee, and trainers watching from the backside rail.

Only this was the Derby. Workouts were no longer a private affair. Even as exercise boys roused themselves from bed, reporters were setting up equipment. Television, newspapers, magazines all wanted features; all wanted that definitive interview, that perfect picture.

Kelsey knew what hers would have been.

The soft dawn, that most magical time for horse and horseman, with mist rising, blurring color, muffled sound. And the signature twin spires of the track spearing up through it. Tubs of hot water added steam. Birds sang their morning song.

Spring had come to Louisville, but there was still a vague chill at this hour, bracing, exciting. It touched off more white steam from the flanks and shoulders of horses returning from a gallop. Pampered and pushed, they slipped through the mists as magically as any Pegasus rising from hooves to wings.

But they were athletes. It was easy to forget that these half-ton creatures balanced on breadstick legs had been born to run.

Of the thousands of Thoroughbreds foaled every year, only a few, a special few, would ever walk through the morning fog at this track, on this week. Only one would stand on Saturday with a blooming blanket of red roses over its glistening back.

Grooms carried the tubs and the wrappings, moving through the thinning swirl among the horses while the sun streamed softly, burning away the dawn, turning dew to diamonds. A cat meowed, boot heels crunched. And then the sound of hooves on dirt, eerily disembodied at first, then growing, swelling as the grayish mists parted like water, a colt swimming through them.

That was her picture, the memory Kelsey would take with her, quiet and comforting amid all the colors and the pageantry.

"What are you doing?"

Kelsey said nothing at first, simply took Gabe's hand in hers. She should have known he would walk into the scene and make himself part of the memory. "Taking a picture. I don't want all this to get lost with the parties and the press and the pressure."

"You're up early for someone who couldn't have gotten to bed before two."

"Who can sleep?"

In answer, Gabe nodded toward a stableboy who was leaning back against the barn wall, dozing. She laughed and took a deep gulp of air, swallowing the scents of horse, liniment, leather, manure.

"It's too new to me. I saw your jockey working Double this morning. They looked good."

"I saw you, leaning on the backstretch rail. You looked good."

"I don't know how you have the energy to flirt with all that's going on. This is like Mardi Gras, a Kiwanian convention, and the Super Bowl rolled into one."

She began to walk. "Parades, hot-air balloon races, owners' dinners, trainers' dinners. That steamboat race yesterday. I've never seen anything like it."

"I won five thousand."

She snorted. "Figures. Who was foolish enough to bet against you?"

He grinned. "Moses."

She tugged down the brim of her cap. "Well, with his ten percent of Saturday's purse, he can afford it."

"You're getting cocky, darling."

"I've always been cocky. You're going to the museum for the draw, aren't you?"

"Wouldn't miss it." He hadn't missed the drawing of the field in five years. His presence, or lack of it, would make no difference as to which position his colt was assigned, but it was his colt. "There's breakfast in the old paddock before. Hungry?"

Moaning, she pressed a hand to her stomach. "I've done more grazing than a holstein since I got to Louisville. I think I'll skip it. If you . . ." She trailed off, noting his attention had wandered. No, she realized; it was more than that. It had focused, frozen, beamed in like a laser on something back at the shedrow. "Something wrong?"

"No." For an instant he'd thought he'd seen his father. That familiar swagger, the pastel suit so out of place among denim and cotton. But it had been only a glimpse. And surely Rich Slater wouldn't be wandering around the barns at Churchill Downs at an hour past dawn. "No," he said again, and shook off the automatic dread. "If you don't want to eat, come watch me."

He didn't think any more about it. Before the morning was over, Gabe was busy analyzing his colt's number-three position with Jamison and his jockey.

"We got the rail." Kelsey stood with Boggs in the barn, nibbling on one of the apples she had in her pockets while the old groom hooked wraps on a line. "It's a sign from God."

Boggs took one of the clothespins clipped to his pant leg and meticulously hooked a royal blue wrap. "I figure God watches the Derby, like everybody. Probably got His favorite." He ran his fingers over a saddle, well worn, the irons rubbed and polished by his own hand. "I might just put some of these dead presidents I got in my pocket down on that colt."

"I thought you never bet."

"Don't." With the same slow care, he draped a blanket over the line. "Not since April '73."

He shot her a look to see if she realized that was the year her mother had killed Alec Bradley. When there was nothing in her eyes but mild interest, he continued.

"Was at Keeneland, too. Over to Lexington for the Stakes race. Three Willows had a Derby hopeful then, too. Fine colt. I loved that colt more'n I ever loved a woman. Name was Sun Spot. I guess I got me a fever, 'cause I put a month's pay on him. He came out of the gate like a whirlwind, like he could already see the wire. At the first turn, the colt beside him stumbled, bumped him hard. Spot went down. Knew as soon as I saw him go he'd not race again. Shattered his near foreleg. Nothing to do but put him down. Your ma put the gun behind his ear herself. Was her colt, and she cried when she did it, but she did what had to be done." He sighed, gustily. "So I ain't never bet since. Maybe it's bad luck if I do."

She put an arm around Boggs and together they studied the tools of his trade, the drying wrappings, the blinkers, the blankets and cotton padding. "Nothing's going to happen to Pride."

He nodded, taking the apple Kelsey offered him. "It's a mistake to love a horse, Miss Kelsey." He polished the apple on his shirt and handed it back to her. "They break your heart one way or another."

She only smiled, tossed the apple up, caught it. "Is this for me, Boggs, or for Pride?"

His gummy grin split his face. "He does like his apples."

"Then I'd better go give it to him."

When she started out, Boggs shifted, then scratched his throat. "You know, I saw somebody today I ain't seen in a while. Somebody I knew back in that spring of '73."

"Oh?"

Stalling, Boggs took the apple from her and twisted it in his gnarled hands so that it came apart in two neat halves. "Mr. Slater's old man."

"Gabe's father? You saw him here?"

"Thought I did. But my eyes aren't what they were. Funny he'd be here. I recollect he was around the day Spot went down. Kicked up a fuss, too, like as if Miss Naomi had planned to lose the race and the horse that day. 'Course he was drunk. But Rich Slater's persuasive. They checked the horse for drugs."

Kelsey stood, the sun at her back, her face in shadow. "And what did they find?"

"They didn't find nothing in that colt. The Chadwicks run clean. But they found them in the colt that bumped him. Amphetamines."

"Who owned the colt?"

"Cunningham." He spat on the ground. "Funny, isn't it? Fingers pointed at Cunningham at first, but it turned out the jockey'd done it. Benny Morales, damn good rider he was. Left a note that said so before he hung himself in Cunningham's tack room."

"God, that's horrible."

"There's plenty that don't smell so sweet around racehorses, Miss Kelsey. Rich Slater, he had it figured that the Chadwicks bribed Benny to drug his horse, so's even if he won, he'd be disqualified if'n they found out. That's pure shit, of course, but a man like that's got to point the blame at somebody. Thing was, most everybody lost that day. Probably wasn't him I saw, but I figured if it was, you might want to keep your distance."

"I will."

Rich Slater had no intention of crossing paths with anyone from Three Willows. He was there as a spectator. And although it would certainly have been wiser for him to be well away from Louisville on Saturday, he wanted a front-row seat.

He was on a roll. A wad of bills in his pocket, a willing woman in his bed, and a raucous round of parties at his fingertips. He'd made it, finally, to the big time. And the best part, the sweetest part, was the people who would go down as he went up.

He had to admit, he was brilliant—and he made sure he didn't get drunk enough to share that opinion with anyone but himself. Not only would he pay off an old debt and slap down his ungrateful son, he would also make a small fortune doing it.

And really, he was doing nothing at all. He'd simply put the right instrument in the right hands.

The Chadwick bitch would pay. Naked, he padded over to the honor bar to raid the stingy bottles of liquor. His companion for Derby week was passed out on the bed, her tight little body sprawled on the tangled sheets. He'd proved his manhood there, he told himself, and toasted the reflection in the mirror.

He still had it.

With the glass in his hand, Rich preened in front of the mirror. His vanity was blind to the loose flesh sagging at his waist. He saw the body of a thirty-year-old, trim and tough. The body he'd passed on to his son, who had blown him off with a five-thousand-dollar check.

Wouldn't let your dad spend a night under your roof? I'll own the fucking roof when I'm done.

He tossed back the whiskey and watched his throat ripple as he swallowed. The boy thought he was better than anybody. Always had. In a couple of days he wouldn't be so high and mighty. In a couple of days, the worm would have turned.

He really had to thank circumstances, past and present, for giving him the opportunity. Cunningham was a bonus, one that had fallen beautifully into his lap. Of course the man was a fool, but fools were the best birds to pluck.

And he was going to be plucking Cunningham for many years to come. A nice steady sideline of blackmail would bring in a nice steady income. But the payoff, oh, the payoff would come just before six P.M. on Saturday. A job, he was sure everyone would agree, well done.

He opened another bottle, poured another drink. He wondered if Naomi Chadwick would remember him. If he walked right up to her, took a handful of that pretty little butt, would she remember him? He was tempted to try it, to walk right up and give her a quick squeeze and a wink.

He didn't like the idea that a woman, any woman, could forget Rich Slater.

He remembered her, all right. He remembered that fancy, spoiled bitch, advertising herself in low-cut dresses or skin tight jeans. Strutting around the track like a filly in heat, spreading her legs for any man who could still get a hard-on.

He'd wanted her, bad. Wanted to lift those frilly skirts and dive in. Show her what a real man could do. But when he'd offered, she'd looked at him as though he were something smeared on the bottom of her boot after a walk through the paddock. And she'd laughed at him. Laughed until he'd wanted to smash his fist into that beautiful face.

Maybe he would have, Rich thought, absently pounding one clenched hand into the palm of the other. Maybe he would have if that half-breed Jew hadn't come along.

"Problem here, Miss Naomi?"

"No, Moses, no problem. Just a track rat. How's our boy doing?"

She'd sashayed off, flicking her tail, too coo over her prize colt. And Rich had had no choice but to go home to the dingy rooms he'd rented and smash his fist into his wife's pale, homely face instead.

Thought she was too good for him. She'd cost him his pride that day, but he'd cost her a great deal more later when he'd fixed the race. That hadn't been his intention, of course. Nobody could have predicted Morales would lose control of his hyped-up horse and knock into hers so hard.

But then again, he thought now. Then again, it had turned out fine. Better than fine, because he'd been smart, he'd been cagey, and he'd used the circumstances against her. He'd paid her back, all right. But he wasn't through.

The ten years she'd spent in prison had been only partial payment. The rest of the debt was coming due Saturday.

Kelsey passed on the Derby day breakfast at the governor's mansion. Not only couldn't she eat, she couldn't bear the idea of being so far away from the track.

Post time for the first race was precisely eleven-thirty. Like the grooms, jockeys, and trainers, Kelsey was there by six. The idea of going back to the hotel at noon for a nap was impossible. Instead, she stayed with Boggs and some of the other crew, nibbling on the fried chicken she'd bought.

"Still here?" Moses dropped down on the ground beside her and poked in the bucket for a thigh.

"Where else?" She was eating from nerves rather than hunger, and washed down the chicken with ginger ale.

"You could sit in your box. It's already a hell of a show. The infield's packed, grandstand's filling up."

"Too nervous. Besides, some reporter will just stick a microphone or a camera in my face."

"You won't avoid them here, either. Your mama's got pull. You could hide out in the Matt Winn Room."

"Uh-uh." Kelsey licked her fingers. "That's for businessmen. Might as well be sitting in a boardroom. That's no place to watch the race. How's Naomi?"

"Wired. You wouldn't know it to look at her, but she's wound tight. Half of that's you being here. She wants you holding that trophy with her."

"We could do it, couldn't we?"

"I'm not going to tempt the gods and say so." He squinted up at the sky. "Good day. Dry, clear. We've got a fast track."

"I was out there earlier while they were prepping it. It's beautiful, all those neat furrows. I was going to watch some of the early races, but it just made me jittery." Because her stomach still had too much room to flutter, she chose another piece of chicken. "Have you seen Gabe?"

"He's sharing the box with Naomi. He'll be back around to harass Jamie and stand in the paddock while his colt's saddled."

"Things were so busy yesterday, I barely saw him." And never alone. "I didn't know whether to bring it up, since I have a pretty good idea how he feels, but Boggs mentioned that he thought he saw Gabe's father."

"When?" Moses asked so quickly, Kelsey was flustered.

"Well, uh, Thursday, late morning. He said he wasn't sure. Moses?" She scrambled to her feet because he'd already gotten up and was heading toward the barn.

"The man's trouble," he spat out. "Bad medicine."

"Bad medicine?" She wanted to smile, but she couldn't make her lips obey. "Come on, Moses."

"Some people carry trouble with them, and like to pass it out. Rich Slater's like that." He moved quickly to Pride's box, satisfying himself, then forcing himself to relax. Horses picked up on emotions. He wanted Pride edgy, revved, but not spooked. "If he's around, I don't want him near here."

"The guards won't let anyone in who isn't authorized. Boggs wasn't even certain. Besides, what trouble could he cause?"

"None." Moses stroked the colt's nose, murmured to him softly. "Guess I'm wired, too. Slater's old news. Bad news, but old."

"Boggs told me about the race in Lexington, when Sun Spot broke down."

"Hard. That was hard on her. Slater tried to stir up a hornet's nest there, but they stung the wrong person. Benny Morales was a good jockey. He was making a comeback that year. He'd been out for a while with a broken back. Cunningham put him up on his colt. I was never sure if Benny doctored that colt because he needed the money that bad, or if he just needed to beat the Chadwick colt."

It hardly mattered why, Moses thought now. The worst had happened.

"He'd been riding for Three Willows when he took a bad spill at a morning workout. It was a year and a half before he was back on his feet. Mr. Chadwick offered him a job, assistant trainer. But Benny wanted to ride, wanted to prove himself. So Cunningham put him up."

"Was he capable?"

"I can't say. He ate a lot of painkillers. Worked himself to death to get back down to weight. There weren't a lot of takers, so Cunningham bought him cheap.

It ended up costing a lot more than a cut of the purse. Well"—he stroked Pride again—"that's old news. We've got a new race here. *The* race. It's almost time to take our boy to the paddock."

A horse would take this walk from barn to paddock on the first Saturday in May only once. Less than three years before, he would have frolicked cheerfully alongside his mother in green pastures. One of the first steps in a dream. As a yearling he might have danced in meadows, raced his companions, or his own shadow. Training, growing as muscle and bone developed, learning the poetry and power of movement that was exclusive to the breed. He would come to the bridle eager, or fitful, feel the first weight of man on his back in a dawn-washed stall.

One day he would be walked to an iron gate and urged to accept the confinement. He would have trained on the longe, on the practice oval. He would learn the scent of his groom, feel heat in his legs and the crop on his back.

He would do what he had been born to do. He would run.

But he would take this walk, to this race, only once. There was no second chance.

At 5:06 they were in the paddock, Pride moving into his stall to be saddled. Tattoos were checked, as were the colors and markings of each of the seventeen entrants. No different from any other race, and different from any other.

There had been only one scratch. No one mentioned the colt from California who had broken down at the morning workout with an injured foot.

Bad luck.

Inside the jockeys' quarters, riders stepped on scales. One hundred and twenty-six pounds, no more, no less, including tack. Reno stepped up, watched the scale, and smiled. The hours in the steam room had been worth it. Moments later, the silks bright, riders made their way from the second floor of their quarters to the paddock.

The waiting was nearly over.

In the stands people grew restless, excited, jubilant. Celebrations continued in the infield, some of them heated from liquor smuggled inside hollowed loaves of bread or diaper bags.

The odds board flickered, and the betting windows were packed.

It was 5:15. The horses were saddled, their lead ponies outfitted brightly with braided tails and flowers. Despite the powder-puff clouds riding high overhead, the air was thick. Tension had weight.

"Don't worry about taking the lead." Moses told Reno. "Let the Kentucky colt set the pace through the first turn. Pride runs well in the pack."

"He'll thread like a needle," Reno agreed. Though his voice was cool, casual, he was sweating under his silks.

"And talk to him. Talk to him. He'll run his heart out if you ask him to."

Reno nodded, struggling to keep his cocky smile in place. There was so much riding on that quick two minutes.

"Riders up!"

At the paddock judge's announcement. Moses slapped a hand on Reno's shoulder, then vaulted him into the saddle. They would head back through the tunnel now, on the way to the track.

"Ready?" Naomi clasped a hand over Kelsey's.

"Yeah." She took a deep breath, then another. "Yeah."

"Me too." After two steps, Naomi shook her head. "Wait one minute." In her trim red suit and elegant pearls, she made a dash across the paddock. She was laughing when she caught up with Moses, threw her arms around him, and kissed him.

"Naomi." Blushing with a combination of pride and embarrassment, like a schoolboy caught pinching the head cheerleader, he wiggled away. "What's wrong with you? There's—"

"People watching," she finished, and kissed him again. "The hell with your reputation, Moses."

She was still laughing as she dashed back to Kelsey. "Well, that settles that."

Amused, and oddly touched, Kelsey fell into step with her. "Does it?"

"A running argument we've had for more years than I care to count. He hasn't wanted our relationship made public because it's unseemly for a woman in my position." She tossed back her hair. God, she felt young and free and incredibly happy. "Nothing but male pride, of course, which they all wear in their jockstraps."

Kelsey snorted out a laugh. "Why don't you just marry him?"

"He's never asked me. And I suppose I have too much female pride to ask him. Speaking of males." She saw Gabe walking toward them. "I'd like to say, before he can hear me, that there is one of the most gorgeous examples of the species that I've ever seen."

"There's something about the eyes," Kelsey murmured. "And the mouth. And the cheekbones." Her smile curved slyly. "And of course, there's that incredible butt."

"I've noticed." Naomi giggled. "Just because I'm nearly old enough to be his mother doesn't mean I've lost my eyesight."

"Ladies." Gabe cocked his head. When two women had gleams like that in their eyes, something was up. "Want to share the joke?"

They looked at each other, and shook their heads in unison. "Nope."

Each hooked an arm through one of his and strolled to their box to the strains of "My Old Kentucky Home."

Deep in the stands, surrounded by picture hats and silk jackets, Rich Slater swirled his third mint julep. The seats Bill Cunningham had arranged for him weren't choice, but he'd sprung for a new pocket-size set of binoculars. With them, he watched Gabe escort the women up to their glitzy box.

Quite a picture they made, he thought. Naomi in her flashy red suit, the daughter in her flashy blue, both blond heads gleaming. Like a couple of sexy bookends for the tall dark man between them.

He wondered if the boy had taken them both to bed yet. A blond sandwich with four milky legs and arms. He'd bet they could fuck like rabbits.

"Look, honey, aren't they the cutest things with the flowers in their hair?"

Cherri, who'd lasted out the week with him due to tireless sex and a high tolerance for sloe gin fizzes, tugged on his arm. Dutifully, Rich shifted his attention back to the game at hand.

"They sure are, baby. Cute as can be."

The entrants were ponied around the track, their flower-bedecked escorts carrying liveried riders. The Arkansas colt danced and tried to nip at the colt in front of him. The pony rider helped the jockey calm him.

The entrants cantered around the track to the cheers of the crowd.

"It's incredible," Kelsey said. "All of it. Just incredible." She shook her head at Gabe's offer of a drink. "I can't swallow. I can hardly breathe. Oh, God, they're loading them in the gate."

Everyone was in place, horses, jockeys, assistants, officials. In the stewards' stand, two judges stood outside, peering through binoculars, waiting for the start. A third remained in the stewards' room, with two television monitors. Others were stationed at poles and the finish line.

From the announcer's booth: "It is now post time."

Once they started the Derby with a whip. Now it was the press of a button, and the words everyone had waited for.

"And they're off!"

A plunge through the gate, the roar of the crowd, and the first feet of the race were eaten up by flashing hooves. Kelsey's heart leaped to her throat and stayed there.

So much color, so much sound, could be lost in the blur of dazzled eyes and speeding pulse. The pack swept past the grandstands for the first time, around the clubhouse turn. The first quarter whizzed by in a fraction more than twenty-two seconds with the Kentucky-bred favorite in the lead.

With her binoculars all but glued to her eyes, Kelsey searched the pack for Pride. His colors blazed as he began to surge forward, almost hoofbeat to hoofbeat with Gabe's colt. Cunningham's game Big Sheba thundered between them.

"He's moving up! He's moving up!" She was screaming but didn't know it. Her voice was lost in the wall of sound. Naomi's fingers were on her arm, digging in.

Pride nosed out Midnight Hour at the half-mile, in forty-five seconds flat, Reno curved over his back.

She could see the turf fly, the swing of silk as bats were whipped, the incredible power of long, slender legs bunching, reaching, lifting.

Midnight Hour dropped back to fourth, horse and rider battling for the rail.

At three-quarters, Pride inched ahead, a neck, a half-length, but the Longshot colt dug in and stole back the distance. A two-horse race, some would say, with the valiant filly behind by two lengths at the mile.

The Arkansas colt surged from the pack, making a bid for a come-from-behind that had the crowd frenzied.

Then that last sprint for the wire, all or nothing.

It happened fast, just before the sixteenth pole. Pride stumbled, those plunging forelegs folding like toothpicks. Reno, balanced in the irons, sailed over his head and rolled like a stone into the infield. As horses and riders fought and veered in the dust cloud to prevent a collision, the colt made one fitful attempt to rise, then crumpled on his ruined legs and stayed down.

Double or Nothing sailed under the wire in two minutes, three and three-quarter seconds as grooms scurried from everywhere onto the track to aid the injured champion.

16

There was no thrill of victory for Gabe in the winner's circle. A gold trophy, a blanket of roses the color of blood. Cameras whirled, capturing the Derby winner, the champion Virginia colt with his red-and-white silks stained with dirt and sweat. The jockey leaned forward over Double's glistening neck to accept his own dozen blooms, his face grim rather than triumphant as he stroked the colt.

"Mr. Slater," was all he could say when Gabe gripped his hand. "Ah, Christ, Mr. Slater."

Gabe only nodded. "You ran a good race, Joey. A Derby record."

Joey's eyes, circled by the grime where his goggles had shielded them, registered no pleasure at the news. "Reno? Pride?"

"I don't know yet. Take your moment, Joey. You and the colt earned it." Gabe's arms went around the colt's neck, ignoring the sweaty dirt. "We'll deal with the rest later." He turned to Jamison, trying to block the cameras aimed at him, the questions hurled. "You were closer, Jamie. Could you tell what happened?"

His face nearly translucent with shock, his eyes glazed with it, Jamison stared down at the roses in his arms. "He broke down, Gabe. That sweet colt just broke." He looked up then, a flare of desperation burning through the shock. "Double would've taken him. He'd have nipped him at the wire." His voice was a plea. "I know it. I feel it."

"It doesn't matter now, does it?" But Gabe laid a hand on his shoulder in support. The taste of victory might have been bitter, but he couldn't refuse it.

The guards kept the press and the fans at bay. Kelsey could hear the tide of their voices from behind the privacy screen, see the shadows moving on it. There were cheers, there were questions, there were demands. But all that was another world behind the thin white wall between life and death. Here, there was only her mother's quiet weeping.

"Moses." He rocked Naomi, stroking her hair, holding on to her and her grief. "Oh, Moses, why?"

"I shouldn'ta bet." Boggs stood, tears streaming down his face, Pride's saddle clutched to his heaving chest. "I shouldn'ta."

Gently, Kelsey ran her hand over Pride's neck. So soft, she thought. So still. Dirt streaked his coat, a testament to the effort. He should be washed, she thought dimly. He should be washed and brushed and pampered with the apples he loved so much.

She lingered over one last caress, then forced herself to rise. Kelsey picked up the dirt-streaked blinders and laid them gently over the saddle. "Take his things back to the barn, Boggs."

"It ain't right, Miss Kelsey."

"No, it isn't." And her heart was aching with the horrible wrongness of it. "But you take care of his things, like always. We need to get my mother away from here."

"Somebody's got to stay—somebody's got to see to him."

"I'm going to stay."

Eyes blurred with tears, he stared at her, then nodded. "That's fittin'." Like a page bearing away his warrior's sword and shield, he turned and left them.

Holding on to her own control, Kelsey crouched. "Moses, she needs you. Will you take her back to the hotel?"

"There's a lot to handle here, Kelsey."

"I'll handle what I can. The rest will have to wait." She put a hand on Naomi's back and gently moved it up and down as if to smooth out the trembles. "Mom." Only Moses was aware it was the first time Kelsey had used the term. "Go with Moses now."

Ravaged by guilt and grief, Naomi rose limply when Moses lifted her to her feet. She looked back down at the colt. Virginia's Pride, she thought. Her pride. "He was only three," she murmured. "Maybe I can't hang on to anything longer than that."

"Don't." Though she had her own demons to fight, Kelsey gripped Naomi's hand. "There are a lot of people out there. You have to get through them."

"Yes." Her eyes went blind. "I have to get through them."

Kelsey walked her past the screen and winced at the sudden press of bodies and sound. She knew she would remember this all of her life—the thrill of the race, the shock of the fall. The cheers and screams of the crowd that had fallen into sudden, terrible silence. The way the grooms had raced toward the fatal spot, and all the confusion and movement of getting both horse and rider from the field.

How many times would she close her eyes and see the way Pride's legs had buckled at that crazy angle?

Or hear her mother's soft, breathy weeping.

"Kelsey." Gabe had rushed from the winner's circle to the stables, holding on to one thin thread of hope. It snapped the moment he saw her face. "Goddammit." He pulled her against him, held on. "They had to put him down?"

She allowed herself one moment, just one with her face pressed against his chest. "No. He was already gone. Boggs reached him first, but it was already over."

"I'm sorry. Christ, I'm sorry. Reno?"

She drew in a steadying breath. "They've taken him to the hospital. The paramedics don't think it's serious, but we're waiting for word." She straightened, then brushed the tears from her cheeks. "I have to deal with the rest of this now."

"Not alone."

She shook her head. If she let herself lean, she'd crumble. "I need to do it. For my mother. For the colt. I'll see you back at the hotel later."

"I'm not leaving you here."

"I have Boggs, the rest of the crew."

The heat died from his eyes. He stepped back, increasing the distance, nodded briskly. "I'll get out of your way. If it turns out you need anything, Jamie will be around."

"Thank you."

It was a nightmare. When Kelsey staggered back to the hotel near midnight her emotions were like a raw wound. She knew the officials had already spoken with Moses and her mother. They'd told her. They'd told her she hadn't just lost a prized colt. It hadn't simply been chance or fate, or Boggs's bad luck.

It had been murder.

Pride had been injected with a lethal dose of amphetamines. A drug that had overworked his heart, one that, as he'd galloped valiantly around turns, down the stretch, had fed off his own adrenaline and sped greedily through his nervous system until, at the sixteenth pole, that heart had stopped.

Now, Three Willows and everyone involved would face questions, speculation, investigation. Had they drugged their horse, misjudging the dose, gambling somehow that the drug wouldn't be found in Pride's saliva?

Or had someone else, a competitor, doctored the horse, and the odds? Someone who wanted to win so badly he would assassinate the colt and risk the life of the man on his back.

She hesitated in front of the door to her mother's suite. What else could be said there? Naomi had Moses to comfort her, to reassure her.

She turned to her own room but couldn't face it. Under the fatigue was a ruthless energy that continued to whip at her mind. Riding it, she walked quickly down the hall and knocked on Gabe's door.

He wasn't sleeping. He hadn't expected her, not after she'd sent him away. Certainly not after he'd gotten the news about Pride. But she was there, her eyes shadowed, her face so delicately pale he thought he could pass his hand through it. He simply stepped back and let her in.

"You've heard?"

"Yes, I heard. Sit down, Kelsey, before you collapse."

"I can't. I'm afraid if I sit still I'll never get moving again. Someone killed him, Gabe. That's what it comes down to. Someone wanted Pride out of the running so badly, they murdered him."

He crossed the parlor to the wet bar and busied himself opening a bottle of mineral water. "My colt won."

"Yes, I'm sorry I haven't even congratulated you, but—" Then she saw his eyes, and stopped cold. "Do you think I came here to accuse you? Even to ask if you had something to do with it?"

While his blood raged, his hands were steady, casually pouring sparkling water over ice. "It's a logical step."

"The hell with that. And the hell with you if you think so little of me."

"I think so little of you?" His laugh was quick and harsh. "What I think of you, and about you, Kelsey, is hardly the point. The facts are your horse is dead, and mine raced me to somewhere in the neighborhood of a million dollars in just over two minutes. That's a pretty good motive for murder, and you won't be alone in thinking it."

"So." She shoved away the glass he offered to her, spilling water onto the carpet. "Facts and logic, then. You forgot an ingredient, Slater. Character."

"So I did." He set her glass aside and sipped leisurely from his own. "Well, mine's black enough."

"Let me tell you something about yourself, Gabriel Slater, high roller, tough guy. You're a marshmallow about those horses. You're as dazzled by and devoted to them as any twelve-year-old girl dreaming about Black Beauty." She tossed back her head, delighted to see those carefully controlled eyes widen in shock.

"Excuse me?"

"You love them. You fucking love them. Did you think it wouldn't get around that you tried to buy Cunningham's filly because you were worried she was being mishandled?"

The shield dropped down again, but she'd seen behind it and plowed on.

"You think your crew doesn't talk to ours about how you play with the foals like they were puppies, or sit up at night when you've got a sick horse? You're a sucker, Slater."

"I've got an investment."

"You've got a love affair. And another thing," she continued, poking a finger into his chest. "I don't appreciate you telling me what you think I should think when I *know*. You wanted to win that race as much as I did, and fixing a race isn't winning. For somebody who's spent his life playing the odds, you should know that. So if you're going to stand here feeling sorry for yourself when you should be feeling sorry for me, I'll just leave you to it."

"Hold on." He grabbed her arm before she could storm out. "You've got a fast trigger, darling." Setting his own glass aside, he rubbed his chest. "And a hell of an aim. You got me, okay? So can we sit down now?"

"You can sit. I still need to walk this off."

Not entirely sure if he was embarrassed or amused by her accuracy, he lowered himself to the arm of the sofa. "I'm sorry, Kelsey. I know that doesn't cover much, but I'm so goddamned sorry."

"I'm trying not to think about how bad I feel right now. I'm worried about Naomi."

"She'll fight back."

"I guess we all will." She paced by the table, picked up one of the glasses, and soothed her scratchy throat. "It was horrible when they told me about the drug. It was like losing him all over again. They're checking the sharps boxes. Every needle, but even if they find something, what difference will it make? Pride's dead."

"If the Racing Commission finds the needle that killed him, it might lead to who used it."

She shook her head. "No, I don't think so. I can't believe anyone would be careless enough to toss it into a sharps box, or if they did, to leave fingerprints or any other evidence." Restless, she stuffed her hands in her pockets, then pulled them out again. "When I find out who—and I will find out—I want them to suffer." She picked up her drink again, looked down into the glass, and watched the tiny bubbles rise. "He raced his heart out, literally raced it out." She shuddered once, then pulled back the grief. "Reno dislocated his shoulder, snapped a collarbone, but that's all. Thank God."

"Joey let me know. You'll have him up again in a few weeks, Kelsey."

"Maybe by the Preakness." Shift gears, she ordered herself. Think about tomorrow. "You know our colt High Water. He could make a decent showing."

"Atta girl," he murmured.

She smiled. "We'll have a lot of work to do. I watched them take Pride away today, and it hurt. I've never lost anyone I cared about. I didn't realize the first time I did it would be a horse. And I did care."

"I know."

"So did you." She walked over and laid a hand on Gabe's cheek. "I'm sorry if I was cold when you offered to stay with me. I'd have fallen apart if you had, but I knew I could get through it by myself."

"I figured you didn't want me around, reminding you I'd won."

"I'm glad you won. It's the only bright spot in the day. If I could have, I'd have watched you walk into the winner's circle. I'd love to have seen them hand you the trophy." On a quick laugh, she reached into her pocket. "God, I forgot. See?" She showed him two tickets, one on Pride, one on Double. "I hedged my bets."

He stared at the tickets, as touched by them as he would have been by a declaration of undying love. "Same money on each horse."

"I guess they both mattered the same amount to me."

He looked up. The color her earlier temper had brought to her cheeks had faded again, leaving her face as pale and delicate as fine glass. The hand in his had toughened with work, but was long and narrow and elegant. She still wore the trim blue silk and slim heels she'd donned for the race.

He lifted a hand and ran it over the hair that was escaping from the intricate French braid. It was the color of wheat struck by afternoon sunlight.

The touch and the sudden silence had her pulse jumping. She was tired, she reminded herself. Drained. She'd spent hours facing reporters, avoiding them. Answering questions, fighting off speculation in what promised to be only the first course of a media feeding frenzy. So why did she feel so energized?

"It's late. I should go." She hadn't meant to jerk back, but she found herself in retreat when he rose. "I should check on Naomi."

"She has Moses."

"Nonetheless."

Now he smiled, slowly, his eyes warming on hers. "Nonetheless," he repeated. "It's been a long day."

"The longest. The kind that stirs up every emotion and wrings it out to dry. Do you know how arousing it is to watch everything you're feeling on your face?" He moved closer, but didn't touch her. "Nerves, needs, doubts . . . urges."

How could they not be on her face when they were storming through her like gale winds? "I'm no good at this, Gabe. You might as well know that up front."

"No good at what?"

"At—" She bumped into a chair, cursed, skirted around it. "At this seduction, surrender, satisfaction business. And the timing—"

"Sucks," he agreed. "The timing sucks." He could step back and let her go. He'd suffer, but he could do it. "You're going to have to tell me you don't want me. Right now. You're going to have to say yes or no, Kelsey. Right here."

"I'm trying to, if you'd just let me think." She jerked back again when he pressed his palms to the wall on either side of her head.

"You figure it's risky, and you haven't quite figured the odds." The old familiar recklessness was moving through him now, churning like an engine. Win or lose, he'd let it race. "The stakes are high, and it's always safer to fold. Is that what you want? To be safe?"

Hardly aware she was moving, she shook her head, slowly, from side to side. Because her eyes never left his, she saw the quick flare of triumph in them.

"The hell with the odds." He pulled her against him. "Let's gamble."

She tossed aside logic and caution. She didn't want them now. She wanted exactly what he was giving her, a hungry mouth, urgent hands. Whatever the risks, she'd already lost herself in the game.

Her breath caught in a gasp of shock when he shoved her back to the wall and dragged her jacket from her shoulders. She hadn't expected this hair-trigger urgency from him. From herself. But her own fingers were tearing at his shirt, rending cloth and buttons in a heedless race for that basic feel of skin.

Then he was under her hands, the taut muscles, the narrow planes. On a surge of greed she locked her mouth on his and fought for more.

She didn't want soft words, slow hands. Something was erupting inside her, and she wanted it to happen fast, to happen hot. Take me. That thought, only that pounded in her brain, in her blood. She heard her own laugh, husky, breathless, and strange, when his mouth seared a line of fire down her throat, over the shoulder bared by her crumpled blouse.

It was the sound of it that snapped whatever thin hold he had on the civilized. With what was nearly a snarl, he grasped her hands and pulled them above her head. She was trembling, but her eyes were almost black with passion and challenge.

With her wrists trapped beneath his fingers, he tore her blouse down the center, sending tiny gold buttons flying. Her body quivered, like a string rudely plucked, but her gaze never faltered.

There was silk beneath the silk, a sheer little fancy that barely covered her breasts before skimming down to disappear beneath her skirt. He watched her face as he skimmed a hand up her leg and found the top of her stocking, the lace-edged hem of the silk. He watched her eyes unfocus as he cupped the fire he'd ignited. As he plunged recklessly into it.

She cried out, shocked, shattered, bucking frantically against his probing hand like a mustang with the first weight of man on her back. Sensations slapped at her, smothered her, staggered her with heat and light and a grinding, glorious need that clenched its sweaty fist in her stomach. Panicked, pleasured, she shook her head while her body exploded.

Her release was like a geyser, boiling from deep inside, thundering up, closer and closer to the surface. Unstoppable. When she was sure she was drained, when even the colors kaleidoscoping behind her eyes began to dim, he drove her up again.

His hands, ruthless and rough, tugged at her skirt. His mouth worked eagerly at the silk dipping over her breasts, then beneath until she was caught, hot inside it. The flavor of her flesh was exotic, spiced with sweat and soft as water. He could hear her quick thirsty pants, the dazed whimpers that caught time after time in her throat while her heart plunged desperately under his hand, his mouth.

There was the sheer animal pleasure of her nails scraping down his back, of her body straining, shuddering, pumping against his greedy hands.

Those hands tangled with hers in a frantic race to yank away his slacks.

The instant he was free, he drove himself into her, hard, deep, his fingers digging bruises into her hips. Twin moans trembled on the air when he mounted her, dragging her legs up to open her fully. Then his mouth was on hers again, swallowing gasps as they rode each other to the hot, sweaty finish.

Her head drooped onto his shoulder. Her body, so filled with frenzied energy, went limp as wet paper. If he hadn't been pressed against her with the wall solid at her back, she would have slid bonelessly to the floor.

"Who won?" she managed.

With what breath he had left, he laughed. "A dead heat. Good Christ, you're amazing."

She didn't have the energy to question that. As her mind began to clear it occurred to her that she'd just made violent, frantic love standing up, and what was left of her clothes, and his, were scattered ruined at their feet.

"This has never happened to me before. Nothing like this has ever happened to me."

"Good." Realizing they could spend the night leaning against the wall like drunks, he scooped her up.

"No, I mean . . ." She trailed off, noting hazily that she still wore one strappy high heel. Carelessly, she kicked it off. "I mean ever. When I was married, we just . . . I mean. Never mind."

"Don't stop there." He carried her into the bedroom. "I love comparisons. When they're in my favor."

"That's the only one I have. Other than Wade—there wasn't anyone other than Wade."

He stopped in the process of lowering her to the bed. His eyes focused. "There was no one before him?"

This was her problem in the bedroom, Kelsey thought grimly. She talked too much. "So?"

"So." Gabe straightened and kissed her again. Maybe it was a dated male fantasy to imagine yourself the only one. But he decided to eliminate Wade and enjoy it. He dropped her onto the bed from a high-enough perch to make her bounce twice before settling. "Your ex wasn't just a bastard. He was an idiot."

"Thanks, I guess." When he continued to look down at her she started to tug on the strap of her camisole—only to discover it was broken. "I think you're going to have to lend me a robe or something so I can get back to my room."

He was smiling when he climbed onto the bed and covered her.

"Really, Gabe, I can't walk down the hall wearing this." She felt the wrinkled ruin of silk bunch between them. "What's left of this," she corrected.

"It looks incredible on you." He skimmed his hand up until her breast was snuggled in his palm. "But this time I figure I'll get you all the way out of it."

"This time?" Her heart stuttered as he stroked his thumb lazily over her nipple. "I couldn't possibly. You couldn't possibly."

His brow arched as he lowered his grinning mouth to hers. "Wanna bet?" She'd have lost. Several times. By the time dawn began to seep through the windows she was sprawled over him, her body still quivering from the last assault, her mind too numb to sleep.

"I have to go. I need to get to the track."

"You need to sleep, then you need to eat. Then we'll go to the track."

"Can we get coffee?" Her words were beginning to slur as fatigue sneaked through to overpower everything else.

"Sure. In a little while." He stroked her hair, her back, not to arouse now, but to lull. "Turn it off for now, darling."

"What time is it?"

He glanced at the clock and lied without compunction. "About four," he said although it was past six.

"Okay. Couple hours." She felt herself drift down a widening tunnel, light as a feather. "Just a quick nap."

He shifted her gently, brushing the hair away from her face, spreading the tangled sheet over her. Her face was still pale, the shadows under her eyes like flaws on marble. For a few minutes he watched her sleep. And watching her sleep, he fell in love.

Uneasy with the sensation, he backed away from it, and the bed. He reminded himself that great sex, no matter how much affection was involved, was a long way from love.

He'd wanted her. Now he had her. That didn't mean he had to know precisely what happened next. She needed a friend every bit as much as she needed a lover. Since he intended to be both, he'd better get started on being a friend.

Gabe took a shower, and when he came back to dress, she hadn't moved. Without a thought to her sensibilities, he walked into the parlor and picked up her purse. Her wallet, a palm-size pack of tissues, a leather appointment book, and, he discovered to his amusement, a hoof pick. Her key was tucked inside a little zippered pocket along with a lipstick, a small vial of perfume—which he indulged himself by sniffing—and a twenty-dollar bill. Items, he supposed, a woman like Kelsey wanted to keep handy.

He slipped her key into his own pocket and left her sleeping alone.

His initial stop was Naomi's room. Moses opened the door at the first knock. He looked strained and tired, but he offered Gabe a hand and a genuine smile. "I didn't get a chance to congratulate you. Your colt ran a beautiful race."

"He had top competition. It wasn't the way I wanted to win."

"No." Moses led him inside with a slap on the back. "It's a hard one, Gabe, for all of us. Now that we know something about how it happened, well, it's harder yet."

"There's no more news, I take it?"

"The investigation's rolling. And Three Willows will roll one of its own." In his seamed face, his eyes were hard as onyx. "All I know is somebody meant that horse to die. Goddamned waste."

"Whatever I can do—whatever anyone at Longshot can do—you have only to say the word. I want the answers every bit as much as you do." Gabe glanced toward the bedroom door as it opened.

Naomi stepped out. If she'd been a boxer, he might have said she was in fighting trim. None of the frailty that had haunted her the day before showed now. She wore a dark purple suit, as close to mourning as she had available, and a look of grim determination.

As Gabe had said, she'd fought back.

"I'm glad you're here." She crossed to him, put her arms around him, and rested her cheek against his. "This is hard on both of us." She drew back, keeping her hands on his shoulders. "A lot of the talk's going to circle around you, too. I want a united front."

"So do I."

"I hate what happened. I hate it for me, for you, and I hate it for racing. But we're going to deal with it. I've just scheduled a press conference. I'd like you to be there."

"Where and when?"

She smiled, then touched his cheek. "At noon, at the track. I think it's important that we do it there. We'll be taking Pride home immediately after the autopsy." She paused, took a long breath. "We should both be prepared for a lot of press in the coming weeks—and with the Preakness, even more speculation." Her eyes hardened. "You damn well better win that one, Gabe."

"I intend to."

Satisfied, she nodded. "I'm going to give Kelsey another hour or so before I call her room. She took on a lot yesterday. I hate to ask her for more."

"She's got more." The nerves that trickled down his back struck him as ridiculous. He slipped his hands into his pockets, fingered Kelsey's room key. "Kelsey stayed with me last night. She's sleeping now. I'm going to get some things for her out of her room, then make sure she eats."

The silence dragged on. Five seconds. Ten. Naomi broke it with a sigh. "I'm glad you were with her. I'm glad it's you."

"You might not be when I tell you it's going to stay me."

She arched a brow. "Are you talking about marriage, Gabe?" For the first time in hours, she laughed. "Ah, the face pales. Such a man thing." She patted his arm as he continued to stare at her. "You'd better get out of here, honey, before I start to ask you more embarrassing questions. If you could have Kelsey here by eleven, we could all go out to the track together. Oh, and get her the navy suit with the coral blouse."

Naomi nudged him out the door, closed it, then rested back against it. "Oh, Moses, what a horrendous twenty-four hours this has been. And now, for just a minute, I feel so good. Do you think she knows he's in love with her?"

All Kelsey knew was that she was furious with him. Not only had he let her oversleep, but he'd taken off—with her key. She was stuck, without a decent stitch of clothing, in his room.

She stepped out of a frigid shower, which had done little to cool her off, and wrapped herself in the hotel robe hanging on the back of the door. With her hair bundled in a towel, she paced from bedroom to parlor and back again.

She debated calling Naomi's suite, but shied away from the idea of explaining that she was essentially naked and marooned in Gabe's room.

When she heard the parlor door open, she marched in, fire on her tongue. "I'd like to know what the hell you think you're—oh."

She and the room service waiter stared at each other with equal parts of distress. "I'm sorry, miss. The gentleman said I should come right in and set up breakfast quietly because you were sleeping."

"Oh. Well. That's all right. I'm up." She folded her hands, and her dignity. "And where is the gentleman?"

"I can't say, miss. I only had my instructions. Would you prefer I come back later?"

"No." She wasn't letting that coffee out of the room. "No, this is fine. I'm sorry I startled you."

While he set up, she debated whether to gather up the scattered clothes or to pretend not to notice them. Opting for the latter, she accepted the check, added a tip she hoped would make Gabe bleed, and signed it with a flourish.

"Thank you, miss. Enjoy your breakfast."

She was pouring her first cup of coffee when Gabe strolled in. "So, you're awake."

"You pig." She gulped the coffee black and hot enough to blister her tongue. "Where's my key?"

"Right here." He drew it out of his pocket, then laid her suit over a chair. "I think I got everything. You're an organized hotel guest. Cosmetics, toothbrush. By the way, you've got great underwear. I figured this little navy thing went with the suit." He held up a teddy and grinned. "Want to put it on?"

She snatched it out of his hand. "You've been pawing through my things."

"I collected your things. Your mother suggested the suit."

"My—" Kelsey gritted her teeth and prayed for patience. "You've been to see her?"

"She's doing fine. More than ready to handle the backlash. She's set up a press conference at the track for noon. How's the coffee?" He poured some for himself. "We're to meet her at eleven in her room, and go out together. She suggested the suit, but not whatever baubles you wanted to go with it. So I picked what I liked."

"She told you what clothes to get for me?" Kelsey drew in air, then expelled it slowly. "Which means you told her I was here."

He sat, then lifted the silver dome from a plate to reveal ham and eggs. "I told her you were with me last night." His gaze flicked up. "Is that a problem?"

"No, but... No." Giving up, she pressed a hand to her temple. "My head's spinning."

"Sit down and eat, you'll feel better." When she did, he reached over and closed a hand firmly over hers. "We're in this together. Got that?"

She stared down at their joined hands. He hadn't meant the press conference, not just the press conference, and they both knew it. Another risk, Kelsey thought, but she lifted her eyes until they were level with his.

"Yeah, I got it."

17

"You never said you were going to kill the horse." Cunningham mopped his sweaty face. It seemed he spent all his time sweating these days. In front of the cameras with a big sloppy grin on his face. At celebration parties where people thumped him on the back and bought him drinks. In bed, staring up at the dark ceiling, reliving that final stretch of the Derby over and over.

He'd wanted to win, but had gratefully settled for second place. Yet the cost had ballooned into more than he'd ever expected to pay.

"You never said," he repeated, while sweat soaked his shirt and pooled nastily at the base of his spine. "Disqualify him, you said, so Sheba would have a chance to place."

"You wanted the details left up to me," Rich reminded him. He was drinking top-grade Kentucky bourbon now and enjoying the view of D.C. from a lofty hotel suite. He could afford it. He could afford a great many things now. "And you got what you wanted. Your filly placed at the Derby. Nobody's going to call you a sucker now, are they? Nobody's going to snicker behind your back."

"You were just supposed to see the colt was disqualified."

"I did." Rich grinned. "Big time. The Chadwicks lose, suspicion points at them, at my cocky young son, and you, Billy boy, come out smelling like a rose." He chose a candied almond from a bowl. "Now, let's be honest here, Billy. You don't mind giving Gabe a backhanded slap, do you? After all, he cost you the family farm and a good dose of your dignity five years ago."

"No, I don't mind taking him down a peg. But—"

"Both of us know that filly of yours didn't have a chance in holy hell of winning that race," Rich continued. "Likely with Three Willows and Longshot in the running, she maybe takes third if she's beat all the way to the wire—more likely fourth or fifth. That wasn't good enough, was it?"

Not with the hole he'd dug himself, Cunningham thought. "No, but—"

"No." Rich crunched down on another almond, his face as earnest as any used-car salesman's. "You needed an edge, and I supplied it. Now, truth is, I didn't expect her to do better than show, but that girl ran with her heart. She'll breed champs," he said with a wink. "That's the bottom line, right? You'll syndicate her now and make yourself a pot of money as long as she'll lift her tail for a handsome stud."

It was true, all true, but Cunningham's glands were still in overdrive. "If it comes out, Rich, I'll be ruined."

"How's it going to come out? Am I going to tell somebody?" He grinned again. "You haven't been bragging to that pretty little piece in bed, have you? Some men can't keep their mouths shut once they've dipped their wick."

"No." Cunningham swiped a hand over his mouth. "I haven't told her anything." Not that he thought she'd notice. Marla was more interested in spending his money than how he came by it. "But people are asking questions. And the press is hounding me."

"Of course they are," Rich said heartily. "All you have to do is shake your head and look sad and reap some free publicity. You can always add a little flourish about how you know Naomi Chadwick and Gabriel Slater, and can't imagine either of them would stoop so low. You make sure you link Gabe's name in there. I'd appreciate that."

Cunningham licked his lips, inched forward. "How'd you do it, Rich?"

"Now, now, Billy boy, that's my little secret. And the less you know, the better. Right? You're just a lucky guy who picked up a horse at a claiming race and carried her through to the Derby."

"The Preakness is in two weeks."

Rich grinned, brows wiggling. "That's greedy, friend. And dangerous. You know how risky it is to race that horse again."

"She has another in her." He forgot his guilt, and his fears. He forgot the men who had died and the sight of the colt falling at the sixteenth pole. "I only need her to show."

"No can do." Chuckling, Rich wagged a finger in the air. "Even if you put her in, and she didn't break down, that leg of the Triple Crown has to run clean. Otherwise they might start looking at you, Billy boy. And who knows—if they look at you, they might start looking *for* me. That happens, and, well . . ." He rattled the ice in his glass. "We wouldn't be friends anymore."

"A lot of money's at stake."

"You want more money? Bet on the Longshot colt. I know my boy. He'll put everything he's got into winning. Vindicate himself." Rich's grin turned sour. He poured more bourbon into the melting ice. "Always had a tight ass about winning clean. Taught him every trick I know, every fucking one, but he figures he's better than me, see? Too good to salt the game." His eyes narrowed, went hard as he drank. "We'll see who comes out on top this time. We'll see."

There wasn't any use arguing, not when Rich started pouring with a free hand. "What am I supposed to do?"

"You scratch her from Pimlico, Billy. Say she pulled up lame in a workout and you don't want to risk her. Look disappointed and righteous, then put her out to pasture until it's time to choose her a lover."

"You're right." It hurt, but Cunningham put aside his greed. "Better not take the chance. I'm going to syndicate her, get the bitch pregnant next spring." He smiled a little. "I might even make a deal with your boy, Rich, to breed her with his Derby colt in a few years."

"Now you're talking." He leaned forward and slapped a hand on Cunningham's knee. "I've worked out a little bonus, Billy."

"Bonus?" Instantly wary, Cunningham drew back. "We had a deal, Rich. I kept my part."

"No argument there. Not a one. But look here, Billy, you raked in a bundle at that race, between the purse and the betting window. I've got to figure your take at three, maybe four hundred grand." His smile widened as Cunningham began to sweat again. "And with the syndication deal, the foals she's going to drop in oh, say, the next ten years, you'll be sitting real pretty. Couldn't've done it without me, could you?"

"I paid you—"

"You did indeed, but let's tally up the cost here. I had to pay Lipsky."

"That was your idea. I had nothing to do with it."

"I'm like a subcontractor, Billy," Rich explained patiently. "What I do all leads back to you. You don't want to forget that. Now, Lipsky took out that old groom, and I took out Lipsky. Now, we won't get into details about the others on my payroll, but they're necessary expenses, and I have to pass them on. We've got ourselves two dead men and a dead horse, and what's standing between them and you is me." He beamed, ticking off murder on his fingers. "So, keeping me happy's got to be pretty important to you. It ought to be worth another hundred thousand."

"A hundred—That's bullshit, Rich! Just plain bullshit. I've got all the expenses. Do you know what it costs to keep a Thoroughbred? Even just one fucking horse? Plus the entry fees."

"You don't want to nickel-and-dime me, Billy boy. You really don't." Rich's smile was as friendly as a death's-head. He kept his hand on Cunningham's knee, squeezing. As Rich intended to squeeze his wallet for some time to come. "A hundred thousand's a bargain. Take my word. I'll give you another week to figure out how to cook your books. You bring it on by here the day before the Preakness. In cash." He sat back, delighted with himself. "I've got a hankering to lay down a bet on my boy's colt. Family ties, you know."

He was laughing as he dumped more bourbon into his glass.

Her own family ties had given Kelsey a splitting headache. She'd expected the trip to Potomac to be difficult, but it had been much more than that. Her father had been furious, as angry as Kelsey had ever seen him. It had hardly mattered that his temper hadn't been directed at her. As Candace had coolly pointed out, she was the cause of the problem.

Milicent had made good on her threat. She hadn't been able to break the terms of Kelsey's grandfather's will, but she had altered her own. In Victorian and melodramatic terms, Milicent no longer had a granddaughter.

With her car still idling in the drive at Three Willows, Kelsey rested her aching head on the steering wheel. It had been a horrible, horrible scene. Milicent's cold fury as she made the announcement, her father's shock, then his outrage. And Candace, already prepared, aiming little darts of blame toward Kelsey's heart.

On a quiet moan of pain, Kelsey straightened and turned off the ignition. She hadn't realized it would hurt so much. She and Milicent had been at odds for so long, it would have made more sense to be relieved.

But she wasn't relieved. She was wounded.

Wearily, she got out of the car, thinking aspirin at least would take care of her throbbing head.

She heard the music, the hard, driving beat of vintage Stones. Mick and the boys were grinding out their sympathy for the devil. Kelsey followed them around the side of the house.

There was a splattered drop cloth over the stones of the patio. A boom box belched out rock and roll from the glass-topped table. At an easel, her hair pulled back in a stubby ponytail, an oversize man's shirt hanging to her knees, Naomi fenced with a crimson-tipped brush.

She might have been wielding a sword, Kelsey thought. Dueling with the canvas that had already exploded with color and shape. Her face, turned in profile, was set in stone, her eyes spewing smoke.

It seemed a very intimate battle, and Kelsey started to back away. But Naomi's head whipped around, and those angry eyes pinned her.

"I'm sorry," Kelsey began, drowned out by the music. Naomi reached over and turned it down to a pulsing throb. "I didn't mean to disturb you."

"It's all right." The passion was fading quickly from her eyes, as if when not facing the canvas she was calm again. "I'm just having a private tantrum." She set down her brush, then picked up a cloth to wipe her hands. "I haven't painted in a while."

"It's wonderful." Kelsey stepped closer, studying the streaks of violent color, the still glistening brushstrokes. "So primal."

"Exactly. You're upset."

"Dammit." Kelsey shoved her hands into her pockets. "I'm beginning to think I have a sign on my forehead that broadcasts my feelings."

"You have an expressive face." So had she, Naomi remembered. Once. "I take it the family meeting didn't go well."

"It went down the toilet. I've caused a rift between my father and my grandmother. A big one. And, I think, a smaller but no less difficult one between him and Candace."

"By staying here."

"By being who I am." She picked up the neglected glass of iced tea Naomi had brought out with her, and drank. "Milicent has not only cut me out of her will, but out of her mind and heart. As far as she's concerned, I no longer exist."

"Oh, Kelsey." Naomi laid a hand on her arm. "I'm sure she doesn't mean it."

Glass clinked against glass as she set the tea down. "Are you?"

Sympathy and concern hardened into fury. "Of course she means it. It's just like her. I'm sorry I've caused you this kind of trouble."

"*I* caused," Kelsey exploded. "This is mine. It's time everyone started to understand that I can think and act and feel for myself. If I didn't want to be here, I wouldn't be. I'm not here to spite them or to placate you. I'm here for me."

Naomi took a deep breath. "You're right. Absolutely right."

"If I wanted to be somewhere else, I'd be somewhere else. But I won't be threatened or bribed or guilted into giving up something that's important to me. My family is important to me. Three Willows is important to me. And so are you."

"Well." Naomi reached for the glass herself, and her hand was unsteady. "Thank you."

Kelsey resisted, barely, the urge to kick a pot of geraniums. "It's hardly a matter for gratitude. You're my mother. I care about you. I admire what you've been able to do with your life. Maybe I'm not satisfied about all the years between, but I like who you are. I'm certainly not going to go scrambling back and pretend you don't exist because Milicent would prefer it."

To keep herself from buckling into a chair, Naomi braced a hand on the table. "You can't imagine, can't possibly imagine what it's like to hear from a grown daughter that she likes who you are. I love you so much, Kelsey."

Her anger skidded to a halt. "I know."

"I didn't know who you would be when I saw you again. All the love I had was for that little girl I'd lost. Then you came here, and you gave me a chance. I'm so dazzled by the woman you are. So proud of you. If you left tomorrow and never came back, you'd still have given me more than I ever thought I'd have again."

"I'm not going anywhere." Leading with her heart, Kelsey stepped forward and opened her arms. "I'm exactly where I want to be."

With her eyes tightly closed, Naomi absorbed the feel, the scent of her daughter. "I want to say I'll make it up to you. That I'll find a way to soften her heart."

"Don't. It's not for you to worry about." Steadier, she eased back. "You can be mad with me. I'm so goddamned mad." Riding on the mood swings, she whirled away to pace. "And hurt. I can't believe how much it hurt. For her to think I cared about her money. For her to use it, and my feelings, against me. To try to control me with them."

"Control is essential to Milicent. It always has been."

"She couldn't break my grandfather's trust. I bet that burned her. Not having the power to change that. And Dad was so upset. He shouted at her. He's never raised his voice to her."

"Yes, he has." There was a grim satisfaction in Naomi's smile. "It's probably been some time. I'm glad he stood up for you."

"I wish I could say I was. It was horrible to see them fight that way. And to see the distance all this has put between him and Candace. To know, right or wrong, that I'm responsible. Grandmother's so unbending, so unwilling to see someone else's side." And hadn't the same been said about her? Kelsey remembered. And shuddered.

"Then she has two choices," Naomi put in. "She'll bend, or she'll die lonely."

"I have to believe they'll make up," Kelsey murmured. "I have to. I'm not sure

Grandmother and I will ever come to terms again. Not after today. She actually used Pride against me. She said that you'd probably gotten one of your hoodlum friends—her exact words, by the way—to drug the horse. After all, if you'd killed a man ..." Appalled, Kelsey trailed off.

"Why would I stop at the idea of killing a horse?" Naomi finished. "Why indeed?"

"I'm sorry." Disgusted with herself, she rubbed at her still aching temples. "I'm wound up."

"It doesn't matter. I'm sure she's not the only one who's had the thought. One of the reasons I'm out here, venting," she said, gesturing toward the canvas, "is that a rumor's circulating that I might have arranged for Pride's death to collect the insurance."

Kelsey dropped her hands, then balled them into fists. "That's hideous! No one who knows you would believe that."

"It's not an unheard-of practice, unfortunately. There's a lot of ugliness in this world, too, Kelsey. The rumor will pass." She picked up her brush again, contemplating. "Simple arithmetic will scotch it eventually. Even though he was heavily insured, Pride was worth a good deal more alive, at the track and at stud, than he is dead. But it stirs memories. Mine. Others."

Calmer, she began to paint again. "This was my therapy in prison. More, it was a way to survive, a way to channel emotions. You don't want to bring attention to yourself inside. With anger, grief, with fear. Especially not with fear."

"Can you tell me about it?" Kelsey asked quietly. "What it was like?"

For a moment Naomi continued to paint in silence. She'd wondered when Kelsey would ask. Not if. The need to know the answers, to find the solutions were as much a part of her daughter's makeup as the color of her eyes.

So she would paint another picture, with words rather than with her brush.

"They strip you." She said it quietly, reminding herself it was done, over. "Not just your clothes, though that's one of the first humiliations. They take everything away from you. Your clothes, your freedom, your rights, your hope. You have only what they give you. The tedious routine of it. You're told when to get up in the morning, when to eat, when to go to bed at night. It doesn't matter what you feel, or what you want."

Kelsey stepped up beside her. The birds were singing now, celebrating spring. The air was ripe with flowers and paint.

"You eat what they give you," Naomi continued, "and after a while, you get used to it. You forget what it's like to go out to a restaurant, or just to wake up at night and go down to the kitchen." She let out a little sigh without realizing it. "It's easier if you forget. If you keep too much of the outside with you, it'll drive you crazy. Because you know it's not yours anymore. You can see the mountains, flowers, trees, the seasons changing. But they're all outside, and really have nothing to do with you. You can't be who you were anymore. And even if you ache for companionship, you don't get too close to anyone. Because people come and go."

She changed brushes and began to paint with the energy that was boiling up inside. "Some of the women kept calendars, but I didn't. I wasn't going to think about the days passing into weeks, the weeks into months, the months into years. How could I? Some had pictures of their family, their children, and liked to talk about them. Or what they would do when they got out. I didn't do that. I couldn't do that. It was simpler for me to focus on the routine."

"But you were lonely," Kelsey murmured. "You must have been so lonely."

"That's the deepest punishment. The loneliness, and the conflicting lack of privacy. It's not the bars. You think it's going to be the bars, closing you in. But it's not."

She took a deep breath, and made herself continue. "If you had free time, you read, or you watched TV. Fashion magazines were big, but I stopped looking at them after the first couple of years. It was too hard to watch the way things were changing, even something as frivolous as hemlines."

"Did you have visitors?"

"My father. Moses. Nothing I could say would stop either one of them from coming. God knows I wanted to see them, no matter how I suffered after they were gone. I watched my father grow old. I suppose that was the hardest part, watching the years pass on his face. That was my calendar. My father's face.

"The last year was the hardest. I was coming up for parole, and it looked as though I'd get it. Knowing freedom was almost within reach—and yet being afraid to be cut off from the world you'd lived in for so long, that was hard. How would you know what to do now, and when to do it? The days dragged, giving you too much time to think, to hope again, to sweat out those last months. Then they let you put on civilian clothes. My father brought me a new suit. Gray pinstripes, very lawyerish. My hands shook so badly I couldn't button the blouse. The sun hurt my eyes when I walked out. It wasn't as if they'd kept us in a hole. It was a decent prison, with decent people in charge, at least for the most part. But the sun was different that day, stronger, brighter. I couldn't see anything through it. And then I saw too much."

She exchanged brushes again, her eyes focused on her work. "Do you really want to hear the rest of this?"

"Go on," Kelsey murmured. "Finish."

"I saw my father, how frail and old he was. The new Cadillac, blindingly white, he drove me home in. I know he spoke to me, and I to him, but I can't remember any of it. Only that everything seemed to move too fast, and the roads were so crowded. And I was afraid, afraid they would take me back. Afraid they wouldn't. We stopped and ate at a restaurant. Linen napkins, wine, flowers on the table. He had to order for me, as if I were a child. I couldn't remember what I liked. And I started to cry. And he cried. So we sat and wept on the white linen cloth because I couldn't remember what it was like to sit in a restaurant and order a meal.

"I slept most of the rest of the drive, exhausted from freedom. Then I woke up and he was turning through the gates. I could see that the trees had grown.

The dogwoods that had been saplings, the ones I'd planted myself, were adult trees that had bloomed year after year without me. New paint in the living room, a vase that hadn't been there before. Every little change terrified me.

"I didn't go down to the barn, not for days, until Moses came to the house and bullied me into it. There was a foal I'd helped birth. Now he was sixteen hands high and at stud. New equipment, new men. New everything. I stayed in the house for a week after that. Slept with the light on and my door open. At first I couldn't stand for a door to be closed. But after a while it got better. I had to learn to drive again. I was terrified, but I did it. The first time I went out alone, I drove to your school. I watched the baby I'd left behind as a young girl, learning to flirt with boys. I made myself accept that you'd learned to live without me. And I tried to start over."

Naomi set her brush down, and stepped back. "It's done."

Kelsey wasn't certain of that. The painting might have been finished, but not the emotion behind it. Nor, as far as she was concerned, was the story done. It wasn't a matter of clearing Naomi's name. A man had been killed, and a woman had paid the price. But she wanted to see that the pieces fit.

Still it was a shock to find Charles Rooney's name in the phone book. The private investigator whose evidence had weighed most heavily in Naomi's trial still had an office in Virginia. Alexandria, now. The discreet ad in the yellow pages declared Rooney Investigative Services handled criminal, domestic, and custody. Licensed and bonded and confidential. The first consultation was free.

Perhaps, she thought, she'd take advantage of that.

"Miss Kelsey." When Gertie hurried into the kitchen, Kelsey quickly slapped the phone book closed.

"You startled me."

"Sorry. That policeman's here again." Her homely face expressed simple and loyal annoyance. "Says he's got some more questions."

"I'll see him. Naomi's down at the barn. No need to bother her."

"You want me to make coffee?"

Kelsey hesitated only a moment. "No, Gertie. Let's get him in and out."

"Sooner the better," Gertie muttered under her breath.

Rossi stood when Kelsey entered the sitting room. He had to admire the way she wore jeans, though he'd been equally impressed with the clip from the press conference, and the way she and her mother had looked, trim and blond in their silk suits.

"Ms. Byden, I appreciate the time."

"I don't have much of it, Lieutenant, but I'm willing to stretch it if you have news for us."

"I wish I did." He had nothing but frustration. No unaccounted-for prints in Lipsky's motel room, no witnesses, no trail. "I'd like to offer my sympathies for your loss at the Derby. I'm not much of a horse lover, but even cops watch that race. It was a terrible thing."

"Yes, it was. My mother's devastated."

"She looked sturdy enough at the press conference."

With a frigid nod, Kelsey sat, and gestured for Rossi to join her. "Did you expect her to fall apart, publicly?"

"Actually, no. But I did find it interesting that Slater sat in on it."

"We're neighbors, Lieutenant. And friends. Gabe is also an owner. And the fact that his colt won, under such tragic circumstances, made it difficult for all of us. We asked him there to show our support, and he accepted to show his."

"You'll excuse me, Ms. Byden, but from what I've seen in the press, you and Mr. Slater seem to be more than friends."

The Byden genes swam to the surface, adding a cool, arrogant tilt to her head. "Is that an official statement, Lieutenant?"

"Just an observation. It's natural enough; you're both attractive people with mutual interests." She didn't rise to the bait. But he hadn't expected her to. "I was hoping you could help me out with the details of what happened at Churchill Downs."

"I thought you weren't interested in horses, Lieutenant."

"Murder interests me, even in horses." He waited a beat. "Particularly if it ties in with a homicide case I want to close."

"You think what happened to Pride is tied in with Old Mick's murder? How? Lipsky's dead."

"Exactly. From what I'm told, it's not easy to get to a Derby entrant."

"No, it's not. The security is tight. We have guards." Her brow furrowed. "It was Gabe's colt Lipsky was after, not ours. And I was under the impression Lipsky's death was considered a suicide. You think it was murder?"

"There's debate on that" was all he would say. "I'd like to snip any loose ends. If you could tell me who had official access to the colt before the race?"

"I would, of course. My mother, Moses, Boggs, Reno." She blew out a breath. "The official who checks identification, the handlers at the gate. The outrider, the one who ponied him onto the track. That was Carl Tripper. The other members of the crew." She ticked off names.

"The guards?"

"Well, yes, I suppose."

"And unofficially?"

She shook her head, but her mind was working. "You'd have to be very slick to get through security on Derby day, Lieutenant. It may look like a free-for-all on television, but the horses are closely watched."

"The drug. It's hard to tell when it was given to the horse."

"That's part of the problem." She took a steadying breath. It was still hard to talk about it. "Pride had traces of digitalis and epinephrine in his bloodstream. It killed him, overworked his heart. He was edgy, but he usually is before a race. Moses keeps him that way."

"Now, why would that be?"

"Some horses run better when they're wired up. Others need to be soothed and calmed. Pride ran best wired."

"How do you go about that?"

"A lot of it comes from the horse. They know when they're going to race. They're not fed as much, they're prepped differently. There's atmosphere. And you might hold them back at the workout when they're itchy to have their head."

"No chemicals?"

Her face went very still. "No drugs, Lieutenant. We don't doctor our horses here with anything that isn't approved and necessary for their health. What someone gave Pride pumped up his heart rate, his adrenaline. The race, the strain of driving him hard for more than a mile, killed him."

Which was precisely what the colt's autopsy report had told him. "Shouldn't the jockey have known something was wrong?"

Her jaw tightened. She wouldn't permit anyone to blame Reno. Not after what he'd been through. She'd seen for herself the way he'd suffered. The way he'd continued to suffer.

"Pride ran because that's what he was born to do, what he'd been trained to do since he took his first steps. He didn't falter. He didn't fight Reno. You only have to look at the tape to see he was putting everything he had into winning that race. And killed himself trying. Reno was lucky he wasn't killed as well."

Rossi studied his notebook. He'd watched the tape of the race over and over, slowing the speed, freeze-framing. Finally, he nodded. "I've got to agree with that. If he'd have gone onto the track instead of the infield, I don't see how he'd have escaped being trampled. And the way he went down, I figured a broken neck."

"So did I. As it is, he won't be up for another month, at the earliest."

"That should do it for now. I'm going to want to talk to some of the names you gave me. Check out their perspective."

"I appreciate your interest, Lieutenant. I'd rather you didn't question my mother, unless it's vital."

"It was her horse, Ms. Byden."

"I think you understand what I'm saying." She rose, ready to defend. "You're perfectly aware of the background here, and how difficult it is for my mother to undergo police interrogation."

"A few questions—"

"Amounts to the same thing, for her. And whether you can understand it or not, she's grieving. You can ask me anything you like, or you can go to the Racing Commission."

"I can't make any promises, but there's no need to disturb her at this time."

"Thank you." She started to walk him to the door. "Lieutenant, you weren't involved in my mother's case, were you?"

"No. I was still at the police academy back then. Green as iceberg lettuce."

"I was curious who was in charge."

"That would have been Captain Tipton. Jim Tipton, retired now. I served under him when he was a lieutenant, and after he made captain. A good cop."

"I'm sure he was. Thank you, Lieutenant."

"Thank you, Ms. Byden." Rossi walked back to the car, nibbling on the seed of an idea. Kelsey Byden had something on her mind, he mused. It wouldn't hurt to do a little digging back himself.

18

"Why do I get the feeling the only place I'm going to get you in bed is in a hotel?"

"Mmmm." Kelsey twirled her bouquet of black-eyed Susans, part of the centerpiece Gabe had stolen for her from their last Preakness party. "I suppose things have been a little hectic. And you have been busy—giving interviews."

"I'm going to give more of them tomorrow."

"That's what I like. A confident man." They strolled across the lobby to the elevators. "And Double is being housed in stall forty. The base of Secretariat, Affirmed, Seattle Slew. Are you superstitious, Slater?"

"Damn right I am." He stepped into the elevator and tugged her in behind him. His mouth was hot on hers before the doors whispered shut.

"The button," she managed, crushing flowers as she pawed her way under his shirt. "You forgot to push the button."

He groped, swore, and managed to press the right floor. "I didn't think I was ever going to get you alone. Two weeks is two weeks too long, Kelsey."

"I know." She let out a breathless laugh when his teeth scraped her neck. "Naomi needed me. And there's hardly been time to think with the investigation, and trying to get the colt ready for tomorrow. I've wanted to be with you."

The doors opened, and she jerked back. Her cocktail dress was a great deal more than off the shoulder. She tugged it back into place, amazed that she'd lose control in an elevator, and grateful that the hall beyond was empty.

"You don't know whether to be pleased with yourself or embarrassed."

She fluffed her hair back into place. "Stop reading my mind," she ordered, and caught the doors before they shut again.

"Your room or mine?"

It was as simple as that, she realized. They'd both been waiting all evening for the chance to pick up where they'd left off in Kentucky.

"Mine," she decided. "This time you can wake up in the morning without any decent clothes to wear."

"Is that a promise to rip them off me?"

She swiped her key card through the slot and tried to come up with a suitable answer. Even as the light beeped from red to green, the phone began to ring. "Hold that thought," she told him, and dashed to answer.

"Hello?" She tossed the crushed flowers onto a coffee table, tugged off one earring, then passed the phone to the unadorned lobe. Her fingers went still as they closed over the second sapphire cluster. "Wade? How did you know I was here?" Very carefully, very deliberately, she removed her other earring and set it down on the table. "I see. I didn't realize you kept in touch with Candace.... Of course. That's cozy, isn't it?... Yes, I'm being sarcastic."

Her eyes flashed to Gabe, then dropped. Without a word he crossed to the minibar, opened a bottle of Chardonnay, and poured her a glass.

"Wade. You didn't call at"—she checked her watch—"eleven-fifteen to make small talk, and I really have no intention of discussing my mother with you. So if that's all..."

Miserably, she accepted the glass from Gabe. Of course that wasn't all. It was never all with Wade.

"Do you want my blessing?... No, I'm not going to be gracious, and this is as civilized as it gets." She thought about swallowing her venom, but instead let it spew as his oh-so-reasonable voice nattered in her ear. "Does the lucky bride know that you have a habit of boffing your associates on business trips?... Yeah, I'm real good at holding a grudge. You bastard, you oily, self-centered jerk. How dare you call me up on your wedding eve to soothe your conscience!... How's this?... No, I don't forgive you. No, I refuse to share in the blame.... That's right, Wade, I'm as rigid and unforgiving as ever, but I have stopped wishing you'd die a long, painful, and ugly death. Now I just want you to get hit by a truck while you're crossing the street. If you want absolution, find a priest."

She hung up, slamming the receiver hard enough to strike a whining ring.

"Well," Gabe murmured into the silence, "that's telling him." He toasted her with a can of Coke. "Does he make a habit of calling you?"

"Every couple of months." She kicked the table, then ripped her shoes off her aching toes and heaved them across the room. "To chat. If you can believe that. We can't be married, but why can't we be friends? I'll tell you why. Because nobody cheats on me. Nobody."

"I'll keep that in mind." Gabe watched her, wondering if he should let her cool down, or if he should just scoop her off to bed and help her expel some of that energy.

"He's getting married tomorrow. He thought I should hear it straight from him, so he called Candace. They still belong to the same club, you know." She gulped down wine, found she didn't have the taste for it. "She told him where I was. She told him, as if he had some unbreakable right to know. As if I give a damn about him getting married."

"Do you?" Gabe reached out to keep the glass she'd slammed down from tipping over onto the rug.

"No." She needed something to throw, anything, and settled on the complimentary travel guide. "I care that he can call me out of the blue and make me feel, even for an instant, that it was my fault he was with another woman. I care that when he does, I think back and remember how perfect it was supposed to be. A nice young couple, from good families, having their splashy society wedding, the romantic two-week honeymoon in the Caribbean, the charming little row house in Georgetown. The right friends, the right clubs, the right parties. And I hate when I look back and I realize I never loved him."

Her voice broke and she fisted her hands at her temples. "I didn't even love him. How could I have married him, Gabe? How could I have when I didn't feel even a fraction for him what I feel for you?"

His eyes flashed, then the light narrowed down to a pinpoint of heat. "Be careful, Kelsey. I don't cheat, but that doesn't mean I play fair. I don't give a damn that you're upset. If you say too much, I'll hold you to it."

"I don't know what I'm saying." Unnerved, trembling, she dropped her hands. "I only know that when I listened to him just now, I realized I'd married him because everyone said he was right for me. And because it seemed like the next natural step. I wanted it to work. I tried to make it work. But how could it? He never once made me feel the way you do." Her voice dropped to a whisper. "No one's ever made me feel the way you do."

He set down his drink, suddenly aware that his fingers had pressed dents in the can. "Everyone will tell you I'm wrong for you."

"I don't care."

"I hate country clubs. I'm not going to take you to spring balls."

"I'm not asking you to."

"I could get the urge tomorrow and put everything I've got on one spin of the wheel."

Her hands relaxed at her sides. She could almost see him doing it. "I think the wheel's already spinning, Slater. Maybe you're not enough of a gambler to put it on the line."

"You don't know what you feel for me." Clawed by his own emotions, he grabbed her, nearly lifting her off the floor. "You're working on it. Christ, I can almost see the gears turning in that head of yours. But you don't know."

"I want you." Her heart was lodged in her throat, pounding. "I've never wanted anyone the way I want you."

"I'll make you give me more. And once I've got hold, Kelsey, you won't shake me loose. If you were smart, you'd take a good look at what you're getting into with me, and you'd run."

She started to shake her head, but he swept her up.

"Too late."

"For you, too," she murmured, and shifted just enough so that her lips could reach his throat. "I'm not running away, Gabe. I'm running after."

And she knew what to expect now, what to anticipate, what to yearn for. Heat and speed and frenzy. She wanted the ache, knowing he could soothe it away, then incite it again until every pulse throbbed like a wound. And she reveled in knowing it was the same for him, that breathless, burning need, the panic, the thrill that they brought to each other from the first greedy touch.

Tumbling over the bed, groping, gasping, they fought with buttons and snaps until clothes scattered like fallen leaves. The quest was for flesh, the taste of it, the feel and scent that was a prelude to that most basic of desires.

He traced his hands over her, the firm, silky-skinned breasts, the narrow rib cage and hips. In the dark he could see her with his fingertips, every inch, every curve and muscle. Like a blind man seeking texture and shape, he explored the body he already knew.

She was everything he'd ever wanted, ever fought for. Ever gambled for. And she was quivering beneath him, ready, eager. Amazingly his.

Her body surged up, agile, quick. When their positions were reversed, she straddled him. In one fluid move, she imprisoned him inside those hot wet walls, arching back to take him hard to the hilt. Her hands groped for, then grasped his, their fingers tightly interlacing as she rocked them both toward madness.

His last thought was that it was indeed too late. Much too late for both of them.

Morning dawned dreary. Heavy clouds thickened the sky and the air, muting all the color to a gunmetal gray. Occasionally rain pricked its way through the layers and fell in sharp darts that stung and chilled. Men and machines raked the track, turned it up anew, sleeked it with furrows. Pimlico drained well, and its groomsmen attended it as carefully, as tenderly, as a man might tend a much-loved horse.

Rain didn't deter the crowds, or the press. By post time for the first race the stands were full. Brightly colored umbrellas seemed to float like balloons on a gray sea. Inside the clubhouse, people stayed dry, feeding on crabs and beer while they watched the action on monitors.

The weather had Kelsey opting for jeans and boots rather than the linen dress she'd expected to wear. It gave her an excuse to linger at the barn and weave black-eyed Susans through Justice's blond mane, to decorate him for his regal task of ponying High Water to the track.

And, in her opinion, there was nothing like a rainy day to make you stop and think.

Six months earlier, she hadn't known Naomi existed. She'd taken no more than a passing glance at the world she was now a part of. She'd been drifting, haunted by a failed marriage, and what she had begun to see as her own failed sexuality. Her job had amused her, nearly satisfied her, yet she'd been thinking of moving on.

There was always another job, another course to take, another trip to plan. She liked to tell herself she'd made all those restless, lateral moves to stimulate her mind. But in reality she'd done so simply to fill holes. Holes she hadn't wanted to acknowledge. Holes she certainly hadn't understood.

She had considered, carefully, whether she was doing the same now, using Naomi, the farm, even Gabe to plug those cracks in her life. Would she, as her family seemed to think, become disenchanted, dissatisfied with the routine, and move on yet again?

Or could she trust the feelings that were blooming inside her? The growing attachment to her mother, a simple, almost quiet evolution from anger and suspicion to affection and respect. Why not just accept that she'd found, and perhaps begun to earn, a place on the farm?

And Gabe? Wasn't it possible to relax and enjoy what was happening between them? She'd had no doubts the night before when they'd tumbled into bed. No doubts when she'd turned lazily to him at dawn and made slow, languid love.

Perhaps it was that inflexible sense of values, her own unwavering perception of right and wrong. How could she allow Naomi to depend on her when she couldn't be certain how long she'd stay? How could she take a lover and glory in lovemaking when neither of them had so much as whispered a word about love?

Maybe she was too rigid. If she couldn't take pleasure in the moment without questioning every motive, what did that say about her own makeup? And was she sulking, just a little, because her ex-husband was being married, perhaps had already taken those vows a second time while she braided flowers into a gelding's mane?

It was time to push that aside once and for all, she warned herself. Time to look forward. She wasn't drifting now. She had a purpose—and questions that needed to be answered. She'd deal with them logically, starting at a twenty-year-old root. First thing Monday morning, she promised herself, she would make that call to Charles Rooney.

The rain had stopped again when they walked to the paddock. Watery sunlight sneaked through breaks in the clouds and fell on dripping eaves. Gutters rang musically and turned the ground to mud.

Kelsey sneaked a look at Boggs. He seemed old, more frail than he had two weeks before. She knew he'd been assigned as High Water's groom as much for his skill as to help heal the wounds.

"The rain's a plus," she said, hoping to lift the shadows from his eyes. "High Water likes a wet track." And so, she remembered, did Double.

"He's a good colt." Absently, Boggs patted his neck. "Steady and kind. Might be he'll surprise us all today."

"Last word, he was five to one."

Boggs shrugged. He'd never paid much heed to the odds. "He ain't run much this year, so they haven't seen what he can do. Still, he's finished in the money more times than not. He'll move if he's asked."

But he's no Pride. Boggs didn't have to say it. Kelsey understood.

"Then I'll ask him." Kelsey went to the colt's head and held his bridle so that she could look in his eyes. They seemed so wise to her, and as Boggs had said, kind. "You'll run, won't you, boy? You'll run as hard and as fast as you can. And that's enough for anyone."

"You're not going to ask him to win?" Naomi laid a hand on Kelsey's shoulder, a small gesture that still touched both of them.

"No. Sometimes the winning isn't as important as the trying." She spotted Reno standing to the side, his arm in a sling, his face haunted and pale. "I'll meet you in the box in a minute."

Kelsey crossed to him and took his free hand. "I was hoping I'd see you."

"Couldn't stay away." He'd wanted to. The last thing he'd wanted was to stand on the sidelines and watch. "I figured to stay home, maybe catch the race on the tube. But I found myself in the car, driving out here."

"We'll have you up again soon, Reno."

A spasm crossed his face. He looked away from her, away from the horses, away from the track. "I don't know if I have the heart for it. That colt deserved better."

"So did you," she said quietly.

"I've spent most of my life dreaming about a Derby win. You can ride dozens of horses, cross dozens of wires, but the Derby's the one. That's gone now."

"There's another Derby next year," she reminded him. "There's always another Derby."

"I don't know if I want another chance." His face tightened when he saw a figure over her shoulder. "Good luck today," he said, and hurried away.

Rossi noted the jockey's quick retreat, and filed it. Despite the lack of welcome on Kelsey's face, he walked to her.

"Miserable day."

"It seemed to be clearing up, until a moment ago."

He smiled, acknowledged the thrust. "I was hoping for a few tips while I was wandering around."

"You're unlikely to get any, Lieutenant." She began walking, resigned to the fact that he fell into step beside her. "You look like what you are. A cop."

"An occupational hazard. I don't claim to know a lot about horses, Ms. Byden, but that one of yours seemed a little on the small side."

"He is. Just over fourteen hands. But I don't think you're here to talk horses."

"You're wrong. Horses are right at the center of this." He offered her his bag of peanuts, then cracked another for himself when she declined. "I've been doing some research. There are a lot of ways to kill a horse, Ms. Byden. Some of which are on the gruesome side."

"I'm aware of that." Much too aware now, she thought. It had been Matt who'd told her when she'd pressed for answers. Told her of electrocution. Putting a horse in standing water, then killing him with live battery cables. A cruel and clever murder, sometimes overlooked. Unless a vet spotted burn marks in the nostrils. Worse, she thought, was suffocating them with Ping-Pong balls, thrust up the nose. They were impossible for a horse to expel, causing a slow, hideous death.

"Your Derby colt," Rossi continued, "he wasn't just killed, he was killed in full view of millions of people. Risky. It's my belief that when someone takes a risk, a particularly unnecessary one, it's because he's anxious to make a point. Who'd want to slap down your mother in public, Ms. Byden?"

"I have no idea." But she stopped. The statement shifted the suspicion from Naomi and instead made her a victim. "Is that what you think this is about?"

"It's an avenue worth exploring. She had the colt insured, heavily. But there's no cash-flow problem at Three Willows, and in the long term, that colt could have generated a lot more. Your mother appears to be a sensible businesswoman. Now, there's Slater."

"He had nothing to do with it."

"That's an emotional response." And precisely what he'd expected. "Backing off that a minute, he reaped the reward. You always want to look at who benefits from murder, Ms. Byden. Any kind of murder. The problem with that is it puts a cloud over him, and his Derby win. So I ask myself, would it be worth it to him? He had a good chance of winning anyway, so would it be worth it to him to stack the deck in so obvious a way? He doesn't strike me as an obvious man."

"An emotional response, Lieutenant?"

"An observation, Ms. Byden. He's not the only one who benefited. There's his trainer, his jockey. They both got a piece of the pie. And there's anyone who bet."

She gave a short laugh, looking around at the crowds. "That certainly narrows the field."

"More than you think." He scanned the crowd as well, enjoying himself. "If it ties in with my two homicides, it narrows it a lot more than you think. Who did Lipsky trust enough—or who was he afraid enough of—to let get close enough to kill him? Someone he worked with, worked for? There were a lot more than two horses in that race, Ms. Byden, and a lot more riding on the Derby than a blanket of flowers."

She stopped, then turned to study his face. "Why are you telling me all of this?"

"You're new to the game. You might see a lot more than people think." He paused to crack open another nut. "And you're involved. Your relationship with your mother isn't making everyone happy."

So, he'd been prying into her personal life as well. She should have expected it. "That's family business, Lieutenant, and has nothing to do with murder."

"I could quote you statistics that would show you family business leads to murder more often than any other kind. I'm just asking you to keep your eyes open."

"They're open, Lieutenant." She stood her ground, unwilling to have him walk into view of the boxes. There was no point in upsetting Naomi moments before the race. "Now, if you'll excuse me, I have to join my mother."

"Good luck," he called out, and chose another nut. He had a feeling Kelsey Byden would be much harder to crack.

Kelsey stepped into the box just as the horses were being loaded into the gate.

"I was afraid you wouldn't make it."

"Ran into someone," Kelsey muttered, and glanced from her mother to Gabe. It was like him, she thought, to be here. To stand with them when this was so completely his moment. She took his hand and gave it a quick squeeze. "Side bet, Slater."

"You still owe me from the first one."

"Double or nothing, then. It's apropos." She studied the field through her binoculars. "Your horse by two lengths. The track's sloppy, but I'll say he runs it in a minute fifty-eight tops. Our colt takes third in two and twelve."

He lifted a brow. "That's a hard bet for a man to turn down. Since there's no way to lose."

The starting gun fired. From the first plunge, Double and his rider took the lead. It was as if, Kelsey thought, they both knew they had something to prove. This was a champion, bursting from the pack in a heartbeat with no need to feel the bat on his back to pour it on. By the first turn he was a half-length in the lead, with the Arkansas colt and the Kentucky roan fighting for second.

Again Kelsey lost herself in the grandeur of it. With her binoculars in place, she urged the horses on, not seeing, as she'd been afraid she would, an overlapping image of Pride going down. There was only the mud-splattered athletes, riders and ridden, thundering around the oval.

There was rain in the air, another misty, steady drizzle that blurred her vision and soaked her skin.

A full length now, and moving out, his red wrappings smeared brown, his rider balanced like a toy in the irons. She heard herself laughing at the glory of it.

Then, like an arrow from a bow, High Water shot up the outside. Kelsey's breath caught at the suddenness of the move. He was gaining, digging in, kicking up turf. Fighting, she thought, dazed, for honor.

Down the stretch, Double lengthened his lead. The crowd roared for him, a flood of sound that overwhelmed everything else. Then for High Water, the five-to-one shot that streaked into third and kept gaining during that heart-stopping final three-sixteenths.

"My God, look at him! My God, Mom, just look at him!"

"I am." Tears mixed with the rain running down Naomi's face. She wrapped her arm tight around Kelsey's waist as they finished 5-7-2. Double had the black-eyed Susans, but High Water had edged out Arkansas for second.

"He did it!" Kelsey let her binoculars drop. "The little guy did it!" She hugged Naomi first, laughing out the victory. "Nobody believed it. None of us believed it." She whirled and with a whoop launched herself into Gabe's arms. "Congratulations! What was the time? What was his time?"

Gabe held up the stopwatch, amused when Kelsey snatched it from him. A minute fifty-seven and a quarter.

She laughed again, rain dripping from her hair onto her face. "Gabriel Slater, you've just won the second jewel in the Triple Crown. What are you going to do now? And I know you're not going to Disney World."

"I'm going to Belmont." He lifted her high, spun her around once, then kissed her. "*We're* going to Belmont."

Inside the clubhouse, Rich Slater toasted the image of his son and Kelsey on the monitor, then downed the aged scotch. A handsome couple, he thought. A very handsome couple they made, much as he and Naomi would have done if she hadn't turned her icy nose up at him.

But there were other matters to contemplate. Other matters to celebrate.

He'd put ten of the hundred thousand he'd bled out of Cunningham on Double's nose. He was quite satisfied with the profits.

For now.

"I hope you don't mind." Kelsey opened the champagne with a cheery *pop.* She'd already had several glasses in her mother's suite, but the night was young. "I'm going to finish this entire bottle. And I may get considerably drunk."

Gabe sat, crossing his feet at the ankles. He'd been fantasizing about a long, hot, very steamy shower for two. But he could wait. It might be interesting to see how many more inhibitions Kelsey let fly after a bottle of Dom.

"Just because I don't drink doesn't mean I wouldn't enjoy watching you indulge yourself."

"I'm going to." She poured, then watched the bubbles froth recklessly over the lip of the flute. "You know, I've never really been drunk. I've been close, but I always pulled myself back." She took a long swallow, waved her hand. "Breeding. Don't want to get too loose at the club—people will talk. Don't want to get too loose at a party—other people will talk." This time she waved the bottle. "Bydens do not solicit gossip."

"What do they solicit?"

"Respect, admiration, and, above all, discretion." She closed one eye to narrow her vision and poured more wine. "The hell with that. Let 'em talk. We won. Isn't it incredible?"

"Yes, it is." He smiled at her. She was barefoot now, and her hair had dried in a glorious tangle of pale gold.

"Everyone was so down before. Trying not to be, but it was so hard. I saw Reno in the paddock, and it just broke my heart." She drank again, sighed, and decided she liked the way champagne made the room circle. Glass in hand, she executed two slow pirouettes to help it along.

"Do that again." He wanted the pleasure of watching the way her hair flowed out, settled, flowed out, settled.

With a giddy laugh, she obliged him. "See, those lessons were good for something. Taught me discipline, too, mental and physical. You know, you could break bricks on this body."

"I'm sure I can find more interesting things to do with it."

She laughed again, knowing he could. Would. "We were talking about the race. I hope it made Reno feel better. You could see how happy Naomi and Moses were. Even Boggs. Poor old Boggs, blaming himself 'cause he bet on Pride. It had nothing to do with it. People are always looking for ways to tie things together. Like Rossi."

"Rossi?"

"Mmmm." She poured another glass, then absently began to unbutton her shirt. It was getting warmer by the swallow. "He was there, at the race. I talked to him. Or he talked to me. He seems to be there every time you turn around, watching, working out his theories. Why should anyone want to hurt Naomi, or make people wonder?"

Gabe adjusted his focus. Her shirt was open to the first sweet curve of breast. But he wanted to concentrate on her words. "Is that what he thinks?"

"Who knows?" She gave a careless shrug. "I don't think he really tells you what he thinks. If you follow me," she said after a moment. "He just says things to sort of plant them in your mind and drive you crazy. But at least he doesn't seem to be looking at Naomi as some sort of horse assassin." She smiled winningly. "He's still got one eye on you, Slater."

"I never doubted it."

"But only one eye." She closed one of her own to demonstrate. "He doesn't think you're obvious."

"Quite a compliment, coming from that source." He decided he could concentrate on Kelsey's emerging flesh after all. "You've got a couple more buttons there, darling."

"I'm getting them. I've never stripped for a man before."

"Let me be the first."

She chuckled, and with her eyes half closed, fumbled open the snap of her jeans. "It irritated me, seeing him there. Rossi, I mean. It started me thinking back over the Derby. All the things that happened. Watching the horses come back through the mist after morning workout. The smells, the sounds, the nerves. Boggs hanging up Pride's wrappings and talking about his last bet. How he thought he saw your father."

"What?" The blood Kelsey's careless striptease had been heating froze like a river of ice. "What did you say about my father?"

"Oh, Boggs thought he saw him at Churchill Downs. He thought it was bad luck. But I don't suppose he was there, or he'd have let you know."

"Kelsey." Gabe rose, took her glass out of her hand, and set it aside. "What did Boggs say about the old man?"

"Nothing much." She blew out a long breath. Her head was spinning, a lovely feeling, but Gabe's eyes were so intense they burned through the fog. "Just that he thought he'd seen him around the shedrow."

He had her arms now. "When?"

"Sometime that morning. But he wasn't sure. He said he only got a glimpse and his eyes aren't good anymore." She shook her head, trying fruitlessly to clear it. "What difference does it make?"

"None," Gabe said, gentling his hold. Or all. All the difference in the world. "I just wondered."

"The past has a way of squeezing the throat." She lifted a hand to his face. "We shouldn't let it. We have now."

"Yes, we do." It could wait, Gabe told himself. Odds were it was nothing, but whatever it was, he would deal with it when they returned home. "Let's see." He cupped her chin, studied her flushed face and blinking eyes. "Darling, you're going to have one hell of a headache come morning."

"Well, then." She hooked her arms around his neck. In one lithe leap she encircled his waist, legs locked. "Then we'd better make it worth it, right?"

"It's the least I can do. Let's go into the shower." He lowered his head and nipped at her bare shoulder. "I'll show you what I have in mind."

19

She thought about telling Gabe. Certainly it wasn't a matter of dependence to tell a man you were so intimately involved with about your intentions. It wouldn't have been weak to ask him to come with her, to lend a little moral support when she faced her past.

But she hadn't told him. Because, intellect aside, it felt dependent. It felt weak. And it was, when you scraped away all of the excess, her problem.

In any case, he hardly had a minute he could call his own. It wasn't every year there was a viable contender for the Triple Crown who had two jewels already in place. His hands were full with the press, his mind full of tensions and possibilities, and his days full overseeing the interim three weeks of training before the Belmont Stakes.

She didn't want to distract him from the goal. A goal, she'd begun to realize, that meant a great deal more to him than money and prestige. To Gabe, the Triple Crown would be proof that he had taken something and not only made it his own, but made it extraordinary.

Underlying that, she didn't want him to toss her own advice back in her face. It wasn't wise to let the past strangle you.

But she couldn't break free of it, not completely. The longer she knew Naomi, the more she grew to care for her, the less Kelsey could believe that her mother had coldly killed a man. Or hotly, for that matter.

There was no disputing the fact that Naomi had pulled the trigger. That she had ended a life. Not only did Naomi admit it, not only had a jury convicted her, but there had been a witness.

Kelsey decided she couldn't lay the past to rest until she'd spoken with Charles Rooney.

She enjoyed the drive. It was difficult not to appreciate, no matter how crowded the highway, the green banks and bursting blooms of full spring. She had the top down and Chopin soaring. The better, she'd decided, to keep her mind off what she was about to do.

She hadn't lied, precisely, in giving Rooney's secretary the name "Kelsey Monroe" when she'd made the appointment. It was merely a precaution, a way to be certain Rooney didn't immediately connect her with Naomi.

A bending of those stiff codes of right and wrong, she thought. She'd always been amused by and disdainful of people who considered white lies acceptable. Or convenient. And here she was, using that same slippery rope to climb to her own ends.

Evaluate later, she told herself.

Nor had she been completely truthful when she'd made excuses to take the afternoon off. Errands and appointments had simply been evasions. She knew Naomi assumed she was going to meet the family. And she'd let Naomi think just that.

Whatever the outcome of the afternoon, Kelsey doubted she'd pass it along to her mother. For the first time since they'd lost Pride, Naomi seemed relaxed again. No one expected High Water to repeat his Preakness performance in the grueling mile and a half at Belmont.

The point had been made, the victory won. Now they could reap the rewards. And she could steal a few hours and dig into the muck of the past.

She'd already mapped out her route in and through the city. Though she wasn't very familiar with Alexandria, she found the building easily enough, and slipped into an empty spot in the underground garage.

Nerves pressed on her, irritating her with damp hands and a skittish stomach. She took her time, deliberately setting the brake, locking the car, tucking her keys into the zippered compartment of her purse.

What could be worse? she asked herself. What could be worse than knowing your mother killed a man? Whatever Charles Rooney told her couldn't be much of a shock. It was only that she, somehow, wanted it to come together tidily in her mind. Then, once and for all, she would be able to accept the woman Naomi had become and stop dwelling on the woman she had been.

The elevator took her to the fifth floor, up from the echoing concrete of the garage to the hushed, carpeted hallways. Glass doors and windows etched with names flanked both sides. Inside them, people worked, with all appearance of industry, at word processors and telephones.

It made her shudder. How would it feel to be on display all through working hours to anyone who happened to wander down the hall? How would it feel to be trapped behind that glass with spring rioting outside?

Struck by her own thoughts, she shook her head. It hadn't been so very long ago that she'd been inside, and just as much on display as the exhibits she'd taken her little tour groups to see in the museum.

How completely a few short months had changed her outlook, and her desires.

Rooney Investigation Services took up the south corner of the building. It was not, as she had assumed, a small operation, nor did it convey that vaguely seamy atmosphere so often created in television and movie portrayals of detective agencies.

No rye in the file cabinets here, she decided, as she entered the glass doors into soft background music and the scent of gardenias.

The romantic fragrance wafted from the waxy blooms tumbling out of jardinieres on either side of a pastel sectional sofa. There were prints of Monet's floating water lilies on the walls and a reproduction Queen Anne coffee table fanned with glossy copies of *Southern Homes.*

The woman seated at the circular ebony workstation in the center of the room was as polished as the furnishings. She glanced up from her monitor and aimed a professional but surprisingly warm smile at Kelsey.

"May I help you?"

"I have an appointment with Mr. Rooney."

"Ms. Monroe? Yes, you're a few minutes early. If you'd just take a seat, I'll see if Mr. Rooney is ready to see you."

Kelsey sat next to the gardenias, picked up a magazine, and for the next ten minutes pretended to be absorbed in the fussy decor of an antebellum mansion outside of Raleigh. All the while her nerves and her conscience pricked at her.

She shouldn't have come. She certainly shouldn't have given a name she no longer used or wanted. She had no business poking fingers in Naomi's affairs. She should get up and tell the stunning and efficient receptionist that she'd made a mistake.

Surely she wouldn't be the first person to make a panicked dash from a detective's office. And even if she were, what did it matter?

She should be back at the barn, working with Honor, not sitting here smelling gardenias and staring at a picture of someone's overly decorated living room.

But she didn't get up, not until the receptionist called her name again and offered to show her in.

There were several doors on either side of the inner corridor. No glass here, Kelsey noted. Whatever went on inside those rooms was private. Discretion would be an integral part of the business.

And because it was, why did she expect Charles Rooney to tell her anything, even after twenty-three years?

Because she had the right, she told herself, and straightened her shoulders. Because she was Naomi Chadwick's daughter.

"Mr. Rooney, Ms. Monroe to see you." The receptionist opened one half of the double oak doors, scooted Kelsey inside, then retreated.

It was a simple room, furnished more like a den than an office, with glassy-eyed big game fish mounted on the walls, models of ships lining shelves. The man who rose from behind the desk might have been everyone's favorite uncle. Slightly paunchy, slightly bald, round-faced and narrow-shouldered. His tie was slightly askew, as if he'd recently tugged against the restriction.

He had a quiet, friendly voice meant to put the most nervous client at ease.

"I'm sorry I kept you waiting, Ms. Monroe. Would you like some coffee?" He gestured toward a Krups coffeemaker on the table behind him. "I keep a pot in here, to keep the juices flowing."

"No, thank you, nothing. But you go ahead." She made herself sit, using the time he gave her while pouring his own mug to study him and his milieu.

Such an ordinary man, she thought, in an ordinary place. How could he have had such a devastating influence on so many lives?

"Now, Ms. Monroe, you indicated you needed some help with a custody case." He seated himself, idly stirring his spoon around and around in the mug. Already a fresh legal pad was waiting for his notes. "You're divorced?"

"Yes."

"And the child? Who, at this time, has primary custody?"

She drew in a long breath. Now that she was in the door, it was time for the truth. "I am the child, Mr. Rooney." With her hands clutching her bag, she kept her eyes on his. "Monroe was my married name. I don't use it anymore, as I've taken back my maiden name. It's Byden. I'm Kelsey Byden."

She knew the instant it clicked. His hand hesitated, his rhythmic stirring skipped a beat. His pupils widened, so that for a moment his eyes seemed black instead of green.

"I see. You'd expect me to remember that name, and that case. Of course I do. You look remarkably like your mother. I should have recognized you."

"I hadn't thought of that. You'd have seen her quite a lot back then. You had her under surveillance."

He didn't miss the faint distaste in her tone. "It's part of the job."

"This particular job took a sharp turn. My father hired you, Mr. Rooney?"

"Ms. Byden—Kelsey—it's difficult for me not to think of you as Kelsey," he said, measuring her and his own heart rate as he spoke. "Custody suits are never pleasant. You were, fortunately, young enough not to be involved in the more difficult aspects. I was hired, as I'm sure you know, to document your mother's . . . lifestyle in order to strengthen your father's case for full custody."

"And what did you discover about her lifestyle?"

"That isn't something I feel free to discuss."

"A great deal of it's public record, Mr. Rooney. I can't believe you're bound by client confidentiality after all this time." Hoping to influence him, she leaned forward, let some of the emotion she was feeling leak into her voice. "I need to know. I'm not a child who needs to be protected from those difficult aspects any longer. You must understand that I feel I have a right to know exactly what happened."

How, he wondered, had he looked at that face and not seen? Looked into those eyes and not known this was Naomi's child? "I sympathize, but there's very little I can tell you."

"You followed her. You took pictures, notes, you made reports. You knew her, Mr. Rooney. And you knew Alec Bradley."

"Knew them?" He inclined his head. "I never exchanged a word with Naomi Chadwick or Alec Bradley."

She wasn't about to be put off with so shallow a technicality. "You saw them together—at parties, at the track, at the club. You saw them together that night, when he came to the house. You were, technically, trespassing when you took the pictures that convicted her."

He hadn't forgotten it. He hadn't forgotten any of it. "I walked a thin line, agreed. And perhaps I crossed it in my zeal to do my job." He offered a small smile while his memories swarmed through his mind. "With today's technology, I could accomplish the same thing without the question of trespass." He paused, took a moment to lift his mug. "But the line still gets crossed, Kelsey. It's crossed every day."

"You formed an opinion of her. I imagine part of your job would be to remain objective, but it would be impossible not to form an opinion of someone when you're monitoring her life."

He began to stir his coffee again, even though the heaping spoonful of sugar he'd added had long since dissolved. "It was over twenty years ago."

"You remember her, Mr. Rooney. You wouldn't have forgotten her, or anything that happened."

"She was a beautiful woman," he said slowly. "A vibrant woman who got in over her head."

"With Alec Bradley."

Annoyed with himself, Rooney set the spoon aside, staining his blotter. "With him, yes. In the public record you spoke of, Naomi Chadwick was arrested for the murder of Alec Bradley, and convicted."

"And your photo of the shooting helped convict her."

"It did." He remembered, vividly, hoisting himself up into the tree, his camera bumping against his chest, his heart pounding. "You could say I was in the right place at the right time."

"She called it self-defense. She claimed that Alec Bradley threatened her, intended to rape her."

"I'm aware of her defense. The evidence didn't support it."

"But you were there! You must have seen if she was afraid, if he seemed threatening."

He folded his hands on the edge of the desk, like a man about to recite a well-rehearsed prayer. "I saw her let him into the house. They had a drink together. They argued. I can't now as I couldn't then testify to what was said between them. They went upstairs."

"She went up," Kelsey corrected. "He followed her."

"Yes, as far as I could tell. I took a chance and used the tree, thinking they would go to her bedroom."

"Because he'd been in there before?" Kelsey asked.

"No. Not that I had observed. But this was only the third night I had gone onto the property, and the first that I knew the rest of the household was absent."

He kept his hands linked, his eyes calm and level on hers. "Several minutes passed. I nearly climbed down again. But then they came into the bedroom. She entered first. It appeared that they were still arguing."

He remembered the look on Naomi's face, the way it had filled his viewfinder with beauty, with anger, with disdain. And yes, he remembered, with fear.

"Her back was to me for a short time." He cleared his throat. "Then she spun around. When she came back into view she had a gun. I could see them both, framed in the window. He put his hands up, backed away. And she fired."

The chill ran through Kelsey like a blade. "And then?"

"And then, Kelsey, I froze. I'm not proud of it, but I was young. I'd never seen . . . I froze," he repeated. "I watched her go to where he'd fallen and lean over. And I watched her go to the phone. I got out of there and sat in my car until I heard the sirens."

"You didn't call the police?"

"No, not immediately. It was foolish of me. It could have cost me my license. But I did go to them, took in the film, made my statement." He loosened his hands, abruptly aware that his fingers were aching from the pressure. "I did my job."

"And all you saw was a beautiful, vibrant woman who got in over her head and shot a man."

"I wish I could tell you different. Your mother served her time. It's over."

"Not for me." Kelsey rose. "What if I hired you, Mr. Rooney. Right now. Today. I want you to go back twenty-three years, take another look at the case. I want to know all there is to know about Alec Bradley."

Fear sprinted up his spine, stiffening it. "Let it rest, Kelsey. Nothing can be solved, and certainly nothing can be changed, by picking at old wounds. Do you think your mother will thank you for making her relive all of that?"

"Maybe not. But I intend to go back, step by step, until I understand. Will you help me?"

He studied her, but it was another woman he saw, a woman sitting pale and composed in a crowded courtroom. Composed, he remembered, except for the eyes. Those desperate eyes.

"No, I won't. I'm going to ask you to think this through, consider the consequences."

"I have thought it through, Mr. Rooney. And I keep coming back to one conclusion. My mother was telling the truth. I'm going to prove it, with or without your help. Thank you for your time."

He sat where he was long after the door closed behind her, long after he'd willed his hands to stop trembling. When he was steady, he picked up the phone and dialed.

Her next stop was the university. The long wait in her father's cramped office calmed her considerably. It was always a balm to be surrounded by books, the scents and sounds of academia. That was why it always lured her back, she supposed. In this world learning was the primary goal. And every question had an answer.

Philip entered, chalk dust on his fingertips. "Kelsey. What a wonderful way to lift my day. I'd have been here sooner, but my seminar ran over a bit."

"I didn't mind waiting. I was hoping you'd have a few minutes free."

"I have the next hour." Which he'd been planning to use to prepare for his final lecture of the day. But that could wait. "If you can spare the rest of the afternoon, I'll treat you to an early dinner when I'm finished."

"Not tonight, thanks. I still have another stop to make. Dad, I need to talk to you."

"I don't want you to worry about your grandmother. I'll deal with that."

"No, I'm not worried about that. It's not important."

"Of course it is." He took her by the shoulders, his hands moving up and down her arms. "I won't tolerate this kind of a breach, nor her using your heritage against you." Furious all over again, he turned to pace the narrow confines of his office, as he would while contemplating a thesis. "Your grandmother is an admirable woman, Kelsey. And a formidable one. Her blind side is the family, and her tendency to confuse her own set of standards with love."

"You don't have to explain her to me, or excuse her. I know that, in her way, she loves me. It's just that her way hasn't always been easy." Had never been easy, Kelsey corrected. "I also know she isn't used to being crossed. This time, she'll either come to accept what I'm doing with my life, or she won't. I can't let it influence me."

He paused, picked up a smooth glass paperweight from his desk. "I don't want you to be at odds."

"Neither do I."

"If you and I went to see her, together . . ."

"No."

Sighing, he took off his glasses, polishing the lenses out of habit rather than need. "Kelsey, she's no longer young. She's your family."

Oh, she thought, the buttons loved ones push. "I'm sorry I can't compromise on this. I know you've been shoved right into the middle of it, and I'm sorry for that, too. She can't have what she wants, Dad. And if we're honest, I've never been what she wanted."

"Kelsey—"

"I'm Naomi's daughter, and she's always resented it. I can only hope that in time she'll come to accept that I'm just as much your daughter."

Carefully, he folded his glasses and set them on his cluttered desk beside a timeworn copy of *King Lear*. "She loves you, Kelsey. It's the circumstances she's fighting."

"I am the circumstances," she said quietly. "I'm the motive, the reason, the child two people wanted long after they didn't want each other. There's no getting past that."

"It's ridiculous to blame yourself."

"Not blame. That's the wrong word. But do I feel a certain sense of responsibility? Yes, I do," she said when he shook his head. "To you, and to her. That's why I'm here. I need you to tell me what happened."

Suddenly weary, he sat, rubbing his fingers over his forehead. "We've done this, Kelsey."

"You gave me an outline, a sketch. You fell in love with someone. Despite some family disapproval on your side, you married her. You had a child with her. Somewhere along the line things went wrong between you."

She moved over to his side, hating to hurt, needing the truth. "I'm not asking you to explain all of that. But you knew the woman you married, you had feelings for her. If you were willing to fight her for the child, to go to court, to hire lawyers and detectives, there had to be a reason. A strong one. I want to know what it was."

"I wanted you," he said simply. "I wanted you with me. Selfishly perhaps, not altogether reasonably. You were the best part of us. I didn't believe growing up in the atmosphere your mother thrived in was right for you. Was best for you."

Had he been wrong? he asked himself. Had he been wrong? How many times had he asked himself that one question, even after everything that had happened had borne him out?

"Your grandmother and I discussed it at great length," Philip continued. "She was violently opposed to Naomi having primary custody of you. In the end, I agreed with her. It wasn't an easy decision, but it was one I believed in. Part of it was selfishness, yes, I can't deny it."

He looked up at her, at the woman, and remembered the child. "I didn't want to give you up, to become a weekend father who would eventually be replaced by the next man in Naomi's life. And the way she lived during those months after the separation seemed deliberately designed to challenge me. Her attorneys must have advised her to behave discreetly, so she did precisely the opposite. She courted the press, incited gossip. I detested the idea of hiring a detective, but the documentation was needed. I left that matter up to the attorneys."

"You didn't hire Rooney directly?"

"No, I—How do you know his name?"

"I've just come from his office."

"Kelsey." He reached out and gripped her hand. "What is the purpose of this? What do you hope to gain?"

"Answers. One answer in particular." She tightened her fingers on his. "I'll ask you. Do you believe Naomi murdered Alec Bradley?"

"There isn't any doubt—"

"That she killed him," Kelsey said tersely. "But murder. Did she murder him? Was the woman you knew, the woman you loved, capable of murder?"

He hesitated, feeling his daughter's fingers threaded through his. "I don't know," he said at last. "I wish with all my heart that I did."

. . .

Kelsey's final meeting of the day was with her mother's lawyers. She'd gleaned little more there, coming up hard against the unassailable wall of attorney-client privilege. She left the plush offices dissatisfied and determined.

There was always another avenue, she reminded herself. Every problem had a solution. All you needed were the factors, the formula, and the patience to see it through. A pity, she thought, that she'd always done so much better in philosophy and the arts than in math and science.

If she was discouraged, it was because she was tired. Too tired, she had to admit, to face Naomi with made-up tales of how she'd spent her afternoon.

She drove through the gates of Longshot instead.

If Gabe wasn't home, she'd go on to Three Willows and make some excuse—a headache, perhaps—and retreat to her room.

Another white lie, Kelsey? she asked herself grimly. If she kept it up much longer, she'd not only become good at it, she'd accept it as normal behavior.

She started toward the house, but instead of knocking, she simply sat down on the front steps and watched the evening bloom.

There would be sunlight for another hour or two, she mused. She wondered if the whippoorwill that sang outside the window of her room had a mate nearby. The call would come simultaneously with dusk—sweet, liquid longing.

The flowers were thriving here, bursting through their bed of mulch to color and scent the air. Dainty primroses, sassy pansies, a trellis that would soon be covered with the spicy perfume of sweet peas. Lilac bushes were heavy with blooms and fragrance, their petals littering the grass with deep purple.

Such a quiet spot, such a lovely spot, for a man of such energy and passion.

She heard the door open behind her, then his footsteps. In a move that was as natural as the flowers blooming beside the deck, she leaned against him when he sat and draped an arm around her.

"I saw your car."

"Who planted the flowers?"

"I did. It's my land."

"My father gardens. In Georgetown I had a lovely little courtyard in the back. So, naturally, I took a course in horticulture and landscape design. It was quite a showplace when I got done with it, but it never looked quite as lovely, quite as intimate as my father's. There are some things you can't get out of books."

"I plant what appeals to me."

"If I had it to do over, that's just how I'd approach it."

"I've been thinking about a rock garden, out there." He gestured toward the slope of the hill. "Why don't you do it with me?"

She smiled, turning her face into his throat where the skin was warm and welcoming. "I'd head straight for the library. I couldn't stop myself."

"So, we'd argue about logic and whim, then raid the nursery." He tipped a finger under her chin to lift her face to his. "What's troubling you, Kelsey?"

She could tell him, she realized. Of course she could. There was nothing she couldn't tell him. "I started something today, and I know I'm not going to stop.

Everyone's told me I should let it alone, but I can't. I won't." She took a deep breath and eased back until they were no longer touching. "Do you believe my mother murdered Alec Bradley?"

"No."

She blinked, shook her head. "Just no? Without hesitation, without qualification?"

"You asked, I answered." He leaned over to snap off a spray of freesia and handed it to her. "Isn't it more important what you believe?"

She shook her head again, then dropped it into her hands. "You can say no, simply no, when you didn't even know her."

"Not really."

"Not really?" She lifted her head again. "What does that mean?"

"I knew of her. I'd seen her around." He angled his head and toyed with the ends of her hair. "I've been a track rat a long time, Kelsey. I remember seeing her at Charles Town, Laurel, here and there."

"You'd have been a child."

"Not the way you mean. But it's true, I didn't know her, didn't form a solid impression. But I know her now."

"And?"

She needed specifics, he thought. She always would. He wasn't certain he could give them to her. "And I've made my living reading people. Faces, intonations, gestures. Gamblers, psychics, cops, shrinks. We all have that skill in common or we don't last long. Naomi pulled the trigger, but she didn't commit murder."

With her eyes closed, she leaned against his body again. The flower he'd given her wafted out a delicate scent. "I believe that, Gabe. Part of me is afraid I do simply because I don't want to accept that my mother could have done what she was convicted of. But that doesn't dilute the belief. I went to see the detective today. The one who testified against her."

His voice remained light. She wondered how she could have so often missed the steel beneath it. "It didn't occur to you to ask me to go with you?"

"It did. I wanted to do it alone." She shrugged. "It didn't accomplish much. He wouldn't tell me anything I didn't already know. And he wouldn't, when I tried to hire him, help me find out more about Alec Bradley."

"What do you want to know?"

"Anything. Everything. My mother's only part of this." She moved away. "What kind of a man was he? Where did he come from? What did he want? Naomi says he became abusive, tried to rape her. What triggered it?"

"Have you asked her?"

"I don't want to do that unless I have to. She'll close up, Gabe. She'd tell me what she knew, but it could bring whatever progress we've made to a dead stop. I don't want to risk that."

"She wasn't the only one who knew him."

Kelsey had already considered that, and rejected it. "I can't start asking questions around the track, pumping the other owners or crews. Whatever I'd learn wouldn't be worth the talk it would generate."

"What's your option?"

"I have the name of the officer who investigated my mother's case. He's retired now, lives in Reston."

"You've been doing your homework."

"I've always been a good student. I'm going to go see him."

Gabe took her hand and pulled her to her feet. "*We're* going to go see him."

She smiled. "Okay."

20

"Been a while, Roscoe." Tipton slapped hands with Rossi. "How come you don't have my old job yet?"

"I'm working on it, Captain."

"Well, take a seat, and we'll work on these brews." Tipton eased himself into the porch rocker. He had a small Igloo cooler beside it, chilling a six-pack of Bud. "How's the wife?"

Rossi accepted the can Tipton offered, and popped it. "Which one?"

"Oh yeah, forgot. You're a two-time loser." With a chuckle, Tipton smacked his can against Rossi's and guzzled down. "Divorce is almost part of the job, isn't it? I got lucky."

"How's Mrs. Tipton?"

"Sassy as ever." Very simple, very basic affection colored his grainy voice. "Two weeks after I retire, she gets a job." Amused, Tipton shook his head. "Tells me it's busywork, now that the kids are grown. Hell, we both know it's to keep her from killing me with a blunt instrument. So I got me my hobby shop in the back, and she's selling shoes down at the mall." He smiled, drank again. "I got lucky, Roscoe. Not every woman can live with a cop, active or retired."

"Tell me about it." Two wives and two divorces in twelve years had taught Rossi that particular lesson too well. "You're looking good, Captain."

It was true. Tipton had put on a little weight in his three years off the force, but it agreed with him. The few pounds had filled out some of the lines the job had dug into his face. He looked relaxed and at peace in a work shirt and jeans. An Orioles cap covered what was left of wiry hair that was a mix of ginger and gray.

"A lot of people don't take to retirement," Tipton commented. "Makes them old. Me, I'm loving it. I got my workshop—built this chair, you know."

"Really?" Rossi tucked his tongue in his cheek as he examined the rickety rocker. The fact that Tipton had painted it a dazzling blue didn't disguise the way it listed to the left. "It must be rewarding."

"Oh, it is. I've got three grandchildren now, too. And time to enjoy them. The wife and I are talking about taking a cruise this fall. Up the St. Lawrence. Foliage."

"Sounds like you've got it all, Captain."

"Damn right." And if he had much more, Tipton was sure he'd run screaming into the night. "A long, peaceful retirement's a man's reward for a job well done."

"No one can argue about the job well done." Rossi sipped at the beer. He preferred imported but knew better than to say so. "I don't guess you pay much attention to what's going down now. But you might have read about a case I'm working on."

"Oh, I glance at the headlines now and again." Pored over them, greedy for any glimpse of murder and mayhem.

"The groom who was murdered at Charles Town, back in March."

"Stabbed. Trampled on top of it. You closed that," Tipton remembered. "Another groom, wasn't it? Lipsky. Suicide."

"That one's open." Rossi leaned back and watched a trio of starlings fluttering around an obviously homemade bird feeder on the front lawn. An orange striped cat sat below, eyeing them patiently. On the porch, he thought, they were just two men, passing the time with shoptalk. "No note, no predisposition to suicide. And the method doesn't fit. Here's how it shakes down."

He explained, as precisely as a written report, the events, from Lipsky's firing to his death. "We've got a picture here of a man with a quick fuse, a violent one, who knows his way around horses. Not a man who makes friends or rises in his chosen profession. One who's had a few scrapes with the law. Battery. Assault. D and D."

"A picture of a man who'd run, not who'd pour himself a cocktail of gin and horse poison." Tipton chewed on that awhile. "But he could probably get his hands on it."

"He could, someone else could. He was after Slater's horse. Now, could be that was personal. He was pissed about being fired, so he goes for the payback. The old man catches him at it, he panics. Now he's got a dead man on his hands. Why didn't he run, Captain? Why does he hunker down in a motel not an hour from Charles Town?"

"Because he's waiting for somebody. Somebody to tell him what to do next."

"And somebody poured him one hell of a drink. There were no prints on the gin bottle. It was wiped clean."

That particular angle had Tipton smiling. Small mistakes, he thought. He had always been fond of small mistakes. He watched his old cat waiting for one of the starlings to make one, and understood precisely.

"And you've got an open case of homicide. Have you taken a good look at this Slater?"

"Oh, I've looked at him. An interesting man. Lots of currents. Did some time."

"For?"

"Illegal gambling. If it had been a couple of months earlier, he'd have ended up in juvie instead of a cell." Absently Rossi tapped his fingers on the arm of his chair. "He's been clean since, so far as the record shows. Grew up mostly on the streets. Mother died when he was a kid. The father slid his way out of trouble. Had some arrests—fraud, forgery, passing bad checks. Mostly con games. Pounded on a working girl in Taos a few years ago. But nothing sticks. Slater slipped out of the system at about fourteen, tripped up and served his time, then kept his nose clean. I can't say he wouldn't have done Lipsky, but he'd have been more direct about it."

"Who else have you got?"

"Nobody who clicks. Did you catch the Derby on TV, Captain?"

"Roscoe, there's only one sport. That's baseball." He tipped his cap. "I did hear something about a horse breaking its leg."

"The horse was drugged, Captain. Overdosed. And it was Slater's ride that won the race."

"Well." Tipton mused over the last swallow of beer. "Where are you circling to, Roscoe?"

"I'm not sure about that, but it's a big circle. It goes back twenty-three years. Naomi Chadwick, Captain. What can you tell me about her?"

"Funny." Tipton set the empty can under his shoe, then crushed it flat. "That's the second time I've heard that name today. The daughter called me this morning." He glanced at his watch. "She should be here soon."

"Kelsey Byden's coming here?"

"She wants to talk to me about her mother." Tipton leaned back in the rocker, enjoying the way it creaked. "That does take me back."

"You should have stayed on the farm," Kelsey muttered. "There's barely a week until Belmont."

"Jamie can handle things without me." Gabe smiled as he negotiated a turn. "In fact, he prefers it."

"I don't feel right about taking you away from work now. I could have done this alone."

"Kelsey." With patience, Gabe picked up her hand, kissed it. "Shut up."

"I can't. I'm too nervous. This is the man who arrested my mother, who questioned her, who put her in jail. Now I'm going to ask him to help me prove he made a mistake. And I lied to Naomi. Again. I told her we were going for a drive."

"We are driving."

"That's not the point," she snapped. "I'm deceiving her, and Moses. Everyone. And for what? So I can satisfy this idiotic need to assure myself I don't spring from a line of murderers?"

"Is that what this is about?"

"No." She rubbed a hand over her eyes. "I don't know. Some of it. Heredity's a scary thing." As soon as she'd said it, she winced. "I don't mean to imply that heredity's the only factor in the makeup of character. Environment . . ." She trailed off, defeated.

"I lose on both counts," he murmured. "I wondered when you'd add it up."

"That's not what I'm doing. That's not what I've done." She hissed out a breath and cursed herself. "I don't know what I'm doing. It has nothing to do with you, or the way I feel about you."

"Let's backtrack a minute." It had been a gamble, a foolish one, to hope this moment would never come. If he was going to lose, he intended to lose big. "You have doubts about yourself because of your family history. Don't," he said when she started to interrupt. "Let's lay the cards down. You have doubts about me because of mine."

He was driving fast now, laying on the curves on the back roads, letting speed eat up some of the tension.

"That's not true, Gabe. I couldn't have slept with you if I'd had doubts."

"Yes, you could. It's easy to ignore logic and doubts in the heat of the moment. And we're good in bed. We're better than good in bed. But sooner or later, logic clicks in again. I've got bad blood, Kelsey, and there's no draining it out."

His eyes stayed on the road, though he was very aware that hers were on his face, studying, considering.

"Where you come from always stays with you. You can clean it up, dress it up, but it's always underneath. I've seen things and done things that would shake that moral code of yours right down to the foundation. I don't cheat and I don't lean on the bottle, but that's about all I can say I haven't done. The simple facts are I wanted what Cunningham had, and I found a way to get it. I wanted you in bed, and I would have done whatever it took to get you there."

"I see." Now she stared straight ahead. The speed didn't frighten her, but he did. "Is it just sex?"

He didn't answer for a moment. They both watched the road twist ahead. "No. I wish to Christ it was."

She closed her eyes on a quiet, shuddering sigh. "Pull over," she murmured. When he ignored her, she straightened in her seat. "Pull over, Slater," she said firmly, "and stop the damn car."

The tires screeched when he slapped a foot on the brakes and jerked the wheel to the shoulder where gravel spat. "If you think I'm letting you get out here, you're a goddamned idiot. I'll take you into Reston, or I'll take you back home."

"I've no intention of getting out here."

"Fine, that's fine. You'd better understand I have no intention of letting you go, not here. Not anywhere. I gave you your chance to run."

She'd never seen him so completely unnerved. "No, you didn't."

He snatched her lapels and jerked her around in her seat. "It's all the chance you're getting. Fuck your right and wrong, Kelsey, and your country club upbringing and anything else that's in my way. You're not walking out on me without a fight."

Her own temper began to rumble. "Fine. Since you're going to take that insulting, Neanderthal attitude, it hardly seems appropriate for me to tell you I'm in love with you."

His hands went limp. For an instant every muscle in his body went numb. Her eyes were on his, sulky, signaling fight in progress. But he was already down for the count.

"You don't know what you are."

She hit him. Both gasped in surprise when her fist jabbed just under his heart.

"I'm not tolerating that." She smacked his hands aside. "I'm not tolerating that attitude. I'm sick to death of people I care about assuming I don't know my own mind or heart. I know it very well. And though at this particular moment it galls me, I'm in love with you. Now start this damn car and let's get this over with."

He couldn't have driven a tricycle. "Give me a minute."

She huffed out a breath, crossed her legs, and folded her arms. "Fine. Take your time. It'll give me the opportunity to plan several ways to make you suffer."

"Come here."

She jabbed out, and connected with her elbow when he reached for her. "Hands off."

"Okay. I just imagined I'd be touching you when I told you I love you."

Not particularly mollified, but thoughtful, she turned her head a fraction. "Have you been imagining it for long?"

"A while. I thought it would pass. Like a virus." He held up both hands when she jerked around. "Are you going to hit me again?"

"I might." Damned if she was going to laugh, no matter how much his eyes tempted her. "A virus?"

"Yeah. Only there's this thing about viruses I'd forgotten. They don't go away. They just sneak into some corner of your system and kick back in when your defenses are down." He took her hand, fisted it in his, and brought it to his lips. "I've been trying to get used to this one."

"And how are you doing?"

"Better now." He lowered his brow to hers. "Christ, what timing. We should be home, alone."

"It doesn't matter." She tilted her head so that her lips brushed his. "We'll make up for it when we are." When he deepened the kiss, she sank into it. "How can everything be such a mess, and this be so right?"

"Luck of the draw." He eased back, and looked into her eyes. "We'll make sure it stays right."

"This is enough for now." Gently, she lifted a hand to his cheek. "This is better than enough."

The first thing Tipton noticed when the couple climbed out of the fancy foreign car in his driveway was that they were lovers. The man did no more than lay a hand on the woman's shoulder. She did no more than glance up, smile. But Tipton pegged it.

The second thing he noticed was that the woman was almost a dead ringer for Naomi. Or the Naomi he had put behind bars.

Oh, there were subtle differences, and his trained eye nailed them as well. The daughter's mouth was softer, a tad more generous. The cheekbones were slightly less prominent, the walk more fluid. Naomi's gait had been an energetic, even a nervous scissoring of legs. One that had drawn the eye of every male within a mile of her.

But all in all, he was glad Kelsey Byden had called first. It would have been a shock to have glanced up and seen her strolling up his walk like the ghost of the woman he'd never forgotten.

"Captain Tipton." Her smile was fleeting as her gaze shifted. "Lieutenant Rossi. I wasn't expecting to see you here."

"Small world, isn't it?" Irritating her only amused him, and he helped himself to another beer. He wasn't on duty, after all. "Why don't I make the introductions. Kelsey Byden and Gabriel Slater, my former commanding officer, Captain James Tipton."

"Roscoe here was always one for procedure." Tipton grinned as Kelsey lifted a brow at the nickname. "Sit down, have a beer?"

"Mr. Slater doesn't drink," Rossi put in.

"Oh, well. I think the wife brewed up some iced tea. Why don't you go on in, Roscoe, and pour our company a couple of glasses?"

"That would be nice." Pleased to put Rossi in the position of serving, Kelsey made herself comfortable on the top step. "I appreciate your taking the time to see us, Captain."

"No problem. I got nothing but time. How's your mother getting on?"

"Very well. You remember her, then?"

"I'm not likely to forget." But he shifted tactics, preferring to get a lay of the land. "Roscoe tells me congratulations are in order, Mr. Slater. You've got a horse that might cop the Triple Crown. Not that I know a lot about it. Baseball's my game."

Gabe knew something about tactics as well. "My money's on the Birds this year. They've got a solid pitching rotation, and an infield so tight you can barely squeeze a mosquito through it."

"They do." Delighted, Tipton slapped his knee. "By sweet Jesus, they do. You see them tromp the Jays last night? Goddamned Canadians."

Gabe grinned, slipped out a cigar. "I caught the last couple of innings." He offered one to Tipton, lit it for him. "That last triple took fifty out of my assistant trainer's pocket and put it into mine."

Tipton puffed. "I'm not a betting man myself."

Gabe flicked on his lighter at the tip of his own cigar, watched Tipton over the flame. "I am." He blew out smoke, nodded when Rossi came back with two tall glasses. "Thanks."

"Roscoe's a football fan. I never could educate him into the thinking-man's sport."

"I'm beginning to develop an interest in the sport of kings." Rossi took his seat again. "I'll have my eye on the Belmont, Mr. Slater."

"A lot of us will."

"Now, the lady didn't come out here to talk sports." Tipton offered Kelsey a friendly smile. "You're here about murder."

"What can you tell me about Alec Bradley, Captain?"

He pursed his lips. She'd surprised him. He'd been sure she would focus on her mother. Intrigued, he shifted gears and turned back the clock. "Alec Bradley, thirty-two, formerly of Palm Beach. He'd been married once to a woman, oh, fifteen years his senior. She paid him off with a nice settlement in the divorce. Apparently he'd worked his way through most of it by the time he met your mother."

"What did he do?"

"Charmed the ladies." Tipton shrugged. "Sponged off acquaintances. Played the horses when he could. He owned his own tuxedo." Tipton paused for a sip of beer. "He was killed in it."

"You didn't like him," Kelsey commented.

To amuse himself, and to help align his thoughts with his words, Tipton blew three smoke rings. "He was dead when I met him, but no. From what the investigation turned up on him, he wasn't the kind of man I'd ask home for dinner. He made dallying with married women—*rich* married women—a profession. They'd pay him off with money and presents, introductions to other restless married women. If they didn't pay him enough, he'd use blackmail. In my day we called them gigolos. I don't know what you call them now."

"Slime," Gabe said pleasantly, and earned an approving nod from the captain.

Slater had taste, he decided. In women and cigars. "That says it well enough. The man had a way about him. Fancy manners, fancy education, a family line that went back to some puffed-up English earl. And he had that way with women, married women who couldn't afford scandal."

"My mother was separated, Captain."

"And in the middle of a custody suit. She couldn't afford the carryings-on with Bradley to come out if she wanted to win it."

"But she saw him publicly."

"Socially," Tipton agreed. "It didn't seem to bother her that people assumed they were lovers. No one could prove it." He tapped cigar ashes into the crushed can of Bud. "There were rumors about Bradley sniffing expensive white powder up his nose. No one proved that either. Until he was dead."

"Drugs." Kelsey paled but continued. "My mother said nothing about drugs. I didn't read anything about them in the newspaper reports."

"No drugs at Three Willows." Tipton sighed. Her eyes, so much like her mother's, were taking him back. "The place was clean. Your mother was clean. Bradley had a mixture of alcohol and cocaine in his system when he died."

"If that's true, he could have been irrational, violent, just as my mother said."

"There weren't any signs of struggle. The lace of your mother's nightgown was torn." He touched a hand to his chest. "She had a couple of bruises. Nothing she couldn't have done herself."

"If she did that herself, why didn't she knock over a few tables, break some lamps?"

Smart girl, he thought. "I asked myself, and her, that same question."

"And what did she say?"

"The first time, we were sitting downstairs. They were still taking pictures in the bedroom. She'd put on a big robe over her nightgown." As if she'd been cold, Tipton remembered. As if she'd been shivering under that heavy quilted material. "When I asked her, she snapped right back, 'Maybe I didn't think of it.' "

He smiled, shook his head. "Pissed at me is what she was. Those were the kind of answers she gave until her lawyers shut her up. The second time I asked her was in the interrogation room. She was smoking, one cigarette after the other. Practically eating them whole. When I asked her again, she said she wished she had thought of it. She wished she had because then someone might believe her."

He set his beer aside and sighed deeply. "And you know, Ms. Byden, the thing was—just like I told Roscoe here before you drove up—I did believe her."

Kelsey unfolded legs she could no longer feel, and forced herself to stand. "You believed her? You believed she was telling the truth, but you sent her to prison."

"I believed her," Tipton repeated, and his eyes narrowed, focused. Cop's eyes. "But the evidence was against her. I spent a lot of sleepless nights looking for something to weigh on the other side. All I had was my gut. I did my job, Ms. Byden. I arrested her. I booked her. I presented the evidence at her trial. That's what I had to do."

"Is that how you live with it?" Kelsey held her fists at her sides. "You knew she was telling the truth."

"I believed," Tipton corrected. "That's a long way from knowing."

"Well, Roscoe, that took me back a few." Tipton watched the Jaguar back out of the drive, then set his chair to creaking again. "How many times do you see real gray eyes? No green in them, no blue, just smoke. You don't forget eyes like that."

"Naomi Chadwick got to you, Captain. That doesn't mean she was telling the truth."

"Oh, she got to me. I was a happily married man, Roscoe, never once caught any action on the side. But I thought about Naomi Chadwick. Did I believe her because she played some elemental tune on my libido?" He sighed, shrugged, and crushed his second can of beer. "I don't know. I was never sure. The D.A. was pushing for an arrest. He wanted that trial. And the evidence was there, so I did my job."

Rossi studied his second Bud. "What did you think of Charles Rooney?"

"The P.I.? He was a hotdogger. There were plenty of fancy names on his client list back then. Mostly divorce cases. I leaned on him, and he stuck to his story. He had the film, he had his reports, and the Bydens' lawyers backed him up."

"He witnessed a murder and didn't report it."

"We pressed that button. Claimed he was shaken up. A guy thinks he's going to snap pictures of a bout of hot sex, gets murder instead. Allegedly he was still sitting in his car when the black-and-whites arrived. He logged the time down to the minute."

"Then waited three days to bring in the film."

Tipton wiggled his wiry eyebrows. "How deep are you digging here, Roscoe?"

"As deep as it takes." He set the half-full beer on the porch between his feet and leaned forward, hands on knees. "Twenty-three years ago, you've got a dead horse in a race, drugs, a suicide, and a murder. Now we've got a murder, a suspicious death with the earmarks of suicide, a dead horse in a race, and drugs. Does the pendulum swing like that, Captain? Or does it get a shove?"

"You're a good cop, Roscoe." Like a veteran firehorse, Tipton quivered at the sound of the bell. "How many of the players are around on this swing?"

"That's what we need to find out. Maybe you could take some time out from your workshop and give me a hand with the research."

Tipton's smile was slow, and settled comfortably on his round face. "I could probably work it into my schedule."

"That's what I'd hoped you'd say. The jockey who hanged himself? Benedict Morales. Benny. Maybe you could flesh him out for me."

Kelsey straightened in her seat when Gabe drove through the gates at Longshot. "Gabe, I should just go home. I'm not good company."

"No, you're not." He braked, turned off the ignition. "And I figure you might as well have your explosion here rather than at Three Willows where you'd have to explain it to Naomi."

"I'm just so angry." She bounded out of the car and slammed the door. "He believed her, but he sent her to prison."

"Cops don't send you to prison, darling, juries do. Believe me, I've been there."

"The point is she spent ten years behind bars. Isn't that the point?"

"The point," he said, taking her arm and steering her into the house, "is that that part's done. You can't change it. How much are you willing to risk to turn back the clock and prove it was a mistake?"

Stunned, she stared at him. "Risk? What's the matter with you? The risk doesn't count—it doesn't matter! What happened to her was wrong. It has to be put right."

"Black and white?"

There was a twist in her gut, one quick churn. "And if it is?"

"Then it is," he said simply. "But don't overlook the gray areas, Kelsey. Not everything you find out if you go on with this is going to fit neatly into one column or the other."

She stepped back from him, and the distance was much wider than the simple movement. "You want me to stop."

"I want you to be prepared."

"For?"

Deliberately he closed the distance, cupping her stiff shoulders in his hands. "Not everyone you care about is perfect. And not everyone who matters to you is going to thank you for sweeping away two decades' worth of dust."

She shrugged irritably in a fruitless attempt to dislodge his hands. "I'm aware that Naomi wasn't—isn't—a saint. I don't expect perfection, Slater, or look for it. But I want the truth."

"Fine. As long as you can handle it when you get it. No use trying to shake me off," he said, and smiled when she shoved at his hands. "The first truth you're going to have to swallow is that you're stuck with the cards you've been dealt. You and I are going to play out this hand."

"I'm not trying to shake you off. I just need to think about what to do next."

"I can help you with that." He urged her closer, those clever hands slipping down her back, cruising up again. "You're going to relax, take a swim."

"I don't have a suit with me."

"Darling, I'm counting on that." He was kissing her now in a way that always turned her mind to fluff. "After, I'm going to talk you into trying out some of those culinary skills you once bragged about."

Relaxing seemed like an excellent idea. With a little murmur of pleasure, she turned her head to ease his access to her neck. "You want me to cook for you?"

"I do. Then I want to take you upstairs and seduce you."

"What are you doing now?"

"This is just a preview. Tomorrow, when you're relaxed and your mind's clear, we'll start thinking again."

"It sounds sensible."

He nipped his way back up to her mouth. It wasn't particularly fair, he knew, to keep certain ideas to himself. But he wanted to clear the tension out of her face. And to celebrate the fact that they'd found each other. For one night, he wanted them both to concentrate on only that.

"Let's be sensible." He stepped back, sliding his hands down her arms until they were linked with hers. "I love you."

Her heart took one long, slow turn in her breast. "How can I argue with that?"

21

In the rosy light of dawn, Moses watched the mares lead their babies to water. He knew the pecking order as well as they. Big Bess, with an arrogant swish of her tail, was first, always. Then Carmen, the hardheaded red, followed by Trueheart, and so on down the line until shy, self-effacing Sunny.

The foals scampered with them, frisky and secure. Unaware, Moses thought, that in a few short weeks they would be weaned and separated from Mama in the next step toward their destinies.

Some would be trained for the track; some would be sold at yearling auctions. One might show a different promise and be culled out as a jumper, or for the show ring. Moses wasn't much on show horses himself. It seemed as shallow to his mind as beauty pageants. Some would be gelded, others bred.

And one, maybe one, would show the mark of a true champion. There was always another Derby, he told himself. Always another chance for that win.

Maybe that one, the little chestnut with the blaze. The one with the cocky tilt to his head. Naomi had named him Tomorrow's Arrogance because of it. He had the lines, the breeding, and time would tell if he had the heart.

In his own breast, Moses's heart was heavy. He'd put too much on the line at the Derby. He knew better. Both sides of his heritage warned against testing the gods. Yet he had tested them, putting all of his hopes, all of his heart, into one two-minute race.

And the cost had been staggering.

"They're beautiful, aren't they?" Kelsey murmured from behind him. "It's hard to believe that in another year they'll be ready for the saddle."

Moses tucked his hands into his front pockets and kept his eyes on the foals. "So, you decided to show up."

"I'm sorry. I'm a little late."

"A little late today. Half a day yesterday, and the day before that."

"There were some things I had to take care of."

"Things." He turned to her, knowing he was about to take out some of his frustration on her. Certain she deserved it. "Only one thing comes first for anybody who works here, and that's the horses."

He strode off toward the barn with Kelsey trotting guiltily after him. "I'm sorry, Moses, really. It was unavoidable—"

Her heels dug in when he stopped abruptly in front of her and swung about. "Listen, little girl, this isn't one of your playgrounds. You don't get to call time here and tie your shoe. What you do is you pull your weight, all day, every day. Because if you don't, someone else has to pick up the slack. That's not the way I run things. Just what were you doing yesterday when you should have been with your horse, when you should have been taking your orders from the yearling manager?"

"I was . . ." Kelsey all but sawed at her tongue. "It was personal business."

"From now on you get your hair fluffed and your nails painted on your own time. I'm not wasting mine. You've got stalls to muck."

"But I—I need to work with Honor."

"She's already on the longe. You can cool her off when she's done. Now get a shovel."

He strode away, disappearing inside his office. Grooms and stable hands who'd stopped to listen immediately got back to work. Everyone enjoyed a public flogging, but no one liked to get caught watching one.

"Well, you've been accepted." Naomi stepped up to Kelsey and ran a comforting hand up and down her spine. "He wouldn't have spoken to you that way unless he considered you part of the team."

"He might have slapped me down privately," Kelsey muttered. "And goddammit, I wasn't getting my hair done. Look at these." Incensed, she fanned out her fingers, the nails short, clipped, unpolished. "Does it look like I've had a manicure recently? I'm not here to play. Just because I needed a few hours off—" She stopped, swore again. "It was important to me."

"Sometimes we can forget there's anything else going on in the world that doesn't happen right here. You're under no obligation to throw yourself into this. The fact is, most owners aren't nearly so involved with the day-to-day work. If you'd rather—"

"You don't think I can handle it." Color bloomed and rode high on Kelsey's cheeks. "You don't think I can see it through."

"I'm not saying that, Kelsey."

"Aren't you? Why should this be any different? I've always moved from job to job, interest to interest. Why should anyone believe that I can stick, that this means any more than writing ad copy, or explaining Impressionist art to tour groups? If I can give up on everything else, why shouldn't I give up on this?" She tossed back her hair. "Because it is different. Because everything's different."

Turning on her heel, she stalked to the barn.

Naomi only sighed. It was, she realized, a surefire way to forget your own troubles when two people you loved dumped their own at your feet. Gauging temperaments, she decided that Kelsey could use some time wielding a pitchfork to cool off. So she started with Moses.

He was at his desk, barking on the phone to Reno's agent. "No, I'm not putting him up at Belmont. He's not ready, and Corelli rode High Water to place in the Preakness. He knows the colt and he deserves the ride. Yeah, that's final."

He slammed the phone down, cutting off the voice yammering through the receiver.

"I'm not putting up a spooked jockey with a bum shoulder."

"I agree with you." Ready to placate, she sat on the corner of his desk. "And so does Reno. He knows he's not ready." In a gesture she hoped would serve as truce, she covered his hand with hers. "Weren't you a little rough on Kelsey out there?"

His face closed, and Moses drew his hand away. "Are you here as the owner, or as her mother?"

"I'm here, Moses," she said, and left it at that. "I know she's taken some time off recently. Just as I know that something's troubling her. Just," she continued quietly, "as I know something's troubling you."

"Let's stick with one issue, Naomi." He pushed back from the desk. "She's been slacking off. So maybe the bloom's faded."

Puzzled, she studied his face. Not just annoyed, she realized, but worried. "And maybe she just had some loose ends to tie up. We can't forget the fact that she's had to make a lot of adjustments in a very short time. I thought you were happy, even impressed with her work up until now."

"Up until now," he agreed. "I've been anything but happy and impressed the last few days. She needed a shot, and I gave her one. Maybe you've forgotten that's one of the things I do around here. If you want her treated differently—"

"I didn't say that." Annoyance snapped into her voice. "But I know you, Moses. You don't slap someone down like that in public for a couple of infractions So, who's decided to treat her differently?"

He turned so that they faced each other with the desk between them. "As far as I see it, that's a girl who's gotten pretty much everything she wants her whole life. She's spoiled, she's reckless, and she's used to coming and going as she pleases."

"Just like I was."

He acknowledged that with a nod. "Some. But you finished what you started, Naomi."

"Maybe this is the first time she's found something worth finishing."

"And maybe she's getting bored and is going to pack her bags. Do you think I don't know what it's going to do to you if she turns away now?"

The chill had Naomi hugging her arms. "You're the one who told me she wasn't going to do that."

"Maybe I was wrong. Maybe I was just so damn happy to see you smile all the way again. Everything seemed to be moving in the right direction. And then . . ." Disgusted, he dropped back down into the chair, scrubbed his hands over his face. "Goddammit. She got in my way at the wrong time."

"What is it, Moses?" She reached for him again. This time he gripped her hand.

"The gods laugh, Naomi. Especially when you forget that they can step in at any time and snatch away what you want most. I've had my heart broke before." He looked up at her again, smiled a little. "You did it first. But it's been a while. I'd forgotten how much it hurts."

"Pride," she murmured. "You let me do all the grieving over him."

Miserable, he looked down at the joined hands. "I missed something, Naomi. I had myself so revved up about winning that I had to be careless, even for a minute. It cost too much."

"You can grieve, Moses, but you can't take the blame."

"That was my horse, Naomi." His eyes cut back to hers. "Your name might be on the papers, but he was mine. And I lost him. I wasn't looking in the right place at the right time. I didn't sense what I should have sensed. Even now, I go back over that day. I go back and back and back, and I can't see it. It had to be under my nose." He rapped a fist against the desk. "Under my fucking nose."

There was, she knew, only one way to handle him in a mood like this. "Okay, Whitetree, it was all your fault. You were in charge. I pay you to train my horses, to know them, to understand them, and to guide them from birth to death. I also pay you to oversee the men, to hire and fire, and to decide which team works for which horse for which race. It looks as though I've also been paying you to foretell the future." She cocked her head. "Since that's the case, I don't know whether to fire you or give you a raise."

"I'm serious about this."

"So am I." She rose and skirted the desk to knead his knotted shoulders. "I want to know what happened, Moses. I want to know who did it, and I want them to pay. What I don't want, and can't afford, is to have you, someone I love and depend on, losing heart. We've got less than eleven months to the first Saturday in May."

"Yeah." He blew out a stream of breath. "I guess I should go apologize to that girl of yours."

"Leave it. She can take a lump."

He smiled again. "She wanted to give me a few. Christ, she's got your eyes. I don't have a lot of regrets about things I haven't done, Naomi. In fact, I can count the big ones on one hand. I've never made a pilgrimage to Israel, never walked in the footsteps of my ancestors on either side. And I never made a child with you."

Her hands stopped, and he reached back and gripped them hard. "I'm sorry."

"No." She lowered her head so that her cheek rested on his hair. "Don't be. Why are there so seldom second chances on the big ones, Moses?"

Rich was thinking the same thing. Second chances were as rare as hens' teeth. It was a lucky man who could snare one. Rich Slater was a lucky man.

He put two grand on the trifecta at Laurel and moseyed back to the bar. Mostly, trifectas were a sucker's game, but he was on a roll.

Sticking with the ponies, he thought. The hell with cards, fuck point spreads. The horses were his babies now.

He ordered another bourbon, his new, sentimental drink of choice, then drew out a five-dollar cigar.

The lighter that flared under it caused his brows to rise. Rich puffed the cigar into life, then swiveled to smile affably at his son. "Well now, just like old times. Bring my boy here one of the same," he ordered the bartender.

Gabe merely held up a finger. "Coffee, black."

"Shit." Rich drew the word out to three syllables. "Don't be such a pussy, boy. I'm buying."

"Coffee," Gabe repeated, then studied his father. He knew the signs: flushed cheeks, bright eyes, big toothy smile. Rich Slater was not only half drunk, but he had money in his pocket.

"I thought you had trouble coming out from Chicago."

"Got that all straightened out. Don't you worry about me, Gabe. Everybody knows old Rich Slater's good for his markers."

"Oh?" Gabe lifted a brow. "I thought the trouble had something to do with dealing from the bottom of the deck."

Was that what he'd told the boy? Rich wondered, and searched back through his soggy memory. Well, it didn't matter. "Just a difference of opinion, that's all. All tidied up now. This here's my race." He gestured toward the monitor. "Number three," he muttered. "Yeah, number three."

Gabe glanced up at the screen just as the gate sprang open. "I've heard you've been playing the track again."

"Come on, baby, hug that rail. Where'd you hear that?"

"Here and there. Somebody spotted you at Churchill Downs on Derby day."

Rich continued to watch the race, urging his horse on with little jerks of his body. His mind was working, though, picking carefully through the minefield Gabe was setting for him.

"He's got it. He's got it! Now, come on, wire. Ha! Son of a bitch, I can pick 'em." Pleased that the first horse on his ticket had come in a winner, he signaled for another drink. "I've got the touch, Gabe, I've always had the touch."

"What kind of touch did you have in Kentucky last month?"

"Kentucky." The broad, amiable grin only widened. "I haven't been down in Kentucky for oh, five, six years or more. Shoulda stuck with the horses, though, that's the truth."

"I saw you myself, the morning of the race."

Not by a flicker did Rich show reaction. His eyes stayed on his son's. "I don't think so, buddy boy. I've got me a nice set of rooms outside Baltimore. All the action I need is within an easy drive. Pimlico, Laurel, Charles Town. Now, maybe you're thinking of Pimlico, the Preakness. I was there. Sure was." He winked. "Had some money down on your colt, too. You didn't let me down. Maybe, seeing as I'm rolling hot, I'll take a trip up to Belmont. Think you can cop the whole Crown, do you, Gabe? You do, we'll have ourselves a real celebration."

"There was trouble at the Derby."

"I know about that. Shocked I was, too, sitting in my room watching it on TV. Crying shame to see a horse go down that way." He shook his head sadly over his drink. "Damn shame. But then, it didn't hurt you any, did it?"

"Somebody helped that horse go down."

Lips pursed around his cigar, Rich nodded. "Now, I heard about that, too. Nasty business. Christ knows it happens." He reached for the beer nuts, popped two in his mouth. Gabe noticed he was wearing a ring on his pinky, little diamonds shaped into a dollar sign.

"Oh, not as much as it used to," Rich went on. "Harder to get away with pumping a horse up with chemicals these days." He puffed out smoke, amusing himself by stringing Gabe along. "Now, back in the days when your granddaddy and me used to play the ponies, there were plenty of tricks. Didn't have so many tests then, so many fucking rules on the horses and the jocks. But that was forty years ago and more." He sighed reminiscently. "Too bad you never got to know your granddaddy, Gabe."

"Too bad he got a bullet in the brain over a . . . difference of opinion."

"That's the truth," Rich said, with no sarcasm. He was a man who'd loved his daddy. "It's like I always tried to teach you, son, sometimes cheating's just part of the game. It's a matter of skill and timing."

"And sometimes it's a matter of murder. A horse, a man. One's not so different from the other to some people."

"Some horses I've liked better than some men."

"I remember another race, in Lexington. I was just a kid." Gabe picked up his cooling coffee, watching his father over the rim. "But I remember you were nervous. It wasn't that hot. The Bluegrass Stakes is in the spring. But you were sweating a lot. You had me working the stands, looking for loose change, panhandling. A horse broke down that day, too."

"Happens." He turned back to the monitor. Despite the chill from the air-conditioning, the back of his neck was damp. "I've seen it happen plenty in my day."

"It was a Chadwick horse then, too."

"No shit? Well, that's bad luck. Hey, can't you see I'm dry here?" Rich slapped a hand on the bar.

"A jockey hanged himself over it. As I recall, we didn't stick around long after that race. A few days, that's all. That was funny, too, because our room was paid up."

"Itchy feet. I've always had them."

"You were flush after that. The money didn't last long. It never did, but you had a nice fat roll when we headed out."

"I must have bet some winners that day."

"You're on a roll now, too, aren't you? New suit, gold watch, diamond ring." He picked up Rich's hand. "Manicure."

"You got a point here, boy?"

Braced against the stench of bourbon, Gabe leaned closer. His voice was low, icily controlled. "You'd better hope I don't find out you were in Kentucky on the first Saturday in May."

"You don't want to threaten me, Gabe."

"Oh yes, I do."

With fear and rage circling through his system, Rich picked up his fresh drink. "You want to back off is what you want to do. You want to let things lie and get your mind on that horse you're running next week. Keep your mind on that and on that pretty blond filly you're banging."

In a flash, Gabe had a hand wrapped around the knot of his father's new silk tie. The bartender hustled over.

"We don't want any trouble here."

"No trouble." Rich grinned into Gabe's face. "No trouble at all. Just a family discussion. That's a prime piece you're putting it to, son. Blue blood. I bet a thoroughbred like that's got plenty of kick, and lots of endurance. Maybe it's time she met your dear old daddy."

Gabe's hand ached with the pressure of making a fist. The fist ached to connect. Yet no matter how repugnant, there was no escaping the fact that the man was his father. "Keep away from her," Gabe said quietly.

"Or?"

"I'll kill you."

"We both know you haven't got the guts for that. But we'll make a deal. You keep out of my business, I keep out of yours." Rich smoothed down his tie when Gabe allowed him to jerk free. "Otherwise I might just have me a nice long talk with your pretty lady. I'd bet we'd have lots to talk about."

"Keep away from what's mine." Gabe took out a bill and put it on the counter beside the coffee he'd barely tasted. "Keep far away from what's mine."

"Kids." Rich beamed a fresh smile at the nervous bartender when Gabe strode away. "They just never learn respect." He picked up his drink, tried to ignore the fact that his hand was unsteady. "Sometimes you just got to pound it into them," he muttered.

Nursing his drink, he turned back to the monitor and waited for his horse to come in.

It was nearly dusk when Kelsey walked out of the barn for the last time. She'd put in a backbreaking twelve hours, hauling manure and straw, scrubbing down concrete, polishing tack. Now every muscle in her body was weeping. All she wanted was a blissfully hot bath and oblivion.

"Want a beer?" Moses sat on a barrel, two cold bottles dangling from his fingers. He'd been waiting for her.

"No." She gave him a nod as frosty as the brews. "Thanks."

"Kelsey." He held a bottle up. "I couldn't find my peace pipe."

Reluctant, she gave in and accepted one. She'd have preferred a gallon of water, but the beer washed away the taste of dirt and sweat just as well.

Moses narrowed his eyes at the purpling bruise on her upper arm. "What happened there? Pacer take a bite?"

"That's right. So?"

"You're not going to be able to stay pissed off at me for long. I'm too charming."

Kelsey drank again. "No, you're not."

"Works with your mother," he grumbled. "Listen, I think you screwed up, and I let you know it. Now I'm telling you you've done a good job. And not just today. For the most part."

"For the most part?"

"That's right. You learn fast, and you don't make the same mistake twice, but you still need somebody looking over your shoulder. You've got a temperament problem, but we're used to that around here, between the horses and your mother."

"My—" Her jaw dropped. "My mother."

"She can be a mule when it suits her. Not that she flies off the handle much now the way she did when she was younger. I'm sorry about that sometimes." He looked down at his boots. "Damn sorry about that. It's not that they broke her, but they changed her. Toughened her, I guess, so she learned how to pull in. I came down on you today more because of her than because of the job."

"I don't understand."

"If you turn away from her now, it'll kill her. She wouldn't want me to say it, but I'm saying it. There's nothing that means more to me in this world than Naomi. I don't want to see her hurt again."

"I'm not turning away. I'm not trying to hurt her. That may be a lot for you to take on faith, but I wish you would. I wish you could."

"You know, I figure anybody who can purge a horse and not run for cover's got to be trusted. See you in the morning."

"Sure." She started away, then looked over her shoulder. "It's a pretty evening."

"It is that."

"Women like to walk in the moonlight."

"I've heard that."

"There should be plenty of it in a couple of hours." Satisfied, Kelsey continued toward the house. She'd done her job, all around, she decided. Now she was going to let Gertie stuff her with anything available in the kitchen, then soak out all the aches in a marathon bath.

An hour later, she was dozing amid a swirl of bubbles and scent. Her world had smoothed out again. She was in the middle of a lazy yawn when the door opened.

"Gabe." Flustered, she scooted up, spewing froth dangerously close to the rim of the tub. "What are you doing?"

"Gertie told me I'd find you up here." He hooked his thumbs in his belt loops and simply enjoyed the view. "I was going to get you and bring you home with me. But it doesn't look like you're dressed for the ride."

"I often bathe naked. It's a habit of mine."

"How about I wash your back, and any other hard-to-reach places?"

"I can handle it." She pushed her hair out of her eyes and struggled not to give in to the urge to cross her arms over her bubble-bedecked breasts. "Listen, why don't you wait downstairs until I'm finished?"

He considered, then shook his head and began unbuttoning his shirt. "Nope. I'm coming in."

"You are not. We're in my mother's house, for God's sake."

"She's not here."

"That's not the point." Hurriedly, she scooped her bangs out of her eyes. "Keep that shirt on, Slater. Gertie's downstairs," she hissed.

"She'll have to stay there. There isn't room in that tub for the three of us." He tossed his shirt aside and sat down to pry off his boots.

"It's not a joke. It's just not appropriate."

"I need you, Kelsey."

Her protest turned into a sigh. She could see it now, the tension in the set of his shoulders. It was all but coming off him in waves. "Dammit," she murmured. "Lock the door."

"I already did."

His jeans joined hers on the floor, then he was easing himself into the steamy water behind her. His arms encircled her waist. He buried his face in her hair.

"God." He drew in her scent, wallowed in her texture while he fought off the fury that had roiled inside him since the confrontation with his father.

He needed it to go away, just for an hour. She could do that for him. She could do anything for him.

"Gabe, tell me what's wrong."

"Ssh." He slicked his hands up to the slippery curve of her breasts, skimmed wet fingertips over her nipples. "Just let me touch you. I only need to touch you."

He drowned her in tenderness. He'd never been so gentle before, so patient, so careful. With her leaning against him he did only what he'd said he'd needed. Only touched her. Fingers sliding along a long thigh, skimming down from knee to calf, flowing up again to dip inside her so that the heat melted her bones.

Shuddering, she tried to turn to face him, but he pressed her back. "Not yet." His mouth danced over her glistening shoulder, along the nape of her neck where falling tendrils curled damply.

So she surrendered, more completely than she had before, letting his hands take her where he chose. Water lapped, bubbles dissolved. Each time she climaxed, felt her body tighten, tremble, explode, she was sure it was the last. Yet he slowly, patiently, quietly, built a new fire.

She could float on the smoke of it, drift, deaf to her own throaty moans. When at last he shifted her, letting water spill carelessly over the rim, over the tiles, she sank back through the clouds of smoke, into the flames.

22

That horse was not going to win. Rich helped himself to Cunningham's scotch. After all, a man shouldn't get himself hung up on one kind of liquor. Or one kind of woman. Or one kind of game.

The boy had never understood that, he thought as he downed a double and poured another. He'd never been able to teach that little son of a bitch anything.

Well, he was going to teach him now. Good and proper.

There would be no Triple Crown this year. No, indeed. He was going to see to that. He'd come to do a job, and if it turned out it had the benefit of a little personal revenge, so much the better.

He settled into Cunningham's easy chair, propped his shiny new Gucci loafers on the footstool. And smiled. This was the life for him, all right. Lord of the manor. A fine house in the country, a couple of spiffy cars in the garage, a hungry woman in bed.

He was going to have it too. Once he tied up this last loose end, he was taking his winnings out to Vegas. They knew him in Vegas. Yes, sir, they knew good old Richie Slater in that town. He'd be a high roller, penthouse suite at Caesars, a top-heavy babe hanging on his arm.

When he'd cleaned up there, he'd buy himself a house. Maybe right in Nevada, come to that. One of those fancy digs with cactus and palm trees and a pool in the backyard. Then when the urge struck him, or the level got low in his billfold, he'd just slip on into town and clean up again.

He sat there, dreaming a bit about a wheel that always spun to his tune and cards that fell like angels into his hand.

"What the hell are you doing?" Flushed and breathless, Cunningham stood in the doorway. Rather than the commanding tone he'd hoped for, his voice came out in a squeak.

"Hey there, Billy boy. All finished talking with your partners? Word is you're syndicating that filly for a million flat."

"That's my business." The deal was nearly set, and nothing, *nothing,* he promised himself, was going to interfere. There was a loan to pay off, and it was nearing deadline. "You got your money, Slater. You and I are done."

Lips puckered, Rich contemplated his last swallow of scotch. "Now, that's downright unfriendly, Billy."

"What are you doing in my house?"

"Can't an old pal drop by for a visit?" He grinned guilelessly. "That pretty little bed-warmer of yours was a lot more welcoming when she let me in. On her way out shopping, she said. Down to Neiman Marcus. Needless Markup, that is. Get it?" He chuckled at his own wit.

"Marla," Cunningham said with what dignity he could muster, "is my wife."

"No shit?" After slapping himself on the knee, Rich rose to pour another drink. "Got yourself a ball and chain with first-class tits, did you? Well, congratulations, Billy boy. You're a bigger fool than anybody could've guessed."

If he wasn't a fool now, Cunningham thought, he'd certainly been one when he'd slid back into a deal with Rich Slater. But now, and from now on, everything was legitimate. The syndication deal, which Cunningham had just shaken hands on down at his barn, was every bit as big as Rich had heard. So it was time, way past the time, to cut old ties. All of them.

"I'm going to ask you to leave, Rich. We're square, you and me, and it isn't smart for us to be seen together."

"Nobody here but you and me." Rich winked and settled back in the chair again. Oh, he knew what Cunningham was thinking. Yes, indeed, he did. Billy boy figured he didn't need good old Rich anymore. "Now, don't you worry. I'm not here to squeeze you for more money. You just rest easy on that."

It pacified him, a little. "What is it, then?"

"A favor, that's all. Just a favor between old friends and former business associates. There's a horse that needs to be taken care of, Bill." He lifted his glass, enjoying the way the sun burst through the window and struck the facets.

"I don't want any part of it."

"What you want and what you've got are two different things." He shifted his eyes from his glass to Cunningham. "I'm going to take out my son's colt, Billy. And you're going to help me."

"You're crazy." Shaken, Cunningham swiped at the sweat beading on his upper lip. "You're crazy, Rich, and I don't want anything to do with it."

"Let's talk about that," Rich said, and smiled.

Kelsey's suitcases were neatly packed and lined up next to Gabe's by the bedroom door. They would leave for New York at seven A.M. sharp. Six hours from now, she thought as she gazed up through the skylight over the bed.

She sighed, shifted, and snuggled up against Gabe. It struck her, amazed her, as it always did, to find him there. Warm, solid. Hers. That body. She skimmed her fingers down his chest, up again. Long and hard and tireless. The face that could make her toes curl every time he looked at her.

And that was only the shell.

A terrific shell, she mused, tracing his jaw with her fingertip. But what was inside it was equally impressive. The strength, the kindness, the courage. He'd already beaten the odds, time and time again. Overcoming a birthright of misery and meanness to make it on his own.

Right now, sleeping in his place of honor in the barn was a horse who had the same kind of strength and courage. Together, they were going to make history.

"It's no use," she murmured, nuzzling her lips against his throat.

"Hmm ?" Automatically he stroked a hand down her back. He'd been enjoying the lazy caress of her fingertips for some time.

"I can't sleep. I'm too revved."

"Well, then." Always willing to accommodate, he rolled her over so that she was stretched on top of him. "Enjoy yourself."

She chuckled, wiggling away. "That's not what I meant." Kneeling, she looked down at him, letting herself linger over the long silhouette. "Not that it isn't a tempting offer." Leaning down, she gave him a smacking kiss. "I'll take you up on it when I get back."

He made a grab, but she was already scrambling off the bed. "Get back from where?"

"I need to walk. I want to look in on Double."

She tugged jeans over naked legs and hips, made his mouth water. "Darling, it's one o'clock in the morning."

"I know." Her head popped out of the opening of a baggy T-shirt. "In a little over eight hours, we'll be at Belmont. So who can sleep?" Tossing back her hair, she pulled on boots.

He could have, but it seemed a moot point. "I'll come with you."

"You don't have to. I won't be long."

He sat up, raked a hand through his hair. "I'll come with you."

"Okay. Catch up with me." She dashed out the door and down the stairs.

It was a perfect June night. Warm, just a little breezy, star-scattered. She heard the long, double-toned hoot of an owl, smelled roses and night-blooming jasmine. Moonlight showered on the outbuildings, lending them a timeless, fairy-tale aura.

Perhaps this was her fairy tale, she thought. Her personal happily-ever-after. It was true that tragedy had brought her here, opened the door to her future. But fairy tales were rife with tragedy. Orphans and spellbound princes, betrayals and sacrifices, evil intent and lost loves.

But right always triumphed. Maybe that was why the analogy appealed to her. If this was her fairy tale, she would see that right triumphed. She wouldn't give up on finding the truth.

She would see Captain Tipton again, and Charles Rooney. She would talk to Gertie, to Moses, and yes, to Naomi. To anyone who had had even the smallest role in the events leading to Alec Bradley's death. She would convince Naomi to allow her lawyers to speak freely.

But for now, for the next week, there was only the Belmont. And she was a part of it. With a quiet laugh, Kelsey lifted her face toward the sky. She had a place in the grandeur and the grit, the sweat and the seduction of racing's finest hour.

In a week's time, she promised herself, she would watch Gabe and his spectacular colt accept the last jewel in the Crown.

A barn cat dashed across the path, his long sleek form a gray bullet that shot her heart to her throat. Chuckling at herself, she rubbed a hand there as if to ease it back into her chest again.

The stable door opened with a thin squeak. The smells came first, old friends rushing at her through the dark. Horse, leather, liniment, manure. Rather than turn on the lights and disturb those sleeping, she groped along the wall from memory and found a flashlight. Its beam cut a narrow swath. Her boot heels clicked after it.

From the second stall a pair of eyes gleamed goblinlike from the shadows. Her breath caught; the beam bobbled. Fairy tales, indeed, she thought, and was grateful Gabe wasn't with her to see how she jumped at a couple of barn cats.

She smiled when she saw the cot pulled in front of Double's box. The security system aside, a warrior like this merited a personal guard. Well, she wouldn't disturb the groom, she promised herself. Just one quick peek over the cot and into the box, and she'd leave them both sleeping.

But the cot, she saw with some surprise, was empty. Alarmed, she shone her light into the box. Double was there, fully awake, staring back at her.

"Sorry, fella. I guess I'm jumpy. Did your friend here go off for a smoke, or a call of nature? Are you all packed ?" She laughed and reached for the box door.

It wasn't latched, was open fully three inches.

"Oh, God." A movement behind her had her swinging about, flashlight gripped like a weapon. The blood thundered in her ears as she zigzagged the beam and cursed the cats who hunted at night.

But a cat, however quick and clever, hadn't unlatched and opened the stall door. Her one clear thought was to protect, to defend. Kelsey shoved the door open and rushed to the colt's side. Even as she pivoted, to shine her light into the corners of the box, the blood in her ears exploded.

She was aware of one vivid flash of pain, the high, alarmed whinny from the colt. Then nothing.

While the figure dashed from the box, breath harsh and panicked, the colt danced, lethal hooves arching over Kelsey's unconscious form.

Halfway between the house and the barn, Gabe balanced two mugs of tea. It appeared to him that they were going to be up most of the night, but the herbal brew Kelsey preferred was a better idea than coffee at this hour. Particularly if he could coax her back into bed and channel her nervous energy into a more intimate arena.

They hadn't been wasting much time on sleep in any case, he thought. Not since the night he'd joined her in her tub. It had been tricky to convince her to move in with him for a few days. He'd shamelessly used the race as a reason for it—his need for some moral support.

It worked, he reminded himself, grinning as he sipped from his mug. He intended for it to continue working, stage by stage, until it was a permanent condition. But he'd calculated that a woman still raw from a divorce needed to be eased into the idea of a second marriage.

The biggest surprise was that *he* hadn't needed to be eased into the idea at all.

It had simply appeared, full-blown, in his mind. Or maybe in his heart. He'd never given a great deal of thought to the traditional boundaries of marriage, wife, family. With an upbringing like his, the idea of it was absurd, even destructive.

But not with Kelsey. With her he wanted the promise, the future. The chance.

Together they would share all of this. He skimmed his gaze over the outbuildings, the hills, the fences. Together they would make more.

And maybe, while they were doing it, they could help each other bury the past.

The shrill, frenzied cry of the colt split the quiet. Both mugs shattered on the gravel as Gabe lunged forward. With Kelsey's name bursting from his lips, he dragged at the barn door, slapped the lights. Ice-edged panic chased him between the boxes, sliced nastily into his spine.

She was sprawled on the straw, facedown, the colt backed into the rear of the box, eyes rolling as he pawed his bedding. The world upended, draining the blood from Gabe's head out through the soles of his feet.

He moved like lightning, shielding her with his own body as he gathered her up. He took a blow to the shoulder, unfelt as he lifted her. Her face was corpse white, her body limp as rags. Ignoring the flailings of the colt, he laid her on the cot. His fingers trembled as he pressed them to the pulse at her throat.

"Please, baby. Please."

It was there, that quick flutter of life. He kept his fingers pressed to it, as if by removing them that life beat would drain away, and buried his face in her hair.

There was only panic and relief, panic and relief, a bright and giddy pendulum swinging inside him. He stayed as he was, his fingers at her throat, his face in her hair, one arm cradling her.

"Gabe. Jesus Christ, Gabe."

The frightened voice of his trainer snapped him back. He lifted his head and watched the somehow dreamlike movements of Jamison stepping into the box to calm the colt.

"Easy, boy. Easy now." Jamison dragged the colt's head down, using his voice and his hands to soothe. "Settle down." But his eyes were anything but calm when they focused on Gabe. "What happened here? Where's Kip? He's supposed to be bunking outside the box."

"I don't know where the hell he is. But you're going to find him. Find him and the fucking night watchman." Forcing himself to move slowly, Gabe ran his hands over Kelsey, checking for broken bones. He located the knot at the back of her head. His fingers lingered there, gentle as a kiss, while his eyes sliced back to Jamison and burned. "Call a doctor, and the cops. Now."

"She's hurt." Jamison continued to stroke the quivering colt. "How bad?"

"I don't know. Call, goddammit!"

As if in answer, Kelsey stirred under his hand and moaned.

"Kelsey." He had to yank himself back from snatching her up. "Kelsey, take it slow."

"Gabe." Her eyes fluttered open, but her vision swam, touching off nausea. "God." She closed them again, struggling to breathe evenly.

"Don't try to move yet."

"I'm not. Believe me." She concentrated on moving air in and out of her lungs. When it seemed she had that down, she cautiously opened her eyes again. This time, she brought his face into focus. There was murder in his eyes, she thought dimly. Then remembered. "The colt. Someone was in with the colt."

"It's all right. He's all right." Gabe cursed viciously when she winced in pain. "I'm going to take you up to the house now. I'm going to take care of you."

"Somebody was in there. The groom was gone. The door was open. But I couldn't see who it was. Did they hurt him?"

"No." Gabe glanced at Jamison, who was sliding the box door closed. "Make the calls, Jamie. I want Lieutenant Rossi. I want Gunner, too. See that he gets out here and checks the colt over.

"He looks fine," Jamison began, but was already nodding. His eyes were bloodshot and strained. "I'll get him here, Gabe. Take her on up, do what you can for her. I'll sit up myself with the colt tonight."

"I want two men on him." Gabe lifted Kelsey as carefully as a man handling spun glass. "No less than two at any time. Is that understood?"

"It is."

"And find Kip. I want to talk to him."

"All right." With a heavy heart Jamison watched Gabe carry Kelsey outside. He turned to the colt, rubbed his weary eyes, then went to make the calls.

"I'm all right, really." But Kelsey kept her eyes closed on the trip from barn to house. "Just a headache."

"Be quiet," Gabe told her, fighting to keep his voice light. "Just rest."

His jaw tightened as his boots crunched over bits of the shattered mugs. If he hadn't stopped to make the goddamned tea. If he'd been with her . . .

"Are you sure Double's all right? I didn't have a chance to see."

"Will you stop worrying about the fucking horse? It exploded out of him, and unlocked the gates. "Do you think I give a damn about that horse right now? I'd have killed him myself if he'd have hurt you."

"Gabe—"

"Shut up! Goddammit!" His face a mask of rage, he shoved the door open. She cringed, chiefly because his shouting caused her head to swim.

"There's no need to yell. You're entitled to be upset, but—"

"Upset?" He laid her down on the couch in the living room. The way his muscles were beginning to tremble, he wasn't certain he could carry her up the stairs. "Is that what you think I am, upset? A little out of sorts maybe because someone knocked you senseless? Yeah, that's right. I'm upset."

He fisted his hand and worked off a fraction of the emotions boiling inside him by ramming it into the wall.

The words she'd been about to speak slid soundlessly down Kelsey's throat. She stared from the dent in the wall to his battered knuckles.

"I guess I'm upset because I found you unconscious in a stall with a panicked horse who might have trampled you to death at any minute."

She hadn't thought of that, and the image it presented made her stomach lurch. She began to tremble. "Gabe. Don't."

"I was a little upset because I thought, for a minute, the longest minute of my life, that you were already dead."

The tears began to spill over. One, then two, then a stream. "I guess 'upset' was the wrong word."

"Christ." Abruptly hollowed out, he rubbed his hands over his face. But it didn't help. He went to her then, gathering her close, holding her when she curled into a ball on his lap. "Christ, Kelsey, I lost my mind." He kissed her, gently now, drying her cheeks with his lips. "I'm sorry. Let me get you some ice."

"No, don't go. Just don't go."

"Okay. Let me see if you're hurt anywhere else."

"It's just my head. He must have been behind me. It was stupid to rush in that way, but I wasn't thinking. I saw the cot was empty, then that the stall door was open. All I could think of was what had nearly happened to him before. What happened to Pride."

"Next time think what would happen to me." He tipped her face up. "I couldn't handle losing you."

She took his hand, pressed his torn knuckles to her lips. "I guess we could both use some ice."

"Yeah."

But they stayed where they were until Rossi knocked on the door.

An hour later, Gabe walked back from the barn again, this time with Rossi at his side. "You've got a hole in your security, Mr. Slater."

"I'm aware of that." A hole big enough, he thought, for someone to slip through when the night watchman made his hourly outside rounds.

"Somebody could have come in from the outside. Somebody who knows your setup here. You've got a lot of land, a lot of ways in and out."

Rossi scanned through the dark. He didn't envy Gabe that. He much preferred his tidy apartment, the claustrophobia and comfort of the city.

"I like taking the easy way," he continued, "and looking at the inside."

Gabe was looking at the inside as well, at every hand he'd inherited from Cunningham, at every man and woman who had been hired on, or fired, in the ensuing five years.

"You've already got a list of everyone who works for me. Do whatever you have to do with it."

"I intend to."

"I've arranged to have two men with the colt at all times. I'd be one of them myself, but I'm not willing to leave Kelsey any longer than necessary.

"I can't blame you for that." Rossi paused. It was a pretty night, what was left of it. He might as well enjoy the breeze. "She's toughing this out pretty well. I'd say she's taking her knock on the head better than your groom's taking his."

"Could be her head's harder." They'd found Kip groaning back to consciousness in the empty box adjoining Double's. "We didn't have any trouble shipping him off to the hospital."

"She'll be fine." Curious, Rossi brushed a shard of china with the toe of his shoe.

"I was carrying a couple of mugs when I heard the horse," Gabe explained. "Guess I dropped them."

"Mmm. Like I said, she'll be fine. You're favoring your right shoulder."

Instinctively, Gabe straightened it. "It's nothing. The colt caught me."

If it hadn't been his shoulder, it might have been Kelsey. Her head, her face. The thought roiled in his stomach. "You've done a background check on me, haven't you, Rossi?"

"Standard procedure."

"Then you know a little something about my father."

"Enough to know he wouldn't win any Daddy of the Year awards."

"He's in town. Has been for several weeks." Gabe spoke without inflection. He might have been discussing the weather. "I'd say I was one of his first stops. I brushed him off with some money. Not nearly as much as he wanted. That tends to make him surly. He knows his way around the track, around the shedrow."

"You think your father would try to hit at you this way?"

"He hates my guts," Gabe said simply. "He'd hit at me any way he could, especially if he could make a profit at it. I thought I saw him at Churchill Downs during Derby week. So did one of the grooms at Three Willows. I tracked him down at Laurel a couple of days ago. He denied it." Gabe reached for a cigar he didn't have. "He's lying."

Understanding the gesture, Rossi took out a pack of cigarettes, offered one. "I'll check it out."

"You do that, Lieutenant." Gabe's eyes glowed steady in the flare of the match. "And keep this in mind while you do. The odds are he knew Lipsky. Rich Slater's a man who likes to cheat. Winning the game's more fun for him that way—and he's been winning. He's flashing money around."

"I'll see if I can find out where he came by it."

"There was another race, when I was a kid. A horse from this farm was running against a horse from Three Willows." Gabe drew smoke into his lungs, watched it drift away on the breeze when he exhaled. "The Three Willows colt stumbled, shattered his legs. They had to put him down. My father flashed some money after that race, too."

"That would have been in Lexington. Spring of '73."

Gabe eyed Rossi through a cloud of smoke. "That's right. That's exactly right."

"Funny you didn't mention this before."

"He didn't hurt Kelsey before."

"Excuse me." Matt Gunner strode up to them. His hair was still in sleep tufts. "The colt's fine, Gabe."

"Good. I appreciate your coming out."

"That's no problem." Matt glanced toward the house. "Kelsey?"

"She's resting. The doctor advised a trip to the hospital, but she won't budge."

"I'd like to look in on her, when she's up to it."

"Sure." He said his good nights, then turned back to Rossi. "You'd better find him before I do."

"You don't have any proof your father was involved in any of this."

Gabe tossed down the cigarette, crushed it out. "I don't need to prove anything."

Kelsey heard him coming up the steps and gingerly shifted to a sitting position. The pills the doctor had given her had smoothed the edges, but she wasn't taking any chances.

"Double?" she said the minute Gabe came into the room.

"Matt gave him a thumbs-up." And he had personally discarded the colt's night feed bag and replaced it.

She sighed, relaxed. "Thank God. I've been sitting here thinking of all the possibilities."

"You're supposed to be resting." He sat on the bed, careful not to shake the mattress. "You've got shadows under your eyes again." Gently, he traced them with his thumb. "Why do I always find that so sexy?"

"Machismo looking for vulnerability." She smiled. "Come to bed. Maybe we can both get a couple of hours' sleep before we have to leave."

"I want you to stay here, Kelsey. Not here," he corrected, "at Three Willows. You're not up to the trip, and it would be safer and smarter for you to stay with Gertie. Rossi can arrange for a couple of men."

"Gabe." She framed his face, touched her lips to his, then spoke softly. "No way in hell."

"Listen to me."

"I could," she agreed. "I could listen to you, and you could listen to me, and we could bat this ball back and forth until morning. I'd still go. So why don't we just pretend we've argued and discussed?"

"You're being selfish." He pushed himself off the bed and began to undress. "You don't want to miss the race, so it doesn't matter that I won't be able to concentrate or enjoy it myself."

Slowly, she ran her tongue over her teeth. "That was a good one. And guilt usually works with me, but not this time. You'll worry whether I'm there or not. And I'm going to be there for you, Gabe. All the way."

"Goddamned mule."

"That won't work either. Though name calling is an acceptable stage in a good fight. I could counter that by calling you an overprotective ass, but I'll refrain because I'm a lady. So—" Her breath caught on a hiss. "Oh, God, what did you do to your back?"

He twisted his head but could get only a marginal glimpse at the dark, spreading bruise on his shoulder. "Took a kick."

"When? It wasn't there before . . ." She trailed off, realizing just when and just how he'd come by it. "Now I will call you an ass. What kind of numb-headed heroics is this? The doctor was just here. He could have treated it."

"It wasn't heroics, numb-headed or otherwise. I was distracted." Cautiously he rotated his shoulder. The sting wasn't so bad, but the throb went deep and had teeth. "Just needs some liniment."

"Jerk."

He started to snap back, then sighed, defeated. "I love you too." Slipping into bed, he cradled her against him.

"What are you doing?"

"Getting some sleep. I'm supposed to check on you every couple of hours. We don't have much more than that anyway."

"The liniment."

"Later. I just want to hold you."

Content with that, she brushed his hair from his brow. "Gabe. I'm going with you."

"I know. Go to sleep."

23

No one would let her work. For her first two days in New York, Kelsey was all but barred from the track, outnumbered and outflanked by everyone from Gabe down to the scruffiest stableboy. It seemed the trip itself was to be her only victory.

With too much time on her hands, and too much of it spent alone, she decided she had two options. She could go quietly mad, or she could treat the enforced inactivity as a short vacation.

The vacation seemed healthier.

She made use of the hotel facilities, swimming each morning to keep the muscles she'd developed over the past few months in shape. She shopped, began a love-hate relationship with the Nautilus equipment in the health club, and generally fought off boredom.

It helped that Gabe had decided to give a pre-race party, using the hotel ballroom on the evening before the Belmont. It gave Kelsey the opportunity to plot out the details, talk strategy with the florist and the hotel caterer. Gabe, after one look at the yards of lists, took the coward's route, and left the entire matter in her hands.

Nothing could have pleased her more.

She spent hours with the hotel manager, the concierge, the chef, debating and dissecting what could and couldn't be done. As Gabe had put no ceiling on the budget, she had already decided there was nothing that couldn't be done, and set about convincing the staff.

"I'd have been smarter handing you a pitchfork and letting you clean out stalls all week." Gabe grabbed a quick cup of coffee and watched Kelsey pore over the final menu for the evening. "You'd have gotten more rest."

"Stop fussing. You're the one who started this."

"I thought a party would be a good idea." He moved over to stand behind her, rubbing her shoulders as she muttered over her papers. "A little food, some music, an open bar. I didn't realize I'd be backing a David O. Selznick production." He narrowed his eyes. "*How* much champagne is that?"

"Go away." But she rolled her shoulders under his hands. "You're not going to drink it anyway. You gave me carte blanche, Slater, and I'm using it. Just be in your tuxedo by eight."

"More like Captain Bligh than Selznick," he muttered.

"Now you sound like the caterer. Go meet your reporters."

"I'm sick of reporters."

"You're just jealous because they put Double on the cover of *Sports Illustrated* instead of you."

"I got the spread in *People*," he reminded her, and entertained himself by nibbling on her ear. "This is a great spot right here," he murmured, nipping his way up her left lobe. "I could be temperamental and miss the interview."

The quick, delicious shivers distracted her. Gabe took advantage and had the first two buttons of her blouse undone before she shook herself free.

"Stop that! I have an appointment in fifteen minutes."

"I'll work fast."

"I mean it." Breathless, she squirmed away, scrambled out of the chair. "I'm getting my hair done."

He grinned. Just now it was tumbling out of the bright, cloth-covered elastic. He'd done that. "I like your hair exactly the way it is."

"Keep your distance, Slater. The rest of my day is booked, minute by minute, and I didn't schedule any time for you to chase me around the desk."

"Adjust."

"This may be just a party for you." As ridiculous as it was, she scooted so that the desk was between them. "But putting it together has kept me sane all week. I have an emotional investment."

"So do I." He put his palms down on the desk, leaned forward. "Come here."

"Absolutely not."

"I've got something for you."

"Oh, please." She'd have rolled her eyes if she'd dared take them off him. "That's very lame."

He straightened, cocked a brow. "A present." He took a small velvet box out of his pocket. "Now aren't you ashamed?"

"A present?" Despite the instant flare of pleasure, she eyed it warily. "Is this a trick?"

"Open it. I was going to give it to you after the race, but I thought it would be better luck for you to have it before."

It lured her. She came around the desk to take it from him, then lifted her mouth to his for a kiss. "Thank you."

"You haven't opened it yet."

"For the thought first."

Her breath sighed out when she snapped the top open. The horse glowed against the black velvet, caught forever in mid-gallop, airborne and magnificent. The pin was fashioned of ruby jade, carved so intricately, so delicately that she almost expected to feel the bunch and flow of muscles as she ran a fingertip over it. The diamond eye glistened with triumph.

"It's beautiful. It's perfect." She looked up at him. "So are you."

"That was my line." He slipped his arms around her waist, bringing her closer. "You're welcome," he said as his mouth closed over hers.

Of course, she was late. Kelsey dashed into the beauty salon babbling apologies. She was checking her watch anxiously by the time the manicurist was trying to do something elegant with her neglected nails.

"Honey, why don't we go for some tips?"

"No, I'll just break them off." Her hair was bundled in huge foam rollers, her face coated with a pale green cream she'd somehow allowed herself to be talked into, and time was ticking away. "Just shape up what's there and slap on some clear polish."

"Don't you want something a little snazzier?"

Kelsey stole a peek at the manicurist's lethally long, carmine-slicked nails. "No, I'll stick with subtlety."

With a shake of her head, the woman dunked Kelsey's right hand in warm water. "Whatever you say, honey."

"It's Kelsey, isn't it?" A woman at the next station smiled at her. "I'm Janet Gardner. Overlook Farms, Kentucky?"

"Oh, yes, Mrs. Gardner." Kelsey decided not to say she hadn't recognized the woman, not with the flame-colored hair coated with glistening blue cream and her face plastered with shocking pink. "It's nice to see you again."

"A face-lift without the scalpel, they tell me." Janet laughed as she tapped a finger to the drying pink mask. "We'll see about that. Yours?"

"Oh, something about relaxing. Apparently I looked harried."

"Who doesn't by the Belmont? My Hank and I are going to sleep for two weeks when we get back home. We promised ourselves."

Kelsey remembered Hank now—the stringy man she'd danced with the night before. He'd had sun-scored cheeks, a pencil-thin mustache, and a voice as rich as molasses. He'd wanted to teach her to tango.

"Give your husband my best. He's a terrific dancer."

"Oh, that's my Hank." Janet chuckled and preened. "All the ladies want a turn around the floor with him. He likes to tell people I married him for his feet."

Obliging the manicurist, Janet slipped off an emerald ring that could have doubled for a paperweight.

"I saw your mother today at the track. It's hard to believe we've been making the rounds together for . . . Well, that would be telling."

"You've known Naomi a long time."

"Since I married into this horse race. Of course, she was born into it." Much more interested in gossiping than in the fashion magazine she'd been thumbing through with her free hand, Janet set it aside. Her eyes brightened with curiosity. "You were, too."

"Belatedly."

"Oh, I think it's more that you came back to it belatedly. I remember seeing you at the track when you were in diapers."

"Really?"

"Oh, goodness, yes. Naomi was prouder of you than of any wall full of blue ribbons. We used to call you Naomi's thoroughbred. But you wouldn't remember that."

Naomi's thoroughbred. The idea both pleased and saddened her. "No, I don't."

"I met your father once or twice. Poor dear, he always looked so lost. He was a librarian?"

"My father is the head of the English department at Georgetown University."

"Oh, yes," Janet bubbled on, oblivious of the stiffness in Kelsey's voice. Obligingly she dunked her fingers in the soaking bowl for her own manicure. "I knew it had something to do with books. Naomi doted on him. We all thought it was a shame things didn't work out. But then, it happens all the time, doesn't it?"

"According to the statistics."

"Hank and I are the lucky ones. Twenty-eight years this September."

"Congratulations." Since there was no escape, Kelsey tried a shift in topic. "You have children?"

"Three. Two boys and a girl. Our DeeDee's married now, and has two little girls of her own." If she'd had a hand free, Janet would have gone straight for the pictures in her wallet. "My boys tell me they're still looking. Of course, my youngest is barely twenty. He's studying structural engineering. Not that I know anything about that."

She went on about her children at some length until Kelsey relaxed into the rhythm.

"But there's something special between a mother and daughter," Janet said, cagily veering back. "Don't you think? I mean, even after all these years of separation, you and Naomi look so sweet together. To tell you the truth, it's been so long a lot of people forget she even had a daughter, if they knew in the first place."

Janet held up one hand, examined the first coat of mauve polish. "Yes, dear, that's very nice." When she shifted her attention back to Kelsey, her voice took on a confidential air. "I hope you won't be offended if I tell you that most of us who knew Naomi, and the situation, were rooting for her. I mean, the idea of taking a child from its mother just seems unnatural."

Well aware that both manicurists had their ears pricked, Kelsey kept her voice cool. "I'm sure Naomi appreciated it."

"Not that it did any good. I'm sorry to say she was her own worst enemy during that trying time. I've always thought it was anger at your father that made her behave so recklessly. And the social scene was a bit . . . wilder back then. Still, Alec Bradley." She clucked her tongue. "Naomi should have known better than to flirt in that direction. Oh." As if she'd just remembered the outcome of that flirtation, Janet blinked and squirmed. "Oh, dear, I'm sorry. That would be a sore point."

The idea of a shooting death and a decade in prison being termed a sore point might have amused Kelsey under different circumstances. But she backtracked to the one statement that had caught her attention. "Did you know Alec Bradley?"

"Oh, yes. Most of us back then at least knew of him. He was drop-dead gorgeous, as my DeeDee would say. Tall, dark, and handsome, with a smile that could melt a woman's heart. He knew it, too. Believe me, he knew it and he used it. He even fluttered around me a bit—but Hank put a stop to that." She giggled girlishly. "I admit I was a little flattered, even knowing his reputation."

"What reputation was that?"

"Well, dear"—eagerly she scooted forward in her chair—"his family would barely acknowledge him. They may have had some financial reversals, but the blood was still blue. And there was that scandal with his first wife." She hunkered still closer, assuming the gossip position. "He had a taste for older women, you know. Wealthy older women. Everyone knew his first wife settled on him generously in the divorce to save face. Not that it helped, really, because everyone knew he'd been, well, servicing the fillies, shall we say?"

"So, he was a womanizer."

"Oh, a champion. And the buzz was, he charged for the service."

"He—women paid him, for sex?"

Another giggle, slightly embarrassed. Janet preferred cagey euphemisms. "I don't know if it was quite that blunt, but it was common knowledge that he could be bought. As an escort. There are a lot of single women, even in racing. Unmarried, divorced, between husbands. Alec could be hired to fill the gap. A handsome arm to hold for a party, at the track. He was, as I said, quite charming. And he tended to bet heavily. And badly."

When she smiled, pink flakes cracked from her face and drifted onto her black-and-gold bib like colorful dandruff. "Now, no one thought it was a business deal between him and your mother, dear. A woman like Naomi could have had any man she wanted. Still could. Alec seemed quite besotted with her. Though he did continue to indulge in the side flirtations. Naomi wasn't one to put up with that sort of nonsense. They argued heatedly about that, and she gave him the boot."

This time Janet's flustering was quite genuine. "That is—I mean—"

"You were there that night." Not interested in evasions or a sudden attack of conscience, Kelsey pressed. "The night he died?"

"Yes, I was." Janet moistened her lips, surprised and a bit unnerved by Kelsey's direct question. "Hank and I were in Virginia on business. A number of racing people were at the country club for a party. There now, looks like I'm done." She held up her hands. "And speaking of parties, I'm so looking forward to tonight. That handsome young man of yours has us all on the edge of our seats."

"They argued." Kelsey ignored the squawk of protest from her manicurist when she shot out a hand and gripped Janet's arm. "That night, they argued."

"Yes, dear." Sorry now that she'd let her yen for gossip sink her over her head, Janet spoke kindly. "Several of us were questioned about it after the . . . difficulties. They argued quite audibly, and Naomi told him, in blunt terms, that their relationship was finished. They'd both been drinking perhaps a little more than was wise. Words flew. Naomi dashed a glass of champagne in his face, and walked out. It was the last I saw of her for a very long time."

In the bright clown mask, Janet's eyes softened. "I was fond of Naomi. I still am. The man wasn't worth it, dear. He simply wasn't worth one minute of her time. I think the real crime is she didn't realize it until it was too late."

For the rest of the afternoon, Kelsey struggled to put the conversation in the back of her mind. She wanted to take it out again, to examine each and every word separately. It made a difference, didn't it? Somehow it made a difference that Alec Bradley had been for hire.

But however it altered the puzzle she so badly wanted to piece together, there was too much interference to concentrate.

Whatever her mood, she had no intention of spoiling Gabe's moment, or her mother's contentment.

She dressed early, and left Gabe a note in the center of the bed for him to meet her in the ballroom at precisely eight.

Final details required her attention, whether the caterer, the florist, and the hotel staff agreed or not. It was to be perfect. And as she stood in the center of the huge, chandelier-lit room, it was.

The red-and-white colors of Longshot predominated. In tablecloths, candles, flowers. To honor the three jewels in the Triple Crown, banks of red roses, sunny black-eyed Susans, and white carnations spilled from tables, tumbled from baskets. Black-suited waiters were lined up for inspection while the catering staff put the finishing touches on three enormous buffet tables.

But her inspiration, her pièce de résistance, and her biggest headache had been the gambling.

Oversize play money was available for purchase, and all for charity, but the details had kept her racing for days with the bureaucracy. Naomi's thoroughbred had nipped all opposition at the wire.

Now she could stand and study the roulette wheels, the dice and blackjack tables, and know she was presenting Gabe with the party of the season. And one, she thought, that would suit him like a second skin.

While the orchestra tuned up she walked over and gave the wheel a reckless spin.

"I'll take red."

With a laugh, she turned around and smiled at Gabe. "You're on time."

"You're beautiful." He didn't cross to her, not yet. He just wanted to look. She wore glimmering white, a column that shimmered from the curve of her breasts to her ankles. His gift was pinned at her heart. Her hair was a tumble of curls, scooped back with glittering clips, falling over bare shoulders. Diamond and ruby drops dripped from her ears. "Really incredibly beautiful."

"Your colors." She held out her hands to his. "What do you think?"

"I think you astonish me." Still holding her at arm's length, he scanned the room. "What have you done here?"

"Besides driving every merchant and city official within fifty miles insane? I've given you a casino for the night. Slater's."

"And the proceeds?"

"There's a shelter for abused women and children in D.C."

His eyes darkened, then lowered to their joined hands. "You humble me, Kelsey."

"I love you, Gabe."

Moved, he lifted her hands to his lips. "What spin of the wheel brought you to me?"

"The luckiest one of your life." She glanced down, smiled at the silver ball nestled in its slot. "Red," she murmured. "You win again. You know, Gabe, this isn't just for you."

"No?"

"No." She inched closer, slipping her arms around his neck. "I want to watch you work here tonight. I have a feeling I'm going to find it very arousing."

And she did. Hours later when the room was crowded with people, the buffet tables decimated, the dance floor spinning with couples, she stood at Gabe's shoulder and studied his technique.

She'd thought she'd understood blackjack. A simple card game of luck and logic where you tried to get as close as possible to twenty-one. If you went over, you lost. But she couldn't for the life of her understand why Gabe held and won on a measly fifteen one hand and hit, and won, on sixteen the next.

"It's just numbers," he told her. "Nothing but numbers, darling."

That's exactly what she'd thought. Until she'd seen him play. "There's no way you can possibly remember all the numbers, the combinations."

He only smiled, tapped his cards, and added a four to his seventeen for twenty-one. "Here." He pushed a stack of red and white chips at her. "You play for a while."

"All right, I will." She took the seat he vacated, then glanced up when Naomi sat down beside her.

"I've just lost a bundle at craps. I'm giving this game ten minutes before I nag Moses into dancing with me." She tucked a sweep of golden hair behind her ear, then crossed her legs. After pushing out some chips, she scanned the room. "Quite a party."

"Your daughter's amazing."

"I know." Naomi's brow furrowed as she studied her cards. "Hit me," she instructed, then huffed out a breath. "Busted."

"It's all for a good cause. Losing should warm your heart." Nibbling her lip, Kelsey contemplated her eight and five. "Okay, I'll take one. An eight! Another eight! I won!" She was chuckling as she raked in her chips, until she caught Naomi's narrowed eye. "Well, winning warms the heart, too. Dance with my mother, Gabe, and I'll see how much of your money I can lose."

"How could I turn down an offer like that?" He held out a hand, curling his fingers around Naomi's. "You look wonderful tonight," he said when they matched steps on the dance floor.

"How would you know? You haven't looked at anyone but Kelsey."

He said nothing for a moment. "I don't seem to have a smooth answer to that."

Tilting her head back, she studied him carefully. "I'd be disappointed if you did. I like watching what she feels for you rush into her face. And I like knowing what you feel for her causes you to miss a step. In an odd way you've both been so structured. You trip each other up."

"But you're worried."

"Not about what's between the two of you. About everything else." She glanced back to where Kelsey sat laughing at the blackjack table, shoving more chips forward. "I know she tried to brush off what happened the other night. But it terrifies me."

His eyes went cool, deceptively so. "It should never have happened. I should have been with her."

"No, it should never have happened," Naomi agreed, but she was still looking at her daughter, not at Gabe. "I think she should stay at Three Willows—or better yet, go back to her father until this is settled."

He'd thought the same, but hearing it didn't make it easier. "Even if she agreed to that, we don't know how long it will take to settle any of it."

"Any of it?"

He cursed himself, another misstep. As far as Naomi knew, there was only the current trouble over the horses. "Who broke through my security, and what they intended to do. On the other hand, it might be over tomorrow, after the race is run."

"I'm going to count on that. I couldn't stand for anything to happen to her, Gabe. I hate the idea that she's been touched by any of the ugliness—just the kind of sordid business Milicent always claimed was part and parcel of racing."

She shook her head back, her eyes flashing. "But it's not. It's not what it's about. Not what we're about. But when it happens, it's all people remember."

"Are you worried about Milicent Byden's opinion?"

"Hell, no." The old defiance came back. "But I won't let her be right. And I'll be damned if I let her smirk over another blot on my honor. So I want this over. For Kelsey, for you. And for myself."

The room was cool and dark when Kelsey woke. She shifted lazily while images from the night before flowed through her mind. Color and light, voices, music. The dizzying spin of the wheel, the lightning toss of dice. She'd lost half of Gabe's winnings at cards; he'd doubled them back at craps.

Most of all, she remembered how he'd looked, dark and dangerous in evening clothes, those mouthwatering and unreadable blue eyes following the spin of the wheel, the fall of the cards. Then the way they would suddenly lock on hers and stop her breath.

And when they'd been alone, when the evening and the noise and the crowds had been behind them, he'd lowered her to the bed. Those clever hands had played her then, teasing out moans, tempting out darker and darker needs.

He had done things to her, done things for her she'd never imagined allowing, much less demanding.

Now, waking, her body felt soft and tender, bruised and cherished. Eyes closed, she skimmed her hand over the sheet, wanting him. Groggy, she pushed herself up in bed and found herself alone.

He wasn't getting away that easily, she told herself. Still half dreaming, she crawled out of bed. She stumbled out into the parlor of the suite, belting her robe.

She grimaced as the light through the open drapes blinded her. Shielding her eyes, she braced a hand on the doorjamb.

"God. What time is it?"

"Just past ten." Naomi poured a cup of coffee from the pot on the room service tray. "Your timing's good, Kelsey. Breakfast just arrived."

"Breakfast? Ten?" She squinted through her splayed fingers. "Gabe?"

"Oh, at the track since dawn."

"But—" Fully awake now, she dropped her hand. "That jerk! He promised he wouldn't go without me this morning. Of all mornings."

"Mmm." Naomi poured a second cup for her daughter. "According to him, you were an ill-disposed lump who told him to go away when he suggested it was time to get up."

"I did not." She took a sip of coffee. "Did I? He's probably making it up."

"He probably wanted you to get a little rest."

"He's my lover, not my keeper." Then she flushed. However unusual the relationship, Naomi was still her mother. She cleared her throat and sat down. "What are you doing here? I thought you'd be at the track."

"It's not a big race for us. A mile and a half." She shrugged and spread blackberry jam on a triangle of toast. "We'd just like to see High Water hold his own. I guess we could get lucky since the Arkansas colt is scratched."

"Scratched? When? What happened?"

"Oh, he pulled up lame in yesterday's workout. A sprained foreleg. I guess I forgot to tell you."

Pouting, Kelsey bit into a slice of bacon. "I feel like I'm outside the party, with my face pressed against the window while everyone else eats the cake."

"I'm sorry, honey. You'll just have to tolerate all of us being worried about you. When I think of what could have happened—" She sighed, spread more jam. "All right, all right, we won't get into it. I know that butt-out look on your face. I've seen it in the mirror often enough."

"It didn't mean butt out," Kelsey said with a smile. "It meant don't worry."

"It goes with the territory, even for a come-from-behind mother. So, eat your breakfast. I have instructions to see that you do."

"Gabe again."

"I imagine you know he loves you."

"Yes, I do."

"Do you know he's besotted?"

This time the smile crept onto Kelsey's face. "Do you think so?"

Naomi only laughed. "Never mind, you already know it. It's thrilling, isn't it, and terrifying to have a man tangled up over you that way."

"Yes. And twice as thrilling and terrifying when you're just as tangled up over him. I know it might seem soon to be this involved with someone after the divorce, but—"

"Kelsey, not only am I not in a position to criticize, but I'm going to point out that you and your ex-husband were separated for two years."

"Still—" Kelsey shook her head. "I'm second-guessing myself because it doesn't seem right. It only feels right." She toyed with her breakfast, hoping she wasn't choosing the wrong moment. "When you separated from Dad, did you still love him? I'm sorry." She lifted her eyes. "Someone said something to me yesterday that made me wonder. If you'd rather not answer, I understand."

"I told you once that whatever you asked I'd try to answer." But this one was hard. It wrenched at an old wound in the heart, an almost forgotten one. "Yes, I still loved him. I loved him for a long, long time after it was foolish to do so. And because I did I was angry, with him, with myself, and determined to prove it didn't matter."

"Is that why you..."

"Threw myself into parties?" Naomi continued. "Enjoyed fanning gossip about myself and other men? Courted small scandals? Yes, at least partly. I wasn't about to admit I'd failed. I wanted Philip to suffer, to have sleepless nights thinking about me reveling in my freedom. And because I undoubtedly succeeded in that, I drove him further and further away until what I wanted most was impossible for me to have."

"You wanted him back."

"Desperately. I was vain enough to think I could have him on my terms, and my terms only."

"And Alec Bradley?" She saw Naomi flinch, and forced herself to finish. "Was he someone you used to make Dad suffer?"

Naomi switched from coffee to water. "He was a kind of final gauntlet flung. A man with as sterling and blooded a pedigree as Philip's, but with a faintly unsavory reputation."

Kelsey's stomach knotted. She had to know, and to know, she had to ask. "Did you hire him?"

The discomfort in Naomi's eyes vanished. "Hire him?" she repeated, blank.

"I've heard that he put certain skills on the market." She gulped at her coffee. "So to speak."

The last reaction Kelsey had expected was laughter. But it came now, rich and delighted across the table. "Christ, what a thought. What a thought! The very last thing I wanted from Alec was stud service." Her amusement fled. "The very last thing."

"I'm sorry, that was a stupid question. I didn't mean it precisely as it sounded. I was thinking more of public displays than private ones."

"No, I didn't hire him. Though I did lend him money a time or two. He was always in between deals, you see," she said dryly. "Always in the midst of a little cash-flow problem. It might be vanity again, coming back to color memory, but as I recall, he pursued me. Not that I evaded," she added, and chose a single raspberry from a bowl. "I wanted the attention. I needed it, and he was very charming. Even when you knew differently, he could make you believe you were the only woman in the room. I was certainly aware of his reputation, of the fact that he could be bought. That added to the appeal, I suppose. The fact that he was with me, charming me, hoping to conquer me, because he couldn't help himself, did wonders for my ego." And a great deal of it, she remembered, had been simple ego. "In the end, he refused to accept, or wasn't able to accept, that I didn't choose to be conquered. And that's what killed him."

"But rape isn't about sex."

"No." She'd once thought it was, or had wanted to believe it was, because sex was easier. "He wanted to hurt me. To humiliate me. I've never really understood why he seemed so desperate that night. There wasn't passion in his eyes. There wasn't lust. I think I could have fought them, have outmaneuvered them. It was the desperation in his eyes that made me reach for the gun."

Naomi shuddered once, then cleared out her clogged lungs with a long quiet breath. "I'd forgotten that."

"I'm sorry I made you remember." Though she promised herself she would think everything through later, Kelsey covered Naomi's hand with hers. "Let it go. We'll both let it go. This is a day to look forward, not back. Why don't you come check out the outfit I bought for the race? If I don't get into it soon, we'll miss the first post."

24

Reno wore a slate-gray suit and maroon tie. His soft Italian boots shone like mirrors. The pencil-slim woman on his arm was a head taller than he, and kept her artfully painted face tilted toward the cameras.

He knew it was a pathetic cliché, the short man proving his masculinity by latching on to tall, stunning women. He didn't give a damn. Right now he needed something to prove his manhood, his worth. His *cojones.*

The sling on his arm precisely matched the silk of his tie. They were, he knew, the only silks he'd be wearing that day.

He smiled and preened for the cameras, as eager for the attention as the woman posed with him. Beneath the bravado, the quick, sassy answers about his next ride, his next season, he was a whirlwind of nerves and misery.

He watched the jockeys stride to the paddock, knew what each and every one of them was feeling, thinking. The concentration, the little mental games to keep the adrenaline up.

Only one would win, but others could prove their mettle with the ride. Some would come back, another race, another year. Others would fade—gain weight, lose interest, take a fall. They might choose to headline in the sticks, preferring second-rate wins to first-rate losses. The great ones would stay on one circuit, getting rich, drawing their own following, avoiding or overcoming the broken bones and bad spills.

The middling ones would move from track to track, following trainers, harassing agents, disappearing perhaps to resurface as a groom or valet, or as an assistant trainer on some tiny farm in the boondocks.

But none of that showed now. Now they were warriors, soldiers, showmen, eyes tensed and narrowed behind the plastic goggles, bodies lean and tight and limber under the silks, their feet encased in supple, dainty boots. The helmets were in place beneath the cloth Eton caps, the post-position number a cardboard garter on the arm.

Some of them would have risen at dawn to work their partners themselves. Others would have slept late, their relationship with their horse purely business and unemotional. Fear of the scale would have kept most of them away from food, seduced them into another hour sweating in steam.

Now they were weighed and ready. Reno watched them with grinding envy and despair.

He should be the one listening, with the air of narrowed focus, to the trainer's final instructions. It should be him garnering the praise, admiration, and hopes of the owners.

It should have been him flying down the track with the whip between his teeth.

His worst fear was that it would never be him again.

He forced himself forward, that quick, cocky smile fastened to his face.

"Miss Naomi."

"Reno." Automatically Naomi reached out, clasping his good arm. "You look great."

"I'd rather be wearing your colors."

"You will, soon." She glanced toward the woman he'd left entertaining some reporters. "Pretty girl. She looks familiar."

"You might have caught her in a couple of commercials. Shampoo and toothpaste, mostly. She's trying to break into movies." He shrugged his date off, and looked at the colt. "He'll run for you, Miss Naomi."

"Yes, I know he will."

"Just the man I wanted to see." Kelsey stepped forward. "I was hoping you'd have some time in the next couple of weeks to look at my yearling again, Reno. Honor needs a rider who can coax the best out of her."

His stomach churned once, hard. "Sure. Sure, I'll do that. I got nothing but time. I'm going to go give Joey a send-off."

"Did I say the wrong thing?" Kelsey murmured when he hurried off.

"I don't know." Distracted, Naomi looked toward Moses. "He's probably just strung out like everyone else."

"I'm sure you're right. I'm going to go wish Gabe good luck. Meet you in the box."

"Make history for me, Joey." Gabe shook hands with his jockey.

Joey flexed his fingers, cracked his knuckles. "I'm going to do that, Mr. Slater."

"You hold him back, like I told you," Jamison added. "I don't want him to drive until the head of the stretch. We're not looking for a record here. We're looking for a win."

"Me and Double here, we could get you both." He grinned and saluted when Reno joined them. "Get yourself a front-row seat, pal. And have some of that fancy champagne you like waiting."

"I'm going to do that." Reno kept his smile in place as he nodded to Gabe. "Good luck today, Mr. Slater. You've got a horse in a million here." His hand grew sweaty in his pocket. "I'd like a chance to go up on him myself one of these days."

"We'll talk about that when you're back to a hundred percent."

"A man gets spoiled riding the kind of horse I've been riding the past year or two." His eyes locked on Jamison's. "That's the way it is, isn't it, Jamie? We get spoiled."

"You could say that, Reno." Jamison kept a hand around Double's bridle.

"I won the Belmont for you two years back, remember? Everybody called it an upset, an apprentice jockey and a long-shot colt. But the truth was, it was my day. My horse. My race." Inside his pocket, his damp fingers opened and closed, opened and closed. "People forget, though. They forget all the races, all the wins. It's the Derby they remember. It's the Derby that puts you on top."

His hand trembled when he took it out of his pocket, when he laid it flat-palmed on the colt's neck. "Well, you got yourself the Derby, and a lot more." He forced a laugh. "Win or lose, they won't forget this Belmont. So you win it. You win it big."

"Riders up!"

At the call, Reno stepped back. His face was white, sheened with sweat. Turning quickly, he strode away. Kelsey snatched at his arm as he passed her.

"Reno?"

"I'm sorry" was all he said before shaking her off and rushing away from the paddock.

"Jockeys." Jamison launched Joey into the saddle. "Temperamental."

"He looked ill," Kelsey murmured, but there was no time to worry, barely any time to think. After the race, she promised herself, she'd try to find him and see if she could help. But now it was Gabe's moment. She wasn't about to have it spoiled.

"Even though you went off without me this morning, I'm going to wish you luck."

"It would have taken a crowbar to get you out of bed at dawn." And he'd wanted the morning to himself, to search for signs of his father. But he'd found none. More relaxed, Gabe tilted his head to study her. Her hair was scooped up under a white straw hat, its wide brim tipped flirtatiously over one eye. Her short, snug red dress was topped by a waist length white jacket. His pin galloped over her breast.

"Now that I see what a few hours' extra sleep did for you, I'm glad I didn't have a crowbar handy."

"A very clever way of sliding out of it, Slater."

"I thought so." He tucked her arm through his. "You're wearing my colors."

"Today they're the only colors worth wearing." She pressed a hand to her heart as they walked to his box. "Why aren't you nervous?"

"Nerves won't change anything."

"Tell that to my stomach," she muttered, and dug in her bag for her binoculars. "I'm beginning to think I want this more than you do."

"No, you don't."

He kept a hand on hers as the horses were led to the gate.

The odds were locked in, the betting windows closed. Overhead the sky was the clear dreamy blue of summer. The oval, the mile and a half of meticulously tended turf, was fast today. The crowd that massed in the grandstands was on its feet, setting up a steady drone punctuated by shouts and cheers.

It was easy to forget how huge it all was. For those who had seen the sport only on a television screen it would seem small, intimate, rather than the world that it was.

It had, through ambition, through luck, and through a steady inner drive, become Gabe's world. Now, all the work, the disappointments, the triumphs, and the hopes came down to this single race. This single horse.

He watched Double being loaded, and remembered the night he had been born. The way the laboring mare had wheezed, the way the wind had blown, keening against the walls of the foaling barn. The snow and sleet hurling down, the endless wait while the mare strained and labored.

Then the first sight, the terrifyingly fragile legs stabbing their way free in a gush of blood. And the mare's cry, eerily human, heralding that last pang of birth.

That small, wet life had lain on the soiled straw, taking the first breath that would lead Double or Nothing, out of Bold Courage, to the starting gate at Belmont Park, Long Island.

And now, three years later, Gabe remembered the thrill that had passed through him, arrow bright, when he had looked into the foal's eyes.

"I love that horse."

He didn't realize he'd spoken aloud until Kelsey's fingers tightened on his. "I know you do."

The gate opened with a scream of metal. Almost at once there was a gasp from the crowd as Double swerved to the right from his number six post position, nearly unseating his rider. Whatever had spooked him, the disastrous move had placed him behind a wall of horses with his jockey fighting for balance.

All of Jamison's careful instructions on how to run the race became useless in the space of a heartbeat. Joey's only goal now was to get Double or Nothing back into the Belmont.

There was a split-second decision, whether to fight through the field or go around it. Rider and horse made it together, swinging wide, in a move—depending on the outcome—that would be seen as either valiant or foolish. As if he knew what had to be done, the colt bore down.

He charged down the field, eating up the distance with wild speed. When they passed the wire the first time he was a length behind the leader, and gaining.

From his position in the box, Gabe kept his binoculars in place. He was focused on only one horse. The race itself was nearly forgotten, shadowed under the bright flash of admiration. There was more than beauty there. There was courage. Win or lose, he wouldn't forget it.

The half mile went in forty-six seconds flat, with Double and the leader pulling steadily away from the pack. The crowd roared, a frenzy of sound. But Gabe heard only Kelsey's voice beside him, quietly murmuring encouragement. It might have been only the two of them, standing hand in hand, watching a single horse.

At the far turn Double made his challenge, battling for advantage as they hit the top of the stretch. It was here, in its demanding, heartbreaking homestretch, that the Belmont tested valor. The Kentucky-bred colt was rallying from behind, shooting toward the leaders like a spear.

But it was too late. What had been born in the Longshot colt that windy night in late winter, what Gabe had seen in his eyes during those first wonderful moments of life, drove him faster than the whip laid across his back.

With heart, with honor, he thundered across the wire two lengths in the lead to take the Belmont Stakes, and the Triple Crown.

For a moment, Gabe could only stare. The emotions swirling inside him came too fast, too hard to sift out only the thrill of victory. That was his horse, cantering easily now, with its rider high in the irons. That was his dream, covered with sweat and dirt and glory. Whatever happened now, no one could ever take away from him, or the spectacular colt, this dazzling moment.

"That's a hell of a horse," Gabe murmured in a voice that felt rusty. Dazed, he looked down at Kelsey, saw her cheeks wet with tears. "That's one hell of a horse."

"Yes." Even as the tears rolled, a laugh bubbled up in her throat. She lifted her arms, circled Gabe's neck. "Congratulations, Slater. You've done it."

"Christ." No amount of control could hold back the foolish grin that spread over his face. "Jesus Christ, we did it!" He swung her up and around, oblivious of the cameras. She was still laughing when he covered her mouth with his.

In his room a few hundred miles away, Rich stared at the television screen. He hadn't gone to New York. With what he'd expected to happen, it was smarter, safer, for him to stay behind.

He nodded as the cameras cut from the victorious colt to its owner. "Enjoy it while you can, boy," he muttered, and toasted himself with twelve-year-old scotch. A smirk twisted his lips over the celebrational kiss, the announcer's breathless voice identifying Gabriel Slater and Kelsey Byden as very friendly rivals.

Rich sat back and waited for the chaos. The colt would be led to the spit bucket, as he would be after any race. And then, Rich thought, and then Gabe wouldn't be smiling so big. Even better this way, he decided. Even better to snatch away the prize after it had been granted.

Things had worked out perfectly. Thanks to Naomi's pretty little girl. If she hadn't come out to the barn that night and interrupted what was planned for the colt, he'd never have raced.

But he had raced, and he'd won. Now, moments from now, the shocking announcement would be made that Double or Nothing had an illegal drug in his system.

Not only would Gabe lose, but he would face scandal, derision, and shame.

Preparing for his own victory, Rich topped off his drink. Liquor slopped, spilled by a jerk of his hand as the official announcement was made.

Nine. Five. Two.

His shocked brain didn't take in the nattering about purses and payoffs. He gaped as the screen filled with the horse and rider, each blanketed with white carnations. He saw Gabe, his arm possessively around Kelsey's shoulders, congratulating his rider, then lean in, as sentimental as a movie cowboy, to kiss the sweaty colt.

His glass struck the screen, and both shattered. The air reeked of liquor as he lunged out of the chair. For a minute he lost his mind, kicking and beating the television until his knuckles ran red, then he heaved it off the table. His only motive was to destroy it, to somehow destroy the machine that showed him such images.

When he finally stopped, gasping and drained, the air stank of smoke and scotch and his own violent sweat. His knuckles were bleeding, and his breath was coming in shuddering rasps. He tripped over a broken chair and righted the bottle of scotch. Most had pooled on the rug, but there was enough to clear the bile from his throat when he chugged from the bottle. Enough to clear his mind again.

Heads will roll, he promised himself. And since he apparently could trust no one to carry out a simple task, he'd have to take care of things himself.

In the week that followed Double's Triple Crown win, there was barely time to think. The routine at Three Willows had to continue, despite the celebrity of their neighbor. The racing season didn't stop at Belmont, nor did the daily care and training of horses allow for sitting on laurels.

And Kelsey had her own ambitions, not the least of which was to mold her own champion. She'd been given her opportunity with Honor, and she was determined to make the most of it.

She had not forgotten her goal of piecing together the puzzle of the past. Charles Rooney might have refused to take or return her calls, but she had every intention of running him to ground. He would talk to her again eventually. She would visit Captain Tipton again as well. And if necessary, she would go to her father and ask him to relive those months of his life day by day until a clear picture emerged.

For the one that was taking shape now was of a woman who had loved her husband. One who had certainly made mistakes, mistakes of pride and vanity and stubbornness in trying to force his hand. But no matter how coolly, how calmly she tried, Kelsey had yet to find the piece that turned a willful, even reckless young woman into a murderer.

"Hey, sis."

"Channing." Kelsey turned, sponge in hand, to kiss him. "I haven't had five minutes to tell you how glad I am you're here."

"Despite the ache in my back, I've only been here a couple of hours." His shirt was already streaked with sweat. "Moses put me to work so fast it feels as if I never left."

"I didn't think you were coming back." With careful strokes, Kelsey sponged off her yearling's face. "We're midway through June."

"It took me a while to work it out."

"Candace is still against your being here?"

"We can safely say she's not too happy with me. We had a hell of a battle."

"I'm sorry.

"No, it was good. A lot came out that had been festering. In me, anyway. She wanted me to carry on the family tradition. All my life that's been a given. I'd be a brilliant surgeon like my father, like his father, and so forth. She expected it. I let her expect it."

"It isn't what you want?"

"I'm going into veterinary medicine." His eyes held steady, as if he expected a protest, or worse, a quick, indulgent laugh. Instead, she stepped forward and kissed both cheeks.

"Good."

"That's it?"

"I could give you the routine about how impossible and how frustrating it is to try to live up to other people's expectations. Especially family. In the past few months I've had firsthand experience with that. But I figure you already know. She'll come around, Channing. She loves you, and under it all, she only wants what you want."

"Maybe." He shuffled straw under his foot. "I hated fighting with her. I guess I hate knowing I'd have backed down if the Prof hadn't stood up for me."

"Dad? Really?"

"It was like having the Seventh Cavalry charge in—without the bugles and blazing guns." He grinned. "He just talked, in that slow, patient way of his. I've never seen him go against her that way. I think it was the shock that he took my part instead of hers that turned the tide."

"He loves you too." Nibbling her lip, she went back to her work. "Are they having problems, Channing?"

"Things are a little strained between them. But with me here, they'll have the time and the privacy to work it out. Anyway, she blames you more than the Prof."

Kelsey made a face. "I guess I'd better patch things up there."

"Mom's not the one to hold a grudge. Not for long, anyway. Her sense of order's been shaken, that's all. It's going to take her a while to get used to it."

"Excuse me." Reno stood at the opening of the box.

"Reno, hi." Kelsey shifted, her hands still busy brushing the yearling. "You remember Channing, my brother."

"Sure. How's it going?"

"Good. How's the shoulder?"

Instinctively, Reno rotated it. "It's coming along. I'll be ready to get up in a couple of weeks. I've got some offers to ride the European circuit this season."

"I heard Moses mention it," Kelsey said. "We're sending High Water over in a few weeks. I hope you take him up on it."

"Might. That's Honor, isn't it? Naomi's Honor."

"It sure is. What do you think of her?"

"I'll let you two talk horse," Channing cut in. "If Moses catches me loitering, he'll dock my pay. Good seeing you, Reno."

"Yeah. See you around." He stepped into the box and crouched. A Thoroughbred's legs always came first. He said nothing, circled the horse, ran his hands along the chest, the flanks, the withers before coming around to examine the eyes and teeth.

"She's a pretty one," Reno said at last. "Terrific form, lots of heart room. You've had her in the gate?"

"Yeah. She doesn't have any trouble there. She spooks sometimes, but since we started using a shadow roll, she's settled." The colt nudged her arm, and obliging, Kelsey took a carrot out of her pocket. "She's gentle, but there's fire in there. Moses thinks we should try her out in a couple of races next year. Are you interested?"

"She's a pretty one," Reno said again, and felt twin tremors of hope and despair. "Why do you want to put me up on her?"

"I've seen you ride, for one. And I like the fact that you don't just mount a horse for a race. You come to workouts, you come to the barn. You treat it like a partnership." She hesitated, nuzzling the horse. "I know you loved Pride, Reno. It showed, the way you felt about him, and how you thought about him. That's the kind of rider I want for Honor."

He looked away, fighting the urge to curl up in the straw and weep. Her words were like small, sharp knives slicing at him. "I did love that horse." He couldn't steady his voice, and gave up trying. "He'd have done anything for me. He broke his heart for me."

"Reno, you can't blame yourself for what happened."

"I wouldn't have hurt him. How were we supposed to know the race would kill him?" He stared blindly into Kelsey's face. "How were we supposed to know?"

"You couldn't," she said gently. "Sooner or later we'll find out who wanted to hurt him."

He let out a trembling breath. "Sooner or later." He took a step in retreat. "That's a fine horse."

"Will you ride her?"

Reno gave her a look of such crushing despair that she moved toward him. But as she reached out, he made one low, animal sound in his throat, and fled.

25

"I tell you, Gabe, it broke my heart."

Kelsey cupped her wineglass in both hands and tucked her legs up under her on his long, comfortable sofa. It was a lovely evening, the doors and windows wide open to welcome the flower-drenched breeze. But she could still see Reno's face, the utter hopelessness of it, washed in the striped sunlight of Honor's box.

"He needs to get up again."

Gabe was stretched out on the same sofa, puffing smoke at the ceiling, his feet in Kelsey's lap. It wasn't that he didn't sympathize with Reno's plight, but he was, quite simply, exhausted. Who could have known that the rapid-fire round of publicity, meetings, phone calls, and requests would be more tiring than a week's ditch digging?

At the moment he'd have preferred a shovel and a sweaty back to the mind-numbing figures and futures tallied by lawyers, accountants, and brokers.

Just that afternoon he'd had to turn down an offer for the rights to his life story, and Double's, for a TV movie-of-the-week.

"I don't know," Kelsey continued, while Gabe's thoughts wandered. "I thought that, too, that he just needed to get up for another race. Until . . ." She rested her head against a cushion. Gabe had put on Mozart, for her. She knew he preferred basic rock or the wail of blues to the classic melding of piano and orchestra. "It wasn't just an altruistic gesture, you know, my asking him to ride Honor. I want the best, but I did think it would help him. Instead, I made things worse."

"You can't know that."

"You didn't see his face. When I think it through, I know what losing Pride did to me. How much it hurt. And even though I loved that colt, I couldn't have been nearly as attached as Reno was. He's blaming himself, Gabe, because he was on the colt when they went down." She toyed with her wine. "I'm thinking of asking Naomi if she could persuade him to find some therapy. Do you think . . ." She glanced toward Gabe. His eyes were closed. "Am I keeping you up?"

"Sorry." He opened one eye. "I was drifting."

"No, I'm sorry." She shifted, began to rub his feet. "You're worn out. I saw that when I walked in the door. I should be asking you how your meetings went today instead of trying out my Psych 101 theories on you."

"If you keep rubbing my feet, you can try out anything you want on me."

She chuckled, then set her glass aside so she could do a better job of it. "So, how did the meetings go? Should we be celebrating a new record for syndication?"

"No." It was fascinating, he thought, and rewarding, to discover just how many erogenous zones there were on the sole of a foot. "I'm not syndicating Double."

"You're not?" Her hands paused. "But, Gabe, the last set of figures you mentioned were astronomical."

"I don't want to share him." His eyes opened again, fastened on hers. "I listened to all the advice, the offers, the numbers, and I decided to do what I want. When something's mine, it's mine."

"That's a very impractical, emotional decision."

"What's your point?"

She shook her head. "Well, there goes my plan to scoop up some shares of a Triple Crown winner."

"That depends." He used all of his willpower to keep his muscles relaxed, to keep his voice light. "You can have half of him."

"Half?" Her brows rose as she pressed her fingers to Gabe's instep. "I think that's a bit more than I can afford."

"A lot of people will tell you you're right. You can't afford the terms."

That had her lips moving into a pout. "I think I'm a better judge of what I can or can't afford. Okay. What are the terms?"

"There's just one." His eyes flashed to hers. "All you have to do is marry me."

Reno went to the barn first. The barn that had once been Cunningham's. No one stopped him. The guards, the grooms all knew Reno. He had a meeting with Jamison, he told them, and they accepted it. They accepted him.

He had a need to see horses again, to smell them, to touch them. He did give some thought to going to Jamison, to pouring out body and soul. But what difference would it make? Nothing could be changed. Nothing could be fixed.

He'd spent a great deal of time during the last weeks blasting out scattershots of blame. But in the end, he understood that they all ricocheted back to him. He'd been the one who had taken the syringe. He'd been the one to plunge that poison into a beautiful, courageous athlete.

It didn't matter how the instrument had come into his hands. He understood that now. He accepted that now. He'd murdered something he'd loved, and in doing so, he'd destroyed himself.

Like father, like son. Reno leaned against a patient mare and wept. It came through the blood, he thought. It came through the breeding. The excuses he'd used were smoke and mirrors. Had he really believed he'd been trying to avenge the father he'd never known? That was the weapon used against him as surely as he'd used the needle on the horse.

Weak. He was weak as his father had been weak. And damned, as his father had been damned.

So, there was only one thing left to do.

He would end it as his father had ended it. Complete the cycle begun by a man he'd known only through photographs and grainy news clips. The man whose ghost he had honored above even his own dignity.

As if in a dream, Reno left the barn and the soothing scent of horses. He walked to the tack room. The tack room that had once been Cunningham's.

It was a full ten seconds before Kelsey could find her voice. It was, she supposed, a typical-enough proposal from a man like Gabe. Challenging, cool-blooded, and risky. Very deliberately she shifted his foot out of her lap and picked up her wine.

"If I marry you, I get a half share of Double."

"That's right." He'd been expecting, at least hoping for, a different kind of reaction. "A half share of Longshot, and all that goes with it."

She sipped, studying him. "And a half share of you, Slater?"

That irritated him. The amused patience in her voice, in her eyes. He swung his legs off the couch and stood. "I'm not Wade, Kelsey. We go into this, we take each other whole. This won't be a tidy, make-the-best-of-a-bad-hand deal with an option to fold."

"I see. Once I ante up, I'm stuck."

"That's it exactly. Since I'm naming the stakes, I'll show you the cards I'm playing with. I want you. That's my high card. It's going to take a lot for you to beat that. Maybe you figure the odds are tilted. You got stung once before, and you don't want it to happen again. But this is a different game, with different players, and from where I'm standing, the stakes are a lot higher."

She kept her eyes on her wine. And he'd said she couldn't bluff, she thought with some pride. Still, she knew better than to let him get a good look at her face until she was ready to call.

"You think I'd back off from marriage, shy away from a full commitment because I lost once before? That's incredibly insulting. Nearly as insulting as this half-assed proposal you're stumbling through."

"You want flowers and candlelight, a ring in my pocket?" He'd meant to give them to her. The fact that he'd rushed his fences only infuriated him more. "I'm not giving you anything he gave you."

Her eyes lifted then, with just enough temper in them to mask her heart. "Oh, now who's hobbled by the past, Slater?" She slapped her glass on the table and rose. "Why don't you just drag me off to—to Vegas? That would be a perfect milieu, wouldn't it? We can say our I dos over a crap table."

He nodded stiffly. "Fine. If that's what you want."

"What I want is a simple, straightforward question to which I can give a simple, straightforward answer. So, you can either ask me, or you can go to hell."

Narrow-eyed, he studied her, but for once he couldn't read her face. How could he, he realized, when for the first time in his life someone else held all the cards?

"Will you marry me?"

"Yes," she said. "Absolutely."

Gauging her, he let out some of the breath he hadn't been aware he'd been holding. "That's it?"

"That's it," she agreed. "So, who gets to rake in the chips?"

His lips curved slowly. "This seems like a good time to start splitting the pot." He stepped toward her, combing his hands through her hair, taking a firm hold. "I love you, Kelsey."

"You must, or you'd never have flubbed that so badly."

"Flubbed, hell." He kissed her, hard. "I've got you, don't I?"

"Yeah." With a laugh, she threw her arms around him. "Yeah, you do."

He scooped her off her feet. "About that trip to Vegas."

"No."

"You're not considering the possibilities." With only one goal in mind now, he headed for the stairs. "It's quick, convenient, colorful. We could spend our wedding night in a big heart-shaped bed under a full-length mirror."

"As appealing as that sounds, I'm going to pass. Why don't we—"

The crash at the back of the house had Gabe dropping her to her feet. "Stay here," he ordered, and he shoved her toward the stairs. Before he could get halfway toward the sound, one of his grooms stumbled in, white-faced and wide-eyed.

"Mr. Slater. Jesus, Mr. Slater, you've got to come. It's Reno. Oh, my God, I think he's dead."

There was no doubt of that. Though someone had had the courage and compassion to cut him down from where he had swung from a rope tied to a beam, there was no mistaking the sight of death.

Kelsey couldn't take her eyes from it, the limp body decked out in riding silks, the horrible angle of the head with its livid bruises around the neck.

"Call the police," Gabe ordered. He turned Kelsey around roughly. "Get out of here. Go home."

"No. I'm staying. I'm all right. I'm staying with you."

He didn't have time to argue. "Wait outside, goddammit!" he exploded when she remained stubbornly beside him. "Wait outside!"

She only shook her head. She did look away from Reno and found her eyes locked on Jamison's. His were glazed, with devastation or shock, she couldn't be sure. But she walked to him, gently leading him to a chair.

"Sit down now, Jamie."

"I found him. Somebody told me he was around and looking for me. I don't know why I came in here, I don't know why, except I did. And I found him. Just like last time. I found him."

"Last time?"

"Benny. Just like Benny. Oh, God." He buried his face in his hands. "Oh, God, when will it stop?"

"There's a note, Mr. Slater." A young stableboy crept closer. He whispered, as though death had ears. "There's a note on the bench there. I didn't touch it," he added. "They always say you're not supposed to touch anything."

"That's right. Go wait outside for the police, will you?"

"Sure, Mr. Slater." He hesitated. "We cut him down," he blurted out. "Maybe we weren't supposed to, but we couldn't just leave him like that. We had to get him down."

"You did the right thing." Gabe put a hand on the boy's shoulder. "Wait outside now." Already dreading what he would find, Gabe walked over to the bench, to the single sheet of paper, handwritten.

I'm sorry. It's the coward's way, but the only way I know. I'll never ride a horse again. I killed the best horse I ever had under me. As God is my witness, I didn't know it was a lethal dose. It was supposed to disqualify him, that's all. And settle a score. I never believed my father was guilty. Until now. What he did, I did. What he did, I'll do. Bad blood. There's no fighting bad blood.

Gabe turned from the note and looked at his trainer. "Did you know, Jamie?"

Tears dripped onto Jamison's hands as he nodded. "I knew. I knew Reno was Benny Morales's son. God help him."

The pieces fit perfectly once they were turned to the light. Benny Morales, disgraced, despairing, had hanged himself, leaving behind a young, pregnant widow. She'd fled Virginia and had settled in Kansas, secluding herself and the infant son she bore from the scandal.

When Reno was five, she married again. Reno took his stepfather's name, but he never stopped dreaming of his real father. From Benny he inherited his small stature, his quick hands, and his love of horses. So he followed in his father's footsteps, working his way up from hot-walker to exercise boy and to apprentice jockey.

Obsessed with his father's memory, he moved to Virginia. He trusted only Jamison, his father's closest friend, with his secret. And Jamison kept it.

"He had scrapbooks on his father." Two days after the suicide, Rossi shared some of the details with Gabe. "Almost a library of them. Several of them were dedicated to the accusations made against his father, the investigation, and the suicide. His mother and stepfather are coming out today from Kansas to claim the body. I can tell you from my talk with her that she supports the fact that he had an unhealthy obsession with his father. Reno saw him as a hero and a scapegoat, and he was determined to right the old wrong."

"By drugging the Chadwick colt," Gabe said softly. "Disqualifying it from the Derby."

"Morales was riding for the Chadwicks when he took the fall that kept him out of racing for more than a year." Rossi didn't need his notes, but he flipped through his book out of habit. "Then, when the horse, Sun Spot, had to be put down at Keeneland, Matthew Chadwick was one of the most outspoken against Benny Morales. He had, after all, lost a valuable investment due to the tampering."

"Bad blood." Gabe set his teeth. "There's still a matter of where Reno got the drug. I think we can figure he injected the horse sometime after weigh-in and before they were loaded in the gate. Most probably while they were in the tunnel. But how did he get it, and from whom?"

"It doesn't seem it would be that difficult for a man in his position, Mr. Slater. Reno'd been around tracks since he was a teenager. He'd have known the right people. And the wrong ones."

"If he'd gotten the drug himself, he wouldn't have mistaken the dose. He didn't intend to kill the horse, Lieutenant. That's clear to me."

"He made a mistake."

"Or he was duped. Have you looked up my father?"

"This is a real family affair, isn't it? No," he said when Gabe remained silent. "He's moved out of his rooms, no forwarding address. The only reason I have to pursue that particular thread is your instinct. I'm trusting that, Mr. Slater. If he shows up around the track, anywhere in the area, we'll bring him in for questioning."

"He'll show. He's too vain to know when to cut his losses."

He hadn't believed in his father's guilt. Kelsey stood at her bedroom window, fresh from a late-afternoon shower, and stared out over the hills. Reno hadn't believed in his father's guilt and so had spent most of his life pursuing that ghost. Wanting to vindicate it, to avenge it. In the end, he had discovered something about the man whose blood ran through him, and about himself, that he had not been able to live with.

It was always a risk to pry open doors to the past. She was encouraging Gabe to shrug off his own yoke of inheritance and be who he was. Yet she couldn't.

Wasn't she risking everything she'd built with Naomi over the past months by probing, poking, prodding at that door? And when she opened it, when she found what was lurking in the dust behind it, would she be able to live with it?

Let it go, she ordered herself. Why pick at something everyone wants locked? She had her whole life ahead of her. A life with Gabe. Fresh new beginnings everywhere. All she had to do was turn away from the shadows and accept what was.

"Miss Kelsey?"

Kelsey answered without looking around. "Yes, Gertie?"

"Mr. Lingstrom's office is on the phone. He wanted to speak with Miss Naomi, but since she's out, he'll talk to you."

"All right, Gertie. I'll take it downstairs."

She took the call in her mother's office, on the business line. She listened, managed to make the appropriate comments. When the call was complete, Kelsey replaced the receiver carefully. She was still sitting at the desk when Naomi walked in.

"God save me from those foolish, time-wasting luncheons. I don't know what makes me think I'm obliged to go. The only bright spot was that I happened to go into this little boutique near the restaurant when it was over. There was the most incredible dress, absolutely perfect for a simple garden wedding. They'll hold it for twenty-four hours if you . . ."

She trailed off, the impetus that had carried her straight through the house to her daughter fading. Kelsey was staring at her, her hands locked together tightly on the desk.

"What is it?" Naomi asked. "Is it about Reno? Is there something else?"

"No, it's not about Reno." She watched the relief flutter over Naomi's face. "Your lawyer just phoned."

"Oh?" Fresh nerves had Naomi lifting a hand to toy with the starshaped pin at her lapel.

"He wanted you to know that the documents you requested he draft are ready for your signature." She paused. "The ones transferring half of Three Willows into my name."

"Well, then. That's fine."

"Why would you do something like that?"

"It's something your grandfather and I discussed before he died. It was always my intention, Kelsey, and his. I'm just making it legal."

"Without telling me."

"I didn't want it to have the tone of an obligation," Naomi said carefully. "On either my part or yours. There hasn't been a lot I've been able to give you. This is something I can. My father left the when and how up to me, but basically this comes down to you through him. I felt this was the right time, and the right way. This isn't a rope to tie you here, Kelsey. Or to tie you to me."

"You must know I'm already tied here, and to you. You gambled that I would be when you asked me to come."

"Yes, I did. I couldn't guess, or even hope that you'd feel anything for me. But I was sure you'd feel it for Three Willows."

"One's very much the same as the other."

A ghost of a smile moved over Naomi's lips. "So I've been told."

"It's very difficult to love and respect one without loving and respecting the other." She rose, holding out her hands across the desk. "I haven't been able to do that. I don't see why I should."

"Not everyone would have given me the chance." Naomi took Kelsey's hands, and gripped hard.

Not everyone had, Kelsey thought. But she would take the risk, and try to change that.

It was nearly five when she pulled up in Tipton's driveway behind his dusty late-model pickup. The neighbor's dog sent up a din, racing back and forth along the chain-link fence that separated the lawns as if to warn her his ground was sacrosanct. A woman leaned out of an upstairs window and shouted the dog down before eyeing Kelsey.

"Looking for Jim?"

"Yes, I am. Is he home?"

"In the shop." She pointed, shook her head. "Can't you hear the racket?"

Indeed she could, now that the dog had quieted to low, throaty snarls. She followed the high-pitched whine of a power saw into the backyard. There was a small shed, one that could be put together from a kit bought at most lumberyards.

Kelsey knocked on a door that hung crookedly on its jamb. At the slight tap it swung wide and banged against the inner wall.

Tipton stood at a bench, safety glasses and ear protectors in place, his Orioles cap turned into the catcher's position. Sawdust flew as he sheared off a two-by-four. Kelsey decided it was safer for both of them if she waited for the blade to stop whirling.

"Gotcha, you son of a bitch," Tipton muttered as a chunk of wood hit the ground.

"Captain Tipton?"

He whirled around, looking very much like something out of a B horror movie, his eyes shaded by amber-toned plastic, his ear protectors bulging and gray, and red splotches dotting his shirt.

"Oh, God, you've cut yourself."

"Where? What?" Alarmed, Tipton checked to make sure all his fingers were in place as Kelsey dashed across the shed. "Oh, this." Grinning, he patted his chest. "Cranberry juice. The wife doesn't like me to work in good clothes."

Kelsey leaned weakly against the bench and swore.

"Scared you, huh?" Still chuckling, he pulled off his ear guards and pushed up his goggles. "Want to sit down?"

"No, I'm fine."

"I'm building some shelves." He picked up a wide, flat board, sighted down it for warping. "The wife and I have this little game. I build shelves and she fills them up with doodads. Keeps us both happy."

"That's nice. I wonder if you could spare a few minutes."

"I might be able to squeeze you in. Lemonade?" Without waiting for her assent, he hefted a big plastic jug and poured two paper cups. "You had some more trouble out your way, I hear."

"Yes. It's an odd coincidence, isn't it? That Reno should so completely mirror his father's life. And death."

"The world's full of odd coincidences, Ms. Byden." But he wasn't happy about this one. He'd completed his background check on Benny Morales, and had gathered all the details only hours before Reno's suicide. Another twenty-four hours, he thought, and events might have taken a different turn. "It solves one of your problems, though. You know who did your horse."

"Reno didn't mean to kill him. I'm certain of that." She sipped the lemonade, found it tart and swimming with pulp. His wife, she thought, must squeeze her own. "Someone used him, Captain. There's a lot of that in the world, too. People using people."

"Can't argue with you there."

"My mother was using Alec Bradley to make my father jealous, to prove her own independence, even to incite gossip. I wonder, though, how had Alec Bradley been using her?"

The girl had a nice, tidy mind, Tipton decided. He picked up a square of sandpaper and began to rub it over a curved slat of wood. "She's a beautiful woman."

"This isn't about sex, Captain. Rape isn't about sex."

He huffed out a breath. "Maybe not. We only ever had her word about the attempted rape."

"I believe her. So did you. Did you ever ask yourself why—if she was telling the truth—why Alec Bradley chose that particular night to attack her? They'd been seeing each other for weeks. She's not the kind of woman who could continue to see a man who abused her. Or who threatened to abuse her."

Tipton continued to sand the wood. It would be a rocking chair for his granddaughter on her birthday in September.

"If she was telling the truth, Ms. Byden. If. He'd been drinking. They'd had a public scene. She'd given him his walking papers and a faceful of French champagne. That kind of combination could push a certain kind of man in the wrong direction." He blew lightly at the wood dust. "But, like I said, there was no evidence to support it."

"Her nightgown was torn. She had bruises." Kelsey let out an impatient sound at his shrug. "All right, as easily self-inflicted as not. But if we say not, if we believe not, how do you prove it? You checked his background, certainly. If there was another woman, someone else he'd abused or attacked, that would weigh on Naomi's side, wouldn't it?"

"I never found one. A lot of rapes go unreported. Especially the kind you're talking about. The date-rape kind."

He didn't like that particular term. Date rape, acquaintance rape. It made the vicious act seem much too friendly.

"And back twenty years ago, people had a different attitude. Bradley had a reputation, but violence wasn't part of it. He had some heavy debts," Tipton continued, almost to himself. "About the time he started seeing your mother, he paid off some of them. About twenty thousand dollars' worth. But he needed at least that much again to pull himself out."

"So he needed money. My mother had money."

"He never asked her for more than a couple of grand." Tipton set the wood aside. "That's her own statement. He never asked her for big money. And that's one of the things I found odd. Because it was his pattern to sponge off women."

"He might have been biding his time. Or . . . he might have been expecting it from another source."

"That was a thought." Tipton pulled a Baby Ruth bar from his back pocket, snapped it in half, and offered a share to Kelsey. "I never tracked it down, though. I always wondered where he got that twenty grand. Could've won it at the track. But the word there was that he lost as much as he won, and most of it was penny-ante. He talked big," Tipton added with a mouthful of chocolate. "Let a lot of people know he had a deal in the works. Just talk, as far I could find."

"But if he did, if it had something to do with my mother." Kelsey began to pace the shop as she worked it out. "She was through with him, told him it was over. So he panicked, tried to force her. If she cut him loose, the deal was dead. He needed money. A lot of people knew he needed money. But who would have used him to get to my mother?"

As the answer swam into her mind, she stopped. The hand holding the paper cup tightened, crushing it into a damp blob.

"That's the trouble when you turn over rocks," Tipton said kindly. "You hardly ever like what you find under them. I never linked your father to Alec Bradley. And I tried. I subpoenaed your father's bank records, went over them with a fine-tooth comb looking for that twenty-thousand-dollar payment. He was clean. Phone records, too. No calls came from or to Alec Bradley's number from the house in Potomac or his office at the university."

"He would never have done such a thing." But Kelsey's lips were stiff and cold. "My father would never have done such a thing."

"The way it looks, you're right. Of course that puts the heat back on your mother."

"There's another answer." Kelsey whirled back. "I know there's another answer."

"You want another answer," Tipton said gently. "Maybe you'll find it. Maybe you won't like it." He sighed and reached out to take the squashed cup from her hand. "I only had one thing linking Philip Byden with what happened that night at Three Willows. That was Charles Rooney."

26

It was obvious something was wrong. She'd come to him after dark, saying only that she wanted to be with him. Gabe wanted to believe it was as simple as that. As true as that.

But her eyes were distant, her smile too bright, with strain at the edges. Her needs, always a delight to him, were frenzied. She'd torn into sex with a wild abandon that couldn't quite mask the desperation.

As if she'd been purging herself, he thought now that she lay quiet beside him. His body had responded, and in that most elemental link they had met, clashed, and joined. But, he thought now, as the silence stretched out between them, neither of them had been satisfied.

"Are you ready now?" he asked her.

She turned her head, looking for a cooler place to rest her cheek on the warm sheets. "Ready?"

"To tell me what's eating you."

"What should be eating me?" Her voice was dull, tired. "A man I knew and like killed himself a few days ago."

"This isn't about Reno. It's about you."

She turned on her back, staring up at the dark skylight. No moon tonight, she thought. The clouds masked it like smoke. It really took very little to hide so much.

"He loved his father," she began. "He didn't even know him, but he loved him. Believed in him. Everything Reno did circled back to that love and belief. Blind, unquestioning love and belief." She sighed once. "And when he realized it had been misplaced, at least the belief had been misplaced, he couldn't live with it."

She shifted restlessly, the sound of her skin against the sheets a whisper in the darkness.

"It would have been better if he'd turned away from it, wouldn't it? Better for him, better for everyone, if he'd left what happened all those years ago alone. What's to be proved, Gabe, what's to be solved by insisting on looking back?"

"It depends on how badly you need to look. And what you find." He touched her hair, let it sift through his fingers. "This is about you, isn't it, Kelsey? About you and Naomi."

"She considers it over. Why can't I? There's no turning back the clock, giving her back those years we lost. That we both lost. She killed Alec Bradley. I should accept that. I shouldn't let it matter so much why."

Kelsey moved again, pushing herself up, drawing in her knees, circling them with her arms in a move of such poignant defense it tore at his heart.

"Then let it go."

"Let it go," she repeated. "It's the sensible thing. After all, whatever wrong she did, whatever mistakes she made, she's paid for. I didn't know her then, or don't remember knowing her. What makes me think I can go back and sort it out? Or that I should? She's happy. My father's happy. Neither of them would thank me for digging into it. I've no right to scrape open old wounds just to satisfy my own ridiculous need for truth, for justice."

Squeezing her eyes tight, she pressed her face to her knees. "They're not always the same, are they? Truth and justice?"

"They should be. One of the most admirable things about you is that you want them to be." He brushed a hand over her shoulder, felt the knots of tension, and began to massage them out. "What stirred this up, Kelsey?"

She took a long, steadying breath and told him about her visit to Tipton. He didn't interrupt, and tried to deal with his own knee-jerk anger that she had gone without him.

"And now you're worried that your father was somehow involved."

"He couldn't have been." Her head shot up. In the dark her eyes shone with defiance and a plea for understanding. "He couldn't have been, Gabe. You don't know him."

"No, I don't." Annoyed with himself, Gabe drew away and reached for a cigar on the night table. "We've skipped that little amenity."

She passed a weary hand through her hair. Somehow she'd managed to hurt him. "This has all happened so fast, everything between you and me has happened at double time. And the situation, my family situation, is on very rocky ground. It isn't that I've kept you from him."

"Forget it." He snapped on his lighter and scowled into the flame. "Forget it," he said again, more quietly. "It's hardly the point. And it's not what's annoying me. I would have gone with you today. I should have been with you."

"It was an impulse." That was the truth, she thought, but only half the truth. "Maybe I wanted to go alone. Maybe I needed to. I don't want to be protected, Gabe. All my life I've been protected without even knowing it. I can't live the rest of it that way."

"There's a difference between being protected and being supported. I need you to lean on me, Kelsey. Just like I need to know I can lean on you."

After a moment she took his hand. "Do you have to be right?"

"I prefer it that way." He lifted her fingers to his lips. "What do you want to do?"

"What I want is to forget it. To let it all alone and go from here. But I can't. I have to know. And when I do I have to live with whatever I find out." She measured her palm against his, then laced fingers. "I'm going to go see Rooney tomorrow afternoon. Will you come with me?"

More lies, Kelsey thought. Of the little white variety.

"You're going to love the dress." Naomi held out the pale lavender business card. "The clerk's name's on the back. Ilsa. They do alterations right there."

"That's great."

"If it doesn't suit you, I'm sure you'll find something else. It's a wonderful shop. Oh, and I spoke to the caterer at the club. I know you want to keep the wedding simple, but you have to have food. He's going to work up a couple of menus for you to choose from. And . . ." She snatched up another list. "I know Gabe has a wonderful garden, and he's got an innate touch with flowers, but you'll want some patio plants and cut arrangements to fill things out. Once you decide on your colors, we can order what you like."

"That's fine."

"Listen to me." Laughing at herself, Naomi set the lists back on her desk. "I've fallen headfirst into the mother-of-the-bride trap. I'm annoying myself."

Kelsey forced her lips to curve, tried to make the smile reflect in her eyes. "No, I appreciate it, really. Even with a small, informal wedding at home, there are dozens of details."

"That you're perfectly capable of handling yourself," Naomi finished. "I know you've had the big splashy wedding, Kelsey, and that you want this to be different."

"I do, yes." Kelsey turned the business card over in her hand, then stuck it guiltily in her pocket. "Candace orchestrated that. I barely had to do more than show up." Hearing herself, she hissed out a breath. "That sounds ungrateful. I'm not. She was wonderful."

"But you'd like to handle this one yourself."

"Let's just say I'd like more of a hand in it. But I don't mind delegating."

"I never thought I'd have this chance. Planning my daughter's wedding." Determined, she pushed all her lists into a pile, topped them with a brass paperweight. "Just yank me back when I threaten to go overboard. And . . ." She eased a hip onto the corner of the desk. "About the dress. I promise I won't say a word if you don't love it. But you will. Now, you'd better go before I nag you into letting me go along with you instead of Gabe."

"We'll shop for your dress together," Kelsey said as guilt piled over guilt. "Maybe over the weekend."

"I'd like that." Breezily, Naomi linked her arm through Kelsey's as she walked Kelsey to the door. "It'll give me a chance to harass you about photographers. Now, go enjoy yourself."

Kelsey mumbled something and walked outside just as Gabe pulled up in the drive.

"We have to make a stop first," Kelsey told him, pulling out the business card after she'd settled into the passenger seat.

He lifted a brow. "Shopping?"

"Soothing my conscience."

It didn't work. Even when it turned out that Naomi had been completely right about the dress. Or, perhaps, because of it.

Under any other circumstances the dress would have lifted her spirits. The pale rose color of the silk, the elegant tea length, the simple lines enhanced by raindrops of seed pearls. It was a wish of a dress that Ilsa assured her might have been made with Kelsey in mind. And didn't they have the sweetest hat to go with it? the clerk expounded. A little whimsy with a flirty fingertip veil so perfect for an intimate outdoor wedding.

Shoes, of course. Classic satin pumps that could be dyed to match. What flowers was she going to carry? She didn't know? White roses would be lovely, she was assured. A bride was entitled to white. Now, did she want to take the dress and hat along with her, or have them sent?

She took them along, moving through the transaction as if in a dream. It was so strange. And so simple.

"You didn't model it for me," Gabe commented as he walked with her back to the car.

"Bad luck," she said absently. Then she stopped, pressing her hands to her flushed cheeks. "God, did I just buy a wedding dress?"

"Apparently." He took her shoulders, turned her to face him. "Second thoughts?"

"No. No, not about you, us. This. It's just moving so quickly. I just bought my wedding dress, and a hat. I actually bought a hat. I'm having shoes dyed. And I haven't even told my family."

"You can rectify that today. If it's what you want." He put the boxes in the trunk.

"Okay." She nodded, and reached for the door handle. Gabe closed his hand over hers, then drew it back.

"Let's try this on for luck, then." He slipped a ring on her finger, a single square-cut diamond centered in a gold band crusted with tiny rubies. "My colors. Our colors, now. That's official."

Tears pricked at her eyes. They may have been standing in a parking lot with the summer sun beating down, but to her, the moment was as romantic as a cruise down a moonlit stream. "It's beautiful, Gabe. I didn't need it."

"I did."

Across the lot, Rich huddled in his car and watched the exchange, the embrace. He took a nip from his flask. And what a handsome couple they make, he thought bitterly. His son, and the slut's daughter.

It was Gabe's fault he was on the run again, that he was going to have to fold his tent and slink off. There would be no triumphant drive to Vegas now. The cops were asking questions. Rich had dragged that much out of Cunningham when he'd squeezed the man for another two thousand.

Let them ask, he thought, switching on his ignition when the Jaguar's roared to life. He wouldn't be around to answer. No, sir, Rich Slater was taking the high road all the way to Mexico, just as soon as he took care of a little business.

He slipped out of the lot, keeping the Jaguar in sight.

"We're going to have to be obnoxious." Kelsey told Gabe as they wove their way through Alexandria's traffic. "Rooney refused to take any of my calls."

"So, we'll be obnoxious."

"You think I'm wasting my time."

"What's important is what you think. You want to talk to him, we'll talk to him."

She shifted in her seat, wishing they could hurry up, wishing they could take forever. "I suppose I want to know how involved my father was in Rooney's investigation. If Dad knew Alec Bradley or just of him. I need to clear it in my mind. I don't suppose it changes anything that happened that night, but I need to know."

"You could ask your father."

"I'll have to, sooner or later. For now I'd . . ." Her voice trailed off. Abruptly she straightened in her seat and leaned forward as Gabe turned into the parking garage beneath Rooney's building.

"What is it?"

"That car, the one that just pulled out."

Gabe flicked a glance at his rearview mirror in time to see the car turn left and join the flow of traffic. "The black Lincoln?"

"My grandmother." Kelsey rubbed at the chill on her arms. "That was my grandmother's car. It was her driver at the wheel. I recognized him."

"There are a lot of offices in this building, Kelsey."

"And life's full of odd coincidences. No." She shook her head, staring straight ahead when Gabe pulled the car into an empty space. "I don't believe it. She was here to see Rooney. I'm going to find out why."

As they crossed to the elevator, Gabe took her arm. She was all but vibrating with temper and nerves. "If you go in guns blazing, you'll just spook him."

"Whatever it takes." She stepped in, then jabbed the button for Rooney's floor.

She might have been packing six-guns, Gabe thought, the way she stalked the receptionist in Rooney's plush outer office.

"Kelsey Byden and Gabriel Slater, to see Mr. Rooney."

The woman's professional smile flashed. "Do you have an appointment?"

"No."

"I'm sorry, Ms. Byden, Mr. Slater—"

"Don't be," Kelsey interrupted, and leaned on the desk in a manner that had the professional smile dimming considerably. "Just tell him we're here. And we're not leaving until we see him. Oh, and you might mention that I just saw my grandmother leaving. Milicent Byden."

It turned the key. Within ten minutes they were being ushered into Rooney's office. He didn't rise from his desk this time, but greeted them both with a single terse nod.

"You've caught me at a bad time. I'm afraid I can't spare more than five minutes."

"We might have managed a more convenient time, Mr. Rooney, if you'd taken any of my calls."

"Ms. Byden." Trying to exude patience, Rooney folded his hands on the desk. He succeeded in looking like a man begging. "I've tried to save both of us time and trouble. I can't help you."

"Why were you there that night, Mr. Rooney? You see, that's a question I keep returning to. Maybe it's because it all happened so long ago and I see it from a different perspective from those who were involved in the heat of the moment. But why that night? That particular night of all nights?"

"I was on routine surveillance. It's just as viable to ask yourself why your mother chose that particular night to shoot Alec Bradley."

"I know the answer to that," Kelsey returned steadily. "I'm wondering if you do. How much did you really see?"

"That's a matter of record." He rose, dismissing them. "I can't help you."

"How far did my father tell you to go? Did he approve your decision to sneak onto my mother's property and spy through her windows?"

"I'm paid to use my own judgment."

"You must have come to know my mother and Alec Bradley very well in those weeks that you followed them. Did you ever follow only him? See who he met, who he spoke with, who might have given him money?"

He could barely swallow, then realized it wasn't necessary. The saliva in his mouth had dried up. "I was hired to investigate your mother."

"But he was part of your investigation. How well did my father know him?"

Rooney's jaw tightened. "To my knowledge, they were not acquainted."

Outwardly cool, Kelsey merely lifted a brow. "He had no interest in the man his wife was allegedly having an affair with ?"

"Estranged wife, and no, at that point in time Philip Byden was only interested in one thing. His child."

"But when you reported to him—"

"I reported to his lawyers. Whether or not he read the copies they sent him, I can't say. He didn't want to be involved." A small smile touched Rooney's mouth. "He felt the idea of hiring an investigator was undignified."

"But he did hire you?"

"Perhaps he felt the ends justified the means. I have another appointment. You'll have to excuse me."

"Why did my grandmother come here today?"

"That's confidential."

"She's a client?"

"I can't help you," he said, spacing his words. But his eyes flicked to Gabe, then away.

Alone, Rooney sat behind his desk, steadying his breathing. He reached into his pocket and thumbed out a Tums that would do little to ease the burning in his gut.

How could it come back like this? After all these years. He'd gone by the book. He'd followed the book to the letter for twenty-three years. How could one night so long ago spring back at him like a tiger?

He started at the sound of his buzzer, then cursed himself. He wouldn't help the situation if he let nerves rattle him. He answered the buzzer.

"Mr. Rooney. There's a gentleman to see you. He doesn't have an appointment, but he claims to be an old friend. I'm to tell you it's old Rich."

"I don't know any..." His mouth went dry again, his palms damp. For one frantic moment, Rooney looked around his office for a route of escape. There was none, he realized. He was as terminally hooked as the glass-eyed swordfish on his wall.

"Send him in, and hold my calls, please."

"Yes, sir."

Rich was beaming when he stepped into Rooney's office. "Long time no see."

"What do you want?"

Rich sat, propped his feet on the desk. "You've put on a little weight, Charlie. Looks good on you, though. Used to look a little like a scarecrow. Why don't you buy an old pal a drink?"

"What do you want?" Rooney repeated.

"Well, you can start by telling me what my boy and that pretty lady of his wanted with you." Rich drew out a cigarette. "We'll work from there."

. . .

"I don't feel a whole lot better," Kelsey said when they climbed back into the car. "Am I supposed to be glad that my father hired that man but kept himself distant so he wouldn't soil his dignity? Or should I be relieved that he had nothing to do with Rooney, or Alec Bradley?"

"Maybe you should spend some time wondering why Rooney was so nervous."

"Nervous? He seemed cold, remote, and annoyed, but not nervous."

"He had his hands locked together to keep them still." Gabe backed out of the parking space. "The air-conditioning was blasting in that office, but he was sweating. His jaw was locked so tight he had a tic at the corner of his mouth. He was bluffing his way through it." Gabe paid the attendant, then eased back into the street. "But little things kept giving him away. And his eyes. He had the look of a man who's holding trash but keeps bumping the pot."

Curious, and fascinated, Kelsey studied him. "You get all that from gambling?"

"It's a gift. Something's got him spooked."

"All we have to do is find out what." She sighed. "I need a phone booth, Gabe. I think it's time I rounded up the family."

Milicent accepted the sherry her son poured her and, feeling magnanimous, patted his hand. "She's finally come to her senses. Don't look so concerned, Philip. I'm quite willing to put these past few months behind us. She's a Byden, after all." She sat back, sighed, sipped. "Blood will tell."

"I certainly hope she's brought Channing with her." Candace paced to the window and flicked the lace curtain impatiently. "I see no reason why he should stay at that place if Kelsey's coming home."

"Channing's doing what's right for him." Philip put a gentle hand on Candace's shoulder. Part of her wanted to shrug it off, but another, deeper part couldn't bear the thought of any more harsh words between them.

"I want him to be happy, Philip. You know I do."

"Of course you do."

"The boy will come around," Milicent assured them. "It's just youthful defiance, that's all. And sentiment. A vet? Really, now. That will pass."

She flicked Channing's dream aside with one elegant hand. "Why, there was a time, if you can imagine it, when Philip was a boy—do you remember, dear?—and he wanted to be a baseball player. Of all things."

"I remember," he murmured. He'd been sixteen, eager, and despite his bookish appearance, he'd had an arm like a rocket. Of course, that dream had been aborted in its embryonic state. A Byden didn't play professional sports. A Byden *was* a professional.

"Channing will listen to reason, just as Philip did. Your mistake, Candace dear, was in not asserting your authority."

"Channing's over twenty-one," Candace said stiffly.

"A mother is always a mother." Milicent's smile settled comfortably when the doorbell chimed. "Ah, that will be the prodigal daughter now. Let her apologize first, Philip. She'll feel better for it. Then we'll have Cook kill the fatted calf."

But Kelsey didn't look apologetic when she entered the sitting room with Gabe at her side. She did smile at her father and go to him for a greeting kiss. Hoping to mend fences, she embraced Candace before turning to her grandmother.

"Thank you for seeing me." She leaned down and kissed Milicent's lightly powdered cheek. "Grandmother, Dad, Candace, this is Gabriel Slater. Gabe, Milicent, Candace, and Philip Byden."

"It's nice to meet you." Philip offered a hand.

"I don't mean to be rude"—Milicent's eyes were cold as they lingered on Gabe—"but I had the impression there was family business to be discussed."

"Yes, there is. Old and new. I suppose I should start with the new. Gabe and I are going to be married."

There was a moment of stunned silence before Philip recovered. "Well, that's . . . a surprise. A happy one."

"A bombshell," Candace corrected. "And just like you, Kelsey." But she softened at the idea of orange blossoms. "Now I suppose sherry won't do. We'll have to have champagne."

"I won't have it." Milicent spoke, her face bone-white beneath her rouge. "I won't have this insulting behavior in my home."

"Mother—" Philip began tentatively.

"My home," she said again, thumping a fist on the arm of her chair. "Is this a slap at me?" she demanded of Kelsey. "A subtle insult? You would bring this person into my home, threaten to bring him into this family?"

Even knowing Milicent, Kelsey was shocked at the reaction. "It's not a slap, an insult, or a threat. It's a fact. We're getting married in a few weeks, at Gabe's home in Virginia. I'd like it very much if all of you would be there."

"Of course we will." Eager to smooth over the rough edges, Candace stepped in. "We're all just a little flustered by the suddenness of the announcement, but we wouldn't miss it for the world. I hope you'll let me help you with some of the details."

"Enough!" Milicent slammed her sherry down with a force that snapped the fragile stem. The remaining drops of amber liquid dripped down to spot the rug. "There is most certainly not going to be a wedding. Apparently, Kelsey, you've allowed yourself to be swayed by an attractive face. That's foolish but not irrevocable."

With an effort, she steadied her breathing and maintained her self-control. "There's been no public announcement, so there will be nothing to tidy up. You"—she pointed at Gabe—"you can save yourself some embarrassment now by leaving."

"I don't think so," he said evenly. "Embarrass me."

"We'll both go." Trembling with rage, Kelsey took his hand. "This was a mistake. Whatever else I have to say to my grandmother I can say at another time. I shouldn't have brought you here and subjected you to this."

"Stop it." Gabe brought their joined hands to his lips, kissed hers just above the ring. "Let her finish."

"I'm going to ask you to let me apologize." Philip moved between his mother's chair and his daughter. "Certainly this has come as a surprise. It might be best if we talk about it later."

"Don't shield the girl." Milicent rose and walked to a glossy Chippendale desk. "You've done that long enough. It's time she learned to face facts."

"I have been," Kelsey murmured. "For some time now."

"Then deal with these." She drew out a file from the desk. "I've compiled quite a bit of information on you, Mr. Slater. Quite a bit. Professional gambler, ex-convict. The son of an itinerant drunkard with no visible means of support and a cleaning woman. A runaway who lived on the streets and spent time in jail for illegal gambling."

She kept the file clutched in her hand as she studied Gabe with cold, condemning eyes. "You may have developed a taste for the finer things, and amassed some of them, but it doesn't change who you are."

"No, it doesn't," Gabe agreed. "Just as being born with them doesn't change who you are."

She slapped the file back on the desk. "Get out of my house."

"Wait." Kelsey's hand closed convulsively around Gabe's arm. "How dare you do this! How dare you pry into Gabe's personal life! And mine!"

"I'll do whatever is necessary to protect the Byden name. And you, despite this sudden attachment you've developed for that woman, are a Byden."

"That woman is my mother. Did you put a dossier together on her as well?" she demanded. "Did you search for nasty little secrets to throw in my father's face to try to keep him from marrying her?"

"It was, to my regret, one of the few times in his life he didn't listen to me."

The scene had been all too similar to this, Milicent remembered. Philip had actually shouted at her, and given her the ultimatum of accepting that woman or losing her own son.

"No, he didn't listen," she repeated. "And the results were disastrous."

"I'm one of the results," Kelsey tossed back. "Is that what you were doing in Rooney's office this afternoon?"

Milicent used one arm to brace herself against the desk. "I don't know what you're talking about."

"I saw you. You hired him again, didn't you? To spy on Gabe, to pry into his past."

"It was just a necessary evil to compile information that would bring you to your senses," Milicent defended.

"Well, you wasted your money. It doesn't make any difference to me. I already know all of it."

"Then you're more your mother than I wanted to believe. You deserve what becomes of you."

"You're right." Kelsey turned to her father. "Did you fall out of love with her, Dad? Or did you allow yourself to be shoved out of it?"

"Kelsey," he said, his voice hoarse, because all at once he wasn't sure of the answer, "what happened then, happened. I apologize with all my heart for this." Rigid with shock and embarrassment, he looked at Gabe. "To both of you."

"Apologize?" Milicent spat out. "I've told you the kind of man he is, the kind of man she's using to humiliate this family, and you apologize."

"Yes." With sorrow in his eyes, Philip looked at his mother. "I apologize for you, for the fact that you've used the family name like a whip. A name that has always meant more to you than something as simple as happiness."

Pale as death, Milicent gripped the edge of the desk. "I will not be spoken to like that, by my son, in my own home." Her eyes flashed back to Kelsey. "She's at the root of this. Naomi is the root of this."

Kelsey nodded slowly. "Perhaps she is. I'm sorry. I won't be back. Let's go home, Gabe."

"Kelsey." Flushed pink, Candace dashed after them, stopping them at the door. "Please, don't blame your father."

"I'm trying not to."

"He would never have allowed this to happen if he'd known... surely you know what kind of man he is."

Kelsey looked into Candace's worried eyes. "Yes, I do. You know, I always thought how well you and Dad were suited. How you complemented each other, filled in the blanks." Leaning forward, she kissed Candace softly on the cheek. "I didn't realize until right now how much you love him. I should have. Tell him I'll call him later, all right?"

"Yes. Yes, I will. And, Kelsey?" Her smile was a little crooked, but it was there. "Best wishes, to both of you."

27

"Quite a family you've got there, darling."

"Okay, Gabe." Once he'd parked in the drive at Three Willows, Kelsey got out of the car and closed her door with deliberate care. "This isn't the time to get cute."

"No, I mean it. I let you rant half the way home, and stew the other half. That ought to finish it."

She wasn't nearly finished. "It wasn't just about me. It wasn't really about me at all. It was about you."

"Hell." In an easy motion, he swung an arm around her shoulder. "I've had a lot worse tossed at me. She didn't bring up the showgirl in Reno, or the business in El Paso."

"That's hardly the point." She stopped dead on the first step. "What showgirl?"

"Got your attention." He gave her an almost brotherly squeeze. "Anyway, I liked your father, and your stepmother. That's two for three."

Baffled, she could only stare up at him. "You're not even angry. You're not even angry over what she did. Gabe, she hired a detective to pry into your life, to put together a file on you as though you were some kind of criminal."

"And what did she accomplish, Kelsey? You already knew the worst of me, and you defended even that. It makes my laying my cards out on the table up front the best gamble I ever took."

"It doesn't excuse what she did."

"But it makes what she did meaningless. Look, maybe I understand, a little, because I never had a family name to defend."

Now she stopped in her tracks. "You're standing up for her?"

"No. But I figure she made the wrong move. And it ended up costing her a lot more than it cost me."

She blew at her bangs. "Maybe I need a little more time to be open-minded. Get my dress out of the car, will you? At least we can make one person happy today when I show it to Naomi."

"Why don't I take you both out to dinner?" He rubbed his thumb over the ring on her finger. He liked seeing it there. "Celebrate?"

"Why don't you? I'll go tell her."

She hurried into the house, giving herself one quick shake, a gesture to toss off the worst of the day. She was halfway up the stairs when Naomi called her.

"Oh, there you are." One hand trailing along the banister, Kelsey rushed down again. "You were absolutely right about the dress. Gabe's getting it out of the car, then he's going to take us out to dinner. Should we see if we can drag Moses away from the barn?"

Naomi stood in the foyer, her hands clasped. "We need to talk. It might be better if we sat down."

"What is it? Oh, God, not one of the horses. Justice was a little wheezy, but I dosed him the way Moses told me."

"It's not one of the horses, Kelsey. Please, come in and sit down."

The stranger was back. That cool, controlled woman who had first invited her to tea. Baffled, Kelsey followed her through the doorway. "You're angry with me about something."

"No, I don't think 'angry' is the appropriate word." She glanced over when Gabe came through the door. "It might be best if we discussed this privately."

"No, there's nothing you can't say to me in front of Gabe."

"All right, then." Naomi walked to the window, faced out. She needed all her control now, all the self-reliance she'd had to learn to survive in prison. "You had a call while you were out. Gertie took the message. She left it on the desk in your room. I went in there a few minutes ago, to take in a guest list I'd been putting together."

Her face expressionless, she turned around. "I'll apologize for reading it. It wasn't intentional. It was simply there, and my eye fell on it."

"Why don't you just tell me who called?"

"Charles Rooney. The message was marked urgent. He wants you to contact him as soon as possible."

"Then I'd better see what it's about."

"Please." Naomi held up a hand. "After more than twenty years, I can't believe it could be so urgent. You've been to see him."

"Yes, twice."

"For what purpose, Kelsey? Haven't I answered your questions?"

"Yes, you have. That's one of the reasons I went to see him. Because you've answered my questions."

"And you?" She turned to Gabe, a flash of temper sneaking through the cracks. "You encouraged her in this?"

"It wasn't a matter of encouragement. But I understand."

"How could you understand?" she demanded, bitter. "How could either of you possibly understand? You can't imagine what went through me when I saw his name on the desk. I've spent more than a decade of my life trying to forget. I made myself dredge it up again, relive it again. A payment, I thought—I hoped—to bring my daughter back. But it's not enough?"

"I didn't go to see him to hurt you. I'm sorry I have. I went because I wanted to help, because I hoped I would find something that would change things."

"They can't be changed."

"If he saw something that night he didn't tell the police. If he held something back."

Stunned, Naomi sank to the arm of the sofa. "Did you think, really think you could find something to clear my name? Is that what this is about, Kelsey? A belated bath for the dirty family linen?" With a weak laugh, Naomi rubbed her eyes. "God. What possible difference could it make now? You can't give me back one second of the time I lost. You can't take away one whisper, one sneer, one sidelong look. It's done," she said, dropping her hands. "It's as dead and buried as Alec Bradley."

"Not to me. I did what I thought was right. And if Rooney called me, there's a reason. He didn't want to talk to me today. He was nervous, maybe even afraid."

"Just leave it alone."

"I can't do that." She stepped forward, gripping Naomi's cold hands in hers. "There's more. What happened to Pride, and Reno. It's so much like what happened all those years ago. Your horse, Benny Morales. It's like this terrible echo that's taken this long to catch up. And it hasn't stopped yet. Even the police wonder if there's a connection."

"The police." What color remained in Naomi's cheeks washed away. "You've spoken with the police?"

Kelsey released her mother's hands and stepped back. "I've been to see Captain Tipton."

"Tipton." The shudder came before she could stop it. "Oh, God."

"He believed you." Kelsey watched Naomi lift her head. "He told me he believed you."

"That's bull." Trembling, she sprang up. "You weren't there, in that horrible room with the questions pounding at you, over and over and over. No one believed me, certainly not Tipton. If he had, why did I go to prison?"

"He couldn't prove it. The photographs—"

"Back to Rooney," Naomi interrupted. "Do you really think you can turn this around? Discover some long-overlooked clue that proves I was defending my honor?" The hurt throbbed in her heart, in her voice. "Well, you can't. And even if you want to help, you won't be able to. Because I can't survive going through it again. I just can't."

She walked from the room and hurried up the stairs. Moments later they heard the sound of a door slamming.

"What a mess." Kelsey dropped into a chair, closed her eyes. "What a mess I've made of things."

"No, you haven't. You've stirred things up. Maybe they needed to be stirred up."

"We'd come a long way. She and I had come such a long way, Gabe. I've ruined that."

"Do you really believe that?"

"I don't know." She lifted her hands, then let them fall. "I started off telling myself I was asking questions for me. Because I had a right to know. Somewhere along the line I twisted that, convinced myself I was doing it for her. But I think I was right in the first place. I wanted to tidy it all up. Make it clean. If I believe her, everyone should believe her."

"That doesn't make you a villain, Kelsey." He crossed over and sat on the arm of her chair. "Tell me what you want to do."

She drew in a deep breath, expelled it. "I'm going to call Charles Rooney. I have to finish it."

They met him at a bar. Not a seedy, gin-soaked dive that might have added atmosphere to a clandestine meeting, but a plant-filled lounge that catered to white-collar professionals. Rooney had used every skill, every trick along his route to make certain he hadn't been followed.

When he saw them come in, he finished off his first gin and tonic. He was done, and knew it. He'd spent the hours since Rich Slater had left his office making plans to disappear. He had the knowledge, the contacts, and now, he had the motive.

"Mr. Rooney."

"Sit down. I can recommend the house wine."

"Fine," Kelsey said, and nodded to the hovering waitress.

"Coffee," Gabe ordered. "Black. You said urgent," he reminded Rooney.

"So I did." He tapped his glass to indicate another. One more for the road, he thought. By morning, he planned to be sipping a mimosa in Rio. "I'm afraid I was a little rattled when I made that call. It was a day for unexpected visitors at my office. The last one was unpleasant. I've been an investigator for over twenty-five years. A long time. I've had a lot of interesting cases. I've never once discharged a weapon." He gave the table two brisk knocks. "I enjoy my work, always have. It's difficult to build up the right clientele. A certain class of people, the right class of people, generally don't care to have an overt association with someone in my line of work. They hire us with the same kind of dismay and disgust that they hire someone to exterminate their roaches. They want the results, of course, but they rarely want to discuss the execution. There are some who prefer a more hands-on approach."

He paused as their drinks were served.

"This is fascinating, Rooney," Gabe commented, "but hardly urgent."

"Milicent Byden," he said, and watched Kelsey's mouth tighten. "She's a woman accustomed to directing servants, giving orders, making certain they're carried out to her specifications."

"We know she hired you to investigate Gabe." Kelsey washed the bad taste out of her mouth with wine. "I hope you got a hefty retainer, Mr. Rooney. Believe me, she's far from satisfied with the results."

"Tossed them back in her face, did you?" He found that amusing and chuckled into his drink. "Maybe there's some justice in the world. She was satisfied with the results the first time she hired me. More than satisfied."

"The first time?"

"It was your grandmother who hired me for the custody suit."

"My information is that you were hired by my father's lawyers."

"*Her* lawyers, Ms. Byden. You should remember they were her lawyers, too. And that's the way she wanted it to shake down."

He took the lime wedge from his drink and squeezed the juice into the glass.

"I'd done a job for an acquaintance of hers. Divorce. She must have figured I'd done a good one, a discreet one. And I fit the bill. Ambitious, still young enough to be impressed by who she was—who her husband was—and the size of her check."

He shrugged that out and dipped into the bowl filled with pretzels shaped like Chinese characters.

"I don't see that it makes a large difference where your retainer came from," Kelsey commented.

"Oh, but it did. I never even met your father. I saw him at the trial, but we never had a one-on-one. That's the way your grandmother wanted it. And she was good at getting things done her way. She wanted your mother out, all the way out of his life, and yours. And she'd worked out a very simple plan to accomplish it. My job was to follow Naomi, take pictures, make reports. That's all Milicent Byden told me. But I'm a good investigator, Ms. Byden. Even then I was good, and I found out more."

"More?" Kelsey felt that door creak open a little wider, and was afraid, very much afraid, of what she would see beyond it.

"It's easy enough to rub some elbows at the track. One of my sources had the goods on Bradley. Knew he'd played deep and was in debt to the wrong people. Bradley wasn't good at keeping secrets, and he'd talked. Talked about the big deal he was working on. All he had to do was make time with a beautiful woman, and he'd be set. Bradley and my source got chummy. They didn't run in the same circles, but they were cut pretty much from the same cloth. Bradley talked too much, my source put the arm on him for more, then passed the information on to me, for a fee."

"You're taking a long time to circle around to the wire, Rooney," Gabe said.

"Then let me make it simple." He loosened his constricting tie. "The custody suit was leaning toward Naomi. Courts don't like to take a kid from its mother. Maybe she liked to party, maybe she liked men, but she didn't fool with either when the kid was around. She had the money, and the means, and there were plenty of people willing to testify that she was a good mother, a devoted one. So, the Bydens needed something to tip the scales in their favor. Milicent found it in Alec Bradley."

"My . . ." Kelsey took a moment to steady her voice. "My grandmother knew Alec Bradley."

"Yes, she knew him, knew his parents. Knew his character. She hired Bradley to seduce your mother. To lure her into a compromising situation, the kind of situation that would make her appear anything but moral and maternal."

Beneath the table, Kelsey gripped Gabe's hand. "You're saying that my grandmother paid Alec Bradley. Paid him to—why should I believe you?"

"You believe what you want." Rooney didn't give a damn. He was just clearing his desk, so to speak, before he retired. "You came after the answers, Ms. Byden. Don't blame me if they don't suit you. She gave him twenty thousand dollars, up front."

Kelsey made a small sound as the figure clicked.

"The trouble was, Naomi wasn't playing the game. Not the way Bradley and your grandmother wanted. She was keeping him on a leash. The way the custody suit was heating up, your grandmother needed action. So she found another element to stir into the mix. There was some trouble at the track. A dead horse, a dead jockey. The publicity on that boomeranged in the Chadwicks' favor."

Gabe held up a hand. "Are you saying that's connected?"

"It's all connected. Bradley needed cash, but Milicent was keeping her wallet slammed shut until he produced results. So Bradley and his pal at the track worked out a little deal. When the horse went down, Bradley picked up some loose change, but he didn't get the bonus he'd hoped for when the sympathy went with Naomi. Milicent gave him a deadline."

Rooney studied what was left of his drink, debated indulging in another. With less than two hours until his flight, he opted to keep a clear head.

"She told me to have my camera and plenty of film. To be outside the house. I went to the club first, and watched Bradley stage the jealousy scene."

"Stage?" Kelsey repeated.

"It's easier to see through an act when you're not involved. Plus my source had alerted me. This was going to be the night. Bradley wanted to rile her. I don't think he expected her to cut him loose. He thought too much of himself when it came to the ladies. When your mother left, I was right behind her. There was nobody else in the house. Not until Bradley got there. My instructions were to take pictures, but only pictures that weighed in on the side of the Bydens."

"Your instructions," Kelsey said dully, "from my grandmother."

"That's right. It looked promising at first, her opening the door in that nightgown, letting him in. They had another drink, and he was pouring on the charm. I got a good shot through the window of them kissing. I didn't bother to take one of her shoving him away. That wasn't my job. They started to argue. I could hear snatches through the window when she shouted loud enough. She was telling him to get out. That they were through. He grabbed her, pawed at her."

Rooney lifted his eyes to Kelsey's. "There was a minute there when I thought about going in, breaking it up. She was in trouble. There was no way to mistake what kind of trouble. But I didn't go in. I had my job to do. In any case, she fought him off. She was pissed, still more pissed than scared. She shouted at him, made a move for the phone, but he came after her again. I don't think she had any doubt about what was going to happen. She ran."

Rooney paused, wiped a hand over his mouth. "He knew I was there. The son of a bitch knew I was there. He looked right out the window and he pointed, like this." Rooney jerked a finger at the ceiling. "Upstairs, he was telling me. I'm going to take care of it upstairs. So I did what I'd been hired to do. I went up the tree. I couldn't hear anything, not the way my heart was pounding. I didn't let myself think. I had a job, a big one, one that was going to lead to a lot of others. And she'd asked for it, hadn't she? That's what I told myself. She'd asked for it, the way she'd been stringing him along."

"You knew he would rape her," Kelsey managed. "You knew. And you did nothing."

"That's right." Rooney downed the rest of his drink. "She came into the bedroom, came running in. She was scared then, but she was mad, too. That filmy robe she'd been wearing was falling off her shoulder where it was torn. He came in after her, and he smiled. He looked friendly, even apologetic. The way they were framed in the window, facing each other, so completely focused on each other, with her clothes falling off, and the shirt of his tux undone. It looked provocative. Even sexy. I don't know what he was saying to her, but she was shaking her head and backing up. He reached down, like he was going to unhook his pants. She slapped him." Rooney moistened his lips. "I got that on film. He slapped her back. I didn't take that shot."

He had to stop again. He hadn't realized how going through that night step by step would affect him. Then he'd felt small, and scared. Now he simply felt small.

"She made a dive. She was out of my view for a minute. He put his hands up. He was still smiling, but it didn't look so friendly now. Then I could see her again, and I saw the gun.

"I started taking pictures fast then. I was scared. I kept taking them after she shot him, even when there was nothing to see."

"It was self-defense." Kelsey's fingers dug into Gabe's. "Just as she said all along."

"Yeah, it was. Maybe, maybe she could have held him off once she had the gun. But she was scared. She was trapped. If all the facts had come out, I don't think they'd have charged her with so much as manslaughter. They sure as hell wouldn't have convicted her."

"But the facts didn't come out."

"No, I took them straight to Milicent Byden. I wasn't thinking, going to her house in the middle of the night, getting her out of bed. She poured me a brandy herself, told me to sit down. Then she listened to what I had to tell her. From beginning to end. She said it had worked out for the best. She instructed me to wait a day or two before going to the police."

"She knew," Kelsey whispered. "So, she knew everything."

"She orchestrated it. If Naomi hadn't been arrested by then, I was to take the film to the cops and give my statement. I was to tell them what I saw, only what I saw, not what I assumed, not what I interpreted. Then she told me what I'd seen. A woman, provocatively dressed, welcoming her lover into an empty house. They shared a drink, an embrace. Then they quarreled. The woman was jealous. That was obvious after the scene at the club. She went upstairs, her lover following to make apologies, amends, perhaps a seduction. And in a jealous rage, the woman took out a gun and killed him. She gave me another five thousand cash that night, and the promise of several references."

White-faced, Kelsey slid from the booth. With one hand pressed to her heaving stomach, she dashed toward the rest rooms.

Gabe watched her go. He found that his fists were balled under the table. "You're a revolting specimen, Rooney. A few thousand dollars and some fancy names on a client list. For that, you watched an attempted rape, then helped see that the victim was locked away."

"There's more," Rooney said. "We'll wait for Kelsey."

"Tell me this. Why did you decide to come out with all of this now? A few hours ago you had nothing to say."

"It's getting complicated. I don't like being squeezed from two sides." Rooney shrugged. "When this comes out, and I've decided it will, my reputation's shot. It looks to me like I'm about to retire a few years early. I might as well do it with a clean slate."

"I'm wondering," Gabe began, and his voice was cool, deceptively detached, "if I should take you outside and beat you to a pulp. Or if I should just let you live with this."

Rooney picked up his glass and sipped the melted ice cubes slowly. "We all make our choices, Slater. You're a gambler. When you know the house has stacked the deck, are you going to bet against it?"

"Some games you just don't play." He rose as Kelsey walked back to the booth.

"I'm all right. I'm sorry." She was still white around the lips, but her hand was steady when it gripped Gabe's.

"You hang on for a minute." He gave his attention back to Rooney. "Let's have the rest."

"You're not going to like it. Milicent Byden didn't hire me just to compile your dossier, Mr. Slater. That came later. She put me on retainer months ago, right after Kelsey contacted Naomi Chadwick."

Kelsey pressed her lips together, praying for her stomach to settle. "I don't understand." But she thought she did, she was terrified that she did.

"Flat out," Rooney continued, "she didn't want you there. Didn't want to take any chances that you and Naomi would click."

"How did she intend to prevent it?"

"Well, since there wasn't anything to smear Naomi with since she'd been released from prison, Milicent made use of the past. After Alec Bradley was shot, I took her my files. All of my files. There was a lot of detail in them. Not just about Naomi. I'm thorough, you see. I had documentation on Bradley and his associate. The race fix, my suspicions on Cunningham's involvement. When she gave you a yank, Kelsey, and you didn't come to heel, she put that information to use."

"How?" Kelsey braced herself. "You'd better tell me how."

"She had me look up Bradley's old friend and lure him back to the area with the promise of a job. She didn't tell me what that job would be, but it didn't take long to figure it out. Not with history repeating itself. A fixed race, a dead colt. Gossip and suspicion circled around Naomi, and you." He jabbed a finger at Gabe. "Milicent didn't want you anywhere near her blood kin. Kelsey was supposed to see just how unsavory racing was, how ruthless. And she was supposed to run back home."

"But I didn't." Kelsey could feel tears burning at her eyes, but she wouldn't free them. Not now. Not yet. "You're telling me that she was behind it? Behind Pride's death? And, God, Mick's?"

"Even a woman like Milicent can't control a man with no ethics. You could say that her hireling momentarily got away from her. She was steamed after the groom's murder. Read me the riot act as if I'd stabbed the poor bastard myself." He shook his head, remembering. "The horse, now, that's what she wanted. A re-creation of crimes, a scandal to teach her granddaughter a lesson."

"Because of me," Kelsey murmured. Her hand lay limply under Gabe's. "All of it because of me."

"You're the last of the Byden line," Rooney pointed out. "She sets store by that. And she hates Naomi with a kind of cold-blooded passion that doesn't dilute with time. If she could ruin her again, and keep control over you, it would all be worth it. She lent Cunningham enough money to buy that horse, Big Sheba. More than enough to keep him under her thumb and persuade him to work with her button man. Not that she liked it," Rooney added. "Associating, even from a distance, with that type. But the ends justify."

"I don't think I know the woman you're talking about," Kelsey said slowly. "I don't think I recognize her. How could she ruin so many lives?"

"Control them," Rooney corrected. "She never considered any of it more than necessary control. And I went along with it." He rubbed a hand between his eyes. "The first time I was young, eager, impressionable. This time I felt trapped. And, hell, it was just a job. My last visitor of the day changed things." He studied Gabe's face for a long moment. "Maybe I'm getting old. Christ knows I'm tired. So when he showed up, trying to make a new deal, I cut my losses. And, maybe, I like to think that I figured it was time for a little atonement."

Rooney's eyes sharpened. "Do you want to know how Benny Morales's son did the Chadwick colt? How somebody nearly did one of yours, Slater? Look to your own organization, and look to your old man. That's right," he said, smiling a little. "Rich Slater wormed plenty of secrets out of Alec Bradley. And he was more than happy to use them, and repeat the sequence when Milicent Byden sent for him. Revenge and control, revenge and money. Her motives, and his. Makes a hell of a combination."

28

"Pull over, will you?"

A half mile from Longshot, Gabe swung to the shoulder of the road. "Are you feeling sick again?"

"No." She was, but not in the way he meant. "I just need to walk for a minute. Can we walk?" Without waiting for his answer, she pushed out of the car.

The perfect night, she thought. The classic midsummer night in the country with a diamond-bright dome of sky, stars, and moon. Not even a wisp of a cloud to spoil it. The air smelled of the honeysuckle that was patiently burying the fence along the rolling field to the right. The high grass that grew beyond it was alive with the chirp of crickets. As she walked, the soft shoulder gave under Kelsey's feet.

"It's too much," she murmured. "It's just too much to take in. How can I tell her, Gabe?" She spun around, her hands reaching for his, for a solution. "How can I tell my mother that it was all planned? That everything that happened was all part of some scheme to keep her away from me?"

"First"—he reached up to tuck her hair behind her ear—"you stop blaming yourself."

"I'm not." She stopped, turning to lean on the fence, to look out over the shadowy hills. "But I'm angry that I was used, like a pawn. She wasn't even thinking of me as a child. I can see that. Not as a child, certainly not as a person.

Progeny," Kelsey said bitterly. "That's all I was. All I am to her. Just the next Byden."

He started to speak, to offer some sort of comfort, then stopped. Sometimes it was kinder simply to listen.

"I think," Kelsey continued, "I really think she wanted to love me, that she tried, even succeeded for stretches of time. But the way she felt about my mother, and maybe—God, I hope—the guilt she lived with over what she'd done made it almost impossible. She wanted me to be a credit to the family name. Educated at the best schools, knowledgeable about the arts, competent in music and other acceptable pastimes. My friends had to be from the right families. Maybe that's why I never made any who were really close to me. And every small rebellion, every flash of my own personality or needs was seen as a mirror of the woman she'd ruined."

Kelsey plucked some honeysuckle from the vine and began slowly, systematically to shred the fragile white blossoms.

"When I turned twelve, she wanted me to go to boarding school in England. My father refused. It was one of the few times I'd ever seen them quarrel. I needed discipline, I needed guidance. My father said I needed childhood."

With a sigh, she rubbed the tattered petals between her fingers, stinging the air with scent. "Did she realize that she was using him, too? Another pawn. How responsible is she, Gabe, for destroying their marriage, whatever chance they had of making it work? That's the least of it, though," she murmured, and let the blossoms fall. "Now I have to find a way to tell my mother why, and how, and who. And my father. I'll have to tell him too, won't I? He has a right to know everything she did then. Everything she's done now."

She turned to him then, pressing her face to his chest, grateful that his arms were there to wrap around her. "So much waste. So many lives lost or ruined. And it all trickles down to some horribly misplaced family pride."

"And a few more of the deadly sins," he said quietly, thinking of his own father. "Envy, greed, lust. I've always believed more in luck than fate. But it's more than luck that brought this full circle." He drew her back so he could see her face. "You and me, Kelsey. We've both been a part of it right from the beginning."

"And maybe we wouldn't be so close to ending it if we hadn't found each other. You'll want to find him now, won't you? Your father?"

"I'll have to find him."

"You could leave it to Rossi." Her grip tightened suddenly, urgently. "Gabe. He wants to hurt you. If he went to Rooney's office so soon after we did, he was probably following us. He's looking for a way to get to you."

"So, I'll find him first. That's my circle, Kelsey. I need to close it."

"But if we went to the police—"

"Why haven't we already called them?"

She looked away. He saw her heart, her needs too clearly. "All right. I need to talk to Naomi first, and you need to find your father. Then we'll end it. I guess you'd better take me home."

. . .

When they pulled up at Three Willows, she declined his offer to come in with her. She would do this alone. He waited until she went inside, until the front porch light went dark.

Gabe had his own demons to face. And the first wasn't his father.

Inside, Kelsey glanced up the stairs. It was late. Undoubtedly Naomi was in bed. Wait until morning, she thought. It's waited so long already, surely it could wait one more night. But that was cowardice. With a sigh, she headed toward the kitchen. She would brew a pot of tea first. That would give her a chance to sort out exactly how she would begin.

"Gertie?" Kelsey was surprised to find the housekeeper up, loading the dishwasher.

"Oh, Miss Kelsey, you gave me such a start." The woman pressed a hand to the bodice of her pink chenille robe.

"It's after midnight. You shouldn't be working so late."

"Oh, I was just putting my dishes in. There was a Bette Davis movie on the TV tonight, *Now, Voyager*. I had me some lemon cake and a good cry." She sighed happily over the thought of it. "They just don't make movies like that these days, Miss Kelsey."

"No, they don't." Struggling to hold a conversation, Kelsey moved to the range, her movements mechanical as she picked up the kettle and walked to the sink to fill it. "Is everyone else in bed?"

"You want some tea? Let me do that." Territorial, Gertie brushed her aside and set the kettle on to boil. "Channing's out with Matt Gunner. That Tennessee Walker of the Williamses got a case of the strangles. They don't know if he'll make it until morning."

"Oh, I'm sorry."

"Well, it's a shame, that's the truth." Gertie busied herself warming a china pot while waiting for the kettle to boil. "But I have to say Channing was mighty excited at the idea of sitting up half the night in a barn. I told him I'd leave the kitchen door unlatched for him, and there's a nice cold plate of chicken in the fridge."

"Then undoubtedly he'll be in heaven."

"It's a pleasure having him around here."

"For me, too. I need two cups, Gertie. I want to take a cup up to my mother."

"Oh, she's sleeping, honey." Gertie chose the chamomile and measured the leaves out by sight. "Fact is, she looked so tired out and upset about something, that I had her take a sleeping pill just an hour ago."

"A sleeping pill?"

"She said I was fussing, but she didn't look well to me. All drawn out and pale. A good night's sleep is what she needed, and I told her so. I was going to check on her before I went to bed."

"I'll do it." Kelsey looked at the teapot with a mixture of resignation and relief. "Just one cup then, Gertie, thanks. I'll talk to her in the morning."

"She'll be fine then. Just overtired, I expect." Gertie put the pot on a tray, arranged the cup and saucer. "She's looked better, happier these past few months than she has in a long, long time. That's your doing. It don't matter what else goes on, a mother pines for her child."

"I'm here now."

"I know it, honey. Don't you stay up too late."

"I won't. Good night, Gertie."

Kelsey carried the tray upstairs, setting it in her room before going to look in on her mother. In the slant of moonlight through the window, she could see Naomi sleeping, deeply.

So it would be in the morning after all, she thought, and slipped into her own room to wait for the dawn.

Gabe didn't bother to stop in at the house, but drove straight to the barn. He saw the light above the tack room and grimly circled around and climbed the stairs. He didn't knock.

Jamison sat at his desk, paperwork in neat, organized piles, a single glass of brandy at his elbow. He looked up, blinking owlishly.

"Gabe. What brings you up here so late?"

"I could ask you the same."

"Oh, well." With a tired smile, Jamison gestured at the stacks of papers. "There's always something needs dealing with. It's easier to concentrate at night, when things are quiet. There's a jar of instant coffee over there," he added. "You can heat up the pot on the hot plate."

"No." Gabe studied his trainer, his friend, in the yellow light of the desk lamp. The past months of strain and worry had taken their toll. The shadows under his eyes were like bruises, the lines bracketing his mouth so sharp and deep they might have been carved by a knife.

Not the face of a man who had recently trained a horse to the Triple Crown.

"I used to hang around the barn a lot when I worked here, didn't I, Jamie? Tagged after you or Mick."

"That you did." Jamison relaxed the shoulders that had gone tense under Gabe's scrutiny. "Or you'd hustle us into a poker game and hose us out of a week's pay."

"Cunningham never gave you much peace, as I remember. If you had one winner, he wanted two. Always a bigger race, a bigger purse. I remember he was always saying Moses over at Three Willows knew how to turn out champions. And if you didn't, he'd find someone who could."

"He was a hard man to work for. I trained good horses for him, won a lot of races. Had Horse of the Year back in the eighties with Try Again. But I never satisfied him."

"He wanted a Derby winner. You never pulled that off. Even after the Chadwicks lost that colt at Keeneland back in—what was it? Seventy-three—and Cunningham's was the favorite, you didn't pull it off."

Gabe's voice was quiet, cool. "That colt came in third, as I remember. A disappointing third. That must have been hard to take after all you'd gone through to see him under the wire first."

The memory had Jamison's mouth twitching. "A show at the Derby's no shame. The colt didn't run his best that day, lost it in the last furlong. And things were hard around here, mighty hard." He lifted his brandy, drank. "After Benny hung himself."

"You and Benny were tight."

"We were good friends."

"Yeah. Good friends." Gabe turned a chair around, straddled it. "How much did you have to do with it, Jamie? Then and now?"

"What are you getting at?"

"You and Benny were close. Did you talk him into fixing the race, or did you just go along with it? I'll tell you what I think," Gabe continued, without waiting for an answer. "I think you asked him to help you out. Give the colt a little edge. Cunningham was pushing you for that edge. Maybe he offered you a bigger cut of the purse. Maybe he just kept the pressure on you until you broke. And when you broke, you took Benny Morales along with you."

His eyes never left Jamison's face. "A Derby win, Jamie. Something you've always wanted, and up until now, never quite pulled off."

"That's foolish talk, Gabe. You've known me too long."

"I have, Jamie. I've known you too long not to know that nothing goes on in that barn that you don't have a hand in. I didn't put you together with what happened to the Three Willows colt this time, or what nearly happened to mine. My mistake," he said, watching Jamison's eyes drop. "Never figured you'd kill a horse just to win a race. Any race."

Gabe took out a cigar, studying it from tip to tip while Jamison remained silent. "That's what blinded me, Jamie, until Reno. He didn't know it was a lethal dose. Neither did you. You were just giving my colt the edge, weren't you, by seeing that Pride was eliminated? Is that how my father put it to you, Jamie? Give yourself the edge."

"I wanted my own place," Jamison whispered. "A man deserves his own after so many years of tending someone else's. Any other year that colt would've won the Derby laughing. Why was it Moses should have one that could match him? Why was it?"

"Bad luck." Gabe lit his cigar. He'd stopped feeling sorrow. He'd stopped feeling grief.

"You wanted that win, Gabe. Don't tell me you didn't."

"Yeah, I wanted it. I won't tell you I didn't."

"Are you going to tell me you wouldn't have looked the other way if you'd known?"

Gabe's eyes flashed up. No, it wasn't sorrow in them. And it was a long way from grief. "If you thought that, why did you hide it from me?"

"You were a wild card. That's how Rich put it. You were a wild card, and you couldn't be trusted. Look how that colt ran, Gabe," he said, desperate. "Think about that. He took the three jewels and nothing could stop him."

"At what cost? It's not just a dead horse, Jamie. It's Mick, and it's Reno."

Jamison's eyes filled, swam with tears. "That wasn't my doing. Jesus God, Gabe, you can't believe that was my doing. Lipsky went off on his own. I didn't even know about it until after. Then it was too late."

His voice broke. For a moment there was only the sound of his labored breathing. With an effort, he pulled himself back. "Rich wanted to give you something to think about, but he didn't tell me until after. I didn't know he was going to go after Double, Gabe. God is my witness. It was to be the Three Willows colt. A scandal, a disqualification."

He shuddered, waiting for Gabe to speak, veering closer to the edge when there was only silence. "You've got to figure that Rich and Cunningham worked it out, Gabe. You've got to figure it."

"That's right. I've got to figure it."

"The disqualification wasn't enough for Rich. The money he got for fixing it wasn't enough. He's greedy, you know that. He used us to kill that colt. I suffered when that horse went down. When I knew what he'd had us do. And Reno." He buried his face in his hands. "I cared about that boy. Afterward, I told him it wasn't his fault, but he wouldn't listen. It's Rich who's responsible. For all of it. Then he comes around here, and he changes the rules."

"How?"

Jamison dropped his hands, wiped the back of one over his mouth. He picked up the brandy again, drank it like medicine.

"He didn't want you to win the Triple Crown, Gabe. It was eating him inside out to think you could. He told me it was a job, just a little side bet he had going. But it was money he wanted. He had me, don't you see? He had me and Reno both. But I wasn't going to hurt Double, you have to believe that. I got the drug myself this time. It was only going to be enough to eliminate him."

Gabe's eyes narrowed down into points of flame. "The night Kelsey came into the barn. It was you, wasn't it? You're the one who hurt her."

"I didn't do her any real harm. I just had to get out before she saw me. I got Kip out of the way. Didn't do more than give him a headache. Then, when she came in, I couldn't finish. I just—"

"I could break you in half for that alone, Jamie." Quick as a snake, Gabe's hand shot out, closed around Jamison's throat. "For that alone," he murmured, squeezing.

"I panicked, Gabe." Terrified, Jamison clawed at Gabe's iron grip. "Jesus, I was half out of my mind. Can't you see?"

"I see a lot of things." Disgusted, Gabe released him.

The ugly mottled red began to fade from Jamison's face as he gulped in air. "He had me trapped. Don't you see? I told Rich I wouldn't do it but he said if it wasn't done, we were going to pay. So I tried, even though it was breaking my heart, I tried. But it didn't work. Reno was supposed to do it the day of the Belmont, but he couldn't. Jesus, Gabe, he hung himself. A horse isn't worth dying for."

"But it's worth killing for?"

"I told you, I didn't—"

"Tell yourself," Gabe spat out. "Tell yourself you were a victim, Jamie. That you were used. That what happened to Benny Morales, and Mick, and Reno, and even to Lipsky was just the luck of the draw. Then see if you can live with it." He rose, kicking the chair aside.

"I did what I had to do. And I stood up to him. Just tonight I stood up to him."

Gabe's head jerked up. "What are you talking about?"

"Rich was here. Not an hour ago. Drunk, mean. He was talking wild. About killing the horses, burning the barn. Christ knows what he'd have done if I hadn't held him off."

Gabe whirled and was bounding down the steps with Jamie shouting after him. He hit the lights in the barn, choking back fear as he systematically checked every box.

"I told you I didn't let him in here," Jamison said. "I told him to get out, to go sleep it off. That we were finished. I wasn't doing his dirty work anymore. Not after Reno. No matter what."

Gabe stood outside Double's box. The colt sidled forward, nuzzled lazily at his hand. "You're finished, Jamie. Pack up and get out tonight."

"A man's entitled to a place of his own. You should know that."

"Yeah, I know that. But yours isn't here, not anymore."

Within twenty minutes, Gabe had roused three grooms and posted them in the barn. Until he ran his father to ground, there would be a twenty-four-hour watch. He'd be back, Gabe thought, as he strode toward the house. The combination of greed and hate would draw him back.

Nothing would satisfy Rich Slater except his son's total misery. What was most important, most cherished, had to be destroyed.

But this time it would be different. This time... The blood drained out of Gabe's face as his own thoughts circled back in his head. What was most important. Most cherished.

Kelsey.

Gertie tried out a new night cream she'd ordered from one of the shop-at-home channels, a guilty pleasure she sometimes indulged in on the kitchen television. The young and perky saleswoman on the screen had touted the cream as something akin to a rebirth.

Gertie didn't expect miracles, only a temporary reprieve from the lines that seemed to bloom on her face with increasing regularity.

Vanity, she clucked at her mirrored reflection. Foolish vanity for a woman who had lived on this earth for more than half a century. But when she looked closely, she thought maybe, just maybe she could spot a slight softening around the eyes where the crow had dug his feet in the deepest.

Satisfied with the new nightly ritual, she stood to remove her robe, then smiled when she heard the sound of the kitchen door creaking open.

That boy would raid the refrigerator for sure, she thought, and likely leave a mess. Boys Channing's age never chased down crumbs. She'd just go along and fix him a plate herself, see that he washed it down with milk instead of that soda pop he was always guzzling.

"I hear you out there," she said as she swung into the kitchen from her adjoining room. "No use sneaking around. You just sit yourself down, and I'll . . ." She stopped, frowning. In the glow of the range light she'd left on for Channing, the kitchen was quiet, spotless, and empty. "Ears playing tricks on me," she muttered. "Maybe they'll start selling something for that on the TV."

She started to turn, then pain burst in her head. She managed one tiny, birdlike cry as she crumpled to the tile.

Rich stood over her, grinning. Coshed the skinny old bitch with her own rolling pin, he thought, and tapped the smooth heavy marble against his palm. He toed at her side, lightly, catching himself when the one-footed stance had him weaving.

Need a little balance, he decided, and reached into his back pocket for his flask. When no more than a few miserly drops hit his tongue, he swore. Stuffing the empty flask back into his pocket, he stepped over the unconscious Gertie. They were bound to have some liquor around here, he thought. Prime stuff, too. Once he'd fueled himself up, he'd hunt up Gabe's pretty little pigeon.

Upstairs, Kelsey drank another cup of tea while she paced her room. She wished Channing would get home. At least then she'd be able to talk to someone. And who would understand better than he this horrible conflict of family loyalties? Even Gabe, for all his support, didn't share the same memories, the same affections and frustrations. Channing, when the trouble was real, was a rock.

In the morning, in a few short hours, she would tell Naomi everything she'd learned. Once the story was told, Kelsey knew she would be freeing one woman she loved, and condemning another.

For under all the bitterness, the anger, and the painful disappointment, she still loved her grandmother.

The Magnificent Milicent, she thought, shutting her eyes. How would she survive the scandal, let alone the legal consequences? And there were bound to be consequences.

And how, Kelsey asked herself, would she be able to live with the fact that what she'd done, and what she would do, could send her own grandmother to prison?

A tinkling crash of glass from downstairs had her biting back a gasp. Channing, she thought, setting down her cup. She hadn't heard him drive up, but he was obviously down there, fumbling through the dark in a very poor attempt not to wake the rest of the house.

Relieved, Kelsey hurried out of her room and down the stairs to find him.

"Channing, you idiot. What did you break? If that was one of Naomi's crystal horses, there will be hell to pay."

At the base of the stairs she stopped, listening. The house was quiet now. Quiet enough to run a chill up her arms. Stop it, she ordered herself, and rubbed them warm. "Come on, Channing, I'm not in the mood to play games. I really need to talk to you."

She snapped on the light in the foyer.

"Look, I know you're down here. Your catlike grace always gives you away. It's important, Channing."

Annoyed now, she marched into the sitting room. In the glow of moonlight she saw the glint of shattered glass on the rug.

"Dammit! It was one of the horses. Nice going, ace." She hurried over, kneeling down to pick up shards.

"All the queen's horses," Rich said, and switched on the lights. "All the queen's men." He grinned down at Kelsey. "But can the queen's lovely daughter put any of them back together again?"

He threw back his head and laughed at the sheer poetry of it.

29

Kelsey gasped in surprise and pain as her hand contracted around a sliver of glass. Blood welled on her palm.

"Careful there, honey pie." Rich sauntered over. "You could slice yourself to ribbons." He tut-tutted over the cut on her hand, then gallantly offered her a handkerchief. "Didn't mean to give you such a start, but I thought it was time we had ourselves a chat. Seeing as you're warming my boy's bed most nights."

"You're Gabe's father." Kelsey scrambled to her feet, but not quickly enough. Rich's hand shot out, locked around her arm.

"There's a family resemblance, isn't there? The ladies always said we made a handsome pair, me and my boy." His eyes, bright with liquor and anticipation, skimmed over her face. "Why, you're even prettier close up, doll face. It isn't hard to see why my boy's been sniffing around you. No indeedy. It isn't hard at all. Here now." He stuffed the handkerchief into her bleeding hand. "You wrap that up."

She obeyed automatically. "If you're looking for Gabe—" She broke off, reevaluated quickly. "He's—upstairs," she said. "I'll go up and tell him you're here."

"The one thing I never tolerated from a woman was a lie." With one flick, he shoved her into a chair hard enough to snap her head back. "You'd better get that straight right now." He leaned over the chair, trapping her between his arms. "Gabe's not upstairs, now, is he? I saw him drop you off out of his fancy car just a little while ago. Don't know why he'd go home to a cold bed when he has something like you. But I always had a hard time teaching the boy anything."

He patted her cheek, pleased with the swell of power when she cringed back. "But this works out real cozy. Just you and me, getting acquainted. Whoops. What's this here?" Chuckling, he pinched his fingers at her wrist, forced her hand up. "That's a whopper now, isn't it?" he said, eyeing her ring. "Is that what I think it is?" He wagged his finger in front of her face. "Is my boy going to make an honest woman out of you, honey pie? Well, you're a real step up from most of the sluts he's snuggled with before. No offense."

"No," she said, hoping to play the game out. "No offense taken. Gabe and I are going to be married in August. I hope you'll be there."

She cried out in shock when the back of his hand swiped across her face. His genial expression never altered. "Now, what did I tell you about lying? What you and that boy of mine would like is for me to drop dead on the spot. Wouldn't you?"

She blinked to clear her vision. "I don't know you," she said carefully. But she knew enough to be afraid, and her trembling gave her away.

"You know me. I'll give you odds my loving son's told you all about me. Your mama, too." The thought of Naomi soured his grin. "She'd have something to say about good old Rich Slater."

Kelsey anchored her chin to keep it from trembling. "I'm sorry. She's never mentioned you."

His smile thinned. "Bitch. Always was a bitch. You take right after her."

"In some ways. You're hurting me, Mr. Slater."

"Rich, honey. Or better yet, you call me Daddy. Since we're going to be family." The idea of it had him hooting with laughter until tears filled his eyes. "One big happy family. I bet that old icicle's fuming over that. Did I mention I know your grandma? I know her real well. She must be foaming at the mouth at the idea of her hoity-toity granddaughter playing house with a son of mine. She hated your mama, you know. Hated her right down to the ground."

"I know."

"You know what I think?" He reached up, pinched Kelsey's throbbing cheek hard enough to make her gasp. "I think you should fix us both a nice drink. Then we'll get to know each other."

"All right." When he stepped back, Kelsey eased out of the chair. Her eyes darted to the patio doors, to the doorway that led to the foyer. If she could get out of the room, she was sure she could outrun him.

"You don't want to try that, honey." He pinched her arm again, his fingers digging down to the bone. "You don't want to."

"There's brandy in the cabinet there. Napoleon."

"Well, that's just fine and dandy." He kept his hand on her arm and dragged her to it. "Pour us both a couple of healthy swallows."

He was already drunk, she thought frantically. If she poured with a generous-enough hand, she might slip past his guard. "Gabe said you've done a lot of traveling."

"I've been here and there."

"I like new places." She smiled and handed him a snifter. "Cheers." She tapped her glass to his.

"You're a cool one." Rich tossed back the brandy, then let out a long, pleased sigh. "That's one of the things that appealed to me most about your mother. She was one long, cool drink of water, that Naomi. She never would give me a sip, though. Let plenty of others drink great big gulps, but she never let good old Rich have one little sip. Maybe she will now. I bet I can make her change her mind. Is she upstairs?"

"She's not home." Before the words were out, Kelsey was reeling back. The blow had stars bursting in front of her eyes as she fell.

"Lying bitch." With a thin smile, Rich drank more brandy. "Cold-eyed lying bitch, just like your ma. Maybe you'd rather I had a taste of you instead." He laughed until his sides ached at the expression of animal terror on her face. "No, no, that wouldn't be proper, poking in where my boy's already been. Besides, I prefer a more . . . mature woman. And Naomi, she's been around the track a time or two, now, hasn't she? Now, maybe if your grandma had hired me instead of the coke-snorting Bradley, things would be different. Why don't we go ask Naomi if she'd like to give Rich a try now?"

"Stay away from her." Her head spun sickeningly as she lurched to her feet. Her vision was blurred where the blow had struck her eye. "I'll kill you if you touch her."

"Yeah, just like your ma. Kill a man for doing what comes natural."

"We know all about you." Dizzy, she leaned against the cabinet. She just needed a minute, she told herself. To clear the pain from her head, to get some feeling back in her watery legs. "Gabe's not here because he went for the police. They'll be here any minute."

She teetered back, nearly falling when he lifted his hand again.

"You want to tell the truth to me, honey pie. Or I'm going to spoil that pretty face of yours."

"It is the truth. We met Charles Rooney tonight. He called after you came to his office. He told us everything." Praying for time, she began to list the details. He believed her now; she could see it in his face. And what she saw there told her he could do worse, a great deal worse than slap her again.

"They'll find you here if you stay," she continued. "They'll find you and they'll put you in prison. The way they put my mother in prison. You could probably still get away. They might not catch you if you ran."

"They've got nothing on me. Nothing." He took her untouched brandy and drank it down. "It's all air. And you're forgetting Grandma."

"No, I'm not. They put my mother away with lies. It'll be easy to put you away with the truth."

"He'd turn me in." Enraged, Rich tossed the snifter, shattering the glass on the hearth in a parody of celebration. "My own flesh and blood would turn me in. We'll have to make him sorry for that. Real sorry."

He lunged. Panic and youth had Kelsey spinning to the side so that he caught nothing more than the sleeve of her blouse. As the seam ripped, she tore away, making a dash for the doorway.

He caught her, bringing her down in a lumbering tackle that radiated pain down to the bone. Panting out sobs, she kicked out blindly, landing a glancing blow off his shoulder, another off his chest as she clawed her way inch by desperate inch over the rug.

He was going to kill her now, she was sure of it. Beat her or choke her with those big bruising hands. And when he was done, he'd go after Naomi.

She screamed once when he yanked her head back by the hair. Light flashed in front of her eyes, wheeled like comets fired by the hideous pain. If she had found her voice she might have begged then, pleaded and begged. But the air was searing in and out of her throat.

"Gotcha, don't I? Gotcha. Thought you were such a smart little bitch."

Her fingers dug into the carpet, reached, then closed over an inch-long shard of crystal. Mindless with terror and pain, she swung out.

Then it was he who screamed, rearing back, the blood spurting out of his cheek where the delicate foreleg of the glass Thoroughbred had pierced his flesh.

Whimpering, she dragged herself up and raced from the room in a panicked, limping run while his curses chased after her.

She fell on the stairs, fighting for breath, struggling to clear enough of the fear from her mind so that she could think. When she called out, trying to warn her mother, only little mewling sounds escaped. With blood and fear stinging her mouth, she clawed her way up, gaining her feet and the top of the stairs just as she heard Rich charging up behind her.

"No!" She snatched a vase of lilies and hurled it down at him. The crash and a grunt of pain bought her a few precious seconds, wasted as she fumbled with bloody hands at the knob of her mother's bedroom door. "Mom! Oh God, Mom!" With one blind burst of strength, she shoved through the door and slammed it behind her. "Mom! Get up!" She was weeping as she fought the lock with fingers gone numb with terror. "For God's sake, get up!"

In a lunge she was at the bed, dragging Naomi up by the shoulders, shaking, pleading.

"Wha—?" Groggy from the sleeping pill, Naomi pushed her daughter's hand away, annoyed. "What is it?"

"He's coming. Wake up! We have to get out. Do you understand me?"

"Who's coming?" Naomi blinked open heavy eyes. "Kelsey? What is it?"

"He'll kill us! Get out of bed, goddammit!" She screamed again when Rich hurled his weight against the door. "Get out of bed!" Breath coming in hot gasps, she turned terrified eyes to the door. "It's not going to hold. Sweet Jesus, it won't hold. The gun. Do you still have the gun?"

She babbled out little prayers as she clawed open the nightstand drawer. It was there, the chrome glinting in the moonlight.

"What are you doing?" Sleepy and dazed, Naomi managed to fight her way through the mists to kneel in bed. "Good God, Kelsey, what are you doing? Who's at the door?"

But as the wood splintered, Kelsey stared straight ahead. She held the gun in both hands, struggling to keep it from slipping out of her shaking fingers.

He burst in, blood glistening on his cheek. And saw only Naomi, kneeling in the bed with the thin silk gown sliding from her shoulders. His teeth flashed as he leaped forward. Kelsey felt the gun buck like a live thing, sending vibrations singing up to her shoulders.

She never heard the shot.

"Alec?" The wooziness floated over Naomi's mind, sliding images of past and present.

"It's not Alec." Kelsey heard her own voice, small with distance. "It's Gabe's father. I've killed Gabe's father."

"Slater?" Half dreaming, Naomi crawled out of bed and, as she had done so many years ago, bent over a dead man. Mechanically she checked his pulse before straightening again. "Rich Slater?" Confused, she rubbed her hands over her eyes. "What in God's name is happening here?"

"I killed him." Kelsey dropped her arm, the gun dangling from her fingers.

Naomi looked up into her daughter's face. She recognized the shock, the disbelief, and the fear. She forced her trembling legs to move forward.

"Sit down, Kelsey. That's right, sit down." She eased her gently onto the side of the bed. Nothing mattered now, nothing but Kelsey.

"Let me have the gun. Okay." Naomi set it aside for the moment. It would take no time at all to deal with it. "Put your head between your legs now and breathe."

"I can't. I can't breathe."

"Yes, you can. Slow and deep. That's it, honey." As Kelsey tried to obey, Naomi outlined her plan. "Now, I'm going to tell you what we're going to do, and I want you to listen very carefully and do exactly, just exactly what I tell you. Understand?"

"He was going to kill me, and you. He would have killed us both. But I killed him. I don't remember pulling the trigger, but I must have." Her teeth began to chatter. "Because I shot him."

"No, *I* shot him. Look at me. Kelsey." Gently, Naomi lifted Kelsey's ravaged face. "Oh, God." She shuddered, dug her nails into her palms until the pain cleared some of the shock. "Listen to me, baby. He broke in, and he..." She brushed at a cut on Kelsey's cheek. "And he hurt you. So I got the gun, and I shot him."

"No, that's wrong. I couldn't wake you up."

"No, no, honey. I woke up when you came in. You came in here to get away from him. Then he broke down the door and I shot him. I'm going to call the police now, and that's exactly what we're going to tell them."

"I don't"—Kelsey lifted a hand to her spinning head—"I don't—" She jerked around and screamed at the sound of feet pounding up the stairs.

"Jesus God." Gabe took one look at his father, then stared at the two women huddled on the bed. "Kelsey!" In one leap he was crouched in front of her, holding her wounded hands. "He hurt you. Look at your face." He jumped up, his eyes hard, deadly. "I'll kill him myself."

"I already have," Naomi said calmly. "Gabe, get her out of here. Take her to her room. I'll call the police."

"I'm all right," Kelsey insisted, but the room faded out as she pushed herself to her feet.

"You just need to lie down." Gabe picked her up. "I'll take care of you." He looked back at Naomi. "I'll take care of her."

"Make her stay in there until I've finished this." Naomi lifted the bedside phone.

"He was just there," Kelsey murmured, shivering as Gabe carried her to her room and laid her on the bed. "He was just there. He broke the horse."

"Just lie still." He wanted to hold her. He wanted to crush something, someone into dust. Instead he whipped the bedspread over her. She was shaking badly, her pupils contracted to pinpoints with shock. And her face... Gabe's hands balled helplessly at his sides. Her face was bruised and bleeding. He couldn't think; just then he couldn't allow himself to think that his own father had done that to her.

He went quickly into the bathroom, dampened a washcloth, and filled a cup with water.

"Here, baby." Gently, he curved an arm under her and brought the cup to her lips. "Drink some of this."

"He was downstairs." Her fingers fretted at the bedspread. "It wasn't Channing. The little horse was shattered, and he was just there. He kept smiling. He kept hitting me and smiling."

The hand on the wet cloth clenched until the knuckles went white. "He won't hurt you anymore." With fingers no more steady than hers, he washed away the blood. "Hold on to me, Kelsey. No one's going to hurt you anymore."

"I couldn't bluff." Shivering, she curled against him. She was cold, so cold, and he held the heat. "I tried, but I was so scared, and so angry. And he knew, and he'd hit me again." She turned her battered face into Gabe's throat. "He has such big hands."

And preferred to use them, Gabe thought grimly, on women. "I'd have killed him for this," he murmured. "Killed him with my own hands for touching you."

"It wasn't me." Suddenly she was so tired, so horribly, horribly tired. "It was you. He wanted to hurt you."

"I know." He turned his head just enough to brush his lips over her brow, then he eased her back on the pillows. "It's over now."

She let her eyes close for a moment. As the worst of the shock ebbed, the pain crept back. Her body felt trampled. "You came." Blindly she groped for his hand, found it.

"Yeah." He looked down at their joined hands. "A hunch. The trouble was I moved on it too late."

Her eyes opened again, fresh panic flashing. "Naomi."

"She's fine. If you'd been alone..." The thought of that had talons of fear clawing through his gut. "Kelsey, I'm going to give you an out. Right now."

"An out?" Though she wasn't sure she would like what she found, she lifted a hand to probe at her throbbing face.

"If I were fair, I'd do the walking."

"Walking?" The heavy fog was lifting. She could see him clearly now. The strain that tightened his face, the swirl of emotion in his eyes. "Gabe." She touched a hand to his cheek as if to brush some color and calm into it. "Don't. I'm all right now."

"He battered your face. He tore your clothes. He terrified you." Deliberately he pried her clutching hand from his and rose. "He was my father. It doesn't matter that I've worked all my life to rid myself of any part of him. It's blood, and it'll always be there. I've got no place in your life, Kelsey. The biggest favor I could do for you is to walk out of it."

With some effort, she pushed herself up. Pain was singing in every bone now. "Did I ask you for a damn favor?" she snapped out. She winced as the scream of sirens sliced through the night and into her throbbing head. "If you want to do me one, then get me a bottle of aspirin, and keep your ridiculous grand gestures to yourself."

He nearly smiled. "I'm trying to be noble."

"Well, you're no good at it. And I don't like noble. I like you." She brushed her hair back, eyed him narrowly. "Do you think you can sneak out of this when I'm down? We had a deal, Slater, and you're not going to welsh."

"I never welsh." He sat on the edge of the bed again, and placed his hands lightly on her shoulders. "And that's my last shot at nobility. A hell of a hero I make anyway. It should have been me who killed him, Kelsey."

She crossed a hand over her body to clasp his. "Don't. You couldn't know that he would be here, that he would do this. And still you came." Her brow furrowed. "Why did you come?"

"It doesn't matter now. But it should have been me. It should have been me and not Naomi who killed him."

Kelsey drew back, her face paling again. "It wasn't you," she said slowly. "And it wasn't Naomi. I killed your father, Gabe."

. . .

Naomi sipped the brandy slowly. She was sitting in the kitchen. The lights were very bright, and hurt her eyes. Her hands were trembling.

But she could deal with it. Would deal with it.

All she could think was that her daughter was upstairs, hurt, terrorized. And Gertie, sweet Gertie was in an ambulance on her way to the hospital.

"He must have come in this way," she said. "Hit Gertie. She'll be all right, won't she?" Control slipped a notch, and her lips trembled. "She's so small and she's so harmless."

"The paramedics said she was lucid, Ms. Chadwick." Rossi kept his voice low. The woman looked as though she would shatter into bits at any moment. "We'll check on her once they've had time to get her to the hospital."

"Moses should have gone with her. I should have made him go."

"He's not going to leave you. We're having a hard-enough time keeping him outside. Just tell me what happened."

Naomi drew in a deep breath and began. "He got in the house. I don't know how. I was upstairs in bed, sleeping. A noise woke me. Before I could get up, Kelsey ran into my room. She was terrified, hysterical. Her face...I could see where he'd hit her."

She pressed a hand to her mouth. She'd slept through that. Slept while he'd beaten her child.

"Then there was banging at the bedroom door. As if someone were throwing himself against it. I got the gun out of the drawer beside the bed. When he broke in, I shot him."

Rossi watched her as she lifted her glass, cupping her other hand over it to try to keep it steady as she drank.

"You were in bed when you shot him, Ms. Chadwick?"

"Yes. No." She set the glass down. She had to be careful. She had to be very careful. "I was in front of the window. I'd gotten up. It happened very fast."

"You say a noise woke you, but your daughter ran in before you could get up and see what it was?"

"Yes." Why did they always repeat what she said? They'd done that before, she remembered. It didn't matter what she said. It never mattered.

"Have you been into the sitting room, Ms. Chadwick, since you notified the police?"

"No." She pressed her lips together. If it was a trick, she couldn't see it. "I didn't come down. I stayed upstairs until you came."

"You've got a hell of a mess in there. Blood, broken furniture. I'd say that much damage took some time to accomplish. Time enough for anyone to get out of bed and check things out."

"I—I was frightened." Should she tell him she'd taken a sleeping pill? Yes. No. "I stayed in my room because I was frightened."

"With a phone right beside you, and a gun in the drawer?"

She looked up, met his eyes. "He broke into my bedroom," she said evenly. "And I shot him."

"No, she didn't." Kelsey stepped into the kitchen. Though she was grateful for the support of Gabe's arm, she made herself move away from it. "She didn't kill anyone."

"You shouldn't be down here." Panicked, Naomi pushed away from the table. "Take her back upstairs, Gabe. You can see she's hurt." She clamped a desperate hand on Rossi's arm. "You can see she's hurt. Look what that bastard did to her. Look what he did to my child. She's in shock. She doesn't know what happened."

"Stop it." Kelsey stepped up to the table. In the strong light her cuts and bruises stood out in stark relief against her pale skin. "I'm not going to let you do this. It isn't necessary. And it isn't right."

"Why don't you sit down, Ms. Byden?" Rossi invited. "And tell me what happened."

"No!" In a lunge Naomi rounded the table and gripped Kelsey's arms. "Listen to me, Kelsey. You're hurt, you're confused. Gabe will take you to the hospital, and I'll handle this."

"No." She shook her head, moving in to draw Naomi close. "Mom, no."

"I'm not going to let you go through this. I won't!" Trembling now, she hugged Kelsey tight. "You don't know what it's like. It won't matter what you say. It won't matter what happened. They'll take you away, Kelsey. Please, please, listen to me!"

"It does matter," Kelsey murmured. "It's not like before."

But it was, Naomi thought. Of course it was. "My fingerprints are on the gun." Stone-faced, Naomi turned back to Rossi. "The gun was in my room. He was killed in my room. That should be enough for you."

"Naomi," Gabe said gently, "sit down."

"You said you'd take care of her." She turned to him. "You said you would. Now make her go upstairs."

"Ms. Chadwick." Rossi studied her eyes. "There's a very simple test that will prove whether it was you or your daughter who discharged the weapon."

"I don't give a damn about your tests. You're not putting my daughter in a cell."

"I think we can agree on that. Sit down. Please," Rossi added.

"Come on." Kelsey draped an arm over Naomi's shoulders. "There's nothing for you to worry about. I promise."

"Would you like some brandy, Ms. Byden?" Rossi asked when she was settled at the table.

Kelsey looked down at the snifter and shuddered. "No. I've lost my taste for it." She drew a deep breath. "I heard glass breaking downstairs," she began.

30

There was dew sparkling on the grass. From her chair on the patio, Kelsey watched it gleam, knowing the sun would soon be strong enough to burn it away.

Down at the barn, horses were being worked, stalls cleaned, troughs filled. Her body still ached enough to prevent her from resenting the fact that she'd been banned from the routine for a week.

She glanced around as the door opened behind her, and she smiled at her mother. "Gertie?"

"She's feeling better. She's fussing." With a sigh, Naomi sat, stretched out her legs. She thought about pouring coffee from the pot Kelsey had on the table, but she felt entirely too lazy. "I'm using guilt to keep her in bed for another day or two. If she gets up, I'll worry."

"Sneaky."

"Whatever works. Right now she's buying out the shopping channels. How are you feeling?"

"I'm fine, until I look in the mirror." She grimaced. Over the last two days some of the bruises had faded, but others had blossomed. "Until I do, it all seems almost like a dream. I don't know if it's just a stage I'm stuck in. I know I killed a man, but I can't seem to feel the horror of it."

"Don't try. You did what you had to do to protect yourself. And me." Naomi lifted her face to the sun. "I don't even remember him, Kelsey. Not really. I suppose I saw him around the track now and then. Maybe even spoke to him. But I don't really remember. I keep thinking I should, that it all should be vivid in my mind. How can I not remember a man who had so much to do with the way my life turned out?"

"He never mattered to you. And he knew it. That was part of the anger that built up in him. He found a way to make you pay, and to make a profit." She pushed the plate of croissants toward Naomi.

"Sun Spot," Naomi murmured. "God, I loved that horse. Yes, he certainly made me pay."

"She—Grandmother—used Alec Bradley for that, for a lot of things. And Cunningham."

"Bill." On a long breath, Naomi shook her head. "He's so much more of a fool than I guessed. And what good did it do him, Kelsey, then or now?"

"He didn't pay before. But he'll pay now. The police, the Racing Commission, they'll see that Cunningham pays for what he did to Pride, and to Sun Spot."

"All those years ago. No one ever put it together."

"It might have ended there, with the lies and the misery, if Gabe hadn't come back. If he hadn't drawn an inside straight." She smiled as Naomi tore off a corner of a roll. "If he hadn't made himself into the man he is."

"And if you hadn't fallen in love with him. That's something that smooths away the worst of it, Kelsey. When I think of what could have happened—"

"It didn't. Rich Slater paid the price for his part in it. And the case is closed. Self-defense."

"I suppose it was foolish of me to lie to the police." She tossed the bite of roll aside. "He didn't believe me. It's ironic, isn't it? Once I told the truth, once I lied. Neither worked."

"You were trying to protect me." It was time to say it, Kelsey told herself, and she hoped the full meaning would be understood. "You tried to protect me before, when I was a child. You were wrong both times. And you were right both times."

"No easy answers."

"It's taken me a long time to realize there isn't always only one." She pressed her lips together before continuing. "I'm grateful for what you're doing for Milicent. No, please don't stiffen up on me. I'm grateful, even though I can't resolve it in my heart, even though it's a lie. I'm grateful."

"What difference would it make now, Kelsey? To have the whole story come out and destroy what's left of her life?" The birds were singing, and the sound was comforting. "It wouldn't give me back those years. It wouldn't change what happened to Mick, to Pride, to Reno."

"She's responsible for that, for all of it." Shame and bitterness warred inside Kelsey. "No matter that she couldn't have meant anyone to die, she's responsible. Hiring other people to do what she considered necessary to protect the family name? What name does she have now?" Kelsey demanded. "What honor?"

"And that's what she has to live with. I don't do this for her."

"I know."

Naomi lifted a brow. "It's not entirely unselfish, either. I don't want to go through it, to live through the press, the police. And I have the gift of knowing you believed me. You believed in me enough to stick."

"I wasn't the only one who believed you. And everyone would know what happened with Alec Bradley, what happened with Pride and all the rest if the story came out."

"I don't care about everyone." Naomi decided she'd pour coffee after all. "I talked it over with Moses last night, and we're agreed." She smiled, adding cream to her coffee. "When a woman has a man who'll stand by her through the worst, the rest is easy."

Naomi glanced over at the sound of a car pulling into the drive. "That's probably Gabe."

"It better be. We were supposed to go over these menus for the reception over breakfast."

"Then I'd better leave you two alone to do it."

"No, why don't you stay? That way you can agree with what I've already decided and give me the edge."

Kelsey leaned forward, took her mother's hand. "I love you."

Emotions swirled up, then settled beautifully. "I know."

Kelsey rose and started across the patio to greet him. Her eyes widened as they shifted from Gabe's to her father's, then back again. "Dad?"

"Oh, Kelsey." Instinctively Philip framed her face with his hands. Nothing Gabe had told him had prepared him. "Oh, sweetheart."

"I'm all right, really. It looks much worse than it is. I was going to come see you in a couple of days." When she looked more presentable, she thought, and shot Gabe a telling look.

"Your young man was right to tell me the whole story. The whole story," he repeated, staring into her eyes. "You left out a great many details when you phoned me, Kelsey."

Another kind of lie, she thought. The sin of omission. "I thought it best. I only wanted you to know I was all right before the papers reported it. And I am all right."

"So I'm told." He looked back at Gabe, then his gaze shifted, locked over Kelsey's shoulder. She moved aside and stood between her parents.

"Dad wanted to see that I was all right," she began.

"Of course he did." Naomi nodded, and kept her hands at her sides. "Hello, Philip."

"Naomi. You look well."

"So do you."

"Ah..." Kelsey groped for some way to ease past the awkwardness. "Channing's down at the barn. Why don't you walk down with me, Dad? You'll get a kick out of seeing him work, and he can show off for you." She looked helplessly at Gabe.

"I'm sure you'd like to talk with Kelsey," Naomi said. "I was just on my way down to the barn myself. I'll tell Channing you're here."

"No, I—" Philip began, then composed himself. "Actually, I'd like to speak with you. If you have the time."

"All right."

"Let's take a walk," Gabe murmured, and grasped Kelsey's hand.

"I don't know where to begin, Naomi. Gabe told me everything. Everything," Philip repeated, heartsick. "He was kind enough to wait for me when I went to see her. I had to see her," he added, "before I came here."

"I understand."

"Understand?" Unbearably weary, he slipped his fingers under his glasses and pressed them to his eyes. "I can't. I can't understand. All that she did, all the pain she caused. And when I confronted her, she was unbending. Unshakable," he said, and dropped his hands. "She sees nothing that she did as anything but necessary. Men died, but she feels no responsibility. Not to them, not to you."

"And that surprises you?"

He winced. "She remains my mother, Naomi. Even knowing all I know. I've thought of hundreds of ways to try to apologize, and none of them begins to cover it. What she did. What I did." He took off his glasses, rubbed his eyes again, then replaced them. "And the simple fact is, I don't know what to say to you."

"It's over, Philip."

"I let you down. All those years ago, I let you down."

"No. There was a time I thought that. It helped, but it wasn't really true. I wasn't what you wanted me to be. Whatever she's done, Milicent wasn't responsible for that. Only for making sure you realized it."

"She could have prevented you from going to prison."

"Yes."

"And what she did now, to you—to Kelsey." His breath caught as the image of his daughter's bruised face swam into his mind. "My God, Naomi. She might have been killed."

"She protected herself. And me." She studied him, the pain in his eyes, the baffled disbelief behind it. "I can't tell you not to feel what you're feeling now. Kelsey was hurt, was forced to defend herself by taking a life. And you and I will never forget it. We'll never forget who started the chain of events. Maybe," she said slowly, "that's enough punishment for Milicent."

"There's nothing I can do."—Philip's voice faltered, broke—"nothing I can do to make up for it."

"There's nothing you have to do. Despite everything, Kelsey has what she wants. And so do I." Her lips curved softly. "I have everything I want. The farm, a man who loves me. My daughter. You did a wonderful job with her, Philip. I always knew you would."

"She's so like you." He studied the woman who had been his wife. So much had changed, and so little. "Good God, Naomi, if I could go back, do something. Anything."

"You can't." He'd always been so fair, she thought. So honorable. Now he suffered because no amount of fairness, no amount of honor could wipe away the pain. "We wanted things from each other that neither of us could give. And we made mistakes, mistakes we used against each other, and that other people used against us. We were both victims of someone else's needs, Philip."

"You paid dearly for it."

"I've gained, too. She loves me. It's just that simple. Just that marvelous. So let's leave the rest where it belongs. Closed." She drew a breath. "You know, I always wondered how I'd feel if I saw you again."

"I wondered, too. How do you feel, Naomi?"

"I'm glad to see you, Philip."

"Do you think we should leave them alone for so long?"

"Yes, I do." To prove it, Gabe gave her a helpful nudge. "They have old business to settle."

"But—" Kelsey looked back over her shoulder. They were still standing, yards apart. "He looked so sad."

"His world's been shaken, badly. It'll settle again. Maybe not quite in the same way, but it'll settle."

"Candace won't let him brood for long." Still, she dragged her feet. "Gabe, what made you bring him here?"

"We're closing the circle," he said, "before we start our own."

"I like the sound of that." She tipped her head toward his shoulder. "You're awfully smart, Slater. And sneaky, too, going behind my back to bring him here."

"Going to see him was my idea. Coming here was his. He needs to make his peace with Naomi."

"He will." She smiled to herself. It was, after all, her personal fairy tale. "I love it here," she murmured. "I love everything about here. Think of the champions we'll make, Gabe."

"Are we talking horses?"

She shook her head and laughed up at him. "Not only horses. Is that okay with you?"

"That's just fine with me."

He walked her away from the barn, from the crews, toward the rising hills where mares grazed with their foals, and horses raced their shadows.

"Next spring, a foal will be born. His dam from Three Willows, his sire from Longshot." He turned her into his arms. "I'll remember the day he was conceived, how I looked at you and wanted you to belong to me."

"And I do." She linked her arms around his neck. "So, what's next?"

"We've got a fresh deck." He tapped his pocket. "Anything can happen."

"Anything? Well . . ." She drew his mouth down to hers. "Deal them."

Montana Sky

The world stands out on either side
No wider than the heart is wide;
Above the world is stretched the sky,—
No higher than the soul is high.
The heart can push the sea and land
Farther away on either hand;
The soul can split the sky in two,
And let the face of God shine through.
But East and West will pinch the heart
That can not keep them pushed apart;
And he whose soul is flat—the sky
Will cave in on him by and by.

—Edna St. Vincent Millay

To family

Part One
Autumn

The beautiful and death-struck year

—A. E. Housman

1

Being dead didn't make Jack Mercy less of a son of a bitch. One week of dead didn't offset sixty-eight years of living mean. Plenty of the people gathered by his grave would be happy to say so.

The fact was, funeral or no funeral, Bethanne Mosebly muttered those sentiments into her husband's ear as they stood in the high grass of the cemetery. She was there only out of affection for young Willa, and she had bent her husband's tired ear with that information as well all the way up from Ennis.

As a man who had listened to his wife's chatter for forty-six years, Bob Mosebly simply grunted, tuning her and the preacher's droning voice out.

Not that Bob had fond memories of Jack. He'd hated the old bastard, as did most every living soul in the state of Montana.

But dead was dead, Bob mused, and they had sure come out in droves to send the fucker on his way to hell.

This peaceful corner of Mercy Ranch, set in the shadows of the Big Belt Mountains, near the banks of the Missouri, was crowded now with ranchers and cowboys, merchants and politicians. Here where cattle grazed the hills and horses danced in sunny pastures, generations of Mercys were buried under the billowing grass.

Jack was the latest. He'd ordered the glossy chestnut coffin himself, had it custom-made and inscribed in gold with the linked *M*s that made up the ranch's brand. The box was lined with white satin, and Jack was inside it now, wearing his best snakeskin boots, his oldest and most favored Stetson, and holding his bullwhip.

Jack had vowed to die the way he had lived. In nose-thumbing style.

Word was, Willa had already ordered the headstone, according to her father's instructions. It would be white marble—no ordinary granite for Jackson Mercy—and the sentiments inscribed on it were his own:

HERE LIES JACK MERCY.
HE LIVED AS HE WANTED, DIED THE SAME WAY.
THE HELL WITH ANYBODY WHO DIDN'T LIKE IT.

The monument would be raised once the ground had settled, to join all the others that tipped and dotted the stony ground, from Jack Mercy's great-grandfather, Jebidiah Mercy, who had roamed the mountains and claimed the land, to the last of Jack's three wives—and the only one who'd died before he could divorce her.

Wasn't it interesting, Bob mused, that each of Mercy's wives had presented him with a daughter when he'd been hell-bent on having a son? Bob liked to think of it as God's little joke on a man who had stepped on backs—and hearts—to get what he wanted in every other area of his life.

He remembered each of Jack's wives well enough, though none of them had lasted long. Lookers every one, he thought now, and the girls they'd birthed weren't hard on the eyes either. Bethanne had been burning up the phone lines ever since word came along that Mercy's two oldest daughters were flying in for the funeral. Neither of them had set foot on Mercy land since before they could walk.

And they wouldn't have been welcome.

Only Willa had stayed. There'd been little Mercy could do about that, seeing as how her mother had died almost before the child had been weaned. Without any relations to dump the girl on, he'd passed the baby along to his housekeeper, and Bess had raised the girl as best she could.

Each of the women had a touch of Jack in her, Bob noted, scanning them from under the brim of his hat. The dark hair, the sharp chin. You could tell they were sisters, all right, even though they'd never set eyes on each other before. Time would tell how they would deal together, and time would tell if Willa had enough of Jack Mercy in her to run a ranch of twenty-five thousand acres.

She was thinking of the ranch, and the work that needed to be done. The morning was bright and clear, with the hills sporting color so bold and beautiful it almost hurt the eyes. The mountains and valley might have been painted fancy for fall, but the chinook wind had come in hot and dry and thick. Early October was warm enough for shirtsleeves, but that could change tomorrow. There'd already been snow in the high country, and she could see it, dribbling along the black and gray peaks, slyly coating the forests. Cattle needed to be rounded up, fences needed to be checked, repaired, checked again. Winter wheat had to be planted.

It was up to her now. It was all up to her. Jack Mercy was no longer Mercy Ranch, Willa reminded herself. She was.

She listened to the preacher speak of everlasting life, of forgiveness and the welcome of heaven. And thought that Jack Mercy would spit on anyone's welcome into a place other than his own. Montana had been his, this wide country of mountain and meadow, of eagle and wolf.

Her father would be as miserable in heaven as he would in hell.

Her face remained calm as the fancy coffin was lowered into the newest scar in the earth. Her skin was pale gold, a legacy from her mother and her Blackfoot blood as much as the sun. Her eyes, nearly as black as the hair she'd hurriedly twisted into a braid for the funeral, remained fixed on the box that held her father's body. She hadn't worn a hat, and the sun beamed like fire into her eyes. But she didn't let them tear.

She had a proud face, high cheekbones, a wide, haughty mouth, dark, exotic eyes with heavy lids and thick lashes. She'd broken her nose falling off an angry wild mustang when she was eight. Willa liked to think the slight left turn it took in the center of her face added character.

Character meant a great deal more to Willa Mercy than beauty. Men didn't respect beauty, she knew. They used it.

She stood very still, the wind picking up strands from her braid and teasing them into a dance. A woman of average height and tough, rangy build in an ill-fitting black dress and dainty black heels that had never been out of their box before that morning. A woman of twenty-four with work on her mind, and a raging, tearing grief in her heart.

She had, despite everything, loved Jack Mercy. And she said nothing, not one word, to the two women, the strangers who shared her blood and had come to see their father buried.

For a moment, just one moment, she let her gaze shift, let it rest on the grave of Mary Wolfchild Mercy. The mother she couldn't remember was buried under a soft mound of wildflowers that bloomed like jewels in the autumn sun. Adam's doing, she thought, and looked up and into the eyes of her half brother. He would know as no one else could that she had tears in her heart she could never let free.

When Adam took her hand, Willa linked fingers with his. In her mind, and heart, he was all the family she had now.

"He lived the life that satisfied him," Adam murmured. His voice was quiet, peaceful. If they had been alone Willa could have turned, rested her head on his shoulder, and found comfort.

"Yes, he did. And now it's done."

Adam glanced over at the two women, Jack Mercy's daughters, and thought something else was just beginning. "You have to speak with them, Willa."

"They're sleeping in my house, eating my food." Deliberately she looked back at her father's grave. "That's enough."

"They're your blood."

"No, Adam, you're my blood. They're nothing to me." She turned away from him and braced herself to receive the condolences.

. . .

Neighbors brought food for death. There was no stopping the bone-deep tradition, any more than Willa could have stopped Bess from cooking for three days straight to provide for what the housekeeper called the bereavement supper. And that was a double pile of horseshit in Willa's mind. There was no bereavement here. Curiosity, certainly. Many of the people who packed into the main house had been invited before. More, many more, had not. His death provided them entry, and they enjoyed it.

The main house was a showplace, Jack Mercy style. Once a cabin of log and mud had stood there, but that had been more than a hundred years before. Now there was a sprawling, rambling structure of stone and wood, of glistening glass. Rugs from all over the world spread over floors of gleaming pine or polished tile. Jack Mercy had liked to collect. When he'd become master of Mercy Ranch he had spent five years turning what had been a lovely home into his personal palace.

Rich lived rich, he liked to say.

So he had. Collecting paintings and sculpture, adding rooms where the art could be displayed. The entrance was a towering atrium, floored with tiles in jewel tones of sapphire and ruby in a repeating pattern of the Mercy Ranch brand. The staircase that swept to the second floor was polished oak, shiny as glass, with a newel post carved in the shape of a howling wolf.

People gathered there now, many of them goggling over it as they balanced their plates. Others crowded into the living room with its acre of slick floor and wide curve of sofa in cream-colored leather. On the smooth river rock of the wall-spanning fireplace hung a life-size painting of Jack Mercy astride a black stallion. His head was cocked, his hat tipped back, a bullwhip curled in one hand. Many felt that those hard blue eyes damned them as they sat drinking his whiskey and toasting his death.

For Lily Mercy, the second daughter Jack had conceived and discarded, it was terrifying. The house, the people, the noise. The room the housekeeper had given her the day before when she'd arrived was so beautiful. So quiet, she thought now as she moved closer to the rail of the side porch. The lovely bed, the pretty golden wood against the silky wallpaper.

The solitude.

She wanted that now, so very much, as she looked out toward the mountains. Such mountains, she thought. So high, so rough. Nothing at all like the pretty little hills of her home in Virginia. And all the sky, the shuddering and endless blue of it curving down to more land than could possibly exist.

The plains, that wild roll of them, and the wind that seemed never to stop. And the colors, the golds and russets, the scarlets and bronzes of both hill and plain exploding with autumn.

And this valley, where the ranch spread in a spot of such impossible strength and beauty. She'd seen deer out the window that morning, drinking from a stream that glowed silver in the dawn. She'd heard horses, the voices of men, the crow of a rooster, and what she thought—hoped—might have been an eagle's cry.

She wondered whether, if she found the courage to walk into the forest that danced up those foothills, she would see the moose, the elk, the fox that she had read about so greedily on the flight west.

She wondered if she would be allowed to stay even another day—and where she would go, what she would do, if she was asked to leave.

She couldn't go back east, not yet. Self-consciously she fingered the yellowing bruise she'd tried to hide with makeup and sunglasses. Jesse had found her. She'd been so careful, but he'd found her, and the court orders hadn't stopped his fists. They never had. Divorce hadn't stopped him, all the moving and the running hadn't stopped him.

But here, she thought, maybe here, thousands of miles away, in a country so huge, she could finally start again. Without fear.

The letter from the attorney informing her of Jack Mercy's death and requesting her to travel to Montana had been like a gift from God. Though her expenses had been paid, Lily had cashed in the first-class airfare and booked zigzagging flights across the country under three different names. She wanted desperately to believe Jesse Cooke couldn't find her here.

She was so tired of running, of being afraid.

She wondered if she could move to Billings or Helena and find a job. Any job. She wasn't without some skills. There was her teaching degree, and she knew how to use a keyboard. Maybe she could find a small apartment of her own, even just a room to start until she got on her feet again.

She could live here, she thought, staring out at the vast and terrifying and glorious space. Maybe she even belonged here.

She jumped when a hand touched her arm, barely stifled the scream as her heart leaped like a rabbit into her throat.

Not Jesse, she realized, feeling the fool. The man beside her was dark, where Jesse was blond. This man had bronzed skin and hair that streamed to his shoulders. Kind eyes, dark, very dark, in a face as beautiful as a painting.

But then Jesse was beautiful, too. She knew how cruel beauty could be.

"I'm sorry." Adam's voice was as soothing as it would have been if he'd frightened a puppy or a sick foal. "I didn't mean to startle you. Iced tea." He took her hand, noting the way it trembled, and wrapped it around the glass. "It's a dry day."

"Thank you. I didn't hear you come up behind me." In a habit she wasn't even aware of, Lily took a step aside, putting distance between them. Running room. "I was just . . . looking. It's so beautiful here."

"Yes, it is."

She sipped, cooling her dry throat, and ordered herself to be calm and polite. People asked fewer questions when you were calm. "Do you live nearby?"

"Very." He smiled, stepped closer to the rail, and gestured east. He liked her voice, the slow, warm southern flavor of it. "The little white house on the other side of the horse barn."

"Yes, I saw it. You have blue shutters and a garden, and there was a little black dog sleeping in the yard." Lily remembered how homey it had looked, how much more welcoming than the grand house.

"That's Beans." Adam smiled again. "The dog. He has a fondness for refried beans. I'm Adam Wolfchild, Willa's brother."

"Oh." She studied the hand he offered for a moment, then ordered herself to take it. She could see the points of resemblance now, the high, slashing cheekbones, the eyes. "I didn't realize she had a—That would make us . . ."

"No." Her hand seemed very fragile, and he let it go gently. "You shared a father. Willa and I shared a mother."

"I see." And realizing that she'd given very little thought to the man they'd buried today, she felt ashamed. "Were you close, to him . . . your stepfather?"

"No one was." It was said simply and without bitterness. "You're uncomfortable here." He'd noticed her keeping to the edges of groups of people, shying away from contact as if the casual brush of shoulders might bruise her. Just as he'd noticed the marks of violence on her face that she tried to hide.

"I don't know anyone."

Wounded, Adam thought. He had always been drawn to the wounded. She was lovely, and injured. Dressed neatly in a quiet black suit and heels, she was only an inch or so shorter than his five ten and too thin for her height. Her hair was dark, with a sheen of red, and it fell in soft waves that reminded him of angel wings. He couldn't see her eyes behind the sunglasses, but he wondered about their color, and about what else he would read in them.

She had her father's chin, he noticed, but her mouth was soft and rather small, like a child's. There had been the faint hint of a dimple beside it when she'd tried to smile at him. Her skin was creamy, very pale—a fragile contrast to the marks on it.

She was alone, he thought, and afraid. It might take him some time to soften Willa's heart toward this woman, this sister.

"I have to check on a horse," he began.

"Oh." It surprised her that she was disappointed. She had wanted to be alone. She was better when she was alone. "I won't keep you."

"Would you like to walk down? See some of the stock?"

"The horses? I—" Don't be a coward, she ordered herself. He isn't going to hurt you. "Yes, I'd like that. If I wouldn't be in your way."

"You wouldn't." Knowing she'd shy away, he didn't offer a hand or take her arm, but merely led the way down the stairs and across the rough dirt road.

Several people saw them go, and tongues wagged as tongues do. Lily Mercy was one of Jack's daughters, after all, though, as was pointed out, she hardly had a word to say for herself. Something that had never been Willa's problem—no, indeed. That was a girl who said plenty, whatever and whenever she wanted.

As for the other one—well, that was a different kettle of fish altogether. Snooty, she was, parading around in her fancy suit and looking down her nose. Anybody with eyes could see the way she'd stood at the gravesite, cold as ice. She was a picture, to be sure. Jack had sired fine-looking daughters, and that one, the oldest one, had his eyes. Hard and sharp and blue.

It was obvious she thought she was better than the rest of them with her California polish and her expensive shoes, but there were plenty who remembered her ma had been a Las Vegas showgirl with a big, braying laugh and a bawdy turn of phrase. Those who did remember had already decided they much preferred the mother to the daughter.

Tess Mercy couldn't have cared less. She was here in this godforsaken outback only until the will couldn't be read. She'd take what was hers, which was less than the old bastard owed her, and shake the dust off her Ferragamos.

"I'll be back by Monday at the latest."

She carried the phone along as she paced about with quick, jerky motions, nervous energy searing the air around her. She'd closed the doors of what she supposed was a den, hoping to have at least a few moments of privacy. She had to work hard to ignore the mounted animal heads that populated the walls.

"The script's finished." She smiled a little, tunneled her fingers through the straightedge swing of dark hair that curved at her jaw. "Damn right it's brilliant, and it'll be in your hot little hands Monday. Don't hassle me, Ira," she warned her agent. "I'll get you the script, then you get me the deal. My cash flow's down to a dribble."

She shifted the phone and pursed her lips as she helped herself to a snifter of brandy from the decanter. She was still listening to the promises and pleas of Hollywood when she saw Lily and Adam stroll by the window.

Interesting, she thought, and sipped. The little mouse and the Noble Savage.

Tess had done some quick checking before she'd made the trip to Montana. She knew Adam Wolfchild was the son of Jack Mercy's third and final wife. That he'd been eight when his mother had married Mercy. Wolfchild was Blackfoot, or mostly. His mother had been part Indian. The man had spent twenty-five years on Mercy Ranch and had little more to show for it than a tiny house and a job tending horses.

Tess intended to have more.

As for Lily, all Tess had discovered was that she was divorced, childless, and moved around quite a bit. Probably because her husband had used her for a punching bag, Tess thought, and made herself clamp down on a stir of pity. She couldn't afford emotional attachments here. It was straight business.

Lily's mother had been a photographer who'd come to Montana to snap pictures of the real West. She'd snapped Jack Mercy—for all the good it had done her, Tess thought.

Then there was Willa. Tess's mouth tightened as she thought of Willa. The one who had stayed, the one the old bastard had kept.

Well, she owned the place now, Tess assumed, shrugging her shoulders. And she was welcome to it. No doubt she'd earned it. But Tess Mercy wasn't walking away without a nice chunk of change.

Looking out the window, she could see the plains in the distance, rolling, rolling endlessly, as empty as the moon. With a shudder, she turned her back on the view. Christ, she wanted Rodeo Drive.

"Monday, Ira," she snapped, annoyed with his voice buzzing in her ear. "Your office, twelve sharp. Then you can take me to lunch." With that as a good-bye, she replaced the receiver.

Three days, tops, she promised herself, and toasted an elk head with her brandy. Then she'd get the hell out of Dodge and back to civilization.

"I shouldn't have to remind you that you got guests downstairs, Will." Bess Pringle stood with her hands on her bony hips and used the same tone she'd used when Willa was ten.

Willa jerked her jeans on—Bess didn't believe in little niceties like privacy and had barely knocked before striding into the bedroom. Willa responded just as she might have at ten. "Then don't." She sat down to pull on her boots.

"Rude is a four-letter word."

"So's work, but it still has to be done."

"And you've got enough hands around this place to see to it for one blessed day. You're not going off somewhere today, of all days. It ain't fittin'."

What was or wasn't fitting constituted the bulk of Bess's moral and social codes. She was a bird of a woman, all bone and teeth, though she could plow through a mountain of hotcakes like a starving field hand and had the sweet tooth of an eight-year-old. She was fifty-eight—and had changed the date on her birth certificate to prove it—and had a head of flaming red hair she dyed in secret and kept pulled back in a don't-give-me-any-lip bun.

Her voice was as rough as pine bark and her face as smooth as a girl's, and surprisingly pretty with moss-green eyes and a pug Irish nose. Her hands were small and quick and able. And so was her temper.

With her fists still glued to her hips, she marched up to Willa and glared down. "You get your sassy self down those stairs and tend to your guests."

"I've got a ranch to run." Willa rose. It hardly mattered that in her boots she topped Bess by six inches. The balance of power had always tottered back and forth between them. "And they're not my guests. I'm not the one who wanted them here."

"They've come to pay respects. That's fittin'."

"They've come to gawk and prowl around the house. And it's time they left."

"Maybe some of them did." Bess jerked her head in a little nod. "But there's plenty more who are here for you."

"I don't want them." Willa turned away, picked up her hat, then simply stood staring out her window, crushing the brim in her hands. The window faced the mountains, the dark belt of trees, the peaks of the Big Belt that held all the beauty and mystery in the world. "I don't need them. I can't breathe with all these people hovering around."

Bess hesitated before laying a hand on Willa's shoulder. Jack Mercy hadn't wanted his daughter raised soft. No pampering, no spoiling, no cuddling. He'd made that clear while Willa had still been in diapers. So Bess had pampered and spoiled and cuddled only when she was certain she wouldn't be caught and sent away like one of Jack's wives.

"Honey, you got a right to grieve."

"He's dead and he's buried. Feeling sorry won't change it." But she lifted a hand, closed it over the small one on her shoulder. "He didn't even tell me he was sick, Bess. He couldn't even give me those last few weeks to try to take care of him, or to say good-bye."

"He was a proud man," Bess said, but she thought, Bastard. Selfish bastard. "It's better the cancer took him quick rather than letting him linger. He would've hated that and it would've been harder on you."

"One way or the other, it's done." She smoothed the wide, circling brim of her hat, settled it on her head. "I've got animals and people depending on me. The hands need to see, right now, that I'm in charge. That Mercy Ranch is still being run by a Mercy."

"You do what you have to do, then." Years of experience had taught Bess that what was fitting didn't hold much water when it came to ranch business. "But you be back by suppertime. You're going to sit down and eat decent."

"Clear these people out of the house, and I will."

She started out, turning left toward the back stairs. They wound down the east wing of the house and allowed her to slip into the mudroom. Even there she could hear the beehive buzz of conversations from the other rooms, the occasional roll of laughter. Resenting all of it, she slammed out the door, then pulled up short when she saw the two men smoking companionably on the side porch.

Her gaze narrowed on the older man and the bottle of beer dangling from his fingers. "Enjoying yourself, Ham?"

Sarcasm from Willa didn't ruffle Hamilton Dawson. He'd put her up on her first pony, had wrapped her head after her first spill. He'd taught her how to use a rope, shoot a rifle, and dress a deer. Now he merely fit his cigarette into the little hole surrounded by grizzled hair and blew out a smoke ring.

"It's"—another smoke ring formed—"a pretty afternoon."

"I want the fence checked along the northwest boundary."

"Been done," he said placidly, and continued to lean on the rail, a short, stocky man on legs curved like a wishbone. He was ranch foreman and figured he knew what needed to be done as well as Willa did. "Got a crew out making repairs. Sent Brewster and Pickles up the high country. We lost a couple head up there. Looks like cougar." Another drag, another stream of smoke. "Brewster'll take care of it. Likes to shoot things."

"I want to talk to him when he gets back."

"I expect you will." He straightened up from the rail, adjusted his mud-colored dishrag of a hat. "It's weaning time."

"Yes, I know."

He expected she did, and nodded again. "I'll go check on the fence crew. Sorry about your pa, Will."

She knew those simple words tacked onto ranch business were more sincere and personal than the acres of flowers sent by strangers. "I'll ride out later."

He nodded, to her, to the man beside him, then hitched his bowlegged way toward his rig.

"How are you holding up, Will?"

She shrugged a shoulder, frustrated that she didn't know what to do next. "I want it to be tomorrow," she said. "Tomorrow'll be easier, don't you think, Nate?"

Because he didn't want to tell her the answer was no, he tipped back his beer. He was there for her, as a friend, a fellow rancher, a neighbor. He was also there as Jack Mercy's lawyer, and he knew that before too much more time passed he was going to shatter the woman standing beside him.

"Let's take a walk." He set the beer down on the rail, took Willa's arm. "My legs need stretching."

He had a lot of them. Nathan Torrence was a tall one. He'd hit six two at seventeen and had kept growing. Now, at thirty-three, he was six six and lanky with it. Hair the color of wheat straw curled under his hat. His eyes were as blue as the Montana sky in a face handsomely scored by wind and sun. At the end of long arms were big hands. At the end of long legs were big feet. Despite them, he was surprisingly graceful.

He looked like a cowboy, walked like a cowboy. His heart, when it came to matters of his family, his horses, and the poetry of Keats, was as soft as a down pillow. His mind, when it came to matters of law, of justice, of simple right and wrong, was as hard as granite.

He had a deep and long-standing affection for Willa Mercy. And he hated that he had no choice but to put her through hell.

"I've never lost anybody close to me," Nate began. "I can't say I know how you feel."

Willa kept walking, past the cookhouse, the bunkhouse, by the chicken house where the hens were going broody. "He never let anyone get close to him. I don't know how I feel."

"The ranch . . ." This was dicey territory, and Nate negotiated carefully. "It's a lot to deal with."

"We've got good people, good stock, good land." It wasn't hard to smile up at Nate. It never was. "Good friends."

"You can call on me anytime, Will. Me or anyone in the county."

"I know that." She looked beyond him, to the paddocks, the corrals, the outbuildings, the houses, and farther, to where the land went into its long, endless roll to the bottom of the sky. "A Mercy has run this place for more than a hundred years. Raised cattle, planted grain, run horses. I know what needs to be done and how to do it. Nothing really changes."

Everything changes, Nate thought. And the world she was speaking of was about to take a sharp turn, thanks to the hard heart of a dead man. It was better to do it now, straight off, before she climbed onto a horse or into a rig and rode off.

"We'd best get to the reading of the will," he decided.

2

Jack Mercy's office, on the second floor of the main house, was big as a ballroom. The walls were paneled in yellow pine lumbered from his own land and shellacked to a rich gloss that lent a golden light to the room. Huge windows provided views of the ranch, the land and sky. Jack had been fond of saying he could see all a man needed to see from those windows, which were undraped but ornately trimmed.

On the floor were layered the rugs he'd collected. The chairs were leather, as he'd preferred, in rich shades of teal and maroon.

His trophies hung on the walls—heads of elk and bighorn sheep, of bear and buck. Crouched in one corner as though poised to charge was a massive black grizzly, fangs exposed, glassy black eyes full of rage.

Some of his favored weapons were in a locked display case. His great-grandfather's Henry rifle and Colt Peacemaker, the Browning shotgun that had brought down the bear, the Mossberg 500 he'd called his dove duster, and the .44 Magnum he'd preferred for handgun hunting.

It was a man's room, with male scents of leather and wood and a whiff of tobacco from the Cubans he liked to smoke.

The desk, which he'd had custom-made, was a lake of glossy wood, a maze of drawers all hinged with polished brass. Nate sat behind it now, fiddling with papers to give everyone present time to settle.

Tess thought he looked as out of place as a beer keg at a church social. The cowboy lawyer, she thought with a quick twist of her lips, duded up in his Sunday best. Not that he wasn't appealing in a rough, country sort of fashion. A young Jimmy Stewart, she thought, all arms and legs and quiet sexuality. But big, gangling men who wore boots with their gabardine weren't her style.

And she just wanted to get this whole damn business over with and get back to LA. She rolled her eyes toward the snarling grizzly, the shaggy head of a mountain goat, the weapons that had hunted them down. What a place, she mused. And what people.

Besides the cowboy lawyer, there was the skinny, henna-haired housekeeper, who sat in a straight-backed chair with her knobby knees tight together and modestly covered with a perfectly horrible black skirt. Then the Noble Savage, with his heartbreakingly beautiful face, his enigmatic eyes, and the faint odor of horses that clung to him.

Nervous Lily, Tess thought, continuing her survey, with her hands pressed together like vises and her head lowered, as if that would hide the bruises on her face. Lovely and fragile as a lost bird set down among vultures.

When Tess's heart began to stir, she deliberately turned her attention to Willa.

Cowgirl Mercy, she thought with a sniff. Sullen, probably stupid, and silent. At least the woman looked better in jeans and flannel than she had in that baggy dress she'd worn to the funeral. In fact, Tess decided she made quite a picture, sitting in the big leather chair, her booted foot resting on her knee, her oddly exotic face set like stone.

And since she'd yet to see a single tear squeeze its way out of the dark eyes, Tess assumed Willa had no more love for Jack Mercy than she herself did.

Just business, she thought, tapping her fingers impatiently on the arm of her chair. Let's get down to it.

Even as she had the thought, Nate lifted his eyes, met hers. For one uncomfortable moment, she felt he knew exactly what was going through her mind. And his disapproval of her, of everything about her, was as clear as the sky spread in the window behind him.

Think what you want, she decided, and kept her eyes cool on his. Just give me the cash.

"There's a couple ways we can do this," Nate began. "There's formal. I can read Jack's will word for word, then explain what the hell all that legal talk means. Or I can give you the meaning, the terms, the options first." Deliberately he looked at Willa. She was the one who mattered most, to him. "Up to you."

"Do it the easy way, Nate."

"All right, then. Bess, he left you a thousand dollars for every year you've been at Mercy. That's thirty-four thousand."

"Thirty-four thousand." Bess's eyes popped wide. "Good Lord, Nate, what am I supposed to do with a fat lot of money like that?"

He smiled. "Well, you spend it, Bess. If you want to invest some, I can give you a hand with it."

"Goodness." Overwhelmed at the thought of it, she looked at Willa, back at her hands, and at Nate again. "Goodness."

And Tess thought: If the housekeeper gets thirty grand, I ought to get double. She knew just what *she'd* do with a fat lot of money.

"Adam, in accordance with an agreement Jack made with your mother when they married, you're to receive a lump sum of twenty thousand, or a two percent interest in Mercy Ranch, whichever you prefer. I can tell you the percentage is worth more than the cash, but the decision remains yours."

"It's not enough." Willa's voice snapped out, making Lily jump and Tess raise an eyebrow. "It's not right. Two percent? Adam's worked this ranch since he was eight years old. He's—"

"Willa." From his position behind her chair, Adam laid a hand on her shoulder. "It's right enough."

"The hell it is." Fury for him, the injustice of it, had her shoving the hand away. "We've got one of the finest strings of horses in the state. That's Adam's doing. The horses should be his now—and the house where he lives. He should have been given land, and the money to work it."

"Willa." Patient, Adam put his hand on her again, held it there. "It's what our mother asked for. It's what he gave."

She subsided because there were strangers' eyes watching. And because she would fix the wrongness of it. She'd have Nate draw up papers before the end of the day. "Sorry." She laid her hands calmly on the wide arms of the chair. "Go on, Nate."

"The ranch and its holdings," Nate began again, "the stock, the equipment, vehicles, the timber rights . . ." He paused, and prepared himself for the unhappy job of destroying hopes. "Mercy Ranch business is to continue as usual, expenses drawn, salaries paid, profits banked or reinvested with you as operator, Will, under the executor's supervision for a period of one year."

"Wait." Willa held up a hand. "He wanted you to supervise the running of the ranch for a year?"

"Under certain conditions," Nate added, and his eyes were already full of apology. "If those conditions are met for the course of a year, beginning no later than fourteen days from the reading of the will, the ranch and all its holdings will become the sole property and sole interest of the beneficiaries."

"What conditions?" Willa demanded. "What beneficiaries? What the hell is going on, Nate?"

"He's left each one of his daughters a one-third interest in the ranch." He watched the color drain from Willa's face and, cursing Jack Mercy, continued with the rest. "In order to inherit, the three of you must live on the ranch, leaving the property for no longer than a one-week period, for one full year. At the end of that time, if conditions are met, each beneficiary will have a one-third interest. This interest cannot be sold or transferred to anyone other than one of the other beneficiaries for a period of ten years."

"Hold on a minute." Tess set her drink aside. "You're saying I've got a third interest in some cattle ranch in Nowhere, Montana, and to collect, I've got to move here? Live here? Give up a year of my life? No way in hell." She rose, gracefully unfolding her long legs. "I don't want your ranch, kid," she told Willa. "You're welcome to every dusty acre and cow. This'll never stick. Give me my share in cash, and I'm out of your way."

"Excuse me, Ms. Mercy." Nate sized her up from his seat behind the desk. Mad as a two-headed hen, he thought, and cool enough to hide it. "It will stick. His terms and wishes were very well thought out, very well presented. If you don't agree to the terms, the ranch will be donated, in its entirety, to the Nature Conservancy."

"Donated?" Staggered, Willa pressed her fingers to her temple. There was hurt and rage and a terrible dread curling and spreading inside her gut. Somehow she had to get beyond the feelings and think.

She understood the ten-year stipulation. That was to keep the land from being tax-assessed at the market price instead of the farm rate. Jack had hated the government like poison and wouldn't have wanted to give up a penny to it. But to threaten to take it all away and give it to the type of organization he liked to call tree huggers or whale kissers didn't make sense.

"If we don't do this," she continued, struggling for calm, "he can just give it away? Just give away what's been Mercy land for more than a century if these two don't do what it says on that paper? If I don't?"

Nate exhaled deeply, hating himself. "I'm sorry, Willa. There was no reasoning with him. This is the way he set it up. Any one of the three of you leaves, it breaks the conditions, and the ranch is forfeited. You'll each get one hundred dollars. That's it."

"A hundred dollars?" The absurdity of it struck Tess straight in the heart, flopped her back into her chair laughing. "That son of a bitch."

"Shut up." Willa's voice whipped out as she got to her feet. "Just shut the hell up. Can we fight it, Nate? Is there any point in trying to fight it?"

"You want my legal opinion, no. It'd take years and a lot of money, and odds are you'd lose."

"I'll stay." Lily fought to regulate her breathing. Home, safety, security. It was all here, just at her fingertips, like a shiny gift. "I'm sorry." She got to her feet when Willa rounded on her. "It's not fair to you. It's not right. I don't know why he did this, but I'll stay. When the year's over, I'll sell you my share for whatever you say is fair and right. It's a beautiful ranch," she added, trying to smile as Willa only continued to stare at her. "Everyone here knows it's already yours. It's only a year, after all."

"That's very sweet," Tess spoke up. "But I'm damned if I'm staying here for a year. I'm going back to LA in the morning."

With her mind whirling, Willa sent her a considering look. However much she wanted both of them gone, she wanted the ranch more. Much more. "Nate, what happens if one of the three of us dies suddenly?"

"Funny." Tess picked up her brandy again. "Is that Montana humor?"

"In the event one of the beneficiaries dies within the transitory year, the remaining beneficiaries will be granted half shares of Mercy Ranch, under the same conditions."

"So what are you going to do, kill me in my sleep? Bury me on the prairie?" Tess flicked her fingers in dismissal. "You can't threaten me into staying here, living like this."

Maybe not, Willa thought, but money talked to certain types of people. "I don't want you here. I don't want either one of you, but I'll do what has to be done to keep this ranch. Miss Hollywood might be interested to know just how much her dusty acres are worth, Nate."

"At an estimate, current market value for the land and buildings alone, not including stock . . . between eighteen and twenty million."

Brandy slopped toward the rim of the snifter as Tess's hand jerked. "Jesus Christ."

The outburst earned Tess a hiss from Bess and a sneer from Willa. "I thought that would get through," Willa murmured. "When's the last time you earned six million in a year . . . sis?"

"Could I have some water?" Lily managed, and drew Willa's gaze.

"Sit down before you fall down." She gave Lily a careless nudge into a chair as she began to pace. "I'm going to want you to read the document word for word after all, Nate. I want to get this all straight in my head." She went to a lacquered liquor cabinet and did something she'd never done when her father had been alive. She opened his whiskey and drank it.

She drank quietly, letting the slow burn move down her throat as she listened to Nate's recital. And she forced herself not to think of all the years she had struggled so hard to earn her father's love, much less his respect. His trust.

In the end, he had lumped her in with the daughters he'd never known. Because in the end, she thought, none of them had really mattered to him.

A name Nate mumbled had her ears burning. "Hold it. Hold just a damn minute. Did you say Ben McKinnon?"

Nate shifted, cleared his throat. He'd been hoping to slide that one by her, for the time being. She'd had enough shocks for one day. "Your father designated myself and Ben to supervise the running of the ranch during the probationary year."

"That chicken hawk's going to be looking over my shoulder for a goddamn year?"

"Don't you swear in this house, Will," Bess piped up.

"I'll swear the damn house down if I want. Why the hell did he pick McKinnon?"

"Your father considered Three Rocks second only to Mercy. He wanted someone who knows the ins and outs of the business."

McKinnon can be mean as a snake, Nate remembered Mercy saying. And he won't take any shit off a damn woman.

"Neither of us will be looking over your shoulder," Nate soothed. "We have our own ranches to run. This is just a minor detail."

"Bullshit." But Will reined it in. "Does McKinnon know about this? He wasn't at the funeral."

"He had business in Bozeman. He'll be back tonight or tomorrow. And yes, he knows."

"Had a hell of a laugh over it, didn't he?"

Had nearly choked with laughter, Nate remembered, but now he kept his own eyes sober. "This isn't a joke, Will. It's business, and temporary at that. All you have to do is get through four seasons." His lips curved. "That's what all of us have to do."

"I'll get through it. God knows if these two will." She studied her sisters, shook her head. "What are you trembling about?" she asked Lily. "You're facing millions of dollars, not a firing squad. For Christ's sake, drink this." She thrust the whiskey glass into Lily's hand.

"Stop picking on her." Incensed, instinctively moving to protect Lily, Tess stepped between them.

"I'm not picking on her, and get out of my face."

"I'm going to be in your face for a goddamn year. Get used to it."

"Then you better get used to how things run around here. You stay, you're not going to sit around on your plump little ass, you're going to work."

At the "plump little ass" remark, Tess sucked air through her nose. She'd sweated and starved off every excess pound she'd carried through high school, and she was damn proud of the results. "Remember this, you flat-chested, knock-kneed bitch, I walk, you lose. And if you think I'm going to take orders from some ignorant little pie-faced cowgirl, you're a hell of a lot more stupid than you look."

"You'll do exactly what I say," Willa corrected. "Or instead of having a nice cozy bed in this house you'll be pitching a tent in the hills for the next year."

"I've got as much right to be under this roof as you do. Maybe more, since he married my mother first."

"That just makes you older," Will tossed back, and had the pleasure of seeing that nice shaft strike home. "And your mother was a bottle-blonde showgirl with more tits than brains."

Whatever Tess would have done or said in retaliation was broken off when Lily burst into tears.

"Happy now?" Tess demanded, and gave Willa a hard shove.

"Stop." Tired of the sniping, Adam seared them both with a look. "You should both be ashamed of yourselves." He bent down, murmuring to Lily as he helped her to her feet. "You want fresh air," he said kindly. "And some food. You'll feel better then."

"Take her for a little walk," Bess told him, and got creakily to her own feet. Her head was hammering like a three-armed carpenter. "I'll put dinner on. I'm ashamed enough for both of you," she said to Tess and Willa. "I knew both of your mas. They'd expect better of you." She sniffed and, with dignity, turned to Nate. "You're welcome to stay for dinner, Nate. There's more than plenty."

"Thanks, Bess, but . . ." He was getting the hell out while he still had all of his skin. "I've got to get on home." He gathered his papers together, keeping a wary eye on the two women who remained in the room, scowling at each other. "I'm leaving three copies of all the documents. Any questions, you know where to reach me. If I don't hear from you I'll check back in a couple days, and see . . . And see," he ended. He picked up his hat and his briefcase and left the field.

In control again, Willa took a cleansing breath. "I've put sweat and I've put blood into this ranch from the day I was born. You don't give a damn about that, and I don't care. But I'm not losing what's mine. You figure that puts me over a barrel, but I know you're not walking away from more money than you've ever seen before, or hoped to. So that makes us even."

With a nod, Tess sat on the arm of a chair and crossed her silky legs. "So, we define terms of our own for living through the next year. You think it's a snap for me to give up my home, my friends, my life-style for a year. It's not."

Tess gave a quick, sentimental thought to her apartment, her club, Rodeo Drive. Then she set her jaw. "But no, I'm not walking away from what's mine, either."

"Yours, my ass."

Tess merely inclined her head. "Whether either one of us likes it, and I doubt either one of us does, I'm as much his daughter as you are. I didn't grow up here because he tossed me and my mother aside. That's fact, and after being here for a day, I'm beginning to be grateful for it. But I'll stick the year out."

Thoughtfully, Willa picked up the whiskey Lily hadn't touched. Ambition and greed were excellent motivators. She'd stick, all right. "And at the end of it?"

"You can buy me out." The image of all that money made her giddy. "Or failing that, you can send the checks for my share of profits to LA. Which is where I'll be one day after the year is up."

Will sampled the whiskey again and reminded herself to concentrate on now. "Can you ride?"

"Ride what?"

With a snort, Will drank. "Figures. Probably don't know a hen from a cock either."

"Oh, I know a cock when I see one," Tess drawled, and was surprised to hear Willa laugh.

"People live here, they work here. That's another fact. I've got enough to do handling the men and cattle without worrying with you, so you'll take your orders from Bess."

"You expect me to take orders from a housekeeper?"

Steel glittered in Willa's eyes. "You'll take orders from the woman who's going to feed you, tend your clothes, and clean the house where you'll be living. And the first time you treat her like a servant will be the last time. I promise you. You're not in LA now, Hollywood. Out here everybody pulls their weight."

"I happen to have a career."

"Yeah, writing movies." There were probably less useful enterprises, but Willa couldn't think of any. "Well, there're twenty-four hours in a day. You're going to figure that one out fast enough." Tired, Will wandered to the window behind the desk. "What the hell am I going to do with the little lost bird?"

"More like a crushed flower."

Surprised at the compassion in the tone, Willa glanced back, then shrugged. "Did she say anything to you about the bruises?"

"I haven't talked to her any more than you have." Tess struggled to push away the guilt. Noninvolvement, she reminded herself. "This isn't exactly a family reunion."

"She'll tell Adam. Sooner or later everyone tells Adam what hurts. For now at least, we'll leave the wounded Lily to him."

"Fine. I'm going back to LA in the morning. To pack."

"One of the men will drive you to the airport."

Dismissing Tess, Willa turned back to the window. "Do yourself a favor, Hollywood, and buy some long underwear. You'll need it."

Will rode out at dusk. The sun was bleeding as it fell behind the western peaks, turning the sky to a rich, ripe red. She needed to think, to calm herself. Beneath her, the Appaloosa mare pranced and pulled on the bit.

"Okay, Moon, let's both run it off." With a jerk of the reins, Will changed directions, then gave the eager mare her head. They streaked away from the lights, the buildings, the sounds of the ranch and into the open land where the river curved.

They followed its banks, riding east into the night where the first stars were already gleaming and the only sounds were the rush of water and the thunder of hooves. Cattle grazed and nighthawks circled. As they topped a rise, Will could see mile after mile of silhouette and shadow, trees spearing up, the waving grass of a meadow, the endless line of fence. And in the distance in the clear night air the faint glint of lights from a neighboring ranch.

McKinnon land.

The mare tossed her head, snorted, when Will reined in. "We didn't run it out, did we?"

No, the anger was still simmering inside her just as the energy simmered inside her mount. Willa wanted it gone, this tearing, bitter fury and the grief that boiled under it. It wouldn't help her get through the next year. It wouldn't help her get through the next hour, she thought, and squeezed her eyes tight.

Tears would not be shed, she promised herself. Not for Jack Mercy, or his youngest daughter.

She breathed deep, drew in the scent of grass and night and horse. It was control she needed now, calculated, unbending control. She would find a way to handle the two sisters who had been pushed on her, to keep them in line and on the ranch. Whatever it took, she would make certain that they saw this through.

She would find a way to deal with the overseers who had been pushed on her. Nate was an irritant but not a particular problem, she decided as she set Moon into an easy walk. He would do no more and no less than what he considered his legal duty. Which meant, in Willa's opinion, that he would stay out of the day-to-day business of Mercy Ranch and play his part in broad strokes.

She could even find it in her heart to feel sorry for him. She'd known him too long and too well to think even for an instant that he would enjoy the position he'd been put in. Nate was fair, honest, and content to mind his own business.

Ben McKinnon, Will thought, and that bitter anger began to stir again. That was a different matter. She had no doubt that he would enjoy every minute. He'd push his nose in at every opportunity, and she'd have to take it. But, she thought with a grim smile, she wouldn't have to take it well and she wouldn't have to make it easy for him.

Oh, she knew what Jack Mercy had been about, and it made her blood boil. She could feel the heat rise to her skin and all but steam off into the cool night air as she looked down at the lights and silhouettes of Three Rocks Ranch.

McKinnon and Mercy land had marched side by side for generations. Some years after the Sioux had dealt with Custer, two men who'd hunted the mountains and taken their stake to Texas, bought cattle on the cheap, and drove them back north into Montana as partners. But the partnership had severed, and each had claimed his own land, his own cattle, and built his own ranch.

So there had been Mercy Ranch and Three Rocks Ranch, each expanding, prospering, struggling, surviving.

And Jack Mercy had lusted after McKinnon land. Land that couldn't be bought or stolen or finessed. But it could be merged, Willa thought now. If Mercy and McKinnon lands were joined, the result would be one of the largest, certainly the most important, ranches in the West.

All he had to do was sell his daughter. What else was a female good for? Willa thought now. Trade her, as you would a nice plump heifer. Put her in front of the bull often enough and nature would handle the rest.

So, since he'd had no son, he was doing the next best thing. He was putting his daughter in front of Ben McKinnon. And everyone would know it, Will thought as she forced her hands to relax on the reins. He hadn't been able to work the deal while he lived, so he was working the angles from the grave.

And if the daughter who had stood beside him her entire life, had worked beside him, had sweated and bled into the land wasn't lure enough—well, he had two more.

"Goddamn you, Pa." With unsteady hands, she settled her hat back onto her head. "The ranch is mine, and it's going to stay mine. Damned if I'll spread my legs for Ben McKinnon or anyone else."

She caught the flash of headlights, murmured to her mare to settle her. She couldn't make out the vehicle, but noted the direction. A thin smile spread as she watched the lights veer toward the main house at Three Rocks.

"Back from Bozeman, is he?" Instinctively she straightened in the saddle, brought her chin up. The air was clear enough that she heard the muffled slam of the truck's door, the yapping greeting of dogs. She wondered if he would look over and up on the rise. He would see the dark shadow of horse and rider. And she thought he would know who was watching from the border of his land.

"We'll see what happens next, McKinnon," she murmured. "We'll see who runs Mercy when it's done."

A coyote sang out, howling at the three-quarter moon that rode the sky. And she smiled again. There were all kinds of coyotes, she thought. No matter how pretty they sang, they were still scavengers.

She wasn't going to let any scavengers on her land.

Turning her mount, she rode home in the half-light.

3

"The son of a bitch." Ben leaned on his saddle horn, shaking his head at Nate. His eyes, shielded by the wide brim of a dark gray hat, glittered cold green. "I'm sorry I missed his funeral. My folks said it was quite the social event."

"It was that." Nate slapped a hand absently against the black gelding's flanks. He'd caught Ben minutes before his friend was taking off for the high country.

In Nate's opinion, Three Rocks was one of the prettiest spreads in Montana. The main house itself was a fine example of both efficiency and aesthetics. It wasn't a palace like Mercy, but an attractive timber-framed dwelling with a sandstone foundation and varying rooflines that added interest, with plenty of porches and decks for sitting and contemplating the hills.

The McKinnons ran a tidy place, busy but without clutter.

He could hear the bovine protests from a corral. Calves being separated from their mamas for weaning didn't go happily. The males'll be unhappier yet, Nate mused, when they're castrated and dehorned.

It was one of the reasons he preferred working horses.

"I know you've got work to see to," Nate continued. "I don't want to hold you up, but I figured I should come by and let you know where we stand."

"Yeah." Ben did have work on his mind. October bumped into November, and that shaky border before winter didn't last long. Right now the sun was shining over Three Rocks like an angel. Horses were cropping in the near pasture, and the men were going about their duties in shirtsleeves. But drift fences needed to be checked, small grains harvested. The cattle that weren't to be wintered over had to be culled out and shipped.

But his gaze skimmed over paddocks and pastures to the rise, toward Mercy land. He imagined Willa Mercy had more than work on her mind this morning. "Nothing against your lawyering skills, Nate, but that legal bullshit isn't going to hold up, is it?"

"The terms of the will are clear, and very precise."

"It's still lawyer crap."

They'd known each other too long for Nate to take offense. "She can fight it, but it'll be uphill and rough all the way."

Ben looked southwest again, pictured Willa Mercy, shook his head. He sat as comfortably in the saddle as another man would in an easy chair. After thirty years of ranch life, it was more his natural milieu. He didn't have Nate's height, but stood a level six feet, his wiry build ropey with muscle. His hair was a golden brown, gilded by hours in the sun and left long enough to tease the collar of his chambray shirt. His eyes were as sharp as a hawk's and often just as cold in a face that had the weathered, craggy good looks of a man comfortable in the out-of-doors. A horizontal scar marred his chin, a souvenir of his youth and a slip of the hand when he'd been playing mumblety-peg with his brother.

Ben ran his hand over the scar now, an absentminded, habitual gesture. He'd been amused when Nate had first informed him of the will. Now that it was coming into effect, it didn't seem quite so funny.

"How's she taking it?"

"Hard."

"Shit. I'm sorry for that. She loved that old bastard, Christ knows why." He took off his hat, raked his fingers through his hair, adjusted it again. "And it's got to stick in her craw that it's me."

Nate grinned. "Well, yeah, but I think it'd sit about the same with anybody."

No, Ben mused, not quite. He wondered if Willa knew that her father had once offered him ten thousand acres of prime bottomland to marry his daughter. Like some sort of fucking king, Ben thought now, trying to merge kingdoms.

Mercy would give it away, he thought, squinting into the sun. He'd give it away rather than ease his hold on the reins.

"She doesn't need either one of us to run Mercy," Ben said. "But I'll do what it says to do. And hell . . ." His grin spread slow, arrogant, and shifted the planes on his face. "It'll be entertaining to have her butting heads with me every five minutes. What are the other two like?"

"Different." Thoughtful, Nate leaned back on the fender of his Range Rover. "The middle one—that's Lily—she spooks easy. Looks like she'd jump out of her skin if you made a quick move. Her face was all bruised up."

"She have an accident?"

"Looked like she'd accidentally run into somebody's fists. She's got an ex-husband. And she's got a restraining order on him. He's been yanked in a few times for wife battering."

"Fucker." If there was one thing worse than a man who abused his horse, it was a man who abused a woman.

"She jumped on staying," Nate continued, and in his quiet, methodical way began to roll a cigarette. "I have to figure she's looking at it as a good place to hide out. The older one, she's slicker. Hails out of LA, Italian suit, gold watch." He slipped the pouch of Drum back in his pocket, struck a match. "She writes movies and is royally pissed at the idea of being stuck out in the wilderness for a year. But she wants the money it'll bring her. She's on her way back to California to pack up."

"She and Will ought to get along like a couple of she-cats."

"They've already been at each other." Nate blew out smoke contemplatively. "Have to admit, it was entertaining to watch. Adam simmered them down."

"He's about the only one who can simmer Willa down." With a creak of leather, Ben shifted in the saddle. Spook was growing restless under him, signaling his wishes to be off with quick head tosses. "I'll be talking to her. I've got to check on a crew we sent up to the high country. We're getting some storms. Mom's got coffee on at the main house."

"Thanks, but I've got to get back. I've got work of my own. See you in a day or two."

"Yeah." Ben called to his dog, watching as Nate climbed into his Range Rover. "Nate—we're not going to let her lose that ranch."

Nate adjusted his hat, reached for his keys. "No, Ben. We're not going to let her lose it."

It was a good ride across the valley and up into the foothills. Ben took it at an easy pace, scanning the land as he went. The cattle were fat; they'd be cutting out some of the Angus for finishing in feedlots before winter. Others they would rotate from pasture to pasture, hold over for another year.

The choices, and the selling, had been his province for nearly five years, as his parents were gradually turning over the operation of Three Rocks to their sons.

The grass was high and still green, glowing against the paintbrush backdrop of trees. He heard the drone overhead and looked up with a grin. His brother Zack was doing a flyover. Ben lifted the hat off his head, waved it. Charlie, the long-haired Border collie, raced in barking circles. The little plane tilted its wings in a salute.

It was still hard for him to think of his baby brother as a husband and a father. But there you were. Zack had taken one look at Shelly Peterson and had fallen spurs over Stetson. Less than two years later, they'd made him an uncle. And, Ben thought, made him feel incredibly old. It was beginning to feel as though there were thirty rather than three years separating him and Zack.

He adjusted his hat and guided his horse uphill through a stand of yellow pine. The air freshened and cooled. He saw signs of deer, and another time might have given in to the urge to follow the tracks, to bring fresh venison home to his mother. Charlie was sniffing hopefully at the ground, glancing back now and then for permission to flush game. But Ben wasn't in the mood for a hunt.

He could smell snow. He was still far below the snow line, but he could smell it teasing the air. Already he'd seen flocks of Canadian geese heading south. Winter was coming early, and he thought it would come hard. Even the rush of water from the creek spurting downhill sounded cold.

As the trees thickened, the ground roughened, he followed the water. The forest was as familiar to him as his own barnyard. There, the dead larch where he and Zack had once dug for buried treasure. And there, in that little clearing, he had brought down his first buck, with his father standing beside him. They'd fished here, plucking trout from the water as easily as plucking berries from a bush.

On those rocks he'd once written the name of his love in flint. The words had faded and washed away with the years. And pretty Susie Boline had run off to Helena with a guitar player, breaking Ben's eighteen-year-old heart.

The recollection still brought him a tug, though he'd have suffered torments of hell before admitting he was a sentimental man. He rode past the rocks, and the memories, and climbed, keeping to the beaten path through trees as lively with color as women at a Saturday night dance.

As the air thinned and chilled and the scent of snow grew stronger, he whistled between his teeth. His time in Bozeman had been productive, but it had made him yearn for this. The space, the solitude, the land. Though he'd told himself he'd brought a bedroll only as a precaution, he was already planning on camping for a night. Maybe two.

He could shoot himself a rabbit, fry up some fish, maybe hang with the crew for the night. Or camp apart. They'd drive the cattle down to the low country. This much snow in the air could mean an early blizzard, and disaster for a herd grazing in the high mountain meadows. But Ben thought they had time yet.

He paused a moment, just to look out over a pretty ridgetop meadow dotted with cows, bordered by a tumbling river, to enjoy the wave of autumn wildflowers, the call of birds. He wondered how anyone could prefer the choked streets of a city, the buildings crowded with people and problems, to this.

The crack of gunfire made his horse shy and cleared his own mind of dreamy thoughts. Though it was a country where the snap of a bullet usually meant game coming down, his eyes narrowed. At the next shot, he automatically turned his horse in the direction of the sound and kicked him into a trot.

He saw the horse first. Will's Appaloosa was still quivering, her reins looped over a branch. Blood had a high, sweet smell, and scenting it, Ben felt his stomach clutch. Then he saw her, holding the shotgun in her hands not ten feet away from a downed grizzly. A growl in his throat, the dog streaked ahead, coming to a quivering halt at Ben's sharp order.

Ben waited until she'd glanced over her shoulder at him before he slid out of the saddle. Her face was pale, he noted, her eyes dark. "Is he all the way dead?"

"Yeah." She swallowed hard. She hated to kill, hated to see blood spilled. Even seeing a hen plucked for dinner could cause her gorge to rise. "I didn't have any choice. He charged."

Ben merely nodded and, taking his rifle out of its sheath, approached. "Big bastard." He didn't want to think what would have happened if her aim had been off, what a bear that size could have done to a horse and rider. "She-bear," he said, keeping his voice mild. "Probably has cubs around here."

Willa slapped her shotgun back in its holder. "I figured that out for myself."

"Want me to dress her out?"

"I know how to dress game."

Ben merely nodded and went back for his knife. "I'll give you a hand anyway. It's a big bear. Sorry about your father, Willa."

She took out her own knife, the keen-edged Bowie a near mate to Ben's. "You hated him."

"You didn't, so I'm sorry." He went to work on the bear, avoiding the blood and gore when he could, accepting it when he couldn't. "Nate stopped by this morning."

"I bet he did."

Blood steamed in the chilly air. Charlie snacked delicately on entrails and thumped his tail. Ben looked over the carcass of the bear and into her eyes. "You want to be pissed at me, go ahead. I didn't write the damn will, but I'll do what has to be done. First thing is I'm going to ask you what you're doing riding up here alone."

"Same thing as you, I imagine. I've got men up in the high country and cattle that need to come down. I can run my business as well as you can run yours, Ben."

He waited a moment, hoping she'd say more. He'd always been fascinated by her voice. It was rusty, always sounding as though it needed the sleep cleared out of it. More than once Ben had thought it a damn shame that such a contrary woman had that straight sex voice in her.

"Well, we've got a year to find that out, don't we?" When that didn't jiggle a response out of her, he ran his tongue over his teeth. "You going to mount this head?"

"No. Men need trophies they can point to and brag on. I don't."

He grinned then. "We sure do like them. You might make a nice trophy yourself. You're a pretty thing, Willa. I believe that's the first time I've said that to a woman over bear guts."

She recognized his warped way of being charming and refused to be drawn in. Over the last couple of years, refusing to be drawn to Ben McKinnon had taken on the proportions of a second career. "I don't need your help with the bear or the ranch."

"You've got it, on both counts. We can do it peaceable, or we can do it adversarial." He gave Charlie an absent pat when the dog sat down beside him. "Don't matter much to me either way."

There were shadows under her eyes, he noted. Like smudged fingerprints against the golden skin. And her mouth, which he'd always found particularly appealing, was set in a hard, thin line. He preferred it snarling—and figured he knew how to bring that about.

"Are your sisters as pretty as you?" When she didn't answer, his lips twitched. "Bet they're friendlier. I'll have to come calling, see for myself. Why don't you invite me to supper, Will, and we can sit ourselves down and discuss plans for the ranch." Now her eyes flashed up to his, and he grinned hugely. "Thought that would do it. Christ Almighty, you've got a face, and nothing suits it better than pure orneriness."

She didn't want him to tell her she was pretty, if that's what he was doing. It always made her insides fumble around. "Why don't you save your breath for getting this carcass up to bleed out?"

Rocking back on his heels, he studied her. "We can get this whole thing over quick. Just get ourselves married and be done with it."

Though her hand clenched on the bloody knife, she took three slow, easy breaths. Oh, he was riding her, and she knew he'd like nothing better than to watch her scream and shout and stomp her feet. Instead she angled her head, and her voice was as cool as the water in the nearby stream.

"There's about as much chance of that as there is of what's left of this bear rearing up and biting you on the ass."

He rose as she did, circled her wrist with his fingers, and ignored her quick jolt of protest. "I don't want you any more than you want me. I just thought it would be easy on everybody if we got it out of the way. Life's long, Willa," he said more gently. "A year isn't much."

"Sometimes a day's too much. Let go of me, Ben." Her gaze lifted slowly. "A man who hesitates to listen to a woman with a knife in her hand deserves whatever he gets."

He could have had the knife out of her hand in three seconds flat, but he decided to leave it where it was. "You'd like to stick me, wouldn't you?" The fact that he knew it to be true both aroused and irritated him. But then, she usually managed to do both. "Get it through your head: I don't want what's yours. And I don't plan on being bartered for more land and more cattle any more than you do." She went pale at that, and he nodded. "We know where we stand, Will. Could be I'll find one of your sisters to my taste, but meanwhile, it's just business."

The humiliation of it was as raw as the blood on her hands. "You son of a bitch."

He shifted his grip to her knife hand, just in case. "I love you too, sweetheart. Now, I'll hang the bear. You go wash up."

"I shot it, I can—"

"A woman who hesitates to listen to a man with a knife in his hand deserves what she gets." He smiled again, slow and easy. "Why don't we try to make this business go down smooth for both of us?"

"It can't." All the passion and frustration that whirled inside her echoed in the two words. "You know it can't. How would you take it if you were standing where I am?"

"I'm not," he said simply. "Go wash the blood off. We've got a ways to ride yet today."

He let her go, crouched again, knowing she was standing over him fighting to regain control. He didn't fully relax until she'd stomped off toward the stream with his dog happily at her heels. Blowing out a breath, he looked down at the exposed fangs.

"She'd rather a bite from you than a kind word from me," he muttered. "God-damn women."

While he finished the gruesome task, he admitted to himself that he'd lied. He did want her. The puzzle of it was, the less he wanted to, the more he did.

It was nearly an hour before she spoke again. They wore sheepskin jackets now against the cold and wind, and the horses were plodding through nearly a foot of snow, with Charlie happily blazing the trail.

"You take half the bear meat. It's only right," Willa said.

"I'm obliged."

"Being obliged is the problem, isn't it? Neither of us wants to be."

He understood her, he thought, better than she might like. "Sometimes you have to swallow what you can't spit out."

"And sometimes you choke." One of the wounds in her heart split open. "He left Adam next to nothing."

Ben studied her profile. "Jack drew a hard line." And Adam Wolfchild wasn't blood, Ben thought. That would have been uppermost in Jack's mind.

"Adam should have more." Will have more, she promised herself.

"I'm not going to disagree with you when it comes to Adam. But if I know anyone who can take care of himself and make his own, it's your brother."

He's all I've got left. She nearly said it before she caught herself, before she remembered it would be a mistake to open any part of her heart to Ben. "How's Zack? I saw his plane this morning."

"Checking fences. I'd have to say he's happy, the way he goes around grinning like a fool day and night. He and Shelly dote on that baby." They all did, Ben thought, but he wasn't going to mention the fact that he couldn't keep his hands off his infant niece.

"She's a pretty baby. It's still hard to see Zack McKinnon settling down to family life."

"Shelly knows when to yank his reins." Unable to resist, Ben grinned at her. "You're not still carrying a torch for my baby brother, are you, Will?"

Amused, she shifted and smiled sweetly. There had been a brief time when they were teenagers that she and Zack had made calf's eyes at each other. "Every time I think of him, my heart goes pitty-pat. Once a woman's been kissed by Zack McKinnon, she's spoiled for anyone else."

"Honey . . ." He reached over, flipped her braid behind her back. "That's because I've never kissed you."

"I'd sooner kiss a two-tailed skunk."

Laughing, he shifted his horse just enough so that his knee bumped Willa's. "Zack'd be the first to tell you, I taught him everything he knows."

"Maybe so, but I think I can live without either one of the McKinnon boys." She jerked a shoulder, then turned her head slightly. "Smoke." There was relief in that, in the sign of people and the near end of her solitary ride with Ben. "The crew's probably in the cabin. It's dinnertime."

With another woman, any other woman, Ben thought, he could have reached over, pulled her close, and kissed her breathless. Just on principle. Since it was Willa, he eased back in the saddle and kept his hands to himself.

"I could eat. I'm going to want to round up the herd, get them down. More snow's coming."

She only grunted. She could smell it. But there was something else in the air. At first she wondered if it was the sensory echo from the bear and the blood on her hands, but it lingered, seemed to grow stronger.

"Something's dead," she murmured.

"What?"

"Something's dead." She straightened in the saddle, scanned the ridges and trees. It was dead quiet, dead still. "Can't you smell it?"

"No." But he didn't doubt she could, and he turned his horse as she did. Already on the scent, Charlie was moving ahead. "It's the Indian in you. One of the hands probably shot dinner."

It made sense. They would have brought provisions, and the cabin was always stocked, but fresh game was hard to resist. Still, that didn't explain the dread in her stomach or the chill along her spine.

There was the scream of an eagle overhead, the wild, soul-stirring echo of it, then the utter silence of the mountains. The sun glittered off the snow, blinding. Following instinct, Willa left the rough path and walked her horse over broken, uneven ground.

"We don't have a lot of time for detours," Ben reminded her.

"Then go on."

He swore, reaching around to check that his rifle was within easy reach. There were bear here, too. And cougar. He thought of camp, hardly more than ten minutes away, and the hot coffee that would be boiling to mud on the stove.

Then he saw it. His nose might not have been as sharp as hers, but his eyes were. Blood was splattered and pooled over the snow, splashed against rock. The black hide of the steer was coated with it. The dog stopped circling the mangled steer and raced back to the horses.

"Well, shit." Ben was already dismounting. "Made a mess of it."

"Wolves?" It was more than the market price to Willa. It was the waste, the cruelty.

He started to agree, then stopped short. A wolf didn't kill, then leave the meat. A wolf didn't hack and slice. No predator but one did.

"A man."

Willa drew a sharp breath as she stepped closer, saw the damage. The throat had been slit, the belly disemboweled. Charlie pressed against her legs, shivering. "It's been butchered. Mutilated."

She crouched, and thought of the bear. No choice there but to kill, and the field dressing had been done efficiently with the tools at hand. But this—this was wild and vicious and without purpose.

"Almost within sight of the cabin," she said. "The blood's frozen. It was probably done hours ago, before sunup."

"It's one of yours," Ben told her after checking the brand.

"Doesn't matter whose." But she noted the number on the yellow ear tag. The death would have to be recorded. She rose and stared over at the stream of smoke rising. "It matters why. Have you lost any cattle this way?"

"No." He straightened to stand beside her. "Have you?"

"Not until now. I can't believe it's one of my men." She took a shallow breath. "Or yours. There must be someone else camping up here."

"Maybe." He was frowning down at the ground. They stood shoulder to shoulder now, linked by the waste at their feet. She didn't jerk away when he ran a hand down her braid, or when he laid that hand companionably on her arm. "We had more snow, a lot of wind. The ground's pretty trampled up, but it looks like some tracks heading north. I'll take some men and check it out."

"It's my cow."

He shifted his eyes to hers. "It doesn't matter whose," he repeated. "We have to get both herds rounded up and down the mountain, and we have to report this. I figure I can count on you for that."

She opened her mouth, closed it again. He was right. She was next to useless at tracking, but she could organize a drive. With a nod, she turned back to her horse. "I'll talk to my men."

"Will." Now he laid a hand over hers, leather against leather, before she could mount. "Watch yourself."

She vaulted into the saddle. "They're my men," she said simply, and rode toward the rising smoke.

She found her men about to have their midday meal when she came into the cabin. Pickles was at the little stove, sturdy legs spread, ample belly spilling over the wide buckle of his belt. He was barely forty and balding fast, compensating for it with a ginger-colored moustache that grew longer every year. He'd earned his name from his obsessive love of dill pickles, and his personality was just as sour.

When he saw Willa, he grunted in greeting, sniffed, and turned back to the ham he was frying.

Jim Brewster sat with his booted feet on the table, enjoying the last of a Marlboro. He was just into his thirties with a face pretty enough for framing. Two dimples winked in his cheeks, and dark hair waved to his collar. He beamed at Willa and sent her a cocky wink that made his blue eyes twinkle.

"Got us company for dinner, Pickles."

Pickles gave another sour grunt, belched, and flipped his ham. "Barely enough meat for two as it is. Get your lazy ass up and open some beans."

"Snow's coming." Willa tossed her coat over a hook and headed for the radio.

" 'Nother week easy."

She turned her head, met Pickles's sulky brown eyes. "I don't think so. We'll start rounding up today." She waited, holding his gaze. He hated taking his orders from a female, and they both knew it.

"Your cattle," he muttered, and turned the ham out onto a platter.

"Yes, they are. And one of them's been butchered a quarter mile east of here."

"Butchered?" Jim paused in the act of handing Pickles an open can of beans. "Cougar?"

"Not unless cats are carrying knives these days. Someone opened one up, hacked it to pieces, and left it."

"Bullshit." Eyes narrowed, Pickles took a step forward. "That's just shit, Will. We've lost a couple to cougar. Jim and me tracked a cat just yesterday. She musta circled around and got another cow, that's all."

"I know the difference between claws and a knife." She inclined her head. "Go look for yourself. Dead east, about a quarter mile."

"Damned if I won't." Pickles stomped over for his coat, muttering about women.

"Sure it couldn't have been a cat?" Jim asked the minute the door slammed.

"Yeah, I'm sure. Get me some coffee, would you, Jim? I'm going to radio the ranch. I want Ham to know we're heading down."

"McKinnon's men are up here, but—"

"No." She shook her head, pulled out a chair. "No cowboy I know does that."

She contacted the ranch, listening to static, waiting for it to clear. The coffee and the crackling fire chased the worst of the chill away as she made arrangements for the drive. She was on her second cup when she finished passing the information along to the McKinnon ranch.

Pickles slammed back in. "Son of a bitching bastard."

Accepting this as the only apology she'd get, Willa moved to the stove and filled her plate. "I rode up with Ben McKinnon. He's following some tracks. We're going to help get his herd down with our own. Has either of you seen anyone around here? Campers, hunters, eastern assholes?"

"Came across a campsite yesterday when we were tracking the cat." Jim sat again with his plate. "But it was cold. Two or three days cold."

"Left goddamn beer cans." Pickles ate standing up. "Like it was their own backyard. Oughta be shot for it."

"Sure that cow wasn't shot?" Jim looked to Pickles for confirmation, a fact that Willa struggled not to resent. "You know how some of those city boys are—shoot at anything that moves."

"Wasn't shot. Ain't no tourist done that." Pickles shoved beans into his mouth. "Fucking teenagers what it is. Fucking crazy teenagers all doped up."

"Maybe. If it was, Ben'll find them easy enough." But she didn't think it had been teenagers. It seemed to Willa it took a lot more years to work up that kind of rage.

Jim pushed the barely warm beans around on his plate. "Ah, we heard about how things are." He cleared his throat. "We radioed in last night, and Ham, he figured he should, you know, tell us how things are."

She pushed her plate away and stood. "Then I'll tell you just how things are." Her voice was very cool, very quiet. "Mercy Ranch runs the way it always has. The old man's in the ground, and now I'm operator. You take your orders from me."

Jim exchanged a quick look with Pickles, then scratched his cheek. "I didn't mean to say different, Will. We were just sorta wondering how you were going to keep the others, your sisters, on the ranch."

"They'll take their orders from me too." She jerked her coat off the hook. "Now, if you've finished your meal, let's get saddled up."

"Goddamn women," Pickles muttered as soon as the door was safely closed behind her. "Don't know one that isn't a bossy bitch."

"That's 'cause you don't know enough women." Jim strolled over for his coat. "And that one *is* the boss."

"For the time being."

"She's the boss today." Jim shrugged into his coat, pulled out his gloves. "And today's what we've got."

4

In dealings with her mother—and Tess always thought of contacts with Louella as dealings—Tess prepped herself with a dose of extra-strength Excedrin. There would be a headache, she knew, so why chase the pain?

She chose mid-morning, knowing it was the only time of day she would be likely to find Louella at home in her Bel Air condo. By noon she would be out and about, having her hair done, or her nails, indulging in a facial or a shopping spree.

By four, Louella would be at her club, Louella's, joking with the bartender or regaling the waitresses with tales of her life and loves as a Vegas showgirl.

Tess did her very best to avoid Louella's. Though the condo didn't make her much happier.

It was a lovely little stucco in California Spanish with a tiled roof, graceful shrubbery. It could, and should, have been a small showplace. But as Tess had said on more than one occasion, Louella Mercy could make Buckingham Palace tacky.

When she arrived, promptly at eleven, she tried to ignore what Louella cheerfully called her lawn art. The lawn jockey with the big, stupid grin, the rearing plaster lions, the glowing blue moonball on its concrete pedestal, and the fountain of the serene-faced girl pouring water from the mouth of a rather startled-looking carp.

Flowers grew in profusion, in wild, clashing colors that seared the eyes. There was no rhyme or reason to the arrangement, no plot or plan. Whatever plants caught Louella's eye had been plunked down wherever Louella's whim had dictated. And, Tess mused, she had a lot of whims.

Standing amid a bed of scarlet and orange impatiens was the newest addition, the headless torso of the goddess Nike. Tess shook her head and rang the bell that played the first bump-and-grind bars of "The Stripper."

Louella opened the door herself and enfolded her daughter in draping silks, heavy perfume, and the candy scent of discount cosmetics. Louella never stepped beyond her own bedroom door in less than full makeup.

She was a tall woman, lushly built, with mile-long legs that still could—and did—execute a high kick. The natural color of her hair had been forgotten long ago. It had been blond for years, as brassy a tone as Louella's huge laugh, and worn big, in a teased and lacquered style admired by TV evangelists. She had a striking face despite the troweled-on layers of base and powder and blush, with strong bones and full lips, slicked now with high-gloss red. Her eyes were baby blue, as was the shadow that decorated their lids, with the brows above them mercilessly plucked and stenciled into dark, thin brackets.

As always, Tess was struck with conflicting waves of love and puzzlement. "Mom." Her lips curved as she returned the embrace, and her eyes rolled as the two yapping Pomeranians her mother adored set up an ear-piercing din in their excitement at having company.

"Back from the Wild West, are you?" Louella's East Texas twang had the resonance of plucked banjo strings. She kissed Tess on the cheek, then rubbed away the smear of lipstick with a spit-dampened finger. "Well, come tell me all about it. They sent the old bastard off in proper style, I hope."

"It was . . . interesting."

"I'll bet. Let's have us some coffee, honey. It's Carmine's morning off, so we'll have to fend for ourselves."

"I'll make it." She preferred brewing the coffee herself to facing her mother's studly houseboy. Tess tried not to imagine what other services the man provided Louella.

She moved through the living area, decorated in scarlets and golds, into a kitchen so white it was like being snow-blinded. As usual, there wasn't a crumb out of place. Whatever else Carmine did during his daily duties, he was tidy as a nun.

"Got some coffee cake around here, too. I'm hungry as a bear." With her dogs scrambling around her feet, Louella rummaged in cupboards, through the refrigerator. Within minutes there was chaos.

Tess's lips twitched again. Chaos followed her mother around as faithfully as the yapping Mimi and Maurice did.

"You meet your kin out there?"

"If you mean the half sisters, yes." With trepidation, Tess eyed the coffee cake her mother had unearthed. Louella was slicing it into huge slabs with a steak knife. Being transferred to a plate decorated with gargantuan roses were approximately ten billion calories.

"Well, what are they like?" With the same generous hand, Louella cut a piece for her dogs, setting the china plate on the floor. The dogs bolted cake and snarled at each other.

"The one from wife number two is quiet, nervous."

"That's the one with the ex who likes to use his fists." Clucking her tongue, Louella slid her ample hips onto the counter stool. "Poor thing. One of my girls had that kind of trouble. Husband would as soon beat the shit out of her as wink. We finally got her into a shelter. She's living up in Seattle now. Sends me a card now and again."

Tess made a small sound of interest. Her mother's girls were anyone who worked for her, from the waitresses to the bartenders, the strippers to the kitchen help. Louella embraced them all, lending money, giving advice. Tess had always thought Louella's was part club, part halfway house for topless dancers.

"How about the other one?" Louella asked as she attacked her coffee cake. "The one that's part Indian."

"Oh, that one's a real cowgirl. Tough as leather, striding around in dirty boots. I imagine she can punch cattle, literally." Amused at the thought, Tess poured out coffee. "She didn't trouble to hide the fact that she didn't want either of us there." With a shrug, she sat down and began to pick at her cake. "She's got a half brother."

"Yeah, I knew about that. I knew Mary Wolfchild—at least I'd seen her around. She was one beautiful woman, and that little boy of hers, sweet face. Angel face."

"He's grown up now, and he's still got the angel face. He lives on the ranch, works with horses or something."

"His father was a wrangler, as I recall." Louella reached in the pocket of her scarlet robe, found a pack of Virginia Slims. "How about Bess?" She let out smoke and a big, lusty laugh. "Christ, that was a woman. Had to watch my *p*'s and *q*'s around her. Had to admire her—she ran that house like a top and didn't take any crap off Jack either."

"She's still running the house, as far as I could tell."

"Hell of a house. Hell of a ranch." Louella's bright-red lips curved at the memory. "Hell of a country. Though I can't say I'm sorry I only spent one winter there. Goddamn snow up to your armpits."

"Why did you marry him?" When Louella arched a brow, Tess shifted uncomfortably. "I know I never asked before, but I'm asking now. I'd like to know why."

"It's a simple question with a simple answer." Louella poured an avalanche of sugar into her coffee. "He was the sexiest son of a bitch I'd ever seen. Those eyes of his, the way they could look right through you. The way he'd cock his head and smile like he knew just what he'd be up to later and wanted to take you along."

She remembered it all perfectly. The smells of sweat and whiskey, the lights dazzling her eyes. And the way Jack Mercy had swaggered into the nightclub when she'd been onstage in little more than feathers and a twenty-pound headdress.

The way he'd puffed on a big cigar and watched her.

Somehow she'd expected that he'd be waiting for her after the last show. And she'd gone with him without a thought, from casino to casino, drinking, gambling, wearing his Stetson perched on her head.

Within forty-eight hours, she'd stood with him in one of those assembly-line chapels with canned music and plastic flowers. And she'd had a gold ring on her finger.

It was hardly a surprise that the ring had stayed put for less than two years.

"Trouble was, we didn't know each other. It was hot pants and gambling fever." Philosophically, Louella crushed out her cigarette on her empty plate. "I wasn't cut out for life on a goddamn cattle ranch in Montana. Maybe I could've made a go of it—who knows? I loved him."

Tess swallowed cake before it stuck in her throat. "You loved him?"

"For a while I did." With the ease of years and distance, Louella shrugged. "A woman couldn't love Jack for long unless she was missing brain cells. But for a while, I loved him. And I got you out of it. And a hundred large. I wouldn't have my girl, and I wouldn't have my club if Jack Mercy hadn't walked in that night and taken a shine to me. So I owe him."

"You owe the man who kicked you, and his own daughter, out of his life? Cut you off with a lousy hundred thousand dollars?"

"A hundred K went a lot farther thirty years ago than it does today." Louella had learned to be a mother and a businesswoman from the ground up. She was proud of both. "And from where I'm sitting, I got a pretty good deal."

"Mercy Ranch is worth twenty million. Do you still think you got a good deal?"

Louella pursed her lips. "It was his ranch, honey. I just visited there for a while."

"Long enough to make a baby and get the boot."

"I wanted the baby."

"Mom." Most of Tess's anger faded at the words, but the injustice of it remained hot in her heart. "You had a right to more. I had a right to more."

"Maybe, maybe not, but that was the deal at the time." Louella lit another cigarette, decided to be late for her afternoon session at the beauty parlor. There was more here, she thought. "Time goes on. Jack ended up making three daughters, and now he's dead. You want to tell me what he left you?"

"A problem." Tess took the cigarette from Louella's hand and indulged in a quick drag. Smoking was a habit she didn't approve of—what sensible person did? But it was either that or the several million calories still on her plate. "I get a third of the ranch."

"A third of the—Good Jesus and little fishes, Tess, honey, that's a fortune." Louella bounced up. She might have been five ten and a generous one-fifty, but she'd been trained as a dancer and could move when she had to. She moved now, skimming around the counter to crush her daughter's ribs in an enthusiastic hug. "What are we doing sitting here drinking coffee? We need ourselves some French champagne. Carmine's got some stashed somewhere."

"Wait. Mom, wait." As Louella tore into the fridge again, Tess tugged on her robe. "It's not that simple."

"My daughter the millionaire. The cattle baron." Louella popped the cork, spewing champagne. "Fucking A."

"I have to live there for a year." Tess blew out a breath as Louella cheerfully clamped her mouth over the lip of the bottle and sucked up bubbles. "All three of us have to live there for a year, together. Or we don't get zip."

Louella licked champagne from her lips. "You have to live in Montana for a year? On the ranch?" Her voice began to shake. "With the cows? You, with the cows."

"That's the deal. Me, and the other two. Together."

One hand still holding the bottle, the other braced on the counter, Louella began to laugh. She laughed so hard, so long that tears streamed down her face, running with Maybelline mascara and L'Oréal ivory base.

"Jesus H. Christ, the son of a bitch always could make me laugh."

"I'm glad you think it's so funny." Tess's voice cracked like ice. "You can chuckle over it nightly while I'm out in bumfuck watching the grass grow."

With a flourish, Louella poured champagne into the coffee cups. "Honey, you can always spit in his eye and go on just as you are."

"And give up several million in assets? I don't think so."

"No." Louella sobered as she studied her daughter, this mystery she had somehow given birth to. So pretty, she mused, so cool, so sure of herself. "No, you wouldn't. You're too much your father's daughter for that. You'll do the time, Tess."

And she wondered if her daughter would get more out of it than a third interest in a cattle ranch. Would the year soften the edges, Louella wondered, or hone them?

She lifted both cups, handed one to Tess. "When do you leave?"

"First thing in the morning." She sighed loud and long. "I've got to go buy some goddamn boots," she muttered, then with a small smile toasted herself. "What the hell. It's only a year."

While Tess was drinking champagne in her mother's kitchen, Lily was standing at the edge of a pasture, watching horses graze. She'd never seen anything more beautiful than the way the wind blew through their manes, the way the mountains rose behind, all blue and white.

For the first time in months, she had slept through the night, without pills, without nightmares, lulled by the quiet.

It was quiet now. She could hear the grind of machinery in the distance. Just a hum in the air. She'd heard Willa talking to someone that morning about harvesting grain, but she had wanted to stay out of the way. She could be alone here with the horses, bothering no one, with no one bothering her.

For three days she'd been left to her own devices. No one said anything when she wandered the house, or went out to explore the ranch. The men would tip their hats to her if they passed by, and she imagined there were comments and murmurings. But she didn't care about that.

The air here was sweet to the taste. Wherever she stood, it seemed, she could see something beautiful—water rushing over rocks in a stream, the flash of a bird in the forest, deer bounding across the road.

She thought a year of this would be paradise.

Adam stood for a moment, the bucket in his hand, watching her. She came out here every day, he knew. He'd seen her wander away from the house, the barn, the paddocks, and head for this pasture. She would stand by the fence, very still, very quiet.

Very alone.

He'd waited, believing she needed to be alone. Healing was often a solitary matter. But he also believed she needed a friend. So now he walked toward her, careful to make enough noise so that she wouldn't be startled. When she turned, her smile came slow and hesitant, but it came.

"I'm sorry. I'm not in the way here, am I?"

"You're not in anyone's way."

Because she was already learning to be relaxed around him, she shifted her gaze back to the horses. "I love looking at them."

"You can have a closer look." He didn't need the bucket of grain to lure any of the horses to the fence. Any of them would come for him at a quiet call. He handed the bucket to Lily. "Just give it a shake."

She did, then watched, delighted, as several pairs of ears perked up. Horses trotted over to crowd at the fence. Without thinking, she dipped a hand into the grain and fed a pretty buckskin mare.

"You've been around horses before."

At Adam's comment, she pulled her hand back. "I'm sorry. I should have asked before I fed her."

"It's all right." He was sorry to have startled that smile away from her face. That quick light that had come into eyes that were somewhere between gray and blue. Like lake water, he thought, caught in the shadows of sunset. "Come along, Molly."

At her name, the roan mare pranced along the fence toward the gate. Adam led her into a corral and slipped a bridle over her head.

Self-conscious again, Lily wiped grain dust on her jeans, took one hesitant step closer. "Her name's Molly?"

"Yes." He kept his eyes on the horse, giving Lily a chance to settle again.

"She's pretty."

"She's a good saddle horse. Kind. Her gait's a bit rough, but she tries. Don't you, girl? Can you ride Western, Lily?"

"I—what?"

"You probably learned on English." Keeping it light, Adam spread the blanket he'd brought along over Molly's back. "Nate keeps some English tack if you'd rather. We can borrow a saddle from him."

Her hands reached for each other, as they did when her nerves jittered. "I don't understand."

"You want to ride, don't you?" He slid one of Willa's old saddles onto Molly's back. "I thought we'd go up in the hills a little way. Might see some elk."

She found herself caught between yearning and fear. "I haven't ridden in—It's been a long time."

"You don't forget how." Adam estimated the length of her legs and adjusted the stirrups accordingly. "You can go alone once you know your way around." He turned then, noting the way she kept glancing back toward the ranch house. As if gauging the distance. "You don't have to be afraid of me."

She believed him. That was what she was afraid of—that it was so easy to believe him. How often had she believed Jesse?

But that was done, she reminded herself. That was over. Her life could begin again, if she'd let it.

"I'd like to go, for a little while, if you're sure it's all right."

"Why wouldn't it be?" He moved toward her, stopping instinctively before she shied again. "You don't have to worry about Willa. She has a good heart, and a generous one. It's just hurting right now."

"I know she's upset. She has every right to be." Unable to resist, Lily lifted a hand to stroke Molly's cheek. "Even more upset since they found that poor cow. I don't understand who would do something like that. She's so angry. And she's so busy. She's always got something to do, and I'm, well, I'm just here."

"Do you want something to do?"

With the horse between them, it was easy to smile. "Not if it involves castrating cows. I could hear them this morning." She shuddered, then managed to laugh at herself. "I got out of the house before Bess could make me eat breakfast. I don't think I'd have held it down for long."

"It's just one of the things you get used to."

"I don't think so." Lily exhaled, barely noticing how close her hand was to Adam's on the mare's head. "Willa's natural with all of it. She's so sure and confident. I envy that, that knowing just who you are. To her I'm just a nuisance, which is why I haven't been able to work up the courage to talk to her, to ask if there's something I could do around here to help."

"You don't have to be afraid of her, either." He brushed his fingertips against hers, continuing to stroke the mare even when Lily's hand slid out of reach. "But meanwhile, you could ask me. I can use some help. With the horses," he added, when she only stared at him.

"You want me to help you with the horses?"

"It's a lot of work, more when winter gets here." Knowing he'd planted the seed, he stepped back. "Think about it." Then he cupped his hands, smiled again. "I'll give you a leg up. You can walk her around the corral, get acquainted, while I saddle up."

Her throat was closed so that she had to swallow hard to clear it. "You don't even know me."

"I figure we'll get acquainted too." He stood as he was, hands linked in a cup, his eyes patient on hers. "You just have to put your foot in my hands, Lily, not your life."

Feeling foolish, she grabbed the saddle horn and let him boost her into the saddle. She looked down at him, her eyes solemn in her battered face. "Adam, my life is a mess."

He only nodded as he checked her stirrups. "You'll have to start tidying it up." He rested a hand on her ankle a moment, wanting her to grow easy to his touch. "But today, you just have to take a ride into the hills."

The little bitch, letting that half-breed paw her. Sniveling little whore thought she could get rid of Jesse Cooke, figured she could run and he wouldn't catch her. Put the cops on his ass. She was going to pay for that.

Jesse stared through the field glasses while little bubbles of fury burst in his blood. He wondered if the half-breed horse wrangler had already gotten Lily on her back. Well, the bastard would pay too. Lily was Jesse Cooke's wife, and he was going to be reminding her of that soon enough.

Stupid little cunt thought she was real clever hightailing it to Montana. But the day Jesse Cooke couldn't outwit a woman was the day the sun didn't rise in the east.

He'd known she wouldn't make a move without contacting her dear old mama. So he'd just camped himself within sight of the pretty house in Virginia. And every morning he'd gotten to the mail and checked through it for a letter from Lily.

Persistence had paid off. The letter had come, as he'd known it would. He'd taken it back to the motel room, steamed it open. Oh, Jesse Cooke was nobody's fool. He'd read it, seen where she was going, what she was up to.

Going to cash in on an inheritance, he thought bitterly. And cut her own husband out of his share of the pie. Not in this lifetime, Jesse mused.

The minute the letter had been resealed and put back in the box, he'd headed for Montana. And had gotten there, he thought now, two full days before his idiot wife. Long enough for a man as smart as Jesse Cooke to get the lay of the land and get himself a job on Three Rocks.

A miserable fucking job, he thought now, keeping machines in repair. Well, he knew his way around engines, and there was always a rig that needed fine-tuning. When he wasn't doing that, they had him out checking fences day and night.

But that came in handy, damn handy, like now. A man out riding in a four-wheel to check fences could take a little detour and check out what else was going on.

And he saw plenty.

Jesse rubbed his fingers over the moustache he'd grown and dyed like his hair, medium brown. Just a precaution, he thought, just a temporary disguise, in case Lily blabbed about him. If she did, they'd have their eye out for a clean-shaven man with blond hair. He had let his hair grow too, and would keep on letting it grow. Like a fucking pansy, he thought, resenting the necessity of giving up his severe Marine Corps crew cut.

It would all be worth it in the end. When he had Lily back, when he reminded her who was boss. Who was in charge.

Until that happy day he would stay close. And he would watch.

"You have a good time, bitch," Jesse muttered, his eyes narrowing behind the high-powered lenses as Lily walked her mount beside Adam's. "Payback time's coming."

Most of the day had died out of the sky by the time Willa got back to the ranch house. Dehorning and castrating cattle was a messy, miserable job, and a tedious one. She knew she was pushing herself, and knew she would continue to push. She wanted the men to see her at every angle, at every job. Shifting operators under the best of circumstances could be a rough transition. And these were far from the best of circumstances.

Which is why she'd been on hand when a herd of elk had trampled through a fence, creating havoc. And why she'd personally headed the crew to chase them off again, to repair the fence.

Now with the work done for the day and the hands settling down for supper and cards in the bunkhouse, she wanted nothing more than a hot bath and a hot meal. She was halfway up the steps to get the first when the knock sounded on the door. Knowing that Bess was likely in the kitchen, Willa stomped back down to answer.

She greeted Ben with a scowl. "What do you want?"

"A cold beer would go down good."

"This isn't a saloon." But she swung away from the door and into the living room to the cold box behind the bar. "Make it fast, Ben. I haven't had my supper."

"Neither have I." He took the bottle she handed him. "But I don't expect I'm going to get an invitation."

"I'm not in the mood for company."

"I've never known you to be in the mood for company." He tipped back the beer and drank deep. "I haven't seen you since we were up in the high country. Thought I should let you know I didn't find anything. Trail died out on me. I'd have to say whoever was up there knew his way around tracking."

She took a beer for herself, and since her feet were aching, dropped down beside Ben on the sofa. "Pickles thinks it was kids. Doped up and crazy."

"And you?"

"I didn't." She moved a shoulder. "Now that sounds like the best explanation."

"Maybe. There's not much use going back up. We've got the cattle down. Is your sister back from LA?"

Willa stopped rolling her head to loosen her shoulders and frowned at him. "You're awfully interested in Mercy business, McKinnon."

"That's part of my job now." He liked reminding her of it, just as he liked looking at her, with her hair falling out of her braid and her boots propped beside his. "Have you heard from her?"

"She'll be here tomorrow, so if that concludes your prying into my business, you can—"

"Going to introduce me?" To please himself he reached out to toy with her hair. "Maybe I'll take a shine to her and keep her occupied and out of your way for a while."

She knocked his hand aside, but he only brought it back. "Do women always fall at your feet?"

"All but you, darling. And that's just because I haven't found the right way to tip your balance." He skimmed a fingertip down her cheek, watched her eyes narrow. "But I'm working on it. What about the other one?"

"The other what?" Willa wanted to shift over a couple of inches, but she knew it would make her look like a fool.

"The other sister."

"She's around. Somewhere."

He smiled, slowly. "I'm making you nervous. Isn't that interesting?"

"Your ego needs pruning again." But she started to rise. He stopped her with a hand on her shoulder.

"Well, well," he murmured, feeling her vibrate under his hand. "It looks like I haven't been paying close enough attention. Come here."

She concentrated on evening her breathing, slowly changed her grip on the beer she held. Oh, he looks so arrogant, she thought. So cocky. So sure I'll melt if he bothers to push the right button.

"You want me to come there," she purred, watching his eyes widen slightly in surprise at the warm tone. "And what'll happen if I do?"

He might have called himself a fool—if there'd been any blood left in his head to allow him to think. But all he could do at that moment was feel the gradual simmer of lust set off by that husky voice.

"I'd say it's long past time we found out." He curled his fingers into her shirt, tightened his grip, and pulled her against him. If his gaze hadn't drifted down from hers to lock onto her mouth, he would have seen it coming. Instead he found himself an inch away from that mouth and soaked from the beer she dumped over his head.

"You're such a jerk, Ben." Pleased with herself, she leaned forward to set the empty bottle on the table. "You think I could live on a ranch surrounded by randy men all my life and not see a move like that a mile off?"

Slowly, he dragged a hand through his wet hair. "Guess not. But then again—"

He moved fast. When she found herself trapped under him, Willa thought, even a snake rattles before he strikes. Now she could only be disgusted with herself for being pressed into the couch by a wiry male with blood in his eye.

"You didn't see that coming." He handcuffed her wrists, hauled her arms over her head. Her face was flushed, but he didn't think it was only temper. Temper didn't make her tremble, didn't put that sudden female awareness in her eyes. "Are you afraid to let me kiss you, Willa? Afraid you'll like it?"

Her heart was beating too fast, felt as though it would shatter through her ribs. Her lips were tingling, as if the nerves centered there were revving up for action. "If I want your mouth on me, I'll tell you."

He only smiled, leaned down closer to her face. "Why don't you tell me you don't? Go ahead, tell me." His voice thickened as he nipped lightly at her jaw. "Tell me you don't want me to taste you. Just once."

She couldn't. It would have been a lie, but lying didn't worry her. She simply couldn't get a word through her dry throat. So she took the other option, and brought her knee up, fast and hard.

She had the pleasure of seeing him go dead pale before he collapsed on her.

"Get off me. Get off, you goddamn idiot. You're crushing my lungs." Desperate for air, she arched, bucked, making him moan. She managed to gasp in a breath before she grabbed a handful of his hair and yanked.

They rolled off the couch and crashed to the floor. She saw stars as her elbow hit the edge of the table. It was pain and fury that had her tearing into him. Something shattered on the floor as they wrestled over it, grunting and cursing.

He was trying to defend himself, but she was obviously out for blood. And proved it by biting his arm just under the shoulder. Yelping, certain that she was going to take a chunk out of him, he managed to get a grip on her jaw and squeeze. Under the pressure the tear of her teeth loosened.

They rolled, boots clattering and digging for purchase, elbows jabbing, hands grappling. Willa didn't realize she was laughing until he had her pinned. She kept right on laughing, helpless even to stop for breath as he stared down at her.

"You think it's funny?" He had to squint, then huff out a breath to get the hair out of his eyes. But all in all, he was grateful she hadn't managed to tear it out of his head by the handful. "You bit me."

"I know." Her voice hitched as she ran a tongue over her teeth. "I think I've got some of your shirt in my mouth. Turn me loose, Ben."

"So you can bite me again, or try to kick my balls into my throat?" Since they were still aching—more than a little—he narrowed his eyes, sneered. "You fight like a girl."

"So what? It works."

His mood was shifting again. He could feel that hot, slick transition from temper to lust, from insult to interest. The way they'd ended up, her breasts were pressed nicely against his chest, and her legs were spread with his snugged between them.

"Yeah, it does. You being female seems to suit the situation."

She saw the change in his eyes, teetered between panic and longing. "Don't." His mouth was barely an inch from hers now, and her breath was gone again.

"Why not? It's not going to hurt anybody."

"I don't want your mouth on me."

He lifted a brow, and he smiled. "Liar."

And she shuddered. "Yeah."

His mouth was only a whisper from hers when she heard the first piercing screams.

5

Ben rolled, gained his feet. This time, as Willa ran behind him she could admire the speed with which he could move. The screams were still echoing when he wrenched open the front door.

"Christ." He muttered it even as he stepped over the bloody mess on the porch and gathered Lily in his arms. "It's all right, honey." Automatically he shifted so that he blocked her view and, with his hands stroking easy down her back, looked over her head into Willa's eyes.

The shock was there, but it wasn't the quaking, glassy-eyed horror of the woman he held. This one was fragile, he thought, whereas Willa would always be sturdy.

"You ought to get her inside," he said to Willa.

But Willa was shaking her head, staring down now at the mangled and bloody mess at her feet. "Must be one of the barn cats." Or it had been, she thought grimly, before someone had decapitated it and cut its guts open and left it like a gory gift at her front door.

"Take her inside, Will," Ben repeated.

The screams had brought others running. Adam was the first to reach the porch. The first thing he saw was Lily weeping in Ben's arms. The quick hitch in his gut had almost as much to do with that as what he saw spread on the porch.

Instinctively he stepped up, laid a hand on her arm, soothing when she jerked. "It's all right, Lily."

"Adam, I saw..." Nausea churned a storm in her stomach.

"I know. You go on inside now. Look at me," he murmured, carefully easing her away from Ben and leading her around and toward the door. "Willa's going to take you inside."

"Look, I've got—"

"Take care of your sister, Will," Adam interrupted, and taking her hand, placed it firmly over Lily's.

Willa lost the battle when Lily's hand trembled under hers. With a mumbled oath she tugged. "Come on. You need to sit down."

"I saw—"

"Yeah, I know what you saw. Forget it." Willa closed the door with a decisive click, leaving the men to ponder the headless corpse on the porch.

"Christ, Adam, is that a cat?" Jim Brewster swiped a hand over his mouth. "Somebody sure did a number on it."

Adam glanced back, studying each man in turn: Jim, face pale, Adam's apple bobbing; Ham tight-lipped; Pickles with a rifle over his shoulder. There was Billy Vincent, barely eighteen and all eager eyes, and Wood Book, stroking his silky black beard.

It was Wood who spoke, his voice calm. "Where's the head? Don't see it there." He stepped closer. It was Wood who oversaw the planting, tending, and harvesting of grain, and his wife, Nell, who cooked for the ranch hands. He smelled of Old Spice and peppermint candy. Adam knew him to be a steady man, as implacable as the Rock of Gibraltar.

"Whoever did this might like trophies." Adam's words stopped the murmurs. Only Billy continued to babble.

"Jee-sus Christ, you ever seen anything like that? Spread the guts all over hell and back, didn't he? Now who'd do that to some stupid cat? What do you think—"

"Shut the hell up, Billy, you asshole." The weary order came from Ham. He sighed once, took out his pack of smokes. "Get on back to supper, all of you. Nothing for you to do here now but gawk like a bunch of old ladies at a fashion show."

"Don't have much appetite," Jim murmured, but he and the others drifted back.

"Sure is a sorry mess," Ham commented. "Guess a kid might do this. Wood's boys are a little wild, but they're not mean. You ask me, it takes mean to do this. But I'll talk to them."

"Ham, mind if I ask if you know what the men have been up to for the past hour?"

Ham studied Ben through a haze of smoke. "Been here and there, washing up for supper and the like. I haven't had my eye on them, if that's what you're asking. The men that work here don't go cutting up a cat for frolic."

Ben merely nodded. It wasn't his place to ask more, and they both knew it. "It had to have happened in the last hour. I've been here a while, and this wasn't here before."

Ham sucked in more smoke, nodded. "I'll talk to Wood's boys." He gave one last look at what lay on the porch. "Sure is a sorry mess," he repeated, then walked away.

"You've had two animals torn up in a week, Adam."

Adam crouched down, laid his fingertip on the bloody fur. "His name was Mike. He was old, mostly blind in one eye, and should have died in his sleep."

"I'm sorry about that." Ben understood the affection, even the intimacy, with animals well and dropped a hand on Adam's shoulder. "I think you've got a real problem here."

"Yeah. Wood's boys didn't do this. They've got no harm in them. And they weren't up in the hills slaughtering a steer either."

"No, I wouldn't say they were. How well do you know your men?"

Adam lifted his gaze. Whatever the grief, it was hard, direct. "The men aren't my territory. The horses are." Still warm, he thought as he stroked the matted fur. Cooling fast, but still warm. "I know them well enough. All but Billy have been here for years, and he signed on last summer. You'd have to ask Willa, she'd know more." He looked down again and grieved for an old half-blind tom who had still liked to hunt. "Lily shouldn't have seen this."

"No, she shouldn't have." Ben sighed and wondered how close she'd come to seeing who it was. "I'll help you bury him."

Inside, Willa paced the living room. How the hell was she supposed to take care of the woman? And why had Adam pushed such a useless task on her? All Lily did was cower in the corner of the sofa and shake.

She'd given Lily whiskey, hadn't she? She'd even patted her head for lack of anything better. She had a problem on her hands, for God's sake, and she didn't need some weak-stomached Easterner to add to it.

"I'm sorry." Those were the first words she'd managed since she'd come inside. Taking a deep breath, Lily tried them again. "I'm sorry. I shouldn't have screamed that way. I've never seen anything . . . I'd been with Adam, helping with the horses, and then I . . . I just—"

"Drink the damn whiskey, would you?" Willa snapped, then cursed herself as Lily cringed and obediently lifted the glass to her lips. Disgusted with herself, Willa rubbed her hands over her face. "I expect anybody would have screamed coming across something like that. I'm not mad at you."

Lily hated whiskey, the burn of it, the smell. Jesse had favored Seagram's. And as the level in the bottle dropped, his temper rose. Always. But now she pretended to drink. "Was it a cat? I thought it was a cat." Lily bit down hard on her lip to keep her voice steady. "Was it your cat?"

"The cats are Adam's. And the dogs. And the horses. But they did it to me. They didn't leave it on Adam's porch. They did it to me."

"Like—like the steer."

Willa stopped pacing, glanced over her shoulder. "Yes. Like the steer."

"Here's a nice pot of tea." Bess hurried in, carrying a tray. The minute she set it down, she began fussing. "Will, what are you thinking of, giving the poor thing whiskey? It's just going to upset her stomach is all." Gently, Bess took the glass from Lily and set it aside. "You drink some tea, honey, and rest yourself. You've had a bad shock. Will, stop that pacing and sit down."

"You take care of her. I'm going out."

Though she poured the tea with a steady hand, Bess gave Willa's retreating back a hard look. "That girl never listens."

"She's upset."

"Aren't we all."

Lily lifted the cup with both hands, felt the warmth spread at the first sip. "She takes it deeper. It's her ranch."

Bess cocked her head. "Yours too."

"No." Lily drank again, gradually grew calmer. "It'll always be hers."

The cat was gone, but there was still blood pooled over the wood. Willa went back for a bucket of soapy water, a scrub brush. Bess would have done it, she knew, but it wasn't something she would ask of another.

On her hands and knees, in the glow of the porch light, she washed away the signs of violence. Death happened. She had believed she accepted and understood that. Cattle were raised for their meat, and a chicken who stopped laying ended up in the pot. Deer and elk were hunted and set on the table.

That was the way of things.

People lived, and died.

Even violence wasn't a stranger to her. She had sent a bullet into living flesh and dressed game with her own hands. Her father had insisted on that, had ordered her to learn to hunt, to watch a buck go down bleeding. That she could live with.

But this cruelty, this waste, this viciousness that had been laid at her door wasn't part of the cycle. She erased it, every drop. And with the bloody bucket beside her, she sat back on her heels and stared up into the sky.

A star died, even as she watched, blazing its white trail across the night and falling into oblivion.

From somewhere near an owl hooted, and she knew prey would be scrambling for cover. For tonight there was a hunter's moon, full and bright. Tonight there would be death—in the forest, in the hills, in the grass. There was no denying it.

It should not have made her want to weep.

She heard the footsteps and hastily composed herself. She was getting to her feet as Ben and Adam came around the side of the house.

"I would have done that, Will." Adam took the bucket from her. "There was no need for you to do this."

"It's done." She reached out, touched his face. "I'm sorry, Adam, about Mike."

"He used to like to sun himself on the rock behind the pole barn. We buried him there." He glanced toward the window. "Lily?"

"Bess is with her. She'll do her more good than I would."

"I'll get rid of this, then check on her."

"All right." But she kept her hand on his cheek another moment, murmured something in the language of their mother.

It made him smile, not the comforting words as much as the tongue. She rarely used it, and only when it mattered most. He stepped away and left her with Ben.

"You've got a problem on your hands, Will."

"I've got several of them."

"Whoever did that did it while we were inside." Wrestling, he thought, like a couple of idiot children. "Ham's going to talk to Wood's kids."

"Joe and Pete?" Will snorted, then rocked on her heels to comfort herself. "No way in hell and back, Ben. Those boys like to run wild around here and regularly beat the hell out of each other, but they aren't going to torture some old cat."

He rubbed the scar on his chin. "Saw that, did you?"

"I've got eyes, don't I?" She had to take a steadying breath as her stomach tipped again. "Cut little pieces off of him, and it looked like burns, probably from a cigarette on the fur. It wasn't Wood's boys. Adam gave them a couple of kittens last spring. They spoil those cats like babies."

"Adam piss anybody off lately?"

She didn't look down at him. "They didn't do it to Adam. They did it to me."

"Okay." Because he saw it the same way, he nodded. And he worried. "You piss anybody off lately?"

"Besides you?"

He smiled a little, climbed up a step until they were eye to eye. "You've been pissing me off all your life. Hardly counts. I mean it, Willa." He closed a hand over hers, linked fingers. "Is there anybody you can think of who'd want to hurt you?"

Baffled by the link, she stared down at their joined hands. "No. Pickles and Wood, they might have their noses a little out of joint now that I'm in charge. Pickles especially. It's the female thing. But they haven't got anything against me personally."

"Pickles was up in high country," Ben pointed out. "Would he do something like this to get at you? Scare the female?"

She sneered out her pride. "Do I look scared?"

"I'd feel better if you did." But he shrugged. "Would he do it?"

"A couple of hours ago I'd have said no. Now I can't be sure." That was the worst of it, she realized. Not being sure who to trust, or how much to trust them. "I wouldn't think so. He's got a temper and he likes to bitch and stew, but I can't see him killing things for no reason."

"I'd say there's a reason here. That's what we have to figure out."

She angled her chin. "Do we?"

"Your land marches with mine, Will. And for the next year you're part of my responsibilities." He only tightened his grip when she tugged at her hand. "That's a fact, and I imagine we'll both get used to it. I aim to keep my eye on you, and yours."

"You keep it too close, Ben, it's liable to get blackened."

"I'll take that chance." But just in case, he took her other hand, held them both at her sides. "I have a feeling I'm going to find the next year interesting. All around interesting. I haven't wrestled with you in . . . must be twenty years. You filled out nice."

Knowing she was outweighed and outmuscled, she stood still. "You've got a real way with words, Ben. Like poetry. You should feel my heart thudding."

"Honey, I'd love to, but you'd just try to deck me."

She smiled and felt better for it. "No, Ben. I *would* deck you. Now go away. I'm tired and I want my supper."

"I'm going." But not quite yet, he thought. He slid his hands up to her wrists and was intrigued to find her pulse hammering there. You wouldn't have known it from her eyes, so cool and dark. You wouldn't know a lot, he decided from just a quick look at Willa Mercy. "Aren't you going to kiss me good night?"

"I'd just spoil you for all those other women you like to play with."

"I'd take my chances on that, too." But he backed off. It wasn't the time, or the place. Still, he had a feeling he'd be looking for both very soon. "I'll be back."

"Yeah." She dipped her hands into her pockets as he climbed into his rig. Her pulse was still drumming. "I know."

She waited until his taillights disappeared down the long dirt road. Then she glanced over her shoulder at the house, at the lights. She wanted that hot bath, that hot meal, and a long night's sleep. But all of that would have to wait. Mercy Ranch was hers, and she had to talk to her men.

As operator, she tried to stay away from the bunkhouse. She believed the men were entitled to their privacy, and this wood-framed building with its rocking chairs on the porch was their home. Here they slept and ate, read their books if reading was what pleased them. They played cards and argued over them, watched television and complained about the boss.

Nell would cook the meals in the bungalow she shared with Wood and their sons, then cart the food over. She didn't serve the men, and one of them was assigned cleanup duty every week. That way they could eat as they pleased. They might eat dusty from work, or in their underwear. They could lie about women or the size of their cocks.

It was, after all, their home.

So she knocked and waited to be hailed inside. They were all there but Wood, who was eating his supper at home with his family. The men ranged around the table, Ham at the head, his chair tipped back since he'd just finished his meal. Billy and Jim continued to shovel in chicken and dumplings like a pair of wolves vying for meat. Pickles washed his back with beer and scowled.

"I'm sorry to interrupt your meal."

"We're about done here," Ham told her. "Billy, get to the dishes. You eat any more, you'll bust. You want some coffee, Will?"

"I wouldn't mind." She walked to the stove herself, poured a cup, and left it black. She understood that this was a delicate matter and she'd have to be both tactful and direct. "I can't figure who would slice up that old cat." She sipped, let it stew. "Anybody have an idea?"

"I checked on Wood's boys." Ham rose to pour coffee for himself. "Nell says they were in the house with her most of the evening. Now they both have pocketknives, and Nell had them fetch them to show me. They were clean." He grimaced as he drank. "The younger one, Pete, he busted out crying when he heard about old Mike. Tall boy, Pete. You forget he's only eight."

"I heard about kids doing shit like that." Pickles sulked in his beer. "Grow up to be serial killers."

Willa spared him a glance. If anybody found a way to make things worse, it was Pickles. "I don't think Wood's boys are John Wayne Gacys in training."

"Coulda been McKinnon." Billy clattered dishes in the sink and hoped Willa would notice him. He was always hoping she'd notice him; his crush on her was as wide as Montana. "He was here." He jerked his head to flop his straw-colored hair out of his eyes. Scrubbed harder than necessary at dishes so the muscles on his arms would flex. "And his men were up in the hills when the steer got laid open."

"You ought to think before you start flapping your lips, you asshole." Ham made the statement without heat. Anyone under thirty, in his mind, had the potential to be an asshole. Billy, with his eager eyes and imagination, had more potential than most. "McKinnon isn't a man who'd cut up some damn cat."

"Well, he was here," Billy said stubbornly, and slanted his eyes sideways to see if Willa was listening.

"He was here," she agreed. "And he was inside with me. I let him into the house myself, and there wasn't anything on the porch then."

"Nothing like this happened when the old man was around." Pickles tipped back his beer again and flicked a glance at Willa.

"Come on, Pickles." Uncomfortable, Jim shifted in his creaking chair. "You can't blame Will for something like this."

"Just stating fact."

"That's right." Willa nodded equably. "Nothing like this happened when the old man was around. But he's dead, and I'm in charge now. And when I find out who did this, I'll take care of them personally." She set her cup down. "I'd like all of you to think about it, to see if you remember anything, or saw anything, anyone. If something comes to you, you know where to find me."

When the door closed behind her, Ham kicked at Pickles's chair and nearly sent it out from under him. "Why do you have to be such a damn fool? That girl's never done anything but her best."

"She's a female, ain't she?" And that, he thought, was that. "You can't trust them, and you sure as hell can't depend on them. Who's to say whoever cut up a cow and a cat won't try it on a man next?" He swigged his beer while he let that little seed root. "Are you going to look to her to watch your back? I know I'm not."

Billy bobbled a dish. His eyes were huge and filled with glassy excitement. "You think somebody'd try to do that to one of us? Try to knife us?"

"Oh, shut the hell up." Ham slammed down his cup. "Pickles is just trying to get everybody worked up 'cause his pecker's in a twist at having a woman in charge. Killing cows and some old flea-bitten cat isn't like doing a man."

"Ham's right." But Jim had to swallow, and he wasn't interested in the rest of the dumpling on his plate. "But maybe it wouldn't hurt to be careful for a while. There are two more women on the ranch now." He pushed away his plate as he rose. "Maybe we should look after them."

"I'll look after Will," Billy said quickly, and earned a quick cuff on the ear from Ham.

"You'll do your work like always. I'm not having a bunch of pussies jumping at shadows over a cat." He topped off his coffee, picked up the cup again. "Pickles, if you haven't got anything intelligent to say, keep your mouth shut. That goes for the rest of you too." He took a moment to aim a beady eye at every man, then nodded, satisfied. "I'm going to watch *Jeopardy*."

"I tell you this," Pickles said under his breath. "I'm keeping my rifle close and a knife in my boot. If I see anybody acting funny around here, I'll take care of them. And I'll take care of myself." He took his beer and stalked outside.

Jim bypassed the coffeepot for a beer himself, glancing at Billy's pale face along the way. Poor kid, he thought, he'll be having nightmares for sure. "He's just blowing it out his ass, Billy. You know how he is."

"Yeah, but—" He wiped a hand over his mouth. It was just a cat, he reminded himself. Just an old, mangy cat. "Yeah, I know how he is."

Willa had nightmares. They woke her in a cold sweat with her heart pounding against her ribs and a scream locked in her throat. She fought her way out of the tangle of sheets, struggling for air. Alone and shivering, she sat in the center of the bed as the moonlight streamed through her windows and a fitful little breeze tapped slyly on the glass.

She couldn't remember clearly what had haunted her sleep. Blood, fear, panic. Knives. A headless cat stalking her. She tried to laugh over it, dropped her head on her drawn-up knees, and tried hard to laugh at herself. It came perilously close to a sob.

Her legs threatened to buckle when she climbed out of bed, but she made herself walk into the bath, switched on the light, lowered her head over the sink, and ran the water icy cold into her cupped hands. It was better then, with the clammy sweat washed off. Lifting her head, she studied herself in the mirror.

It was still the same face. That hadn't changed. Nothing had changed, really. It had simply been a hellish night. Didn't she have the right to be shaken, just a little, by all that was going on? Worry was like lead on her shoulders, and she had to carry it alone. There was no passing it off, no sharing the load.

The sisters were hers, and the ranch, and whatever was plaguing it. She would handle it all.

And if there was a change inside her, something irksome, something she recognized as essentially female, she would handle that as well. She didn't have the time or the temperament to play mating games with Ben McKinnon.

Oh, he was just trying to rile her anyway. She brushed the hair away from her damp cheeks, poured cold water into a glass. He'd never been interested in her. If he was now, it was only for the hell of it. Which was just like Ben. She nearly smiled as she let the water cool her throat.

She thought she might kiss him after all. Just to get it out of the way. A kind of test. She might sleep better for it. That might chase him out of her dreams and nightmares. And once she stopped wondering, stopped thinking about what kept stirring inside her, she would be able to concentrate more fully on the ranch.

She looked toward the bed, shuddered. She needed to sleep, but she didn't want to see the blood again, to see the mangled bodies. So she wouldn't.

She took a deep breath before climbing back into bed. She'd will them away, think of something else. Of spring that was so far off. Of flowers blooming in meadows and warm breezes floating down from the hills.

But when she dreamed, she dreamed of blood and death and terror.

6

From Tess Mercy's journal:

After two days of life on the ranch, I've decided I hate Montana, I hate cows, horses, cowboys, and most particularly chickens. I've been assigned the chicken coop by Bess Pringle, the scrawny despot who runs the house where I'm being held prisoner. I learned of this new career move after dinner last night. A dinner, I might add, of roast hunk of bear. It seems Danielle Boone went up in the hills and shot herself a grizzly. It was yummy.

Actually, it was quite good until I learned what I'd been eating. I can report that grizzly does not, despite what may have been stated by others, taste remotely like chicken. Whatever else I could say about Bess—and I could say plenty, given the way she eyeballs me—the woman can cook. I'm going to have to watch myself or I'll be back to the tubby stage I lived through in my youth.

There's been some excitement around the Ponderosa while I was back in the real world. Apparently someone butchered a cow up in what they call high country. When I said I thought that's what you did with cows, Annie Oakley did her best to wither me with a look. I have to admit she's got some good ones. If she wasn't such a tight-assed know-it-all, I might actually like her.

But I digress.

The cow butchering was more in the way of a mutilation and has caused some concern among the rank and file. The night before my return, one of the barn cats was decapitated and left on the front porch. Poor Lily found it.

I don't know whether to be concerned that this isn't a usual event around here or to pretend it is and make sure my door is locked every night. But the cowgirl queen looks worried. Under other circumstances, that would give me a small warm glow of satisfaction. She really gets under my skin. But with the way things stand, and thinking—or trying not to think—of the long months ahead of me, I find myself uncomfortable.

Lily spends a lot of her time with Adam and his horses. The bruises are fading, but her nerves are alive and well. I don't think she has a clue that the gorgeous Noble Savage is developing a case on her. It's kind of fun to watch. I can't help but like Lily, she's so harmless and lost. And after all, the two of us are in the same boat, so to speak.

The other characters in the cast include Ham; he's perfect, straight out of Central Casting. The bowlegged, grizzled cattleman with a beady eye and a callused hand. He tips his hat to me and says little.

Then there's Pickles. I have no idea if the man has another name. He's a sour-faced, surly character who looks like a bloated string in pointy-toed boots and is nearly hairless but for an enormous reddish moustache. He scowls a lot, but I did see him working with the cattle, and he seems to know his stuff.

There's the Book family. Nell cooks for the hands and has a sweet, homely face. She and Bess get together to gossip and do women-on-the-ranch things I don't want to know about. Her husband is Wood, which I've discovered is short for Woodrow. He has a lovely black beard, a very nice smile and manner. He calls me ma'am and suggested very politely that I should get myself a proper hat so as not to burn my face when I'm out in the sun. They have two boys, about ten and eight, I'd say, who love to run around whooping and pounding on each other. They're awfully pretty. I saw them practicing their spitting behind one of the outbuildings. They seemed to be quite skilled.

There's Jim Brewster, who seems to be one of the good ol' boy types. He's the lanky, I'm getting to it, boss sort. He's very attractive, looks appealing in jeans with that little round outline in the back pocket, which I'm sure is something revolting like chewing tobacco. He's given me a few cocky grins and winks. So far I have been able to resist.

Billy is the youngest. He looks barely old enough to drive and has his puppy eyes on our favorite cowgirl. He's a big talker and is constantly being told by anyone within hearing distance to shut up. He takes it well and rarely listens. I feel almost maternal toward him.

I haven't seen the cowboy lawyer since my return and have yet to meet the infamous Ben McKinnon of Three Rocks Ranch, who appears to be the bane of Willa's existence. I'm sure I'll like him enormously for that alone. I believe I'll have to find a way to soften Bess up in order to get all the dish on the McKinnons, but meanwhile I have a date in the chicken coop.

I'm going to try to think of it as an adventure.

Tess didn't mind rising early. She was invariably up by six in any case. An hour at the gym, perhaps a breakfast meeting, then she would hunker over her work until two. Then she'd take a dip in the pool, or take another meeting, perhaps do a little shopping. Maybe she'd have a date or maybe she wouldn't, but her life was hers and ran just as she liked.

Rising early to deal with a bunch of chickens had an entirely different flavor.

The chicken house was big, and certainly looked clean. To Tess's untrained eye, the fifty hens Mercy boasted seemed a legion of beady-eyed, ominously humming predators.

She dumped the feed as Bess had instructed, dealt with the water, then dusted off her hands and eyed the first roosting hen.

"I'm supposed to get the eggs. I believe you may be sitting on one, so if you don't mind..." Gingerly she reached out, her eyes locked on the hens. It was immediately apparent who was in charge. Yelping as beak nipped flesh, Tess jumped back. "Look, sister, I've got my orders."

It was an ugly battle. Feathers flew, tempers snapped. The henhouse erupted with clucking and squawking as neighboring hens joined the fray. Tess managed to get her hand around a nice warm egg, wrenched it clear, then stepped back red-faced and panting.

"That's quite a technique you got there."

At the voice behind her, Tess let loose of the egg. It spurted out of her fingers and fell splat on the floor. "Goddamn it! After all that."

"I spooked you." The commotion inside the henhouse had lured Nate. Instead of heading on to see Willa, he'd detoured and found the California connection—in her designer jeans and shiny new boots—battling chickens. He could only think she made a picture. "Looking for breakfast?"

"More or less." She pushed her hair back from her face. "What are you looking for?"

"I've got some business with Will. Your hand's bleeding," he added.

"I know it." In a bad temper, she sucked on the wounds on the back of her hand. "That vicious birdbrain attacked me."

"You're just not going about it right." He offered her a bandanna to wrap around her hand, then stepped up to the next roost. And managed, Tess noted, to look graceful despite the necessity of stooping and bending to keep from bashing his head on the ceiling. "You've just got to go in like it's natural. Make it quick but not abrupt." He demonstrated, slipping a hand under the roosting hen and pulling it out with an egg. Not a feather stirred.

"It's my first day on the job." Pouting only a little, she held up the bucket. "I like to find my chicken in the freezer section, wrapped in cellophane." As he walked along, gathering eggs, she followed behind. "I suppose you keep chickens."

"Used to. I don't bother with them now."

"Cattle?"

"Nope."

She raised an eyebrow. "Sheep? Isn't that a risk? I've seen all those western movies, the range wars."

"I don't raise sheep either." He settled an egg in the bucket. "Just horses. Quarter horses. You ride, Miz Mercy?"

"No." She tossed her hair back with a shrug. "Though I'm told I'd better learn. And I suppose it would give me something to do around here."

"Adam would teach you. Or I could."

"Really?" She smiled slowly with a flutter of lashes. "And why would you do that, Mr. Torrence?"

"Just being neighborly." She sure had a nice smell about her, he thought. Something just a little dark, just a little dangerous. And all female. He set another egg inside the bucket. "It's Nate."

"All right." Her voice warmed to a purr, and her eyes slanted up a sly look under thick, spiky lashes. "Are we neighbors, Nate?"

"In a manner of speaking. My place is east of here. You smell good, Miz Mercy, for someone who's been fighting with chickens."

"It's Tess. Are you flirting with me, Nate?"

"Just flirting back." His smile was slow and easy. "That's what you were doing, wasn't it?"

"In a manner of speaking. Habit."

"Well, if you want advice—"

"And lawyers are full of it," she interrupted.

"We are. My advice would be to tone down the power. The boys around here aren't used to women with as much style as you've got."

"Oh." She wasn't sure if she'd been complimented or insulted, but she decided to give him the benefit of the doubt. "And are you used to women with style?"

"Can't say I am." He gave her a long, thoughtful look out of quiet blue eyes. "But I recognize one. You'll have them crazy and thinking of killing each other within a week."

Now that, she decided, *was* a compliment. "That ought to liven things up."

"From what I hear, they've been lively enough."

"Dead cats and cows." She grimaced. "A nasty business. I'm glad I missed it."

"You're here now. That seems to be the lot," he added, and she looked down in the bucket.

"Plenty of them. And Christ, they're filthy." It was liable to put her off omelets for quite a while.

"They'll wash." He took the bucket from her and started out. "You settling in?"

"As best I can. It's not my milieu—my usual environment."

He tucked his tongue in his cheek. "Folks from your—what was it?—milieu come out here all the time. Not that they stay." Automatically he ducked down to avoid rapping his head on the low doorway of the henhouse. "Those Hollywooders come charging out, buying up land, plunking down houses that cost the earth and more. Think they're going to raise buffalo or save the mustangs or God knows what."

"You don't like Californians?"

"Californians don't belong in Montana. As a rule. They go running back to their restaurants and nightclubs soon enough." He turned, studied her. "That's what you'll do when your year's up."

"You bet your ass. You can keep your wide-open spaces, pal. I'll take Beverly Hills."

"And smog, mudslides, earthquakes."

She only smiled. "Please, you're making me homesick." She figured she had his number. Montana-born and -bred, a slow, thorough thinker who liked his beer cold and his women modest. The sort who would have kissed his horse at the end of the last reel in any B western.

But my, oh my, he was cute.

"Why the law, Nate? Somebody sue your horses?"

"Not lately." He continued to walk, shortening his stride to let her keep pace. "It interested me. The system. And it helps keep the ranch going. Takes time and money to build up a solid herd and a reputation."

"So you went to law school to supplement your ranch income. Where? University of Montana?" Her mouth was smug and amused. "There is a university in Montana, isn't there?"

"I've heard there is." Recognizing the sarcasm, he slid his gaze down to hers. "No, I went to Yale."

"To—" As she'd stopped dead, he was well ahead of her before she recovered. She had to scramble to catch up. "Yale? You went to Yale and came back here to play range lawyer for a bunch of cowboys and ranch hands?"

"I don't play at the law." He tipped his hat in good-bye and circled around to a corral beside the pole barn.

"Yale." She said it again, shook her head. Fascinated now, she shifted the bucket he'd handed back to her and scurried after him. "Hey, listen. Nate—"

She stopped. There was a great deal of activity in the corral. Two men and Willa were doing something to a small cow. Something the cow didn't appear to appreciate. Tess wondered if they were branding, and thought she'd like to see how that little trick was done. Besides, she wanted to talk to Nate again, and he was moving to the action.

She hefted her bucket, strode up to the gate and through it. No one bothered to look at her. They were focused on their work and the cow had all their attention. Lips pursed, Tess stepped closer, leaned forward to check out the activity over Willa's shoulder.

When she saw Jim Brewster quickly, neatly, and efficiently castrate the calf, her eyes rolled back in her head and she fainted dead away, with barely a sound. It was the crash of the bucket and breaking eggs that made Willa glance around.

"Well, Jesus Christ, will you look at that?"

"She's done passed out cold, Will," Jim informed her, and earned a bland scowl.

"I can see that. Deal with the calf." She straightened, but Nate was already lifting Tess into his arms. "Looks like a handful."

"She's not a featherweight." He grinned. "Your sister's built just fine, Will."

"You can enjoy that little benefit while you haul her into the house. Damn it." She scooped up the bucket. "She busted damn near every egg. Bess'll have a fit." Disgusted, she looked back at Jim and Pickles. "You two keep at it. I'm going to have to see to her first. As if I've got nothing better to do than find smelling salts for some brainless city girl."

"You shouldn't be so hard on her, Will," Nate began as he carried Tess across the road toward the ranch house. His lips twitched. "She's out of her milieu."

"I wish to hell she'd get back in it and out of mine. I've got this one fainting on me, and the other one tiptoeing around as if I'd shoot her between the eyes if she looked at me."

"You're a scary woman, Will." He glanced down as Tess stirred in his arms. "I think she's coming around."

"Dump her somewhere," Willa suggested, pulling open the door of the house. "I'll get some water."

He had to admit Tess was an interesting armful. Not one of the bony, pencil-thin California types but a soft, round woman who had her weight distributed just where it belonged. She groaned, and her lashes fluttered as he carried her toward a sofa. Her eyes, blue as cornflowers, stared blankly into his.

"What?" was the best she could manage.

"Take it easy, honey. You just had yourself a swoon, that's all."

"A swoon?" It took a moment for her brain to get around to the word and its meaning. "I fainted? That's ridiculous!"

"Went down real graceful too." She'd toppled like a tree, he remembered, but didn't think she'd appreciate the analogy. "Didn't hurt your head, did you?"

"My head?" Still dazed, she lifted a hand to it. "I don't think so. I..." And then she remembered. "Oh, God, that cow. What they were doing to that cow. What are you grinning at?"

"I'm imagining what it was like for you to see a bull turned into a steer for the first time. Guess you don't see much of that in Beverly Hills."

"We keep all our cattle in the guest house."

He nodded appreciatively. "There now, you're coming around."

She was, indeed. Enough to realize she was being cradled against his chest like a baby. "Why are you carrying me?"

"Well, it didn't seem neighborly to drag you by the hair. Your color's coming back."

"Haven't you put her down yet?" Willa demanded as she strode back into the room holding a glass of water.

"I like it this way. She smells pretty."

The exaggerated drawl made Willa chuckle and shake her head. "Stop playing with her, Nate, and dump her. I've got work to do."

"Can't I keep her, Will? I don't have me a female out on the ranch. Gets lonely."

"You two are a riot." Striving to restore some dignity, Tess swiped the hair out of her eyes. "Put me down, you idiot beanpole."

"Yes'm." From a considerable height, he dropped her onto the leather couch. She bounced once, scowled, and pushed herself up.

"Drink this." With little sympathy, Willa thrust the glass of water into Tess's hand. "And stay away from the corrals."

"You can be sure I will." Furious with herself, and the fact that she was still shaky, Tess drank. "What you were doing out there was revolting, barbaric, and cruel. If mutilating a helpless animal isn't illegal, it should be." She set her teeth when Nate beamed at her. "And stop grinning at me, you fool. I don't imagine you'd appreciate having your balls snipped off with pruning shears."

He felt them draw up, cleared his throat. "No, ma'am, I can't say I would."

"We don't castrate the men around here till we're through with them," Willa said dryly. "Look, Hollywood, weaning and castration are part of ranch life. Just what do you think would happen if we left every cow with his works? We'd have bulls humping everything."

"Cattle orgies every night," Nate put in, then backed off at the searing looks delivered by both women.

"I don't have time to explain the facts of life to you," Willa continued. "Just get over it and stay away from the corral for the next couple of days. Bess'll find work for you inside the house."

"Oh, joy."

"I don't see what else you're good for. You can't even gather eggs without breaking the lot of them." When Tess hissed at her, she turned to Nate. "You wanted to talk to me?"

"Yeah, I did." He hadn't expected quite so much entertainment. "First, I wanted to see if you were all right. I heard about the trouble you've been having."

"I'm all right enough." Willa took the glass of water out of Tess's hand and drank the rest of it down herself. "There doesn't seem to be a lot I can do about it. The men are a little spooked, and they're keeping their eyes out." She set the empty glass down, pushed her hat back. "You haven't heard about this sort of thing happening to anyone else?"

"No." And it worried him. "I don't know what I can do to help, but if there is anything, just ask."

"I appreciate it." Willa took his hand and squeezed it, a gesture that caused Tess to purse her lips thoughtfully. "Were you able to deal with that other business we talked about?"

Her will, he thought, naming Adam as beneficiary. And the papers transferring his house, the horses, and half of her interest in Mercy to him at the end of the year. "Yeah, I'll have a draft to you on all of it by the end of the week."

"Thanks." She released his hand, adjusted her hat. "You can talk to her if you've got time to waste on it." She sent Tess a wicked smile. "I've got cows to castrate."

As Willa strode out, Tess folded her arms and tried to settle her temper. "I could learn to hate her. It wouldn't take any effort at all."

"You just don't know her."

"I know she's cold, rude, unfriendly, and riding on a power trip. That's more than enough for me." No, she realized as she got to her feet, the temper wasn't going to settle. "I haven't done a damn thing to deserve that attitude from her. I didn't ask to be stuck out here, and I sure as hell didn't ask to be related to that gnat-assed witch."

"She didn't ask for it either." Nate sat on the arm of a chair, methodically rolled a cigarette. He had a little time and thought there were things that needed to be said. "Let me ask you something. How would you feel if you suddenly found out your home could be taken away? Your home, your life, everything you've ever loved?"

His eyes were mild as he struck a match, held it to the tip of the cigarette. "To keep it, you have to rely on strangers, and even if you manage to hold on, you won't keep it all. Good chunks of it are going to belong to those strangers. People you don't know, never had the opportunity to know, are living in your house with as much legal right as you. There's nothing you can do about it. Added to that, you've got all the responsibility, because these strangers don't know squat about ranching. It's up to you to hold it together. All they have to do is wait, and if they wait, they'll get as much as you, even though you were the one to work, to sweat, to worry."

Tess opened her mouth, closed it again. Put that simply, it changed the hue. "I'm not to blame for it," she said quietly.

"No, you're not. But neither is she." He turned his head, studied the portrait of Jack Mercy above the fireplace. "And you didn't have to live with him."

"What was he—" She broke off, cursed herself. She didn't want to ask. Didn't want to know.

"What was he like?" Nate blew out smoke. "I'll tell you. He was hard, cold, selfish. He knew how to run a ranch better than anyone I know. But he didn't know how to raise a child." Remembering that, thinking of that, fired him up. Now his voice was clipped. "He never gave her an ounce of affection or, as far as I know, one single word of praise, no matter how she worked her skin off for him. She was never good enough, or fast enough, or smart enough to suit him."

Guilt wasn't going to work, Tess told herself. He wasn't going to make her feel guilt or sympathy. "She could have left."

"Yeah, she could have left. But she loved this place. And she loved him. You don't have to grieve for your father, Tess. You lost him years ago. But Willa's grieving. It doesn't matter that he didn't deserve it. He didn't want her any more than he wanted you, or Lily, but she wasn't lucky enough to have a mother."

All right, guilt was going to work. A little. "I'm sorry about that. But it doesn't have anything to do with me."

He took a slow drag on his cigarette, then crushed it out carefully as he rose. "It has everything to do with you." He studied her, and his eyes were suddenly cool and detached and uncomfortably lawyerlike. "If you don't understand that, you've got too much of Jack Mercy in you. I'll be going." He touched the brim of his hat in farewell and walked out.

For a long time, Tess stood where she was, staring up at the portrait of the man who'd been her father.

Miles away on three rocks land, Jesse Cooke whistled between his teeth as he changed the points and plugs in an old Ford pickup. He was feeling fine, pumped up from the conversation over breakfast about the animal mutilations at Mercy. What was more rewarding, what was so damn perfect, was that Lily had come across that headless cat.

He only wished he could have seen it.

But Legs Monroe had it straight from Wood Book over at Mercy that the little city woman with the black eye had screamed her head off.

Oh, that was sweet.

Jesse whistled a country tune as his clever fingers made adjustments. He'd always hated country music, the whiny women sobbing over their men, dickless men moaning over their women. But he was adjusting. Every damn one of his bunkhouse mates was a fan, and it was all anyone listened to. He could handle it. In fact, he was beginning to think Montana was the place for him.

It was a land for real men, he'd decided. Men who knew how to handle themselves and keep their women in line. After he'd taught Lily a proper lesson, they'd settle down here. She was going to be rich.

The thought of that had him chuckling and tapping his foot to his own tune. Imagine dumb-ass Lily inheriting a third of one of the top ranches in the state. Worth a fucking fortune, too. All it was going to take was a year.

Jesse pulled his head out from under the hood and looked around. The mountains, the land, the sky—they were all hard. Hard and strong, like him. So this was his place, and Lily was going to learn that her place was with him. Divorce didn't mean shit in Jesse Cooke's book. The woman belonged to him, and if he had to use his fists to remind her of that from time to time, well, that was his right.

All he had to do was be patient. That was the hard part, he admitted, wiping a greasy hand over his cheek. If she found out he was close, she'd run. He couldn't afford to let her run until the year was up.

That didn't mean he wasn't going to keep his eye on her, no, indeedy. He was going to keep watch over his useless stick of a wife.

It was easy enough to make friends with a couple of the asshole hands over at Mercy. Drink a few beers, play some cards, and pump them for information. He could wander over to the neighboring ranch at will, as long as he didn't let Lily see him.

And the day Jesse Cooke, ex-Marine, let a woman outwit him was the day they'd eat cherry Popsicles in hell.

Ducking under the hood again, he got back to work. And reviewed his plans for his next visit to Mercy.

7

Sarah McKinnon flipped flapjacks on the griddle and enjoyed the fact that her older son was sitting at her kitchen table drinking her coffee. More often than not these days, he brewed his own in his quarters over the garage.

She missed him.

Fact was, she missed having both of her boys underfoot, squabbling and picking on each other. God knew there'd been times she'd thought they would set her crazy, that she would never have a moment's peace again.

Now that they were grown and she had that peace, she found herself yearning for the noise, the work, the tempers.

She'd wanted more children. With all her heart she'd wanted a little girl to fuss over in her houseful of men. But she and Stu had never had any luck making a third baby. She'd comforted herself that they'd made two healthy, beautiful boys, and that was that.

Now she had a daughter-in-law she loved, and a granddaughter to dote on. She would have more grandchildren, too. If she could ever push Ben toward the right woman.

The boy was damn particular, she mused, slanting a look toward him as he frowned over the morning paper. He wasn't still single at thirty for lack of opportunity. Lord knew there'd been women in and out of his life—and his bed too, but she didn't care to dwell on that.

But he'd never stumbled over a woman, and Sarah supposed it was just as well. You had to stumble before you could fall, and falling in love was a serious business. When a man chose carefully, he usually chose well.

But, damn it, she wanted those grandchildren.

With a plate heaped with flapjacks in her hand, she paused a moment by the kitchen window. Dawn had broken through the eastern sky, and she watched it bloom, going rosy with light and low-lying clouds.

In the bunkhouse the men would be up and at their own breakfast. Within moments, she would hear her husband's feet hit the floor above her head. She'd always risen before him, hoarding these first cozy moments to herself in the core of the house. Then he would come down, all fresh-shaven and smelling of soap, his hair damp. He'd give her a big morning kiss, pat her bottom, and slurp up that first cup of coffee as if his life depended on it.

She loved him for his predictability.

And she loved the land for its lack of it.

She loved her son, this man who had somehow come from her, for his combination of both.

As she set the plate on the table, she ran her hand over the thick mop of Ben's hair. Remembered, with odd and sudden clarity, his first paid-for haircut, at the age of seven.

How proud he'd been. And how foolishly she'd wept at those gilded curls hitting the barbershop floor.

"What's on your mind, fella?"

"Hmm?" He set the paper aside. Reading at the table was allowed, until the food was on it. "Nothing much, beautiful. What's on yours?"

She sat, cradled her coffee cup. "I know you, Benjamin McKinnon. The gears are turning in there."

"Ranch business mostly." To buy time, he started on his breakfast. The flapjacks were so light they should have been floating an inch off his plate, and the bacon was crisp enough to crack. "Nobody cooks like my ma," he said, and grinned at her.

"Nobody eats like my Ben." She settled back and waited.

He said nothing for a while, enjoying the food, the smells, the light glowing through the window as morning spread. Enjoying her. She was as dependable as the sunrise, he thought. Sarah McKinnon, with her pretty green eyes and her shiny strawberry blond hair. She had the milky-white Irish complexion that defied the sun. There were lines on it, he mused, but they were so soft, so natural, you didn't even see them. Instead you saw that smile, warm and confident.

She was a slip of a woman, slim in her jeans and plaid shirt. But he knew the strength in her. Not just the physical, though she had lifted him off his feet with her hand on his rump many a time, could ride tirelessly on horse or tractor through the bitter cold or the merciless heat, and could heft a fifty-pound bag of feed on her shoulder like a woman lifting a cooing baby.

But what was inside, where it counted most, was iron. She never faltered. In all his life, he'd never seen her turn her back on a challenge, or a friend.

If he couldn't find a woman as strong, as kind, as generous, he'd live his life a bachelor.

The idea of that would have rocked Sarah's heart.

"I've been thinking about Willa Mercy."

Sarah's brows lifted, perked by a kernel of hope. "Oh? Have you?"

"Not that way, Ma." Though he had. He very much had. "She's in a bad spot."

The dancing light in her eyes faded. "I'm sorry for that. She's a good girl, doesn't deserve this heartache. I've been thinking of riding over, paying a call. But I know how busy she is just now." Sarah's lips curved. "And I'm dying of curiosity about the others. I didn't get much time to look them over at the funeral."

"I think Will would appreciate a visit." Biding his time, he forked up more flapjacks. "We've got things under control around here. I think I could spare a little extra time over at Mercy. Not that Will would like it, but having an extra man around there, now and again, might smooth things out some."

"If you wouldn't poke at her so much, you'd get along better."

"Maybe." He lifted a shoulder. "The fact is, I don't know how much of the managing she did before the old man died. You have to figure she can handle it, but with Mercy dead, they're a man short. I haven't heard anything about her hiring another hand."

"There was some speculation she'd hire someone out of the university as foreman." That was how gossip ran from ranch to ranch—speculations over the phone wires. "A nice young man with experience in animal husbandry. Not that Ham doesn't know his business, but he's getting on in years."

"She won't do it. She's got too much to prove, and too much fondness for Ham. I can give her a hand," he continued. "Not that she thinks much of my college degree. I thought I'd ride over later this morning, feel her out."

"I think that's very kind of you, Ben."

"I'm not doing it to be kind." He grinned over the rim of his cup, and it was the same wicked devil of a grin he'd had since childhood. "It'll give me the chance to poke at her again."

She chuckled and rose to fetch the coffeepot. She'd heard her husband's feet hit the floor. "Well, that'll help keep her mind off her troubles."

. . .

She could have used a distraction. Wood's boys had snuck into the bull pasture to play matador with their mother's red Christmas apron. They'd escaped with their lives, and only one sprained ankle between them. She'd rescued them herself, hauling a dazed and clammy-faced Pete over the fence and leaving an angry, fire-eyed bull behind.

The ensuing lecture she'd delivered to two hanging heads had given her no pleasure—nor had the bone-shaking fear that the incident had shot through her. She ended up playing accessory after the fact by taking the red apron and agreeing to launder it herself before Nell could notice it was missing.

This earned her undying and desperate admiration from the culprits. And, Willa hoped, instilled enough fear in them to keep them from shouting *"Toro"* at a snorting black Angus bull again anytime in the near future.

One of the tractors had thrown a rod, and she'd had to ship Billy off to town for parts. Elk had broken through a portion of the northwest fence again, and now there were cattle to round up.

Bess was down with a cold, Tess had broken most of the eggs for the third time this week, and Lily the mouse was in temporary charge of the kitchen.

To top it all off, her men were bickering.

"A man plays poker and has a run of luck, I say he sticks around to give the rest of the table a chance to even the score." Pickles adjusted the annoyed calf's horns in the squeeze shoot and popped them off to the tune of Tammy Wynette backed up by insulted moos.

"You can't afford to lose," Jim shot back, "you don't play."

"A man's got a right to get back his own."

"And a man's got a right to turn in when he wants. Ain't that right, Will?"

She medicated the cow, plunging the needle in swiftly and efficiently. It was cooler today, autumn coming in strong. But the jacket she'd started out with was now slung over a rail as she sweated through her shirt. "I'm not getting in the middle of your petty feuds."

Pickles's frown carved vertical lines between his brows and set his moustache quivering. "Between Jim and that cardsharp over to Three Rocks, they took me for two hundred."

"J C's not a cardsharp." More to spite Pickles than anything else, Jim flew to his new friend's defense. "He just played better than you. You couldn't bluff a blind man on a galloping horse. And you're just pissed off because he fixed Ham's rig and had it purring like a kitten."

Because it was true, down to the ground, Pickles's chin jutted like a lance. "I don't need some a-hole from over to Three Rocks coming 'round and fixing our rigs and taking my money at cards. I'da fixed the rig when I had the chance."

"You've been saying that for a week."

"I'da got to it." Grinding his teeth, Pickles got to his feet. "I don't need somebody coming around taking over. I don't need somebody changing the way things are. I've been working this ranch for eighteen years come next May. I don't need no Johnny come lately a-holes telling me what's what."

"Who're you calling an a-hole?" Eyes hot, Jim sprang to his feet, pushed his face into Pickles's. "You want to take me on, old man? Come ahead."

"That's enough." Even as fists raised, white-knuckled, Willa stepped between them. "I said enough." Using both hands she shoved the men apart. One sweeping glance dared either one to take a punch. "As far as I can see, there are two assholes right here who don't have the sense to keep their minds on their work when they're hip-deep in it."

"I can do my work." Pickles's jaw clenched as he glared down at her. "I don't need him, or you, to tell me what has to be done."

"That's fine, then. And I don't need you to start a pissing contest when we're hip-deep in balls and horns. You go cool off. And when you've cooled off, you ride out and check on the fence crew."

"Ham doesn't need anybody checking on him, and I've got work right here."

Willa stepped closer, bumped her temper against his. "I said go cool off. Then get your butt in your rig and check fences. You do it, and do it now, or you pack up your gear and pick up your last paycheck."

His color rose high, as much in anger as at the humiliation of being ordered around by a woman half his age. "You think you can fire me?"

"I know I can, and so do you." She jerked her head toward the gate. "Now get moving. You're in my way here."

They stared at each other for ten humming seconds. Then he stepped aside, spat on the ground, and stalked toward the gate. Beside Willa, Jim blew out a breath between his teeth.

"You don't want to lose him, Will. He's ornery, Christ knows, but he's a hell of a cowboy."

"He's not going anywhere." If she had been alone, she could have pressed a hand against her jittery stomach. Instead, she crouched and prepared the next hypo. "Once he clears the mad out, he'll be all right. He didn't mean to swipe at you, Jim. He likes you as well as he likes anybody."

Grinning now, Jim hauled a cow toward the squeeze shoot. "That ain't saying much."

"I guess not." She smiled herself. "Prickly old bastard. How much you win off him last night?"

"About seventy. Got my eye on some pretty snakeskin boots."

"You're such a dude, Brewster."

"I like to look sharp for the ladies." He winked at her and the routine fell back into place. "Maybe you'll come dancing with me sometime, Will."

It was an old joke, and cleared more tension. Willa Mercy didn't dance. "And maybe you'll lose the seventy back to him tonight." She wiped sweat off her forehead and kept her voice causal. "This guy from Three Rocks?"

"J C. He's okay."

"Did he have any news from over there?"

"Not much." As Jim worked he recalled that J C had been more interested in the workings of Mercy. "He said how John Conner's girl broke things off, and John got himself shit-faced drunk and passed out in the toilet."

It was easier now, and again routine. Old gossip, familiar names. "Sissy breaks up with Conner every other week, and he always gets shit-faced."

"Just so you know things are as usual."

They grinned at each other, two people hunkered down in blood and manure with the cool breeze blowing the stink everywhere. "Twenty says he'll buy her a bauble and she'll take him back by Monday."

"No bet. I ain't no greenhorn."

They worked together for another twenty minutes, communicating with grunts and hand signals. When they paused long enough to cool dry throats, Jim shifted his feet. "Will, Pickles didn't mean to ride you, either. He's missing the old man is all. Pickles had a powerful respect for him."

"I know." She ignored the nagging ache in her heart as she squinted her eyes. The line of dust coming down the road meant Billy was back. She thought she'd go hunt down Pickles, soothe his ruffled feathers, and give him the tractor to repair. "Go on and get your dinner, Jim."

"My favorite words."

She took her own meal with her, climbing into the cab of her Land Rover and eating the roast beef sandwich one-handed as she negotiated the dirt road, crisscrossed with tire tracks and hoofprints. The path cut through pastures, toward hillocks, then rose, and gave her a breathless view of autumn color.

It was passing its peak, she mused, going soft as it faded and leaves were stripped from the trees. But she could hear a meadowlark's high, insistent call as she left the window down to the play of the wind. It should have soothed her, that familiar music. She wanted it to soothe her, and she couldn't understand why it didn't.

With a careful eye she studied the fencing she passed, satisfied that it was, for now, in good repair. Cattle grazed placidly, a cow occasionally raised its head to stare with marked disinterest at the passing rig and driver.

To the west the sky was growing dark and bad-tempered, casting shadow and eerie light on the peaks. She imagined there'd be snow in the mountains and rain here in the valley before evening. God knew they could use the rain, she thought, but she had little hope it would be the slow, serene soaker that the land would absorb. Likely as not, it would come in hard, brittle drops that would batter the crops and bounce like bullets off the ground.

Already she yearned to hear it pound on the roof like angry fists, to be alone with that violent sound and her own thoughts for a few hours. And to look out her window, she thought, at a wall of mean rain that masked everything and everyone.

Maybe it was the coming storm that was making her so restless, so edgy, she thought, as she caught herself checking her rearview mirror for the fourth time.

Or maybe she was just annoyed that she'd come across evidence of the fence crew and not the crew themselves.

No rig, no sound of hammer, no men walking the fence line in the distance. Nothing but road and land and hills rising into a bruised sky.

She felt too alone. And that made no sense to her. She liked being alone on her own land. Even now she was longing for time by herself with no one asking her questions, demanding answers, or listing complaints.

But the nerves remained, jumping like trout in her stomach, crawling over the back of her neck like busy ants. She found herself reaching behind her, laying her fingers on the stock of the shotgun in her gun rack. Then, very deliberately, stopping the rig and stepping out to scan the land for signs of life.

It was risky. He knew it was risky, but he had a taste for it now and couldn't stop himself. He thought he'd chosen his time and place well enough. There was a storm brewing, and the fence crew had finished in this section. He imagined they were back at the ranch yard by now, hunting up their dinner.

It didn't give him much of a window, but he knew how to make the best of it. He'd chosen a prime steer out of the pasture, one that was fat and sleek and would have brought top money at market.

He'd chosen his spot carefully. Once he was finished, he could ride fast and soon be back at the ranch yard, or on a far point of Mercy land. One edge of the road butted the rising hills that went rocky under a cloak of trees.

No one would come upon him from that direction.

The first time he'd done it, his stomach had revolted at the first spurt of blood. He'd never cut into anything so alive, so big before. But then—well, then it had been so . . . interesting. Cutting into such a weighty living thing, feeling the pulse beat, then slow, then fade like a clock run down.

Watching the life drain.

Blood was warm, and it pulsed. At least it pulsed at first, then it just pooled, red and wet, like a lake.

The steer didn't fight him. He lured it with grain, then led it with a rope. He wanted to do it dead center of the ranch road. Sooner or later someone would come along, and my, oh, my, what a surprise. The birds would circle overhead, drawn by the smell of death.

The wolves might come down, lured by it.

He'd had no idea how seductive death could smell. Until he'd caused it.

He smiled at the steer munching from the bucket of grain, ran a hand over the coarse black hide. Then tugging at the plastic raincoat to be sure it covered him well, he raked the knife over the throat in one smooth move—he really thought he was getting better at it—and laughed delightedly as blood flew.

"Get along, little dogie," he sang as the steer crumpled to the ground.

Then he got to the interesting work.

. . .

Pickles was having a fine time sulking. As he drove along the fence line, he played several conversations in his head. He and Jim. He and Willa. Then he tried out the words he'd use when he complained to Ham about how Willa had gotten in his face and threatened to fire him.

As if she could.

Jack Mercy had hired him, and as far as Pickles was concerned nobody but Jack Mercy could fire him. As Jack was dead—God rest his soul—that was that.

Could be he'd just up and quit. He had a stake laid by, growing interest in the bank down at Bozeman. He could buy his own ranch, start out slow and easy and build it into something fine.

He'd like to see what that bossy female would do if she lost him. Never make it through the winter, he thought sourly, much less through a whole damn year.

And maybe he'd just take Jim Brewster along with him, Pickles thought, conveniently forgetting he was mighty put out at Jim. The boy was a good hand, a hard worker, even if he was an a-hole most of the time.

He might just do it, buy him some land up north, raise some Herefords. He could take Billy along, too, just for the hell of it. And he'd keep the ranch pure, he thought, adding to his fantasy. No damn chickens or small grains, no pigs, no horses but what a man needed as a tool. This diversifying shit was just that. Shit. As far as he was concerned, it was the only wrong turn Jack Mercy had ever made.

Letting that Indian boy breed horses on cattle land.

Not that he had anything against Adam Wolfchild. The man minded his business, kept to himself, and he trained some fine saddle horses. But it was the principle. The girl had her way, she and the Indian would be running Mercy shoulder to shoulder.

And in Pickles's opinion, they'd run it straight into the ground.

Women, he told himself, belonged in the goddamn kitchen, not out on the land ordering men around. Fire him, his ass, he thought with a sniff, and turned onto the left fork to see if Ham and Wood had finished up.

Storm brewing, he thought absently, then spotted the rig stopped in the road. It made him smile.

If a rig had broken down, he had his toolbox in the back. He'd show anybody in southwest Montana with sense enough to scratch their butt that he knew more about engines than anybody within a hundred miles.

He stopped his rig and, tucking his thumbs in the front pockets of his jeans, sauntered over. "Got yourself some trouble here?" he began, then stopped short.

The steer was laid wide open, and there was enough blood to bathe in. The stink of it had his nostrils flaring as he stepped closer, barely glancing at the man crouched beside the body.

"We got us another one? Jesus fucking Christ, what's going on around here?" He bent closer. "It's fresh," he began, then he saw—the knife, the blood running off the blade. And the eyes of the man who held it. "God Almighty, you? Why'd you do it?"

"Because I can." He watched knowledge come into the man's eyes and saw them dart quickly toward the rig. "Because I like it," he said softly. With some regret, he jerked the knife up and plunged it into Pickles's soft belly. "Never killed a man before," he said, and yanked the knife upward with a steady, nerveless hand. "It's interesting."

Interesting, he thought again, studying the way Pickles's eyes went from shocked, to pained, to dull. He kept the knife moving up, toward the heart, leaning with the body as it fell, then straddling it.

All his fascination with the steer was forgotten. This, he realized, was far bigger game. A man had brains, he mused, pulling his knife free with a wet, sucking sound. A cow was just stupid. And a cat, while clever, was just a small thing.

Considering, he leaned back, wondering how to make this moment, this new step, something special. Something people would talk about everywhere, and for a long, long time.

Then he smiled, giggled until he had to press his bloody hand to his mouth. He knew just how to make his mark.

He turned the knife in his hand and went cheerfully to work.

When Willa saw the rider galloping over her pasture, she stopped the rig. She recognized the big black that Ben rode, and the dog Charlie, who was bounding along beside Spook like a shadow. Relief was the first reaction, and one she didn't welcome. But there was something eerie in the air, and she'd have been grateful to see the devil himself riding up.

Though it was an impressive sight, she sniffed, the way he and the black gelding sailed over the fence with a careless bunch and flow of muscle.

"You make a wrong turn, McKinnon?"

"Nope." He reined in his horse beside the rig. Charlie, in happy welcome, lifted a leg and peed on Willa's front tire. "You get that fence fixed?" He smiled when she stared at him. "Zack saw you had one down when he went up this morning. The elk have been a real pain in the ass this year."

"They always are. I expect Ham's dealt with it by now. I was going to ride by and check."

He swung off the horse, then leaned in the window. "Is that a sandwich over there?"

She glanced at the second half of her dinner. "Yeah. So?"

"You going to eat it?"

With a sigh, she picked it up and handed it to him. "Did you hunt me down for a free meal?"

"That's just a side benefit. I'm going to be shipping some cattle down to the feedlot in Colorado, but I thought you might want to take a couple hundred head off my hands to finish." Companionably, he broke off a corner of the sandwich, tossed it to the hopeful dog.

She watched the dog gulp down bread and beef, then grin. The grin, she mused, wasn't so far off from his master's arrogant, self-satisfied smirk. "You want to dicker over price here?"

"I thought we could do it friendlier. Over a drink later." He reached a hand through the window to toy with the hair that had come loose from her braid. "I still haven't met your oldest sister."

Will shoved the jeep in gear. "She's not your type, Slick, but you come ahead by if you want." She watched him mow through the last bite of sandwich. "*After* supper."

"Want me to bring my own bottle too?"

She only smiled and eased on the gas. After a moment's thought, Ben remounted and trotted after her. They both knew she was keeping her speed slow enough so that he could.

"Adam going to be around?" Ben raised his voice so she could hear it clearly over the engine. "I'm interested in a couple new saddle ponies."

"Ask him. I'm too busy to socialize, Ben." To irritate him, she accelerated, spewing dust in his face. Still, she was disappointed when she took the left fork and he turned and rode off in the opposite direction.

She wished she could have fought with him about something, made him mad enough to grab hold of her again. She'd been thinking quite a bit about the way he'd grabbed hold of her.

She didn't do a lot of thinking about men—not that way. But it was certainly diverting to think—that way—about Ben. Even if she didn't intend to do anything about it.

Unless she changed her mind.

She grinned to herself. She might just change her mind, too, just to see what it was all about. She had a feeling that Ben could show her more clearly and more thoroughly than most just what a man could do with a woman.

Maybe she'd irritate him into kissing her tonight. Unless he got distracted by big-busted Tess and her fancy French perfume. At that idea she gunned the engine, then braked hard as she spotted Pickles's rig on the curve of the road.

"Well, shit, found him." And now, she thought, she'd have to placate him. She climbed out, scanning the fence line and the pasture on either side. She didn't see any sign of him, or any reason why he would have left his rig across the road.

"Gone off somewhere to sulk," she muttered, and moved toward the cab of the rig to sound the horn.

Then she saw him, him and the steer stretched out in front of the rig, side by side in a river of blood. She didn't know why she hadn't smelled it, not with the way the air was thick and raw with death. But the smell reared up and slammed into her gut now, and she stumbled toward the side of the road and violently threw up her dinner.

Her stomach continued to heave painfully as she staggered toward her own rig and lay hard on the horn. She kept her hand pressed down, her head against the window frame as she fought to get her breath.

Turning her head, she tried to spit out the taste of sickness clawing in her throat, then rubbed her hands over her clammy face. When her vision grayed and wavered, she bit down hard on her lip. But she couldn't make herself walk back down the road, couldn't make herself look again. Giving in, she folded her arms and laid her head down. She didn't lift it even when she heard the thunder of hoofbeats and Charlie's high barks.

"Hey." Ben slid off his horse, the rifle slung by its strap over his shoulder. "Willa."

A springing wildcat wouldn't have surprised him as much as her turning, burying her face in his chest. "Ben. Oh, God." Her arms came around him, clung. "Oh, God."

"It's all right, darling. It's all right now."

"No." She squeezed her eyes tight. "No. In front of the rig. The other rig. There's . . . God, the blood."

"Okay, baby, sit down. I'll see to it." Grim-faced, he eased her down on the running board of the rig, frowning when she put her head between her knees and shuddered. "Just sit there, Will."

By the look on her face, and the din his dog was sounding, Ben thought it must be another steer, or one of the ranch dogs. He was already furious before he stepped up to the abandoned rig. Before he saw it was more, much more, than a steer.

"Sweet Jesus."

He might not have recognized the man, not after what had been done to him. But he recognized the rig, the boots, the hat covered with blood lying near the body. His stomach twisted with both sickness and fury. One thought broke through both as he gave Charlie a sharp order to silence: Whoever did this wasn't simply mad, he was evil.

He turned quickly at the sound behind him, then spread out an arm to block Willa's path. "Don't." His voice was rough, and the hand on her arm firm. "There's nothing you can do, and no need for you to see that again."

"I'm all right now." She put a hand on Ben's and stepped closer. "He was mine, and I'll look at him." She rubbed the heels of her hands under her eyes. "They scalped him, Ben. For God's sake. For God's sweet sake. They cut him to pieces and scalped him."

"That's enough." His hands weren't gentle as he turned her around, forced her head back until their eyes met. "That's enough, Willa. Go back to your rig, radio the police."

She nodded, but when she didn't move, he wrapped his arms around her again, cradled her head on his chest. "Just hold on a minute," he murmured. "Just hold on to me."

"I sent him out here, Ben." She didn't just hold, she burrowed. "He pissed me off and I told him to ride out here or pack up and pick up his check. I sent him out here."

"Stop it." Alarmed by the way her voice fractured on each word, he pressed his lips to her hair. "You know you're not to blame for this."

"He was mine," she repeated, then shuddering once, drew away. "Cover him up, Ben. Please. He needs to be covered up."

"I'll take care of it." He touched her cheek, wishing he could rub color back into it. "Stay in the rig, Will."

He waited until she was back in the vehicle, then pulled the grease-stained tarp out of the bed of Pickles's truck. It would have to do.

8

From the kitchen window Lily could see the forest and the climb of mountains into the sky. Night was coming more quickly as October gave way to November. From the window, she could watch the sun drop toward the peaks. It had hardly been two weeks since she'd come to Montana, but already she knew that once the sun fell behind those shadowy hills night would come swiftly and the air would quickly chill.

The dark still frightened her.

She looked forward to the dawns. To the days. There was so much to do, she could spend hours on the chores. She was grateful to be useful again, to feel a part of something. In so short a time she had come to depend on seeing that wide spread of sky, the rise of mountains, the sea of land. She'd come to count on hearing the sounds of horses, cattle, and men. And the smell of them.

She loved her room, the privacy of it, and the grace, and the house with all its space and polished wood. The library was stuffed with books, and she could read every night if she chose to, or listen to music, or leave the TV murmuring.

No one cared what she did with her evenings. No one criticized her small mistakes, or raised a hand to her.

Not yet.

Adam was so patient. And he was gentle as a mother with the horses. With her as well, she admitted. When he guided her hands down a horse's leg to show her how to check for strains, he didn't squeeze. He'd shown her how to use a dandy brush, how to medicate a split hoof, how to mix supplements for a pregnant mare.

And when he'd caught her feeding an apple to a yearling on the sly, he hadn't lectured. He'd just smiled.

The hours they worked together were the best of her life. This new world that had opened up for her had given her hope, a chance for a future.

Now that could be over.

A man was dead.

She shuddered to think of it, to be forced to admit that murder had slunk into her bright new world. In one vicious stroke, a man's life was over, and she was once again helpless to control what happened next.

It shamed her that she thought more of herself and what would happen to her than of the man who had been killed. It was true that she hadn't known him. With the skill of the hunted, Lily had easily avoided the men of Mercy Ranch. But he had been part of her new world, and it was selfish not to think of him first.

"Christ, what a mess."

Lily jumped as Tess swung into the kitchen, and her hand tensed on the dishrag she'd forgotten she was holding. "I made coffee. Fresh. Are they . . . is everyone still here?"

"Will's still talking to the cowboy cops, if that's what you mean." Tess wandered to the stove, wrinkled her nose at the coffeepot. "I stayed out of the way, so I don't know what's going on, exactly." She walked to the pantry, opening and closing the door in jerks. "Anything stronger than coffee around here?"

Lily twisted the dishrag in her hands. "I think there's wine, but I don't think we should disturb Willa to ask."

Tess just rolled her eyes and wrenched open the refrigerator. "This adequate, if slightly inferior, bottle of Chardonnay is as much ours as hers." Taking it out, Tess asked, "Got a corkscrew?"

"I saw one earlier." She made herself put down the cloth. She'd already wiped the counters clean twice. Opening a drawer, she took out a corkscrew and handed it to Tess. "I, ah, made some soup." She gestured toward the pot on the stove. "Bess is still running a fever, but she managed to eat a bowl of it. I think—I hope she'll be feeling better by tomorrow."

"Uh-huh." Tess searched out wineglasses herself, poured. "Sit down, Lily. I think we should talk."

"Maybe I should take out some coffee."

"Sit down. Please." Tess slipped onto the wooden bench of the breakfast nook and waited.

"All right." Lily sat down across the polished table and folded her hands in her lap.

Tess slid the wineglass over, lifted her own. "I suppose eventually we should get into the story of our lives, but this doesn't seem to be the right time." From her pocket she took the single cigarette she'd slipped out of her secret emergency pack, twirling it in her fingers before reaching for the book of matches. "This is a pretty ugly business."

"Yes." Automatically Lily rose, fetched an ashtray, and brought it back to the table. "That poor man. I don't know which one he was, but—"

"The balding one, with the big moustache and bigger belly," Tess told her, and with a shrug for willpower, lit the cigarette.

"Oh." Now that she had a face to focus on, Lily felt the shame grow. "Yes, I've seen him. He was stabbed, wasn't he?"

"I think it was worse than that, but I don't have a lot of the details other than Will found him on one of those roads that go all over the ranch."

"It must have been horrible for her."

"Yeah." Tess grimaced, picked up her wine. She might not have been fond of her youngest half sister, but she wouldn't have wished this particular experience on anyone. "She'll handle it. They breed them tough out here. Anyway . . ." She sipped, found the wine not quite as inferior as she'd thought. "What about you? Are you staying or going?"

More out of a need to do something with her hands than a desire for wine, Lily reached for her glass. "I don't really have anyplace else to go. I suppose you'll be going back to California."

"I've thought about it." Tess leaned back, studied the woman across from her. Keeps her eyes down, Tess mused, and her hands busy. She'd been certain that shy Lily would already have booked a flight to anywhere. "I figure it this way. People are murdered every day in LA. Kids regularly whack each other for painting graffiti in the wrong territory. There are drug hits every time you blink. Shootings, knifings, muggings, bludgeonings." She smiled. "God, I love that town."

Catching Lily's appalled expression, Tess threw back her head and laughed. "Sorry," she managed after a moment, pressing a hand to her heart. "My point is that as bad as this is, as close as it is, it's only one murder. Comparatively, it just isn't that big a deal, certainly not big enough to chase me away from collecting what's mine."

Lily drank again, struggled to gather her thoughts. "You're staying. You're going to stay."

"Yeah, I'm going to stay. Nothing's changed."

"I thought—" Closing her eyes, Lily let the relief run through her and twine with the shame. "I was sure you wouldn't, and then I'd have to leave." She opened her eyes again, soft, quiet blue with hints of haunted gray. "That's horrible. That poor man's dead, and all I've been able to think about is how it affects me."

"That's just honest. You didn't know him. Hey." Because there was something about Lily that tugged at her, Tess reached for her sister's hand. "Don't beat yourself up over it. We've all got a lot at stake here. We're entitled to think about what's ours."

Lily looked down at the joined hands. Tess's were so pretty, she thought, with the glitter of rings and the enviable strength and confidence in the fingers. She lifted her gaze. "I didn't do anything to deserve this place. Neither did you."

Tess merely nodded and, withdrawing her hand, lifted her glass again. "I didn't do anything to deserve being ignored my entire life. And neither did you."

Willa came into the kitchen, stopped short when she saw the women at the table. Her face was still pale, her movements still jerky. After all the questions, the going over and over her discovery of the body, she'd been more than happy to see the police on their way.

"Well, this is cozy." She slipped her hands into her pockets as she stepped toward the table. Her fingers still tended to shake. "I figured the two of you would be packing, not sitting around having a chat."

"We've been talking about that." Tess lifted an eyebrow but made no comment when Will picked up her wineglass and drank. "We're not going anywhere."

"Is that so?" Because wine seemed like a fine idea, Willa crossed to the cupboards and took out a tumbler. Then she just stood there, unable to move, barely able to think.

She hadn't been able to fully consider the loss of the ranch. It had been there, in the back of her mind, the certainty that the two women who had been pushed on her would run. And with them would go her life. But it wasn't until now, until she knew they would stay, that it hit her. And it hit hard.

Giving in, she rested her head against the cupboard door and closed her eyes.

Pickles. Dear God, would she see him for the rest of her life, what had been done to him, what had been left of him? And all that blood, baking in the sun. The way his eyes had stared up at her, the horror frozen in them.

But the ranch, for now, was safe.

"Oh God, oh God, oh God."

She didn't realize she'd moaned it out loud until Lily laid a tentative hand on her shoulder. Shrinking from the touch, Willa straightened quickly.

"I made soup." Lily felt foolish saying it but could think of nothing else. "You should eat something."

"I don't think I could handle food right now." Willa stepped back, afraid that too much comfort would break her. She walked back to the table and, under Tess's fascinated eye, filled the tumbler full of wine.

"That's good," Tess murmured, watching in admiration as Willa gulped wine like water. "That's damn good. How long can you do that and still stand up?"

"We'll have to find out." She turned when the kitchen door opened, drew a steadying breath when Ben came in.

She didn't want to berate herself for leaning on him, for collapsing in his arms, for letting him do the dirty work while she had sat by, too ill to function. But it was hard to swallow.

"Ladies." In a gesture that mimicked Willa's habit, he took the glass from her hand and sipped. "Here's to the end of a lousy day."

"I'll drink to that." Tess did, as she studied him. The gilded cowboy, she mused. And a mouthwaterer. "I'm Tess. You must be Ben McKinnon."

"Nice to meet you. Sorry it isn't under more pleasant circumstances." He lifted a hand to Willa's chin, turned her face to his. "Go lie down."

"I have to talk to the men."

"No, you don't. What you have to do is go lie down and turn this off for a while."

"I'm not going to pull the covers over my head because—"

"There's nothing you can do," he interrupted. She was trembling. He could feel just how hard she was fighting it, but the tremors came through and into his fingertips. "You're sick and you're tired, and you've just had to relive an ugly experience half a dozen times. Adam is taking the cops down to talk to the men in the bunkhouse, and there's nothing for you to do but try to get some sleep."

"My men are—"

"Who's going to pull them together tomorrow—and the day after—if you break down?" He inclined his head when she shut her mouth. "Now you can go up and lie down under your own steam, Will, or I'll take you myself. Either way, that's what you're going to do. Right now."

Tears burned the back of her eyes, bubbled hot in her throat. Too proud to shed them in front of him, she shoved his hand aside, swiveled on her heel, and stalked out.

"I'm impressed," Tess murmured when the kitchen door slammed. "I didn't think anyone could push her around."

"She'd have pushed back, but she knew she'd break. Will won't let herself break." He frowned into his wine, wishing he'd been able to gentle her into it instead of browbeating her. "I don't know many who could have gotten through what she did today without breaking."

"Should she be alone?" Lily pressed her fingers to her lips. "I could go up with her, but . . . I don't know if she'd want that."

"No, she's better off alone." But Ben smiled, pleased that she'd offered. "This hasn't exactly been a weekend at a dude ranch resort for either of you, but I'll say welcome to Montana anyway."

"I love it here." The minute she'd said it, Lily flushed and scrambled to her feet as Tess chuckled. "Would you like something to eat? I made soup, and there's plenty of fixings for sandwiches."

"Angel, if that's your soup I'm smelling, I'd be grateful to have a bowl."

"Good. Tess?"

"Sure, why the hell not?" Since Lily seemed eager to serve, Tess stayed where she was, tapping her fingers on the table. "Do the police think it was someone from the ranch who did it?"

Ben slid in across from her. "I imagine they'll concentrate here, first anyway. There's no public access to the ranch, but that doesn't mean someone from outside couldn't have found the way out there. A horse, a jeep." He moved his shoulders, skimmed a hand through his hair. "It's easy enough access from Three Rocks to Mercy land. Hell, I was there myself."

He lifted an eyebrow at Tess's speculative look. "Of course, I can tell you I didn't do it, but you don't know me. It's also possible to get there through the Rocking R Ranch, or Nate's place, or the high country."

"Well"—Tess poured herself more wine—"that certainly narrows things down, doesn't it?"

"I'll tell you this—anyone who knows the mountains, the land around here, could hide out for months, go pretty much wherever the hell he pleased. And be damn hard to find."

"We appreciate your easing our minds." She flicked a glance at Lily as she set steaming bowls on the table. "Don't we, Lily?"

"I'd rather know." Lily sat on the edge of the bench next to Tess and folded her hands again. "You can take precautions better if you know."

"That's exactly right. I'd say a good precaution would be for neither of you to wander far from the house here alone, for the time being."

"I'm not much of a wanderer." Though her stomach suddenly felt uneasy, Tess spooned up soup. "And Lily sticks pretty close to Adam." She looked at Ben. "Is he a suspect?"

"I don't know what the police think, but I can tell you that Adam Wolfchild would no more gut and scalp a man than he'd sprout wings and fly to Idaho." He glanced over when Tess's spoon crashed onto the table. He'd have cursed himself if it would have done any good. "I'm sorry. I thought you knew the details."

"No." Tess went for the wine rather than the soup. "We didn't."

"She saw that?" Lily twisted her hands in her lap. "She found that?"

"And she'll live with that." They both would, Ben thought, for it was an image he knew would never completely fade from his memory. "I don't want to scare you, I just want you to be careful."

"You can count on it," Tess promised him. "But what about her?" She jerked a thumb toward the ceiling. "You're not going to keep her close to the house without shackles."

"Adam will keep an eye on her. And so will I." Hoping to ease the tension, he spooned up more soup. "And hanging around here isn't going to be much of a hardship if this is the kind of cooking I'm in for."

Both women jumped when the outside door opened. Adam came in, along with the night chill. "They're done with me for now."

"Join the party," Tess invited. "Soup and wine is our menu tonight."

He gave her a solemn look before studying Lily. "I think I'd go for coffee. No, sit," he added when Lily started to get up. "I can get it myself. I just came by to check on Willa."

"Ben made her go up and lie down." Nerves and relief had words bubbling out before Lily could stop them. "She needed to rest. I can fix you some soup. You should eat something, and there's plenty."

"I can get it. Sit down."

"There's bread. I forgot to put the bread out. I should—"

"You should sit." He spoke very quietly as he ladled up soup. "And try to relax." He filled a second bowl, brought both to the table. "And you should eat. I'll get the bread."

She stared at him, baffled, while he moved competently around the kitchen. None of the men in her life had so much as picked up a dish unless it was to ask for seconds. She flicked a glance at Ben, looking for the sneer, but he continued to eat as though there was nothing unusual at all about having a man serve food.

"Do you want me to stay over, Adam, give you a hand with things for a day or two?"

"No. Thanks anyway. We'll have to take it a step at a time." He sat down across from Lily and looked her in the eye. "Are you all right?"

She nodded, picked up her spoon, and tried to eat.

"Pickles didn't have any family," Adam continued. "I think there was a sister maybe, down in Wyoming. I guess we'll try to find her, if she's still around, but I'd say we'll handle the arrangements once they release the body."

"You ought to have Nate do that." Ben broke off a hunk of bread. "Willa will pass that to him if you suggest it."

"All right, I'll do that. I don't think she'd have gotten through this without you. I want you to know that."

"I just happened to be there." It still unnerved him, the way she'd all but crawled into his arms. And the way she'd fit when she had. "Once she's over the shock, she'll likely be sorry it was me who was."

"You're wrong. She'll be grateful, and so am I." He turned his hand over, palm up, where there was a long, thin scar between the lines of heart and head. "Brother."

Ben's lips twitched as he looked at the similar mark on his own hand. And he remembered when two young boys had stood on the banks of a river in the half-light of a canyon and solemnly mixed their blood in brotherhood.

"Uh-oh, male ritual time." Absurdly touched, Tess nudged Lily so that she could slide out. "That's my cue to leave you gentlemen to your port and cigars while I go up and do something exciting like paint my toenails."

Appreciating her, Ben grinned. "I bet they're real pretty, too."

"Sweetheart, they are awesome." It was simple to decide she liked him. And not a very large step from there to decide to trust him. "I guess I'll range myself with Adam and say I'm grateful you were here. Good night."

"I'll go too." Lily reached down for Tess's half-eaten bowl of soup.

"Don't go." Adam laid a hand over hers. "You haven't eaten."

"You'll want to talk. I can take it up with me."

"Don't run off on my account." Pretty sure that he saw how the wind blew here, Ben slid off the bench. "I've got to get home. I appreciate the meal, Lily." He reached up to touch her cheek, felt her instinctive wince of defense. Smoothly, he dropped his hand, as if the moment hadn't happened. "You eat while it's hot," he advised. "I'll be around tomorrow, Adam."

"Good night, Ben." Adam kept his hand over Lily's, giving it a coaxing tug until she sat again. Then he took her other hand, linked his fingers in hers, and waited until she lifted her eyes to his. "Don't be afraid. I won't let anything happen to you."

"I'm always afraid."

Her hands flexed under his, but he judged it was time to take the chance, so he continued to hold them. "You came to a strange place, with only strangers around you. And you stayed. There's courage there."

"I only came to hide. You don't know me, Adam."

"I will when you let me." He released one of her hands, lifted his own, and brushed his thumb over the faded bruise beneath her eye. She went very still, watched him warily as he traced his thumb down to the marks on her jaw. "I want to know you, Lily, when you're ready."

"Why?"

His eyes smiled and stirred her heart. "Because you understand horses, and you sneak kitchen scraps to my dogs." The smile moved to his mouth when she flushed. "And because you make good soup. Now, eat," he said, and released her hand. "Before it's cold."

Watching him from under her lashes, she picked up her spoon and ate.

Upstairs, armed with a book she'd chosen from the library and a bottle of mineral water she'd taken from behind the bar, Tess walked toward her room. She had decided to read until her eyes crossed, hoping that it would bring her undisturbed and dreamless sleep.

Her imagination was much too vivid, she thought. It was the very reason she was beginning to make her mark as a screenwriter. And the very reason that the details Ben had provided were going to shift and stir until they formed many ugly visions in her head.

She had great hope that the thick paperback romance whose cover promised plenty of passion and adventure would steer her mind to other venues.

Then she passed Willa's door and heard the bitter, broken weeping. She hesitated, wished to hell she'd thought to come up the other stairs. More, wished the helpless sobbing didn't touch a chord in her. When a strong woman wept, she thought, the tears came from the deepest and darkest corners of the heart.

She lifted a hand to knock, then on an oath just laid her palm on the wood. Perhaps if they had known each other, or if they had been complete strangers, she could have gone in. If they had had no ghosts between them, no harbored resentments, she could have opened that door and offered . . . something.

But she knew she wouldn't be welcomed. There could be no woman-to-woman comfort here, much less sister to sister. And realizing she was sorry for that, very sorry, she continued to her own room, carefully closed, carefully locked the door behind her.

But she no longer thought her dreams would be undisturbed.

In the dark, in the middle of the night when the wind kicked up and threatened and the rain came hard and vicious, he lay smiling. Reliving every moment of the kill, second by second, brought a curious thrill.

It had been like being someone else while it was happening, he realized. Someone with vision so clear, with nerves so steady, he was barely human.

He hadn't known he'd had that inside him.

He hadn't known he would like it so much.

Poor old Pickles. To keep from laughing aloud, he pressed both hands to his mouth like a child giggling in church. He hadn't had anything against the old fart, but he'd come along at the wrong time, and needs must.

Needs must, he thought again, snorting into his hands. That's what his dear old ma had always said. Even when she'd been stoned, she'd been happy to dispense such homilies. Needs must. A stitch in time. Early to bed and a penny saved. Blood's thicker than water.

Recovered, he let out a breath and dropped his hands on his belly.

He remembered how the knife had slid into Pickles's belly. All those layers of fat, he mused, patting himself. It had been like stabbing a pillow. Then there had been that sucking sound, the kind you could make giving a woman a nice fat hickey to brand her.

But the best, the very best, had been lifting what was left of Pickles's hair. Not that it made much of a trophy, all thin and straggly, but the way the knife had made that wicked flap had been so fascinating.

And the blood.

Good Jesus, did he bleed.

He wished he could have taken more time with it, maybe done a little victory dance. Now the next time . . .

He had to stifle another chuckle. For there would be a next time. He was through with cattle and pets. Humans were much more challenging. He'd have to be careful, and he'd have to wait. If he took another one too quick, it would spoil the anticipation.

And he wanted to choose the next one, not just stumble over someone.

Maybe he should do a woman. He could take her into the trees, where he had hidden his trophies. He could cut her clothes away while she was begging him not to hurt her. Then he could rape the shit out of her.

He grew hard thinking of it, idly stroked himself while he planned. It would certainly add a new thrill to be able to take his time over it, to watch his prey, watch the eyes bulge with fear as he explained every little thing he was going to do.

It had to be even better that way. When they knew.

But he would need to practice. A woman would be the next stage, and he hadn't perfected this one yet.

No rush, he thought dreamily, and began to masturbate in earnest. No rush at all.

Part Two
Winter

They that know the winters of that country
know them to be sharp and violent. . . .

—William Bradford

9

Even murder couldn't stop work. the men were jumpy, but they took orders. Now that they were another hand short, Willa pushed herself to take up the slack. She rode fences, drove out to the fields to check on the harvest, manned the squeeze shoot herself, and huddled over the record books at night.

The weather turned, and turned fast. The chill in the air threatened winter, and there was frost on the pastures every morning. What cattle wouldn't be wintered over had to be shipped to feed pens for finishing—Mercy's own outside of Ennis or down to Colorado.

If she wasn't on horseback or driving a four-wheeler, she went up with Jim in the plane. She'd considered getting her pilot's license, but had quickly discovered that air travel didn't suit her. She didn't care for the noise of the engine or how the quick dips and turns affected her stomach.

Her father had loved to buzz the land in the little Cessna. The first time she'd flown with him, she'd been miserably ill. It had been the last time he had taken her up.

Now that there was only Jim qualified to pilot—and he had a tendency to hotdog—she wondered if she'd have to reconsider. An operation like Mercy needed a backup pilot, and maybe if she were at the controls she wouldn't get lightheaded or nauseous.

"Pretty as a picture from up here." Grinning, Jim dipped the wings, and Willa felt her breakfast slide greasily toward her throat. "Looks like we got another fence down." Cheerfully he dropped altitude to get a closer look.

Willa gritted her teeth and made a mental note of their position. She forced herself to scan the cattle, take a broad head count. "We need to rotate those cows before they take the grass down." She hissed between her teeth when the plane angled sharply. "Can't you fly this damn thing straight?"

"Sorry." He tucked his tongue in his cheek to hold back a chuckle. But when he got a look at her face, he leveled off gently. She was a pale shade of green. "You oughtn't to come up, Will, leastwise without taking some of those airsick pills first."

"I took the damn things." She concentrated on her breathing, wished she could appreciate the beauty of the land, the pastures green and glinting with frost, the hills thick with trees, the peaks white with snow.

"Want me to take us down?"

"I'm handling it." Barely. "We'll finish."

But when she looked down again, she saw the road where she had found the body. The police had taken the body away, had even taken the mutilated carcass of the steer. They'd combed the area looking for and gathering evidence. And the rain had washed away most of the blood.

Still, she thought she could see darker patches on the dirt that had soaked in deep. She couldn't tear her eyes away, and even when they flew past and over pasture, she could still see the road, the dark patches.

Jim kept his eyes trained on the horizon. "The police came by again last night."

"I know."

"They haven't found anything. It's been damn near a week, Will. They don't have squat."

The anger in his voice cleared her vision, helped her turn her eyes away and toward his face. "I guess it's not like the TV shows, Jim. Sometimes they just don't get the bad guy."

"I keep thinking how I won that money off him the night before it happened. I wish I hadn't won that money off him, Will. I know it doesn't mean a damn, but I wish I hadn't."

She reached over, gave his shoulder a quick squeeze. "And I wish I hadn't had words with him. That doesn't mean a damn either, but I wish I hadn't."

"Goddamn bitchy old fart. That's what he was. Just a goddamn bitchy old fart." His voice hitched, and Jim cleared his throat. "I—we heard you were maybe going to bury him in Mercy cemetery."

"Nate hasn't been able to locate his sister, or anyone. We'll bury him on Mercy land. I guess Bess would say that was fittin'."

"It is. It's good of you, Will, to put him where there's only family." He cleared his throat again. "The boys and me were talking. We thought maybe we could be like the pallbearers and we'd pay for his stone." His color rose when he caught Willa staring at him. "It was Ham's idea, but we all agreed to it. If you do."

"Then that's the way we'll do it." She turned her head, stared out the window. "Let's go down, Jim. I've seen enough for now."

. . .

When Willa drove back into the ranch yard, she spotted Nate's rig, and Ben's. Deliberately, she stopped in front of Adam's little white house. She needed time before she faced anyone. Her legs weren't much steadier than her stomach. There was a headache, brought on, she supposed, by the incessant humming of the plane, kicking behind her eyes.

She climbed out, stepped through the gate of the picket fence, and indulged herself by squatting down to pet Beans. He was fat as a sausage, with floppy ears and huge mop paws. Elated to see her, he rolled over to offer his belly for a rub.

"You fat old thing. You going to lie here and sleep all day?" He thumped his tail in agreement and made her smile. "Your back end's wide as a barn."

Her voice brought Adam's spotted hound, Nosey, racing around the side of the house. With his ears perked up and his tail waving like a flag, he trotted over and pushed himself under Willa's arm.

"Been up to no good again, haven't you, Nosey? Don't think I don't know you've had your eye on my chickens."

He grinned at her, and in his attempt to lick her hands, her face, stepped on his buddy. When the two dogs began to wrestle and dance, Willa got to her feet. She felt better. Maybe it was just being in Adam's yard, where the fall flowers were still stubbornly blooming and dogs had nothing better to do than play.

"You finished fooling with those useless dogs?"

She looked over her shoulder. Ham stood on the other side of the gate, a cigarette dangling from his mouth. His jacket was buttoned and he wore leather gloves, making her think perhaps he felt the cold more these days.

"I reckon I am."

"And you're finished flying around in that death trap?"

She ran her tongue over her teeth as she walked toward him. In his sixty-five years, Ham had never been inside a plane of any kind. And he was damn proud of it. "Seems like. We need to rotate cattle, Ham. And we've got another fence down. I want those cows moved from the southmost pasture today."

"I'll put Billy on it. Only take him twice as long to do it as anybody with half a brain. Jim can handle the fencing. Wood's got his hands full down at the fields, and I've gotta get the shipment down to the feedlot."

"Is this your not-so-subtle way of telling me we're running thin?"

"I'm going to talk to you about that." He waited until she came through the gate, took his time enjoying his smoke. "We could use another hand, two would be best. But it's my thinking you should wait, till spring at least, to hire on."

He flicked the miserly butt of his cigarette away, watched it fly. Behind them, Beans and Nosey whined at the gate, hoping for more attention. "Pickles was a pain in the ass. The man would bitch if the sun was shining or if a cloud covered it up. He just liked to complain. But he was a good cowboy and a halfway good mechanic."

"Jim told me that you and the men want to buy his stone."

"Only seems right. Worked with the picky old bastard damn near twenty years." He continued to stare out at middle distance. He'd already looked into her face, seen what was there. "You ain't helping anybody, blaming yourself for what happened to him."

"I sent him out."

"That's crap, and you know it. You may be a stiff-necked temperamental female, but you ain't stupid."

She nearly smiled. "I can't get past it, Ham. I just can't."

He knew that, understood that because he knew her. Understood her. "Finding him the way you did, that's going to prey on you. Nothing much to do about that but wait it out." He looked back at her again, shifted his disreputable hat against the angle of the sun. "Working yourself into the ground isn't going to make it go away any quicker."

"We're two hands short," she began, but he only shook his head.

"Will, you ain't sleeping much and you're eating less." Beneath the grizzled beard, his lips curved slightly. "Bess being back on her feet, I get plenty of the news from inside the main house. That woman can talk the ears off a rabbit. And even if she wasn't rattling away at me every chance she gets, I could see it for myself."

"I've got a lot on my mind."

"I know that." His voice roughened with his own brand of affection. "I'm just saying you don't have to have your hand in every inch of this ranch. I've been here since before you were born, and if you don't trust me to do my job, well, maybe you should be looking for three new hands come spring."

"You know I trust you, it's not—" She broke off, sucked in a breath. "That's low, Ham."

Pleased with himself, he nodded. Yeah, he knew her all right. He understood her.

And he loved her.

"As long as it makes you stop and think. We can get through the winter the way things are. That oldest boy of Wood's is coming along fine. He'll be twelve before long, and he can pull his weight. The younger one's a goddamn farmer." Baffled by it, Ham took out another cigarette, rolled fresh that morning. "Rather bale hay than sit a horse, but he's a good worker, so Wood claims. We'll do well enough through winter with what we've got."

"All right. Anything else?"

Again, he took his time. But since he had her attention, he figured he might as well finish up. "Them sisters of yours. You might tell the short-haired one to buy her some jeans that don't fit like skin. Every time she walks by, that fool Billy drops his tongue on his boots. He's going to hurt himself."

It was the first laugh she'd had in days. "And I don't suppose you look, do you, Ham?"

"I look plenty." He blew out smoke. "But I'm old enough not to hurt myself. The other one sits a horse real pretty." He squinted, gestured with his cigarette. "Well, you can see that for yourself."

Willa looked down the road, saw the riders heading east. Adam sat on his favored pinto, hatless and flanked by two riders. Willa had to admit that Lily handled the roan mare well, moving as smooth as silk with the mare's gait. On the other hand, Tess was jogging in the saddle atop a pretty chestnut. Her heels were up rather than down, her butt bouncing against leather in quick, jerky slaps that had to hurt, and she appeared to be gripping the saddle horn for dear life.

"Christ, will she be sore tonight." Amused, Willa leaned on the gate. "How long has that been going on?"

"Last couple days. Seems she took it in her mind to learn to ride. Adam's been working with her." He shook his head as Tess nearly slid out of the saddle. "Don't know if even that boy can do anything with her. You could saddle Moon and catch up with them."

"They don't need me."

"That's not what I said. You should take yourself a nice long ride, Will. It's always what worked best for you."

"Maybe." She thought about it, a nice long gallop with the wind slapping her face and clearing her mind. "Maybe later." For another moment she watched the three riders and envied them the easy camaraderie. "Maybe later," she repeated, and climbed back in her rig.

Willa wasn't surprised to find both Nate and Ben in the kitchen, enjoying Bess's barbecued beef. To keep Bess from scolding her for not eating, she took a plate herself, pulled up a chair.

"About time you got back." A bit disappointed that she hadn't been able to order the girl to eat, Bess fell onto the next best thing. "Past dinnertime."

"Food's still warm," Willa commented, and made herself take the first bite. "Since you're busy feeding half the county, you shouldn't have missed me."

"Got worse manners than a field hand." Bess plopped a mug of coffee at Willa's elbow, sniffed. "I've got too much work to do to stand around here trying to teach you better." She flounced out, wiping her hands on a dish towel.

"She's been watching for you for the past half hour." Nate pushed his empty plate away, picked up his own coffee. "She worries."

"She doesn't need to."

"She will as long as you keep riding out alone."

Willa spared Ben a look. "Then she'll have to get over it. Pass the salt."

He did so, slapping it in front of her. On the opposite end of the table, Nate rubbed the back of his neck. "I'm glad you got back, Will. I've got some papers for you."

"Fine. I'll look at them later." She drizzled salt over her beef. "That explains why you're here." She looked pointedly at Ben.

"I had business with Adam. Horse business. And I stuck around in my supervisory capacity. And for the free meal."

"I asked Ben to stay," Nate put in before Willa could snarl. "I talked to the police this morning. They'll be releasing the body tomorrow." He waited a moment for Willa to nod, to accept. "Some of the papers I have for you deal with the funeral arrangements. There's also some financial business. Pickles had a small passbook savings account and a standard checking. Combined, we're only talking about maybe thirty-five hundred. He owed nearly that on his rig."

"I'm not worried about the money." She couldn't have eaten now if there'd been a gun to her head. "I'd appreciate it if you'd just handle the details and bill the ranch. Please, Nate."

"All right." He took a legal pad out of the briefcase at his feet, scribbled some notes. "As to his personal effects. There's no family, no heirs, and he never had a will made."

"There wouldn't be much anyway." Misery settled over her, heavy and thick. "His clothes, his saddle, tools. I'll leave that to the men, if that's all right."

"I think that's the way it should be. I'll handle the legal points." He touched a hand to hers, let it linger briefly. "If you think of anything, or you have any questions, just give me a call."

"I'm obliged."

"No need to be." He unfolded himself and stood. "If you don't mind, I'm going to borrow a horse, ride out after Adam to ah..."

"You're going to have to think faster than that," Ben told him, "if you're going to lie about sniffing after a woman."

Nate only grinned and took his hat from the hook by the back door. "Thank Bess for the meal. I'll be around."

Willa frowned at the door Nate closed behind him. "Sniffing after what woman?"

"Your big sister wears some mighty pretty perfume."

She snorted, picked up her plate, and took it to the counter beside the sink. "Hollywood? Nate's got more sense than that."

"The right perfume can kick the sense right out of a man. You didn't eat your dinner."

"Lost my appetite." Curious, she turned back, leaned on the counter. "Is that what yanks your chain, Ben? Fancy perfume?"

"It doesn't hurt." He leaned back in his chair. "Of course, soap and leather on the right kind of skin can do the same damn thing. Being female's a powerful and mysterious thing." He picked up his coffee, watching her over the rim of the cup. "But I guess you'd know that."

"Doesn't matter around a ranch which way your skin stretches."

"Like hell. Every time you go within five feet of young Billy, his eyes cross."

She smiled a little because it was pure truth. "He's eighteen and randy as they come. Saying the word 'breast' around him drains all the blood out of his head into his lap. He'll get over it."

"Not if he's lucky."

Feeling friendlier, she crossed her feet at the ankles. "I don't know how you men tolerate it. Having your ego, your personality, and your idea of romance all dangling between your legs."

"It's a trial. Are you going to sit down and finish your coffee?"

"I've got work."

"That's what you've said every time *I've* come within five feet of you the last couple of days." He picked up her mug, rose, and carried it to her. "You keep working and not eating, Willa, you're going to end up flat on your face." He took her chin in his hand and gave her a long, long look. "And the face isn't half bad."

"You're grabbing onto it enough lately." She jerked her head, struggling to remain cool when his fingers stayed put. "What's your problem, McKinnon?"

"I don't have one." To test them both, he skimmed a finger up and over her mouth. It had a shape to it, he mused, even in a snarl, that made a man want a bite. "But you seem to have one. I've been noticing you're jumpy around me lately. Used to be you were just mean."

"Maybe you can't tell the difference."

"Yeah, I can." He shifted, boxing her neatly between the counter and his body. "You know what I think, Will?"

He had broad shoulders, long legs. Lately she'd been entirely too aware of the size and shape of him. "I'm not interested in what you think."

Being a cautious man with a good memory, he pressed against her to block a well-aimed knee. "I'll tell you anyway." He took his hand off her chin and gathered up the hair she'd left loose that morning. "You do smell of soap and leather, now that I'm close enough to tell."

"Any closer, you'd be on the other side of me."

"Then there's all this hair, a good yard of it. Straight as a pin and soft as silk." He kept his eyes on hers, drew her head back a fraction more. "Your heart's pounding. And there's this little pulse right here in your throat." He used his free hand to trace it, feel it skitter. "Jumping so hard it's a wonder it doesn't come right through the skin and bounce into my hand."

She wasn't entirely sure it wouldn't happen if he didn't give her room to breathe. "You're irritating me, Ben." It took every ounce of effort to keep her voice even.

"I'm seducing you, Willa." He all but purred it, in words like honey. And his smile came slow and potent when she trembled. "That's what you're afraid of, to my way of thinking. That I could, and I will, and you won't be able to do a damn thing about it."

"Back off." Her voice wasn't steady now, nor were the hands she lifted to his chest.

"No." He tugged her hair again. "Not this time."

"You said yourself not long ago that you don't want me any more than I want you." What was happening inside her? she wondered in panic. The shivering and shakes, the long, liquid pulls. "There's no point in playing like you do just to annoy me."

"I was wrong. What I should have said was that I want you every bit as much as you want me. I was irritated over it. You're just scared of it."

"I'm not scared of you." What was happening inside her was frightening. But not because of him. She promised herself it wasn't because of him.

"Prove it." Those eyes of his, sharp green and close, lit with challenge. "Right here. Right now."

"Fine." Accepting the dare, afraid not to, she grabbed a handful of his hair and dragged his mouth down to hers.

He had the McKinnon mouth, she realized. Like Zack's, it was full and firm. But there the similarity ended. None of the dreamy kisses she'd shared with Zack years before compared to this burst, this shock of having a man's skillful lips devouring hers. Or the hot, impatient way he used tongue and teeth to simply overpower, to focus every thought, every feeling, every need into that point where mouth met mouth.

The edge of the counter bit into her back. The fingers she'd twined through his hair curled into a hard, taut fist. And the primal male taste of him coursed through her body and left it in ruins. He hadn't given her even a moment to defend herself.

He didn't intend to.

He felt her body jerk, stiffen against the onslaught. And wondered if what was battling through her was even close to what was battling through him. He'd expected heat, or cold. She had both in her. He'd expected power, for she was anything but weak. He'd hoped to find pleasure, as her mouth seemed to have been created to give and to take it.

He hadn't known he'd find them all, a rage of all that would slam into him like bare-knuckled fists and leave him reeling.

"Goddamn it." He dragged his mouth away, stared into her eyes, so big and dark and shocked. "Goddamn it all to hell."

And his mouth came down on hers again to feed.

She moaned, a sound trapped in her throat, a sound he could feel when he closed his hand over that smooth column and squeezed lightly. He wanted to taste there, just there where that pulse jumped and that moan sounded, but for the life of him he couldn't get enough of her mouth. And she was holding him now, holding hard, moving against him, hips grinding.

He closed a hand over her breast, so firm through the flannel. When it wasn't enough, not nearly enough, he yanked her shirt free of her jeans and streaked under to flesh.

The feel of his hand, hard and callused and strong on her, had the muscles in her thighs going loose, the tension in her stomach pushing toward pain. His thumb flicked over her nipple, ricocheting bullets of heat from point to point through her overtaxed system.

She went limp, might have slid through his arms like vapor if he hadn't changed his grip. That sudden and utter surrender aroused him more than all the flash and fire.

"We need to finish this." He cupped her breast, fingers skimming, stroking as he waited for her eyes to open and meet his. "And though it's tempting to go right on with it here, Bess might be miffed if she came in and found us waxing her floor the way I have in mind."

"Back off." She fought to suck in air. "I can't breathe, back off."

"I'm having some trouble with that myself. We'll breathe later." He lowered his head, nipped at her jaw. "Come home with me, Willa, let me have you."

"I'm not going to do that." She struggled free, stumbled to the table, and braced her palms on it for balance. She had to think, had to. But she could only feel. "Keep away," she snapped when he moved toward her. "Keep away and let me breathe."

It was the lick of real panic in her voice that had him leaning back against the counter. "All right, breathe. It isn't going to change anything." He reached for the mug of coffee beside him and, when he noted his hands weren't steady, left it where it sat. "I don't know if I'm too pleased about this either."

"Fine. That's just fine." Steadier, she straightened, faced him. "You think because you've talked a dozen women onto their backs you can just come in here and talk me onto mine. Easy pickings, too, since I've never done it before."

"Can't be more than ten women by my count," he said easily. "And I didn't have to—" He broke off, eyes going wide, jaw dropping. "Never done what, exactly?"

"You know damn well what, exactly."

"Ever?" He pushed his hands into his pockets. "At all ever?"

She merely stared, waiting for him to laugh. Then she'd have the perfect excuse to kill him.

"But I figured you and Zack..." He trailed off again, realizing that might not have sat too well with him under the circumstances.

"Did he say I did?" Her eyes narrowed to slits as she poised, ready to spring.

"No, he never—no." At a loss, Ben dragged a hand out of his pocket and raked it through his hair. "I just figured, that's all. I just figured you... at some time or other. Well, hell, Willa, you're a grown woman. Of course I figured you'd—"

"Slept around?"

"No, not exactly." Hand me a shovel, he thought. I'm getting tired of digging this hole for myself with my bare hands. "You're a good-looking woman," he began, and winced, knowing he could have done better than that. Would have, too, if his tongue wasn't so tangled up. "I just assumed that you'd had some experience in the area."

"Well, I haven't." Temper was clearing just enough to let in flickers of embarrassment. "And it's up to me when and if I want to change that, and who I want to change it with."

"Absolutely. I wouldn't have pushed if I'd realized..." He couldn't take his eyes off her, the way she stood there all flushed and rumpled, with that sexy mouth swollen from his. "Or maybe I'd have pushed different. I've been thinking about you that way for a while."

Suspicion flickered in her eyes. "Why?"

"Damned if I know. It just is. Now that I've had my hands on you, I'd have to say I'm going to be thinking more. You've got a nice feel to you, Willa." The humor came back, curving his lips. "And you were doing a damn fine job of kissing me back, for an amateur."

"You're not the first man I've kissed, and you won't be the last."

"That doesn't mean you can't practice on me—when you get the urge." He walked over to take his hat and jacket from the pegs by the door. If either of them noticed that he gave her a wide berth, neither commented. "What are friends for?"

"I don't have any trouble controlling my urges."

"You're telling me," he said, with feeling, and fit his hat on his head. "But I have a notion I'm about to have a hell of a time controlling mine where you're concerned."

He opened the door, gave her one long last look. "You've got one hell of a mouth, Willa. One hell of a mouth."

He shut the door, shrugged into his jacket. As he circled around the house toward his rig, he let out a whistling breath. He'd thought a little nuzzling in the kitchen would take both of their minds off the trouble hanging over Mercy. It had done a hell of a lot more than that.

He rubbed a hand over his belly, knowing the knots twisting inside would be there for quite a while yet. She'd gotten to him, and gotten to him hard. And the fact that she had no idea what they could do to each other in the dark only made it more terrifying.

And arousing.

He'd always chosen women who knew the ropes, who understood the pleasures, the rules and the responsibilities. Women, he admitted, who didn't expect more than a good, healthy ride where nobody got hurt, nobody got hobbled.

He glanced back at the house as he climbed behind the wheel, turned the key in the ignition. It wouldn't be so simple with Willa, not when he'd be her first.

He drove away from Mercy without a clue to what he would do about her. All he knew for certain was that Willa was going to have to accept that Ben McKinnon was going to be the one she'd change things with.

He glanced toward the bunkhouse as he drove past and thought of everything she'd been through in the past few weeks. Enough, he thought, to break anyone to bits. Anyone but Willa.

Letting out a long sigh, he headed for his own land. He'd be there for her, whether she liked it or not. And he'd take it slow in that certain area. He'd even try his hand at being gentle.

But he'd be there.

10

Snow came hard and fast and early. It buried the pastures and had the drift fences groaning. Men worked day and night to see that the cattle—too stupid to dig through the snow to grass—were fed and tended.

November proved to be a poor boundary against winter, and before the end of it, the valley was socked in.

Skiers came, flocking to Big Sky and other resorts to schuss down slopes and drink brandy by roaring fires. Tess gave some thought to joining them for a day or two. Not that she'd ever been much on skiing, but the brandy sounded fine. In any case there would be people, conversations, perhaps flirtations, certainly civilization.

It might be worth strapping herself to a couple of slats of wood and tumbling down a mountain.

She talked to her agent constantly, using Ira more as a bridge to her life than a representative of her work. She wrote, making progress with a new screenplay and detailing daily life in her journal.

Not that she considered the routine on the ranch much of a life.

She continued to take charge of the chickens and was actually rather pleased that she had a handle on the job now and could slip an egg from under a broody hen without so much as a peck.

She had a bad moment, very bad, one day when she strolled behind the coop and walked into Bess, quickly, competently, ruthlessly wringing the neck of one of Tess's flock.

There'd been a lot of squawking then—though not from the chickens. Two of them lay dead as Judas on the ground while the women shouted at each other over the corpses.

Tess had skipped dinner that night—chicken pot pie—but it had taught her the error of assigning names to her beaked and feathered friends.

Every evening she made use of the indoor pool with its curved-glass wall and southern exposure. And she'd decided there was something to be said for looking at snow while she lounged in her personal lake with steam rising around her.

Yet every morning she rose, crossed her eyes at the view of snow out her window, and dreamed of palm trees and lunching at Morton's.

She kept up her horseback riding out of sheer stubbornness. It was true that she didn't climb whimpering out of the saddle with muscles screaming now. And she'd developed a certain wary affection for Mazie, the mare Adam had assigned her. Still, riding out into the wind and the cold wasn't her idea of high entertainment.

"Jesus. Jesus Christ." Tess stepped outside, hunched inside the thick wool jacket, and wished she'd pulled on two pairs of long underwear. "It's like breathing broken glass. How does anyone stand this?"

"Adam says it makes you appreciate spring more."

To ward off the wind, Lily wrapped her scarf more securely around her neck. Yet she appreciated the winter—the majestic, powerful sweep of it, the way the snow seemed to freeze the peaks into sharp relief against the sheer wall of sky. The dark belt of trees that clung to the rising foothills was so prettily draped with snow, and the silver of rock and ridge formed shadows and contrasts, like folds in a stunning blanket.

"It's so beautiful. Miles and miles of white. And the pines. The sky's so blue it almost hurts your eyes." She smiled at Tess. "It's nothing like a city snow."

"I don't have much experience with snow, but I'd say this is nothing like anything." She flexed her fingers in her gloves as they walked toward the horse barn.

At least the ranch yard was negotiable, Tess thought. Paths to and from paddocks and corrals had been plowed. And the roads had been scraped off as well with a blade attached to one of the four-wheelers. Young Billy had done that, she remembered. He'd appeared to be having the time of his life.

She watched her breath plume out in front of her and was tempted to complain again. But it was beautiful, coldly beautiful. The sky was such a hard, brittle blue she expected it to crack at any moment, and the mountains that speared into it were so well defined in the clear air that they seemed to have been painted. Sunlight danced off the fields of snow in glittering sparks, and when the wind rushed, it lifted that snow and those dancing lights into the air in thin drifts.

Palm trees, warm beaches, and mai tais seemed light-years away.

"What's she up to today?" Tess pulled out sunglasses and put them on.

"Willa? She went out early in one of the pickups."

Tess's mouth thinned. "Alone?"

"She almost always goes alone."

"Asking for trouble," Tess muttered, and stuck her hands in her pockets. "She must think she's invincible. If whoever killed that man is still around . . ."

"You don't think that, do you?" Alarmed, Lily began to scan the fields as if a madman might rise up out of one of the drifts like a grinning gnome. "The police haven't come up with anything. I thought it had to be someone camped in the hills. With this weather, he couldn't still be here. And it's been weeks since—since it happened."

"Sure, that's right." Though she was far from convinced, Tess saw no reason to set Lily's nerves more on edge. "Nobody'd camp out in this cold, especially some itinerant maniac. I guess she just gets under my skin." She narrowed her eyes at the rig heading toward the ranch from the west road. "Speak of the devil."

"Maybe if you—" Lily broke off, shook her head.

"No, go ahead. Maybe if I what?"

"Maybe if you didn't try so hard to irritate her."

"Oh, it's not so hard." Tess's lips curved in anticipation. "In fact, it's effortless." She changed directions as the rig pulled up. "Been out surveying the lower forty?" Tess asked, as Willa rolled down her window.

"Are you still here? I thought you were going to Big Sky to soak in a Jacuzzi and hustle men."

"I'm thinking about it."

Willa shifted her attention to Lily. "If Adam's taking you out, go soon and don't stay long. Snow's coming in." She flicked her eyes toward the sky, the telltale clouds piling together in thick layers. "You may want to tell him I spotted a herd of mule deer northwest of here. About a mile and a half. You might like to see them."

"I would." She patted her pocket. "I have my camera. Can you come with us? Bess sent plenty of coffee along."

"No, I've got things to do. And Nate's coming by later."

"Oh?" Tess lifted an eyebrow, struggled to sound casual. "When?"

Willa slid the gearshift into first. "Later," she repeated, and drove away toward the house.

She knew very well that Tess had her eye on Nate, and she didn't intend to encourage it. As far as she was concerned, Nate would be completely out of his depth with a slick Hollywood piranha.

And maybe he had his eye focused right back, but that was only because men always got dopey around beautiful, stacked women. Grabbing her thermos of coffee from the seat beside her, Willa climbed out of the rig. Tess was beautiful and stacked, she admitted, with just a quick twinge of envy. And confident and quick-tongued. So sure of herself and her control over her own femininity. And her power over men.

Willa wondered if she'd be more like that if she'd had a mother to teach her the ropes. If she'd been raised in a different environment, where there were females giggling over hairdos and hemlines, over lipstick shades and perfume.

Not that she wanted that, she assured herself, as she stepped inside and pulled off her gloves. She wasn't interested in all that fussing and foolishness, but she was beginning to think those very things could add to a woman's confidence around men.

And she wasn't feeling as confident as she wanted to. At least not around one man.

She shucked her coat and hat, then carried the thermos with her to the office upstairs. She'd changed nothing inside it yet. It was still Jack Mercy's domain with its trophy heads and whiskey decanters. And entering, walking over, seating herself at his desk, always brought a quick twist to her gut.

Grief? she wondered. Or fear. She just wasn't sure any longer. But the office itself brought on a swarm of unpleasant and unhappy emotions, and memories.

She had rarely come in there when he was alive. If he sent for her, ordered her to take a chair across from that desk, it was to criticize or to shuffle her duties.

Girl, he'd called her. He'd rarely used her name. Girl, you fucked up good this time.

Girl, you better start pulling weight around here.

You'd better get yourself a husband, girl, and start having babies. You're no use otherwise.

Had there ever been kindness in this room? she asked herself, and rubbed hard at her temples. She wanted badly to remember even one moment, one incident when she came in here and found him sitting behind this desk and smiling. One time, only one time when he'd told her he was proud of what she'd done. Of anything she'd done.

But she couldn't. Smiles and kind words hadn't been Jack Mercy's style.

And what would he say now? she wondered. If he walked in here and saw her, if he knew what had happened on the land, to one of his men, while she'd been in charge.

You fucked up, girl.

She rested her head in her hands a moment, wishing she had an answer for that. In her mind she knew she'd done nothing to cause a vicious murder. But in her heart, the responsibility weighed heavy.

"Done and over," she murmured. She opened a drawer, took out record books. She wanted to check them over, the careful detailing of number of head, of weight. The pasture rotations, the additives and grain. She'd make sure there was not one figure out of place before Nate came later today to look over her accounts.

Burying her resentment that he, or anyone, had power over Mercy, she got to work.

Nearly two miles from the ranch house, Lily happily snapped pictures of mule deer. It made her laugh to look at them with their shaggy winter coats and bored eyes. The prints would likely be out of focus—she knew she hadn't inherited her mother's skill with a camera—but they would please her.

"I'm sorry." She let the camera dangle from the strap around her neck. "I'm taking too long. I get caught up."

"We've got some time yet." After a brief study of the clouds, Adam shifted in the saddle and turned to Tess. "You're riding well. You learn."

"Self-defense," she claimed, but felt a warm spurt of pride. "I never want to hurt the way I did those first couple of days. And I need the exercise."

"No, you're enjoying it."

"All right, I'm enjoying it. But if it gets much colder than this, I won't be enjoying it till spring."

"It'll get colder than this. But your blood'll be thicker. Your mind tougher." He leaned down to stroke the neck of his mount. "And you'll be hooked. Every day you don't ride, you'll feel deprived."

"Every day I can't stroll down Sunset Boulevard I feel deprived. I manage."

He laughed. "When you get back to Sunset Boulevard, you'll think of the sky here, and the hills. Then you'll come back."

Intrigued, she tipped down her sunglasses, peered at him over the tops. "What is this? Indian mysticism and fortune-telling?"

"Nope. Psychology one-oh-one. Can I use the camera, Lily? I'll take a picture of you and Tess."

"All right. You don't mind, do you?" she asked Tess.

"I never turn away from a camera." She walked her horse around Adam's, turned her—rather smoothly, she thought—and came close to Lily's right. "How's this?"

"It's good." He lifted the camera, focused. "Two beautiful women in one frame." And snapped, twice. "When you look at these, you'll see how much you share. The shape of the face, the coloring, even the way you sit in the saddle."

Automatically, Tess straightened her shoulders. She felt what she considered a mild affection for Lily, but she was far from ready for sisterhood. "Let's have the camera, Adam. I'll take the two of you. The Virginia Magnolia and the Noble Savage."

The minute it was out of her mouth, she winced. "Sorry. I tend to think of people as characters. No offense."

"None taken." Adam passed her the camera. He liked her, the way she went after what she wanted, said what was on her mind. He doubted very much she'd appreciate being told those were two of his favorite qualities about Willa. "How do you think of yourself?"

"Shallow Gal. That's why my screenplays sell. Smile."

"I like your movies," Lily said when Tess lowered the camera. "They're exciting and entertaining."

"And play to the least common denominator. Nothing wrong with that." She handed the camera back to Lily. "You write for the masses, you take off your brain and keep it simple."

"You're not giving yourself or your audience enough credit." Adam flicked his gaze toward the trees, scanned.

"Maybe not, but..." Tess trailed off as a movement caught her eye. "There's something back there in the trees. Something moved."

"Yes, I know. It's upwind. I can't smell it." Casually, he laid his hand on the butt of his rifle.

"Bears are hibernating now, right?" Tess moistened her lips and tried not to think of a man and a knife. "It wouldn't be a bear."

"Sometimes they wake up. Why don't you start heading home? I'll take a look."

"You can't go up there alone." Instinct made Lily reach over, grab his reins. At the abrupt movement his horse shied and kicked up snow. "You can't. It could be anything. It could be—"

"Nothing," he said calmly, and soothed his horse. A few innocent flakes danced into the air. He didn't think they'd stay innocent for long. "But it's best to see."

"Lily's right." Shivering, Tess kept her eyes trained on the tree line. "And it's starting to snow. Let's just go. Right now."

"I can't do that." Adam locked his dark, quiet eyes on Lily's. "It's probably nothing." He knew better by the way his horse was beginning to quiver beneath him, but kept his voice easy. "But a man was killed barely a mile from here. I have to see. Now head back, and I'll catch up with you. You know the way."

"Yes, but—"

"Please, do this for me. I'll be right behind you."

Knowing she was useless in an argument, Lily turned her horse.

"Stay together," Adam told Tess, then rode toward the tree line.

"He'll be all right." Her teeth threatened to chatter as Tess made the reassurance. "Hell, Lily, it's probably a squirrel." Too much movement for a squirrel, she thought. "Or a moose or something. We'll have to tease him about saving the womenfolk from a marauding moose."

"And what if it's not?" Lily's quiet southern voice fractured like glass. "What if the police and everyone are wrong and whoever killed that man is still here?" She stopped her horse. "We can't leave Adam alone."

"He's the one with the gun," Tess began.

"I can't leave him alone." Quaking at the prospect of defying an order, Lily nonetheless turned and started back.

"Hey, don't—oh, hell. This'll make a dandy scene in a script," Tess muttered, and trotted after her. "You know, if he shoots us by mistake, we're going to be really sorry."

Lily only shook her head and, veering off the road, started into the hills, following Adam's tracks. "You know how to get back if you had to ride quickly?"

"Yeah, I think, but—Christ, this is insane. Let's just—"

The gunshot split the air and echoed like thunder. Before Tess could do more than cling to her skittish horse, Lily was galloping headlong into the trees.

Nate didn't come alone. Ben drove up behind him, with his sister-in-law and his niece. Shelly came into the house chattering and immediately began unwrapping the baby.

"I should have called, I know, but when Ben said he was coming by I just grabbed Abigail and jumped into the rig. We've been dying for company. I know you've got business to tend to, but Abby and I can visit with Bess while you're talking. I hope you don't mind."

"Of course I don't. It's good to see you."

It was always good to see Shelly, with her happy chatter and sunny smile. She was, Willa had always thought, perfect for Zack. They meshed like butter on popcorn, both lively and entertaining.

With the baby happily kicking on the sofa, Shelly peeled off her hat and fluffed her sunny blond hair. The short, sassy cut suited her pixie face and petite build, and her eyes were the color of fog in the mountains.

"Well, I didn't give Ben much choice, but I swear I'll stay out of your way until you've finished."

"Don't be silly. I haven't been able to play with the baby in weeks. And she's grown so. Haven't you, sweetheart?" Indulging herself, Willa lifted Abby and hefted her high over her head. "Her eyes are turning green."

"She's going to have McKinnon eyes," Shelly agreed. "You'd think she'd have the gratitude to take after me a bit, since I'm the one who carried her around for nine months, but she looks just like her pa."

"I don't know, I think she's got your ears." Willa brought Abby close to kiss the tip of her nose.

"Do you?" Shelly perked up immediately. "You know she's sleeping right through the night already. Only five months old. After all the horror stories I heard about teething and walking the floor, I figured I'd—" She held up both hands as if to signal herself to stop. "There I go, and I promised I'd stay out of the way. Zack says I could talk the bark off a tree."

"Zack'll talk you blind," Ben put in. "Surprises me that with the two of you as parents, Abby didn't pop out talking." He reached out to tweak the baby's cheek and grinned at Willa. "She's a pretty handful, isn't she?"

"And sweet-natured, which proves she isn't all McKinnon." With some regret, Willa passed the cooing baby back to her mother. "Bess is back in the kitchen, Shelly. I know she'd love to see you and Abby."

"I hope you have time for a little visit when you're done, Will." Shelly laid a hand on Willa's arm. "Sarah wanted to come by, too, but she couldn't get away. We've been thinking about you."

"I'll be down soon. Maybe you can talk Bess into parting with some of the pie she's been making for supper. Everything's up in the office," she added to the others, and started upstairs.

"You understand this is just for form's sake, Will," Nate began. "Just so there's no question about adhering to the terms of the will."

"Yeah, no problem." But her back was stiff as she led the way into the office.

"Didn't see your sisters around."

"They're out riding with Adam," Willa told him, moving behind the desk. "I don't imagine they'll be out too much longer. Hollywood's blood's too thin for her to handle the cold for more than an hour or so."

Nate sat, stretched out his legs. "So, I see you two are still getting along beautifully."

"We stay out of each other's way." She handed him a record book. "It works well enough."

"It's going to be a long winter." Ben eased a hip onto the edge of the desk. "You two ought to think about making peace, or just shooting each other to get it done."

"The second part doesn't seem quite fair. She wouldn't know the difference between a Winchester and a posthole digger."

"I'll have to teach her," was Nate's comment as he scanned figures. "Things all right around here otherwise?"

"Well enough." Unable to sit, Will pushed away from the desk. "From what I can tell, the men are convinced that whoever killed Pickles is long gone. The police haven't been able to prove any different. No signs, no weapon, no motive."

"Is that what you think?" Ben asked her.

She met his eyes. "That's what I want to think. And that's what I'll have to think. It's been three weeks."

"That doesn't mean you should let your guard down," Ben murmured, and she inclined her head.

"I've no intention of letting my guard down. In any area."

"Everything here looks in perfect order to me." Nate passed the record book to Ben. "All things considered, you've had a good year."

"I expect the next will be even better." She paused. She didn't clear her throat, but she wanted to. "I'm going to be sowing natural grasses come spring. That was something Pa and I disagreed on, but I figure there's a reason for what grows native to this area, so we're going back to it."

Intrigued, Ben flicked a glance at her. He'd never known her to talk about change when it came to Mercy. "We did that at Three Rocks more than five years ago, with good results."

She looked at Ben again. "I know it. And once we're reseeding, we'll be rotating more often. No more than three weeks per pasture." Pacing now, she didn't notice that Ben set the book aside to study her. "I'm not as concerned as Pa was with producing the biggest cattle. Just the best. Past few years we've had a lot of trouble at birthing time with oversized calves. It might change the profit ratio at first, but I'm thinking long term."

She opened the thermos she'd left on the desk and poured coffee, though it was no more than lukewarm by now. "I've talked to Wood about the cropland. He's had some ideas about it that Pa wasn't keen on. But I think it's worth some experimenting. We've got a little more than six hundred acres cultivated for small grains, and I'm going to give Wood control of them. If it doesn't work, it doesn't, but Mercy can carry some experimentation for a year or two. He wants to build a silo. We'll ferment our own alfalfa."

She shrugged. She knew what some would say about the changes, and her interest in crops and silos and her other plans to ask Adam to increase the string of horses: She was forgetting the cattle, forgetting that Mercy had been pure for generations.

But she wasn't forgetting anything. She was looking ahead.

She set her cup down. "Do either of you, in your supervisory capacity, have a problem with my plans?"

"Can't say that I do." Nate rose. "But then, I'm not a cattleman. I think I'll go on down and see if there's pie, leave you two to discuss this."

"Well?" Willa demanded when she faced Ben alone.

"Well," he echoed, and picked up her cup. "Damn, Will, that's cold." He winced as he swallowed it down. "And stale."

"I didn't ask your opinion on the coffee."

He stayed where he was, sitting on the edge of the desk, and leveled his eyes to hers. "Where'd all these ideas come from?"

"I've got a brain, don't I? And an opinion."

"True enough. I've never heard you talk about changing so much as a blade of grass around here. It's curious."

"There wasn't any point talking about it. He wasn't interested in what I thought or had to say. I've done some studying up," she added, and stuck her hands in her pockets. "Maybe I didn't go to college like you, but I'm not stupid."

"I never thought you were. And I never knew you wanted to go to college."

"It doesn't matter." With a sigh, she walked to the window and stared out. Storm's coming, she thought. Those first pretty flecks of white were only the beginning. "What matters is now, and tomorrow and next year. Winter's planning time. Figuring-things-out time. I'm starting to plan, that's all." She went stiff when his hands came down on her shoulders.

"Easy. I'm not going to jump you." He turned her to face him. "If it matters, I think you're on the mark."

It did matter, and that was a surprise in itself. "I hope you're right. I've been getting calls from the vultures."

He smiled a little. "Developers?"

"Bastards jumped right in. They'd give me the moon and the sun to sell the land so they can break it up, make a fancy resort or fucking vanity ranches for Hollywood cowboys." If she'd had fangs, they would have been gleaming. "They'll never get their fat fingers on a single acre of Mercy land while I'm standing on it."

Automatically he began to knead her shoulders. "Sent them off scalded, did you, darling?"

"One called just last week. Told me to just call him Arnie. I told him I'd see him skinned and staked out for the coyotes if he set a foot on my property." The corner of her lip quirked. "I don't think he'll be coming by."

"That's the way."

"Yeah. But the other two." She turned, looked out again at the snow and the hills and the land. "I don't think they understand yet just how much money's involved, what those jackasses'll pay to get hold of a ranch like this. Hollywood, she'll figure it out sooner or later. And then . . . they've got me two to one, Ben."

"The will holds the land for ten years."

"I know what it said. But things change. With enough money and enough pressure they could change quicker." And ten years was nothing, she thought, in the grand scheme of things. Her grand scheme to turn Mercy into not *one* of the best but *the* best. "I can't buy them out after the year's up. I've figured it every way it can be figured, and I just can't. There's money, sure, but most of it's in the land and on the hoof. When the year's up, they'll own two-thirds to my one."

"No point worrying over what can't be changed, or what may or may not happen." He stroked a hand down her hair once, then a second time. "Maybe what you need is a distraction. Just a little one."

He turned her again, then shook his head. "Don't go shying off. I've been thinking a lot about this since the first time." He touched his lips to hers, a teasing brush. "See? That didn't hurt anything."

Her lips were vibrating, but she couldn't claim it was painful. "I don't want to get all started up again. There's too much going on for distractions."

"Darling." He leaned down, toyed with her lips again. "That's just when you need them most. And I'm willing to bet this makes us both feel a lot better."

His eyes stayed open and on hers as he gathered her close, as he lowered his head, rubbed lip to lip. "It's working for me already," he murmured, then quick as lightning, deepened the kiss.

The jolt, the heat, the yearning all melded together to swim in her head, through her whole body. And she forgot, when the sensations seized her, to be worried or tired or afraid. It was easy to move into him, to press close and let everything else fall away.

And harder, much harder than she'd anticipated, to pull back and remember.

"Maybe I've been thinking about it, too." She raised a hand to keep the distance between them. "But I haven't finished thinking about it."

"As long as I'm the first to know when you do." He twined her hair around his finger, released it. "We'd better go downstairs before I give you too much to think about."

The riders coming in fast caught his eye. With one hand resting on Willa's shoulder, he stepped closer to the window. "Adam's back with your sisters."

She saw them, and more. "Something's wrong. Something's happened."

He could see for himself the way Adam helped Lily out of the saddle, and held on to her. "Something's happened," he agreed. "Let's go find out."

They were halfway down the stairs when the front door swung open. Tess strode in first. The cold had whipped strong color into her cheeks, but her eyes were huge, her lips white.

"It was a deer," she said. "Just a deer. Bambi's mom," she managed, and a tear slipped out of her eye as Nate came down the hall from the kitchen. "Oh, God, why would anybody do that to Bambi's mom?"

"Ssh." Nate draped an arm over her shoulders. "Let's go sit down, honey."

"Lily, let's go in with Tess."

She shook her head and kept her hand gripped tight in Adam's. "No, I'm all right. Really. I'm going to make some tea. It would be better if we had some tea. Excuse me."

"Adam." Willa watched Lily hurry toward the kitchen. "What the hell happened? Did you shoot a doe while you were out?"

"No, but someone had." Revolted, he peeled off his coat, tossed it over the newel post. "They'd left it there, torn to pieces. Not for the game, not even for the trophy, just to kill. The wolves were at it." He rubbed his hands over his face. "I fired to scatter them and get a better look, but Lily and Tess rode up. I wanted to get them back here."

"I'll get my coat."

Before Willa could turn, Adam stopped her. "There's no point. There won't be much left by now, and I saw enough. She'd been shot clean, in the head. Then she'd been gutted, hacked, left there. He cut off her tail. I guess that was enough trophy this time around."

"Like the others, then."

"Like the others."

"Can we track him?" Ben demanded.

"Snow's come in since it was done, a day ago at least. More's coming in now. Maybe if I could have set off right then, I'd have had some luck." Adam moved his shoulder, a gesture that communicated both frustration and acceptance. "I couldn't go off and leave them to get back here alone."

"We'd better have a look anyway." Ben was already reaching for his hat. "Ask Nate to drive Shelly home, Willa."

"I'm coming with you."

"There's no point, and you know it." Ben took her shoulders. "No point."

"I'm coming anyway. I'll get my coat."

11

The snow came down in sheets, white and wild and wicked. By nightfall, there was nothing to see from the windows but a constant fall of thick flakes that built a wall between the glass and the rest of the world.

Lily stared at it, tried to stare through it, while the heat from the blazing logs in the fire licked at her back and worry ate at her nerves.

"Will you sit down?" Tess snapped, and hated the edge in her voice. "There's nothing you can do."

"They've been gone a long time."

Tess knew how long they'd been gone. Exactly ninety-eight minutes. "Like I said, there's nothing you can do."

"You could use some more tea. This is cold." Even as Lily turned to gather the tray, Tess leaped to her feet.

"Will you *stop?* Just stop waiting on me—on everyone. You're not a servant around here. Just sit the hell down, for Christ's sake."

She shuddered once, pressed her fingers to her eyes, and took a long, deep breath. "I'm sorry," she murmured, as Lily stood where she was, hands locked together, eyes blank. "I've got no business yelling at you. I've never seen anything like that. Never seen anything like that."

"It's all right." Empathy eased the tension in her fingers. "It was horrible. I know. Horrible."

They sat, on either end of the long leather couch, silent for a full thirty seconds while the wind beat at the windows with vicious gusts. Tess found herself holding back a sickly laugh.

"Oh, hell." She blew out a breath and repeated, "Oh, hell. What have we got ourselves into here, Lily?"

"I don't know." The wind sent a demon howl down the chimney. "Are you scared?"

"Damn right I'm scared. Aren't you?"

Eyes sober and steady, Lily pursed her lips in consideration. She lifted a fingertip, rubbed it lightly over her bottom lip. It tended to quiver, she knew, when fear had a grip on her.

"I don't think I am. I don't understand it, not really, but I'm not scared, not the way I expect to be. Just sorry and sad. And worried," she added, as her eyes were pulled back to the window and her mind drew a picture of three riders, lost in whirling white. "About Adam and Willa and Ben."

"They'll be all right. They live here."

Nerves bouncing, Tess rose to pace. The sharp snap of a flame in the fireplace made her jump. Swear. "They know what they're doing." If they didn't, she thought, who the hell did? "Maybe that's why I'm so scared right now. I don't know what the hell I'm doing. And I always do, you know. It's one of my best things. Set the goal, form the plan, take the steps. But this time I don't know what I'm doing."

Turning, she sent Lily a thoughtful look. "You do. You know what you're doing with your tea trays and soup simmering and fire building."

Lily shook her head, forced herself to keep her eyes away from the windows. "Those aren't important things."

"Maybe they are," Tess said softly, then stiffened when she saw the glare of lights through the curtain of snow. "Someone's here."

Because she once again didn't know what to do—run? hide?—Tess turned deliberately and walked into the foyer, to the front door to open it. Moments later, Nate appeared, coated with white.

"Get back inside," he ordered, nudging her out of the way as he closed the door behind him. "Are they back yet?"

"No. Lily and I . . ." She gestured toward the living area. "What are you doing here?"

"It's a bad one," he said. "I got Shelly and the baby home all right, but barely made it back." He took off his hat, shook off snow. "It's been two hours now. I'll give them a few more minutes before I head out after them."

"You're going out again. In that?" She'd never experienced a blizzard, but was certain she was living through one now. And blizzards killed. "Are you insane?"

He merely gave her shoulder an absent pat—a man with his mind obviously elsewhere. "Got any coffee hot? I could use a cup. And a thermos to go."

"You're not going out in that." In a gesture she knew to be foolish even as she made it, she stepped between Nate and the door. "No one's going out in that."

He smiled, traced a fingertip down her cheek. He didn't see her gesture as foolish, but as sweet. "Worried about me?"

Terrified was closer to it, but she'd think about that later. "Frostbite, hypothermia. Death." She snapped off the words like frozen twigs. "I'd be worried about anyone who didn't have the good sense to stay inside during a storm like this."

"Three of my friends are out in it." His voice was quiet, the purpose behind them unshakable. "Coffee would help, Tess. Black and hot." Before she could speak, he held up a hand, cocked his head. "There. That should be them."

"I didn't hear anything."

"They're back," Nate said simply, and settling his hat again, went out to meet them.

He was right, which made Tess decide Nate had the ears of a cat. They came in out of the howling wind layered with snow. Gathered in the living room, drinking coffee Bess had delivered within minutes, they thawed out.

"Too much snow to see anything." Ben sank into a deep chair as Adam sat cross-legged in front of the fire. "We got out all right, but there was already a couple new inches down. No way to track."

"But you saw." Tess perched on the arm of the sofa. "You saw what was there."

"Yeah." With a quick glance at Adam, Willa moved her shoulders. She didn't see any point in adding that the wolves had come back. "I'll talk to the men about it in the morning. There's enough to do now."

"To do now?" Tess echoed.

"They're already out rounding up the herd, getting them into shelter. I'll find Ham."

"Wait." Certain that she was the only sane person left, Tess held up a hand. "You're going back out in this. For cows?"

"They'd die in this," Willa said briskly.

As Tess watched in amazement, everyone but her and Lily shrugged back into outdoor gear and headed out. With a shake of her head, she reached for the brandy. "For cows," she muttered. "For a bunch of stupid cows."

"They'll be hungry when they get back." Lily didn't look out the window this time, nor did she listen for the engine of the four-wheeler. "I'll go help Bess with supper."

She could be irritated, Tess thought, or resigned. She decided that being resigned was easier on the system. "I'm not going to sit here alone." But she took the brandy with her as she caught up with Lily. "Do you get storms like this back east?"

Distracted, Lily shook her head. "We get our share of snow in Virginia, but I haven't seen anything quite like this. It comes in so quickly, with so much wind. I can't imagine having to be out in it, to work in it. I expect Nate will stay the night, don't you? I'll have to ask Bess if there's a room ready for him."

She pushed open the kitchen door and found Bess already at the stove nursing an enormous pot steaming fragrantly. "Stew," Bess announced, sampling from a wooden spoon. "Enough for an army. Needs an hour or two yet to simmer."

"They've gone out again." Automatically, Lily went to the pantry to take an apron from a peg. Tess raised an eyebrow at the ease of the gesture. Already routine, she realized.

"Figured as much," said Bess. "I'm going to put together an apple cobbler here." She glanced at Tess, sniffed at the brandy in her hand. "You looking to be useful?"

"Not particularly."

"The woodboxes are half empty," Bess told her, and hauled a basket of apples out of the pantry. "The men don't have time to bring in fuel."

Tess swirled the brandy in her hand. "You expect me to go outside and bring in wood?"

"The power goes out, girl, you'll want to keep your butt warm just like the rest of us."

"The power." At the idea of losing power, of being stuck in the cold, in the dark through the night, her color drained.

"We got a generator." Bess moved her shoulders as she began briskly paring apples. "But we can't waste it on heating bedrooms when we got plenty of fuel. You want to sleep warm, you bring in wood. You give her a hand, Lily. She needs it more than I do. There's a rope leading from that door there to the woodpile. You follow that, and bring it in by hand. You won't be able to push the wheelbarrow through the snow, and there's no use shoveling the path out until it's done falling. Get bundled up good, take a flashlight."

"All right." Lily took one look at Tess's annoyed face. "I can bring it in. Why don't you stay inside, and you can carry wood up to the bedrooms?"

It was tempting. Very. Even now Tess could hear the frigid howl of the wind threatening the kitchen windows. But the smirk on Bess's face caused her to set her snifter aside. "We'll both bring it in."

"Not with those fancy lady's gloves," Bess called out as they started out. "Get yourself some work gloves from the mudroom after you've got the rest of your gear on."

"Hauling in wood," Tess muttered on her way to the foyer closet. "There's probably enough inside already to last a week. She's just doing this to get to me."

"She wouldn't ask us to go out if it wasn't necessary."

Tess dragged on her coat, then shrugged. "She wouldn't ask you," she agreed, then plopped down at the base of the steps to tug on her boots. "The two of you seem to be pretty chummy."

"I think she's great." Lily wound the knit scarf around her neck twice before buttoning her coat over it. "She's been nice to me. She'd be nice to you too, if you'd . . ."

Squashing a ski cap onto her head, Tess nodded. "No, don't spare my feelings. If I'd what—?"

"Well, it's just that you're a little abrasive with her. Abrupt."

"Well, maybe I wouldn't be if she wasn't always finding some idiotic chore for me to do, then complaining that I don't do it to her specifications. I'll get frostbite bringing in this damn wood, and she'll say I didn't stack it right. You wait and see."

Miffed, she headed back down the hall again, went through the kitchen without a word and into the mudroom to hunt up a pair of thick, oversized work gloves.

"Ready?" Lily grabbed a flashlight and prepared to follow Tess.

The minute Tess opened the door, the wind slapped ice-edged snow into their faces. Wide-eyed, they stared at each other; it was Lily who took the first step into the wolf bite of the wind.

They grabbed the leading rope, pulling themselves along as the wind shoved them rudely back a step for every three they took. Boots sank knee-deep into snow, and the flashlight bobbled along through the dark like a drunken moonbeam. They all but stumbled over the tarp-covered woodpile.

Tess kept a grip on the flashlight and held her arms out while Lily filled them with wood. Legs spread to hold her balance, the tip of her nose tingling, Tess gritted her teeth. "Hell has nothing to do with fire," she shouted. "Hell is winter in Montana."

Lily smiled a little and began to fill her own arms. "Once we're inside and warm, with the fires going, we'll look out and think it's pretty."

"Bullshit," Tess muttered as they fought their way back to the house to dump the first load. "How bad do you want a warm bed?"

Lily looked toward the toasty kitchen, then back out into the thundering storm. "Pretty bad."

"Yeah." Tess sighed, rolled her shoulders. "Me too. Once more into the breach."

They repeated the routine three times, and Tess began to get into the swing of it. Until she lost her footing and fell headlong and face first into a three-foot drift. The flashlight buried itself like a mole in topsoil.

"Are you all right? Did you hurt yourself?" In her rush to help, Lily leaned over, lost her balance, overcompensated, and sat down hard on her butt. With her breath gone, she stayed where she was, sunk to the waist, while Tess rolled over and spat out snow.

"Fuck, fuck, fuck." Struggling to sit up, Tess narrowed her eyes at Lily's giggles. "What's so goddamn funny? We'll be buried any minute, and they won't find us until the spring thaw." But she felt her own laughter bubbling up as she studied Lily, sitting in a deep throne of snow like some miniature ice queen. "And you look like an idiot."

"So do you." Breath hitching, Lily pressed a snow-coated glove to her heart. "And you're the one with a beard."

Philosophically, Tess swiped the snow off her chin and tossed it into Lily's face. It was all they needed. Despite the mule kick of the wind, they scooped snow into lopsided balls and pummeled each other. Shrieking now, scrambling to their knees, they heaved and tossed and dodged. They were no more than a foot apart, so aim wasn't a factor in the battle. Speed was all that mattered. As snow slapped her face and snuck down the collar of her coat, Tess had to admit that Lily had her there. She might appear delicate, but she had an arm like a bullet.

There was only one way to even the odds.

Tess tackled her and sent them both rolling. Laughing like hyenas, white as snowmen, they plopped on their backs to catch their breath. Flakes drifted down on them, huge and heavy, with the iced edges smoothed out.

"We used to make snow angels when I was a kid," Lily said, and lazily demonstrated by skimming her arms and legs over the snow. "And once it snowed enough for us to be out of school for two days. We built a snow fort and an army of snow people. My mother came out and took pictures of it."

Tess blinked up, trying to see the black sky through the curtain of white. "The one and only time I went skiing, I decided snow and I weren't compatible." She mimicked Lily's moves. "I guess it's not so bad, really."

"It's beautiful." Then she laughed. "I'm freezing."

"I'll buy you a huge mug of coffee laced with brandy."

"I'll take it." Still smiling, Lily sat up. Then her heart leaped into her throat, blocking the scream. Her hand clamped over Tess's as the shadow moved, became a man. Came closer.

"Did you all take a tumble?"

Tess's head jerked around, her pulse roaring in her ears. They were alone, she thought in panic, too far from the house for a shout to carry over the wind. The image of the butchered deer reared up in her mind, turning her to helpless mush.

The flashlight, she thought, as her eyes darted right and left. He had one, the beam strong enough to blind her while keeping him in silhouette. She wanted to run, ordered herself to run, to drag Lily with her, but she couldn't seem to move.

"You shouldn't be out here in the dark," he said, and stepped closer.

Now she moved, survival instincts springing free like a cat out of a cage. She bounded up, snatched a log from the woodpile, and prepared to swing. "Stay back," she ordered, and despite her shaking hands the order was strong and firm. "Lily, get up. Get up, goddamn it."

"Hey, I didn't mean to spook you." He angled the light so that it played along the snow. "It's Wood, Miss Tess. Billy and me just got in, and the wife thought you might need some help up here."

His voice was easy, nonthreatening—even, Tess thought, slightly amused. But they were alone, basically helpless, and he was a strong man with his face still in shadow. Trust no one, she decided, and took a firmer grip on the log.

"We're fine. Lily, go inside and tell Bess that Wood's here. Tell her," she hissed, and Lily finally snapped into action and moved.

"No need to put Bess to any trouble." Wood angled the flashlight toward the woodpile, skimmed the beam over the trampled path to the house. "The wife's got supper on for me, but I can haul some logs in for you. Power's bound to go before long."

Completely alone with Wood now, Tess prayed that Lily was inside and alerting Bess. Fear licked along her spine with a sharp-edged tongue. She took one step back, then two. "We've already taken some in."

"Can't have too much in this kinda storm." He held the flashlight out to her, and she jerked back, visualizing a knife. "You want to take this," he said gently, "I'll load up."

Still poised to run, Tess reached out, took the light. Wood bent to the pile as Lily came flying back. "Bess has coffee on." Her voice rose and fell like an arpeggio. "She said there was plenty if Wood wanted a cup."

"Well, now, I appreciate that." He continued to stack logs competently in the crook of one arm. "But I'll get one back to home. The wife's waiting on me. You all go back in, use that light now. I can find my way well enough."

"Yes, let's go in. Let's go inside, Tess." Shivering, Lily tugged on Tess's arm. "Thank you, Wood."

"Don't mention it," he murmured, shaking his head as they backed down the path. "Women," he said to himself.

"I was so scared," Lily managed. The moment they were inside the mudroom she threw her arms around Tess. "You were so brave."

"I wasn't brave. I was terrified." As fresh realization set in, she clutched Lily and shook violently. "How could we have forgotten? How could we be playing out there like a couple of idiots after everything that's happened? God! God, it could be anyone. Why did it take so long for that to sink in?" She drew back, met Lily's eyes. "It could be anyone."

"Not Adam." After tearing her gloves off, Lily rubbed her chilled hands together. "He couldn't hurt anyone, or anything. And he was with us when we—when we found it today."

Tess opened her mouth, closed it again. What point was there in speculating that Adam could have gone out before dawn, done what had been done, then led them to it, taken them to see what he'd wanted them to see?

"I don't know, Lily. I just don't know. But if we're going to stay here, get through this winter, we'd better start thinking, and we'd better start watching our backs." She pulled off her hat, her coat. "I can't imagine Adam doing that. Or Ben, or Nate. Hell, I can't imagine anyone doing it, and that's the problem. We have to start imagining it."

"We're safe here." Lily turned her back, carefully hung her coat. "We're safe. I haven't felt safe in a long time, and I'm not going to let anything spoil it."

"Lily." Tess laid a hand on her shoulder. "Staying safe means staying careful. And staying smart. We both want something here," she continued as Lily turned back. "And we want it badly enough to risk being here. The way I see it, we have to look out for each other. And we have to trust each other. If I see anything odd, I'm going to tell you, and you're going to do the same. Anything that doesn't feel right, anyone who doesn't act right. Agreed?"

"Yes, I'll tell you. And Willa." She shook her head before Tess could protest. "She deserves that, Tess. She has every bit as much at stake. She has more at stake."

Exactly, Tess thought, then shrugged. "Okay, we'll play it that way. For now, anyway. Now I want that coffee."

They had coffee. And waited. They ate stew. And waited.

The wind screamed at the windows, the fire snapped in the grate, and the grandfather clock in the study bonged the hours away.

It was past midnight when Willa came in, and she came in alone.

Tess stopped pacing the living room and studied her. Willa's face was sheet-white with exhaustion, those dark, exotic eyes bruised with it. She walked directly to the fire, trailing snow and wet behind her over the exquisite rugs and gleaming floors.

"Where are the others?" Tess asked her.

"They had to get back. They've got their own worries."

With a nod, Tess went to the whiskey decanter and poured a generous glass. She'd have preferred having Nate and Ben in the house, but she was learning that Montana was filled with little disappointments. She handed the glass to Willa.

"Cows all tucked in for the night?"

Without bothering to answer, Will tossed back half the whiskey, shuddered hard.

"I'll run you a bath."

With her mind too weary to focus, Willa blinked at Lily. "What?"

"I'm going to run you a hot bath. You're frozen and exhausted. You must be starving. There's stew on the stove. Tess, you fix Willa a bowl."

Willa had just enough energy left to be amused. Her baffled smile followed Lily out of the room. "She's going to run me a bath. Can you beat that?"

"Our resident domestic expert. Anyway, you could use one. You smell."

Willa sniffed, winced. "Guess I do." Because the first blast of whiskey had her head reeling, she set the glass aside. "I'm too tired to eat."

"You need something. You can eat in the tub."

"In the tub. Eat in the tub?"

"Why the hell not?"

Willa spared Tess one smirking glance. "Why the hell not?" she agreed, and stumbled her way upstairs to strip.

Lily had the water steaming and frothy with bubbles. Naked, Willa stared down at it for a full ten seconds. A bubble bath, she thought. She couldn't remember the last time she'd had a bubble bath. The big scarlet tub had been one of her father's indulgences, and she'd rarely used it. And then only when he'd been away.

He was away now, she reminded herself. Dead away.

She swung a leg over the side, hissed as hot water met chilled skin. Then with an enormous sigh, she lowered herself to the chin.

She emptied her mind of snow, of wind, of the raging dark, the brutal fight to round up cattle. They would have missed some, and they would lose some.

That was inevitable. The blizzard had come in too fast and too mean to prevent that. But they had done their best.

Her muscles wept as she laid her head back, closed her eyes. Can't think, she realized as her mind clicked on and off. Had to think. What to do. Every movement, every chore, every decision made come morning would be instinctive. She knew what to do there. It wasn't her first blizzard, nor would it be her last.

But murder—murder and butchery.

What to do.

"Fall asleep in there and you'll drown," Tess said from the doorway.

Willa sat up, scowling. She wasn't particularly modest. The scowl was for the intrusion, even if it did include the heavenly scent of stew. "You ever try knocking?"

"You left the door open, champ." Rather amused at her role of server, Tess settled the tray across the tub. "I want to talk to you."

Willa only sighed. She scooted up enough to manage the meal, dipped a spoon into the stew while bubbles melted off her breasts. "So talk."

Tess sat on the wide ledge of the tub. Quite a bathroom, she mused. It was as plush as any movie star's fantasy with its ruby, sapphire, and white tiles, its forest of ferns in brass and copper pots. The separate shower was walled in clear glass, boasted half a dozen showerheads at different angles and heights. And the tub where Willa was lounging was easily big enough for a small, tasteful orgy.

Idly she dipped a finger into the bubbles, sniffed at them. "Violets," she commented. "Must be Lily's."

"You want to talk about bubble baths?" Willa scooted up higher as she gained more enthusiasm for the meal. She could have eaten a truckload of stew.

"We'll leave the girl stuff for later." She glanced over as Lily came to the doorway, her gaze politely fixed inches above Willa's head. "I've got your robe, for when you're finished. I'll just hang it on the back of the door."

"Come on in, have a seat," Willa invited with a wave of her hand. "Tess wants to talk." When Lily hesitated, Willa rolled her eyes. "We've all got tits here, Lily."

"And hers are barely noticeable, anyway," Tess added with a smug smile. "Have a seat," she ordered. "You're the one who wanted to bring her in on all of this."

"All of what?" Willa demanded with her mouth full.

"Let's just say Lily and I are a little nervous. Wouldn't you agree with that, Lily?"

Flushing, Lily lowered the lid on the toilet and sat. "Yes."

Despite the heat of the water, Willa's skin chilled. "You two planning to bolt?"

"We're not cowards." Tess inclined her head. "Or fools. The three of us have equal interest in getting through this year. I assume we all have equal interest in getting through it in one piece. Somebody, very possibly somebody on this ranch, is—let's say knife happy. How do we deal with it?"

Willa's mouth went stubborn. "I know my men."

"We don't," Tess pointed out. "Maybe we should start by you filling us in.

Telling us what you know about each one of them. As appealing as it sounds, the three of us can't travel in a pack twenty-four hours a day for the next nine or ten months."

"You're right."

The careless agreement caused Tess's mouth to drop open. "Well, well, I must mark this day on my calendar. Willa Mercy agrees with me."

"I still can't stand you." Scraping her bowl, Willa continued. "But I do agree. The three of us need to cooperate if we're going to get through this. Until the police, or we, find out who killed Pickles, I don't think either of you should wander around alone."

"I can defend myself. I've taken classes."

Tess's announcement made Willa snort.

"I could take you down," Tess tossed out. "In ten seconds I'd have you on your back seeing stars. But that's beside the point." She had a low-grade urge for a cigarette, and promised herself she'd indulge it soon. "Lily and I can't very well attach ourselves to each other at the hip."

"I'm with Adam most of the day. With the horses."

Willa nodded at Lily and slid back into the water. "You can depend on Adam. And Bess. And Ham."

"Why Ham?" Tess wanted to know.

"He raised me," Willa said shortly. "The weather's going to keep the two of you close to the house for the next little while anyway."

"What about you?" Lily asked.

"I'll worry about me." Willa submerged, holding her breath under the water, then came up feeling nearly human again. "I haven't had the benefit of Hollywood's self-defense courses, but I know the men, I know the land. If either one of you is nervous, you can saddle up and go to work with me. Now, unless one of you wants to scrub my back, I'd like some privacy."

Tess rose, and as an afterthought reached down for the tray. "Being cocky isn't much protection against a knife."

"A Winchester is." And satisfied with that, Willa reached for the soap.

She slept poorly. Exhaustion, as powerful as it was, couldn't beat back the nightmares. Willa tossed and turned, fighting for sleep as images of blood and gore raced through her head.

When that thin winter light crept through the wall of steadily falling snow, she shivered and wished there was something, someone, to hold on to. For just a little while.

Someone else woke in that same stingy light with those same images running like a river through his head.

But they made him smile.

12

From Tess's journal:

I'm beginning to like snow. Or I'm going slowly insane. Each morning when I look out my bedroom window, there it is, white and shiny. Miles of it. I can't say I care for the cold. Or the fucking wind. But the snow, particularly when I'm inside looking out, has a certain appeal. Or maybe I'm beginning to feel safe again.

It's a week before Christmas, and nothing has happened to interrupt the routine. No murdered men, no slaughtered wildlife. Just the eerie quiet of snow-smothered days. Maybe the cops were right after all, and whoever killed that poor bald guy was a psychotic hiker. We can only hope.

Lily is big into the holiday spirit. Funny, sweet woman. She's like a child about it, hustling bags into her bedroom, wrapping presents, baking cookies with Bess. Great cookies, which means I've been adding an extra fifteen minutes to my morning workouts.

We took a trip into Billings, for what it's worth, to do some Christmas shopping. Lily was easy enough. I found a pretty brooch of a rearing horse, very delicate and feminine. Figured I had to come up with something for sour-face Bess, and settled on a cookbook. Lily approved it, so I suppose I'm safe. The cowgirl's another matter. I still haven't pinned her down.

Is this woman fearless or stupid?

She goes out every day, more often than not alone. She works her ass off, swaggers down to the old bunkhouse every evening to talk to her men. When she's in the house, she's often buried up to her eyeballs with ledgers and cow reports.

I'm afraid I'm starting to admire her, and I'm not sure I like it. I got her a cashmere sweater, I don't know why. She never wears anything but flannel. But it's screaming siren red, very soft and female. She'll probably end up tossing it on over her long underwear and castrating cows in it. Hell with it.

For Adam, because he appeals to me on a surprisingly fraternal level, I found a lovely little watercolor of the mountains. It reminded me of him.

After much debate with myself, I decided to spring for a token gift for both Ben and Nate, since they spend so much time around here. I picked up a video of Red River *for Ben, kind of a gag that I hope will be taken in the proper spirit.*

And after some subtle probing, I learned that Nate has a weakness for poetry. He's getting a volume of Keats. We'll see.

Between the shopping, the smells from the kitchen, and the decorating, I'm getting in the holiday mood myself. Just shipped off a ton of presents for Mom. With her, it's not the quality but the quantity, and I know she'll be happily ripping off shiny paper for hours.

The damnedest thing, I miss her.

Despite all the Santa Clausing, I'm antsy. Too many hours indoors, I think. I'm using this extra time—winter is chock-full of time around here since it's dark before five in the evening—to play with an idea for a book. Just for fun, just to pass the time during these incredibly long nights.

And speaking of long nights . . . Since all seems quiet again, I'm taking one of the jeeps—I mean rigs—and driving over to Nate's to deliver my gift. Ham gave me directions to Nate's—what would I call it—spread, I suppose. I've been waiting weeks for an invitation to his house, and for him to make a move. I guess it's up to me to start the ball rolling.

I can't decide how subtle I should be about getting him into bed, and so will play it by ear. At the rate he's going, it could be spring before I get laid.

The hell with that, too.

"Going somewhere?" Willa demanded as Tess glided downstairs.

"As a matter of fact." She tilted her head, took in Willa's usual uniform of flannel and denim. "You?"

"I just got in. Some of us don't have time to primp in front of a mirror for an hour." Willa's brow furrowed. "You're wearing a dress."

"Am I?" Feigning surprise, Tess looked down at the simple, form-fitting blue wool that skimmed above her knees. "Well, how did that happen?" With a snicker, she came down the rest of the way and walked to the closet for her coat. "I have a Christmas present to deliver. You remember Christmas, don't you? Even with your busy schedule you must have heard of it."

"There was a rumor." Sexy dress, heels, fuck-me perfume, Willa mused, and narrowed her eyes. "Who's the present for?"

"I'm dropping in on Nate." Tess swirled on her coat. "I hope he has some wassail handy."

"Should have figured it," Willa muttered. "You're going to break your neck getting to the rig in those ice picks."

"I've got excellent balance." With a careless wave, Tess glided out. "Don't wait up. Sis."

"Yeah. Good balance," Willa repeated, watching as Tess made her way gracefully to the rig. "I hope Nate's got good balance."

She turned away, walked into the living room, and stretched out on the sofa. After one long look at the tall, elaborately decorated tree framed in the front window, she buried her face in the leather.

Christmas had always been a miserable time of year for her. Her mother had died in December. Not that she remembered, but she knew it, and it had always put a cloud over the holidays. Bess had tried, God knew, to make up for it with decorations and cookies, with silly presents and carols. But there had never been family gathered around the piano, or family huddled under the tree opening gifts on Christmas morning.

She and Adam had exchanged theirs on Christmas Eve, always. After her father was rip-roaring drunk and snoring in his bed.

There had been presents under the tree with her name on them. Bess had seen to that, and for years had put Jack's name on them. But when Willa had turned sixteen, she'd stopped opening those. They were a lie after all, and after a couple of further attempts, Bess had given up the pretense.

Christmas morning had meant hangovers and bad temper, and on the one occasion she'd been brave enough to complain, a stinging backhand.

She'd stopped looking forward to the holidays a long time ago.

And now she was tired, so damn tired. The winter had come so soon, and so brutally. They'd lost more cows than she'd expected, and Wood was worried they hadn't gotten the winter wheat in soon enough. The market price per head had dipped—not enough for panic, but enough for worry.

And she found herself waiting, every day waiting, to find something, or someone, slaughtered on her doorstep again.

No one to talk to, she thought. So she kept her worries to herself. She didn't want Lily and Tess terrified every minute of the day, but neither could she relax and ignore it. She made certain that either she or Adam or Ham kept an eye on both of them when they were out of the house.

Now Tess was gone, driving off, and Willa hadn't had the energy or the wisdom to stop her.

Call Nate, she told herself. Get up and call Nate to tell him she's coming. He'll look out for her. But she didn't move, just couldn't seem to swing her legs down and sit up. To sit up and face that brightly, pitifully cheerful tree with the pretty presents under it.

"If you're going to sleep, you should go to bed."

She heard Ben's voice, resigned herself to it. "I'm not sleeping. I'm just resting a minute. Go away."

"I don't know; when I come over here you don't tell me to leave again." So he sat down, settling in the middle of the sofa. "You're wearing yourself out, Will." Reaching down, he turned her face away from the back of the sofa. The tears on it made him drop his hand as if she'd burned him. "You're crying."

"I am not." Humiliated, she pressed her face into leather again. "I'm just tired. That's all." Then her voice hitched, broke, and disgraced her. "Leave me alone. Leave me alone. I'm tired."

"Come here, darling." Though he had little experience with weeping females, he figured he could handle this one. As easily as if she'd been a child, he lifted her up, cradled her on his lap. "What's the matter?"

"Nothing. I'm just . . . Everything," she managed, and let her head rest on his shoulder. "I don't know what's wrong with me. I'm not crying."

"Okay." Deciding they were both better off pretending she wasn't, he gathered her closer. "Let's just sit here awhile anyway. You're a comfortable armful for a bony woman."

"I hate Christmas."

"No, you don't." He pressed his lips to the top of her head. "You're just worn out. You know what you should do, Will? You and your sisters should take a few days off and go to one of those fancy spas. Get yourself pampered and pummeled, take mud baths."

She snorted, felt better. "Yeah, right. Me and the girls swapping gossip in the mud. That's my style, all right."

"Better yet, you could go with me. We could get a room with one of those big bubble tubs, a heart-shaped bed with a mirror over it. That way you can see what's going on when we make love. You'll learn faster that way."

It had a certain decadent, dizzying appeal, but she shrugged. "I'm not in any hurry."

"I'm getting to be in one," he muttered, then tilted her head back. "Haven't done this in a while." And closed his mouth over hers.

She didn't pretend to resist or protest, not when it was exactly what she needed. The warmth, the steady hand, the skilled mouth. Instead, she slid her arms around his neck, turned into him, and let all those worries and doubts and bad memories fade away.

Here was comfort and, regardless of anything, someone who would listen, and perhaps even care. She sank into that, into the wanting of that as much as the wanting of him.

He felt the need he'd kept carefully reined strain at its tether. The unexpected sweetness of her, the surprising and arousing pliancy, the little licks of heat that hinted of passion simmering beneath innocence.

The combination came close to snapping that straining tether.

So it was he who drew back, she who protested. Struggling to temper instinct with sense, he shifted her again, settled her head once more in the curve of his shoulder. "Let's just sit here a while."

She felt his heart beat, fast, under her hand. Heard her own pound in her head. "You get me stirred up. I don't know why it's you who gets me stirred up, Ben. I just can't figure it."

"Well, I feel heaps better now." He sighed once, then rested his head against hers. "This isn't so bad."

"No, I guess it isn't." So she sat in his lap while her feelings settled again. She watched the twinkle of the lights on the tree, and the fall of light snow, just a whisper of white, through the window beyond. "Tess went over to Nate's," she said at length.

He heard the tone, knew her well enough to interpret it. "You're worried about that?"

"Nate can handle himself. Probably." She made a restless movement, then gave up and let her eyes drift closed.

"It's Tess you're worried about."

"Maybe. Some. Yes. Nothing's happened for weeks now, but . . ." She exhaled. "I can't watch her every minute of the day and night."

"No, you can't."

"She thinks she knows all the answers. Miss Big City Girl with her self-defense courses and her snappy clothes. Shit. She's as lost out here as a mouse in a roomful of hungry she-cats. What if the rig breaks down, or she runs off the road?" She drew a deep breath and said what was most on her mind. "What if whoever killed Pickles is still around, watching?"

"Like you said, nothing's happened in weeks. Odds are he's long gone."

"If you believe that, why are you here most every day, using every lame excuse in the book to drop by?"

"They aren't so lame," he muttered, then shrugged. "There's you." He didn't bother to scowl when she snorted. "There is you," he repeated. "And there's the ranch. And yeah, I think about it." He tilted her head up again and kissed her hard and quick. "Tell you what, I'll just ride by Nate's and make sure she got there."

"Nobody's asking you to check up on my problems."

"Nope, nobody is." He lifted her, set her aside, then rose. "One day you might just ask me for something, Willa. You might just break down and ask. Meanwhile I'll do things my own way. Go on to bed," he told her. "You need a decent night's sleep. I'll see to your sister."

She frowned after him as he walked out, and wondered what he was waiting for her to ask.

Tess got there. She considered it a fine adventure to drive through the light snowfall in the deep country dark. She had the radio turned up to blast, and by some minor miracle she found a station that played downright rock. She wailed along with Rod Stewart as she approached the lights of Nate's ranch.

Tidy as a Currier and Ives painting, she decided. The well-plowed dirt road with its fresh sprinkle of white, the neat outbuildings and rectangles of fence, the rising shadows of trees.

Her headlights must have stirred the horses, as three trotted out of the barn and into the corral to watch her drive by.

Pretty as a painting themselves, she thought, with their flowing tails and dancing hooves. One of them loped over to the fence, luring her into slowing down to study its trim lines and glossy color.

She drove on, taking the gentle curve in the road that led to the main house. It, too, was pretty and neat. Unpretentious, she decided, a boxy two stories with a generous covered porch, white shutters against dark wood, double chimneys with smoke pumping into the snowy sky. Simple, she mused, hold the pretenses and fancywork. Just like the man who lived there.

She was smiling as she gathered up her bag, the gift, and climbed out of the rig. And managed, barely, to hold back the scream when she spotted the wildcat.

She took three stumbling steps back, rapped up hard against the rig. The cat's eyes stared into hers. It was dead, stone cold dead and draped over the hitching rail. But it gave her a very bad moment.

The fangs and claws were lethally sharp and told her exactly what would happen to a woman careless enough to stumble onto a live one. It hadn't been mutilated, and the lack of blood settled her thundering heart. It was simply draped, like a rug, she thought in wonder, over the rail. With a shudder, she gave it a wide berth and climbed the steps to the front door.

What kind of people, she wondered, draped the carcass of a wildcat over their front entrance? With a nervous laugh, she looked down at the gift in her hand. Then read Keats?

Jesus, what a country.

Even as she lifted her hand to knock, the door opened. In the mood she was in, Tess was pleased she didn't add a shriek to her jolt.

The short, dark woman studied her solemnly. She was nearly as wide as she was tall, wrapped now in a thick black coat and many scarves. Her black hair was bundled under yet another scarf, but Tess could see it was salted with gray.

"Señorita," she said in a gorgeous, fluid voice. "May I help you?"

The liquid, sexy voice coming out of the tiny, wrinkled face fascinated Tess, and she immediately started casting character. Her smile spread and brightened. "Hello, I'm Tess Mercy."

"Yes, Señorita Mercy." At the Mercy name, the woman opened the door wider, stepping back in invitation.

"I'd like to see Nate, if he's free."

"He's in his office. Just down the hall. I will show you."

"You're on your way out." And Tess didn't want her arrival announced. "I can find it. Señora . . . ?"

"Cruz." She blinked a moment at Tess's offered hand, then took it in a brisk grip. "Mister Nate will be pleased to see you."

Will he? Tess thought, but she continued to smile. "I have a little gift for him," she said, and held up the brightly wrapped book. "A surprise."

"That is very generous. It is the third door on the left." The ghost of a smile around the woman's mouth told Tess that the underlying reason for her visit was all too obvious. At least to another female. "Good night, Señorita Mercy."

"Good night, Señora Cruz." And Tess chuckled to herself as the door closed between them and she was left alone in the quiet hall.

Bright geometric-patterned rugs over dark wood floors, clever pen-and-ink sketches on ivory-toned walls. Lovely dried-flower arrangements in brass urns—that would be the señora's touch, Tess assumed as she wandered.

A fire was burning nicely in the living room, simmering in a stone hearth beneath a stone mantel on which stood pewter candlesticks and a collection of intriguing paperweights. The furniture was wide and deeply cushioned and masculine. Dark colors to contrast with light walls and the bright rugs.

An interesting mix, Tess decided. Simple, male, yet pleasing to the eye.

She caught the low strains of a Mozart concerto as she walked closer to the open office door.

And there he was, all gangling and sexy and Jimmy Stewart-ish in a high-backed leather chair behind a big oak desk. The desk lamp slanted light over his hands as he made notations on a yellow legal pad. His brow was knotted, his tie loose, his hair, all that thick gold of it, mussed. From his own hands, she noted, as he raked his fingers through it.

Well, well, she thought, just feel my heart go pitty-pat. Amused at herself, she watched him another minute, pleased to be able to study him when he was working and unaware of her.

The room was filled with books, and a single mug of coffee sat at his elbow while the lovely music murmured in the background.

Nate, she decided, giving her hair a brief stroke, you're a goner.

"Well, good evening, Lawyer Torrence." Well aware that she was posed in the doorway, she smiled slowly as his head jerked up, as his eyes cleared of business, then surprise, and focused.

"Well, hello, Miz Mercy." Tension whipped into him as he saw her there, snow still lightly dusted over her hair and the shoulders of her coat. That tension increased when he saw the secret female smile on her lips, but he leaned back in his chair like a man perfectly at ease. "This is a pleasant surprise."

"I hope so. And I hope I'm not interrupting something vitally important."

"Not vital." The notes he'd been taking had already gone completely out of his mind.

"Señora Cruz let me in." She started toward the desk, thinking of the wildcat. She would take a page from the feline book and toy with her prey before moving in for the kill. "Your housekeeper."

"My keeper." He was quite simply baffled. Should he get up, offer her a drink, stay where he was? Why the hell was she looking at him as though she was already licking the remains of him from her lips? "Maria and her husband, Miguel, keep things running around here. Is this a social visit, Tess, or do you need a lawyer?"

"Social, for the moment. Completely social." She slipped off her coat and watched his eyes flicker. Yes, she concluded, the dress was definitely a success. "To be honest, I needed to get out of the house." She draped her coat over the back of a chair, then eased a hip onto the corner of his desk, letting the skirt slide sneakily up her thigh. "A little cabin fever."

"It happens." He hadn't forgotten her legs, but it had been a while since he'd seen them in anything but jeans or thick wool pants. Displayed in sheer hose to well above the knee, they made his mouth go dry. "Can I get you a drink?"

"That would be lovely." She crossed her legs, slowly. Another sneaky slide. "What have you got?"

"Ah . . ." He couldn't remember, and felt like an idiot.

Better and better, she decided, and slithered off the desk. "I'll just see for myself, shall I?" She walked to the decanters on a cabinet across the room and chose vermouth. "Would you like one?"

"Sure, thanks." He nudged the coffee aside. Caffeine sure as hell wasn't going to get him through this. "I haven't been able to get over for a couple of days. How are things?"

"Quiet." She poured two glasses, brought them to the desk. After handing Nate his, she slipped onto the desk again, on his side. "Though festive." She leaned down, just a bit, tapped her glass to his. "Happy holidays. In fact . . ." She took a small sip. "That's one of the reasons I came by." Reaching over, she picked up the package she'd put on the desk. "Merry Christmas, Nate."

"You got me a present?" He narrowed his eyes at the package, expecting a slam.

"Just a little one. You've been a good friend, and counselor." She smiled over the last word. "Do you want to open it now, or wait till Christmas morning?" She touched her tongue to her top lip, and all the blood drained out of his brain into his lap. "I can come back."

"I'm a sucker for presents," he told her, and ripped the paper off. When he saw the book he teetered between being faintly embarrassed and gently moved. "I'm a sucker for Keats, too," he murmured.

"So I hear. I thought when you read it, you might think of me."

He lifted his eyes to hers. "I manage to think of you without visual aids."

"Do you?" She inched closer, leaning down so that she could take hold of his loosened tie. "And what do you think?"

"I think, at the moment, you're trying to seduce me."

"You're so quick, so smart." She laughed and slid into his lap. "And so right." One quick tug on the tie and she had his mouth on hers.

Like the house, like the man, the hunger was simple and without pretense. His hands closed over her breasts, the warm, full weight of them. And when she shifted to straddle him, his hands moved around to cup her bottom.

She had already tossed his tie aside and was working on his shirt before he'd taken the first breath.

"If I'd had to go another week without your hands on me, I'd have screamed." She fastened her teeth low on his neck. "I'd rather scream with them on me."

He still hadn't managed to breathe, but his hands were busy enough, pushing that short, snug skirt of the dress up her hips, finding the delight of firm bare skin over the lacy tops of stockings. "We can't—here." He went back to her breasts, unable to decide where he needed to touch first. "Upstairs," he managed as he savaged her mouth. "I'll take you upstairs."

"Here." She threw back her head as his lips ran down her throat. He had a wonderful mouth. She'd been sure of it. "Right here, right now." On the verge of exploding already, she dragged at his belt. "Hurry. The first time fast. We'll worry about finesse later."

He was with her there. Hard as steel, aching, desperate. He struggled with the zipper in the back of her dress as she struggled with his. "I haven't got any... Christ, you're built." He dragged the dress down far enough to find those lovely, full breasts spilling over the top of a low-cut black bra. He nipped the bra down with his teeth, then used them on her.

It was a shock. She'd always considered herself healthily sexual. But when that busy mouth on her flesh shot her over the edge without a net, her body bucked, her mind spun. "God. Oh, my God." Letting her head fall back, she absorbed that first, delightful orgasm. "More. Now."

She'd exploded over him—wildly, gorgeously—and dazed him. With his hands full of her, he pressed his lips to hers and tried to think. "We have to go upstairs, Tess. I don't generally have sex at my desk. I'm not prepared for it."

"That's okay." She let her brow rest against his, drew three deep breaths. Lord, she was quaking like a schoolgirl. "I am."

Reaching back, she fumbled over the surface of the desk, knocking a number of things to the floor as he took advantage of the thrust of her breast and suckled. She heard her breath wheeze, swore she could feel her eyes cross as she groped behind her for her bag. She opened it, tossed it aside, and let a trail of condoms spill out.

He blinked. A quick guess told him there were at least a dozen. So Nate cleared his throat. "I don't know whether to be afraid or flattered."

It made her laugh. Sitting there, half naked and aroused to hell and back, she let loose a low, rocking laugh. "Consider it a challenge."

"Good call." But when he reached for them, she drew them teasingly out of reach.

"Oh, no. Allow me."

With her eyes on his, she ripped a packet off, tore it open. Mozart continued to play with grace and dignity as she freed Nate from his slacks, gave a feline hum of anticipation, and slowly, torturously protected them both.

His lungs clogged, his fingers dug into the arms of the chair. Her hands were clever, delicate as a rose. And he was suddenly terrified that he would disgrace himself like a teenage virgin. "Goddamn, you're good."

She smiled, shifted. "I've been thinking about this since the first time I saw you."

He gripped her hips as she rose over him, held her there while both of them quivered. "Yeah? Well, that makes two of us."

She braced her hands on his shoulders, let her fingers dig in for purchase. "Why'd we wait so long?"

"Damned if I know." Slowly, his eyes locked on hers, he lowered her, pierced her, filled her. She shuddered once, moaned low and long in her throat, and didn't move a muscle. Her eyes closed, then opened.

"Yes," she said, and smiled again.

"Yes." His hands stayed fastened on her hips as she rode him, hard and fast and well.

Later, when she was limp in his arms, he managed to reach the phone. She moaned a little as he shifted her, dialed.

"Will? It's Nate. Tess is here . . . Yeah. She'll be staying here tonight." He turned his head, nipped at her bare shoulder, and realized he'd never gotten that dress completely off. Plenty of time for that, he thought, and tuned back in to Willa's voice. "No, she's fine. She's great. She'll be back in the morning. 'Bye."

"That was considerate of you," Tess murmured. She'd popped a few of the buttons off his shirt somewhere along the line, and now enjoyed the smooth bare skin of his chest under her lazy fingertips.

"She'd worry." He worked the bunched-up dress from around her waist and pulled it over her head. Now she wore nothing but lace-topped stockings, sexy high heels, and a satisfied smirk. The smirk was the only thing he wanted to see slip off her. "How do you feel?"

"I feel wonderful." Tossing back her hair, she linked her hands behind his neck. "And you?"

He slipped his hands under her bottom, lifting her as he rose. "Lucky," he told her, and laid her back on his desk. He took a moment to toss the legal pad that rested beside her head over his shoulder. "And about to get luckier."

Surprised, interested, she grinned. "My, my, round two already?"

"Just hold on, honey." He ran his hands up and over her, pleased when she trembled. "And hold on tight."

It didn't take long for her to take the warning seriously.

13

The temperature rose on New Year's Eve. One of El Niño's wild weather patterns that make sense only to God brought bright blue skies, sunlight, and warm air. Though it would mean mud and slop—and ice when the wind blew capriciously again—it was a moment to be enjoyed.

Willa rode fences in a light denim jacket, whistling as she made repairs. The mountains were snowcapped, the white lacing deep in the folds and waves. The chinook had teased patches of ground and grass through the white in pastures, while the snowpack along the ranch roads was still higher than a rig. But the cottonwoods had lost their ermine trim and stood bare and black with wet while the pines rose sassily green.

She thought it was Lily's simple happiness that was influencing her mood. The woman's holiday mood was still in high gear, and only a true grinch could have resisted it.

Why else, Willa thought, had she agreed to Lily's hesitant request for a New Year's Eve party? All those people in the house, Willa mused, having to dress up, make conversation. With everything else on her mind, it should have been a misery.

But she could admit, at least to herself, that she was looking forward to it.

Even now, Lily and Bess and Nell were huddled in the kitchen creating the feast. The house had been scrubbed raw and polished blind, and Willa had orders to be bathed and dressed by eight sharp. She would do it, Willa realized, for Lily.

Somehow over the months she'd fallen in love with the stranger who had become her sister.

Who wouldn't? she asked herself as she mounted Moon and rode on. Lily was sweet and kind and patient. And vulnerable. No matter how hard she'd tried to maintain a distance between them, they had grown closer and closer until now she couldn't imagine Mercy without Lily's touch.

Lily liked to gather twigs, stick them in old bottles. And somehow she made them look cheerful and charming. She hunted up old bowls out of cupboards, filled them with fruit, or dumped pinecones into straw baskets. She snuck plants out of the pool house and scattered them through the rooms.

When no one complained, she'd foraged for more, digging candlesticks out of closets, buying scented candles and lighting them in the evening so that the house smelled of vanilla and cinnamon and lord knew what else.

But it was pleasant. It was, Willa decided, homey.

And anyone with eyes could see that Adam was in love with her. A little afraid of that vulnerability Lily carried around, Willa mused, but quietly in love. It could work, she supposed, with time and care. She doubted that Lily realized just how deep Adam's feelings went. As far as Willa could see, Lily thought he was being kind.

Dismounting, she began to repair more broken wire.

Then there was Tess. Willa couldn't claim to be in love with Miss Hollywood, but she might have become slightly less resentful. For the most part, Tess stayed out of her way, closeting herself for several hours a day with her writing or phone calls to her agent. She did the chores assigned to her. Not cheerfully, and not often well, but she did them.

Willa was fully aware of what was going on between Tess and Nate. She just didn't choose to dwell on it. That, she concluded, would never work. The minute the time was up, Tess would be on a flight back to LA and would never give Nate another thought.

She only hoped he was prepared for it.

And what about you, Will? she wondered. Leaning on a fence post, she looked up into the mountains, wished for a moment that she could mount Moon and ride off, up and up until she lost herself in snow and trees and sky. The quiet that was there. The utter peace of it, the music of water thawing and forcing its way through ice, over rocks, the sweep of wind through pine, and that glorious scent that was the land just breathing.

No responsibilities, just for a day. No men to order, no fence to ride, no cattle to feed. Just a day to do nothing but stare at the sky and dream.

Of what? she asked herself, and shook her head. With all the love and longing, the sex and snapping air around her, would she dream of that? Would she indulge herself in a little fantasy about what it would be like to let Ben show her what a man could do to a woman? And for her?

Or would she dream of blood and death, of failure and guilt? Would she ride into those hills and find something, or someone else, slaughtered because she'd let down her guard?

She couldn't take the chance.

Turning back to Moon, she laid a hand over her rifle, sighed once, then mounted.

She saw the rider and hoped it was Ben galloping toward her, with Charlie running by his side. And it shamed her that she was disappointed, even for an instant, that it was Adam.

How beautiful he is, she thought. And how sturdy.

"Don't see you riding alone much these days," she called out.

He grinned, reining in. "God, what a day!" He drew a deep breath of it, lifting his face to the sky. "Lily's party planning, and she's rooked Tess into it."

"So you settled for me." She watched his face, laughed at his stunned and guilty expression. "I'm only teasing, Adam. And even though I know it's no hardship on you, I'm grateful you're keeping an eye on them."

"Lily's put it out of her mind. All of it." He turned his mount to ride alongside Willa. "I imagine it's how she dealt with her marriage. I don't know if it's healthy, but it seems to give her peace of mind."

"She's happy here. You make her happy."

He understood that Willa would know his deepest feelings. She always did. "She needs time yet, to feel safe. To trust that I can want her and not hurt her because of it."

"Has she told you anything about her ex-husband?"

"Bits and pieces." Adam shrugged his shoulders restlessly. He wanted more, he wanted all of it. And it was difficult to wait. "She was teaching when she met him, and they got married very quickly. It was a mistake. She says little more than that. But inside, she's still afraid. If I move too quickly, turn abruptly, she jumps. It breaks my heart."

It would, she thought. The wounded always broke his heart. "I've seen her change in the short time she's been here. Been with you. She smiles more. Talks more."

He angled his head. "You've grown fond of her."

"Some."

He smiled. "And the other one. Tess?"

" 'Fond' isn't the word I'd use," she said dryly. "I'm working on 'tolerate.' "

"She's a strong woman, smart, focused. More like you than Lily."

"Please, don't insult me."

"She is. She confronts things, makes them work for her. She hasn't your sense of duty, and perhaps her heart isn't as soft, but she has both duty and heart. I like her very much."

Her brow knit as she turned to look at him. "Do you really?"

"Yes. When I was teaching her to ride, she fell off, several times. She would get up, brush off her jeans, and climb right back on." With a look on her face, he remembered, that was the mirror of the one Willa wore when she was fighting to conquer a new problem. "That takes courage and determination. And pride. She makes Lily laugh. She makes me laugh. And I'll tell you something she doesn't know."

"Secrets?" Grinning, Willa nudged her horse closer to his, dropping her voice, though there was no one for miles. The sun was easing down toward the western peaks, softening the light. "Tell all."

"She's fallen for the horses. She doesn't know it, or isn't ready to admit it, but I see it. The way she touches them, talks to them, sneaks them sugar when she thinks I don't see."

Willa pursed her lips. "We'll be into foaling season soon. Let's see how well she likes birthing."

"I think she'll do well. And she admires you."

"Bullshit."

"You aren't ready to see that, but I do." He squinted, gauged the distance back home. "Race you to the barn."

"You're on." With a whoop, she kicked Moon into action and hustled back at a dead run.

She walked into the house with color in her cheeks and a gleam in her eye. No one beat Adam on horseback, but she'd come close. Damn close, and it had lifted her mood—which plummeted immediately when Tess came down the stairs.

"There you are. Upstairs, Annie Oakley. Party time, and your eau de sweat won't do for tonight."

"I've got two hours."

"Which may be barely enough time to transform you into something resembling a female. Hit the showers."

She'd intended to do just that, but now her back was up. "I've got some paperwork."

"Oh, you can't." Lily came up behind her, hands fluttering. "It's already six."

"So? Nobody's coming that I need to impress."

"Nobody's coming you need to offend either." With a sigh, Tess took her arm and began to haul her up the stairs.

"Hey!"

"Come on, Lily. This is going to take both of us."

Biting her lip, Lily took Willa's other arm. "It's going to be so nice, really it is, to see people. You've been working so hard. Tess and I want you to enjoy yourself."

"Then take your damn hands off me." She dislodged Lily easily enough, but Tess tightened her grip and steered Willa into the bedroom. "Five more seconds, and I deck you if you don't—" She broke off, staring at the dress laid out on the bed.

"What the hell is that?"

"I went through your closet, and as there's nothing in it remotely resembling party wear—"

"Hold on." This time Willa jerked free, spun around. "You went through my clothes?"

"I didn't see anything in there to be proprietary about. In fact, I thought I'd stumbled into the rag bin, but Bess assured me it was indeed your wardrobe."

Though her palms had gone damp, Lily stepped between them. "We altered one of Tess's dresses for you."

"Hers?" With a sneer, Willa looked Tess up and down. "You'd have had to lose half the material to make that work."

"True enough," Tess shot back. "And all in the bust. But it turns out that Bess is very clever with a needle. It's possible that even with your toothpick legs and flat chest you might look oddly attractive in it."

"Tess." Lily hissed the word and nudged her older sister aside. "It's a beautiful color, don't you think? You'd look so dramatic in jewel tones, and this shade of blue is just made for you. It was so generous of Tess to let it be altered for you."

"I never really cared for it," Tess said carelessly. "One of those little fashion mistakes."

Lily closed her eyes briefly and prayed for peace. "I know I'm putting you to a lot of trouble with this party, Will. I appreciate so much that you'd let me plan it, and all but take over the house the last couple of days. I know it's an inconvenience for you."

Done in, Willa dragged a hand through her hair. "I don't know who's better at getting to me, but the hell with it. Just get out, both of you. I can manage to shower and put on some stupid hand-me-down dress all by myself."

Accepting victory, Tess took Lily's arm and urged her toward the door. "Wash your hair, champ."

"Go to hell." Willa kicked the door shut behind them.

She felt like a fool. A fool who would undoubtedly freeze her ass off in this excuse for a dress before the evening was over. As she stood in front of her mirror, Willa tugged at the hem. That little action had the effect of moving it down close to an inch, while the low-cut neckline dipped distressingly in reaction, toward her navel.

Tits or ass, she thought, scratching her head—which did she want to cover more?

The dress did have sleeves, which was something. But they began at mid-shoulder, and nothing she tried seemed to convince them to settle a bit closer to her neck. Whatever the dress was made of was thin and soft and clung like a second skin.

Grudgingly she stepped into her heels and got a quick lesson in physics. As she went up, so did the hemline.

"Oh, screw it." Stepping closer to the mirror, she decided she might as well go all out and use her miserly hoard of cosmetics. It was, after all, New Year's Eve.

And the dress, what there was of it, was a pretty color. Electric blue, she supposed. Maybe she didn't have much cleavage, despite the best efforts of that dipping, clinging V neck, but her shoulders weren't half bad. And damned if her legs were toothpicks. They were long, sure, but they were muscled, and the dark-toned panty hose she struggled into hid the couple of new bruises she'd discovered after her shower.

She refused to fuss with her hair. She wasn't any good with curls or complicated styles in any case, so she left it straight, spilling down her back. Which would at least keep the flesh warm that the plunge back bared.

She remembered earrings only because Adam had given them to her for Christmas, and she fixed the pretty dangling stars on her lobes.

Now if she could manage to stay on her feet all night—since sitting down in that dress wasn't an option—she'd be fine.

"Oh, you look wonderful" were the first words out of Lily's mouth when Willa came downstairs. "Just wonderful," she repeated, dancing to the landing in something floaty and winter white. "Tess, come see. Willa looks fabulous."

Tess's comment was a grunt as she stepped out of the room looking dangerous in basic black. "Not half bad," she decided, secretly thrilled with the results as she tapped her pearl choker and circled Willa. "A little makeup and you'll do."

"I have makeup on."

"Christ, the woman has eyes like a goddess and doesn't know how to use them. Come on."

"I'm not going back up there and glopping gunk on my face," Willa protested as Tess dragged her back up the stairs.

"Honey, for what I pay, it's first-class gunk. Hold the fort, Lily."

"All right. Don't be long, though." And she beamed after them, flushed with the warmth of sisterhood.

She wished they could see how much fun they were together, from her point of view. Squabbling, just as she imagined sisters would. And now sharing clothes, makeup, dressing for a party together.

She was so grateful to be a part of it all. Giving in to the thrill, she spun in a circle, then stopped short when she saw Adam standing in the hall behind her.

"I didn't hear you come in."

"I came in the back." He could have looked at her endlessly, the dark-haired fairy in a floating white dress. "You look beautiful, Lily."

"Thank you."

She felt very nearly beautiful. But he, he was so outrageous, so perfect in every detail, she could barely believe he was real. A thousand times over the past months she'd longed to touch him. Not just a hand, a brush of shoulders, but to touch him. Part of her was certain he would be offended or amused, and that she wouldn't risk.

"I'm glad you're here," she said, speaking too quickly now. "Tess took Will back up for some last-minute touches, and people will start coming any minute. I don't do very well playing hostess. I never know what to say."

She stepped back as he stepped forward, then made herself stop. Her heart turned over when he brushed his fingers down her cheek. "You'll be fine. They won't know what to say either, once they look at you. I don't."

"I—" Oh, she would make a fool of herself now, she was certain, with this need to fling herself into his arms and be held close. Just to be held. "I should help Bess. In the kitchen."

"She's got everything under control." He kept his eyes on hers and his moves slow as he reached for her hand. "Why don't we pick out some music? We might even squeeze in a dance before anyone comes."

"I haven't danced in a long time."

"You'll dance tonight," he promised, and led her into the great room.

They'd no more than made their initial selections and filled the CD player when the first headlights glanced off the window.

"Promise me the midnight dance," he said, twining their fingers together again.

"Of course. I'm nervous," she admitted with a quick smile. "Stay close, won't you?"

"As long as you need me." He glanced over as Tess and Willa came down, sniping at each other. Because it was expected, and warranted, Adam let out a heartfelt whistle. Tess winked. Willa scowled.

"I'm going to want a drink, as soon as possible." Hissing through her teeth, Willa strode to the door and greeted the first guests.

Within an hour, the house was filled with people and voices and clashing scents. Apparently no one was too weary to attend another holiday party, too jaded to drink another glass of champagne, or too restrained to refrain from discussing politics and religion. Or their neighbors and friends.

Willa remembered why she didn't care for socializing when Bethanne Mosebly sidled up to her and began to pump her for details of the murder.

"We were all shocked to hear about what happened to John Barker." Bethanne inhaled champagne between sentences with such fervor that Willa was tempted to offer her a straw. "Must have been a terrible shock for you."

Though Willa didn't immediately snap to John Barker and Pickles being one and the same, Bethanne's greedily excited eyes tipped her off. "It's not an experience I'm looking to repeat. Excuse me, I'm just going to—"

That was as far as she got before Bethanne's hand clamped down on her arm. "They said he was cut to pieces." She toasted the fact with another gulp of champagne, leaving her small bird's mouth wet and gleaming. "Just hacked to ribbons." The long needle fingers pinched harder. "And scalped."

It was the glee that sickened her, even more than the image that burst full-blown into her brain. Even knowing that Bethanne had no harm in her other than an overly well-developed affection for chatter and gossip, Willa had to fight off a shudder.

"He was dead, Bethanne, and it was brutal. Too bad I didn't have my video camera for pictures at eleven."

The disgust and sarcasm couldn't puncture the avid interest. Bethanne inched closer, giving Willa an unwelcome whiff of wine, Scope, and Obsession. "They say it could have been anyone, anyone at all who did it. Why, you could be murdered in your own bed any night of the week. Why, I was just telling Bob on the drive here how much it's been on my mind."

Willa forced her lips into a thin smile. "I'll sleep easier knowing you're so worried about it. You're out of champagne, Bethanne. The bar's that way."

Willa ducked away, then kept moving. Her one thought was to find air. How could anyone breathe with so many people gulping up the oxygen? she wondered. She pushed her way into the hall and didn't stop until she reached the front door, wrenched it open, and found herself face-to-face with Ben.

He gawked at her, and she fumbled. Recovering before he did, she shoved past him and strode over to lean on the porch rail. It was cold enough now to send her breath steaming in clouds, to make the chill bumps rise on her skin. But the air was fresh as a wish, and that was exactly what she needed.

When his hands came to her shoulders and turned her around, she ground her teeth. "The party's inside."

"I wanted to make sure I wasn't hallucinating."

No, he thought, she was real enough. Cool, bare skin shivered a bit under his hands. Those big doe eyes seemed even darker, even larger. The bold blue of the dress gleamed in the starlight and clung intimately to every curve and angle before it stopped dead, teasingly high on long, firm thighs.

"God Almighty, Will, you look good enough to eat in three quick bites. And you're going to freeze your pretty butt off standing out here."

His coat was already open. He made use of it by stepping forward and wrapping it around her, enjoying the added benefit of having that tight little body pressed up hard to his.

"Turn me loose." She squirmed, but he had her caught, arms pinned, body trapped. "I came out here to be alone for five damn minutes."

"Well, you should've put on a coat." Pleased with the situation, he sniffed at her—more like a dog than a lover—and heard her muffling a chuckle. "Smell good."

"That idiot Tess, spraying stuff on me." But she was beginning to relax again in the warmth. "Gunking up my face."

"It looks good gunked." He grinned when she tipped it back to his, eyeing him pityingly.

"What's wrong with men, anyway, that they fall for this kind of stuff? What's so hot about looks that come out of pots and tubes?"

"We're weak, Will. Weak and foolish and easy. Wanna neck?" He rooted at her throat and made her laugh.

"Cut it out, McKinnon. You ass." But her arms were around his waist now, comfortable, and she'd forgotten what had put her in such a foul mood. "You're late," she added. "Your parents are already here, and Zack and Shelly. I thought you weren't coming."

"I got hung up." He kissed her before she could duck, drew the kiss out when she forgot to protest. "Miss me?"

"No."

"Liar."

"So?" Because he was grinning just a bit too smugly, she looked over his shoulder, through the brightly lit window at the crowd of people. "I hate parties. Everybody just stands around and yaks. What's the point?"

"Social and cultural interaction. A chance to dress up, drink for free, and ogle each other. I'm planning on ogling you once we're back inside. Unless you'd rather go off to the horse barn and let me get you out of that pretty dress."

More intrigued with the prospect than she wanted to be, she lifted a brow. "Are those my only choices?"

"We could use my rig, but it wouldn't be as cozy."

"Why do men think about sex day and night?"

"Because thinking's the closest thing to doing. You got anything on under this?"

"Sure. I had to slick myself down with oil to get it on."

He winced, tried not to moan. "I deserved that. Let's go inside and stand around and yak."

When he stepped back, the cold hit her like a slap. She shivered her way to the door. Still, she stopped with her hand on the knob, turned to him. "Ben, why have you suddenly developed this thing about getting my clothes off?"

"There's nothing sudden about it."

He opened the door himself, nudged her inside. Very much at home, he shrugged out of his coat and tossed it over the newel post. Unlike Willa, he liked parties just fine, the noise and fuss and smells of them. People deep in conversation were sitting on the staircase with plates of food. Others jammed into the hall, spilled back through the open doors of other rooms. Most had a greeting for him, or a few words to exchange as he kept one hand firmly on Willa's arm to prevent her escape.

Escape was what she had in mind, he knew, but he had a point to make. He was going to make it to her, and to everyone—including several duded-up cowhands who had their eye on her. The end of the old year, the beginning of the new with all its mysteries and possibilities seemed like the perfect time.

"If you'd turn loose of me a minute," she muttered close to his ear, "I could—"

"I know what you could. I'm hanging on. Get used to it."

"What the hell's that supposed to mean?" She could only swear under her breath as he tugged her into the great room.

Guests had moved back, making room for dancing. Ben grabbed a beer on his way and watched with pleasure as his parents executed a quick, intricate two-step.

"You can tell something about people who dance together that way," he said.

Willa looked up at him. "What?"

"They know each other inside and out. And like what they see on both sides. Now, take them." He inclined his head toward Nate and Tess, who were swaying—you couldn't call it dancing—on the edge of the crowd and grinning at each other. "They don't know each other yet, not all the way, but they're having a hell of a good time finding out."

"She's just using him for sex."

"And he looks all broken up about it, doesn't he?" With a chuckle, Ben set his beer aside. "Come on."

Horrified, she pulled back, trying to dig in those unfamiliar heels as he towed her to the dance floor. "I can't. I don't want to. I don't know how."

"So learn." He put a firm hand on her waist, positioned hers on his shoulder.

"I don't dance. Everybody knows I don't dance."

He merely propped the hand she'd taken away back on his shoulder again. "Sometimes you can go a long way following someone who knows where he's going."

He swung her around so it was either move her feet or fall on her butt. She felt miserably clumsy, embarrassingly spotlighted. And held herself rigid as a board.

"Relax," he murmured in her ear. "It doesn't have to hurt. Look at Lily there. Pretty as a picture with her face all flushed and her hair mussed. Brewster's having the time of his life teaching her to two-step."

"She looks happy."

"She is. And Jim Brewster'll be half in love with her before the dance is over. Then he'll partner up with another woman and fall half in love with her." Because she was thinking about that and forgetting to pull back, he eased her a little closer. "That's the beauty of dancing. You get your hands on a woman, get the feel of her, the scent of her."

"And move on to the next."

"Sometimes you do. Sometimes you don't. Look here a minute, Willa."

She did, saw the flicker in his eye, and barely had time to blink in shock before his mouth was on hers. He kissed her slow and deep, a stunning contrast to the quick moves of the dance. Her heart circled giddily in her chest, then seemed to plop over and thud to bursting.

She was moving with him when he lifted his head. "Why did you do that?"

The answer was simple, and he planned to be honest. "So all the men eyeing you know whose brand you're wearing these days." And he wasn't disappointed in her reaction. Her eyes went wide with shock, then narrowed with fury. Her skin went rosy with it. Even as she hissed, he clamped his lips to hers again. "You might as well get used to that, too," he told her. Then he stepped back. "I'll get you a drink."

He figured by the time he got back with it, she wouldn't be tempted to throw it in his face.

Willa was thinking more about shredding his face, layer by layer, when Shelly bustled up to her. "You and Ben. I didn't have a clue. That man can keep secrets from God." As she spoke, she steered Willa toward a corner. "When did all this start? What's going on?"

"It hasn't. Nothing." Temper percolated dangerously. She could feel it, physically feel it, bubble under her skin. "That son of a bitch. Branding me. He said he was branding me."

"He did?" A romantic through and through, Shelly patted a hand to her heart. "Oh, my. Zack never said anything like that to me."

"Which is why he's still breathing."

"Are you kidding? I'd love it." She burst out laughing at Willa's stunned gape. "Come on, Will, macho arrogance is sexy in small doses. I get all gooey inside when Zack flexes his muscles."

Willa shifted, looked hard into Shelly's eyes. "How much have you had to drink?"

"I'm not drunk, and I'm not kidding. And sometimes he just scoops me up and tosses me over his shoulder. With the baby it's not quite as spontaneous, but boy, does it work."

"For you, maybe. I don't like pushy men."

"I know. It was horrible the way everyone just stood around while you were beating Ben off." Shelly drawled it out, dipped a finger in her wine, licked it off. "Anyone could see how much you detested being kissed brainless."

Willa searched for an intelligent, pithy response. "Shut up, Shelly" was the best she could do before she stalked off.

"The cowgirl's got a bur up her butt," Tess commented.

"Ben likes to irritate her."

Tess raised an eyebrow at Nate. "I think he'd like to do more than that."

"Looks like. Speaking of doing more than that." He leaned down and whispered a suggestion in her ear that made her blood pressure spike. "Lawyer Torrence, you do have a way with words."

"We could slip out, go to my place, and see the new year in more . . . privately. Nobody'd miss us."

"Um." She turned so that her breasts nestled against his chest. "Too far. Upstairs. My room. Five minutes."

His eyes widened. "With all these people in the house?"

"And a nice sturdy lock on the door. Top of the stairs turn left, make the first right, three doors down on the right." She skimmed her fingertips over his jaw. "I'll be waiting."

"Tess, I think—"

But she was already gliding away, with one smoldering look back over her shoulder. He could have sworn he heard his brain cells die. He took two steps after her, stopped, and tried to be sensible.

The hell with it. He hadn't been sensible since she'd swaggered into his office with sex on her mind. It didn't even matter that he was falling headlong in love and she wasn't even close to tripping. They fit. Whether she saw it or not, it had clicked for him.

Hoping to be discreet, he snagged a bottle of champagne and two glasses. And made it as far as the base of the stairs.

"Private party?" Ben asked, then chuckled at the flush that spread up Nate's throat. "Give Tess a Happy New Year's kiss from me."

"Get your own woman."

"I aim to."

But he took his time cooking her out and pinning her down again. His goal was to have her firmly planted in his arms at midnight. He gave her plenty of rope, and as the countdown began, firmly reeled her in.

"Don't you start on me again."

"Only a minute to go," he said easily. "I always think of that last minute between years as untime." When her brow furrowed, he knew he had her attention and slid his arms around her. "Not now, not then. Not anything. If we were alone, I could do what I want with you for those sixty seconds. But it wouldn't be real. So I'm going to wait till it is. Put your arms around me. It doesn't count yet. Not for seconds yet."

She couldn't hear anything but his voice, none of the noise, the laughter, the excited countdown of time penetrated. As if in a dream, she lifted her arms, wound them around his neck.

"Tell me you want me," he murmured. "It doesn't count. Not yet."

"I do. But I don't—"

"No buts. It doesn't matter." He slid a hand up, over her bare back, under her hair. "Kiss me. It's not real, not yet. You kiss me, Willa. Just once, you kiss me."

She angled in, kept her eyes open and her mind blank as she fit her lips to his. So warm, so welcoming, so unexpectedly gentle that she shuddered in reaction. And time ran out on her.

Cheers echoed somewhere in the back of her head. People jostled her in their hurry to exchange New Year's greetings. And as the seconds slid away from the end to the beginning, her heart ached with it.

"It is real." It was as much accusation as statement when she drew away. Her eyes glittered with the fresh awareness, and the fear of it. "It is."

"Yeah." He stunned her by taking her hand, bringing it to his lips. "Starting now." He slid an arm around her waist, kept her close to his side. "Look there, darling." He shifted her just a little. "That's a pretty sight."

Even through her own confusion, she had to admit it was. Adam, with his hands cupped on Lily's face, and Lily's fingers holding his wrists.

See how their eyes meet and hold, she thought. How her lips tremble just a little, how gently he brushes them with his. And how they stay there, just so, fixed in that bare whisper of a kiss.

"He's in love with her," Willa murmured. Emotions churned inside her. Too much to feel, she thought with a hand pressed to her stomach. Too much to think, too much to wonder. "What's going on? I wish I could understand what's going on. Nothing's the same anymore. Nothing's simple anymore."

"They can make each other happy. That's simple."

"No." She shook her head. "No, it won't be. Can't you feel it? There's something . . ." She shuddered again, because she could feel it. And it was cold, and vicious and close. "Ben, there's something—"

That was when the screaming started.

14

There wasn't much blood. The police would conclude that she had been killed elsewhere, then brought to the ranch. No one recognized her. Her face was largely unmarred. Just a bruise under the right eye.

Her hair was gone.

Her skin was faintly blue. That Willa had seen for herself when she rushed outside and found young Billy struggling to calm Mary Anne Walker after they'd stumbled over the body. She was naked, and her skin had crisscrossing slashes in it like hatch marks on a drawing.

Very little blood, and what there was had dried on that pale blue skin.

Mary Anne had been sick right there on the front steps. And Billy had soon followed suit, chucking up his share of the beer he'd guzzled in the rig while he was busy getting Mary Anne's panties down to her ankles.

Willa had gotten them both back inside and ordered everyone who was crowding out on the porch, gawking and talking at once, to come back inside. She told herself she would think about the woman later, the woman with the blue skin and no hair who was dead at the foot of the steps.

She would think about that later.

"Bess has already called the police." Adam laid a hand on her arm, waiting until her eyes shifted to his. The voices around them were too loud, too frightened. "I should go out there with Ben, stay with—stay with her until the police come. Can you handle this?"

"Yes." She looked up in relief as Nate came rushing down the stairs. "Yes, go on. Outside," she said, reaching for Nate's hand. "Please, go out with Ben and Adam. There's . . . there's another."

She turned and started into the great room. Stu McKinnon had already shut off the music, was using his strong, soothing voice to calm the guests. Willa let him take charge for the moment, while she just stood there staring at her father's portrait over the fireplace. Those cold blue eyes stared back at her. She could almost see him sneering at her, blaming her.

Barefoot, her dress not quite zipped, Tess barreled down the steps just as Lily came rushing down the hall. "What happened? Someone was screaming."

"There's been another murder." Lily gripped Tess's hand hard. "I didn't see. Adam wouldn't let me go out, but it's a woman. No one seems to know who she is. She was just there. Just there in front of the house."

"Oh, my God." Tess pressed her free hand to her mouth, forced herself to stay in control. "Happy fucking New Year. Okay." She took a deep breath. "Let's do whatever comes next."

They stepped up to Willa, instinctively flanking her. None of them was fully aware that they had linked hands.

"I don't know her," Willa managed. "I don't even know her."

"Don't think about it now." Tess tightened her grip on Willa's hand. "Don't think about it. Let's just get through this."

Hours later, just as dawn broke, she felt a hand on her shoulder. She'd fallen asleep, God knew how, in front of the living room fire. She jerked away, struggled away as Ben tried to lift her.

"I'm taking you upstairs. You're going to bed."

"No." She got to her feet. Her head was eerily light, her body numb, but her heart was pounding again. "No, I can't." Dazed, she stared around the room. The remnants of the party were all there. Glasses and plates, food going stale, ashtrays overflowing. "Where—"

"Everyone's gone. The last of the police left ten minutes ago."

"They said they wanted to talk to me again."

Take me into the library again, she thought, question me again. Take me through the steps again. And again. All leading to that moment when she had rushed outside to see two terrified teenagers and a dead woman with pale blue skin.

"What?" She pressed a hand to her head. Ben's voice was like a buzz in the front of her brain.

"I said I told them they could talk to you later."

"Oh. Coffee? Is there any coffee left?"

He'd already had a good look at her, curled in the chair, her white face a hard contrast to the dark shadows under her eyes. She might be standing at the moment, but he knew it was only sheer will that kept her on her feet. And that was simple enough to deal with. He lifted her off them and into his arms.

"You're going to bed. Now."

"I can't. I have . . . things to do." She knew there were dozens of things to do but couldn't seem to think of even one. "Where . . . my sisters?"

His eyebrows lifted as he carried her up the steps. He figured she was too punchy to realize it was the first time she'd called Lily and Tess her sisters. "Tess went up an hour ago. Lily's with Adam. Ham can handle whatever needs to be done today. Go to sleep, Will. That's all you need to do."

"They asked so many questions." She didn't protest, couldn't, when he laid her on her bed. "Everybody asking questions. And the police, taking people into the library, one at a time."

She looked at him then, into his eyes—cold green now, she thought. Cold and hard and unreadable. "I didn't know her, Ben."

"No." He slipped off her shoes, debated with himself briefly, then gritted his teeth and turned her over to unzip her dress. "They'll check missing persons reports, check her prints."

"Hardly any blood," she murmured, quiet as a child as he slid the dress down. "Not like before. She didn't seem real, not like a person at all. Do you think he knew her? Did he know her when he did that to her?"

"I don't know, darling." And as tenderly as if she'd been a child, he tucked her under the blankets. "Put it away for now." Sitting on the edge of the bed, he stroked her hair. "Just let it go and sleep."

"He blames me." Her voice was thick and drunk with exhaustion.

"Who blames you?"

"Pa. He always did." And she sighed. "He always will."

Ben left his hand on her cheek a moment. "And he was always wrong."

When he rose and turned, he saw Nate in the doorway.

"She out?" Nate asked.

"For now." Ben laid the dress over a chair. "Knowing Will, she won't sleep long."

"I talked Tess into taking a pill." He smiled wanly. "Didn't take much talking." He gestured down the hall. Together they walked to Willa's office, shut the door. "It's early," Nate said, "but I'm having whiskey."

"Hate to see you drink alone. Three fingers," he added when Nate poured. "Don't think she was from around here."

"No?" Neither did he, but Nate wanted Ben's take. "Why?"

"Well." Ben sipped, hissed through his teeth at the lightning bolt of liquor. "Fingernails and toenails painted up with some shiny purple polish. Tattoos on her butt and her shoulder. Looked like three earrings in each ear. That says city to me."

"Didn't look more than sixteen. That says runaway to me." Nate drank, and drank deep. "Poor kid. Could have been riding her thumb, or working the streets in Billings or Ennis. Wherever this bastard found her, he kept her a while."

Ben's attention sharpened. "Oh?"

"I got a little out of the cops. Abrasions around the wrists and ankles. She'd been tied up. They couldn't say for sure until they run the tests, but they seemed fairly sure she'd been raped, and that she'd been dead at least twenty-four hours before he left her here. That adds up to being kept somewhere."

Ben paced it off for a moment, the frustration and disgust. "Why here? Why dump her here?"

"Someone's focused on Mercy."

"Or on someone at Mercy," Ben added, and saw by the look in Nate's eyes that they agreed. "All this started after the old man died, after Tess and Lily came here. Maybe we should start looking closer at them and who'd want to hurt them."

"I'm going to talk to Tess when she wakes up. We know there's an ex-husband in Lily's past. One who liked to knock her around."

Ben nodded and absently rubbed the scar across his chin. "It's a long jump from wife abuse to slicing up strangers."

"Maybe not that long a jump. I'd feel better knowing where the ex is, and what he's up to."

"We feed his name to the cops, hire a detective."

"We're on the same beam there. You know his name?"

"No, but Adam will." Ben downed the rest of the whiskey, set the glass aside. "Might as well get started."

They found him in the stables, examining a pregnant mare. "She's going to foal early," Adam said, as he straightened up. "Another day or two." After a last stroke, he stepped out of the foaling stall, slid the door closed. "Will?"

"Sleeping," Ben told him. "For the moment."

He nodded, moved down the concrete aisle to the grain bin. "Lily's in on my couch. She wanted to help with the morning feeding, but she dropped off while she was waiting for me to change. I'm glad she didn't see it. Tess either." His usual fluid movements were jerky with tension and fatigue. "I'm sorry Will did."

"She'll get through it." Ben moved to a hay net, filled it with fresh. "How much do you know about Lily's ex-husband?"

"Not a lot." Adam continued to work, as unsurprised by the assistance as the question. "His name's Jesse Cooke. They met when she was teaching, got married a couple months later. She left him about a year after that. The first time. She hasn't told me much more, and I haven't been pushing."

"Does she know where he is?" Ignoring his best suit, Nate filled a feeding trough.

"She thinks back East. That's what she wants to think."

For the next few minutes they worked in silence, three men accustomed to the routine, the smells, the work. The stables were lit with the morning sun trailing through the open corral door with hay motes dancing cheerfully in every slanting beam. Horses shifted on fresh bedding, munched on feed, blew an occasional greeting.

From the chicken house a rooster called, and there was the jangle of boots on hard-packed dirt as men went about their chores in the ranch yard. No radio played tinny country this morning, nor was the winter silence broken by the voices of men at work. If glances were tossed toward the main house, the porch, the space beneath, no one commented.

An engine gunned; a rig headed out. And the silence came back, a lingering guest at a party gone wrong.

"You may have to push her a bit now," Ben said at length. "It's an angle we can't afford to ignore. Not after this."

"I've already thought of that. I want her to get some rest first. Goddamn it." The grain scoop Adam held snapped at the handle with the quick flex of his hands. "She should be safe here."

The temper he rarely acknowledged swirled up so fast, so huge it choked his words. He wanted to pound something, rip something to shreds. But he had nothing. Even his hands were empty now.

"That was a child out there. How could someone do that to a child?"

He whirled on them, his hands in fists, his eyes dark and burning with rage. "How close was he? Was he out there, looking through the windows? Or was he inside with us? Did the son of a bitch touch her, dance with her? If she'd walked outside to get a breath of air, would he have been there?"

He looked down at his hands, opened them to stare at the palms. "I could kill him myself, and it would be easy." His gaze shifted, skimmed both men. "It would be so easy."

"Adam." Lily's voice was hardly a whisper, quiet fear at the edge of his black rage. With her arms crossed, her fingers digging hard into her shoulders, she stepped closer.

"You should be sleeping." His muscles quivered with the effort to hold back the fury. "We're nearly done here. Go on home to bed."

"I need to talk to you." She'd heard enough, seen enough to know the time had come. "Alone, please." She turned to Ben and Nate. "I'm sorry. I need to speak with Adam alone."

"Take her inside," Nate suggested. "Ben and I can finish this. Take her in," he repeated. "She's cold."

"You shouldn't have come out here." Adam moved to her, careful not to touch. "Let's go in, have some coffee."

"I put some on before I came out." She noted that he stayed an arm's length away, and it made her ashamed. "It should be ready now."

He walked her out the back, across the corral fence and to his rear door. From habit, he scraped his boots before going inside.

The kitchen smelled cozily of coffee just brewed, but the light was thin and stingy, and it prompted him to flip the switch and fill the room with hard artificial light.

"Sit down," she began. "I'll get it."

"No." He stepped in front of her as she reached for the cupboard door. Still he didn't touch her. "You sit."

"You're angry." She hated the tremor in her voice, hated the fact that anger from a man, even this man, could turn her knees to water. "I'm sorry."

"For what?" It snapped out of him before he could stop it. Even when she backed up a step, he couldn't block it all. "What the hell have you got to apologize to me for?"

"For everything I haven't told you."

"You don't owe me explanations." The cupboard door slammed against the wall as he wrenched it open. And out of the corner of his eye he saw her jerk in reaction. "Don't flinch from me." He leveled his breathing, kept his eyes on the cups set neatly in rows on the shelves. "Don't do that, Lily. I'd cut off my hands before I'd use them on you that way."

"I know." Tears swam into her eyes and were blinked brutally back. "I know that, in my heart. It's my head, Adam. And I do owe you." She walked to the round kitchen table with its simple white bowl of glossy red apples. "More than explanations. You've been my friend. My anchor. You've been everything I've needed since I came here."

"You don't pay someone back for friendship," he said wearily.

"You wanted me." Her breath hitched once as he turned slowly to face her. "I thought it was just . . . just the usual." Her nervous hands brushed at her hair, at the thighs of the jeans she'd pulled on before leaving the main house that morning. "But you never touched me that way, or pressured me, or made me feel obliged. You can't know what it's like to feel obliged to let someone have you just to keep peace. How degrading that is. I have things to tell you."

She couldn't look at him, turned her face away. "I'll start with Jesse. Could I cook breakfast?"

He held a cup in his hand as he stared at her. "What?"

"It will be easier for me if I have something to do while I talk. I don't know if I can get it out just sitting here."

Since it was what she wanted, he set the cup down, walked to the table, and sat. "There's bacon in the refrigerator. And eggs."

She let out a long, unsteady breath. "Good." She went to the coffee first, poured him a cup. But her gaze avoided his. "I told you a little," she began as she went to the refrigerator. "About how I was teaching. I was never as smart or as creative as my mother. She's amazing, Adam. So strong and vital. I didn't know until I was twelve how much he'd hurt her. My father. I heard her talking to a friend once, crying. She'd just met my stepfather, and she was, I realize now, afraid of her feelings for him. She was talking about preferring to be alone, about never wanting to be vulnerable to a man again. About how my father had turned her out, and she'd been so much in love with him. He'd turned her out, she said, because she hadn't given him a son."

Adam said nothing as she arranged bacon in a black iron frying pan and set it to sizzle. "So it was because of me that she was alone and afraid."

"You know better than that, Lily. It was because of Jack Mercy."

"My heart knows it." She smiled a little. "It's my head again. In any case, I never forgot that. She did marry my stepfather two years later. And they're very happy. He's a wonderful man. He was strict with me. Never harsh, but strict, and a bit remote. It was my mother he wanted, and I came with the package. He wanted the best for me, gave me all he could, but he could never give me the kind of easy affection there might have been between a father and daughter. It was, I guess, too late in starting for us."

"And you were hungry for that easy affection."

"Oh, starved." She whipped eggs in a bowl. "I got a lot of this out of therapy and counseling much later. It's so easy to see it now. I'd never had a warm, loving relationship with a male figure. I'd never had a man focused on me. And I was shy, crushingly shy in school, with boys. I didn't date much, and I was very serious about my studies."

Her smile was a bit more natural as she grated cheese into the eggs. "Terribly serious. I couldn't see things the way my mother could, so I rooted myself in facts and figures. And I was good with children, so teaching seemed a natural course. I was twenty-two and teaching fifth grade when I met Jesse. In a coffee shop near my apartment. My first apartment, the first month I was out on my own. He was so charming, so handsome, so interested in me. I was dazzled."

Automatically she sprinkled dill in the beaten eggs, ground a hint of pepper over them. "I suppose he picked me up. That was a new experience for me. We went to the movies that same evening. And he called me every day after school. Brought me flowers and little gifts. He was a mechanic, and he tuned up this pitiful car I had."

"You fell in love with him," Adam concluded.

"Oh, yes, completely, blindly in love. I never looked past the surface with Jesse, didn't know I should. Later I could pick out the lies he'd told me. About his family, his past, his work. His mother, I found out later, was in an institution. She'd beaten him as a child, she drank and used drugs. So did he, but I never knew until we were married. The first time he hit me . . ."

She trailed off, cleared her throat. For a moment there was only the sound of grease crackling as she took bacon out of the pan.

"It was about a month after we were married. One of my friends at school was having a birthday, and we were going to go to one of those clubs. Silly. Where the men dance and women tuck dollar bills into their jockstraps. Just foolishness. Jesse seemed to think of it that way too, until I was dressing to go. Then he started on what I was wearing, the dress, the hair, the makeup. I laughed, sure that he was teasing me. Suddenly he grabbed my purse, emptied it out, tore up my driver's license. I was so shocked, so angry, I grabbed it back from him. And he knocked me down. He was slapping me, shouting, calling me names. He tore my clothes and he raped me."

With surprisingly steady hands, she poured eggs into the pan. "He cried afterward, like a baby. Huge, racking sobs." She let out a little breath because it was too easy to remember, to see it all again. "Jesse had been in the Marines—he was so proud of that, of his discipline and strength. You can't imagine what it was like to see someone I'd thought was so strong cry that way. It was shocking, and devastating, and in a terrible way empowering."

Strength, Adam thought, had nothing to do with uniforms or biceps. He hoped she'd learned that as well.

"He begged me to forgive him," Lily went on. "Said he'd gone crazy with jealousy, thinking about other men being near me. He said that his mother had left his father when he was a child. Ran off with another man. Before, he had told me she'd died. Both were lies, but I believed him, and I forgave him."

It wasn't easy to be honest, all the way honest, but she wanted to be. "I forgave him, Adam, because it made me feel strong, in that moment. And because I thought if he'd lost control that way it had to be because he loved me. That's part of the trap—the cycle. He didn't hit me again for eight weeks."

Slowly, and with great concentration, she stirred the bubbling eggs. "Doesn't matter what it was over. It was a pattern that I refused to see, that I was just as much responsible for as he was. He started to drink, and he lost his job, and he beat me. I forgot the toast," she said matter-of-factly, and walked over to the bread box.

"Lily—"

She shook her head. "I let him convince me it was my fault. Every time my fault. I wasn't smart enough, sexy enough, quiet enough, loose enough. Whatever the situation called for. It went on for over a year. Twice he put me in the hospital and I lied and said I'd fallen. Then one day I looked at myself in the mirror. I saw what my friends had been seeing all those months, what they saw when they tried to talk to me about it, to help me. The bruises, that animal look in the eye, the bones sharp in my face because I couldn't keep weight on."

She went back to the eggs, turning them gently as they set. "I walked out. I don't remember exactly. I know I didn't take anything, and that I went home to my mother, just like the cliché. I know I was afraid, because he'd told me he would never let me go. That if I ever left, he'd come after me. But I knew I'd kill myself if I stayed even another day. I had thought about it, planned how I would do it. With pills, because I'm a coward."

She arranged the eggs, the toast, the bacon on a plate and brought it to the table. "He came after me," she said, and for the first time looked into Adam's face. "He was waiting for me one day when I went out, and he dragged me to his car. He choked me, screaming at me. He drove off with me half unconscious beside him. He was calmer then, explaining things to me the way he'd always done. Why I was wrong, why I needed to be taught how a wife was supposed to behave. I was more terrified then than I'd ever been before. When he was calm, I was more afraid of what he would do—could do to me."

She steadied herself, because the fear could sneak back at any time, peck away at her faltering courage. "He had to slow down for traffic, and I jumped out. The car was still moving, but I didn't fall. I always thought it was a miracle. I went to the police and got a restraining order. I started to move around. He always found me. The last time, the time before I came here, he found me again, and I think he would've killed me that time, but a neighbor heard me screaming and beat at the door. Started breaking in the door. And Jesse ran."

She sat, folded her hands on the table. "So did I. I didn't think he could find me here. I've barely contacted my mother because I was afraid he'd get to me through her. But I spoke with her this morning, before I came out to the stables. She hasn't seen him or heard from him." She drew a deep breath. "I know that you and Ben and Nate are going to talk to the police about this. I'll answer any questions about him. But he never hurt anyone but me that I know of. And he only ever used his hands. It seems that if he had found me, he would have come after me."

"He'll never hurt you again." He nudged the plate aside so he could cover her hands with his. "Whatever the answers are, Lily, he'll never touch you again. I swear it."

"If it is him . . ." She squeezed her eyes tight. "If it is, Adam, then I'm responsible. I'm responsible for two people's lives."

"No, you're not."

"If it is him," she continued calmly, "I have to face that, and live with it. I've been hiding here, Adam, using you and Will and this place to keep all the bad things away. It doesn't work." She sighed, turned her hands over in his. "I have to face it. I learned that in therapy too. I don't have courage, not the natural kind like Will and Tess have. What I have has been learned, practiced. I was afraid to tell you all this, and now I wish I had told you right from the start. It would make the rest of this easier."

"There's more?"

"Not about Jesse, and not about the horrible things, but it's hard."

"You can tell me anything."

"With all that happened last night, my mind keeps coming back and rerunning this one moment." With a nervous laugh, she drew her hands out from under his. "I wish you'd eat. It's going cold."

"Lily." Baffled, he pressed his fingers to his eyes, then obediently shifted his plate, lifted his fork. "What one moment?"

"It's just that I thought, as I was saying before, that you wanted me, that it was the usual. I didn't see how it could be anything but, well, that knee-jerk sort of response men have. Pheromones." She glanced up, wary as he choked. "It seemed that way," she said, defensive now. "And you never said or did anything to indicate otherwise. Until last night. And that moment when you took my face in your hands, and you looked at me. And everything went away but you when you kissed me. Everything went away except you, then it all went wrong, but for that moment, just that one moment, it was so lovely."

She rose quickly, hurried to the stove. "I know it was New Year's. People kiss at midnight, and it doesn't mean—"

"I love you, Lily."

The words slid through her like hope. She caught them, held them to her, and turned. He stood now, only a step behind her, the thin winter sunlight on his hair, and his eyes only for her.

"I fell in love the minute I saw you. But then, I'd been waiting for you all my life. Just for you." He held out a hand. "Only for you."

Joy broke through the hope, a hot, bubbling geyser through a calm pool. "It's so simple really." She took his hand. "When it's right, it's so simple." And went into his arms. "I don't want to be anywhere but with you."

"We're home here." He buried his face in her hair. "Stay with me."

"Yes." She turned her lips to his throat, caught the first sharp flavor of him. "I've wanted you to touch me. Adam, touch me now."

He cupped her face, as he had before. Kissed her, as he had before. But this time her arms came around him, and her response was soft and sweet and shy. When he drew her away, he didn't have to ask, but led her out of the kitchen into the bedroom with its tidily made bed and simple window shades.

Then he touched her hair, stepped back to give her room to decide. "Is it too soon?"

The wanting trembled inside her. "No, it's perfect. You're perfect."

Turning, he pulled the shades so that the sun pulsed gold behind them and turned morning into dusk inside the small room. She took the first step, and it was easier than she could have imagined. She sat on the side of the bed, the color high in her cheeks as she removed her boots. He sat beside her, did the same, then kissed her, quietly.

"Are you afraid?"

It was a wonder to her that she wasn't. Nervous, yes, but without real fear. She knew the flavor of real fear, and its bitter aftertaste, well. Shaking her head, she rose and lifted her hands to the buttons of her shirt.

"I just don't want you to be disappointed."

"The woman I love is going to lie with me. How could I be disappointed?"

Watching him, alert for every response, she slipped the shirt off her shoulders. For a moment, she held it bunched in front of her breasts. She would remember this, Lily thought, every moment of this. Every word, every movement, every breath.

He stood, walked to her. A hand on her shoulder first, a light stroke along the curve, his eyes on hers. Gently, he took the shirt from her, let it fall. His gaze lowered, as did his hands, both skimming softly over the tops of her breasts.

She let her eyes close as his fingers trailed, dipped, traced. Then she opened them slowly to unfasten the buttons of his shirt, draw the flannel aside, then watch the pale skin of her hands glide over the smooth copper of his chest.

"I want to feel you against me." He murmured it as he unhooked her bra, slid the straps down, let it slip to the floor between them. Gathering her close, he held her. A tremor rippled through him, a calm lake disturbed by a lazy finger. "I won't hurt you, Lily."

"No." Of that she could be certain. Of that she could be sure, as his lips lowered to test the skin of her shoulders, her throat. There would be no pain here, not even that of embarrassment. Here there was trust, and desire could be kind.

She didn't jump when his fingers tugged at the snap of her jeans. She shuddered, but not with fear, as he slid the denim down over her hips, murmuring to her as he helped her step free.

Her heart quaked when he stripped off his own jeans, but it quaked in delight and wonder and keen anticipation.

He was so beautiful, that golden skin taut over lean muscles, that sleek, shiny hair skimming strong shoulders. And he wanted her, wanted to belong to her. It was, to Lily, a fine, glittering miracle.

"Adam." She sighed out his name as they lowered themselves to the bed. "Adam Wolfchild." With the good, solid weight of him pressing her into the mattress, she wrapped her arms tight around his neck, drew his mouth down to hers. "Love me."

"I do. I will."

. . .

While they celebrated life in a shadowy room, another celebrated death in the daylight. Deep in the forest, alone and gleeful, he studied the trophies he'd so carefully arranged in a metal box. Prizes of the kill, he thought, stroking the long golden hair of a young girl who'd taken a wrong turn.

Her name was Traci; she'd told him when he'd offered her a ride. Traci with an *I*. She claimed to be eighteen, but he'd seen the lie in that. Her face was pudgy still with baby fat, but her body, when he took her into the hills later and stripped her, was female enough.

It had been so easy. A young girl with her thumb out along the side of the road. A purple knapsack slung over her shoulders, tight jeans showing off her short legs. And that bright gold hair, out of a bottle, of course, but it had gotten his attention, gleaming like gilded fire in the sun. Her fingernails had been painted to match the knapsack, a bright, unnatural purple.

Later, he'd seen that her toes were accented with the same color.

He'd let her ramble a while, he remembered as he stroked the hair. Getting out of Dodge, she said, and laughed. That's where she was from—Dodge City, Kansas.

"You're not in Kansas anymore," he told her, and nearly fell over laughing at his own wit.

He'd let her ramble a while, he thought again, about how she was going to work her way up to Canada, and see some of the world. She took gum out of her sack, offered him some. He found four neatly rolled joints in it later, but had she offered him any of that? No, indeedy.

He knocked her unconscious, one quick fist to the cheek that had rolled her eyes back white. And he took her up into the hills, to where it was quiet, and private, and he could do whatever he liked.

He liked to do quite a lot.

He raped her first. A man had his priorities. Tied her up good and tight so she couldn't use those purple nails to scratch. She screamed herself hoarse, bucking and squiggling on that narrow cot while he did things to her, used things on her.

Smoked her pot and did it all again.

She begged and pleaded with him to let her go. Then she begged and pleaded some more when she saw he was going to leave her there, tied up and naked.

But a man had responsibilities, and he wasn't able to stay.

When he came back, twenty-four hours later, he could have sworn she was happy to see him, the way she cried. So he did her again, and when he told her to say how much she liked it, she agreed that she had. She told him everything he wanted to hear.

Until she saw the knife.

It had taken him more than an hour to clean up the blood, but it had been worth it. Well worth it. And the best part, the very best part, had been the inspiration of dumping what was left of Traci with an *I* from Dodge City, Kansas, right at the doorstep of Mercy Ranch.

Oh, that had been sweet.

Tenderly, he kissed the bloodied hair, placed it carefully in the box.

They were all running scared now, he thought as he put the box back in its hole, rebuilt the small cairn over it. All of them trembling in their shoes. Afraid of him.

When he rose, lifted his face to the cold winter sun, he knew he was the biggest man in Montana.

15

If anyone had told Tess she would spend a frigid January night in a horse stall kneeling in blood and birth fluid and enjoy every minute of it, she would have given them the name of her agent's psychiatrist.

But that's exactly what she had done. For the second night running. She had seen two foals born, even had a small part in it. And it thrilled her.

"Sure as hell gets your mind off your problems, doesn't it?" She stood back with Adam and Lily as the newborn struggled to gain its feet for the first time.

"You've got a nice touch with horses, Tess," Adam told her.

"I don't know about that, but it's keeping me sane. Everybody's so jumpy. I came out of the chicken house yesterday and walked right into Billy. I don't know which of us jumped higher."

"It's been ten days." Lily rubbed her hands together to warm them. "It's starting to seem unreal. I know Will has talked to the police several times, but there's still nothing."

"Look." Adam slid an arm around her shoulders, drew her to his side as the foal began to nurse. "That's real."

"And so's the ache in my back." Tess pushed a hand to it. It was as good an excuse as any to leave them alone. And she thought a hot bath and a few hours' sleep would set her up for a visit to Nate's. "I'm going in."

"You were a big help, Tess. I appreciate it."

Grinning, she picked up her hat, settled it on her head. "Christ. If my friends could see me now." She chuckled over the idea as she walked out of the stables and into the wild cold of the morning.

What would they say at her favorite beauty salon if she walked in like this, with God knew what under her nails, jeans and flannel smeared with afterbirth, her hair . . . well, that didn't bear thinking of, and not a lick of makeup.

She imagined that Mr. William, her stylist, would topple over in a dead faint on his pink carpet.

Well, she thought, the entire experience was going to make for some fascinating cocktail conversation once she was back in LA. She visualized herself at some tony party in Beverly Hills, regaling her hostess with tales of shoveling manure, gathering eggs, castrating cows—that part she would embellish—and riding the range.

A far cry, Tess mused, from the fancy vanity ranches some of the Hollywood set indulged in. Then she would add that there'd also been some psychopath on the loose.

She shuddered and drew her coat closer. Put it out of your mind, she told herself. Doesn't help to think about it.

Then she saw Willa on the porch, just standing on the second step staring out at the hills. Frozen, Tess thought, like Midas's daughter at his touch. Not a clue, Tess realized, what a picture she made. Willa was the only woman in Tess's acquaintance who had no real concept of her own power as a female. For Willa it was all work, the land, the animals, the men.

She was working at perfecting a sarcastic comment when she drew up close enough to see Willa's face. Devastated. Her hat dangled at her back over that black waterfall of loose hair. Her back was straight as an arrow, her chin angled. She should have appeared confident, even arrogant. But her eyes were haunted and blind with what might have been guilt or grief.

"What is it?"

Willa blinked, the only movement she made. She didn't turn her head, didn't shift her feet. "The police were just here."

"Now?"

"Just a little while ago." She'd lost track of the time already, couldn't have said how long she'd been standing there in the cold.

"You look like you need to sit down." Tess came up one step, then two. "Let's go in."

"They found out who she was." Willa still didn't move, but her gaze shifted until it rested on the space at the bottom of the steps. "Her name was Traci Mannerly. She was sixteen. She lived in Dodge City with her parents and her two younger brothers. She'd run away from home, this was the second time, about six weeks ago."

Tess shut her eyes. She hadn't wanted a name, she hadn't wanted details. It was easier to get through the day without them. "Let's go in."

"They told me she'd been dead at least twelve hours before we found her here. She'd been tied up, at the wrists and the ankles. There were rope burns and abrasions where she'd tried to get free."

"That's enough."

"And she'd been raped. They said repeatedly, and sodomized. And she was... she was two months pregnant. She was pregnant and she was sixteen and she was from Kansas."

"That's enough," Tess said again. There were tears spilling out of her eyes as she wrapped her arms around Willa.

They swayed there, on the step, weeping and holding tight and hardly aware of it. A hawk screamed overhead. The clouds bundled up to block the sun and threaten snow. They stood together, clutched by the fear and grief only women fully understand.

"What are we going to do?" Tess shuddered out a breath. "Oh, God, what are we going to do?"

"I don't know. I just don't know anymore." Willa didn't pull away. Even as she realized they were holding tight to each other in the rising wind, she stayed where she was. "I can run this place. Even with all this I can do it. But I don't know if I can stand thinking about that girl."

"It doesn't do any good to think about it. We can think about why, why he brought her here. We can think about that. But not about her. And we can think about us." She eased back, scrubbed the tears from her face. "We'd better start thinking about us. I think Lily and I need lessons in how to handle a gun."

Willa stared at her a moment, began to see more than the glossy Hollywood façade. "I'll teach you." She took a steadying breath, slipped her hat back into place. "We'll get started now."

"It's a worrisome thing," Ham commented over his midday bowl of chili.

Jim helped himself to a second bowl and winked at Billy. "What's that, Ham?"

The answer waited, and the sound of gunfire echoed. "A woman with a gun," Ham said in his slow, dry voice. "More worrisome is three women with three guns."

"Tell you the truth"—Jim dumped a biscuit into his bowl and took a hefty bite—"that Tess looks mighty sexy with a rifle on her shoulder."

Ham eyed him pityingly. "Boy, you ain't got enough work to occupy you."

"No amount of work ought to keep a man from looking at a pretty woman. Right, Billy?"

"Right."

Though, for himself, Billy hadn't given women much thought since the night of the New Year's party. Bouncing on Mary Anne in the rig had been just fine and dandy. But the awful experience of finding the body with her had put a pall over the entire event.

"Scary, though," he said with his mouth full. "They've been at it better than a week, and I ain't seen Tess hit a target yet. Makes a man leery of going out of doors while the shooting's going on."

"Tell you what I think." Jim thumped a burp out of his chest and rose. "I think what they need is a man to show them how it's done. I got a few minutes."

"Nobody needs to show Will what to do with a gun." Quick pride peppered Ham's voice. After all, he'd been the one to teach her how to shoot. "She can outshoot you or anybody else in Montana with one eye closed. Why don't you leave those women alone?"

"I ain't going to touch." Jim shrugged into his coat. "Unless I get the chance."

He stepped outside, and spotted Jesse climbing out of a rig. "Hey, J C." Grinning, he threw up a hand. "Haven't seen you for a couple weeks."

"Been busy." He knew he was taking a chance, a big one, coming over to Mercy in the daylight hours. He visited there as often as he could at night, in the shadows. Often enough to know that his whore-bitch of a wife was spreading her legs for Wolfchild.

But that could wait.

"I was down at Ennis picking up some parts. You had an order come in." He tossed a package at Jim, then skimmed a finger over his moustache. He was beginning to like the feel of it. "Brought it by for you."

"Appreciate it." Jim set the package on the rail. " 'Bout time for poker, I'd say."

"I'm up for it. Why don't you and your boys come around to Three Rocks tonight?" He grinned charmingly. "I'll send you back lighter in the pocket."

"Might just do that." He glanced over at the sound of gunshots, chuckled. "We got us three females at target practice. I was about to give them some pointers."

"Women ought to stay away from guns." Jesse took out a pack of cigarettes, shook one out, offered it.

"They're spooked. You'd have heard about the trouble here."

"Sure." Jesse blew out smoke, wondered if he could risk a glimpse of Lily in the daytime. "Bad business. Kid, wasn't it? From Nebraska?"

"Kansas, I hear. Runaway. Got the shit killed out of her."

"Young girls ought to stay home where they belong." Eyes narrowing, Jesse studied the flame of his cigarette. "Learn how to be wives. Women want to be men these days, you ask me." This time his grin was just a little mean. " 'Course, maybe that don't bother you, seeing as you got a woman for a boss."

Jim's back went up, but he nodded easily enough. "Can't say I care for it much, generally. But Will knows what's what."

"Maybe. The way I hear it, by next fall you'll have three women bosses."

"We'll see." His pleasant anticipation of showing off in front of the women faded. He picked up the package. "Appreciate you dropping this off."

"No problem." Jesse turned back to the rig. "You come on by tonight, and bring money. I'm feeling lucky."

"Yeah." Soured, Jim adjusted his hat, watched the rig drive off. "Asshole," he muttered, and went back in the bunkhouse.

On the makeshift target range, well behind the pole barn, Lily shuddered.

"Getting cold?" Tess asked.

"No. Just a chill." But she caught herself looking over her shoulder, peering against the sun at the glint of it on the chrome of a departing rig. "Someone walked over my grave," she murmured.

"Well, that's cheery." Resuming her stance, Tess drew a bead on the tin can with the little Smith & Wesson Ladysmith—what Willa called a pocket pistol—and fired. Missed by a mile. "Shit."

"You can always beat him over the head with it." Will stepped behind her again, steadied Tess's arm. "Concentrate."

"I was concentrating. It's just a little bullet. If I had a bigger gun, like yours—"

"You'd fall on your ass every time you fired it. You'll use a girl gun until you know what you're doing. Come on, even Lily hits the mark five times out of ten."

"I just haven't found my groove." She fired again, scowled. "That was closer. I know that was closer."

"Yeah, at this rate, you'll be able to hit the side of a barn in a year." Willa drew the single-action Army Colt out of the holster riding low on her hip. The .45 was a lot of gun—weighty and mean—but she preferred it. Showing off only a little, she picked off six cans with six shots.

"Annie Fucking Oakley." Tess sniffed and hated the surge of admiration and envy she felt. "How the hell do you do that?"

"Concentration, a steady hand, and a clear eye." Smiling, she slid the gun back into its sheath. "Maybe you need something more. Hate anybody?"

"Besides you?"

Willa merely raised an eyebrow. "Who was the first guy to dump you and break your heart?"

"No one dumps me, champ." Then her lips pouted. "There was Joey Columbo in sixth grade. Little son of a bitch led me on, then two-timed me with my best friend."

"Put his face over that can standing on the fence rail there and plug one between his eyes."

Teeth set, Tess shifted, aimed. Her finger trembled on the trigger. Then she lowered the gun with a laugh. "Christ, I can't shoot a ten-year-old."

"He's all grown up now, living in Bel Air, and still laughing about the chubby dork he dumped in junior high."

"Bastard." Now her teeth bared as she took her shot. "I nipped it." She shouted it, dancing a bit, and Willa cautiously removed the gun from her hand before Tess could shoot herself in the foot. "It moved."

"Probably the wind."

"Hell it was. I killed Joey Columbo."

"Just a flesh wound."

"He's lying on the ground, watching his life pass in front of his eyes."

"You're starting to enjoy this too much," Lily decided. "I just pretend I'm in one of those arcades at the carnival and I'm trying to win the big stuffed teddy bear." Her cheeks flushed when her sisters both turned and stared at her. "Well, it works for me."

"What color?" Willa asked after a moment. "What color teddy bear?" she elaborated.

"Pink." Lily slanted her eyes left at Tess's chortle of laughter. "I like pink teddy bears. And I've won a good dozen of them while you've been shooting thin air."

"Oh, now she's getting nasty. I think we should have a contest. Not you, killer," Tess said, nudging Willa aside. "Just me and the teddy bear lover." She leaned closer to Lily. "Let's see if you can handle the pressure, sister."

"Then I suggest you reload." Willa bent down for the ammo. "You're both going to be shooting empty."

"What's the winner get?" Carefully reloading, Tess hunkered down. "Besides satisfaction. We need a prize. I do best with clear, set goals."

"Loser does the laundry for a week," Willa decided. "Bess could use a break."

"Oh." Lily rose. "I'd be happy to—"

"Shut up, Lily." With a shake of her head, Willa looked at Tess. "Agreed?"

"Everyone's laundry. Including delicates?"

"Including your fancy French panties."

"By hand. No silks in the washing machine." Satisfied with the deal, Tess stepped back. "You go first," she told Lily.

"Twelve shots each, in two rounds of six. When you're ready, Lily."

"Okay." She took a breath, replayed everything Willa had taught her about stance, breathing. It had taken her days to stop slamming her eyes shut as she squeezed the trigger, and she was proud of her progress. She fired slowly, steadily, and watched four cans fly.

"Four out of six. Not too shabby. Guns down, ladies," Willa ordered as she walked over to reset the targets.

"I can do that." Tess straightened her shoulders. "I can hit all of them. They're all that freckle-faced bastard Joey Columbo. I bet he's on his second divorce by now. Two-timing Kool-Aid swiller."

She shocked everyone, including herself, by knocking three cans from their perch. "I hit that other one. I heard it ping."

"It did," Lily agreed, generously. "We're tied."

"Reload." Enjoying herself, Willa strolled over to reset. When she turned and spotted Nate heading their way, she lifted an arm in salute.

"Hold your fire." He stopped short and threw his hands up when Lily and Tess turned. "I'm unarmed."

"Want to put an apple on your head?" Fluttering her lashes, Tess stepped closer and met him with a kiss.

"Not even for you, Dead Eye."

"We're in the middle of a shoot-off," Willa informed him. "Lily, you're up. I see a giant pink teddy bear in your future." She laughed and set her hands on her hips. "You had to be here," she told Nate, then whooped when Lily hit five out of six. "Sign her up for the Wild West Show. Beat that, Hollywood."

"I can do it."

But her palms were sweaty. She caught a whiff of horses and cologne that was Nate and rolled her tensed shoulders. She took aim, squeezed the trigger, and missed all six shots.

"I was distracted," she claimed as Willa cheered and pulled Lily's hand up over her head. "You distracted me," she told Nate.

"Honey, you're a wonder. Not everybody can hit thin air six times out of six." Nate cautiously took the gun, unloaded or not, out of her hand and gave her a hard kiss in consolation.

Willa smirked. "Don't forget to separate the whites, laundry girl. And pick up your spent shells."

Lily moved close as she and Tess gathered up shells. "I'll help you," she whispered.

"The hell you will. A bet's a bet." Tess cocked her head. "But next time, we arm wrestle."

"I'm heading into Ennis for some supplies." Nate rocked back on his heels and tried, too obviously, not to stare at the denim straining over Tess's butt as she picked up spent shells from the ground. "Thought I'd stop by and see if you needed anything."

Like hell, Willa thought, noting just where his eyes kept wandering. "Thanks, but Bess went in a couple days ago and stocked up."

Tess straightened. "Want some company on the ride?"

"That'd be good."

Her eyes stayed on his as she dumped her handful of shells into Willa's open palm. "I'll just get my purse." She tucked her arm through Nate's and shot a sly look over her shoulder. "Tell Bess I won't be back for dinner."

"Just be back for wash day," Willa shouted after her. "She's got a clamp on his balls all right."

"I think they're nice together," Lily said. "Handsome and easy. His smile just breaks out whenever he sees her."

"That's because he knows his pants are going to end up around his ankles." She laughed at Lily's disapproving look. "Good for them. I just don't get the sex thing, that's all."

"Are you afraid of it?"

The question was so unexpected, considering the source, Willa could only gape. "Huh?"

"I was. Before Jesse, with him. After." Automatically Lily walked over to stack the target cans. "I think it's natural, before, you know. When you just can't know how things will be, whether you'll do something wrong or make a fool of yourself."

"It's pretty basic stuff. What could you do wrong?"

"A lot of things. I did a lot of things wrong. Or thought I did. But I wasn't afraid with Adam. Not when I realized he cared for me. I wasn't afraid at all with Adam."

"Who could be?"

A smile played around Lily's mouth, then she sobered. "You haven't said anything about . . . I know that you know that I'm—with him." She let out a breath, watched it fog in the chilly air, then disappear. "That I'm sleeping with him."

"Really?" Willa tucked her tongue in her cheek. "I thought he waited for you at the side door every night, then walked you back at dawn because you were holding a secret canasta tournament. You mean you're having sex? I'm shocked."

The smile came back. "Adam said we wouldn't fool anyone."

"Why would you want to?"

"He . . . he asked me to move into his house, but I didn't know how you'd feel about it. He's your brother."

"You make him happy."

"I want to." She hesitated, then slipped a chain from under her shirt, keeping her fingers closed around something that dangled from it. "He wants . . . He gave me this."

Stepping closer, Willa looked at what rested in Lily's open palm. It was a simple ring, Black Hills gold etched with a diamond pattern. "It was my mother's," Willa whispered as her throat closed. "Adam's father gave it to her when they were married." She lifted her eyes to Lily. "Adam asked you to marry him."

"Yes." He'd done so beautifully, Lily remembered, with simple words and quiet promises. "I couldn't give him an answer yet. It didn't feel right. I made such a mess of things before—" She broke off, cursed herself. "I was in such a mess before," she corrected. "And I've only been here a few months. I felt I had to speak with you first."

"It has nothing to do with me. It doesn't," Willa insisted when Lily began to protest. "This is between you and Adam, completely. I only have the benefit of being tremendously happy. Take it off the chain, Lily, put it on, and go find him. No, don't cry." She leaned forward and kissed Lily's cheek. "He'll think something's wrong."

"I love him." Lily slipped the chain over her head, slid the ring off. "With everything I have, I love him. It fits," she managed as she put the ring on her finger. "He said it would."

"It fits," Willa agreed, "beautifully. Go on and tell him. I'll finish up here."

As they bumped along the access road, Tess stretched luxuriously.

"You're looking awfully smug for someone who just lost a shoot-out."

"I'm feeling smug. I don't know why." Lowering her arms, she scanned the scenery, the snow-covered mountains, the long lay of the land. "Life's a mess. There's a mad killer still at large and I haven't had a manicure in two months. I'm actually thrilled with the prospect of going into some little bumfuck town and window-shopping. God help me."

"You like your sisters." Nate shrugged at her arch look. "You've gone ahead and bonded despite yourselves. I watched the three of you out there, and I'm telling you, Tess, I saw a unit."

"A common goal, that's all. We're protecting ourselves, and our inheritance."

"Bull."

She scowled, folded her arms. "You're going to wreck my fine mood, Nate."

"I saw the Mercy women. Teamwork, affection."

"The Mercy women." She laughed carelessly, then pursed her lips. It has a ring, doesn't it? she mused. "Maybe I don't think Will's quite as big a pain in the butt as I did. But that's because she's adjusting."

"And you're not?"

"Why would I have to? There was nothing wrong with me." She trailed a finger up his thigh. "Was there?"

"Other than being stuck-up, ornery, and hardheaded, not a thing." He hissed through his teeth when her fingers streaked up, found his weakness, and pinched.

"And you love it." Inspired, she struggled out of her coat.

"Too warm?" Automatically he reached down to adjust the heater.

"It's going to be," she promised, and tugged her sweater over her head.

"What are you doing?" Shock made him nearly run off the road. "Put that back on."

"Uh-uh. Pull over." And she flicked the front hook of her bra so that her breasts spilled out like glory.

"It's a public road. It's broad daylight."

She reached over, tugged down his zipper, and found him hard and ready. "And your point is?"

"You're out of your mind. Anybody could come along and . . . Christ Jesus, Tess," he managed as she slid her head under his arm and clamped her mouth on him. "I'll kill us."

"Pull over," she repeated, but the teasing note had fled. Now there was hoarse and husky need as she tore open his shirt. "Oh, God, I want you inside me. All the way in. Hard, fast. Now."

The rig rocked, the wheels spun, but he managed to get to the shoulder of the road without flipping them over. He jerked on the brake, fought himself free of the seat belt. In one rough move he had her on her back, all but folded on the seat while he struggled with her jeans.

"We'll be arrested," he panted.

"I'll risk it. Hurry."

"We—oh, God." There was nothing under the denim but her. "You should have frozen." Even as he said it he was dragging her hips free. "Why aren't you wearing long johns?"

"I must be psychic." Right now she was simply desperate, and she arched up. Her moan was deep and throaty and melded with his as he rammed himself into her.

Then there were only gasps and groans and pants. The windows steamed, the seat squeaked, and they came almost in unison in less than a dozen thrusts.

"Good God." He would have collapsed on her if there'd been room. "I must be crazy."

She opened her eyes, then started to laugh. Her ribs were aching before she could control it. "Nate, the respected attorney and salt of the earth, how the hell are you going to explain my bootprints on the ceiling of your truck?"

He looked up, studied them, and sighed. "Pretty much the same way I'm going to explain the fact that I no longer have a single button on this shirt."

"I'll buy you a new one." She sat up, managed to locate her bra and snap it on. Giving her hair a quick shake, she boosted her hips to get her sweater. "Let's go shopping."

16

"You got a minute, Will?"

Willa looked up from the papers spread over the desk, pulled herself out of the figures. Christ, grass seed was dear, but if they were going to rebroadcast she wanted to start now. Birth and wean weights circled in her head as she closed a ledger.

"Sorry. Sure, Ham. Problem?"

"Not exactly."

He held his hat in his hands and eased himself into a chair. The winter had been hard on his bones. Age was hard on the bones, he corrected, and he was starting to feel the years more with every passing wind.

"I went down to the feedlot like you wanted. Looks good. Ran into Beau Radley from over High Springs Ranch?"

"Yes, I remember Beau." She rose to put another log on the fire. She knew Ham's bones as well as he did. "Lord, Ham, he must be eighty."

"Eighty-three this spring, so he tells me. When you can get a word in." Ham set his hat on his lap, tapped his fingers on the arms of the chair.

It was odd sitting there, where he'd sat so many times. Seeing Willa behind the desk, with coffee at her elbow, instead of the old man with a glass of whiskey in his hand.

Jumping up Jesus, that man could drink.

Willa struggled with impatience. Ham took his time, and everyone else's, when he had a point to make. She often thought conversations with him were like watching a glacier move. Generations were born and died before you got to the end of it.

"Beau Radley, Ham?"

"Uh-huh. You know his young'un moved on down to Scottsdale, Arizona. Must be twenty, twenty-five years ago. That'd be Beau Junior."

Who would be, by Willa's estimation, about sixty. "And?"

"Well, Beau's missus, that's Heddy Radley. She makes those watermelon pickles that always take first prize at the county fair? Seems she's got the arthritis pretty bad."

"I'm sorry to hear that." If they got a break in the weather early, Willa thought as her mind wandered, she would see if Lily wanted to start a kitchen garden. A real one.

"Winter's been hard," Ham commented. "Don't seem to be letting up, and it's coming to calf-pulling time."

"I know. I'm thinking about adding another pole barn."

"Might be an idea," Ham said noncommittally, then took out his tobacco and began to meticulously roll a cigarette. "Beau's selling out and moving down with his boy to Scottsdale."

"Is he?" Willa's attention snapped back. High Springs had excellent pastureland.

"Done made him a deal with one of those developers." Ham laid his tongue over the paper, spat lightly. Whether it was a comment on developers or tobacco in his mouth, Willa couldn't have said. "Going to break it up, put in some cussed dude ranch resort and raise frigging buffalo."

"The deal's already made?"

"Said it was, paid him three times what the land's worth for ranching. Goddamn city jackals."

"Well, that's that. We'd never match the price." She blew out a breath, rubbed her hands over her face, then lowered them as another idea came to her. "What about his equipment, his cattle, horses?"

"I'm getting to it."

Ham blew out smoke, watched it drift to the ceiling. Willa imagined cities being built, leveled, new stars being born, novas.

"He's got a new baler. Barely three seasons old. Wood sure would like to have it. Don't think much of his string of horses, but he's a good cattleman, Beau is." He paused, smoked some more. Oaks grew from acorns. "Told him I thought you'd pay two-fifty a head for what he had on the feedlot. He didn't seem insulted by it."

"How many head?"

"About two hundred, good Hereford beef."

"All right. Make the deal."

"All right. There's more." Ham tapped his cigarette out, settled back. The fire was warm, the chair soft. "Beau's got two hands. One's a college boy he just signed on last year out of Bozeman. One of those animal husbandry fellas. Beau says he's got highfalutin ideas but he's smart as a whip. Knows to beat all about cross-breeding and embryo transplants. The other's Ned Tucker, known him ten years easy. Good cowboy, steady worker."

"Hire them," Willa said into the next pause. "At whatever wage they were getting at High Springs."

"Told Beau I figured that. He liked the idea. Feels warm toward Ned. Wants him to be settled at a good spread." He started to rise, then settled back again. "I got something else to say."

Her brow raised. "So say it."

"Maybe you think I can't handle my job no more."

Now it was shock, plain and simple, on her face. "Why would I think that? Why would you think that?"

"Seems to me you're doing your work and half of mine besides, with a little of everybody else's tossed in. If you ain't in here going over your papers, then you're out riding fence, checking pasture, looking at the equipment, doctoring cows."

"I'm operator now, and you know damn well I couldn't run this place without you."

"Maybe I do." But it had been an opening and had gotten her full attention. "And maybe I been asking myself what the hell you're trying to prove to a dead man."

She opened her mouth, closed it, swallowed. "I don't know what you're talking about."

"Hell you don't." Anger hastened his words and brought him out of the chair. "You think I don't see, I don't know. You think somebody who tanned your hide when you needed it and bandaged your hurts don't know what's inside your head? You listen to me, girl, 'cause you're too big and mean for me to turn over my knee like I used to. You can beat yourself into the ground from here to the Second Coming and it don't mean a damn to Jack Mercy."

"It's my ranch now," she said evenly. "Or a third of it is."

He nodded, pleased to hear the echo of resentment in her tone. "Yeah, and he slapped you with that too, just like he slapped you all your life. He didn't do what was right for you, what was fitting. Now, maybe I think more of those two girls than I did when they first came around, but that ain't the point. He did what he did to you 'cause he could, that's all. And he brought in overseers from outside Mercy."

Even as her temper simmered to the surface, she realized something she'd overlooked. "It should have been you," she said quietly. "I'm sorry, Ham. It never even occurred to me. It should have been you supervising the ranch through this year. I should have thought of that before, and realized how insulting it was."

Insulting it was, but insults—some insults—he could live with. "I ain't asking you to think of it. And I ain't particularly insulted. It was just like him."

"Yeah." She sighed once. "It was just like him."

"I don't have anything against Ben and Nate, they're good men. Fair. And it would take a brainless moose not to see what Jack was up to, bringing Ben around here. Around you. But I ain't talking about that." He waved a hand at her as she scowled. "You got nothing to prove to Jack Mercy, and it's time somebody said so to your face." He nodded briskly. "So I am."

"I can't just push it away. He was my father."

"We pump sperm out of a bull and stick it in a cow, that don't make that bull a father."

Stunned, she got to her feet. "I never heard you talk about him like this. I thought you were friends."

"I had respect for him as a cattleman. Never said I respected the man."

"Then why did you stay on, all these years?"

He looked at her, shook his head slowly from side to side. "That's a damn fool question."

For me, she thought, and felt both foolish and humbled. Unable to face him, she turned, stared out the window. "You taught me to ride."

"Somebody had to." His voice went rusty, so he cleared it. "Before you broke your fool neck climbing on when nobody was looking."

"When I fell and broke my arm when I was eight, you and Bess took me to the hospital."

"The woman was too flustered to be driving you herself. Likely have wrecked the rig." Uneasy, he shifted in his chair, drummed his stubby fingers.

If his wife had lived past their first two years of marriage, he might have had kids of his own. He'd stopped thinking of that, and the lack, because there'd been Willa to tend to.

"And I ain't talking about all that. I'm talking now. You gotta back off a little, Will."

"There's so much going on. Ham, I keep seeing that girl, and Pickles. If I let my mind go clear, I see them."

"Nothing you can do to change what happened, is there? And nothing you did to make it happen. This bastard, he's doing what he's doing 'cause he can."

It was too close to what he'd said about her father—it made her shudder. "I don't want another death on my hands, Ham. I don't think I could stand it."

"Goddamn it, why don't you listen?" The furious shout made her turn, stare at him. "It's not on your hands, and you're a big-headed fool if you think so. What happened happened, and that's that. This ranch don't need you to be fussing over every acre of it twenty hours a day, either. It's about time you tried being a female for a while."

Her mouth fell open. Shouting wasn't his way unless he was riled past patience. And never could she recall him referring to her gender. "Just what does that mean?"

"When's the last time you put on a dress and went out to kick up your heels?" he demanded, even though it made him flush to say it. "I'm not counting New Year's and whatever that thing was you were almost wearing that had the boys spilling drool out their mouths."

She laughed at that and, intrigued, slid a hip onto the corner of the desk. "Is that so?"

"If I'd been your pa, I'd have sent you back upstairs for a proper dress, with your ears ringing, too." Embarrassed by his outburst, he crushed his hat onto his head. "But that's done, too. Now I'm saying why don't you get that McKinnon boy to take you out to a sit-down dinner or a picture show or some such thing instead of you spending every waking hour in a pair of muddy boots? That's what I'm saying."

"And you've certainly had a lot to say this afternoon." Which meant, she reflected, that he'd been storing it up. "Just what makes you think I'd be interested in a sit-down dinner with Ben McKinnon?"

"A blind man coulda seen the way you two were plastered together pretending to be dancing." He decided not to mention the fact that at the poker game at Three Rocks the week before, Ben had pumped him dry for information on her. Conversation over five-card stud was as sacrosanct as that in a confessional. "That's all I have to say about it."

"Sure?" she asked sweetly. "No observations on my diet, my hygiene, my social skills?"

Oh, she's a sassy one, he thought, and bit back a smile. "You ain't eating enough to fill a rabbit, but you clean up good enough. Far as I can see, you ain't got any social skills." He was pleased to have worked a fresh scowl out of her. "I got work to do." He started out, then paused. "I hear Stu McKinnon is feeling poorly."

"Mr. McKinnon's ill? What's wrong with him?"

"Just a flu bug, but he ain't feeling up to snuff. Bess made a sweet potato pie. Be nice if you took it over. He's got a partiality for sweet potato pie, and for you. Be neighborly."

"And I could work on my lack of social skills." She glanced at the desk, the papers, the work. Then looked back at the man who'd taught her everything worth knowing. "All right, Ham. I'll run over and see him."

"You're a good girl, Will," he said, and sauntered out.

He'd given her plenty to think about on the drive over. Two new men, another two hundred head of cattle. Her own stubborn need to prove herself worthy to a man who had never cared.

And, perhaps, her lack of sensitivity to a man who had always cared, and had always been there for her.

Had she been infringing on Ham's territory the last few months? Probably. That, at least, she could fix. But his words on the murder, however steady and sensible, couldn't wipe out her sense of responsibility.

Or her fear.

She shivered, bumped up the heater in the rig. The road was well plowed, easily navigated. Snow was heaped on the sides so that it was like driving through a white tunnel with white peaks spearing up into a hard blue sky.

There'd been an avalanche to the northwest that had buried three skiers. And some hunters camped in the high country had gotten caught in a blizzard and had to be brought out by copter and treated for frostbite. A neighboring ranch had lost some of its range cattle to wildcat looking for food. And two hikers climbing in the Bitterroots had been lost.

And somewhere, despite the brutal nature of winter, was a killer.

The Big Sky ski area was doing record business. More fortunate hunters claimed game was so plentiful this year that they hardly needed a weapon. Foals were already being dropped, and cattle were growing fat in feedlots and basin pastures.

Regardless of life and prosperity, death was lurking much too close.

Lily was flushed with love and planning a spring wedding. Tess had nudged Nate into a weekend away at one of the tony resorts. And Ham wanted her to put on her dancing shoes.

She was terrified.

And hit the brakes, hard, to avoid running into an eight-point buck. She swerved, skidded, ended up sideways across the road, as the buck simply lifted his head and watched the show with bored eyes.

"Oh, you're a beauty, aren't you?" Laughing at herself, she rested her head on the steering wheel while her heart made its way slowly out of her throat and back to her chest. It took a fast leap back up when someone tapped on her window.

She didn't recognize the face. It was a good one, angelically handsome, framed with curly golden-brown hair under a dung-brown hat. As his lips, accented with a glossy moustache, tipped up in smile, she slid a hand under her seat toward the .38 Ruger.

"You okay?" he asked when she rolled down the window an inch. "I was behind you, saw you skid. Did you hit your head or anything?"

"No. I'm fine. Just startled me. I should have been paying more attention."

"Big bastard, isn't he?" Jesse turned his head to watch as the buck walked regally to the side of the road, then leaped over the mound of snow. "Wish I had my thirty-thirty. A rack like that'd go fine on the bunkhouse wall." He looked back at her, amused to see fear and suspicion in her eyes. "Sure you're okay, Miz Mercy?"

"Yes." She slid her fingers closer to the gun. "Do I know you?"

"Don't think so. I've seen you around here and there. I'm J C, been working at Three Rocks the past few months."

She relaxed a little, but kept the window up. "Oh, the poker ace."

He flashed a grin, and it was as formidable a weapon as the Ruger. "Got me a rep, do I? Gotta say it's a pure pleasure taking your money, indirectly, that is, through your boys. You're a little pale yet."

He wondered what her skin would feel like. She was part Indian, he remembered, and had the look of it. He'd never had a half-breed before. And wouldn't that just fix Lily's butt if he went and fucked her sister?

"You ought to take a minute to get your breath back. If you hadn't had good reflexes, I'd be digging you out of the drifts now."

"I'm fine, really." He had gorgeous eyes, she mused. Cold, but beautiful. They shouldn't have made her insides curl up in defense. "I'm on my way to Three Rocks, as it happens," she continued, determined to work on those social skills. "I'm told Mr. McKinnon's under the weather."

"Flu. Put him down hard the last couple days, but he's feeling some better. You've had your own problems over to Mercy."

"Yes." She drew back instinctively. "You'd better get back in your rig. It's too cold to be standing out there."

"Wind's got a bite, all right. Like a healthy woman." He winked, stepped back. "I'll follow you in. You be sure to tell old Jim I'm up for a game anytime."

"I'll do that. Thanks for stopping."

"My pleasure." Chuckling to himself, he tipped his hat. "Ma'am."

He chuckled out loud when he climbed back into his rig. So that was Lily's half-breed half sister. He'd bet she would give a man a hard ride. He might have to find out. He hummed all the way into Three Rocks, and when Willa took the turn toward the main house, tooted his horn cheerfully and waved her on.

Shelly opened the door, with the baby on her shoulder. "Will, what a surprise. Pie!" Her eyes went huge and just a little greedy. "Come in, grab a fork."

"It's for your father-in-law." Willa held it out of reach. "How's he feeling?"

"Better. Driving Sarah crazy. That's why I'm here instead of home. Trying to give her a hand. Take off your coat, come on back to the kitchen." She patted the gurgling baby on the back. "Truth is, Will, I'm spooked staying home alone. I know it's stupid, but I keep thinking someone's watching me. Watching the house, looking through the windows. I've had Zack up three times this week to check locks. We never locked up before."

"I know. It's the same at Mercy."

"You haven't heard any more from the police."

"No, nothing helpful."

"We won't talk about it now." Shelly lowered her voice as they approached the kitchen. "No use getting Sarah upset. Look who I found," she announced as she swung through the door.

"Willa." Sarah put down the potatoes she was peeling for stew, wiped her hands. "How wonderful to see you. Sit down. There's coffee on."

"Pie." Though she was never quite sure how to respond to the spontaneous affection, Willa smiled when Sarah kissed her cheek. "For the invalid. Bess's sweet potato."

"Maybe that'll keep him busy and out of my hair. You tell Bess how much I appreciate it. You sit down now, have some cake with that coffee and talk to us. Shelly and I have about talked each other out. I swear winter gets longer and meaner every year."

"Beau Radley's selling out and moving to Arizona."

"No." Sarah pounced on the nibble of gossip like a starving mouse on cheese. "I hadn't heard that."

"Sold to developers. They're going to put in a resort. Dude ranch. Buffalo."

"Oh, my." Sarah whistled through her teeth as she poured coffee into her company cups. "Won't Stu have six fits when he hears."

"Hears what?" Silver hair flowing, bathrobe comfortably ratty, Stu strolled in. "We got company and nobody calls me?" He winked at Willa, gave her a quick pat on the head. "And pie? We got pie and you leave me up there moldering in bed?"

"You won't stay in it long enough to molder. Well, sit then. We'll have pie instead of cake with coffee."

He pulled up a chair, eyed his daughter-in-law. "Going to let me hold my baby yet?"

"Nope." Shelly swiveled Abby around. "Not until you're germ-free. Look but don't touch."

"I'm being run into the ground by women," he told Willa. "Sneeze a couple of times and you find yourself strapped in bed having pills forced down your throat."

"He was running a fever. One-oh-one." Clucking, Sarah slid pie under his nose. "Eat that and stop complaining. Babies are less trouble when they're ailing than any grown man I know. I can't count the number of times I've been up and down those stairs in the past three days."

Even as she said it, she was cupping his chin, studying his face. "Color's better," she murmured, letting her hand linger. "You can have your pie and a visit, but then you go back and take a nap."

"See?" Stu gestured with his fork. "She can't wait until I'm feeling off to start bossing me around." He brightened considerably when the door opened and Zack came in. "Now we'll even the odds a bit. Come on in, boy, but don't think you're getting any of my pie."

"What kind? Hey, Will." Zack McKinnon was a slimly built man who stopped just shy of lanky. He'd inherited his mother's wavy hair and his father's squared-off jaw. His eyes were green, like Ben's, but dreamier. He was a man who liked to spend his days in the clouds. The minute he was out of coat and hat, he kissed his wife and picked up his daughter.

"Did you wipe your feet?" his mother demanded.

"Yes'm. Is that sweet potato?"

"It's mine," Stu said darkly, then nudged the pie closer possessively as the door opened again.

"The piebald mare's looking ready to—" Ben spotted Willa and his smile came slow. "Hey, Will."

"She brought pie," Zack said, eyeing it avariciously. "Dad won't share."

"What kind?" Ben dropped into a chair beside Willa and began to play with her hair.

"Your father's kind," she said, and brushed his hand away.

"Thata girl." Stu scooped up another forkful, then looked crushed when his wife sliced two more pieces. "I thought I was sick."

"You'll be sick if you eat all this yourself. Give Shelly the baby, Zack, and pour the coffee. Ben, stop fussing with Will and let the girl eat."

"Nag, nag, nag," Stu muttered, then beamed when Willa winked and slid her piece of pie from her plate to his.

"Stuart McKinnon, shame on you." Sarah put her hands on her hips as her husband dug in to the second piece.

"She gave it to me, didn't she? How are those pretty sisters of yours, Will?"

"They're fine. Ah . . ." Neither Lily nor Adam had asked that it be kept secret. In any case, Willa imagined tongues were already starting to wag. "Adam and Lily are engaged. They're going to be married in June."

"A wedding." Shelly bounced as happily as the baby. "Oh, that's wonderful."

"Adam's getting married." Sarah let out a sigh as her eyes went sentimentally moist. "Why, I can remember when he and Ben used to tramp off to the stream with fishing poles." She sniffed, dabbed her eyes. "We'll help you with the shower, Willa."

"Shower?"

"The bridal shower," Shelly said, gearing up. "I can't wait. They'll live in that adorable little house of his, won't they? I wonder what kind of dress she's looking for. I'll have to tell her about this wonderful shop in Billings where I found mine. And they have gorgeous bridesmaids' dresses too. I hope she wants vivid colors for you."

Willa set her cup down before she choked. "For me?"

"I'm sure you and Tess will be her attendants. Both of you want strong colors. Rich blue, dark pink."

"Pink?"

At the desperate look in her eyes, Ben howled. "You're scaring her bloodless, Shelly. Don't worry, Will. I'll look after you. I'm going to be best man." He toasted her with his coffee. "I just talked to Adam this morning. You beat me to the announcement."

With his plate scraped clean, Zack came up for air. "Better let me talk to him. I've still got the scars from our wedding." As Shelly's eyes narrowed, he grinned. "Remember those monkey suits we had to wear, Ben? Thought I'd strangle before I could say 'I do.' " He bent to his coffee when Shelly smacked the back of his head. "Of course, I had a lump in my throat when I looked down the aisle and saw this vision coming toward me. The most beautiful sight any man sees in his life."

"Good save, son," Stu commented. "I don't mind weddings myself, though your mom and I did it the easy way and eloped."

"That was only because my father wanted to shoot you. You tell Lily to let us know if there's anything we can do to help, Will. Just thinking about a wedding makes spring seem closer."

"I will. I know she'll appreciate it. I have to get back."

"Oh, don't go yet." Shelly reached out to grab her hand. "You've hardly been here at all. I can have Zack go down to the house and get my stack of *Bride's* magazines and the photo album. It might give Lily some ideas."

"I'm sure she'd like to come over herself and huddle with you." Now the idea of a wedding was making her shoulder blades itch. "I'd stay if I could, but the light's already going."

"She's right," Sarah murmured, shooting an uneasy glance out the window. "It's no time for a woman to be out on the road alone at night. Ben—"

"I'll ride over with her." Ignoring Willa's protests, he rose and fetched his hat and coat. "One of your men can drive me back, or I'll borrow a rig."

"I'd rest easier," Sarah put in before Willa could refuse again. "It's a shameful thing what's happened here. We'd all rest easier knowing Ben's with you."

"All right, then."

Once the good-byes were said, with the rest of the McKinnons walking them to the door, Will climbed behind the wheel of the rig. "You're a lucky man, McKinnon."

"Why is that?"

She shook her head and stayed silent until they'd left the ranch house behind. "You can't know, you can't possibly understand how lucky you are because it just is for you. It's just the way it is and always has been."

Baffled, he shifted in his seat to study her profile. "What are you talking about?"

"Family. Your family. I sat there in that kitchen. I've sat there before, but I don't know if it all sank in. It did today. The ease and affection, the history, the bond. You wouldn't know what it's like not to have any of that. It's just yours."

It was true enough, and he didn't know if he'd ever thought it through. "You've got sisters now, Willa. There's a bond there, and it's easy to see."

"Maybe there's the beginnings of something, but there's no history. No memories. I've seen you start a story and Zack finish it. I've heard your mother laugh over something stupid the two of you did as boys. I never heard my mother laugh. I'm not being maudlin," she said quickly. "It just hit me, sitting there today, watching you and your family. That's the way it's supposed to be, isn't it?"

"Yeah, I'd say it is."

"He stole that from us. I'm just beginning to realize how much he stole from all three of us. Not just me. I'm going to make a detour."

When they came to the boundary of Mercy land, she shifted into four-wheel drive and swung onto a winter-rutted access road. He didn't ask where she was heading. He'd already figured it out.

Snow was mounded over the graves, burying the headstones, smothering the wild grass and tender flowers. She thought it looked like a postcard, so perfect, so undisturbed, with only Jack Mercy's stone, higher, brighter than all the rest, thrusting up out of the snow toward the darkening sky.

"Do you want me to go with you?"

"No, I'd rather you didn't. If you could just wait here. I won't be long."

"Take your time," he murmured as she climbed out.

She sank knee-deep in snow, trudged her way through it. It was cold, bitterly, with the wind slapping the air, sending snow swirling from its bed. She saw deer, a small herd of doe on the rise of a hill, like sentinels for the dead.

There was no sound but the wind, and the wind was like the first stars groaning as she made her way to her father's grave.

The headstone was carved as he'd ordered, carved as he'd lived his life. Without a thought to anyone but himself. What did it matter? she wondered, for he was as dead as her mother, who was said to have lived kind, and gentle.

She had come from that, Willa thought, from the kind and the cruel. What it made her she couldn't say. Selfish on some levels. Generous on others, she hoped. Proud and filled with self-doubt. Impatient, but not without compassion.

Neither kind, she decided, nor cruel, and that wasn't so bad, all in all.

What she did understand, standing there in the rough wind, in the rougher silence, was that she had loved them both. The mother she had never known, and the father she had never touched.

"I wanted you to be proud of me," she said aloud. "Even if you couldn't love me. To be . . . satisfied with me. But it never happened. Ham was right today. You slapped me all my life. Not just the physical slaps—there wasn't much punch behind those because you didn't really give a damn. Emotionally. You hit me emotionally more times than I can count. And I just came back, my head lowered like a kicked dog, so you could do it again. I guess I'm here to tell you I'm done with that. Or I'm going to try to be."

She was going to try, very hard.

"You thought you'd pit the three of us against each other. I see that now. Doesn't look like we're going to oblige you. We're keeping the ranch, you selfish son of a bitch. And I think we may just keep each other too. We're going to make it work. To spite you. We may not be much of a family now, but we're not done yet."

She walked away the way she'd come.

He hadn't taken his eyes off her, and was grateful for the lack of tears. Still, he hadn't expected the smile, even the grim one that firmed her lips as she got back into the rig.

"You okay?"

"I'm fine." She drew a deep breath, pleased that it didn't hitch. "I'm just fine. Beau Radley's selling off," she said as she maneuvered the rig around. "I'm buying some of his equipment, a couple hundred head from the feedlot, and taking on two of his men."

The lack of segue left him a little muddled, but he nodded slowly. "Okay."

"I didn't tell you that for your approval, but so you can note it in your supervisory capacity." She swung onto another access road to shortcut it to the ranch. Quick gusts of wind that would drag the temperature down to unbearable rattled gleefully at the windows.

"I'll have the monthly report up to date by tomorrow so you can go over it."

He scratched his ear, wary of the trap. "That's fine."

"That's business." Her smile relaxed a bit as she saw the lights of the ranch house peek through the distance. "On a personal level, why haven't you ever asked me out for a sit-down dinner or a picture show instead of just trying to get my pants down?"

His mouth fell open so far he nearly had to use his hand to shove his jaw up again. "Excuse me?"

"You come sniffing around, get your hands on me when I let you, ask me to bed often enough, but you never once asked me out on a date."

"You want me to take you to dinner?" He'd never thought of it. He would have with another woman, but this was Willa. "To a movie?"

"Are you ashamed to be seen in public with me?" She stopped the rig again, left the engine running as she swiveled in the seat to face him. His face was in shadows now, but it was still light enough for her to read the stunned look in his eyes. "I'm all right to go rolling around in the horse barn with, but not good enough for you to put on a clean shirt and invest fifty bucks in a meal?"

"Where'd you get a damn fool idea like that? In the first place, I haven't rolled around in the horse barn with you because you're not ready, and in the second place, I never figured you were interested in sitting down in a restaurant and eating with me. Like a date," he finished lamely.

Maybe feminine power was fiercer than she'd imagined, Willa mused, if wielding just a hint of it caused a man like Ben McKinnon to flop like a trout on the hook. "Well, maybe you're wrong."

It was a trick, he thought, as she drove on. There was a trap here somewhere, and it would snap its teeth on his ankle as soon as he took a wrong step. He watched her narrowly, ready for signs as she pulled up in front of the main house, turned off the engine.

"Go on and drive this back," she said easily. "I can send someone over to get it tomorrow. Thanks for the company."

Damn it, he could almost hear the snap of the spring as he stepped a toe into the trap. "Saturday night. Six o'clock. Dinner and a movie."

Her stomach muscles quivered with laughter, but she nodded soberly. "Fine. See you then." And stepped out, shut the door in his face.

17

Winter clung like a bur to the back of Montana. Temperatures remained brutal, and when they rose to tolerable, snow tumbled from the sky in frosty sheets. Twice, access roads at Mercy were blocked by ten-foot drifts, piled into glossy white mountains by the unforgiving wind.

Cows went into labor despite the weather. In the pole barn, Willa sweated through her shirt with the muscle-straining effort of pulling calves. An expectant mother mooed bitterly as Willa reached into the birth canal, grabbed hold. Still in the birth sac, the calf was slippery and stubborn. Willa dug in, hissing as the next contraction vised painfully on her hands.

Her arms would carry bruises to the elbow before it was done.

She waited it out, timed her pull, and dragged the first half of the cow out.

"Coming on the next," she called out as blood and amniotic fluid soaked her arms. "Let's go, baby, let's go." Like a diver going under, she took a quick breath to fill her lungs with air, then dragged hard with the next contraction. The calf popped out like an oiled cork.

Her boots were slimy, her thick cord pants stained. Her back was screaming. "Billy, stand by with the injections," she ordered. "Keep an eye on them."

If things went well, mother would clean baby up. If not, that task would also fall to Billy. In any case, she had trained him carefully over the past few weeks, with a hypo and an orange, until she was confident that he could inject the newborns with the necessary medication.

"I'm going on to the next one," she told him as she wiped an arm over her sweaty forehead. "Ham?"

"Coming along." He watched eagle-eyed as Jim pulled another calf.

It was always a worry that even with human assistance a calf would prove too large, or be turned wrong, and make the birthing process lethal for both baby and mother. Willa still remembered the first time she'd lost this battle, the blood and the pain and the helplessness. The vet could be called, if they knew in time. But for the most part, the calf-pulling season of February and March was the province of the cattleman.

Steroids and growth hormones, she thought as she examined the next laboring cow. The price per pound had seduced ranchers into producing bigger calves, turning what should have been a natural process into an unnatural one that required human hands and muscle.

Well, she would be cutting back on that, she thought as she sucked in a breath and plunged her cramping hands into the cow. And they would see. If her attempt to return to more natural ranching proved a failure in the long run, she would have only herself to blame.

"Ladies and gentlemen, coffee is served." Tess's entrance was spoiled when she went white and gagged. The air in the pole barn was thick with the mingling smells of sweat and blood and soiled straw. Visions of a slaughterhouse danced in her head as she turned straight around and gulped in the icy air.

"Jesus, Jesus, Jesus." No good deed goes unpunished, she thought, and waited for the dizziness to pass.

Bess had known, certainly Bess had known exactly what she would walk in on when she'd casually asked Tess to take the thermoses of coffee out to the pole barn. With a shudder Tess made herself turn back around.

That little deed would require punishment as well, she decided. Later.

"Coffee," she repeated, staring, fascinated despite herself as Willa wrenched a calf partially out of a cow's vagina. "How can you do that?"

"Upper-body strength," Will said easily. "Go ahead and pour some." She spared her sister an arch look. "My hands are full."

"Yeah." Tess wrinkled her nose as the calf squirted out. It wasn't a pretty sight, she mused. At one time she would have said that no birth could be. But the horses . . . she'd been charmed and humbled by the sight of a foaling mare.

But this was nasty, she thought, and messy and almost assembly-line cold. Pull 'em out, clean 'em up. Maybe it was because they were destined to be steaks on a platter, she considered. Then she shook her head and handed a cup of coffee to Billy. Or maybe she just didn't like cows.

They were, in her opinion, too big, too homely, and too desperately uninteresting.

"Wouldn't mind a cup of that," Jim said, and his eyes twinkled at her. "We could switch places a minute. It's not as hard as it looks."

"I'll pass, thanks." And she smiled back at him, giving him a steaming cup so he could take a breather. It no longer insulted her to be considered an ignorant greenhorn. In fact, at the moment Tess thought it was a distinct advantage.

"How come they can't just push the calves out themselves?" she asked him.

"Too big." Grateful, he gulped down the coffee. Even the burning of his tongue was welcome.

"Well, horses have pretty big foals, and when we're in the foaling stall we mostly just stand by and watch."

"Too big," he reiterated. "With the growth hormones we give them, cows can't throw off calves by themselves. So we pull 'em."

"But what if it happens when nobody's around to . . . pull?"

"Bad luck." He handed back an empty cup. She didn't want to think about what was smeared on the outside.

"Bad luck," she repeated. Because that didn't bear thinking about either, she left the thermoses and cups and went outside again.

"Your sister's all right, Will."

Willa shot a half smile at Jim and took a moment to pour herself coffee. "She's not all bad."

"Wanted to puke when she walked in," he pointed out. "I figured she'd haul ass back to the house, but she didn't."

"Maybe she could help out in here." Billy grinned. "I can't see her sticking her hands in a cow's hole, but she might could use a needle."

Willa rolled her shoulders. "I think we'll leave her to play with the chickens. For now, anyway." And now was what mattered, she decided, as she watched a newborn calf begin to nurse for the first time.

"And she was up to her elbows inside a cow." Tess shuddered over her brandy. Evening had come in cold and clear, there was a fire roaring in the grate, and Nate had come to dinner. The combination made her brave enough to recount the experience. "Inside, dragging out another cow."

"I thought it was fascinating." Lily enjoyed her tea, and the warmth of Adam's hand over hers. "I'd have stayed longer, but I was in the way."

"You could have stayed." Willa had a combo of coffee laced with brandy. "We'd have put you to work."

"Really?" Though Tess moaned at Lily's simple enthusiasm, Lily just smiled. "I'd love to help tomorrow."

"You haven't got enough brawn to pull, but you could medicate. Now you," Willa continued, giving Tess a long, considering look, "you're a big, strapping woman. Bet you could pull a calf without losing your breath."

"Just her lunch," Nate put in, and earned chuckles from everyone but Tess.

"I could handle it." Gracefully, she skimmed back her hair, making the rings glitter on her pretty manicured fingers. "If I wanted to handle it."

"Twenty says you'd chicken before you were in to the wrists."

Damn it, Tess realized. Cornered. "Make it fifty, and you're on."

"Done. Tomorrow. And Mercy Ranch adds another ten for every calf you pull."

"Ten." Tess sniffed. "Big deal."

"Pull enough and you'd be able to pay for your next fancy haircut in Billings."

Tess flipped her hair again. She was about due for another trim. "All right, then. I say you're going to be springing for a facial as well." She raised an eyebrow. "You could use one of those yourself. And a paraffin wax on those hands. Unless, of course, you like skin that resembles leather."

"I don't have time to waste in some silly salon."

Tess swirled her brandy. "Chicken." She hurried on before Willa could hiss out a response. "I say I'll pull as many as you, and if so, Mercy Ranch treats all three of us—you, me, and Lily—to the works. A weekend at a spa in Big Sky. You'd like that, wouldn't you, Lily?"

Torn between loyalties, Lily fumbled. "Well, I—"

"And we could do some shopping for the wedding. Check out a couple shops Shelly talked about."

"Oh." The thrill of that had her looking dreamily at Adam. "That would be lovely."

"Bitch," Willa murmured at Tess without rancor. "You're on. But if you lose, you're back on laundry detail."

"Oops." Nate took the coward's way out and studied his brandy when Tess snarled at him.

"Meanwhile, I've got to finish recording the birth information from today." Willa rose, stretched. Then froze. Had that been a shadow at the window? Or a face? Slowly she lowered her arms, struggled to keep her features composed. "I wouldn't stay up too late," she said to Tess as she started out of the room. "You're going to need your strength tomorrow."

"I'm really going to love hearing you scream during your bikini wax," Tess called out, and had the satisfaction of seeing Willa's head jerk around and her face register sheer horror. "I love having the last word," she murmured.

"Excuse me a minute." Adam rose and followed Willa. He found her in the library, loading a rifle. "What is it?"

So much for the poker face, she thought, snapping the chamber closed. "I thought I saw something outside."

"So you're going out alone." As he spoke he chose a shotgun, loaded it.

"No use spooking everyone. It might have been my imagination."

"You don't have a well-developed imagination."

She shook her head at that and decided it was hard to be insulted by the truth. "Well, it won't hurt to do a quick walk around. We'll go out the back."

They bundled into their outdoor gear in the mudroom. Though it was Willa's instinct to go out first, Adam beat her to it, gently easing her aside.

Someone watched them. It was cold, and bitter, but Jesse stood in the shadows, watching while his hand flexed eagerly on the weapon he carried. He dreamed of using it, on the man, taking out the man, leaving him bleeding.

And just taking the woman, dragging her away, using her until he was done with her. Then killing her, of course. What other choice would he have?

He wondered if he dared risk it, here, now. They were armed, and he'd seen how many people were in the house. He'd seen exactly. He'd seen Lily laughing, cozying up to that half-breed.

Maybe it was best to wait—wait, and watch for the right moment. It could come anytime.

It could come if they walked over to the pole barn. He knew what they would find there. He'd already been there.

"Around by the front windows." If she couldn't lead the way, at least she could move side by side. "It was just a flash, after I stood up to go. I thought it might have been a face, someone looking in at us, but it was too dark to be sure. And it was gone fast."

Adam only nodded. He knew Willa too well to believe she would jump at shadows. There were prints in the snow alongside the walkway, but that was to be expected. With all the activity in the pole barn over the last couple of days, the snow on the lawn would hardly be undisturbed. There had been melt and refreezing, so the surface was brittle and gave way with a crackle under their boots.

"Might have been one of the men," Willa said while she studied the ground. "But it's unlikely. They would just have knocked."

"Don't see why they'd have gone through the flower beds to peek in the window either." Adam gestured toward tracks close to the house between evergreen shrubs where flowers would bloom late in the spring.

"So I did see something."

"I never doubted it." From where he stood, Adam could see clearly through the window into the lights of the front room. He watched Lily laugh, sip her tea, then rise to offer Nate more brandy. "Someone was watching us. Or one of us."

Willa shifted her gaze away from the lights in the window, toward the dark. "One of us?"

"Lily's ex-husband, Jesse Cooke. He's not in Virginia."

Instinctively Willa looked back to the window, shifted her grip on her rifle. "How do you know?"

"Nate did some checking for me. He hasn't shown up at his job or paid his rent since October."

"You think he's come after her? How would he know where to look?"

"I don't know." He moved back, away from the house. "Just speculating. That's why I don't see any point in bringing it up to her."

"I won't say anything to her. But I think we should tell Tess. That way one of us can keep our eye out for him. And for Lily. Do we know what he looks like?"

"No, but I'll see what I can find out."

"All right. Meanwhile, we'd better look around. I'll go this way, and—"

"We'll stick together, Will." He laid a hand on her arm. "Two people are dead. Maybe this was just a pissed-off ex-husband wanting to get back at his wife. Or maybe it was something else. We stick together."

In silence they moved through the wind, circling the house. Overhead the sky was clear as glass, with diamond-chip stars wheeling and a three-quarter moon casting pale blue light on the snow at their feet. Cottonwood trees loomed and seemed to shiver under their coating of ice.

In the frigid quiet, Willa heard the call of cattle. A mournful sound, she thought while her breath fumed out in front of her and was whisked away by the wind. Odd—such a sound had always seemed comforting to her before; now it was eerie.

"They're awfully stirred up for this late at night." She looked in the direction of the pole barn, the corral beyond. "Maybe we've got some cows in labor. I'd better check."

Adam thought uncomfortably of his horses, unattended in the stables. It wasn't easy to turn his back on them and go with Willa to the cattle.

"Hear that?" She stopped, ears straining. "Hear that?" she repeated in a whisper.

"No." But he turned so they were guarding each other's backs. "I don't hear anything."

"I don't hear it now either. It sounded like someone whistling 'Sweet Betsy from Pike.' " She shook it off, tried to laugh at herself. "Just the wind, and the creeps. Hell, it has to be twenty below with the windchill. Anybody out here whistling tunes would have to be . . ."

"Crazy?" Adam finished, and fought to see through the shadows.

"Yeah." Willa shivered inside her sheepskin. "Let's go."

She'd intended to go straight into the pole barn, but the thick huddle of cattle at the far end of the corral drew her attention. "That's not right," she said half to herself. "Something's off here."

She walked to the gate, shoved it open.

At first she didn't believe it, thought her eyes were dazzled by moonlight on snow. But the smell—she recognized the smell of death too well by now.

"Oh, God, Adam." With her free hand she covered her mouth, fought back the gorge that rose like a fountain in her throat. "Oh, sweet God."

Calves had been slaughtered. It was impossible at first to tell how many, but she knew she'd brought some of them into the world herself, only hours before. Now, instead of huddling against their mamas for warmth, they lay tossed into the snow, throats and bellies slit.

Blood glittered on the ground, rich and red, in a hideous pool already crusting in the cold.

It was weak, but she turned away from the carnage, lowered her rifle, and leaned on the fence until her insides settled into place.

"Why? Why in God's name would anyone do something like this?"

"I don't know." He rubbed her back, but he didn't turn away. He counted eight infant calves, mutilated. "Let's get you back to the house. I'll deal with this."

"No, I can deal with it. I can." She wiped a gloved hand over her mouth. "The ground's too hard to bury them. We'll have to burn them. We'll have to get them out of here, away from the other calves and the females, and burn them."

"Nate and I can do that." He struggled not to sigh at her set expression. "All right, we'll all do it. But I want to get you back inside for a few minutes. Will, I have to check on the horses. If—"

"Jesus." Her own misery faded in fear for him, and his. "I didn't even think. Let's go. Hurry."

She didn't head back to the house, but half ran toward the horse barn. The fear raced giddily in her head that she would fling open the door and be met again with that hideous smell of death.

They hit the door together, wrenched it open. She was already prepared to grieve, prepared to rage. But all that met her was the scents of hay and horse and leather.

Nonetheless, by tacit agreement they checked every stall, then the corral beyond. They left lights burning behind them.

Adam moved to his house next, to look in on his dogs. He'd started locking them in at night right after the incident with the barn cat. They greeted him happily, tails thumping. He suspected, with a mixture of amusement and worry, that they would have greeted an armed madman with the same friendly enthusiasm.

"We can call the main house from here, ask Nate to meet us at the pole barn. You want Ham, too."

Willa bent down to scratch an eager Beans between the ears. "Everyone. I want everyone out there. I want them to see what we're up against." Her eyes hardened. "And I want to know what everyone's been doing for the last couple hours."

. . .

The task wasn't physically arduous, but it was painful. Dragging butchered newborns into a pile on the snow-covered ground. There were plenty of hands to help, and there was no conversation.

Once Willa caught Billy surreptitiously wiping a hand over his eyes. She didn't hold the tears against him. She would have wept herself if it would have done any good.

When it was done, she took the can of gasoline from Ham. "I'll do it," she said grimly. "It's for me to do this."

"Will—" He cut off his own protest, then nodded before gesturing the men to move back.

"How can she stand it?" Lily murmured, shivering with Tess beyond the corral fence. "How can she stand it?"

"Because she has to." Tess shuddered as Willa sloshed gas on the small heap. "We all have to," she added, draping an arm over Lily's shoulders. "Do you want to go inside?"

More than anything in the world, Lily thought, but she shook her head fiercely. "No, we'll stay till it's finished. Until she's finished."

Willa adjusted the bandanna she'd tied over her nose and mouth and took the box of matches from Ham. It took her three attempts to get a flame to hold in her cupped hand, and with the teeth of the wind snapping against her, she had to crouch low and close to start the fire.

It burned high and fast, spewing heat. In only seconds, the odor of roasting meat was thick, and sickening. Smoke whipped out toward her, making her eyes water and her throat clog. She stepped back, one step, then two before she could hold her ground.

"I'll call Ben." Nate shifted to her side.

She kept her eyes on the flames. "For what?"

"He'll want to know. You're not alone in this, Willa."

But she felt alone, and helpless. "All right. I appreciate your help, Nate."

"I'll be staying the night."

She nodded. "No sense in me asking Bess to make up a guest room, is there?"

"No. I'll do a shift on guard, and use Tess's room."

"Take whatever gun you want." Turning, she moved to Ham. "I want a twenty-four-hour watch, Ham. Two men at a time. Nate's staying, so that makes six of us tonight. I want Wood to stay home with his family. They shouldn't be alone. Billy and I'll take the first, you and Jim relieve us at midnight. Nate and Adam will take over at four."

"I'll see to it."

"Tomorrow I want you to find out how soon we can sign on the two hands from High Springs. I need men. Offer them a cash bonus if you have to, but get them here."

"I'll see they're on within the week." In a rare show of public affection, he squeezed her arm. "I'm gonna tell Bess to make coffee, plenty of it. And you be careful, Will. You be careful."

"No one's killing any more of mine." Her face set, Willa turned, studied the women huddled together at the corral fence. "You get them inside for me, will you, Ham? Tell them to stay inside."

"I'll do that."

"And tell Billy to get a rifle."

She shifted again and watched the flames shoot into the black winter sky.

A little Madness in the Spring . . .

—Emily Dickinson

18

Ben looked over the operation at Mercy, the steady activity in the pole barn, so like the activity he'd left back at Three Rocks, the piled and tattered snow in the corrals, the gray puffs of smoke from chimneys.

Except for the blackened circle well beyond the paddock, there were no signs of the recent slaughter.

Unless you looked closely at the men. Faces were grim, eyes were spooked. He'd seen the same looks in the faces and in the eyes of his own hands. And like Willa, he had ordered a twenty-four-hour guard.

There was little he could do to help her, and the frustration of that made his own mouth tight as he gestured her away from the group.

"Don't have much time for chatting." Her voice was brisk. He didn't see fear in her eyes, but fatigue. Gone was the woman who had flirted him into a date, who had laughed with him over a white tablecloth and wine, shared popcorn at the movies. He wanted to take her away again, just for an evening, but knew better.

"You hired on the two men from High Springs."

"They came on last night."

Turning, she studied Matt Bodine, the younger of the two new hands, already dubbed College Boy. His carrot-colored hair was covered by a light gray Stetson. He had a baby face, which he'd tried to age with a straight line of red hair over his top lip. It didn't quite do the job, Willa thought.

Though they were nearly the same age, Matt seemed outrageously young to her, more like Billy than herself. But he was smart, had a strong back and a well of fresh ideas.

Then there was Ned Tucker, a lanky, taciturn cowboy of indeterminate age. His face was scored with lines from time and sun and wind. His eyes were an eerily colorless blue. He chewed on the stubs of cigars, said little, and worked like a mule.

"They'll do," she said after a moment.

"I know Tucker well enough," Ben began, then wondered if he knew anyone well enough. "Got a hell of a hand with a lasso, wins at the festival every year. Bodine, he's new." He shifted so that his eyes as well as the tone of his voice indicated his thought. "Too new."

"I need the help. If it's one of them who's been fucking with me, I'd just as soon have him close by. Easier to watch." She let out a little breath. They should have been talking about the weather, the calf pulling, not about murder. "We lost eight calves, Ben. I'm not losing any more."

"Willa." He laid a hand on her arm before she could walk away. "I don't know what I can do to help you."

"Nothing." Sorry for the snap in her voice, she slipped her hands into her pockets and softened her tone. "There's nothing anyone can do. We've got to get through it, that's all, and things have been quiet the last couple days. Maybe he's finished, maybe he's moved on."

She didn't believe it, but it helped to pretend she did.

"How're your sisters handling it?"

"Better than I could have expected." The tightness around her mouth eased as she smiled. "Tess was out here pulling calves. After the first couple, and a lot of squealing, she did okay."

"I'd have paid money to see that."

For an instant the smile spread into a grin. "It was worth the price of a ticket, especially when her jeans split."

"No shit? You didn't take pictures, did you?"

"Wish I'd thought of it. She cussed a lot, and the men—well, I got to say they appreciated the moment. We got her a pair of Wood's cords." Willa glanced over as Tess approached, in the cords, a borrowed hat, and one of Adam's cast-off coats. "They fit her a sight better than that sprayed-on denim she was wearing."

"Depends on your viewpoint," Ben said.

"Morning, Rancher McKinnon."

"Morning, Rancher Mercy."

Tess grinned at him, adjusted her hat to a rakish angle. "Lily's brewing up a few gallons of coffee," she told Willa. "Then she'll be out to help stick needles into cow butts."

"You gonna pull some more calves?"

Tess eyed Ben, then Willa. From the expressions on their faces, she could see that her reputation had preceded her. "I figured I could give it another day, seeing as I'm going to be spending the weekend at the spa in Big Sky."

Willa's grin fell off her face. "What the hell are you talking about?"

"Our little bet." Gotcha, Tess thought, and smiled sweetly. "I pulled two more calves than you the other day. Ham was doing the counting for me."

"What bet?" Ben wanted to know, and was ignored as Willa stepped into Tess's face.

"That's bull."

"No, it was calves. Of course, some of them might have been bulls, but you'll fix that in a few months—and that's something I won't lend a hand with. Mercy Ranch owes us a weekend at the resort. I've already made the reservations. We leave first thing Friday morning."

"The hell with that. I'm not leaving the ranch for two days to go sit in some stupid mud bath."

"Welsher."

Willa's eyes slitted dangerously, causing Ben to clear his throat and move, subtly he hoped, out of range. "It has nothing to do with welshing. After the trouble around here, I was hardly thinking about some lame bet. I had calls to make, the cops came out. I didn't pull calves for more than a couple hours all day."

"I did. And I won." Tess shifted forward until the toes of their boots bumped. "And we're going. You try to back out, I'll make sure everyone within a hundred miles knows your word isn't worth diddly."

"My word's solid, and anybody who says different is a liar."

"Ah, ladies . . ."

Willa's head whipped around, and her eyes seared Ben where he stood. "Back off, McKinnon."

"Backing off," he murmured, spreading his hands as he did so. "Backing way off."

"You want to go when we're hip-deep in this mess," Willa continued, and poked Tess hard in the shoulder, "you go. I've got a ranch to run."

"You're going." Tess poked her right back. "Because that was the deal. Because you lost the bet, and because Lily's counting on it. And because it's time you started thinking of the people around here with as much respect as you give the goddamn cows. I busted my ass to fix this. I've been stuck on this godforsaken ranch for nearly six months because some selfish son of a bitch wanted to play games beyond the grave."

"And in another six months you'll be gone." Why that—simply that—should infuriate her, Willa couldn't have said.

"Damn straight," Tess tossed back. "The minute my sentence is up, I'm gone. But meanwhile I've been playing the game, sticking to the rules. You're, by Christ, going to stick to them too. We're going if I have to beat you senseless, tie you up, and toss you in the nearest jeep."

"Rig." Willa angled her chin up as if inviting a fist. "It's a rig, Hollywood, and you couldn't whip a blind three-legged dog."

"Fuck your rigs." Fed up, Tess gave her a hard shove. "And fuck you."

That snapped it. The temper was there and full-blown before Willa could suck it in. Her fist was there, in full swing before she could pull it. It snapped Tess's head back, left an ugly red mark on the side of her jaw, and sent her butt first onto the slushy ground.

Even as Ben swore and stepped forward, Willa was apologizing. "I'm sorry. I shouldn't have done that. I—"

Then her breath pushed out of her lungs in a whoosh as Tess bulleted up and rammed her, full body. They tumbled to the ground in a flurry of arms and legs and shrieks.

It took Ben about five seconds to decide to keep his own skin whole and stay out of it.

They wrestled into the piled snow, back onto the wet ground, grunting and punching. He expected hair pulling, and he wasn't disappointed. Tipping his hat back on his head, he held up a hand as men came out of the pole barn to see what the excitement was about.

"Well, goddamn my ass," Ham said wearily. "What finally set them off?"

"Something about a bet, a mud bath, and a rig."

Ham took out his tobacco while the men formed an informal circle. "Will's outweighed, but she's mean." He winced when a fist connected with an eye. "Taught her better than that," he said with a shake of his head. "Will shoulda seen that coming."

"Think they'll start scratching?" Billy wondered. "Jeez."

"I think they'd both turn on anyone who got in the middle." Ben stuck his hands in his pockets. "That Tess has mighty long nails. I don't want them raking over my face."

"I say Will takes her." Jim nipped back as the two women rolled dangerously close to his boots. "I'll put ten on her."

Ben considered, shook his head. "Some things you're better off not betting on."

It was the fury that made Tess forget all her self-defense courses, her two years of karate training, made her just fight like a girl in a playground brawl. The red haze over her eyes darkened every time Willa landed a blow. Here there was no defensive padding, no rules, no instructor calling time.

She had her face pushed into wet, muddy snow and spat it out of her mouth on an oath.

Willa saw stars explode in glorious color as Tess yanked her hair. Tears of pain and rage burned her eyes as she wriggled around and fought for leverage. She heard something rip and had time to pray it was cloth and not her hair coming out at the roots.

It was only pride that prevented her from using her teeth.

She regretted the pride when she found herself flipped headlong into the snow. Tess had remembered her training and decided to combine it with inspiration—she sat on her sister.

"Give it up," Tess shouted, fighting to stay aboard as Willa bucked. "I'm bigger than you."

"Get your—fat—ass—off!" With one concentrated effort, Willa managed to shove Tess backward. She pushed herself away, swiveled, and struggled to sit up.

As the men stayed respectfully silent, the two women panted, gasped, and stared at each other. It was some satisfaction to Willa, as she wiped blood from her chin, to see the sleek, sophisticated Tess covered with dirt, her hair mashed and dripping into her eyes, and her mouth swollen and bleeding.

Now that she had time to breathe, Tess began to feel. Everything hurt, every bone, every muscle, every cell. She gritted her teeth, her gaze on Willa's face. "I say it's a draw."

However huge her relief, Willa nodded slowly, then flicked a glance at the fascinated, grinning men. She saw money changing hands and swore under her breath. "Am I paying you worthless cowboys to stand around scratching your butts?"

"No, ma'am." Judging it to be safe, Jim stepped forward. He started to offer a hand before he saw by the glint in Willa's eyes that it was premature. "I guess break's over, boys."

At the jerk of Ham's head, the men wandered back into the pole barn. The conversation and laughter came rolling out within seconds.

"You finished now?" Ham demanded.

Shrinking a little at the tone, Willa scrubbed at the dirt on her knee and nodded.

"That's fine, then." Ham tossed down his cigarette, ground it out with his heel. "Next time you want to get into a catfight, try to do it where you won't distract the men. Ben," he added, with a flip of a finger on the brim of his hat.

A wise man, Ben suppressed the grin as Ham strode off. "Ladies," he said, with what he hoped was appropriate sobriety, "can I help you up?"

"I can get up myself." Willa didn't quite swallow the groan as she struggled to her feet. She was wet, freezing, filthy, her shirt was torn, and her left eye was throbbing like a bad tooth.

Thinking of teeth, she ran her tongue over them and was relieved to find them all in place.

"I'll take a hand." Like a princess at a ball, Tess held out her hand, let Ben pull her out of the heap of muddy snow. She wanted to shudder at what she was going to see in the mirror but managed a cool smile. "Thank you. And," she added, aiming the smile at Willa, "I'd say that the matter is now settled. Friday morning, and pack a decent dress for dinner."

Too furious to speak, recognizing the danger in uttering a single word, Willa spun on her heel and stalked into the pole barn. The laughter inside instantly cut off into silence.

"She'll go." Ben said it quietly, took out a bandanna, and gently dabbed at the blood at the corner of Tess's mouth. "You got her on pride and honesty. She can buck just about anything but those."

"Ouch." She closed her eyes a moment, then gingerly fingered the rising lump on her temple. "It cost me more than I bargained for. That's the first real fight

I've been in since ninth grade, when Annmarie Bristol called me Wide Load. I cleaned her clock, then I went on a diet-and-exercise program."

"It worked." He bent down and picked up her crushed hat. "All around."

"Yeah." Tess set the hat on her dirty, wet hair. "I'm in damn good shape. Never figured she'd be so hard to take down."

"She's lean, but she's tough."

"Tell me about it," Tess murmured, nursing her swollen lip. "She needs to get away from here. More than I do, more than Lily does."

"I think you're right about that."

"I don't know when she sleeps. She's up before anyone else in the morning, spends half the night in the office, or out here." Then she shrugged. "What the hell do I care?"

"I think you know."

"Maybe." She looked back at him, arched a brow. "I tell you what else she needs. A good, sweaty, mind-emptying bout of sex. What the hell are you waiting for?"

It wasn't something he cared to discuss. But even as propriety urged him to shut up, instinct tugged in a different direction. He glanced back toward the barn, took Tess's arm, and led her farther away.

"Willa, you know . . . she's never . . . she's never," he repeated, and then shut his mouth.

"Never what?" The narrowed, impatient look in his eyes tipped her off. Tess stopped dead. "She's never had sex? Good God." She blew out a breath, readjusted her thoughts. "Well, that puts a different light on the matter, doesn't it?"

Despite her throbbing lip, she pressed a light kiss to his cheek. "You're a patient, considerate man, Ben McKinnon. I think that's lovely, and very sweet."

"Hell." He shuffled his feet. "I'm thinking maybe she never had anybody to talk to about, to explain things to her."

Tess caught the drift instantly and shook her head. "Oh, no, uh-uh. No way."

"I just thought maybe, you know, being sisters—"

"Oh, yeah, Will and I are like this." Sarcasm dripping, Tess crossed two fingers. "Just how do you think she'd take to me giving her a crash course in Sexual Relations one-oh-one?"

"Yeah. You're right."

And you're a frustrated, hungry man, Tess thought, and patted his cheek. "Just keep working on her, big guy. And maybe I'll think of something. I'm going to go soak in the Jacuzzi for a day or two." With a hand pressed to her sore ass, Tess limped off to the house.

"Oh, my." It was all Lily could say, almost all she'd managed to say since they'd driven to the Mountain King Spa and Resort.

She'd never seen anything like it.

The main lodge spread for acres, glass and wood and clever pebbled paths through snow-dipped evergreens and heated pools where steam curled in dreamy mists.

She'd clutched the strap of her purse tightly as they checked in, her head swiveling in wonder around the plush lobby with its double fireplace, atrium ceiling, and lush plants. Her heart had begun to thunder as she'd thought of the expense, for surely any place so beautiful, so quietly sumptuous, would cost the earth even for an overnight stay.

But Tess had greeted the desk clerk with a friendly smile, called him by name, and chatted easily about how much she and her companion had enjoyed their stay earlier in the season.

He'd all but simpered over her, calling up a bellman to take care of their luggage and guide them to their private cabin nestled on a ridge behind curtaining pines.

Then the cabin itself had simply wiped her mind clean.

A huge wall of glass opened up the living area to the majesty of the mountains, offered a tempting peek at the private hot tub built cleverly into the rocks.

There was a fire already set and burning in a stone hearth, flowers, fresh and dewy, exploding out of pottery vases, a deep, curving seating area in buff, accented by jewel-toned pillows in front of an entertainment center complete with big-screen TV, VCR, and stereo.

A charming dining room set in dark wood was arranged conveniently near a sleek little kitchenette.

"Oh, my," she said, but under her breath this time, as the bellman led the way into a bedroom with its own glass doors leading to a stone terrace. Two double beds were made up neatly with thick pillows and quilts, and the bath beyond—she only managed a quick look—had a mile of ivory counter, an oversized jet tub, and a separate glassed-in shower. And surely that was a bidet.

A bidet. Imagine it.

She could barely think as Tess instructed the bellman. "These bags in here, thank you. You can take hers . . ." Tess sent Willa a steely look. "In the other bedroom. You don't mind sharing the room with me, do you, Lily?"

"What? No, no, of course not, I—"

"Good. Go ahead and get settled. Our first treatment's in an hour."

"Treatment? But what—"

"Don't worry," Tess said, as she sailed out after the bellman. "I took care of it. You'll love it."

All Lily could do was sink down on the side of the bed and wonder if she'd wandered into someone else's dream.

"What happened to your eye, honey?"

The technician, therapist, consultant, whatever the hell she was called, made a long, sympathetic study of Willa's shiner. Willa didn't shrug. It was tough shrugging when you were buck naked on a padded table in a small, dim room.

"Wasn't watching where I was going."

"Ummm. Well, we'll see what one of our skin consultants can do about it. Just relax," she ordered, and began to wrap Willa in something warm and damp. "Is this your first visit to Mountain King Spa?"

"Yeah." And her last, she promised herself.

The claustrophobia came quickly, unexpectedly, as the wrappings snugged her arms close to her body. She felt her heart pound, her breathing shorten, and she began to struggle.

"No, no, just relax, take slow, quiet breaths." A warm, heavy blanket went over the wrappings. "A lot of clients have that initial reaction to an herbal wrap. It'll pass if you just clear your mind, let yourself go. Now, these cotton balls are soaked in our Eye-Lax solution. It'll probably help a bit with that swelling as well as the puffiness. You haven't been sleeping enough."

Swell. Now she was blind as well as trapped. Willa wondered if she would be the first client to tear herself free of herb-soaked restraints and run naked and screaming out of the Ladies' Treatment Center.

Since she didn't want the distinction, she fought to relax, let herself go. It was no more than she deserved, she supposed, for keeping her mouth so stubbornly shut on the drive down.

Music was playing, she realized. Or it wasn't music really, but the sounds of water falling into water and birds chirping. She took one of those slow, quiet breaths and reminded herself she only had just over forty-eight more hours to suffer.

In less than five minutes, she was sound asleep.

She awoke groggily twenty minutes later with the consultant murmuring to her.

"Huh? What? Where?"

"We're getting all those toxins out of your system." Efficiently the consultant removed the layers of herbal wrap. "I want you to be sure to drink plenty of water. Nothing but water for the next few hours. You have a gommage in ten minutes. So relax. I'll help you with your robe and slippers."

Still half asleep, Willa let herself be bundled into her robe and slid her feet into the plastic slippers the spa provided. "What's a gommage?"

"You'll love it," the consultant promised.

So she was naked again, on yet another table with yet another woman in a pale pink lab coat fiddling with her. At the first rough swipe with a damp loofah over bare skin slicked with a fine sandy cream, Willa yelped.

"Was I too rough? I'm terribly sorry."

"No, it just caught me by surprise."

"Your skin's going to be like silk."

Willa shut her eyes, mortified, as the woman rubbed her bare butt. "What the hell is that stuff you're putting on me?"

"Oh, it's our special exfoliator. Skin-Nu. All our products are herbal-based and available in our salon. You have fabulous skin, the coloring . . . but where did you get all these bruises?"

"Pulling calves."

"Pulling . . . oh, you work on a ranch. That's exciting, isn't it? Is it a family operation?"

Willa gave up, let the layers of skin be scraped away. "It is now."

The next time Willa saw Tess, she, Willa, was flat on her back again, naked again, unless you counted the warm, thick brown mud that was being slowly smoothed all over her. Tess poked a head in the door, took one look, and burst into deep, bubbling laughter.

"You're going to pay for this, Hollywood." Christ, the woman was painting hot mud on her tits. On her tits!

"Correction, Mercy's already paying. And you've never looked lovelier."

"I'm sorry, ma'am," the new consultant said, "these are private rooms."

"It's okay, we're sisters." Tess leaned against the doorjamb, looking right at home in her white terry-cloth robe and plastic slippers. "I've got a facial in five. Just thought I'd see how you were holding up."

"I've been lying down since I got here."

"You really want to try the steam room if you have time between treatments. What have you got on next?"

"I have no idea."

"I believe Ms. Mercy is scheduled for a facial next as well. The one-hour Bio Treatment."

"Oh, that's a honey," Tess remembered. "Well, enjoy. Lily's getting the full-body facial in the next room. She's whimpering in pleasure right now. See you."

"You came with your sisters," the consultant said when Tess closed the door.

"So to speak."

The consultant smiled and painted mud on Willa's face. "Isn't that nice."

Willa gave up and closed her eyes. "So to speak."

Willa got back to the suite after six, all but crawling, as her legs were so limp and loose they didn't seem willing to hold weight. She could have whimpered herself and hated to admit that it, too, would have been from pleasure. Her body felt so light, so pampered, so relaxed that her mind simply had no choice but to follow suit.

Maybe the fifteen-minute steam bath with a bunch of other naked women after her full hour massage had been a bit of overkill. But she'd lost her head.

"There you are." Tess was just popping the cork on a bottle of champagne when Willa walked in. "Lily and I had just decided we wouldn't wait for you."

"Oh, you look wonderful." Still wrapped in her robe, Lily got up from the sofa and clasped her hands together. "You're positively glowing."

"I don't think I can move. That guy, that massage guy, Derrick, I think he did something to me."

"You had a man?" Eyes wide, Lily hurried over to lead Willa to the couch. "For a full-body massage?"

"Wasn't I supposed to?"

"My massage therapist was a woman, I just assumed..." She trailed off as Tess handed her a flute.

"I ordered a female for you, Lily. I thought you'd be more comfortable." She passed another flute to Willa. "And I requested a male for Willa because I thought she should start getting used to what it feels like to have a man get his hands on her—even in perfectly professional surroundings."

"If I wasn't afraid I'd melt if I tried to stand up again, I'd punch you for that."

"Honey, you should be thanking me." With her own glass, Tess eased onto the arm of the sofa. "So was it great or what?"

Willa sipped the wine. She'd downed enough water to sink a battleship and the change to bubbles with a kick was glorious. "Maybe." She sipped again, let her head fall back. "He looked like Harrison Ford, and he rubbed my feet. God. And there was this place just above my shoulder blades." She shuddered. "He used his thumbs. He had incredible thumbs."

"You know what they say about thumbs on a man." Smirking, Tess lifted her glass, toasted when Willa bothered to open one eye. "I've noticed that Ben has very... large... thumbs."

"Isn't noticing Nate enough for you?"

"Sleeping with Nate's enough for me. But I'm a writer. Writers notice details."

"Adam has wonderful thumbs." The minute Lily heard herself say it, she choked and went beet-red. "I mean, he has good hands. That is, I mean, they're very..." She snickered at herself, gave up. "Long. Could I have some more?"

"You bet." Tess bounced up, grabbed the bottle. "A couple more and maybe you'll tell us all about Adam's wonderful long thumbs."

"Oh, I couldn't."

"I've got another bottle."

"Don't tease her about it," Willa said, but there wasn't any sting in the words. "Not everybody likes to brag about their bedroom activities."

"I'd like to," Lily said, and flushed again. "I'd like to brag and strut and tell everyone because it's never been like this for me. I never knew it could. I never knew I could." Though she had no head for liquor, she knocked back her second glass with abandon. "And Adam is so beautiful. I mean his face and his heart, but his body. Oh, my God."

She pressed a hand to her breast and held out her glass, which Tess obligingly filled. "It's like something carved out of amber. It's perfect, and I get all loose and fluttery inside just looking at him. And he's so gentle when he touches me. And then he's not, and I don't care because I want him, and he wants me, and everything goes wild and I feel so strong, as if I could make love with him for hours, for days. Forever. And sometimes I have three or four orgasms before we're finished, and with Jesse I hardly ever had even one, and then—"

She broke off, blinked, swallowed. "Did I just say that?"

Tess took a slow, labored breath, a long drink. "Are you sure you want to stop? Another few minutes, and I might just come myself."

"Oh." Hurriedly, Lily set her glass down, clasped her hands to her hot cheeks. "I've never said things like that to anyone. I didn't mean to embarrass you."

"You didn't." Willa's own stomach was fluttering as she reached over to pat Lily's arm. "I think it's wonderful for you, and for Adam."

"I couldn't say things like that to anyone before." Lily's voice broke, and the tears swam. "I couldn't to anyone except the two of you."

"Now, Lily, don't—"

"No." Lily cut off Tess's concern with a shake of her head. "Everything's changed for me. It started changing when I first met both of you. I started changing. Even with all the horrible things that have happened, I'm so happy. I found Adam, and both of you. I love all of you so much. I love you so much. I'm sorry," she said, and sprang up to rush to the bathroom.

Moved, flummoxed, Willa sat where she was and listened to the sound of water rushing into the bathroom sink. "Should one of us go in there?"

"No." Feeling misty-eyed herself, Tess filled Willa's glass again, then dropped onto the couch beside her. "We'll give her a minute." Thoughtfully she selected a perfect Granny Smith apple from the complimentary basket on the table. "She's right, you know. As bad as things are, there's a lot of good stuff trying to balance the scales."

"I guess." Willa looked down into her glass, then lifted her gaze to Tess's. "I guess I'm glad I got to know you. I don't have to like you," she added before things got sloppy. "But I'm glad we got to know each other."

Tess smiled, tapped her glass to Willa's. "I'll drink to that."

19

"What's the point?" Willa asked as she frowned down at her toenails, currently being painted Poppy Pink by a technician. "Nobody sees them but me, and I don't pay much attention to my toenails."

"Which was quite obvious," Tess returned, pleased with her Ravage Red polish. "Before Marla worked her magic on you, your toenails looked like they'd been groomed with a lawn mower."

"So?"

Willa hated the fact that she was actually enjoying most of the process—which had included her new favorite, foot massage. She turned to the opposite side of the padded pedicure bench where Lily was beaming down at her half-painted toes.

"You really think Adam's going to go for—what is it"—Willa cocked her head to read the label on the bottle of polish—"Calypso Coral?"

"It makes me feel pretty." Smiling, Lily admired her nails, already shaped and slicked with matching lacquer. "Grown-up and pretty." She looked over at Tess. "I guess that's the point, isn't it?"

"There." As if after a long classroom lecture a student had finally grasped the formula, Tess clapped, careful to guard her nails against smears. "At last some simple common sense. A smart woman doesn't dress up and decorate herself for a man. She does it for herself first. Then for other women, who are the only species that really notices the details. Then, coming up in the rear, for men, who, if a woman's lucky, see the big picture."

Amused at all of them, Tess wiggled her brows, lowered her voice an octave. "Ugh. Looks good. Smells good. Me wanna mate."

She was rewarded for this insight by a snorting chuckle from Willa. "You don't think much of men, do you, Hollywood?"

"*Au contraire,* dimwit, I think a great deal about men and find them, on the whole, an interesting diversion from the day-to-day routine of life. Take Nate."

"You appear to have already done that."

"Yes." Tess's smile turned smug and feline. "Nathan Torrence, an enigma at first. The slow-talking Montana rancher with the law degree from Yale who likes Keats, Drum tobacco, and the Marx brothers. A combination like that, well, it presents both a challenge and an opportunity."

She lifted her completed foot and preened. "I like challenges, and I never miss an opportunity. But I'm getting my toenails painted because it makes me feel good. If he gets a charge out of it, that's just a bonus."

"It makes me feel exotic," Lily put in, "like—what was the name of that woman in the sarong? The one in the old black-and-white movies?"

"Dorothy Lamour," Tess told her. "Now take Adam, a different type of man altogether."

"He is?" Since they'd moved to her favorite topic, Lily perked up. "How?"

"Don't encourage her, Lily. She's playing at expert here."

"I don't have to play at it, when it comes to men, champ. Adam," Tess continued, wagging a finger. "Serious, solid, and yet vaguely mysterious. Probably the most gorgeous man I've ever seen in my short, if illustrious, career of male tracking, with this—the only word I can think of is 'goodness'—sort of beaming out of those yum-yum eyes."

"His eyes," Lily said with a sigh that made Willa roll her own.

"But—" Tess made her point with a shake of her finger. "It doesn't make him boring, as goodness sometimes can, because there's this simmering, controlled passion in there too. And as far as you're concerned, Lily, you could shave your head and paint your face Calypso Coral, and he'd still adore you."

"He loves me," Lily said with a foolish grin.

"Yes, he does. He thinks you're the most beautiful woman in the world, and if you woke up some morning and some wicked witch had put a spell on you and turned you into a hag, he'd still think you were the most beautiful woman in the world. He sees past the physical, appreciates it but sees past it to everything you are inside. That's why I think you're the luckiest woman in the world."

"Maybe that wasn't such a bad take," Willa commented, "for a Hollywood writer."

"Oh, I'm not done. We have to complete our triad." Delighted with herself, Tess leaned back. "Ben McKinnon."

"Don't start," Willa commanded.

"Obviously you're hot for him. We'll just sit here a minute and dry," she told the technicians, then reached for her glass of sparkling mineral water. "A woman would have to be dead two weeks not to have a pulse spike around Ben McKinnon."

"How much has your pulse been spiking?"

Pleased with the reaction, Tess moved a lazy shoulder. "I'm otherwise involved. If I wasn't . . . In any case, I haven't been dead for two weeks."

"Could be arranged."

"No, don't get up and stalk around yet, you'll smear." Tess put a restraining hand on Willa's arm. "Back to Ben—his sexuality is right out there, striding along a foot in front of him. Raw, hot, unapologetic sex in a tough male package. You watch him ride a horse and you just know he'd ride a woman with the same power. He's also intelligent, loyal, honest, and looks fabulous in Levi's. As a student of such matters, I'd have to say Ben McKinnon has the best buns in denim east or west of the Pecos. Not a bad distraction," she finished, taking a slow sip of water, "from the day-to-day routine."

"I don't know why you're looking at his butt when you've already got a guy," Willa muttered.

"Because it's a fine butt, and I have excellent eyesight." Tess skimmed her tongue over her teeth. "Of course, a woman would have to be brave enough, strong enough, and smart enough to match him in power and style."

There, Tess thought, as Willa sulked beside her, challenge issued, Ben. That's the best help I can give you.

It wasn't until Willa was back at Mercy and unpacking that she realized that through the last twenty-four hours of her stay at the spa, she hadn't thought of the ranch, of her troubles, her responsibilities at all. And now that she did realize it, there was a quick wash of guilt that it should have been so easy to leave it all behind, to immerse herself in the pampering and pleasure.

Like walking into an alternate reality, she supposed, and grimaced as she tumbled pretty gold boxes onto her bed. Which might explain why she'd barely put up a struggle when Tess and Lily had urged her to buy creams, lotions, scents, shampoo.

Christ Almighty, hundreds of dollars' worth of female foolishness that she was unlikely to remember to use.

So she'd give the lot of them to Bess, she decided, to go with the fancy perfumed soaps and bubble bath she'd bought her.

In any case, it was good to be getting back into jeans, she thought, tugging them on. It was better to have Adam tell her there'd been no whisper of trouble over the weekend. The men were starting to relax again, though the round-the-clock guard remained in effect. Calf-pulling season was winding down, and the calendar insisted that spring was on the way.

You wouldn't know it, she mused, trailing her shirt from her fingers as she walked to the window. The air swooping down from Canada was as bitter as an old woman with gout. There was no snow in the sky, and for that she was grateful. Still, Willa knew the vagaries of March—and April, for that matter. The reality of spring remained as distant as the moon.

And she longed for it.

That surprised her as well. Normally she was content in any season. Winter was work, certainly, but it also offered, even demanded, periods of rest. For the land, for the people on it.

Spring might be a time of rebirth and rejoicing, but it was also a time of mud, of drought or impossible driving rain, of aching muscles, fields to be planted, cattle to be separated and led to range.

But she longed for it, longed to see even one single bud bloom—the flower of the bitterroot, triumphing out of the mud; a laurel, springing up miraculously in the thickening forest; wild columbine teasing a mountain ridge.

Amazed at herself, she shook her head and stepped back from the window. Since when had she started dreaming of flowers?

It was Tess's doing, she imagined. All that talk about romance and sex and men. Just a natural segue into spring, flowers—and mating season.

Chuckling, she studied the scatter of gold boxes over the simple quilt on her bed. And what were those, she admitted, but expensive mating lures?

At the sound of footsteps she called out and began to gather the boxes up. "Bess? Got a minute? I've some other things in here you might want. I don't know why I—"

She broke off as Ben, not Bess, stepped into the room.

"What the hell are you doing here? Don't you knock?"

"Did. Bess let me in." His brows went up, and the eyes under them lit with appreciation. "Well, hell, Willa, look at you."

She was grateful she'd pulled on jeans at least and also very aware she was shirtless but for the thin, clinging silk of her thermal undershirt. Her nipples hardened traitorously even as she snatched up the flannel shirt she'd tossed aside.

"I'm not back an hour," she complained as she punched her arms through shirtsleeves, "and you're in my face. I don't have time to chat or go over reports. I've already lost a whole weekend."

"Doesn't appear you lost a thing." He was understandably disappointed when she buttoned up the plaid shirt but intrigued by the busy, businesslike way her fingers executed the task. Eventually he'd like to see them go in reverse.

"You look fine." He came closer. "Rested. Pretty." And lifted a hand to the spiraling curls raining over her shoulders. "Sexy. I had a couple of bad moments when Nate told me about the place you were going. Figured you might come back with your face all tarted up and your hair chopped off like one of those New York models trying to look like a teenage boy. Why do you suppose they want to do that?"

"I couldn't say."

"How'd they get all that hair of yours into those corkscrews?"

"You hand those people enough money, they'll do anything." She tossed back the curls, faintly embarrassed by them. "What do you want, Ben, to stand here and talk about salon treatments?"

"Hmm?" It was the damnedest thing, he mused, toying with her hair again. All those wild curls, and it was still as soft as duck down. "I like it. Gives me ideas."

She was getting that picture clearly enough, and slipped strategically out of reach. "It's just hair curls."

"I like it curled." His grin spread as he maneuvered her toward the wall. "I like it straight too, the way it just swings down your back, or when you twist it back in a pigtail."

She knew the dimensions of her room well enough to judge she'd be rapping into the wall in another two steps. So she held her ground. "Look, what do you think you're doing?"

"Is your memory that poor?" He took hold of her, pleased that she'd stopped retreating. "I didn't figure a few days away would have you forgetting where we left off. Hold still, Willa," he said patiently when she lifted her arms to push him off. "I'm just going to kiss you."

"What if I don't want you to?"

"Then say, 'Get your hands off me, Ben McKinnon.'"

"Get—"

That was as far as she got before he cut off her opportunity. And his lips were hungry, not nearly as patient as his voice had been. The arms that held her tightened possessively, stole her breath, had her parting her lips to gasp for air. . . .

And her mouth was invaded by his quick and clever tongue.

It was like being swallowed, she thought hazily. Like being eaten alive with a greed that incited greed. Hearts pounding. That was his, she realized, as well as hers. Racing wild. Dangerously fast. And she wondered if they continued to ride this course, at this speed, how soon one or both of them would fly headlong over the saddle and into the air.

"Missed you."

He said it so quietly as his lips trailed down to sample her throat that she thought she'd imagined it.

Missed her? Could he?

Those lips cruised up again, along the side of her throat, behind her ear, doing things to her skin that made her giddy and weak inside.

"You smell good," he murmured.

He'd said she looked good, she remembered, as her knees trembled. Smelled good. Did that mean he had the big picture? And what came next was . . . She thought of Tess's lightly cynical remark and swallowed hard.

"Wait. Stop." She couldn't have pushed a mound of feathers away, much less an aroused man, but at her breathy voice and the flutter of her hands he changed the tone.

"Okay." He still held her, but easy now, his hand stroking up her back to soothe. She was shaking, he realized, and cursed himself for it. Innocent, innocent, he repeated like a mantra, until his breathing began to level.

He'd only meant to indulge in a couple of teasing tastes, not a flurry of half-mad gulps. But days, weeks—hell, years—of frustration and wanting, he admitted, were boiling up and threatening to blow.

And what he wanted to do, what he'd imagined doing to her in that room, on that bed, wasn't the way a civilized man should initiate a virgin.

"Sorry." He eased back to study her face. Fear and confusion and desire swirled in her eyes. He could have done without the fear. "I didn't mean to spook you, Will. I forgot myself a minute." To lighten the mood, he flicked a finger at a curl. "Must be the hairdo."

He was sorry, she realized, more than a little stunned. And something else was in his eyes. It couldn't be tenderness, not from him, but she was certain it was a softer emotion than lust. Maybe, she thought—and smiled a little—maybe it was affection.

"It's okay. I guess I forgot myself for a minute too. Must have been the way you were gulping me down like two quarts of prime whiskey."

"You've got a tendency to be as potent," he muttered.

"I do?"

The stunned female response got his blood moving again. "Don't get me started. I really came up to let you know that Adam and I are riding up into high country to take a look around. Zack says the north pass is blocked by snow. And he thought some hunters might be making use of your cabin."

"Why does he think that?"

"On one of his flyovers he caught sight of tracks, other signs." Ben shrugged it off. "Wouldn't be the first time, but since I want to see how bad the pass is blocked, Adam and I thought we'd swing up and check it out."

"I'll go with you. I'll be ready in fifteen minutes."

"We're getting a late start. Odds are we won't make it back tonight. We can radio you from the cabin."

"I'm going. Ask Adam to saddle Moon for me, and I'll pack my gear."

It was good to ride, Willa thought. Good to be in the saddle, out in the air that crisped with the climb. Moon loped easily through the snow, apparently pleased to be out herself. Her breath plumed ahead and her harness jingled.

The sun shone bright, dazzling light off the untrod snow, adding glitter to the draped trees. Here in high country, spring would come late and last hardly more than a precious moment.

A falcon called, a scream in the silence, and she saw signs of deer, of other game, of predators that hunted the hills. Perhaps she had enjoyed her weekend of pampering, but this was her world. The higher she climbed, the more thrilled she was to be back.

"You look pleased with yourself." Ben flanked her left and, keeping an easy hand on the reins, studied her face. "What did they do to you up there at that fancy spa?"

"All sorts of things. Wonderful things." She tilted her head, sent him a sly smile. "They waxed me. All over."

"No kidding?" He felt a pleasant little thrumming in his loins. "*All* over?"

"Yep. I've been scraped down, oiled up, waxed and polished. It was pretty good. You ever had coconut oil rubbed over your entire body, Ben?"

The thrumming increased considerably. "You offering, Willa?"

"I'm telling you. At the end of the day this guy would rub—"

"Guy?" He shot straight arrow in the saddle. The sharp tone of his voice had Charlie scampering back from his scouting mission and whining. "What guy?"

"The massage guy."

"You let a guy rub your—"

"Sure." Satisfied with his reaction, she turned to Adam. The gleam in his eye assured her that her brother knew just what game she was playing. "Lily had something called aromatherapy. It seemed to me to be a lot like our mother's people have been doing for centuries. Using herbs and scents to relax the mind, and the body. Now they've slapped on a fancy name and charge you an arm and a leg for it."

"White men," Adam said with a grin. "Always seeking profit from nature."

"That was my thought. In fact, I asked Lily's massage therapist why she figured—"

"She?" Ben interrupted. "Lily had a woman massage lady?"

"That's right. So I asked her why it was she figured her people had come up with all these treatments when the Indians had been using mud and herbs and oils before there were whites within a thousand miles of the Rockies."

"How come Lily had a woman and you didn't?"

Willa glanced over at Ben. "Lily's shy. Anyway, some of the treatments seemed very basic. And the oils and creams not unlike what our grandmother would have brewed up in her own lodge."

"They put it in fancy bottles and make it theirs," Adam added.

Ben knew when his chain was being pulled, and now he shifted in the saddle. "They use bear grease on you, too?"

Willa bit off a smile. "Actually I suggested they look into it. You should tell Shelly to take a weekend there when the baby's weaned. Tell her to ask for Derrick. He was amazing."

Adam coughed into his hand, then clucked to his horse and took the lead, with Charlie trotting happily in his wake.

"So you let this guy, this Derrick guy, see you naked?"

"He's a professional." She flicked back her curling hair, no longer embarrassed a bit. "I'm thinking of getting regular massages. They're very . . . relaxing."

"I bet." Reaching over, Ben put a hand on her arm, slowing both their mounts. "I've just got one question."

"What is it?"

"Are you trying to drive me crazy?"

"Maybe."

He nodded. "Because you figure it's safe since we're out here and Adam's just up ahead."

The smile got away from her. "Maybe."

"Think again." He moved fast, leaning into her, dragging her into him and fixing his mouth hard on hers. When he let her jerk back, control her frisking mount, he was smiling. "I'm going to buy me some coconut oil, and we'll see how you look in it."

Her heart stuttered, settled. "Maybe," she said again. She started to kick Moon into a trot.

The shot crashed and echoed, a high-pitched, shocking sound. Too close, was all Willa had time to think before Adam's horse reared, nearly unseating him.

"Idiots," she said between her teeth. "Goddamn citified idiots must be—"

"Take cover." Ben all but shoved her out of the saddle, swinging his mount to her other side as a shield. He had his rifle out in a lightning move even as he plunged knee-deep into the snow. "Use the trees, and stay down."

But she'd seen now, the blood that stained the sleeve of Adam's jacket. And seeing it, she was running toward her brother, in the open. Ben swore ripely as he tackled her, used his body to cover hers as another shot exploded.

She fought bitterly, bucking and clawing in the snow. Terror was a hot, red haze. "Adam—he's shot. Let me go."

"Keep down." Ben's face was close to hers, his voice cold and calm as he held her under him. Charlie barked like thunder, quivering for the signal to hunt. He subsided only when Ben gave him the terse order to stay.

Still covering Willa, Ben shifted his eyes as Adam bellied toward them. "How bad?"

"Don't know." The pain was bright, a violent song up his arm to the shoulder. "I think he got more of the coat than me. Will, you're not hit?" He rubbed a snow-coated glove over her face. "Will?"

"No. You're bleeding."

"It's okay. His aim was off."

She closed her eyes a moment, willing herself to calm. "It was deliberate. It wasn't some stupid hunter."

"Had to be a long-range rifle," Ben murmured, lifting his head enough to scan the trees, the hills. He slid a hand over his dog's vibrating back to calm him. "I can't see anything. From the direction, I'd guess he's holed up in that gulch, up there in the rocks."

"With plenty of cover." Willa forced her breath slowly in, slowly out. "We can't get to him."

Trust her, Ben thought, to think first of attack. He slid off Willa, steadied his rifle. "We're almost to the cabin. You and Willa make for it, keep to the trees. I can draw his fire here."

"The hell with that. I'm not leaving you here." She started to scramble up, but Ben pushed her flat again. In the seconds that his eyes held Adam's, the men agreed how to handle it.

"Adam's bleeding," Ben said quietly. "He has to be looked after. You get him to the cabin, Will. I'll be right behind you."

"We can make a stand in the cabin if we have to." Blocking out the pain, Adam walked his way through the details. "Ben, we can cover you from up ahead. When you hear our fire, start after us."

Ben nodded. "Once I get to that stand of rocks where we used to have that fort, I'll fire. That'll give you time to make it to the cabin. Fire again so I'll know you made it."

Now she had to choose, Willa realized, between one man and the other. The blood staining the snow gave her no choice at all. "Don't do anything stupid." She took Ben's face in her hands, kissed him hard. "I don't like heroes."

Keeping low, she grabbed the reins of her horse. "Can you mount?" she said to Adam.

"Yeah. Stay in the trees, Willa. We're going to move fast." With one last look at Ben, Adam swung into the saddle. "Ride!"

She didn't have time to look back. But she would remember, she knew she would remember always, the way Ben knelt alone in the snow, the shadows of trees shielding his face and a rifle lifted to his shoulder.

She'd lied, she thought when she heard him fire once, twice, three times. She had an open heart for heroes.

"There's no return fire," she called out as she and Adam pulled up behind a tower of rock. "Maybe he's gone."

Or maybe he was waiting, Adam thought. He said nothing as Willa unsheathed her rifle. She fired a steady half dozen rounds. "He'll be all right, won't he, Adam? If the sniper tries to circle around and—"

"Nobody knows this country better than Ben." He said it quickly to reassure both of them. He'd left his brother behind, was all he could think. Because it was all that could be done. "We've got to keep moving, Willa. We can give Ben the best cover from the cabin."

She couldn't argue, not when Adam's face was so pale, not when the cabin, warmth, and medical supplies were only minutes away. But she knew what none of them had said: There was no cover for the last fifty yards. To get inside, they would have to ride in the open.

The sun was bright, the snow dazzling. She had no doubt that they stood out against that white like deer in a meadow. In the distance she could hear the frigid sound of water forcing its way over ice and rock and, closer, the rapid sound of her own breathing.

Rocks punched out of snow, trees crouched. She rode with her rifle in her hand, prepared for some faceless gunman to leap out at any moment and take aim. Overhead an eagle circled and called out in triumph. She counted the seconds away by her heartbeats, and bit down hard on her lip when she heard the echo of Ben's rifle.

"He made it to the stand of rocks."

She could see the cabin now, the sturdy wooden structure nestled on rocky ground. Inside, she thought, was safety. First aid for Adam, a radio to signal for help. Shelter.

"Something's wrong." She heard herself say it before it became completely clear. A picture out of focus, a puzzle with pieces missing. "Someone's shoveled a path," she said slowly. "And there are tracks." She took a deep breath. "I can still smell smoke." Nothing puffed from the chimney, but she could catch the faint whiff of smoke in the air. "Can you?"

"What?" Adam shook his head, fought to stay conscious. "No, I..." The world kept threatening to gray on him. He couldn't feel his arm now, not even the pain.

"It's nothing." Moving on instinct, Willa shoved her rifle back in its sheath, took Adam's reins with her free hand. In the open or not, they would have to move quickly before he lost any more blood. "Nearly there, Adam. Hold on. Hold on to the horn."

"What?"

"Hold on to the horn. Look at me." She snapped it out so that his eyes cleared for a moment. "Hold on."

She kicked Moon into a gallop, shouting to urge Adam's mount to keep pace. If Adam fell before they reached safety, she was prepared to leap down, drag him if necessary, and let the horses go.

They burst into a flash of sunlight, blinding. Snow flew up from racing hooves like water spewing. She rode straight in the saddle, using her body to defend her brother's. And every muscle was braced for that quick insult of steel into flesh.

Rather than taking the cleared path, she drove the horses toward the south side of the cabin. Even when the shadow of the building fell over them, she didn't relax. The sniper could be anywhere now. She dragged her weapon free, jumped the saddle, then fought the nearly waist-high snow to reach Adam as he swayed.

"Don't you pass out on me now." Her breath burned in her lungs as she struggled to support him. His blood was warm on her hands. "Damned if I'm carrying you."

"Sorry. Hell. Just give me a second." He needed all his concentration to beat back the dizziness. His vision was blurred around the edges, but he could still see. And he could still think. Well enough to know they wouldn't be safe until they were inside the cabin walls. And even then...

"Get inside. Fire off a shot to let Ben know. I'll get the gear."

"The hell with the gear." Willa steadied him against her side and dragged him toward the door.

Too warm, she thought the minute she was inside the door. Pulling Adam toward a cot, she glanced at the fireplace. Nothing but ash and chunks of charred wood. But she could smell the memory of a recent fire.

"Lie down. Hold on a minute." Hurrying back to the door, she fired three times to signal Ben, then closed them in. "He'll be right along," she said, and prayed it was true. "We have to get your coat off."

Stop the bleeding, get a fire started, clean the wound, radio the ranch, worry for Ben.

"I haven't been much help," Adam said, as she removed his coat.

"Next time I'm shot you can be the tough one." She choked off a gasp at the blood that soaked the sleeve of his shirt from shoulder to wrist. "Pain? How bad?"

"Numb." With a tired and objective eye, he studied the damage. "I think it passed through. I don't think it's so bad. Would've bled more if it hadn't been so cold."

Would've bled less, Willa thought, ripping the sleeve aside, if they hadn't been forced to ride like maniacs. She tore through the thermal shirt as well, felt her stomach heave mightily at the sight of torn and scored flesh.

"I'm going to tie it up first, stop the bleeding." She pulled out a bandanna as she spoke. "I'm going to get some heat in here, then we'll clean it out and see what's what."

"Check the windows." He laid a hand on hers. "Reload your rifle."

"Don't worry." She tied the makeshift bandage snugly. "Lie back down before you faint. You're beginning to look like a paleface."

She tossed a blanket over him, then rushed to the woodbox. Nearly empty, she noted, while her heart thudded. With trembling hands she set the kindling, arranged logs, set them to blaze.

The first aid kit was in the cupboard over the sink. Setting it on the counter, she flipped the lid to be sure it was fully stocked. With that small relief, she crouched down to the cabinet below for bandages, pushed through containers of cleaning supplies.

And felt her bowels turn to water.

The bucket kept below the sink was just where it should have been. But it was heaped with rags and stiffened towels. And the rusty stain coating all of them was blood. Old blood, she thought, as she gingerly reached out. And much too much blood to have been the result of some casual kitchen accident.

Too much blood to be anything but death.

"Will?" Adam struggled to sit up. "What is it?"

"Nothing." She closed the cupboard door. "Just a mouse. Startled me. I can't find bandages." Before she turned back, she schooled the revulsion out of her face. "We'll use your shirt."

She clattered a basin into the sink, filled it with warm water. "I'd say this is going to hurt me more than it's going to hurt you, but it won't."

She set the basin and first aid kit beside him, then went into the bathroom for clean towels. She found one, only one, and indulged herself by pressing her clammy face against the wall.

When she came back, Adam was up, swaying at the window. "What the hell are you doing?" she barked, pulling him back to the cot.

"Can't let our guard down yet. Will, we've got to call the ranch." There were bees buzzing in his ears, and he shook his head to scatter them. "Let them know. He could head down there."

"Everyone at the ranch is fine." Willa removed the bandanna and began to clean the wound. "I'll call as soon as I've got you settled. Don't argue with me." Her voice took on a trembling edge. "You know I don't do well with blood to begin with, and this is my first gunshot. Give me a break here."

"You're doing fine. Shit." He hissed through his teeth. "I felt that."

"That's probably good, right? Looks like it went in here just under the shoulder." Nausea churned, was ignored. "And came out here in the back." Raw, torn flesh with blood still seeping. "You must have lost a pint, but it's slowing down. I don't think it hit bone. I don't think." She gnawed her lip as she opened the bottle of alcohol. "This is going to burn like hellfire."

"Indians are stoic in pain, remember. Holy shit!" He yelped once, jerked, and his eyes watered as the antiseptic seared.

"Yeah, I remember." She tried to chuckle, nearly sobbed. "Go ahead and yell all you want."

"It's okay." His head spun, stomach churned. He could feel the clammy sweat pop out in small beads on his skin. "I got it out. Just get it done."

"I should have given you pain pills first." Her face was as white as his now, and she spoke quickly, words tumbling out to keep them both from screaming. Tears were falling. "I don't know if we have anything but aspirin anyway. Probably like trying to piss out a forest fire. It's clean, Adam, it looks clean. I'm just going to smear this stuff on it now and wrap it up."

"Thank Christ."

They sweated their way through the last of it, then each sighed heavily and studied the other. Their faces were dead pale and sheened with sweat. Adam was the first to smile.

"I guess we didn't do half bad, considering it was the first gunshot wound for both of us."

"You don't have to tell anybody I cried."

"You don't have to tell anybody I screamed."

She mopped her damp face, then his. "Deal. Now lie back and I'll . . ." She trailed off, buried her face against his leg. "Oh, God, Adam, where's Ben? Where's Ben? He should be here."

"Don't worry." He stroked her hair, but his eyes were trained on the door. "He'll be here. We'll radio the ranch, get the police."

"Okay." She sniffled, lifted her head. "I'll do it. Just sit there. You've got to get your strength back." She rose and walked to the radio, switched it on. There was no familiar hum, no light. "It's dead," she said, and her voice reflected her words. A cursory look made her stomach drop. "Someone's pulled out the wires, Adam. The radio's dead."

Tossing down the mike, she strode across the room, hefted her rifle. "Take this," she ordered, and laid the gun across his knees. "I'll use yours."

"What the hell are you doing?"

She picked up her hat, wound the scarf around her throat again. "I'm going after Ben."

"The hell you are."

"I'm going after Ben," she repeated. "And you're in no shape to stop me."

His eyes on hers, he rose, steadied himself. "Oh, yes, I am."

It was a matter for debate, but at that moment they both heard the muffled sound of hooves in snow. Unarmed, Willa whirled toward the door and dragged it open. With Adam only steps behind her, she raced out. Her knees didn't buckle until Ben slid out of the saddle.

"Where the hell have you been? You were supposed to be right behind us. We've been here nearly thirty minutes."

"I circled around. Found some tracks but—Hey!" He dodged the fist she'd aimed at his face, but misjudged the one to his gut. "Jesus, Will, are you crazy? You—" He broke off again when she threw her arms around him. "Women," he muttered, nuzzling her hair. "How you holding up?" he asked Adam.

"Been better."

"Me too. I'll tend to the horses. See if there's any whiskey around here, would you?" He gave Willa a friendly pat on the back and turned her toward the door. "I need a drink."

20

"Campsite a little north of where we got ambushed was cold. Signs somebody dressed some game. Looked like three people on horseback, with a dog." He patted Charlie on the head. "Two days, maybe three. Tidied the place up, so I'd say they knew what they were doing."

He dug into the canned stew Willa had heated. "Anyhow, there were fresh tracks. One rider, heading north. My guess is that would be our man."

"You said you'd be right behind us," Willa said again.

"I got here, didn't I? Charlie and I wanted to poke around first." He set what was left of the stew on the floor for the grateful dog and resisted rubbing his hand over his stomach where her fist had plunged. "The way I see it, the guy takes a couple of shots, then rides off. I don't think he waited around to see what we'd do."

"He may have been staying here," Adam put in. "But that doesn't explain why he sabotaged the radio."

"Doesn't explain why he tried to shoot us, either." Ben shrugged his shoulders. "The man we've been worried about for the past few months uses a knife, not a gun."

"There were three of us," Willa pointed out. At Charlie's thumping tail she managed a small smile. "Four. A gun's a safer bet."

"You got a point." Ben reached for the coffeepot, topped off all three cups.

Willa stared at hers, watched the steam. They had food in their bellies, the kick of caffeine in their blood. It was all the time she could give the three of them to recover.

"He's been here." Her voice was steady. She'd been working on that. "I know the police checked the cabin after that woman was killed, and they didn't find anything to indicate she'd been held here. But I think she was. I think she was held right here, killed right here. And then he cleaned up after himself."

She got up, went to the base cupboard, dug out the bucket. "I think he mopped up her blood with these, then stuck it back under the sink."

"Let me have that." Ben took the bucket from her, then eased her into a chair. "We'd better take this back with us." He set it aside near the woodbox, out of her range of vision.

"He killed her here." Willa was careful to keep her voice from bobbing along with her heart. "He probably tied her to one of the bunks. Raped her, killed her. Then he cleaned up the mess so if anybody checked in, things would look just as they should. He'd have had to bring her down on horseback, most likely at night. I guess he could have hidden the body somewhere for a few hours, even a day, then he dumped what was left of her at the front door. Just dumped her there with less care than you would a butchered deer."

She closed her eyes. "And every time I begin to think, to hope, that it's over, it comes back. He comes back. And there's no figuring the why."

"Maybe there is no why." Ben crouched in front of her, took her hands in his. "Willa, we've got two choices here. It's going to be dark in an hour. We can stay until morning, or we can use night as a cover and head back. Either way it's a risk. Either way it's going to be hard."

She kept her hands in Ben's, looked at Adam. "Are you up to the ride?"

"I can ride."

"Then I don't want to stay here." She drew a deep breath. "I say we head out at dusk."

It was a cold, clear night with just a hint of fog crawling low on the ground. A hunter's moon guided them. Just, Willa thought, as that same hunter's moon spotlighted them for whatever predator stalked them. The dog trotted ahead, his ears pricked up. Beneath her, Moon quivered as her nerves were transmitted to the mare.

Every shadow was a potential enemy, every rustle in the brush a whispered warning. The hoot of an owl, the quick whoosh of wings on a downward flight, and the scream of something hunted well and killed quickly were no longer simply sounds of the mountains at night but reminders of mortality.

The mountains were beautiful with the pale blue cast that moonlight made on snow, the dark trees outlined in fluffy ermine, the unbowed rock jutting up to challenge the sky.

And they were deadly.

He would have come this way, she thought, riding steadily east with his trophy strapped over his saddle. Wasn't that what that poor girl had been to him? A trophy. Something to show how skilled he was, and how clever. How ruthless.

She shuddered, hunched her shoulders against the kick of the wind.

"You okay?"

She glanced at Ben. His eyes gleamed in the dark like a cat's. Sharp, watchful. "I thought, on the day of my father's funeral when Nate read off how things were, would be, I thought nothing would ever be as hard, as hurtful as that. I thought I'd never feel that helpless, that out of control. That it was the worst that could happen to me."

She sighed, carefully guided her horse down an uneven slope where the shadows were long and the ground began to show through in patches. Thin fingers of mist parted like water.

"Then when I found Pickles, when I saw what had been done to him, I thought that was the worst. Nothing could be more horrid than that. But I was wrong. I just keep being wrong about how much worse it can get."

"I won't let anything happen to you. You can believe that."

There in the distance, the first glimmer of light that was Mercy. "You were a damn fool today, Ben, going out tracking on your own. I told you I didn't like heroes, and I think less of fools." She nudged her horse forward, toward the lights.

"Guess she told me," Ben murmured to Adam.

"She was right." Adam tilted his head at Ben's quick frown. "I wasn't any good to you, and she was too busy making sure I didn't bleed to death to do anything else. Going looking on your own didn't help things."

"You'd have done the same in my place."

True enough. "We're not talking about me. She cried."

Uncomfortable now, Ben shifted, shot a look toward Willa as she rode a few paces ahead. "Oh, hell."

"Promised I wouldn't tell, and I wouldn't have if all the tears had been for me. But there were plenty for you. She was about to go out after you."

"Well, that's just—"

"Foolish." Adam's lips curved. "I'd have tried to stop her, but I doubt I'd have managed it. Maybe you'd better think of that next time."

He tried to ease his stiffening shoulder. "There's going to be a next time, Ben. He isn't finished."

"No, he isn't finished." And Ben quietly closed the distance to Willa.

. . .

The damn sight on the rifle had been off. Stinking expensive biathlon sight, and it had been defective.

That's what Jesse told himself as he relived every moment of the ambush. It had been the rifle, the sight, the wind. It hadn't been him, hadn't been his aim, hadn't been his fault.

Just bad fucking luck, that was all.

He could still see the way the half-breed, wife-stealing bastard's horse had reared. He'd thought, oh, for one sweet moment he'd thought he nailed the target.

But the sight had been off.

It had been impulse, too. He hadn't planned it out. If he'd planned it out instead of having it all just happen, Wolfchild would be cold and dead—and maybe McKinnon would be dead too. And maybe he'd have taken a taste of Lily's half sister for good measure.

Jesse blew out smoke, stared into the dark, and cursed.

He'd get another chance, sooner or later, he'd get another chance. He'd make sure of it.

And wouldn't Lily be sorry then?

Every night for a week Willa woke in the grip of a nightmare, drenched in sweat, with screams locked in her throat. Always the same: She was naked, wrists bound. Night after night she struggled to free herself, felt the cord bite into her flesh as she whimpered and writhed. Smelled her own blood as it trickled down her bare arms.

Always, just before she pulled herself awake, there was the glint of a knife, that shimmering arc as the blade swept down to work on her.

Every morning she shoved it away, knowing that, like a rat, it would gnaw free in the night.

The signs of spring, those early hesitant signs, should have thrilled her. The brave glint of crocus her mother had planted scattered such hopeful color. There was the growing spread of earth where the snow melted back to thinning patches, the sounds of young cattle, the dance of foals in pasture.

The time to turn the earth was coming, to plant it and watch it grow. And the time when the cottonwoods and aspens and larches would take on a lovely haze of green. The lupine would bloom, and even the high meadows would be bright with it, with the neon signs of Indian paintbrush, with the sunny faces of buttercups.

The mountains would show more silver than white, and the days would be long again and full of light.

It was inevitable that winter would whisk back at least once more. But spring snows were different; they lacked the brutal harshness of February's. Now that the sun was smiling, bumping the temperature up to the balmy sixties, it was easy to forget how quickly it could change again. And easy to cherish every hour of every bright day.

From the window of her office, Willa could see Lily. She was never far from Adam these days, had rarely left his side since the night they had come back from high country. Willa watched Lily touch Adam's shoulder, as she often did, fussing with the sling he wore.

He was healing. No, she thought, they were healing each other.

How would it be to have someone that devoted, that much in love, that blind to everything but you? How would it be to feel exactly that same way about someone?

Scary, she thought, but maybe it would be worth those jiggles of fear and doubt to experience that kind of unfettered emotion. It would be an exhilarating trip, that wild ride on pure feeling, pure need. And more, she realized, beyond the moment, the promise and permanence that was so easily read on the faces of Lily and Adam when they looked at each other.

The little secret smiles, the signals that were so personal. So *theirs*. What a thrill, she mused, and what security to know there was someone who would be there for you, always. To have someone who thought of you first, and last.

Silly, she told herself, and turned away from the window. Daydreaming this way with so much to be done, so much at stake. And she would never be the kind of woman a man thought of first. Even her own father hadn't thought of her first.

She could admit that now, here in his office that still held so much of him trapped in the air, like a scent ground into the fibers of carpet. He had never thought of her first, and he had certainly not thought of her last.

And what was she? Deliberately Willa sat in the chair that was still his, laid her hand on the smooth leather arms where his had rested countless times. What had she ever been to him? A substitute. A poor one at that, she thought, certainly by Jack Mercy's standards.

No, not even a substitute, she thought as her hands curled into fists. A trophy, one of three that he hadn't even bothered to keep a memento of. Something easily discarded and forgotten, not even worth the space of a snapshot on his desk.

Not worth as much as the heads of the game kills mounted on the walls.

The fury, the insult of it was rising up in her so quick, so huge, she didn't fully realize what she was doing until she'd done it. Until she was up and yanking the first glassy-eyed head from the wall. The left antler of the six-point buck cracked as it hit the floor, and the sound, almost like a gunshot, mobilized her.

"The hell with it. The hell with him. I'm not a fucking trophy." She scrambled onto the sofa, tugged at the bighorn sheep that stared at her with canny eyes. "It's my office now." Grunting, she heaved the head aside and attacked the next. "It's my ranch now."

Later, she might admit she went a little insane. Pulling, pushing, dragging at the mountings, a macabre task, stripping the walls of those disembodied heads, breaking nails as she pried them loose. Her lips were peeled back in a snarl matching that of the mountain cat she wrestled from its perch.

For a moment Tess just watched from the doorway. She was too stunned to do much more as she saw the grisly heap growing on the floor, and her sister muttering oaths as she muscled the towering grizzly out of its corner.

If she hadn't known better, Tess would have said Willa was locked in a life-and-death battle, with the bear in the lead. Since she did know better, she wasn't certain whether she should laugh or run away.

Instead of either, she pushed the hair back from her face, cleared her throat. "Wow. Who opened the zoo?"

Willa whirled, her face contorted in rage, her eyes alive with it. The bear lost the edge of gravity and toppled like a tree. "No more trophies," Willa said, and panted to get her breath. "No more trophies in this house."

Sanity seemed called for. Hoping to instill it, Tess leaned negligently against the doorjamb. "I can't say that I've ever cared for the decor in here, or elsewhere. *Field and Stream* isn't my style. But what brought on this sudden urge to redecorate?"

"No more trophies," Willa repeated. Desperation had cemented into conviction. "Not them. Not us. Help me get them out." She took a step, held out a hand. "Help me get them the hell out of our house."

When realization came, it was sweet. Stepping forward, Tess rolled up her sleeves, and there was a gleam in her eyes now. "My pleasure. Let's evict Smokey here first."

Together they heaved and dragged the stuffed and snarling bear to the doorway, then through it. They'd made it to the top of the steps before Lily came running up them.

"What in the world—For a minute I thought—" She pressed a hand to her speeding heart. "I thought you were about to be eaten alive."

"This one had his last meal some time ago," Willa managed to say, and tried for a better grip.

"What are you doing?"

"Redecorating," Tess announced. "Give us a hand with this bastard. He's heavy."

"No, screw it." Willa blew out a breath. "Back off," she warned, and when the stairs were clear she began to shove. "Come on, help me push."

"Okay." Tess made a show of spitting on her hands, then put her back into it. "Push, Lily. Let's dump this big guy together."

When he went, he went with a flourish, tumbling down the staircase with the noise of a thunderclap, dust puffing, claws clattering. At the din, Bess came rushing out from the kitchen, her face red with the effort and her hand on the .22 Baretta she'd taken to keeping in her apron pocket.

"Name of God Almighty." Huffing for air, Bess slapped her hands on her hips. "What are you girls up to? You've got a bear in the foyer."

"He was just leaving," Tess called out, and began to whoop with laughter.

"I'd like to know who's going to clean up this mess." Bess nudged the trophy with her toe, considering it every bit as nasty dead as alive.

"We are." Willa swiped her palms over her jeans. "Just consider it spring cleaning." She turned on her heel and marched back into the office.

Now, with the first thrust of fury deadened, she could see clearly what she'd done. Heads and bodies were strewn all over the room like bomb victims after a blast. Wooden mountings were cracked or chipped where she'd thrown them. Eerily, a loosened glass eye stared up at her from the beautiful pattern of the carpet.

"Oh, my God." She let out one long breath, then another. "Oh, my God," she said again.

"You sure showed them, pal." Tess gave her a light thump on the back. "They didn't have a chance against you."

"It's—" Lily pressed her lips together. "It's horrible, isn't it? Really horrible." She hiccuped, turned away, pressed her lips tighter. "I'm sorry. It's not funny. I don't mean to laugh." She struggled to hold it back by crossing her arms hard over her stomach. "It's just so awful. Like a wildlife garage sale or something."

"It's hideous." Tess lost her slippery hold on composure and began to giggle. "Hideous and morbid and obscene, and—oh, Jesus, Will, if you'd seen yourself when I first walked in. You looked like a madwoman doing the tango with a stuffed bear."

"I hate them. I've always hated them." Her own laughter bubbled up until she simply sat on the floor and let it go.

Then the three of them were sprawled on the floor, howling like loons amid the decapitated heads.

"They're all going," Willa managed, and pressed a hand to her aching side. "As soon as I can stand up, they're all going."

"Can't say I'll miss them." Tess wiped her streaming eyes. "But what the hell are we going to do with them?"

"Burn them, bury them, give them away." Willa moved her shoulders. "Whatever." She took a cleansing breath and pushed herself to her feet. "Clean sweep," she announced, and hauled up a mounted elk's head.

They carted them out—elk, moose, deer, sheep, bear. There were stuffed birds, mounted fish, lonely antlers. As the pile in front of the porch began to build, the men wandered over to make a fascinated and baffled audience.

"Mind if we ask what you ladies are doing?" As unofficial liaison, Jim stepped forward.

"Spring cleaning," Willa told him. "You think Wood can fire up the backhoe and dig a hole big enough to dump these in, give them a decent burial?"

"You're just going to dump them in a hole?" Shocked, Jim turned back as the men began to mumble. It took only a few minutes in a huddle to come to an agreement. This time Jim cleared his throat. "Maybe we could have a few for down to the bunkhouse and thereabouts. It's a shame just to bury 'em. That buck there'd look fine over the fireplace. And Mr. Mercy, he put store by that bear."

"Take what you want," Willa said.

"Can I have the cat, Will?" Billy hunkered down to admire it. "I sure would appreciate it. He's a beauty."

"Take what you want," she repeated, and shook her head as the men began to argue, debate, and lay claim.

"Now you've done it." Ham moseyed over while four of the men muscled the bear into the back of a rig. "I'm going to have that damn ugly bastard staring at me every morning and every night. They'll be storing what don't fit on the walls in one of the outbuildings, too, mark my words."

"Better there than in my house." Willa cocked her head. "I thought you liked that bear, Ham. You were with him when he took it down."

"Yeah, I was with him. Don't mean I harbor an affection for it. Jesus. Billy, you're going to break that rack you keep that up. Have a care, for God's sake. Be hanging their hats from it," he muttered as he stalked over to supervise. "Damn idiot cowboys."

"Now everybody's happy," Tess observed.

"Yep. Library's next."

"I can give you an hour." Tess glanced at her watch. "Then I've got to get ready. I've got a hot date."

She had some new lingerie, delivered just that afternoon from Victoria's Secret. She wondered how long it would take Nate to get her out of it.

Not long, she speculated. Not long at all.

She let her thoughts circle back to Will. "And isn't this the night for you and Ben to take in your weekly picture show?" she said with her tongue in her cheek.

"I guess it is."

"Lily's fixing a fancy dinner for Adam tonight."

Distracted, Willa glanced back. "Oh?"

"Well, it's sort of the anniversary of when we first . . . first," Lily finished, and blushed.

She'd gotten a delivery from Victoria's Secret too.

"And it's Bess's night off." Casually, Tess studied her nails. Evicting wildlife had been tough on her manicure. "I heard she was going down to Ennis to spend the night with her gossipmate Maude Wiggins. Since I'm planning on staying at Nate's, you'll have the house all to yourself."

"Oh, you shouldn't be alone," Lily jumped in. "I can—"

"Lily." Tess rolled her eyes. "She won't be alone unless she's incredibly slow or incredibly stupid or just plain stubborn. A quick woman, a smart one, a flexible one, would get herself all polished and perfumed and suggest a quiet evening in."

"Ben would think I'd lost my mind if I got all dressed up, then said I wanted to stay in."

"Wanna bet?"

At Tess's slow smile, Willa felt her own lips curving. "Things are too complicated now. I've got too much on my mind to be thinking of wrestling with Ben."

"When aren't things complicated?" Tess took Willa's arms, turned her face-to-face. "Do you want him or not? Yes or no."

Willa thought of the flutter that had been in her stomach all day. Because he'd been on her mind. "Yes."

Tess nodded. "Now?"

"Yeah." Willa let out a breath she hadn't been aware of holding. "Now."

"Then leave the rest of the spring cleaning for tomorrow. It'll take Lily and me at least an hour to find something halfway sexy in that closet of yours."

"I didn't say I wanted you to dress me again."

"It's our pleasure." Mind on her mission, Tess pulled Willa back inside. "Isn't it, Lily? Hey, where are you going?"

"Candles," Lily called out as she dashed across the road. "Willa doesn't have nearly enough candles in her room. I'll be right there."

"Candles." Willa dragged her feet. "Fancy clothes, pretending I don't want to see a movie, candles in my bedroom. It feels like I'm setting a trap."

"Of course it does, because that's exactly what you're doing."

At the doorway of Willa's room, Tess stopped, put her hands on her hips. There was work to be done here, she determined, if the scene was to be properly set. "And I guarantee, he's not only going to love being caught, he's going to be grateful."

21

"I feel like an idiot."

"You don't look like an idiot." Tess tilted her head and studied Willa from top to toe.

Yes, the hair swept up was a good touch—Lily's. With only a few pins anchoring all that mass, it would tumble down satisfactorily at a man's impatient handling.

Then there was the long dress—simple, full-skirted, nipped just a bit at the waist. Too bad it wasn't white, Tess mused, but Willa's limited wardrobe hadn't run to long white dresses. And the pale gray was quiet, almost demure. Except that Tess had left the long line of front buttons undone to the thigh.

The tiny silver hoops at Willa's ears were Lily's contribution again. The makeup was Tess's, and she knew Willa had been relieved that she'd used a light hand. But she didn't think Willa understood the power of innocence on the verge.

"You look," Tess finally decided, "like a virgin eager to be sacrificed."

Willa rolled her eyes. "Oh, God."

"That's a good thing." Woman to woman, she patted Willa's cheek. "You'll destroy him."

Then the guilt hit. Had she pushed this moment? Tess wondered. Had she finagled it before Willa was ready? It was easy to forget that Willa was six years younger than she. And untouched.

"Listen . . ." Tess caught herself wringing her hands and dropped them to her sides. "Are you sure you're ready for this? It's a natural step, but it's still a big one. If you're not absolutely sure, Nate and I can stay. We can make it a double date, keep things simple. Because—"

"You're more nervous than I am." Since that was such a surprise, and oddly sweet, Willa grinned.

"Of course not. I'm just—hell." It wasn't just Lily, who had left half an hour before blinking back tears, who was sentimental, Tess discovered. While Willa's eyes widened in shock, Tess leaned forward and kissed her gently on both cheeks.

Absurdly touched, Willa felt her stomach flutter and her color rise. "What was that for?"

"I feel like a mommy." And she was going to start bawling in a minute, so she turned quickly for the door. "I put condoms in your nightstand drawer. Use them."

"For heaven's sake, he'll think I'm—"

"Prepared, smart, self-aware. Damn it." Even as she heard the sound of the rig pull up outside, Tess gave up. Turning back, she rushed up to Willa and hugged her hard. "See you tomorrow," she managed, and raced out.

Grinning hugely, Willa stayed where she was. She heard Tess's voice rise, and Nate, who'd been waiting downstairs, answered. Then the door, and Ben's easy greeting. Her stomach jumped again, so she sat on the edge of the bed and pressed her hand to it. The conversation trailed off, then the door opened and closed again. An engine roared to life.

She was alone with Ben.

She could always change her mind, she reminded herself. There was no obligation here. She would play it by ear. She made herself rise. Starting now.

He was in the great room, studying the newly blank stone above the fireplace. "I took it down," she said, and he turned, and he studied her. "We took it down today," she corrected. "Lily, Tess, and I. We haven't decided what we want to put up in place of his portrait, so we're living with nothing for a while."

She's taken down Jack Mercy's portrait, Ben thought. By the tone in her voice, he knew she understood just what a step she'd taken. "It changes the room. The focus of it."

"Yes, that was the idea."

He stepped forward, stopped. "You look great, Will. Different."

"I feel different." She smiled. "Great. And how are you?"

He'd been feeling easy before he turned and saw her in that long mist-colored dress, the flowing skirt with the teasing hint of leg. That slim neck revealed by the pinned-up hair. She looked too soft, too touchable, too everything.

"Fine. The same. Seems like I should take you to something fancier than a movie, the way you look."

"Lily and Tess get a charge out of going through my closet and criticizing my wardrobe. I'm told this is about the only decent thing I own." She plucked at the skirt and his blood pressure spiked as the unbuttoned material gave way to more leg. "They've threatened to take me shopping."

Stop babbling, she ordered herself, and moved behind the bar. "Want a drink?"

"I'm driving."

"Actually, I was thinking we could just stay in." There, now she'd done it.

"In?"

"Yeah, I don't get the house to myself often anymore. Bess is staying with a friend tonight, and Tess and Lily are . . . well."

"Nobody's here?" Something lodged in his throat, something hot and not easily swallowed.

"Nobody's here." She opened the cold box behind the bar, found the champagne Tess had directed her to serve. "So, I thought we could just . . . stay in. Relax." The bottle clinked hard on wood when she set it down. "Tess has a suitcase full of videos if we want a movie, and there's food."

Since he made no move to do so, Willa tore off the foil, twisted the wire free. "Unless you'd rather go out."

"No." He focused on the bottle when she popped the cork. "Champagne? Are we celebrating?"

"Yeah." If she could just manage to get a grip on the glasses. "Spring. I saw wildflowers today, and the bulbs are sprouting. Birds are building a nest in the pole barn again." She passed him his glass. "We'll start inseminating cows soon."

His lips twitched as he took the glass. "Yeah, it's that time of year."

"Oh, the hell with this." She muttered it, then downed the bubbly wine in her glass in two long gulps. "I'm no good at games. This is Tess and Lily's idea, anyway." Debating another, she set her empty glass down, looked him dead in the eye. "Look, the point is, Ben, I'm ready."

"Okay." Baffled, he took a sip of champagne. "You want to go out after all?"

"No, no." She pressed her fingers against her eyes, took a breath. "I'm ready to have sex with you."

He choked, managed to wheeze in air, sputter it out. "Excuse me?"

"Why dance around all this?" She came out from behind the bar. "You want me to go to bed with you, and I'm ready to. So, let's go to bed."

He took another drink—a mistake, as each individual bubble took on an edge and ripped its way down his throat. "Just like that?"

The horror in his voice had her fumbling. What if he'd just been stringing her along, teasing her the way he had since childhood?

Why, then, she thought, he'd have to die.

"It's what you said you wanted," she snapped at him. "So?"

"So." She'd always done him in with angry eyes and impatience. Made him want to bite her—in all sorts of interesting places. But she was changing the game, he thought. And the rules. "Just, I'm ready now so yippee?"

"What's wrong with that?" She jerked a shoulder. "Unless you've changed your mind."

"No, I haven't changed my mind. It's not a matter of changing my mind, it's . . . Jesus, Will." He set the glass on the bar before he could bobble it and make a fool of himself. "You've thrown me off stride."

"Oh." The confusion faded from her eyes and her mouth curved into a smile. "Is that all?"

"What do you expect?" His voice shot out, filled with male frustration. "You stand there all prettied up, shove champagne at me, and tell me you want to have sex. How am I supposed to keep my rhythm?"

Maybe he had a point, though she couldn't quite see it. But he looked sort of cute, all flustered and embarrassed. So she'd humor him.

"Okay." She closed the distance, wound her arms around his neck. "Let's see if we can get your rhythm back." Pressed her mouth hard to his.

His reaction was quick, and satisfying. The way his arms came up, banded her, the way his mouth angled and fed, the quick intake and release of his breath. Then, when his lips gentled, the way he murmured her name.

"Your gait seems steady enough to me." Now her voice was shaky. The muscles in her thighs were vibrating like harp strings. "I want you, Ben. I really want you." She proved it by locking her mouth to his again, then tearing it away to rain kisses over his face. "We don't have to go upstairs. The couch."

"Hold on. Slow down." Before I rip your clothes off and ruin it. "Slow down," he repeated, holding her close before the last of the blood could drain out of his head. "I've got to get my feet back under me, and you've got to be sure. It's going to be really tough to back off if you change your mind."

With a laugh, she boosted herself up, wrapped her legs around his waist. "Do I look like I'm going to change my mind?"

"No, guess not." But if she did, it was on him to hold himself back. He thought such an eventuality might kill him. "I want you, Willa." He brushed his lips over hers. "I really want you."

Her heart did a neat somersault. "Sounds like a deal."

"Upstairs." He managed to walk even as she tightened her grip and started nibbling at his jaw. "The first time should be in a bed."

"Was yours?"

"No, actually." He got to the stairs, wondered why he'd never noticed how long they were. "It was in a rig in the middle of winter and I nearly froze my . . . never mind."

She chuckled, nuzzled at his throat. "This'll be better, won't it?"

"Yeah." For him, without a doubt. For her . . . he was going to do his best. He stopped in the doorway of her room. He wasn't sure how many more shocks he could survive in one night.

Candles burned everywhere, and the fire glowed low. The bed was turned down, inviting with dozens of pillows.

"Tess and Lily," Willa explained. "They really got into this."

"Oh." Nothing like being showcased, Ben thought as his nerves jumped. "Did they . . . has anyone talked to you about . . . things?"

"McKinnon." She eased back to grin at him. "I run a ranch."

"It's not exactly the same." He set her on her feet, backed off a step. "Listen, Willa, this is kind of a first for me, too. I've never—the others weren't—" He had to shut his eyes a minute, gather his scattered wits. "I don't want to hurt you. And I, well, I haven't had anyone in a while. I set my sights on you damn near a year ago, and I haven't had anyone else since."

"Really?" That was interesting. "Why?"

He sighed, sat on the edge of the bed. "I have to get my boots off."

"I'll give you a hand." She obligingly turned her back to him, hefted one booted foot between her legs. He nearly groaned. "A year?" She glanced over her shoulder as she tugged.

"Maybe more, if it comes down to it." Struggling to be amused, he planted a foot on her butt and pushed.

"You were never particularly nice to me." She took his other foot, pulled at the boot.

"You scared the hell out of me."

She stumbled forward as the boot came off, then turned, still holding it. "I did?"

"Yeah." Irritated with himself, he pushed a hand through his hair. "And that's all I'm going to say about it."

It was enough to think about, she supposed. "Oh, I forgot." She hurried to the table by the window and fiddled with Tess's CD player. "Music," she explained. "Tess claims it's mandatory."

He couldn't hear anything over the knocking of his own heart. Her hair was falling down, just a little, and the firelight streamed through that long, thin skirt every time she moved.

"That should do it. Unless we should have the champagne up here."

"That's all right." His throat was closing again, snapping like a bear trap. "Later."

"Okay." She lifted her hands, began to undo the buttons of the dress while his mouth fell open. Her busy fingers flipped open six before he could get his tongue off his toes.

"Hold it. Slow down. If you're going to strip for a man, you should pace yourself."

"Is that so?" Intrigued, she stopped, watched his gaze dip to her fingers, then began again. "I'm not wearing a stitch under here," she said conversationally. "Tess said something about contrast and impact."

"Oh, good Jesus." He wasn't sure how he got to his feet when he couldn't feel them. But he stepped to her. "Don't take it off." His voice had thickened, and the sound of it had her eager fingers pausing, trembling. "Let me finish it."

"All right." Odd, her arms were so heavy now. She let them fall to her sides as he slipped the rest of the buttons free. It was a lovely sensation, she thought, the skim of his knuckles over her skin. "Shouldn't you be groping me or something?"

A laugh, even a weak one, soothed some of the nerves. "I'll get to it." The dress was open now, with light and shadow playing over that lovely line of bare flesh. "Just stand there," he said quietly, and touched his mouth to hers. "Can you do that?"

"Yeah. But my knees are going to start knocking."

"Just stand there," he repeated, touching only mouth to mouth as he undid his shirt. "Let me taste you a while. Here." His lips cruised over her jaw. "Here." Up to her ear. "You can trust me."

"I know." Now her eyes were heavy, she felt the lids drooping as his mouth toyed with hers. "Whenever you chew on my lip that way, I can't get my breath."

"Want me to stop?"

"No, I like it." She said it dreamily. "I can breathe later."

He tossed his shirt aside. "I want to see you, Willa. Let me look at you."

Slowly, he slid the dress from her shoulders, let it drift to the floor. She was long and slim, subtle curves and strong angles, her skin glowing gold in the dancing light. "You're beautiful."

It was an effort not to lift her hands to cover herself. No one had ever said that to her. Not once in her life. "You always said skinny."

"Beautiful." He cupped a hand to the back of her neck, drew her slowly toward him. His fingers combed up, her hair tumbled down. He experimented with the weight of it, lifting it, letting it fall while his mouth rubbed over hers. "I always wanted to play with your hair, even when you were a kid."

"You used to pull it."

"That's what boys do when they want girls to pay attention to them." He gathered it, gave it a tug, and had her head jerking back. "Mmm." He sampled the exposed line of her throat, nibbled lazily where the pulse was rabbiting. "Paying attention?"

"Yeah." She shuddered, couldn't stop. "Or I'm trying to, but I keep losing my focus. All this stuff's happening inside me."

"I want to be inside you." Her eyes opened at that, and in them he saw nerves gloriously mixed with needs. "But there's more first. I have to touch you."

He skimmed a hand down to her breast, circled with a fingertip, forced a moan through her lips as his thumb scraped over her nipple. She felt an answering tug, deep inside. An echo of shock and pleasure. Then his hand slid down, over her hip, his fingers trailing lightly toward her center, brushing, awakening, then retreating.

Her eyes were huge, focused on his. Her hands came to his shoulders for balance and found smooth skin, taut muscles, an old scar. Her fingers dug in once as she tried to absorb and analyze the sensation of those callused hands stroking her flesh.

She hadn't expected this. She'd thought it would be fast, a grappling match full of grunts and howls. How could she have known there would be tenderness mixed with the heat? And the heat was huge.

"Ben?"

"Hmm?"

"I don't think I can stand up anymore."

His lips curved against her shoulder. "Just another minute. I haven't quite finished."

So this was what it was like to awaken a woman. To know that your hands were the first hands. To know you were the first to bring that flush to the skin, that weakness to the limbs, that quiver to the muscles. He could be careful with her, would be careful with her, no matter how that very innocence made his blood surge.

When her eyes drooped this time, he lifted her into his arms, laid her on the bed.

"You still have your pants on."

He covered her, letting her grow accustomed to his weight. "It'll be better for both of us if I keep them on a while yet."

"Okay." His hands were roaming again, and she was beginning to float. "Tess—in the drawer there—condoms."

"I'll take care of it. Let go for me, Will." He trailed a line of kisses down her throat. "Just let it all go." And with a shudder of his own he took her breast in his mouth.

She arched, the breath exploding through her lips. Sensation careened through her system, flashing with heat, urging her hips to grind with the rhythm he set. He bit lightly, but the sensation was no kin to pain. Her hands were fisted in his hair, urging him to feed.

He heard her sigh, and gasp and murmur. Her response to every touch was as free and open as any man could wish. Beneath his her body was agile, limber one moment, taut the next as she flowed with him. The flavor of her filled him, threatened to drive him mad if he didn't stop, if he didn't take more. Her scent—soap and skin—aroused him more than any perfume.

He took her mouth again, needed it like he needed breath. Her tongue tangled with his in an avid dance. Somewhere in the back of his mind, he could hear the quiet thrum of music.

He stroked a hand up that long length of leg, stopping just short of the heat, retreating. Her breath came quickly now, fast and shallow while her nails bit into him.

"Look at me." He brushed her, lightly, found her erotically hot, wet. But even as she arched, he retreated again. "Look at me. I want to see your eyes the first time. I want to see what it does to you."

"I can't." But her eyes were open, wide and blind. Her body was on the edge of something, like a high cliff where the wind both pulled and pushed. "I need—"

"I know." God, that voice of hers—straight sex. And now even throatier, rustier, and quivering with little gasps. "But look at me." He cupped her, watched her eyes go dark with fear and passion.

The first time, he thought. "Let go."

What choice did she have? His fingers stroked her to flash point, and everything happened at once. Her body tightened like a fist. Lights whirled in front of her eyes, spinning to the roar of sound in her head that was her own frantic heartbeat.

And this pleasure was kin to pain, an eruption that had her helplessly crying out while her body bucked, shuddered, then went slack.

Her skin was dewed with sweat now, her lips soft with surrender when he sought them again. Weakness warred, then gave way to fresh energy as he patiently, ruthlessly worked her back into a frenzy. Her system overcharged, reeled, imploded. She rocked against him, wildly greedy for more. And he gave more until she was pliant again, body still quivering in reaction, breath coming slow and thick.

When he rolled off her she couldn't even manage a protest, but lay sprawled in the hot, tangled sheets.

He had to pray he wouldn't fumble now, though his hands shook when he tugged at the snap of his jeans. He'd wanted her sated and satisfied before he took her, wanted her to remember the pleasure if he was unable to prevent the pain.

"I feel like I'm drunk," she murmured. "I feel like I'm drowning."

He knew the feeling. His blood was singing a siren's song in his head, and his loins were screaming for release. Stripping away his jeans, he tossed them aside before he remembered what he carried in his wallet, snugged into the back pocket.

Blessing Tess, he dug into Willa's nightstand drawer.

"Don't fall asleep," he begged as he heard her sigh. "For God's sake don't fall asleep."

"Uh-uh." But this state of floaty relaxation was the next best thing. She stretched, and the firelight danced over her, rippling golds and reds and ambers. Ben tore his gaze away and finished the business at hand. "Are you going to touch me again?"

"Yeah." He had to get the nerves under control. The hunger was one thing, he could keep it chained, but the nerves fluttered through his stomach as he ranged himself over her. "I need you." It wasn't an easy admission, not the same as want, and he gave it to her as his mouth closed over hers. "Let me have you, Willa. Hold on to me and let me have you."

And her arms came around him as he slid into her.

Oh, God, so tight, so hot. He had to use every ounce of control not to plunge mindlessly into her like a stallion covering a ready mare. Battling to go slowly, he fisted his hands on either side of her head, watched her face. Watched it so intently, so closely that he saw those first flickers of shock, of acceptance, and finally, that lovely glaze of dark pleasure.

"Oh, it's wonderful." She breathed the words out as he moved inside her. "Really wonderful."

She gave up her innocence without regret, with a smile bowing her lips as she matched him stroke for slow stroke. In his eyes she saw the need he had spoken of, the need focused only and fully on her. When she looked deeper, she saw herself reflected back in them, lost in them.

And this, she thought, when he finally buried his face in her hair and emptied himself into her, was beauty.

"I didn't know it would be like that." Still pinned beneath him, still joined, Willa lazily played with his hair. "I might have been ready sooner."

"I'd say the timing worked just fine." He had fantasies already working. Pouring champagne over that lovely golden body and licking it off. Drop by drop.

"I always thought people set too much store by sex. I guess I've changed my mind."

"It wasn't sex." He turned his head, nibbled at her temple. "We'll have sex some other time. This was making love. And you can't set too much store by either."

She stretched her arms up, then lowered them so that her hands could knead his bottom. "What's the difference?"

He was still half aroused, and well aware it wouldn't take much to finish the job. "You want me to show you?" Lifting his head, he grinned down at her. "Right now?"

She chuckled and, feeling sentimental, stroked his cheek. "Even a bull needs recovery time."

"I ain't no bull. Just stay right there."

"Where are you going?" My, oh, my, she thought, she hadn't taken nearly enough time to look at that body of his. It was . . . an education.

"I'll be right back," he told her, and strode out without bothering with his jeans.

Well, well. She stretched again, then shifted so that she was cradled by pillows. It seemed the night wasn't over. Experimentally, she laid a hand on her breast. Her heart was bumping along at a normal rate now rather than with that snare drum riff it had reached when he'd nuzzled just there.

It was an odd feeling, she thought, to have a man suckling you, to have him pull you inside him. And to experience those mirror tugs in the womb.

Everything he'd done had made her body feel different—tighter then looser, lighter then heavier.

She wondered if she looked different—to herself, to him. There was no denying that she felt different.

With all the pain, all the grief and fear in her life over the past months, she had found an oasis. For tonight, if only for tonight, there was only this room. Nothing outside of this room mattered. No, not even murder. She wouldn't let reality in.

Tomorrow was soon enough for worries, for the fear of what was haunting her ranch, her mountains, her land. Just for tonight she would be only a woman. A woman, she decided, who, this once, would be content to let a man hold the reins.

So she was smiling when he walked back in. And for a moment, just looked.

She'd seen him shirtless before, countless times, and knew those broad shoulders, that strong back. One memorable day she'd caught him and Adam and Zack skinny-dipping in the river, so she'd seen him naked.

But she'd been twelve then, and she wasn't thinking like a twelve-year-old now. And she wasn't looking at a teenager, but a man. A powerful one. One that had her stomach flopping around in delighted reaction.

"You look good naked," she said conversationally.

He stopped pouring the glass he'd brought in with him, turned to stare at her. "You don't look so bad yourself."

The fact was, she looked stunning, sprawled over the rumpled sheets without a hint of modesty. Her hair was tumbled, her eyes glowed in the candlelight, and she had one hand low on her belly, idly tapping along with the music.

"You sure as hell don't look like a novice," he told her.

"I learn fast."

Now his smile came, slow, dangerous. "I'm counting on that."

"Yeah?" She loved a challenge. "So, what have you got there, McKinnon?"

"Your champagne." He set the bottle on her dresser, where candles flickered. "Have a glass." The one he brought her was full to the rim. "You may want to be a little drunk for this."

"Really?" The smile widened into a grin, but with a shrug, she sipped. "Aren't you having any?"

"After."

She chuckled, sipped again. "After what?"

"After I take you. That's what I'm going to do this time." He trailed a finger from her throat down to her quivering belly. "I'm going to take you. And you're going to let me."

The breath backed up in her lungs and it took an effort to push it out. He didn't look tender now, or flustered. Now with those eyes so dark, so green, so focused. He looked ruthless. Exciting.

"Am I?"

"Yeah." He could see that pulse in her throat begin to beat and flutter. "It's not going to be slow, but it's going to take a long time. Drink the champagne down, Willa. I'll taste it on you."

"Are you trying to make me nervous?"

He climbed onto the bed, straddled her, watched her blink in surprise. "Darling, I'm going to make you crazy." He took the glass, dipped a finger in the wine, then traced it over her nipple. "I'm going to make you scream. Yeah." He nodded slowly, repeating the process on her other breast. "You should be afraid. In fact, I like you being just a little afraid this time."

He trickled the last few drops over her belly, then set the glass aside. "I'm going to do things to you that you can't even imagine. Things I've been waiting to do."

She swallowed hard as a new and fascinating chill ran over her skin. "I think I am afraid." She shuddered out a breath. "But do them anyway."

22

It wasn't easy to track Willa down once April hit its stride, and with it the spring breeding season. As far as Tess could see, everything was focused on mating, people as well as animals. If she hadn't known better, she would have sworn she'd caught Ham flirting with Bess. But she imagined he had been trying to wrangle a pie.

Young Billy was eye-deep in love with some pretty little thing who worked a lunch counter in Ennis. His former liaison with Mary Anne had hit the skids, left him brokenhearted for about fifteen minutes.

The way he strutted around, Tess could see he thought of himself as a man of the world now.

Jim had some slap and tickle going with a cocktail waitress, and even the longtime-married Wood and Nell were exchanging winks and sly grins.

With nothing disturbing the peace and pastoral quality of the air, everyone seemed ready to fall into a routine of work, flirtations, and giggling sex.

There was Lily, of course, with wedding preparations in full swing. And Willa, when she stood still long enough, had a dopey grin on her face.

It seemed to Tess that the cows were trying to keep pace with the humans. Though she couldn't see anything particularly romantic about a man shooting bull sperm into a cow.

She sincerely doubted the bull was thrilled with the arrangement either, but he was allowed to cover a few, just to keep him happy. And the first time Tess witnessed the coupling was enough of a shock to make her wish it her last. She refused to believe that the bull's chosen *innamorata* had been mooing in sexual delight.

She'd watched Nate and his handler breed his stallion too. She had to admit there had been something powerful, elemental, and a little frightening in that process as well. The way the stallion had trumpeted, reared, and plunged. The way the mare's eyes had rolled in either pleasure or terror.

She wouldn't have called the process romantic, and it certainly hadn't been anything to giggle about. The smells of sweat and sex and animal had been impetus enough for Tess to drag Nate off at the first decent opportunity and jump him.

He hadn't seemed to mind.

Now it was another glorious afternoon, with the temperature warm enough for shirtsleeves. The sky was so big, so blue, so clear, it seemed that Montana had stolen every inch of it for itself.

If she looked toward the mountains—as she often caught herself doing—she would see spots of color bleeding through the white. The blues and grays of rock, the deep, dark green of pine. And if the sun angled just so, a flash that was a river tumbling down fueled with snowmelt.

She could hear the tiller running behind Adam's house. She knew Lily was planning a garden and had cajoled Adam into turning the earth for the seedlings she'd started. Though he'd warned Lily it was too early to plant, he was indulging her.

As, Tess mused, he always would.

It was a rare thing, she decided, that kind of love, devotion, understanding. With Adam and Lily, it was as solid as the mountains. As often as she wrote about people, watched them so that she could do just that, she'd never grasped the simple and quiet power of love.

She could write about it, make her characters fall in or out of it. But she didn't understand it. She thought perhaps it was like this land that she'd lived on, lived with for so many months now. She had learned to value and appreciate it. But understand it? Not a bit.

Cattle and horses dotted the hills where grass was still dingy from winter, and men worked in the mud brought on by warming weather to repair fencing, dig posts, and drive cattle to range.

They would do it over and over again, year after year, season after season. That, too, she supposed, was love. If she felt a stir herself, she blocked it off, reminded herself of palm trees and busy streets.

She had, Tess thought with a sigh, survived her first—and she hoped last—Montana winter.

"There you are." Tess started forward, but Willa rode straight past her toward the near pasture. "Damn it." Refusing to give up, Tess broke into a trot and followed. She was only slightly out of breath by the time she caught up. "Listen, we've got to get into town tomorrow. Lily's fitting our attendant dresses."

"Can't." Willa uncinched Moon, hauled off the saddle. "Busy."

"You can't keep avoiding this." She winced as Willa thoughtlessly tramped on the infant wildflowers perking up around the fence posts.

"I'm not avoiding it." After dropping the saddle over the fence, Willa removed the saddle blanket and bit. "I've resigned myself to the fact that I'm going to be wearing some lame dress, probably have posies in my hair. I just can't take off for the day right now."

Pulling a pick out of her pocket, she leaned into Moon, lifted the mare's near hind leg, and went to work on her hoof.

"If you don't go, Lily and I will have to choose the dress for you."

Willa snorted, skirted Moon's tail, and lifted the next hoof. "You're going to pick it out anyway, so it doesn't matter if I'm there or not."

True enough, Tess thought, and with an ease she wouldn't have believed possible even a few months before, she stroked and patted Moon. "It would mean a lot to Lily."

This time Willa sighed and moved to the foreleg. "I'd like to oblige her. Really. I'm swamped right now. There's a lot to get done while the weather holds."

"Holds what?"

"Holds off."

"What do you mean holds off?" Tess frowned up at the clear, perfect blue of the sky. "It's the middle of April."

"Hollywood, we can get snow here in June. We ain't done with it yet." Willa studied the western sky, the pretty, puffy clouds that clung to the peaks. She didn't trust them. "A spring snow's a fine thing, gives us moisture when we need it and melts off quick enough. But a spring blizzard." She shrugged, pocketed the pick. "You never know."

"Blizzard, my butt. The flowers are blooming." Tess looked down at the trampled blooms. "Or were."

"We grow them hardy here—those that we grow. I wouldn't put that long underwear away just yet. Hold, Moon." With that order, she hefted the saddle again and carried it toward the stable.

"There's other things." Determined to finish, Tess dogged her heels. "I haven't had a chance to talk to you alone in days."

"I've been busy." In the dim stable, Willa stored her tack and took up a grooming brush.

"With this and that."

"Which means?"

"Look, so you're making up for lost time with Ben. That's fine, glad you're happy. And you're busy impregnating unsuspecting cows all day, or ruining your hands with barbed wire, but I need to know what's going on."

"About?"

"You know very well." Cursing under her breath, Tess walked back outside, where Willa began brushing Moon. "It's been quiet, Will. I like it quiet. But it's also making me edgy. You're the one who talks to the cops, to the men, and you haven't been passing things along."

"I figured you were too busy playing with one of your stories and talking to your agent all day to worry about it."

"Of course I'm worried about it. All Nate says is there's nothing new. But you still have guards on."

Willa blew out a breath. "I can't take any chances."

"And I don't want you to." To soothe herself, Tess stroked Moon's cheek. "Though I admit I've had a few bad moments waking up at night hearing people walking around outside. Or you pacing around in."

Willa kept her eyes on Moon's smooth coat. "I have nightmares."

More surprised by the admission than the fact, Tess moved closer. "I'm sorry."

She hadn't been able to talk about it, and wondered now if that was a mistake. So she would see. "They've gotten worse since going up to the cabin. Realizing that girl was killed there. No doubt of that now that they've matched her blood to the towels and rags I found under the sink."

"Why the hell didn't the cops find them?"

Willa shrugged her shoulders and continued to groom her horse. "It's not the only cabin, the only shelter in the hills. They looked around, saw nothing out of place, everything as it should be. They didn't see any point in poking into dark corners and overturning buckets, I guess. They sure as hell have gone over the place now, every inch. Hasn't helped. Anyway, I think about that, and the time up in the hills with Adam shot, and bleeding, and not knowing."

She gave Moon a slap on the flank to send her into the pasture. "Just not knowing."

"Maybe it is over," Tess put in. "Maybe he's gone off. Sharks do that, you know. Cruise one area for a while, then go off to another feeding ground."

"I'm scared all the time." It wasn't hard to admit it, not when she watched Lily walk around the side of the house laughing up at Adam. Fear and love, she'd discovered, went hand in hand. "Work helps, keeps the fear in the back of the mind. Ben helps. You can't think at all when a man's inside you."

Yes, you can, Tess mused. Unless it's the right man.

"It's that three o'clock in the morning thing," Willa continued. "When there's nobody there, and nothing to hold it off. That's when the fear creeps up and snaps at my throat. That's when I start wondering if I'm doing the right thing."

"About?"

"The ranch." It spread out around her, her life. "Having you and Lily stay on when we can't be sure if it's safe."

"You don't have any choice." Tess hooked a boot in the fence, leaned back into it. She couldn't see the land through Willa's eyes, doubted she ever would. But she'd come to admire the pull of it, and the power. "We have minds of our own. Agendas of our own."

"Maybe."

"I'll tell you what mine is. When my time's up here, I'm going back to LA. I'm going shopping on Rodeo Drive and I'm having lunch at whatever the current hot spot is." Which, she knew, would certainly not be the hot spot she'd lunched in that past autumn. "And I'm taking my share of the profits from Mercy and putting it toward a place in Malibu. Near the ocean so I can hear the waves day and night."

"Never seen the ocean," Willa murmured.

"No?" It was hard to imagine. "Well, maybe you'll come visit sometime. I'll show you what civilized people do with their days. Might just add a chapter to my book. Willa in Hollywood."

Grinning, Willa rubbed her chin. "What book? I thought you were writing another movie."

"I am." Flustered, Tess dipped her hands in her pockets. "I'm just playing with a book. Just for fun."

"And I'm in it?"

"Pieces of you."

"It's set here, in Montana? On Mercy?"

"Where else am I going to set it?" Tess muttered. "I'm stuck here for a year. It's nothing." Her fingers began to drum against the rail. "I haven't even told Ira. It's just something I'm fooling around with when I'm bored."

If that was true, Willa thought, she wouldn't be so embarrassed. "Can I read it?"

"No. I'm going to go tell Lily you're dodging the shopping trip tomorrow. And don't complain if you have to wear organdy."

"The hell I will." Willa turned around and studied the mountains again. Her mood had lifted considerably, but as she watched more clouds roll in, gather, and cling, she knew it wasn't over. Not winter, not anything.

The dinner party was Lily's idea. Just a small, intimate, casual dinner, she'd promised. Just the three sisters, and Adam, Ben, and Nate. Her family, as she thought of them now.

Small, intimate, and casual perhaps, but exciting for her. She would be hostess, a position she'd never held in her life, at a party in her own home.

Her mother had always planned and managed social events when Lily was growing up. And so efficiently, so cleverly that Lily's input or assistance simply hadn't been necessary. During the brief time she'd lived on her own, she hadn't had the funds or the means to host dinners. And her marriage certainly hadn't been conducive to social occasions.

But now things had changed. She had changed.

She spent all day preparing for it. Cleaning the house was hardly a chore. She loved every inch of it, and Adam wasn't a man to toss clothes everywhere or leave beer bottles cluttering the tables. He didn't mind the touches she'd added—the little brass frog she'd ordered from a catalogue, the pretty glass ball of melting blues she'd fallen in love with at first sight in a shop in Billings. In fact, he seemed to appreciate them. He often said the house had been too simple, too empty, before she'd come to him.

She'd pored over recipes with Bess and settled on a rib roast, which she was just sliding into the oven when Bess poked her head in the kitchen doorway.

"Everything under control in here?"

"Absolutely. I prepared it just as you told me. And look." Proud as a mother with twins, Lily opened the refrigerator to show off her pies. "Didn't the meringue turn out nice? All those pretty sugar beads."

"Most men got a fondness for lemon meringue." Bess approved them with a nod. "You did just fine there."

"Oh, I wish you'd change your mind and come."

Bess waved a hand. "You're a sweet girl, Lily, but when I got a choice between putting my feet up and watching my movies and sitting around with a roomful of young people, I'm putting my feet up. Now, you want a hand, I'll give you one."

"No. I want to do it myself. I know that sounds silly, but—"

"Doesn't." Bess wandered over to the window where Lily had herb pots started from seed. Coming along well, she thought, just like Lily. "A woman's got a right to lord it over her own kitchen. But you call me if you run into any problem." She winked. "Nobody has to know you had a little help."

Bess turned as the back door opened again. "Wipe your feet," she ordered Willa. "Don't you be tracking mud in here on this clean floor."

"I'm wiping them." But under those eagle eyes, Willa gave them a few extra swipes on the mat.

"Oh, aren't those lovely!" Lily pounced on the wildflowers Willa was clutching. "That was so sweet of you to think of it, to pick them for me."

"Adam did." Willa passed them over and considered her mission complete. "One of the horses pulled up with a strain, so he's busy treating it. He didn't want them to wilt."

"Oh, Adam did." Lily sighed, and her heart melted as she buried her nose in the tiny blooms. "Is the horse all right? Does he need help?"

"He can handle it. I've got to get back."

"Couldn't you come in for a minute, have coffee? There's fresh."

Before Willa could refuse, Bess jabbed an elbow in her ribs. "Sit down and have coffee with your sister. And take off your hat in the house. I've got laundry to do."

"Bossy old thing," Willa complained when Bess shut the door behind her. But she already had her hat off. "I guess I've got time for a cup, if it's already hot."

"It is. Please, sit down. I just want to put these in water."

Willa sat at the round maple table, drummed her fingers on the wood. The dozens of chores still on her list raced through her head. "Smells good in here."

"It's the herbs, and this potpourri I made."

"Made it?" Willa drummed a little faster. "You're a regular little homemaker, aren't you?"

Lily kept her eyes on the stems she carefully slid into an old glass bottle. "It's all I'm good at."

"No, it's not. And I didn't mean it to sound that way." Annoyed with herself, Willa squirmed in her chair. "You've made Adam so happy he looks like he could float. And it's so neat and pretty in here." She scratched the back of her neck and felt like an awkward rube. "I mean, like that big white bowl there with the shiny red and green apples. I'd never think of something like that. Or putting stuff in those bottles you've got on the counter. What is that stuff?"

"Flavored vinegars." Lily glanced toward the long-necked bottles where sprigs of basil and rosemary and marjoram floated. "You use them for cooking, for salad. I like the way they look."

"Shelly does stuff like that too. I could never figure it."

"That's because you have to look at the big picture, the foundation and not the fancywork. I admire you so much."

Willa stopped frowning at the bottles and gaped. "Huh?"

"You're so smart and strong and capable." Lily set a pretty blue cup and saucer on the table. "You scared me to death when I first came here."

"I did?"

"Well, everything did. But especially you." Lily took her own cup, added a hefty measure of cream to make it palatable to her taste. Then she sat, deciding it was time to confess all. "I watched you the day of the funeral. You'd lost your father, and you were hurting, but you were also coping. And later, when Nate read the will, and everything that was yours, that should have been yours, was taken out of your control, you dealt with it."

Willa remembered, too. Remembered she hadn't been kind. "I didn't have much choice."

"There's always a choice," Lily said quietly. "Mine was usually running away. I'd have run that day if there'd been any place left to go. And I don't think I would have had the courage to stay when the horrible things started to happen if not for you."

"I didn't have anything to do with it. You stayed for Adam."

"Adam." Everything about Lily softened—voice, eyes, mouth. "Yes. But I wouldn't have had the courage to go to him, to let myself feel for him. I looked at you, at everything you were doing, had done, and thought, She's my sister and she's never run from anything. There must be something inside me that matches what's in her. So I dug for it. It's the first time in my life I've stuck when things got rough."

Willa pushed her coffee aside and leaned forward. "Look, I grew up the way I wanted to, did what I wanted to. I never found myself trapped in a relationship where someone used me for a punching bag."

"Didn't you?" Lily gathered her courage again when Willa said nothing. "Bess told me how hard our father was on you."

Bess talked too damn much, was all Willa could think. "An occasional backhand from a parent isn't the same as a fist in the face from a husband. Running from that wasn't cowardly, Lily. It was right and it was smart."

"Yes. But I never fought back. Not once."

"Neither did I," Willa murmured. "I may not have run from my father, but I never fought back either."

"You fought back every time you got on a horse, pulled a calf, rode a fence." Lily kept her eyes steady when Willa's flicked over her face. "You made Mercy yours. That's how you fought back. You dug your roots. I didn't know him, and he never chose to know me. But, Willa, I don't think he knew you either."

"No." Her voice was soft and slow with the realization. "I don't suppose he did."

Lily drew a deep breath. "I'd fight back now, and that's in very large part because of you, because of Tess, because of the chance I've had here. Jack Mercy didn't give me that chance, Will. You did. You should have hated us. You had every right to hate us. But you don't."

She'd wanted to, Willa remembered. It just hadn't been possible. "Maybe hate just takes too much energy."

"It does, but not everyone understands that." Lily paused, toyed with her cup. "When Tess and I were shopping the other day, I thought—for a minute I thought I saw Jesse. Just a flash, just a glimpse."

"You saw him in Ennis?" Willa bolted straight up in her chair, fists curled.

"No." Dazzled by her, Lily smiled a little. "See, that's your first reaction, fight back. Mine was to run. I used to think I saw him everywhere, I could imagine him everywhere. It hasn't happened in a while. But the other day, some face in the crowd, the tilt of a head . . . But I didn't run. I didn't panic. And I think if I ever had to, really had to, I'd fight back. I owe that to you."

"I don't know, Lily. Sometimes running's a fine choice."

It went so well Lily could hardly believe it was her life. Her new life. People she had grown to love were sitting in the cozy dining room, taking second helpings of food she'd prepared, laughing with each other like friends. Arguing with each other like family.

It was Tess who had started that, quite deliberately, Lily realized, by telling Willa the dress they'd picked out for her was a fuchsia organdy with a six-flounce skirt and puffed sleeves. With a bustle.

"You're out of your mind if you think you'll get me into something like that. What the hell is fuchsia anyway? Isn't that pink? No way I'm wearing pink flounces."

"You'll look so sweet in it," Tess purred. "Especially with the hat."

"What hat?"

"Oh, it's adorable, matching color, enormous floppy brim decked in a garden of spring flowers. English primroses. And the crown's cut out so we can dress your hair up high. Then there's the gloves. Elbow length, very chic."

Because Willa had gone dead pale, Lily took pity on her. "She's just teasing you. The dress is lovely. Pale blue silk with pearl buttons at the back and just a touch of lace on the bodice. It's very simple, very classic. And there's no hat or gloves."

"Spoilsport," Tess muttered, then grinned at Willa. "Gotcha."

"At this rate, Will's going to have a dress on more times this year than I've seen in her whole life." Ben toasted her. "I used to figure she slept in Levi's."

"Like to see you drive cattle in a dress," Willa tossed back.

"So would I." With a chuckle, Nate nudged his plate aside. "Lily, that was a fine meal. Adam's going to have to start buying bigger belts with you cooking for him."

"You have to have room for pie." Beaming with pleasure, Lily rose. "Why don't we have it in the living room?"

"That girl can cook," Ben commented as he settled into a wing chair in the living room. "Adam's a lucky son of a bitch."

"Is that how you gauge a man's fortune in a wife, McKinnon?" Willa chose the floor in front of the fire and folded her legs. "By how she cooks?"

"Couldn't hurt."

"A clever woman hires a cook." Tess groaned a little as she sat with Nate on the sofa. "And only eats this way once a year. I'm going to have to do fifty extra laps in the pool tomorrow."

Willa thought of several snide comments, but let them pass. She shot a quick look toward the kitchen, where Adam and Lily were busy readying dessert. "Before they come in, did Lily say anything to you about seeing her ex while you were shopping the other day?"

"No." Tess sat up quickly. "Not a word."

"In Ennis?" Nate's eyes narrowed, and he stopped playing with Tess's fingers.

"She said she was mistaken. Said it was an old habit to imagine him wherever she went, but it worried me."

"She got quiet for a while." Pursing her lips, Tess thought back. "We were window-shopping at a lingerie store, and I thought she was dreaming of her wedding night. She seemed nervous for a couple minutes, but she never said a thing."

"You ever get that picture of him?" Ben asked Nate.

"Just a couple of days ago. There was some sort of holdup back East." He, too, sent a cautious look toward the kitchen. "Looks like a frigging altar boy. Pretty face and a jarhead haircut. I haven't seen him around. I should have brought it over with me, got it to Adam."

"I want to see it," Willa said. "We'll talk about it later," she added, when she heard Adam's voice. "I don't want to spoil this for her."

To cover the gap, Ben rose and strolled over as Lily carried in a tray. "Now, that's pie." He leaned over, sniffed, like a man who had nothing more on his mind than his next bite. "So what have you got for everybody else?"

They kept the evening light, and when Nate gave Tess a subtle signal by a quick squeeze of her hand, he rose. "I'd better head on before you have to roll me out the door. Lily." He bent to kiss her. "You set one fine table."

"I'm so glad you came."

"I'll walk out with you." Tess feigned a yawn. "All that food, I'm going to sleep like a log."

By tacit agreement Ben and Willa gave them five minutes after hugs and good-byes before they made their own exit.

When they were alone, Adam turned Lily into his arms. "Who do they think they're fooling?"

"What do you mean?"

Finding her incredibly sweet, he pressed a kiss to her brow. "Did you hear a rig start up?"

She blinked, understood, and laughed. "No, I don't suppose I did."

"I think they've got the right idea." He swept Lily up, headed for the steps.

"Adam, all the dishes."

"They'll still be here in the morning." He kissed her again. "And so will we."

. . .

In her bed, in the dark, Willa let out a long throaty moan. The sound of that always aroused him, spurred him to quicken the pace. He loved to watch her when she rode him, the way her hair rained down off her shoulders, so lush and dark. He could see those flashes, those flickers of pleasure on her face as she lost herself. And when he took her breasts in his hands, when he reared up to replace his hands with his hungry mouth, she wrapped herself around him like a silky vine, all clinging arms and legs so he could feast on her.

No matter how much she gave, he wanted more.

"Go over." He panted out the demand, pressed his hand where they joined, and found her, drove her.

Her moan came again, a rusty sound of delight that pumped through his blood like good whiskey. He felt her give, and flood, then sob again before her teeth closed over his shoulder.

So he let her set the pace now, let her shudder back into control. Now she leaned over him, her hair curtaining his face, her hands braced on either side of it.

"I want to make you crazy." She lowered her head until her lips were a breath from his. "I want to make you beg."

Her pace was slow, torturous, and her mouth took his in quick, nipping kisses that gradually deepened and heated. When his hands were fisted in her hair, his breath heaving, she released his mouth, eased back. Quickened the rhythm, skimmed her hands over him, watched his eyes.

She saw what she wanted. They were wild and blind and desperate, mirroring the emotions raging inside her. His hands had moved, gripped her hips now, gripped them hard. She'd have bruises. Branding, she thought in triumph.

Her body bowed back, shuddered while Ben's fingers dug into her pumping hips. She knew what to expect now, that explosion of pleasure ramming into pleasure, the assault on the system that could come like lightning or linger like dew. Yet still it was always a shock, this violent intimacy and the need that always, always bloomed.

She felt him erupt, the final hard drive of him into her, and the glorious burst of heat. The orgasm struck like an arrow winging through her system, and pinned to him, filled with him, she welcomed it.

"Willa." Ben drew her down so they could tremble, slick flesh to slick flesh. When he could speak more than her name, he turned his lips to her throat. "I've wanted to hold you like this all night."

A little foolishness like that always warmed her, and tied her tongue. "You were too busy eating to think about this."

"I'm never to busy to think about this. Or you. I do think about you." He lost his hands in her hair as he turned her mouth to his. "More all the time. And I worry about you."

"Worry?" Beautifully relaxed, she braced herself on her elbows and looked down at him. She loved to find his face in the dark, pick out feature by feature. "About what?"

"I don't like not being right on hand with all this going on."

"I can take care of myself." She brushed the hair back from his face. Funny, she thought, how the tips of it always looked as if they'd been dipped in wet gold dust. Funnier still how her fingers always itched to touch it these days. "And I can take care of the ranch."

"Yeah." Almost too well, he thought. "But I worry anyway. I could stay tonight."

"We've been through that. Bess likes to pretend she doesn't know what's going on up here. I like to let her. And . . ." She kissed him before she rolled lazily to her back. "You've got your own ranch to run." She stretched. "Saddle up, McKinnon. I'm done with you."

"Think so?" He rolled atop her to prove her wrong.

When a man tiptoes out of a darkened house, he mostly feels like a fool. Or very lucky. Nate was debating which course to take when he opened the front door and came face-to-face with Ben.

They stared at each other, cleared throats. "Nice night," Nate said.

"One of my best." Ben gave up, flashed a grin. "So, where'd you park your rig?"

"Back of the pole barn. You?"

"Same. Don't know why we bother. There's not a man on this spread who doesn't know what we're up to with those women." They stepped off the porch, headed toward the barn. "I keep wondering if I'm going to get shot at."

"Adam and Ham have this shift," Nate pointed out. "I try to time it that way. They're not so trigger-happy." He glanced back toward the main house, Tess's window. "And it might be worth dodging a couple bullets."

"I worry about a man who says that."

"I'm thinking I'll marry her."

Ben stopped dead. "Something's buzzing in my ear. I don't think I heard you right."

"You heard me right enough. She's banking on going back to California in the fall." Nate shrugged. "I'm banking she won't."

"You tell her that?"

"Tell Tess." Amused at the thought, Nate let out a muffled hoot of laughter. "Hell, no. You have to be cagey with a woman like that. Used to running the show. So you make her think everything's her idea. She doesn't know she's in love with me, but it'll come to her."

Talk of love and marriage was making Ben's gut churn. "What if it doesn't? Come to her. What if she packs up and goes? You just going to let her?"

"Can't lock her up, can I?" Nate took out his keys, jiggled them in his palm. "But I'm betting she stays. And I've got some time yet to work on it."

Ben thought of Willa, and how he'd react if she suddenly got it in her head to pull up stakes. He'd have her hog-tied in record time. "Don't think I could be as reasonable."

"Well, push hasn't come to shove yet. I've got court the next day or two," he added when he climbed into his rig. "Soon as I'm able, I'll swing by with that picture."

"You do that." Ben paused by his own rig, looked back toward the main house. No, he didn't think he could be reasonable if he was in love. On the drive home he told himself, several times, that it was a good thing he wasn't.

23

Jesse had it all worked out. Oh, he'd been willing to wait, be patient. Be reasonable. After all, if he held out till fall, he could sweep up a lot of money along with his wife.

But now the little bitch thought she could go off and marry that Indian bastard. He'd studied on it and knew that if he let that happen, legally he'd get zilch. So he couldn't let it happen.

If his aim had been a little more true, he'd have taken care of Adam Wolfchild already. The opportunity had been there, but the son of a bitch had gotten lucky. And since Wolfchild hadn't been alone, Jesse hadn't risked waiting around for another chance at him.

He was sure there'd be another opportunity. Just a little window of luck was all he'd need. But spring work, and that damn slave driver Ben McKinnon, kept him tied at Three Rocks while his adulterous wife was out buying wedding finery.

So if he couldn't get to Wolfchild, he would damn well get to Lily. He'd have to make her sorry she'd messed with him and ruined his plans for cashing in on her inheritance, but that would be a pleasure.

He'd hoped to cash in on a lot of things, he thought as he drew another queen to go with his other two ladies. But it was time to move on. And he was taking Lily with him.

"I'll see your five," Jesse said, smiling easily at Jim across the poker table. "And bump it five."

"Too rich for me." Ned Tucker tossed in his cards, belched, and got up to get a fresh beer. He was comfortable at Mercy; he found Willa a fair boss and enjoyed the company of the men. He gave the bear the men had wrestled into the corner a rub on the head for luck. Not, Ned thought, that it had done him a damn bit of good at the table that night.

He shook his head as Jesse pulled in another pot. "Sumbitch can't seem to lose," he said to Ham.

"Got enough luck to shit gold nuggets." But Ham decided to try his own. "Deal me in this hand. I've gotta take over for Billy outside in an hour. Might as well lose some money first."

An hour, Jesse thought, as he took his turn at deal. Billy and that know-it-all college boy were on shift now. Neither one of them would be much challenge to him. He would give the game another ten minutes, then make his move.

He lost one hand, folded on another, then pushed back from the table. "Deal me out. Gonna get some air."

"Make sure Billy don't shoot you," Jim called out. "That boy's mind's on town pussy and he spooks easy."

"Oh, I can handle Billy," Jesse said, and shrugging into his jacket, he strolled out.

He checked the time. He'd studied the workings of Mercy carefully enough to know that Adam would be giving his horses a final look for the night. The main house would be settled down, and Lily would be alone. He took the Colt out from under the seat of his rig. You could never be too careful. Tucked it into his belt and moved through the shadows toward the pretty white house.

It would go like clockwork, he mused. Lily would cry and plead, but she'd come easily enough. She always did what she was told. If not quick enough, after the first smack.

He was looking forward to that first smack. It had been much too long.

He tapped his belt, moved quietly toward the rear of the house.

"That you, J C?" Cheered by the prospect of company on his shift, Billy came forward, rifle lowered and on safety. "You skinning the guys back at the bunkhouse again? What are you doing out here?"

Jesse smiled at him, slid the gun from his belt. "Taking what's mine," he said, and smashed the butt of the Colt down. "No reason to shoot you," Jesse said as he dragged Billy into the bushes. "And it makes too much noise. You just stay out of my way now, or I might change my mind."

He crept to the back door, quiet as a snake, and looked through the glass.

And there she was. Sweet little Lily, he thought. Sitting at the table drinking tea and reading a magazine. Waiting for her Indian lover to come stick it to her. Faithless bitch.

The rumble of thunder threw him off a moment, made him look up at the starless sky. Even the weather was on his side, he thought with a grin. A nice rain would be fine cover on the trip south.

He turned the knob slowly, stepped in.

"Adam, there's an article in here about wedding cakes. I wonder . . ." She trailed off, her gaze still glued to the page, but her heart thudding. Beans was growling under the table. And she knew, even before she gathered the courage to turn, she knew.

"Keep that dog quiet, Lily, or I'll kill him."

She didn't doubt it. He looked the same—even with the darker hair, the length of it, the moustache, he looked exactly the same to her. Those beautiful eyes slitted mean, his mouth frozen in a dangerous smile. She managed to get to her feet, put herself between Jesse and the dog.

"Beans, hush now. It's all right." When he continued to growl, she watched in horror as Jesse took a gun from his belt. "Don't, please, Jesse. He's just an old dog. And they'll hear you. They'll hear if you shoot. People will come."

He wanted to kill something, felt the urge bubbling up. But he wanted it quiet more. "Then shut him up. Now."

"I—I'll put him in the other room."

"You move slow, Lily, and don't try to run." He liked the feel of the gun in his hand, the way the butt curled neatly into his palm. "I'll hurt you bad if you do. Then I'll sit right here and wait for that Indian you've been spreading your legs for. And I'll kill him when he walks in."

"I won't run." She took Beans by the collar, and though his pudgy body was tense and he strained against her, she dragged him to the door and through it. "Please put the gun away, Jesse. You know you don't need it."

"Guess I don't." Still smiling, he slid it back in his belt. "Come here."

"This is no good, Jesse." She struggled hard to remember everything she'd learned in therapy, to stay calm, to think clearly. "We're divorced. If you hurt me again, they'll put you in jail."

He laid a hand on the butt of the gun again. "I said come here."

Closer to the door, she thought. There might be a way to get through. She had to get through to warn Adam, everyone. "I'm trying to start over," she said as she walked toward him. "We can both start fresh. I never did anything but disappoint you, and—" She cried out, not in shock but in pain, when he slapped her backhanded across the face.

"I've been waiting to do that for more than six months." And since it felt so good, he did it again, hard enough to send her to her knees. "I've been right here, Lily." He gripped her hair, yanked her to her feet by it. "Watching you."

"Here?" The pain was too sickeningly familiar, made it too hard to think. But she did think. Of murder, of madness. "You've been here. Oh, God."

Now the fear was paralyzing. He used his fists, she told herself. Just his fists. He wouldn't rip people apart.

But all she saw when she looked in his eyes was blind rage.

"Now you're coming with me, and you're going to be quiet and do just what I say." In case she didn't understand his meaning, he gave her hair another vicious yank. "You mess with me, Lily, I'll hurt you and anybody else that gets in the way." He continued to talk, his face close to hers. In the other room the dog was barking wildly, but neither paid attention. "We're going to take a nice long trip. Mexico."

"I'm not going with you." She took the next blow, reeled from it, then shocked them both by leaping forward, attacking with nails, teeth, fists.

The force of her headlong rush rammed him back against the counter, and pain bloomed in his hip where it struck the edge. He howled when she drew blood from his cheek, too stunned to strike back until she'd raked his face a second time. "Fucking cunt!" He knocked her back into the table, sent her pretty teacup flying.

The dogs howled like wolves and scratched madly at the door.

"I'll kill you for that. I'll fucking kill you."

And he nearly did. The gun was in his hand, his finger on the trigger vibrating. But she was staring up at him, not with fear, not with pleading in her eyes. But with hate.

"Is that what you want?" He dragged her up again, held the barrel to her temple. "You want me to kill you?"

There had been a time she might, out of sheer weariness, have said yes. But she thought of her life here, with Adam, with her sisters. Her home and family.

"No, I'll go with you." And wait, she promised herself, for the first chance to escape, or to fight.

"Damn right you will." He closed a hand over her throat, shook her as blood stung his eyes. "I haven't got time to make you pay now, but you wait. You just wait."

He was trembling as he pulled her to the door. The shock of her hurting him, actually hurting him until the blood ran down his face, had rocked him badly. The time he'd wasted dealing with her when she could have come along docile as a cow left him jittery.

He barely noticed that it wasn't rain falling from that dark sky, but snow. While the thunder still raged. Thick, heavy flakes danced in front of his eyes so that he didn't see Adam until they were nearly face-to-face and he was looking at a rifle.

"Let go of her." Adam's voice was calm as a lake, without any of the fury or fear rippling the surface. "Lily, step away from him."

Jesse shifted his grip to her throat, his arm over her windpipe. The gun, still in his hand, was at her head. There was no calm in him. He was screaming, "She's my goddamn fucking wife! Get the hell out of my way. I'll kill her. I'll put a bullet in her brain."

He heard a gun cock and saw Willa step forward, coatless, snow covering her hair. "Take your hands off my sister, you son of a bitch."

It was wrong, everything was wrong, and the panic made Jesse's finger tremble. "I'll do it. Her brains'll be splattered on your shoes if you take one step. You tell them, Lily. Tell them I'll kill you here and now."

She could feel the steel pressed into her temple. Imagine the flash of explosion. She could barely breathe through the grip on her throat. To stay alive, she kept her eyes on Adam. "Yes, he will. He's been here, all the time, he's been here."

Jesse's eyes fired. He looked like a monster with the blood oozing down his face and his lips peeled back in a wide, challenging grin. "That's right. I've been here, right along. You want me to do to her what was done to the others, you just stay in my way." His lips curved in a dazzling smile. He was in charge again. He was in control. "Maybe I won't gut her, I won't lift her hair, but she'll still be dead."

"So will you," Adam said, and sighted.

"I can snap her neck like a twig." Jesse's voice rolled and pitched. "Or put a bullet in her ear. And maybe I'll get lucky." He increased the pressure on Lily's throat so that her hands came up in defense to drag at the obstruction. "Maybe I'll get off one more shot, right into your sister's gut."

"He's bluffing, Adam." Willa's finger twitched on the trigger. She'd put a bullet in his brain, she thought grimly. If Lily would just move her head another inch, just shift over an inch, she could risk it. But the damn snow was blowing like a curtain. "He doesn't want to die."

"I'm a fucking Marine!" Jesse shouted. "I can take two of you out before I go down. And Lily's first."

Yes, Lily was first. "You won't get away." But Adam lowered his rifle. Rage, pride, weren't worth Lily's life. "And you'll pay for every minute she's afraid."

"Back off, bitch," he ordered Willa, and tightened his grip so Lily's eyes rolled up white. "I can break her neck as easy as blinking."

Helpless, every instinct raging against it, Willa stepped back. But she didn't lower the gun. One clear shot, she promised herself. If she had one clear shot, she'd take it.

"You get in the rig." He pulled Lily with him, moving backward, his eyes jumping from side to side. "Get in the fucking rig, behind the wheel." He pushed her in, shoved her across the seat, keeping the gun high and in plain sight. "You come after us," he shouted, "I kill her, slow as I can. Start the goddamn thing and drive."

Lily had one last look at Adam's face as she turned the key. And she drove.

With hands that trembled, Willa lowered the rifle. She hadn't taken the shot. There'd been a moment, just an instant, and she'd been afraid to risk it.

"God. Dear God. They're heading west." Think, she ordered herself. Think. "The cops can put up a roadblock, stop them if he tries for the main road. If he's smart, he'll figure that and go into the hills. We can be after them inside twenty minutes, Adam."

"I let her go. I let him take her."

Willa gave him a hard shake. "He'd have killed her, right in front of us. He was panicked and crazy. He'd have done it."

"Yes." Adam drew in a breath, let it out. "Now I'll find them. And I'll kill him."

Willa nodded once. "Yes. You call the police, I'll get the men. Those of us going into the hills will need horses and gear. Hurry."

She started off in a spring, nearly tripped over Billy, who'd managed to crawl, groaning, onto the road. "Jesus." The blood covering his face made her certain he'd been shot. "Billy!"

"He hit me. Hit me with something."

"Just sit tight. Stay right here." She headed toward the main house at a dead run. "Bess! Get the first aid kit. Billy's over in front of Adam's. He's hurt. Get him in here."

"What the hell's going on?" Annoyed at having her evening session at her computer interrupted, Tess came to the head of the stairs. "First dogs barking like maniacs, now you yelling down the roof. What happened to Billy?"

"Jesse Cooke. Hurry," she ordered as Bess scooted by her. "I don't know how bad he's hurt."

"Jesse Cooke." Alarmed, Tess raced down the stairs. "What are you talking about?"

"He's got Lily. He's got her," Willa repeated, overriding Tess's babbled questions. "My guess is he's taking her into high country. We've got a thunder blizzard in the works, and she didn't even have a coat." The first bubble of hysteria was her last as Willa clamped down hard on emotion. "He's panicked and he's got to be half crazy, more. You call Ben, Nate, anyone else you can think of, tell them we need a search party and fast. We're riding after them."

"I'll get warmer gear together." Tess's fingers stayed white on the newel post. "And for Lily. She'll need it when we find her."

"Make it fast."

Within ten minutes Willa was organizing the men. They were armed, prepared to set out in rigs or on horseback with supplies to last two days.

"He doesn't know the area like most of us," she continued. "He's only had a few months. And Lily will throw him off, slow him down as much as she can. We'll spread out. There's a chance he'll take her up to the cabin, so Adam and I will head there. The weather's going to make it rough on him, but it isn't going to help us either."

"We'll get the son of a bitch." Jim slapped his rifle into its sheath. "And we'll get him before morning."

"There won't be any tracking in this, so . . ." She trailed off as she saw Ben's rig drive recklessly into the ranch yard. She wanted to buckle then, needed to, so she stiffened her spine. "So we spread out over a wide area. You all have your targets. The cops are covering the main roads, and they're sending more men. Search and Rescue will be out at first light. I want her back by then. As for Cooke—" She drew a breath. "Whatever it takes. Let's move."

"Which are you taking?" It was the only question Ben asked.

"I'm going with Adam, up the west face toward the cabin."

He nodded. "I'm with you. I need a horse."

"We've got one."

"I'm going too." Eyes ready to brim over with tears, Tess stepped next to Adam. "I can ride."

"You'll slow us down."

"Goddamn you." Tess gripped Willa's arm and spun her around. "She's my sister too. I'm going."

"She can ride" was all Adam said. He swung into the saddle and, with his young hound beside him, galloped off.

"Wait for Nate," Willa ordered. "He knows the way." She mounted quickly. "He'll need someone to fill him in on the rest of it."

Knowing she had to be satisfied with that, Tess nodded. "All right. We'll catch up with you."

"We'll bring her home, Tess," Ben murmured as he hoisted into the saddle, whistled for Charlie.

"Bring them both home," Tess said, as she watched them ride away.

Adam said nothing until they found the abandoned rig. His mind was too dark for words, his heart too cold. They stopped long enough to look carefully for signs. The rig was plunged to the wheel wells in snow, leaning drunkenly against a tree.

The thick, wet snow covered everything, and the dogs scouted through it, noses buried.

"He'd hit her." Adam wrenched open the driver's-side door, terrified that he'd find blood. Or worse. "There were bruises already on her face where he'd hit her."

The rig was empty, with a few drops of blood near the far door. Not Lily's, he thought. Cooke's.

"There was blood running down his face," Willa reminded him. "She'd given it back, in spades."

When Adam turned, his eyes were blank as a doll's. "I told her, I promised her, no one would ever hurt her again."

"There was nothing you could do. He won't hurt her now, Adam. She's his only way out of this. He won't do to her what—"

"What he did to the others?" Adam bit the words off, buried the thought. Without another word he mounted and rode ahead.

"Let him have some distance." Ben laid a hand over Willa's. "He needs it."

"I was standing right there too. I had a gun on him. I'm a better shot than Adam, better than anyone on Mercy, but it didn't do any good. I was afraid to risk—" Her voice broke and she shook her head.

"What if you'd risked it, and she'd moved, jerked? You might have hit her instead."

"Or she might be safe now. If I had it to do over again, I'd shoot the son of a bitch right between the eyes." She made herself shake it off. "Doubling back on it doesn't help either. It could be he's heading toward the cabin, the direction's right enough. He'd think he could make a stand there."

Willa swung onto her horse. "She tried to fight him this time. Maybe running would have been better."

Lily would have run if she could have. She was freezing, her shirt soaked through, but she would have taken her chances with the storm and the hills, if running had been an option.

He'd put the gun away, but after she ran the rig into the tree, he changed strategies. She'd aimed for the tree, hoping the impact on his side would jar him enough to buy her a lead. It had only earned her a headlong toss into the snow.

And then he tied her hands and looped the slack around his waist so that she was tethered to him. She stumbled a lot, deliberately at first to slow him down. But he only jerked her upright again.

The snow was monstrous. The higher they climbed, the more vicious it became, with bellowing bursts of thunder following the eerie sky-cracking lightning. And the wind was so fierce she could barely hear him cursing her.

The world was white—swirling, howling white.

He had a knapsack over his shoulders. She wondered if there was a knife in it, and what he might do to her in the end.

The cold had sapped her strength, leached into her bones so that they felt like brittle sticks, ready to snap. Fighting him was no more than a fantasy now, running a fading hope. Where could she run when there was nothing but a blinding wall of snow?

All she could do was survive.

"Thought they had me, didn't they?" He jerked the rope so she fell against him. He had the collar of his sheepskin jacket turned up, but still the wet snow snuck in and down his neck and irritated him. "Your horseshit shoveler and half-breed bitch of a sister thought they had the upper hand. I got what I wanted." He squeezed her breast hard through her shirt. "Always did, always will."

"You don't want me, Jesse."

"You're my fucking wife, aren't you? Took vows, didn't you? Love, honor, and obey. Till death." He pushed her into the snow for the hell of it and rode on the power of that. "They'll come after us, but they don't know what they're up against, do they, Lily? I'm a goddamn Marine."

He could plow through this snow just like he'd plowed through basic training, he thought. He could plow through anything and still kick ass.

"I've been planning this for a long time." He took out a cigarette, flicked on the Zippo he'd turned up to maximum flame. "I've been taking the lay of the land. I've been working at Three Rocks since I got here, practically right on your skinny ass."

"At Three Rocks. For Ben."

"Ben Bigshot McKinnon." He let smoke pour out between his teeth. "The same who's been bouncing on your sister lately. I've given some thought to that myself." He studied Lily, shivering in the snow. "She'd be a hell of a lot more interesting in bed than you. A fucking tree would be, but you're my wife, right?"

She pushed herself up. It would be too easy to just lie there and give up. "No, I'm not."

"No lousy piece of paper's going to tell me different. You think you can run out on me, go to some freaking lawyer, call out the cops? They put me in a cell because of you. I got a lot of payback coming."

He studied her again. Pale, beaten. His. Taking one last drag, he flicked his cigarette into the snow. "You look cold, Lily. Maybe I'll just take a minute or two to warm you up. We got time," he continued, pulling the rope to drag her to him. "The way they're going to be tripping over themselves trying to track me. Couldn't track an elephant in this."

He pushed his hand between her legs. When all he saw in her eyes was revulsion, he pushed harder until the first flicker of pain bloomed. "You like to pretend you don't like it rough, but you're a whore like all the rest. You used to tell me it was just fine, didn't you? 'That's just fine, Jesse. I like what you do to me.' Didn't you used to say that, Lily?"

She stared into his eyes, fought to ignore the humiliation of his hand on her. "I lied," she said coolly. She didn't wince from the pain as he dug into her. Wouldn't let herself.

"Castrating bitch, I can't even get a hard-on with you." She'd never used to back-talk him. Not after the first couple licks. Unsettled, he shoved her back, then shifted his pack. "No time for this anyway. When we get to Mexico, it'll be different."

Changing directions, he took her south.

She lost track of time, and distance, and direction. The snow had slowed, though the occasional boom of thunder still rolled over the peaks. She put one foot in front of the other, mechanically, each step a survival. She was certain now that he wasn't going to the cabin, wondered where Adam was, where he was looking, what he was feeling.

She'd seen murder in his eyes at that last glimpse of his face. He would find her, she knew he would find her. All she had to do was live until he did.

"I need to rest."

"You'll rest when I say." Worried that he'd lost his way in the storm, Jesse took out his compass. Who could tell where the hell they were going in this mess?

It wasn't his fault.

"Not much farther anyway." He pocketed the compass and headed due east now. "Just like a woman—bitch, moan, and complain. Never known you not to whine about something."

She'd have laughed if she'd had the strength left. Perhaps she had whined once upon a time about the paychecks that had gone missing, the whiskey bottles, the forgotten promises. But it seemed a far cry from whining about dying of exposure in the Rockies.

"It'll be harder for you if I collapse from exhaustion, Jesse. I need a coat, something hot to drink."

"Shut up. Just shut the hell up." He stared through the dark and the lightly falling snow, shielding his flashlight with his hand. "I've got to think."

He had his direction. He had that, all right. But the distance was another matter. None of the landmarks he'd been careful to memorize seemed to materialize. Everything looked different in the dark. Everything looked the same.

It wasn't his fault.

"Are we lost?" She had to smile. Wasn't that just like him? Big-talk Jesse Cooke, ex-Marine, lost in the mountains of Montana. "Which way is Mexico?"

And she did laugh, weakly, even when he whirled on her, fists raised. He would have used them, just to relieve his frustration, but he saw what he was looking for. "You want to rest? Fine. This is as far as we go for now."

He pulled her again through a snowdrift that reached the top of her thighs and toward the mouth of a small cave.

"This was Plan B. Always have a Plan B, Lily. I scouted this place out more than a month ago." And he'd meant to lay in extra supplies, just in case, but hadn't had the chance. "Hard to spot. Your Indian isn't going to find you here."

It was still cold, but at least it was out of the wind. Lily sank to her knees in relief.

Delighted now that he'd reached the next stage of his plan, Jesse shrugged off his pack. "Got us some jerky in here. Bottle of whiskey." He took that out first, drank deeply. "Here you go, sweetheart."

She took it, hoping that even false heat would slow the shivering. "I need a blanket."

"So happens I got one. You know I'm always prepared, don't you?"

He was pleased with the survival gear he'd packed—the food and the flashlight, the knife, the matches. He tossed her a blanket, amused when she gathered it awkwardly with her bound hands and struggled to wrap it around herself. He crouched on the floor of the cave.

"We'll get a little sleep. Can't risk a fire, though I imagine those boys are way north of here." He took out another cigarette. God knew a man deserved a drink and a smoke after putting in a long day. "In the morning, we'll head out. I figure we get to one of these bumfuck towns and I can hot-wire a car. Then we're on our way to sunny Mexico." In celebration, he blew smoke rings. "Can't be soon enough for me." He bit off a piece of jerky, chewed thoughtfully. "Montana sucks."

He stretched out his legs, rested his back on the wall of the cave while she let herself drowse in the stingy warmth of the blanket. "I'm going to make me a pile of money down there. I wouldn't have had to worry about that if you'd behaved yourself. Your share of Mercy, that was big bucks for me, Lily, and you had to fuck it up by thinking you could go off and get married. We're going to talk about that later. A lot."

He took the bottle back and drank deeply again. "But a smart man like me, one who's got luck at cards, he can do just fine down there with those greasers."

She needed to sleep, had to sleep to pull her strength back until Adam found her. Until she could get away. She curled against the side wall, as far away as the tether would allow, and wrapped the blanket tight around her.

He would drink now. She knew the pattern. He would drink until he was drunk, and then she'd have a better chance of getting away from him.

But she had to sleep. It was closing in on her like a fog and the chills were racking her so hard she thought her bones would crack. She listened to the whiskey slosh in the bottle as he lifted it, felt herself drift.

"Why did you kill those people, Jesse? Why did you do all those things?"

The bottle clinked, sloshed. He chuckled a little, as if at a small private joke. "A man does what he's got to."

It was the last thing she heard him say.

24

On a cold, windy ridge, Adam stood, staring into the dark, trying to see into it as he might a mirror. The only relief from that dark was the strong beam of the flashlight in his hand and the beams behind him.

"He's veered off from the cabin." Ben studied the sky, measured the hours until dawn. He wanted the sun, damn it. The morning might bring signs other than the scent the dogs were pursuing. Morning would bring the planes, and his own brother would be up, scanning every tree and rock.

"He's got someplace else he's taking her." Adam kept his face to the wind, as if it might tell him something. Anything. "He knows someplace else. He'd have to be past crazy to take the mountain on foot at night without a shelter."

The man who had ripped two people to pieces was past crazy, Ben thought grimly. But it wasn't what Adam needed to hear. "He's gone to ground somewhere. We'll find him."

"Snow's let up some. Storm's moved east. She wasn't dressed for a night in the cold." Adam stared straight ahead, had to stare into the dark and make himself breathe no matter how his insides shook. "She gets cold at night. Bird bones. Lily's got little bird bones."

"He can't be that far ahead of us." Because it was all he could do, Ben laid a hand on Adam's shoulder, left it there. "They're on foot. They'll have to stop and rest."

"I want you to leave me alone with him. When we find them, I want you to take Lily and Will, and leave him to me." Adam turned now, and the eyes that were always so gentle, so quiet, were hard and cold as the rock on which he stood. "You leave him to me."

There was civilized, Ben thought, and there was justice. "I'll leave him to you."

From her post by the horses, Willa watched them. She had lived and worked and survived in a man's world her entire life. Perhaps she understood better than most that there were times a woman couldn't cross the line. Whatever they spoke of wasn't for her, and she accepted that. What was between them on that ridge wasn't just between men, but between brothers.

Her sister's fate was in their hands. And hers.

When they started back toward her, she took Lily's blouse and gave both dogs the scent fresh. Shuddering with excitement, they whined and headed due south.

"Sky's clearing," she said, as they mounted and Adam rode ahead. She could see stars, just a sprinkle of them glinting through. "If the clouds move off we'll have a half-moon and some light."

"It'll help." Ben gave her a quick study. She rode straight as an arrow with no sign of flagging. But he couldn't see her eyes, not clearly enough. "You holding up?"

"Sure. Ben . . ."

He slowed a bit, thinking she might be close to breaking, need him to comfort. "You need a minute, we can hang back."

"No, no. Damn it, it's been working at my mind for hours. There was something familiar about the bastard. Something . . . like I'd seen him somewhere before. But it was dark, and there was blood all over his face where Lily must have scratched him." She pushed her hat back, suddenly irritated by the weight of it. "I dumped Billy on Bess so fast. I didn't take time to ask him any questions. I should have. Maybe we'd have a better idea of his moves."

"You had other things on your mind."

"Yeah." But it nagged at her, that memory that circled, then dipped just out of reach. "Doesn't matter now." She settled her hat back on her head, nudged Moon into a quick trot. "Finding Lily's what matters." Finding her alive, she thought, but couldn't say it.

The cave was dark. She was burning up, then freezing, then burning again, tossed in fever and dreams and terrors. Her hands were cold, sore to numbness at the wrists where the rope abraded her skin. She curled tight into herself, dreamed of curling tight into Adam, having his arm drape over her as it did during the night to pull her close. And warm. And safe.

She whimpered a little as the rocks scattered across the floor of the cave bit into her shoulder, her back, her hip. Every time she shifted, she hurt, but it was a distant pain, a dream pain. No matter how she struggled she couldn't quite bring herself to the surface of it.

When the light burned over the back of her eyelids, she turned away from it. She so wanted to sleep, to drop away from everything. She murmured a little, as the fever began to brew inside her.

Footsteps, she thought dimly. Adam's home. He'd crawl into bed beside her now. His body would be a bit chilled but would warm quickly. If she could just turn, just wake enough to turn to him, his mouth would be soft on hers, and he would make love to her, slow and sweet, as he often did when he came in late from his shift.

They wouldn't even have to speak, just sigh perhaps. They wouldn't need words, just touch and taste and that steady rhythm of bodies finding each other. Then sleep again . . .

As she started to drift again, she thought she heard a scream, cut quickly off. Like a mouse caught in a trap. Adam would take it away before she saw it. He understood things like that.

Sinking into unconsciousness, she never felt the knife slip between her wrists to cut the rope, or the heavy warmth of Jesse's coat spread over her. But she said Adam's name as the man who stood over her, blood dripping from his hands, sheathed his knife.

It had been quick work, and he regretted that. He hadn't had time for finesse. He'd gotten lucky finding them before any of the others did. Luckier still to find the bastard drunk and stupid. He'd died easier than he deserved. Like a pig slaughtered with only one surprised squeal.

But he'd taken the hair nonetheless. It was traditional now, and he'd even thought to bring a plastic bag to hold it. In case he got lucky.

He'd have to leave the woman as she was, for others to find. Or circle around, stumble across the cave a second time when there was someone with him, to make it seem all nice and proper.

He scanned the light around the cave again, then smiled when it shone on a small stack of twigs. Well, he could take time for that, couldn't he? A little fire close to the opening, smoke to bring one of the search parties along quicker.

What a picture they'd find, he thought, chuckling. He simply couldn't help but laugh as he built the fire quickly, set it to flame. Couldn't help but laugh as the flames danced over the body slumped against the wall of the cave and the blood pooling like a red river.

When he rode off, he rode east, zigzagging through the trees and picking his way down and up rock until he caught the flash of another searcher's light. All he had to do then was turn his mount and melt in among the men who fanned out over the hills, looking to be heroes.

He was the only one who knew a hero's work was already done.

"Smoke." Willa was the first to catch the scent. Her saddle creaked as she rose in it, concentrated. "There's smoke." And with it the first true tug of hope pulled at her heart. "Adam?"

"Up ahead. I can't see it, but it's there."

"He built a fire," Ben murmured. "Stupid bastard."

Though they hadn't discussed it, they moved into a trot and now rode three abreast. And the first thin light broke in the east.

"I know this place. Adam, we did some rock climbing in the ravine near here." Ben's jaw tightened. "Caves, lots of little caves. Decent shelter."

"I remember." Only the memory of the gun against Lily's temple kept Adam from breaking into a gallop. His eyes had grown accustomed to the dark, and they narrowed now against the gently growing dawn. And they were sharp. "There!" He pointed ahead at the thin gray column of smoke just as Charlie's high, frantic barking echoed.

"Found them." Before Willa could speak, Ben blocked her mount with his. "Stay here."

"The hell I will."

"Do what you're told for once, goddamn it."

He knew that bark. It wasn't the excitement of a find, it was the signal for a kill. He could already tell from the set of her chin that she wasn't going to obey any order. But she might listen to a plan.

"He's armed," Ben reminded her. "Maybe we can flush him. If we do, we need you back here, with your rifle. You're a better shot than Adam. Damn near as good as me. Odds are he's not expecting we brought a woman, so he'll be focused on us."

Because it made sense, she nodded. "All right. We try it that way first." She looked over at Adam as she pulled out her gun. "I'll cover you."

He dismounted, met Ben's eyes. "Remember" was all he said.

They parted there, one to the left, one to the right to flank the opening of the cave where the small fire was down to fading smoke. Willa steadied Moon with her knees and waited, watched them. They moved in sync, men who had hunted together since childhood and knew each other's thoughts. A hand signal, a nod, and the pace changed, quick, but not rushed.

Her heart began to knock against her ribs as they neared the cave. Her breath caught in her lungs, clogged there as she braced for the shattering sound of gunfire, of screams, or of the horrific sight of blood splattering over snow.

She prayed, the words repeating over and over in her head in English, in her mother's tongue, then in a desperate mixture of both as she pleaded with any god who would listen to help.

Then she drew a breath, forced it out. Steadying herself, she lifted her rifle and drew a bead on the mouth of the cave.

It was Lily who stumbled out into the crosshairs.

"My God." She forgot her duty, her post, and kicked Moon forward in a gallop. Lily was already in Adam's arms, being rocked in the trampled snow, when Willa slid off her horse. "Is she hurt? Is she all right?"

"She's burning up. Fever." Desperate, Adam pressed his face to hers as if to cool it. Even thoughts of vengeance vanished as she shuddered against him. "We've got to get her back quickly."

"Inside," Lily managed, and burrowed into Adam. "Inside. Jesse. Oh, God."

"Inside?" Willa's head whipped up, and all the fear came roaring back. "Ben?" She said his name the first time, then shouted it as she ran toward the cave.

He was quick, but not quite quick enough to stop her from getting in, from seeing what was spread out on the floor of the cave.

"Get out." He blocked her view with his body, took her hard by the shoulders. "Go out now."

"But how?" Blood, a sea of it. The gaping throat, the split belly, the brutal lifting of the trophy of hair. "Who?"

"Get out." He turned her roughly, shoved her. "Stay out."

She made it as far as the opening, then had to lean on the rock. Sweat had popped cold to her skin, and her stomach heaved viciously. She sucked in air, each breath a rasping sob until she was sure she wouldn't faint or be sick.

Her vision cleared, and she watched Adam bundling Lily into his coat. "I have a thermos of coffee in my saddlebags. It should still be warm." Willa straightened, ordered her legs to hold her weight. "Let's try to get some into her, then we'll take her home."

Adam rose, lifting Lily into his arms. When his eyes met Willa's, the sun flashed into them as it would on the edge of a sword. "He's already dead, isn't he?"

"Yes, he's already dead."

"I wanted it on my hands."

"Not like that you didn't." Willa turned and went to her horse.

Willa paced the living room of Adam's house. She was useless in a sickroom and knew it. But she felt worse than useless out of it. They'd barely been back an hour, and she'd already been dismissed. Bess and Adam were upstairs doing whatever needed to be done for Lily. Ben and Nate were dealing with the police, and her men were taking the rest of the morning to recover after the long night.

Even Tess had been given an assignment and was in the kitchen heating up pots of coffee or tea or soup. Something hot and liquid anyway, Willa thought, as she paced past the window again.

At least she'd had something to do before. Streaking down from the high country to alert the police, to call off Search and Rescue, to tell Bess to ready a sickbed. Now there was nothing but useless waiting.

So when Bess came down the stairs, Willa pounced. "How is she? How bad is it? What are you doing for her?"

"I'm doing what needs to be done." Worry and lack of sleep made her voice sharp and testy. "Now go on home and go to bed your own self. You can see her later."

"She should be in a hospital," Tess replied, as she came in with a tray, the bowl of soup she'd been ordered to heat steaming in the center.

"I can tend her well enough here. Fever doesn't break before long, we'll have Zack fly her into Billings. For now she's better off in her own bed, with her man beside her." Bess snatched the tray away from Tess. She wanted both of these girls out of her hair, where she wouldn't have to worry about them as well as the one upstairs in bed. "Go about your business. I know what I'm doing here."

"She always knows what she's doing." Tess scowled after Bess, who flounced back up the stairs. "For all we know Lily might have frostbite, or hypothermia."

"Wasn't cold enough for either," Willa said wearily. "And we checked for frostbite anyway. It's exposure. She's caught a bad chill and she's banged up some. If Bess thinks it's worse, she'll be the first to send her to the hospital."

Tess firmed her lips and said what she'd been harboring in her heart for hours. "He might have raped her."

Willa turned away. It had been one more fear, a woman's fear, that she'd lived with during the long night. "If he had, she would have told Adam."

"It isn't always easy for a woman to talk about it."

"It is when it's Adam." Willa rubbed her gritty eyes, dropped her hands. "Her clothes weren't torn, Tess, and I think there was more on his mind than rape. There'd have been signs of it. Bess would have seen them when she undressed her. She'd have said."

"All right." That was one hideous little terror she could put aside. "Are you going to tell me what happened up there?"

"I don't know what happened up there." She could see it, perfectly. It was imprinted on her mind like all the others. But she didn't understand it. "When we found them Lily was delirious, and he was dead. Dead," she repeated, and met Tess's eyes, "like the others were. Pickles and that girl."

"But—" Tess had been sure that Adam had killed him. That they would put a spin on it for the police, but that Adam had done it. "That doesn't make any sense. If Jesse Cooke killed the others . . ."

"I don't have any answers." She picked up her hat, her coat. "I need air."

"Willa." Tess laid a hand on her arm. "If Jesse Cooke didn't kill the others?"

"I still don't have any answers." She shook her arm free. "Go to bed, Hollywood. You look like hell."

It was a weak parting shot, but she wasn't feeling clever. It felt as though her legs were filled with water as she trudged across the road. She would have to talk to the police, she thought. She would have to bear that one more time. And she would have to think, to get her mind in order and think of what to do next.

Too many rigs in the yard, she thought, and paused to study the official seals on the sides of the cars flanking Ben's truck. If there had ever been a police rig on the ranch when her father had been alive, she couldn't recall it. She didn't care to count how many times one had been there since his death.

Gathering her forces, she climbed the steps to the porch and went inside. By the time she'd removed her hat, hung it on the hall rack, Ben was coming down the stairs.

He'd seen her from the office window, watched her almost staggering progress toward the house, her deliberate squaring of shoulders as she saw the police cars.

And he'd had enough.

"How's Lily?"

"Bess won't let anyone but Adam near her." Willa took her coat off slowly, certain that any sudden move would bang her aching bones together. "But she's resting."

"Good. You can follow suit."

"The police will want to talk to me."

"They can talk to you later. After you've gotten some sleep." He took her arm and towed her firmly up the stairs.

"I've got responsibilities here, Ben."

"Yeah, you do." When they reached the top of the stairs and she turned in the direction of the office, he simply picked her up bodily and carried her toward her room. "The first is not to end up in a sickbed yourself."

"Let go of me. I don't appreciate the caveman routine."

"Neither do I." He kicked her door shut behind him, strode to the bed, and dumped her. "Especially when you're playing the caveman." She bounced up, he shoved her down again. "You know I've got you outmuscled, Will. I'm not letting you out of here until you've had some sleep."

Maybe she couldn't outwrestle him, but she thought she could outshout him. "I've got cops in my office, a sister too sick to say two words to me, a bunkhouse full of men who are speculating on just what the hell happened up in high country, and a ranch nobody's running. What the hell do you expect me to do, let it all go to hell while I take a nap?"

"I expect you to bend." She'd been wrong, he could outshout her too. The explosion might have knocked her back if she hadn't already been down. "Just once in your damn life, bend before you break. The cops can wait, your sister's being taken care of, and your men are too damn tired to speculate on anything but who's snoring the loudest. And the ranch isn't going to fall apart if you turn off for a couple hours."

He grabbed her boot, wrenched it off, then heaved it across the room. She reached for the second, gripped the top in what would have been a comic struggle if his eyes hadn't been so raw with temper. "What the hell crawled up your butt?" she demanded. "Just cut it out, Ben."

The second boot slid out of her fingers and went flying. "You think I didn't see your face when you walked into that cave? That I don't know what it did to you, or how you were holding yourself together by your fingernails all the way back down?" He grabbed her shirtfront, and for a moment she was certain he intended to haul her off the bed and toss her after her boots. "I'm not having it."

She was stunned enough that she didn't react until he'd unbuttoned her shirt and yanked it off her shoulders. "Just take your hands off me. I can undress myself when I'm ready. You're an overseer around here, McKinnon, but you don't run my life, and if you don't—"

"Maybe you need somebody to run it."

He lifted her off the bed—clean off, she thought in wonder, as her feet dangled inches above the polished wood floor. And she realized he was as furious as she'd ever seen him, and she'd seen him red-eyed furious plenty. She'd never seen him like this.

He added a quick, teeth-rattling shake. "Maybe you need to listen to somebody besides yourself now and again."

It was the shake that snapped it. The humiliation of it. "If I do, it won't be you. And the only place you're going to be running is for cover if you don't turn me loose—" Her hand was fisted and ready when he dropped her onto her feet.

"Take a swing at me." He ground out the dare. "Go ahead, but you're going to bed if I have to tie you to the headboard."

She grabbed the hands that grabbed at her shirt. "I'm warning you—"

"He worked for me."

That stopped her, stopped them both as they struggled with her thermal shirt. "What?" Now her hands covered his, dug in. "Jesse Cooke?"

And her hands went limp as she remembered. That day on the road to Three Rocks, that pretty, smiling face at the window of her rig. They'd been that close, as close as Ben and she were now, with only that thin shield of glass between them.

What would he have done, she wondered, if her door hadn't been locked, her window up?

"That's where I saw him." She shuddered when she thought of how he'd flashed that grin at her, called her by name. "I couldn't put it together. He was right there all along. He's been here, playing poker with the men. Right down in the bunkhouse playing cards."

She shook herself, looked at Ben, and saw the weight he was carrying. Not anger so much as guilt, she thought. And she knew the sharp edge of it too well. "It's not your fault." She touched his face, and her words were as gentle as fingertips. "You couldn't know."

"No, I couldn't know." He'd chewed over that until it had made him as ill as spoiled beef. "But it doesn't change it. I had him work on Shelly's rig. She had him in for coffee—her and the baby alone with him. He fixed my mother's bathroom sink. He was in the house with my mother."

"Stop." She did bend, enough to put her arms around him, to draw him down until he sat beside her. "He's done now."

"He's done, but it's not." He took her by the shoulders, turning her so they faced each other on the edge of the bed. "Whoever killed him, Willa, works for you, or for me."

"I know that." She'd thought of it, thought of it constantly on the racing ride back from the cave, during her helpless pacing of Adam's living room. "Maybe it was payback, Ben, for the others. Maybe Jesse killed the others, and whoever found him did it for them. Lily wasn't hurt. She was alone, and sick, but he didn't touch her."

"And maybe one at a time's enough for him. Will, the chances that we've got two men who do that with a knife are slim. Cooke carried a small boot knife, a four-inch blade hardly bigger than a toy. You don't do that kind of damage with an undersized blade."

"No." It all played back in her head. "No, you don't."

"Then there's that first steer we found, up toward the cabin. No way he did that. I'd barely signed him on. He didn't know his way around high country then."

She had to moisten her lips, they'd become so dry. "You've told all this to the police."

"Yeah, I told them."

"Okay." She rubbed her fingers dead center of her brow. There wasn't a headache there yet, just intense concentration. "We go on the way we have. Keep the guards, the men working in teams and shifts. I know my men." She rapped a fist on her knee. "I know them. The two new ones I just hired on—Christ, I shouldn't have taken on any new hands until this was done."

"You have to stop riding out alone."

"I can't take a damn bodyguard every time I've got cattle to check."

"You stop riding out alone," he said evenly, "or I'll use the old man's will to block you. I'll put down that I consider you incompetent as operator. I can convince Nate to go along with me."

What little color she had left drained out of her face as she got to her feet. "You son of a bitch. You know goddamn well I'm as competent as any rancher in the state. More."

He rose as well, faced her. "I'll say what I need to say, and I'll do what I have to do. You butt against me on this, you risk losing Mercy."

"Get the hell out of here." She whirled away, balled fists at her sides. "Just get the hell out of my house."

"You want to keep it your house, you don't ride out without Adam or Ham. You want me out, you get into bed and get some sleep."

He could have forced her down again. It would have been easier than saying what he had to say. "I care about you, Willa. I've got feelings for you, and they go pretty deep." It was harder yet when she turned and stared at him. "Maybe I don't know what the hell to do with them, but they're there."

Her heart hurt all over again, but in a way she didn't expect. "Threatening me is sure a damn fool way of showing them."

"Maybe. But if I asked you nice, you wouldn't listen."

"How do you know? You never ask nice."

He dragged a hand through his hair, regrouped. "I've got to get through my day too. Worrying about you's putting a hitch in my stride. If you'd do this one thing for me, it'd make it easier."

This was interesting, she thought. When her mind was clear again, she'd have to ponder it. "Do you ride out alone, Ben?"

"We're not talking about me."

"Maybe I've got feelings too."

That was unexpected—and something worth considering. So he considered it, sticking his hands in his pockets and rocking back on his heels. "Do you?"

"Maybe. I don't want to punch you every time I see you these days, so maybe I do."

His mouth curved up. "Willa, you do have a way of flushing a man's ego and then shooting it down. Let's take it forward a step." He came toward her, tilted her face up with his finger under her chin, and brushed his lips against hers. "You matter to me. Some."

"You matter to me too. Some."

She was softening. He knew she wasn't aware of it, but he was. Under different circumstances it would have been time to make gentle love to her, perhaps say more. Perhaps say nothing. Because he knew that was just what she'd expect, he kissed her again, let it deepen, let himself sink into her, into that sensation of intimate isolation.

Her arms came up, circled his neck. Her body went pliant as he gathered her closer. The muscles he stroked, kneaded, began to relax under his hands. This time, when he lifted her onto the bed, she sighed.

"You'd better lock that door," she murmured. "We could have the cops in here. Get ourselves arrested."

He kissed her eyes closed as he unfastened her jeans. He kissed her curved lips as he drew the jeans down her legs. Then he threw a blanket over her, got up, and lowered the shades. Her eyes were heavy, smiling lazily as she watched him move back to her, bend down, touch that warm mouth to hers again.

"Get some sleep," he ordered, then straightened and strode to the door.

She popped up like a string. "You son of a bitch."

"I love it when you call me that." With a chuckle, he closed the door.

Steaming, she plopped back on the pillows. How was it he always seemed to outmaneuver her? He'd wanted her flat on her back in bed, and by God, that's just where she was. It was mortifying.

Not that she was staying. In just a minute she would get up, take a bracing shower. Then she'd get back to work.

In just a minute.

She wasn't closing her eyes, wasn't going to sleep. If she did, she was certain she'd be back in that cave, back in the horror. But that wasn't the reason, she assured herself as she struggled to force her eyelids open again. It wasn't fear that was pushing her along. It was duty. And as soon as she got her second wind, she was getting up to fulfill that duty.

She wasn't going to sleep just because Ben McKinnon told her to. Especially since he'd told her to.

She fell like a rock and slept like a stone.

Part Four
Summer

Rough winds do shake the darling buds of May,
And summer's lease hath all too short a date.

—Shakespeare

25

There wasn't a dish in the sink, not a crumb on the counter or a scuff mark on the floor. Lily stared at the spotless kitchen. Adam had beaten her to it. Again. She stepped to the back door, through it. The gardens she'd planned were tilled, with the hardier vegetables and flowers already planted.

Adam and Tess. Lily hadn't even gotten soil on her garden gloves. And oh, how she'd wanted to.

She struggled not to resent it, to remember that they were thinking of her. She'd been ill for two weeks, and for another, too weak to handle her regular chores without periodic rests. But she was recovered now, fully, and growing weary of being worried over and pampered.

She knew the freezer was stuffed to overflowing with dishes that Bess or Nell had prepared. Lily hadn't cooked a meal since the night Jesse had come through the door where she now stood looking out at the tender green buds on the trees, feeling the gentle warmth of the May air on her face.

It seemed like years since that cold and bitter night. And there were blank spots still, areas of gray she didn't care to explore. But she was to be married in three short weeks, and her life was more out of her control than it had ever been before.

She hadn't even been permitted to address her own wedding invitations. It had been discovered, to everyone's surprise, that Willa possessed the neatest handwriting among them. So Tess had assigned the job to Willa, with Lily playing only a minor role.

They'd let her lick the stamps.

The flowers were ordered, the photographer and music settled on. And she'd let them, all of them, lovingly step over and around her to handle the details.

It had to stop. It was going to stop. Closing the door firmly at her back, she marched toward the stables. Or she began in a march and ended up with dragging feet. Every time she ventured toward stables or pasture, Adam found a way of whisking her home again. Never touching her, she thought. Or touching her so dispassionately it was more like doctor to patient than lover to lover.

He stepped out of the stables as she approached, which made her think, not for the first time, that he had some sort of radar where she was concerned. He smiled, but she saw that his eyes remained sober, and searching.

"Hi. I'd hoped you'd sleep longer."

"It's after ten. I thought I'd work with a couple of the yearlings today, on the longe line."

"There's plenty of time for that." As usual, he guided her away from the stables, his hand barely touching her elbow. "Did you have breakfast?"

"Yes, Adam, I had breakfast."

"Good." He resisted picking her up and carrying her back to the house, tucking her away where she'd be safe and close. "Did you finish that new book I brought you? It's a pretty morning, maybe you could sit on the porch and read. Get a little sun."

"I nearly finished it." Had barely started it. It made her guilty, knowing he'd made a special trip into town to buy her books, magazines, the little candied almonds she was so fond of.

And she hated the book, the magazines, the almonds. Even the flowers he was constantly bringing home to cheer her.

"I'll bring the radio out for you. And a blanket. It can get cool when you're just sitting." He was terrified she'd catch a chill, lie shivering in bed again with her hand limp in his. "I'll make you some tea, then—"

"Stop it!" The explosive shout stunned them both. In the time he stared at her, she realized she'd never really shouted at anyone before. It was a powerful and thrilling experience. "Stop it, Adam. I'm tired of this. I don't want to sit, I don't want to read. I don't want you bringing me tea and flowers and candy and treating me like a piece of cracked glass."

"Lily, there's no need to get upset. You'll make yourself sick again, and you're barely out of bed."

For the first time in her life she understood the wisdom of counting to ten before speaking. Another time, she decided, she might even try it.

"I am out of bed. I would have been out of bed days before I was if you hadn't been hovering around me. And I am sick. I'm sick of not being allowed to wash my own dishes or plant my own garden or run my own life. I'm sick to death of it."

"Let's go inside." He treated her as he would a fractious mare, with great patience and compassion. "You just need to rest. With the wedding only weeks away you've got a lot on your mind."

That tore it. She whirled on him. "I do not need to rest, and I do not need to be placated like a cranky child. And there isn't going to be any wedding, not until I say differently."

She stalked off, leaving him stunned, speechless, and staggered.

She rode on the temper, the unfamiliar and exciting kick of it all the way to the main house, up the stairs, and into the office, where Willa was arguing with Tess.

"If you don't like the way I'm setting things up, why the hell did you dump the job on me? I've got enough to do without fussing with this reception."

"I'm dealing with the flowers," Tess shot back. "I'm dealing with the caterer—if you can call some bucktoothed jerk whose specialty is pigs in a blanket a caterer." She threw up her hands, then fisted them on her hips. "All you have to do is arrange for tables and chairs for the alfresco buffet. And if I want striped umbrellas, then the least you can do is find me striped umbrellas."

Now Willa's fists rode her hips as well, and she went nose to nose with Tess. "And where in God's name am I supposed to come up with fifty blue-and-white-striped umbrellas—much less this canopy thing you're so hot for. If you'd just . . . Lily, aren't you supposed to be resting?"

"No. No, I am not supposed to be resting." She was surprised sparks didn't fly from her fingertips as she marched to the desk and swept all the lists and folders and invoices onto the floor in an avalanche of paper. "You can toss every bit of paper that has to do with the wedding in the trash. Because there's not going to be any wedding."

"Honey." Tess broke out of her shock, slid an arm around Lily's shoulder, and tried to nudge her into a chair. "If you're having second thoughts—"

"Don't 'honey' me." Lily wrenched away, fuming. "And don't pretend you give me credit for having second thoughts when no one gives me credit for having the first ones. It's my wedding, damn it. Mine. And you've all just taken it over. If you want to plan a wedding so badly, then *you* get married."

"I'll get Bess," Tess murmured, and sent Lily into a fresh tantrum.

"Don't you dare get Bess and have her up here clucking over me. The next person, the very next person who clucks over me, I'm slapping them. I mean it. You." She jabbed a finger at Tess. "You planted my garden. And you." She spun on Willa. "You addressed my wedding invitations. Between the two of you, you've taken everything. And what slips through your fingers, Adam snaps up so quickly I can't even grab for it."

"Well, fine." Willa threw up her hands. "Excuse us for trying to help you through a difficult time. I can't tell you how much I enjoyed getting writer's cramp with this one here breathing down my neck."

"I was not breathing down your neck," Tess said between her teeth. "I was supervising."

"Supervising, my butt. You've got your nose in everything and sooner or later someone's going to pop you in it."

"Oh, and that would be you, I suppose."

"Shut up, both of you. Just shut the hell up."

They did, though their mouths hung open when Lily lifted a vase and sent it flying. "The two of you can argue till your tongues fall out, but not over my business. Not over me. Do you understand? I'm not going to be used anymore. I'm not going to be controlled. I'm not going to be brushed aside. I want everyone to stop looking at me as if I'm going to fall to pieces at any moment. Because I'm not. I'm *not!*"

"Lily." Adam stepped into the doorway. He wasn't sure how to approach her now, so he stood back and hoped a soothing tone would work. "I didn't mean to upset you. If you need time to—"

"Oh, don't you start on me." Vibrating with fury, she kicked at the papers scattered at her feet. "That's just what I'm talking about. Don't anyone upset Lily. Don't anyone treat Lily like a normal woman. Poor thing, poor Lily. She might shatter."

She spun around so she could fire a stream of frustrated rage at all of them. "Well, I'm the one Jesse abused. He held a gun to *my* head. I'm the one he dragged into the hills and kicked into the snow and pulled along on a rope like a dog. And I got through it. I survived it. It's about time you did too."

It was Adam who shattered, at the image that flashed into his brain. "What do you want me to do? Forget it? Pretend it never happened?"

"Live with it. I am. You haven't asked any questions." Her voice hitched, but she steadied it. No, she promised herself, she wasn't going to shatter. And she wasn't going to cry. "Maybe you don't want the answers. Maybe you don't want me the way things are."

"How can you say that?"

Now she drew herself up, made her voice as cool and reasonable as she could with her heart pounding so hard it hurt her ribs. "You haven't touched me, Adam. Not once since it happened have you touched me." She shook her head as Willa and Tess started to leave the room. "No, stay. This isn't just between Adam and me. That's only part of it. You haven't talked about it either, so let's talk about it now. Right now."

She wiped a tear from her cheek. Damn it, that would be the last one that fell. "Why haven't you touched me, Adam? Is it because you think he did, and you don't want me now?"

"I don't know how." He stepped forward, stopped. His hands felt clumsy, outsized, as they had for weeks. "I didn't stop him. I didn't protect you. I didn't do what I promised you. And I don't know how to touch you, or why you'd want me to."

She closed her eyes a moment. Why hadn't she seen that before? He was the fragile one now. He was the lost one. "You came for me." She said it softly, hoping he could understand just how much that mattered. "Yours was the first face I saw when I stumbled out of that cave, away from . . . away from it. You were the first thing I saw, and that's one of the reasons I can live with it."

She took one unsteady breath, tried again, and found that the next one came more easily. "And all the time he had me, I knew you'd come. That's one of the reasons I got through it. And I fought back."

She looked at her sisters. They, too, had to know how much it mattered. "I fought back and I held on just as you would have done. He had the gun, and he was stronger, but he didn't have control. Not really. Because I didn't give up. I drove into that tree. To slow him down, to make it harder for him."

"Oh, Lily." Undone, Tess sat down and began to weep. "Oh, God."

"And when he tied my hands, I kept falling down." A calm settled over her now, a calm that came from surviving the worst. "Because that would slow him down too. I knew he wouldn't kill me. He'd hurt me, but he wouldn't kill me. But then it was so cold, and I couldn't fight back anymore. But I held on."

Saying nothing, Willa walked over, poured a glass of water, and brought it to Tess. Lily took a deep breath. She would finish now, say it all, everything that hadn't been said.

"I thought he might rape me, and I could survive that. He'd done it before. But he wasn't in control this time, and he was afraid. Every bit as much as I was, maybe more. When we got to the cave, I was so tired, and I knew I was sick. Nothing he did to me then would have mattered because all I had to do was get through it. And get back here."

She walked to the window, looked out. And gathering her strength because she had gotten back, she had made it through, she turned around once more. "He had whiskey, and I took some because I thought it might help. He drank a lot. I fell asleep, or passed out, listening to him drinking and boasting, just like he used to. I listened to the whiskey sloshing in the bottle, and in part of my mind I thought he might get drunk enough, just drunk enough, and I might be strong enough, just strong enough, to get away. Then someone came."

She crossed her arms over her chest, hugged her elbows. "It's not clear." If any part of the ordeal still frightened her, it was this. The nebulous, fever-soaked memories. "I must have had a fever by then and I suppose I was delirious. I thought it was you," she told Adam. "I thought I was home, in bed, and you were coming in, sliding in next to me. I could almost feel it. And feeling it, I fell asleep again, and slept while whoever was there killed Jesse and cut the rope on my hands. I was only a few feet away, but—"

That quick, high-pitched scream that had snapped off. She could still hear it if she let herself. "When I woke up," she continued, steadily, "Jesse's coat was over me. There was blood on it, all over it. So much blood. I saw him. The light was just coming in through the opening of the cave, and I could see him. Seeing Jesse like that was worse somehow than when he'd held the gun to my head. The need to get away from him was worse. Every time I took a breath, I breathed in the smell of him, and what had been done to him while I'd been a few feet away, sleeping. And I was more frightened in those few moments than I'd been through all the rest of it."

She stepped forward, just one step, toward Adam. "But then I crawled out into the sunlight, and you were there. You were there when I needed you most. And I knew you would be."

Purged, she walked over, poured a glass of water for herself. "I'm sorry I shouted at all of you. I know everything you've done was out of concern. But I need to take my life back now. I need to go on."

"You should've yelled sooner." Composed again, Tess rose. "You're right, Lily. You're absolutely right about all of it. I got carried away planning things for you. I'm sorry. I'd have hated being shoved to the background this way."

"It's all right. It's been a bad habit of mine to let myself be shoved. And I might ask for help planting the rest of the garden."

"Maybe I should plant my own. I didn't know I'd like it so much. I'll be downstairs." She started out, shot a telling glance at Willa.

"If you want to start taking things back," Willa said, nudging the papers with her foot. "You can start by picking these up and getting them out of here." She smiled. "I don't like hunting up printed cocktail napkins."

Taking a chance, she grasped Lily's shoulders, leaned in close so that her whisper could be heard. "He'd have crawled through hell if that's what it took to get you back. Don't punish him for loving you too much."

Easing back, she glanced at Adam. "You've got a couple hours off," she told him, "to get your life straightened out." Walking out, she closed the door behind her.

"I must seem ungrateful," Lily began, but he only shook his head, so she crouched down and began to gather the papers. "I threw a vase. I've never done anything like that before. I didn't know I'd want to. It was difficult to go back to feeling unnecessary."

"I'm sorry I made you feel that way." He crossed to her, gathered papers himself. He picked up the list of acceptances for the wedding, then lifted his eyes to hers. "Nothing in my life is more necessary than you, or more precious. If you want to call off the wedding..." No, he couldn't be patient or reasonable about this. All he could say was "Don't."

And nothing he could have said, Lily realized, could have been more perfect. "After Tess and Will have gone to all this trouble? That would be rude." She started to smile, nearly did, but he covered his face with his hands. Covered it, but not before she'd seen the stricken look in his eyes, and the hurt she'd put there.

"I let him take you."

"No."

"I thought he would kill you."

"Adam."

"I thought if I touched you it would make you think of it, of him."

"No, no, Adam. Never." So it was she who held him. "Never. Never. I'm sorry. I'm sorry. I didn't mean to hurt you. I was just so angry, so frustrated. I love you, I love you, I love you. Oh, hold me, Adam. I won't break."

But he might. Even as his arms came around her, his grip tightened convulsively, he thought he might shatter like thin glass. "I wanted to kill him." His voice was muffled against her throat. "I would have. And living with the wanting isn't nearly as hard as living with the fact that I didn't. And worse is living with the thought that I nearly lost you."

"I'm here. And it's over." When his mouth found hers, she poured herself into it, her hands soothing him as he had always soothed her. "I need you so much. And I need you to need me back."

He framed her face. "I do. I always will."

"I want to plant gardens with you, Adam, and raise horses, paint porches." Cupping his face in turn, she drew his head back and said what was trembling in her heart. "I want to make children. I want to make a child with you, Adam. Today."

Staggered, he lowered his brow to hers. "Lily."

"It's the right time." She lifted his hand, pressed it to her lips. "Take me home, Adam, to our bed. Make a child with me today."

From the side window, Tess watched Lily and Adam walk toward the white house. It made her think of the first time she'd seen them walk together, on the day of the funeral. "Check it out," she called to Willa.

"What?" A little impatient, Willa joined her at the window, then smiled. "That's a relief." Moments later, the shades on the bedroom windows of the white house came down, and she grinned. "Looks like we've still got a wedding going."

"I still want those striped umbrellas."

"You're such a bitch."

"Ah, that's what they all say. Will." In a surprising move, she laid a hand on Willa's shoulder. "Are you still driving cattle up to high country tomorrow?"

"That's right."

"I want to come."

"Very funny."

"No, I mean it. I can ride, and I think it might be an interesting experience, one I can use in my work. And since Adam's going, Lily should too. It's important that we stick together. It's safer that way."

"I was going to have Adam stay behind."

Tess shook her head. "You need people you can trust. Adam won't stay behind even if you ask him. So Lily and I go too."

"Just what I need. A couple of greenhorns." But she'd already thought of it herself, and had weighed the pros and cons. "The McKinnons will be moving their herd up as well. We'll take one man with us, leave Ham in charge of the rest. Better get your beauty sleep tonight, Hollywood. We ride out at dawn."

The only thing missing, Tess thought as she yawned in the saddle at daybreak, was the theme from *Rawhide.* So she hummed it to herself, struggled to remember the words that were vaguely familiar only because of the bar scene in *The Blues Brothers.*

Was it "Cut 'em in" or "Head 'em out"?

"Head 'em out" was the obvious winner, as that was exactly what Willa called into the misty morning air.

It was rather magnificent, Tess mused. The sea of cattle swarming forward, the riders skimming the edges of the herd on horses fresh and eager. All of them surged through the curtain of mists, the low-lying river of fog, tearing it into delicate fingers while the sun glinted off dewy grass.

And westward, the mountains rose like gods, all silver and white.

Then Willa turned in the saddle, shouted out for Tess to move her ass. Why, Tess thought with a grin, that just completed a perfect picture. Belatedly she kicked her horse forward to catch up as the drive began.

No, something was still missing, she realized as the noise of hooves on hard-packed dirt, of braying moos, of riders clucking and calling filled the air. Nate. For once she wished he had cattle as well as horses; then maybe she'd be riding along with him.

"Don't just ride," Willa called out as she trolled up alongside. "Keep 'em in line. You lose one, you go after it."

"Like I could lose a big fat cow," Tess muttered, but she tried to mimic Willa's herding whistle and the way her sister slapped her looped rope on the saddle.

Not that Tess had been given a rope, or would know what to do with one, but she used her hand, then as the hundreds of marching hooves kicked up dust, her bandanna.

"Oh, for Christ's sake." Rolling her eyes, Willa circled back. "Not like that, you idiot. You may need that hand." She took the bandanna from Tess, who was holding it over her nose, and after a few quick trips, leaned over to tie it on. "That's an improvement," she decided when it was secured and hung down over half of her sister's face. "Never seen you look better."

"Just go play trail boss."

"I am trail boss." With that Willa kicked Moon into a gallop and rode to the rear of the herd to check for stragglers.

It was an experience, Tess decided. Maybe not quite like driving longhorns north from Texas or whatever cowboys had once done. But there was a kind of majesty in it, she supposed. A handful of riders controlling so many animals, driving them along past pastures where other cattle watched the procession with bored eyes, nipping potential strays back in with a quick movement of horse.

Season after season, she mused, year after year and decade after decade, in a manner that changed little. The horse was the tool here, as it had always been. A four-wheeler couldn't travel the forests, over the rivers, up and down the rocky ravines.

The pastures of the high country were rich, and so the cattle were taken up to graze on thick meadow grass, to laze through the summer and into the early fall under the wide sky with eagle and mountain sheep and each other for company.

And summer was coming, like a gift. The trees grew greener, the pines lusher, and she could hear the cheerful bubble of water moving quick and cool. Wildflowers dotted a near meadow, a surprising shower of color, teased out by the strong sun. Birds darted through the trees like arrows, over the hills like kites. And the mountains rose, creamy white at the peaks, with the deep green belt of trees darkening, and the ridges and folds that were valleys and canyons shimmering shadowlike.

"How you holding up?" Jim paced his horse beside her and made her grin. He looked as cocky and raw as anything that had ridden out of the Wild West.

"Holding. Actually it's fun."

He winked. "Be sure to tell that to your back end at the end of the day."

"Oh, I stopped feeling that an hour ago." But she stretched up just to check. No, her butt was as dead as a numbed tooth. "I've never been up this high before. It's gorgeous."

"There's a spot just up ahead. You look out thataway"—he gestured—"it's a picture."

"How long have you been doing this, Jim? Taking the herd up in the spring?"

"For Mercy? Shit, about fifteen years, give or take." He winked again, saw Willa riding up, and knew she'd give him the look that meant he was lollygagging. "Keeps me outta pool halls and away from wild women." He trotted back to point, leaving Tess chuckling.

"Don't flirt with a cowboy on a drive," Willa told her.

"We were having a short, civilized conversation. When I flirt I—oh, oh, my God." Tess reined in her horse, looked out in the direction Jim had just indicated. Understanding, Willa stopped behind her.

"Nice view."

"It's like a painting," Tess whispered. "It doesn't seem real." It couldn't be real, the way the colors and shapes, the size and scope all swept together.

The peaks shot up against the sky, tumbled down to a wide, silvery canyon where a river ran blue and trees grew thick and green. Somewhere along the way, it seemed miles to Tess, the river took a curve and vanished into rock. But before it vanished it spewed white, crashed over rock, then settled to serene.

A hawk circled in the distance, arching around and around that curving river, amid rugged rocks, under spearing silver peaks, above green trees.

"Good fishing there." Willa leaned on her saddle horn. "People come from all over hell and back to fly-fish in this river. Me, I'm not big on it, but it's a sight to see. The way the lines dance and whip through the air, and land with barely a sound or a ripple. Farther down, around the curve, there's some wild white water. People plunk themselves in rubber rafts and have a high old time riding it. I'll stick with horses."

"Yeah." But Tess wondered what it would be like. It surprised her that she wondered not in cool writer's fashion but in hot, thrilling anticipation of what it would feel like to chase that river, to fly down it.

"It'll be here when we come back." Willa turned her horse. "Montana's funny that way. It mostly stays put. Come on, we're falling behind."

"All right." Tess carried that view with her, along with countless others, as they drove the herd on.

The air cooled to a snap, and patches of snow appeared under the trees, around rocks. And still there were flowers, the sprawl of mountain clematis, the sassy purple of wild delphinium. A meadowlark sang a spring song.

When they stopped to rest the horses and grab a quick lunch, jackets came out of saddlebags.

"For Christ's sake, don't tie your horse." With another roll of the eyes for the greenhorn, Willa took the reins from Tess, gave her mount an easy slap that sent it trotting away.

"What the hell did you do?" Tess took two running steps before she realized the horse would outdistance her. "Now what am I supposed to do? Walk?"

"Eat." Willa shoved a sandwich in her face.

"Oh, fine, just fine. I'll have a little roast beef while my horse goes trotting back home."

"He's not going far. You can't go tying your horse up around here, then wandering off to sit under a tree and have your lunch." Then she grinned as she spotted Ben riding up. "Hey, McKinnon, haven't you got enough to do without looking for handouts?"

"Thought there might be an extra sandwich." He slid off his horse, gave it the same absent pat as Willa had given Tess's. Speechless, Tess watched his mount mosey off.

"What, are you all crazy? There won't be a horse left to ride at this rate."

Ben took the sandwich Tess held, bit into it, and winked at Willa. "She try to tie hers up?"

"Yep. Tenderfoot."

"You don't tie horses up in high country," he said between bites. "Cats. Bears."

"What are you—cats?" Eyes popping, Tess spun around in a circle, trying to look everywhere at once. "You mean mountain lions? Bears?"

"Predators." Willa took what was left of the sandwich from Ben, finished it off. "A horse hasn't got a chance if it's tethered. How far back's your herd, Ben?"

"About a quarter mile."

"But—" Tess thought of her rifle that was still in her saddle holster. "What chance have *we* got?"

"Oh, fair to middling," Ben drawled, and Willa roared with laughter.

"Lily's probably got that coffee hot by now."

He tugged Willa's hat over her eyes. "How do you think I found you, kid? I followed the scent."

Tess stood frozen to the spot as they wandered toward the little campfire where Lily heated the pot. At a faint rustle in the brush behind her she sprinted forward like a runner off the mark. "Wait. Wait for me."

"Your sister's got a powerful love for coffee," Ben commented as Tess barreled by.

"You should have seen her face when I set her horse loose. It was worth bringing her along just for that."

"Everything all right otherwise?"

"Quiet." She slowed her pace. "Normal. Or as quiet and normal as you'd expect with wedding plans gearing up."

"I wouldn't like to see anything spoil that."

"Nothing's going to." She stopped completely now, turned her back on the group by the fire so that she faced only Ben. "I talked to the police again," she said quietly. "They're investigating my men. Every one of them."

"Mine too. It's necessary, Willa."

"I know it. I left Ham back, and it worries me, not knowing. He and Bess, Wood's two boys. As far as it goes, Ben, they're alone."

"Ham can handle himself, so can Bess if it comes to that. And nobody's going to hurt those kids, Will."

"I wouldn't have thought so before. Now I just don't know. I wanted Nell to take them, go stay with her sister for a while. She won't leave Wood. Of course if it is Wood, then she and the boys are probably safe."

Playing back her own words in her head, Willa blew out a breath. "I can't believe what I think sometimes, Ben. If it's Wood, if it's Jim, if it's Billy. Or one of your men. I've known most of them my whole life. And then I think, maybe Jesse Cooke was the last of it. Maybe it'll stop with him and we won't have to deal with it anymore. Thinking that way's like shoving Pickles and that girl aside."

"Thinking that way's human." He touched her cheek. "I've wondered if it might stop with Cooke."

"But you don't believe it."

"No, I don't believe it."

"Is that why you're here? Is that why you're driving your herd up the same day I'm driving mine?"

He'd been afraid it hadn't been a very subtle move, and now he rubbed a hand over the scar on his chin. "You could say I've got an investment in you. I look after what's mine."

Her brows rose. "I'm not yours, Ben."

He bent down, gave her a quick, casual kiss. "Look again," he suggested, and went after his coffee.

26

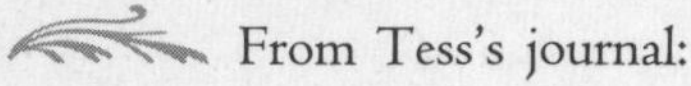
From Tess's journal:

Driving cattle is in no way similar to driving a Mercedes 450 SL—which is a little something I believe I'll treat myself to when I get back to the bright lights and big city.

Driving cattle is an adventure perhaps akin to whizzing along the highway in a spiffy sports car. You go places, you see things, and the wind is in your hair. But it is also a painful business.

My butt is so sore I've got to sit on a pillow to write. I suppose, all in all, it was worth it. The Rockies are a grabber, absolutely. Even finding snow underfoot this late in the year couldn't spoil it. The air's different in high country. Purer is the closest I can come to describing it. It's like the clearest of spring waters in a fine crystal glass.

We stopped on a rocky plateau and I swear I thought I could see all the way to Nate's ranch.

It made me miss him a little—well, more than a little. An odd feeling. I can't recall ever missing a man before. Sex, sure, but that's a different matter.

In any case, the cattle seem to drive themselves for the most part, trudging along with only the occasional complaint. Adam says it's because many of them have made the trip before and know the drill, and the others just tag along. Still, they make quite a noise with all that clopping and mooing, and the occasional maverick has to be rounded up.

I watched Will rope a cow and I was impressed. The woman looks more natural on horseback than she does on her own two feet. I'd have to say regal, though I'd never say it to her. Her head's quite big enough as it is. She's a natural boss, and I'd have to admit that's a necessary attribute in her position. She works like a stevedore, again admirable, but I don't appreciate her cracking the whip in my direction.

I suspect we meandered a bit on our way up. I have to give her credit for that as well. I have no doubt she lengthened the route for my and Lily's benefit. It was quite a trip. We saw elk and mule deer, moose, bighorn sheep, and huge, gorgeous birds.

I did not see a bear. I am in no way disappointed by this.

Lily took rolls of pictures. She's recovered so completely you could almost forget all the horror that happened to her. Almost. I think of scales when I think of Lily, with her balancing tragedy and happiness on either end. She's found a way to weight down that happiness end. I admire that, too.

But forgetting all the way just isn't possible. Beneath the tough, focused exterior, Will is a bundle of nerves. We've all homed in on the wedding, all seem determined to have nothing spoil it. But there's worry here. It's in the air.

On another front, I'm whipping through the rewrites on my script. Ira's very pleased with the deal, and the progress. I expect to be inundated with meetings when I get back to LA in the fall. And I finally decided to tell him about the book. He was pretty jazzed, which surprised me, so I shot off the first couple chapters to him to give him a taste. We'll see.

At the moment, I'm squeezing in writing time between wedding preparations. The shower's coming up, and we're all pretending Lily doesn't know we're planning one. Should be a boot.

. . .

"So what are you men planning for the bachelor party?" Tess sat on the corral fence at Nate's and watched him take a yearling through his paces.

"Something dignified, of course."

"How many strippers?"

"Three. Any more isn't dignified." He reined in, backed the yearling up, then squeezed gently with his knees. The yearling broke into an easy trot. "That's the way. Smart boy."

Look at him, Tess thought, all lanky and lean with his hat pulled low and those long, narrow hands as sexy as a concert pianist's.

He quite literally made her mouth water. "I ever tell you how good you look on a horse, Lawyer Torrence?"

"A time or two." It still made heat crawl up his neck. "But you can tell me again."

"You look good. When am I going to see you in court?"

Surprised, he circled the horse. "Didn't know you wanted to."

Neither had she. "Well, I do. I like looking at you in your lawyer suit, all sober and serious. I like looking at you."

He slid off, looped the reins around the rail, and began to uncinch the saddle. "Hasn't been much time for looking or anything else just lately, has there?"

"Busy time. Only ten days until the wedding, and Lily's parents are coming in tomorrow. After things settle, maybe you can take me into town, let me watch you ride the court. Then . . . we could stay in a hotel for the night and play." She ran her tongue around her teeth. "Wanna play with me, Nate?"

"Your rules or mine?"

"No rules at all." With a laugh, she hopped off the fence and grabbed him into a hot, lengthy kiss. "I've missed you."

"Have you?" That was progress he hadn't expected quite so soon. "That's nice."

She glanced toward the house, thought of bed. "I don't suppose we could . . ."

"I don't think Maria could stand the shock of that, middle of the day and all. Maybe you could stay the night."

"Mmm. Wish I could, but I'm already AWOL. And I don't like to stay away long, after what happened."

His eyes went cold as he turned to lift the saddle off the yearling. "I wish I'd been there sooner that night, to back Adam up."

"It wouldn't have mattered. There was nothing Adam or Will could do to stop it. Nothing you could've done if you'd been there."

"Maybe not." But he'd had some bad moments thinking of it, imagining it. Wondering what he would have done if it had been Tess with a gun at her head. Because the light had gone out of her eyes as well, he moved on impulse and swung up on the horse's bare back. "Come on, take a ride with me."

"Without a saddle?" She blinked, then laughed and stepped back. "I don't think so. I like having the horn to grab onto."

"Tenderfoot." He held out a hand. "Come on. You can grab me."

Intrigued but wary, Tess eyed the horse. "He's awfully big for a yearling."

"Just a baby and anxious to please." Nate cocked his head and waited for her to take the offered hand.

"All right. But I really hate falling off." She let him grip her hand and with little grace clambered on behind him. "Different," she decided, but found a definite advantage in being able to snuggle close behind Nate, her arms circling his waist. "Sexy. Adam rides bareback quite a lot. He looks like a god."

Nate chuckled, clucked the horse into a walk. "Puts you more in tune with your mount."

It also, Tess realized when they slid into a trot, put her more in tune with her lust. And when they smoothed out into a gallop she was grinning like a fool. "This is great. More."

"That's what you always say." He circled the corral again, enjoying the sensation of those firm, generous breasts pressed into his back. His eyes crossed when she slid her hands down below his belt.

"Figured as much," she said, when she found him hard. "Ever do it on horseback?"

"Nope." The idea provided a fascinating visual—Tess laid back in front of him on the horse's neck, her legs wrapped tight around his waist as they mated to the rhythm of the horse. "We'd break our necks when he caught the scent of sex and bucked us off."

"I'm ready to risk it. I really want you, Nate."

He stopped, steadied the horse, then turning, hauled her in front of him with a great deal of gasping and groping. "No." He could barely get the word out of his busy mouth as her fingers zoomed in on his belt buckle. "This'll have to hold us for now. Just hold on to me, Tess. Just hold on and let me kiss you a while."

She would have been reckless, but he held her close, pinning her arms to her sides as he assaulted her mouth. Her hat fell off, landed in the dirt, and her heart went wild, the echoes of it pounding everywhere at once. Then it changed, everything changed and became gentle, sweet, pure as the air in high country.

From desperation to tenderness he eased her until her pulse slowed and went thick, until her throat ached from it and her eyes stung.

"I love you." He hadn't meant to say it, but it was too much, too huge to keep trapped inside. His lips formed the words against hers, slowly.

"What?" Dazed, dreaming, she stared into his eyes. "What did you say?"

"I'm in love with you."

She dropped out of her floaty state and hit reality with a thud. She'd heard the words before. They were easy for some to toss off, just another line. But not from him, she realized. Not from a man like Nate.

"That's getting a little carried away." She wanted to smile, keep it light. Couldn't. "Nate, we're just . . ."

"Lovers?" he added, and didn't bother to curse himself for finishing her sentence. "Convenient bed partners? No, we're not, Tess."

She took a steadying breath and spoke firmly. "I think we'd better get down."

Instead he took her chin in his hand so that her eyes stayed level with his.

"I'm in love with you, have been for a while now. I'll make what adjustments I have to to make it work for you, but it comes down to this: I want you to stay with me, marry me, raise a family with me here."

The first shock paled beside the rest of it. "You know I can't possibly—"

"You got a while to get used to the idea." With this, he dismounted. "There's not much I've wanted in life," he said, studying her stunned face. "My law degree, this place, a good string of horses. I got them. Now I want you."

It helped, she thought, the unmitigated insult and arrogance of that helped shift shock into temper. "You may want to take notes, Lawyer Torrence. I'm not a law degree, a ranch, or a brood mare."

"No, you're not." A smile flirted around his mouth as he plucked her off the horse. "You're a woman, a tough-minded, ambitious, and frustrating woman. And you're going to be mine."

"Would you care to hear what I think of this sudden cowboy mentality of yours?"

"I've got a pretty good picture." He slid the bridle off the yearling, slapped its flank to send it trotting away. "You'd better get home, take some time to think it through."

"I don't need time to think it through."

"I'll give it to you anyway." He looked up at the sky. The sun was just beginning to drop toward the western peaks, blushing red against blue. "Going to rain tonight." He said it casually as he leaped over the fence and left Tess gaping after him.

"I don't know what bur's up your butt, Willa muttered, "but yank it out. Lily's going to be back here with her folks any minute."

"You're not the only one who's allowed to have things on her mind." Tess crammed a petit four in her mouth.

The house was full of chattering women, gaily wrapped gifts, and white streamers. It had been Tess's idea to serve champagne punch for the wedding shower, and though Bess had clucked her tongue over it for the sake of form, she was enjoying a cup herself while she gossiped with neighbors.

Everybody's happy as clowns, Tess thought, and snagged another petit four. Celebrating the ridiculous idea of two people chaining themselves together for the rest of their lives. She pouted, debated another cake, then went for a cigarette instead.

No way was Nate Torrence going to make her split another pair of jeans. She grabbed a cup of punch and decided to get drunk instead.

By the time the bride-to-be came in, Tess had gulped down three cups and was feeling more celebratory. She got a kick out of the way Lily feigned surprise. The shower hadn't been a secret since the first invitation had been sent. Now there were gifts to be oohed and aahed over, everything from whisk brooms to peignoirs.

Tess watched Lily's mother blink back tears and slip outside.

An interesting woman, Tess decided, pouring herself another cup. Attractive, well presented, well spoken. What the hell had she ever seen in a son of a bitch like Jack Mercy?

When Bess poured two cups and slipped out too, Tess shrugged and tried to work up the proper enthusiasm for a set of embroidered napkins.

"Here you go, Adele." Bess settled herself on the glider, handed Adele a cup while the woman dabbed at her eyes. "Been some time since we sat here."

"I didn't know how I would feel coming back. It's hardly changed."

"Oh, here and there. You haven't changed much yourself."

Vanity was a small weakness, and Adele automatically touched a hand to her carefully groomed hair. It was cut sleek and short, kept a subtle shade of deep blond.

"Lines," she said with a weak laugh. "I never know where they come from, but there are new ones in my mirror every morning."

"Just life." Bess took stock. Adele still had a pretty, almost delicate face, the features small and well proportioned. She'd kept in shape, too, Bess mused. Trim, easing toward lanky, and her eye for color and line hadn't changed either. She looked good in the rose-toned slacks and ivory blouse.

"You've got a fine daughter, Adele. You did a good job with her."

"I could've done better. I should have. Seeing her now, I look back to when she was a little girl. The hours I should have spent with her that I didn't."

"You had work, and your own life too."

"I did." To soothe herself, Adele sipped her drink. "And a lot of pain, the first few years anyway. I hated Jack Mercy more than I ever loved him, Bess."

"That's natural. He didn't do right by you or the girl. But I'd say you found the better man."

"Rob? He's a good man. Set in his ways, he always has been. But they're good ways." Her lips softened. They'd had a good life, she thought. "Rob's not, well, overtly affectionate, but he loves Lily. I wonder now if we didn't expect too much from her. If we both didn't. But we love her."

"It shows."

She rocked awhile in silence. "God, the view. I've never forgotten it. I missed this place. I've been happy back East—the green, the gentleness of the land. But I have missed this place."

"You'll come back, now that Lily's living here."

"Yes. We'll come back. Rob's enchanted. He loves to travel. We've avoided this part of the country, but now . . . He's down with Adam, looking at the horses." She sighed, smiled. "He's a good man too, isn't he, Bess? Lily's Adam."

"One of the finest I know, and he'd walk through fire for her."

"She's been through so much. When I think about it—"

"Don't." Bess covered Adele's hand with hers. "It's behind her now. Just like Jack Mercy's behind you. She's going to be a beautiful bride, and a happy wife."

"Oh." It brought the tears again. They were falling down her cheeks when Willa stepped out.

"Excuse me." Automatically, she started back inside.

"No, don't." Sniffling, Adele rose, reached out a hand. "I'm just being sentimental. I haven't had a chance to really talk to you. Every letter Lily wrote me was full of you, and Tess."

A woman's tears always disarmed her. Willa shifted, tried to smile. "I'm surprised there was room with Adam in there."

"You have the same eyes, you and your brother." Dark and wise, Adele thought. And steady. "I knew your mother, a little. She was a beautiful woman."

"Thank you."

"I've been frightened." Adele cleared her throat. "I realize this isn't a good time to bring it up, but I've been so worried. I know Lily toned down a great deal of what's happened here in her letters and calls to me. But when Jesse—when those things happened with Jesse, there were reports back East. I wanted to say that I'm still worried, but I feel easier now that I've met you, and Adam."

"She's stronger than you think. Than any of us thought."

"You may be right," Adele agreed, then braced herself. "And I want to thank you for your hospitality, for inviting Rob and me to stay here in your home. I know it must be awkward for you."

"I thought it would be. It's not. My sister's parents are always welcome at Mercy."

"Not much of Jack in you." Adele paled, appalled at herself. "I'm sorry."

"Don't be." Willa's eyes shifted as she spotted the gleam of sun on chrome. And her lips curved slowly. "And here comes the next surprise." She flicked a glance at Adele. "I hope this one's not awkward for you."

"What have you done, girl?" Bess asked.

Willa only continued to smile, and poked her head back inside. "Hey, Hollywood, come on out here a minute."

"What?" Carrying a cup in one hand, Tess wandered to the door. "We're playing parlor games. How many words can you make out of 'honeymoon'? I think I'm ahead. There's a basket of bath stuff riding on it."

"I've got a better prize for you."

Tess looked over, cleared her fuzzy eyes enough to recognize Nate's rig as it pulled up. "Don't wanna talk to him now. Arrogant cowboy lawyer. Just tell him I'm . . . Oh, Jesus bleeding Christ."

"Don't you blaspheme at a wedding shower," Bess ordered, then popped up with a mile-wide grin as the side door of the rig opened and a vision burst out. "Louella Mercy, as I live and breathe, you're a sight for sore eyes."

"I'm a sight, period." With a braying laugh, Louella raced forward on red stiletto heels and embraced her staggered daughter. "Surprise, baby." She kissed Tess, smudged away the smear of lipstick from her cheek, then whirled to catch Bess in a bear hug. "Still kicking butt around here?"

"As best I can."

"And this must be Jack's youngest." She twirled to Willa, squeezed hard enough to crack her ribs. "Lord, you look just like your mama. Never saw anyone to match Mary Wolfchild for straight good looks."

"I—thanks." Dazzled, Willa only stared. Why, the woman looked like a glamour queen and smelled like a perfume counter. "I'm so glad you could come," she added, and meant it. "I'm so glad to meet you."

"That goes double for me, honey. Could've knocked me over with a feather when I got your letter inviting me out." Keeping an arm tight around Willa's shoulders, she turned and beamed at Adele. "I'm Louella, wife number one."

A little stunned, Adele stared. Was the woman actually wearing a gold lamé blouse in the middle of the afternoon? "I'm Lily's mother."

"Wife number two." With another earsplitting laugh, Louella embraced Adele like a sister. "Well, the bastard had good taste in women, didn't he? Where's your girl? Must take more after you than Jack, as Tess tells me she's pretty as a picture and sweet as they come. I've got presents."

"Should I take them in for you, Louella?" At the base of the steps, Nate stood grinning, Louella's wriggling pocket dogs in his arms.

Focusing on him fully for the first time, Tess all but writhed in horror. "Oh, God, Mom, you didn't bring Mimi and Maurice!"

"Of course I did. Couldn't leave my precious babies at home all alone." She took them from Nate and made kissy noises. "Is this a prime hunk, ladies?" She gave Nate a proprietary kiss on the cheek and left a clear imprint of her lips behind. "I swear my heart's been going pitty-pat ever since I laid eyes on him. You just take everything right on inside, sweetie."

"Yes, ma'am." He shot Tess a quick, amused look before he turned back to unload the rig.

"So what are we all doing out here?" Louella demanded. "I hear there's a party going on, and I could sure use a drink. You don't mind if I take a look around the place, do you, Willa?"

"Not at all. I'd love to show you around myself. Nate, Louella's things go in the room next to Tess's. The pink room."

"Wait until Mary Sue sees you," Bess began as she led Louella inside. "You remember Mary Sue Rafferty, don't you?"

"Is she the one with the buck teeth or the one with the lazy eye?"

Carefully, Tess set her empty cup on the porch rail. "Your idea?"

"Mine and Lily's." Willa beamed. "We wanted to surprise you."

"You did. You definitely did. And we'll have a nice talk about it later." Tess grabbed Willa by the shirtfront. "A nice, long talk about it."

"Okay. I'm going to make sure she gets that drink."

"Your ma sure packs for the duration." Nate hauled the last of five suitcases out of the back of the rig. Each one of them weighed like a yard of wet concrete.

"She packs nearly that for a weekend in Vegas."

"She sure makes a statement."

Mortification aside, Tess squared her shoulders and prepared to defend her mother. "Meaning?"

"Meaning she's right there, no pretenses. It's all Louella. After five minutes, I was crazy about her." Curious, he angled his head. "What did you think I meant?"

She moved her tense shoulders but couldn't quite relax them. "People have varying reactions when it comes to my mother."

He nodded slowly. "Apparently you do. You ought to be ashamed of yourself." And while she was gaping, he carried two of the suitcases past her.

With a snarl, Tess hauled one up herself and followed him. "Just what was that supposed to mean?" She huffed her way up the stairs. Louella didn't believe in packing light.

"I mean you've got one in a million there." He set the cases on the bed, turned, and walked out.

Tess dumped the third case on the bed, flexed her arms, and waited. "I know what I've got," she said the minute he walked back in with the rest of the luggage. "She's my mother. Who else would come to a wedding shower in Montana wearing Capri pants and gold lamé? Oh, wipe that lipstick off your cheek. You look like an idiot."

She struggled with the straps of a suitcase, flipped the top back, and rolled her eyes at the contents. "Who else would pack twenty pairs of high heels to spend a couple weeks on a cattle ranch? And this." She pulled out a sheer lavender robe trimmed in purple feathers. "Who wears things like this?"

He eyed the robe as he tucked his bandanna back in his pocket. "Suits her. You're too concerned with appearances, Tess. That's your biggest problem."

"With appearances? For God's sake, she paints her dogs' toenails. She has concrete swans in her front yard. She sleeps with men younger than I am."

"And I imagine they consider themselves lucky." He leaned against one of the bed's four posts. "Zack flew her to my spread and nearly wrecked his plane, he was laughing so hard. He told me she kept him howling since they took off from Billings. She asked me if she could come back and see my horses later. She wanted to see them, but she couldn't wait to get here and see you first. Thirty seconds after she hugged the life out of me, we were friends. She talked about you most all the way here, made me tell her half a dozen times that you were all right, safe. Happy. I guess it took her about ten miles to figure out I was in love with you. Then I had to stop so she could fix her makeup because it made her cry."

"I know she loves me." And she was ashamed. "I love her. It's just—"

"I'm not finished," Nate said coolly. "She told me she didn't hold anything against Jack Mercy because he'd given her something special. And having you changed her life. It made her a mother and turned her into a businesswoman. She was glad to be coming back, to take another look, to meet your sisters. To see you here and know you were getting what you had a right to."

He straightened, kept his eyes on hers. "So I'll tell you what my reaction is to Louella Mercy, Tess. Pure admiration—for a woman who took a kick in the face and stood right back up again. Who raised a daughter on her own, made a home for her, ran a business to see that her child never went without. Who gave that daughter backbone and pride and a heart. I don't care if she wears cellophane to church, and neither should you."

He walked out on her. Tess sat on the edge of the bed feeling a little drunk and very weepy. Carefully she laid the robe over the bed, then rose and began to unpack for her mother.

When Louella bounced in fifteen minutes later, the chore was nearly half done. "What in the world are you fooling with this for? We're having a party."

"You never finish unpacking. I thought I'd give you a head start."

"Don't fuss with it now." Louella grabbed her hands. "I'm working on getting Bess plowed. She'll sing when she's plowed."

"Really?" Tess set aside a sundress in eye-popping cerise. "I wouldn't want to miss that." Then she turned and laid her head on Louella's shoulder. A shoulder, she thought, that had always been there, without question, without qualification. "I'm glad to see you, Mom. I'm glad you came." Her voice hitched. "Really glad."

"What's all this?"

"I don't know." Tess sniffed and stood back. "Stuff. Things. I don't know."

"It's been a scary time for you." Louella took out a lace-trimmed hanky and dried her daughter's face.

"Yeah, in a lot of ways. I guess I'm shakier than I realized. I'll get through it."

"Of course you will. Now come on down and join the party." With her arm around Tess's waist, Louella started out. "Later, we'll pop open a bottle of French bubbly and catch up."

"I'd like that." Tess's arm slid around Louella's waist in turn. "I'd like that a lot."

"Then you can fill me in on that long, cool drink of water you've got your eye on."

"Nate doesn't like me very much right now." It was going to make her weepy again to think of it. "I'm not sure I like me very much either."

"Well, that can be fixed." Louella paused on the stairs, listened to the sounds of women. "I like both of you."

"I should have asked you to come," Tess murmured. "I should have asked you to visit months ago. It shouldn't have been Willa inviting you. Partly I didn't because I thought you'd be uncomfortable. And partly I didn't because I thought I would be. I'm sorry."

"Sweetie, you and me, we're as different as Budweiser and Moët. Doesn't mean they don't both have their points. God knows, I've scratched my head over you as often as you've scratched yours over me."

Louella gave Tess a quick squeeze. "Listen to that hen chatter. Reminds me of my chorus girl days. I've always had a fondness for women carrying on. Can't be uncomfortable with that, or with a wedding in the works. And I sure do like your sisters, honey."

"So do I." Tess firmed her chin. "Nothing's going to spoil the wedding for us."

. . .

He was thinking the same thing. He could hear the sound of women's laughter, of women's voices, pretty as music. It made him smile. He liked to think of Lily inside, in the center of it, soft and sweet. She'd be dead if not for him, and he'd been hugging his secret heroics to his heart for weeks.

He'd saved her life, and he wanted to see her married.

When those pretty images paled, he could always bring the picture of what he'd done to Jesse Cooke to the front of his mind. Sometimes he liked to fall asleep with that replaying through his head. A fine, colorful dream, scented with blood.

He'd been very careful since then, and when the lust for killing became overpowering, he cooled it in the hills and buried his prey. It was odd how much stronger that lust was now, more than the need for food, for sex. Soon, he knew, soon, it wouldn't be satisfied by rabbit or deer or a calf from pasture.

It would have to be human.

But he would hold it back, he would control it until after Lily was safely married. He was bound to her now, and where he was bound, he was loyal.

He feared she was worried that something would happen. But he had fixed that as well. He'd printed the note with great care, pondered the words like an exercise. Now that he had written it, now that he had slipped it under her kitchen door, he was lighter of heart.

She wouldn't worry now. She would know someone was looking out for her. Now he could relax and enjoy the sounds of the female ritual. Now he could dream of wedding bells that would herald the breaking of his fast for blood.

As the sky washed with red over the western peaks and the party broke up, some of the women who drove past waved. He lifted a hand in return. And he wondered whom he would choose to hunt when the time was right.

27

"I think you should see this."

Her brow arched, Willa took the sheet of notepaper from Lily's hand. She'd been ready to turn in after a long day of socializing when Lily had come to her room. It took only the first glance to wash the fatigue away.

I don't want you to worry. I won't let anything happen to you, or Adam, or your sisters. If I had known what J C was up to, I would have killed him sooner, before he scared you. You can rest easy now and have a nice wedding. I'll be there, looking out for you and yours. Best wishes, a friend.

"Christ." The chill sent a shudder through her. "How did you get this?"

"It was under the door in the kitchen."

"You showed it to Adam?"

"Yes, right away. I don't know how to feel about this, Will. The person who sent this killed Jesse. And the others." She took the paper back from Willa, folded it. "Yet he seems to be trying to reassure me. There's no threat here, and yet I feel threatened."

"Of course you do. He was practically in your house." She began to pace, her stockinged feet soundless. "Goddamn it. Goddamn it! We're back to the center again. This was put there today, dozens of people coming and going. It could have been anyone. No matter what I do I can't narrow it down."

"He doesn't mean to hurt me, or you, or Tess." Lily drew a calming breath. "Or Adam. I'm holding on to that. But, Will, he'll be at the wedding. He'll be there."

"You're to let me worry about this. I mean it," she continued, putting her hands firmly on Lily's shoulders. "Give me the note. I'll deal with it, see that it gets to the police. You're getting married in a few days. That's all you have to think about."

"I'm not going to tell my parents. I thought about it, talked it over with Adam, and decided not to tell anyone but you. Whoever you think should know is fine with me. But I don't want to upset my mother and father."

"This won't touch them." Willa took the note, set it on her dresser. "Lily, the wedding means almost as much to me as it does to you. I've got, I guess you could say, a double interest." She tried to smile, but it wouldn't quite gel. "Not everyone can say their brother and sister are getting married. At least not in Montana. Just concentrate on being a bride. It'd mean a lot to me."

"I'm not afraid. I don't seem to be afraid of much anymore." She pressed her cheek to Willa's. "I love you."

"Yeah. Same goes."

She closed the door behind Lily, then stared at the folded note. What the hell was she going to do now? The answer wasn't going to bed for a good night's sleep. Instead, she picked up her boots and walked to the phone.

"Ben? Yeah, yeah, we saved you some cake. Listen, I need a favor. You want to call that cop who's working this case and ask him to meet me at your place? I have something I need to show him, and I don't want to do it here. No." She cradled the phone between her ear and shoulder, tugged on a boot. "I'll explain when I get there. I'm on my way. I don't have time for that," she said when he started to argue. "I'll lock the doors of the rig and carry a loaded rifle on the seat, but I'm leaving now."

She hung up before he could shout at her.

"Damn, stubborn, pigheaded woman."

Willa had stopped counting the number of times Ben had called her that, or a similar name, over the past two hours. "It had to be dealt with, and it's done." She appreciated the wine he'd poured her, though it had been a surprise. She hadn't thought Ben went in for wine, or that he would be playing host after the session with the police.

"I'd have come for you."

"You damn near did," she reminded him. "You were nearly halfway to Mercy when I ran into you. I told you I'd be all right. You read the note yourself. It wasn't a threat."

"The fact that it was written at all is threat enough. Lily must be frantic."

"No, actually, she was very calm. More concerned that her parents not be upset by it. We're not telling them about it. I guess I'll have to tell Tess. She'll tell Nate, but that's as far as we'll take it."

She sipped again while he paced. She supposed his quarters suited a muscle-flexing type of man. The walls were paneled in honey-toned wood, the floors matching and uncluttered by carpet or rug. The furniture was big, heavy, and deeply cushioned in unadorned navy. There wasn't a single fussy pillow or feminine knickknack in sight.

There were, though, framed photos of his family crowding the pine mantel over the fireplace, a set of antique spurs, and a pretty hunk of turquoise on a shelf where books leaned against each other drunkenly.

There was a hoof pick tossed on a table along with a bone-handled pocketknife and some loose change.

Simple, basic. Ben, she decided, then decided further that she had let him pace and complain long enough.

"I appreciate you helping me handle this right away. We could get lucky and the cops could do cop things with the note and figure out who wrote it."

"Sure, if this was a Paramount production."

"Well, it's the best I can do for now." She set the half-full glass aside and rose. "I've got a wedding in less than a week and a houseful of company, so—"

"Where do you think you're going?"

"Home. Like I said, I've got a houseful of company, and morning comes early." She took out her keys; he snatched them out of her hand. "Look, McKinnon—"

"No, you look." He tossed her keys over his shoulder, and they rattled into a corner. "You're not going anywhere tonight. You're staying right here where I can keep an eye on you."

"I've got the midnight shift."

He merely picked up the phone, punched in numbers. "Tess? Yeah, it's Ben. Willa's here. She's staying. Call Adam and tell him to adjust guard duty accordingly. She'll be back in the morning." He hung up without waiting for an assent. "Done."

"You don't run Mercy, Ben, or me. I do." She took a step toward her keys and found the room revolving as she was slung over his shoulder. "What the hell's gotten into you?"

"I'm taking you to bed. I handle you better there."

She swore at him, kicked, and when that failed wiggled into position to take a bite out of his back. He hissed through his teeth, but kept going.

"Girls bite," he said when he dumped her on his bed. "I expected better from you."

"If you think I'm going to have sex with you when you treat me like a maverick calf, you're dead wrong."

His back throbbed where her teeth had dug in just enough to make him mean. "Let's see about that." He shoved her back, pinned her, and handcuffed her hands over her head. "Fight me." It was a pure dare delivered in steel tones. "We never tried that before. I might like it."

"You son of a bitch." She bucked, twisted, and when he lowered his mouth to hers, bit again. He rolled with her, careful to keep her hands—and nails—away from his exposed flesh.

Her aim with her knee was off just enough to make him grateful, close enough to make him sweat.

He used his free hand to rip her shirt, then the thin cotton beneath, but didn't touch her. It was the grapple, the excuse for violence he thought they both needed to scare away the fears.

And when she lay still beneath him, panting, her eyes closed, he thought he knew what they both needed next.

"Turn me loose, you coward."

"I'll tie you to the headboard if I have to, Willa, but you're staying. And when we're done, you'll sleep. Really sleep." He touched his lips to her temple, then her cheek, her jaw in a sudden shift to tender.

"Let me go."

He lifted his head. Her hair was tumbled over the dark green corduroy spread of his bed. There were flags of angry color riding high across her cheekbones. Her eyes burned so hot he was surprised his skin didn't blister.

"I can't." He lowered his forehead to hers, wondering if either of them would be able to accept it. "I just can't."

His mouth found hers again, quietly, slowly, deeply, until she felt something inside of her quake to the point of shivering apart. "Don't." She turned her face away, tried to struggle back to level. "Don't kiss me that way."

"It's rough on both of us." He turned her face back, saw her eyes were damp and dark now, the heat burned out of them. "It may get rougher yet." His mouth met hers again, lingered so that the shock swept through him. "God, I need you, Will. How the hell did this happen?"

He dragged her where he was bound to go, making her head reel and her heart break open to pour out secrets she'd kept even from herself. She sobbed out his name, then simply lost her grip on the slippery ledge she'd clung to for longer than she'd known.

When he lifted his head again, she stared into his face, one she'd known her whole life, and saw fresh and new. "Let go of my hands, Ben." She didn't struggle, didn't shout, but only said again, "Let go of my hands."

So he did, gentling his grip, then releasing it. When he started to lever himself away, those hands came to his face, framed it, and brought him back. "Kiss me again," she murmured. "The way I told you not to."

So he did, deepening the moment, then drowning in it.

He pushed aside her tattered shirt to find her, claim her, his hands sure and slow. She surrendered to it, the sensation of those hands gliding, scraping, stroking. Gave in to it, the taste of that mouth drawing and drinking from hers. Yielded against it, the heat of that body, the hard angles pressed into the curves of hers.

Whatever he wanted tonight, she would give. Whatever he seemed to need, she'd find. The quiet, unspoken desperation seeped from him into her, and the pleasure of knowing she possessed whatever it was he searched for.

The violence was spent. Now there were only sighs and murmurs, the whisper of flesh sliding over flesh, the quick moans of surprised delight.

The moon rose, unnoticed, and the night birds sang to the light. Wind, gentle with full spring, teased the curtains and wafted like water over their heated skin.

There was the long, long groan of that first lazy climax, one that shimmered through her as silver as the moonlight and left her glowing. He drew her up so they were torso to torso, so that he could lose his hands in her hair, sweep the weight of it back from her face. When her lips curved, so did his.

He held her like that, just held her, with their hearts pounding together, her head on his shoulder, his hands in her hair. And still holding her, he laid her back and slipped inside her.

Slow and deep, so that each thrust was like a velvet slap. He watched her come, watched it happen, the darkening eyes, the trembling lips, the sudden racking shudder. The silky movements quickened, driving them both toward the brink.

This time when she fell, he let her drag him with her.

It was a perfect day for a wedding, laced with warm breezes that teased the scent of pine down to the valley, stirred the perfume of the potted flowers Tess had ordered arranged in banks around the porches and terraces of the main house, Adam and Lily's house, even the outbuildings.

There wasn't a hint of rain, or the hail that had come so fiercely forty-eight hours before and sent Tess and Lily into a tailspin of worry. The willow tree by the pond that Jack Mercy had ordered built, stocked with Japanese carp, then forgotten, was delicately green.

There were tables with striped umbrellas, a snowy white canopy to shade the wedding feast, and a wooden platform that the men had cheerfully constructed to stand as a dance floor.

It was a perfect day, Willa mused, if she ignored the fact that cops would be sprinkled among the guests.

"Gosh, look at you." Misty-eyed, Willa reached up to adjust the tie of Adam's tux. "You look like a picture out of a magazine." Unable to keep her hands off him, she brushed at his shirtfront. "Big day, huh?"

"The biggest." He caught a tear off her lashes, pretended to put it in his pocket. "I'll save it. You hardly ever let them fall."

"The way they keep backing up on me, I have a feeling plenty are going to fall today." She took the tiny lily of the valley boutonniere—his own request—

and carefully pinned it on for him. "I know I'm supposed to let your best man do all this, but Ben's got those big hands."

"Yours are shaking."

"I know." She laughed a little. "You'd think I was getting married. This whole thing didn't make me nervous until this morning when I had to put this get-up on."

"You look beautiful." He took her hand, laid it on his cheek. "You've been in my heart, Willa, since before you were born. You'll always be there."

"Oh, God." Her eyes welled again. She gave him a hasty kiss, then whirled. "I've got to go." In her blind rush out the door, she barreled into Ben. "Move."

"Just hold on, let me look." Ignoring the teary eyes, he turned her in a circle, admiring the flow and fit of the slim blue gown. "Well, well, well. Pretty as a bluebell in a meadow." He brushed a tear from her cheek. "With dew still on it."

"Oh, save your fancy talk and go do what you're supposed to do with Adam. Make man noises and tell bad jokes or something."

"That's what I'm here for." He kissed her before she could wriggle free. "The first dance is mine. And the last," he added, as she dashed away.

It wasn't fair, Willa told herself as she hurried toward the main house. It wasn't fair that he had her stirred up this way. She had too much on her mind, too much to do. She damn well didn't want to be in love with Ben McKinnon.

Probably wasn't, she thought, and swiped a hand under her nose.

It was just so embarrassingly female, this reaction of hers. Imagining herself in love with him just because they went to bed together, because he said those fancy words now and again or looked at her in a certain way.

She'd have to get over it, that was all. Get herself back in gear before she made herself the biggest joke in the county. Or crowded her mind with it so she started doing something stupid like pining away, or dogging his heels, or picturing herself in a wedding dress.

She stopped outside the door, pressed a hand to her fluttering stomach. As composed as possible, she strode inside and was met by the sight of Adele weeping and leaning on Louella's arm as they came down the steps.

"What's wrong? Did something happen?" Willa was braced to rush to the gun rack when Louella smiled.

"Nothing's wrong. Adele's just having a mother-of-the-bride moment."

"She looked so beautiful, didn't she, Louella? Like an angel. My baby."

"The most beautiful bride I've ever seen. You and me, honey, we're going to open a bottle of that bubbly early and drink to her." She patted Adele as they walked. "Will, you go on up. Lily asked if you would when you came back."

"I should find Rob."

"Men just don't get moments like this, Addy." Louella steered her toward the kitchen. "We'll hunt him up after we've toasted the bride. A time or two. Get upstairs, Will. Lily's waiting for you."

"All right." But she had to shake her head a moment, baffled and amused by the bond that these two very different wives of Jack Mercy had forged.

She was still shaking it when she opened the door to Lily's temporary bedroom and was struck dumb.

"Isn't it great?" Tess bubbled over as she fussed with the veil. "Isn't she fabulous?"

"Oh, my—oh, Lily. You look like a fairy tale. Like a princess."

"I wanted the white gown." Dazzled by herself, Lily turned in front of the cheval glass. The woman who beamed back at her was beautiful, draped in billowing skirts of white satin, nipped into a bodice romantic with lace and tiny gleaming pearls. "I know it's my second marriage, but—"

"No, it's not." Tess brushed a hand down the long, snug sleeves of the bridal gown. "It's the only one that matters, so it's your first."

"My first." Lily smiled, touched her fingers to the veil that drifted over her shoulders. "I'm not even nervous. I was sure I would be, but I'm not."

"I've got something." Nervous enough for all of them, Willa brought out the small velvet box she'd held behind her back. "You don't have to use them. You've probably already got the old and new and all of that stuff taken care of. But when Tess told me there were pearls on your dress, I remembered these. They were my grandmother's. Our grandmother's," she corrected, and held the box out.

Lily could only sigh as she opened the lid. The pearls were fashioned into fragile teardrops with old-fashioned and lovely filigree settings. Without hesitation she removed the earrings she'd bought to match the dress and replaced them with the gift.

"They're so beautiful. They're so perfect."

"They look good." Made for the delicate, like Lily, she thought with a tangle of pride and envy. Not the sturdy like herself. "I figured she'd like you to have them. I didn't know her or anything, but . . . hell, I'm going to start leaking again."

"We all are, but I can fix that." Tess stuffed a tissue into Willa's hand. "I stole a bottle of champagne and hid it in the bathroom so Bess wouldn't know. I'd say we deserve a glass."

Willa chuckled as Tess hurried into the adjoining bath. "Takes after her ma."

"Thank you, Willa." Lily touched the drops at her ears. "Not just for these, for everything."

"Don't start on me, Lily. I'm running out of fingers to plug the dam. I've got a reputation around here, and it's not as a sniveler." She heard the pop of the cork echo off the bathroom tile with great relief. "The men figure out I'm a soft touch, there'll be no living with them."

"Here we go." Tess brought in three flutes and a bottle foaming at the lip. "What'll we drink to?" She poured generously, passed out glasses. "To true love and connubial bliss?"

"No, first . . ." Lily lifted her glass. "To the ladies of Mercy." She touched her glass to Willa's, Tess's. "We've come a long way in a short time."

"That I can drink to." Tess lifted a brow. "Will?"

"So can I." Willa bumped the rim of her flute against Tess's, grinned at the celebratory ring of crystal. Leave it to Hollywood to pick the best glasses.

Smiling, Lily touched the glass to her lips. "But I can only take a sip. Alcohol isn't good for the baby."

"Baby?" Tess and Will choked in unison.

Savoring the moment, Lily wet just the tip of her tongue with the champagne. "I'm pregnant."

Later, Willa would think she'd never seen anything more magical than Lily gliding across the dusty ranch road in her fairy-tale dress on the arm of the man who had become her father, toward the man who became her husband.

And as the vows were said and the promises made, she let herself forget there was anything in the air but beauty. And as the first kiss was exchanged between husband and wife and the cheers rose up, she cheered along.

She thought of the child, and the future.

"How far'd you travel this time?" Ben murmured in her ear.

Startled, she looked up and nearly stumbled over his feet. "What?"

"You keep going away."

"Oh. You know I have to concentrate when I'm dancing. I lose the count."

"Wouldn't if you'd let a man do the leading and just go along. Anyway, that's not it." He eased her closer. "You worried about him being here?"

"Of course I am. I keep looking at faces that I know, people I think I know, and wondering. If it wasn't for this damn will, Adam and Lily could go off for a couple weeks on a real honeymoon. I'd have two less to worry about."

"If it wasn't for the damn will they might not have gotten as far as postponing a honeymoon," he reminded her. "Put it aside, Will. Nothing's going to happen here today."

"I mostly have. They look so happy." She turned her head so that she could see the bride and groom again, circling in each other's arms. "Funny, a year ago they'd never met. And now they're married."

"And starting a family."

This time she did trip. "How do you know?"

"Adam told me." He grinned and, since he was tired of having his feet trounced on, led her over to the buffet table. "I think if he was any happier he'd have to split in two parts to hold it."

"I want them to stay that way." She resisted reaching down to pat the derringer she had strapped to her thigh. It was a pitiful, girlish weapon, but she felt better knowing it was there. "You'd better start spreading yourself out, Ben, dancing with some of the ladies here. People are going to talk otherwise."

He chuckled, lifted her chin. For someone as clear-eyed as Willa, she was dead blind when it came to herself. "Darling, people already are." He enjoyed the way she scowled at that, scanning the crowd as if she would catch someone whispering behind a hand. "Doesn't bother me any."

"I don't like people gossiping over their fences about me." She jerked her chin toward Tess and Nate. "What are they saying about that?"

"That Nate's caught himself a slippery one, and he'll have to be sure-handed to hold on. Now, there's a woman who can dance." He snagged two glasses from a passing waiter, gestured with one toward Louella.

She was poured into a hot-pink dress and kicking up her skyscraper heels with Ben's father. At least a dozen cowboys pounded their feet and waited their turn. "That's your father."

"Yep."

"Look at him go."

"He'll be sore for a week, but he'll be happy."

Laughing, Willa grabbed Ben's hand and hustled over for a better view. As they watched, a cowboy from a neighboring ranch cut in and spun Louella into a spirited two-step. Stu McKinnon took out his bandanna and mopped his flushed face.

"She'll outlast all of them," Tess predicted.

Nate winked at Ben and watched Stu hobble off for a beer. "She teach you how to dance like that?"

"I haven't had enough to drink yet to dance like that." Taking Willa's glass, Tess drank deep, handed back the empty. "Give me time."

"Oh, I'm a patient man. Best wedding I've been to in my life, Will. You and the ladies have done yourselves proud." Then he grunted when Louella slammed into him.

"Your turn, handsome."

"Louella, I couldn't keep up with you if I had four feet. You must keep everything hopping at that restaurant of yours."

"Restaurant, hell." She howled and grabbed his hands. "I run a strip joint, honey. Now, let me show you some moves."

"A strip joint?" Willa arched an eyebrow as Nate was dragged onto the dance floor.

"Oh, shit." Tess sighed long and hard. "Get me another drink, Ben. I need it."

"Coming up."

"A strip joint?" Willa repeated.

"So what? It's a living."

"What's it like? I mean, do they take everything off and dance around buck naked?" Her eyes popped wide, not in shock but fascination. "Does Louella—"

"No." Tess grabbed the glass from Ben, drank again. "At least, not since she bought her own place."

"I've never been to one." And wouldn't it be interesting, Willa mused. "Does she have men, too? Naked dancing men?"

"Oh, good God." Tess passed the drink to Willa. "Only on ladies' night. I'm going to rescue Nate before she puts him in traction."

"Ladies' night." The very idea was marvelous to Will. "I guess I'd pay to see a man dance naked." Speculating, she turned her head, shot Ben a look.

"No, not for any amount of money."

She thought she could come up with another kind of payment and, laughing, slid an arm around his waist and watched the show.

He watched too. And was happy. The bride was beautiful, glowing, just as a bride should be in her white gown and veil. The music was loud, and food and drink were plentiful.

It made him feel sentimental, heart strong and proud all at once.

The day had happened because of him, and he hugged that knowledge, and the giddy pleasure of it, to himself. There had been so much out of his control, all of his life, just beyond his reach. But he'd accomplished this.

Perhaps no one could ever know. He might have to keep the secret all of his life. Like a hero in a book—a kind of Robin Hood who took no personal credit.

They'd see about that.

Saving Lily had changed his direction, his purpose. But not his means.

It amused him that the police were wandering through the crowds of guests. Looking for him. Thinking they could spot him.

They never would.

He imagined himself going on for years, forever. Killing for pleasure. Strictly for pleasure now. Revenge, even harbored resentments, seemed very pale and weak beside pleasure.

Someone bumped into him. A pretty woman, flirting. He flirted back, making her laugh and blush, leading her into a dance.

And thinking, all the while wondering if she might be the next one.

Her pretty red hair would make a nice trophy.

28

He got a redheaded whore because she reminded him of the pretty redheaded girl he'd danced with at Lily's wedding. A whore wasn't much of a challenge, and he was disappointed in that.

But he'd waited so long.

He'd waited, considerately, until Lily's parents and Tess's mother had gone on home. It hadn't seemed right to him to cause all that excitement with company around.

Lily's folks had stayed on a week after the wedding, and Louella ten days. Everybody agreed they were going to miss Louella particularly with her big, wide laugh, her knee-slapping jokes.

And those tight skirts she liked to wear.

The woman was a caution, and he hoped she came back to visit real soon. He felt a tie to her now, to all of them. The in-laws and the outlaws, as his ma used to say. That had always made him laugh.

The in-laws and the outlaws.

But now the company had cleared out, and the ranch was back to routine. The weather was holding fine, and he was pleased by it. The crops were coming along well, though they could use some rain. But God knew, and so did he, that rain in Montana was usually feast or famine.

There'd been some thunder headed to the west a time or two, but June had stayed bone-dry thus far. The streams were running well, and the snowmelt was plentiful, so he wasn't worried.

The cattle were fattening in pasture, with the spring calves coming along just as they should. There'd been some elk nosing around, which was always a worry. Damn varmints tore up the fences and could carry disease into the herd, but Willa stayed on top of those matters.

He'd studied on her new ideas, the reseeding of natural grass, the gradual cutting back of chemicals and growth hormones and found that he approved. He'd decided that most anything she did that the old man hadn't, he approved of.

It had taken him some time, and some hard soul-searching, but he now believed it had been right and just that she'd been given the reins of Mercy. It still burned that McKinnon and Torrence had a say in things, at least for a few more months, but Willa handled them well enough, too.

He'd come to care for Lily and Tess, but blood was thicker than water, he'd always said. He now visualized both of them settled on Mercy, all the family rooted on the ranch.

Family stuck by family. He'd been taught that from the cradle, had done his best to live by it. It had only been grief and rage that had caused him to want to bring them pain, as he had pain. But now he'd put that solidly at the old man's door, where it belonged.

He'd left a sign there too, one that had made him weep and laugh all at once.

Now it was time for bigger game, so he hunted the redheaded whore.

He picked her up in Bozeman, a twenty-dollar street hooker he didn't figure would be missed. She was bone-thin and dumb as a post, but she had a mouth like a suction cup and knew how to use it. When they were in the cab of his rig and her face was buried in his lap she worked off the first twenty, and he ran his fingers through her long red hair.

It was probably dyed, but that didn't matter. It was a fine bright color, and it was clean. Dreaming of what was to come, he laid his head back, closed his eyes, and let her earn her keep.

"You're hung like a bull, cowboy," she said when it was done. "I shoulda charged you by the inch." It was her standard line after a blow job and usually earned a quick grin if not a modest tip. She wasn't disappointed when he flashed his teeth and bumped his hips up to reach for his wallet.

"I got another fifty here, sweetheart. Let's take a little ride."

She was cautious, a woman in her profession had to be. But her gaze latched greedily on the dead president he held between forefinger and thumb. "Where to?"

"I'm a country boy, towns crowd me. Let's find us a nice quiet spot and we'll set the springs in this old rig creaking." When she hesitated, he reached out, twirled her hair around his finger. "You sure are pretty. What'd you say your name was?"

Mostly johns didn't care about names, and she liked him better for asking. "It's Suzy."

"How about it, Suzy Q? Want to take a ride with me?"

. He seemed harmless, and she did have the loaded twenty-five-caliber pistol in her bag. She smiled, her thin face going sly. "You gotta wear a slicker, cowboy."

"Sure." He'd no more have dipped his wick into a street whore without protection than slit his own wrists. "Can't be too careful these days."

With a wink, he watched his fifty disappear into her shiny vinyl handbag. He started the engine and drove out of Bozeman.

It was a pretty night, and the road was clear, tempting him to push the gas pedal to the floor. But he drove moderately, humming along with Billy Ray Cyrus on the radio. And as the dark became country dark, he was a happy man.

"This is far enough for fifty." It made her nervous, the quiet, the lack of light and people.

Not far enough, he thought, and smiled at her. "I know a little place, just a couple miles up." Steering with one hand, he reached under the seat, amused at the way she shrank back and reached for her bag. He pulled out a bottle of the cheap wine he'd doctored. "Drink, Suzy?"

"Well . . . maybe." Her johns didn't usually offer her wine, or call her pretty, or use her name. "Just a couple more miles, cowboy," she said, and tipped back the bottle. "Then we'll ride."

"Me and my pal here are more than ready." He patted his crotch, turned up the radio. "Know this one?"

She drank again, giggled, and sang along with him and Clint Black.

She was a little thing, barely a hundred pounds. It took less than ten minutes for the drug to work. He nipped the bottle neatly from her limp fingers before it could spill. Whistling now, he pulled to the side of the road.

She was slumped in the corner, but he lifted an eyelid to be certain, then nodded. Climbing out, he dumped the rest of the drugged wine out, then heaved the bottle, sending it in a long, flying arc into the dark.

He heard it shatter as he walked to the bed of the rig and got out the rope.

"You don't have to do this, Will." Adam studied his sister as they walked their horses through a narrow stream.

"I want to. For you." She paused, let Moon drink. "For her. I know I haven't come to her grave very often. I let other things get in the way."

"You don't have to go to our mother's grave to remember her."

"That's the problem, isn't it? I can't remember her. Except through you."

She tipped back her head. It was a gorgeous afternoon and she was pleasantly tired, her shoulders just a little achy from unrolling wire and hammering fence.

"I didn't come, very often, because it always seemed morbid. Standing there, looking down at a piece of earth and a carved stone, having no memories of her to pull out and hold on to." She watched a bird flit by, chasing the breeze. "I've started thinking of it differently. It was seeing Lily with her mother, and Tess with hers. It's thinking of the baby Lily's carrying. The continuity."

She turned to him, and her face was relaxed. "It was always the land that was continuity to me, the seasons, the work that had to be done in each one of them. When I thought of yesterday or of tomorrow, it was always the ranch."

"It's your heart, Willa, your home. It's you."

"Yeah, that'll always be true. But I'm thinking of the people now. I never really did before—except for you." She reached out, closed a hand over his. "You were always there. My memories are of you. Picking me up, me riding your hip, your voice talking to me and telling me stories."

"You were, and always will be, a joy to me."

"You're going to be such an amazing father." She gave his hand a last squeeze, began to walk Moon again. "I've been thinking. It's not just the land that continues, not just the land we owe. I owe her my life, and I owe her you, and I owe her the child I'll be aunt to."

He was silent a moment. "It's not just her you owe."

"No, it's not." Adam would understand, she thought. He always did. "I owe Jack Mercy, too. The anger's gone now, and so is the grief. I owe him my life, and the lives of my sisters, and so the child I'll be aunt to. I can be grateful for that. And maybe, in some way I owe him what I am. If he'd been different, so would I."

"And what about the tomorrows, Will? What about your tomorrows?"

She could only see the seasons, and the work that had to be done in each one of them. And the land, waiting endlessly. "I don't know."

"Why don't you tell Ben how you feel about him?"

She sighed and wished for once there could be some corner of her heart secret from Adam. "I haven't made up my mind how I feel."

"Your mind has nothing to do with it." His lips curved as he kicked his horse into a trot. "Neither does his."

And what the hell was that supposed to mean? she wondered. Her brow knit, she clicked to Moon and galloped after him. "Don't start that cryptic business with me. I'm only half Blackfoot, remember. If you have something to say—"

She broke off as he held up a hand. Without question she pulled up and followed his gaze toward the tilting stones of the cemetery. She smelled it too.

Death. But that was to be expected here; it was another of the reasons she so rarely came.

But then she knew, even before she saw, she knew. Because old death had a quiet and dusty murmur. And new death screamed.

They walked the horses slowly again, dismounted in silence with only the wind in the high grass and the haunting song of birds.

It was her father's grave that had been desecrated. What rose up in her was disgust, chased by superstition. To mock and insult the dead was a dangerous matter. She shuddered, found herself murmuring a chant in her mother's tongue to calm restless spirits.

Then to calm her own, she turned away and stared over the land that rolled and waved to forever.

Not a very subtle message, she thought, as the healing rage took over. The mutilated skunk had been spread over the grave, its blood staining the mound of new grass. The head had been removed, then placed carefully just under the headstone.

The stone itself had been smeared with blood, going brown now in the sun. And words had been printed over the deep carving:

DEAD BUT NOT FORGOTTEN

She jerked when Adam laid a hand on her shoulder. "Go back to the stream, Willa. I'll take care of this."

Her weak legs urged her to do as he asked, to crawl back onto her horse and ride. But the rage was still here, and beneath that, the debt she had come to acknowledge.

"No, he was my father, my blood. I'll do it." Turning, she fumbled with the clasps on her saddlebags. "I can do it, Adam. I need to do it."

She took out an old blanket, spent some of her temper ripping it. After digging for her gloves, she tugged them on. Her eyes were bright and hard. "Whatever he was, whatever he'd done, he didn't deserve this."

She took a piece of the blanket and, kneeling beside her father's grave, began the filthy task of removing the corpse from it. Her stomach revolted, but her hands stayed steady. Her gloves were stained with gore when she finished, so she stripped them off, tossed them into the heap. Tying the blanket securely, she set it aside.

"I'll bury it," Adam murmured.

She nodded, rose. Using her canteen, she soaked another piece of the blanket, then knelt again to wash the stone.

She couldn't get it clean, no matter how she scrubbed. She would have to come back with something more than water and a makeshift rag. But she did her best and sat back on her heels, her hands raw and cold.

"I thought I loved you," she murmured. "Then I thought I hated you. But nothing I ever felt for you was as deep or as deadly as this." She closed her eyes and tried to clear her lungs of the stench. "It's been you all along, I think. Not me, but you it's been aimed at. Dear God, what did you do, and who did you do it to?"

"Here." Adam reached down to lift her to her feet. "Drink a little," he said, and offered her his canteen.

She drank, gulping deep to wash the nasty taste from her throat. There were flowers blooming on her mother's grave, she realized. And blood staining her father's.

"Who hated him this much, Adam? And why? Who did he hurt more than me, and you? More than Lily and Tess? Who did he hurt more than the children he ignored?"

"I don't know." He worried only about Willa now, and gently led her back to her horse. "You've done all you can do here. We'll go home."

"Yes." Her legs felt brittle, like ice ready to crack. "We'll go home."

They rode west, toward Mercy and a sky stained red as the grave.

The Fourth of July meant more than fireworks. It meant roping and riding, bronco busting and bull riding. For more than a decade, Mercy and Three Rocks had held a competition for cowboys on their ranches and any of the neighboring spreads who didn't choose to go farther afield for holiday entertainment.

It was Mercy's turn to host. Willa had listened to Ben's request that they move the competition to Three Rocks that year, to Nate's advice that they cancel it altogether. She'd considered, then ignored.

She was Mercy, and Mercy continued.

So people crowded corral fences, cheering on their picks. Cowboys brushed off their butts as they were tossed out of the saddle, into the air, and onto the ground. In a near pasture, the barrel-racing competition entered its second phase. Near the pole barn, hooves thundered and ropes flew through the air.

A bandstand was set up, draped with bunting of red, white, and blue. Music was interrupted periodically as names and places were announced. Gallons of potato salad, truckloads of fried chicken, and barrels of beer and iced tea were consumed.

Hearts were broken, along with a few bones.

"I see we're up against each other in the target shooting," Ben commented, slipping an arm around Willa's waist.

"Prepare to lose."

"Side bet?"

She angled her head. "What do you have in mind?"

"Well." He tucked his tongue in his cheek, leaned down close so their hats bumped, and whispered something that made her eyes round.

"You're making that up," she decided. "No one could live through that."

"Not chicken, are you?"

She straightened her hat. "You want to risk it, McKinnon, I'll take you on. You're in this round of bronc busting, aren't you?"

"I'm on my way over."

"I'll go with you." She smiled sweetly. "I've got twenty on Jim."

"You bet against me?" He wobbled between insult and shock. "Hell, Willa."

"I've been watching Jim practice. Ham's been coaching him." She sauntered away. No point in telling him she'd bet fifty on Ben McKinnon. It would just go to his head.

"Hey, Will." A little blood drying on his chin, his arm around a blonde in girdled-on jeans, Billy beamed at her. "Jim's in the chute."

"That's what I'm here for." She propped a boot on the rail beside his. "How'd you do?"

"Aw, shit." He rolled a sore shoulder.

"That good, huh?" With a laugh she squeezed over to make room for Ben. "Well, you're young yet, kid. You'll still be breaking bronc when geezers like McKinnon here are riding their rocking chairs. You get Ham to work with you."

She looked up, saw her foreman was standing on the outside wall of the chute, snapping last-minute instructions to Jim.

"I was thinking maybe you could. You ride better'n anybody on Mercy except for Adam. And he won't bust broncs."

"Adam's got a different way of taming them. We'll see," she added, then let out a whoop as the chute opened and horse and rider shot out. "Ride that devil, Jim!"

He careened by in a cloud of dust, one hand thrown high.

When the eight-second bell clanged, he jumped clear, rolled, then gained his feet to the wild cheers of the onlookers.

"Not bad," Ben said. "I'm coming up." With manhood and pride at stake, he cupped his hands under Willa's elbows, lifted her up, and kissed her. "For luck," he said, then swaggered off.

"Think he'll take our Jim, Will?" Billy wanted to know.

She thought Ben McKinnon could take damn near anything. "He'll have to ride like a hellhound."

Though the blonde shifted under his arm in a bid for attention, Billy tugged Willa's sleeve. "You're up against him in the target shooting, aren't you?"

"That's right."

"You'll take him, Will. We all put money on you. All the boys."

"Well, I wouldn't want you to lose it." She watched Ben climb over the chute. He tipped his hat to her, a cocky move that made her grin back at him.

When his horse leaped out of the door, her heart did a foolish little roll in her chest. He looked . . . magnificent, she decided. Riding straight on that furious horse, one hand grabbing for the sky, the other locked to the saddle. She caught a glimpse of his eyes, the dead-focused concentration in them.

They look like that when he's inside me, she realized, and her heart did another roll, quicker. She didn't even hear the bell clang, but watched him jump down, the horse still kicking furiously. He stayed on his feet, boots planted. And though the crowd cheered, he looked straight at her. And winked.

"Cocky bastard," she muttered. And I'm hip-deep in love with him.

"Why do they do that?" Tess asked from behind her.

"For the hell of it." Grateful for the excuse to think of something else, Willa turned. Tess had turned herself out for the day. Tight jeans, fancy boots, a bright blue shirt with silver trim that matched the band on her snowy-white hat. "Well, ain't you a picture. Hey, Nate. Ready for the race?"

"It's a tight field this year, but I'm hopeful."

"Nate's helping out with the pie-eating contest." Tess chuckled and tucked an arm through his. "We were hunting up Lily. She wanted to watch, since she helped make the pies."

"I saw her . . ." Willa narrowed her eyes and searched the crowds. "I think she and Adam were helping out with the kids' games. Egg toss, maybe, or the three-legged races."

"We'll find her. Want to tag along?"

"No, thanks." Willa shrugged off Tess's invitation. "I may catch up later. I need a beer."

"You're worried about her," Nate murmured as they zigzagged through the crowd.

"I can't help it. You didn't see her the day she came back from the cemetery. She wouldn't talk about it. Usually I can goad her into talking about anything, but not this."

"It's been over two months since Jesse Cooke was murdered. That's something to hang on to."

"I'm trying." Tess shook herself. There was music, people, laughter. "It's a hell of a party. You do throw amazing parties out here."

"We can start throwing our own anytime you say."

"Nate, we've been there. I'm going back to LA in October. There's Lily." Desperate for the distraction, Tess waved wildly. "I swear, she glows all the time now. Pregnancy certainly agrees with her."

Nate thought it might agree with Tess as well. That was something else they could start—once he'd finished pecking away at this stubborn idea of leaving.

The first fireworks exploded at twenty minutes past dusk. Color leaped over the sky, shadowed the stars, then bled down like tears. Willa let herself be cuddled back against Ben to watch the show.

"I think your daddy likes sending those bombs off more than the kids like to watch."

"He and Ham argue over the presentation and order every blessed year." Ben grinned as a gold starburst bloomed overhead with a crackling boom. "Then they cackle like hens, taking turns lighting fuses. Never would let Zack or me have a hand in it."

"It's not your time," she murmured. That, too, would come. That, too, was continuity. "It was a good day."

"Yeah." He covered her hands with his. "Real good."

"Not miffed 'cause I beat you shooting?"

It still stung, a little, but he shrugged his shoulders. The two of them had whittled away the rest of the competitors until they'd gone head to head in the final round. Then head to head in two tie-breaking rounds. And there she'd squeaked past him.

"By a lousy half an inch, tops."

"Doesn't matter by how much." She looked over, up at him, and grinned. "Matters who won. You're a good shot." She wiggled her brows. "I'm better."

"Today you were better. Anyway, I cost you twenty when I beat out Jim. Serves you right."

Laughing, she turned in his arms. "I made back the fifty I put on you." When his brow lowered, she laughed again. "Do I look like a fool?"

"No." He tipped her face up. "You look like a smart woman who knows how to hedge her bets."

"Speaking of bets." Despite the crowd that gasped and cheered at every burst of light, she wrapped herself around him, pressed her mouth warm and firm to his. "Let's go inside and see if we live till morning."

"You going to let me stay till morning?"

"Why not? It's a holiday."

Later, when the fireworks were done, the crowds gone, and the night quiet, they turned to each other again. Her dreams hadn't been full of blood and death and fear this time. Finding him there, warm, solid, ready to hold her, she knew there'd be no shaking dreams that night.

Someone else dreamed of a redheaded whore and shivered, thrilled with the memory. It had been so easy, so smooth, and every detail played back so clearly.

He'd watched her come back to consciousness, the glassy eyes, the muffled whimper. He'd driven her far from Bozeman, into the sheltering dark of trees.

Not on Mercy land. Not this time, and never again. He was done with punishing Mercy. But he couldn't be done with killing.

He'd tied her hands behind her back, and he'd gagged her. He wouldn't have minded hearing her scream, but he didn't want her to be able to use her teeth on him. He'd cut her clothes away but had been careful, very careful, not to cut her flesh.

He was very, very good with a knife.

While she'd slept, he had taken his money back, and the rest of hers, which had been pathetically little. He'd bided his time, toying with her little pistol, her tube of red lipstick.

Now that she was awake, now that her eyes were wide and she was struggling in the dirt, making noises like a trapped animal, he took the tube back out of her cheap purse.

"A whore should be painted up proper," he told her, and aroused himself by stroking the lipstick over her nipples until they were bright, blood red. "I like that. Yes, indeed." Since her cheeks were pale, he colored them as well, in round circles like a doll's happy blush.

"Were you going to shoot me with this toy of yours, sweetheart?" He pointed the pistol playfully at her heart and watched her eyes roll white. "Guess a woman in your line a work's gotta protect herself in more ways than one. Told you I'd wear a rubber."

He set the pistol aside, then tore open the foil package. "Love to have you suck me off again, Suzy Q. I do believe that was the finest blow job I ever paid for. But you might bite this time." He pinched her red nipples painfully. "We can't have that, can we?"

He was already hard, throbbing hard, but made himself slide the condom on slowly. "I'm going to fuck you now. You can't rape a whore, but since I ain't going to pay for it, I guess technically we could call it that. So we'll say I'm going to rape you now." He levered himself over her, smiling as she tried to draw her legs up to protect herself. "Now, honey, don't be shy. You're going to like it."

In two rough jerks, he pulled her legs straight, spread them, locked them. "You're damn well going to like it. And you're going to tell me how much you love it. You can't say much with that rag stuffed in your whore-sucking mouth, but you're going to moan and groan for me. I want you to groan now. Like you can't wait for it. Now."

When she didn't respond, he released one of her legs and slapped her. Not hard, he thought, just enough to let her know who was boss. "Now," he repeated.

She managed a sob, and he settled for it. "You make noise for me, plenty of noise. I like plenty of noise with my sex."

He rammed himself into her. She was dry as dust and as unwelcoming as a tomb, but he pumped furiously, working up a sheen of sweat that gleamed on his back under the scatter of stars. Her eyes rolled in pain and fear, the way a horse's did when you dug in spurs and drew blood.

When he was finished, he rolled off her, panting. "That was good. That was good. Yeah, I'm going to do that again in just a minute or two."

She was curled into a ball and, weeping, tried to crawl. Lazily, he picked up the gun, fired a shot at the sky. It stopped her cold. "You just rest there, Suzy Q. I'm going to see if I can work up the gumption for another round."

He sodomized her this time, but it wasn't as good. It took him too long to get hard, and the orgasm was small and unsatisfying. "Guess that's it for me." He gave her a friendly slap on the rump. "And for you."

He thought it was a shame he couldn't keep her a couple days like he had little Traci with an *I*. But that kind of game was too risky now.

And there would always be another whore.

He opened his pack, and there it was, waiting. Lovingly he slipped the knife from its oiled-leather sheath, admired the way the starlight caught the metal and glimmered.

"My daddy gave me this. Only thing he ever gave me. Pretty, ain't it?" After shoving her onto her back, he held it in front of her face so that she could see it. He wanted her to see it.

And smiling, he straddled her.

And smiling, he went to work on her.

Now there was a trophy of red hair in his box of secrets. He doubted anyone would find her where he'd left her. Or if they did, if they would be able to identify what was left of her once the predators had done with what he'd left behind for them.

He didn't need the fear and the fame any longer. It was enough that he knew.

29

Summers in Montana were short and fierce, and August could be cruel. Sun baked the dirt and dried the trees to kindling and made men pray for rain.

A match flicked the wrong way or a well-aimed bolt of lightning would turn pasture into fire, crops into tears.

Willa sweated through her shirt as she surveyed a field of barley. "Hottest summer I remember."

Wood merely grunted. He spent most of his time scowling at the sky or worrying over his grain. His boys should have been there worrying with him, but he'd gotten tired of their spatting and sent them off to bother their mother.

"Irrigation's helping some." He spat, as if that drop of moisture would make a difference. Mercy was both joy and worry to him, and had been for too many years to count. "Water table's dead low. Couple more weeks of this, we'll be in trouble."

"Don't sugarcoat it for me," she said wearily, and remounted. "We'll get through it."

He grunted again, shook his head at her as she rode off.

The ground bounced heat back at her relentlessly. The cattle she passed stood slack-legged, with barely enough energy to swish tails. Not even the stingiest breeze stirred the grass.

She saw a rig well out along a fence line, and the two men unrolling wire. Changing directions, she galloped out.

"Ham, Billy." She dismounted, walked over to the two-gallon jug in the bed of the rig, and poured herself a cup of icy water.

"Ham says this ain't hot, Will." Sweating cheerfully, Billy strung wire. "He says he recollects when it was so hot it fried eggs still in their shells."

She smiled at that. "I expect he does. You get as old as Ham here, you've seen everything twice." She took off her hat, wiped an arm over her brow. She didn't like Ham's color. The red flush that stained his face looked hot enough to explode. But she knew to tread carefully.

Pouring two cups, she walked over, held them out. "Hot work. Take a break."

"Be done soon," Ham said, but his breath was puffing.

"You got to keep the fluid in. You told me that often enough that I have to take it as truth." She all but shoved the cup into his hand. "You boys take your salt tablets?"

"Sure we did." Billy gulped the water down, his Adam's apple bobbing.

"Ham, I'm going to finish here with Billy. You take Moon back for me."

"What the hell for?" His eyes were running from squinting into the sun. Under his soaked shirt, his heart pounded like a hammer on an anvil. But he finished any job he started. "I said we're about done here."

"That's fine, then. I need you to take Moon back and get me those stock reports. I'm falling behind, and I want to catch up on them tonight."

"You know where the damn reports are."

"And I need them." Casually, she took her gloves out of her saddlebags. "And see if you can sweet-talk Bess into making some peach ice cream. She'll do it for you, and I've got a yen for some."

He wasn't a fool, knew just what she was doing. "I'm stringing wire here, girl."

"No." She hefted the roll as Billy watched, wide-eyed and fascinated. "I'm stringing wire here. You're going to take Moon back in, get those stock reports in my office, and see about peach ice cream."

He tossed his cup on the ground, planted his feet. "The hell with that. Take her back yourself."

She set the roll down. "I run Mercy, Ham, and I'm telling you what I want you to do. You got a problem with that, we'll take it up later. But now, you ride back and do what I'm telling you."

His face was redder now, making her pulse skittish, but she kept her eyes cool and level with his. After ten humming seconds, with the heat crippling both of them, he turned stiffly away and mounted.

"You think I can't do the job this half-assed boy can do, then you get my paycheck ready." He kicked the horse, sent Moon into a surprised rear, then galloped off.

"Jeez" was all Billy could think of.

"Damn it, I should have handled that better." She rubbed her hands over her face.

"He'll be all right, Will. He doesn't mean it. Ham'd never leave you or Mercy."

"That's not what I'm worried about." She blew out a breath. "Let's get this damn wire strung."

She waited until nightfall, canceled a date with Ben, and sat out on the front porch. She heard the thunder, watched lightning flash, but the sky was too clear for rain.

Despite the heat she had no taste for the ice cream Bess had churned. Even when Tess came out with a bowl heaped full of it, Willa shook her head.

"You've been sulking since you came in today." Tess leaned against the porch rail and tried to imagine cool ocean breezes. "Want to talk about it?"

"No. It's a personal problem."

"They're the most interesting." Philosophically, Tess spooned up some ice cream and sampled it. "Ben?"

"No." Willa gave an irritated shrug. "Why is it people think every personal thought in my head revolves around Ben McKinnon?"

"Because women usually do their best sulking over a man. You didn't have a fight with him?"

"I'm always fighting with him."

"I mean a real fight."

"No."

"Then why did you cancel your date?"

"Jesus Christ, can't I choose to stay home on my own porch one night without answering a bunch of questions?"

"Guess not." Tess dug out another spoonful. "This is great stuff." Licked the spoon clean. "Come on, try it."

"If it'll get you off my back." With little grace, Willa grabbed the bowl and scooped some up. It was sheer heaven. "Bess makes the best peach ice cream in the civilized world."

"I tend to agree with you. Want to eat ice cream, get drunk, and take a swim? Sounds like a great way to cool off."

Willa's eyes slitted with suspicion. "Why are you so friendly?"

"You look really bummed. I guess I'm feeling sorry for you."

It should have annoyed her. Instead it touched her. "I had words with Ham today. He was out stringing wire and I got spooked. He looked so old all of a sudden, and it was so blasted hot. I thought he'd have a stroke or something. A heart attack. I made him come back in, and that slapped his pride flat. I just can't lose anybody else," she said quietly. "Not right now. Not yet."

"His pride will bounce back. Maybe you dented it a little, but he's too devoted to you to stay mad for long."

"I'm counting on it." Soothed, she handed the bowl back to Tess. "Maybe I'll come in shortly and take that swim."

"All right." Tess opened the screen, shot back a grin. "But I'm not wearing a suit."

Chuckling, Willa eased back in the rocker, let it creak. Thunder rumbled, a little closer now. And she heard the crunch of boots on stone. She sat up, one hand going under the chair where her rifle rested. She brought it back up, laid it in her lap when Ham stepped into the light.

"Evening," she said.

"Evening. You got my check?"

Stubborn old goat, she thought, and gestured to the chair beside her. "Would you sit down a minute?"

"I got packing to do."

"Please."

Bandy legs stiff as a week-old wishbone, he climbed the steps, lowered himself into the next rocker. "You took me down in front of that boy today."

"I'm sorry." She folded her hands in her lap, stared down at him. It was the sound of his voice, raw with hurt and wounded pride, that scraped at her. "I tried to make it simple."

"Make what simple? You think I need some girl I used to paddle coming out and telling me I'm too old to do my job?"

"I never said—"

"Hell you didn't. Plain as day to me."

"Why do you have to be so stubborn?" She kicked at the porch rail out of sheer frustration. "Why do you have to be so hardheaded?"

"Me? Never in my life did I see a more rock-headed female than the one I'm sitting beside right now. You think you know it all, girl? You think you got all the answers? That every blessed thing you do is right?"

"No!" She exploded with it, leaped up. "No, I don't. I don't know half the time if it's right, but I have to do it anyway. And I did what I had to do today, and it *was* right. Goddamn you, Ham, you were going to have heatstroke in another ten minutes, and then where the hell would I be? How the hell could I run this place without you?"

"You're already doing just that. You took me off the job today."

"I took you off the fences. I don't want you riding fence in this heat. I'm telling you I'm not having it."

"You're not having it." He rose too, went nose to nose with her. "Who the hell do you think you are, telling me you're not having it? I've been riding fence in every kind of weather since before you were born. And you nor nobody's telling me I can't do it until I say I'm done."

"I'm telling you."

"Then cut me my last check."

"Fine." She swung to the door, pushed by temper. Her hand fisted on the edge, then whipped it back in a slam that shook the wood under her feet. "I was scared! Why can't I be allowed to be scared?"

"What in hell are you scared of?"

"Losing you, you mule-headed son of a bitch. You were all red-faced and sweaty and your breath was puffing like a bad engine. I couldn't stand it. I just couldn't. And if you'd just gone in like I asked you, it would've been fine."

"It was hot," he said, but his voice was weak now, and a little ashamed.

"I know it was hot. Goddamn it, Ham, that's the point. Why'd you make me push you that way? I didn't want to embarrass you in front of Billy. I just wanted you to get out of the sun. I know who my father was," she said furiously, and made his head come up, his eyes meet hers again. "And I haven't buried him yet. Not the one who really counted when I needed him to count. I don't want to bury him for a long time."

"I could've finished." He bumped his toe on the rail, stared at it. "Hell, Will, I was making the boy do most of the work. I know my limits."

"I need you here." She waited for her system to calm again. "I need you, Ham. I'm asking you to stay."

He moved his shoulders, kept his eyes on his feet. "I guess I got no place better to be. I shouldn'ta bucked you. I guess I knew you were thinking of me." He shifted his feet, cleared his throat. "You're doing a fine job around here, all in all. I'm, ah . . . I'm proud of you."

And that's why he was the one who counted, she thought. The father of her blood had never said those words to her. "I can't do it alone. You want to come in?" She opened the door again. "Have some of that peach ice cream. You can tell me all the things I'm doing wrong."

He scratched his beard. "Maybe. I guess there's a few things I could straighten you out on."

When he left, his belly was full and his heart considerably lighter. He strolled toward the bunkhouse, light of step. He heard the sounds, the disturbed braying of cattle, the click of boot heels.

Who the hell was on guard duty? He couldn't quite place it. Jim or Billy, he thought, and decided to wander over to check things out.

"That you, Jim? Billy? What are you playing with the penned head for this time of night?"

He saw the calf first, bleeding, eyes rolling in fear and pain. He'd taken two running steps before he saw the man rise up out of the shadows.

"What the devil's this? What the hell have you done?"

And he knew, before he saw the knife arch up, but there was no time to scream.

The panic came first. With the knife dripping in his hand, he stared down at Ham, the blood. Wiped a hand over his mouth. He'd just needed a quick fix, that was all. One calf. He'd meant to drag it away from the ranch yard, but the knife had just leaped into his hand.

And now Ham. He'd never meant to hurt Ham. Ham had trained him, worked with him, paid attention when attention needed to be paid. He'd always felt Ham had known the truth about where he'd come from and who he was.

And Ham was loyal.

But now there was no choice. It had to be finished. He crouched down, prepared, just as Willa rushed out of the night.

"Ham? Is that you? I forgot to tell you about the—" Her boots skidded. Lightning flashed, bursting light onto the men all but at her feet. "Oh, sweet God, what happened to him? What happened?" She was already on her knees, turning him over into her arms. "Did he—" And there was blood on her hands.

"I'm sorry, Will. I'm sorry." He turned the knife on her, held it to her throat. "Don't call out. I don't want to hurt you. I swear I don't want to hurt you." He took a deep, shuddering breath. "I'm your brother."

And bringing his fist up, he knocked her cold.

Ham woke to pain. Fiery, blinding pain. He couldn't pinpoint it, couldn't find the source, but he tasted blood in his mouth. Groaning, he tried to sit up, but couldn't move his legs. He turned his head, saw that the calf had bled out. Its eyes were dead.

Soon, he thought, he'd bleed out too.

There was something else on the ground that caught his eye. He stared at it a long time, watched it come and go as his vision cleared and blurred. Then hissing, he crawled toward it, brushed the tip with his fingers.

Willa's hat.

He had to carry her. He should have gone for a rig, knew he should have, but he'd been so shaken he hadn't been able to think clearly. Now he laid her as gently as he could on the ground near the pasture and with a trembling hand rattled a bucket of oats.

They'd go on horseback. It was probably best. He wanted to get her away, into the hills a ways so that he could explain everything to her. She'd understand once he had.

Blood was thicker than water.

He saddled the paint pony that nosed into the bucket, then the roan that tried to nuzzle through.

Oh, he hated to do it, even temporarily, but he tied Willa's hands, tied her feet, then strapped her across the saddle. She'd come to shortly, he thought, and she'd try to get away before he could explain.

She had to understand. He prayed she'd understand as he vaulted into the saddle, took both pairs of reins. If she didn't, he'd have to kill her.

Thunder stalked closer as he rode into the hills.

Ham clutched the hat in his hand, staggered to his feet. He managed two drunken steps before he went to his knees. He called out, and though his voice boomed in his ears, it was barely a whisper.

He thought of Willa, hardly more than a baby with a milky mouth, grinning at him as he plopped her into the saddle in front of him. A little girl, all braids and eyes, begging him to let her ride out to pasture with him. An adolescent, gawky as a colt, running wire with him and chattering his ears off.

And the woman who had looked at him tonight, her heart in her eyes when she'd told him he was the one who counted.

So he bit back the pain that was eating through him like cancer and fought his way to his feet again.

He could see the main house, the lights in the windows circling in front of his eyes. Blood dripped through his fingers and onto her hat. He didn't feel the ground when it jumped up to meet him.

She came to slowly, her jaw throbbing. Her eyes focused on the ground bumping and falling beneath her. She tried to shift, found herself snugly secured, lying across the saddle with her head dangling. She must have moaned, or made some sound, for the horses stopped quickly.

"It's okay, Will. You're okay." He loosed the straps, the restraints on her legs, but kept her hands secured. "Need to ride a little further. Can you handle it?"

"What?" Still groggy, she felt herself lifted, then she was sitting in the saddle, shaking her head to clear it while her hands were strapped tight to the horn.

"You just catch your breath. I'll lead your horse."

"What are you doing?" It leaped back into her mind but refused to root there. "Ham?"

"Couldn't help it. Just couldn't help it. We'll talk this through. You just—" He broke off, dragging her down by the hair when she sucked in her breath. "Don't you scream. Nobody's going to hear you, but I don't want you screaming." Mumbling to himself, he tugged out his bandanna, tied it quickly over her mouth. "I'm sorry I have to do it this way, but you just don't understand yet."

Trying not to be angry with her, he strode back to his horse, swung on, and rode into the trees.

Well, Willa had missed her swim, Tess thought as she tied the belt of a short terry robe. She ran her fingers through her hair to smooth it back and wandered out of the pool house toward the kitchen.

Probably still sulking, she decided. Willa took everything in and worried over it. It might be a good idea to try to teach her a few relaxation techniques—though Tess couldn't quite visualize Willa meditating or experimenting with imaging.

Rain would make her happy, Tess supposed. Lord, everyone around here lived their life by the weather. Too wet, too dry. Too cold, too hot. Well, in two months, she would say farewell, scenic Montana, and hello, LA.

Lunch alfresco, she mused. Cartier's. God knew, she deserved to treat herself to some ridiculously expensive bauble after this yearlong banishment from the real world.

The theater. Palm trees. Traffic-choked highways and the familiar haze of smog.

God bless Hollywood.

Then she pouted a little because it didn't sound quite as wonderful as it had a month before. Or a month before that.

No, she'd be glad to get back. Thrilled. She was just feeling broody, that was all. Maybe she'd buy a place up in the hills rather than on the beach, though. She could have a horse up there, and the trees, the grass. That would be the best of both worlds, after all. A brisk, exciting drive from the excitement and crowds of the city home to the pleasure she'd come to enjoy of the country.

Well, not exactly country, by Montana standards, but the Hollywood hills would do just fine.

She could probably persuade Nate to come out and visit. Off and on. Their relationship would fade after a while. She expected and, damn it, accepted that. So would he. This wild idea of his to have her settle down here, get married, and start breeding was ridiculous.

She had a life in LA. A career. She had plans, big, juicy plans. She would be thirty-one years old in a matter of weeks, and she wasn't tossing those plans aside at this stage of her life to be a ranch wife.

Any kind of a wife.

She wished she had brought down a cigarette, but she swung into the kitchen in search of other stimulation.

"You've had your share of ice cream."

Tess wrinkled her nose at Bess's back. "I didn't come in for ice cream." Though she would have enjoyed one or two spoonfuls. She went to the refrigerator, took out a pitcher of lemonade.

"You been skinny-dipping again?"

"Yep. You ought to try it."

Bess's mouth twitched at the idea. "You put that glass in the dishwasher when you're finished. This kitchen's clean."

"Fine." Tess plopped down at the table, eyed the catalogue Bess was thumbing through. "Shopping?"

"I'm thinking. Lily might like this here bassinet. The one we used for you girls wasn't kept after Willa. He got rid of it."

"Oh." It was an interesting thought, the idea of her and Lily and Willa sharing something as sweet as a baby bed. "Oh, it's adorable." Delighted, Tess scraped her chair closer. "Look at the ribbons in the skirt."

Bess slanted her eyes over. "I'm buying the bassinet."

"All right, all right. Oh, look, a cradle. She'd love a cradle, wouldn't she? One to sit by your chair and rock."

"I expect she would."

"Let's make a list."

Bess's eyes softened considerably and she pulled out a pad she'd stuck under the catalogue. "Got one started already."

They made cooing noises over mobiles and stuffed bears, argued briefly over the right kind of stroller. Tess rose to get them both more lemonade, then glanced at the kitchen door when she heard footsteps.

"I wasn't expecting anyone," she whispered, her nervous hand going to her throat.

"Me either." Calm as ice, Bess pulled her pistol out of her apron pocket and, standing, faced the door. "Who's out there?" When the face pressed against the screen, she laughed at herself. "God Almighty, Ham, you nearly took a bullet. You shouldn't be sneaking around this time of night."

He fell through the door, right at her feet.

The pistol clattered as it hit the table. Tess was on the floor with her before Bess could lift Ham's head in her lap. "He's bleeding bad here. Get some towels, press them down hard."

"Bess . . ."

"Quiet now. Let's see what's what here."

Tess ripped the shirt aside and pressed down hard on the wound. "Call for an ambulance, a helicopter. He needs help quickly."

"Wait." Ham grabbed for Bess's hand. "He's got . . ." He squeezed until he could find the breath to speak again. "He's got her, Bessie. He's got our Will."

"What?" Straining to hear, Tess pushed her face close. "Who has Will?"

But he was unconscious. When her eyes lifted, latched onto Bess's, they were ripe with fear. "Call the police. Hurry."

He was ready to stop now. He'd circled, backtracked, followed a stream down its center, then moved onto rock. He had no choice but to tether the horses, but he kept them close.

Willa watched his every move. She knew the hills, and he wouldn't find the hunt easy even if she had to go on foot once she got loose.

He hauled her down first, retied her ankles. After getting his rifle, he sat across from her, laid it across his lap. "I'm going to take the gag off now. I'm sorry I had to use it. You know it won't do any good to scream. They may come after us, but not for a while, and I covered the trail."

He reached over, put his hand on the cotton. "We're just going to talk. Once you hear me out, we'll get back to the way things were." He tugged the gag down.

"You murdering bastard."

"You don't mean that. You're upset."

"Upset?" Fury carried her, had her pulling furiously to try to break her bonds. "You killed Ham. You killed all the others. You slaughtered my cattle. I'll kill you with my own hands if I get the chance."

"Ham was an accident. I'm as fond of him as I can be, but he saw me." Like a boy caught with the shards of a cookie jar at his feet, he lowered his head. "The cattle was a mistake. I shouldn't have done that to you. I'm sorry."

"You're—" She shut her eyes, balled her helpless hands into fists. "Why? Why have you done these things? I thought I could trust you."

"You can. I swear you can. We're blood, Willa. You can trust your own blood."

"You're no blood of mine."

"Yes, I am." He knuckled a tear away, such was his joy in being able to tell her. "I'm your brother."

"You're a liar and a murderer and a coward."

His head snapped up, his hand flew out. The sting of flesh striking flesh sang up his arm, and he regretted it immediately. "Don't say things like that. I got my pride."

He rose, paced, worked himself back under control. Things didn't go well when you lost control, he knew. But stay in charge, stay on top, and you could handle anything that came along.

"I'm as much your brother as Lily and Tess are your sisters." He said it calmly as the sky split and fractured with swords of electric light. "I want to explain things to you. I want to make you see why I did what I did."

"Fine." The side of her face burned like hellfire. He'd pay for that too, she promised herself. He would pay for everything. "Okay, Jim, explain it to me."

Ben slammed his rifle into its sheath, snagged his gunbelt, strapped it on. The .30 carbine he shot into the holster was a brute of a revolver, and he wanted a mean gun. He wouldn't allow himself to feel, or he might sink shaking to his knees. He could only allow himself to move.

Men were saddling up fast, with Adam shouting orders. Ben wasn't giving any orders, not this time. Nor was he taking them. He took Willa's hat, gave it to Charlie to scent. "You find her," he murmured. "You find Willa." Stuffing the hat in his saddlebag, he swung into the saddle.

"Ben." Tess grabbed the bridle. "Wait for the others."

"I'm not waiting. Move aside, Tess."

"We can't be sure where—or who." Though there was only one man missing.

"I'll find the where. I don't have to know who." He jerked his horse's head out of her grip. "I just have to kill him."

Tess raced over to Adam, put both arms around Lily, and held tight. "Ben rode off. I couldn't stop him."

Adam merely nodded, gave the signal to ride. "He knows what he's doing. Don't worry." Turning, he embraced them both. "Go inside," he told Lily, and laid his hand on her gently rounded belly. "Wait. And don't worry."

"I won't worry." She kissed him. "You found me. You'll find her. Bring her back safe." It was a plea as much as a statement, but she stepped back to let him mount.

"Take Lily inside, Tess." Nate reined in, steadied his eager mount. "Stay inside."

"I will." She laid a hand on his leg, squeezed. "Hurry" was all she could say.

The horses drove west, and she and Lily turned, started back toward the house to begin the painful process of waiting.

30

"My mother served drinks in a bar down in Bozeman." Jim sat cross-legged as he told his tale, like a true storyteller should. "Well, maybe she served more than drinks. I expect she did, though she never said. But she was a good-looking woman, and she was alone, and that's the kind of thing that happens."

"I thought your mother came from Missoula."

"Did, original. Went back there, too, after I was born. Lots of women go home after something like that, but it never worked out for her. Or me. Anyhow, she served drinks and maybe more for the cowboys who passed through. Jack Mercy, he passed through plenty back in those days, looking to kick ass, get piss-faced drunk, find a woman. You ask anybody, they'll tell you."

He picked up a stick, ran it over the rock. Behind her back Willa twisted her wrists, working them against the rope. "I've heard stories," she said calmly. "I know what kind of man he was."

"I know you do. You used to turn a blind eye to it. I saw that too, but you knew. He took a shine to my mother back then. Like I said, she was a good-looking woman. You see the ones he married. They all had something. Looks, sure. Louella, she had flash. And Adele, seemed to me, seeing her, she'd have been classy and smart. And your ma, well she was something. Quietlike, and special, too. Seemed she could hear things other people couldn't. I was taken with your ma."

It made her blood chill to hear it, to think of him anywhere near her mother. "How did you know her?"

"We paid some visits. Never stayed long in the area, never at Mercy either. I was just a kid, but I got a clear memory of your ma, big and pregnant with you, walking with Adam in the pasture. Holding his hand. It's a nice picture." He mused on it for a while. "I was a bit younger than Adam, and I skinned my knee or some such, and your ma, she came up and got me to my feet. My mother and Jack Mercy were arguing, and your ma took me into the kitchen and put something cool on my knee and talked real nice to me."

"Why were you at the ranch?"

"My ma wanted me to stay here. She couldn't take care of me proper. She was broke and she got sick a lot. Her family'd kicked her out. It was drugs. She had a weakness for them. It's because she was alone so much. But he wouldn't have me, even though I was his own blood."

She moistened her lips, ignored the pain as the rope bit in. "Your mother told you that?"

"She told me what was." He pushed back his hat, and his eyes were clear. "Jack Mercy knocked her up one of the times he was down in Bozeman and looking for action. She told him as soon as she knew, but he called her a whore and left her flat." His eyes changed, went glassy with rage. "My mother wasn't a whore. She did what she had to do, that's all. Whores are no damn good, worthless. They spread their legs for anybody. Ma only went on her back for money when she had to. And she didn't do it regular until after he'd planted me and left her without a choice."

Hadn't she told him that, tearfully, time and time again throughout his life? "What the hell was she supposed to do? You tell me, Will, what the hell was she supposed to do? Alone and pregnant, with that son of a bitch calling her a filthy lying whore."

"I don't know." Her hands were trembling now from the effort, from the fear. Because his eyes weren't clear any longer, nor were they glassy. They were mad. "It was difficult for her."

"Damn near impossible. She told me time and time again how she begged and pleaded with him, how he turned his back on her. On me. His own son. She could've gotten rid of me. You know that? She could've had an abortion and been done with it, but she didn't. She told me she didn't because I was Jack Mercy's kid and she was going to make him do right by both of us. He had money, he had plenty, but all he did was toss a few lousy dollars at her and walk out."

She began to see, too well, the bitterness of the woman planting the bitter seeds in the child. "I'm sorry, Jim. Maybe he didn't believe her."

"He should've!" He slammed his fist on the rock. "He'd done it with her. He'd come to her regular, promised her he'd take care of her. She told me how he promised her, and she believed him. And even when she had me, took me to him to show him I had his eyes, and his hair, he turned her away so she had to go back to Missoula and beg her family to help her out. It's because he was married to Louella then, snazzy Louella, and he'd just got her pregnant with Tess. So he didn't want me. He figured he had a son coming. But he was wrong. I was the only son he was going to get."

"You had a chance to hurt Lily. In the cave, when Cooke had her." He was too good with a rope, she thought. She couldn't budge the knots. "You didn't."

"I wouldn't hurt her. I thought about it, sure. Early on when I first found out what he'd done in his will. I thought about it, but they're kin." He drew a deep breath, rubbed the side of his hand where he'd bruised it on the rock. "I promised my ma I'd come back to Mercy, I'd get what was mine by right of birth. She was sickly, having me made her sickly. That's why she needed the drugs to help her get through the day. But she done her best for me. She told me all about my father, all about Mercy. She'd sit for hours and tell me about all of it, and what I'd do when I was old enough to go right up to his face and tell him I wanted what was mine."

"Where's your mother now, Jim?"

"She died. They said the drugs killed her, or she used them to kill herself. But it was Jack Mercy who killed her, Will, when he turned her away. She was dead from then on. When I found her lying there, cold, I promised her again I'd come to Mercy and do what she wanted."

"You found her." There was sweat pouring down her face now. The heat had eased from the air, but sweat ran and dribbled into the raw skin of her wrists to sting. "I'm sorry. So sorry." And she was, desperately.

"I was sixteen. We were in Billings then, and I did some work at the feedlots when I could. She was stone dead when I came home and found her, lying there in piss and vomit. She shouldn't have died that way. He killed her, Will."

"What did you do then?"

"I figured on killing him. That was my first thought. I'd had a lot of practice killing. Stray cats and dogs mostly. I used to pretend they had his face when I carved them up. Only had a pocketknife to work with back then."

Her stomach rolled, rose up to her throat, and was swallowed down. "Your family, your mother's family?"

"I wasn't going to go begging there, after they'd pushed her aside. Hell with them." He picked up the stick, stabbed it at the rock. "Hell with them."

She couldn't hold off the shudders as he stabbed the rock, over and over, repeating that phrase while his face twisted. Then he stopped, his face cleared, and he tapped the stick musically like a man keeping time.

"And I'd made a promise," he continued. "I went to Mercy, and I faced him down. He laughed at me, called me the bastard son of a whore. I took a swing at him, and he knocked me flat. He said I wasn't no son of his, but he'd give me a job. If I lasted a month, he'd give me a paycheck. He turned me over to Ham."

A fist squeezed her heart. Ham. Had someone found him? Was anyone helping him? "Did Ham know?"

"I always figured he did. He never spoke of it, but I figured it. I look like the old man, don't you think?"

There was such hope, such pathetic pride in the question. Willa nodded. "I suppose you do."

"I worked for him. I worked hard, I learned, and I worked harder. He gave me a knife when I turned twenty-one." He slid it out of its sheath, turned it under the moonlight. A Crocodile Bowie, with an eight-inch blade. The sawtooth top glittered like fangs.

"That means something, Willa, a man gives his son a fine knife like this."

And the sweat on her skin turned to ice. "He gave you the knife."

"I loved him. I'd have worked the skin off my hands for him, and the bastard knew it. I never asked him for a thing more, because in my heart I knew when the time came he'd give me what was mine by right. I was his son. His only son. But he gave me nothing but this knife. When the time came, he gave it all to you, to Lily and to Tess. And he gave me nothing."

He inched forward, closer to her, the knife gleaming in his hand, his eyes gleaming in the dark. "It wasn't right. It wasn't fair."

She closed her eyes and waited for the pain.

. . .

Charlie raced through the hills, nose to the ground, ears at alert. Ben rode alone, grateful for the moonlight, praying that the clouds that gathered thick in the west would hold off. He couldn't afford to lose the light.

He could almost swear he smelled her himself. That scent of hers, soap and leather and something more that was only Willa. He wouldn't picture her hurt. It would cloud his mind, and he needed all his senses sharp. This time his quarry knew the land as well as he. His quarry was mounted and knew all the tricks. He couldn't depend on Willa slowing him down or leaving signs, because he couldn't be sure she was . . .

No, he wouldn't think of that. He would only think of finding her, and what he would do to the man when he did.

Charlie splashed into a stream and whined as he lost the scent. Ben walked his horse into the water, stood for a moment listening, plotting, praying. They'd follow the water for a while, he decided.

That's what he would have done.

They walked through the stream, the water level stingy from the lack of rain. Thunder rumbled, and a bird screamed. Ben clamped down on the urge to hurry, to kick his horse into a run. He couldn't afford to rush until they'd picked up the trail again.

He saw something glint on the bank, forced himself to dismount. Water ran cold over his boots as he walked through the stream, bent, picked it up.

An earring. Plain gold hoop. The breath whooshed out of his lungs explosively as his fist clutched it. She'd taken to wearing baubles lately, he remembered. He'd found it charming and sweet, that little touch of female added to her denim and leather. He'd enjoyed telling himself it was for his benefit.

He tucked it into his front pocket, swung back on his horse. If she was clearheaded enough to leave him signs, he was clearheaded enough to follow them. He took his horse up the bank and let Charlie pick up the trail.

"He shouldn't have done what he did." Voice shaking, Jim sawed at the rope tying her ankles. "He did it just to show me he didn't give a rat's ass about me. About you, either."

"No." The tears that sprang to her eyes weren't pity, but sheer relief. With her bound hands she reached forward to massage her legs. They were horribly cramped. "He didn't care about either of us."

"It made me crazy at first. Me and Pickles were up at the cabin when I heard, and I just went crazy. That's why I killed the steer that way. I had to kill something. Then I started thinking. I had to get back at him, Will, make him pay. I wanted you to pay too, at first. You and Tess and Lily. I didn't figure they had any right to what was mine. What he should've left to me. I thought I'd scare them off. Nobody'd get anything if I scared them off. I left the cat on the porch. I liked seeing Lily scream and cry over it. I'm sorry about that now, but I wasn't thinking of her as kin then. I just wanted her to go away, back where she'd come from. And for Mercy to go to hell."

"Can you cut my hands loose, Jim? Please, my arms are cramped."

"I can't. Not yet. You just don't understand it all."

"I think I do." The feeling was back in her legs. They were stinging as the blood surged back, but she could run if she saw an opening. "He hurt you. You wanted to hurt him back."

"I had to. What kind of man would I be if I took that from him? But the thing is, Will, I like killing things. I figure that's from him too." He smiled and a flash of lightning haloed him like a fallen saint. "Nothing much you can do about what comes down through the blood. He liked killing too. Remember that time he had you raise that calf, right from pulling it clear of its mother? You raised it up like a pet, even named it."

"Blossom," she murmured. "Stupid name for a cow."

"You loved that dumb cow, won blue ribbons with it. I remember how he took you out that day. You were twelve, maybe thirteen, and he made you watch while he killed it for beef. Teaching you ranch life, he said, and you cried, and you went off and got sick. Ham damn near came to blows with the old man over it. You never had a pet since."

He took out a cigarette, struck a match. "You had an old dog then, died about a year after all that. You never got another."

"No, I never did." She brought her knees to her chest, pressed her face to them as the memory washed over her.

"I'm just telling you so you'll see, so you'll understand what's in the blood. He liked being the boss, making people dance to his tune. You like being the boss too. It's in the blood."

She could only shake her head, will herself not to break. "Stop it."

"Here now." He rose, got the canteen he'd filled at the stream, and brought it to her. "Drink a little. I didn't mean to get you so worked up. I'm just trying to make you understand." He stroked her hair, his baby sister's pretty hair. "We're in this together."

Charlie surged forward, clamoring over rocks. He didn't bark or howl, though his body vibrated often. Ben listened for the sounds of men, of horses, more dogs. If he was on track, then so was Adam. He could be sure of that. But he heard nothing but the night.

He found the second earring lying on rock where wildflowers struggled through cracks. He retrieved it, touched it to his lips before tucking it away. "Good girl," he whispered. "Just hang on a little longer."

He looked toward the sky. The clouds were sneaking toward the moon, and half the stars were gone. Rain, so long prayed for, was coming too soon.

. . .

She drank, watched his eyes. There was affection in them. Terrifying. "You could have killed me, months ago. Before anyone else."

"I never wanted to hurt you. You'd gotten the shaft, just like me. I always figured that one day, we'd run Mercy. You and me. I didn't even mind you being in charge. You've got a real knack for it. I do better when someone else points the way."

He sat back again, took a drink himself, capped the canteen. He'd lost track of time. It was soothing, sitting here with her, under the wide sky, reminiscing.

"I didn't plan on killing Pickles. Didn't have a thing against him, really. Oh, he could be a pain in the butt with his complaining and argumentative ways, but he didn't bother me any. He just happened along. I never figured he'd come rolling up there just then. Thought I had more time. I'd just planned on doing another steer, leaving it out where one of the boys would come across it and get things heated up. Then I had to do it. And, Will, to tell the truth and shame the devil, I got a taste for it."

"You butchered him."

"Meat's meat when it all comes down to it. Damn, I could go for a beer right now. Wouldn't a beer go down smooth?" He sighed, took off his hat to fan his face. "Cooled off some, but goddamn, it's close. Maybe we're in for that rain we've been waiting for."

She looked up at the sky, felt a jolt of alarm. They were going to lose the moon. If anyone was coming after her, they'd be coming blind as bats. She tested her legs again and thought they would do.

And he tapped the knife on the toe of her boot. "I don't know why I scalped him. Just came to me. Kind of a trophy, I guess. Like hanging a rack on the wall of the den. I've got a whole box of trophies buried east of here. You know where those three cottonwood trees stand across from the far pasture?"

"Yeah, I know." She fought to keep her eyes on his, and off the knife.

"I did all those calves that night. Seemed to me that would send those city girls running off, and that would be that. But they stuck. Had to admire that. Started me thinking a little, but I just couldn't get past the mad of it." He shook his head at his own stubbornness. "So when I picked up that kid, hitchhiking, I used her. I wanted to do a woman."

He moistened his lips. Part of him knew it wasn't proper to talk of it with his little sister, but he couldn't stop himself. "I'd never done a woman before. I had a yen to do Shelly, you know, Zack's wife."

"Oh, my God."

"She's a pretty thing, pretty hair. Couple times I went over to Three Rocks to play poker with the boys there, I studied on it. But I did that girl, and I left her there, right at the front door, just to show Jack Mercy who was boss. That was before the calves," he said dreamily. "I remember now. That was before. They get all mixed up in my head, until Lily they do. It was Lily that changed things. She's my sister. I got that into my head when J C treated her like that, hurt her like that. She might've died if I hadn't taken care of her. Isn't that right?"

"Yes." She wouldn't be sick, refused to be. "You didn't hurt her."

"I wouldn't have harmed a hair on her head." He caught the joke, slapped the rock, and howled. "A hair on her head. Get it? That's a good one." He sobered, the change abrupt and frightening. "I love her, Will. I love her and you and Tess just like a brother should. And I'll look out for you. And you have to look out for me. Blood's thicker than water."

"How do you want me to look out for you, Jim?"

"We got to have a plan, get our stories together here. I figure I'll take you back and we'll tell everybody that somebody dragged you off. You didn't see, but I went off after you. Didn't have time to send out the alarm. We'll say I chased him off, scared him off. I'll fire a couple of shots." He patted the rifle. "He ran off into high country, and I got you away safe. That'll work, won't it?"

"It could. I'll tell them I never saw his face. He hit me. I've probably got a bruise anyway."

"I'm sorry about that, but it works out real good. We'll go back to the way things were, all right. Couple months more and the ranch is free and clear. I can be foreman now." He saw her eyes flicker, her instinctive cringe. "You don't mean it. You're lying."

"No, I'm just thinking it over." Her heart began to thud at the rapid change of his moods. "We have to make sure it sounds right or else—"

"You're lying!" He screamed it so that the rocks echoed. "You think I can't see it? You think I'm too stupid to see what's going on in your head? I take you back, you'll tell them everything. You'll turn me over, your own brother. Because of Ham."

Wild with fury, he sprang to his feet, the knife in one hand, the rifle in the other. "It was an accident. There wasn't anything I could do. But you'll turn me over. You care more about that old man than your own family."

He'd never let her go. And he'd kill her before she got two yards. So she pushed herself to her feet, teetered once until she could brace them apart, and faced him. "He was my family."

He tossed the rifle down, grabbed her by the shirtfront with his free hand, and shook her. "I'm your blood. I'm the one who matters. I'm a Mercy, same as you."

Out of the corner of her eye she saw the knife wave. And the clouds smothered the moon and killed the glint. "You'll have to kill me, Jim. And once you do, you won't be able to run fast enough or hide deep enough. They'll hunt you. If Ben or Adam finds you first, God help you."

"Why won't you listen?" His shout boomed over rock and hill and hung in the heavy air. "It's Mercy that counts. I just want my share of Mercy."

She closed her aching hands into fists, stared into his desperate eyes. "I haven't got any mercy to give you." Rearing back, she thrust her stiffened hands into his stomach and whirled to run.

He caught her by the hair, yanking back until stars erupted in front of her eyes. Sobbing in pain, she rammed back with her elbow, caught him hard. But his grip stayed firm. Her feet slid out from under her and she would have gone down but for the hold on her hair.

"I'll make it quick," he promised. "I know how."

Ben stepped out of the shadows. "Drop the knife." His pistol was cocked, aimed, ready. "You so much as break the skin on her, I'll blow you to hell."

"I'll do more than break skin." Jim angled the knife under her chin. His voice was dead calm again. He felt the control seep back into him, the command. He was in charge. The woman pressed against him was no longer his sister but just a shield. "All I do is jerk my wrist, and she's dead before she hits the ground."

"So are you."

Jim's eyes flickered over. His rifle was just out of reach. Cautious, he moved back a step, keeping the knife edge at Willa's throat. "You give me five minutes' start, and when I'm clear, I'll let her go."

"No, he won't." She hissed as the knife bit in and the first trickle of blood oozed down her throat. "He'll kill me," she said calmly, kept her eyes on Ben's. "It's just a matter of when."

"Shut up, Will." Jim flicked the knife under her chin. "Let the men handle this. You want her, McKinnon, you can have her. But you put down the gun, and you step back until we're mounted. Otherwise, I do her here, and you watch her die. Those are your choices."

Ben skimmed his gaze from Jim's face to Willa's. Lightning shot overhead like lances, illuminated the three of them standing on silvered rock.

He held the look until he saw her nod slowly in acknowledgment. And he hoped, in understanding.

"Are they?" He pulled the trigger. The bullet hit just where he'd aimed it, dead between the eyes. God bless her, he thought, as his hand finally shook. She didn't flinch. Even when the knife clattered to the ground, she didn't flinch.

She felt herself sway and rock now that no one was holding her up. She saw the sky reel just as rain started to fall. And she saw Ben rushing toward her.

"Good shot," she managed, and to her mortification and relief, she fainted.

She came to in his arms, with her face wet and his mouth rushing over it. "Just lost my balance."

"Yeah." He was kneeling in the dirt, rocking her like a baby as rain flooded down on them. "I know."

Her ears were ringing like church bells. Though she knew it was cowardly, she turned her face into his shoulder rather than turn it toward the body that must be sprawled beside them. "He said he was my brother. He did it because of Mercy, because of my father, because of—"

"I heard him clear enough." He pressed his lips to her hair, then took off his hat and put it on her in a fruitless attempt to keep her dry. "Damn idiot woman, you were begging him to kill you. I lost three lives listening to you goading him while I was climbing up."

"I didn't know what else to do." Fear she'd battled back opened wide and devoured her. "Ham?"

"I don't know." She was shaking now, and he gathered her closer. "I don't know, darling. He was alive when I rode out."

"Okay." Then there was hope. "My hands. Oh, Jesus, Ben, my hands."

He began to curse then, hard and fast, as he pulled out his knife and cut the rope away from the raw flesh. "Oh, baby." It broke his heart and left him shattered. "Willa."

He was still rocking her, kneeling in the pouring rain, when Adam found them.

31

"You're going to eat when I tell you to eat, and eat what I tell you to eat." Bess stood over the bed and scowled.

"Can't you leave me be for five damn minutes?" Huddled in the bed, as miserable as a scalded cat, Ham shoved at the tray she set over his lap.

"I do, and you're climbing out of bed. Next time you do, I'm stripping you naked so you can't get past the door."

"I spent six weeks flat on my back in the hospital. And I've been out of that cursed hospital for over a week. I'm alive, for Christ's sake."

"Don't you use the Lord's name to me, Hamilton. The doctor said two full weeks of bed rest, with one hour, twice a day, of walking." Her chin jutted, her head angled, and she looked down her pug nose at him. "Need I remind you you had a knife stuck in your thick hide and you bled all over my clean kitchen floor?"

"You remind me every time you walk in here."

"Well, then." She looked over in approval as Willa stepped in. "Good. You can try dealing with him. I've got work to do."

"Giving her grief again, Ham?"

He glowered as Bess flounced out of the room. "The woman doesn't stop fussing over me, I'm tying these sheets together and climbing out the window."

"She needs to fuss just a little while longer. We all do." She sat on the edge of the bed, gave him a thorough study. He had good color again, and some of the weight he'd lost in the hospital was coming back on. "You look pretty good, though."

"I feel fine. No reason I couldn't be up in the saddle." His hands fumbled when she laid her head on his chest and cuddled. Awkward, he patted her hair. "Come on now, Will, I ain't no teddy bear."

"Grizzly bear's more like it." She grinned and kissed his whiskered cheek despite his embarrassed wriggles.

"Women, always after a man when he's down."

"It's the only time you're going to let me pet you." She sat back, took his hand. "Has Tess been in?"

"She was in a while back. Came to say good-bye." She'd been blubbering over him too, he remembered. Hugging and kissing. He'd nearly blubbered himself. "We're going to miss seeing her strut around here in those fancy boots."

"I'm going to miss her too. Nate's already here to take her to the airport. I've got to go see her off."

"You okay . . . with everything?"

"I'm living with everything. Thanks to you and Ben, I'm living." She gave his hand a last squeeze before going to the door. "Ham." She didn't turn back, but spoke, staring out into the hallway. "Was he Jack Mercy's son? Was he my brother?"

He could have said no, and just let it die. It would've been easier for her. Or it might have been. But she'd always been a tough one. "I don't know, Will. The God's truth is, I just don't know."

She nodded and told herself she would live with that, too. The never knowing.

When she got outside, she saw Lily, already in tears and holding on to Tess for dear life.

"Hey, you'd think I was going to Africa to become a missionary." Tess squeezed back her own tears. "It's only California. I'll be back for a visit in a few months." She patted Lily's growing belly. "I want to be here when Junior comes."

"I'll miss you so much."

"I'll write, I'll call, hell, I'll send faxes. You'll hardly know I've left." She closed her eyes and hugged Lily fiercely. "Oh, take care of yourself. Adam." She reached out for his hands, then went into his arms. "I'll see you soon. I'll be calling you for advice in case I end up buying that horse." He murmured something. "What did that mean?"

He kissed her cheeks. "My sister, in my heart."

"I'll call," she managed to choke out, then turned and nearly bumped into Bess.

"Here." Bess pushed a wicker basket into her hands. "It's a ride to the airport, and with that appetite of yours, you'll never make it."

"Thanks. Maybe I'll lose this five pounds you put on me."

"It doesn't hurt you any. You give my best to your ma."

"I will."

With a sigh, Bess touched her cheek. "You come back soon, girl."

"I will." She turned blindly and stared at Willa. "Well," she managed, "it's been an adventure."

"Sure has." Thumbs tucked in her front pockets, Willa came the rest of the way down the stairs. "You can write about it."

"Some of it." She swallowed hard to steady her voice. "Try to stay out of trouble."

Willa lifted a brow. "I could say the same to you, in the big, bad city."

"It's my city. I'll, ah, drop you a postcard so you can see what the real world looks like."

"You do that."

"Well." She turned. "Hell." Shoved the basket at Nate and spun to walk into Willa's open arms. "Damn it, I'll really miss you."

"Me too." Willa tightened her grip, clung. "Call."

"I will, I will. God, wear some lipstick once in a while, will you? And use that lotion I left you on your hands before they turn into leather."

"I love you."

"Oh, God, I've got to go." Weeping, Tess stumbled toward the rig. "Go castrate a cow or something."

"I was on my way." With a little hitching breath, Willa took out her bandanna and blew her nose as the rig rumbled away. " 'Bye, Hollywood."

Tess was sure she'd gotten hold of herself by the time she'd checked her bags in the terminal. An hour-long cry was good enough for anyone, she thought, and Nate had been considerate enough to let her indulge in it.

"You don't have to come to the gate." But she kept his hand clutched in hers.

"I don't mind."

"You'll keep in touch."

"You know I will."

"Maybe you'll fly in for a weekend, let me show you around."

"I could do that."

Well, he was certainly making it easy, she thought. It was all so easy. The year was up, she had what she wanted. Now it was back to her life. The way she wanted.

"You'll keep me up with the gossip. Fill me in on Lily and Willa. I'm going to miss them like crazy."

She looked around, busy people coming and going, and wished desperately for her usual excitement at the prospect of getting into the air and flying.

"I don't want you to wait." She made herself look up at him. Into those patient eyes. "We've already said good-bye. This only makes it harder."

"It can't be any harder." He put his hands on her shoulders, ran them down her arms, up again. "I love you, Tess. You're the first and last for me. Stay. Marry me."

"Nate, I . . ." Love you too, she thought. Oh, God. "I have to go. You know I do. My work, my career. This was only temporary. We both knew that."

"Things change." Because he could read her feelings on her face, he shook her gently. "You can't look me in the eye and tell me you're not in love with me, Tess. Every time you start to say you're not, you look away and don't say anything."

"I have to go. I'll miss my plane." She broke away, turned, and fled.

She knew what she was doing. Exactly what she was doing. She rushed past gate after gate telling herself that. How was she supposed to live on a horse ranch in Montana? She had her career to think of. Her laptop bumped against her hip. She had a new screenplay to start, a novel to work on. She belonged in LA.

Swearing, she spun around and ran back, pushing through other people who rushed in the opposite direction. "Nate!" She saw his hat, on the downward glide of the escalator, and doubled her pace. "Nate, wait a minute."

He was already at the bottom when she clambered her way down. Out of breath, she stood in front of him, a hand pressed to her speeding heart. She looked into his eyes. "I'm not in love with you," she said without a blink, watched his eyes narrow. "See that, smart guy? I can look right at you and lie."

And with a laugh, she jumped into his arms. "Oh, what the hell. I can work anywhere."

He kissed her, set her on her feet again. "Okay. Let's go home."

"My bags."

"They'll come back."

She looked over her shoulder and said a spiritual good-bye to LA. "You don't seem very surprised."

"I'm not." He scooped her out the door, then up into his arms and into a wild circle. "I'm patient."

Ben found Willa running wire along the fence line that separated Three Rocks from Mercy. It made him realize he should have been doing the same. Still, he dismounted, strolled over to her. "Need a hand?"

"No, I've got it."

"I was wondering how Ham was getting on."

"He's cranky as a constipated bear. I'd say he's coming along fine."

"Good. Let me do that for you."

"I know how to run fence."

"Just let me do it for you." He yanked the wire from her.

Stepping back, she set her hands on her hips. "You've been coming around here a lot, wanting to do things for me. It's got to stop."

"Why?"

"You've got your own land to worry about. I can run Mercy."

"Run every damn thing," he muttered.

"The term of the will's done, Ben. You don't have to check things over around here anymore."

His eyes weren't friendly when they flickered under the brim of his hat. "You think that's all there is to it?"

"I don't know. You haven't been interested in much else lately."

"What's that supposed to mean?"

"What it says. You haven't exactly been a regular visitor in my bed the last few weeks."

"I've been occupied."

"Well, now I'm occupied, so go run your own wire."

He braced his legs apart much as she'd braced her own and faced her between the fence posts. "This line's as much mine as yours."

"Then you should've been checking it, same as me."

He tossed the wire down between them, like a boundary between them, between their land. "Okay, you want to know what's going on with me, I'll tell you." He tugged two thin gold hoops out of his pocket and shoved them into her hand.

"Oh." She frowned down at them. "I'd forgotten about them."

"I haven't." He'd kept them—God knew why, when every time he looked at them he relived the night, the dark, the fear. And each time he looked at them he wondered if he'd have found her in time if she hadn't been smart enough, strong enough, to leave a trail.

"So, you found my earrings." She tucked them in her own pocket.

"Yeah, I found them. And I climbed up that ridge listening to him screaming at you. Saw him holding a knife to your throat. Watched a line of blood run down your skin where he nicked you."

Instinctively she pressed her hand to her throat. There were times when she could still feel it there, the keen point of the knife her father had put in a killer's hand.

"It's done," she told him. "I don't much like going back there."

"I go back there plenty. I can see that flash of lightning, your eyes in that flash of lightning when you knew what I was going to do. When you trusted me to do it."

She hadn't closed her eyes, he remembered. She'd kept them open, level, watching as he squeezed the trigger.

"I put a bullet in a man about six inches from your face. It's given me some bad moments."

"I'm sorry." She reached for his hand, but dropped her own when he pulled back, stayed on his own land. "You killed someone for me. I can see how that would change your feelings."

"That's not it. Well, maybe it is. Maybe that's what did it." He turned away, paced, looked up at the sky. "Maybe it was always there anyway."

"All right, then." She was grateful his back was to her so he couldn't see the way she had to squeeze her eyes tight, bite down on her lip to keep from weeping. "I understand, and I'm grateful. There's no need to make this hard on either of us."

"Hard, hell, that doesn't come close." He tucked his hands in his back pockets and contemplated the long line of fence. It was all that separated them, he mused, those thin lines of barb-edged wire. "You've been underfoot and causing me frustration most all of my life."

"You're on my land," she shot back, wounded. "Who's under whose feet?"

"I guess I know you better than most. I know your flaws well enough. You've got a bundle of them. Ornery, mean-tempered, exasperating. You've got brains, but your guts get in the way of them half the time. But knowing the flaws is half the battle."

She kicked him, hard enough to make him stumble into his own horse. He picked up the hat she'd knocked off his head, brushed it over the leg of his jeans as he turned. "Now I could wrestle you down for that, and it'd probably turn into something else."

"Just try it."

"You see, that's the damnedest thing." He shook a finger at her. "That look right there, the one you're wearing on your face right now. When I think it through, that's the one that did it to me."

"Did what?"

"Had me falling in love with you."

She dropped the hammer she'd picked up to hit him with. "In what?"

"I figure you heard me the first time. You got ears like a damn alley cat." He scratched his chin, settled his hat back into place. "I think you're going to have to marry me, Willa. I don't see a way around it. And I tell you, I've been looking."

"Is that so?" She bent down, picked up the hammer again, and tapped it against her palm. "Have you?"

"Yeah." He eyed the hammer, grinned. He didn't think she'd use it. Or if she tried, he figured he'd be quick enough to avoid a concussion. "I'd have found one if there'd been a way. You know"—he started toward her, circling—"I used to think I wanted you to distraction because you were so contrary. Then when I had you, I decided I still wanted you because I didn't know how long I'd keep you."

"Keep coming on," she said coolly, "and you'll have a dent in your big head."

He kept coming on. "Then it kept creeping up on me, why no one ever pulled at me the way you do. Ever made me miss them five minutes after I walked out the door the way you do. When you weren't safe, I was crazy. Now that you are, I figure the only way to handle things is to marry you."

"That's your idea of a proposal?"

"You've never had better. And with your prickly attitude, you won't get better." He timed it, grabbed the hammer out of her hand, and tossed it over the fence. "No point in saying no, Will. I've got my mind set on it."

"That's what I'm saying." She crossed her arms. "Until I get better."

He sighed, heavily. He'd been afraid it would come to this. "All right, then. I love you. I want you to marry me. I don't want to live my life without you. Will that do?"

"It's some better." Her heart was so full she was surprised it wasn't spilling over. "Where's the ring?"

"Ring? For God's sake, Will, I don't carry a ring around with me riding fence." Perplexed, he pushed back his hat. "You never wear rings anyway."

"I'll wear the one you give me."

He opened his mouth to complain, shut it again, and grinned. "Is that a fact?"

"That's a fact. Damn, Ben, what took you so long?"

She stepped over the wire and into his arms.

Sanctuary

To the Ladies of the Lounge

Part One

When weather-beaten I come back . . .
My body a sack of bones; broken within . . .
—John Donne

1

She dreamed of Sanctuary. The great house gleamed bride-white in the moonlight, as majestic a force breasting the slope that reigned over eastern dunes and western marsh as a queen upon her throne. The house stood as it had for more than a century, a grand tribute to man's vanity and brilliance, near the dark shadows of the forest of live oaks, where the river flowed in murky silence.

Within the shelter of trees, fireflies blinked gold, and night creatures stirred, braced to hunt or be hunted. Wild things bred there in shadows, in secret.

There were no lights to brighten the tall, narrow windows of Sanctuary. No lights to spread welcome over its graceful porches, its grand doors. Night was deep, and the breath of it moist from the sea. The only sound to disturb it was of wind rustling through the leaves of the great oaks and the dry clicking—like bony fingers—of the palm fronds. The white columns stood like soldiers guarding the wide veranda, but no one opened the enormous front door to greet her.

As she walked closer, she could hear the crunch of sand and shells on the road under her feet. Wind chimes tinkled, little notes of song. The porch swing creaked on its chain, but no one lazed upon it to enjoy the moon and the night.

The smell of jasmine and musk roses played on the air, underscored by the salty scent of the sea. She began to hear that too, the low and steady thunder of water spilling over sand and sucking back into its own heart.

The beat of it, that steady and patient pulse, reminded all who inhabited the island of Lost Desire that the sea could reclaim the land and all on it at its whim.

Still, her mood lifted at the sound of it, the music of home and childhood. Once she had run as free and wild through that forest as a deer, had scouted its marshes, raced along its sandy beaches with the careless privilege of youth.

Now, no longer a child, she was home again.

She walked quickly, hurrying up the steps, across the veranda, closing her hand over the big brass handle that glinted like a lost treasure.

The door was locked.

She twisted it right, then left, shoved against the thick mahogany panel. *Let me in,* she thought as her heart began to thud in her chest. *I've come home. I've come back.*

But the door remained shut and locked. When she pressed her face against the glass of the tall windows flanking it, she could see nothing but darkness within.

And was afraid.

She ran now, around the side of the house, over the terrace, where flowers streamed out of pots and lilies danced in chorus lines of bright color. The music of the wind chimes became harsh and discordant, the fluttering of fronds was a hiss of warning. She struggled with the next door, weeping as she beat her fists against it.

Please, please, don't shut me out. I want to come home.

She sobbed as she stumbled down the garden path. She would go to the back, in through the screened porch. It was never locked—Mama said a kitchen should always be open to company.

But she couldn't find it. The trees sprang up, thick and close, the branches and draping moss barred her way.

She was lost, tripping over roots in her confusion, fighting to see through the dark as the canopy of trees closed out the moon. The wind rose up and howled and slapped at her in flat-handed, punishing blows. Spears of saw palms struck out like swords. She turned, but where the path had been was now the river, cutting her off from Sanctuary. The high grass along its slippery banks waved madly.

It was then she saw herself, standing alone and weeping on the other bank.

It was then she knew she was dead.

Jo fought her way out of the dream, all but felt the sharp edges of it scraping her skin as she dragged herself to the surface of the tunnel of sleep. Her lungs burned, and her face was wet with sweat and tears. With a trembling hand, she fumbled for the bedside lamp, knocking both a book and an overfilled ashtray to the floor in her hurry to break out of the dark.

When the light shot on, she drew her knees up close to her chest, wrapped her arms around them, and rocked herself calm.

It was just a dream, she told herself. Just a bad dream.

She was home, in her own bed, in her apartment and miles from the island where Sanctuary stood. A grown woman of twenty-seven had no business being spooked by a silly dream.

But she was still shaking when she reached for a cigarette. It took her three tries to manage to light a match.

Three-fifteen, she noted by the clock on the nightstand. That was becoming typical. There was nothing worse than the three A.M. jitters. She swung her legs over the side of the bed and bent down to pick up the overturned ashtray. She told herself she'd clean up the mess in the morning. She sat there, her oversized T-shirt bunched over her thighs, and ordered herself to get a grip.

She didn't know why her dreams were taking her back to the island of Lost Desire and the home she'd escaped from at eighteen. But Jo figured any first-year psych student could translate the rest of the symbolism. The house was locked because she doubted anyone would welcome her if she did return home. Just lately, she'd given some thought to it but had wondered if she'd lost the way back.

And she was nearing the age her mother had been when she had left the island. Disappeared, abandoning her husband and three children without a second glance.

Had Annabelle ever dreamed of coming home, Jo wondered, and dreamed the door was locked to her?

She didn't want to think about that, didn't want to remember the woman who had broken her heart twenty years before. Jo reminded herself that she should be long over such things by now. She'd lived without her mother, and without Sanctuary and her family. She had even thrived—at least professionally.

Tapping her cigarette absently, Jo glanced around the bedroom. She kept it simple, practical. Though she'd traveled widely, there were few mementos. Except the photographs. She'd matted and framed the black-and-white prints, choosing the ones among her work that she found the most restful to decorate the walls of the room where she slept.

There, an empty park bench, the black wrought iron all fluid curves. And there, a single willow, its lacy leaves dipping low over a small, glassy pool. A moonlit garden was a study in shadow and texture and contrasting shapes. The lonely beach with the sun just breaking the horizon tempted the viewer to step inside the photo and feel the sand rough underfoot.

She'd hung that seascape only the week before, after returning from an assignment on the Outer Banks of North Carolina. Perhaps that was one reason she'd begun to think about home, Jo decided. She'd been very close. She could have traveled a bit south down to Georgia and ferried from the mainland to the island.

There were no roads to Desire, no bridges spanning its sound.

But she hadn't gone south. She'd completed her assignment and come back to Charlotte to bury herself in her work.

And her nightmares.

She crushed out the cigarette and stood. There would be no more sleep, she knew, so she pulled on a pair of sweatpants. She would do some darkroom work, take her mind off things.

It was probably the book deal that was making her nervous, she decided, as she padded out of the bedroom. It was a huge step in her career. Though she knew her work was good, the offer from a major publishing house to create an art book from a collection of her photographs had been unexpected and thrilling.

Natural Studies, by Jo Ellen Hathaway, she thought as she turned into the small galley kitchen to make coffee. No, that sounded like a science project. *Glimpses of Life?* Pompous.

She smiled a little, pushing back her smoky red hair and yawning. She should just take the pictures and leave the title selection to the experts.

She knew when to step back and when to take a stand, after all. She'd been doing one or the other most of her life. Maybe she would send a copy of the book home. What would her family think of it? Would it end up gracing one of the coffee tables where an overnight guest could page through it and wonder if Jo Ellen Hathaway was related to the Hathaways who ran the Inn at Sanctuary?

Would her father even open it at all and see what she had learned to do? Or would he simply shrug, leave it untouched, and go out to walk his island? Annabelle's island.

It was doubtful he would take an interest in his oldest daughter now. And it was foolish for that daughter to care.

Jo shrugged the thought away, took a plain blue mug from a hook. While she waited for the coffee to brew, she leaned on the counter and looked out her tiny window.

There were some advantages to being up and awake at three in the morning, she decided. The phone wouldn't ring. No one would call or fax or expect anything of her. For a few hours she didn't have to be anyone, or do anything. If her stomach was jittery and her head ached, no one knew the weakness but herself.

Below her kitchen window, the streets were dark and empty, slicked by late-winter rain. A streetlamp spread a small pool of light—lonely light, Jo thought. There was no one to bask in it. Aloneness had such mystery, she mused. Such endless possibilities.

It pulled at her, as such scenes often did, and she found herself leaving the scent of coffee, grabbing her Nikon, and rushing out barefoot into the chilly night to photograph the deserted street.

It soothed her as nothing else could. With a camera in her hand and an image in her mind, she could forget everything else. Her long feet splashed through chilly puddles as she experimented with angles. With absent annoyance she flicked at her hair. It wouldn't be falling in her face if she'd had it trimmed. But she'd had no time, so it swung heavily forward in a tousled wave and made her wish for an elastic band.

She took nearly a dozen shots before she was satisfied. When she turned, her gaze was drawn upward. She'd left the lights on, she mused. She hadn't even been aware she'd turned on so many on the trip from bedroom to kitchen.

Lips pursed, she crossed the street and focused her camera again. Calculating, she crouched, shot at an upward angle, and captured those lighted windows in the dark building. *Den of the Insomniac,* she decided. Then with a half laugh that echoed eerily enough to make her shudder, she lowered the camera again.

God, maybe she was losing her mind. Would a sane woman be out at three in the morning, half dressed and shivering, while she took pictures of her own windows?

She pressed her fingers against her eyes and wished more than anything else for the single thing that had always seemed to elude her. Normality.

You needed sleep to be normal, she thought. She hadn't had a full night's sleep in more than a month. You needed regular meals. She'd lost ten pounds in the last few weeks and had watched her long, rangy frame go bony. You needed peace of mind. She couldn't remember if she had ever laid claim to that. Friends? Certainly she had friends, but no one close enough to call in the middle of the night to console her.

Family. Well, she had family, of sorts. A brother and sister whose lives no longer marched with hers. A father who was almost a stranger. A mother she hadn't seen or heard from in twenty years.

Not my fault, Jo reminded herself as she started back across the street. It was Annabelle's fault. Everything had changed when Annabelle had run from Sanctuary and left her baffled family crushed and heartbroken. The trouble, as Jo saw it, was that the rest of them hadn't gotten over it. She had.

She hadn't stayed on the island guarding every grain of sand like her father did. She hadn't dedicated her life to running and caring for Sanctuary like her brother, Brian. And she hadn't escaped into foolish fantasies or the next thrill the way her sister, Lexy, had.

Instead she had studied, and she had worked, and she had made a life for herself. If she was a little shaky just now, it was only because she'd overextended, was letting the pressure get to her. She was a little run-down, that was all. She'd just add some vitamins to her regimen and get back in shape.

She might even take a vacation, Jo mused as she dug her keys out of her pocket. It had been three years—no, four—since she had last taken a trip without a specific assignment. Maybe Mexico, the West Indies. Someplace where the pace was slow and the sun hot. Slowing down and clearing her mind. That was the way to get past this little blip in her life.

As she stepped back into the apartment, she kicked a small, square manila envelope that lay on the floor. For a moment she simply stood, one hand on the door, the other holding her camera, and stared at it.

Had it been there when she left? Why was it there in the first place? The first one had come a month before, had been waiting in her stack of mail, with only her name carefully printed across it.

Her hands began to shake again as she ordered herself to close the door, to lock it. Her breath hitched, but she leaned over, picked it up. Carefully, she set the camera aside, then unsealed the flap.

When she tapped out the contents, the sound she made was a long, low moan. The photograph was very professionally done, perfectly cropped. Just as the other three had been. A woman's eyes, heavy-lidded, almond-shaped, with thick lashes and delicately arched brows. Jo knew their color would be blue, deep blue, because the eyes were her own. In them was stark terror.

When was it taken? How and why? She pressed a hand to her mouth, staring down at the photo, knowing her eyes mirrored the shot perfectly. Terror swept through her, had her rushing through the apartment into the small second bedroom she'd converted to a darkroom. Frantically she yanked open a drawer, pawed through the contents, and found the envelopes she'd buried there. In each was another black-and-white photo, cropped to two by six inches.

Her heartbeat was thundering in her ears as she lined them up. In the first the eyes were closed, as if she'd been photographed while sleeping. The others followed the waking process. Lashes barely lifted, showing only a hint of iris. In the third the eyes were open but unfocused and clouded with confusion.

They had disturbed her, yes, unsettled her, certainly, when she found them tucked in her mail. But they hadn't frightened her.

Now the last shot, centered on her eyes, fully awake and bright with fear.

Stepping back, shivering, Jo struggled to be calm. Why only the eyes? she asked herself. How had someone gotten close enough to take these pictures without her being aware of it? Now, whoever it was had been as close as the other side of her front door.

Propelled by fresh panic, she ran into the living room, and frantically checked the locks. Her heart was battering against her ribs when she fell back against the door. Then the anger kicked in.

Bastard, she thought. He wanted her to be terrorized. He wanted her to hide inside those rooms, jumping at shadows, afraid to step outside for fear he'd be there watching. She who had always been fearless was playing right into his hands.

She had wandered alone through foreign cities, walked mean streets and empty ones, she'd climbed mountains and hacked through jungles. With the camera as her shield, she'd never given a thought to fear. And now, because of a handful of photos, her legs were jellied with it.

The fear had been building, she admitted now. Growing and spiking over the weeks, level by level. It made her feel helpless, so exposed, so brutally alone.

Jo pushed herself away from the door. She couldn't and wouldn't live this way. She would ignore it, put it aside. Bury it deep. God knew she was an expert at burying traumas, small and large. This was just one more.

She was going to drink her coffee and go to work.

By eight she had come full circle—sliding through fatigue, arcing through nervous energy, creative calm, then back to fatigue.

She couldn't work mechanically, not even on the most basic aspect of darkroom chores. She insisted on giving every step her full attention. To do so, she'd had to calm down, ditch both the anger and the fear. Over her first cup of coffee, she'd convinced herself she had figured out the reasoning behind the photos she'd been receiving. Someone admired her work and was trying to get her attention, engage her influence for their own.

That made sense.

Occasionally she lectured or gave workshops. In addition, she'd had three major shows in the last three years. It wasn't that difficult or that extraordinary for someone to have taken her picture—several pictures, for that matter.

That was certainly reasonable.

Whoever it was had gotten creative, that was all. They'd enlarged the eye area, cropped it, and were sending the photos to her in a kind of series. Though the photos appeared to have been printed recently, there was no telling when or where they'd been taken. The negatives might be a year old. Or two. Or five.

They had certainly gotten her attention, but she'd overreacted, taken it too personally.

Over the last couple of years, she had received samples of work from admirers of hers. Usually there was a letter attached, praising her own photographs before the sender went into a pitch about wanting her advice or her help, or in a few cases, suggesting that they collaborate on a project.

The success she was enjoying professionally was still relatively new. She wasn't yet used to the pressures that went along with commercial success, or the expectations, which could become burdensome.

And, Jo admitted as she ignored her unsteady stomach and sipped coffee that had gone stone cold, she wasn't handling that success as well as she might.

She would handle it better, she thought, rolling her aching head on her aching shoulders, if everyone would just leave her alone to do what she did best.

Completed prints hung drying on the wet side of her darkroom. Her last batch of negatives had been developed and, sitting on a stool at her work counter, she slid a contact sheet onto her light board, then studied it, frame by frame, through her loupe.

For a moment she felt a flash of panic and despair. Every print she looked at was out of focus, blurry. Goddamn it, goddamn it, how could that be? Was it the whole roll? She shifted, blinked, and watched the magnified image of rising dunes and oat grass pop clear.

With a sound somewhere between a grunt and a laugh she sat back, rolled her tensed shoulders. "It's not the prints that are blurry and out of focus, you idiot," she muttered aloud. "It's you."

She set the loupe aside and closed her eyes to rest them. She lacked the energy to get up and make more coffee. She knew she should go eat, get something solid into her system. And she knew she should sleep. Stretch out on the bed, close everything off and crash.

But she was afraid to. In sleep she would lose even this shaky control.

She was beginning to think she should see a doctor, get something for her nerves before they frayed beyond repair. But that idea made her think of psychiatrists. Undoubtedly they would want to poke and pry inside her brain and dig up matters she was determined to forget.

She would handle it. She was good at handling herself. Or, as Brian had always said, she was good at elbowing everyone out of her way so she could handle everything herself.

What choice had she had—had any of them had when they'd been left alone to flounder on that damned spit of land miles from nowhere?

The rage that erupted inside her jolted her, it was so sudden, so powerful. She trembled with it, clenched her fists in her lap, and had to bite back the hot words she wanted to spit out at the brother who wasn't even there.

Tired, she told herself. She was just tired, that was all. She needed to put work aside, take one of those over-the-counter sleeping aids she'd bought and had yet to try, turn off the phone and get some sleep. She would be steadier then, stronger.

When a hand fell on her shoulder, she ripped off a scream and sent her coffee mug flying.

"Jesus! Jesus, Jo!" Bobby Banes scrambled back, scattering the mail he carried on the floor.

"What are you doing? What the hell are you doing?" She bolted off the stool and sent it crashing, as he gaped at her.

"I—you said you wanted to get started at eight. I'm only a few minutes late."

Jo fought for breath, gripped the edge of her worktable to keep herself upright. "Eight?"

Her student assistant nodded cautiously. He swallowed hard and kept his distance. To his eye she still looked wild and ready to attack. It was his second semester working with her, and he thought he'd learned how to anticipate her orders, gauge her moods, and avoid her temper. But he didn't have a clue how to handle that hot fear in her eyes.

"Why the hell didn't you knock?" she snapped at him.

"I did. When you didn't answer, I figured you must be in here, so I used the key you gave me when you went on the last assignment."

"Give it back. Now."

"Sure. Okay, Jo." Keeping his eyes on hers, he dug into the front pocket of his fashionably faded jeans. "I didn't mean to spook you."

Jo bit down on control and took the key he held out. There was as much embarrassment now, she realized, as fear. To give herself a moment, she bent down and righted her stool. "Sorry, Bobby. You did spook me. I didn't hear you knock."

"It's okay. Want me to get you another cup of coffee?"

She shook her head and gave in to her knocking knees. As she slid onto the stool, she worked up a smile for him. He was a good student, she thought—a little pompous about his work yet, but he was only twenty-one.

She thought he was going for the artist-as-college-student look, with his dark blond hair in a shoulder-length ponytail, the single gold hoop earring accenting his long, narrow face. His teeth were perfect. His parents had believed in braces, she thought, running her tongue over her own slight overbite.

He had a good eye, she mused. And a great deal of potential. That was why he was here, after all. Jo was always willing to pay back what had been given to her.

Because his big brown eyes were still watching her warily, she put more effort into the smile. "I had a rough night."

"You look like it." He tried a smile of his own when she lifted a brow. "The art is in seeing what's really there, right? And you look whipped. Couldn't sleep, huh?"

Vain was one thing Jo wasn't. She shrugged her shoulders and rubbed her tired eyes. "Not much."

"You ought to try that melatonin. My mother swears by it." He crouched to pick up the broken shards of the mug. "And maybe you could cut back on the coffee."

He glanced up but saw she wasn't listening. She'd gone on a side trip again, Bobby thought. A new habit of hers. He'd just about given up on getting his mentor into a healthier lifestyle. But he decided to give it one more shot.

"You've been living on coffee and cigarettes again."

"Yeah." She was drifting, half asleep where she sat.

"That stuff'll kill you. And you need an exercise program. You've dropped about ten pounds in the last few weeks. With your height you need to carry more weight. And you've got small bones—you're courting osteoporosis. Gotta build up those bones and muscles."

"Uh-huh."

"You ought to see a doctor. You ask me, you're anemic. You got no color, and you could pack half your equipment in the bags under your eyes."

"So nice of you to notice."

He scooped up the biggest shards, dumped them in her waste can. Of course he'd noticed. She had a face that drew attention. It didn't matter that she seemed to work overtime to fade into the background. He'd never seen her wear makeup, and she kept her hair pulled back, but anyone with an eye could see it should be framing that oval face with its delicate bones and exotic eyes and sexy mouth.

Bobby caught himself, felt heat rise to his cheeks. She would laugh at him if she knew he'd had a little crush on her when she first took him on. That, he figured, had been as much professional admiration as physical attraction. And he'd gotten over the attraction part. Mostly.

But there was no doubt that if she would do the minimum to enhance that magnolia skin, dab some color on that top-heavy mouth, and smudge up those long-lidded eyes, she'd be a knockout.

"I could fix you breakfast," he began. "If you've got something besides candy bars and moldy bread."

Taking a long breath, Jo tuned in. "No, that's okay. Maybe we'll stop somewhere and grab something. I'm already running behind."

She slid off the stool and crouched to pick up the mail.

"You know, it wouldn't hurt you to take a few days off, focus on yourself. My mom goes to this spa down in Miami."

His words were only a buzzing in her ear now. She picked up the manila envelope with her name printed neatly on it in block letters. She had to wipe a film of sweat from her brow. In the pit of her stomach was a sick ball that went beyond dread into fear.

The envelope was thicker than the others had been, weightier. *Throw it away,* her mind screamed out. *Don't open it. Don't look inside.*

But her fingers were already scraping along the flap. Low whimpering sounds escaped her as she tore at the little metal clasp. This time an avalanche of photos spilled out onto the floor. She snatched one up. It was a well-produced five-by-seven black-and-white.

Not just her eyes this time, but all of her. She recognized the background—a park near her building where she often walked. Another was of her in downtown Charlotte, standing on a curb with her camera bag over her shoulder.

"Hey, that's a pretty good shot of you."

As Bobby leaned down to select one of the prints, she slapped at his hand and snarled at him, "Keep away. Keep back. Don't touch me."

"Jo, I..."

"Stay the hell away from me." Panting, she dropped on all fours to paw frantically through the prints. There was picture after picture of her doing ordinary, everyday things. Coming out of the market with a bag of groceries, getting in or out of her car.

He's everywhere, he's watching me. Wherever I go, whatever I do. He's hunting me, she thought, as her teeth began to chatter. He's hunting me and there's nothing I can do. Nothing, until...

Then everything inside her clicked off. The photograph in her hand shook as if a brisk breeze had kicked up inside the room. She couldn't scream. There seemed to be no air inside her.

She simply couldn't feel her body any longer.

The photograph was brilliantly produced, the lighting and use of shadows and textures masterful. She was naked, her skin glowing eerily. Her body was arranged in a restful pose, the fragile chin dipped down, the head gently angled. One arm draped across her midriff, the other was flung up over her head in a position of dreaming sleep.

But the eyes were open and staring. A doll's eyes. Dead eyes.

For a moment, she was thrown helplessly back into her nightmare, staring at herself and unable to fight her way out of the dark.

But even through terror she could see the differences. The woman in the photo had a waving mass of hair that fanned out from her face. And the face was softer, the body riper than her own.

"Mama?" she whispered and gripped the picture with both hands. "Mama?"

"What is it, Jo?" Shaken, Bobby listened to his own voice hitch and dip as he stared into Jo's glazed eyes. "What the hell is it?"

"Where are her clothes?" Jo tilted her head, began to rock herself. Her head was full of sounds, rushing, thundering sounds. "Where is she?"

"Take it easy." Bobby took a step forward, started to reach down to take the photo from her.

Her head snapped up. "Stay away." The color flashed back into her cheeks, riding high. Something not quite sane danced in her eyes. "Don't touch me. Don't touch her."

Frightened, baffled, he straightened again, held both hands palms out. "Okay. Okay, Jo."

"I don't want you to touch her." She was cold, so cold. She looked down at the photo again. It was Annabelle. Young, eerily beautiful, and cold as death. "She shouldn't have left us. She shouldn't have gone away. Why did she go?"

"Maybe she had to," Bobby said quietly.

"No, she belonged with us. We needed her, but she didn't want us. She's so pretty." Tears rolled down Jo's cheeks, and the picture trembled in her hand. "She's so beautiful. Like a fairy princess. I used to think she was a princess. She left us. She left us and went away. Now she's dead."

Her vision wavered, her skin went hot. Pressing the photo against her breasts, Jo curled into a ball and wept.

"Come on, Jo." Gently, Bobby reached down. "Come on with me now. We'll get some help."

"I'm so tired," she murmured, letting him pick her up as if she were a child. "I want to go home."

"Okay. Just close your eyes now."

The photo fluttered silently to the floor, facedown atop all the other faces. She saw writing on the back. Large bold letters.

DEATH OF AN ANGEL

Her last thought, as the dark closed in, was Sanctuary.

2

At first light the air was misty, like a dream just about to vanish. Beams of light stabbed through the canopy of live oaks and glittered on the dew. The warblers and buntings that nested in the sprays of moss were waking, chirping out a morning song. A cock cardinal, a red bullet of color, shot through the trees without a sound.

It was his favorite time of day. At dawn, when the demands on his time and energy were still to come, he could be alone, he could think his thoughts. Or simply be.

Brian Hathaway had never lived anywhere but Desire. He'd never wanted to.

He'd seen the mainland and visited big cities. He'd even taken an impulsive vacation to Mexico once, so it could be said he'd visited a foreign land.

But Desire, with all its virtues and flaws, was his. He'd been born there on a gale-tossed night in September thirty years before. Born in the big oak tester bed he now slept in, delivered by his own father and an old black woman who had smoked a corncob pipe and whose parents had been house slaves, owned by his ancestors.

The old woman's name was Miss Effie, and when he was very young she often told him the story of his birth. How the wind had howled and the seas had tossed, and inside the great house, in that grand bed, his mother had borne down like a warrior and shot him out of her womb and into his father's waiting arms with a laugh.

It was a good story. Brian had once been able to imagine his mother laughing and his father waiting, wanting to catch him.

Now his mother was long gone and old Miss Effie long dead. It had been a long, long time since his father had wanted to catch him.

Brian walked through the thinning mists, through huge trees with lichen vivid in pinks and red on their trunks, through the cool, shady light that fostered the ferns and shrubby palmettos. He was a tall, lanky man, very much his father's son in build. His hair was dark and shaggy, his skin tawny, and his eyes cool blue. He had a long face that women found melancholy and appealing. His mouth was firm and tended to brood more than smile.

That was something else women found appealing—the challenge of making those lips curve.

The slight change of light signaled him that it was time to start back to Sanctuary. He had to prepare the morning meal for the guests.

Brian was as contented in the kitchen as he was in the forest. That was something else his father found odd about him. And Brian knew—with some amusement—that Sam Hathaway wondered if his son might be gay. After all, if a man liked to cook for a living, there must be something wrong with him.

If they'd been the type to discuss such matters openly, Brian would have told him that he could enjoy creating a perfect meringue and still prefer women for sex. He simply wasn't inclined toward intimacy.

And wasn't that tendency toward distance from others a Hathaway family trait?

Brian moved through the forest, as quietly as the deer that walked there. Suiting himself, he took the long way around, detouring by Half Moon Creek, where the mists were rising up from the water like white smoke and a trio of does sipped contentedly in the shimmering and utter silence.

There was time yet, Brian thought. There was always time on Desire. He indulged himself by taking a seat on a fallen log to watch the morning bloom.

The island was only two miles across at its widest, less than thirteen from point to point. Brian knew every inch of it, the sun-bleached sand of the beaches, the cool, shady marshes with their ancient and patient alligators. He loved the dune swales, the wonderful wet, undulating grassy meadows banked by young pines and majestic live oaks.

But most of all, he loved the forest, with its dark pockets and its mysteries.

He knew the history of his home, that once cotton and indigo had been grown there, worked by slaves. Fortunes had been reaped by his ancestors. The rich had come to play in this isolated little paradise, hunting the deer and the feral hogs, gathering shells, fishing both river and surf.

They'd held lively dances in the ballroom under the candle glow of crystal chandeliers, gambled carelessly at cards in the game room while drinking good southern bourbon and smoking fat Cuban cigars. They had lazed on the veranda on hot summer afternoons while slaves brought them cold glasses of lemonade.

Sanctuary had been an enclave for privilege, and a testament to a way of life that was doomed to failure.

More fortunes still had gone in and out of the hands of the steel and shipping magnate who had turned Sanctuary into his private retreat.

Though the money wasn't what it had been, Sanctuary still stood. And the island was still in the hands of the descendants of those cotton kings and emperors of steel. The cottages that were scattered over it, rising up behind the dunes, tucked into the shade of the trees, facing the wide swath of Pelican Sound, passed from generation to generation, ensuring that only a handful of families could claim Desire as home.

So it would remain.

His father fought developers and environmentalists with equal fervor. There would be no resorts on Desire, and no well-meaning government would convince Sam Hathaway to make his island a national preserve.

It was, Brian thought, his father's monument to a faithless wife. His blessing and his curse.

Visitors came now, despite the solitude, or perhaps because of it. To keep the house, the island, the trust, the Hathaways had turned part of their home into an inn.

Brian knew Sam detested it, resented every footfall on the island from an outsider. It was the only thing he could remember his parents arguing over. Annabelle had wanted to open the island to more tourists, to draw people to it, to establish the kind of social whirl her ancestors had once enjoyed. Sam had insisted on keeping it unchanged, untouched, monitoring the number of visitors and overnight guests like a miser doling out pennies. It was, in the end, what Brian believed had driven his mother away—that need for people, for faces, for voices.

But however much his father tried, he couldn't hold off change any more than the island could hold back the sea.

Adjustments, Brian thought as the deer turned as a unit and bounded into the concealing trees. He didn't care for adjustments himself, but in the case of the inn they had been necessary. And the fact was, he enjoyed the running of it, the planning, the implementing, the routine. He liked the visitors, the voices of strangers, observing their varying habits and expectations, listening to the occasional stories of their worlds.

He didn't mind people in his life—as long as they didn't intend to stay. In any case, he didn't believe people stayed in the long run.

Annabelle hadn't.

Brian rose, vaguely irritated that a twenty-year-old scar had unexpectedly throbbed. Ignoring it, he turned away and took the winding upward path toward Sanctuary.

When he came out of the trees, the light was dazzling. It struck the spray of a fountain and turned each individual drop into a rainbow. He looked at the back end of the garden. The tulips were rioting dependably. The sea pinks looked a little shaggy, and the . . . what the hell was that purple thing anyway? he asked himself. He was a mediocre gardener at best, struggling constantly to keep up the grounds. Paying guests expected tended gardens as much as they expected gleaming antiques and fine meals.

Sanctuary had to be kept in tiptop shape to lure them, and that meant endless hours of work. Without paying guests, there would be no means for upkeep on Sanctuary at all. So, Brian thought, scowling down at the flowers, it was an endless cycle, a snake swallowing its own tail. A trap without a key.

"Ageratum."

Brian's head came up. He had to squint against the sunlight to bring the woman into focus. But he recognized the voice. It irritated him that she'd been able to walk up behind him that way. Then again, he always viewed Dr. Kirby Fitzsimmons as a minor irritation.

"Ageratum," she repeated, and smiled. She knew she annoyed him, and considered it progress. It had taken nearly a year before she'd been able to get even that much of a reaction from him. "The flower you're glaring at. Your gardens need some work, Brian."

"I'll get to it," he said and fell back on his best weapon. Silence.

He never felt completely easy around Kirby. It wasn't just her looks, though she was attractive enough if you went for the delicate blond type. Brian figured it was her manner, which was the direct opposite of delicate. She was efficient, competent, and seemed to know a little about every damn thing.

Her voice carried what he thought of as high-society New England. Or, when he was feeling less charitable, damn Yankee. She had those Yankee cheekbones, too. They set off sea-green eyes and a slightly turned-up nose. Her mouth was full—not too wide, not too small. It was just one more irritatingly perfect thing about her.

He kept expecting to hear that she'd gone back to the mainland, closed up the little cottage she'd inherited from her granny and given up on the notion of running a clinic on the island. But month after month she stayed, slowly weaving herself into the fabric of the place.

And getting under his skin.

She kept smiling at him, with that mocking look in her eyes, as she pushed back a soft wave of the wheat-colored hair that fell smoothly to her shoulders. "Beautiful morning."

"It's early." He stuck his hands in his pockets. He never knew quite what to do with them around her.

"Not too early for you." She angled her head. Lord, he was fun to look at. She'd been hoping to do more than look for months, but Brian Hathaway was one of the natives of this little spit of land that she was having trouble winning over. "I guess breakfast isn't ready yet."

"We don't serve till eight." He figured she knew that as well as he did. She came around often enough.

"I suppose I can wait. What's the special this morning?"

"Haven't decided." Since there was no shaking her off, he resigned himself when she fell into step beside him.

"My vote's for your cinnamon waffles. I could eat a dozen." She stretched, linking her fingers as she lifted her arms overhead.

He did his best not to notice the way her cotton shirt strained over small, firm breasts. Not noticing Kirby Fitzsimmons had become a full-time job. He wound around the side of the house, through the spring blooms that lined the path of crushed shells. "You can wait in the guest parlor, or the dining room."

"I'd rather sit in the kitchen. I like watching you cook." Before he could think of a way around it, she'd stepped up into the rear screened porch and through the kitchen door.

As usual, it was neat as a pin. Kirby appreciated tidiness in a man, the same way she appreciated good muscle tone and a well-exercised brain. Brian had all three qualities, which was why she was interested in what kind of lover he'd make.

She figured she would find out eventually. Kirby always worked her way toward a goal. All she had to do was keep chipping away at that armor of his.

It wasn't disinterest. She'd seen the way he watched her on the rare occasions when his guard was down. It was sheer stubbornness. She appreciated that as well. And the contrasts of him were such fun.

She knew as she settled on a stool at the breakfast bar that he would have little to say unless she prodded. That was the distance he kept between himself and others. And she knew he would pour her a cup of his really remarkable coffee, and remember that she drank it light. That was his innate hospitality.

Kirby let him have his quiet for a moment as she sipped the coffee from the steaming mug he'd set before her. She hadn't been teasing when she'd said she liked to watch him cook.

A kitchen might have been a traditionally female domain, but this kitchen was all male. Just like its overseer, Kirby thought, with his big hands, shaggy hair, and tough face.

She knew—because there was little that one person on the island didn't know about the others—that Brian had had the kitchen redone about eight years before.

And he'd created the design, chosen the colors and materials. Had made it a working man's room, with long granite-colored counters and glittering stainless steel.

There were three wide windows, framed only by curved and carved wood trim. A banquette in smoky gray was tucked under them for family meals, though, as far as she knew, the Hathaways rarely ate as a family. The floor was creamy white tile, the walls white and unadorned. No fancy work for Brian.

Yet there were homey touches in the gleam of copper pots that hung from hooks, the hanks of dried peppers and garlic, the shelf holding antique kitchen tools. She imagined he thought of them as practical rather than homey, but they warmed the room.

He'd left the old brick hearth alone, and it brought back reminders of a time when the kitchen had been the core of this house, a place for gathering, for lingering. She liked it in the winter when he lighted a fire there and the scent of wood burning mixed pleasurably with that of spicy stews or soups bubbling.

To her, the huge commercial range looked like something that required an engineering degree to operate. Then again, her idea of cooking was taking a package from the freezer and nuking it in the microwave.

"I love this room," she said. He was whipping something in a large blue bowl and only grunted. Taking that as a response, Kirby slid off the stool to help herself to a second cup of coffee. She leaned in, just brushing his arm, and grinned at the batter in the bowl. "Waffles?"

He shifted slightly. Her scent was in his way. "That was what you wanted, wasn't it?"

"Yeah." Lifting her cup, she smiled at him over the rim. "It's nice to get what you want. Don't you think?"

She had the damnedest eyes, he thought. He'd believed in mermaids as a child. All of them had had eyes like Kirby's. "It's easy enough to get it if all you want is waffles."

He stepped back, around her, and took a waffle iron out of a lower cabinet. After he'd plugged it in, he turned, and bumped into her. Automatically he lifted a hand to her arm to steady her. And left it there.

"You're underfoot."

She eased forward, just a little, pleased by the quick flutter in her stomach. "I thought I could help."

"With what?"

She smiled, let her gaze wander down to his mouth, then back. "With whatever." What the hell, she thought, and laid her free hand on his chest. "Need anything?"

His blood began to pump faster. His fingers tightened on her arm before he could prevent it. He thought about it, oh, he thought about it. What would it be like to push her back against the counter and take what she kept insisting on putting under his nose?

That would wipe the smirk off her face.

"You're in my way, Kirby."

He had yet to let her go. That, she thought, was definite progress. Beneath her hand his heartbeat was accelerated. "I've been in your way the best part of a year, Brian. When are you going to do something about it?"

She saw his eyes flicker before they narrowed. Her breathing took on an anticipatory hitch. *Finally,* she thought and leaned toward him.

He dropped her arm and stepped back, the move so unexpected and abrupt that this time she did nearly stumble. "Drink your coffee," he said. "I've got work to do here."

He had the satisfaction of seeing that he'd pushed one of her buttons for a change. The smirk was gone, all right. Her delicate brows were knit, and under them her eyes had gone dark and hot.

"Damn it, Brian. What's the problem?"

Deftly, he ladled batter onto the heated waffle iron. "I don't have a problem." He slanted a look at her as he closed the lid. Her color was up and her mouth was thinned. Spitting mad, he thought. Good.

"What do I have to do?" She slammed her coffee cup down, sloshing the hot liquid onto his spotless counter. "Do I have to stroll in here naked?"

His lips twitched. "Well, now, that's a thought, isn't it? I could raise the rates around here after that." He cocked his head. "That is, if you look good naked."

"I look *great* naked, and I've given you numerous opportunities to find that out for yourself."

"I guess I like to make my own opportunities." He opened the refrigerator. "You want eggs with those waffles?"

Kirby clenched her fists, reminded herself that she'd taken a vow to heal, not harm, then spun on her heel. "Oh, stuff your waffles," she muttered and stalked out the back door.

Brian waited until he heard the door slam before he grinned. He figured he had come out on top of that little tussle of wills and decided to treat himself to her waffles. He was just flipping them onto a plate when the door swung open.

Lexy posed for a moment, which both she and Brian knew was out of habit rather than an attempt to impress her brother. Her hair was a tousled mass of spiraling curls that flowed over her shoulders in her current favorite shade, Renaissance Red.

She liked the Titian influence and considered it an improvement over the Bombshell Blonde she'd worn the last few years. That was, she'd discovered, a bitch to maintain.

The color was only a few shades lighter and brighter than what God had given her, and it suited her skin tones, which were milky with a hint of rose beneath. She'd inherited her father's changeable hazel eyes. This morning they were heavy, the color of cloudy seas, and already carefully accented with mascara and liner.

"Waffles," she said. Her voice was a feline purr she'd practiced religiously and made her own. "Yum."

Unimpressed, Brian cut the first bite as he stood, and shoveled it into his mouth. "Mine."

Lexy tossed back her gypsy mane of hair, strolled over to the breakfast bar, and pouted prettily. She fluttered her lashes and smiled when Brian set the plate in front of her. "Thanks, sweetie." She laid a hand on his cheek and kissed the other.

Lexy had the very un-Hathaway-like habit of touching, kissing, hugging. Brian remembered that after their mother had left, Lexy had been like a puppy, always leaping into someone's arms, looking for a snuggle. Hell, he thought, she'd only been four. He gave her hair a tug and handed her the syrup.

"Anyone else up?"

"Mmm. The couple in the blue room are stirring. Cousin Kate was in the shower."

"I thought you were handling the breakfast shift this morning."

"I am," she told him with her mouth full.

He lifted a brow, skimmed his gaze over her short, thin, wildly patterned robe. "Is that your new waitress uniform?"

She crossed long legs and slipped another bite of waffle between her lips. "Like it?"

"You'll be able to retire on the tips."

"Yeah." She gave a half laugh and pushed at the waffles on her plate. "That's been my lifelong dream—serving food to strangers and clearing away their dirty plates, saving the pocket change they give me so I can retire in splendor."

"We all have our little fantasies," Brian said lightly and set a cup of coffee, loaded with cream and sugar, beside her. He understood her bitterness and disappointment, even if he didn't agree with it. Because he loved her, he cocked his head and said, "Want to hear mine?"

"Probably has something to do with winning the Betty Crocker recipe contest."

"Hey, it could happen."

"I was going to be somebody, Bri."

"You are somebody. Alexa Hathaway, Island Princess."

She rolled her eyes before she picked up her coffee. "I didn't last a year in New York. Not a damn year."

"Who wants to?" The very idea gave him the creeps. Crowded streets, crowded smells, crowded air.

"It's a little tough to be an actress on Desire."

"Honey, you ask me, you're doing a hell of a job of it. And if you're going to sulk, take the waffles up to your room. You're spoiling my mood."

"It's easy for you." She shoved the waffles away. Brian nabbed the plate before it slid off the counter. "You've got what you want. Living in nowhere day after day, year after year. Doing the same thing over and over again. Daddy's practically given the house over to you so he can tromp around the island all day to make sure nobody moves so much as one grain of his precious sand."

She pushed herself up from the stool, flung out her arms. "And Jo's got what she wants. Big-fucking-deal photographer, traveling all over the world to snap her pictures. But what do I have? Just what do I have? A pathetic résumé with a couple of commercials, a handful of walk-ons, and a lead in a three-act play that closed in Pittsburgh on opening night. Now I'm stuck here again, waiting tables, changing other people's sheets. And I hate it."

He waited a moment, then applauded. "Hell of a speech, Lex. And you know just what words to punch. You might want to work on the staging, though. The gestures lean toward grandiose."

Her lips trembled, then firmed. "Damn you, Bri." She jerked her chin up before stalking out.

Brian picked up her fork. Looked like he was two for two that morning, he thought, and decided to finish off her breakfast as well.

Within an hour Lexy was all smiles and southern sugared charm. She was a skilled waitress—which had saved her from total poverty during her stint in New York—and served her tables with every appearance of pleasure and unhurried grace.

She wore a trim skirt just short enough to irritate Brian, which had been her intention, and a cap-sleeved sweater that she thought showed off her figure to best advantage. She had a good one and worked hard to keep it that way.

It was a tool of the trade whether waitressing or acting. As was her quick, sunny smile.

"Why don't I warm that coffee up for you, Mr. Benson? How's your omelette? Brian's an absolute wonder in the kitchen, isn't he?"

Since Mr. Benson seemed so appreciative of her breasts, she leaned over a bit further to give him full bang for his buck before moving to the next table.

"You're leaving us today, aren't you?" She beamed at the newlyweds cuddling at a corner table. "I hope y'all come back and see us again."

She sailed through the room, gauging when a customer wanted to chat, when another wanted to be left alone. As usual on a weekday morning, business was light and she had plenty of opportunity to play the room.

What she wanted to play to was packed houses, those grand theaters of New York. Instead, she thought, keeping that summer-sun smile firmly in place, she was cast in the role of waitress in a house that never changed, on an island that never changed.

It had all been the same for hundreds of years, she thought. Lexy wasn't a woman who appreciated history. As far as she was concerned, the past was boring and as tediously carved in stone as Desire and its scattering of families.

Pendletons married Fitzsimmonses or Brodies or Verdons. The island's Main Four. Occasionally one of the sons or daughters took a detour and married a mainlander. Some even moved away, but almost invariably they remained, living in the same cottages generation after generation, sprinkling a few more names among the permanent residents.

It was all so . . . predictable, she thought, as she flipped her order pad brightly and beamed down at her next table.

Her mother had married a mainlander, and now the Hathaways reigned over Sanctuary. It was the Hathaways who had lived there, worked there, sweated time and blood over the keeping of the house and the protection of the island for more than thirty years now.

But Sanctuary still was, and always would be, the Pendleton house, high on the hill.

And there seemed to be no escaping from it.

She stuffed tips into her pocket and carried dirty plates away. The minute she stepped into the kitchen, her eyes went frigid. She shed her charm like a snake sheds its skin. It only infuriated her more that Brian was impervious to the cold shoulder she jammed in his face.

She dumped the dishes, snagged the fresh pot of coffee, then swung back into the dining room.

For two hours she served and cleared and replaced setups—and dreamed of where she wanted to be.

Broadway. She'd been so sure she could make it. Everyone had told her she had a natural talent. Of course, that was before she went to New York and found herself up against hundreds of other young women who'd been told the same thing.

She wanted to be a serious actress, not some airheaded bimbo who posed for lingerie ads and billed herself as an actress-model. She'd fully expected to start at the top. After all, she had brains and looks and talent.

Her first sight of Manhattan had filled her with a sense of purpose and energy. It was as if it had been waiting for her, she thought, as she calculated the tab for table six. All those people, and that noise and vitality. And, oh, the stores with those gorgeous clothes, the sophisticated restaurants, and the overwhelming sense that everyone had something to do, somewhere to go in a hurry.

She had something to do and somewhere to go too.

Of course, she'd rented an apartment that had cost far too much. But she hadn't been willing to settle for some cramped little room. She treated herself to new clothes at Bendel's, and a full day at Elizabeth Arden. That ate a large chunk out of her budget, but she considered it an investment. She wanted to look her best when she answered casting calls.

Her first month was one rude awakening after another. She'd never expected so much competition, or such desperation on the faces of those who lined up with her to audition for part after part.

And she did get a few offers—but most of them involved her auditioning on her back. She had too much pride and too much self-confidence for that.

Now that pride and self-confidence and, she was forced to admit, her own naïveté, had brought her full circle.

But it was only temporary, Lexy reminded herself. In a little less than a year she would turn twenty-five and then she'd come into her inheritance. What there was of it. She was going to take it back to New York, and this time she'd be smarter, more cautious, and more clever.

She wasn't beaten, she decided. She was taking a sabbatical. One day she would stand onstage and feel all that love and admiration from the audience roll over her. Then she would be someone.

Someone other than Annabelle's younger daughter.

She carried the last of the plates into the kitchen. Brian was already putting the place back into shape. No dirty pots and pans cluttered his sink, no spills and smears spoiled his counter. Knowing it was nasty, Lexy turned her wrist so that the cup stacked on top of the plates tipped, spilling the dregs of coffee before it shattered on the tile.

"Oops," she said and grinned wickedly when Brian turned his head.

"You must enjoy being a fool, Lex," he said coolly. "You're so good at it."

"Really?" Before she could stop herself, she let the rest of the dishes drop. They hit with a crash, scattering food and fragments of stoneware all over. "How's that?"

"Goddamn it, what are you trying to prove? That you're as destructive as ever? That somebody will always come behind you to clean up your mess?" He stomped to a closet, pulled out a broom. "Do it yourself." He shoved the broom at her.

"I won't." Though she already regretted the impulsive act, she shoved the broom back at him. The colorful Fiestaware was like a ruined carnival at their feet. "They're your precious dishes. You clean them up."

"You're going to clean it up, or I swear I'll use this broom on your backside."

"Just try it, Bri." She went toe-to-toe with him. Knowing she'd been wrong was only a catalyst for standing her ground. "Just try it and I'll scratch your damn eyes out. I'm sick to death of you telling me what to do. This is my house as much as it is yours."

"Well, I see nothing's changed around here."

Their faces still dark with temper, both Brian and Lexy turned—and stared. Jo stood at the back door, her two suitcases at her feet and exhaustion in her eyes.

"I knew I was home when I heard the crash followed by the happy voices."

In an abrupt and deliberate shift of mood, Lexy slid her arm through Brian's, uniting them. "Look here, Brian, another prodigal's returned. I hope we have some of that fatted calf left."

"I'll settle for coffee," Jo said, and closed the door behind her.

3

Jo stood at the window in the bedroom of her childhood. The view was the same. Pretty gardens patiently waiting to be weeded and fed. Mounds of alyssum were already golden and bluebells were waving. Violas were sunning their sassy little faces, guarded by the tall spears of purple iris and cheerful yellow tulips. Impatiens and dianthus bloomed reliably.

There were the palms, cabbage and saw, and beyond them, the shady oaks where lacy ferns and indifferent wildflowers thrived.

The light was so lovely, gilded and pearly as the clouds drifted, casting soft shadows. The image was one of peace, solitude, and storybook perfection. If she'd had the energy, she'd have gone out now, captured it on film and made it her own.

She'd missed it. How odd, she thought, to realize only now that she'd missed the view from the window of the room where she'd spent nearly every night of the first eighteen years of her life.

She'd whiled away many hours gardening with her mother, learning the names of the flowers, their needs and habits, enjoying the feel of soil under her fingers and the sun on her back. Birds and butterflies, the tinkle of wind chimes, the drift of puffy clouds overhead in a soft blue sky were treasured memories from her early childhood.

Apparently she'd forgotten to hold on to them, Jo decided, as she turned wearily from the window. Any pictures she'd taken of the scene, with her mind or with her camera, had been tucked away for a very long time.

Her room had changed little as well. The family wing in Sanctuary still glowed with Annabelle's style and taste. For her older daughter she'd chosen a gleaming brass half-tester bed with a lacy canopy and a complex and fluid design of cornices and knobs. The spread was antique Irish lace, a Pendleton heirloom that Jo had always loved because of its pattern and texture. And because it seemed so sturdy and ageless.

On the wallpaper, bluebells bloomed in cheerful riot over the ivory background, and the trim was honey-toned and warm.

Annabelle had selected the antiques—the globe lamps and maple tables, the dainty chairs and vases that had always held fresh flowers. She'd wanted her children to learn early to live with the precious and care for it. On the mantel over the little marble fireplace were candles and seashells. On the shelves on the opposite wall were books rather than dolls.

Even as a child, Jo had had little use for dolls.

Annabelle was dead. No matter how much of her stubbornly remained in this room, in this house, on this island, she was dead. Sometime in the last twenty years she had died, made her desertion complete and irrevocable.

Dear God, why had someone immortalized that death on film? Jo wondered, as she buried her face in her hands. And why had they sent that immortalization to Annabelle's daughter?

DEATH OF AN ANGEL

Those words had been printed on the back of the photograph. Jo remembered them vividly. Now she rubbed the heel of her hand hard between her breasts to try to calm her heart. What kind of sickness was that? she asked herself. What kind of threat? And how much of it was aimed at herself?

It had been there, it had been real. It didn't matter that when she got out of the hospital and returned to her apartment, the print was gone. She couldn't let it matter. If she admitted she'd imagined it, that she'd been hallucinating, she would have to admit that she'd lost her mind.

How could she face that?

But the print hadn't been there when she returned. All the others were, all those everyday images of herself, still scattered on the darkroom floor where she'd dropped them in shock and panic.

But though she searched, spent hours going over every inch of the apartment, she didn't find the print that had broken her.

If it had never been there . . . Closing her eyes, she rested her forehead on the window glass. If she'd fabricated it, if she'd somehow wanted that terrible image to be fact, for her mother to be exposed that way, and dead—what did that make her?

Which could she accept? Her own mental instability, or her mother's death?

Don't think about it now. She pressed a hand to her mouth as her breath began to catch in her throat. Put it away, just like you put the photographs away. Lock it up until you're stronger. Don't break down again, Jo Ellen, she ordered herself. You'll end up back in the hospital, with doctors poking into both body and mind.

Handle it. She drew a deep, steadying breath. Handle it until you can ask whatever questions have to be asked, find whatever answers there are to be found.

She would do something practical, she decided, something ordinary, attempt the pretense, at least, of a normal visit home.

She'd already lowered the front of the slant-top desk and set one of her cameras on it. But as she stared at it she realized that was as much unpacking as she could handle. Jo looked at the suitcases lying on the lovely bedspread. The thought of opening them, of taking clothes out and hanging them in the armoire, folding them into drawers was simply overwhelming. Instead she sat down in a chair and closed her eyes.

What she needed to do was think and plan. She worked best with a list of goals and tasks, recorded in the order that would be the most practical and efficient. Coming home had been the only solution, so it was practical and efficient. It was, she promised herself, the first step. She just had to clear her mind, somehow—clear it and latch on to the next step.

But she drifted, nearly dreaming.

It seemed like only seconds had passed when someone knocked, but Jo found herself jerked awake and disoriented. She sprang to her feet, feeling ridiculously embarrassed to have nearly been caught napping in the middle of the day. Before she could reach the door, it opened and Cousin Kate poked her head in.

"Well, there you are. Goodness, Jo, you look like three days of death. Sit down and drink this tea and tell me what's going on with you."

It was so Kate, Jo thought, that frank, no-nonsense, bossy attitude. She found herself smiling as she watched Kate march in with the tea tray. "You look wonderful."

"I take care of myself." Kate set the tray on the low table in the sitting area and waved one hand at a chair. "Which, from the looks of you, you haven't been doing. You're too thin, too pale, and your hair's a disaster of major proportions. But we'll fix that."

Briskly she poured tea from a porcelain teapot decked with sprigs of ivy into two matching cups. "Now, then." She sat back, sipped, then angled her head.

"I'm taking some time off," Jo told her. She'd driven down from Charlotte for the express purpose of giving herself time to rehearse her reasons and excuses for coming home. "A few weeks."

"Jo Ellen, you can't snow me."

They'd never been able to, Jo thought, not any of them, not from the moment Kate had set foot in Sanctuary. She'd come days after Annabelle's desertion to spend a week and was still there twenty years later.

They'd needed her, God knew, Jo thought, as she tried to calculate just how little she could get away with telling Katherine Pendleton. She sipped her tea, stalling.

Kate was Annabelle's cousin, and the family resemblance was marked in the eyes, the coloring, the physical build. But where Annabelle, in Jo's memory, had always seemed soft and innately feminine, Kate was sharp-angled and precise.

Yes, Kate did take care of herself, Jo agreed. She wore her hair boyishly short, a russet cap that suited her fox-at-alert face and practical style. Her wardrobe leaned toward the casual but never the sloppy. Jeans were always pressed, cotton shirts crisp. Her nails were neat and short and never without three coats of clear polish. Though she was fifty, she kept herself trim and from the back could have been mistaken for a teenage boy.

She had come into their lives at their lowest ebb and had never faltered. Had simply been there, managing details, pushing each of them to do whatever needed to be done next, and, in her no-nonsense way, bullying and loving them into at least an illusion of normality.

"I've missed you, Kate," Jo murmured. "I really have."

Kate stared at her a moment, and something flickered over her face. "You won't soften me up, Jo Ellen. You're in trouble, and you can choose to tell me or you can make me pry it out of you. Either way, I'll have it."

"I needed some time off."

That, Kate mused, was undoubtedly true; she could tell just from the looks of the girl. Knowing Jo, she doubted very much if it was a man who'd put that wounded look in her eyes. So that left work. Work that took Jo to strange and faraway places, Kate thought. Often dangerous places of war and disaster. Work that she knew her young cousin had deliberately put ahead of a life and a family.

Little girl, Kate thought, *my poor, sweet little girl. What have you done to yourself?*

Kate tightened her fingers on the handle of her cup to keep them from trembling. "Were you hurt?"

"No. No," Jo repeated and set her tea down to press her fingers to her aching eyes. "Just overwork, stress. I guess I overextended myself in the last couple of months. The pressure, that's all."

The photographs. Mama.

Kate drew her brows together. The line that formed between them was known, not so affectionately, as the Pendleton Fault Line. "What kind of pressure eats the weight off of you, Jo Ellen, and makes your hands shake?"

Defensively, Jo clasped those unsteady hands together in her lap. "I guess you could say I haven't been taking care of myself." Jo smiled a little. "I'm going to do better."

Tapping her fingers on the arm of the chair, Kate studied Jo's face. The trouble there went too deep to be only professional concerns. "Have you been sick?"

"No." The lie slid off her tongue nearly as smoothly as planned. Very deliberately she blocked out the thought of a hospital room, almost certain that Kate would be able to see it in her mind. "Just a little run-down. I haven't been sleeping well lately." Edgy under Kate's steady gaze, Jo rose to dig cigarettes out of the pocket of the jacket she'd tossed over a chair. "I've got that book deal—I wrote you about it. I guess it's got me stressed out." She flicked on her lighter. "It's new territory for me."

"You should be proud of yourself, not making yourself sick over it."

"You're right. Absolutely." Jo blew out smoke and fought back the image of Annabelle, the photographs. "I'm taking some time off."

It wasn't all, Kate calculated, but it was enough for now. "It's good you've come home. A couple of weeks of Brian's cooking will put some meat on you again. And God knows we could use some help around here. Most of the rooms, and the cottages, are booked straight through the summer."

"So business is good?" Jo asked without much interest.

"People need to get away from their own routines and pick up someone else's. Most that come here are looking for quiet and solitude or they'd be in Hilton Head or on Jekyll. Still, they want clean linen and fresh towels."

Kate tapped her fingers, thinking briefly of the work stretched out before her that afternoon. "Lexy's been lending a hand," she continued, "but she's no more dependable than she ever was. Just as likely to run off for the day as to do what chores need doing. She's dealing with some disappointments herself, and some growing-up pains."

"Lex is twenty-four, Kate. She should be grown up by now."

"Some take longer than others. It's not a fault, it's a fact." Kate rose, always ready to defend one of her chicks, even if it was against the pecks of another.

"And some never learn to face reality," Jo put in. "And spend their lives blaming everyone else for their failures and disappointments."

"Alexa is not a failure. You were never patient enough with her—any more than she was with you. That's a fact as well."

"I never asked her to be patient with me." Old resentments surfaced like hot grease on tainted water. "I never asked her, or any of them, for anything."

"No, you never asked, Jo," Kate said evenly. "You might have to give something back if you ask. You might have to admit you need them if you let them need you. Well, it's time you all faced up to a few things. It's been two years since the three of you have been in this house together."

"I know how long it's been," Jo said bitterly. "And I didn't get any more of a welcome from Brian and Lexy than I'd expected."

"Maybe you'd have gotten more if you'd expected more." Kate set her jaw. "You haven't even asked about your father."

Annoyed, Jo stabbed out her cigarette. "What would you like me to ask?"

"Don't take that snippy tone with me, young lady. If you're going to be under this roof, you'll show some respect for those who provide it. And you'll do your part while you're here. Your brother's had too much of the running of this place on his shoulders these last few years. It's time the family pitched in. It's time you were a family."

"I'm not an innkeeper, Kate, and I can't imagine that Brian wants me poking my fingers into his business."

"You don't have to be an innkeeper to do laundry or polish furniture or sweep the sand off the veranda."

At the ice in her tone, Jo responded in defense and defiance. "I didn't say I wouldn't do my part, I just meant—"

"I know exactly what you meant, and I'm telling you, young lady, I'm sick to death of that kind of attitude. Every one of you children would rather sink over your heads in the marsh than ask one of your siblings for a helping hand. And you'd strangle on your tongue before you asked your daddy. I don't know whether you're competing or just being ornery, but I want you to put it aside while you're here. This is home. By God, it's time it felt like one."

"Kate," Jo began as Kate headed for the door.

"No, I'm too mad to talk to you now."

"I only meant . . ." When the door shut smartly, Jo let the air out of her lungs on a long sigh.

Her head was achy, her stomach knotted, and guilt was smothering her like a soaked blanket.

Kate was wrong, she decided. It felt exactly like home.

. . .

From the fringes of the marsh, Sam Hathaway watched a hawk soar over its hunting ground. Sam had hiked over to the landward side of the island that morning, leaving the house just before dawn. He knew Brian had gone out at nearly the same hour, but they hadn't spoken. Each had his own way, and his own route.

Sometimes Sam took a Jeep, but more often he walked. Some days he would head to the dunes and watch the sun rise over the water, turning it bloody red, then golden, then blue. When the beach was all space and light and brilliance, he might walk for miles, his eyes keenly judging erosion, looking for any fresh buildup of sand.

He left shells where the water had tossed them.

He rarely ventured onto the interdune meadows. They were fragile, and every footfall caused damage and change. Sam fought bitterly against change.

There were days he preferred to wander to the edge of the forest, behind the dunes, where the lakes and sloughs were full of life and music. There were mornings he needed the stillness and dim light there rather than the thunder of waves and the rising sun. He could, like the patient heron waiting for a careless fish, stand motionless as minutes ticked by.

There were times among the ponds and stands of willow and thick film of duckweed that he could forget that any world existed beyond this, his own. Here, the alligator hidden in the reeds while it digested its last meal and the turtle sunning on the log, likely to become gator bait itself, were more real to him than people.

But it was a rare, rare thing for Sam to go beyond the ponds and into the shadows of the forest. Annabelle had loved the forest best.

Other days he was drawn here, to the marsh and its mysteries. Here was a cycle he could understand—growth and decay, life and death. This was nature and could be accepted. No man caused this or—as long as Sam was in control—would interfere with it.

At the edges he could watch the fiddler crabs scurrying, so busy in the mud that they made quiet popping sounds, like soapsuds. Sam knew that when he left, raccoons and other predators would creep along the mud, scrape out those busy crabs, and feast.

That was all part of the cycle.

Now, as spring came brilliantly into its own, the waving cordgrass was turning from tawny gold to green and the turf was beginning to bloom with the colors of sea lavender and oxeye. He had seen more than thirty springs come to Desire, and he never tired of it.

The land had been his wife's, passed through her family from generation to generation. But it had become his the moment he'd set foot on it. Just as Annabelle had become his the moment he'd set eyes on her.

He hadn't kept the woman, but through her desertion he had kept the land.

Sam was a fatalist—or had become one. There was no avoiding destiny.

The land had come to him from Annabelle, and he tended it carefully, protected it fiercely, and left it never.

Though it had been years since he'd turned in the night reaching out for the ghost of his wife, he could find her anywhere and everywhere he looked on Desire.

It was both his pain and his comfort.

Sam could see the exposed roots of trees where the river was eating away at the fringe of the marsh. Some said it was best to take steps to protect those fringes. But Sam believed that nature found its way. If man, whether with good intent or ill, set his own hand to changing that river's course, what repercussions would it have in other areas?

No, he would leave it be and let the land and the sea, the wind and the rain fight it out.

From a few feet away, Kate studied him. He was a tall, wiry man with skin tanned and ruddy and dark hair silvering. His firm mouth was slow to smile, and slower yet were those changeable hazel eyes. Lines fanned out from those eyes, deeply scored and, in that oddity of masculinity, only enhancing his face.

He had large hands and feet, both of which he'd passed on to his son. Yet Kate knew Sam could move with an uncanny and soundless grace that no city dweller could ever master.

In twenty years he had never welcomed her nor expected her to leave. She had simply come and stayed and fulfilled a purpose. In weak moments, Kate allowed herself to wonder what he would think or do or say if she simply packed up and left.

But she didn't leave, doubted she ever would.

She'd been in love with Sam Hathaway nearly every moment of those twenty years.

Kate squared her shoulders, set her chin. Though she suspected he already knew she was there, she knew he wouldn't speak to her unless she spoke first.

"Jo Ellen came in on the morning ferry."

Sam continued to watch the hawk circle. Yes, he'd known Kate was there, just as he'd known she had some reason she thought important that would have brought her to the marsh. Kate wasn't one for mud and gators.

"Why?" was all he said, and extracted an impatient sigh from Kate.

"It's her home, isn't it?"

His voice was slow, as if the words were formed reluctantly. "Don't figure she thinks of it that way. Hasn't for a long time."

"Whatever she thinks, it *is* her home. You're her father and you'll want to welcome her back."

He got a picture of his older daughter in his mind. And saw his wife with a clarity that brought both despair and outrage. But only disinterest showed in his voice. "I'll be up to the house later on."

"It's been nearly two years since she's been home, Sam. For Lord's sake, go see your daughter."

He shifted, annoyed and uncomfortable. Kate had a way of drawing out those reactions in him. "There's time, unless she's planning on taking the ferry back to the mainland this afternoon. Never could stay in one place for long, as I recall. And she couldn't wait to get shed of Desire."

"Going off to college and making a career and a life for herself isn't desertion."

Though he didn't move or make a sound, Kate knew the shaft had hit home, and was sorry she'd felt it necessary to hurl it. "She's back now, Sam. I don't think she's up to going anywhere for a while, and that's not the point."

Kate marched up, took a firm hold on his arm, and turned him to face her. There were times you had to shove an obvious point in Sam's face to make him see it, she thought. And that was just what she intended to do now.

"She's hurting. She doesn't look well, Sam. She's lost weight and she's pale as a sheet. She says she hasn't been ill, but she's lying. She looks like you could knock her down with a hard thought."

For the first time a shadow of worry moved into his eyes. "Did she get hurt on her job?"

There, finally, Kate thought, but was careful not to show the satisfaction. "It's not that kind of hurt," she said more gently. "It's an inside hurt. I can't put my finger on it, but it's there. She needs her home, her family. She needs her father."

"If Jo's got a problem, she'll deal with it. She always has."

"You mean she's always had to," Kate tossed back. She wanted to shake him until she'd loosened the lock he had snapped on his heart. "Damn it, Sam, be there for her."

He looked beyond Kate, to the marshes. "She's past the point where she needs me to bandage up her bumps and scratches."

"No, she's not." Kate dropped her hand from his arm. "She's still your daughter. She always will be. Belle wasn't the only one who went away, Sam." She watched his face close in as she said it and shook her head fiercely. "Brian and Jo and Lexy lost her, too. But they shouldn't have had to lose you."

His chest had tightened, and he turned away to stare out over the marsh, knowing that the pressure inside him would ease again if he was left alone. "I said I'd be up to the house later on. Jo Ellen has something to say to me, she can say it then."

"One of these days you're going to realize you've got something to say to her, to all of them."

She left him alone, hoping he would realize it soon.

4

Brian stood in the doorway of the west terrace and studied his sister. She looked frail, he noted, skittish. Lost somehow, he thought, amid the sunlight and flowers. She still wore the baggy trousers and oversized lightweight sweater that she'd arrived in, and had added a pair of round wire-framed sunglasses. Brian imagined that Jo wore just such a uniform when she hunted her photographs, but at the moment it served only to add to the overall impression of an invalid.

Yet she'd always been the tough one, he remembered. Even as a child she'd insisted on doing everything herself, on finding the answers, solving the puzzles, fighting the fights.

She'd been fearless, climbing higher in any tree, swimming farther beyond the waves, running faster through the forest. Just to prove she could, Brian mused. It seemed to him Jo Ellen had always had something to prove.

And after their mother had gone, Jo had seemed hell-bent on proving she needed no one and nothing but herself.

Well, Brian decided, she needed something now. He stepped out, saying nothing as she turned her head and looked at him from behind the tinted lenses. Then he sat down on the glider beside her and put the plate he'd brought out in her lap.

"Eat," was all he said.

Jo looked down at the fried chicken, the fresh slaw, the golden biscuit. "Is this the lunch special?"

"Most of the guests went for the box lunch today. Too nice to eat inside."

"Cousin Kate said you've been busy."

"Busy enough." Out of habit, he pushed off with his foot and set the glider in motion. "What are you doing here, Jo?"

"Seemed like the thing to do at the time." She lifted a drumstick, bit in. Her stomach did a quick pitch and roll as if debating whether to accept food. Jo persisted and swallowed. "I'll do my share, and I won't get in your way."

Brian listened to the squeak of the glider for a moment, thought about oiling the hinges. "I haven't said you were in my way, as I recollect," he said mildly.

"In Lexy's way, then." Jo took another bite of chicken, scowled at the soft-pink ivy geraniums spilling over the edges of a concrete jardiniere carved with chubby cherubs. "You can tell her I'm not here to cramp her style."

"Tell her yourself." Brian opened the thermos he'd brought along and poured freshly squeezed lemonade into the lid. "I'm not stepping between the two of you so I can get my ass kicked from both sides."

"Fine, stay out of it, then." Her head was beginning to ache, but she took the cup and sipped. "I don't know why the hell she resents me so much."

"Can't imagine." Brian drawled it before he lifted the thermos and drank straight from the lip. "You're successful, famous, financially independent, a rising star in your field. All the things she wants for herself." He picked up the biscuit and broke it in half, handing a portion to Jo as the steam burst out. "I can't think why that'd put her nose out of joint."

"I did it by myself for myself. I didn't work my butt off to get to this point to show her up." Without thinking, she stuffed a bite of biscuit in her mouth. "It's not my fault she's got some childish fantasy about seeing her name in lights and having people throw roses at her feet."

"Your seeing it as childish doesn't make the desire any less real for her." He held up a hand before Jo could speak. "And I'm not getting in the middle. The two of you are welcome to rip the hide off each other in your own good time. But I'd say right now she could take you without breaking a sweat."

"I don't want to fight with her," Jo said wearily. She could smell the wisteria that rioted over the nearby arched iron trellis—another vivid memory of childhood. "I didn't come here to fight with anyone."

"That'll be a change."

That lured a ghost of a smile to her lips. "Maybe I've mellowed."

"Miracles happen. Eat your slaw."

"I don't remember you being so bossy."

"I've cut back on mellow."

With what passed as a chuckle, Jo picked up her fork and poked at the slaw. "Tell me what's new around here, Bri, and what's the same." Bring me home, she thought, but couldn't say it. Bring me back.

"Let's see, Giff Verdon built on another room to the Verdon cottage."

"Stop the presses." Then Jo's brow furrowed. "Young Giff, the scrawny kid with the cowlick. The one who was always mooning over Lex?"

"That's the one. Filled out some, Giff has, and he's right handy with a hammer and saw. Does all our repair work now. Still moons over Lexy, but I'd say he knows what he wants to do about it now."

Jo snorted and, without thinking, shoveled in more slaw. "She'll eat him alive."

Brian shrugged. "Maybe, but I think she'll find him tougher to chew up than she might expect. The Sanders girl, Rachel, she got herself engaged to some college boy in Atlanta. Going to move there come September."

"Rachel Sanders." Jo tried to conjure up a mental image. "Was she the one with the lisp or the one with the giggle?"

"The giggle—sharp enough to make the ears bleed." Satisfied that Jo was eating, Brian stretched an arm over the back of the glider and relaxed. "Old Mrs. Fitzsimmons passed on more than a year back."

"Old Mrs. Fitzsimmons," Jo murmured. "She used to shuck oysters on her porch, with that lazy hound of hers sleeping at her feet beside the rocker."

"The hound passed, too, right after. Guess he didn't see much point in living without her."

"She let me take pictures of her," Jo remembered. "When I was a kid, just learning. I still have them. A couple weren't bad. Mr. David helped me develop them. I must have been such a pest, but she just sat there in her rocker and let me practice on her."

Sitting back, Jo fell into the rhythm of the glider, as slow and monotonous as the rhythm of the island. "I hope it was quick and painless."

"She died in her sleep at the ripe old age of ninety-six. Can't do much better than that."

"No." Jo closed her eyes, the food forgotten. "What was done with her cottage?"

"Passed down. The Pendletons bought most of the Fitzsimmons land back in 1923, but she owned her house and the little spit of land it sits on. Went to her granddaughter." Brian lifted the thermos again, drank deeply this time. "A doctor. She's set up a practice here on the island."

"We have a doctor on Desire?" Jo opened her eyes, lifted her brows. "Well, well. How civilized. Are people actually going to her?"

"Seems they are, little by little, anyway. She's dug her toes in."

"She must be the first new permanent resident here in what, ten years?"

"Thereabouts."

"I can't imagine why..." Jo trailed off as it struck her. "It's not Kirby, is it? Kirby Fitzsimmons? She spent summers here a couple of years running when we were kids."

"I guess she liked it well enough to come back."

"I'll be damned. Kirby Fitzsimmons, and a doctor, of all things." Pleasure bloomed, a surprising sensation she nearly didn't recognize. "We used to pal around together some. I remember the summer Mr. David came to take photographs of the island and brought his family."

It cheered her to think of it, the young friend with the quick northern voice, the adventures they'd shared or imagined together. "You would run off with his boys and wouldn't give me the time of day," Jo continued. "When I wasn't pestering Mr. David to let me take pictures with his camera, I'd go off with Kirby and look for trouble. Christ, that was twenty years ago if it was a day. It was the summer that..."

Brian nodded, then finished the thought. "The summer that Mama left."

"It's all out of focus," Jo murmured, and the pleasure died out of her voice. "Hot sun, long days, steamy nights so full of sound. All the faces." She slipped her fingers under her glasses to rub at her eyes. "Getting up at sunrise so I could follow Mr. David around. Bolting down cold ham sandwiches and cooling off in the river. Mama dug out that old camera for me—that ancient box Brownie—and I would run over to the Fitzsimmons cottage and take pictures until Mrs. Fitzsimmons told Kirby and me to scoot. There were hours and hours, so many hours, until the sun went down and Mama called us home for supper."

She closed her eyes tight. "So much, so many images, yet I can't bring any one of them really clear. Then she was gone. One morning I woke up ready to do all the things a long summer day called for, and she was just gone. And there was nothing to do at all."

"Summer was over," Brian said quietly. "For all of us."

"Yeah." Her hands had gone trembly again. Jo reached in her pockets for cigarettes. "Do you ever think about her?"

"Why would I?"

"Don't you ever wonder where she went? What she did?" Jo took a jerky drag. In her mind she saw long-lidded eyes empty of life. "Or why?"

"It doesn't have anything to do with me." Brian rose, took the plate. "Or you. Or any of us anymore. It's twenty years past that summer, Jo Ellen, and a little late to worry about it now."

She opened her mouth, then shut it again when Brian turned and walked back into the house. But she was worried about it, she thought. And she was terrified.

Lexy was still steaming as she climbed over the dunes toward the beach. Jo had come back, she was sure, to flaunt her success and her snazzy life. And the fact that she'd arrived at Sanctuary hard on the heels of Lexy's own failure didn't strike Lexy as coincidence.

Jo would flap her wings and crow in triumph, while Lexy would have to settle for eating crow. The thought of it made her blood boil as she raced along the tramped-down sand through the dunes, sending sand flying from her sandals.

Not this time, she promised herself. This time she would hold her head up, refuse to be cast as inferior in the face of Jo's latest triumph, latest trip, latest wonder. She wasn't going to play the hotshot's baby sister any longer. She'd outgrown that role, Lexy assured herself. And it was high time everyone realized it.

There was a scattering of people on the wide crescent of beach. They had staked their claims with their blankets and colorful umbrellas. She noted several with the brightly striped box lunches from Sanctuary.

The scents of sea and lotions and fried chicken assaulted her nostrils. A toddler shoveled sand into a red bucket while his mother read a paperback novel in the shade of a portable awning. A man was slowly turning into a lobster under the merciless sun. Two couples she had served that morning were sharing a picnic and laughing together over the clever voice of Annie Lennox on their portable stereo.

She didn't want them—any of them—to be there. On her beach, in her personal crisis. To dismiss them, she turned and walked away from the temporary development, down the curve of beach.

She saw the figure out in the water, the gleam of tanned, wet shoulders, the glint of sun-bleached hair. Giff was a reliable creature of habit, she thought, and he was just exactly what the doctor called for. He invariably took a quick swim during his afternoon break. And, Lexy knew, he had his eye on her.

He hadn't made a secret of it, she mused, and she wasn't one to resent the attentions of an attractive man. Particularly when she needed her ego soothed. She thought a little flirtation, and the possibility of mindless sex, might put the day back on track.

People said her mother had been a flirt. Lexy hadn't been old enough to remember anything more than vague images and soft scents when it came to Annabelle, but she believed she'd come by her skill at flirtation naturally. Her mother had enjoyed looking her best, smiling at men. And if the theory of a secret lover was fact, Annabelle had done more than smile at at least one man.

In any case, that's what the police had concluded after months of investigation.

Lexy thought she was good at sex; she had been told so often enough to consider it a fine personal skill. As far as she was concerned, there was little else that compared to it for shouldering away tension and being the focus of someone's complete attention.

And she liked it, all the hot, slick sensations that went with it. It hardly mattered that most men didn't have a clue whether a woman was thinking about them or the latest Hollywood pretty boy while it was going on. As long as she performed well and remembered the right lines.

Lexy considered herself born to perform.

And she decided it was time to open that velvet curtain for Giff Verdon.

She dropped the towel she'd brought with her onto the packed sand. She didn't have a doubt that he was watching her. Men did. As if onstage, Lexy put her heart into the performance. Standing near the edge of the water, she slipped off her sunglasses, let them fall heedlessly onto the towel. Slowly, she stepped out of her sandals, then, taking the hem of the short-skirted sundress she wore, she lifted it, making the movements a lazy striptease. The bikini underneath covered little more than a stripper's G-string and pasties would have.

Dropping the thin cotton, she shook her head, skimmed her hair back with both hands, then walked with a siren's swagger of hips into the sea.

Giff let the next wave roll over him. He knew that every movement, every gesture Lexy made was deliberate. It didn't seem to make any difference. He couldn't take his eyes off her, couldn't prevent his body from going tight and hard and needy as she stood there, all luscious curves and pale gold skin, with her hair spiraling down like sun-kissed flames.

As she walked into the water, and it moved up her body, he imagined what it would be like to rock himself inside her to the rhythm of the waves. She was watching him too, he noted, her eyes picking up the green of the sea, and laughing.

She dipped down, rose up again with her hair shiny and wet, water sliding off her skin. And she laughed out loud.

"Water's cold today," she called out. "And a little rough."

"You don't usually come in till June."

"Maybe I wanted it cold today." She let the wave carry her closer. "And rough."

"It'll be colder and rougher tomorrow," he told her. "Rain's coming."

"Mmm." She floated on her back a moment, studying the pale blue sky. "Maybe I'll come back." Letting her feet sink, she began to tread water as she watched him.

She'd grown accustomed to his dark brown eyes watching her like a puppy when they were teenagers. They were the same age, had grown up all but shoulder to shoulder, but she noticed there had been a few changes in him during her year in New York.

His face had fined down, and his mouth seemed firmer and more confident. The long lashes that had caused the boys to tease him mercilessly in his youth no longer seemed feminine. His light brown hair was needle-straight and streaked from the sun. When he smiled at her, dimples—another curse of his youth—dented his cheeks.

"See something interesting?" he asked her.

"I might." His voice matched his face, she decided. All grown-up and male. The flutter in her stomach was satisfying, and unexpectedly strong. "I just might."

"I figure you had a reason for swimming out here mostly naked. Not that I didn't enjoy the view, but you want to tell me what it is? Or do you want me to guess?"

She laughed, kicking against the current to keep a teasing distance between them. "Maybe I just wanted to cool off."

"I imagine so." He smiled back, satisfied that he understood her better than she could ever imagine. "I heard Jo came in on the morning ferry."

The smile slid away from her face and left her eyes cold. "So what?"

"So, you want to blow off some steam? Want to use me to do it?" When she hissed at him and started to kick out to swim back to shore, he merely nipped her by the waist. "I'll oblige you," he said as she tried to wiggle free. "I've been wanting to anyway."

"Get your hands—" The end of her demand was lost in a surprised grunt against his mouth. She'd never expected reliable Giff Verdon to move so quickly, or so decisively.

She hadn't realized his hands were so big, or so hard, or that his mouth would be so . . . sexy as it crushed down on hers with the cool tang of the sea clinging to it. For form's sake she shoved against him, but ruined it with a throaty little moan as her lips parted and invited more.

She tasted exactly as he'd imagined—hot and ready, the sex kitten mouth slippery and wet. The fantasies he'd woven for over ten years simply fell apart and reformed in fresh, wild colors threaded with helpless love and desperate need.

When she wrapped her legs around his waist, rocked her body against his, he was lost.

"I want you." He tore his mouth from hers to race it along her throat while the waves tossed them about and into a tangle of limbs. "Damn you, Lex, you know I've always wanted you."

Water flowed over her head, filled it with roaring. The sea sucked her down, made her giddy. Then she was in the dazzling sunlight again with his mouth fused to hers.

"Now, then. Right now." She panted it out, amazed at how real the need was, that tight, hot little ball of it. "Right here."

He'd wanted her like this as long as he could remember. Ready and willing and eager. His body pulsed toward pain with the need to be in her, and of her. And he knew if he let that need rule, he would take her and lose her in one flash.

Instead he slid his hands down from her waist to cup and knead her bottom, used his thumbs to torment her until her eyes went dark and blind. "I've waited, Lex." And let her go. "So can you."

She struggled to stay above the waves, sputtered out water as she gaped at him. "What the hell are you talking about?"

"I'm not interested in scratching your itch and then watching you walk off purring." He lifted a hand to push back his dripping hair. "When you're ready for more than that, you know where to find me."

"You son of a bitch."

"You go work off your mad, honey. We'll talk when you've had time to think it through calm." His hand shot out, grabbed her arm. "When I make love with you, that's going to be it for both of us. You'll want to think about that too."

She shoved his hand away. "Don't you touch me again, Giff Verdon."

"I'm going to do more than touch you," he told her as she dove under to swim toward shore. "I'm going to marry you," he said, only loud enough for his own ears. He let out a long breath as he watched her stride out of the water. "Unless I kill myself first."

To ease the throbbing in his system, he sank under the water. But as the taste of her continued to cling to his mouth, he decided he was either the smartest man on Desire or the stupidest.

Jo had just drummed up the energy to take a walk and had reached the edges of the garden when Lexy stormed up the path. She hadn't bothered to towel off, so the little sundress was plastered against her like skin. Jo straightened her shoulders, lifted an eyebrow.

"Well, how's the water?"

"Go to hell." Breath heaving, humiliation still stinging, Lexy planted her feet. "Just go straight to hell."

"I'm beginning to think I've already arrived. And so far my welcome's been pretty much as expected."

"Why should you expect anything? This place means nothing to you and neither do we."

"How do you know what means anything to me, Lexy?"

"I don't see you changing sheets, clearing tables. When's the last time you scrubbed a toilet or mopped a damn floor?"

"Is that what you've been doing this afternoon?" Jo skimmed her gaze up Lexy's damp and sandy legs to her dripping hair. "Must have been some toilet."

"I don't have to explain myself to you."

"Same goes, Lex." When Jo started to move past, Lexy grabbed her arm and jerked.

"Why did you come back here?"

Weariness swamped her suddenly, made her want to weep. "I don't know. But it wasn't to hurt you. It wasn't to hurt anybody. And I'm too tired to fight with you now."

Baffled, Lexy stared at her. The sister she knew would have waded in with words, scraped flesh with sarcasm. She'd never known Jo to tremble and back off. "What happened to you?"

"I'll let you know when I figure it out." Jo shook off the hand blocking her. "Leave me alone, and I'll do the same for you."

She walked quickly down the path, took its curve toward the sea. She barely glanced at the dune swale with its glistening grasses, never looked up to follow the flight of the gull that called stridently. She needed to think, she told herself. Just an hour or two of quiet thought. She would figure out what to do, how to tell them. If she should tell them at all.

Could she tell them about her breakdown? Could she tell anyone that she'd spent two weeks in the hospital because her nerves had snapped and something in her mind had tilted? Would they be sympathetic, ambivalent, or hostile?

And what did it matter?

How could she tell them about the photograph? No matter how often she was at sword's point with them, they were her family. How could she put them through that, dredging up the pain and the past? And if any of them demanded to see it, she would have to tell them it was gone.

Just like Annabelle.

Or it had never existed.

They would think her mad. Poor Jo Ellen, mad as a hatter.

Could she tell them she'd spent days trembling inside her apartment, doors locked, after she'd left the hospital? That she would catch herself searching mindlessly, frantically, for the print that would prove she wasn't really ill?

And that she had come home, because she'd finally had to accept that she was ill. That if she had stayed locked in that apartment alone for another day, she would never have found the courage to leave it again.

Still, the print was so clear in her mind. The texture, the tones, the composition. Her mother had been young in the photograph. And wasn't that the way Jo remembered her—young? The long waving hair, the smooth skin? If she was going to hallucinate about her mother, wouldn't she have snapped to just that age?

Nearly the same age she herself was now, Jo thought. That was probably another reason for all the dreams, the fears, the nerves. Had Annabelle been as restless and as edgy as her daughter was? Had there been a lover after all? There had been whispers of that, even a child had been able to hear them. There'd been no hint of one, no suspicion of infidelity before the desertion. But afterward the rumors had been rife, and tongues had clucked and wagged.

But then, Annabelle would have been discreet, and clever. She had given no hint of her plans to leave, yet she had left.

Wouldn't Daddy have known? Jo wondered. Surely a man knew if his wife was restless and dissatisfied and unhappy. She knew they had argued over the island. Had that been enough to do it, to make Annabelle so unhappy that she would turn her back on her home, her husband, her children? Hadn't he seen it, or had he even then been oblivious to the feelings of the people around him?

It was so hard to remember if it had ever been different. But surely there had once been laughter in that house. Echoes of it still lingered in her mind. Quick snapshots of her parents embracing in the kitchen, of her mother laughing, of walking on the beach with her father's hand holding hers.

They were dim pictures, faded with time as if improperly fixed, but they were there. And they were real. If she had managed to block so many memories of her mother out of her mind, then she could also bring them back. And maybe she would begin to understand.

Then she would decide what to do.

The crunch of a footstep made her look up quickly. The sun was behind him, casting him in shadow. A cap shielded his eyes. His stride was loose and leggy.

Another long-forgotten picture snapped into her mind. She saw herself as a little girl with flyaway hair racing down the path, giggling, calling, then leaping high. And his arms had reached out to catch her, to toss her high, then hug her close.

Jo blinked the picture away and the tears that wanted to come with it. He didn't smile, and she knew that no matter how she worked to negate it, he saw Annabelle in her.

She lifted her chin and met his eyes. "Hello, Daddy."

"Jo Ellen." He stopped a foot away and took her measure. He saw that Kate had been right. The girl looked ill, pale, and strained. Because he didn't know how to touch her, didn't believe she would welcome the touch in any case, he dipped his hands into his pockets. "Kate told me you were here."

"I came in on the morning ferry," she said, knowing the information was unnecessary.

For a difficult moment they stood there, more awkward than strangers. Sam shifted his feet. "You in trouble?"

"I'm just taking some time off."

"You look peaked."

"I've been working too hard."

Frowning, he looked deliberately at the camera hanging from a strap around her neck. "Doesn't look like you're taking time off to me."

In an absent gesture, she cupped a hand under the camera. "Old habits are hard to break."

"They are that." He huffed out a breath. "There's a pretty light on the water today, and the waves are up. Guess it'd make a nice picture."

"I'll check it out. Thanks."

"Take a hat next time. You'll likely burn."

"Yes, you're right. I'll remember."

He could think of nothing else, so he nodded and started up the path, moving past her. "Mind the sun."

"I will." She turned away quickly, walking blindly now because she had smelled the island on him, the rich, dark scent of it, and it broke her heart.

Miles away in the hot red glow of the darkroom light, he slipped paper, emulsion side up, into a tray of developing fluid. It pleased him to re-create the moment from so many years before, to watch it form on the paper, shadow by shadow and line by line.

He was nearly done with this phase and wanted to linger, to draw out all the pleasure before he moved on.

He had driven her back to Sanctuary. The idea made him chuckle and preen. Nothing could have been more perfect. It was there that he wanted her. Otherwise he would have taken her before, half a dozen times before.

But it had to be perfect. He knew the beauty of perfection and the satisfaction of working carefully toward creating it.

Not Annabelle, but Annabelle's daughter. A perfect circle closing. She would be his triumph, his masterpiece.

Claiming her, taking her, killing her.

And every stage of it would be captured on film. Oh, how Jo would appreciate that. He could barely wait to explain it all to her, the one person he was certain would understand his ambition and his art.

Her work drew him, and his understanding of it made him feel intimate with her already. And they would become more intimate yet.

Smiling, he shifted the print from the developing tray to the stop bath, swishing it through before lifting it into the fixer. Carefully, he checked the temperature of the wash, waiting patiently until the timer rang and he could switch on the white light and examine the print.

Beautiful, just beautiful. Lovely composition. Dramatic lighting—such a perfect halo over the hair, such lovely shadows to outline the body and highlight skin tones. And the subject, he thought. Perfection.

When the print was fully fixed, he lifted it out of the tray and into the running water of the wash. Now he could allow himself to dream of what was to come.

He was closer to her than ever, linked to her through the photographs that reflected each of their lives. He could barely wait to send her the next. But he knew he must choose the time with great care.

On the worktable beside him a battered journal lay open, its precisely written words faded from time.

The decisive moment is the ultimate goal in my work. Capturing that short, passing event where all the elements, all the dynamics of a subject reach a peak. What more decisive moment can there be than death? And how much more control can the photographer have over this moment, over the capturing of it on film, than to plan and stage and cause that death? That single act joins subject and artist, makes him part of the art, and the image created.

Since I will kill only one woman, manipulate only one decisive moment, I have chosen her with great care.

Her name is Annabelle.

With a quiet sigh, he hung the print to dry and turned on the white light to better study it.

"Annabelle," he murmured. "So beautiful. And your daughter is the image of you."

He left Annabelle there, staring, staring, and went out to complete his plans for his stay on Desire.

5

The ferry steamed across Pelican Sound, heading east to Lost Desire. Nathan Delaney stood at the starboard rail as he had once before as a ten-year-old boy. It wasn't the same ferry, and he was no longer a boy, but he wanted to re-create the moment as closely as possible.

It was cool with the breeze off the water, and the scent of it was raw and mysterious. It had been warmer before, but then it had been late May rather than mid-April.

Close enough, he thought, remembering how he and his parents and his young brother had all crowded together at the starboard rail of another ferry, eager for their first glimpse of Desire and the start of their island summer.

He could see little difference. Spearing up from the land were the majestic live oaks with their lacy moss, cabbage palms, and glossy-leaved magnolias not yet in bloom.

Had they been blooming then? A young boy eager for adventure paid little attention to flowers.

He lifted the binoculars that hung around his neck. His father had helped him aim and focus on that long-ago morning so that he could catch the quick dart of a woodpecker. The expected tussle had followed because Kyle had demanded the binoculars and Nathan hadn't wanted to give them up.

He remembered his mother laughing at them, and his father bending down to tickle Kyle to distract him. In his mind, Nathan could see the picture they had made. The pretty woman with her hair blowing, her dark eyes sparkling with amusement and excitement. The two young boys, sturdy and scrubbed, squabbling. And the man, tall and dark, long of leg and rangy of build.

Now, Nathan thought, he was the only one left. Somehow he had grown up into his father's body, had gone from sturdy boy to a man with long legs and narrow hips. He could look in a mirror and see reflections of his father's face in the hollow cheeks and dark gray eyes. But he had his mother's mouth, firmly ridged, and her deep brown hair with hints of gold and red. His father had said it was like aged mahogany.

Nathan wondered if children were really just montages of their parents. And he shuddered.

Without the binoculars he watched the island take shape. He could see the wash of color from wildflowers—pinks and violets from lupine and wood sorrel. A scatter of houses was visible, a few straight or winding roads, the flash of a creek that disappeared into the trees. Mystery was added by the dark shadows of the forest where feral pigs and horses had once lived, the gleam of the marshes and the blades of waving grasses gold and green in the streaming morning sunlight.

It was all hazed with distance, like a dream.

Then he saw the gleam of white on a rise, the quick wink that was sun shooting off glass. Sanctuary, he thought, and kept it in his sights until the ferry turned toward the dock and the house was lost from view.

Nathan turned from the rail and walked back to his Jeep. When he was settled inside with only the hum of the ferry's engines for company, he wondered if he was crazy coming back here, exploring the past, in some ways repeating it.

He'd left New York, packed everything that mattered into the Jeep. It was surprisingly little. Then again, he'd never had a deep-seated need for things. That had made his life simpler through the divorce two years before. Maureen had been the collector, and it saved them both a great deal of time and temper when he offered to let her strip the West Side apartment.

Christ knew she'd taken him up on it and had left him with little more than his own clothes and a mattress.

That chapter of his life was over, and for nearly two years now he'd devoted himself to his work. Designing buildings was as much a passion as a career for him, and with New York as no more than a home base, he had traveled, studying sites, working wherever he could set up his drawing board and computer. He'd given himself the gift of time to study other buildings, explore the art of them, from the great cathedrals in Italy and France to the streamlined desert homes in the American Southwest.

He'd been free, his work the only demand on his time and on his heart.

Then he had lost his parents, suddenly, irrevocably. And had lost himself. He wondered why he felt he could find the pieces on Desire.

But he was committed to staying at least six months. Nathan took it as a good sign that he'd been able to book the same cottage his family had lived in during that summer. He knew he would listen for the echo of their voices and would hear them with a man's ear. He would see their ghosts with a man's eyes.

And he would return to Sanctuary with a man's purpose.

Would they remember him? The children of Annabelle?

He would soon find out, he decided, when the ferry bumped up to the dock.

He waited his turn, watching as the blocks were removed from the tires of the pickup ahead of him. A family of five, he noted, and from the gear he could see that they would be camping at the facility the island provided. Nathan shook his head, wondering why anyone would choose to sleep in a tent on the ground and consider it a vacation.

The light dimmed as clouds rolled over the sun. Frowning, he noted that they were coming in fast, flying in from the east. Rain could come quickly to barrier islands, he knew. He remembered it falling in torrents for three endless days when he'd been there before. By day two he and Kyle had been at each other's throats like young wolves.

It made him smile now and wonder how in God's name his mother had tolerated it.

He drove slowly off the ferry, then up the bumpy, pitted road leading away from the dock. With his windows open he could hear the cheerfully blaring rock and roll screaming out of the truck's radio. Camper Family, he thought, was already having a great time, impending rain or not. He was determined to follow their example and enjoy the morning.

He would have to face Sanctuary, of course, but he would approach it as an architect. He remembered that its heart was a glorious example of the Colonial style—wide verandas, stately columns, tall, narrow windows. Even as a child he'd been interested enough to note some of the details.

Gargoyle rainspouts, he recalled, that personalized rather than detracted from the grand style. He'd scared the piss out of Kyle by telling him they came alive at night and prowled.

There was a turret, with a widow's walk circling it. Balconies jutting out with ornate railings of stone or iron. The chimneys were soft-hued stones mined from the mainland, the house itself fashioned of local cypress and oak.

There was a smokehouse that had still been in use, and slave quarters that had been falling to ruin, where he and Brian and Kyle had found a rattler curled in a dark corner.

There were deer in the forest and alligators in the marshes. Whispers of pirates and ghosts filled the air. It was a fine place for young boys and grand adventures. And for dark and dangerous secrets.

He passed the western marshlands with their busy mud and thin islands of trees. The wind had picked up, sending the cordgrass rippling. Along the edge two egrets were on patrol, their long legs like stilts in the shallow water.

Then the forest took over, lush and exotic. Nathan slowed, letting the truck ahead of him rattle out of sight. Here was stillness, and those dark secrets. His heart began to pound uncomfortably, and his hands tightened on the wheel. This was something he'd come to face, to dissect, and eventually to understand.

The shadows were thick, and the moss dripped from the trees like webs of monstrous spiders. To test himself he turned off the engine. He could hear nothing but his own heartbeat and the voice of the wind.

Ghosts, he thought. He would have to look for them there. And when he found them, what then? Would he leave them where they drifted, night after night, or would they continue to haunt him, muttering to him in his sleep?

Would he see his mother's face, or Annabelle's? And which one would cry out the loudest?

He let out a long breath, caught himself reaching for the cigarettes he'd given up over a year before. Annoyed, he turned the ignition key but got only a straining rumble in return. He pumped the gas, tried it again with the same results.

"Well, shit," he muttered. "That's perfect."

Sitting back, he tapped his fingers restlessly on the wheel. The thing to do, of course, was to get out and look under the hood. He knew what he would see. An engine. Wires and tubes and belts. Nathan figured he knew as much about engines and wires and tubes as he did about brain surgery. And being broken down on a deserted road was exactly what he deserved for letting himself be talked into buying a friend's secondhand Jeep.

Resigned, he climbed out and popped the hood. Yep, he thought, just as he'd suspected. An engine. He leaned in, poked at it, and felt the first fat drop of rain hit his back.

"Now it's even more perfect." He shoved his hands in the front pockets of his jeans and scowled, continued to scowl while the rain pattered on his head.

He should have known something was up when his friend had cheerfully tossed in a box of tools along with the Jeep. Nathan considered hauling them out and beating on the engine with a wrench. It was unlikely to work, but it would at least be satisfying.

He stepped back, then froze as the ghost stepped out of the forest shadows and watched him.

Annabelle.

The name swam through his mind, and his gut clenched in defense. She stood in the rain, still as a doe, her smoky red hair damp and tangled, those big blue eyes quiet and sad. His knees threatened to give way, and he braced a hand on the fender.

Then she moved, pushed back her wet hair. And started toward him. He saw then that it was no ghost, but a woman. It was not Annabelle, but, he was sure, it was Annabelle's daughter.

He let out the breath he'd been holding until his heart settled again.

"Car trouble?" Jo tried to keep her voice light. The way he was staring at her made her wish she'd stayed in the trees and let him fend for himself. "I take it you're not standing here in the rain taking in the sights."

"No." It pleased him that his voice was normal. If there was an edge to it, the situation was cause enough to explain it. "It won't start."

"Well, that's a problem." He looked vaguely familiar, she thought. A good face, strong and bony and male. Interesting eyes as well, she mused, pure gray and very direct. If she were inclined to portrait photography, he'd have been a fine subject. "Did you find the trouble?"

Her voice was honey over cream, gorgeously southern. It helped him relax. "I found the engine," he said and smiled. "Just where I suspected it would be."

"Uh-huh. And now?"

"I'm deciding how long I should look at it and pretend I know what I'm looking at before I get back in out of the rain."

"You don't know how to fix your car?" she asked, with such obvious surprise that he bristled.

"No, I don't. I also own shoes and don't have a clue how to tan leather." He started to yank down the hood, but she raised a hand to hold it open.

"I'll take a look."

"What are you, a mechanic?"

"No, but I know the basics." Elbowing him aside, she checked the battery connections first. "These look all right, but you're going to want to keep an eye on them for corrosion if you're spending any time on Desire."

"Six months or so." He leaned in with her. "What am I keeping my eye on?"

"These. Moisture can play hell with engines around here. You're crowding me."

"Sorry." He shifted his position. Obviously she didn't remember him, and he decided to pretend he didn't remember her. "You live on the island?"

"Not anymore." To keep from bumping it on the Jeep, Jo moved the camera slung around her neck to her back.

Nate stared at it, felt the low jolt. It was a high-end Nikon. Compact, quieter and more rugged than other designs, it was often a professional's choice. His father had had one. He had one himself.

"Been out taking pictures in the rain?"

"Wasn't raining when I left," she said absently. "Your fan belt's going to need replacing before long, but that's not your problem now." She straightened, and though the skies had opened wide, seemed oblivious to the downpour. "Get in and try it so I can hear what she sounds like."

"You're the boss."

Her lips twitched as he turned and climbed back into the Jeep. No doubt his male ego was dented, she decided. She cocked her head as the engine groaned. Lips pursed, she leaned back under the hood. "Again!" she called out to him, muttering to herself. "Carburetor."

"What?"

"Carburetor," she repeated and opened the little metal door with her thumb. "Turn her over again."

This time the engine roared to life. With a satisfied nod, she shut the hood and walked around to the driver's side window. "It's sticking closed, that's all. You're going to want to have it looked at. From the sound of it, you need a tune-up anyway. When's the last time you had it in?"

"I just bought it a couple of weeks ago. From a former friend."

"Ah. Always a mistake. Well, it should get you where you're going now."

When she started to step back, he reached through the window for her hand. It was narrow, he noted, long, both elegant and competent. "Listen, let me give you a lift. It's pouring, and it's the least I can do."

"It's not necessary. I can—"

"I could break down again." He shot her a smile, charming, easy, persuasive. "Who'll fix my carburetor?"

It was foolish to refuse, she knew. More foolish to feel trapped just because he had her hand. She shrugged. "All right, then." She gave her hand a little tug, was relieved when he immediately released it. She jogged around the Jeep and climbed dripping into the passenger seat.

"Well, the interior's in good shape."

"My former friend knows me too well." Nathan turned on the wipers and looked at Jo. "Where to?"

"Up this road, then bear right at the first fork. Sanctuary isn't far—but then nothing is on Desire."

"That's handy. I'm heading to Sanctuary myself."

"Oh?" The air in the cab was thick and heavy. The driving rain seemed to cut them off from everything, misting out the trees, muffling all the sound. Reason enough to be uncomfortable, she told herself, but she was sufficiently annoyed with her reaction to angle her head and meet his eyes directly. "Are you staying at the big house?"

"No, just picking up keys for the cottage I'm renting."

"For six months, you said?" It relieved her when he began to drive, turned those intense gray eyes away from her face and focused on the road. "That's a long vacation."

"I brought work with me. I wanted a change of scene for a while."

"Desire's a long way from home," she said, then smiled a little when he glanced at her. "Anyone from Georgia can spot a Yankee. Even if you keep your mouth shut, you move differently." She pushed her wet hair back. If she'd walked, Jo thought, she'd have been spared making conversation. But talk was better than the heavy, rain-drenched silence. "You've got Little Desire Cottage, by the river."

"How do you know?"

"Oh, everybody knows everything around here. But my family rents the cottages, runs them and the inn, the restaurant. As it happens I was assigned Little Desire, stocked the linens and so forth just yesterday for the Yankee who's coming to stay for six months."

"So you're my mechanic, landlord, and housekeeper. I'm a lucky man. Who exactly do I call if my sink backs up?"

"You open the closet and take out the plunger. If you need instructions for use, I'll write them down for you. Here's the fork."

Nathan bore right and climbed. "Let's try that again. If I wanted to grill a couple of steaks, chill a bottle of wine, and invite you to dinner, who would I call?"

Jo turned her head and gave him a cool look. "You'd have better luck with my sister. Her name is Alexa."

"Does she fix carburetors?"

With a half laugh, Jo shook her head. "No, but she's very decorative and enjoys invitations from men."

"And you don't?"

"Let's just say I'm more selective than Lexy."

"Ouch." Whistling, Nathan rubbed a hand over his heart. "Direct hit."

"Just saving us both some time. There's Sanctuary," she murmured.

He watched it appear through the curtain of rain, swim out of the thin mists that curled at its base. It was old and grand, as elegant as a Southern Belle dressed for company. Definitely feminine, Nate thought, with those fluid lines all in virginal white. Tall windows were softened by arched trim, and pretty ironwork adorned balconies where flowers bloomed out of clay pots of soft red.

Her gardens glowed, the blooms heavy-headed with rain, like bowing fairies at her feet.

"Stunning," Nathan said, half to himself. "The more recent additions blend perfectly with the original structure. Accent rather than modernize. It's a masterful harmony of styles, classically southern without being typical. It couldn't be more perfect if the island had been designed for it rather than it being designed for the island."

Nathan stopped at the end of the drive before he noticed that Jo was staring at him. For the first time there was curiosity in her eyes.

"I'm an architect," he explained. "Buildings like this grab me right by the throat."

"Well, then, you'll probably want a tour of the inside."

"I'd love one, and I'd owe you at least one steak dinner for that."

"You'll want my cousin Kate to show you around. She's a Pendleton," Jo added as she opened her door. "Sanctuary came down through the Pendletons. She knows it best. Come inside. You can dry off some and pick up the keys."

She hurried up the steps, paused on the veranda to shake her head and scatter rain from her hair. She waited until he stepped up beside her.

"Jesus, look at this door." Reverently, Nathan ran his fingertips over the rich, carved wood. Odd that he'd forgotten it, he thought. But then, he had usually raced in through the screened porch and through the kitchen.

"Honduran mahogany," Jo told him. "Imported in the early eighteen-hundreds, long before anyone worried about depleting the rain forests. But it is beautiful." She turned the heavy brass handle and stepped with him into Sanctuary.

"The floors are heart of pine," she began and blocked out an unbidden image of her mother patiently paste-waxing them. "As are the main stairs, and the banister is oak carved and constructed here on Desire when it was a plantation, dealing mostly in Sea Island cotton. The chandelier is more recent, an addition purchased in France by the wife of Stewart Pendleton, the shipping tycoon who rebuilt the main house and added the wings. A great deal of the furniture was lost during the War Between the States, but Stewart and his wife traveled extensively and selected antiques that suited them and Sanctuary."

"He had a good eye," Nathan commented, scanning the wide, high-ceilinged foyer with its fluid sweep of glossy stairs, its glittering fountain of crystal light.

"And a deep pocket," Jo put in. Telling herself to be patient, she stood where she was and let him wander.

The walls were a soft, pale yellow that would give the illusion of cool during those viciously hot summer afternoons. They were trimmed in dark wood that added richness with carved moldings framing the high plaster ceiling.

The furnishings here were heavy and large in scale, as befitted a grand entranceway. A pair of George II armchairs with shell-shaped backs flanked a hexagonal credence table that held a towering brass urn filled with sweetly scented lilies and wild grasses.

Though he didn't collect antiques himself—or anything else, for that matter—he was a man who studied all aspects of buildings, including what went inside them. He recognized the Flemish cabinet-on-stand in carved oak, the gilt wood pier mirror over a marquetry candle stand, the delicacy of Queen Anne and the flash of Louis XIV. And he found the mix of periods and styles inspired.

"Incredible." His hands tucked in his back pockets, he turned back to Jo. "Hell of a place to live, I'd say."

"In more ways than one." Her voice was dry, and just a little bitter. It had him lifting a brow in question, but she added nothing more. "We do registration in the front parlor."

She turned down the hallway, stepped into the first room on the right. Someone had started a fire, she observed, probably in anticipation of the Yankee, and to keep the guests at the inn cheerful on a rainy day if they wandered through.

She went to the huge old Chippendale writing desk and opened the top side drawer, flipped through the paperwork for the rental cottages. Upstairs in the family wing was an office with a workaday file cabinet and a computer Kate was still struggling to learn about. But guests were never subjected to such drearily ordinary details.

"Little Desire Cottage," Jo announced, sliding the contract free. She noted it had already been stamped to indicate receipt of the deposit and signed by both Kate and one Nathan Delaney.

Jo laid the paperwork aside and opened another drawer to take out the keys jingling from a metal clip that held the cottage name. "This one is for both the front and the rear doors, and the smaller one is for the storage room under the cottage. I wouldn't store anything important in there if I were you. Flooding is a hazard that near the river."

"I'll remember that."

"I took care of setting up the telephone yesterday. All calls will be billed directly to the cottage and added to your bill monthly." She opened another drawer and took out a slim folder. "You'll find the usual information and answers in this packet. The ferry schedule, tide information, how to rent fishing or boating gear, if you want it. There's a pamphlet that describes the island—history, flora and fauna—Why are you staring at me like that?" she demanded.

"You've got gorgeous eyes. It's hard not to look at them."

She shoved the folder into his hands. "You'd be better off looking at what's in here."

"All right." Nathan opened it, began to page through. "Are you always this jittery, or do I bring that out in you?"

"I'm not jittery, I'm impatient. Not all of us are on vacation. Do you have any questions—that pertain to the cottage or the island?"

"I'll let you know."

"Directions to your cottage are in the folder. If you'd just initial the contract here, to confirm receipt of the keys and information, you can be on your way."

He smiled again, intrigued at how rapidly her southern hospitality was thinning. "I wouldn't want to wear out my welcome," he said, taking the pen she offered him. "Since I intend to come back."

"Breakfast, lunch, and dinner are served in the inn's dining room. The service hours are also listed in your folder. Box lunches are available for picnics."

The more she talked, the more he enjoyed hearing her voice. She smelled of rain and nothing else and looked—when you looked into those lovely blue eyes—as sad as a bird with a broken wing.

"Do you like picnics?" he asked her.

She let out a long sigh, snatched the pen back from him, and scrawled her initials under his. "You're wasting your time flirting with me, Mr. Delaney. I'm just not interested."

"Any sensible woman knows that a statement like that only presents a challenge." He bent down to read her initials, "J.E.H."

"Jo Ellen Hathaway," she told him in hopes of hurrying him along.

"It's been a pleasure being rescued by you, Jo Ellen." He offered a hand, amused when she hesitated before clasping it with hers.

"Try Zeke Fitzsimmons about that tune-up. He'll get the Jeep running smoothly for you. Enjoy your stay on Desire."

"It's already started on a higher note than I'd expected."

"Then your expectations must have been very low." She slid her hand free and led the way back to the front door. "The rain's let up," she commented, as she opened the door to moist air and mist. "You shouldn't have any trouble finding the cottage."

"No." He remembered the way perfectly. "I'm sure I won't. I'll see you again, Jo Ellen." Will have to, he thought, for a number of reasons.

She inclined her head, shut the door quietly, and left him standing on the veranda wondering what to do next.

6

On his third day on Desire, Nathan woke in a panic. His heart was booming, his breath short and strangled, his skin iced with sweat. He shot up in bed with fists clenched, his eyes searching the murky shadows of the room.

Weak sunlight filtered through the slats of the blinds and built a cage on the thin gray carpet.

His mind stayed blank for an agonizing moment, trapped behind the images that crowded it. Moonlit trees, fingers of fog, a woman's naked body, her fanning dark hair, wide, glassy eyes.

Ghosts, he told himself as he rubbed his face hard with his hands. He'd expected them, and they hadn't disappointed him. They clung to Desire like the moss clung to the live oaks.

He swung out of bed and deliberately—like a child daring sidewalk cracks—walked through the sun bars. In the narrow bathroom he stepped into the white tub, yanked the cheerfully striped curtain closed, and ran the shower hot. He washed the sweat away, imagined the panic as a dark red haze that circled and slid down the drain.

The room was thick with steam when he dried off. But his mind was clear again.

He dressed in a tattered short-sleeved sweatshirt and ancient gym shorts, then with his face unshaven and his hair dripping headed into the kitchen to heat water for instant coffee. He looked around, scowled again at the carafe and drip cone the owners had provided. Even if he could have figured out the proper measuring formula, he hadn't thought to bring coffee filters.

At that moment he would have paid a thousand dollars for a coffeemaker. He set the kettle on the front burner of a stove that was older than he was, then walked over to the living room section of the large multipurpose room to flip on the early news. The reception was miserable, and the pickings slim.

No coffeemaker, no pay-per-view, Nathan mused as he tuned in the sunrise news on one of the three available channels. He remembered how he and Kyle had whined over the lack of televised entertainment.

How are we supposed to watch The Six Million Dollar Man *on this stupid thing? It's a gyp.*

You're not here to keep your noses glued to the TV screen.

Aw, Mom.

It seemed to him the color scheme was different now. He had a vague recollection of soft pastels on the wide, deep chairs and straight-backed sofa. Now they were covered in bold geometric prints, deep greens and blues, sunny yellows.

The fan that dropped from the center pitch of the ceiling had squeaked. He knew, because he'd been compelled to tug on the cord, that it ran now with only a quiet hiss of blades.

But it was the same long yellow-pine dining table separating the rooms—the table he and his family had gathered around to eat, to play board games, to put together eye-crossingly complex jigsaw puzzles during that summer.

The same table he and Kyle had been assigned to clear after dinner. The table where his father had lingered some mornings over coffee.

He remembered when their father had shown him and Kyle how to punch holes in the lid of a jar and catch lightning bugs. The evening had been warm and soft, the hunt and chase giddy. Nathan remembered watching the jar he'd put beside his bed wink and glow, wink and glow, lulling him to sleep.

But in the morning all the lightning bugs in his jar had been dead, smothered, as the book atop the lid had plugged all the holes. He still couldn't remember putting it there, that battered copy of *Johnny Tremaine.* The dark corpses in the bottom of the jar had left him feeling sick and guilty. He'd snuck out of the house and dumped them in the river.

He chased no more lightning bugs that summer.

Irritated at the memory, Nathan turned away from the TV, went back to the stove to pour the steaming water over a spoonful of coffee. He carried the mug out onto the screened porch to look at the river.

Memories were bound to surface now that he was here, he reminded himself. That was why he'd come. To remember that summer, step by step, day by day. And to figure out what to do about the Hathaways.

He sipped coffee, winced a little at its false and bitter taste. He'd discovered that a great deal of life was false and bitter, so he drank again.

Jo Ellen Hathaway. He remembered her as a skinny, sharp-elbowed girl with a sloppy ponytail and a lightning temper. He hadn't had much use for girls at ten, so he'd paid her little attention. She'd simply been one of Brian's little sisters.

Still was, Nathan thought. And she was still skinny. Apparently her temper was still in place as well. The streaming ponytail was gone. The shorter, choppy cut suited her personality if not her face, he decided. The carelessness of it, the nod to fashion. The color of it was like the pelt of a wild deer.

He wondered why she looked so pale and tired. She didn't seem the type to pine away over a shattered affair or relationship, but something was hurting. Her eyes were full of sorrow and secrets.

And that was the problem, Nathan thought with a half laugh. He had a weakness for sad-eyed women.

Better to resist it, he told himself. Wondering what was going on behind those big, sad, bluebell eyes was bound to interfere with his purpose. What he needed was time and objectivity before he took the next step.

He sipped more coffee, told himself he'd get dressed shortly and walk to Sanctuary for a decent cup and some breakfast. It was time to go back, to observe and to plan. Time to stir more ghosts.

But for now he just wanted to stand here, look through the thin mesh of screen, feel the damp air, watch the sun slowly burn away the pearly mists that clung to the ground and skimmed like fairy wings over the river.

He could hear the ocean if he listened for it, a low, constant rumble off to the east. Closer he could identify the chirp of birds, the monotonous drumming of a woodpecker hunting insects somewhere in the shadows of the forest. Dew glistened like shards of glass on the leaves of cabbage palms and palmettos, and there was no wind to stir them and make them rattle.

Whoever chose this spot for the cottage chose well, he thought. It sang of solitude, offered view and privacy. The structure itself was simple and functional. A weathered cedar box on stilts with a generous screened porch on the west end, a narrow open deck on the east. Inside, the main room had a pitched ceiling to add space and an open feel. On each end were two bedrooms and a bath.

He and Kyle had each had a room in one half. As the elder, he laid claim to the larger room. The double bed made him feel very grown-up and superior. He made a sign for the door: Please Knock Before Entering.

He liked to stay up late, reading his books, thinking his thoughts, listening to the murmur of his parents' voices or the drone of the TV. He liked to hear them laugh at something they were watching.

His mother's quick chuckle, his father's deep belly laugh. He'd heard those sounds often throughout his childhood. It grieved him that he would never hear them again.

A movement caught his eye. Nathan turned his head, and where he'd expected a deer he saw a man, slipping along the river bank like the mist. He was tall and lanky, his hair dark as soot.

Because his throat had gone dry, Nathan forced himself to lift his mug and drink again. He continued to watch as the man walked closer, as the strengthening sun slanted over his face.

Not Sam Hathaway, Nathan realized as the beginnings of a smile tugged at his lips. Brian. Twenty years had made them both men.

Brian glanced up, squinted, focused on the figure behind the screen. He'd forgotten the cottage was occupied now and made a note to himself to remember to take his walks on the opposite side of the river. Now, he supposed, he would have to make some attempt at conversation.

He lifted a hand. "Morning. Didn't mean to disturb you."

"You didn't. I was just drinking bad coffee and watching the river."

The Yankee, Brian remembered, a six-month rental. He could all but hear Kate telling him to be polite, to be sociable. "It's a nice spot." Brian stuck his hands in his pockets, annoyed that he'd inadvertently sabotaged his own solitude. "You settling in all right?"

"Yeah, I'm settled." Nathan hesitated, then took the next step. "Are you still hunting the Ghost Stallion?"

Brian blinked, cocked his head. The Ghost Stallion was a legend that stretched back to the days when wild horses had roamed the island. It was said that the greatest of these, a huge black stallion of unparalleled speed, ran the woods. Whoever caught him, leaped onto his back, and rode would have all his wishes granted.

Throughout childhood it had been Brian's deepest ambition to be the one to catch and ride the Ghost Stallion.

"I keep an eye out for him," Brian murmured and stepped closer. "Do I know you?"

"We camped out one night, across the river, in a patched pup tent. We had a rope halter, a couple of flashlights, and a bag of Fritos. Once we thought we heard hooves pounding, and a high, wild whinny." Nathan smiled. "Maybe we did."

Brian's eyes widened and the shadows in them cleared away. "Nate? Nate Delaney? Son of a bitch!"

The screen door squeaked in welcome when Nathan pushed it open. "Come on up, Bri. I'll fix you a cup of lousy coffee."

Grinning, Brian climbed up the stairs. "You should have let me know you were coming, that you were here." Brian shot out a hand, gripped Nathan's. "My cousin Kate handles the cottages. Jesus, Nate, you look like a derelict."

With a rueful smile, Nathan rubbed a hand over the stubble on his chin. "I'm on vacation."

"Well, ain't this a kick in the ass. Nate Delaney." Brian shook his head. "What the hell have you been doing all these years? How's Kyle, your parents?"

The smile faltered. "I'll tell you about it." Pieces of it, Nathan thought. "Let me make that lousy coffee first."

"Hell, no. Come on up to the house. I'll fix you a decent cup. Some breakfast."

"All right. Let me get some pants and shoes on."

"I can't believe you're our Yankee," Brian commented as Nathan started inside. "Goddamn, this takes me back."

Nathan turned back briefly. "Yeah, me too."

A short time later Nathan was sitting at the kitchen counter of Sanctuary, breathing in the heavenly scents of coffee brewing and bacon frying. He watched Brian deftly chopping mushrooms and peppers for an omelette.

"Looks like you know what you're doing."

"Didn't you read your pamphlet? My kitchen has a five-star rating." Brian slid a mug of coffee under Nathan's nose. "Drink, then grovel."

Nathan sipped, closed his eyes in grateful pleasure. "I've been drinking sand for the last two days and that may be influencing me, but I'd say this is the best cup of coffee ever brewed in the civilized world."

"Damn right it is. Why haven't you come up before this?"

"I've been getting my bearings, being lazy." Getting acquainted with ghosts, Nathan thought. "Now that I've sampled this, I'll be a regular."

Brian tossed his chopped vegetables into a skillet to sauté, then began grating cheese. "Wait till you get a load of my omelette. So what are you, independently wealthy that you can take six months off to sit on the beach?"

"I brought work with me. I'm an architect. As long as I have my computer and my drawing board, I can work anywhere."

"An architect." Whisking eggs, Brian leaned against the counter. "You any good?"

"I'd put my buildings against your coffee any day."

"Well, then." Chuckling, Brian turned back to the stove. With the ease of experience he poured the egg mixture, set bacon to drain, checked the biscuits he had browning in the oven. "So what's Kyle up to? He ever get rich and famous like he wanted?"

It was a stab, hard and fast in the center of the heart. Nathan put the mug down and waited for his hands and voice to steady. "He was working on it. He's dead, Brian. He died a couple of months ago."

"Jesus, Nathan." Shocked, Brian swung around. "Jesus, I'm sorry."

"He was in Europe. He'd been more or less living there the last couple of years. He was on a yacht, some party. Kyle liked to party," Nathan murmured, rubbing his temple. "They were tooling around the Med. The verdict was he must have had too much to drink and fallen overboard. Maybe he hit his head. But he was gone."

"That's rough. I'm sorry." Brian turned back to his skillet. "Losing family takes a chunk out of you."

"Yeah, it does." Nathan drew a deep breath, braced himself. "It happened just a few weeks after my parents were killed. Train wreck in South America. Dad was on assignment, and ever since Kyle and I hit college age, Mom traveled with him. She used to say it made them feel like newlyweds all the time."

"Christ, Nate, I don't know what to say."

"Nothing." Nathan lifted his shoulders. "You get through. I figure Mom would have been lost without Dad, and I don't know how either one of them would have handled losing Kyle. You've got to figure everything happens for a reason, and you get through."

"Sometimes the reason stinks," Brian said quietly.

"A whole hell of a lot of the time the reason stinks. Doesn't change anything. It's good to be back here. It's good to see you."

"We had some fine times that summer."

"Some of the best of my life." Nathan worked up a smile. "Are you going to give me that omelette, or are you going to make me beg for it?"

"No begging necessary." Brian arranged the food on a plate. "Genuflecting afterward is encouraged."

Nathan picked up a fork and dug in. "So, fill me in on the last two decades of the adventures of Brian Hathaway."

"Not much of an adventure. Running the inn takes a lot of time. We get guests year-round now. Seems the more crowded and busy life in the outside world gets, the more people want to get the hell away from it. For weekends, anyhow. And when they do, we house them, feed them, entertain them."

"It sounds like a twenty-four/seven proposition."

"Would be, on the outside. Life still moves slower around here."

"Wife, kids?"

"Nope. You?"

"I had a wife," Nathan said dryly. "We gave each other up. No kids. You know, your sister checked me in. Jo Ellen."

"Did she?" Brian brought the pot over to top off Nathan's cup. "She just got here herself about a week ago. Lex is here, too. We're one big happy family."

As Brian turned away, Nathan lifted his eyebrows at the tone. "Your dad?"

"You couldn't dynamite him off Desire. He doesn't even go over to the mainland for supplies anymore. You'll see him wandering around." He glanced over as Lexy swung through the door.

"We've got a couple of early birds panting for coffee," she began. Then, spotting Nathan, she paused. Automatically she flipped back her hair, angled her head, and aimed a flirtatious smile. "Well, kitchen company." She strolled closer to pose against the counter and give him a whiff of the Eternity she'd rubbed on her throat from a magazine sample that morning. "You must be special if Brian's let you into his domain."

Nathan's hormones did the quick, instinctive dance that made him want to laugh at both of them. A gorgeous piece of fluff was his first impression, but he revised it when he took a good look into her eyes. They were sharp and very self-aware. "He took pity on an old friend," Nathan told her.

"Really." She liked the rough-edged look of him, and pleased herself by basking in the easy male approval on his face. "Well, then, Brian, introduce me to your old friend. I didn't know you had any."

"Nathan Delaney," Brian said shortly, going over to fetch the second pot of freshly brewed coffee. "My kid sister, Lexy."

"Nathan." Lexy offered a hand she'd manicured in Flame Red. "Brian still sees me in pigtails."

"Big brother's privilege." It surprised Nathan to find the siren's hand firm and capable. "Actually, I remember you in pigtails myself."

"Do you?" Mildly disappointed that he hadn't lingered over her hand, Lexy folded her elbows on the bar and leaned toward him. "I can't believe I've forgotten you. I make it a policy to remember all the attractive men who've come into my life. However briefly."

"You were barely out of diapers," Brian put in, his voice dripping sarcasm, "and hadn't polished your femme-fatale routine yet. Cheese and mushroom omelettes are the breakfast special," he told her, ignoring the vicious look she shot in his direction.

She caught herself before she snarled, made her lips curve up. "Thanks, sugar." She purred it as she took the coffeepot he thrust at her, then she fluttered her lashes at Nathan. "Don't be a stranger. We get so few interesting men on Desire."

Because it seemed foolish to resist the treat, and she seemed so obviously to expect it, Nathan watched her sashay out, then turned back to Brian with a slow grin. "That's some baby sister you've got there, Bri."

"She needs a good walloping. Coming on to strange men that way."

"It was a nice side dish with my omelette." But Nathan held up a hand as Brian's eyes went hot. "Don't worry about me, pal. That kind of heartthrob means major headaches. I've got enough problems. You can bet your ass I'll look, but I don't plan to touch."

"None of my business," Brian muttered. "She's bound and determined not just to look for trouble but to find it."

"Women who look like that usually slide their way out of it too." He swiveled when the door opened again. This time it was Jo who walked through it.

And women who look like that, Nathan thought, don't slide out of trouble. They punch their way out.

He wondered why he preferred that kind of woman, and that kind of method.

Jo stopped when she saw him. Her brows drew together before she deliberately smoothed her forehead. "You look right at home, Mr. Delaney."

"Feeling that way, Miss Hathaway."

"Well, that's pretty formal," Brian commented as he reached for a clean mug, "for a guy who pushed her into the river, then got a bloody lip for his trouble when he tried to fish her out again."

"I didn't push her in." Nathan smiled slowly as he watched Jo's brows knit again. "She slipped. But she did bloody my lip and call me a Yankee pig bastard, as I recall."

The memory circled around her mind, nearly skipped away, then popped clear. Hot summer afternoon, the shock of cool water, head going under. And coming up swinging. "You're Mr. David's boy." The warmth spread in her stomach and up to her heart. For a moment her eyes reflected it and made his pulse trip. "Which one?"

"Nathan, the older."

"Of course." She skimmed her hair back, not with the studied seductiveness of her sister but with absentminded impatience. "And you did push me. I never fell in the river unless I wanted to or was helped along."

"You slipped," Nathan corrected, "then I helped you along."

She laughed, a quick, rich chuckle, then took the mug Brian offered. "I suppose I can let bygones be, since I gave you a fat lip—and your father gave me the world."

Nathan's head began to throb, fast and vicious. "My father?"

"I dogged him like a shadow, pestered him mercilessly about how he took pictures, why he took the ones he did, how the camera worked. He was so patient with me. I must have been driving him crazy, interrupting his work that way, but he never shooed me away. He taught me so much, not just the basics but how to look and how to see. I suppose I owe him for every photograph I've ever taken."

The breakfast he'd just eaten churned greasily in his stomach. "You're a professional photographer?"

"Jo's a big-deal photographer," Lexy said with a bite in her voice as she came back in. "The globe-trotting J. E. Hathaway, snapping her pictures of other people's lives as she goes. Two omelettes, Brian, two sides of hash browns, one bacon, one sausage. Room 201's having breakfast, Miss World Traveler. You've got beds to strip."

"Exit, stage left," Jo murmured when Lexy strode out again. "Yes," she said, turning back to Nathan. "Thanks in large part to David Delaney, I'm a photographer. If it hadn't been for Mr. David, I might be as frustrated and pissed off at the world as Lexy. How is your father?"

"He's dead," Nathan said shortly and pushed himself up from the stool. "I've got to get back. Thanks for breakfast, Brian."

He went out fast, letting the screen door slam behind him.

"Dead? Bri?"

"An accident," Brian told her. "About three months ago. Both his parents. And he lost his brother about a month later."

"Oh, God." Jo ran a hand over her face. "I put my foot in that. I'll be back in a minute."

She set the mug down and raced out the door to chase Nathan down. "Nathan! Nathan, wait a minute." She caught him on the shell path that wound through the garden toward the trees. "I'm sorry." She put a hand on his arm to stop him. "I'm so sorry I went on that way."

He pulled himself in, fought to think clearly over the pounding in his temples. "It's all right. I'm still a little raw there."

"If I'd known—" She broke off, shrugged her shoulders helplessly. She'd likely have put her foot in it anyway, she decided. She'd always been socially clumsy.

"You didn't." Nathan clamped down on his own nerves and gave the hand still on his arm a light squeeze. She looked so distressed, he thought. And she'd done nothing more than accidentally scrape an open wound. "Don't worry about it."

"I wish I'd managed to keep in touch with him." Her voice went wistful now. "I wish I'd made more of an effort so I could have thanked him for everything he did for me."

"Don't." He bit the word off, swung around to her with his eyes fierce and cold. "Thanking someone for where your life ended up is the same as blaming them for it. We're all responsible for ourselves."

Uneasy, she backed off a step. "True enough, but some people influence what roads we take."

"Funny, then, that we're both back here, isn't it?" He stared beyond her to Sanctuary, where the windows glinted in the sun. "Why are you back here, Jo?"

"It's my home."

He looked back at her, pale cheeks, bruised eyes. "And that's where you come when you feel beat up and lost and unhappy?"

She folded her arms across her chest as if chilled. She, usually the observer, didn't care to be observed quite so clear-sightedly. "It's just where you go."

"It seems we decided to come here at almost the same time. Fate? I wonder—or luck." He smiled a little because he was going to go with the latter.

"Coincidence." She preferred it. "Why are you back here?"

"Damned if I know." He exhaled between his teeth, then looked at her again. He wanted to soothe that sorrow and worry from her eyes, hear that laugh again. He was suddenly very certain it would ease his soul as much as hers. "But since I am, why don't you walk me back to the cottage?"

"You know the way."

"It'd be a nicer walk with company. With you."

"I told you I'm not interested."

"I'm telling you I am." His smile deepened as he reached up to tuck a stray lock of hair behind her ear. "It'll be fun seeing who nudges who to the other side."

Men didn't flirt with her. Ever. Or not that she had ever noticed. The fact that he was doing just that, and she noticed, only irritated her. The inherent Pendleton Fault Line dug between her brows. "I've got work to do."

"Right. Bed stripping in 201. See you around, Jo Ellen."

Because he turned away first, she had the opportunity to watch him walk into the trees. Deliberately she shook her hair so that it fell over her ears again. Then she rolled her shoulders as if shrugging off an unwelcome touch.

But she was forced to admit she was already more interested than she wanted to be.

7

Nathan took a camera with him. He felt compelled to retrace some of his father's footsteps on Desire—or perhaps to eradicate them. He chose the heavy old medium-range Pentax, one of his father's favorites and surely, he thought, one that David Delaney had brought to the island with him that summer.

He would have brought the bulky Hasselblad view camera as well, and the clever Nikon, along with a collection of lenses and filters and a mountain of film. Nathan had brought them all, and they were neatly stored, as his father had taught him, back at the cottage.

But when his father hiked out to hunt a shot, he would most usually take the Pentax.

Nathan chose the beach, with its foaming waves and diamond sand. He slipped on dark glasses against the fierce brilliance of the sun and climbed onto the marked path between the shifting dunes, with their garden of sea oats and tangle of railroad vines. The wind kicked in from the sea and sent his hair flying. He stood at the crest of the path, listening to the beat of the water, the smug squeal of gulls that wheeled and dipped above it.

Shells the tide had left behind were scattered like pretty toys along the sand. Tiny dunes whisked up by the wind were already forming behind them. The busy sanderlings were rushing back and forth in the spume, like businessmen hustling to the next meeting. And there, just behind the first roll of water, a trio of pelicans flew in military formation, climbing and wheeling as a unit. One would abruptly drop, a dizzying headfirst dive into the sea, and the others would follow. A trio of splashes, then they were up again, breakfast in their beaks.

With the ease of experience, Nathan lifted his camera, widened the aperture, increased the shutter speed to catch the motion, then homed in on the pelicans, following, following as they skimmed the wave crests, rose into their climb. And capturing them on the next bombing dive.

He lowered the camera, smiled a little. Over the years he'd gone long stretches of time without indulging in his hobby. He planned to make up for it now, spending at least an hour a day reacquainting himself with the pleasure and improving his eye.

He couldn't have asked for a more perfect beginning. The beach was inhabited only by birds and shells. His footprints were the only ones to mar the sand. That was a miracle in itself, he thought. Where else could a man be so entirely alone, borrow for a while this kind of beauty, along with peace and solitude?

He needed those things now. Miracles, beauty, peace. Cupping a hand over the camera, Nathan walked down the incline to the soft, moist sand of the beach. He crouched now and then to examine a shell, to trace the shape of a starfish with a fingertip.

But he left them where he found them, collecting them only on film.

The air and the exercise helped settle the nerves that had jangled before he'd left Sanctuary. She was a photographer, Nathan thought, as he studied a pretty, weather-silvered cottage peeking out from behind the dunes. Had his father known that the little girl he'd played mentor to one summer had gone on to follow in his footsteps? Would he have cared? Been proud, amused?

He could remember when his father had first shown him the workings of a camera. The big hands had covered his small ones, gently, patiently guiding. The smell of aftershave on his father's cheeks, a sharp tang. Brut. Yes, Brut. Mom had liked that best. His father's cheek had been smoothly shaven, pressed against his. His dark hair would have been neatly combed, smooth bumps of waves back from the forehead, his clear gray eyes soft and serious.

Always respect your equipment, Nate. You may want to make a living from the camera one day. Travel the world on it and see everything there is to see. Learn how to look and you'll see more than anyone else. Or you'll be something else, do something else, and just use it to take moments away with you. Vacations, family. They'll be your moments, so they'll be important. Respect your equipment, learn to use it right, and you'll never lose those moments.

"How many did we lose, anyway?" Nathan wondered aloud. "And how many do we have tucked away that we'd be better off losing?"

"Excuse me?"

Nathan jerked when the voice cut through the memory, when a hand touched his arm. "What?" He took a quick step in retreat, half expecting one of his own ghosts. But he saw a pretty, delicately built blonde staring up at him through amber-tinted lenses.

"Sorry. I startled you." She tilted her head, and her eyes stayed focused, unblinking, on his face. "Are you all right?"

"Yeah." Nathan dragged a hand through his hair, ignored the uncomfortably loose sensation in his knees. Less easily ignored was the acute embarrassment as the woman continued to study him as if he were some alien smear on a microscope slide. "I didn't know anyone else was around."

"Just finishing up my morning run," she told him, and he noted for the first time that she wore a sweat-dampened gray T-shirt over snug red bike shorts. "That's my cottage you were staring at. Or through."

"Oh." Nathan ordered himself to focus on it again, the silvered cedar shakes, the sloping brown roof with its jut of open deck for sunning. "You've got a hell of a view."

"The sunrises are the best. You're sure you're all right?" she asked again. "I'm sorry to poke, but when I see a guy standing alone on the beach looking as if he'd just been slapped with a two-by-four and talking to himself, I've got to wonder. It's my job," she added.

"Beach police?" he said dryly.

"No." She smiled, held out a friendly hand. "Doctor. Doctor Fitzsimmons. Kirby. I run a clinic out of the cottage."

"Nathan Delaney. Medically sound. Didn't an old woman used to live there? A tiny woman with white hair up in a bun."

"My grandmother. Did you know her? You're not a native."

"No, no, I remember, or have this impression of her. I spent a summer here as a kid. Memories keep popping out at me. You just walked into one."

"Oh." The eyes behind the amber lenses lost their clinical shrewdness and warmed. "That explains it. I know just what you mean. I spent several summers here growing up, and memories wing up at me all the time. That's why I decided to relocate here when Granny died. I always loved it here."

Absently, she grabbed her toe, bending her leg back, heel to butt, to stretch out. "You'd be the Yankee who's taken Little Desire Cottage for half a year."

"Word travels."

"Doesn't it just? Especially when it doesn't have far to go. We don't get many single men renting for six months. A number of the ladies are intrigued." Kirby repeated the process on the other leg. "You know, I think I might remember you. Wasn't it you and your brother who palled around with Brian Hathaway? I remember Granny saying how those Delaney boys and young Brian stuck together like a dirt clod."

"Good memory. You were here that summer?"

"Yes, it was my first summer on Desire. I suppose that's why I remember it best. Have you seen Brian yet?" she asked casually.

"He just fixed me breakfast."

"Magic in an egg." It was Kirby's turn to look past the cottage, beyond it. "I heard Jo's back. I'm going to try to get up to the house after the clinic closes today." She glanced at her watch. "And since it opens in twenty minutes, I'd better go get cleaned up. It was nice seeing you again, Nathan."

"Nice seeing you. Doc," he added as she began to jog toward the dunes.

With a laugh, she turned, jogged backward. "General practice," she called out. "Everything from birth to earth. Come in for what ails you."

"I'll keep it in mind." He smiled and watched her ponytail swing sassily as she ran through the valley between the dunes.

Nineteen minutes later, Kirby put on a white lab coat over her Levi's. She considered the coat a kind of costume, designed to reassure the reluctant patient that she was indeed a doctor. That and the stethoscope tucked in its pocket gave the islanders the visual nudge many of them needed to let Granny Fitzsimmons's little girl poke into their orifices.

She stepped into her office, formerly her grandmother's well-stocked pantry off the kitchen. Kirby had left one wall of shelves intact, to hold books and papers and the clever little combo fax and copy machine that kept her linked with the mainland. She'd removed the other shelves, since she had no plans to follow her grandmother's example and put by everything from stewed tomatoes to watermelon pickles.

She'd muscled the small, lovingly polished cherrywood desk into the room herself. It had traveled with her from Connecticut, one of the few pieces she'd brought south. It was outfitted with a leather-framed blotter and appointment book that had been a parting gift from her baffled parents.

Her father had grown up on Desire and considered himself fortunate to have escaped.

She knew both of her parents had been thrilled when she'd decided to follow in her father's footsteps and go into medicine. And they had assumed she would continue to follow, into his cardiac surgery specialty, into his thriving practice, and right along to the platinum-edged lifestyle both of them so enjoyed.

Instead she'd chosen family practice, her grandmother's weather-beaten cottage, and the simplicity of island life.

She couldn't have been happier.

Tidily arranged with the appointment book that bore her initials in gold leaf were a snazzy phone system with intercom—in the unlikely event that she should ever need an assistant—and a Lucite container of well-sharpened Ticonderoga pencils.

Kirby had spent her first few weeks of practice doing little more than sharpening pencils and wearing them down again by doodling on the blotter.

But she'd stuck, and gradually she'd begun to use those pencils to note down appointments. A baby with the croup, an old woman with arthritis, a child spiking a fever with roseola.

It had been the very young or the very old who'd trusted her first. Then others had come to have their stitches sewn, the aches tended, their stomachs soothed. Now she was Doc Kirby, and the clinic was holding its own.

Kirby scanned her appointment book. An annual gyn, a follow-up on a nasty sinus infection, the Matthews boy had another earache, and the Simmons baby was due in for his next immunizations. Well, her waiting room wasn't going to be crowded, but at least she'd keep busy through the morning. And who knew, she thought with a chuckle, there could be a couple of emergencies to liven up the day.

Since Ginny Pendleton was her gyn at ten o'clock, Kirby calculated she had at least another ten minutes. Ginny was invariably late for everything. Pulling the necessary chart, she stepped back into the kitchen, poured the last of the coffee from the pot she'd made early that morning, and took it with her to the examining room.

The room where she'd once dreamed away summer nights was now crisp and clean. She had posters of wildflowers on the white walls rather than the pictures of nervous systems and ear canals that some doctors decorated with. Kirby thought they made patients jumpy.

After sliding the chart into the holder inside the door, she took out one of the backless cotton gowns—she thought paper gowns humiliating—and laid it out on the foot of the examining table. She hummed along with the quiet Mozart sonata from the stereo she'd switched on. Even those who eschewed classical would invariably relax to it, she'd found.

She'd arranged everything she'd need for the basic yearly exam and had finished off her coffee when she heard the little chime that meant the door at the clinic entrance had opened.

"Sorry, sorry," Ginny came in on the run as Kirby stepped into the living room that served as the waiting area. "The phone rang just as I was leaving."

She was in her middle twenties, and Kirby was continually telling her that her fondness for the sun was going to haunt her in another ten years. Her hair was white-blond, shoulder-length, frizzed mercilessly, and crying out for a root job.

Ginny came from a family of fishermen, and though she could pilot a boat like a grinning pirate, clean a fish like a surgeon, and shuck oysters with dizzying speed and precision, she preferred working at the Heron Campground, helping the novice pitch a tent, assigning sites, keeping the books.

For her doctor's appointment, she'd spruced herself up with one of her favored western shirts in wild-plum purple with white fringe. Kirby wondered with idle curiosity how many internal organs were gasping for oxygen beneath the girdle-tight jeans.

"I'm always late." Ginny sent her a sunny, baffled smile that made Kirby laugh.

"And everyone knows it. Go ahead in and pee in the bottle first. You know the routine. Then go into the exam room. Take everything off, put the gown on opening to the front. Just give a holler when you're ready."

"Okay. It was Lexy on the phone," she called out as she scurried down the hall in her cowboy boots and shut the door. "She's feeling restless."

"Usually is," Kirby replied.

Ginny continued chatting as she left the bathroom and turned into the exam room.

"Anyway, Lexy's going to come down to the campground tonight about nine o'clock." There was a thud as the first boot hit the floor. "Number twelve is free. It's one of my favorites. We thought we'd build us a nice fire, knock off a couple of six-packs. Wanna come?"

"I appreciate the offer." There was another thud. "I'll think about it. If I decide to come by, I'll bring another six-pack."

"I wanted her to ask Jo, but you know how huffy Lex gets. Hope she will, though." Ginny's voice was breathless, leading Kirby to imagine she was peeling herself out of the jeans. "You seen her yet? Jo?"

"No. I'm going to try to catch her sometime today."

"Do them good to sit down and tie one on together. Don't know why Lexy's so pissed off at Jo. Seems to be pissed off at everybody, though. She went on about Giff too. If I had a man who looked like Giff eyeing me up one side and down the other the way he does her, I wouldn't be pissed off at anything. And I'm not saying that because we're cousins. Fact is, if we weren't blood-related, I'd jump his bones in a New York minute. All set in here."

"I'd give odds Giff will wear her down," Kirby commented, taking out the chart as she came in. "He's got a stubborn streak as wide as hers. Let's check your weight. Any problems, Ginny?"

"Nope, been feeling fine." Ginny stepped on the scale and firmly shut her eyes. "Don't tell me what it is."

Chuckling, Kirby tapped the weight up the line. One thirty. One thirty-five. Whoops, she thought. One forty-two.

"Have you been exercising regularly, Ginny?"

Eyes still tightly shut, Ginny shifted from side to side. "Sort of."

"Aerobics, twenty minutes, three times a week. And cut back on the candy bars." Because she was female as well as a doctor, Kirby obligingly zeroed out the scale before Ginny opened her eyes. "Hop up on the table, we'll check your blood pressure."

"I keep meaning to watch that Jane Fonda tape. What do you think about lipo?"

Kirby snugged on the BP cuff. "I think you should take a brisk walk on the beach a few times a week and imagine carrot sticks are Hershey bars for a while. You'll lose that extra five pounds without the Hoover routine. BP's good. When was your last period?"

"Two weeks ago. It was almost a week late, though. Scared the shit out of me."

"You're using your diaphragm, right?"

Ginny folded her arms over her middle, tapped her fingers. "Well, most of the time. It's not always convenient, you know."

"Neither is pregnancy."

"I always make the guy condomize. No exceptions. There's a couple of really cute ones camped at number six right now."

Sighing, Kirby snapped on her gloves. "Casual sex equals dangerous complications."

"Yeah, but it's so damn much fun." Ginny smiled up at the dreamy Monet poster Kirby had tacked to the ceiling. "And I always fall in love with them a little. Sooner or later, I'm going to come across the big one. The right one. Meantime, I might as well sample the field."

"Minefield," Kirby muttered. "You're selling yourself short."

"I don't know." Trying to imagine herself walking through those misty flowers in the poster, Ginny tapped her many-ringed fingers on her midriff. "Haven't you ever seen a guy and just wanted him so bad everything inside you curled up and shivered?"

Kirby thought of Brian, caught herself before she sighed again. "Yeah."

"I just love when that happens, don't you? I mean it's so . . . primal, right?"

"I suppose. But primal and inconvenience aside, I want you using that diaphragm."

Ginny rolled her eyes. "Yes, doctor. Oh, hey, speaking of men and sex, Lexy says she got a load of the Yankee and he is prime beef."

"I got a load of him myself," Kirby replied.

"Was she right?"

"He's very attractive." Gently, Kirby lifted one of Ginny's arms over her head and began the breast exam.

"Turns out he's an old friend of Bri's—spent a summer here with his parents. His father was that photographer who did the picture book on the Sea Islands way back. My mother's still got a copy."

"The photographer. Of course. I'd forgotten that. He took pictures of Granny. He made a print and matted it, sent it to her after he left. I still have it in my bedroom."

"Ma got the book out this morning when I told her. It's really nice," Ginny added as Kirby helped her sit up. "There's one of Annabelle Hathaway and Jo gardening at Sanctuary. Ma remembered he took the pictures the summer Annabelle ran off. So I said maybe she ran off with the photographer, but Ma said he and his wife and kids were still on the island after she left."

"It was twenty years ago. You'd think people would forget and leave it alone."

"The Pendletons are Desire," Ginny pointed out. "Annabelle was a Pendleton. And nobody ever forgets anything on the island. She was really beautiful," she added, scooting off the table. "I don't remember her very well, but seeing the picture brought it back some. Jo would look like that if she put some effort into it."

"I imagine Jo prefers to look like Jo. You're healthy, Ginny, go ahead and get dressed. I'll meet you outside when you're done."

"Thanks. Oh, and Kirby, try to make it by the campground. We'll make it a real girls' night out. Number twelve."

"We'll see."

At four, Kirby closed the clinic. Her only emergency walk-in had been a nasty case of sunburn on a vacationer who'd fallen asleep on the beach. She'd spent fifteen minutes after her last patient sprucing up her makeup, brushing her hair, dabbing on fresh perfume.

She told herself it was for her own personal pleasure, but as she was heading over to Sanctuary, she knew that was a lie. She was hoping she looked fresh enough, smelled good enough, to make Brian Hathaway suffer.

She took the beach door. Kirby loved that quick, shocking thrill of seeing the ocean so near her own home. She watched a family of four playing in the shallows and caught the high music of the children's laughter over the hum of the sea.

She slipped on her sunglasses and trotted down the steps. The narrow boardwalk she'd had Giff build led her around the house, away from the dunes. Rising out of the sand was a stand of cypress, bent and crippled by the wind that even now blew sand around her ankles. Bushes of bayberry and beach elder grew in the trough. She added her own tracks to those that crisscrossed the sand.

She circled the edges of the dune swale, islander enough to know and respect its fragility. In moments, she had left the hot brilliance of sand and sea for the cool, dim cave of the forest.

She walked quickly, not hurrying, but simply with her mind set on her destination. She was used to the rustles and clicks of the woods, the shifts of sound and light. So she was baffled when she found herself stopping, straining her ears and hearing her own heart beating fast and high in her throat.

Slowly, she turned in a circle, searching the shadows. She'd heard something, she thought. Felt something. She could feel it now, that crawling sensation of being watched.

"Hello?" She hated herself for trembling at the empty echo of her own voice. "Is someone there?"

The rattle of fronds, the rustle that could be deer or rabbit, and the heavy silence of thickly shaded air. Idiot, she told herself. Of course there was no one there. And if there were, what would it matter? She turned back, continued down the well-known path and ordered herself to walk at a reasonable pace.

Sweat snaked cold down the center of her back, and her breath began to hitch. She clamped down on the rising fear and swung around again, certain she would catch a flash of movement behind her. There was nothing but twining branches and dripping moss.

Damn it, she thought and rubbed a hand over her speeding heart. Someone was there. Crouched behind a tree, snugged into a shadow. Watching her. Just kids, she assured herself. Just a couple of sneaky kids playing tricks.

She walked backward, her eyes darting side to side. She heard it again, just a faint, stealthy sound. She tried to call out again, make some pithy comment on rude children, but the terror that had leaped into her throat snapped it closed. Moving on instinct, she turned and increased her pace.

When the sound came closer, she abandoned all pride and broke into a run.

And the one who watched her snickered helplessly into his hands, then blew a kiss at her retreating back.

Her breath heaving, Kirby pounded through the trees, sneakers slapping the path in a wild tattoo. She gulped in a sob as she saw the light change, brighten, then flash as she burst out of the trees. She looked back over her shoulder, prepared to see some monster leaping out behind her.

And screamed when she ran into a solid wall of chest and arms banded tight around her.

"What's wrong? What happened?" Brian nearly picked her up in his arms, but she clamped hers around him and burrowed. "Are you hurt? Let me see."

"No, no, I'm not hurt. A minute. I need a minute."

"Okay. All right." He gentled his hold and stroked her hair. He'd been yanking at weeds on the outer edge of the garden when he'd heard the sounds of her panicked race through the forest. He'd just taken the first steps forward to investigate when she shot out of the trees and dead into him.

Now her heart was thudding against his, and his own was nearly matching its rhythm. She'd scared the life out of him—that wild-animal look in her eyes when she jerked her head around as if expecting to be attacked from behind.

"I got spooked," she managed and clung like a burr. "It was just kids. I'm sure it was just kids. It felt like I was being stalked, hunted. It was just kids. It spooked me."

"It's all right now. Catch your breath." She was so small, he thought. Delicate back, tiny waist, silky hair. Hardly aware of it, he gathered her closer. It was odd that she should fit against him so well and at the same time seem fragile enough for him to pick up and tuck safely in his pocket.

Christ, she smelled good. He lowered his cheek to the top of her head for a moment, indulged in the scent and texture of her hair as he slowly stroked the tension out of her neck.

"I don't know why I panicked that way. I never panic." And because the sensation was subsiding, she became gradually aware that he was holding her. Very close. That his hands were moving over her. Very smoothly. His lips were in her hair. Very softly.

Her slowing heart rate kicked up again, but this time it had nothing to do with panic.

"Brian." She murmured it, ran her hands up his back as she lifted her head.

"You're all right now. You're okay." And before he knew what he was doing, his mouth was on hers.

It was like a fist in the gut, a breath-stealing blow that sent his brain reeling and buckled his knees. Then her lips were parting under his, so warm and smooth, with sexy little purrs slipping between them and into his mouth.

He went deeper, nipping her tongue, then soothing it while his hands slid down over snug denim to mold her bottom and angle heat against heat.

She stopped thinking the instant his mouth took over hers. The novelty of that experience was a separate, giddy thrill. Always she'd been able to separate her intellect, to somehow step outside herself in a way, to direct and control the event. But now she was swirled into it, lapped by sensation after sensation.

His mouth was hot and hungry, his body hard, his hands big and demanding. For the first time in her life, she truly felt delicate, as though she could be snapped in two at his whim.

For reasons she couldn't understand, the sensation was unbearably arousing.

Murmuring his name against his busy mouth, she hooked her hands over the back of his shoulders. Her head tipped back limply. For the first time with a man she teetered on the brink of absolute and unquestioning surrender.

It was the change, the sudden pliancy, the helpless little moan, that snapped him back. He'd dragged her up to her toes, his fingers were digging into her flesh, and the single image that had lodged in his mind was that of taking her on the ground.

In his mother's garden, for Christ's sake. In the daylight. In the shadow of his own home. Disgusted with both of them, Brian jerked her out to arm's length.

"That's what you wanted, wasn't it?" he said furiously. "You went to a lot of trouble to prove I'm as weak as the next guy."

Colors were still swimming in her head. "What?" She blinked to clear her vision. "What?"

"The damsel-in-distress routine worked. Score one for your side."

She came back to earth with a thud. His eyes were as hard and hot as his mouth had been, but with passion of a different sort. When his words and the meaning behind them registered, her own widened with shocked indignation.

"Do you honestly believe I staged this, made a fool of myself just so you'd kiss me? You arrogant, conceited, self-important son of a bitch!" Insulted to the core, she shoved him away. "I don't have routines, and I'm not now nor will I ever be a damsel of any sort. And furthermore, kissing you is not a major goal in my life."

She pushed her tousled hair back, squared her shoulders. "I came here to see Jo, not you. You just happened to be in the way."

"I suppose that's why you jumped into my arms and wrapped yourself around me like a snake."

She drew a breath, determined to cloak herself in calm and dignity. "The problem here, Brian, is that you wanted to kiss me, and you enjoyed it. Now you have to blame me, accuse me of perpetrating some ridiculous female ruse, because you want to kiss me again. You want to get your hands on me the way you just had them on me, and for some reason that really ticks you off. But that's your problem. I came here to see Jo."

"She's not here," Brian said between his teeth. "She's out with her cameras somewhere."

"Well, then, you just give her a message for me. Heron Campground, nine o'clock, site twelve. Girls' night out. Think you can remember that, or do you want to write it down?"

"I'll tell her. Anything else?"

"No, not a thing." She turned, then hesitated. Pride or no, she simply couldn't face going back into the trees alone just yet. She shifted directions and headed down the shell path. It would more than double the distance home, she thought, but a good sweaty walk would help her work off her temper.

Brian frowned at her back, then into the woods. He had a sudden and certain feeling that none of what had just happened had been a pretense. And that, he decided, made him not only a fool but a nasty one.

"Hold on, Kirby, I'll give you a ride back."

"No, thanks."

"Damn it, I said hold on." He caught up with her, took her arm, and was stunned by the ripe fury on her face when she whirled around.

"I'll let you know when I want you to touch me, Brian, and I'll let you know when I want anything from you. In the meantime..." She jerked free. "I'll take care of myself."

"I'm sorry." He cursed himself even as he said it. He hadn't meant to. And the raised-eyebrow, wide-eyed look she sent him made him wish he'd sawed off his tongue first.

"I beg your pardon, did you say something?"

Too late to back out, he thought, and swallowed the bitter pill. "I said I'm sorry. I was out of line. Let me drive you home."

She inclined her head, regally, he thought, and her smile was smug. "Thank you. I'd appreciate it."

8

"You were supposed to bring a six-pack, not fancy wine, big shot." Already disposed to complain, Lexy loaded her sleeping bag and gear into Jo's Land Rover.

"I like wine." Jo kept her voice mild and her sentences short.

"I don't know why you want to spend the night dishing in the woods anyway." Lexy scowled at Jo's tidily rolled and top-grade sleeping bag. Always the best for Jo Ellen, she thought sourly, then shoved her two six-packs of Coors into the cargo area. "No piano bar, no room service, no fawning maître d'."

Jo thought of the nights she'd spent in a tent, in second-rate motels, shivering in the cab of her four-wheeler. Anything to get the shot. She muscled in the bag of groceries she'd begged off of Brian, shoved her hair back. "I'll survive somehow."

"I set this up, you know. I set it up because I wanted to get the hell away from here for one night. I wanted to relax with friends. My friends."

Jo slammed the rear door, clenched her teeth as the sound echoed like a gunshot. It would be easier to walk away, she thought. Just turn around and go back into the house and leave Lexy to find her own way to the campground.

Damned if she was going to take the easy way.

"Ginny's my friend too, and I haven't seen Kirby in years." Leaving it at that, she circled around to the driver's side, climbed behind the wheel, and waited.

The pleasant anticipation she'd felt when Brian had relayed Kirby's invitation had disappeared, leaving a churning pit in her stomach. But she was determined to follow through, not to be chased away by her sister's bitchiness.

She was bound to have a miserable time now but, by God, she was going. And so, she thought when her sister slammed in beside her, was Lexy.

"Seat belt," Jo ordered, and Lexy let out an exasperated huff of breath as she strapped in. "Listen, why don't we just get drunk and pretend we can tolerate each other for one night? An actress of your astonishing range shouldn't have any trouble with that."

Lexy cocked her head, aimed a brilliant smile. "Fuck you, sister dear."

"There you go." Jo started the engine, reaching for a cigarette out of habit the minute it turned over.

"Would you not smoke in the car?"

Jo punched in the lighter. "My car."

She headed north, her tires singing musically on the shell road. The air rushing in the windows was a beautiful balm. She used it to soothe her raw nerves and made no complaint when Lexy turned the stereo up full blast. Loud music meant no conversation, and no conversation meant no arguments. At least for the drive to camp.

She drove fast, the memory of every curve in the road coming back to her. That too, soothed. So little had changed. Dark still fell quickly here, and the night brought the sounds of wind and sea that made the island seem a huge place to her. A world where the tides ruled dependably.

She remembered driving fast along this road with the wind rushing through her hair and the radio screaming. Lexy had been beside her then too.

The spring before Jo had left the island, a soft, fragrant spring. She would have been eighteen then, she remembered, and Lexy just fifteen. They'd been giggling, and there'd been the best part of a quart of Ernest and Julio between them to help the mood along. Cousin Kate had been visiting her sister in Atlanta, so there'd been no one to wonder where two teenage girls had gone off to.

There had been freedom and foolishness, and a connection, Jo thought, that they'd lost somewhere along the way. The island remained as it was, always. But those two young girls were gone.

"How's Giff?" Jo heard herself ask.

"How should I know?"

Jo shrugged. Even all those years back, Giff had had his eye on Lexy. And even all those years back, Lexy had known it. Jo simply wondered if that had stayed constant. "I haven't seen him since I've been back. I heard he was doing carpentry and whatnot."

"He's a jerk. I don't pay any attention to what he's doing." Lexy scowled out the window as she remembered the way he'd kissed her brainless. "I'm not interested in island boys. I like men." She turned back, shot a challenging look. "Men with style and money."

"Know any?"

"Quite a few, actually." Lexy hooked an arm out the window, easing into a pose of casual sophistication. "New York's bursting with them. I like a man who knows his way around. Our Yankee, for example."

Jo felt her spine stiffen, deliberately relaxed it. "Our Yankee?"

"Nathan Delaney. He has the look of a man who knows his way around... women. I'd say he's exactly my type. Rich."

"Why do you think he's rich?"

"He can afford a six-month vacation. An architect with his own company has to have financial substance. He's traveled. Men who've traveled know how to show a woman interesting pieces of the world. He's divorced. Divorced men appreciate an amiable woman."

"Done your research, haven't you, Lex."

"Sure." She stretched luxuriously. "Yes, indeedy, I'd say Nathan Delaney is just my type. He should keep me from being bored brainless for the next little while."

"Until you can get back to New York," Jo put in. "Shift hunting grounds."

"Exactly."

"Interesting." Jo's headlights splashed the discreet sign for Heron Campground. She cut her speed and took the turn off Shell Road into a land of sloughs and marsh grass. "I always figured you thought more of yourself than that."

"You have no idea what I think about anything, including myself."

"Apparently not."

They fell into a humming silence disturbed only by the shrill peeping of frogs. At a sharp cracking sound, Jo shuddered involuntarily. It was the unmistakable sound of a gator crunching a turtle between its jaws. She thought she understood exactly what that turtle felt in those last seconds of life. The sensation of being helplessly trapped by something large and feral and hungry.

Because her fingers trembled, she gripped the wheel tighter. She hadn't been consumed, she reminded herself. She'd escaped, she'd bought some time. She was still in control.

But the anxiety attack was pinching away at her with insistent little fingers. She made herself breathe in, breathe out, slow, normal. God, just be normal. She turned the radio off.

She passed the little check-in booth, empty now as the sun had set, and concentrated on winding her way through the chain of small lakes. Lights flickered here and there from campfires. Ghost music floated out of radios, then vanished. Where the hillocks of grass parted, she could see the delicate white glow of lily pads in the moonlight.

She would walk back, she told herself, take pictures, focus on the silence and the emptiness. On being alone. On being safe.

"There's Kirby's car."

Too much roaring in the ears, Jo thought, and forced out another breath. "What?"

"The snazzy little convertible there. That's Kirby's. Just park behind it."

"Right." Jo maneuvered the Land Rover into position and found when she cut the engine that the air was full of sound. The humming and peeping and rustling of the little world hidden behind the dunes and beyond the edge of the forest. It was ripe with scent as well, water and fish and damp vegetation.

She climbed out of the car, relieved to step into so much life.

"Jo Ellen!"

Kirby dashed out of the dark and grabbed Jo in a hard hug. Quick, spontaneous embraces always caught Jo off guard. Before she could steady herself, Kirby was pulling back, her hands still firm on Jo's arms, her smile huge and delighted.

"I'm so glad you came! I'm so glad to see you! Oh, we have a million years to catch up on. Hey, Lexy. Let's get your gear and pop a couple of tops."

"She brought wine," Lexy said, pulling open the cargo door.

"Great, we'll pop some corks too, then. We've got a mountain of junk food to go with it. We'll be sick as dogs by midnight." Chattering all the way, Kirby dragged Jo to the back of the Land Rover. "Good thing I'm a doctor. What's this?" She dived into the grocery bag. "Pâté. You got pâté?"

"I nagged Brian," Jo managed to say.

"Good thinking." Kirby hefted the food bag, then hooked Lexy's six-pack. "I've got these. Ginny's getting the fire going. Need a hand with the rest?"

"We can get it." Jo shouldered her camera bag, tucked her bedroll under one arm, and clinked the bottles of wine together. "I'm sorry about your grandmother, Kirby."

"Thanks. She lived a long life, exactly as she wanted to. We should all be that smart. Here, Lexy, I can get that bag." Kirby beamed at both of them, deciding she'd just about cut the edge off the tension that had been snarling in the air when they'd arrived. "Christ, I'm starving. I missed dinner."

Lexy slammed the rear door shut. "Let's go, then. I want a beer."

"Shit, my flashlight's in my back pocket." Kirby turned, angled a hip. "Can you get it?" she asked Jo.

With a little shifting and some flexible use of fingers, Jo pried it out and managed to switch it on. They headed down the narrow path single file.

Site twelve was already set up and organized, a cheerful fire burning bright in a circle of raked sand. Ginny had her Coleman lantern on low and an ice chest filled. She sat on it, eating from a bag of chips and drinking a beer.

"There she is." Ginny lifted the beer can in toast. "Hey, Jo Ellen Hathaway. Welcome home."

Jo dumped her bedroll and grinned. For the first time, she felt home. And felt welcome. "Thanks."

"A doctor." Jo sat cross-legged by the campfire, sipping Chardonnay from a plastic glass. One bottle was already nose down in the sand. "I can't imagine it. When we were kids, you always talked about being an archaeologist or something, a female Indiana Jones, exploring the world."

"I decided to explore anatomy instead." Comfortably drunk, Kirby spread more of Brian's excellent duck pâté on a Ritz cracker. "And I like it."

"We all know about your work, Jo, but is there someone special in your life?" Kirby asked, trying to steer the conversation in Jo's direction.

"No. You?"

"I've been working on your brother, but he isn't cooperating."

"Brian." Jo choked on her wine, sucked in air. "Brian?" she repeated.

"He's single, attractive, intelligent." Kirby licked her thumb. "He makes great pâté. Why not Brian?"

"I don't know. He's . . ." Jo gestured widely. "Brian."

"He pretends to ignore her." Lexy sat up and reached for the pâté herself. "But he doesn't."

"He doesn't?" Kirby looked over, eyes narrowed. "How do you know?"

"An actor has to observe people, their role playing." Lexy waved a hand airily. "You make him nervous, which irritates him. Which means you irritate him because he notices you."

"Really?" Though her head was spinning, Kirby finished off her wine and poured another glass. "Has he said anything about me? Does he—Wait." She held up a hand and rolled her eyes. "This is so high school. Forget I asked."

"The less Brian says about anything, the more it's on his mind," Lexy told her. "He hardly ever mentions your name."

"Really?" Kirby said again and began to perk up. "Is that so? Well, well. Maybe I'll give him another chance, after all."

She blinked as a light flashed in her eyes. "What's that for?" she demanded as Jo lowered her camera.

"You looked so damn smug. Shift over closer to Lex, Ginny. Let me get the three of you."

"Here she goes," Lexy muttered, but she flipped her hair back and posed nevertheless.

It was rare for her to take portraits, even candid ones. Jo indulged herself, letting them mug or preen for the camera, framing them in, adjusting the angle, letting the burst of light from her strobe flash illuminate them.

They were beautiful, she realized, each in her own unique fashion. Ginny, with her bottle-blonde frizz and wide-open smile; Lexy, so self-aware and sulky; Kirby, carelessly confident and classy.

They were hers, Jo thought. Each one of them, for different reasons, was part of her. She'd forgotten that for too long.

Her vision blurred before she knew her eyes had flooded with tears. "I've missed you all. I've missed you so much." She set the camera aside hastily, then rose from her crouch. "I've got to pee."

"I'll go with her," Kirby murmured as Jo rushed out of the clearing. She snagged a flashlight and hurried after. "Jo. Hey." She had to double her pace to catch up, grab Jo's arm. "Are you going to tell me what's wrong?"

"My bladder's full. As a doctor, you should recognize the symptom."

When Jo started to turn, Kirby simply tightened her grip. "Honey, I'm asking as your friend, and as a doctor. Granny would have said you look peaked. I can tell from this brief session that you're run-down and stressed out. Won't you tell me what's wrong?"

"I don't know." Jo pressed a hand to her eyes because they wanted to fill up again. "I can't talk about it. I just need some space."

"Okay." Trust always had to be gained by degrees, Kirby thought. "Will you come and see me? Let me give you a physical?"

"I don't know. Maybe. I'll think about it." Jo steadied herself and managed a smile. "There is one thing I can tell you."

"What?"

"I've got to pee."

"Well, why didn't you say so?" Chuckling, Kirby aimed the light on the path. "You go running out of camp without a light, you could end up gator bait." Cautious, Kirby scanned the thick vegetation fringing the near pond.

"I think I could walk this island blind. It stays with you. I missed it more than I realized, Kirby, but I still feel like a stranger here. It's a shaky line to walk."

"You haven't been home two weeks. Give yourself that time you said you need."

"I'm trying. Me first," Jo said and ducked into the little outhouse.

Kirby started to laugh, then found herself shuddering. The minute Jo closed the door she felt completely alone, completely exposed. The sounds of the slough seemed to rush toward her, over her. Rustles and calls and plops. Clouds drifted slyly over the moon and had her gripping her flashlight in both hands.

Ridiculous, she told herself. It was just a leftover reaction to her experience in the woods that afternoon. She was hardly alone. There were campsites pocketed all through the area. She could even see the flicker of lights from lanterns and fires. And Jo was only a single wooden door away.

There was nothing to be frightened of, she reminded herself. There was nothing and no one on the island that meant her any harm.

And she nearly whimpered with relief when Jo stepped out again.

"You're up," Jo told her, still buttoning her jeans. "Take the flash. I nearly fell in. It's black as death in there, and nearly as atmospheric."

"We could have walked over to the main toilets."

"I wouldn't have needed them by the time I got there."

"Good point. Wait for me, okay?"

Jo hummed assent and leaned back against the door. Then almost immediately straightened when she heard footsteps padding softly to her right. She tensed, told herself that the reaction was a by-product of city living, and watched a light bob closer.

"Hello, there." The male voice was low and pleasant.

She ordered herself to relax. "Hello. We'll be out of your way in a minute."

"No problem. I was just taking a little moonlight walk before I turned in. I'm over at site ten." He took a few steps closer but stayed in the shadows. "Beautiful night. Beautiful spot. I never expected to see a beautiful woman."

"You never know what you'll see on the island." Jo squinted as the light from his lantern reflected into her eyes. "That's part of its charm."

"It certainly is. And I'm enjoying every bit of it. An adventure in every step, don't you think? The anticipation of what's to come. I'm a fan of . . . anticipation."

No, she realized, his voice wasn't pleasant. It was like syrup—too sweet, too thick, and it carried that exaggerated drawl that Yankees insultingly believed mimicked the South.

"Then I'm sure you won't be disappointed in what Desire has to offer."

"From where I'm standing, the offerings are perfect."

If she'd had the flashlight, she would have abandoned manners and shined it in his face. It was the voice coming out of the dark, she told herself, that made it seem so eerie and dangerous. When the door creaked beside her, she turned quickly and reached for Kirby's hand before Kirby had stepped all the way out.

"We've got company," Jo said, annoyed that her voice was too high and too bright. "This is a popular spot tonight. Number ten was just passing through."

But when she looked back, raising Kirby's hand that held the flash, there was no one there. With a panicked sound in her throat, Jo grabbed the flashlight and waved it frantically over the dark grass and trees.

"He was here. There was someone here. I didn't imagine it. I didn't."

"All right." Gently, Kirby laid a hand on Jo's shoulder, concerned by the trembling. "It's all right. Who was he?"

"I don't know. He was just there. He talked to me. Didn't you hear?"

"No, I didn't hear anything."

"He was almost whispering. That's why. He didn't want you to hear him. But he was there." Her fingers gripped Kirby's like a vise, the panic beating like bat wings in her stomach. "I swear he was right over there."

"I believe you, honey, why wouldn't I?"

"Because he's gone, and . . ." She trailed off, rocked herself for a moment to regain her balance. "I don't know. Christ, I'm a mess. It was dark, he startled me. I couldn't see his face." She blew out a breath, dragged her hair back with both hands. "He creeped me out, I guess."

"It's no big deal. I got spooked in the woods today walking to Sanctuary. Ran like a rabbit."

Jo let out a little laugh, scrubbed her clammy palms dry on the thighs of her jeans. "Really?"

"Jumped gibbering into Brian's arms. Made him feel big and male enough to kiss me, though, so it wasn't a complete loss."

Jo sniffled, grateful that she could feel her legs solidly under her again. "So, how was it?"

"Terrific. I believe I'll definitely give him another chance." She gave Jo's hand a squeeze. "Okay now?"

"Yeah. Sorry."

"No problem. Spooky place." Her grin flashed. "Let's sneak back and scare the hell out of Lex and Ginny."

. . .

As they started off, hands linked, he watched them from the shadows. He smiled to himself, enjoying the music of quiet female voices drifting away. It was best, he realized, that she had come with the other one. He might have felt compelled to move to the next stage if Jo Ellen had wandered so neatly into him alone.

And he wasn't ready, not nearly ready, to move from anticipation to reality. There was still so much to prepare, so much to enjoy.

But, oh, how he wanted her. To taste that sexy, top-heavy mouth, to spread those long thighs, to close his hands around that pretty white throat.

He closed his eyes and let the image of it roll through his brain. The frozen image of Annabelle, so still and so perfect, shifted into hot life and became his. Became Jo.

A portion of the journal he carried with him played through his head.

Murder fascinates us all. Some would deny it, but they are liars. Man is helplessly drawn to the mirror of his own mortality. Animals kill to survive—for food, for territory, for sex. Nature kills without emotion.

But man also kills for pleasure. It has always been so. We alone among the animals know that the taking of a life is the essence of control and power.

Soon I'll experience the perfection of that. And capture it. My own immortality.

He shuddered in pleasure.

Anticipation, he mused as he turned on his light again to guide his way. Yes, he was a huge fan of anticipation.

9

The cheerful whistling woke Nathan. As he drifted in that netherworld just under full consciousness, he dreamed of a bird chirping happily on the near branch of the maple tree outside his window. There had been one in his youth, a mockingbird that sang its morning song every day for a full summer, greeting him so reliably that he had named it Bud.

Hazy, hot days filled with the important business of bike riding and ball playing and Popsicle licking.

The insistent wake-up call caused Nathan to greet every morning with a grin and a quick salute to Bud. He'd been devastated when Bud deserted him in late August, but Nathan's mother said that Bud had probably gone off early for his winter vacation.

Nathan rolled over and thought how odd it was that Bud should know how to whistle "Ring of Fire." In the half dream the bird hopped onto the windowsill, a cartoon bird now, a Disney character with sleek black feathers and Johnny Cash's weathered, been-there-done-that face.

When the bird began executing some sharp choreography that included high kicks and fancy spins, Nathan jerked himself awake. He stared at the window, half expecting to see a richly animated cartoon extravaganza.

"Jesus." He ran his hands over his face. "No more canned chili at midnight, Delaney."

He rolled over facedown on the pillow. Then he realized that while the bird wasn't there, the whistling was.

Grunting, he crawled out of bed and stepped into the cutoffs he'd stepped out of the night before. Brain bleary, he blinked at the clock, winced, then stumbled out of the room to find out who the hell was so cheerful at six-fifteen.

He followed the whistling—it was "San Antonio Rose" now—out the screened porch, down the steps. A shiny red pickup was parked behind his Jeep in the short drive. Its owner was under the house, standing on a stepladder and doing something to the ductwork while whistling his heart out. The ropy muscles rippling outside and under the thin blue T-shirt had Nathan readjusting his thoughts of quick murder.

Maybe he could take Whistling Boy, he considered. They looked to be close to the same height. He couldn't see the face, but the gimme cap, the snug jeans, and scruffy work boots said youth to Nathan.

He'd think about killing him after coffee, he decided.

"What the hell are you doing?"

Whistling Boy turned his head, shot a quick, cheerful grin from under the bill of his cap. "Morning. You got some leaks here. Gotta get it up and running right before AC weather hits."

"You're air-conditioning repair?"

"Hell, I'm everything repair." He stepped off the ladder, swiping a hand clean on the seat of his jeans before holding it out to Nathan. "I'm Giff Verdon. I fix anything."

Nathan studied the friendly brown eyes, the crooked incisor, dimples, the shaggy mess of sun-streaked hair spilling out of the cap, and gave up. "You fix coffee? Decent coffee?"

"You got the makings, I can fix it."

"They got some sort of cone thing with a . . ." Nathan illustrated vaguely with his hands. "Pot."

"Drip coffee. That's the best. You look like you could use some, Mr. Delaney."

"Nathan. I'll give you a hundred dollars for a real pot of coffee."

Giff gave a chuckling laugh, slapped Nathan smartly on the back. "You need it that bad, it's free. Let's go fix you up."

"You always start work at dawn?" Nathan asked as he shuffled up the steps behind Giff.

"Get an early start, you enjoy more of the day." He headed directly to the stove, filled the kettle at the sink. "Got any filters?"

"No."

"Well, we'll jury-rig her, then." Giff tore off some paper towels, folded them cleverly, and slipped them into the plastic cone. "You're an architect, right?"

"Yeah."

Nathan ran his tongue over his teeth, thought fleetingly about brushing them. After coffee. Worlds could be conquered, oceans could be crossed, women could be seduced. After coffee. Life would be worth living again. After coffee.

"I used to think I'd be one."

"Used to think you'd be one what?" Nathan prompted as Giff dug into the cabinet over the stove for coffee.

"An architect. I could always see these places in my head, houses mostly, windows, rooflines, shades of brick and siding. Right down to the fancy work." Giff scooped coffee out of the can and into the cone with the careless precision of habit. "I could even walk myself inside, go through the layout. Sometimes I'd shift things around. That stairway doesn't belong over there, it's better over here."

"I know what you mean."

"Well, I could never afford the schooling or the time to go off and study, so I build instead."

In anticipation, Nate got out two mugs. "You're a builder?"

"Well, now, I don't know if I'd say that. Nothing that fancy, really. I do add-ons, fix things up." He patted the tool belt cocked with gunslinger swagger on his hip. "Swing a hammer. Always something needs to be done around here, so I keep busy. Maybe one of these days I'll take one of the houses in my head and build it from the ground up."

Nathan leaned back against the counter and tried not to drool as Giff poured boiling water into the cone. "Have you done any work at Sanctuary?"

"Sure. This and that. I worked on the crew that remodeled the kitchen for Brian over there. Miz Pendleton's got in her mind to add on a little bathhouse. A solarium, like. Something where she can put a Jacuzzi tub and maybe an exercise room. People look for that kind of thing now when they're on vacation. I'm putting together a design for her."

"The south side," Nathan said to himself. "The light would be right, and it could be worked right into the gardens."

"Yep, just what I was figuring." Giff's smile widened. "I guess I'm on the right track there if you thought the same."

"I'd like to see your drawings for it."

"Yeah?" Surprise and pleasure zipped through him. "Great. I'll bring them by sometime when I got them a little more complete. Better payment than a hundred bucks for the coffee. Drip takes time," he added, noting the way Nathan was eyeing the slowly filling pot. "The best things do."

When Nathan was in the shower, sipping his second cup while hot water pounded the back of his neck, he had to agree that Giff was right. Some things were worth the wait. His mind was clear again, his system all but singing with caffeine. By the time he was dressed and had downed cup number three, he was primed for the hike to Sanctuary and set for an enormous breakfast.

Both the pickup and Giff were gone when Nathan walked down the steps again. Off to fix up something else, Nathan decided. He knew Giff had been amused when he'd asked him to write down the instructions for brewing drip coffee, step by step. But Nathan dealt better with a clear outline.

He caught himself whistling "I Walk the Line." Back to Johnny Cash, he thought, with a shake of his head. And he didn't even like country music.

When he stepped into the forest, dim and green, he deliberately slowed his steps and followed the gentle bend of the river under the arching sway of limbs and moss. Because it always struck him as entering a church, he stopped whistling.

A flutter of color caught his eye, and he stopped to watch a sunny yellow butterfly flit along the path. To the left, the lances of palmettos, tangled vines, and twisted trunks formed a wall that reached up and up, giving him glimpses of scarlet from the flowering vine, snatches of vivid blue sky through the forks of branches.

Though it was a detour, he kept to the river path a bit longer, knowing that the water would widen and lead him deeper into the cool stillness.

Then he saw her, crouched beside a fallen log. Her baggy jacket was pushed up past her elbows, her hair was pulled back into a stubby tail. She had one knee on the damp ground, the other foot planted for balance.

He couldn't have said why he found that so attractive. Why he found her so . . . interesting.

But he stayed where he was, and remained silent, watching Jo set up her shot.

He thought he knew what she was after. The play of light on the water, the shadows of trees on the dark surface, the faint breath of mist just fading. A small, intimate miracle. And the way the river curved, just beyond, Nathan thought. The way it disappeared around that bend where the grass was high and wet and the trees thick made one wonder what could be seen, if you only walked on.

When he saw the doe step out to the left, he stepped forward quietly and crouched behind her. She jolted when he laid a hand on her shoulder, so he squeezed.

"Ssh. To the left," he murmured near her ear. "Ten o'clock."

Though her heart had leaped and pounded, Jo shifted the camera. When she focused on the doe, she took a steadying breath and waited.

She caught the doe, head lifted, scenting the air. Then again her shutter clicked as the deer scanned the river and looked across directly at the two humans, crouched and still. Her arms began to ache as seconds passed into minutes. But she didn't move, unwilling to risk losing a shot. The reward came when the doe picked her way gracefully through the grass and the yearling slipped out of the trees and joined her at the verge to drink.

Light slanted down in dreamy white shafts that slid like liquid through the faint, swimming mist, and the deers' tongues sent ripples spreading soft and slow over the dark water.

She would underexpose, just a bit, she thought, to accent that otherworldly aura rather than go for the crisp clarity of reality. The prints should look enchanted, with the faintest of fairy-tale blurs.

She didn't lower her camera until she'd run out of film, and even then she remained silent, watching while the deer meandered downriver and around the bend.

"Thanks. I might have missed them."

"No, I don't think so."

She turned her head, had to will herself not to jerk back. She hadn't realized he was quite that close, or that his hand still made warm connection with her shoulder. "You move quietly, Nathan. I never heard you."

"You were pretty absorbed. Did you get the shot you were working on before the deer?"

"We'll see."

"I've been taking some shots myself. Old hobby."

"Natural that it would be. It'd be in your blood."

He didn't care for the sound of that and shook his head. "No, I don't have a passion for it. Just an amateur's interest. And a lot of equipment."

She never knew whether it was easier to speak of such losses, or say nothing. So she said nothing.

"In any case," he continued, "I've got all the professional equipment now, and a very minor skill." He smiled at her. "Not like yours."

"How do you know I have any skill when you haven't seen my work?"

"Excellent question. I could say the opinion comes from watching you work just now. You have the patience, the silent grace, the stillness. Stillness is an attractive quality."

"Maybe, but I've been still long enough." She started to rise, but he shifted his hand from her shoulder to her elbow and drew her up with him. "I don't want to keep you from your walk."

"Jo Ellen, you keep brushing me off, I'm going to get a complex." She looked more rested, he thought. There was a little color in her cheeks—but that could have been brought on by annoyance. He smiled and lifted the single-lens reflex camera that hung around her neck. "I've got this model."

"Do you?" Remembering his upbringing, she stopped herself from tugging the camera away from him. "As I said, it would be hard for you not to have some interest in photography. Was your father disappointed that you didn't follow in his f-steps?"

"No." Nathan continued to study the Nikon, remembering his father patiently instructing him on aperture, field of vision. "My parents never wanted me to be anything but what I wanted to be. Anyway, Kyle made his living with a camera."

"Oh, I didn't realize." Kyle was dead too, she remembered abruptly and, without thinking, touched a hand to Nathan's. "Look, if it's a tender spot, there's no need to poke at it."

"You can't ignore it either." Nathan shrugged his shoulders. "Kyle based himself in Europe—Milan, Paris, London. He did a lot of fashion photography."

"It's an art of its own."

"Sure. And you take pictures of rivers."

"Among other things."

"I'd like to see."

"Why?"

"We've just established that it's an interest of mine." He released her camera. "I'm going to spend more time on it while I'm here. And I'd like to see your work. Like you said, it's . . . connected to my father."

It was the right tack to take. He could almost see her mind change from automatic refusal to agreement. "I brought some with me. You could take a look sometime, I suppose."

"Good. How about now? I was heading over to Sanctuary anyway."

"All right, but I don't have a lot of time. I'm still on housekeeping duty." She started to bend to pick up her camera bag, but he beat her to it.

"I've got it."

Jo walked with him, dug her cigarettes out of her jacket pocket. "This isn't another come-on, is it?"

"It would be if I'd thought of it. I've still got that steak waiting."

"It's going to get freezer burn." She exhaled, studied him through narrowed eyes. "Why did your wife leave you?"

"What makes you think she left me?"

"Okay—why did you leave her?"

"We left each other." He brushed some low-hanging moss out of their way. "Marriage canceled through lack of interest. Are you trying to gauge what kind of husband I was before you let me grill you a piece of meat?"

"No." But the annoyance in his tone made her lips twitch. "But I would have if I'd thought of it. Why don't we leave that topic, and I'll ask you how you've enjoyed your first week on Desire."

He stopped, turned, looked at her. "Isn't this just about where you fell into the water that summer?"

She lifted a brow. "No, actually, it was quite a bit farther downriver that you *pushed* me into the water. And if you've got a notion to repeat yourself, I'd think again."

"You know, one of the reasons I'm here is to revisit some of those days, and nights." He took a step forward, she took a step back. "Are you sure it wasn't here that you went in?"

"Yes, I'm sure." He backed her up another step. She slapped a hand on his chest but found herself maneuvered nearer the bank. "Just like I'm sure I'm not going in again."

"Don't be too sure." As her feet skidded on the wet grass, he hauled her back and against him. "Oops." And grinning, locked his arms comfortably around her waist. "Not much to you, is there?"

She gripped his arms firmly, just in case. "There's enough."

"I guess I'll have to take your word for that . . . and anticipate finding out for myself. Anticipation's half the fun."

"What?" She felt her blood drain down to the soles of her feet. *I'm a big fan of anticipation.* "What did you say?"

"That I'd take your word for it. Hey." He shifted his weight, pulled her closer as she struggled against him. "Watch out, or we're both going to be taking a morning dip."

He managed to pull her back from the edge. Her face had gone sheet-white, and tremors jerked from her so that her skin seemed to bump against his palms.

"Steady," he murmured and gathered her against him. "I didn't mean to scare you."

"No." The fear had come and gone rapidly, and left her feeling like a fool. Because her heart was still thumping, she let herself be held—wondered how long it had been since anyone had put arms around her and let her rest there. "No, it was nothing. Stupid. There was a guy at the campground a couple of nights ago. He said something similar. He scared me."

"I'm sorry."

She let out a long sigh. "Not your fault, really. My nerves are a little close to the surface these days."

"He didn't hurt you?"

"No, no, he never touched me. It was just creepy."

She left her head against his shoulder, started to close her eyes. It would have been so easy to stay there. Being held. Being safe. But easy wasn't always the right way. Or the smart way.

"I'm not going to sleep with you, Nathan."

He waited a moment, letting himself enjoy the feel of her snug against him, the texture of her hair against his cheek. "Well, then, I may as well drown myself in the river right now. You've just shattered my lifelong dream."

He made her want to laugh, and she squelched down the bubble in her throat. "I'm trying to be up front with you."

"Why don't you lie to me for a while instead? Soothe my ego." He gave her ponytail a little tug, and she lifted her head. "In fact, why don't we start with something simple and work our way up to complications?"

She watched his gaze dip down to her mouth, linger, then slide slowly back up to her eyes. She could almost taste the kiss, feel the hum of it on her lips. It would be simple to close her eyes and let his mouth close over hers. It would be easy to lean forward and meet him halfway.

Instead, she lifted a hand, pressed her fingers to his mouth. "Don't."

He sighed, took her wrist and skimmed his lips over her knuckles. "Jo, you sure know how to make a man work for his pleasures."

"I'm not going to be one of your pleasures."

"You already are." He kept her hand in his and turned to walk to Sanctuary. "Don't ask me why."

Since he didn't seem to expect her to comment on that, or to make small talk, Jo walked in silence. She was going to have to think about this . . . situation, she decided. She wasn't foolish enough to deny that she'd had a reaction to him. That physical, gut-level click any woman recognized as basic lust. It was normal enough to be almost soothing.

She might be losing her mind, but her body was still functioning on all the elemental circuits.

She hadn't felt the click often enough in her life to take it for granted. And when it was so obviously echoed in the man who caused it . . . that was something to think about.

For now, at least, this was something she could control, something she could understand, analyze, and list clear choices about. But she suspected that the trouble with clicks was that they caused itches. And the trouble with itches was that they nagged until she just gave the hell up and scratched.

"We'll have to make this quick," she told Nathan and headed toward the side door.

"I know. You're on bed-making detail. I won't keep you long. I'm planning on sniffing around Brian until he feeds me."

"If you're not busy, you might talk him into getting out afterward. Going to the beach, doing some fishing. He spends too much time here."

"He loves it here."

"I know." She turned into a long hallway where a mural of forest and river flowed over the wall. "That doesn't mean he has to serve Sanctuary every hour of every day." She pressed a hinge, and a section of the mural opened.

"That's an odd way to put it," Nathan commented, following her through the opening and up the stairs into what had once been the servants' quarters and was now the private entrance to the family wing. "Serving Sanctuary."

"It's what he does. I suppose it's what all of us do when we're here."

She turned left at the top of the stairs. As she passed the first open door, she glanced into Lexy's room. The huge old canopy bed was empty. Unmade, naturally. Clothes were scattered everywhere—on the Aubusson carpet, the polished floor, the dainty Queen Anne chairs. The scents of lotions and perfumes and powders hung on the air in female celebration.

"Well, maybe not all of us," Jo muttered and kept walking.

Taking a key out of her pocket, she unlocked a narrow door. Nathan's brows lifted in surprise when he walked in. It was a fully equipped and ruthlessly organized darkroom.

An ancient and threadbare rug protected the random-width-pine floor; thick shades were drawn down and snugly fastened to stay that way over twin windows. Shelves of practical gray metal were lined with bottles of chemicals, plastic tubs. On others were boxes of thick black cardboard, which he assumed held her paper, contact sheets, and prints. There was a long wooden worktable, a high stool.

"I didn't realize you had a darkroom here."

"It used to be a bath and dressing room." Jo hit the white light, then moved around the prints she'd developed the night before that were still hanging on the drying line. "I hounded Cousin Kate until she let me take out the wall and the fixtures and turn it into my darkroom. I'd been saving for three years so I could buy the equipment."

She ran a hand over the enlarger, remembering how carefully she'd priced them, counted her pennies. "Kate bought this for me for my sixteenth birthday. Brian gave me the shelves and the workbench. Lex got me paper and developing fluid. They surprised me with them before I could spend my savings. It was the best birthday I've ever had."

"Family comes through," Nathan said, and noted she hadn't mentioned her father.

"Yes, sometimes they do." She inclined her head at his unspoken question. "He gave me the room. After all, it wasn't easy for my father to give up a wall." She turned away to reach up for a box above her matting machine. "I'm compiling prints for a book I'm contracted for. These are probably the best of the lot, though I still have some culling to do."

"You're doing a book? That's great."

"That remains to be seen. Right now it's just something to be worried about." She stepped back as he walked up to the box, then tucked her thumbs in her back pockets.

It took only the first print for him to see that she was well beyond competent. His father had been competent, Nathan mused, at times inspired. But if she considered herself David Delaney's pupil, she had far outreached her mentor.

The black-and-white print shimmered with drama, the lines so clean, so crisp they might have been carved with a scalpel. It was a study of a bridge soaring over churning water—the white bridge empty, the dark water restless, and the sun just breaking the far horizon.

Another showed a single tree, branches wide and spreading and empty of leaves over a deserted, freshly plowed field. He could have counted the furrows. He went through them slowly, saying nothing, struck time after time at what she could see, and freeze and take away with her.

He came to a night shot, a brick building, windows dark but for the top three, which glowed startlingly bright. He could see the dampness on the brick, the faint mist swirling above black puddles. And could all but feel the chilly, moist air on his skin.

"They're wonderful. You know that. You'd have to be ridiculously neurotic and humble not to know how much talent you have."

"I wouldn't say I'm humble." She smiled a little. "Neurotic, probably. Art demands neuroses."

"I wouldn't say neurotic." Curious, he lowered the last print so that he could study her face. "But lonely. Why are you so lonely?"

"I don't know what you're talking about. My work—"

"Is brilliant," he interrupted. "And heartbreaking. In every one of these it's as if someone's just walked away and there's no one there but you."

Uneasy, she took the print from him, put it back in the box. "I'm not terribly interested in portrait photography. It's not what I do."

"Jo." He touched his fingertips to her cheek, saw by the flicker in her eye that the simple gesture had startled her. "You close people out. It makes your work visually stunning and emotional. But what does it do to the rest of your life?"

"My work is the rest of my life." With a sharp slap, she set the box back on the shelf. "Now, as I said, I've got a full morning."

"I won't take up much more of it." But he turned idly and began to examine the prints on the drying line. When he laughed, Jo hunched her shoulders and prepared to snarl. "For someone who claims to have no interest in portrait photography, you sure hit it dead on."

Scowling, she walked over and saw that he'd homed in on one of the shots she'd taken at the campground. "That's hardly work, it's—"

"Terrific," he finished. "Fun, even intimate. That's the doc with her arm slung around your sister. Who's the woman with the acre of smile?"

"Ginny Pendleton," Jo muttered, trying not to be amused. Ginny's smile was just that, an acre wide, fertile, and full of promise. "She's a friend."

"They're all friends. It shows—the affection and that female connection. And it shows that the photographer's connected, not in the picture maybe, but of it."

Jo shifted uncomfortably. "We were drunk, or getting there."

"Good for you. This is undoubtedly wrong for the theme of the book you're doing now, but you ought to keep it in mind if you do another. Never hurts to mix a little fun in with your angst."

"You just like looking at attractive, half-plowed females."

"Why not?" He tipped a hand under her chin, lifting it higher when she would have jerked away. "I'd love to see what you do with a self-portrait the next time you're feeling that loose."

His eyes were warm and friendly, so damned attractive in the way they looked direct and deep into hers. She felt that little click again, sharper this time.

"Go away, Nathan."

"Okay." Before either of them could think about it, he dipped his head and touched his lips lightly to hers. Then touched them there again, a little longer, a little more firmly. Warmer than he'd expected, he thought, and more arousing, as she'd kept her eyes open and unblinking on his throughout. "You shivered," he said quietly.

"No, I didn't."

He skimmed his thumb over her jawline before he dropped his hands. "Well, one of us did."

And she was mortally afraid she would do so again. "You're not going away."

"I guess not—at least not the way you mean." He pressed his lips to her forehead this time. She didn't shiver, but her heart lurched. "No, definitely not the way you mean."

When he left her, she turned to the window, hurriedly unfastening the shade to throw it up and the window behind it. She wanted air, air to cool her blood and clear her mind. Even as she gulped it in, she saw the figure standing near the edge of the dune swale with the wind breezing through his hair, fluttering his shirt.

Alone, as her father was always alone, with every person who would reach out closed off behind that thin, invisible wall of his own making. With a vicious pull, she slammed the window shut again, shot the shade down.

Damn it, she wasn't her father. She wasn't her mother. She was herself. And maybe that was why there were times when she felt as if she was no one at all.

10

Giff was whistling again. Nathan tried to identify the tune as he tackled his French toast at the breakfast counter, but this one eluded him. He could only assume Giff had wandered too deep into country-western territory for Nathan's limited education to follow.

The man was certainly a cheerful worker, Nathan mused. And apparently he could fix anything. Nathan was certain it had taken absolute faith for Brian to ask Giff to take apart the restaurant's dishwasher in the middle of the breakfast shift.

Now Brian was frying and grilling and stirring, Giff was whistling and tinkering with dishwasher guts, and Nathan was downing a second helping of golden French toast and apple chutney.

He couldn't remember when he'd ever enjoyed a meal more.

"How's it coming, Giff?" Brian stepped around Giff to set a completed order under the warmer.

"Fair to middlin'."

"You don't get that thing up and running by end of shift, Nate here's going to be washing those dishes by hand."

"I am?" Nathan swallowed the next bite. "I only used one."

"House rules. You eat in the kitchen, you pick up the slack. Right, Giff?"

"Yep. Don't think it's going to come to that, though. I'll get her." He glanced over as Lexy swung through the door. "Yep," he said with a grin, "I'll get her, in my own time."

She spared him a sidelong flick of lashes, annoyed that he managed to look so cute in a silly baseball cap and grubby T-shirt. "Two more specials, one with ham, one with bacon. Two eggs over light, bacon, side of grits, wheat toast. Giff, keep your big feet out of the way," she complained, stepping around them to pick up her orders under the warmer.

Giff's grin was already spreading wide as she swung out the door again. "That sister of yours is the prettiest damn thing, Bri."

"So you say, Giff." Brian cracked two eggs, slid them into a skillet.

"She's crazy about me."

"I could tell. The way she bubbled over when she saw you was embarrassing."

Giff snorted, tapped the handle of his screwdriver against his palm. "That's just her way. She wants a man sniffing after her like a puppy, gets her nose up in the air when you don't. She'll come around. You just got to understand how a particular female works, is all."

"Who the hell understands how any females work?" Brian gestured with his spatula at Nathan. "Do you understand, Nate?"

Nathan contemplated the next bite of French toast, watched the syrup drip lazily. "No," he decided. "No, I can't say that I do. And I've done considerable studying on the subject. You could even say I've dedicated a small portion of my life to it, with mixed results."

"It's not a matter of how they all work." Patiently Giff began replacing screws. "You gotta focus in on the one. It's like an engine. One don't necessarily run the same as another, even if they're the same make and model. They've just got their particular quirks. Now, Alexa..."

He trailed off, carefully sending another screw home, selecting the next. "She's almost too pretty for her own good. She thinks about that a lot, worries over it."

"She's got enough glop on her bathroom counter to paint up a Vegas chorus line," Brian put in.

"Some women feel that's a responsibility. Now, Lex, she gets ticked off if a man's not dazzled by her twenty-four hours a day, and if he is dazzled twenty-four hours a day, she figures he's an idiot 'cause he's not seeing anything but the surface. The trick is to find the line, then choose the right time and place to cross it."

Brian flipped eggs onto a plate. It was Lexy to a tee, he mused. Contrary and annoying. "Seems like too much work to me."

"Hell, Bri, women aren't anything but work." Giff flicked up the brim of his hat, dimples flashing. "That's part of the appeal. She'll run for you now," he added, nodding at the dishwasher.

Gauging the time, he calculated that Lexy would be coming back in for her orders any moment. "Ginny and me and some of the others are thinking of having a bonfire on the beach tonight," he said casually. "Down around by Osprey Dunes. I got a lot of scrap wood put by, and it's going to be a clear night." When Lexy pushed through the door, Giff was a satisfied man. "I thought you might want to tell your guests here, let the cottagers and campers know."

"Know what?" Lex demanded.

"About the bonfire."

"Tonight?" Her eyes lit as she set dishes on the counter. "Where?"

"Down around Osprey." Giff carefully replaced his tools in his dented metal box. "You'll come on down, won't you, Brian?"

"I don't know, Giff. I've got some paperwork to catch up on."

"Oh, come on, Bri." Lexy nudged him as she reached for the new orders. "Don't be such a stick. We'll all come." Hoping to irritate Giff, she flashed an inviting smile at Nathan. "You'll come down, won't you? There's nothing like a bonfire on the beach."

"Wouldn't miss it." He slid a cautious glance at Giff, hoping the man had put his hammer away.

"Terrific." She beamed at him as she walked by, the full-candlepower smile she saved for special occasions. "I'll start spreading the word."

Giff scratched his chin as he unfolded himself and rose. "No need to look so uneasy, Nate. Flirting comes naturally to Lexy."

"Uh-huh." Nathan eyed the toolbox, thought of all the potential weapons inside.

"Doesn't bother me any." At home, Giff took a biscuit out of a bowl and bit in. "Man decides to take on a beautiful woman, he's got to expect a little flirting on her side, a lot of looking from other men. So you go right on and look." Giff hefted his toolbox and winked. "Now, you do more than look, we'd have to go around some. See you tonight."

He went off whistling.

"You know, Bri . . ." Nathan picked up his plate to carry it to the sink. "That guy has biceps like rock. I don't believe I'm even going to look."

"Good thinking. Now you can pay for that breakfast by loading the dishwasher."

"I don't feel like socializing, Kate. I'm going to do some darkroom work tonight."

"You're not doing any kind of work." Kate marched over to Jo's dresser, picked up the simple wooden-handled hairbrush, and shook it at her. "You're going to put on some lipstick, fix your hair, and go down to that bonfire. You're going to dance in the sand, drink some wine, and by God, you're going to have a good time."

Before Jo could protest again, Kate held up a hand, traffic-cop style. "Save your breath, girl. I've already had this round with Brian, and won. You might as well just throw in the towel now."

When she tossed the hairbrush, Jo caught it before it beaned her. "I don't see why it matters—"

"It matters," Kate said between her teeth and wrenched open the door on the rosewood armoire. "It matters that people in this house learn how to have a little fun now and then. When I'm through with you, I'm going to go browbeat your father."

Jo snorted, flopped back on the bed. "Not a chance."

"He'll go," Kate said grimly as she studied what there was of Jo's wardrobe. "If I have to knock him unconscious and drag him down to the beach. Don't you have a blouse in here that looks remotely like you care what you have on your back?" Disgusted, she shoved aside hangers. "Something the least bit stylish or attractive?"

Without waiting for an answer, she went to the door, calling out, "Alexa! You pick out a blouse for your sister and bring it down here."

"I don't want one of her shirts." Alarmed now, Jo hopped up. "If I have to go, I'll go in my own clothes. And I'm not going, so it doesn't matter."

"You're going. Put some curl in your hair. I'm tired of seeing it just hang there."

"I don't have anything to put curl in it with if I wanted curl in it, which I don't."

"Hah!" was Kate's only response. "Alexa, you bring that blouse and your hot rollers down here to your sister's room."

"You stay out of here, Lex," Jo shouted. "Kate, I'm not sixteen years old."

"No, you're not." Kate gave a decisive nod, the little gold drops in her ears bobbing at the movement. "You're a grown woman, and a lovely one. It's long past time you took some pride in it. Now, you're going, and you're going to put some effort into your appearance, and I won't take any sass about it. Damn kids, fighting me every which way," she muttered and swung into Jo's bathroom. "Not even a wand of mascara in here. You want to be a nun, enter a convent. Lipstick is not a tool of Satan."

With a blouse slung over her shoulder and a case of hot rollers in her hand, Lexy came in. Her mood was up in anticipation of the night ahead, so she grinned and wiggled her eyebrows at Jo. "On one of her rampages?"

"Big-time one. I don't want my hair curled."

"Oh, loosen up, Jo Ellen." Lexy dumped the rollers on the dresser, then checked out her own appearance in the mirror. She'd kept the makeup subtle to suit the casual event. In any case, firelight was terrifically flattering. Most would be wearing jeans, she knew, so her long, flowing skirt covered with red poppies would make an interesting contrast.

"And I'm not wearing your clothes."

"Suit yourself." Lexy turned, pursed her lips, and gave her sister the once-over. She was feeling just good enough to be companionable. "Hmm. Frills aren't your style."

"Now there's news. Just let me note that down."

Lexy let the sarcasm roll off her perfumed shoulders and walked a slow circle around her sister. "Got a plain black T-shirt that isn't so baggy two of you could slide into it?"

Wary, Jo nodded. "Probably."

"Black jeans?" At Jo's assenting shrug, Lexy tapped her finger to her lips. "That's the way we'll go then. Sleek and hip. Maybe some dangles at the ears and a good belt to accessorize, but that's all. No curls, either."

"No curls?"

"Nope, but you need a new do." Lexy continued to tap her finger, her eyes narrowing, her head nodding. "I can fix that. A little snip here, a little snip there."

"Snip?" Jo put both hands to her hair in defense. "What do you mean, snip? I'm not letting you cut my hair."

"What do you care? It's just hanging there anyway."

"Exactly." Kate breezed back in. "Lexy's got a nice touch with hair. She trims mine up if I can't get over to the mainland. Go wash it, Jo. Lexy, go get your scissors."

"Fine." Defeated, Jo threw up her hands. "Just fine. If she scalps me I won't have to go sit on the sand with a bunch of fools half the night listening to somebody sing 'Kum Ba Yah.' "

Fifteen minutes later, she found herself sitting with a towel bibbed around her and bits of hair falling. "Jesus." Jo squeezed her eyes tight. "I have lost my mind. It's now official."

"Stop squirming," Lexy ordered, but there was a laugh in the order rather than a sting. "I've barely done anything. Yet. And think how long this is going to keep Cousin Kate off your back."

"Yeah." Jo forced her shoulders to relax. "Yeah, there is that."

"You've got great hair, Jo. Good body, a nice natural wave." She pouted a little, studying her own wildly spiraling mane in the mirror. "Don't know why I have to pay such money for curl, myself. My hair's straight as a pin."

With a shrug for life's vagaries, she concentrated again on the job at hand. "A decent cut's all you need. What I'm doing is giving you one that you won't have to do a thing with."

"I already don't do a thing."

"And it looks it. This won't."

"Just don't cut off too . . ." Jo's eyes went huge, her throat closed as she watched three inches of hair flop into her lap. "Christ! Oh, Christ! What have you done?"

"Relax, I'm giving you bangs, that's all."

"Bangs? Bangs? I didn't ask for bangs."

"Well, you're getting them. A nice fringe to the eyebrow. Your eyes are your best feature. This will highlight them, and it's a nice, casual look that suits you." She continued to comb and snip, stood back, scowled, and snipped some more. "I like it. Yes, I like it."

"Good for you," Jo muttered. "You wear it."

"You're going to owe me an apology." Lexy squirted some gel in her palm, rubbed her hands together, then slicked them through Jo's damp hair. "You only need a little of this, about the size of a dime."

Jo scowled at the tube. "I don't use hair gunk."

"You're going to. Just a little," she repeated, then switched on her blow-dryer. "You can air-dry it too, but this'll give it a little more volume. Won't take you more than ten minutes in the morning to fuss with it."

"Doesn't take me more than two now. What's the damn point?" Jo told herself she didn't care about the cut. She was tired of sitting there being fussed with, that was all. She wasn't nervous.

"Fine." Lexy switched off the dryer, tugged out the plug. "All you do is bitch and find fault. Go ahead and look like a hag. I don't give a shit." She stormed out, leaving Jo to tug the towel aside bad-temperedly.

But when she caught her reflection in the mirror, she stopped, stepped closer. It looked . . . nice, she decided, and lifted a hand to brush the tips. Instead of hanging, it skimmed, she supposed, angled over the ears, graduated toward the back. It was sort of . . . breezy, she decided. The bangs weren't such a bad touch after all. Experimentally, she shook her head. Everything fell back into place, more or less. Nothing drooped into her eyes to irritate her.

She picked up her brush, ran it through and watched her hair rise and fall in nice, neat blunt ends. Tidy, she mused. Fuss-free, but with, well, style. She had to admit it had style and the style flattered.

The memory snuck through of sitting on the edge of her bed while her mother brushed her hair.

You've got beautiful hair, Jo Ellen. So thick and soft. It's going to be your crowning glory.

It's the same color as yours, Mama.

I know. And Annabelle laughed and hugged her close. You'll be my little twin.

"I can't be your twin, Mama," Jo whispered now. "I can't be like you."

Wasn't that why she'd never done anything more with her hair than scrape it back into an elastic band? Wasn't that why there was no tube of mascara in the bathroom? Was it stubbornness, Jo wondered, or was it fear, that kept her from spending more than five minutes a day on her appearance? From really looking at herself?

If she was going to keep herself sane, Jo thought, she was going to have to learn how to face what she saw in the mirror every day. And facing it, she realized, she would have to learn to accept it.

Taking a bracing breath, she left her room and walked down to Lexy's.

She found Lexy in the bathroom, choosing a lipstick from among the clutter of cosmetics on the counter.

"I'm sorry." When Lexy said nothing, Jo took the last step forward. "Lexy, I am sorry. You were absolutely right. I was being bitchy, I was finding fault."

Lexy stared down at the little gold tube, watched the slick red stick slide up and down. "Why?"

"I'm scared."

"Of what?"

"Everything." It was a relief to admit it, finally. "Everything scares me these days. Even a new haircut." She managed to work up a smile. "Even a terrific new haircut."

Lexy relented enough to smile back when their eyes met in the mirror. "It is pretty terrific. It would look better if you had some color, fixed up your eyes."

Jo sighed, looked down at the personal department store of cosmetics. "Why not? Can I use some of this stuff?"

"Anything there would work. We're the same coloring." Lexy turned back to the mirror, carefully painted her lips. "Jo . . . are you scared of being alone?"

"No. I do alone really well." Jo picked up blusher, sniffed at it. "That's about all that doesn't scare me."

"Funny. That's about the only thing that does scare me."

The fire speared up, rose out of white sand and toward a black, diamond-studded sky. Like some Druid ritual fire, Nathan thought, as he sipped an icy beer and watched the flames. He could imagine robed figures dancing around it, offering sacrifices to some primitive and hungry god.

And where the hell had that come from? he wondered, and took another swig to wash the image away.

The night was cool, the fire hot, and the beach, so often deserted, was filled with people and sound and music. He just wasn't quite ready to be part of it. He watched the mating dances, the ebb and flow of male and female as basic as the tide.

And he thought of the photos Jo had shown him that morning, those frozen slices of lonely. Maybe it had taken that, he realized, to make him see how lonely he'd become.

"Hey, handsome." Ginny plopped down on the sand beside him. "Whatcha doing over here all by yourself?"

"Searching for the meaning of life."

She hooted cheerfully. "Well, that's easy. It's living it." She offered him a hot dog, fresh out of the fire and burned to a crisp. "Eat up."

Nathan took a bite, tasted charcoal and sand. "Yum."

She laughed, squeezed his knee companionably. "Well, outdoor cooking's not my strong point. But I whip up a hell of a southern-style breakfast if you ever . . . find yourself in my neighborhood."

As a come-on it was both obvious and easy. There was her acre of smile, slightly off center now from the tequila she'd been drinking. He couldn't help but smile back at her. "That's a very attractive offer."

"Well, sugar, it's one every single woman on the island between sixteen and sixty would dearly love to make you. I just figure I'm getting to the head of the line."

Not entirely sure how he was supposed to respond now, Nathan scratched his chin. "I'm really fond of breakfast, but—"

"Now don't you fret over it." This time she squeezed his arm as if testing and approving the biceps. "You know what you've got to do, Nathan?"

"What's that?"

"You've got to dance."

"I do?"

"You sure do." She hopped up, shot down a hand. "With me. Come on, big guy. Let's kick up some sand."

He put a hand in hers, found it so warm and alive it was easy to grin. "All right."

"Ginny's got herself a Yankee," Giff commented, watching Ginny pull Nathan toward the damp sand.

"Looks like." Kirby licked marshmallow off her thumb. "She sure knows how to have a good time."

"It isn't so hard." With a beer dangling between his fingers, Giff scanned the beach. Some people were dancing or swaying, others were sprawled around the blazing fire, still others strolled off into the dark to be alone. Kids whooped and hollered, and the old sat in beach chairs exchanging gossip and watching the youth.

"Not everybody wants to have a good time." Kirby glanced toward the dunes again but saw no one coming over them from the direction of Sanctuary.

"You know, you got your eye cocked for Brian, and I've got mine cocked for Lexy." Giff threw a friendly arm around her shoulder. "Why don't we go dance? We'll keep our eyes cocked together."

"That's a fine idea."

Brian came over the dunes, Lexy on one side, Jo on the other. He paused at the top, took a long, slow survey. "And this, my children, all this, will one day be yours."

"Oh, Bri." Lexy elbowed him. "Don't be such a grump." She spotted Giff immediately and felt little toothy nips of jealousy as she saw him slide Kirby into his arms for a slow dance. "I've got a hankering for some crab," she said lightly and started down toward the beach.

"We could probably escape now," Jo began. "Kate's still dragging Daddy down. We could head north, circle around, and be back home before she gets here."

"She'd only make us pay for it later." Resigned, he jammed his hands in his back pockets. "Why do you suppose we're so bad at social occasions, Jo Ellen?"

"Too much Hathaway," she began.

"Not enough Pendleton," he finished. "Guess Lexy got our share of that," he added, nodding down to where their sister was already in the thick of things, surrounded by people. "Let's get it over with."

They'd barely reached the beach before Ginny raced over and greeted them both with loud kisses. "What took y'all so long? I'm half lit already. Nate, let's get these people some beer so they can catch up." She whirled away to do so, ran into someone, and giggled. "Well, hey, Morris, you wanna dance with me? Come on."

Nathan blew out a breath. "I don't know where she gets the energy. She damn near wore me out. Want that beer?"

"I'll get it," Brian told him and walked off.

"I like your hair." Nathan lifted a finger to brush under Jo's bangs. "Very nice."

"Lexy whacked at it, that's all."

"You look lovely." He skimmed his hand over her shoulder, down her arm until it captured her own hand. "Is that a problem for you?"

"No, I . . . Don't start on me, Nathan."

"Too late." He moved in a little closer. "I already have." Her scent was warm, lightly spicy, intriguing. "You're wearing perfume."

"Lexy—"

"I like it." He leaned in, stunning her by sniffing her hair, her neck. "A lot."

She was having trouble drawing a full breath, and annoyed, she took a step back. "That's not why I wore it."

"I like it anyway. You want to dance?"

"No."

"Good. Neither do I. Let's go sit by the fire and neck."

It was so absurd, she nearly laughed. "Let's just go sit by the fire. If you try anything, I'll have my daddy go get his gun and dispatch you. And you being a Yankee, no one will turn a hair."

He laughed and slipped an arm around her waist, ignoring what he'd come to realize was her instinctive jolt at being touched. "We'll just sit, then."

He got her a beer, poked a stick through a hot dog for her, then settled down beside her. "I see you brought your camera."

Automatically, she laid a hand on the scarred leather bag at her hip. "Habit. I'll wait a while before I take it out. Sometimes a camera puts people off—but after they've had enough beer, they don't mind so much."

"I thought you didn't take portraits."

"As a rule, I don't." Conversation always made her feel pressured. She dipped into her pocket for a cigarette. "You don't have to prime inanimate objects with flattery or liquor to get a shot."

"I've only had one beer." He took the lighter from her, cupped a hand around it to shield it from the wind off the ocean, and lit her cigarette. His eyes met hers over the flame. "And you haven't exactly primed me with flattery. But you can take my picture anyway."

She considered him through the smoke. Strong bones, strong eyes, strong mouth. "Maybe." She took the lighter back and tucked it in her pocket. What would she see through the lens? she wondered. What would what she saw pull out of her? "Maybe I will."

"How uncomfortable will it make you if I tell you I've been waiting here for you?"

Her gaze shifted to his again, then away. "Very. Very uncomfortable."

"Then I won't mention it," he said lightly, "or bring up the point that I watched you stand up there between the dunes, and I thought, There she is. What took her so long?"

Jo anchored the stick between her knees to free up a hand for her beer. And the hand was damp with nerves. "I wasn't that long. The fire hasn't been going more than an hour."

"I don't mean just tonight. And I don't suppose I should mention how incredibly attracted I am to you."

"I don't think—"

"So we'll talk about something else altogether." He smiled at her, delighted with the baffled look in her eyes, the faint frown on that lovely, top-heavy mouth.

"Lots of faces to study around here. You could do another book just on that. The faces of Desire." He shifted slightly so that their knees bumped.

Jo stared at him, amazed at the smoothness of his moves. Certainly that's what they were, just moves. Any man who could get a woman's heart tripping in her chest with no more than a few careless words and a grin must have a trunkful of moves.

"I haven't finished the book I'm contracted for, much less thought about another."

"But you will eventually. You've got too much talent and ambition not to. But for now why don't you just satisfy my curiosity and tell me about some of these people?"

"Who are you curious about?"

"All of them. Any of them."

Jo turned the dog just over the flames, watched the fat rise and bubble. "That's Mr. Brodie—the old man there with the white cap and the baby on his lap. That would be his great-grandchild, his fourth if I'm counting right. His parents were house servants at Sanctuary around the turn of the century. He was born on Desire, raised here."

"And grew up in the house?"

"He'd have spent a lot of time in it, but his family was given a cottage of their own and some land for their long and loyal service. He fought in World War Two as a gunner and brought his wife back from Paris. Her name was Marie Louise, and she lived here with him till she died three years back. They had four children, ten grandchildren, and now four greats. He always carries peppermint drops in his pocket." She turned her head. "Is that what you mean?"

"That's just what I mean." He wondered if she knew how her voice had warmed as she slipped into the story. "Pick another."

She sighed, finding it a little foolish. But at least it wasn't making her nervous. "There's Lida Verdon, cousin of mine on the Pendleton side. She's the tired, pregnant woman scolding the toddler. This'll be her third baby in four years, and her husband Wally's handsome as six devils and just no damn good. He's a truck driver, goes off on long runs. Makes a decent living, but Lida doesn't see much of it."

A child ran by screaming with pleasure, chased by an indulgent daddy. Jo crushed her cigarette out in the sand, buried it. "When Wally's home," she continued, "he's mostly drunk or working on it. She's kicked him out twice now, and taken him back twice. And she's got one baby on leading strings and another under her apron as proof of the reconciliations. We're the same age, Lida and I, born just a couple of months apart. I took the pictures at her wedding. She looks so pretty and so happy and young in them. Now, four years later, she's just about worn out. It's not all fairy tales on Desire," she said quietly.

"No." He slipped his arm around her. "It's not all fairy tales anywhere. Tell me about Ginny."

"Ginny?" With a quick laugh, Jo scanned the beach. "You don't have to tell anything about Ginny. You just have to look at her. See the way she's making Brian laugh? He hardly ever laughs like that. She just brings it out of you."

"You grew up with her."

"Yeah, almost like sisters, though she's closest with Lexy. Ginny was always the first of us to try anything, especially if it was bad. But there was never any harm in it, or in her. It's just a matter of Ginny liking everything, and a lot of it. And—uh-oh. I bet she helped stir that up."

He was too busy looking at Jo to notice. Everything about her had brightened, relaxed. "What?"

"See there?" Jo leaned back against his arm and gestured toward the edge of the water. "Lex and Giff are tangling. They've been blowing hot and cold on each other since they were in diapers. Ginny's mighty fond of both of them and probably did something to have them blowing hot tonight."

"She wants them to fight?"

"No, you pinhead." Laughing, Jo lifted the sizzling hot dog from the fire, anchored the stick in the sand. "She wants them to make up."

Nathan considered, then lifted his brows as Giff scooped Lexy up, hefted her Rhett Butler–style in his arms, and strode—with her kicking and cursing—down the beach. "If that's how it works, I'm going to have to talk to Ginny about stirring things up for me."

"I'm a much harder sell than my sister," Jo said dryly.

"Maybe." Nathan plucked the hot dog off the stick and tossed it from hand to hand to cool it. "But I've already got you cooking for me."

Despite the struggling woman in his arms, Giff kept his pace steady until the bonfire was a flicker in the distance. Satisfied that they were as private as they were going to get, he set her on her feet.

"Who the hell do you think you are?" She shoved him hard with both hands.

"Same person I've always been," he said evenly. "It's time you took a good look."

"I've looked at you before, and I don't see anybody who's got a right to haul me off when I don't want to go." No matter how exciting it had been, she told herself. No matter how romantic. "I was having a conversation."

"No, you weren't. You were coming on to that guy to piss me off. This time it worked."

"I was being polite and friendly to a man Ginny introduced me to. An attractive man from Charleston. A lawyer who's spending a few days on the island camping with some friends."

"A Charleston lawyer who was just about to drool on your shoulder." Giff's normally mild eyes spit fire. "You've had time to sow your oats, Lexy, and I gave you plenty of space to sow them in. Now you're back, and it's time to grow up."

"Grow up." She planted her hands on her hips, ignoring the water that foamed up the sand inches from her feet. "I've been grown, and you're just one of the many who hasn't had the sense to see it. I do what I want when I want, and with whom I want."

She turned on her heel and began to stalk off, her nose in the air. Giff rubbed his chin and told himself he shouldn't have lost his temper, even if Lexy had been sliding herself around some Charleston lawyer. But the damage was done.

He moved fast. By the time she heard him coming and turned, she had time only to squeal before he tackled her.

"Why, you flea-brained idiot, you'll ruin my skirt." Furious now, she used elbows, knees, teeth, rolling with him while the surf lapped up and soaked them both. "I hate you! I hate every inch of you, Giff Verdon."

"No, you don't, Lexy. You love me."

"Hah. You can kiss my ass."

"I'll be glad to, honey." He pinned her arms, levered himself up to grin down at her. "But I believe I'll work my way down to it." He lowered his head, and when she turned hers aside, brushed his lips over the soft skin just below her ear. "This is a fine place to start."

Shudders coursed through her, liquid and hot. "I hate you. I said I hate you."

"I know what you said." He nibbled slowly down to her throat, thrilled with the way her body went lax beneath him. "Kiss me, Lexy. Come on and kiss me."

On a sob, she turned her head, found his mouth with hers. "Hold me. Touch me. Oh, I hate you for making me want you."

"I know the feeling." He stroked her hair, her cheeks, while she trembled and strained beneath him. "Don't fret so. I'd never hurt you."

Desperate, she gripped his hair, dragged him down harder. "Inside me. I need you inside me. I'm so empty." She arched up, groaning.

He closed a hand over her breast, filled his palm with her, then giving in to his hunger, tugged the scooped neck of her blouse down so he could take her into his mouth.

The taste of her, hot, damp, pungent, pumped through his blood like whiskey. He wanted it to be slow and sweet, had waited all his life just for that. But she was moving restlessly beneath him, her hands tugging, pulling, reaching. When he closed his mouth over hers again, he couldn't think, could barely breathe. It was all taste and sound.

He was panting as he fought with her wet skirt, yanking at the thin, clinging material until his hand could skim up her thigh, until he found her, already wet. She jerked against his hand and climaxed before he could do more than moan.

"Jesus. Jesus, Lexy."

"Now. Giff, I'll kill you if you stop. I swear I'll kill you."

"You won't have to," he managed. "I'll already be dead. Get these goddamn clothes off." He tugged at her skirt with one hand, his jeans with the other. "For God's sake, Lexy, help me."

"I'm trying." She was laughing now, trapped in a dripping skirt, still flying on the fast, hard orgasm, her blood singing so high she could barely hear the sea. "I feel drunk. I feel wonderful. Oh, hurry."

"Hell with it." He tossed his jeans aside, dragged off his shirt, and pulled her into the water, skirt and all.

"What are you doing? This is brand-new."

"I'll buy you a new one. I'll buy you a dozen. Only for God's sake, let me have you." He dragged the skirt down by the elastic waist and was inside her almost before she could kick her way clear.

She cried out in shock, in delight. She wrapped her legs around him, dug her fingers into his shoulders and watched his face. Dark eyes, never leaving hers, seeing only her.

When the wave swamped her, outside and in, she burrowed against him, and knew he would always bring her back.

"I love you." He murmured it to her as his body raced toward the edge. "I love you, Lexy."

He let himself go, shuddering with her until they both went limp. Then he gathered her close and let the waves rock them. It had been perfect, he thought, free and simple and right. Just as he'd always known it would be.

"Hey, out there."

He glanced over lazily, spotted the figure on the shore waving both arms. Then he snorted, pressed his lips to Lexy's hair. "Hey, Ginny."

"I see some clothes thrown around here look familiar. Y'all naked out there?"

"Appear to be." He grinned as he felt Lexy chuckle against him.

"Ginny, he drowned my skirt."

"About time, too." She blew them elaborate kisses. "I'm walking a while. Gotta clear my head some. Lexy, Miz Kate got your daddy to drop in down at the bonfire. I'd make sure I had something covering my butt before I went back."

Weaving more than a little, and chuckling herself, Ginny headed down the beach. It made her heart happy to see the two of them together like that. Why, poor old Giff had been pining away for her for years, and Lexy, well, she'd just been chasing her own tail waiting for Giff to catch hold of her.

She had to stop a moment, waiting for her spinning head to settle back on her shoulders. Shoulda skipped the tequila shooters, she told herself. But then, life was too short to go skipping things.

One day she was going to find the right man to catch hold of her too. And until then, she was going to have a high old time looking for him.

As if she'd conjured him, a man walked across the sand toward her. Ginny cocked a hip, aimed a grin. "Well, hey there, handsome. Whatcha doing out here by yourself?"

"Looking for you, beautiful."

She shook her hair back. "Ain't that a coincidence?"

"Not really. I prefer to think of it as fate." He held out a hand and, thinking it was her lucky night, she took it.

Just drunk enough to make it easy, he thought as he led her farther into the dark. And sober enough to make it . . . fun.

Part Two

What wound did ever heal but by degrees?

—Shakespeare

11

For the first time in weeks, Jo woke rested and with an appetite. She felt settled, she realized, and very nearly happy. Kate had been right, Jo decided as she gave her hair a quick finger-comb. She'd needed the evening out, the companionship, the music, the night. And a few hours in the company of a man who apparently found her attractive hadn't hurt a thing. In fact, Jo was beginning to think it wouldn't hurt a thing to spend a bit more time in Nathan's company.

She passed her darkroom on the way downstairs and for once didn't think of the envelope filled with pictures that she'd hidden deep in a file drawer. For once, she didn't think of Annabelle.

Instead she thought of wandering down to the river again and the possibility of bumping into Nathan. Accidentally. Casually. She was getting as bad as Ginny, she decided with a laugh. Plotting ways to make a man notice her. But if it worked for Ginny, maybe it would work for her. What was wrong with a little flirtation with a man who interested her? Excited her.

There now. She paused on the stairs, curious enough to take stock. It wasn't so hard to admit that he excited her—the attention paid, the breezy way he would take her hand, the deliberate way his eyes would meet and hold hers. The cool and confident way he'd kissed her. Just moved in, she recalled, sampled, approved, and backed off. As if he'd known there would be ample opportunity for more at a time and place of his choosing.

It should have infuriated her, she mused. The cocky and blatantly male arrogance of it. And yet she found it appealed to her on the most primitive of levels. She wondered how she would play the game, and if she would show any skill at it.

She smiled, continued downstairs. She had a feeling she might just surprise Nathan Delaney. And herself.

"I'd go, Sam, but I have quite a few turnovers here this morning." Kate glanced over as Jo stepped into the kitchen. Raking a hand through her hair, she sent Jo a distracted smile. "Morning, honey. You're up early."

"So's everyone, it seems." Jo glanced at her father as she headed to the coffee-pot. He stood by the door, all but leaning out of it. The desire to escape was obvious. "Problem?" Jo asked lightly.

"Just a little one. We've got some campers coming in on the morning ferry, and some going out on the return. I just got a call from a family who's packed up and ready to go, and there's no one to check them out."

"Ginny's not at the station?"

"She doesn't answer there, or at home. I imagine she overslept." Kate smiled wanly. "Somewhere. I'm sure the bonfire went on quite late."

"It was still going strong when I left, about midnight." Jo sipped her coffee, frowning as she tried to remember if she'd seen Ginny around before she headed back home.

"Girl got a decent night's sleep, in her own bed," Sam added, "she wouldn't have any trouble getting herself to work."

"Sam, you know very well this isn't like Ginny. She's as dependable as the sunrise." With a worried frown, Kate glanced at the clock. "Maybe she isn't feeling well."

"Hung over, you mean."

"As some human beings are occasionally in their lives," Kate snapped back. "And that's neither here nor there. The point is, we have people waiting to check out of camp and others coming in. I can't leave here this morning, and even if I could I don't know anything about pitching tents or Porta-Johns. You'll just have to give up a couple of hours of your valuable time and handle it."

Sam blinked at her. It was a rare thing for her voice to take on that scathing tone with him. And it seemed he'd been hearing it quite a bit lately. Because he wanted peace more than anything else, he shrugged. "I'll head over."

"Jo will go with you," Kate said abruptly, which caused them both to stare. "You might need a hand." She spoke quickly now, her mind made up. If she could force them into each other's company for a morning, maybe the two of them would hold an actual conversation. "Jo, you can walk over from the campground and check on Ginny. Maybe her phone's just out, or she's really not feeling well. I'll worry about her until we get in touch."

Jo shifted the camera on her shoulder, watched her tentative morning plans evaporate. "Sure. Fine."

"Let me know when you get it straightened out." Kate shooed them to the door and out. "And don't worry about housekeeping detail. Lexy and I will manage well enough."

Because their backs were turned, Kate smiled broadly, brushed her hands together. There, she thought. Deal with each other.

Jo climbed in the passenger seat of her father's aged Blazer, snapped her seat belt on. It smelled of him, she realized. Sand and sea and forest. The engine turned over smoothly and purred. He'd never let anything that belonged to him suffer from neglect, she mused. Except his children.

Annoyed with herself, she pulled her sunglasses out of the breast pocket of her camp shirt, slid them on. "Nice bonfire last night," she began.

"Have to see if that boy policed the beach area."

That boy would be Giff, Jo noted, and was aware they both knew Giff wouldn't have left a single food wrapper to mar the sand. "The inn's doing well. Lots of business for this time of year."

"Advertising," Sam said shortly. "Kate does it."

Jo struggled against heaving a sigh. "I'd think word of mouth would be strong as well. And the restaurant's quite a draw with Brian's cooking."

Sam only grunted. Never in his life would he understand how a man could want to tie himself to a stove. Not that he understood his daughters any better than he understood his son. One of them flitting off to New York wanting to get famous washing her hair on TV commercials, and the other flitting everywhere and back again snapping photographs. There were times he thought the biggest puzzle in the world was how they had come from him.

But then, they'd come from Annabelle as well.

Jo jerked a shoulder and gave up. Rolling down her window, she let the air caress her cheeks, listened to the sound of the tires crunching on the road, then the quick splashing through the maze of duckweed that was life in the slough.

"Wait." Without thinking, she reached out to touch Sam's arm. When he braked, she hopped out quickly, leaving him frowning after her.

There on a hummock a turtle sunned himself, his head raised so that the pretty pattern on his neck reflected almost perfectly in the dark water. He paid no attention to her as she crouched to set her shot.

Then there was a rustle, and the turtle's head recoiled with a snap. Jo's breath caught as a heron rose up like a ghost, an effortless vertical soar of white. Then the wings spread, stirring wind. It flew over the chain of small lakes and tiny islands and dipped beyond into the trees.

"I used to wonder what it would be like to do that, to fly up into the sky like magic, with only the sound of wing against air."

"I recollect you always liked the birds best," Sam said from behind her. "Didn't know you were thinking about flying off, though."

Jo smiled a little. "I used to imagine it. Mama told me the story of the Swan Princess, the beautiful young girl turned into a swan by a witch. I always thought that was the best."

"She had a lot of stories."

"Yes." Jo turned, studied her father's face. Did it still hurt him, she wondered, to remember his wife? Would it hurt less if she could tell him she believed Annabelle was dead? "I wish I could remember all of them," she murmured.

And she wished she could remember her mother clearly enough to know what to do.

She took a breath to brace herself. "Daddy, did she ever let you know where she'd gone, or why she left?"

"No." The warmth that had come into his eyes as he watched the heron's flight with Jo iced over. "She didn't need to. She wasn't here and she left because she wanted to. We'd best be going and getting this done."

He turned and walked back to the Blazer. They drove the rest of the way in silence.

Jo had done some duty at the campground during her youth. Learning the family business, Kate had called it. The procedure had changed little over the years. The large map tacked to the wall inside the little station detailed the campsites, the paths, the toilet facilities. Blue-headed pins were stuck in the sites that were already occupied, red was for reserved sites, and green was for those where campers had checked out. Green sites needed to be checked, the area policed.

The rest room and shower facilities were also policed twice daily, scrubbed out, the supplies renewed. Since it was unlikely that Ginny had done her duty there since before the bonfire, Jo resigned herself to janitorial work.

"I'll deal with the bathrooms," she told Sam as he carefully filled out the paperwork needed to check a group of impatient campers out. "Then I'll walk over to Ginny's cabin and see what's up."

"Go to her cabin first," Sam said without looking up. "The facilities are her job."

"All right. Shouldn't take more than an hour. I'll meet you back here."

She took the path heading east. If she'd been a heron, she thought with a little smile, she'd have been knocking on Ginny's door in a blink. But the way the path wound and twisted, sliding between ponds and around the high duck grass, it was a good quarter mile hike.

She passed a site with a neat little pop-up camper. Obviously no early risers there, she mused. The flaps were zipped tight. A pair of raccoons waddled across the path, eyed her shrewdly, then continued on toward breakfast.

Ginny's cabin was a tiny box of cedar tucked into the trees. It was livened up with two big, bright-red pots filled with wildly colored plastic flowers. They stood by the door, guarded by an old and weathered pair of pink flamingos. Ginny was fond of saying she dearly loved flowers and pets, but the plastic sort suited her best.

Jo knocked once, waited a beat, then let herself in. The single main room was hardly thirty square feet, with the kitchen area separated from the living area by a narrow service bar. The lack of space hadn't kept Ginny from collecting. Knick-knacks crowded every flat surface. Water globes, souvenir ashtrays, china ladies in frilly dresses, crystal poodles.

The walls were painted bright pink and covered with really bad prints—still lifes, for the most part, of flowers and fruit. Jo was both touched and amused to see one of her own black-and-white photos crammed in with them. It was a silly shot of Ginny sleeping in the rope hammock at Sanctuary, taken when they were teenagers.

Jo smiled over it as she turned toward the bedroom. "Ginny, if you're not alone in there, cover up. I'm coming in."

But the bedroom was empty. The bed was unmade and it, as well as a good deal of the floor, was covered with clothes. From the looks of it, Jo decided, Ginny had had a hard time picking out the right outfit for the bonfire.

She looked in the bathroom just to be sure the cabin was empty. The plastic shelf over the tiny pedestal sink was crammed with cosmetics. The bowl of the sink was still dusted with face powder. Three bottles of shampoo stood on the lip of the tub, one of them still uncapped. A doll smiled from the top of the toilet tank, her pink and white crocheted gown spread full over an extra roll of toilet paper.

It was so Ginny.

"Whose bed are you sleeping in this morning, Ginny?" Jo murmured, and with a little sigh, left the cabin and prepared to scrub public rest rooms.

When she reached the facilities, Jo took keys out of her back pocket and opened the small storage area. Inside, cleaning paraphernalia and bathroom supplies were ruthlessly organized. It was always a surprise to realize how disciplined Ginny could be about her work when the rest of her life appeared to be an unpredictable and often messy lark.

Armed with mop and bucket, commercial cleaners, rags, and rubber gloves, Jo went into the women's shower. A woman of about fifty was busily brushing her teeth at one of the sinks. Jo sent her an absentminded smile and began to fill her bucket.

The woman rinsed, spat. "Where's Ginny this morning?"

"Oh." Jo blinked her eyes against the strong fumes of the cleaner as it bubbled up. "Apparently among the missing."

"Overpartied," the woman said with a friendly laugh. "It was a great bonfire. My husband and I enjoyed it—so much that we're getting a very late start this morning."

"That's what vacations are for. Enjoyment and late starts."

"It's hard to convince him of the second part." The woman took a small tube out of her travel kit and, squirting moisturizing lotion on her fingers, began to slather it on. "Dick's a real bear about time schedules. We're nearly an hour late for our morning hike."

"The island's not going anywhere."

"Tell that to Dick." She laughed again, then greeted a young woman and a girl of about three who came in. "Morning, Meg. And how's pretty Lisa today?"

The little girl raced over and began to chatter.

Jo used the voices for background music as she went about her chores. The older woman was Joan, and it seemed she and Dick had the campsite adjoining the one Meg and her husband, Mick, had claimed. They'd formed that oddly intimate vacationers' friendship over the past two days. They made a date to have a fish fry that night, then Meg slipped into one of the shower stalls with her little girl.

Jo listened to the water drum and the child's voice echo as she mopped up the floor. This was what Ginny liked, she realized, collecting these small pieces of other people's lives. But she was able to join in with them, be a part of them. People remembered her. They took snapshots with her in them and slipped them into their family vacation albums. They called her by name, and repeaters always asked after Ginny.

Because she didn't hide from things, Jo thought, leaning on her mop. She didn't let herself fade into the background. She was just like her brightly colored plastic flowers. Cheerful and bold.

Maybe it was time she herself took a few steps forward, Jo thought. Out of the background. Into the light.

She gathered her supplies and walked out of the ladies' section, rounding the building to the door of the men's facilities. She used the side of her fist to knock, giving the wooden door three hard beats, waited a few seconds, and repeated.

Wincing a little, she eased the door open and shouted. "Cleaning crew. Anyone inside?"

Years before when she'd been helping Ginny, Jo had walked in on an elderly man in a skimpy towel who'd left his hearing aid back at his campsite. She didn't want to repeat the experience. She heard nothing from inside—no sound of water running, urinals whooshing, but she made as much noise as possible herself as she clamored in.

As a final precaution, she propped the door open and hung the large plastic KEEPING YOUR REST ROOMS CLEAN sign in plain sight. Satisfied, she hauled her bucket to the sinks and dumped in cleaner. Twenty minutes, thirty tops, and she'd be done, she told herself. To get through it she began to plan the rest of her day.

She thought she might drive up to the north shore. There were ruins there from an old Spanish mission, built in the sixteenth century and abandoned in the seventeenth. The Spaniards hadn't had much luck converting the transient Indians to Christianity, and the settlement that historians suspected had been planned had never come to pass.

It was a nice day for a drive to the north tip, the light would be excellent by mid-morning for photographing the ruins and the terraces of shells accumulated and left by the Indians. She wondered if Nathan would like to go along with her. Wouldn't an architect be interested in the ruins of an old Spanish mission? She could ask Brian to put together a picnic lunch, and they could spend a few hours with the ghosts of Spanish monks.

And who was she fooling? Jo demanded. She didn't give a hang about the monks or the ruins. It was the picnic she wanted, the afternoon with no responsibility, no agenda, no deadline. It was Nathan she wanted. She straightened and pressed a hand to her stomach as it fluttered hard and fast. She wanted the time alone with him, perhaps to test them both. To see what would happen if she found the courage to just let herself go. To be with him. To be Jo.

And why not? she thought. She would call his cottage when she got back home. She'd make it very casual. Impromptu. Unplanned. And whatever happened, happened.

When the lights switched off, she yelped, splashed water all over her feet. She spun around, leading with her mop like a lance, and heard the echo of the heavy door closing.

"Hello?" The sound of her own voice, too thin and too shaky, made her shiver. "Who's there?" she demanded, and in the dim light filtering through the single high and frosted window, she edged toward the door.

It resisted her first shove. Panic reared up toothily and snapped at her throat. She shoved again, then pounded. Then she whirled, heart booming in her ears. She was certain that someone had slipped in and stood behind her.

She saw nothing—just empty stalls, the dull gleam of the wet floor. Heard nothing but her own racing breath. Still, she leaned against the door, terrified to turn her back on the room, and her eyes wheeled left and right, searching for movement in the shadows.

Sweat began to run down her back, icy panic sweat. She couldn't draw enough air, no matter how fast and hard she tried to gulp it in. Part of her mind held firm, lecturing her: You know the signs, Jo Ellen, don't let it win, don't let go. If you break down, you'll be back in the hospital again. Just get a grip. Get a grip.

She pressed a hand to her mouth to hold back the screams, but they came through in whimpers. She could feel herself begin to crack, terror pushing viciously against will until she simply turned her face to the door, slapping it weakly with her palm.

"Please, please, let me out. Don't leave me in here alone."

She heard the sound of feet crunching on the path, opened her mouth to shout. Then the fear grew monstrous, shoved her stumbling back. Her eyes were wide and fixed on the door, her pulse pounding painfully against her skin. There was a scrape and an oath. Her vision spun, grayed, then went blind as the door swung open and brilliant sunlight poured in.

She saw the silhouette of a man. As her knees buckled, she fumbled for the mop again, jabbing it out like a sword. "Don't come near me."

"Jo Ellen? What the hell's going on?"

"Daddy?" The mop clattered to the floor. She nearly followed it, but his hands caught her arms, drew her up.

"What happened here?"

"I couldn't get out. I couldn't. He's watching. I couldn't get away."

At the moment all Sam knew was that she was pale as death and shaking so hard he could almost hear her bones rattle. Moving on instinct, he picked her up and carried her out into the sun. "It's all right now. You're all right, pudding."

It was an old endearment both of them had forgotten. Jo pressed her face to his shoulder, holding tight when he sat on a stone bench with her cradled on his lap.

She was so small still, Sam thought with surprise. How could that be when she always looked so tall and competent? Whenever she'd had nightmares as a child, she'd curled up in his lap just this way, he remembered. She'd always wanted him when her dreams were bad.

"Don't be afraid. Nothing to be afraid of now."

"I couldn't get out."

"I know. Somebody'd braced some wood against the door. Kids, that's all. Playing pranks."

"Kids." She shuddered it out, clung to it as she did to him. "Kids playing pranks. Yes. They turned the lights off, shut me in. I panicked." She kept her eyes closed a moment longer, trained her breathing back to level. "I didn't even have the sense to turn them back on. I just couldn't think."

"You had a scare. Didn't used to scare so easy."

"No." She opened her eyes now. "I didn't."

"Time was you'd have busted down that door and torn the hide off whoever was fooling with you."

It nearly made her smile, his memory image of her. "Would I?"

"Always had a mean streak." Because she'd stopped trembling, and she was a grown woman and no longer the child he'd once comforted, he patted her shoulder awkwardly. "Guess you softened up some."

"More than some."

"I don't know. I thought you were going to run that mop handle clean through me for a minute. Who'd you mean was watching you?"

"What?"

"You said he was watching you. Who'd you mean?"

The photographs, she thought. Her own face. Annabelle's. Jo shook her head quickly and shifted away. Not now, was all she could think. Not yet. "I was just babbling. Scared stupid. I'm sorry."

"No need to be. Girl, you're white as a sheet yet. We'll get you home."

"I left all the stuff inside."

"I'll tend to it. You just sit here until you get your legs back under you."

"I think I will." But when he started to rise, she reached for his hand. "Daddy. Thanks for—chasing the monsters away."

He looked at their joined hands. Hers was slim and white—her mother's hand, he thought with unbearable sadness. But he looked at her face, and saw his daughter. "I used to be pretty good at it, I guess."

"You were great at it. You still are."

Because his hand suddenly felt clumsy, he let hers go and stepped back. "I'll put the things away, then we'll head home. You probably just need some breakfast."

No, Jo thought as she watched him walk away. She needed her father. And until that moment, she hadn't had a clue just how much.

12

Jo wasn't in a picnic mood any longer. Even the thought of food curdled in her stomach. She would go out alone, she decided. Over to the salt marsh, or down to the beach. If she'd had the energy she would have raced down and tried to catch the morning ferry back to the mainland. She could have lost herself in the crowds in Savannah for a few hours.

She washed her face with icy water, pulled a fielder's cap over her hair. But this time when she passed the darkroom she was compelled to go in, to open the file drawer, dig out the envelope. Her hands trembled a little as she spread the pictures out on her workbench.

But the photograph of Annabelle hadn't magically reappeared. There was just Jo, shot after shot. And eyes, those artfully cropped studies of her eyes. Or Annabelle's eyes. How could she be sure?

There had been a photograph of her mother. There *had* been. A death photo. She couldn't have imagined it. No one could imagine such a thing. It would make her insane, it would mean she was delusional. And she wasn't. Couldn't be. She'd seen it, goddamn it, it had been there.

With a snap of will she forced herself to stop, to close her eyes, to count her breaths, slowly, in and out, in and out, until her heart stopped dancing in her chest.

She remembered too clearly that sensation of cracking apart, of losing herself. She would not let it happen again.

The photo wasn't there. That was fact. It had existed. That was fact, too. So someone had taken it. Maybe Bobby had realized it upset her and gotten rid of it. Or someone else had broken into her apartment while she was in the hospital and taken it away. Whoever had sent it had come back and taken it away.

Briskly, Jo stuffed the photos back in the manila envelope. She didn't care how crazy that sounded, she was holding on to that idea. Someone was playing a cruel joke, and by obsessing over it, she was letting them win.

She stuffed the envelope back in the file drawer, closed it with a slam, and walked away.

But she could confirm or eliminate one possibility with a single phone call. Hurrying back to her room, she pulled her address book out of the desk and thumbed through quickly. She would ask, that was all, she told herself as she dialed the number of the apartment Bobby Banes shared with a couple of college friends. She could keep it casual and just ask if he'd taken the print.

Her nerves were straining by the third ring.

"Hello?"

"Bobby?"

"No, this is Jack, but I'm available, darling."

"This is Jo Ellen Hathaway," she said crisply. "I'd like to speak to Bobby."

"Oh." There was the sound of a throat clearing. "Sorry, Miss Hathaway, I thought it was one of Bobby's ah, well . . . He's not here."

"Would you ask him to get in touch with me? I'll give you a number where I can be reached."

"Sure, but I don't know when he'll be back exactly, or exactly where he is, either. He took off right after finals. Photo safari. He was really hot to put together some new prints before next semester."

"I'll leave you the number in any case," she said and recited it. "If he checks in, pass that along, will you?"

"Sure, Miss Hathaway. I know he'd like to hear from you. He's been worried about . . . I mean, wondering. He's been wondering about continuing his internship with you in the fall. Um, how's it going?"

There was no doubt in her mind that Bobby's roommate knew about her breakdown. She'd hoped, but hadn't expected, otherwise. "It's going fine, thanks." Her voice was cool, cutting off the possibility of deeper probing. "If you hear from Bobby, tell him it's important that I speak with him."

"I'll do that, Miss Hathaway. Ah—"

"Good-bye, Jack." She hung up slowly, closed her eyes.

It didn't matter that Bobby had shared her problem with his friends. She couldn't let it matter, couldn't let herself be embarrassed or upset over it. It was too much to expect him to have kept it to himself when his trainer went crazy on him one morning and was carted off to the hospital.

Her pride would just have to stand it, she decided. Shaking off the clinging shame, she headed downstairs. With any luck, Bobby would call within the next couple of weeks. Then she'd have at least one answer.

When she reached the kitchen door, she heard voices inside and paused with her hand on the panel.

"Something's wrong with her, Brian. She's not herself. Has she talked to you?"

"Kate, Jo never talks to anyone. Why would she talk to me?"

"You're her brother. You're her family."

Jo heard the clatter of dishes, caught the lingering odor of grilled meat from the breakfast shift. A cupboard door opening, shutting.

"What difference does that make?" Brian's voice was testy, impatient. Jo could almost see him trying to shrug Kate off.

"It should make all the difference. Brian, if you'd just try, she might open up to you. I'm worried about her."

"Look, she seemed fine to me last night at the bonfire. She hung out with Nathan for a couple of hours, had a beer, a hot dog."

"And she came back from the campground this morning pale as a sheet. She's been up and down like that ever since she got back. And coming back the way she did, out of the blue. She won't talk about what's going on in her life, when she's going back. You can't tell me you haven't noticed how . . . shaky she is."

Jo didn't want to hear any more. She backed away quickly, turned on her heel, and hurried to the front of the house.

Now they were watching her, she thought wearily. Wondering if she was going to snap. If she told them about her breakdown, she imagined there would be sympathetic—and knowing—nods and murmurs.

The hell with it. She stepped outside, into the sunlight, took a long gulp of air. She could handle it. Would handle it. And if she couldn't find peace here, just be left alone to find it, she would leave again.

And go where? Despair washed over her. Where did you go when you'd left the last place?

Her energy drained, bit by bit. Her feet dragged as she descended the stairs. She was too damn tired to go anywhere, she admitted. She walked to the rope hammock slung in the shade of two live oaks and crawled into it. Like climbing into a womb, Jo thought as the sides hugged her and let her sway.

Sometimes on hot afternoons, she had found her mother there and had slipped into the hammock with her. Annabelle would tell stories in a lazy voice. She would smell soft and sunny, and they would rock and rock and look up through the green leaves to the pieces of sky.

The trees were taller now, she mused. They had had more than twenty years to grow—and so had she. But where was Annabelle?

He strode along the waterfront in Savannah, ignoring the pretty shops and busy tourists. It had not been perfect. It had not been nearly perfect. The woman had been wrong. Of course, he'd known that. Even when he'd taken her he'd known.

It had been exciting, but only momentarily. A flash, then over—like coming too soon.

He stood staring at the river and calmed himself. A little game of mental manipulation that slowed his pulse rate, steadied his breathing, relaxed his muscles. He'd studied such mind-over-body games in his travels.

Soon he began to let the sounds in again—piece by piece. The jingle of a passing bicycle, the drone of tires on pavement. The voices of shoppers, the quick laugh of a child enjoying an ice cream treat.

He was calm again, in control again, and smiled out over the water. He made an attractive picture, and he knew it—his hair blowing lightly in the breeze, a man handsome of face and fit of body who enjoyed catching the female eye.

Oh, he'd certainly caught Ginny's.

She'd been so willing to walk with him on the dark beach and over the dunes. Tipsily flirting with him, the southern in her voice slurred with tequila.

She'd never known what hit her. Literally. He had to bite back a chuckle, thinking of that. One short, swift blow to the back of the head, and she'd toppled. It had been nothing to carry her into the trees. He'd been so high on anticipation, she'd seemed weightless. Undressing her had been . . . stimulating. True, her body had been lusher than he'd wanted, but she'd only been practice.

Still, he'd been in too much of a hurry. He could admit that now, he could analyze now. He'd rushed through it, had fumbled a bit with the equipment because he'd been so anxious to get those first shots. Her naked, with hands bound above her head and secured to a sturdy sapling. He hadn't taken the time to fan her hair out just so, to perfect the lighting and angles.

No, he'd been too overwhelmed with the power of the moment and had raped her the instant she regained consciousness. He'd meant to talk to her first, to capture the fear growing in her eyes as she began to understand what he meant to do.

The way it had been with Annabelle.

She struggled, tried to speak. Her lovely, long legs worked, drawing up, pumping. Her back arched. Now I felt that calm, cold control snick into place.

She was subject. I was artist.

The way it had been with Annabelle, he thought again. The way it should have been now, this time.

But the first orgasm had been a disappointment. So . . . ordinary, he thought now. He hadn't even wanted to rape her again. It had been more of a chore than a pleasure, he remembered. Nothing more than an additional step to manipulate the final shot.

But when he'd taken the silk scarf out of his pocket, slipped it around her neck, tightened it, tightened it, watched her eyes go huge, her mouth work for air, for a scream . . .

That had been considerably better. The orgasm then had been beautifully, brutally hard and long and satisfying.

And he thought, the last shot of her, that decisive moment, might be one of his finest.

He'd title it *Death of a Tramp,* for really, what else had she been? Hardly one of the angels. She'd been cheap and ordinary, he decided. Nothing but a throwaway.

That was why it hadn't been even close to perfect. It hadn't been his fault, but hers. It brightened his mood considerably now that it had come clear. She had been flawed—the subject, not the artist.

Yet he had picked her. He'd chosen her, he'd taken her.

He had to remind himself again that she had simply been practice. The entire incident had been no more than a run-through with a stand-in.

It would be perfect next time. With Jo.

With a little sigh, he patted the leather briefcase that held the photographs he'd developed in his rented rooms nearby. It was time to head back to Desire.

Since Lexy was nowhere to be found, again, Brian headed out to the garden to attack more weeds. Lexy had promised to do it, but he was more than certain she'd run off to hunt up Giff and seduce him into a lunchtime roll. He'd seen the two of them the night before from his bedroom window. Soaking wet, sandy, and giggling like children as they came up the path. It had been obvious even to his tired brain that they'd been doing more than taking a midnight swim. He'd been amused, even a little envious.

It seemed so easy for them just to take each other as they were, to live in the moment. Though he imagined that Giff had in mind a great deal more than the moment and that Lexy would do a quick tap dance on his heart on her way.

Still, Giff was a clever and a patient man, and he might have Lexy dancing to his tune before he was done. Brian thought it would be interesting to watch. From a safe distance.

That was really all he wanted, Brian mused. A safe distance.

He glanced down at the columbine, its lavender and yellow trumpets open and celebrational. It was pretty, it was cheerful, and it was up to him to keep it that way. He reached into the pocket of the short canvas apron he'd slung around his waist for the cultivator. And heard the whimper.

He looked over, saw the woman in the hammock. And his heart skipped. Her hair was darkly red in the green shade, her hand, falling limply over the side, slim and pale and elegant. Shock had him taking a step forward, then she turned her head, restless, and he backed off.

Not his mother, for Christ's sake. His sister. It was staggering how much she looked like Annabelle at times. At the right angle, with the right light. It made it difficult to let go of the memories, and the pain. His mother had loved to swing in the hammock for an hour on a summer afternoon. And if Brian came across her there, he would sometimes sit cross-legged on the ground beside her. She would lay a hand on his head, ruffle his hair, and ask him what adventures he'd had that day.

And she would always listen. Or so he'd once thought. More likely she'd been daydreaming while he chattered. Dreaming of her lover, of her escape from husband and children. Of the freedom she must have wanted more than she wanted him.

But it was Jo who slept in the hammock now, and from the looks of her, she wasn't sleeping peacefully.

A part of him—a part he viewed with disdain and something close to hate—wanted to turn around, walk away, and leave her to her own demons. But he went to her, his brow furrowing in concern as she twitched and moaned in her sleep.

"Jo." He laid a hand on her shoulder and shook it. "Come on, honey, snap out of it."

In the dream, whatever it was pursuing her through the forest with its ghost trees and wild wind reached out and dug its sharp nails into her flesh.

"Don't!" She swung out, ripping herself away. "Don't touch me!"

"Easy." He'd felt the wind of her fist brush his face and wasn't sure whether to be concerned or impressed. "I could do without the broken nose."

Her breath ragged, she stared blindly at him. "Brian." The damn shudders won, so she flopped back down and closed her eyes. "Sorry. Bad dream."

"So I gathered." It was concern after all, and more than he'd expected. Kate was right, as usual. Something was very definitely wrong here. He took a chance and eased himself down on the edge of the hammock. "You want something? Water?"

"No." The surprise showed in her eyes when she opened them and looked down at the hand he'd laid over hers. She couldn't remember the last time he'd taken her hand. Or she his. "No, I'm fine. Just a dream."

"You used to have bad ones as a kid too. Wake up hollering for Daddy."

"Yeah." She managed a weak smile. "You don't grow out of everything, I guess."

"Still get them a lot?" He tried to make it sound casual, but he saw the flicker in her eyes.

"I don't wake up hollering for anyone anymore," she said stiffly.

"No, I don't suppose you would." He wanted to get up, move away. Hadn't her problems stopped being his years ago? But he stayed where he was, rocking the hammock gently.

"It's not a flaw to be self-sufficient, Brian."

"No."

"And it's not a sin to want to handle problems on your own."

"Is that what you're doing, Jo? Handling problems? Well, rest easy. I've got enough of my own without taking on yours."

But still he didn't leave, and they rocked together quietly in the green shade. The comfort of it made her eyes sting. Cautious and needy, she took a tentative step. "I've been thinking a lot about Mama lately."

His shoulders tensed. "Why?"

"I've been seeing her, in my mind." The photograph that isn't there. "Dreaming about her. I think she's dead."

The tears had slipped out without either of them realizing it. When he glanced back, saw them sliding down her cheeks, his stomach clutched. "What's the point of this, Jo Ellen? What's the point in making yourself sick over something that happened twenty years ago and can't be changed?"

"I can't stop it—I can't explain it. It's just there."

"She left us, we lived through it. That's just there too."

"But what if she didn't leave. What if someone took her, what if—"

"What if she was abducted by aliens?" he said shortly. "For Christ's sake. The cops kept the case open more than a year. There was nothing, no evidence she'd been kidnapped, no evidence of foul play. She left. That's that. Stop driving yourself crazy."

She shut her eyes again. Maybe that was what she was doing, slowly driving herself toward insanity. "Is it better to think that every time she told us she loved us it was a lie? Is that more stable, Brian?"

"It's better to leave it alone."

"And be alone," she murmured. "Every last one of us. Because someone else might say they love us, and that might be a lie too. Better to leave it alone. Better not to take the chance. Better to be alone than left alone."

It hit close enough to home to make him bristle. "You're the one with the nightmares, Jo, not me." He made his decision quickly and rose before he could change his mind. "Come on."

"Come on where?"

"We're going for a drive. Let's go." He took her hand again, hauled her to her feet, and began to pull her with him to his car.

"Where? What?"

"Just do what you're told for once, goddamn it." He bundled her in, slammed the door, and saw with satisfaction that she was stunned enough to stay put. "I've got Kate on my back," he muttered as he piled in and turned the key. "You crying. I've had just about enough. I've got my own life, you know."

"Yeah." She sniffled, rubbed the back of her hand over her cheeks to dry them. "You're really living it up, Brian."

"Just shut up." The wheels spun as he whipped the car around and headed down the road. "You're going to come back here looking like a sheet-white bag of bones, we're going to get to the bottom of it. Then maybe everybody'll go back to their respective corners and leave me the hell alone."

Eyes narrowed now, she clutched the door handle. "Where are we going?"

"You're going," he corrected, "to the doctor."

"The hell I am." Surprise warred with sick alarm. "Stop this car right now and let me out."

He set his mouth grimly and accelerated. "You're going to the doctor. And if I have to, I'll cart you in. We'll find out if Kirby's half as good as she thinks she is."

"I am not sick."

"Then you shouldn't be afraid to let her look you over."

"I'm not afraid, I'm pissed. And I have no intention of wasting Kirby's time."

He swung up the little drive, squealed to a halt at Kirby's cottage, then clamped a hand on his sister's shoulder. His eyes were hot and dark and level. "You can walk in, or you can embarrass both of us by having me haul you in over my shoulder. Either way, you're going, so choose."

They glared at each other. Jo figured her temper was every bit a match for his. In a verbal battle, she had a decent shot of taking him down. If he decided to get physical—and she remembered from their youth that it was very possible—she didn't have a prayer. Taking the high road, she shifted pride to the forefront.

With a toss of her head, she stepped lightly out of the car and walked up the steps to Kirby's cottage.

They found Kirby at the kitchen counter, slathering peanut butter on bread. "Hi." She licked her thumb and let her greeting smile stay in place as she scanned first one coldly furious face, then the other. Strange, she thought, how suddenly strong the family resemblance. "Want some lunch?"

"Got any time to do a physical?" Brian demanded and gave his sister a firm shove forward.

Kirby took a small bite of the open-faced sandwich as Jo turned and hissed at her brother. "Sure. My next appointment isn't until one-thirty." She smiled brightly. "Which one of you wants to get naked for me today?"

"She's having her lunch," Jo informed Brian grandly.

"Peanut butter's not lunch unless you're six." He gave her another shove. "Go in there and strip. We're not leaving until she's looked you over, head to foot."

"I see this is my first appointment by abduction." Kirby eyed Brian consideringly. She'd hoped he cared enough about his sister to be tough with her, but she hadn't been sure. "Go ahead, Jo, back in my old room. I'll be right in."

"There's nothing wrong with me."

"Good. That'll make my job easier and give you an excuse to punish Brian afterward." She skimmed a hand over her neat French twist and smiled again. "I'll help you."

"Fine." She spun around and stomped down the hall.

"What's all this about, Brian?" Kirby murmured when the door slammed.

"She's having nightmares, she's not eating. She came back from the campground this morning white as a sheet."

"What was she doing at the campground?"

"Ginny didn't show up for work today."

"Ginny? That's not like her." Kirby frowned, then waved it away. That was a different worry. "I'm glad you brought her in. I've been wanting to take a look at her."

"I want you to find out what's wrong with her."

"Brian, I'll give her a physical, and if there's a physical problem, I'll find it. But I'm not a psychiatrist."

Frustrated, he dug his hands into his pockets. "Just find out what's wrong with her."

Kirby nodded, handed him the rest of her sandwich. "There's milk in the fridge. Help yourself."

When she stepped into the examining room, Jo was still fully dressed and pacing. "Look, Kirby—"

"Jo, you trust me, don't you?"

"That has nothing to—"

"Let's just do this, get it done, then everyone will feel better." She picked up a fresh gown. "Go into the bath across the hall, put this on, and pee in the cup." She took out a fresh chart and a form as Jo frowned at her. "I'm going to need some medical history—last period, any physical problems, any prescriptions you're on, any allergies, that sort of thing. You can start filling that out once you've donned the latest fashion there and I'm doing the urinalysis."

She bent over to print Jo's name on the chart. "Better give in gracefully," Kirby murmured. "Brian's bigger than you."

Jo shrugged once, then stalked off to the bathroom.

. . .

"Blood pressure's a little high." Kirby removed the cuff. "Nothing major, and likely due to a slight temper fluctuation."

"Very funny."

Kirby warmed her stethoscope between her palms, then pressed it to Jo's back. "Deep breath in, out. Again. You're a tad underweight, too. Which makes the female in me green with envy and the sensible physician cluck her tongue."

"My appetite's been a little off lately."

"The cooking at Sanctuary should take care of that." And if it didn't, Kirby intended to reevaluate. She took out her ophthalmoscope, began to examine Jo's eyes. "Headaches?"

"Now or ever?"

"Either."

"Now, yes, but I'd say that's a direct result of tangling with Brian the Bully." Then she sighed. "I suppose I've been getting more of them in the last few months than usual."

"Dull and throbbing or sharp and piercing?"

"Mostly the dull and throbbing variety."

"Dizziness, fainting, nausea?"

"I—no, not really."

Kirby leaned back, leaving one hand resting on Jo's shoulder. "No, or not really?" When Jo shrugged, Kirby set the instrument aside. "Honey, I'm a doctor and I'm your friend. I need you to be straight with me, and you need to know that anything you tell me inside this room stays between us."

Jo took a deep breath, clutched her hands hard in her lap. "I had a breakdown." The wind whooshed out of her, part fear, part relief. "About a month ago, before I came back here. I just fell apart. I couldn't stop it."

Saying nothing, Kirby laid both hands on Jo's shoulders, massaged gently. Jo lifted her head and saw nothing but compassion in those soft green eyes. Her own filled. "It makes me feel like such a fool."

"Why should it?"

"I've never felt that helpless. I've always been able to handle things, Kirby, to deal with them as they came. And then everything just piled up, heavier and heavier. And I'm not sure if I was imagining things or if they were really happening. I just don't know. And then I collapsed. Just broke."

"Did you see someone?"

"I didn't have any choice. I fell apart right in front of my assistant. He carted me off to the ER, and they hospitalized me for a few days. A mental breakdown. I don't care if we are nearing the twenty-first century, I don't care how it's intellectualized. I'm ashamed."

"I'm telling you there's nothing shameful about it and that you have every right to feel whatever you want to feel."

Jo's lips curved a little. "So I don't have to be ashamed that I'm ashamed."

"Absolutely not. What was your work schedule like?"

"Tight, but I liked it tight."

"Your social life?"

"Nil, but I liked it nil. And yes, that pretty much goes for my sex life too. I wasn't depressed or pining over a man or the lack of one. I've been thinking about my mother a lot," Jo said slowly. "I'm nearly the same age she was when she left, when everything changed."

And your life fell apart, Kirby thought. "And you wondered, worried, if everything was going to change again, beyond your control. I'm not a shrink, Jo, just an old-fashioned GP. That's a friend's speculation. What was the prognosis when you were released?"

"I don't know, exactly." Jo shifted, crinkling the paper beneath her. "I released myself."

"I see. You didn't note any prescriptions down on your form."

"I'm not taking any. And don't ask me what they prescribed. I never filled anything. I don't want drugs—and I don't want to talk to a shrink."

"All right, for now we'll handle this the old-fashioned way. We'll eliminate any physical cause. I'll prescribe fresh air, rest, regular meals—and some good, safe sex if you can get it," she added with a smile.

"Sex isn't one of my priorities."

"Well, honey, then you are crazy."

Jo blinked, then snorted out a laugh as Kirby dabbed the inside of her elbow with alcohol. "Thanks."

"No charge for insults. And the last part of the prescription is to talk. With me, with your family, with whoever you can trust to listen. Don't let it build up again. You're cared for, Jo. Lean a little."

She shook her head before Jo could speak. "Your brother cares enough to drag you in here—here to a place he's avoided like the plague since I moved in. And if I'm any judge of character, he's out there right now pacing and muttering and worried sick that I'm going to go out and tell him his sister has three weeks to live."

"It would serve him right." Jo sighed heavily. "Even if I do feel better now than I have in weeks." Then her eyes fastened on the syringe and widened. "What the hell is that for?"

"Just need a little blood." Needle poised, Kirby grinned. "Want to scream, and see how long it takes him to run in here?"

Jo averted her eyes, held her breath. "I wouldn't give him the satisfaction."

When Jo was dressed again, Kirby tossed her a fat plastic bottle. "They're just vitamins," she said. "High-potency. If you start eating right, you won't need them. But they'll give you a boost for now. I'll let you know when the blood work comes back from the lab, but everything else is within normal range."

"I appreciate it, really."

"Show it, then, by taking care of yourself and talking to me when you need to."

"I will." It always felt a bit odd for her to make an overtly affectionate move, but she stepped over and kissed Kirby's cheek. "I will. And I meant what I said. I feel better than I have in a long time."

"Good. Follow Doctor Kirby's orders, and you should feel better yet." Keeping her concerns to herself, she led Jo out.

Brian was exactly where she'd expected, restlessly pacing her living room. He stopped and scowled at them both. Kirby met the look with a bright smile.

"You have a bouncing one-hundred-and-ten-pound girl, Daddy. Congratulations."

"Very funny. What the hell's wrong with you?" he demanded of Jo.

She angled her head, narrowed her eyes. "Bite me," she suggested, then strolled to the door. "I'm walking back. Thanks for squeezing this idiot's whims into your schedule, Kirby."

"Oh, I've been working on doing just that for months." She chuckled as the screen door slammed.

"I want to know what's wrong with my sister."

"She's suffering from acute brotheritis at the moment. While extremely irritating, it's rarely fatal."

"I want a fucking straight answer," he said between his teeth, and she nodded approvingly.

"I like you even better when you're human." She turned to the coffeepot, pleased to see he'd made himself useful and had brewed fresh. "All right, straight answers. Would you like to sit down?"

His stomach jittered painfully. "How bad is it?"

"Not nearly as bad as you apparently think. You take it black, don't you? Like a real man." Her breath caught when he closed a hand hard over her arm.

"I'm not in the mood for this."

"Okay, so my witty repartee isn't going to relax you. It'll take a couple of weeks to get full test results back, but I can give you my educated opinion from the exam. Jo's a little run-down. She's edgy and she's stressed and she's annoyed with herself for being edgy and stressed. What she needs is exactly what you've shown me you can give her. Support—even when she kicks against it."

The first trickle of relief loosened the pressure in his chest. "That's it? That's all?"

She turned away to finish pouring the coffee. "There's doctor-patient confidentiality. Jo's entitled to her privacy and to my discretion."

"Jo's my sister."

"Yes, and on a personal level I'm happy to see you take that relationship to heart. I wasn't sure that you did. Here." She pressed the cup into his hand. "She came home because she needed to be home. She needed her family. So be there. That's all I can tell you. Anything else has to come from her."

He paced away, sipping coffee without realizing it. All right, he thought, she wasn't suffering from any of the mysterious and deadly diseases he'd conjured up while he'd been waiting. She'd just run herself out of energy. It wasn't cancer or a brain tumor.

"All right." This time he said it aloud. "I can probably browbeat her into eating regularly and threaten Lexy away from picking fights with her."

"You're very sweet," Kirby murmured.

"No, I'm not." He set the cup down abruptly and stepped back. His worry had faded enough to allow him to see Kirby clearly. The way those mermaid eyes were smiling at him. The way she stood there, all cool and composed, all pink and gold. "I'm just looking out for myself. I want my routine back, and I won't get it until she's steadied out."

Eyes warm, Kirby walked toward him. "Liar. Fraud. Softie."

"Back off."

"Not yet." She reached up to catch his face in her hands. He'd stirred more than her lust this time, and she couldn't resist it. "You booked the physical for her, and you haven't paid the bill." She rose to her toes. "My services don't come cheap." And brushed her lips to his.

His hands were at her waist as the taste of her flooded into him. "I keep telling you to back off." He tilted his head, deepened the kiss. "Why don't you listen?"

Her breath was already starting to back up, clog her lungs. A glorious sensation. "I'm stubborn. Persistent. Right."

"You're aggressive." His teeth nipped into her bottom lip, tugged. "I don't like aggressive women."

"Mmm. Yes, you do."

"No, I don't." He pushed her back against the counter until his body was pressed hard and hot to hers, until his mouth could fix firmly and devour. "But I want you. Happy now?"

She tipped her head back, moaning when his mouth raced down her throat. "Give me five minutes to cancel my afternoon appointments and we'll both be ecstatic. Brian, put your hands on me, for God's sake."

"It's not going to be easy." He nipped at her ear where a little emerald stud winked at the lobe, worked his way restlessly back to her mouth to plunder until her nails dug into his shoulders. He saw himself taking her there, where they stood, just dragging down his fly, dragging down her neat trousers and plunging in until this desperate need, this vicious frustration, was behind him.

But he didn't touch her, didn't take her. Instead, he used the ache churning inside him to control them both. He wrapped his hand around her throat, drew her head back until their eyes met. Hers were the green of restless seas, urging him to dive in.

"It's going to be my way. You're going to have to accept that."

Nerves shuddered through desire. "Listen—"

"No, we're done with that. Done with the games too. You could've backed off, but you didn't. Now it's going to be my way. When I come back, we're going to finish this."

Her breath was coming fast, her blood pumping hot. For a moment she hated him for being able to study her with eyes so cool and controlled. "Do you think that scares me?"

"I don't think you've got sense enough to let it scare you." And he smiled, slowly, dangerously. "But it should. When I come back," he repeated and stepped away from her. "And I won't give a damn if you're ready."

She steadied herself and grabbed for some pride. "Why, you arrogant bastard!"

"That's right." He walked toward the door, praying he could make it out before the aching for her made him groan aloud. He shot her a last look, skimming his gaze over the tousled, sunlit hair, the eyes that sparkled with a range of dangerous emotions, the mouth that was still swollen from his. "I'd go tidy myself up a bit, doc. Your next patient just pulled up."

He let the screen slam behind him.

13

Little Desire Cottage wasn't much of a detour on the way back to Sanctuary. In any case, Jo thought, scrambling to justify it, the walk would do her good.

Maybe she wanted to take some afternoon shots of the river, see how many more wildflowers had bloomed. And since she'd be walking by, it would be rude not to at least stop in.

Besides, it was family property.

She even worked out a little just-passing-by excuse, did some mental rehearsing to perfect just the right casual tone. So it was quite a letdown to get to the cottage and see that Nathan's Jeep was gone.

She stood at the base of the stairs a moment, debating, then quickly mounted them before she could change her mind. There was nothing wrong with slipping in, just for a second, leaving a note. It wasn't as if she would disturb anything or poke around. She just wanted to—Damn it, his door was locked.

It was another minor jolt. People on Desire rarely locked their doors. Too curious now to worry about manners, she pressed her face to the glass panel and peered in.

On the long table that served the kitchen area sat a compact laptop computer, frustratingly and neatly closed. A streamlined printer stood beside it. Long tubes that she assumed held blueprints were stacked nearby. One large square of paper was unrolled and anchored at the corners with a jar of instant coffee, an ashtray, and two mugs. But no matter how she shifted or angled her head, she couldn't make out what was printed on it.

None of my business anyway, she reminded herself, straining to see. At a crash of leaves behind her she stepped back quickly, looked over her shoulder. A wild turkey cut loose with its quick, gobbling call and lumbered into flight. With a roll of her eyes, Jo patted her skipping heart. It would be perfect if Nathan himself strolled out of the trees and caught her spying into his house.

She reminded herself that she had dozens of things she could do, dozens of places she could go. It wasn't as though she'd gone out of her way to see him. By much.

It was probably best that she'd missed him, she told herself, as she jogged back down the stairs and headed home. Taking the Palmetto Trail, she followed the bend of the river into the thick shade where muscadine vines and resurrection ferns turned forest to verdant jungle.

She didn't need the kind of distraction, the kind of complication that Nathan Delaney was bound to bring to her life just now. She was just getting back on her feet.

If she pursued a relationship with him, she'd have to tell him about . . . things. And if she told him, that would be the end of the relationship. Who wanted to get tangled up with a crazy woman on their vacation?

The path twisted, crowded in by the saw palmettos that gave it its name. She heard the turkey call again, and the long, liquid notes of a warbler. Her camera bag thudded at her hip as she quickened her pace and argued with herself.

So, by not starting anything, she was just saving them both time and embarrassment.

Why the hell hadn't he been home?

"Ssh." Giff put a hand over Lexy's mouth when he heard footsteps coming along the path near the clearing that was guarded by thick oak limbs and cabbage palms. "Someone's passing by," he whispered.

"Oh." In a lightning move, Lexy grabbed her discarded blouse and pressed it to her breasts. "I thought you said Nathan had gone over to the mainland for the day."

"He did. I passed him on his way to the ferry."

"Then who—oh." Lexy snickered as she peeked through palm fronds. "It's just Jo. Looking annoyed with the world, as usual."

"Quiet." Giff ducked Lexy's head down with his. "I'd just as soon your sister not catch me with my pants down."

"But you've got such a nice . . ." She made a grab for him, and muffling giggles, they tussled until Jo passed out of sight.

"You're a bad one, Lex." Giff pinned her, grinned down into her face. She still wore her bra—they hadn't quite gotten around to disposing of it—and he enjoyed the sensation of the slick material rubbing against his chest. "Just how would I have explained myself if she'd come over this way?"

"If she doesn't know what's going on, it's time someone showed her."

With a shake of his head, he leaned down to kiss the tip of her nose. "You're too hard on your sister."

"I'm too hard on her?" Lexy snorted. "Let's try that the other way around. It fits much better."

"Well, maybe you're too hard on each other. Looks to me like Jo's had a rough time with something lately."

"Her life's perfect for her," Lexy disagreed, pouting and twirling a lock of Giff's hair around her fingers. "She's got her work, all that traveling. People ooh and aah over her photographs like they were newborn babies. Or they study them like stupid textbooks. And she makes piles of money, enough so that she doesn't have to worry about stingy trust funds."

Love tugged at him as he skimmed his knuckles over her chin. "Honey, it's a pure foolish waste of time for you to be jealous of Jo."

"Jealous?" At the shock of the insult her eyes went dark and wide. "Why in holy hell would I be jealous of Jo Ellen?"

"Exactly." He kissed her, just a little nibbling peck. "The two of you are after the same thing. The way you are and the way you go after it are as different as night and day, but the goal's the same."

"Really?" Her voice was cool and smooth as fresh milk. "And what goal would that be?"

"To be happy. That's what most people want down under the rest of it. And to make their mark. Just because she's made hers before you doesn't make yours less important. And, after all, she had three years' head start."

It didn't placate Lexy in the least. Her voice went from cool to icy. "I don't know why you brought me out here if all you wanted to do was talk about my sister."

"Honey, you brought me." He grinned and kept her pinned under him despite her bad-tempered wiggles. "As I recall, you moseyed on down to Sand Castle Cottage, where I was minding my own business, replacing screens. You whispered a little something in my ear, and as you already had this here blanket in your tote, what was a man to do?"

She lifted her chin, raised a brow. "Why, I don't know, Giff. What is a man to do?"

"I guess I'll have to show you."

He took his time and that left her a little weak and trembling. The night before, everything had poured over her in a hot rush. Need on top of pleasure, pleasure clawing at need. But today, in the cool air and dim light, his hands were slow, calluses scraping gently over her skin, fingers pressing, then skimming. And though his mouth was hot, it didn't hurry. It came back to hers again and again, as if hers was the only flavor he needed.

When she sighed, it came from deep within.

She could be seduced as well as taken. He'd waited a lifetime to do both, to watch her let him do both. There was nothing about her that wasn't precious to him. Now he could show her, inch by inch. One day soon he would tell her, word by word.

When he slipped inside her, her moan of welcome was sweet and silky. He braced himself over her to give more, to take more, and his pace was as lazy as the river that flowed nearby.

She whimpered when he lowered his head to suck gently on her breasts.

"You come first," he murmured. "So I can see you."

She couldn't have stopped herself. She was being carried along like a weightless leaf on the river's current. The orgasm flowed through her, long and lovely and deep. She could barely sigh out his name as it slid through her system.

His mouth came back to hers as it curved, and he emptied himself into her.

"Mmmm." It was all she could manage as he rolled her over and snuggled her head on his chest. She'd never had a climax like that—one that crept up from the toes like silk-dipped fingers.

And he'd seemed so in control, so completely aware of her. Only the thunder of his heart under her cheek proved that he'd been as undone as she.

She smiled again, and turned her lips to his chest. "You must have done a lot of practicing."

He kept his eyes closed, enjoying the air on his face and her hair under his hand. "I'm a strong believer that you keep working on a skill until you get it right."

"I'd say you got it right."

"I've wanted you all my life, Lexy."

It made something inside her shiver to hear him say it, so simple, so easy. Caught in the afterglow, she lifted her head, and when she looked at him, that something shivered again. "I guess, deep down, I've always wanted you too."

When his eyes opened, and the look in them made her mouth go dry, she put on a sassy grin. "But you used to be so skinny."

"You used to be flat-chested." She chuckled when he reached down to cup her breasts. "Things do change."

Scooting up, she straddled him. "And you used to pull my hair."

"You used to bite me. I've still got your teeth marks back of my left shoulder."

Laughing, she shook her hair back. It was going to be painful to brush the tangles out, but she had to admit, it had been well worth it. "You do not."

"Hell I don't. Mama calls it my Hathaway brand."

"Let's just see." She tugged at him until he rolled toward his side. She peered down, squinted, though she could see the faint white scar clearly enough. Her brand. It gave her an odd little thrill to know he carried it. "Where? I don't see anything." She shifted closer. "Oh, you mean that little thing? Why, that's nothing. I can do much better now."

Before he could defend himself, she clamped her teeth on his shoulder. He yelped, flipped her over, and rolled until they were tangled in the blanket. His hands managed to reach here, reach there so that she was as breathless with freshening desire as with laughter.

"I'd say it's time I put my mark on you."

"Don't you dare bite me, Giff." She giggled, struggled, rolled. "Ouch! Damn it."

"I didn't bite you yet."

"Well, something did."

He moved fast, visions of snakes slicing into his brain. He rolled her, gained his feet, and scooped her into his arms in one lightning move. Her jaw dropped open as she watched his eyes, suddenly hard and cold, scan the ground.

"Golly," was all she could manage, as her romantic's heart flopped in her chest.

Nothing slithered or crept or crawled. But he saw a glint of silver. He set Lexy on her feet, turned her around. A faint red scrape marred her delicate shoulder blade. "You just rolled over something, that's all." He kissed the scrape lightly, then bent to pick up the dangle of silver. "Somebody's earring."

Bright-eyed, Lexy reached back to rub absently at the little pain. Why, he'd picked her up as if she weighed nothing at all, she thought dreamily. And he'd stood there, holding her, as if he would have defended her against a fire-breathing dragon.

Images of Lancelot and Guinevere, of misty castles, floated into her head before she managed to focus on the earring Giff was holding. It was a bright trail of small silver stars.

"That's Ginny's." With a slight frown, she reached out and took it from him. "It's from her favorite pair. Wonder how it got here."

Giff lifted his brows, wiggled them. "I guess we're not the first people to use the forest for something other than a nature walk."

With a laugh, Lexy sat on the blanket again, setting the earring carefully beside her before she reached for her bra. "I guess you'd be right. Long detour from the campground and her cottage, though. Was she wearing them last night?"

"I don't pay much mind to my cousin's earbobs," Giff said dryly.

"I'm almost sure . . ."

She trailed off, trying to bring back the picture. Ginny'd been wearing a bright-red shirt with silver studs, tight white jeans cinched with a concho belt. And yes, Lexy thought, almost certainly her favorite silver star dangles. Ginny liked the way they swung and caught the light.

"Well, doesn't matter. I'll get it back to her. If I can find her."

He sat down to pull on his Jockeys. "What do you mean?"

"She must have found herself a hot date at the bonfire last night. She didn't show up for work this morning."

"What do you mean she didn't show up? Ginny always shows up."

"Well, she didn't this morning. I heard the hubbub over it when I came down for the breakfast shift." Lexy dug in her tote for a hair pick and began the arduous process of dragging out the tangles. "Ouch, damn it. We had a bunch of check-ins and -outs over at the campground, and no Ginny. Kate sent Daddy and Jo over to handle it."

Giff pulled on his jeans, rising to snap them. "They checked her cabin?"

"I finished up before they got back, but I'd expect so. I can tell you, Kate was in a tizzy."

"That's not like Ginny. She's wild, but she'd never leave Kate in the lurch that way."

"Maybe she's sick." Lexy rubbed the earring between her fingers before tucking it into the little pocket of the tiny shorts she'd put on to drive Giff crazy. "She was knocking back the tequila pretty steady."

He nodded in agreement, but he knew that even hung over, she'd have done her job or seen to her own replacement. He remembered the way she'd looked, staggering over the beach in the dark, waving at him and Lexy, blowing them kisses. "I'll go check on her."

"You do that." Lexy rose, enjoying the way he watched her legs unfold. "And maybe later..." She slid her arms around him, up his back. "You'll come check on me."

"I was giving that some thought. I was figuring I'd come by, have dinner at the inn. Let you... serve me."

"Oh." Her lips took on a feline curve as she stepped back, slowly pulling the pick through her long corkscrew curls. "Were you figuring that?"

"Yeah. Then I was figuring how about if I just wandered on upstairs afterward, maybe wandered right on into your room. We could try this in a bed for a change."

"Well." She ran her tongue over her top lip. "I might just be available to-night—depending on what kind of tipper you are."

He grinned and captured her just-moistened lips with his in a kiss that rocked her straight back on her heels.

When she could breathe again, she exhaled slowly. "That's a real good start." She bent down to gather the blanket, deliberately turning to tease him with tight buns in tight shorts, then turned her head. "I'm going to give you... excellent service."

By the time Giff was back in his truck and on the road to the campground, his heart rate was nearly back to normal. The woman was potent, he thought, and life with her was going to be a continual adventure. He didn't think she was quite ready to have her notions adjusted to a lifetime with him, but he was going to work on that too.

He smiled to himself, flipped the radio up so Clint Black wailed through the speakers. He had it all planned, Giff mused. The courtship—which was progress-ing just fine in his opinion. The proposal, the marriage, the life.

As soon as he convinced her that he was exactly what she needed, that would be that. Meanwhile, they would give each other a hell of a ride.

He turned into the campground, frowning a little as he saw the teenager inside the booth instead of Ginny. "Hey, Colin." Giff braked, leaned out his window. "Got you manning the post today?"

"Looks like."

"Seen Ginny?"

"Not hide nor hair." The boy tried out a lascivious wink. "She musta caught a live one."

"Yeah." But there was an uncomfortable shift in Giff's gut. "I'm going to look in at her cabin. See what's up."

"Help yourself."

Giff drove slowly, mindful of the possibility that a child might dart out in front of him. With summer just around the corner, he knew more would be coming, stacking up in the campground, the cottages, spreading towels on the beach. Those in the cottages would fry themselves in the sun half the day, then come back and run their ACs to the max. Which usually meant he'd be kept busy replacing coils.

Not that he minded. It was good, honest work. And though he dreamed now and then of taking on something more challenging, he figured his time would come.

He pulled up into Ginny's short drive and climbed out. He hoped to find her in bed, moaning, with her head in a basin. That would explain why it was so damn quiet. When she was home, Ginny always had the radio blaring, the TV on, her voice raised in song or in argument with one of the talk shows she was addicted to. The noises clashed cheerfully. She said it kept her from feeling lonesome.

But he heard nothing except the click of palm fronds in the breeze, the hollow plop of frogs in water. He walked to the door, and because he'd run as tame in her cabin as he did in his own home, he didn't bother to knock.

He nearly jumped out of his skin as he pulled open the door and a man's form filled it. "Jesus Christ Almighty, Bri, you might as well shoot me as scare me to death."

"Sorry." Brian smiled a little. "I heard the truck, thought it might be Ginny." His gaze shifted over Giff's shoulder. "She's not with you, is she?"

"No, I just heard she wasn't at work and came to check."

"She's not here. It doesn't look like she's been around today, though it's hard to tell." He glanced back over his shoulder. "Woman's messy as three teenage girls on a rampage."

"Maybe she's at one of the sites."

Brian scanned the trees that crowded close around the tufts of golden marsh grass. There were a couple of pintail ducks taking a breather in the slough on their trek along the Atlantic flyway. A marsh hawk circled lazily overhead. Near the narrow path, where spiderwort tangled, a trio of swallowtail butterflies flitted gaily.

But he saw no sign of the human inhabitant of this small corner of the island.

"I parked over near number one, circled around to here. I asked after her, but nobody I ran into has seen her since yesterday."

"That's not right." The discomfort in Giff's stomach escalated into dull pain. "Bri, that's just not right."

"I agree with you. It's after two o'clock. Even if she'd spent the night somewhere else she should have surfaced by now." Worry was a fist pressing at the back of his neck. He rubbed it absently as he looked back into the living mess of Ginny's cabin. "It's time we started to make calls."

"I'll go by, tell my mother. She'll have half a dozen calls made before either of us can make one. Come on, I'll drop you back at your car."

"Appreciate it."

"She was pretty drunk last night," Giff added as he slipped behind the wheel. "I saw her—Lexy and I saw her. We were in the water . . . taking a swim," he added with a quick glance over.

"Swimming—right."

Giff waited a beat, tugged at the brim of his cap. "How am I supposed to tell you I'm sleeping with your sister?"

Brian pressed his fingers to his eyes. "I guess that was one way. It's a little difficult for me to get my tongue around the word 'congratulations' under the circumstances."

"You want to know my intentions?"

"I don't." Brian held up a hand. "I really, really don't."

"I'm going to marry her."

"Now I'm never going to be able to say the word 'congratulations' again." Shifting in his seat, Brian aimed a level stare at Giff. "Are you crazy?"

"I love her." Giff slapped the truck into reverse and backed up. "I always have."

Brian got a vividly clear picture of Lexy gleefully kicking Giff's still bleeding heart off a cliff. "You're a big boy, Giff. You know what you're getting into."

"That's right, just like I know that you and everybody else in your family never give Lexy enough credit." Giff's normally mild voice took on a defensive edge that made Brian raise his eyebrows. "She's smart, she's strong, she's got a heart as big as the ocean, and when you shake the nonsense away, she's as loyal as they come."

Brian blew out a long breath. She was also reckless, impulsive, and self-absorbed. But Giff's words had struck a chord and made Brian ashamed. "You're right. And if anyone can polish up her better qualities, I'd say it would be you."

"She needs me." Giff tapped his fingers on the wheel. "I'd appreciate it if you didn't mention any of this to her. I haven't gotten to that part yet."

"Believe me, the last thing I want to discuss with Alexa is her love life."

"Good. Well, I veered off from where I was heading. Like I was saying, I saw Ginny last night. Must have been somewhere around midnight. Wasn't paying much attention to the time. She was walking south on the beach—stopped and waved at us."

"Was she alone?"

"Yeah. Said she needed to clear her head. I didn't notice her walk back, but I was kind of, uh, busy for a while."

"Well, if she passed out on the beach, someone would have come across her by now, so she must have walked back, or cut up over the dunes."

"We found one of her earrings in that clearing on the Sanctuary side of the river."

"When?"

"Little bit ago," Giff said as he pulled up beside Brian's car. "Lexy and I were . . ."

"Oh, please, don't put that image in my brain. What are you, rabbits?" He shook his head. "Are you sure it was Ginny's earring?"

"Lexy was—and she was pretty sure Ginny was wearing it last night."

"That's the kind of thing Lex would notice. But it's a funny way for Ginny to walk if she was heading home."

"That's what I thought. Still, she might have been with someone by then. It's not like Ginny to leave a party before it's over—unless she's got another kind of party planned."

"None of this is like Ginny."

"No, it's not. I'm getting worried, Brian."

"Yeah." He got out of the truck, then turned and leaned in the window. "Go get your mother started on those calls. I'm going to head down to the ferry. Who knows, maybe she met the man of her dreams and eloped to Savannah."

By six there was a full-scale search under way. Through the forest paths, along the rugged hiking trails to the north, down the long curve of beach and around the winding paths that twisted through the sloughs. Some of those who scoured the island remembered another search for another woman.

Twenty years hadn't dimmed the memory. And while they looked for Ginny, many murmured about Annabelle.

Probably she'd taken off just the way Belle had. That was what some thought. She'd gotten an itchy foot and decided to scratch it. The Pendleton girl always had been wild. No, not Annabelle, some said, but Ginny. Annabelle had been still water running deep, and Ginny was all crashing surf.

But both of them were gone, just the same.

Nathan walked in on one of the conversations as he lingered at the dock, tossing his briefcase into the cab, loading his supplies in the back.

It made his heart beat just a little too fast, a little too hard. It made his stomach churn. He heard Annabelle's name tossed back and forth and it made his ears ring. He'd come to face it, Nathan reminded himself, then had tried to ignore it. He wasn't sure how much longer he could do either. Or if he was going to be able to live with whichever path he took.

He drove to Sanctuary.

He saw Jo sitting on the grand front steps, her head resting on her drawn-up knees. She lifted it when she heard his Jeep, and he saw all the ghosts in her eyes.

"We can't find her." She pressed her lips together. "Ginny."

"I heard." Not knowing what else to do, he sat beside her, draped an arm around her shoulders so she could lean against him. "I just came in on the ferry."

"We've looked everywhere. Hours now. She's vanished, Nathan, just vanished, like—" She couldn't say it. Wouldn't say it. And, drawing a breath, slammed the door on even the thought of it. "If she was on the island, someone would have seen her, someone would have found her."

"It's a lot of ground to cover."

"No." She shook her head. "If she was trying to hide, sure, she could keep one step ahead. Ginny knows the island as well as anyone, every trail and cove. But there's no reason for that. She's just gone."

"I didn't see her on the morning ferry. I kicked back and slept most of the way, but she's tough to miss."

"We already checked that. She didn't take the ferry."

"Okay." He ran his hand up and down her arm as he tried to think. "Private boats. There's a number of them around—islanders and outlanders."

"She can pilot a boat, but none of the natives report one missing. No one's reported one missing, or come in to say they took Ginny out."

"A day-tripper?"

"Yeah." She nodded, tried to accept it. "That's what most people are starting to think. She got a wild hair and took off with someone. She's done it before, but never when she was scheduled to work, and never without leaving word."

He remembered the way she'd smiled at him. *Hey, handsome.* "She was hitting the tequila pretty steady last night."

"Yeah, they're saying that too." She jerked away from him. "Ginny's not some cheap, irresponsible drunk."

"I didn't say that, Jo, and I didn't mean that."

"It's so easy to say she didn't care, didn't give a damn. She just left without a word to anyone, without a thought to anyone." Jo sprang up as the words tumbled out. "Left her home and her family and everyone who loved her without a second thought for how sick with worry and hurt they would be."

Her eyes glittered with fury, her voice rose with it. She no longer cared that it was her mother she spoke of now. No longer cared that she could see by the sober and sympathetic look on his face that he knew it.

"I don't believe it." She caught her breath, let it out slowly. "And I've never believed it."

"I'm sorry." He got to his feet, put his arms around her. Though she shoved, strained against him, he kept them firm. "I'm sorry, Jo."

"I don't want your sympathy. I don't want anything from you or anyone else. Let me go."

"No." She'd been let go too often and by too many, Nathan thought. He pressed his cheek to her hair and waited her out.

She stopped struggling abruptly and wrapped her arms tight around him. "Oh, Nathan, I'm so scared. It's like going through it all again, and still not knowing why."

He stared over her head to the rioting garden of snapdragons and Canterbury bells. "Would it make a difference? Would it help to know why?"

"Maybe not. Sometimes I think it would make it worse. For all of us." She turned her face into his throat, pathetically grateful that he was there, that he was solid. "I hate seeing my father remember, and Brian and Lexy. We don't talk about it, can't seem to bring ourselves to talk about it. But it's there. Pushing at us, and I guess it's pushed us away from each other most of our lives." She let out a long sigh, lulled by the steady beat of his heart against hers. "I find myself thinking more about Mama than Ginny, and I hate myself for it."

"Don't." He touched his lips to her temple, her cheekbone, then her mouth. "Don't," he repeated and slid more easily and more deeply into the kiss than he'd intended.

She didn't pull away, but opened to him. The simple comfort he'd meant to offer grew into something with the backbeat of urgency. His hands came up, framed her face, then slid down her in one long, slow caress that made her stomach drop away to her knees.

The need that rose up in her was so sweet, so ripe, so huge. She wanted nothing more than to fall into it. Where did this come from? she thought dizzily. And where could it go? She wished suddenly and with all her heart that they could just be two people drowning each other in this slow, endless kiss while the sun dipped low in the sky and shadows grew long and deep.

"I can't do this," she murmured.

"I have to." He changed the angle of the kiss and took her under again. "Hold on to me again, for just a minute," he said when her arms dropped limply away. "Need me again, for just a minute."

She couldn't resist it, couldn't deny either of them, so she held close and held tight and let the moment spin out around them. Dimly she heard tires spin on the road below. Reality slipped back in and she drew back.

"I have to go."

He reached out, took her by the fingertips. "Come back with me. Come home with me. Get away from this for a while."

Emotions surged into her eyes, filled them, made them intensely blue. "I can't."

She backed up, then rushed up the stairs, closing the door behind her quickly and without looking back.

14

Thirty-six hours after Ginny had failed to show up for work, Brian dragged into the family parlor and stretched out on the ancient davenport. He was exhausted, and there was simply nothing else to be done. The island had been searched in every direction, dozens of calls had been made. Finally, the police had been notified.

Not that they'd seemed terribly interested, Brian thought, as he studied the plaster rosettes edging the coffered ceiling. After all, they were dealing with a twenty-six-year-old woman—a woman with a reputation. A woman who was free to come and go as she pleased, had no known enemies and a predilection for taking strolls on the wild side.

He already knew the authorities would give the matter a glance, do the basics, then file it.

They had done a bit more than that twenty years before, he remembered, when another woman had vanished. They'd worked harder and longer to find Annabelle. Cops prowling the island, asking questions, taking notes, looking soberly concerned. But money had been involved there—trust funds, property, inheritances. It had taken him some time to realize that the police had been pursuing an angle of foul play. And that, briefly, his father had been the prime suspect.

It had scared the hell out of him.

But no evidence of foul play had ever been found, and interest eventually waned. Brian imagined interest would wane in Ginny Pendleton's case much sooner.

And he'd simply run out of things to do.

He thought fleetingly about reaching for the remote, switching on the television or stereo, and just zoning out for an hour. The parlor—or the family room, as Kate insisted on calling it—was rarely used.

It was Kate who'd chosen the casual and comfortable furnishings, mixing the deep, wide chairs, the heavy old tables, the stretch-out-and-nap sofa. She'd tossed in colorful floor pillows, with some idea, Brian imagined, that the room might actually be too crowded now and then for everyone to have a traditional seat.

But most often, the room was occupied by no more than one person at a time.

The Hathaways weren't the gather-together-to-watch-the-evening-news type. They were loners, he thought, every one of them, finding more excuses to be apart than to bond together.

It made life less . . . complicated.

He sat up, but lacked the energy to distract himself with someone else's news. Instead, he rose and went to the little refrigerator behind the mahogany bar. That was another of Kate's stubborn fantasies, keeping that bar and cold box stocked. As if the family might stop in after a long day, share a drink, some conversation, a little entertainment. Brian gave a half laugh as he popped open a beer.

Not bloody likely.

With that thought still lying bitter in his head, he glanced up and saw his father in the doorway. It was a toss-up as to who was more surprised to find himself faced with the other.

Silence hung in the air, the thick and sticky kind that only family could brew. At length Brian tipped back his beer, took a long, cold swallow. Sam shifted his feet, hooked his thumbs in his front pockets.

"You finished for the day?" he asked Brian.

"Looks that way. Nothing else to do." Since just standing there made him feel foolish, Brian shrugged his shoulders and said, "Want a beer?"

"Wouldn't mind."

Brian got another bottle from the fridge, popped the top as his father crossed the room. Sam took a swallow and fell back on silence. It had been his intention to relax his mind with a few innings of baseball, maybe knock back a few fingers of bourbon to help him sleep.

He had no idea at all how to have a beer with his son.

"Rain's come in," he said, groping.

Brian listened to it patter against the windows. "It's been a pretty dry spring."

Sam nodded, shifted again. "Water level's dead low on some of the smaller pools. This'll help."

"The outlanders won't like it."

"No." Sam's frown was a reflex. "But we need the rain."

Silence crept in again, stretched until Brian angled his head. "Well, looks like that uses up the weather as a topic. What's next?" he said coolly. "Politics or sports?"

Sam didn't miss the sarcasm, he just chose to ignore it. "Didn't think you had much interest in either."

"Right. What would I know about such manly subjects? I cook for a living."

"That's not what I meant," Sam said evenly. His nerves were scraped raw, his temper closer to the surface than he liked. He concentrated on not losing it. "I just didn't know you had an interest."

"You don't have a clue what interests me. You don't know what I think, what I want, what I feel. Because that's never interested you."

"Brian Hathaway." Kate's voice snapped as she stepped into the room with Lexy beside her. "Don't you speak to your father in that tone."

"Let the boy have his say." Sam kept his eyes on his son as he set his beer aside. "He's entitled."

"He's not entitled to show disrespect."

"Kate." Sam shot her one quelling look, then nodded at Brian. "You got something in your craw, spit it out."

"It would take years, and it wouldn't change a goddamn thing."

Sam moved behind the bar. He wanted that sour mash after all. "Why don't you just get started anyway?" He poured three fingers of Jim Beam in a short glass, then after a brief hesitation, poured a second and slid it down the bar to Brian.

"I don't drink bourbon. Which probably makes me less of a man as well."

Sam felt a dull pain center in his gut and lifted his own glass. "A man's drink of choice is his own business. And you've been full grown for a time now. Why should it matter to you what I think?"

"It took me thirty years to get here," Brian shot back. "Where the hell were you for the last twenty?" The lock he'd put on the questions, and the misery behind them, gave way to frustration and snapped open as though it had been rusted through and just waiting for that last kick. "You walked away, just like she did. Only you were worse because you let us know, every fucking day of our lives, that we didn't matter. We were just incidentals that you dumped on Kate."

War in her eyes, Kate surged forward. "Now you listen to me, Brian William Hathaway—"

"Leave him be," Sam ordered, his voice cold to mask the hot needles pricking at his throat. "Finish it out," he told Brian. "You've got more."

"What difference will it make? Will it make you go back and be there when I was twelve and a couple of outlander kids beat the hell out of me for sport? Or when I was fifteen and sicked up on my first beer? When I was seventeen and scared shitless because I was afraid I'd gotten Molly Brodie pregnant when we lost our virginity together?"

His fists balled at his sides with a rage he hadn't known lived inside him. "You weren't ever there. Kate was. She's the one who mopped up the spills and held my head. She's the one who grounded me when I needed it and taught me to drive and lectured and praised. Never you. Never once. None of us needs you now. And if you treated Mama with the same selfish disregard, it's no wonder she left."

Sam flinched at that, the first show of emotion during the long stream of bitterness. His hand shook slightly as he reached for his glass again, but before he could speak, Lexy was shouting from the doorway.

"Why are you doing this? Why are you doing this now? Something's happened to Ginny." Her voice shattered on a sob as she raced into the room. "Something terrible's happened to her, I know it, and all you can do is stand here and say these awful things." Tears streaming, she clamped her hands over her ears as if she could block it all out. "Why can't you leave it alone, just leave it all alone and pretend it doesn't matter?"

"Because it does." Furious that even now she wouldn't stand with him, Brian whirled on her. "Because it does matter that we're a pathetic excuse for a family, that you're running off to New York and trying to replace the hole he put in your life with men. That Jo's made herself sick and that I can't be with a woman without thinking I'll end up pushing her away the way he did Mama. It matters, goddamn it, because there's not one of us who knows how to be happy."

"I know how to be happy." Lexy's voice rose and stumbled as she shouted at him. She wanted to scream out the denial, to make it all a lie. "I'm going to be happy. I'm going to have everything I want."

"What the hell's going on here?" Jo braced a hand on the doorjamb and stared. The raised voices had brought her out of her room, where she'd been trying to nap to make up for the sleep she'd lost worrying over Ginny.

"Brian's hateful. Just hateful." On another wild sob, Lexy turned and rushed into Jo's arms.

The shock of that, and the sight of her brother and her father facing each other across the bar like boxers at the bell, had her gaping. Kate stood in the middle, weeping quietly.

"What's happening here?" Jo managed as her head began to throb. "Is it about Ginny?"

"They don't care about Ginny." Lost in grief, Lexy sobbed into Jo's shoulder. "They don't care."

"It's not about Ginny." Sick now with fury and guilt, Brian stepped away from the bar. "It's just a typical Hathaway evening. And I've had enough of it."

He strode out, pausing briefly by Lexy. He lifted a hand as if to stroke her hair, then dropped it again without making contact.

Jo took a quiet, shallow breath. "Kate?"

Kate brushed briskly at the tears on her cheeks. "Honey, will you take Lexy to your room for a bit? I'll be along shortly."

"All right." Jo took a quick glance at her father—the stony face, the enigmatic eyes, and decided it was best to save her questions. "Come on, Lexy," she murmured. "Come on with me now."

When they'd gone, Kate took a hankie from her pocket and blew her nose. "Not that it's any excuse for his behavior," she began, "but Brian's worried sick and exhausted. All of us are, but he's been talking to the police and still running the inn on top of everything else. He's just worn out, Sam."

"He's also right." Sam sipped, wondering if the liquor would wash the harsh taste of shame out of his throat. "I haven't been a father to them since Belle walked out on us. I left it all up to you."

"Sam . . ."

He looked over at her. "Are you going to tell me that's not true?"

She sighed a little, then because her legs just seemed too tired to hold her up another minute, slid onto a stool at the bar. "No, there's no point in lying."

Sam huffed out what passed for a laugh. "You've always been honest to a fault. It's an admirable—and irritating—quality."

"I didn't figure you paid much notice. I've been chorusing a more polite variation on what Brian's just poured out for years." She angled her head, and though her eyes were red-rimmed, they were steady when they met his. "Never made a dent in you."

"It made a few." He set his glass down to rub his hands over his face. Maybe it was because he was tired, and heartsick, and remembering too damn clearly what he'd let fade, but the words he hadn't known he could say were there. "I didn't want them to need me. Didn't want anyone to. And I sure as hell didn't want to need them."

He started to leave it at that. It was more than he'd ever said before, to anyone other than himself. But she was watching him, so patiently, with such quiet compassion, he found the rest of it pouring out.

"The fact is, Kate, Belle broke my heart. By the time I got over it, you were here and things seemed to run smooth enough."

"If I hadn't stayed—"

"They'd have had nobody. You did a good job with them, Kate. I don't know that I realized that until that boy hit me between the eyes just now. It took guts to do that."

Kate shut her eyes. "I'll never understand men, not if I live another half century. You're proud of him for shouting at you, swearing at you?"

"I respect him for it. It occurs to me that I haven't shown him the proper respect a grown man deserves."

"Well, hallelujah," she muttered and picked up Brian's untouched bourbon and drank. And choked.

Sam's lips curved. She looked so pretty, he thought, sitting there thumping a fist to her heart with her face red and her eyes wide. "You've never been one for hard liquor."

She gulped in a breath, hissed it out because it burned like the flames of hell. "I'm making an exception tonight. I'm about worn to the bone."

He took the glass out of her hand. "You'll just get sick." He reached down into the fridge and found the open bottle of the Chardonnay she preferred.

As he poured it for her, she stared at him. "I didn't realize you knew what I like to drink."

"You can't live with a woman for twenty years and not pick up on some of her habits." He heard the way it sounded and felt dull color creep up his neck. "Live in the same house, I mean."

"Hmm. Well, what are you going to do about Brian?"

"Do?"

"Sam." Impatient, she took a quick sip to knock the taste of bourbon out of her mouth. "Are you going to throw this chance away?"

There she was again, was all he could think, poking at him when all he wanted was a little peace. "He's pissed off, and I let him have his say. Now that's done."

"It is not done." She leaned forward on the bar, snagging his arm before he could evade her. "Brian just kicked the door open, Sam. Now you be father enough, you be man enough to walk through it."

"He doesn't have any use for me."

"Oh, that's the biggest pile of bull slop I've ever heard." She was just angry enough not to notice that his cough disguised a chuckle. "The lot of you are so stubborn. Every gray hair I have is a result of Hathaway mule-headedness."

He skimmed a glance over her neat cap of rich russet. "You don't have any gray hair."

"And I pay good money to keep it away." She huffed out a breath. "Now you listen to me, Sam, and keep your ears open for once. I don't care how old those three children are, they still need you. And it's past time you gave them what you stopped giving them and yourself years ago. Compassion, attention, and affection. If Ginny pulling this awful stunt has brought this to a head, then I'm almost glad of it. And I'm not going to stand by and see the four of you walk away from each other again."

She pushed off the stool, snagged her glass. "Now, I'm going to try to calm Lexy down, which should take me half the night. That gives you plenty of time to find your son and start mending fences with him."

"Kate..." When she paused at the door and turned those sparkling eyes back on him, nerves had him reaching for the bottle of Jim Beam, setting it aside again. "I don't know where to start."

"You idiot," she said with such gentle affection that the heat rose up his neck a second time. "You already have."

Brian knew exactly where he was going. He didn't delude himself that he was just taking a long walk to cool off. He could have rounded the island on foot and his blood would still have been hot. He was furious with himself for losing his temper, for saying things it did no good to say. It ripped at him that he'd made both Lexy and Kate cry.

Life was simpler when you kept things inside, he decided, when you just lived with them and went about your business.

Wasn't that what his father had done all these years?

Brian hunched his shoulders against the rain, annoyed that he'd come out without a jacket and was now soaked through. He could hear the sea pounding as he trudged along the soggy sand between the dunes. Lights glowed behind the windows of cottages, and he used them as a compass in the dark.

He heard a drift of classical music as he mounted Kirby's stairs. He saw her through the rain-splattered glass of the door. She wore soft and baggy blue sweats, her feet bare. Her hair swung forward to curtain her face as she bent to poke inside the refrigerator, one dainty foot with sassy pink toenails tapping time to the music.

The quick punch of lust was very satisfying. He opened the door without knocking.

She straightened quickly and with a short, audible gasp. "Oh, Brian. I didn't hear you." Off guard, she balanced a hand on the open refrigerator door. "Is there word on Ginny?"

"No."

"Oh, I thought . . ." Nerves drummed in her fingers as she raked them through her hair from brow to tip. His eyes were dark and direct, with something unquestionably dangerous smoldering in them. Her heart took a rabbit leap into her throat. "You're soaked."

"It's raining," he said and began to walk toward her.

"I, ah—" It didn't matter how ridiculous she told herself it was, her knees were starting to shake. "I was about to have a glass of wine. Why don't you pour some and I'll get you a towel."

"I don't need a towel."

"Okay." She could smell the rain on him now, and the heat. "I'll get the wine."

"Later." He reached out and shut the refrigerator door, then trapped her against it with his body and crushed his mouth to hers in a searing, greedy kiss.

Even as the moan strangled in her throat, his hands snaked under her shirt, closed possessively over her breasts. His teeth nipped at her tongue, shooting tiny thrills of pain and fear through her. Then his hands slid down, around her, cupping her bottom and lifting until she was inches off the floor, and wet, straining denim was pressed against the wicked ache between her thighs.

She managed to shudder out a breath when his lips fastened on her throat. "So much for small talk." Hungrily, she attacked his ear. That quick bite of flesh stirred a craving for more. "The bedroom's down the hall."

"I don't need a bed." His smile sharp-edged and feral, he lifted his head and looked at her. "My way, remember. And I do my best work in the kitchen."

Her feet hit the floor again before she could blink. He pulled her arms over her head, capturing her wrists in one hand as he pushed her back against the door. "Look at me," he demanded, then slid his free hand under the elastic of her pants and plunged his fingers into her.

She gave one choked cry—shock and pleasure colliding in a brutal assault on the system that had her hips jerking against him, matching his ruthless rhythm in primal response. Her vision narrowed, her breath shortened, and she came in an explosive gush.

She'd already been wet. He'd found her slick and ready, and that alone had been brutally arousing. But when her eyes went blind and she flooded into his hand, fists of vicious need pounded at his body. His breath was a snarl as he yanked the shirt over her head, fastened his mouth to her breast.

She was small and firm and tasted of peaches. He wanted to devour her, to feed until he was sated or dead. His murmurs of approval mixed with threats neither of them could comprehend. Her hands were raking through his hair, tugging at his wet shirt, those always competent fingers fumbling in their haste. Her very lack of control was another layer of arousal for him.

"More," he muttered, dragging her pants over her hips. "I want more." When his mouth raced down, she gripped his shoulders and sobbed.

"You can't—I can't. Oh, God. What are you doing to me?"

"I'm having you."

Then his mouth was on her, teeth and tongue relentlessly driving her beyond sanity. Her head fell back against the humming refrigerator door as heat swamped her, as it sucked her down, as it coated her skin with sweat. The force of the climax struck her like a runaway train speeding through the tunnel where he held her trapped and helpless.

Her body went limp, her head lolling back when he lifted her. Nothing shocked her now, not even when he laid her on the kitchen table like a main course he had skillfully prepared for his own appetite.

He stripped off his shirt, his eyes never leaving hers. Bracing one foot on the edge of the table, he pulled off one sneaker, then the other, tossing them both aside. He unbuttoned his jeans, dragged the zipper down.

Her eyes were clearing. Good, he thought. He wanted to watch them go blind again. As he stripped off his jeans, he let his gaze wander over her. Rosy, damp skin, delicate curves, her hair tumbled against dark wood. She was beautiful, breathtaking. When he was sure he could form words, he would tell her. Now he mounted her, and feeling her tremble beneath him, smiled.

"Say, Take me, Brian."

She had to concentrate on pulling in enough air to survive, then let it out on a moan as his thumbs brushed over her nipples.

"Say it."

Mindlessly, she arched for him. "Take me, Brian. For God's sake."

He drove inside her in one fast, hard stroke, holding them both on the edge as he watched those mermaid eyes glaze. "Now, take me, Kirby."

"Yes." She lifted a hand to his face, wrapped her legs around him, and gloried in the fast, dark ride.

He was breathless when he collapsed on her, and for the first time in days both his body and his mind were relaxed. He could feel her still quivering lightly beneath him, the solid aftershocks of good, hard sex.

He rubbed his face in her hair, enjoying the scent of it. "That was just to whet the appetite."

"Oh, my God."

He chuckled, and pushing himself up, was delighted to see her smiling at him. "You tasted like peaches."

"I'd just had a bubble bath before you came around to ravish me."

"Good timing on my part."

She reached up to brush the hair back from his face—a casually affectionate gesture that intrigued them both. "As it turned out, I suppose it was. You looked very dangerous and exciting when you walked in here."

"I was feeling dangerous. We had a family scene at Sanctuary."

"I'm sorry."

"Not your problem. I could use that wine now." He shifted, slid off the table, and went to the refrigerator.

Kirby allowed herself to enjoy the view. As a doctor she could give him high marks for keeping in shape. As his lover, she could be grateful for that long, hard body. "Wineglasses are in the second cabinet to the left," she told him. "I'll get a robe."

"Don't bother," he said as she hitched herself off the table.

"I'm not going to stand around the kitchen naked."

"Yes, you are." He poured two generous glasses before his gaze slid in her direction, roamed over her. "And you won't be standing for all that long, anyway."

Amused, she arched a brow. "I won't?"

"No." He turned, handed her a glass, then tapped his against it. "I figure the counter there will put you at about the right height."

She was grateful she'd yet to sip her wine. "The kitchen *counter*?"

"Yeah. Then there's the floor."

Kirby looked down at the shiny white linoleum her grandmother had been proud to have installed three years before. "The floor."

"I figure we might make it to the bed—if you're set on being traditional—in a couple, three hours." He glanced at the clock on the stove. "Plenty of time. We don't serve breakfast until eight."

She didn't know whether to laugh or gulp. "Awfully confident of your staying power, aren't you?"

"Confident enough. How's yours?"

The thrill of challenge made her smile. "I'll match you, Brian—and more, I'll make sure we live through it." Her eyes laughed at his over the rim of her glass. "After all, I'm a doctor."

"Well, then." He set his glass aside. She squealed when he nipped her around the waist—then yelped when her butt hit the Formica. "Hey, it's cold."

"So's this." Brian dipped a finger into his wine, then let it drip onto her nipple. He bent forward, licked it delicately away. "We'll just have to warm things up."

15

Sam supposed it was a bad sign when a man had to pump up his courage just to speak to his own son. And it was worse when you'd worked yourself up to it, then couldn't find the boy.

The kitchen was empty, with no sign of coffee on the brew or biscuits on the rise. Sam stood there a moment, feeling outsized and awkward, as he always did in what he persisted in thinking of as a woman's area.

He knew Brian habitually took a walk in the morning, but he also knew Brian just as habitually started the coffee and the biscuit or fancy bread dough first. In any case, Brian was usually back by this time. Another half hour, forty minutes, people would be wandering into the dining room and wanting their grits.

Just because Sam didn't spend much time around the house, and as little as possible around the guests, didn't mean he didn't know what went on there.

Sam ran his cap around in his hands, hating the fact that worry was beginning to stir in his gut. He'd woken up on another morning and found a member of his family gone. No preparation then, either. No warning. Just no coffee brewing in the pot and no biscuit dough rising in the big blue bowl under a thick white cloth.

Had he driven the boy off? And would he have more years now to wonder if he was responsible for pushing another out of Sanctuary and away from himself?

He closed his eyes a moment until he could tuck that ugly guilt away. Damned if he'd hang himself for it. Brian was a full-grown man, just as Annabelle had been a full-grown woman. The decisions they made were their own. He tugged his cap onto his head, started toward the door.

And felt twin trickles of relief and anxiety when he heard the whistling heading down the garden path.

Brian stopped whistling—and stopped walking—when he saw his father step through the door on the screened porch. He resented having his mood shoved so abruptly from light to dismal, resented having his last few moments of solitude interrupted.

Brian nodded briefly, then moved past Sam into the kitchen. Sam stood where he was for a minute, debating. It wasn't hard for one man to spot when another had spent the night rolling around with a woman on hot, tangled sheets. Seeing that relaxed, satisfied look on his son's face had made him feel foolish—and envious. And he thought of how much easier it would be all around for him to keep walking and just leave things where they lay.

With a grunt, he pulled off his cap again and went back inside.

"Need to have a word with you."

Brian glanced over. He'd already donned a butcher's apron and was pouring coffee beans into the grinder. "I'm busy here."

Sam planted his feet. "I need a word with you just the same."

"Then you'll have to talk while I work." Brian flicked the switch on the grinder and filled the kitchen with noise and scent. "I'm running a little behind this morning."

"Uh-huh." Sam twisted his cap in his hands and decided to wait until the grinder was finished rather than trying to talk over it. He watched Brian measure out coffee, measure out water, then set the big Bunn Omatic on to brew. "I, ah, was surprised you weren't already in here at this."

Brian took out a large bowl and began to gather the basics for his biscuits. "I don't punch a time clock for anybody but myself."

"No, no, you don't." He hadn't meant it that way, and wished to God he knew how to talk to a man wearing an apron and scooping into flour and lard. "What I wanted to say was about yesterday—last night."

Brian poured milk, eyeballing the amount. "I said all I had to say, and I don't see the point in rehashing it."

"So, you figure you can say your piece, but I'm not entitled to say mine."

Brian snatched up a wooden spoon, cradled the bowl in his arm out of habit, and began to beat. The dreamy afterglow of all-night sex had dulled to lead. "What I figure is you've had a lifetime to say yours, and I've got work to do."

"You're a hard man, Brian."

"I learned by example."

It was a neat and well-aimed little dart. Sam acknowledged it, accepted it. Then, weary of playing the supplicant, he tossed his cap aside. "You'll listen to what I have to say, then we'll be done with it."

"Say it, then." He dumped the dough on a floured board and plunged his hands into it to knead violently. "And let's be done with it."

"You were right." Sam felt the click in his throat and swallowed it. "Everything you said was right, and true."

Wrist-deep in biscuit dough, Brian turned his head and stared. "What?"

"And I respect you for having the courage to say it."

"What?"

"You got flour in your ears?" Sam said impatiently. "I said you were right, and you were right to say it. How long does it take that goddamn contraption to make a goddamn cup of coffee?" he muttered, staring accusingly at the machine.

Slowly, Brian began to knead again, but he kept his eyes on Sam. "You could squeeze off a cup if you need one."

"Well, I do." He opened a cupboard door, then scowled at the glasses and stemware.

"Coffee cups and mugs haven't been kept there for eight years," Brian said mildly. "Two cupboards down to the left—right over the coffee beverage area."

"Coffee beverage area," Sam murmured. "Fancy names for fancy drinks when all a man wants is a cup of black coffee."

"Our cappuccino and lattes are very popular."

Sam knew what cappuccino was, right enough—or was mostly sure. But lattes baffled him. He grunted, then carefully slid the glass carafe out to pour coffee into his mug. He sipped, felt a little better, and sipped again. "It's good coffee."

"It's all in the beans."

"I guess grinding them fresh makes some difference."

"All the difference in the world." Brian dropped the dough in the bowl, covered it, then walked to the sink to wash up. "Now, I believe we have what could pass as an actual conversation for the first time in, oh, most of my life."

"I haven't done right by you." Sam stared down into the rich black liquid in his mug. "I'm sorry."

Brian stopped drying his hands and gaped. "What?"

"Damned if I'm going to keep repeating myself." Sam jerked his head up, and his eyes were filled with frustration. "I'm giving you an apology, and you ought to be big enough to take it."

Brian held up a hand before it all descended into an argument again. "You caught me off guard. Knocked me flat," Brian corrected, and went to the refrigerator for breakfast meats and eggs. "Maybe I could accept it if I knew what you were apologizing for."

"For not being there when you were twelve and getting pounded on. When you were fifteen and sicking up your first beer. When you were seventeen and too stupid to know how to make love to a girl without becoming a father."

More than a little shaky, Brian took out a skillet. "Kate took me over to Savannah and bought me condoms."

"She did not." If the boy had slapped him over the head with the sausage meat, he'd have been less shocked. "Kate bought you rubbers?"

"She did." Brian found himself smiling over the memory as he heated the skillet. "Lectured me up one side and down the other about responsibility and restraint, abstinence. Then she bought me a pack of Trojans and told me if I couldn't control the urge, I'd do a damn sight better to wear protection."

"Sweet Jesus." The chuckle escaped as Sam leaned back on the counter. "I just can't picture it." Then he straightened, cleared his throat. "It should have been me telling you."

"Yes, it should have been you." As if the arrangement were vital, Brian set sausages in the skillet. "Why wasn't it?"

"I didn't have your mother telling me that I'd better go talk to that boy, something was on his mind. Or that Lexy had new dress shoes and wanted to show them off. I saw those things for myself, but I got used to her prodding me on them. Then when I didn't have her, I let it all go." He set the coffee down, shot his hands in his pockets. "I'm not used to explaining myself. I don't like it."

Brian took out another bowl, broke the first egg for pancake batter. "Your choice."

"I loved her." It seared his throat, and Sam was grateful that Brian continued to focus on his work. "It's not easy for me to say that. Maybe I didn't tell her enough—the feeling came a lot easier than the words. I needed her. Serious Sam, she'd call me, and wouldn't let me stay that way for long. She loved being around new people, talking about everything under the sun. She loved this house, this island. And for a while, she loved me."

Brian didn't think he'd ever heard a longer speech from Sam Hathaway. Not wanting to break the flow, he poured the butter he'd melted into the bowl and said nothing.

"We had our problems. I'm not going to pretend we didn't. But we always got through them. The night you were born . . . Jesus, I was scared. Piss-yourself scared, but Belle wasn't. It was all a big adventure to her. And when it was over and she had you cuddled right up in her arms and nursing, she laid back against the pillows, smiling. 'Look what a beautiful baby we made ourselves, Sam. We'll have to make lots more.' A man's got to love a woman like that," Sam murmured. "He doesn't even have a choice."

"I didn't think you did. Love her."

"I did." Sam picked up his coffee again. All the talk had dried out his throat. "It took me a lot of years of being without her to stop loving her. Maybe I did push her away, but I don't know how. The not knowing ate at me bad for a lot of years."

"I'm sorry." He saw the flicker of surprise in his father's eyes. "I didn't think it mattered to you. I didn't think any of it really mattered."

"It mattered. But after a while you learn to live with what you've got."

"And you had the island."

"It was what I could depend on, what I could tend to. And it kept me from losing my mind." He took a deep breath. "But a better man would have been around to hold his son's head when he puked up too much Budweiser."

"Löwenbräu."

"Christ, an import? No wonder I don't understand you."

Sam sighed and took a long look at the man his son had become. A man who wore an apron to work and baked pies. A man, he corrected, with cool and steady eyes, and shoulders strong and broad enough to carry more than his own load.

"We've both had our say, and I don't know as it'll make any difference. But I'm glad we said it." Sam held out a hand and hoped it was the right thing.

Jo walked in on the surprising tableau of her father and brother shaking hands in front of the stove. They both looked at her, identical flickers of embarrassment on their faces. Just then she was too damn tired and irritable to analyze it.

"Lex isn't feeling well. I'll be taking her breakfast shift."

Brian grabbed a kitchen fork and hurriedly scooted the sausage around before it burned. "You're going to wait tables?"

"That's what I said." She grabbed a short apron from a peg and tied it on.

"When's the last time you waited tables?" Brian demanded.

"The last time I was here and you were short-staffed."

"You're a lousy waitress."

"Well, I'm all you've got, pal. Lexy's got a crying jag headache, and Kate's heading over to the campground to straighten out the mess there. So live with it."

Sam picked up his cap and edged toward the door. Dealing with his son was one thing, and that had been hard enough. He wasn't about to take on a daughter in the same day. "I've got things to do," he muttered and nearly winced when Jo shot him a killing look.

"Well, so do I, but I'm waiting tables because the two of you decided to go at each other and Kate and I had to spend half the damn night listening to Lexy cry and carry on. Now the two of you, I see, have shaken hands like real men, so everything's fine and dandy. Where are the damn order pads?"

"Top drawer, under the cash register." Out of the corner of his eye, Brian saw his father slip out the door. Typical, he thought grimly, and drained the sausage. "The computer's new," he told Jo. "You ever work a cash register computer?"

"Why the hell would I? I'm not a sales clerk, I'm not a waitress. I'm a goddamn photographer."

Brian rubbed the back of his neck. It was going to be a long morning. "Go up and pour some aspirin down Lexy's throat and get her down here."

"You want her, you get her. I've had more than my fill of Lexy and her drama queen routine. She was wallowing in it." Jo slapped the pad down on the counter and stalked to the coffeepot. "Center of attention, as always."

"She was upset."

"Maybe she was, until she began to enjoy the role, but it wasn't my fault. And I'm the one who was stuck with her. It was after two before Kate and I got her calmed down and out of my room. Now she's the one who claims to have a headache." Jo rubbed hard at the center of her forehead. "Any aspirin down here?"

Brian took a bottle from a cupboard and set it on the counter. "Take the pot in and make the first rounds. Blueberry pancakes are the special. If you have to scowl, scowl in here. Out there you smile. Tell the customers your name and pretend you can be personable. It should offset the slow service."

"Kiss my ass," she snarled but grabbed the pot and the pad and swung through the door.

It didn't get any better.

Brian was slicing a grapefruit and grinding his teeth at the two orders that had been sitting under the warming light for a full five minutes. Another two, he thought, and he'd have to dump them and start again.

Where the hell was Jo?

"Busy morning." Nathan breezed in the back door. "I got a glimpse of the dining room through the windows. Looks like a pretty full house."

"Sunday morning." Brian flipped what he thought must have been the millionth pancake of the day. "People like a big breakfast on Sundays."

"Me, too." Nathan grinned at the grill. "Blueberry pancakes sound perfect."

"Get in line. Goddamn it, what's she doing out there, building the pyramids? You know computers?"

"I'm the proud owner of three. Why?"

"You're now manning the cash register." Brian jerked a thumb behind him. "Go over there and figure it out. I can't keep stopping what I'm doing to fix it every time she fucks up a bill."

"You want me to work the cash register?"

"You want to eat?"

"Why don't I work the cash register?" Nathan decided, and walked over to study it.

Jo rushed in, her face pink and harassed, her arms loaded down with dishes. "She had to know. She had to know what it would be like today. I'm going to kill her if I live through this. What the hell are you doing here?" she shot at Nathan.

"Apparently I've been put on the payroll." He eyed her as she dumped the dishes in the sink and grabbed the waiting orders. "You look real cute today, Jo Ellen."

"Bite me," she muttered and shouldered out the door.

"I imagine she's been just that pleasant to the customers."

"Don't spoil my fantasy," Nathan told him. "I like to believe she saves those ass kicks just for me."

"Going to push her in the river again?"

"She slipped. And I've got something . . . else in mind for me and Jo."

Brian scrubbed a hand over his face. "I don't want to hear about it. I don't want that particular image in my head either."

"I just figured you should know what direction I'm planning to take." To illustrate, Nathan grabbed her when she swung back through the door. Hauling her against him, he kissed her scowling and surprised mouth.

"Are you crazy?" She shoved an elbow in his gut to free herself, then pushed orders and cash and credit cards into his hands. "Here, figure it out." She darted over to snag a fresh pot of coffee and tossed scribbled orders on the counter. "Two specials, eggs, scrambled, side of bacon, whole wheat toast. One I don't remember, but it's written down there, and we're running low on biscuits and cream. And if that monster kid at table three spills his juice one more time, I'm going to strangle him and his idiot parents."

Nathan grinned as she stalked out again. "Bri, I think it could be love."

"More likely insanity. Now keep your hands off my sister and ring up those orders or I'm not feeding you."

. . .

At ten-thirty, Jo staggered into her room and fell facedown on the bed. Everything hurt. Her back, her feet, her head, her shoulders. Nobody, she thought, nobody who hadn't been there could possibly know how hard waitressing was. She'd hiked up mountains, waded through rivers, spent sweltering days in the desert—and would do so again for the right shot.

But she would slit her wrists with a smile on her face if she ever had to wait another table.

And she hated having to admit that Lexy not only wasn't a lazy malingerer, but she made the job look easy.

Still, if it hadn't been for Lexy, Jo wouldn't have missed that glorious, watery, after-the-rain light that morning. She wouldn't be gritty-eyed from three hours' sleep. And her feet wouldn't be screaming.

She set her teeth when she felt the mattress give under someone's weight. "Get out, Lexy, or I might find the energy to kill you."

"Don't bother. She's not here."

She turned her head, narrowed her eyes at Nathan. "What are you doing here?"

"You keep asking me that." He reached out to tuck her hair behind her ear and clear his view of her face. "Right now, I'm checking on you. Tough morning, huh?"

She groaned, closed her eyes. "Go away."

"Ten seconds into the foot rub and you're going to beg me to stay."

"Foot rub?"

She pulled her leg back, but he closed his fingers around her ankle, holding it steady as he pried off her shoe. "Ten, nine, eight . . ."

And when he ran the heel of his hand firmly up her arch, sheer pleasure shivered through her system and made her groan.

"See, I told you. Just relax. Happy feet are the key to the universe."

"Galileo?"

"Carl Sagan," he said with a grin. "Did you get anything to eat down there?"

"If I so much as look at another pancake, I'll throw up."

"I thought not. I brought you something else."

She blinked one eye open. "What?"

"Hmm. You've got very attractive feet. Long, narrow, an elegantly high instep. One of these days I'm going to start nibbling on them and work my way up. Oh, you meant what did I bring you to eat." He pressed his fingers against the ball of her foot, worked them down to the heel. "Strawberries and cream, one of Brian's miraculous biscuits with homemade jam, and some bacon for protein."

"Why?"

"Because you need to eat." He glanced back at her. "Or did you mean why am I going to nibble on your feet?"

"Never mind."

"Okay. Why don't you roll over, sit up, and eat? Then I can do this right."

She started to say she wasn't hungry—an automatic response. But she remembered Kirby's orders to eat. And the idea of strawberries had some appeal. She sat up, trying not to feel foolish when Nathan settled down cross-legged with her foot cradled in his lap. She took the bowl of strawberries and picked one out with her fingers.

She studied him in silence a moment. He hadn't bothered to shave that morning, and his hair was in need of a trim. But the just a bit unkempt style suited him, as did the gold the island sun was teasing out of his thick brown hair.

"You don't have to go to all this trouble," she told him. "I'm thinking about sleeping with you."

"Well, that's a load off my mind."

She took a bite of a strawberry, and the taste was so sweet and unexpectedly bright, she smiled. "I guess I'm a little out of sorts this morning."

"Are you?" He gripped her toes, worked them gently back and forth. "I hadn't noticed."

"Which is your sly Yankee way of saying I'm always bitchy."

"Not always. And I think the word I'd have chosen would have been 'troubled.' "

"A Hathaway legacy." Because the strawberries had stirred an appetite, she picked up a slice of bacon and bit in. "We had a family brawl last night, which was why Lexy was in bed with her head under the covers and I was waiting tables."

"Do you always pick up the slack?"

Surprised, she shook her head. "No, I wouldn't say I pick up much of anything. I'm rarely here."

"And when you are, you're waiting tables, changing linen, scrubbing toilets."

"How did you hear about that?"

Her voice had gone sharp, puzzling him. "You told me. You were on housecleaning detail here at the inn."

"Oh, that." Feeling foolish, she reached for the biscuit, broke it in half.

"What else?"

"Nothing." She jerked a shoulder. "Just some kids playing a prank a couple of days ago. They locked me in the men's showers over at the campground. I got a little freaked."

"That's not funny."

"No, at the time I didn't find it amusing."

"Did you catch them?"

"No, they were long gone by the time my father came along and got me out. It wasn't a big deal, just annoying."

"So we can add cleaning the men's showers to the list of slack you don't pick up. And in between all that, you're putting a photography book together and finding time to work on new pictures. What about fun?"

"Photography is fun for me." When he only lifted a brow, she sampled another strawberry. "I went to the bonfire."

"And stayed till nearly midnight. You wild woman."

The line formed between her brows. "I'm not much on parties."

"What are you much on besides photography? Books, movies, art, music? This is called the science of getting to know each other," he told her when she said nothing. "It's very handy, especially when one person is thinking about sleeping with the other." He leaned forward, amused when she edged back. "Are you going to share any of those strawberries?"

Jo ordered her pulse to level, and because he was still rubbing her feet, fed him a berry.

He caught the tips of her fingers in his teeth, sucked them in as well. Smiling slowly, he released them. "That's subliminal sensory stimulation. Or what's more commonly known as I'm coming on to you."

"I think I got that."

"Good. Now, movies?"

She tried to think if there was another man who had ever disconcerted her so easily or so often. The answer was a solid no. "I lean to the old black-and-white, especially film noir. The cinematography, the light and shadows are so incredible."

"The Maltese Falcon?"

"The best of the best."

"Look at that." He patted her foot. "Common ground. What about contemporary stuff?"

"There I head for straight action. Art films rarely grab me. I'd rather see Schwarzenegger mow down fifty bad guys than listen to a handful of people expressing their angst in a foreign language."

"This is a big relief for me. We could never have settled down to raise five children and golden retrievers if I'd had to face art films."

It made her laugh, a low, smoky sound he found ridiculously arousing. "If those are my choices, I may reconsider subtitles."

"Your favorite city, anywhere."

"Florence," she said before she'd known it was true. "That bright wash of sunlight, the colors."

"The buildings. The age and grandeur of them. The Pitti Palace, the Palazzo Vecchio."

"I have a wonderful shot of the Pitti, just before sunset."

"I'd love to see it."

"I didn't bring it with me," she said absently, remembering the moment, the slant of light, the quick whoosh of air and noise as a flock of pigeons rose in a wave. "It's back in Charlotte."

"I can wait." Before she had a chance to react, he squeezed her foot. "So, when you've finished breakfast, how about taking me on a real tour of the island?"

"It's Sunday."

"Yeah, I heard a rumor about that."

"No, I mean that's turnover day. Most of the cottages turn over on Sunday. They have to be cleaned and resupplied for incoming guests by three."

"More housekeeping. What the hell did they do when you weren't here?"

"Kate lost the two girls she had on cottage duty the week before I got here.

They took jobs on the mainland. And since I'm here, and so's Lexy, she hasn't bothered to replace them yet."

"How many are on your list?"

"Six."

He considered, nodded, rose. "Well, then, we'd better get started."

"We?"

"Sure. I can handle a vacuum cleaner and a mop. And this way you'll get done faster and we'll have time to find the least occupied spot on the beach and neck for a while."

She shifted, slid her feet—her incredibly happy feet, she had to admit—into her shoes. "Maybe I know a couple of spots—if you're as handy with a vacuum cleaner as you are with reflexology."

"Jo Ellen." He put his hands on her hips in a gesture she found shockingly intimate. "There's something you should know."

He was still married. He was under federal indictment. He preferred bondage to straight sex. She let out a little breath, amazed at herself. She hadn't been aware she possessed that much imagination. "What is it?"

"I'm thinking about sleeping with you too."

She snorted a laugh, backed up. "Nathan, that's been a load *on* my mind since you found your way back to Desire."

He was so happy to be back, to be so close to her. Just watching her brought him that quick zing of anticipation for what was to come. In his own good time.

He thought he might prolong it. After all, he'd planned carefully and money was no problem. He had all the time in the world. It would be even more satisfying to lull her into complacency, to watch her relax, bit by bit. Then he would yank her back, a brisk tug on the chain she wasn't aware linked them.

She'd be afraid. She'd be confused. She would be all the more vulnerable because of the calm he'd provided before he rearranged the composition.

Yes, he could wait. He could enjoy the sun and the surf and before long he would know every minute of her routine. Just the way he'd known her habits in Charlotte.

He would let her drift along, maybe even fall in love a little. And what delicious irony that was.

All the while she would have no idea that he was there to control her fate, to grasp his own destiny. And to take her life.

16

"I don't see why you can't take one day off, just one, and spend some time with me."

Giff put his nail gun down, sat back on his heels, and studied Lexy's sulky face. It was one of those wicked whims of nature, he supposed, that made that pouty look so damned appealing to a man. "Honey, I told you this was going to be a busy week for me. And it's only Tuesday."

"What difference does it make what day it is?" She threw her hands up in the air. "Every day around here is the same as the other."

"Well, I'll tell you what difference it makes to me." He skimmed a hand over the edge of the decking he'd completed. "I told Miss Kate that I'd have this porch addition finished and screened in by Saturday."

"So you'll have it done by Sunday."

"I told her Saturday." That, to Giff, said everything. But since it was Lexy he was talking to, he worked up the patience to spell out the rest. "The cottage is booked for next week. Since she needs Colin at the campground full-time right now, and Jed's got this week of school to finish before the summer break, I've got to see to it on my own."

She didn't care about the damn porch. The floor was nearly finished anyway. How long could it take to put a silly roof on it and screen it in? "Just a day, Giff." She crouched down next to him, letting all her charm slide into her voice as she kissed his cheek. "Just a few hours. We can take your boat over to the mainland. Have a nice lunch in Savannah."

"Lex, I just can't spare the time. Now if I can get this done, we can go next Saturday. I can juggle some things around, and we can take the whole weekend if you want."

"I don't want to go Saturday." Her voice lost its purr and edged toward mulish. "I want to go now."

Giff had a five-year-old cousin who was just as insistent on having her way and having it now. But he didn't think Lexy would appreciate the comparison. "I can't go now," he said patiently. "You can take the boat if you're so antsy to get gone. Go do some shopping."

"By myself?"

"Take your sister, take a friend."

"I can't think of anyone I less want to spend the day with than Jo. And I don't have any friends. Ginny's gone."

He didn't need to see the tears flood her eyes to know that was the root of the problem and the greatest source of her newest discontent. There was nothing he could do about it, just as there was nothing he could do about the raw spot in his own heart since Ginny's disappearance.

"If you want me to go, you have to wait till Saturday. I'll get the weekend clear. We can book a hotel room, and I'll take you out for a fancy dinner."

"You don't understand anything!" She thumped a fist on his shoulder as she sprang to her feet. "Saturday's not today, and I'll go crazy if I don't get away from here. Why won't you make time for me? Why won't you just make time?"

"I'm doing my best." Even his patience could wear thin. Giff picked up the nail gun and shot a bolt home.

"You can't even stop work and pay attention for five minutes. You just shuffle me in between jobs. And now a stupid porch is more important than being with me."

"I gave my word on the porch." He rose and, hefting a new board, laid it across the sawhorse to measure. "I keep my word, Lexy. You still want to go to Savannah on the weekend, I'll take you. That's the best I can do."

"It's not good enough." She jerked her chin up. "And I'm sure I won't have any trouble finding someone who'd be happy to take me today."

He scraped his pencil over the board to make his mark, then looked up at her with cool, narrowed eyes. He recognized the threat, and the very real possibility that she'd make good on it. "No, you won't," he said in calm, measured tones. "And that will be up to you."

It was like a slap. She'd expected him to rage, to have a jealous fit and tell her exactly what he'd do if she looked at another man. Then they could have had a loud, satisfying fight before she'd let him drag her into the empty house for make-up sex.

Then she would have convinced him to take her to Savannah.

The scene she'd already staged in her head dissolved. Because she wanted to cry, she tossed her head and turned away. "Fine then, you go right on and build your porch and I'll do what I have to do."

Giff said nothing as she stalked down the temporary steps. He had to wait until his vision cleared of blind rage before he picked up the skill saw. Temper could cost dearly, he knew, and he didn't want it to cost him a finger. He was going to need all of them, he thought, if she followed through.

It would take four fingers to make the fist he was going to plow into some guy's face.

Lexy heard the saw buzz and gritted her teeth. Selfish bastard, that's all he was. He certainly didn't care about her. She walked fast across the sand, her eyes stinging, her breath short. No one cared about her. No one understood her. Even Ginny . . .

She had to stop a moment as the muscles in her stomach seized. Ginny had left. Just gone away. Everyone she let herself care about left her, one way or another. She never mattered enough to make them stay.

At first she'd been sure something terrible had happened to Ginny. She'd gotten herself kidnapped, or she'd stumbled half drunk into a pond and been eaten by a gator.

That was ridiculous, of course. It had taken her days, but Lexy had resigned herself to the fact that she'd been left behind again. Because no one stayed, no matter how much you needed them to.

But this time . . . She shot a defiant look over her shoulder at the cottage where Giff was working. This time she'd do the leaving first.

She headed for the line of trees. The sun was too hot on her skin, the sand too gritty in her sandals. At that moment she hated Desire and everything on it with a wild and vicious passion. She hated the people who came and expected her to serve them and clean up after them. She hated her family for thinking of her as an irresponsible dreamer. She hated the beach with its blinding white sun and endless lapping waves. And the forest with its pockets of dim shadows and screaming silence.

And most of all she hated Giff because she'd been thinking about falling in love with him.

She wouldn't now. She wouldn't give him the satisfaction. Instead, she thought, as she left sun for shade, she would set her sights on someone else and make Giff suffer.

When she caught sight of Little Desire Cottage, and the figure sitting on the screened porch, she smiled slowly. She didn't know why she hadn't thought of it before. Of him before.

Nathan Delaney. He was perfect. He was successful, sophisticated, educated. He'd been places and done things. He was gorgeous to look at—gorgeous enough that even Jo had taken notice.

She'd bet Nathan Delaney knew how to treat a woman.

Lexy opened the little red bag she wore strapped across her body. After popping a cherry Lifesaver in her mouth to sweeten her breath, she took out her compact, carefully dusted her nose and brow. Her color was up, so her cheeks needed no blusher, but she methodically painted her mouth a young, inviting red. She spritzed on some Joy and fluffed back her hair while calculating exactly how to play the scene.

She wandered closer to the cottage, then looked up with a friendly smile. "Why, hello there, Nathan."

He'd brought his computer out on the picnic table on the porch to enjoy the breeze while he worked. The design he was tinkering with was nearly perfected. At the interruption, he looked up distractedly. And realized his neck had stiffened up again.

"Hello, Lexy." He rubbed at the ache.

"Don't tell me you're working on such a beautiful morning."

"Just fiddling with final details."

"Why, is that one of those little computers? How in the world do you draw whole buildings on that?"

"Painstakingly."

She laughed and, cocking her head, skimmed a finger down her throat. "Oh, now I've interrupted you, and you probably wish I'd scoot."

"Not at all. It gives me an excuse to take a break."

"Really? Would you just hate me if I asked to come up and take a peek? Or are you temperamental and don't like to show your work in progress?"

"My work's just the beginning of progress, so it's tough to be temperamental about it. Sure, come on up."

He glanced at his watch as she turned to go to the steps. He really wanted a couple of hours more to refine the plans. And he had a date at one. A drive up to the north end of the island, a picnic lunch. And some more time to get to know Jo Ellen Hathaway.

Still, he smiled at Lexy—it was impossible not to. She was pretty as a picture, smelled fresher than the spring breeze teasing through the screens. And the short white skirt she wore hinted that she had legs approximately up to her ears.

"Want something cold?"

"Mmm, I'll just have a sip of yours, okay?" She picked up the large insulated glass on the table and sipped slowly. "Iced coffee. Perfect." She detested iced coffee and had never understood why people chilled a perfectly nice hot drink.

She ran her tongue over her top lip and sat companionably beside him. Not too close. A woman didn't want to be obvious. She glanced at the monitor and was so surprised by the complex and detailed floor plan that she nearly forgot the point of the visit.

"Why, isn't that fantastic? How in the world do you do all that with a computer? I thought architects used pencils and slide rules and calculators."

"Not as much as we used to. CAD makes our lives easier. Computer-assisted drawing," he explained. "You can take out walls, change angles and pitch, widen doorways, lengthen rooms, then change your mind and put it all back the way it was. And you don't wear out erasers."

"It's just amazing. Is this going to be someone's house?"

"Eventually. A vacation home on the west coast of Mexico."

"A villa." Images of hot music, exotic flowers, and white-suited servants popped into her mind. "Bri's been to Mexico. I've never been anywhere." She slanted him a look under her lashes. "You've been all over the world, haven't you?"

"I wouldn't say all over, but here and there." A little alarm bell rang in his brain, but he ignored it as foolish and egocentric. "Wonderful cliffs on the west coast, great vistas. This place will look out over the Pacific."

"I've never seen the Pacific Ocean."

"It can be wild down this way. This area here"—he tapped the monitor—"it'll be the solarium. Arched glass, sides and roof—motorized roof. They'll be able to open it for parties or whatever when the weather's right. The pool goes there. We're keeping it free-form and building up the west side with native rock and flora. Small waterfall trickling down here. It'll look like a lagoon."

"A swimming pool, right inside the house." She gave a long, wistful sigh. "Isn't that something. They must be millionaires."

"And then some."

She filled her eyes with dreamy admiration and stared deeply into his. "You must be the very best, then. So important. So successful. Designing Mexican villas for millionaires." She laid her hand on his thigh. "I can't even imagine what it would be like, being able to build such beautiful things."

Uh-oh. The second alarm bell was louder and impossible to ignore. He considered himself a fairly intelligent man. An intelligent man knew when a woman was hitting on him. "A lot of people work on a project like this. Engineers, landscapers, contractors."

Wasn't he sweet? she thought, and slid a little closer. "But without you, they wouldn't have anything to work on. You're the one who makes it happen, Nathan."

Retreat was often the intelligent man's choice, Nathan decided. He shifted, managed to put the best part of an inch between them. "Not if I don't get these plans done." He gave her a quick smile that he hoped wasn't as nervous as it felt. "And I'm running a bit behind on them, so—"

"They look wonderful." Her hand trailed up a little higher on his thigh. Intelligent or not, he was also human. His body reacted as nature dictated.

"Listen, Lexy—"

"I'm just so impressed." She leaned in, inviting. "I'd just love to see more." Her breath fluttered out onto his lips. "Lots more." Deciding he was either too much of a gentleman—or too blockheaded—to make the next move, she pressed her mouth to his and wound her arms around his neck.

It took him a minute. She was warm and tasty, and most of the blood had drained out of his head, making it difficult to think rationally. But he managed to take hold of her wrists, unwind her, and ease away.

"You know . . ." He found it necessary to clear his throat. "You know, Lexy, you're a very appealing woman. I'm flattered."

"Good." Her pulse picked up a little. The image of Giff's face, enraged with jealousy, slipped into her mind and the pulse picked up a bit more. "Then why don't we go inside for a little while?"

"There's this other thing." He drew her arms down, kept his hands firmly over hers. "I really like my face the way it is. I've gotten used to it. Hardly ever cut myself shaving anymore."

"I like it too. It's a wonderful face."

"I appreciate that. And I don't want Giff to feel obliged to try to remodel it for me."

"Oh, what do I care about Giff?" She gave a careless toss of her head. "He doesn't own me."

The edge that came into her voice, and the sulky heat in her eyes amused him, and told him that a lovers' spat was certainly at the root of this current attempt at seduction. "Have a fight, did you?"

"I don't want to talk about Giff. Why don't you kiss me again, Nathan? You know you want to."

Part of him did, a very primal part that was just a little too close to the surface right then. "Okay, we won't talk about Giff. We'll talk about Jo."

"She doesn't own me either."

"No. I'm..." He wasn't quite sure how to put it. "Interested in her," he decided.

"I think you're interested in me." To prove it, she freed a hand and made a beeline for his crotch.

Managing not to yelp, he caught her hand firmly. "Cut that out." His voice took on a lecturing tone that would have made any mother proud. "You're worth more than this, Lexy. A hell of a lot more."

"Why would you want Jo more than me? She's cold and bossy and—"

"Stop it." He gave her captured hands one quick, hard squeeze. "I don't want to hear you talk about her that way. I care about her. And so do you."

"You don't know what I care about. Nobody does."

Because her voice had cracked at the end, he felt suddenly and pitifully sorry for her. Gently he lifted her hands, and when he kissed them had her blinking in surprise. "Maybe that's because you haven't really made up your mind yourself yet." Hoping it was safe, he released one of her hands to brush the hair back from her face. "I like you, Lexy. I really do. That's another reason I'm not taking you up on your very tempting offer."

Shame washed over her, rushing hot to her cheeks. "I made a fool of myself."

"No. I damn near did, though." Steadier at last, he eased back, reached for his now tepid coffee to cool his throat. "Most likely you'd have changed your mind somewhere along the way. Then where would I be?"

She sniffled. "Maybe I wouldn't have. Sex is easy. It's the rest that messes things up."

"Tell me about it." When he offered her the coffee, she managed to smile and shake her head.

"I hate iced coffee. I only drank it to seduce you."

"Nice touch. You want to tell me about your fight with Giff?"

"Doesn't matter." Misery settled over her so heavily she rose and paced, hoping to shake it off. "He doesn't care about me, doesn't care what I do or who I'm with. He couldn't even spare an hour of his precious time for me today."

"Sweetheart, he's crazy about you."

She let out a quick laugh. "Being crazy about somebody's easy too."

"Not always. Not when you're trying to make it all work."

Lips pursed, she looked back at him. "Do you really have feelings for Jo?"

"Apparently."

"She's not easy about anything."

"I'm finding that out."

"Are you sleeping with her?"

"Lexy—"

"Not yet," she decided and her lips curved. "And it's making you twitchy." She came back, sat on the edge of the table. "Want some tips?"

"I don't think it's appropriate for us to discuss..." He trailed off, then simply abandoned dignity. "What kind of tips?"

"She likes to be in charge, in control of things, you know? It's how she works, how she lives. And always, she keeps that little space, that maneuvering room between herself and someone else."

He found himself smiling again, and liking Alexa Hathaway even more. "She'd never guess how well you know her."

"Most people underestimate me," Lexy said with a shrug. "And mostly I let them. But I figure you did me a good turn today, so I'll do you a good turn back. Don't let her maneuver too much. When the time comes, you sweep her away, Nathan. I don't think anybody's ever swept Jo Ellen away, and it's just what she needs."

She gave him a long, measuring, and very female look, then smirked. "I figure you can handle that part just fine. And I also figure you're smart enough not to tell her what went on around here."

"Not in this lifetime."

Then the sassy look faded. "Find out what's wrong with her, Nathan."

"Wrong?"

"Something's eating at her, and whatever it is, she came here to get away from it. But she isn't getting away from it. The first week or so she was here, she'd cry in her sleep, or pace the floor half the night. And now and then there's a look in her eye, like she's afraid. Jo's never afraid."

"Have you talked to her?"

"Me?" She laughed again. "Jo wouldn't talk to me about anything important. I'm the silly little sister."

"There's nothing silly about you, Lexy. And I, for one, don't underestimate you."

Touched, she leaned over and kissed him. "I guess that makes us friends."

"I'd like to think so. Giff's a very lucky man."

"Only if I decide to give him a second chance." She tossed her head and rose. "Maybe I will—after he crawls some and begs a lot."

"As a friend, I'd appreciate it if you didn't mention this to Giff either. He'd feel really bad about pounding me."

"Oh, I won't name names." She sauntered to the door, glanced back. "But I think you'd handle yourself, Nathan. I do believe you'd handle yourself just fine. 'Bye now."

Alone, Nathan rubbed his eyes, his heart, then his stomach. Handling that one, he thought, would be a real challenge. And he wished Giff the very best of luck.

Jo was just loading the picnic hamper when Lexy strolled into the kitchen. Her camera bag sat on the counter, carefully packed. Her tripod leaned against it.

"Going on a picnic?" Lexy asked airily.

"I want to shoot some pictures on the north end, thought I'd make an afternoon of it."

"All by yourself?"

"No." Jo tucked the wine she'd decided on into the basket. "Nathan's going along."

"Nathan?" Lexy hitched herself up on the counter to sit, chose a glossy green apple out of the stoneware fruit bowl. "Why, isn't that a coincidence." Smiling, Lexy polished the apple on her blouse, just between her breasts.

"Is it?"

"I just came from his place."

"Oh?" Though her back went stiff, Jo managed to keep her tone casual.

"Mmm-hmm." Enjoying dancing on the edge, and leading her sister to it, Lexy bit into the apple. "I was passing by the cottage, and there he was, sitting out on the screened porch having some iced coffee. He invited me up."

"You don't like iced coffee."

Lexy tucked her tongue in her cheek. "Tastes do change. He showed me some floor plans he's working on. A Mexican villa."

"I wouldn't think you'd be interested in floor plans."

"Oh, I'm interested in all kinds of things." The devil in her eyes, Lexy took another crunchy bite of apple. "Especially good-looking men. That one's prime beef."

"I'm sure he'd be flattered you think so," Jo said dryly and slapped the lid down on the hamper. "I thought you were going to see Giff."

"I saw him too."

"You've been busy." Jo hefted the hamper, slung her camera bag over her shoulder. "I've got to get going or I'll lose the light."

"Toddle on along then and have a nice picnic. Oh, and Jo? Give Nathan my best, won't you?"

When the door slammed, Lexy wrapped an arm around her stomach and howled with laughter. Another tip, Nathan, she thought—rile up that green-eyed monster a bit, then reap the rewards.

She wasn't going to mention it. She would absolutely not lower herself to bring it up in even the most casual manner. Jo shifted her tripod, then bent to look through the viewfinder to perfect the angle she wanted.

The sea beat more violently here, whipping and lashing at the rough beach below the jutting bluff. Gulls wheeled and screamed, white wings slashing across the sky.

Heat and humidity were soaring, making the air shimmer.

The south wall of the old monastery was still standing. The lintel over the narrow doorway had held. Through it, light and shadow tangled and wild vines flourished. She wanted that abandoned look—the tufts of high grass, the hillocks of sand the wind built, then destroyed.

She wanted no movement and had to wait, judge the instants of stillness between gusts of wind. A broad depth of field, she thought, everything in sharp focus—the textures of the stone, the vines, the sand, all the varying shades of gray.

To accomplish it, she had to stop down, decreasing the aperture, slowing the shutter speed. Tilting her lens slightly more toward horizontal, she framed in, careful to block out the ruin of the remaining walls. She wanted it to look as though the building could be whole, yet was still empty and deserted.

Alone.

She took her shots, then carried tripod and camera to the east corner. The texture was excellent there, the pits and scars that wind and sand and time had dug into the stones. This time she used the tumbled walls, capturing desolation and loss.

When she heard a quiet click, she straightened. Nathan stood just to her left, lowering his camera.

"What are you doing?"

"Taking your picture." He'd managed three before she caught him at it. "You had a nice intense look about you."

Her stomach shuddered. Pictures of her, without her being aware. But she forced her lips to curve. "Here, let me have the camera. I'll take yours."

"Better—set the timer on yours and take both of us. In front of the ruins."

"This type of view camera, this light, they aren't made for portraits."

"So, we won't mat it for your next show. It doesn't have to be perfect, Jo." He set his camera down. "It just has to be us."

"If I had a diffuser..." Turning her head, she squinted into the sun, then, muttering, changed the camera's viewpoint to cut back on shadows, calculated the aperture, adjusted shutter speed. She shrugged her shoulders.

"Jo." It was a struggle not to laugh. "Think of it as a snapshot."

"I will not. Go stand to the left of the opening in the front wall. About two feet over."

She waited until he'd walked to the spot she'd pointed out. Through the viewfinder she watched him grin at her. She could do so much better, she thought, if she had some control, had the necessary equipment to manipulate the light and shadows. She'd have been able to highlight his windblown hair, bring out all those different shades of light and dark.

The light was hard, she decided. It should have been softer, just a little romantic to show off those wonderful eyes, that strong bone structure. With a reflector, some backfill, a diffuser, she could have made this shot sing.

God, he was attractive. Standing against that worn and pitted stone, he looked so strong and alive. So male and capable. So sexy with that plain gray T-shirt over a broad chest, those faded and worn jeans snug over narrow hips.

"I see why you don't do portraits as a rule."

She blinked, straightened. "What?"

"Your model would lapse into a coma waiting for you to set the shot." Smiling, he stretched out his arm, giving her a come-ahead curl with his fingers. "It doesn't have to be art."

"It always has to be art," she corrected. She fussed for another moment, then set the timer and went to stand beside him. "Ten seconds. Hey!"

He shifted, pulled her in front of him, and wrapped his arms around her waist. "I like this pose. Relax and smile."

She did, leaning back against him as the shutter clicked. When she started to move, he nuzzled her hair.

"I still like this pose." He turned her around, arms sliding and continuing to circle as he lowered his mouth to hers. "And this one even more."

"I have to put my equipment away."

"Okay." He simply moved his mouth from hers and skimmed it down her throat.

Nerves and desire did a pitch and roll inside her. "I—the light's changed. It's not right anymore." Because her knees were going to shake, she drew back. "I didn't mean to take so long."

"It's all right. I liked watching you work. I'll help you stow your gear."

"No, I'll do it. I get edgy when anyone fools with my equipment."

"Then I'll open the wine."

"Yeah, that'd be nice." She walked back to her tripod, easing out a long, quiet breath. She was going to have to make up her mind, and very soon, she thought, as to whether she was going to advance or retreat.

She unhooked her camera, carefully packed it away. "Lexy said she'd been with you this morning."

"What?" He could only hope the pop of the cork masked part of the shock in his voice.

"She said she went by your cottage." Jo was already cursing herself for bringing it up, and kept her eyes firmly on her work.

Nathan cleared his throat and suddenly wanted a glass of wine very badly. "Ah, yeah, she did. For a minute. Why?"

"No reason." Jo collapsed the tripod. "She said you'd shown her some plans you were working on."

Maybe he'd underestimated Lexy after all, he mused, and poured two hefty portions of wine. "The Mexico job. I was doing some fine-tuning on it when she . . . dropped in."

Jo carried her equipment over, stacked it neatly at the far edge of the blanket he'd spread over the ground. "You sound a little nervous, Nathan."

"No, just hungry." He handed her the wine, took a deep gulp of his own before sitting down and diving into the basket. "So, what do you have to eat?"

Jo's muscles tensed. "Did something happen with Lexy?"

"Something? Happen?" Nathan pulled out a plastic container of cold fried chicken. "I don't know what you mean."

Her eyes narrowed at the all-too-innocent look on his face. "Oh, don't you?"

"What are you thinking?" When you didn't want to defend, he decided, attack. "You think I . . . with your sister?" Insult coated his voice, all the more effective from the desperation that pushed it there.

"She's a beautiful woman." Jo slapped a covered bowl of sliced fruit down on the blanket.

"She certainly is, so of course that means I jumped her at the first opportunity. What the hell kind of man do you take me for?" Temper snapped out, some of it real and, Nathan felt, all of it justified. "I go after one sister in the morning and switch to the other for the afternoon? Maybe I'll give your cousin Kate a roll before nightfall and make my points off the whole family."

"I didn't mean—I was only asking—"

"Just what were you asking?"

"I..." His eyes were dark and hot, fury streaking out of them. The jitter of alarm came first, which surprised her, then it was smothered quickly by self-disgust. "Nothing. I'm sorry. She was baiting me." Annoyed with herself, Jo dragged a hand through her hair. "I knew she was baiting me. She knew I was coming up here with you, and that I've been seeing you, more or less, and she wanted to get a rise out of me."

She blew out a breath, cursed herself again for not keeping her mouth shut. "I wasn't going to mention it," she went on when Nathan said nothing. "I don't know why I did. It just slipped out."

He cocked his head. "Jealous?"

She would have been relieved that the heat had died out of his eyes, but the question tightened her up all over again. "No. I was just...I don't know. I'm sorry." She reached for his hand, closing the distance. "I really am."

"Let's forget it." Since he had her hand, he brought it to his lips. "It never happened."

When she smiled, leaned over, and kissed him lightly on the mouth, he rolled his eyes skyward, wondering if he should thank Lexy or throttle her.

17

Kirby checked Yancy Brodie's temperature while his mother looked on anxiously.

"He was up most of the night, Doc Kirby. I gave him Tylenol, but the fever was right back up this morning. Jerry had to leave before dawn to go out on the shrimp boat, and he was just worried sick."

"I don't feel good," Yancy said fretfully and looked up into Kirby's eyes. "My mama said you were gonna make me feel better."

"We'll see what we can do about that." Kirby ran a hand over four-year-old Yancy's straw-colored tuft of hair. "Did you go to Betsy Pendleton's birthday party a couple of weeks ago, Yancy?"

"She had ice cream and cake, and I pinned the tail on the jackass."

"Donkey," his mother corrected.

"Daddy calls it a jackass." Yancy grinned, then laid his head on Kirby's arm. "I don't feel good."

"I know, sweetie. And you know what else, Betsy doesn't feel good today either, and neither do Brandon and Peggy Lee. What we've got here is an outbreak of chicken pox."

"Chicken pox? But he doesn't have any spots."

"He will." She'd already noted the rash starting under his arms. "And you've got to try really hard not to scratch when it starts to itch, honey. I'm going to give your mom some lotion to put on you that will help. Annie, do you know if you and Jerry ever had the chicken pox?"

"We both did." Annie let out a long sigh. "Fact is, Jerry gave it to me when we were kids."

"Then it's likely you won't get it again. Yancy's incubating now, so you want to keep his exposure to other kids and adults who haven't had it to a minimum. You're quarantined, buster," she said, tapping Yancy on the nose. "Tepid baths with a little cornstarch will help once it breaks out, and I'm going to give you both topical and oral medications. I've only got samples here, so you'll have to get Jerry to fill some prescriptions over on the mainland. Tylenol for the fever's fine," she added, laying a cool hand on Yancy's cheek. "I'll drop by your place in a few days to take a look at him."

Noting the look of distress on Annie's face, Kirby smiled, touched her arm. "He'll be fine, Annie. The three of you are in for a couple of tough weeks, but I don't foresee any complications. I'll go over everything with you before you take him home."

"I just . . . could I talk to you for a minute?"

"Sure. Hey, Yancy." Kirby removed the stethoscope from around her neck and slipped it around his. "You want to hear your heart go thump?" She eased the earpieces in place, guided his hand. His tired eyes went big and bright. "You listen to that for a minute while I talk to your mom."

She led Annie into the hallway, leaving the door open. "Yancy's a strong, healthy, completely normal four-year-old boy," she began. "You have nothing to worry about. Chicken pox is inconvenient, irritating, but it's very rarely complicated. I have some literature if you'd like."

"It's not . . ." She bit her lip. "I took one of those home pregnancy tests a couple of days ago. It was positive."

"I see. Are you happy about that, Annie?"

"Yeah. Jerry and me, we've been trying to make another baby for the best part of a year now. But . . . is it going to be all right? Is it going to get sick?"

Exposure to the virus during the first trimester carried a slight risk. "You had chicken pox when you were a child?"

"Yeah, my mother put cotton gloves on me to stop me from scratching and scarring."

"It's really unlikely you'd contract it again." If she did, Kirby thought with a tug of worry, they would deal with that when it happened. "Even if you did contract the virus, the odds are the baby will be fine. Why don't you let me run a backup pregnancy test now, just to confirm? And give you a quick look. We'll see how far along you are. And go from there."

"It'd make me feel a lot better."

"Then that's just what we'll do. Who's your regular OB?"

"I went to a clinic over to the mainland for Yancy. But I was hoping you could take care of things this time."

"Well, we'll talk about that. Irene Verdon's in the waiting room. Let's see if she can keep an eye on Yancy for a few minutes. Then I want the two of you to go home and get some rest. You're going to need it."

"I feel better knowing you're looking after us, Doc Kirby." Annie laid a hand on her stomach. "All of us."

By one o'clock, Kirby had diagnosed two more cases of chicken pox, splinted a broken finger, and treated a bladder infection. Such, she thought as she grabbed a jar of peanut butter, was the life of a general practitioner.

She had thirty minutes before her next appointment and hoped to spend it sitting down and stuffing her face. She didn't groan when her door opened, but she wanted to.

This was a stranger. She knew every face on the island now, and she'd never seen this one. She tagged him immediately as a beach rover, one of the type who popped up on the island from time to time in search of sun and surf.

His hair was streaky blond and skimmed his shoulders, his face was deeply tanned. He wore ragged cutoffs, a T-shirt that suggested she sun her buns in Cozumel, and dark-lensed Wayfarer sunglasses.

Late twenties, she judged, clean and attractive. She set her sandwich aside and returned his hesitant smile.

"Sorry." He dipped his head. "Have I got the right place? I was told there was a doctor here."

"I'm Doctor Fitzsimmons. What can I do for you?"

"I don't have an appointment or anything." He glanced at her sandwich. "Should I make one?"

"Why do you need one?"

"I just have this, ah . . ." He shrugged his shoulders, then held out a hand. The palm was badly burned, with a red welt across it oozing with blisters.

"That looks nasty." Automatically she stepped forward, taking his hand gently to examine it.

"It was stupid. Coffee was boiling over and I just grabbed the pot without thinking. I'm down at the campground. When I asked the kid at check-in if there was someplace I could get some salve or something, he told me about you."

"Let's go in the back. I'll clean and dress this for you."

"I'm horning in on your lunch."

"Goes with the territory. So you're camping," she continued as she led him back to the examining room.

"Yeah, I was planning on heading down to the Keys, doing some work. I'm an artist."

"Oh?"

He sat in the chair she indicated, then frowned at his palm. "I guess this will put the skids on work for a couple of weeks."

"Unless you want to paint left-handed," she said with a smile as she washed up, snapped gloves on.

"Well, I was thinking about hanging out here longer anyway. Great place." He sucked in his breath as she began to clean the burn. "Hurts like a bitch."

"I bet it does. I'd recommend aspirin. And a potholder."

He chuckled, then set his teeth against the pain. "I guess I'm lucky there's a doc around. This kind of thing can get infected, right?"

"Mmm. But we'll see that it doesn't. What kind of things do you paint?"

"Whatever strikes me." He smiled at her, enjoying her scent, the way her hair swept down gold over her cheek. "Maybe you'd like to pose for me."

She laughed, then rolled her chair over to a drawer for salve. "I don't think so, but thanks."

"You've got a terrific face. I do good work with beautiful women."

She glanced up. His eyes were hidden by the lenses. Though his smile was wide and friendly, there was something around the edges that made her suddenly ill at ease. Doctor or not, she was a woman and she was alone with a stranger. One who was watching her just a little too closely.

"I'm sure you do. But being the only doctor on the island keeps me pretty busy." She bent her head again to coat the burn with salve.

Foolish, she told herself. She was being ridiculous. He had a second-degree burn on his hand and he was letting a stranger treat it. And he was an artist. Naturally he was watching her.

"If you change your mind, I guess I'm going to be hanging here for a while. Jesus, that feels better." He blew out a long breath, and she felt his hand relax in hers.

Feeling even more foolish now, she offered him a sympathetic smile. "That's what we're here for. I want you to keep this dry. You can put a plastic bag around it when you shower. I wouldn't try swimming for the next week. The dressing should be changed daily. If you don't have someone around to help you with it, just come in and I'll do it."

"I appreciate it. You've got good hands, Doc," he added as she wound gauze around his hand.

"That's what they all say."

"No, I mean it—not just good doctor hands. Artistic hands. Angel hands," he said with another smile. "I'd love to sketch them sometime."

"We'll see about that when you can hold a pencil again." She rose. "I'm going to give you a tube of salve. And I want you to check in with me in two days unless you leave the island. In that case you'll want to have it looked at elsewhere."

"Okay. What do I owe you?"

"Insurance?"

"No."

"Twenty-five for the office visit and ten for the supplies."

"More than fair." He got up, tugged his wallet out of his back pocket with his left hand. Gingerly he plucked bills out with the fingers of his wrapped hand. "Guess it's going to be awkward for a while."

"They'll help you out at the campground if you need it. It's a friendly island."

"So I've noticed."

"I'll get you a receipt."

"No, that's all right." He shifted, and she felt that little jolt of nerves again. "Listen, if you're over that way, maybe you could stop in. You could see some of my work, or we could—"

"Kirby! You back there?"

She felt a warm rush of relief, so fast and full it nearly made her giddy. "Brian. I'm just finishing up with a patient. You be sure to keep that gauze dry," she said briskly and pulled off her gloves. "And don't be stingy with the salve."

"You're the doctor." He sauntered out ahead of her, then lifted his brows at the man who stood in the kitchen with a bloody rag around his left hand. "Looks like you've got a problem there."

"Good eye," Brian said dryly and glanced at the gauze-wrapped hand. "Looks like I'm not the only one."

"Busy day for the doc."

"The doc," Kirby said as she walked in, "hasn't had five minutes to—Brian, what the hell have you done?" Heart in her throat, she leaped forward, grabbed his wrist, and quickly unwrapped the rag.

"Damn knife slipped. I was just—I'm dripping blood all over the floor."

"Oh, be quiet." Her heart settled back when she studied the long slice on the back of his hand. It was deep and bleeding freely, but nothing had been lopped off. "You need stitches."

"No, I don't."

"Yes, you do, about ten of them."

"Look, just wrap it up and I'll get back to work."

"I said be quiet," she snapped. "You'll have to excuse me, I—" She glanced over, frowned. "Oh, I guess he left. Come into the back."

"I don't want you sewing on me. I only came because Lexy and Kate went half crazy on me. And if Lexy hadn't been pestering me, I wouldn't have cut myself in the first place, so just dump some antiseptic on it, wrap it up, and let me go."

"Stop being a baby." Taking his arm firmly, she pulled him into the back. "Sit down and behave yourself. When's the last time you had a tetanus shot?"

"A shot? Oh, listen—"

"That long ago." She washed up quickly, put the necessary tools in a stainless-steel tray, then sat down in front of him with a bottle of antiseptic. "We'll take care of that afterward. I'm going to clean this, disinfect, then I'll give you a local."

He could feel the wound throbbing in time with his heart. Both picked up speed. "A local what?"

"Anesthetic. It'll numb the area so I can sew you back together."

"What is this obsession of yours with needles?"

"Let me see you move your fingers," she ordered. "Good, good. I didn't think you'd cut through any tendons. Are you afraid of needles, Brian?"

"No, of course not." Then she picked up the hypo and he felt all the blood drain out of his face. "Yes. Damn it, Kirby, keep that thing away from me."

She didn't laugh as he'd been dead certain she would. Instead, she looked soberly into his eyes. "Take a deep breath, let it out, then take another and look at the painting over my right shoulder. Just keep looking at the painting and count your breaths. One, two, three. That's it. Little stick, that's all," she murmured and slid the needle under his skin. "Keep counting."

"Okay, all right." He could feel the sweat crawling down his back and focused on the watercolor print of wild lilies. "This is the perfect time for you to make some snotty comment."

"I worked in ER. Saw more blood during that year than a layman does in three lifetimes. Gunshots, knifings, car wrecks. I never panicked. The closest I've ever come to panicking was just now, when I saw your blood dripping onto my kitchen floor."

He looked away from the print and into her eyes. "I'll mop it up for you."

"Don't be an idiot." She grabbed a swatch of surgical paper to make a sterile field, then paused when he touched his hand to hers.

"I care too." He waited until she looked at him again. "I care a lot. How the hell did this happen?"

"I don't know. What do you think we should do about it?"

"It's probably not going to work, you know. You and me."

"No." She picked up the suture. "Probably not. Keep your hand still, Brian."

He glanced down, saw her slide the suturing needle under his skin. His stomach rolled. Taking another deep breath, he looked back at the painting. "Don't worry about making it neat. Just make it fast."

"I'm famous for my ladylike little stitches. Just relax and keep breathing."

Since he figured it would be more humiliation than he could stand to pass out on her, he tried to obey. "I'm not afraid of needles. I just don't like them."

"It's a common phobia."

"I don't have a phobia. I just don't like people sticking needles in me."

She kept her head bent so he wouldn't see her smile. "Perfectly understandable. What was Lexy pestering you about?"

"The usual. Everything." He tried to ignore the slight tug as she drew the edges of the wound together. "I'm insensitive. I don't care about her—or anyone else, for that matter. I don't understand her. No one does. If I was a real brother,

I'd lend her five thousand dollars so she could go back to New York and be a star."

"I thought she'd decided to stay here through the summer."

"She had some sort of go-round with Giff. Since he hasn't come crawling after her, she's gone from the sulky stage—which was our big treat yesterday—to the nasty stage. Are you almost done?"

"Halfway," she said patiently.

"Half. Great. Wonderful." His stomach rolled again. Okay, think about something else. "Who was the beach bum?"

"Hmm? Oh, the burn. Tussle with a coffeepot. Says he's an artist, on his way to the Keys. He may be over at the campground for a while. I never did get his name."

"What kind of an artist?"

"A painter, I think. He wanted me to pose for him. Damn it, be still," she said when his hand jerked.

"What did you tell him?"

"That I was flattered, thank you very much, but didn't have time. He made me nervous."

Brian's free hand shot out and grabbed her shoulder, making her curse. "Only a couple more," she began.

"Did he touch you?"

"What?" No, it wasn't fear or pain in his eyes, she realized. It was fury. And that was wonderfully satisfying. "Why, yes, of course, Brian. One-handed, he wrestled me to the floor in a wild burst of lust and ripped off my clothes."

Brian's fingers dug in. "I want a straight answer. Did he put his hands on you?"

"No, of course he didn't. I just got nervous for a minute because the office was empty and he seemed overly interested. Then it turned out he just wanted to sketch my hands." She fluttered the fingers of her left one. "Angel hands. Now be still before you ruin my work and end up with a nasty scar. Not that your jealousy isn't flattering."

"I'm not jealous." He removed his hand and willed the green haze over his vision to subside. "I just don't want some beach bum hassling you."

"He didn't hassle me, and if he had I could have handled it. One more now." She tugged, knotted, snipped, then examined the neat line of stitches carefully. "A lovely job, if I do say so myself." She rose to prepare his tetanus shot.

"How would you have handled it?"

"Handled what? Oh, we're still on that, are we? With a polite rebuff."

"And if that hadn't worked?"

"One good squeeze on that burn and he'd have been on the floor screaming in pain."

When she turned back, careful to keep the hypo behind her back, she saw Brian smiling. "You would have too."

"Absolutely. I once cooled the ardor of an oversexed patient by pressing ever so gently on his larynx. He quickly decided to stop making obscene suggestions to me and the nursing staff. Now you want to look at the lilies again, Brian."

He paled. "What have you got behind your back?"

"Just look at the lilies."

"Oh, Christ." He turned his head, then a moment later yelped and jerked.

"Brian, that was the alcohol swab. This'll be over in ten seconds. You're going to feel a prick."

He hissed. "A prick, my ass. What are you using, an upholstery needle?"

"There, all done." She smoothed a bandage over the needle prick, then sat down to wrap his hand. "Keep this dry. I'll change the dressing for you when it needs it. In about ten days, two weeks, we'll see about taking the stitches out."

"Won't that be fun?"

"Here." She reached in the pocket of her smock and took out a Tootsie Pop. "For being such a good boy."

"I know sarcasm when I hear it, but I'll take the sucker."

She unwrapped it for him, stuck it in his mouth. "Take a couple of aspirin," she advised. "The local's going to wear off quickly and it's going to hurt some. You want to get ahead of the pain, not chase it."

"Aren't you going to kiss it?"

"I suppose." She lifted his hand, touched her lips lightly to the gauze. "Be more careful with your kitchen tools," she told him. "I like your hands just the way they are."

"Then I don't suppose you'd object if I moseyed on over here later tonight, wrestled you one-handed to the floor, and tore your clothes off."

"I don't suppose I would." She leaned forward until her lips met his, then with a little sigh lingered there. "The sooner the better."

Brian glanced over at the examination table, and his grin spread slowly. "Well, since I'm here now, maybe you should give me a complete physical. Haven't had one in a couple, three years. You could wear your stethoscope. Just your stethoscope."

The idea made a nice curl of lust slide into her stomach. "The doctor is in," she began, then came back to earth when she heard the outside door open. "But I'll have to give you an evening appointment." She eased back, then stood to remove the tray. "I've had a morning full of chicken pox, and that's my next patient."

He didn't want to go, he realized. He wanted to sit there and watch her. He wanted to study her, the competent way she handled her instruments, the brisk and graceful way she moved. So he stalled and did just that.

"Who's got the chicken pox?"

"Who under ten doesn't, is more like it. We're at seven and counting." She glanced around. "Have you had it?"

"Oh, yeah, the three of us got it at the same time. I think I was nine, so that would have made Jo about six, Lex just under three. I guess my mother went through a couple of gallons of calamine."

"Must have been great fun for all of you."

"It wasn't so bad, after the first couple of days. My father went over to the mainland and brought back this huge box of Lincoln Logs, at least a dozen coloring books, and that jumbo box of Crayolas, Barbie dolls, Matchbox cars."

Because the memory made him sentimental, Brian shrugged. "I guess he was desperate to keep us all occupied."

And to give your mother a little peace, Kirby mused. "I imagine three sick kids are pretty hard to handle. Sounds like he had the right idea."

"Yeah, I guess they worked through it together. I used to think that was the way it was with them. Until she took off." Telling himself it didn't matter, he stood up. "I'll get out of your way. Thanks for the repair job."

Because his eyes looked suddenly sad, she framed his face in her hands and kissed him lightly. "I'll bill you. But the physical we've scheduled . . . that's free."

It made him smile. "That's quite a deal."

He turned to the door. He didn't look back at her, and the words just seemed to come out before he considered them or knew they were there. "I think I'm falling in love with you, Kirby. I don't know what we're going to do about that either."

He walked out quickly, leaving her staring. She eased herself down on her stool and decided her next patient was just going to have to wait another moment or two. Until the doctor got her breath back.

Just before sunset, Kirby took a walk on the beach. She needed some quiet time, she told herself, just a little space to think before Brian came back.

He loved her. No, he thought he loved her, she corrected. That was a different level entirely. Still, it was a step she hadn't expected him to take. And one she was afraid of tripping over.

She walked to the water's edge, let the surf foam over her ankles. There, she thought, when the tide swept back and sucked the sand down under her feet. That was exactly the same sensation he was causing in her. That slight and exciting imbalance, that feeling of having the ground shift under you no matter how firmly you planted your feet.

She'd wanted him, and she chipped away at his defenses until she won that battle. Now the stakes had gone up, considerably higher than she'd ever gambled on before.

She'd been very careful to do the picking and choosing in personal relationships. And she'd chosen Brian Hathaway. But somewhere along the way the angle had changed on her.

He wouldn't speak of love lightly, not Brian. She could. But not with Brian, she realized. If she said those words, she would have to mean them. And if she meant them, she would have to build on them. Words were only the foundation.

Home, family. Permanence. She would have to decide if she wanted those things at all, and if she wanted them with him. Then she would have to convince him that he wanted them with her.

It wouldn't be simple. The bruises and scars from his childhood kept anything about Brian from being simple.

She lifted her face to the wind. Hadn't she already decided? Hadn't she known in that split second when she saw him bleeding, when fear swept all professional calm aside, that her feelings for him had gone well beyond lust?

It scared her. She was afraid she would indeed trip over that step. And more, she was afraid to commit to taking it. Better to take it slow, she decided. To be sure of her footing. She handled things better if she was calm and clear-sighted. Certainly something as important as this should be approached with caution and a cool head.

She ignored the little voice snickering inside her head and turned back to walk home. The glint far across the dunes made her frown. The second time it flashed, she realized it was the setting sun's reflection off glass. Binoculars, she thought with a shiver. With a hand shielding her eyes, she could just make out a figure. The distance made it impossible to tell whether it was male or female. She began to walk more quickly, wanting to be inside again, behind closed doors.

It was foolish, she knew. It was just someone watching the beach at sunset, and she simply happened to be on the beach. But the sensation of being watched, of being studied, stayed with her and hurried her steps toward home.

She'd spotted him, and that only made it more exciting. He'd frightened her, just by being there. Chuckling softly, he continued to frame Kirby in the telephoto lens, snapping methodically as she rushed along the beach.

She had a beautiful body. It had been a pleasure to watch the wind plaster her shirt and slacks to it, outline the curves. The sunlight had glowed on her hair, turning it a rich, burning gold. As the sun had dipped lower at his back, all the tones and hues had deepened, softened. He was pleased that he'd used color film this time.

Oh, and that look in her eyes when she'd realized someone was there. The lens had brought her so close, he'd nearly been able to see her pupils dilate.

Such pretty green eyes, he thought. They suited her. Just as the swing of blond hair suited her, and that soft, soothing voice.

He wondered what her breasts would taste like.

She'd be a hot one in the sack, he decided, snapping quickly before she disappeared around the dunes. The small, delicate types usually were, once you got them revving. He imagined she thought she knew all there was to know about anatomy. But he figured he could show her some tricks. Oh, yes, he could show the lady doctor a few things.

He remembered an excerpt from the journal that seemed to fit the moment and his mood. The rape of Annabelle.

I experimented, allowing myself full range to do things to her that I have never done to another woman. She wept, tears streaming down her cheeks and dampening the gag. I had her again, again. It was beyond me to stop. It wasn't sex, was no longer rape.

It was unbearable power.

Yes, it was the power he wanted, the full scope of it, which he had not achieved with Ginny. Because Ginny had been defective, he reminded himself. She had been whore instead of angel, and a poor choice.

If he decided to—if he decided he needed just a little more practice before the main event—Kirby, with her pretty eyes and angel hands, would be a fine subject. She would work out just fine.

Something to think about, he mused. Something to consider. But for now he thought he'd wander toward Sanctuary and see if Jo Ellen was out and about.

It was nearly time to remind her he was thinking about her.

18

As Giff drove up the road to Sanctuary, he saw Lexy. She stood on the second-floor terrace, her long legs prettily displayed in cuffed cotton shorts, her hair bundled messily on top of her head. She was washing windows, which he was sure would have her in one of her less hospitable moods.

As appealing a picture as she made, she would have to wait. He needed to talk to Brian.

She saw Giff park his pickup but barely spared him a glance. Her smile was smug as she polished off the mixture of vinegar and water with newspaper until the windowpane shone. She'd known he would come around, though it had taken him longer than she'd expected.

But she decided to forgive him—after he crawled just a little.

She bent to soak her rag again, turning her head a bit, slanting her eyes over and down. Then sprang straight up when she saw Giff was heading not toward the house and her but toward the old smokehouse, where Brian was painting porch furniture.

Why, that rattlesnake, she thought, slapping the cleaning solution on the next window. If he was waiting for her to come to him, he was going to be sorely disappointed. She'd never forgive him now. Not if she lived to be a thousand years old. He could crawl over hot coals, she thought, furiously polishing the window. He could beg and plead and call her name on his deathbed and she would laugh gaily and walk on.

From this moment on, Giff Verdon meant less than nothing to her.

She picked up her bucket and moved three windows down so she could keep an eye on him.

At the moment, Lexy and her moods weren't at the forefront of Giff's mind.

He caught the oversweet smell of fresh paint, heard the hiss of the sprayer. He worked up a smile as he rounded the stone corner of the smokehouse and saw Brian.

Little dots of sea-blue paint freckled his arms to past the elbows, and polka-dotted the old jeans he wore. An army-green tarp was spread out and covered with chaises and chairs. Brian was giving the old glider a second coat.

"Nice color," Giff called out.

Brian moved the nozzle slowly back and forth another stroke before disengaging it. "You know Cousin Kate. Every few years she wants something different—and always ends up going with blue."

"Freshens them up nice, though."

"It does." Brian flicked the motor off, set the sprayer down. "She's ordered new umbrellas for the tables, pads for the chairs. Should be in on the ferry in another day or two. She wants the picnic tables painted over at the campground, too."

"I can take care of that if you don't have time."

"I'll probably do it." Brian rolled his shoulders free of kinks. "Gets me out in the air. Gives me some daydreaming time." He'd just been having a nice one, too, replaying his night with Kirby.

He knew he would never think of a stethoscope in quite the same way again.

"How's that porch coming?"

"Got the screening in the truck. The weather looks like it's going to hold, so I should be finished by end of the week, like Miss Kate wanted."

"Good. I'll try to come by and take a look at it."

"How's the hand doing?" Giff asked, nodding toward the bandage.

"Oh." Frowning, Brian flexed his fingers. "A little stiff is all." Brian didn't ask how Giff had heard about it. News simply floated on the island's air—especially the juiciest tidbits. The fact was, he considered it a wonder no one knew that he'd spent most of the night on the good doctor's examining table.

"You and Doc Kirby, huh?"

"What?"

"You and Doc Kirby." Giff adjusted his cap. "My cousin Ned was down to the beach early this morning. You know how he collects shells, polishes them up and sells them off to day-trippers down to the ferry. Seems he saw you leaving the doc's this morning about daybreak. You know how Ned runs his mouth."

So much for wonders, Brian mused. "Yeah, I do. How long did it take him to pass the news?"

"Well . . ." Amused, Giff rubbed his chin. "I was heading down to the ferry to see if the screen came in, saw Ned on Shell Road and gave him a lift. That would make it, oh, about fifty minutes, give or take."

"Ned's slowing down."

"Well, he's getting up in age, you know. Be eighty-two come September. Doc Kirby's a fine woman," Giff added. "Don't know anybody on the island doesn't think high of her. Or you, Bri."

"We've spent a few evenings together," Brian muttered and crouched down to rub the nozzle tip with a rag. "People shouldn't start smelling orange blossoms."

Giff lifted a brow. "Didn't say they were."

"We're just seeing each other some."

"Okay."

"Nobody's thinking about making it a permanent relationship, or tangling it up with strings."

Giff waited a moment. "You trying to convince me, Bri, or is somebody else here?"

"I'm just saying—" Brian caught himself, lifting his hands as if to signal himself to call a halt. He straightened again and tried not to be irritated by the bland and innocent smile on Giff's face. "Did you come by here just to congratulate me on sleeping with Kirby, or is there something else on your mind?"

Giff's smile faded. "Ginny."

Brian sighed, discovered that the tension balled dead center at the back of his neck couldn't be rubbed away. "The cops called here this morning. I guess they talked to you, too."

"Didn't have squat to say. I don't think they'd have bothered to call if I hadn't been hassling them. Damn it, Brian, you know they're not looking for her. They're barely going through the motions."

"I wish I could tell you different."

"They said we could make up flyers, hand them out around in Savannah. What the hell good is that?"

"Next to none. Giff, I wish I knew what to say to you. But you know, Ginny's twenty-six years old and free to come and go as she pleases. That's how the cops look at it."

"That's the wrong way to look at it. Ginny has family here, she has a home and friends. No way she'd have taken off without a word to anyone."

"Sometimes," Brian said slowly, "people do things you never expect they would do. Never believe they could do. But they do them just the same."

"Ginny's not your mama, Brian. I'm sorry this brings back a bad time for you and your family. But this is now. This is Ginny. It's not the same."

"No, it's not." Brian forced himself to keep his voice and his temper even. "Ginny didn't have a husband and three children. If she decided to shake the sand out of her shoes, she wasn't leaving lives broken behind her. Now I'll keep talking to the police, I'll see they're called at least once a week to keep Ginny in their heads. We'll make up the flyers for you in the office. I just can't do any more than that, Giff. I'm not having my life turned inside out a second time."

"That's fine." Giff nodded stiffly. "That's fine, then. I'll get out of your way so you can go about your business."

Fury lengthened his stride as he stalked back to the truck. He climbed in, slammed the door behind him. Then just lowered his head onto the steering wheel.

He'd been wrong. All the way wrong. Sniping at Brian that way, going stiff and snooty on him. It wasn't Brian's fault or his responsibility. And it wasn't right, Giff added, as he sat back and closed his eyes, for a friend to cut into another that way. He'd just give himself a moment to calm and to settle, then he'd go back and apologize.

Lexy sauntered out of the house. She'd streaked down the inside stairs, nearly breaking her neck in her hurry to be sure Giff didn't drive off before she could taunt him with what he couldn't have. And her heart was still racing. But she moved slowly now, one hand trailing along the banister, a distant smile on her face.

She moseyed up to the truck and, forgetting that her hands smelled of vinegar, propped them on the bottom of the open window. "Why, hello there, Giff. I was about to take a little walk in the woods to cool off, and saw your truck."

He opened his eyes, looked into hers. "Go on then, Lexy," he murmured and leaned over to turn the key.

"What is it?" The misery in his eyes was a balm for her soul. "You feeling poorly, Giff? Maybe you're feeling blue." She trailed a fingertip up his arm. "Maybe you're wishing you knew how to apologize to me so you wouldn't be so lonely these days."

His eyes remained dark, but the shadows in them shifted from misery to temper. He pushed her hand aside. "You know what, Alexa? Even my limited little world doesn't revolve only around you."

"You've got your nerve, thinking you can talk to me that way. If you think I care what your world revolves around, Giff, you're very mistaken. I couldn't care less."

"Right now that makes two of us. Get away from the truck."

"I will not. Not until I've had my say."

"I don't give a damn what you have to say, now back off before you get hurt."

She did just the opposite, stretching through the open window to turn the key and shut the engine down. "Don't you order me around." She stuck her face in his. "Don't you think for one minute you can tell me what to do, or threaten me into doing it."

She sucked in a breath, prepared to scold him properly. But there was misery in his eyes again, more than she'd ever seen or expected to. Her temper subsided, and she laid a hand on his cheek. "What's the matter, honey? What's hurting you?"

He started to shake his head, but she kept her hand in place. "We can be mad at each other later. You talk to me now. Tell me what's wrong."

"Ginny." He let out an explosive breath that scalded his throat. "Not a word from her, Lexy. Not a single word. I don't know what to do anymore. What to say to my family anymore. I don't even know how to feel."

"I know." She slipped back, opened the door. "Come on."

"I've got work to do."

"You do what I say for once in your life. Now come on with me." She took his hand, tugging until he climbed out. Saying nothing, she led him around the side of the house toward the shade. "Sit down here." She drew him down on the side of the rope hammock and, slipping an arm around him, nudged his head down to her shoulder. "You just rest your mind a minute."

"I don't think about it all the time," he murmured. "You go crazy if you do."

"I know." Reaching around, she took his hand in hers. "It just sneaks up on you now and again, and it hurts so much you don't think you can stand it. But you do, till the next time."

"I know what people are saying. She just got a wild hair and took off. It'd be easier if I could believe that."

"It wouldn't, not really. It hurts either way. When Mama left I cried and cried for her. I figured if I cried enough she'd hear me and come back. When I got older I thought, well, she just didn't care enough about me, so I won't care either. I stopped crying, but it still hurt all the same."

"I keep thinking she'll send some stupid postcard from Disney World or somewhere. Then I could just be mad at her instead of so goddamn worried."

Lexy tried to imagine that, let herself see it. Perfect. Ginny on some colorful, foolish ride, howling with laughter. "It'd be just like her to do that."

"I guess it would." He stared down at their joined hands, watching their fingers interlace. "I just tore a strip off Brian over it. Stupid."

"Don't you worry about that. Brian's hide's thick enough to take it."

"How about yours?" He eased back, absently pushing a loosened bobby pin back into her messy topknot.

"All us Hathaways are tougher than we look."

"I'm sorry anyway." He lifted their joined hands and kissed her knuckles. "Do we have to be mad at each other later?"

"I guess not." She kissed him lightly, then smiled. The birds were singing in the trees above her, and the flowers smelled so nice and sweet on the air. "Since I've been missing you, just a little bit."

Her breath caught as he pulled her close, pressed his face hard against her throat. "I need you, Lexy. I need you."

When she released her breath, it was unsteady, shuddering from lungs to throat to lips. She put her hands on his shoulders, her fingers pressing once into those hard muscles. Then she pulled back, rose, struggling to grip her own emotions as firmly.

She'd turned her back on him. Giff rubbed his hands over his face, then dropped them helplessly. "What did I say now? What is it I do that always makes you take that step back from me?"

"I'm not." She had to press her fingers to her lips to stop them from trembling before she faced him again. When she did, her heart was swimming in her eyes. "In my whole life, my whole life, Giff, no one's ever said that to me. Unless it was a man meaning sex."

He got to his feet fast. "That's not what I meant. Lexy—"

"I know." She blinked impatiently at the tears. She wanted to see him clearly. "I know it's not what you meant. And I'm not stepping back, I'm just trying to get hold of myself before I act like a fool."

"I love you, Lexy." He said it quietly so she would believe him. "I always have and always will love you."

She closed her eyes tight. She wanted it all engraved on her memory. The moment—every sound, every scent, every feeling. Then she was launching herself into his arms, wrapping herself around him, her breath coming in tiny little hitches that made her dizzy.

"Hold me. Hold on to me, Giff, tight. No matter what I do, no matter what I say, don't ever let me go."

"Alexa." Swamped by her, he pressed his lips into her hair. "I've always held on to you. You just didn't know it."

"I love you too, Giff. I can't remember when I didn't. It always made me so mad."

"That's all right, honey." He smiled, snuggled her closer. "I don't mind you being mad. As long as you don't stop."

In her bedroom, Jo carefully hung up the phone. Bobby Banes had finally gotten in touch. And had given her at least one answer.

He hadn't taken the print from her apartment.

But you saw the print, didn't you? It was a nude, mixed in with all the shots of me. It looked like me, but it wasn't. I was holding it. I picked it up. You must have seen it.

She could hear her own voice, pitching into panic, and the concern and hesitation in Bobby's when he answered.

I'm sorry, Jo. I didn't see a print like that. Just those ones of you. Ah . . . there wasn't any nude study. At least I didn't notice.

It was there. I dropped it. It fell facedown on the other prints. It was there, Bobby. Just think for a minute.

It must have been there . . . I mean, if you say you saw it.

His tone had been placating, she thought now. Sympathetic. But it hadn't been convinced.

Sick and shaky, she turned away from the phone, told herself it was useless to wish he hadn't called, hadn't told her. It was better, much better, to have the truth. All she had to do now was live with it.

From her bedroom window, Jo looked down on her sister and Giff. They made a pretty picture, she decided. Two young, healthy people locked in each other's arms, with flowers growing wild and ripe all around them. A man and woman sparkling with love and sexual anticipation on a summer afternoon.

It looked so easy, so natural. Why couldn't she let it be easy and natural for herself?

Nathan wanted her. He wasn't pushing, he didn't appear to be angry that she kept that last bit of distance between them. And why did she? Jo wondered, watching as Giff tipped Lexy's face up to his. Why didn't she just let go?

He stirred her. He brought her pleasure and set something to simmering inside her that hinted the pleasure would spread and deepen if she allowed it.

Why was she afraid to allow it?

In disgust she turned away from the window. Because she questioned everything these days. She watched her own moves, analyzed them clinically. Oh, she felt better physically. The nightmares and slick-skinned panic attacks were fewer and farther between.

But . . .

There was always that doubt, the fear that she wasn't really stable. Why else could she still see in her mind that photograph, the photograph of the dead woman? One minute her mother, the next herself. The eyes staring, the skin white as wax. She could still see the texture of the skin, smooth and pale. The shades and sweep of the hair, that artfully spread wave of it. The way the hand had been draped, elbow bent, arm crossed between the breasts. And the head turned, angled down as in shy slumber.

How could she see it so clearly when it had never existed?

And because she could, she had to believe she was still far from well. She had no business even considering a relationship with Nathan—with anyone—until she was solidly on her feet again.

And that, she admitted, was just an excuse.

She was afraid of him—that was the bottom line. She was afraid he would come to mean more to her than she could handle. And that he would expect more of her than she could give.

He was already drawing feelings out of her that no one else ever had. So she was protecting herself with cowardice that wore a mask of logic.

She was tired of being logical and afraid. Would it be so wrong to take a page out of her sister's book for once? To act on impulse, to take whatever she could get?

God, she needed someone to talk to, someone to be with. Someone who could, even for a little while, crowd out all these self-doubts and worries.

Why shouldn't it be Nathan?

She rushed out of her room before she could change her mind, and for once didn't even bother to grab her camera. She paused impatiently when Kate called out her name.

"I'm just heading out." Jo stopped at the door to the office. Kate was behind a desk covered with papers and brochures.

"Trying to get ahead of the fall reservations." Kate pulled a pencil out from behind her ear. "We've got a request to have a wedding here at the inn in October. We've never done that kind of thing before. They want Brian to do the catering, have the ceremony and reception right here. It would be just wonderful if we could figure out how to do it."

"That would be nice. Kate, I'm really on my way out."

"Sorry." She stuck the pencil back behind her ear and smiled distractedly. "Lost my train again. I've been doing that all morning. I've got your mail here. I was going to drop it off in your room, then the phone rang and I haven't budged from this spot in two hours."

As if to punctuate the statement, the phone jingled again, and behind her the second line beeped, signaling an incoming fax. "If it's not one thing, it's two, I swear. There you go, honey, you got a package there." She picked up the phone. "Sanctuary Inn, may I help you?"

Jo heard nothing but the beehive buzz in her own ears. She stepped forward slowly, could feel the air around her thickening like water. The manila envelope felt stiff in her hand when she reached for it. Her name had been printed on it in block letters in thick black marker.

Jo Ellen Hathaway
Sanctuary
Lost Desire Island, Georgia

The warning in the corner stated clearly: PHOTOS. DO NOT BEND.

Don't open it, she told herself. Throw it in the trash. Don't look inside. But her fingers were already tearing at the seal, ripping open the flap. She didn't hear Kate's exclamation of surprise as she upended the envelope, shaking the photographs out onto the floor. With a little keening sound, Jo dropped to her knees, shoving through them, pushing one after another aside in a desperate search for one. The one.

Without hesitation, Kate hung up on the reservation she was taking and rushed around the desk. "Jo, what is it? Jo Ellen, what's wrong? What is all this?" she demanded, holding Jo under one arm as she stared at dozens of pictures of her young cousin.

"He's been here. He's been here. Here!" Jo scrambled through the photos again. There she was, walking on the beach. Asleep in the hammock, on the edge of the dune swale, setting up her tripod at the salt marsh.

But where was the one? Where was the one?

"It's got to be here. It's got to."

Alarmed, Kate hauled Jo up to her knees and shook her. "Stop it. Now. I want you to stop it this minute." Because she recognized the signs, she dragged Jo over to a chair, pushed her into it, then shoved her head between her knees. "You just breathe. That's all you do. Don't you go fainting on me. You sit right there, you hear me? You sit right there and don't you move."

She rushed into the bathroom to run a glass of water and dampen a cloth. When she dashed back in, Jo was just as she'd left her. Relieved, Kate knelt down and laid the cold cloth on the back of Jo's neck.

"There now, just take it easy."

"I'm not going to faint," Jo said dully.

"That's fine news to me, I'll tell you. Sit back now, slowly, drink a little water." She brought the glass to Jo's lips herself, held it there, grateful when color gradually seeped back into them. "Can you tell me what this is all about now?"

"The photos." Jo sat back, closed her eyes. "I didn't get away. I didn't get away after all."

"From what, honey? From who?"

"I don't know. I think I'm going crazy."

"That's nonsense." Kate made her voice sharp and impatient.

"I don't know that it is. It's already happened once."

"What do you mean?"

She kept her eyes closed. It would be easier to say it that way. "I had a breakdown a few months ago."

"Oh, Jo Ellen." Kate eased down onto the arm of the chair and began to stroke Jo's hair. "Why didn't you tell me you'd been sick, honey?"

"I just couldn't, that's all. Everything just got to be too much and I couldn't hold on anymore. The pictures started to come."

"Pictures like these?"

"Pictures of me. Just pictures of my eyes at first. Just my eyes." Or her eyes, she thought with a shudder. Our eyes.

"That's horrible. It must have frightened you so."

"It did. Then I told myself someone was just trying to get my attention so I'd help them break into photography."

"That's probably just what it was, but it was a terrible way to do it. You should have gone to the police."

"And tell them that someone was sending me, a photographer, pictures?" Jo opened her eyes again. "I thought I could handle it. Just ignore it, just deal with it. Then an envelope like that one came in the mail. Full of pictures of me, and one . . . one I thought was of someone else. But it wasn't," Jo said fiercely. She was going to accept that. If nothing else, she was going to accept that one thing. "I imagined it. It wasn't there at all. Just those pictures of me. Dozens of them. And I fell apart."

"Then you came back here."

"I had to get away. I thought I could get away. But I can't. These are from here, right here on the island. He's been right here, watching me."

"And these are going to the police." Simmering with fury, Kate rose to snatch up the envelope. "Postmark's Savannah. Three days ago."

"What good will it do, Kate?"

"We won't know that till we do it."

"He could still be in Savannah, or anywhere else. He could be back on the island." She ran her hands through her hair, then let them drop into her lap. "Are we going to ask the police to question everyone with a camera?"

"If necessary. What kind of camera?" Kate demanded. "Where and how were they developed? When were they taken? There ought to be a way of figuring some of that out. It's better than sitting here being scared, isn't it? Snap your backbone in place, Jo Ellen."

"I just want it to go away."

"Then *make* it go away," Kate said fiercely. "I'm ashamed you'd let someone do this to you and not put up a fight." Kate snatched up a photo, held it out. "When was this taken? Look at it, figure it out."

Jo's stomach churned as she stared at it. Her palms were damp as she reached out and took the photo. The shot was slightly out of focus, she noted. The angle of light was poor, casting a bad shadow across her body. He was capable of much better work, she thought, then let out a long breath. It helped to think practically, even to critique.

"I think he rushed this one. The marsh at this spot is fairly open. Obviously he didn't want me to know he was taking pictures, so he hurried through it."

"Good. Good girl. Now when were you down there last?"

"Just a couple of days ago, but I didn't take the tripod." Her brow furrowed as she concentrated. "This had to be at least two weeks back. No, three. Three weeks ago, I went out at low tide to do some studies of the tidal pools. Let me see another print."

"I know it's difficult for you, but I like this one." Kate tried a bolstering smile as she offered Jo a photo of herself cradled in Sam's lap. Shade dappled over them in patterns, making the study almost dreamy.

"The campground," Jo murmured. "The day I was locked in the showers and Daddy let me out. It wasn't kids. The bastard. It wasn't kids, it was him. He locked me in there, then he waited around and he took this."

"That was the day Ginny went missing, wasn't it? Nearly two weeks now."

Jo knelt on the floor again, but she wasn't panicking now. Her hands were steady, her mind focused. She went through photo by photo, coolly. "I can't be sure of each and every one, but those I can pinpoint were all taken at least that long ago. So I'll assume they all were. Nothing in the last two weeks. He's held on to them. He's waited. Why?"

"He needed time to print them, to select them. To decide which ones to send. He must have other obligations. A job. Something."

"No, I think he's very flexible there. He had pictures of me on assignment at Hatteras, and others of me in Charlotte. Day-to-day stuff. He isn't worried about obligations."

"All right. Get your purse. We're going to get the boat and go over to the mainland. We're taking this, all of this, to the police."

"You're right. That's better than sitting here being afraid." Very carefully she slipped photo after photo back into the envelope. "I'm sorry, Kate."

"For what?"

"For not telling you. For not trusting you enough to tell you about what happened."

"And you should be." She reached out a hand to help Jo to her feet. "But that's done now, and behind us. From now on you and everyone else in this house are going to remember we're a family."

"I don't know why you put up with us."

"Sweetie pie," Kate smiled and patted Jo's cheek, "there are times when I wonder the selfsame thing."

19

"Hey, where y'all going?" Lexy spotted Kate and Jo as they stepped out the side door. Her eyes were bright, her smile brilliant. She was nearly dancing.

"Jo and I have to run over to the mainland on some business," Kate began. "We'll be back by—"

"I'm going with you." Lexy raced through the door, zipping by before Kate could grab her arm.

"Lexy, this isn't a pleasure trip."

"Five minutes," Lexy called back. "It's only going to take me five minutes to get ready."

"That girl." Kate heaved a sigh. "She's always wanting to be someplace she's not. I'll go tell her she has to stay behind."

"No." Jo tightened her grip on the pair of envelopes she held. "Under the circumstances it might be better if she knows what's going on. I think, until we find out something more, she needs to be careful."

Kate's heart skipped a beat, but she nodded. "I suppose you're right. I'll tell Brian we're going. Don't you worry, sweetie." Kate flicked a hand over Jo's hair. "We're going to take care of this."

Because she was afraid of being left behind, Lexy was true to her word. She knew Kate would have balked at the little shorts she'd had on, so she changed in record time to thin cotton pants. She brushed her hair out, tied it back in a mint-green scarf in anticipation of the boat trip. On the drive to Sanctuary's private dock north of the ferry, she freshened her makeup and chattered.

Jo's ears were ringing by the time they boarded the reliable old cabin cruiser.

Once there had been a glossy white boat with bright red trim. The *Island Belle* had been her father's pride and joy, Jo remembered. How many times had the family piled into it, to sail around the island, to streak out over the waves, to take an impromptu run to the mainland for ice cream or a movie?

She remembered steering it, standing on her father's feet to give her a little more height, with his hands laid lightly over hers on the wheel.

A little to starboard, Jo Ellen. That's the way. You're a natural.

But Sam had sold it the year after Annabelle went away. All the replacements since had gone unnamed. The family no longer took dizzying rides together.

Still, Jo knew the routine. She checked the fuel while Lexy and Kate released the lines. Automatically she adjusted her stance to accommodate the slight sway at the dock. Her hands took the wheel easily, and she smiled when the engine caught with a kick and a purr.

"Daddy still keeps her running smooth, I see."

"He overhauled the engine over the winter." Kate took a seat, and her agitated fingers twisted the gold chain that draped over her crisp cotton blouse.

She would let Jo pilot, she thought. It would help her stay calm. "I've been thinking the inn should invest in a new one. Something spiffier to look at. We could offer tours around the island, stop off at Wild Horse Cove, Egret Inlet, that sort of thing. 'Course that means we'd have to hire on a pilot."

"Daddy knows the island and the water around it better than anyone," Jo pointed out.

"I know." Kate shrugged her shoulders. "But whenever I bring that up, he mutters under his breath and finds something else he has to do. Sam Set-in-His-Ways Hathaway is not an easy man to move."

"You could tell him how he'd be able to keep an eye on things better if he was in charge." Jo glanced at the compass, set her heading, and started across the sound. "He could make sure people didn't trample the vegetation or upset the ecosystem. Put someone else on it, they're not going to care as much, be as vigilant."

"It's a good angle."

"You buy a new boat, he'll have a hard time resisting it." Lexy readjusted the knot in her scarf. "Then you mention how you need to find the right pilot—not only one who's experienced and competent, but somebody who understands the fragility of the environment and how it needs to be explained to the tourists so they understand why Desire has stayed pure all these years."

Both Jo and Kate turned to stare at Lexy in astonishment. Lexy spread her hands. "You just have to know how to work people, is all. You talk about educating the tourists on respecting the island and leaving it as they found it and that sort of thing, he'll not only come around, he'll end up thinking it was his idea to start with."

"You're a sly child, Alexa," Kate told her. "I've always admired that about you."

"The island's what matters to Daddy." Lexy leaned over the rail to let the wind slap her face. "Using that to turn him around isn't sly, it's just basic. Can't you go any faster, Jo? I could swim to Savannah at this rate."

Jo started to suggest that Lexy do just that, then shrugged. Why not? Why not go fast and free for just a little while? She glanced back at the shoreline of Desire, the white house on the hill, then she gunned the throttle. "Hold on, then."

At the burst of speed, Lexy let out a whoop, then threw back her head and laughed. Oh, God, but she loved going places. Going anywhere. "Faster, Jo! You always handled these buckets better than any of us."

"And she hasn't manned a boat in two years," Kate began, then shrieked as Jo whipped the wheel around, shooting the boat into a fast, wide circle. Heart thumping, she grabbed the rail while Lexy shouted out for more.

"Look there, it's Jed Pendleton's fishing boat. Let's buzz them, Jo. Give them a taste of our wake and rock them good."

"Jo Ellen, you'll do no such thing." Kate conquered the laugh that sprang to her throat. "You behave yourself!"

Jo shared a rare grin with Lexy before she rolled her eyes. "Yes, ma'am," she murmured, tongue in cheek, and cut her speed. She sent out a short hail to the fishing boat. "I was just testing her engines and response."

"Well, now you have," Kate said primly. "And I expect it'll be a smooth ride from here on."

"I just want to get there." Lexy turned around and leaned back on the rail. "I'm dying to see people walking around. And I've just got to do some shopping. Why don't we all buy something new and pretty? Party dresses. Then we'll have us a party. Get all dressed up, have music and champagne. I haven't had a new dress in months."

"That's because your closet's already bursting at the seams," Jo said.

"Oh, those are ancient. Don't you ever have to have something new—just have to? Something wonderful?"

"Well, I have been wanting a new dedicated flash," Jo told her dryly.

"That's because you're more interested in dressing your camera than yourself." Lexy tilted her head. "Something bold and blue for you for a change. Silk. With silk undies, too. That way if you ever let Nathan get down to them, he'll have a nice surprise. Bet you would, too."

"Alexa." Kate held up a hand and counted slowly to ten. "Your sister's private life is just that—private."

"What private life? Why the man's been dying to get inside those baggy jeans she wears since he laid eyes on her."

"How do you know he hasn't?" Jo shot back.

"Because," Lexy said with a slow, feline smile, "once he has, you're going to be a whole lot more relaxed."

"If all it takes to relax a woman is a quick roll, you'd be comatose by now."

Lexy only laughed and turned her head back into the wind. "Well, I'm sure feeling serene these days, honey pie. Which is more than I can say for you."

"Lexy, that's enough." Kate spoke quietly, then rose. "And we're not going to the mainland to shop. We're going because your sister's got troubles. She wanted you to come along so she could tell you about it, so those troubles won't touch on you."

"What are you talking about?" Lexy straightened. "What's wrong?"

"Sit down," Kate ordered and picked up the envelopes Jo had stowed. "And we'll tell you."

Ten minutes later, Lexy was going through the photos. Her stomach was tight, but her hands were steady and her mind was working. "He's stalking you."

"I don't know if I'd call it that." Jo kept her eyes on the water, on the faint haze that was the mainland.

"It's exactly that, and that's how you're going to put it to the police. There are laws against it. I knew a woman up in New York. Her ex-boyfriend wouldn't leave her be, kept popping up, calling her, following her around. She lived scared for six months before they did something about it. It's not right you should have to live scared."

"She knew who he was," Jo pointed out.

"Well, you have to figure out who this is." Because the pictures spooked her, Lexy set them aside. "Did you break up with anybody close to the time this started?"

"No, I haven't been seeing anyone in particular."

"You don't have to think it was in particular," Lexy reminded her. "He has to think it. Who were you dating—even one date?"

"Nobody."

"Jo, you had dinner with someone, went to a show, had a quick lunch."

"Not dates."

"Don't be so literal. Problem with you is everything's just black and white in your head. Just like your pictures. Even those have shades of gray, don't they?"

Not entirely sure if she was insulted or impressed by her sister's analogy, Jo frowned. "I just don't see—"

"Exactly." Lexy nodded. "You think up a list, then you think of another for men you turned down when they asked you out. Maybe somebody asked you a couple, three times and you figured he gave up."

"I've been busy this past year. There's hardly anyone."

"That's good. It'll make the odds better on finding the right one." Lexy crossed her legs, put herself into forming the plotline. "Maybe there's someone in your building in Charlotte who tried to draw you out, make conversation when you bumped into each other in the hallway. Open your mind now," Lexy said impatiently. "A woman knows when a man's got an interest in her, even if she's got none in him."

"I haven't paid much attention."

"Well, pay attention now, and think. You're the one who has to stay in control here. You're not going to let him know he's got you scared. You're not going to give him the satisfaction of thinking he can put you in a hospital again." She reached over, gave Jo's shoulder a hard shake. "So you think. You've always been the smartest one of us. Use your head now."

"Let me take the wheel, Jo." Gently, Kate pried Jo's tensed hands away. "You sit down, take a breath."

"She can breathe later. Right now she's going to think."

"Lexy, ease off."

"No." Jo shook her head. "No, she's right. You're right," she said to Lexy, taking a good long look at the sister she'd allowed herself to think of as fluff. This time what she saw was substance. "And you're asking the right questions—ones I never thought to ask myself. When I go to the police, they're going to ask the same ones."

"I expect they are."

"Okay." Jo let out an unsteady breath. "Help me out."

"That's what I'm doing. Let's sit down." She took Jo's arm, sat with her. "Now, first think about the men."

"There aren't many. I don't draw them like bees to honey."

"You would if you wanted to, but that's another problem." Lexy waved it away with a flick of her hand. Something to be solved later. "Maybe there's one you come into contact with regularly. You don't pay much attention, but you see him, he sees you."

"The only man I see regularly is my intern. Bobby was the one who took me to the hospital. He was there when the last package came in the mail."

"Well, isn't that handy?"

Jo's eyes widened. "Bobby? That's ridiculous."

"Why? You said he was your intern. That means he's a photographer too. He'd know how to use a camera, develop film. I bet he knew where you'd be and what your schedule was whenever you were on assignment."

"Of course, but—"

"Sometimes he went with you, didn't he?"

"As part of his training, sure."

"And maybe he has a thing for you."

"That's just silly. He had a little crush at first."

"Really?" Lexy lifted a brow. "Did you accommodate him?"

"He's twenty years old."

"So?" Lexy shrugged it off. "Okay, you didn't sleep with him. He was a regular part of your life, he was attracted to you, he knew where you'd be, he knew your routine and he knew how to use a camera. Goes to the top of the short list, I'd say."

It was appalling, even more appalling than the faceless, nameless possibilities. "He took care of me. He got me to the hospital."

He said he hadn't seen the print, Jo remembered as her stomach muscles fisted painfully. It had been only the two of them there, and he said he hadn't seen it.

"Does he know you came back to Sanctuary?"

"Yes, I—" Jo cut herself off, closed her eyes. "Yes, he knows where I am. Oh, God, he knows where I am. I just talked to him this morning. He just called me."

"Why did he call you?" Lexy demanded. "What did he say to you?"

"I'd left a message for him to get in touch with me. Something I . . . I needed to ask him something. He got back to me today."

"Where was he calling from?" Kate flicked a quick glance over her shoulder.

"I didn't ask—he didn't say." With a supreme effort, Jo reined in the thudding fear. "It doesn't make any sense for Bobby to have sent the prints. I've been working with him for months."

"That's just the kind of relationship the police are going to be interested in," Lexy insisted. "Who else knows where you are—that you're sure of?"

"My publisher." Jo lifted a hand to rub her temple. "The post office, the super at my apartment building, the doctor who treated me at the hospital."

"That means anybody who wanted to know could find out. But Bobby stays top of the list."

"That makes me feel sick, sick and disloyal. And it's logical." Pausing, she squeezed the bridge of her nose between her thumb and fingers. "He's good enough to have taken the shots—if he worked at it, took his time. He's got a lot of potential. He still makes mistakes, though—rushes, or doesn't make the right choices in the darkroom. That could explain why some of the photos aren't as high-quality as others."

"What's wrong with them?" Curious, Lexy slipped some of the prints out again.

"Some of them have hard shadows, or the framing's off. See here?" She pointed to the shadow falling over her shoulder in one. "Or this one. It's not crisp, the tones aren't well defined. Some are mottled in a way I'd say means he used fast film, then overenlarged. Or some are thin—underexposed negatives," she explained. "And others just lack creativity."

"Seems pretty picky to me. You look good in most all of them."

"They aren't as carefully composed, certainly not as artfully composed, as the others, as the ones taken in Charlotte or on Hatteras. In fact . . ."—she began to frown as she went through them again, shot by shot—"if I'm remembering right, it looks to me as though the later the photo was taken, the less professional, the less creative it is. As if he's getting bored—or careless.

"See here, a first-year student with some talent and decent equipment could have taken this shot of me in the hammock. The subject is relaxed, unaware, the light's good because it's filtering through the trees. It's an easy shot. It's already laid out. But this one, the beach shot, he should have used a yellow filter to cut the glare, soften the shadows, define the clouds. That's basic. But he didn't bother. You lose texture, drama. It's a careless mistake. He never made them before."

Quickly, she pulled photos out of the other envelope. "Here's another beach shot, from Hatteras this time. Similar angle, but he used a filter, he took his time. The texture of the sand, the lift of my hair in the wind, the position of the gull just heading out over the waves, good cloud definition. It's a lovely shot, really, a solid addition for a show or gallery, whereas the one from home is washed out."

"Was Bobby on assignment with you there? On Hatteras?"

"No. I worked alone."

"But there's a lot of people on Hatteras, compared to Desire. You might not have noticed him. Especially if he wore a disguise."

"A disguise. Oh, Lexy. Don't you think I'd have clued in if I saw some guy walking around in Groucho glasses and a funny nose?"

"With the right makeup, a wig, different body language, I could walk right up to you on the street and you wouldn't recognize me. It's not that hard to be someone else." She smiled. "I do it all the time. It could have been this intern of yours or half a dozen people you know. Dye the hair, wear a hat, sunglasses. Put facial hair on or take it off. All we know for sure is that he was there, and he was here."

Jo nodded slowly. "And he could be back."

"Yeah." Lexy put a hand over Jo's. "But now we're all going to be watching out for him."

Jo looked at the hand covering hers. It shouldn't have surprised her, she realized, to find it there, to find it firm and warm. "I should have told both of you before. I should have told all of you before. I wanted to handle it myself."

"Now there's news," Lexy said lightly. "Cousin Kate, Jo says she wanted to handle something herself. Can you imagine that, the original 'Get out of my way I'll do it myself' girl wanted to handle something on her own."

"Very clever," Jo muttered. "I didn't give you enough credit either, for being willing to be there."

"More news, Kate." Lexy kept her eyes on Jo's. "Why, the bulletins just keep pouring in. Jo didn't give me enough credit for being an intelligent human being with a little compassion. Not that she or anyone else ever has, but that's the latest flash coming off the wire."

"I'd forgotten how good you are at sarcasm—and since I probably deserved both those withering remarks, I won't ruin it by proving I'm better at sarcasm than you can ever hope to be."

Before Lexy could speak, Jo turned her hand over and linked her fingers with Lexy's. "I was ashamed. Almost as much as I was scared, I was ashamed that I'd had a breakdown. The last people I wanted to know about that were my family."

Sympathy flooded Lexy. Still, she kept a smirk on her face and in her voice. "Why, that's just foolish, Jo Ellen. We're Southerners. We admire little else more than we admire our family lunatics. Hiding crazy relations in the attic's a Yankee trait. Isn't that so, Cousin Kate?"

Amused, and bursting with pride in her youngest chick, Kate glanced back over her shoulder. "It is indeed, Lexy. A good Southern family props up its crazies and puts them on display in the front parlor along with the best china."

Her own quick laugh made Jo Ellen blink in surprise. "I'm not a lunatic."

"Not yet." Lexy gave her hand a friendly squeeze. "But if you keep going you could be right on up there with Great-granny Lida. She's the one, as I recollect, wore the spangled evening dress day and night and claimed Fred Astaire was coming by to take her dancing. Put a little effort into it, you could aspire to that."

Jo laughed again, and this time it was long and rich. "Maybe we'll go shopping after all, and I'll see if I can find a spangled evening dress, just in case."

"Blue's your color." And because she knew it was easier for her than for Jo, Lexy wrapped her arms around her sister and hugged hard. "I forgot to tell you something, Jo Ellen."

"What's that?"

"Welcome home."

It was after six before they got back to Sanctuary. They'd gone shopping after all and were loaded down with the bags and boxes to prove it. Kate was still asking herself how she'd let Lexy talk her into that frantic ninety-minute shopping spree. But she already knew the answer.

After the hour spent in the police station, they'd all needed to do something foolish.

When they came in through the kitchen, she was already prepared for Brian's tirade. He took one look at them, the evidence of their betrayal heaped in their arms, and snarled.

"Well, that's just dandy, isn't it? That's just fine. I've got six tables already filled in the dining room, I'm up to my elbows in cooking, and the three of you go off shopping. I had to drag Sissy Brodie in here to wait tables, and she hasn't got any more than a spoonful of sense. Daddy's mixing drinks—which we're giving them the hell away to make up for the poor service—and I just burned two orders of chicken because I had to go in there and mop up after that pea-brained Sissy dumped a plate of shrimp fettuccine Alfredo on Becky Fitzsimmons's lap."

"Becky Fitzsimmons is in there, and you got Sissy waiting on her?" Tickled down to her toes, Lexy set her bags aside. "Don't you know anything, Brian Hathaway? Sissy and Becky are desperate enemies since they tangled over Jesse Pendleton, who was sleeping with them both nearly at the same time for six months. Then Sissy found out and she marched right up to Becky outside church after Easter services and called her a no-good toad-faced whore. Took three strong men to pull them apart."

Reliving the scene with gusto, Lexy pulled the scarf loose and shook her hair free. "Why, a plate of shrimp fettuccine's nothing. You're lucky Sissy didn't take up one of your carving knives there and go after Becky good and proper."

Brian drew a breath for patience. "I'm counting my blessings right now. Get your pad and get your butt in there. You're already an hour late for your shift."

"It's my fault, Brian," Jo began and braced herself for the attack when he whirled on her. "I needed Lexy, and I suppose we lost track of time."

"I don't have the luxury of losing track of anything, and I don't need you standing in my kitchen taking up for her when she's too irresponsible to do what she's supposed to." He rattled the lid off the chicken breast he was sautéing and flipped the meat. "And I don't want you trying to smooth it all over," he said to Kate. "I don't have time to listen to excuses."

"I wouldn't dream of offering any," Kate said stiffly. "In fact, I wouldn't dream of wasting my breath on someone who speaks to me in that manner." She jerked her chin up and sailed into the dining room to help Sam with bartending duties.

"It was my fault, Brian," Jo said again. "Kate and Lexy—"

"Don't bother." Lexy waved a hand breezily to mask her simmering temper. "He isn't about to listen—he knows all there is to know, anyway." She snatched up a pad and stomped through the door.

"Flighty, irresponsible bubblehead," Brian muttered.

"Don't talk about her that way. She's none of those things."

"What is this? Suddenly the two of you have bonded over the discount rack at the department store? Women buy shoes together and all at once they're soul mates?"

"You don't think much of the species, do you? Well, it was women I needed, and women who were there for me. If we were a little later getting back than suits you—"

"Suits me?" He flipped the chicken onto a plate, clenching his teeth as he concentrated on adding side dishes and garnishes. Damned if he'd have women destroying his presentation. "This isn't about what suits me. It's about running a business, holding on to the reputation we've been building up here for twenty-five years. It's about being left in the lurch with close to twenty people wanting a good meal served in a pleasant and efficient manner. It's about keeping your word."

"All right, you've every right to be angry, but be angry with me. I'm the one who dragged them off today."

"Don't worry." He filled a basket with fresh, steaming hush puppies. "I'm plenty angry with you."

She looked at the pots steaming on the stove, the vegetables already chopped on the cutting board. Dishes were piling up in the sink, and Brian was working awkwardly, hampered by his injured hand.

Left in the lurch was exactly right, she decided. And it had been poorly done by all of them.

"What can I do to help? I could get these dishes—"

"You can stay out of my way," he said without looking at her. "That's what you're best at, isn't it?"

She absorbed the hit, accepted the guilt. "Yes, I suppose it is."

She slipped quietly out the back door. Sanctuary wasn't barred to her, she thought, not as it had been in her dreams. But the road to and away from it was forever rocky and full of potholes.

And Brian was right. She'd always been expert at staying away, at leaving the pleasures and the problems that brewed in that house to others.

She wasn't even sure she wanted it to be otherwise.

She cut through the forest. If someone was watching her, let him watch, let him snap his goddamn pictures until his fingers went numb. She wasn't going to live her life afraid. She hoped he was there. She hoped he was close, that he would show himself. Now. This minute.

She stopped, turned in a slow circle, her face grim as she scanned the deep green shadows. A confrontation would suit her mood perfectly. There was nothing she would enjoy better than a good, sweaty physical fight.

"I'm stronger than you think," she said aloud and listened to the furious tone of her own voice echo back. "Why don't you come out, face-to-face, and find out? You bastard." She grabbed a stick, thudded it against her palm. "You son of a bitch. You think you can scare me with a bunch of second-rate photographs?"

She whipped the stick against a tree, pleased by the way the shock wave sang up her arm. A woodpecker sprang from the trunk above her and bulleted away.

"Your composition sucked, your lighting was awful. What you know about capturing mood and texture wouldn't fill a thimble. I've seen better work from a ten-year-old with a disposable Kodak."

Her jaw set, she waited, eager to see someone, anyone, step out onto the path. She wanted him to charge. She wanted to make him pay. But there was nothing but the whisper of wind through the leaves, the clicking of palmetto fronds. The light shifted, dimming degree by degree.

"Now I'm talking to myself," she murmured. "I'll be as loony as Great-granny Lida before I'm thirty at this rate." She tossed the stick, watched it fly end over end, arcing up, then landing with a quiet thump in the thick brush.

She didn't see the worn sneaker inches from where it landed, or the frayed cuffs of faded jeans. When she walked deeper into the forest, she didn't hear the strained sound of breathing struggling to even out, or the harsh whisper that shook with raw emotion.

"Not yet, Jo Ellen. Not yet. Not until I'm ready. But now I'm going to have to hurt you. Now I'm going to have to make you sorry."

He straightened slowly, considered himself in full control. He didn't even notice the blood that welled in his palms as he clenched his fists.

He thought he knew where she was going and, familiar with the forest, he cut through the trees to beat her there.

Part Three

Love is strong as death;
jealousy is cruel as the grave.
—Song of Solomon

20

Jo didn't realize she'd made up her mind to go to Nathan's until she was nearly there. Even as she stopped, considered changing direction, she heard the pad of footsteps. Adrenaline surged, her fists clenched, her muscles tensed. She whirled, more than ready to attack.

Dusk settled around her, dimming the light, thickening the air. Overhead a slice of twilight moon hung in a sky caught between light and dark. Water lapped slyly at the high grass along the banks of the river. With a rush of wind, a heron rose, soaring away from her and its post.

And Nathan stepped out of the shadows.

He broke stride when he saw her, then stopped a foot away. His shoes and the frayed hem of his jeans were damp from the water grasses, his hair tousled from the quickening breeze. Noting her balls-of-the-feet fighting stance, he raised an eyebrow.

"Looking for a fight?"

She ordered her fingers to uncurl, one by one. "I might be."

He stepped forward, then tapped his fist lightly on her chin. "I say I could take you in two rounds. Want to go for it?"

"Maybe some other time." The blood that was singing in her ears began to quiet. He had broad shoulders, she mused. A nice place to lay your head—if you were the leaning sort. "Brian kicked me out," she said and tucked her hands in her pockets. "I was just out walking."

"Me, too. I'm done walking for a while." The hand he'd fisted uncurled, and the fingers of it brushed over her hair. "How about you?"

"I haven't decided."

"Why don't you come inside..." He took her hand, toyed with her fingers. "Think about it."

Her gaze shifted from their hands to his eyes, held steady there. "You don't want me to come inside and think, Nathan."

"Come in anyway. Had any dinner?"

"No."

"I've still got those steaks." He gripped her hand more firmly and led her toward the house. "Why did Brian kick you out?"

"Kitchen crisis. My fault."

"Well, I guess I won't ask you to help grill the steaks." He stepped inside, switched on the lights to cut the gloom. "About all I have to go with them are some frozen fries and a white Bordeaux."

"Sounds perfect to me. Can I use your phone? I should call, let them know I won't be back for... a little bit."

"Help yourself." Nathan walked to the fridge, got the steaks out of the freezer. She was jumpy as a spring, he thought, taking the meat to the microwave to defrost it. Angry on top, unhappy underneath.

He wondered why he had such a relentless need to find the reason for all three. He listened to the murmur of her voice as he puzzled over the buttons on the microwave. He was about to make an executive decision and hope for the best when she hung up the phone and came over.

"This part I know," she said and punched a series of buttons. "I'm an expert nuker."

"I do better when the package comes with directions. I'll start the grill. I've got some CDs over there if you want music."

She wandered over to the stack of CDs beside the clever little compact stereo on the end table beside the sofa. It seemed he preferred straight, no-frills rock with a mix of those early rebels Mozart and Beethoven.

She couldn't make up her mind, couldn't seem to concentrate on the simple act of choosing between "Moonlight Sonata" and "Sympathy for the Devil."

Romance or heat, she asked herself impatiently. What do you want? Make up your damn mind what it is you want and just take it.

"The fire shouldn't take long," Nathan began as he stepped back in, wiping his hands on his jeans. "If you—"

"I had a breakdown," she blurted out.

He lowered his hands slowly. "Okay."

"I figure you should know before this goes any farther than it already has. I was in the hospital back in Charlotte. I had a collapse, a mental collapse, before I came back here. I may be crazy."

Her eyes were eloquent, her lips pressed tight together. Nathan decided he had about five seconds to choose how to handle it. "How crazy? Like running-down-the-street-naked-and-warning-people-to-repent crazy? Or I-was-abducted-by-aliens crazy? Because I'm not entirely convinced all those abducted-by-aliens types are actually crazy."

Her mouth didn't exactly relax, but it did fall open. "Did you hear what I said?"

"Yeah, I heard you. I'm just asking for clarification. Do you want a drink?"

She closed her eyes. Maybe lunatics were attracted to lunatics. "I haven't run naked in the streets yet."

"That's good. I'd have to think twice about this if you had." Because she started to pace, he decided touching her wasn't the best next move. He went back to the refrigerator to take out the wine and uncork it. "So, were you abducted by aliens, and if so, do they really look like Ross Perot?"

"I don't understand you," she muttered. "I don't understand you at all. I spent two weeks under psychiatric evaluation. I wasn't functioning."

He poured two glasses. "You seem to be functioning all right now," he said mildly and handed her the wine.

"A lot you know." She gestured with the glass before drinking. "I came within an inch of having another breakdown today."

"Are you bragging or complaining?"

"Then I went shopping." She whirled away, stalking around the room. "It's not a sign of stability to teeter on the brink of an emotional crisis, then go out and buy underwear."

"What kind of underwear?"

Eyes narrowed, she glared at him. "I'm trying to explain myself to you."

"I'm listening." He took a chance, raising his hand to skim his fingers over her cheek. "Jo, did you really think I'd react to this by backing off and telling you to go away?"

"Maybe." She let out the air clogging her lungs. "Yes."

He pressed his lips to her brow and made her eyes sting. "Then you are crazy. Sit down and tell me what happened."

"I can't sit."

"Okay." He leaned back against the kitchen table. "We'll stand. What happened to you?"

"I—it was . . . a lot of things. Work-related stress. But that doesn't really bother me. You can use stress. It keeps you motivated, focused. Pressures and deadlines, I've always used them. I like having my time designated, my routine set out and followed. I want to know when I'm getting up in the morning, what I'm doing first and second and last."

"We'll say spontaneity isn't your strong suit, then."

"One spontaneous act and everything else shifts. How can you get a handle on it?"

"One spontaneous act," he commented, "and life's a surprise, more complicated but often more interesting."

"That may be true, but I haven't been looking for an interesting life." She turned away. "I just wanted a normal one. My world exploded once, and I've never been able to pick up the pieces. So I built another world. I had to."

He tensed, straightened, and the wine that lingered on his tongue went sour. "Is this because of your mother?"

"I don't know. Part of it must be. The shrinks certainly thought so. She was about my age when she left us. The doctors found that very interesting. She abandoned me. Was I repeating the cycle by abandoning myself?"

She shook her head and turned back to him. "But it wasn't just that. I've lived with that most of my life. I coped, damn it. I made my choices and I went for it, straight line, no detours. I liked what I was doing, where I was going. It satisfied me."

Knowing his hand wouldn't be steady, Nathan set the glass aside. "Jo Ellen, what happened before, what other people did, no matter who they were to us, can't destroy what we are. What we have. We can't let that happen."

She closed her eyes, relieved and soothed by his words. "That's what I'm telling myself. Every day. I started having dreams. I've always had very vivid dreams, but these unnerved me. I wasn't sleeping well, or eating well. I can't even remember if that started before or after the first pictures came."

"What pictures?"

"Someone started sending me photographs, of me. Just my eyes at first. Just my eyes." She rubbed a hand over her arm to chase away the chill. "It was creepy. I tried to ignore it, but it didn't stop. Then there was a whole package, dozens of photographs of me. At home, on assignment, at the market. Everywhere I went. He'd been there, watching me." Her hand rubbed slowly, steadily over her speeding heart. "And I thought I saw . . . more. I hallucinated, I panicked. And I broke."

Rage whipped through him, one hard, vicious lash. "Some bastard was dogging you, stalking you, tormenting you, and you're blaming yourself for crumbling?" His hands were steady now as he reached out for her, pulled her against him.

"I didn't face it."

"Stop it. How much is anyone supposed to face? The son of a bitch, putting you through that." He stared over her shoulder, wishing viciously he had something to fight, something to pummel. "What's the Charlotte PD doing about it?"

"I didn't report it in Charlotte." Her eyes went wide when he jerked her back. Widened still more when she saw the wild fury in his.

"What the hell do you mean, you didn't report it? You're just going to let him get away with it? Just do nothing?"

"I had to get away. I just wanted to get away from it. I couldn't cope. I could barely function."

When he became aware that his fingers were digging into her shoulders, he let her go. Snatching up his glass, he paced away from her. And he remembered how she'd looked when he first saw her on the island. Pale, exhausted, her eyes bruised and unhappy.

"You needed sanctuary."

Her breath came out in three jerks. "Yes, I suppose I did. Today I learned I hadn't found it. He's been here." Resolutely she swallowed the fresh panic in her throat. "He mailed photos of me from Savannah. Photos he'd taken here on the island."

Fresh fury clawed at him with hot-tipped fingers. Drawing on all of his control, Nathan turned slowly. "Then we'll find him. And we'll stop him."

"I don't even know if he's still on the island. If he'll come back, if...I don't know why, and that's the worst of it. But I'm facing it now, and I'm going to deal with it."

"You don't have to deal with it alone. You matter to me, Jo Ellen. I won't let you deal with it alone. You're going to have to face that too."

"Maybe that's why I came here. Maybe that's why I had to come here."

He set his wine down again so he could take her face in both hands. "I won't let anyone hurt you. Believe that."

She did, a little too easily, a little too strongly, and tried to backpedal. "It's good knowing you're on my side, but I have to be able to handle this."

"No." He lowered his mouth gently to hers. "You don't."

Her heart began to flutter in a different kind of panic. "The police said—"

"You went to the police?"

"Today. I..." She lost her train of thought for a moment as his mouth brushed hers again. "They said they'd look into it, but they don't have a lot to look into. I haven't been threatened."

"You feel threatened." He ran his hands down to her shoulders, over them. "That's more than enough. We're going to make that stop." He skimmed his lips over her cheek, along her temple, into her hair. "I'm going to take care of you," he murmured.

The words revolved in her spinning mind, refused to settle. "What?"

He doubted either one of them was ready to face what he'd suddenly realized. He needed to take care of her, to soothe away those troubles, to ease her heart. And he needed to be sure that whatever he did wouldn't snap the thin threads of the relationship they were just beginning to weave.

"Put it aside for a little while. Take an evening to relax." He ran his fingers up and down her spine once before drawing back to study her. "I've never seen anyone more in need of a rare steak and a glass of wine."

He was giving her time, she realized. That was good. That was best. She managed to smile. "It does sound pretty good. It would be nice not to even think about all of this for an hour."

"Then I'll put the steaks on, you can dig out the fries. And I'll bore you to tears talking about this new project I have in mind."

"You can try, but I don't cry easily." She turned to the freezer, opened it, then closed it again. "I don't like sex."

He stopped one step away from the microwave. It was necessary to clear his throat before he could face her again. "Excuse me?"

"Obviously that's part of the package we're putting together here." Jo linked her hands together. It was best to be up front about it, she thought. Practical. Especially since the words were out and couldn't be taken back.

He really had to stop putting his wine down, Nathan decided, and picking it up again, he took one long, slow sip. "You don't like sex."

"I don't hate it," she said, pulling her fingers apart to wave a hand. "Not like coconut."

"Coconut."

"I really hate coconut—even the smell puts me off. Sex is more like, I don't know, flan."

"Sex is like flan."

"I'm ambivalent about it."

"Uh-huh. Meaning, take it or leave it. If it's there, fine, but why go out of your way?"

Her shoulders relaxed. "That's about it. I thought I should tell you so you wouldn't build up any big expectations if we go to bed."

He ran his tongue over his teeth. "Maybe you haven't had any really well-prepared flan . . . in your experience."

She laughed. "It's all pretty much the same."

"I don't think so." He finished off his wine, set the empty glass down. Her eyes went from amused to wary as he walked toward her. "And I'm compelled to debate the subject. Right now."

"Nathan, that wasn't a challenge, it was just a . . ." The words slid down her throat when he swept her off her feet. "Wait a minute."

"I was on the debate team in college." It was a lie, but he thought it too good a line to miss.

"I haven't said I was going to sleep with you."

"What do you care?" He started down the short hallway. "You're ambivalent, remember?" He laid her on the bed, slid his body over hers. "And a little flan never hurt anybody."

"I don't want—"

"Yes, you do." He lowered his mouth, keeping only a breath between them. "So do I, and I have, right along. You're in an honest mood tonight, aren't you, Jo? Tell me you don't wonder, that you don't want?"

His body was warm and solid, his eyes clear and direct. "I wonder."

"That's good enough." He crushed his mouth to hers.

The taste of it, the sudden, sharp demand of it, pushed the worries out of her head. Grateful, knowing he would expect no more than what she had, she lifted her arms to wrap around him.

"Your mouth." He scraped his teeth over that wonderfully overfull top lip. "Christ, I've wanted that mouth. It drives me crazy."

She would have laughed, nearly did. Then his tongue was tangling hotly with hers, and the unexpected burn streaked down to throb between her thighs. It took only her moan to have him diving deeper.

Staggered, she clenched her fists in his hair. He hadn't kissed her like this before. She hadn't known that the pressure of mouth to mouth could cause a thousand wild aches in a thousand places. His hands stayed cupped around her face, as though everything he wanted centered only there.

She moved under him, a tremble, then an arch of hips. He had to tear his mouth from hers and press it to her throat to keep himself from rushing both of them. The scent of her skin, that zing of some early spring fragrance, was another welcome shock to his system. He lingered there, tormenting them both until the pulse under his tongue was racing.

He was undoing her, knot by knot. Moment by moment her body loosened, the shifts and quakes inside her spreading, building. There was excitement in not being quite able to catch her breath, not being quite sure where his mouth would travel next. Enchanted, she ran her hands over his shoulders, down his back, pleased with the bunch and flow of male muscle under her fingers.

When his mouth came greedily back to hers, she met it gratefully, delighting in the edgy jolts that snapped through her system. She arched again, mildly frustrated with the barriers that prevented her from taking him inside her. The need for physical release was greater than she had imagined.

He caught the lobe of her ear between his teeth and bit. "We're not settling for ambivalent this time."

He eased back, straddling her. The last rays of the sun streaked through the west window and set the air on fire. Her hair haloed around her face, the deep, smoky red of autumn leaves. Her eyes were high-summer blue, her skin the delicate rose of spring.

He lifted her hand, kissing the fingers one by one.

"What are you doing?"

"Savoring you. Your hand's trembling, and your eyes are full of nerves. I like that." He scraped his teeth over her knuckle. "It's exciting."

"I'm not afraid."

"No, you're confused." He lowered her hand, unfastened the first button of her blouse. "That's even better. You don't know what I'm going to make you feel next."

When her blouse was undone, he parted it, then slowly let his gaze slip down. Underneath she wore a bra of electric blue, the sheen of satin dipping low over the milk-pale swell of her breasts.

"Well, well." Though his stomach tightened with the need to devour her, he lifted his gaze back to hers. "Who would have thought it?"

"It's not mine." She cursed herself when he smiled. "I mean, I only bought it and wore it out of the store to stop Lexy from hounding me."

"God bless Lexy." Gently, watching her face, he skimmed his thumbs just above the edge of the satin. Her lashes fluttered, lowered. "You're holding back on me." He skimmed his thumbs a fraction lower. "I won't let you. I want to hear you sigh, Jo Ellen. I want to hear you moan. Then I want to hear you scream."

She opened her eyes, but her breath caught when he scraped his thumb over her nipple. "Oh, God."

"You hide too much, and not just this remarkable body. You hide too much of Jo Ellen. I'm going to see it all, and I'm going to have it all before we're finished."

He flicked the front hook of the bra, watched her breasts spill free. Then lowering his head, devoured them.

She did moan, then the sounds she made were quick, wild whimpers. The ache was unbearable, unreasonable. She moved restlessly beneath him to soothe it and only deepened the throb.

She dragged at his shirt, yanking it over his head and tossing it violently aside so she could feel hot flesh. The storm crashed inside her, tossing her closer and closer to that high, sharp peak, then dragging her back, just inches back, before she could ride it.

His mouth, his hands streaked over her now, daring her to keep pace, making it impossible for her to do anything but stumble blindly. She writhed, tried to roll free. Anywhere there was air, was an anchor to hold her.

But he held her trapped, imprisoned in that terrifying pleasure. And gave her no choice but to endure the violent war of sensation battling sensation. He pulled her slacks over her hips, revealing the blue swatch of satin. His mouth was on her belly, riding low, his labored breathing thickening the air with hers.

She didn't hear herself begging, but he did.

He had only to slide a finger under that satin, had only to touch her to have her explode.

Her body convulsed under his, rocked by wave after molten wave of pleasure. He pressed his face to her belly as it quivered, as his own body shuddered in response.

Thank God, thank God, was all she could think when the tension flooded out of her. Her muscles went lax, and she took one grateful gulp of air. Only to expel it again on a muffled scream as those clever, unmerciful fingers drove her up again.

Did she think that was all? The blood throbbed painfully in his head, his heart, his loins as he tore away the thin barrier. Did she think he would let either of them settle for less than madness now? He yanked her hips high and used his tongue to destroy her.

And she did scream.

Her arms flew back, her fingers bouncing off the glossy painted iron posts of the headboard, then gripping desperately as if to keep her body from being swept away. Behind her closed lids lights pulsed violent red, beneath her skin her blood swam dangerously fast. She shattered again, a thousand pieces of her flying free.

Then his hands gripped hers over the bedposts. He plunged into her, filled her, took her ruthlessly to peak again with long, slow, deliberate strokes. Even as her vision wavered, she could see his eyes, the sharp intensity of them, the pure gray edging toward black.

Helpless, she matched his pace, her breath hitching and tearing when he quickened the tempo. Her hips pumping when he began to thrust inside her, hard and fast.

When his mouth came down on hers, she could do nothing but surrender to it. When her body spun finally and completely out of control, she could do nothing but let herself go.

And he could do nothing but let himself follow.

. . .

She didn't know if she'd slept. She almost wondered if she'd simply slid into a coma. But it was full dark when she opened her eyes. That, Jo thought hazily, or she'd been struck blind.

He lay over her, his head resting between her breasts. She could feel the rapid beat of his heart, hear the quiet sigh of the wind fluttering through the window screens.

He felt her shift, just slightly. "I'll stop crushing you in just a second."

"It's all right. I can almost breathe."

His lips curved as he brushed them over the side of her breast, but he rolled over. Before she could move, he'd wrapped an arm around her and pulled her against him. "Flan, my ass."

She opened her mouth, certain that some pithy comment would come. But there was only laughter. "Maybe I've just been off desserts for a while."

"Then you'll just have to have seconds."

She snuggled up against him without thinking. "If we try for seconds, we'll kill each other."

"No, we won't. We'll get to those steaks first, and I'll get you a little drunk. Which was my original plan, by the way. Then we'll have seconds."

"You planned to get me drunk?"

"That was one of my ideas. Then there was the one about climbing up the trellis to your balcony. Sort of the swashbuckle scenario."

"You'd have broken your neck."

"Nah, Brian and I used to monkey up and down that thing all the time."

"Sure, when you were ten." She rose onto her elbow, shook her hair back. "You're about a hundred pounds heavier now, and I doubt you're as agile."

"This is no time to call my agility into question."

She smiled, lowered her brow to his. "You're absolutely right. Maybe you'll surprise me one night."

"Maybe I will. But now . . ." He gave her hair a tug before he sat up. "I'm going to cook you dinner."

"Nathan." She smoothed a hand over the wrinkled spread while he searched for his jeans. "Why are you going to so much trouble for me?"

He didn't speak for a moment. He couldn't be sure of his moves, or his words. After tugging on his jeans he studied her silhouette in the dark. "It only took seeing you again, Jo Ellen. That's all it took. It knocked the wind out of me, and I still don't have my breath back."

"I'm a mess, Nathan." She swallowed hard and was grateful for the dark so he couldn't see her face. The longing that had geysered inside of her had to show. "I don't know what I think or feel about anything. Anyone. You'd be better off shaking loose."

"I've taken the easy way a few times. It usually ends up being dull. So far you've been anything but dull."

"Nathan—"

"You're really wasting your time arguing with me while you're sitting naked on my bed."

She dragged a hand through her hair. "Good point. We'll argue later."

"Fine. I'll just go dump more charcoal on the grill." And since he planned to have her naked and on his bed again before the evening was over, he didn't think they'd have much time to argue.

21

"Stay." Nathan wrapped his arms around Jo's waist, nuzzled the back of her neck. Her hair was still damp from the shower they'd shared. Smelling his soap on her skin aroused him yet again. "I'll fix you breakfast in the morning."

She hooked her arm around his neck. It amazed her how easy it was to be this close. "You don't have anything to fix."

"Bread. I have bread." He spun her around so he could feast on that wonderful curve of neck and shoulder. "I'm terrific at toast. I'm famous for my toast."

"As incredibly appetizing as that sounds... Nathan." With a sound caught between a laugh and a moan, she tried to wiggle away from his roving hands. "We really will kill each other, and I have to get back."

"It's barely midnight."

"It's after one."

"Well, then, it's practically morning, you might as well stay."

She wanted to. As his mouth found hers, persuasively, she badly wanted to. "I have things to straighten out at home. And I have to make it up to Brian for leaving him in such a mess tonight."

She put her hands to his face, liking the way it felt under her fingers. Cheekbones, jaw, the scrape of beard. Had she ever explored a man's face this way? Or wanted to?

"And I have to think." Firmly, she drew away. "I'm a thinker, Nathan. A planner. This is new territory for me."

He rubbed a thumb over the line that formed between her brows. "You'll just compel me to keep changing directions on you."

Fresh nerves skidded over her skin. "Then I'll have to stay a step ahead. But now, I have to go home."

He could see her mind was made up, and so he forced himself to readjust the pleasant image of waking beside her in the morning. "I'll drive you."

"You don't have to—"

"Jo." He put his hands on her shoulders, and his voice was quiet and final. "You're not going out alone in the dark."

"I'm not afraid. I'm not going to be afraid anymore."

"Good for you. I'm still driving you. Or we can argue about it, I can maneuver you back into the bedroom, and drive you home in the morning. Does your father have a gun?"

She laughed, pushed at her bangs. "It's very unlikely he'd shoot you for sleeping with me."

"If he does, I'm counting on you to nurse me back to health." He took his keys from the counter.

"I'm a Southern woman," she said as they started out the door. "I'll even find a petticoat to tear into bandages."

"It would almost be worth getting shot for that."

As she climbed into his Jeep, she asked, "Ever been shot?"

"No." He slid in beside her and started the engine. "But I had my tonsils out. How much worse could it be?"

"Considerably, I'd imagine."

She stretched out her legs, leaned back, and shut her eyes. She was tired, but deliciously so. Her muscles were loose, her mind pleasantly fogged. The air felt silky on her skin.

"The nights are best on the island," she murmured, "when the quiet just rings in your ears and no one else is awake. You can smell the trees and the water. The sea's a whisper in the background, like a pulse beating."

"You can be alone and not be lonely."

"Mmm. When I was a little girl I used to imagine what it would be like if I were all alone, had the island all to myself just for a few days. It would all be mine, everywhere I walked, everywhere I looked. I thought I would like that. But then I dreamed it, and I was afraid. In the dream I kept running and running, through the house, out into the forest, over the beach. I wanted to find someone, anyone, to be there with me. But I was all alone. And I woke up crying for Daddy."

"Now you take pictures of being alone."

"I suppose I do." She let out a sigh and opened her eyes. And there, through the dark, she saw the glimmer of light. "Kate left a light on for me."

It was comforting, that flicker of home. She watched it dance through the trees, outdo the shadows. Once she'd run away from that light, and once she'd run toward it. She hoped the time would come when she could walk either way without fear.

As they neared the end of the drive, she saw the figure rise from the porch swing. Her stomach did an ungainly roll before Nathan covered her hand with his.

"Stay here. Lock the doors."

"No, I—" She let out a trembling breath. "It's Brian," she said, feeling foolish at the wave of relief that swamped her.

Nathan nodded, also recognizing the figure as Brian stepped into the light. "Okay, let's go."

"No." She gave the hand that covered hers a quick squeeze. "Let's not complicate it. If he needs to yell at me some more, I deserve it, and I don't want the two of you eyeing each other and trying to figure out how to handle the fact that you're friends and you're sleeping with his sister."

"He doesn't appear to be armed."

It made her laugh, as intended. "Go home." She shifted, finding it simple to just lean over and touch her lips to his. "Let Brian and me deal with our family baggage. We're too polite to do a good job of it in front of you."

"I want to see you tomorrow."

She opened the door. "Come for breakfast—unless you're set on having your world-famous toast."

"I'll be here."

She started toward the porch, waiting until she heard his Jeep reverse before she mounted the stairs. "Evening," she said coolly to Brian. "Nice night for porch sitting."

He stared at her a moment, then moved so quickly she nearly shrieked. His arms strapped tight around her. "I'm sorry. I'm so sorry."

Stunned speechless, she started to pat his back, then yelped as he jerked her away and shook her.

"It's your own goddamn fault. So typical, so goddamn Jo Ellen."

"What?" Insult slapped on top of surprise and had her shoving him. "What the hell are you talking about? Stop manhandling me."

"Manhandling? I ought to kick your butt up to your ears. Why the hell didn't you tell somebody what was going on? Why didn't you let me know you were in trouble?"

"If you don't let go of me right now—"

"No, you just go on the way you always have, pushing people out of the way so you can—"

He broke off with a grunt as her fist plowed into his stomach. The blow was quick and forceful enough to catch him off guard. Dropping his hands, he eyed her narrowly.

"That hasn't changed either. You always packed a decent punch."

"You're lucky I didn't aim for that pretty face of yours." Sniffing, she rubbed her hands over her arms where his fingers had gripped. Damned if she wouldn't have bruises, she thought. "Obviously you're in no state to have a reasonable, civilized conversation. So I'm going up to bed."

"You take one step toward that door and I'll haul you over my knee."

She raised herself up on tiptoe and stuck her face in his. "Don't you threaten me, Brian Hathaway."

"Don't you test me, Jo Ellen. I've been sitting here for better than two hours worried sick, so I'm in the mood to take you on."

"I was with Nathan, which you knew very well. And there's no cause for you to worry about my sex life."

He gritted his teeth. "I don't want to hear about it. I don't want to think about it. I'm not talking about you and Nathan being... I'm not talking about that."

Jo bit the inside of her cheek to keep from grinning. Had she known it was so easy to flummox her brother, she would have used that angle years ago.

"Well, then." Pleased with the point scored, she strolled to the porch swing and sat. She cocked her head as she took out a cigarette. "Just what is it you want to hear about, think about, and talk about, Brian?"

"You can't pull off the grand Southern Belle number, Jo. It just doesn't suit you."

She flicked her lighter on. "It's late and I'm tired. If you have something to say, say it so I can go to bed."

"You shouldn't have been alone." His voice had gone quiet and drew her gaze. "You shouldn't have gone through that alone, been in that hospital alone. And I want you to know that the choice of doing that was yours."

She took a slow drag. "Yes, it was my choice. It was my problem."

"That's right, Jo." He took a step forward, hooking his thumbs in his front pockets to keep his hands from curling into fists. "Your problems, your triumphs, your life. You've never seen fit to share any of those things. Why should this be different?"

Her stomach jittered. "What could you have done?"

"I could have been there. I would have been there. Yeah, that shocks the hell out of you, doesn't it?" he said before she lowered her eyes. "I don't care how fucked-up this family is, you wouldn't have gone through that by yourself. And you're not going to go through the rest of it by yourself."

"I've been to the police."

"I'm not just talking about the cops, though any pea brain would have gone to them in Charlotte when this started."

She flicked an ash, took another drag. "You're going to have to make up your mind whether you want to shame me or insult me."

"I can do both."

Annoyed, she flipped the cigarette away, watched the red tip fly through the dark, then disappear into it. "I came home, didn't I?"

"That, at least, was half sensible. You came home looking like something that had been dragged down five miles of bad road, then you don't tell anybody what's wrong. Except Kirby. You told Kirby, didn't you, after I dragged you over there?" His eyes flashed. "I'll deal with her later."

"You leave her alone. I told her about the breakdown and that was all. That's medical, and she's not obliged to tell her lover about her patients' medical histories."

"You told Nathan."

"I told him tonight. I told him all of it tonight, because I thought it was only right and fair." Weary now, she rubbed her forehead. An owl was hooting monotonously somewhere in the cool dark. She wished she could find its tree, climb the branches, and just huddle there in peace.

"Do you want me to go over it all again now, Brian? Do you want chapter and verse and all the little details?"

"No." He let out a sigh and sat beside her. "No, you don't have to go over it again. I guess you'd have told me before if the lot of us weren't so screwed up. I've been thinking about that while I've been sitting out here working myself up to pound on you."

"Couldn't have taken much. You were already mad at me. Kicked me out of the house."

He let out a quick, rough laugh. "Your own fault you let me. It's your house too."

"It's your house, Brian. It always has been more yours than anyone's." It was said gently, with quiet acceptance. "You're the one who cares most, and tends most."

"Does that bother you?"

"No. Well, maybe some, but mostly it's a relief to me. I don't have to worry if the roof's going to leak, because you do."

She tipped her head back, looking up at the glossy white paint of the veranda, then out over the moonlight-sprinkled gardens. The wind chimes were tinkling, the fountain quiet for the night, and the scent of musk roses floated poignantly on the breeze.

"I don't want to live here. For a long time I thought I didn't ever want to be here. But I was wrong. I do. Everything here means more to me than I let myself believe. I want to know I can come back now and then. I can sit here on a warm, clear night like this and smell the sweet peas and the jasmine and Mama's roses. Lexy and me, we just can't stay here the way you do. But I guess we both need to know that Sanctuary stands on the hill like always and nobody's going to lock the door on us."

"No one would."

"I dreamed the doors were locked and I couldn't get inside. No one came when I called, and all the windows were dark and empty." She closed her eyes, wanting it to play back in her mind, wanting to know she could stand against it now. "I lost myself in the forest. I was alone and scared and couldn't find my way. Then I saw myself standing on the other side of the river. Only it wasn't me at all. It was Mama."

"You've always had strange dreams."

"Maybe I've always been crazy." She smiled a little, then looked out into the night. "I look like her, Brian. Sometimes when I see my face in the mirror, it gives me such a jolt. In the end, that's what pushed me over the edge. When those pictures came, all those pictures of me. I thought one of them was Mama. Only she was dead. She was naked and her eyes were open and staring and lifeless as a doll's. I looked just like her."

"Jo—"

"But the picture wasn't there," she said quickly. "It wasn't even there. I imagined it. I've always hated seeing pictures of myself, because I see her in them."

"You may look like her, Jo, but you're not like her. You finish what you start, you stick."

"I ran away from here."

"You got away from here," he corrected. "You went out to make your own life. That's different from leaving a life you'd already started and all the people who needed you. You're not Annabelle." He draped an arm over her shoulder and let the swing slide into motion. "And you're only about as crazy as the rest of us around here."

She laughed. "Well, that's comforting, isn't it?"

It was late when Susan Peters marched out of the rented cottage and stalked toward the cove. She'd had a nasty fight with her husband—and had had to do it in undertones so as not to disturb their friends who'd taken the cottage with them for the week.

The man was an idiot, she decided. She couldn't even think why she'd married him, much less why she'd stayed married to him for three years—not to mention the two they'd lived together before making it legal.

Every time, every single time, she so much as mentioned buying a house, he got that closed-in look on his face. And he started going on about down payments and taxes and maintenance and money, money, money. What the hell were both of them working their butts off for? Was she supposed to live in an apartment in Atlanta forever?

The hell with the conveniences, she thought, and tossed back her curly mop of brown hair. She wanted a yard, a little garden, a kitchen where she could practice cooking the gourmet dishes she'd taken classes for.

But all she got out of Tom was one day. One day. Well, when was one day going to get here?

Disgusted, she plopped down on the beach, slipping off her shoes so she could dig her toes in the sand while she stared out at the quiet water that lapped and lapped against the hull of the little outboard they'd rented.

He didn't have any problems spending money on a silly boat so he could go fishing every stupid day they were on Desire.

They had enough for a down payment. She propped her elbow on her knee and watched sulkily as the moon floated overhead. She'd done all the research on financing and balloon payments and interest rates. She wanted that sweet little house on Peach Blossom Lane.

Sure, it would be tight for the first couple of years, but they could manage. She'd been so positive that when she talked to him about building equity and breaking out of the endless cycle of renting month after month, he would come around.

And, oh, it was just about killing her that Mary Alice and Jim were about to settle on that pretty place in the development. A magnolia tree in the front yard and a little patio off the kitchen.

She sighed and wished she'd waited until they'd gotten back home to start working on Tom again. That would have been smarter. She knew how important timing was when dealing with her husband. But she'd gotten so damned upset, she hadn't been able to stop herself.

When they got back to Atlanta, Tom was going to look at that house on Peach Blossom if she had to drag him by the ear.

She heard the footsteps behind her and stared straight ahead. "No point in coming down here to try to make up, Tom Peters. I'm not nearly finished being mad at you yet. I may never be."

Furious that he didn't attempt to talk her out of it, she wrapped her arms around her knees. "You just go on back up and balance your checkbook, since money is all you want. I don't have another thing to say to you."

As the silence dragged on, she gritted her teeth and turned her head. "Listen here, Tom—Oh." Embarrassment heated her cheeks as she looked up into a stranger's face. "I'm sorry. I thought you were someone else."

He smiled, charmingly, and with a gleam of laughter in his eyes. "That's all right. I'm going to think of you as someone else, too."

Even as the first streak of alarm sent a scream toward her throat, he struck.

It wasn't going to be perfect, he decided, studying her as she lay crumpled at his feet. He hadn't planned on this impromptu practice session, but he hadn't been able to sleep. His mind was so full of Jo, and the sexual need was unexpectedly sharp tonight.

He was very, very annoyed with her. And that only made him want her more.

Then the pretty brunette had just been there, like a gift, sitting all alone by the water under the shifting light of the moon.

A wise man didn't look a gift horse in the mouth. So to speak, he thought with a chuckle as he hauled her up into his arms. They would just move off a bit, he decided. In case old Tom—whoever he might be—wandered down to the cove.

She was a light load, and he didn't mind the exercise. He whistled tunelessly as he carried her over the sand and up through a narrow break in the dunes. He would need the moonlight, so he settled on the verges of the swale. It was picturesque, with the moon-silvered bushes, he thought, as he laid her down.

And it was deserted.

He used his belt to tie her hands and one of the silk scarves he always carried to gag her. He stripped her first, pleased to find that her body was trim and athletic. She moaned a little as he pulled off his jeans.

"Don't worry, darling, you look very pretty, very sexy. And the moonlight flatters you."

He took out his camera—the Pentax single-lens reflex he liked for portraits—pleased that he'd loaded it with slow film. He wanted fine detail now, knife-edged sharpness. Likely he'd have to do some burning in and dodging in the darkroom to get the contrasts and textures just so.

He would look forward to that, to perfecting the prints.

Whistling under his breath, he fixed his flash and ran off three shots before her eyelids fluttered.

"That's right, that's right, I want you to come around now. Slow. A few nice close-ups of that pretty face. The eyes are the best. They always are."

He grew hard as they opened, dulled with pain and confusion. "Beautiful, just beautiful. Look here, look right here now. That's the way, baby. Focus."

Delighted, he captured understanding and fear. He set the camera down as she began to stir. Her movement would blur the shot, and he didn't have any backup film of faster speed. Still smiling, he picked up the gun he'd laid on his neatly folded jeans. And showed it to her.

"Now, I don't want you to move. I want you to stay still, really still, and do everything I tell you. The last thing I want to do is use this. Now you understand that, don't you?"

Tears began to swim in her eyes, then leak out. But she nodded. Terror bubbled in her brain, and though she tried to remain motionless, shudders racked her.

"I'm just going to take your picture. We're having a photo shoot. You're not afraid of having your picture taken, a pretty woman like you."

He exchanged gun for camera and smiled winningly. "Now here's what I want you to do. Bend your knees. Come on now, that's the way, and move them over to your left side. You've got a lovely body. Why don't we show it off to its best advantage?"

She did what he asked, her eyes wheeling over to stare at the gun. The chrome glinted and shone. He just wanted pictures, she told herself, as her breath hitched and shuddered. He would leave her alone then. He'd go away. He wouldn't hurt her.

Terror bulged in her eyes, turned her skin milky white and had him throbbing viciously. His hands began to tremble, signaling him that he could no longer wait for the next stage.

His heart thudded in his head as he carefully set his camera down on his shirt. Very gently he put a hand on her throat and looked deeply into her eyes.

"You're beautiful," he murmured. "And you're helpless. You know that, don't you? There's nothing you can do. I'm in control. I have all the power. Don't I?"

She jerked her head down in a nod, small sobs muffling against the silk. When his hand closed over her breast and squeezed, she moaned out pleas and tossed her head wildly. Her heels dug into the sand as she tried to escape.

He straddled her. "It won't do you any good." He shuddered as she bucked and twisted under him. "The more fight you put up, the better I like it. Try to scream." He squeezed her breasts again, then bent down to bite at them. "Scream, goddamn it. Scream."

A harsh keening sound ripped out of her, burned her throat. Desperate, she fought against the gag, struggled to use her teeth, her tongue, her lips to drag it aside.

He pried her thighs apart, deliberately bruising the flesh. And thought of Jo as he raped her. Thought of Jo Ellen's long legs. Jo Ellen's sexy mouth. Jo Ellen's heavy-lidded blue eyes, while he pounded himself with sweaty violence into her substitute.

The orgasm was towering, brought tears of surprise and triumph to his eyes. So much better than the last one, he realized, and absently closed a hand over her throat, pressing down only until she stopped fighting.

He'd chosen well this time, he thought, as the climax eased off into sweetness. He'd found his practice angel. The breeze cooled his damp skin when he rose for the camera.

He remembered how the process had been outlined in his journal and reminded himself not merely to duplicate but to improve.

"I may rape you again, I may not." He smiled, attractive creases forming around his mouth and eyes. "I may hurt you, I may not. It all depends on how you behave. Now you just lie there, angel, and think about that."

Satisfied that she was quiescent for a while, he changed lenses. Her pupils were enormous black moons with only a sliver of pale brown encircling them, her breathing was short and shallow. He whistled contentedly as he loaded fresh film. He shot the entire roll before he raped her a second time.

And he'd decided to hurt her. After all, the choice, the mood, the control were all completely in his hands.

She stopped fighting him. In all but a physical sense she'd stopped being there. Her body was numb, belonged to someone else. In her mind she was safe, with Tom, sitting together on the patio of their pretty new house on Peach Blossom Lane.

She barely felt him remove the gag. She managed a quiet sob, made a pitiful effort to draw in breath enough to scream.

"You know it's too late for that." He said it gently, almost lovingly, as he wound the scarf around her throat. "You'll be my angel now."

He tightened the scarf, slowly, wanting to draw out the moment. He watched her mouth open, struggle to suck in air. Her heels drummed on the sand, her body jerked.

His breath became labored, the power flooding him, screaming in his head, racing through his blood. He lost track of the times he stopped, let her claw back to consciousness before he took her to the brink again. He would rise, aim the camera again. Not just one decisive moment, he thought. But many. The fear of death, the acceptance, the flicker of hope as life pumped back. The surrender when it blinked out again.

Oh, he regretted the lack of a tripod and remote.

Finally his system roared past control and he finished it.

Gasping, he murmured endearments, kissed her gratefully. She had shown him a new level, this unexpected angel that fate had tossed at his feet. It had been meant to be, of course. He understood that now. He'd had more to learn before he met his destiny with Jo. So much more to learn.

He removed the scarf, folded it, and laid it reverently over the gun. He took time to pose her, adjusting her hands after he'd freed them. The welts on the wrists troubled him a little until he slid her hands under her head like a pillow.

He thought he would title this one *Gift of an Angel.*

He dressed, then bundled her clothes. The marsh was too far, he decided. Whatever the gators and other predators had left of Ginny was buried deep there. He didn't have time for the hike, or energy for the labor.

There were conveniently deep spots in the river, however, and that would do well enough. He would take her to her final resting place, weigh her body down so that it would rest on the slippery bottom.

And then, he decided with a wide yawn, he'd call it a night.

22

When Giff slipped out of Lexy's room and down the back steps, the sky was pearled with dawn. He'd meant to be out of the house and on his way before sunup. But then, he thought with a lazy smile, Lexy had a way of persuading a man to tarry.

She'd needed him. First to work off her mad at Brian, then to tell him about her sister's troubles. They could talk about things like that, and all manner of other things, tucked in her room, their voices hushed with secrets.

That ease of talking, Giff mused, was just one of the advantages of being in love with someone you'd known since childhood.

Then there was the electric jolt, the unexpected sizzle of surprise, as you got to know that very familiar person on other, more intimate levels. Giff puffed out a breath as he reached for the door. It sure wasn't any hardship to study Lexy Hathaway on those other levels. The way she'd looked in that little silk nightie she'd bought in Savannah had been enough to make a strong man sink to his knees and praise God for coming up with the brilliant notion of creating Eve.

Getting her out of that sheer little concoction hadn't been a worrisome task either. In fact, he decided that when he took her to Savannah on Saturday he'd buy her another one, just so he could...

The erotic image of Lexy in buttermilk silk fled as he found himself faced with her father. It was a toss-up as to which one of them was more disconcerted, Lexy's lover, with his hair still tumbled from sex and sleep, or Lexy's father, with a bowl of cornflakes in his hand.

Both cleared their throats.

"Mr. Hathaway."

"Giff."

"I... ah... I was..."

"That plumbing need seeing to again upstairs?"

It was an out, offered as desperately as it was nearly taken. But Giff straightened his shoulders, told himself not to take the coward's way, and met Sam's eyes directly. "No, sir."

Miserably uneasy, Sam set his bowl down and dumped milk onto the cereal. "Well, then," was all he could think to say.

"Mr. Hathaway, I don't want you to think I'm sneaking out of your house." Which of course, Giff admitted, was exactly what he was doing.

"You've been running tame in Sanctuary since you could walk." Leave it alone, boy, Sam prayed. Leave it lie and move along. "You're welcome to come and go as you please, just like you ever were."

"I've been walking a lot of years now, Mr. Hathaway. And for most of them I've been . . . I figure you know how I feel about Lexy. How I always have."

Damn cereal was going to get soggy, Sam thought with regret. "I guess you didn't grow out of it like most thought you would."

"No, sir. I'd say it's more I grew into it. I love her, Mr. Hathaway. My feelings for her are long-standing and steady. You've known me and my family all my life. I'm not feckless or foolish. I've got some savings put by. I can make a good living with my hands and my back."

"I don't doubt it." But Sam frowned. Maybe he'd barely sipped through his first cup of coffee, but his mind was clear enough to catch the drift. "Giff, if you're asking me for permission to . . . call on my daughter, seems to me you've already opened that particular door, walked in, and made yourself to home."

Giff flushed and hoped his swallow wasn't audible. "Yes, sir, I can't deny the truth of that. But it's not that particular door I'm speaking of, Mr. Hathaway."

"Oh." Sam opened a drawer for a spoon, hoping Giff would take the hint and mosey on before things got any stickier. Then he put the spoon down with a clatter and stared. "Sweet Jesus, boy, you're not talking about marrying her?"

Giff's jaw set, his eyes glinted. "I'm going to marry her, Mr. Hathaway. I'd like to have your blessing over it, but either way, I'm having her."

Sam shook his head, rubbed his eyes. Life just flat refused to be simple, he reflected. A man went along, minding his own business, wanting nothing more than for other people to mind theirs in return, but life just kept throwing tacks under your bare feet.

"Boy, you want to take her on, I'm not going to stand in your way. Couldn't anyhow, even if I planted my boots in concrete. The two of you are of age and ought to have the sense to know your own minds." He dropped his hands. "But I've got to say, Giff, as I've always been fond of you, I think you're taking on a sack of trouble there. You'll be lucky to get one moment's peace from the time you say 'I do' till you take your last breath."

"Peace isn't a priority of mine."

"She'll run through every penny you've put by and won't have a clue where she spent it."

"She's not near as foolish as you think. And I can always make more money."

"I'm not going to waste my breath talking you out of something you've got your mind set on."

"I'm good for her."

"No question about it. Fact is, you might be the making of her." Resigned to it, Sam offered a hand. "I'll wish you luck."

Sam watched Giff go off with a spring in his step. He didn't doubt the boy was in love, and if he let himself he could remember what it was like to feel that light in the head, that edgy in the gut. That hot in the blood.

Sam settled in the breakfast nook with his second cup of coffee and his soggy cereal and watched the sky lighten to a bold summer blue. He'd been just as dazed and dazzled by Annabelle as Giff was now with Lexy. It had only taken one look for his heart to jolt straight out of his chest and fall at her feet.

Christ, they'd been young. He was barely eighteen that summer, coming to the island to work on his uncle's shrimp boat. Casting nets, sweating under a merciless sun until his hands were raw and his back a misery.

He enjoyed every second of it.

He fell in love with the island, first glance. The hazy greens, the pockets of solitude, the surprises around every bend of the river or road.

Then he saw Belle Pendleton walking along the beach, gathering shells at sunset. Long golden legs, willowy body, the generous fall of waving red hair. Eyes as clear as water and blue as summer.

The sight of her hazed his vision and closed his throat.

He smelled of shrimp and sweat and engine grease. He wanted a quick swim through the waves to loosen the muscles the day's work had aching. But she smiled at him and, holding a pink-lined conch shell, began to talk to him.

He was tongue-tied and terrified. He'd always been intimidated by females, but this vision who had already captured his heart with one smile left him grunting out responses like an ill-mannered ape. He never knew how he'd managed to stutter out an invitation to take a walk the next evening.

Years later, when he asked her why she'd said yes, she just laughed.

You were so handsome, Sam. So serious and stern and sweet. And you were the first boy—and the last man—to make my heart skip a beat.

She'd meant it. Then, Sam thought. After he had worked enough, saved enough money to satisfy him, he'd gone to her father to ask permission for her hand. A great deal more formal that had been, Sam mused, sipping his coffee, than the meeting just now with Giff. There'd been no sneaking out of Annabelle's bedroom at dawn either. Though there had been stolen afternoons in the forest.

Even when a man's blood had been cool for years, he remembered what it was like to have it run hot. For the first few years that Annabelle was gone, his blood had heated from time to time. He'd taken care of that in Savannah.

It hadn't shamed him to pay for sex. A professional woman didn't require conversation or wooing. She simply transacted business. It had been some time since he'd required that particular service, though. And since AIDS and other potential horrors of impersonal sex scared him, Sam was relieved to have weaned himself away from it.

Everything he needed was on the island. He'd found the peace that young Giff claimed not to want.

Sam sat back to enjoy the rest of his coffee in the quiet. He had to struggle with a hard twinge of irritation when the door opened and Jo walked in. The fact that she hesitated when she saw him and a slight flicker of annoyance moved over her face both shamed and amused him.

Peas in a pod, he decided, who don't much care to share the pod.

"Good morning." Damn it, all she'd wanted was a quick slug of coffee before she went out to work. Not just wander or brood, but work. She'd awakened for the first time in weeks refreshed and focused, and she didn't want to waste it.

"Clear morning," Sam said. "Thunderstorms and strong winds by evening, though."

"I suppose." She opened a cupboard.

Silence stretched between them, long and complete. The trickle of coffee as Jo poured it from pot to cup was loud as a waterfall. Sam shifted, his khakis hissing against the polished wood of the bench.

"Kate told me . . . she told me."

"I imagined she would."

"Um. You're feeling some better now."

"I'm feeling a great deal better."

"And the police, they're doing what they can do."

"Yes, what they can."

"I was thinking about it. It seems to me you should stay here for the next little while. Until it's settled and done, you shouldn't plan on going back to Charlotte and traveling like you do."

"I'd planned to stay, work here, for the next few weeks anyway."

"You should stay here, Jo Ellen, until it's settled and done."

Surprised at the firm tone, as close to an order as she could remember receiving from him since childhood, she turned, lifted her brows. "I don't live here. I live in Charlotte."

"You don't live in Charlotte," Sam said slowly, "until this is settled and done."

Her back went up, an automatic response. "I'm not having some wacko dictate my life. When I'm ready to go back, I'll go back."

"You won't leave Sanctuary until I say you can leave."

This time her mouth dropped open. "I beg your pardon?"

"You heard me right enough, Jo Ellen. Your ears have always been sharp and your understanding keen. You'll stay here until you're well enough, and it's safe enough for you to leave and go about your business."

"If I want to go tomorrow—"

"You won't," Sam interrupted. "I've got my mind set on it."

"You've got your mind set?" Stunned, she strode over to the table and scowled down at him. "You think you can just set your mind on something that has to do with me after all this time, and I'll just fall in line?"

"No. I reckon you'll have to be planted in line and held there, like always.

That's all I have to say." He wanted to escape, he wanted the quiet, but when he started to slide down the bench to get up, Jo slapped a hand onto the table to block him.

"It's not all I have to say. Apparently you've lost track of some time here. I'm twenty-seven years old."

"You'll be twenty-eight come November," he said mildly. "I know the ages of my children."

"And that makes you a sterling example of fatherhood?"

"No." His eyes stayed level with hers. "But there's no changing the fact that I'm yours just the same. You've done well enough for yourself, by yourself, up to now. But things have taken a turn. So you'll stay here, where there are those who can look out for you, for the next little while."

"Really?" Her eyes narrowed to slits. "Well, let me tell you just what I'm going to continue to do for myself, by myself."

"Good morning." Kate breezed in, all smiles. She'd had her ear to the door for the last two minutes and calculated it was time to make an entrance. It pleased her to enter a room in that house and not find apathy or bitterness. Temper, at least, was clean.

"That coffee smells wonderful. I'm just dying for some."

In a calculated move, she brought a cup and the pot to the table, sliding in beside Sam before he could wriggle away. "Just let me top this off for you, Sam. Jo, bring your cup on over here. I swear I don't know the last time we sat down for a quiet cup of coffee in the morning. Lord knows, after that chaos in the dining room last night, we need it."

"I was on my way out," Jo said stiffly.

"Well, honey, sit down and finish your coffee first. Brian'll be coming in soon enough to tell us all to scat. You look like you got a good night's sleep." Kate smiled brilliantly. "Your daddy and I were worried you'd be restless."

"There's no need to worry." Grudgingly, Jo got her coffee and brought it to the table. "Everything that can be done's being done. In fact, I'm feeling so much calmer about it all, I'm thinking about going back to Charlotte." She shot a challenging look at Sam. "Soon."

"That's fine, Jo, if you want to send the lot of us to an early grave with worry." Kate spoke mildly as she spooned sugar into her coffee.

"I don't see—"

"Of course you see," Kate interrupted. "You're just angry, and you have a right to be. But you don't have the right to take that anger out on those who love you. It's natural to do just that," Kate added with a smile, "but it's not right."

"That's not what I'm doing."

"Good." Kate patted her hand, as if the matter were settled. "You're planning to take some pictures today, I see." She glanced over at the camera bag Jo had set on the counter. "I got out that book that Nathan's father did on the island. Put it in the public parlor after I'd looked through it again. My, there are some pretty photographs in there."

"He did good work," Jo muttered, struggling not to sulk.

"He sure did. I found one in there of Nathan, Brian, and I suppose Nathan's younger brother. Such handsome little boys. They were holding up a couple of whopping trout and had grins on their faces that stretched a mile wide. You ought to take a look at it."

"I will." Jo found herself smiling, thinking of Nathan at ten with a trout on the line.

"And you could think about doing a photo book on the island yourself," Kate went on. "It would be just wonderful for business. Sam, you take Jo over to the marsh, that spot where the sea lavender's full in bloom. Oh, and if the two of you go through the forest, along the southwest edge, the path there's just covered with trumpet vine petals. That would make such a nice picture, Jo Ellen. That narrow, quiet little path just dusted with fallen blossoms."

She went on and on, chattering out suggestions without giving father or daughter a chance to interrupt. When Brian trooped in the back door and stared, baffled, at the cozy family group, Kate beamed him a smile.

"We'll be out of your way in just a shake, sweetie. Jo and Sam were just deciding which route they were going to take around the island today for Jo's pictures. Y'all better get started."

Kate got up quickly, gathering Jo's camera bag. "I know how fussy you are about the light and such. You just tell your daddy when it strikes you as right. I can't wait to see what kind of pictures you get. Hurry along now, before Brian starts to fuss at us. Sam, you get a chance, you take Jo down to where those baby terns hatched a while back. Goodness, look at the time. You two scoot."

She all but dragged Sam to his feet, kept nudging and talking until she'd shoved them both out the door.

"Just what the hell was that, Kate?" Brian asked her.

"That, with any luck at all, was the beginning of something."

"They'll go their own ways when they're five feet from the house."

"No, they won't," Kate disagreed as she started toward the ringing phone on the wall. "Because neither one of them will want to be the first to take that step away. While they're each waiting for the other one to back off first, they'll be heading in the same direction for a change. Good morning," she said into the receiver. "The Inn at Sanctuary." Her smile faded. "I'm sorry, what? Yes, yes, of course." Automatically, she grabbed a pencil and began scribbling on the pad by the phone. "I'll certainly make some calls right away. Don't worry now. It's a very small island. We'll help in every way we can, Mr. Peters. I'll come on down there to the cottage myself, right now. No, that's just fine. I'll be right along."

"Mosquitoes getting in through the screen again?" Brian asked. But he knew it was more than that, much more.

"The Peterses took Wild Horse Cove Cottage with some friends for the week. Mr. Peters can't seem to find his wife this morning."

Brian felt a quick stab of fear at the base of his spine. He couldn't ignore it, but told himself it was foolish overreaction. "Kate, it's not quite seven A.M. She probably got up early and took a walk."

"He's been out looking for almost an hour. He found her shoes down by the water." Distracted, she ran a hand through her hair. "Well, it's probably just as you say, but he's terribly worried. I'll run down there and calm him down, help him look around until she comes wandering home."

She managed a thin smile. "I'm sorry, sweetie, but this means I'm going to have to wake Lexy up so she can take the breakfast shift in my place this morning. She's liable to be snappish about it."

"I'm not worried about Lexy. Kate," he added as she headed for the door, "give me a call, will you, when Mrs. Peters gets home?"

"Sure I will, honey. Like as not she'll be there before I make it down to them."

But she wasn't. By noon Tom Peters wasn't the only one on Desire who was worried. Other cottagers and natives joined in the search, Nathan among them. He'd seen Tom and Susan Peters once or twice during their stay and had a vague recollection of a pretty brunette of medium height and build.

He left the others to comb the beach and the cove while he concentrated on the swath of land between his cottage and Wild Horse Cove. There was barely an eighth of a mile between them. The verge of his end forested then, giving way to dune and swale. He covered the ground slowly and saw, when he reached the stretch of sand, the crisscrossing footprints of others who had come that way to look.

Though he knew it was useless, he climbed over the dunes. The cove below was secluded, but anyone there would have been spotted half a dozen times by now by others who were searching.

There was only one figure there now, a man who paced back and forth. "Nathan?"

He turned and, seeing Jo mounting the incline between the dunes, held out a hand to help her up.

"I went by your cottage," she began. "I see you've heard."

"That must be the husband down there. I've seen him a couple of times before."

"Tom Peters. I've been all over the island. I was out working this morning, from about seven. One of the Pendleton kids tracked us down an hour or so ago and told us. He said her shoes were down there, by the water."

"That's what I heard."

"People are thinking she might have gone in to swim, and... The current's fairly gentle here, but if she cramped or just swam out too far..."

It was a grim scenario, one that had already occurred to him. "Shouldn't the tide have brought her in by now if that's what happened?"

"It may yet. If the current carried her along for a while, they could find her down the island at the next tide change. Barry Fitzsimmons drowned like that.

We were about sixteen. He was a strong swimmer, but he went out by himself one night during a beach party. He'd been drinking. They found him the next morning at low tide, half a mile down."

Nathan shifted his gaze to the south, where the waves were less serene. He thought of Kyle, sinking under blue Mediterranean waves. "Where are her clothes, then?"

"What?"

"It seems to me if she'd decided to go swimming, she'd have stripped down."

"I suppose you're right. But she might have come down in her bathing suit."

"Without a towel?" It didn't quite fit, he decided. "I wonder if anyone's asked him if he knows what she was wearing when she left the house. I'm going down to talk to him."

"I don't think we should intrude."

"He's alone and he's worried." Nathan kept her hand in his as he started down. "Or he had a fight with his wife, killed her, and disposed of her body."

"That's horrid and ridiculous. He's a perfectly decent, normal man."

"Sometimes perfectly decent, normal men do the unthinkable."

Nathan studied Tom Peters as they approached. Late twenties, he decided, about five ten. He looked fit in wrinkled camp shorts and a plain white T-shirt. Probably worked out at the gym three or four mornings a week, Nathan thought. He had a good start on his vacation tan, and though the stubble on his chin gave him an unkempt appearance, his dark blond hair had been cut recently, and cut well.

When he raised his head and Nathan saw his eyes, he saw only sick fear.

"Mr. Peters. Tom."

"I don't know where else to look. I don't know what to do." Saying the words out loud brought tears swimming into his eyes. He blinked them back, breathing rapidly. "My friends, they went to the other side of the island to look. I had to come back here. To come back here, just in case."

"You need to sit down." Gently Jo took his arm. "Why don't we go back up to your cottage and you can sit down for a while? I'll make you some coffee."

"No, I can't leave here. She came down here. She came down last night. We had a fight. We had a fight, oh, God, it's so stupid. Why did we have a fight?"

He covered his face with his hands, pressing his fingers against his burning eyes. "She wants to buy a house. We can't afford it yet. I tried to explain to her, tried to show her how impractical it is, but she wouldn't listen. When she stormed out I was relieved. I was actually relieved and thought, Well, now, at least I can get some sleep while she goes out and sulks."

"Maybe she took a swim to cool off," Nathan prompted.

"Susan?" Tom let out a short laugh. "Swim alone, at night? Not hardly. She'd never go in water past her knees anyway. She doesn't like to swim in the ocean. She always says she hears cello music the minute it hits her knees. You know," he said with a faint smile, *"Jaws."*

Then he turned back, staring out at the water. "I know people are thinking she might have gone swimming, she might have drowned. It's just not possible.

She loves to sit and look at the ocean. She loves to listen to it, to smell it, but she won't go in. Where the hell is she? Goddamn it, Susan, this is a hell of a way to scare me into buying a house. I've got to go somewhere, look somewhere. I can't just stand here."

He raced back toward the dunes and sent sand avalanching down as he rushed up and over them.

"Do you think that's what she's doing, Nathan? Putting a scare into him because she's angry?"

"We can hope so. Come on." He slipped an arm around her waist. "We'll take the long way back to the cottage, keep our eyes peeled. Then we'll take a break from this."

"I could use a break. From just about everything."

The wind was rising as they headed through the trough between the surfside dune hummocks and the higher, inland dunes where beach elders and bayberry stabilized the sand. Tracks scored the ground, the scratches from scudding ghost crabs, the three-toed prints from parading wild turkeys, the spots where deer had meandered to feed on seeds and berries.

Human tracks had churned up the sand as well, and the wind would take them all.

Despite the grazing, thousands of white star rush and fragile marsh pinks spread their color.

Would she have walked this way, Jo wondered, alone, at night? It had been a clear evening, and a lonely beach drew troubled hearts as well as contented ones. The wind would have been stiff and fresh. And even after the tide receded, leaving the sand wet, the wind would have chased it along in streamers that scratched at the ankles.

"She could have left her shoes down there," Jo considered. "If she'd wanted to walk. She was angry, upset, wanted to be alone. It was a warm night. She might have headed down the shoreline, just following the water. That's more likely than anything else."

She turned, looking out over the low hillocks to the sea. The wind lifted sand and salt spray, sending the sea oats waving, sifting a fresh coat over the pennywort and railroad vines that tangled.

"Maybe they've found her by now." Nathan laid a hand on her shoulder. "We'll call and check when we get to the cottage."

"Where else would she have gone?" Jo shifted, to stare inland where the dunes crept slowly, relentlessly, toward the trees in smooth curves. "It would have been foolish to wander into the forest. She'd have lost the moonlight—and she'd have wanted her shoes. Would she be angry enough with her husband to stay away, to worry him like this because of a house?"

"I don't know. People do unaccountable things to each other when they're married. Things that seem cruel or indifferent or foolish to outsiders."

"Did you?" She turned her head to study his face. "Did you do cruel, indifferent, and foolish things when you were married?"

"Probably." He tucked the hair blowing across her face behind her ear. "I'm sure my ex-wife has a litany of them."

"Marriage is most often a mistake. You depend on someone, you inevitably lean too hard or take them for granted or find them irritating because they're always there."

"That's remarkably cynical for someone who's never been married."

"I've observed marriage. Observing's what I do."

"Because it's less risky than participating."

She turned away again. "Because it's what I do. If she's out somewhere, walking, avoiding coming back, letting her husband suffer like this, how could he ever forgive her?"

Suddenly she was angry, deeply, bitterly angry. "But he will, won't he?" she demanded, whirling back to him. "He'll forgive her, he'll fall at her feet sobbing in relief, and he'll buy her the fucking house she wants. All she had to do to get her way was put him through hell for a few hours."

Nathan studied her glinting eyes, the high color that temper had slapped into her cheeks. "You may be right." He spoke mildly, fascinated that she could shift from concern to condemnation in the blink of an eye. "But you're heaping a lot of blame and calculation on a woman you don't even know."

"I've known others like her. My mother, Ginny, people who do exactly what they choose without giving a damn for the consequences or what they do to others. I'm sick to death of people. Their selfish agendas, their unrelenting self-concern."

There was such pain in her voice. The echo of it rolled through him, leaving his stomach raw and edgy. He had to tell her, he thought. He couldn't keep blocking it out, couldn't continue to shove it aside, no matter how hard he'd worked to convince himself it was best for both of them.

Maybe Susan Peters's disappearance was a sign, an omen. If he believed in such things. Whatever he believed, and whatever it was he wanted, eventually he would have to tell her what he knew.

Was she strong enough to stand up to it? Or would it break her?

"Jo Ellen, let's go inside."

"Yeah." She folded her arms as clouds rolled over the sun and the wind kicked into a warning howl. "Why the hell are we out here, worrying ourselves over a stranger who has the bitchiness to put her husband and friends through this?"

"Because she's lost, Jo. One way or another."

"Who isn't?" she murmured.

It would wait another day, he told himself. It would wait until Susan Peters had been found. If he was daring the gods by taking another day, stealing another few hours before he shattered both their lives, then he'd pay the price.

How much heavier could it be than the one he'd already paid?

When he was sure she was strong, when he was sure she could bear it, he would tell her the hideous secret that only he knew.

Annabelle had never left Desire. She had been murdered in the forest just west of Sanctuary on a night in high summer, under a full white moon. David Delaney, the father he had grown up loving, admiring, respecting, had been her killer.

Jo saw lightning flash and the shimmering curtain of rain form far out to sea. "Storm's coming," she said.

"I know."

23

The first drops hit the ground with fat plops, and Kirby quickened her pace. The search group she'd joined had parted ways at the fork of the path. She'd chosen the route to Sanctuary, and now she shivered a bit as the rain fell through the overhanging limbs and vines to soak her shirt. By the time she reached the verge it was coming down hard, wind-whipped and surprisingly cold. She saw Brian, hatless, shoulders hunched, trooping up the road to her right.

She met him on the edge of the east terrace. Saying nothing, he took her hand and pulled her onto the screened porch. For a moment they simply stood dripping as lightning stabbed the sky in pitchforks and thunder boomed in answer.

"No word?" Kirby shifted her medical bag from hand to hand.

"Nothing. I just came over from the west side. Giff has a group that took the north." Weary, Brian rubbed his hands over his face. "This is getting to be a habit."

"It's been more than twelve hours since she was seen." Kirby looked out into the driving rain. "That's too long. They'll have to call off the search until the storm passes. God, Brian, we're going to find her washed up after this. It's about the only explanation left. Her poor husband."

"There's nothing to do now but wait it out. You need a dry shirt and some coffee."

"Yeah." She dragged her wet hair away from her face. "I do. I'll take a look at your hand while I'm here and redress it for you."

"It's fine."

"I'll decide that," she said, following him in, "after I take a look."

"Suit yourself. Go on up and get something out of Jo's closet."

The house seemed so quiet, isolated in the violent rain. "Is she here?"

"As far as I know, she's out too." He went to the freezer, took out some black bean soup he'd made weeks before. "She'll take shelter, like everybody else."

When Kirby came back fifteen minutes later, the kitchen smelled of coffee and simmering soup. The warmth eased away the last of the tension in her shoulders. Leaning against the doorway a moment, she indulged herself by watching him work.

Despite his bandaged hand, he was neatly slicing thick slabs from a loaf of brown bread he'd undoubtedly baked himself. His wet shirt clung to him, displaying an attractive outline of muscle and rib. When he looked over at her, his eyes were a cool, misty blue that made her stomach flutter pleasantly.

"It smells wonderful."

"Figured you hadn't eaten."

"No, I haven't—not since a stale Danish this morning." She held out the shirt she'd taken from his closet. "Here, put this on. You shouldn't stand around in wet clothes."

"Thanks." He noted that she'd changed into some of Jo's dull gray sweats. They bagged on her and made her seem all the more delicate. "You look lost in those."

"Well, Jo's a good six inches taller than I am." She lifted a brow as he tugged the wet shirt off over his head. His skin was damp and brown and smooth. "God, you're attractive, Brian." She laughed when his brows drew together in what was obviously confused embarrassment. "I get to appreciate your wonderful build on two levels, as a doctor and as a woman. Better put that shirt on, or I might lose control, on both counts."

"That could be interesting." Letting the shirt dangle from his fingers, he stepped toward her. "Which would come first?"

"I never let personal leanings interfere with professional obligations." She trailed a finger up his arm, then down to his wrist. "Which is why I'm going to examine that wound first thing."

"And second thing?" Before she could answer, he cupped his hands under her elbows and lifted her. When their mouths were level, he leaned forward to toy with her lips.

"Excellent upper body strength." Her voice was just a little breathless as she wrapped her legs around his waist. "Your pulse is a little elevated," she murmured, checking the one at his throat with her mouth. "Just a little fast."

"I've got a case on you, Doc Kirby." Brian turned his face into her hair. It smelled of rain and lemons. "It doesn't seem to be passing. Fact is, I'm starting to think it's terminal." When she went very still, he shifted her until he could see her eyes. "What do you want from me, Kirby?"

"I thought I knew." Her fingers tingled when she skimmed them over his face. "I'm not sure anymore. Maybe whatever case you've got is contagious. Do you have this ache around your heart?"

"Just like it's being squeezed."

"And this lifting and sinking sensation in your stomach?"

"All the time lately. So what's wrong with us, Doc?"

"I'm not sure, but—" She broke off as the screen door slammed. Voices rose and invaded the kitchen. Sighing, Kirby laid her brow against Brian's until he shifted her hips and set her down.

"Sounds like Lexy and Giff are back." He kept his eyes on Kirby. "Some of the others are likely with them, and they'll be looking for a hot meal."

"Then I'll help you dish up some soup."

"I'd appreciate it." He lifted the lid on the pot, letting steam and scent escape. "We're going to have to finish this conversation sometime or other."

"Yes, we are." She opened a cupboard to get bowls. "Sometime or other."

From Nathan's porch, Jo watched the rain and smoked restlessly. He'd tried the television when they came in, hoping for a weather report. The cable was already out, so they settled for the radio. Static hissed out, along with the announcer's listings of small-craft advisories and flash-flood warnings.

They'd lose power if it kept up much longer, she thought. And the ponds and rivers would certainly flood. Already she could see puddles forming and deepening.

"No word yet." Nathan joined her on the porch. "Some of the search party's taken shelter at Sanctuary to wait this out." He laid a towel over her shoulders. "You're shivering. Why don't you come inside?"

"I like to watch." Lightning stabbed the sky and sent an answering jolt into her stomach. "Quick squalls like this are hell to be out in, but they're exciting from the right vantage point." She took a deep breath when the sky went hot and white. The sting of ozone lingered on the air. "Where's your camera? I took mine back home."

"In the bedroom. I'll get it for you."

Impatient, she stabbed out her cigarette in a broken shell. Too much energy, she thought. It was pumping through her, pounding at her. She all but snatched the camera from Nathan when he brought it out. "What kind of film do you have in here?"

"Four hundred," he said quietly, watching as she quickly examined it.

"Good. That's fast. I want fast." She lifted, aimed at the rain-lashed trees, the swinging moss. "Come on, come on," she muttered, then snapped with the next burst of lightning. "Another, I want another." Thunder rattled the air as she changed angles, her finger as itchy as if it were on the trigger of a gun.

"I need to get down, shoot up at that tree."

"No." Nathan bent to pick up the towel that had fallen from her shoulders. The overhang offered little protection. The two of them were rapidly getting soaked. "You're not going out there. You don't know where or when we could have a lightning strike."

"That's half of it, isn't it? The not knowing. The not caring." She tossed back her head. Recklessness streaked through her, glowed dangerously in her eyes. "I don't know what I'm doing with you, or when I might get hit next. I don't seem to care. How much are you going to hurt me, Nathan, and how long will it take me to get over it? And how long before one of us does something cruel, indifferent, or foolish?"

Before he could speak, she grabbed a handful of his hair and dragged his mouth to hers. "I don't care." She dug her teeth into his lip.

"You need to care." Enraged with fate, he caught her face in his hands, pulled her back. His eyes were as dark and violent as the storm whipping the air. "I want you to understand that when I do hurt you, I won't have a choice."

"I don't care," she repeated, pulling his mouth back to hers. "I only want now. Right now. I want you. I don't want to think, I don't want either of us to think. I just want to feel."

His mind was already hazed as they stumbled through the door. She bobbled the camera, laughing and moaning as he tore at her shirt. "Fast," she managed. "I still want fast."

He tumbled with her to the floor, and the camera thudded lightly on the carpet as they ripped off clothes and shoes. Her hands were tangled in her shirt when he thrust inside her. She grappled to free them, the momentary thrill of being helpless and bound adding another layer of excitement. Then she was free, and her fingers dug into his hips to urge him to drive deeper, and harder.

He couldn't stop himself, and let the speed, the heat, the fury of mating rule them both. If her need was frantic, his was desperate. To take her, to have her, to keep her. One more day, one more hour. A dozen lifetimes.

If his punishment for his father's sin was to fall in love, so terribly in love, and lose, he would take every moment he could steal before payment came due.

She cried out in grateful relief when the orgasm stabbed through her. His body plunged violently in hers, then stilled. His breath was ragged as he pushed himself back to stare down at her. "Is that what you wanted?"

"Yes."

"Fast, and heartless."

"Yes."

His hand closed in a fist. It was exactly what he'd given her. "Do you think it's going to stop at that?"

She closed her eyes briefly, then willed herself to open them. "No."

"Good." He relaxed his hand, brushed it over her cheek. Another moment stolen, he thought when her eyes opened and met his. "I'd hate to have to argue with you when I'm still wanting you. Give me more, Jo Ellen." His mouth lowered to tease her. "Don't make me take it this time."

Her arms lifted, wrapped around him. "I'm so afraid of you."

"I know. Give me more anyway. Take a chance."

His mouth stayed gentle, waiting for hers to answer, then to demand. He wanted more, much more, than that rough and edgy release they'd offered each other. More than the animal lunge of hot blood. When she sighed out his name he knew he had the beginnings of it.

Her mouth grew more hungry, her hands began to roam. Fresh need built in her quickly, as though it had never been met. She craved the taste of his skin and took her mouth on a journey over his face and throat. With a murmur of approval, she rolled with him until she stretched across his body with the freedom to do as she pleased.

The wind kicked, rattling the screen door on its hinges. The house shuddered beneath them. In contrast they moved slowly, almost languidly. Touch and taste, sigh and murmur. She lost herself in the easy sway of it, the shift and glide of bodies, rhythms set and matched.

She thought she could float over him, inch by inch, and wonder as she set each separate muscle to quivering.

He eased her back, sitting up to slide her into his lap. It was tenderness he needed for both of them now, to soothe the pain already suffered. And the pain yet to come.

Their eyes held as he lowered his mouth to hers, took the kiss deep, gradually deep so that the warmth from it flushed over her. The intimacy of it shimmered through her. She might have resisted, she lifted a hand to his chest as if to do so. But her limbs went limp, and she was lost.

And she gave him more.

It was surrender he wanted, for both of them. His and hers. A yielding. Soft, liquid kisses filled them both, nudged them lazily toward excitement. When he cupped her, her moan was quiet and ended on a little gasp of pleasure. He took her up slowly so that the orgasm was long and sleek.

They each trembled, and when she reached for him, thrilling to find him hard and ready, her lips curved against his.

"Again," she murmured. "Just like that. Again."

The pleasure rolled through her, layer by layer, to whirl in her head like wine. Still shimmering from it, she shifted, until her body was over his and the thick beat of his heart was under her mouth.

"I love what you can do to me." She slid down, spreading light, open-mouthed kisses down to his belly. "I want to know I can do it to you."

His skin quivered when she closed that hot, generous mouth over him. Dark pleasure blurred his vision, and the roar in his head drowned out the rain. She drove him to the brink, where he clung to pleasure and control and sanity only by slippery fingertips.

She rose up over him, her body glimmering in the murky light. She lowered to him, took him in, arched back, took him deeper. Her arms lifted up, folded behind her head as if in triumph. Her eyes met his, stared intently into that smoky gray as she began to move.

Slowly, torturously. And her body shivered when his hands closed hard and possessive over her breasts. Smoothly, silkily. His breath caught and strangled as she braced her own hands on his chest.

Her head fell back, her body going arrow-taut and her muscles clamping hard around him as she rode herself to peak. Yet even as her heart tripped, her brain staggered, her system revved greedily for more. She couldn't bear it, couldn't stop it. Her body drove, forward, back, racing for new pleasure.

Sweat dewed her skin. When he levered himself up to surround her nipple with his mouth, he tasted salt and heat. She came again, crying out in shock and near panic. Holding tight to her, he let go of the edge and took them both flying.

Her lungs were burning, her throat dry as dust. She tried to swallow, then gave up and dropped her head on his shoulder. When her ears stopped ringing, she heard the silence.

"It's stopped raining."

"Mmm-hmm."

With a laugh she nearly managed to take a full breath. "We're going to have a hell of a time explaining these rug burns." Enjoying the sensation, she ran her hands over his damp back. "I need about a gallon of water."

"I'll get it."

"Okay, I'll wait right here."

"Though it pains me to admit it, I think I'm a little too weak as yet to cart you over to the sink." He shifted her weight and grinned as she rolled limply onto the rug.

He got up to fill a glass, then stopped and looked at her. Her skin was rosily flushed all over, her hair a tangled red halo around her face. Her mouth was soft, still swollen and slightly curved in contentment. On impulse he set the glass down and lifted his camera.

Her eyes flew open when she heard the click of the shutter. She yelped, instinctively crossing her arms over her breasts. "What the hell are you doing?"

Stealing moments, he thought. He was going to need them. "Christ, you look good." He crouched, clicked off another shot as her eyes widened.

"Stop that. Are you crazy? I'm naked."

"You look incredible. All rumpled and flushed and freshly fucked. Don't cover yourself. You've got beautiful breasts."

"Nathan." She only folded her arms more protectively. "Put that camera down."

"Why?" He lowered it but continued to grin. "You can develop them yourself. Who's to see? There's nothing much more artistic and visually stunning than a nude study."

"Fine." Keeping one arm strategically bent, she held out a hand. "Let me take you."

"Sure." He offered the camera, amused to see her frown of surprise.

"You aren't the least bit embarrassed."

"No."

She angled her head toward the camera he still held. "I want that roll of film."

"Well, I wasn't planning on taking it in to Fotomat, darling." He glanced down, checked the number of shots left. "Just one more in here. Let me take it. Just your face."

"Just my face," she agreed and relaxed enough to smile at him. "There. Now I want that film."

"Okay." He moved quickly when she lowered her arm and got off the last shot.

"Damn it, you said it was out."

"I lied." Roaring with laughter, he rose and set the camera on the table. "But it's out now. I'll want to see the contacts so I can pick out the prints I want."

"If you think I'm going to develop that film, you're mistaken." She got up and grabbed the camera.

"The pictures you took of the storm are in there." He said it with a smile on his face that widened as he saw her struggle between the urge to rip out the roll and ruin it and the need to preserve her own shots.

"That was very sneaky, Nathan."

"I thought so. Don't put that back on," he said when she bent down to retrieve her shirt. "It's still damp. I'll get you a dry one."

"Thanks." She watched him walk to the bedroom, pursing her lips as she studied his tight, muscular buns. Next time, she decided as she tugged on her slacks, she'd make sure she had her own camera handy.

And with that thought in mind, she unloaded the film and tucked it into her back pocket.

He tossed her a T-shirt when he came back out, then fastened the dry jeans he'd pulled on. "I'll walk back to Sanctuary with you. We'll check on the status of things."

"All right. The search parties will probably be heading out again." She combed her fingers through her hair to untangle it. "It's going to be a mess out there from the storm. I'd put some boots on if I were you."

He glanced down at her olive-green sneakers. "You're not wearing any."

"I would if I had them handy."

"So we'll both get sloppy." He took her hand and watched surprise flicker into her eyes when he lifted it to kiss her knuckles. "Then tonight, I'll take you out to dinner."

"Out to dinner?"

"Well, in to dinner. We'll sit in the dining room, look at menus, order wine. I'm told people do that all the time."

"It's silly. I live there."

"I don't. I want to have dinner with you. The kind of evening where you sit across from each other at a table, with candles inbetween, have conversation. Where other people pretend they're not watching us and thinking what an attractive couple we make." He picked up a ball cap from the coffee table and snugged it over her hair. "And I can look at you all through the meal and think about making love to you again. It's called romance."

"I'm not any good at romance."

"You said that about sex. You were wrong." He took her hand and walked to the door. "Let's see how this works out. Maybe Brian will whip up some flan."

She had to laugh. "People are going to think it's pretty strange for me to take a table at the inn."

"It'll give them something to talk about." Their feet squelched into the soggy ground when they reached the bottom of the stairs.

The heat was rolling back, sending the steam rising, turning the air thick. The forest looked ripe, fertile, and darkly green. Water dripped and plopped from leaves, sending fresh showers over their heads as they turned toward the river.

"Churned everything up," Jo commented. "Water's running high and fast. It may crest over the banks, but I doubt it'll cause any damage here."

She detoured for a closer look, philosophically accepting ruined shoes as she sank past her ankles in muck. "Daddy'll want to take a look, I imagine, but there's not much to be done. It'll be more worrisome over at the campground. The beach should be fine, though. The winds weren't high enough to take down the dunes. We'll have a nice crop of shells washed up from it."

"You sound like your father's daughter."

Distracted, she looked over her shoulder. "No. I rarely give a thought to what goes on here. During hurricane season I might pay more attention to the weather reports for this area, but we haven't been hit hard that way in years."

"Jo Ellen, you love this place. It shouldn't worry you to admit that."

"It's not the center of my life."

"No, but it matters to you." He stepped closer. "A lot of things, a lot of people can matter to you without taking over your life. You matter to me."

Alarm jingled in her heart, and she took a hasty step back. "Nathan—" She nearly fell as the ground sucked at her feet.

"You're going to end up back in the river." He took her arms in a firm grip. "Then you'll accuse me of pushing you in again. That's not what I'm doing. I'm not pushing you, Jo Ellen. But I'm not going to be sorry if you slip."

"I like keeping my feet under me, and knowing where the ground gives before I step on it."

"Sometimes you've got to try new territory. This is unexplored ground for me, too."

"That's not true. You've been married, you—"

"She wasn't you," he said quietly and Jo went still in his arms. "I never felt about her the way I'm feeling about you, right now. She never looked at me the way you're looking at me. And I never wanted her as much as I want you. That was what was wrong with it all along. I didn't know it, didn't understand how much of it was my fault until I saw you again."

"You're moving too fast for me."

"Then keep up. And goddamn it, Jo Ellen," he said with an impatient sigh as he tipped her head back. "Give in a little."

She tasted the impatience when his mouth met hers, and the need that went deeper than she'd allowed herself to see. The quick flare of panic inside her fought with a shiver of delight. And the warm stream that shimmered in her blood felt like hope.

"Maybe you're not pushing." She didn't resist when he gathered her closer. "But I feel like I'm sinking." She rested her head on his shoulder, willed her brain to clear. "Part of me just wants to let it happen, and another part keeps fighting to kick back to the surface. I don't know which is best, for me or for you."

He needed that glimmer of hope, the whisper in his heart that promised if she loved him enough, if they loved each other enough, they could survive what had happened. And what was to come.

"Why don't you think about which makes you happier instead of which may be best?"

It sounded so simple that she started to smile. She watched the river flow, wondered if it was time for her just to dive in and see where it took her. She could almost see herself riding that current. See herself rushing along it.

Trapped under the surface, staring up. Dragged down away from air and light.

The scream ripped from her throat, had her sinking to her knees before he could catch her.

"Jo, for God's sake!"

"In the water. In the water." She clamped a hand over her mouth to hold back the bubbling hysteria. "Is it Mama? Is it Mama in the water?"

"Stop it." He knelt beside her, dragged her around by the shoulders until her face was close to his. "Look at me. I want you to stop it. I'm not letting you fall apart. I'm not letting it happen, so you just look at me and pull back."

"I saw—" She had to gulp for air. "In the water, I saw—I'm losing my mind, Nathan. I can't hold on to it."

"Yes, you can." Desperately he pulled her close. "You can hold on to me. Just hold on to me." As she shuddered against him, he looked down grimly at the surface of the river.

And saw the pale ghost staring up at him.

"Jesus God." His arms tightened convulsively on Jo. Then he shoved her back and slid heedlessly into the rising river. "She's in here," he shouted, grabbing on to a downed limb to keep himself from being swept clear. "Give me a hand with her."

"What?"

"You're not losing your mind." Panting with the effort, Nathan reached out with his free hand and gripped hair. "There's someone in here! Help me get her out."

"Oh, my God." Without hesitation now, Jo bellied up to the edge, fighting to anchor her toes in the slippery bank. "Give me your hand, Nathan. Try to hold on to her and I'll help pull you up. Is she alive? Is she breathing?"

He'd gotten a closer look now, a clearer look. And his stomach lurched with horror and pity. The river hadn't been kind. "No." He spoke flatly, shifting his grip on the limb. His gaze lifted to Jo's. "No, she's not alive. I'll hold on here, keep her from going downriver. You get to Sanctuary for help."

She was calm now, cold and calm. "We'll get her out together," she said and stretched out her hand.

24

It was a hideous, grisly task. Twice Nathan lost his grip as he tried to free Susan Peters's hair from the spearing branches that had trapped her body. He went under, fiercely blanking out his mind when her arms knocked into his belly. He could hear Jo calling him, concentrated on the desperate calm in her voice, as together they struggled to free what was left of Susan from the river.

Ignoring her lurching stomach, Jo slid farther over the bank, with the water lapping and rushing over her chin when she hooked her arms under the body. Her breath came short and shallow as for one gut-wrenching moment she was face-to-face with death.

She knew the shutter in her mind had clicked, capturing the image, preserving it. Making it part of her forever.

Then she hauled, grunting, digging knees and feet into the soggy ground. She let the body roll, couldn't bear even to watch. She thrust her hands out, felt Nathan's grip them, slip, clutch again. When he was chest-high out of the water, squirming his way free from the river, she rolled away and retched.

"Go back to the cottage." He coughed violently, spat to clear the taste of river and death from his mouth.

"I'll be all right." She rocked back on her heels, felt the first hot tears flow down her icy cheeks. "I just need a minute. I'll be all right."

She had no more color than what they had pulled from the river did, and she was shaking so hard he was surprised he couldn't hear her bones clattering. "Go back to the cottage. You need dry clothes." He closed a hand over hers. "You have to call Sanctuary for help. We can't leave her like this, Jo."

"No. No, you're right." Steeling herself, she turned her head. The body was paste gray and bloated, the hair dark and matted and slick with debris. But she had once been a woman. "I'll get something to cover her. I'll get her a blanket."

"Can you make it on your own?"

She nodded, and though her body felt hollowed out and frighteningly brittle, she pushed herself to her feet. She looked down at him. His face was pale and filthy, his eyes reddened from the water. She thought of the way he'd gone into the angry river, without hesitation, without a thought for anything but what needed to be done.

"Nathan."

He used the heel of his hand to wipe the mud off his chin, and the gesture was sharp. "What?"

"Nothing," she murmured. "Later."

He waited until he heard her footsteps recede, waited until he heard nothing but the roar of the river and the thud of his own laboring heart. Then he pulled himself over to the body, forced himself to turn it, to look. She'd been pretty once—he knew that. She would never be pretty again. Gritting his teeth, he touched her, easing her head to the side until he could see, until he could be sure.

There, scoring her neck, were livid red bruises. He snatched his hand away, drew up his knees and pressed his face into the filthy denim of his jeans.

Sweet Jesus, sweet Jesus. What was happening here?

Fear was worse than grief, sharper than guilt. And when one rolled into the other, it left the soul sickened.

Still, he had himself under control when Jo came back. She hadn't changed her clothes, but he said nothing, just helped her spread the thin yellow blanket over the body.

"They're coming." She scrubbed her fingers over her mouth. "Brian and Kirby. I got Bri on the phone, told him . . . told him. He said he'd bring her, a doctor, but wasn't going to tell anyone else until . . ."

She trailed off, looked helplessly into the trees. "Why would she have come up here, Nathan? Why in God's name would she have gone into the river? Maybe she fell in the dark, hit her head. It's horrible. I was prepared that we'd find her drowned, washed up on the beach. Somehow this is worse."

Only yards from his door, was all he could think. Only yards from where he'd just made love to Jo. Where he had dared the gods, he thought with a hard shudder.

Had the body come downriver, or had it been put in here, so close he could almost have seen it from his kitchen window on a clear afternoon?

She slipped her hand into his, concerned that it was still icy and as lifeless as the body that lay on the bank. "You're soaked through and frozen. Go get into dry clothes. I'll wait for them."

"I'm not leaving. I'm not leaving you. Or her."

Thinking of warmth and comfort, she put her arms around him. "That was the kindest and bravest thing I've ever seen anyone do." She pressed her lips to his throat, wanting to feel him give, respond. "You went in for her. You could have left her, but you went in. Getting her out wouldn't have mattered to some."

"It mattered."

"To you. You're a good man, Nathan. I'll never forget what you did."

He closed his eyes tight, then drew away without touching her. "They're coming," he said flatly. Even as he turned, Brian and Kirby came hurrying down the path.

Kirby took a quick look at both of them. "Go inside, get in a hot shower. I'll take a look at you shortly." She moved past them and knelt by the blanket.

Jo stood her ground. "It has to be Mrs. Peters. She was caught up on that branch. She must have fallen in sometime last night, and the storm brought her downriver."

Jo steadied herself, reached for Nathan's hand again as Brian knelt beside Kirby. Brian nodded grimly when Kirby folded the blanket down.

"That's her. They came in for meals a couple of times. Goddamn it." He sat back on his heels, scrubbed his hands over his face. "I'll go find her husband. We need to take her somewhere—somewhere better than this."

"No, she can't be moved." Kirby fought her words out over the thick beat of her heart. "You need to call the police and tell them to get out here quickly. I don't believe she drowned." Gently, she lifted the chin, exposed the raw bruising. "It looks as though she was strangled. She was murdered."

"How could this be? How could this happen?" Lexy curled up tight in the corner of the couch in the family parlor. She gripped her hands together to keep herself from biting her nails. "People don't get murdered on Desire. People just don't. Kirby has to be wrong."

"We'll find out soon enough." Kate switched the ceiling fan up to high to try to stir the heavy air. "The police will tell us. Either way, that poor woman's dead, and her husband . . . Jo Ellen, stop prowling so and sit, drink that brandy. You're bound to catch a terrible chill."

"I can't sit." Jo continued to pace from window to window, though she couldn't have said what she was looking for.

"I wish you would sit." Lexy spoke plaintively. "You're about to drive me to distraction. I wish Giff was here. I don't see why he has to be down there with the others instead of here with me."

"Oh, stop whining for five minutes," Jo snapped. "Hold your own hand for a change."

"Don't. Don't the two of you start." Kate threw up her hands. "I can't stand it just now."

"And I can't stand this waiting. I'm going back out." Jo walked to the door. "I've got to see what's happening. I've got to do something."

"Jo! Don't go out alone." Kate pressed a hand to her head. "I'm already worried sick. Please don't go out there alone."

Seeing her cousin look suddenly old and shaky, Jo changed her mind. "You're right. None of us should go out. We're just in the way. You sit down, Kate. Come on, now." She took Kate's arm and led her toward the sofa beside Lexy. "You sit down and have a brandy. You're worn out."

"I'll get the brandy," Lexy said.

"Just give her mine," Jo told Lexy as she rose. "I don't want it."

"If fussing over me will keep the two of you from snapping at each other, then fuss away." She took the brandy Lexy offered her and smiled weakly. "We should have fresh coffee for when they come in. I don't know when Brian last made any."

"I'll take care of it." Lexy leaned down to kiss Kate's cheek. "Don't you worry." But when she straightened she saw Giff in the doorway.

"They're coming in. They want to talk to Jo."

"All right." Jo closed a hand gratefully over the one Lexy touched to her arm. "I'm ready."

. . .

"How much longer will they peck at her?" Brian stood on the front porch, listening to the jungle sounds of cicadas and peepers filling the air.

"It can't be much longer," Kirby said quietly. "They've had her in there nearly an hour. They didn't keep Nathan more than an hour."

"She shouldn't have to go through this. It's bad enough she found the body, helped drag it out of the water, without having to go over and over it again."

"I'm sure they'll make it as easy on her as they can." She only sighed when he whirled and scalded her with a look. "Brian, there's nothing else to be done, no other choices to be made. A woman's been murdered. Questions have to be asked."

"Jo sure as hell didn't kill her." He threw himself down on the porch swing. "It's easier for you. Big-city doctor. Seen it all, done it all."

"Maybe that's true." She spoke coolly to mask the hurt. "But easier or harder doesn't change the facts. Someone decided not to let Susan Peters live any longer. They used their hands and they choked the life out of her. Now questions have to be asked."

Brian brooded into the dark. "They'll look toward the husband now."

"I don't know."

"They will. It's the logical step. Something happens to the wife, look to the husband. Odds are, he's the one who did it. They looked to my father when my mother left. Until they were satisfied she'd just . . . left. They'll take that poor bastard into some little room. And questions will have to be asked. Who knows, maybe he's the one who decided not to let Susan Peters live."

He shifted his gaze to Kirby. She stood very straight, very composed under the yellow glow of the porch light. She still wore Jo's baggy sweats. But he'd seen her with the police, watched her relay information, rolling clinical terms off her tongue, before huddling over the body with the team from the coroner's office.

There was nothing delicate about her.

"You should go home, Kirby. There's nothing else for you to do here now."

She wanted to weep. She wanted to scream. She wanted to pound her fists against the clear, thin wall he'd suddenly erected between them. "Why are you shutting me out, Brian?"

"Because I don't know what to do about you. And I never meant to let you in in the first place."

"But you did."

"Did I, Kirby? Or did you just jimmy the door?"

Jo's shadow fell between them before she stepped out. "They're finished here. The police."

"Are you all right?" Kirby moved over to her. "You must be exhausted. I want you to go upstairs and lie down now. I can give you something to help you sleep."

"No, I'm fine. Really." She gave Kirby's hand a quick squeeze. "Better, in fact, for having gone through it step by step. I just feel sad and sorry, and grateful to be whole. Did Nathan go back?"

"Kate talked him into going upstairs." Brian rose, walked closer to study her for himself. She looked steadier than he'd expected. "I don't think it would take much to persuade him to stay here tonight. Cops may be tromping around the river for hours yet."

"Then we'll persuade him. You should stay too," she said to Kirby.

"No, I'll be better at home." She looked at Brian. "There's no need for me here. I'm sure one of the detectives will drive me back. I'll just get my bag."

"You're welcome to stay," Brian told her, but she flicked a cool, composed glance over her shoulder.

"I'll be better at home," she repeated and let the screen door slam shut behind her.

"Why are you letting her go?" Jo asked quietly.

"Maybe I need to see if I can. Might be for the best."

Jo thought of what Nathan had said just before the world had gone mad again. "Maybe we all should start thinking about what makes us happy instead of what might be best. I know I'm going to try, because you start running out of chances after a while. I've got something to say to you that I've passed up plenty of chances to say before."

He shrugged his shoulders, tucked his hands in his pockets in what Jo thought of as his gloomy Hathaway stance. "Spill it, then."

"I love you, Brian." The warmth of saying it was nearly eclipsed by the sheer delight of watching the astonishment on his face.

He decided it was a trick, a feint to distract the eye before she delivered the jab. "And?"

"And I wish I'd said it sooner and more often." She rose on her toes to press a brief, firm kiss on his suspicious mouth. "Of course, if I had I wouldn't have the satisfaction of seeing you goggle like a trout on the line right now. I'm going up and make Kate go to bed so she can pretend not to know Nathan's going to sleep in my room tonight."

"Jo Ellen." Brian found his voice by the time she reached the door, then lost it again when she looked back at him.

"Go ahead." She smiled broadly. "Just say it. It's so much easier than you think."

"I love you too."

"I know. You've got the best heart of all of us, Bri. That's what worries you." She closed the door quietly, then went upstairs to the rest of her family.

She dreamed of walking through the gardens of Sanctuary. The high summer smells, the high summer air. Overhead the moon was as full and clear as a child's cutout. White on black. Stars were a streaming sea of light.

Monkshood and Canterbury bells nodded gently in the breeze, their blossoms glowing white. Oh, how she loved the pure-white blooms, the way they shone in the dark. Fairy flowers, she thought, that danced while mortals slept.

She felt immortal herself—so strong, so vivid. Raising her arms high, she wondered she didn't simply lift off the ground and soar. The night was her time as well. Her alone time. She could drift along the garden paths like a ghost, and the ring of the wind chimes was music to dance by.

Then a shadow stepped out of the trees. And the shadow became a man. Immortal, only curious, she walked toward him.

Now running, running through the forest in the blinding dark, with rain lashing viciously at her face. The night was different now, she was different now. Afraid, pursued. Hunted. The wind was a thousand howling wolves with fangs bared and bloody, the raindrops tiny bright-edged spears aimed to tear the flesh. Limbs whipped at her mercilessly. Trees sprang up to block her path.

She was pathetically mortal now, terrifyingly mortal. Her breath caught on a little sob as she heard her hunter call her name. But the name was Annabelle.

Jo ripped away the sheets that tangled around her legs and bolted upright. Even as the vision cleared away, Nathan laid a hand on her shoulder. He wasn't lying beside her, but standing, and his face was masked in the dark.

"You're all right. Just a dream. A bad one."

Not trusting her voice, she nodded. The hand on her shoulder rubbed it once, absently, then dropped away. The gesture was a distant comfort.

"Do you want something?"

"No." The fear was already fading. "It's nothing. I'm used to it."

"It'd be a wonder if you didn't have nightmares after today." He moved away from her, walked to the window, turned his back.

She could see he'd pulled on his jeans, and when she ran her head over the sheets beside her, she found they were cool. He hadn't been sleeping beside her. Hadn't wanted to, Jo realized. He'd only stayed over at Sanctuary because Kate had made it impossible to refuse. And he was only sharing the bed here because it would have been awkward otherwise.

But he hadn't touched her, hadn't turned to her.

"You haven't slept, have you?"

"No." He wasn't sure he would ever close his eyes peacefully again.

Jo glanced at the clock. 3:05. She'd experienced her share of restless three A.M.s. "Maybe you should take a sleeping pill."

"No."

"I know this was hell for you, Nathan. There's nothing anyone can say or do to make it better."

"Nothing's ever going to make it better for Tom Peters."

"He might have killed her."

Nathan hoped it was true—with all his heart he hoped it. And felt filthy for it.

"They argued," Jo said stubbornly. "She walked out on him. He could have followed her down to the cove. They kept arguing and he snapped. It would only take a minute, a minute of rage. Then he panicked and carried her away. He'd have wanted the distance, so he put her in the river."

"People don't always kill in rage or panic," he said softly. Bitterness rose into his throat, threatening to choke him. "I have no business being in this house.

Being with you. What was I thinking of? Going back. To fix what? What the hell did I think I could do?"

"What are you talking about?" She hated the quaver in her voice. But the sound of his, so hard and cold, chilled her.

He turned back to stare at her. She sat in the big, feminine bed, her knees drawn up defensively, her face a pale shadow. He'd made mistakes all along, he realized. Selfish and stupid mistakes. But the biggest had been to fall in love with her, and to nudge her into love with him. She would hate him before it was done. She would have to.

"Not now. We've both had enough for now." Walking toward her, he thought, was as hard as it would be to walk away. He sat on the side of the bed, ran his hands down her arms. "You need to sleep."

"So do you. Nathan, we're alive." She took his hand, pressed it to her heart. "Getting through and going on—that's important. It's a lesson I learned the hard way." Leaning forward, she touched her lips to his. "Right now, let's just help each other get through the night." Her eyes were dark and stayed on his as she tilted her head to warm the kiss. "Make love with me. I need to hold you."

He let her draw him down, let himself sink. She would hate him before it was done, but for now love would be enough.

In the morning he was gone, from her bed, from Sanctuary, and from Desire.

"He left on the morning ferry?" Jo stared at Brian, wondering how he could fry eggs when the world had just turned upside down again.

"I passed him at dawn, heading back to his cottage." Brian checked his order sheet and spooned up grits. Crises came and went, he thought, but people always managed to eat. "He said he had some business to take care of on the mainland. He'd be a couple of days."

"A couple of days. I see." No good-bye, no see you around. No anything.

"He looked pretty ragged around the edges. And so do you."

"It hasn't been an easy twenty-four hours for anyone."

"No, but I've still got an inn to run. If you want to be useful, you could sweep off the terraces and patios, see that the cushions are put back out."

"Life goes on, right?"

"There's nothing we can do about that." He scooped the eggs up neatly, the glimmering yolks trembling. "You just do what has to be done next."

He watched her drag the broom out of the closet and head outside. And he wondered just what in the hell he was supposed to do next.

"I'm surprised people can eat, the way their mouths are running." Lexy breezed in, exchanged an empty coffeepot for a full one, then slapped down new orders. "One more person asks me about that poor woman, I'm going to scream."

"There's bound to be talk, there's bound to be questions."

"You don't have to listen to them." She gave herself a break, resting a hip against the counter. "I don't think I got more than ten minutes' sleep all night. I don't guess any of us did. Is Jo up yet?"

"She's out clearing off the terraces."

"Good. Keep her busy. Best thing for her." She huffed out a breath when Brian sent her a speculative look. "I'm not brainless, Bri. This has to be harder on her than the rest of us. Harder yet, after what she's already been through. Anything that keeps her mind off it for a five-minute stretch is a blessing."

"I never thought you were brainless, Lex. No matter how hard you pretend to be."

"I'm not going to worry about your insults this morning, Brian. But I am worried about Jo." She turned to peek out the window and was satisfied to see her sister sweeping violently. "Good manual labor should help. And thank God for Nathan. He's just exactly what she needs right now."

"He's not here."

She spun back around so fast that the coffee sloshed to the rim of the pot. "What do you mean he's not here?"

"He went over to the mainland for a few days."

"Well, what in blue hell for? He should be right here, with Jo Ellen."

"He had some business to see to."

"Business?" Lexy rolled her eyes and grabbed the tray of new orders. "Why, isn't that just like a man, just exactly like one? All of you, useless as a three-titted bull, every last one of you."

She stormed out, hips twitching. And for some reason Brian found himself in a much lighter mood. Women, he thought. Can't live with them, can't dump them off a cliff.

An hour later Lexy marched outside. She found Jo opening the last of the patio table umbrellas. "Everything's nice and tidy here, I see. Fine and dandy. Go on up and get a bathing suit. We're going to the beach."

"What for?"

"Because it's there. Go on and change. I've got sunscreen and towels here already."

"I don't want to sit on the beach."

"I don't think I asked what you wanted to do. You need some sun. And if you don't come along with me for an hour, Brian or Kate will find something else for you to sweep up or scrub."

Jo looked at the broom with distaste. "There is that. All right. Why not? It's hot. I could use a swim."

"Get a move on, then, before somebody catches us and puts us to work."

. . .

Jo cut through the breakers, took the roll, then began to swim with the current. She'd forgotten how much she loved being in the ocean—fighting against it, drifting with it. She could hear a girlish squeal in the distance as a couple laughed and wrestled in the surf. Farther out, a young boy, brown as a berry, struggled to catch a wave and ride his inflatable raft back to shore.

When her arms tired, she flipped onto her back. The sun burned down through hazy skies and stung her eyes. It was easy to close them, to float. When her mind drifted to Nathan, she cut it off.

He had a life of his own, and so did she. Maybe she'd started to lean just a little too much. It was good that he'd jerked that shoulder away so abruptly, forced her to regain her own balance.

When he came back—if he came back—she'd be steadier.

With a moan of disgust, she flipped again, letting her face sink into the water.

Goddamn it, she was in love with him. And if that wasn't the stupidest thing she'd ever done, she didn't know what topped it. There was no future there, and why would she even think of futures? She turned her head, gulped in air, and began to swim again.

They had come together by accident, through circumstance, and had simply taken advantage of it. If they'd gotten closer than they intended, that was a matter of circumstance too. And circumstances changed. She'd changed.

If coming back to Sanctuary had brought some pain and some misery, it had also brought back to her a strength and clear-sightedness that she'd been missing for far too long.

She planted her feet, let the sand shift under her as she walked through the waves to shore.

Lexy was posed on a blanket, stretched out to show off her generous curves. She rested lazily on an elbow, turning the pages of a thick paperback novel. On the cover was a bare-chested man with amazing and improbable pecs, black hair that swirled over his gleaming shoulders, and an arrogant smile on his full-lipped mouth.

Lexy gave a low, murmuring sigh and flipped a page. Her own hair rippled in the breeze. The curves of her generous breasts rose in smooth, peach-toned swells over the minuscule bikini top on which neon shades of green and pink warred. Her long legs were slicked with lotion, and her toenails were a glitter of coral.

She looked, Jo decided, like an ad for some sexy resort.

Dropping down beside her, Jo picked up a towel and rubbed it over her hair. "Do you do that on purpose, or is it just instinct?"

"What's that?" Lexy tipped down her rose-lensed sunglasses and peered over the top.

"Arrange yourself so that every male in a hundred yards strains his neck to get a look at you."

"Oh, that." Lips curving, Lexy nudged her glasses back in place. "That's just instinct, sugar. And good luck. You could do the same, but you'd have to put your mind to it some. You've gotten your figure back since you've been home. And that black tank suit's not a bad choice. Looks athletic and sleek. Some men go for that." She tipped her glasses down again. "Nathan seems to."

"Nathan hasn't seen me in this suit."

"Then he's in for a treat."

"If he comes back."

" 'Course he'll come back. You're smart, you'll make him pay just a little for going off."

Jo scooped up a handful of sand, let it drift through her fingers. "I'm in love with him."

"Of course you are. Why wouldn't you be?"

"In love with him, Lexy." Jo frowned at the glittering grains of sand that clung to her hand.

"Oh." Lexy sat up, crossed her pretty legs, and grinned. "That's nice. You sure took your time falling, but you picked a winner."

"I hate it." Jo grabbed more sand and squeezed it into her fist. "I hate feeling this way, being this way. It ties my stomach up in knots."

"It's supposed to. I've had mine tied up dozens of times. It was always real easy to loosen it up again." Her mouth went into a pout as she looked out to sea. "Until now. I'm having a harder time of that with Giff."

"He loves you. He always has. It's different for you."

"It's different for everybody. We're all built different inside. That's what makes it so interesting."

Jo tilted her head. "You know, Lex, sometimes you're absolutely sensible. I never expect it, then there it is. I guess I need to tell you what I told Brian last night."

"What's that?"

"I love you, Lexy." She bent over and touched her lips to her sister's cheek. "I really do."

"I know that, Jo. You're ornery about it, but you always loved us." She let out a breath as she decided to make her own confession. "I guess that's why I got so mad at you when you went away. And I was jealous."

"You? Of me?"

"Because you weren't afraid to go."

"Yes, I was." Jo rested her chin on her knee and watched the waves batter the shore. "I was terrified. Sometimes I'm still scared of being out there, of not being able to do what I need to do. Or doing it but failing at it."

"Well, I failed, and I can tell you, it sucks."

"You didn't fail, Lexy. You just didn't finish." She turned her head. "Will you go back?"

"I don't know. I was sure I would." Her eyes clouded, misted between gray and green. "Trouble is, it gets easy to stay here, let time go by. Then I'll just get old and wrinkled and fat. Oh, what are we talking about this for?"

Annoyed with herself, Lexy shook her head, picked out a cold can of Pepsi from the little cooler beside her. "We should be talking about something interesting. Like, I was wondering . . ."

She popped the top, took a long, cooling sip. Then ran her tongue lazily over her top lip. "Just how is sex with Nathan?"

Jo snorted out a laugh. "No," she said definitely and rolled over to lie on her stomach.

"On a scale of one to ten." Lexy poked Jo's shoulder. "Or if you had to pick one adjective to describe it."

"No," Jo said again.

"Just one little bitty adjective. I mean, would it be 'incredible'?" she asked, leaning down close to Jo's ear. "Or would it be 'fabulous'? Maybe 'memorable'?"

Jo let out a small sigh. " 'Stupendous,' " she said without opening her eyes. "It's stupendous."

"Oh, stupendous." Lexy waved a hand in front of her face. "Oh, I like that. Stupendous. Does he keep his eyes open or closed when he kisses you?"

"Depends."

"He does both? That gives me the shivers. You'd never know which. I just love that. So, how about when he—"

"Lexy." Though a giggle escaped, Jo kept her eyes tightly closed. "I'm not going to describe Nathan's lovemaking technique for you. I'm going to take a nap. Wake me up in a bit."

And to her surprise, she dropped like a stone into sleep.

25

Nathan paced the aging Turkish carpet in the soaring two-level library of Dr. Jonah Kauffman's brownstone. Outside, and two dozen stories down, New York was sweltering under a massive heat wave. Here in the dignified penthouse all was cool and polished and worlds away from the bump and grind of the streets.

It never felt like New York inside Kauffman's realm. Whenever Nathan walked into the grand foyer with its golden woods and quiet colors, he thought of English squires and country houses.

One of Nathan's earliest commissions had been to design the library, to shift walls and ceilings to accommodate Kauffman's enormous collection of books in the understated and traditional style that suited one of the top neurologists in the country. The warm chestnut wood, the wide, intricately carved moldings, the tall sweep of triple windows set back to form a cozy alcove had been Nathan's choices. Kauffman had left it all up to him, chuckling whenever Nathan would ask for an opinion.

You're the doctor on this case, Nathan. Don't ask me to collaborate on the choice of structural beams, and I won't ask you to assist in brain surgery.

Now Nathan struggled to compose himself as he waited. This time around, Kauffman was the doctor, and Nathan's present, his future, every choice, large or small, that he would ever make were in Kauffman's skilled hands.

It had been six days since he'd left Desire. Six desperately long days.

Kauffman strode in, slid the thick pocket doors shut behind him. "Sorry to make you wait, Nathan. You should have helped yourself to a brandy. But brandy's not your drink, is it? Well, I'll have one and you can pretend to join me."

"I appreciate your seeing me here, Doctor. And your doing all . . . this yourself."

"Come now, you're part of the family." Kauffman lifted a Baccarat decanter from a sideboard to pour two snifters.

He was tall, nearly six five, an imposing man both straight and trim after seventy years of living. His hair remained thick, and he allowed himself the vanity of wearing it brushed back like a flowing white mane. He sported a neat beard and moustache that surrounded his somewhat thin mouth. He preferred the no-nonsense lines of British suits, the elegance of Italian shoes, and he never failed to appear perfectly and elegantly turned out.

But it was his eyes that drew the onlooker's attention first, and most often held it. They were dark and keen under heavy lids and sweeping black brows. Those eyes warmed as he offered Nathan a snifter. "Sit down, Nathan, and relax. It won't be necessary to drill into your brain anytime in the foreseeable future."

Nathan's stomach did a long, slow turn. "The tests?"

"All of them, and you requested—rather, you insisted on—quite an extensive battery of tests, are negative. I've gone over the results myself, as you asked. You have no tumors, no shadows, no abnormalities whatsoever. What you have, Nathan, is a very healthy brain and neuro system. Now sit down."

"I will." His legs gave way easily enough, and he sank into the buttery-soft leather of a wingback, man-size chair. "Thank you for all the time and trouble, but I wonder if I shouldn't get a second opinion."

Kauffman raised those dramatic black brows. As he sat down across from Nathan, he automatically lifted the pleats of his trousers so they would fall correctly. "I consulted with one of my associates on your tests. His opinion corroborates with mine. You're welcome, of course, to go elsewhere."

"No." Though he didn't care for brandy, Nathan took a quick swallow and let it slide through his system. "I'm sure you covered all the bases."

"More than. The CT and the MRI scans were both perfectly normal. The physical you underwent, the blood work and so forth, only served to prove that you're a thirty-year-old man in excellent health and physical condition." Kauffman swirled his snifter, brought it to his lips. "Now, it's time you told me why you felt the need to put yourself through such intensive testing."

"I wanted to be sure there wasn't anything physically wrong. I thought I might be having blackouts."

"Have you lost time?"

"No. Well, how would I know? There's a possibility that I've been blanking out, doing . . . something during—what would you call it—a fugue state."

Kauffman pursed his lips. He'd known Nathan too long to consider him an alarmist. "Have you any evidence of that? Finding yourself in places without remembering how you got there?"

"No. No, I haven't." Nathan allowed the relief to trickle through, slowly. "I'm all right, then, physically."

"You're in excellent, even enviable, physical condition. Your emotional condition is another matter. You've had a hideous year, Nathan. The loss of your family is bound to have taken its toll on you. A divorce not long before that. So much loss, so much change. I miss David and Beth so much myself. They were very dear to me."

"I know." Nathan stared into those dark, compelling eyes. Did you know? he wondered. Did you suspect? But all he saw on Kauffman's face was sympathy and regret. "I know they were."

"And Kyle." Kauffman sighed deeply. "So young, his death so unnecessary."

"I've had time to cope, to start to accept that my parents are gone." Even to thank God for it, Nathan thought. "As for Kyle, we hadn't been close in a long time. Their deaths didn't change that."

"And you feel guilty that you don't grieve for him as you do for them."

"Maybe." Nathan set the snifter aside, rubbed his hands over his face. "I'm not sure where the guilt's rooted anymore. Doctor Kauffman, you were friends with my father for thirty years, you knew him before I was born."

"And your mother." Kauffman smiled. "As a man who has three ex-wives, I admired their dedication to each other and their marriage. To their sons. You were a lovely family. I hope you can find comfort in the memory of that."

And that, Nathan thought with a sinking heart, was the crux of it. There could be no comfort in the memories now, and never would be again. "What would make a man, a seemingly normal man living a perfectly normal life, plan and commit an obscene act? An unspeakable act."

The pressure on his chest forced Nathan's heart to beat too hard, too thickly. He picked up the snifter again, but without any desire to drink. "Would he be insane, would he be ill? Would there be some physical cause?"

"I couldn't say, Nathan, on such general speculation. Do you believe your father committed an unspeakable act?"

"I know he did." Before Kauffman could speak, Nathan shook his head and rose to pace again. "I can't—I'm not free to explain it to you. There are others I have to talk to first."

"Nathan, David Delaney was a loyal friend, a loving husband, and a devoted father. You can rest your mind on that."

"I haven't been able to rest my mind on that since the month after he was killed." Emotions swirled in his eyes, turning them to smoke. "I buried him,

Doctor Kauffman, him and my mother. And I'm very tempted to bury the rest. If I could be sure," he said softly, "that it's not happening again."

Kauffman leaned forward. He'd been treating the human condition for half a century and knew there was no healing of the body or the brain without healing of the heart. "Whatever it is you believe he did, you can't bear the weight of it."

"Who else can? Who else will? I'm the only one left."

"Nathan." Kauffman let out a little sigh. "You were a bright, interesting child, and you have become a talented and intelligent young man. Too often when you were growing up, I saw you shoulder the responsibilities of others. You took on your brother's far too often for your own good, or for Kyle's. Don't make that mistake now over something you can neither change nor repair."

"I've been telling myself that for the last couple of months. 'Leave it alone, live your own life.' I'd decided not to dig into the past, to try to concentrate on the present and forge a future. There's a woman."

"Ah." Kauffman relaxed, eased back.

"I'm in love with her."

"I'm delighted to hear it and would love to meet her. Has she been vacationing on that island you took yourself off to?"

"Not exactly. Her family lives there. She's spending some time. She's had... difficulties of her own. Actually I met her when we were children. When I saw her again... well, to simplify, one thing led to another. I could have prevented it." He moved to the window, to the view of Central Park, which was thick and green with summer. "Perhaps I should have."

"Why would you deny yourself happiness?"

"There's something I know that affects her. If I tell her, she'll despise me. More, I don't know what it will do to her, emotionally." Because the park made him think of the forest on Desire, he turned away from it. "Would it be better for her to go on believing something that hurts her but isn't true, or to know the truth and have to live with pain she might not be able to bear? I'll lose her if I tell her, and I don't know if I can live with myself if I don't."

"Is she in love with you?"

"She's beginning to be. If I let things go on as they are, she will be." A ghost of a smile flitted around his mouth. "She'd hate hearing me say that, as if it were inevitable. As if she had no control over it."

Kauffman heard the warmth come back into Nathan's voice. The boy had always been his favorite, he admitted privately. Even among his own grandchildren. "Ah, an independent woman. Always more interesting—and more difficult."

"She's fascinating, and she certainly isn't easy. She's strong, even when she's wounded, and she's been wounded enough. She's built a shell around herself, and since I've seen her again I've watched it crack, watched her open up. Maybe I've even helped that happen. And inside she's soft, giving."

"You haven't once said what she looks like." Kauffman found that to be the telling mark. Physical attraction had led him into three hot marriages, followed by three chilly divorces. More was needed for the long, often sweaty, haul.

"She's beautiful," Nathan said simply. "She'd prefer to be ordinary, but it's impossible. Jo doesn't trust beauty. She trusts competency. And honesty," Nathan finished, staring down into the brandy he'd barely touched, "I don't know what to do."

"Truth is admirable, but it isn't always the answer. I can't tell you what choice to make, but I've always believed that love, when genuine, holds. Perhaps you should ask yourself which would be more loving, giving her the truth or remaining silent."

"And if I remain silent, the foundation we build on will already have a crack. Still I'm the only one alive who can tell her, Doctor Kauffman." Nathan lifted his gaze, and his eyes stormed with emotion. "I'm the only one left."

Nathan didn't return to the island the next day, or the day after. By the third day Jo had convinced herself it didn't matter. She was hardly sitting around waiting for him to sail across the sound and scoop her up like a pirate claiming his booty.

On the fourth day she was weepy, despising herself for wandering down to the ferry twice a day, hoping to catch sight of him.

By the end of a week she was furious, and spent a great deal of her time snapping at anyone who risked speaking to her. In the interest of restoring peace, Kate bearded the lion in Jo's room, where she had gone to sulk after a hissing match with Lexy.

"What in the world are you doing holed up indoors on such a pretty morning?" Moving briskly, Kate whisked back the curtains Jo had pulled over the windows. Sunlight beamed in.

"Enjoying my privacy. If you've come in here to try to convince me to apologize to Lexy, you're wasting your time."

"You and Lexy can fight your own battles, just like always, as far as I'm concerned." Kate put her hands on her hips. "But you'll mind your tone when you speak to me, young lady."

"I beg your pardon," Jo said coolly, "but this is my room."

"I don't care if you're sitting on top of your own mountain, you won't bare your claws on me. Now I've been as patient as I know how to be these last few days, but you've mooned around and snarled around here long enough."

"Then maybe it's time I should think about going home."

"That's your decision to make. Oh, shake yourself loose, Jo Ellen," Kate ordered with a snap in her own voice. "The man's only been gone a week, and he'll certainly be back."

Jo firmed her jaw. "I don't know what, or whom, you're referring to."

Before she could stop herself, Kate snorted. "Don't think you can out la-de-da me. I've been at it more years." Kate sat down on the bed where Jo was sprawled under the pretense of selecting the final prints for her book. "A blind man on a galloping horse could see that Nathan Delaney's got you in a dither. And it's likely the best thing to happen to you in years."

"I am not, in any way, any shape, any form, in a dither."

"You're more than halfway in love with him, and it wouldn't surprise me in the least if he'd gone off like this to nudge you over the rest of the way."

Since that hadn't occurred to her, Jo felt her blood heat to a boil. "Then he's made a very large miscalculation. Going off without a word is hardly the way to win my affections."

"Then do you want him to know you've been moping around here the whole time he's been gone?" Kate lifted a brow as she saw the flush of anger heat Jo's cheeks. "There are plenty who'd be happy to tell him so if you keep this up. I'd hate for you to give him that satisfaction."

"I don't intend to give him so much as the time of day, should he decide to come back."

Kate patted Jo's knee. "I couldn't agree more."

Wary of a trap, Jo narrowed her eyes. "I thought you liked him."

"I do. I like him very much, but that doesn't mean I don't think he deserves a good swift kick in the rear end for making you unhappy. And I'd be mighty disappointed in you if you gave him the opportunity to crow over it. So get up," she ordered, rising herself. "Go on about your business. Take your camera and go along. And when he comes back, all he'll see is that your life went on without him."

"You're right. You're absolutely right. I'm going to call my publisher and give them the final go-ahead on the last prints. Then I'm going to go out, take some new shots. I've got an idea for another book."

Kate smiled as Jo scrambled up and began to pull her shoes on. "That's wonderful. You'll have pictures of the island in it, then."

"All of them. People this time, too. Faces. No one's going to accuse me of being lonely, of hiding behind the lens. I've got more than one facet to me."

"Of course you do, sweetie pie. I'll get out of your way so you can get to work." All but vibrating with the pleasure of success, Kate strolled out. Maybe now, she thought, they'd have some peace.

The adrenaline carried Jo through that day and into the next. It fueled her, this new ambition. For the first time in her career, she hunted up faces with enthusiasm, began to study and dissect them. She thrilled at the way Giff's eyes twinkled under the brim of his cap, the way his hand gripped a hammer.

She hounded Brian in the kitchen, using charm when she could, threats when she couldn't, to draw the right expression, to produce the right body language.

Lexy was easy. She would pose endlessly. But Jo's favorite shot was one of Lexy and Giff, the foolishly happy expressions on their faces as Giff swept Lexy up to spin her in circles just on the edge of the garden.

She even trooped after her father, using silence to lull him into relaxing, then capturing the quiet thoughtfulness in his face as he looked out over the salt marsh.

"It's time you put that thing away." Sam's brows drew together in irritated embarrassment as she aimed the camera at him again. "Run along and play with that somewhere else."

"It stopped being play when they started paying me. Turn just a little to the right and look out toward the water."

He didn't move a muscle. "I don't recollect you ever being such a pest before."

"I'll have you know I'm a very famous photographer. Thousands cheer when I aim my lens." She clicked quickly when a faint smile tugged at his mouth. "You're so handsome, Daddy. And you look so masterful out here."

"You're so damned famous, you shouldn't have to flatter people to get their picture."

She laughed and lowered the camera. "True enough. But you are handsome. I was taking some shots over at Elsie Pendleton's. The Widow Pendleton," Jo added, wiggling her eyebrows. "She made a point to ask after you. Several times."

"Elsie Pendleton's been looking for a man to replace the one she buried since she tossed the first handful of dirt on his coffin. It ain't by any means going to be me."

"For which good sense your family thanks you."

He found his lips trembling again, shook his head as much over the reaction as the cause. "You're awfully chipper today."

"A nice change, don't you think? I got tired of myself." She crouched down to change lenses. "And it occurred to me that a corner needed to be turned. Maybe coming here was the start of it." She paused for a moment, just to look out over the shimmering marsh. "Facing some things, myself included. And realizing that maybe if I didn't feel loved, it was because I hadn't let anyone love me."

She glanced up, saw that he was watching her, searching her face. "Don't look for her in me, Daddy." Jo closed her eyes as the pain stabbed through her. "Don't look for her in me anymore. It hurts me when you do."

"Jo Ellen—"

"All my life I've tried to stop looking like her. In college when the other girls were fussing and primping, I held back. If I fussed I'd have to look in the mirror. And I'd see her, just the way you do when you look at me." Her eyes swam as she straightened. "What do I have to do, Daddy, to make you see who I am?"

"I do see. I can't help but see her too, but I do see you, Jo Ellen. Don't go spilling over on me here. I'm useless with that female stuff." He stuffed his hands in his pockets and turned away. "You get hold of yourself now. It's Lexy who leaks at the drop of a hat, not you. Damn girl'll leak if you look cross-eyed, and if she isn't leaking she's flouncing. She don't marry that Giff soon and get on with things, I'll lose my mind."

Jo gave a watery chuckle. "Why, Daddy, I didn't know you loved her enough to let her drive you crazy."

" 'Course I love her. She's mine, isn't she?" He spoke gruffly and made himself turn back to face Jo. "So are you."

"Yes." She smiled and let the ache pass away. "So am I."

. . .

When the light no longer pleased her, Jo locked herself in her darkroom. There was excitement there as well. From film to negatives, from negatives to contacts. These she pored over, scrutinizing details, flaws, shadows through her loupe.

Out of a dozen she might select one that satisfied her strict requirements. Still, her drying line filled rapidly with prints she felt were worthy. When she came to an unmarked roll of film, she clicked her tongue in annoyance.

Careless of her, she thought. She set the timer, flicked off the lights, and began the developing process. The dark soothed her. She could move competently, even mechanically, by feel alone. Anticipation hummed. What would she see here, what would she find? What frozen moment would be preserved forever simply because she had chosen it?

She turned on the red bulb, washed the room in that eerie workman's lighting. And gave a choked cry that was part shock, part laughter as she stared at the negative of herself, nude, sprawled on Nathan's carpet.

"Jesus, that'll teach me not to mark film."

She held up the roll, studying the other negatives. The ones she'd taken of the storm looked promising. And her mouth pursed as she examined the earlier shots, ones Nathan must have taken along the way.

There was one of dunes, across the meadow where the flowers were blooming and the sea beyond rolled in a high, frothy crest.

Decent composition, she mused. For an amateur. Of course if she bothered to take it to contact stage, she'd undoubtedly find several major flaws.

Her eyes were drawn back to the end of the roll. Her own face, her own body. Even as her hand reached for the scissors to destroy the negatives, she paused. Was she going to be that prudish, that stubborn, and not satisfy her own curiosity?

She was the only one who had to see them, after all.

On impulse, she set back to work. It couldn't hurt to make a set of contacts from the roll. She could destroy the ones of herself later. After she'd taken a good look at them.

She didn't hum along with the radio as she worked now. She felt too uneasy, and too excited, to hear the music that tinkled out.

The sheet was barely dry when she slapped it onto her light table and applied the loupe. She caught her breath as the images enlarged and focused.

She looked so . . . wanton, she supposed would be the word. Her eyes half closed, her lips just curved in obvious sexual satisfaction. Her body looked almost ripe. Apparently she had gotten her figure back without even noticing. She certainly had curves.

In the next her eyes were fully open and round with shock. Her hands were halfway up to her breasts, movement frozen by the fast film. There was no denying that she looked—how had he put it? Rumpled and sexy?

Oh, God, she had never allowed herself to be that exposed to anyone before. She'd let that happen, and now for just a moment, she could admit she wanted to let it happen again.

She wanted to let him touch her, to make her feel desired and reckless. There was a yearning deep in the pit of her stomach to be that woman again, the woman he'd seen and captured on film. To let him take control of her, and to know that she had the power to take control of him.

He'd given that to her, and by preserving that moment, had made her look straight at it and see what she could have with him. And what she could lose without him.

"You bastard, Nathan. I hate you for this."

She got up quickly, stuffed the sheet deep into a drawer. No, she wouldn't destroy it. She would keep it, as a reminder. Whenever she felt herself tempted to trust a man again, to give that much to a man, she would take it back out, study it.

And remind herself how easily they walked away.

"Jo Ellen." Lexy's voice came through the door as her knock sounded sharp and loud.

"I'm working in here."

"Well, I know that. But you might want to finish up quick, fast, and in a hurry. Guess who came in on the late ferry?"

"Brad Pitt."

"Don't I wish? But you might like this better. Nathan Delaney just walked in the kitchen, big as life and twice as handsome. And he's looking for you."

Jo lifted a fist to her heart and firmly shoved it back in place. "Tell him I'm busy."

"I already gave him the cold shoulder for you, sugar. Told him I didn't see why you should drop what you were doing and come running just because he blew back onto Desire like an ill wind."

Jo found her lips curving in appreciation. She could easily visualize the scene, with Lexy playing the chilly Southern Belle to the hilt. "I appreciate it."

"But I have to tell you—oh, open this door, Jo. I'm tired of talking through it."

Because Lexy had just climbed to the top of Jo's most favored list, she obliged, snicking open the lock, and opening the door enough that she could lean on the jamb.

"I'd appreciate it if you'd tell him I'm not interested in adjusting my schedule to suit his whims."

"I will. That's nicely put. But Jo, he looks so windblown and sexy and on the edge of something." Lexy rolled her eyes in pure female appreciation. "It gave my heart a nice flutter just to look at him."

"Well, you can just stop fluttering. Whose side are you on?"

"Yours, honey lamb, absolutely one hundred percent." She kissed Jo's cheek to prove it. "He has to be punished, no doubt about it. And if you need some advice on how to go about it, I'm more than happy to give you some ideas."

"I've got plenty of my own, thanks." But she rolled her shoulders to ease the tension. "Tell him I have no desire to see or speak to him, and that I expect to be busy with a great many more important matters than him for quite some time."

"I wish you'd tell him that yourself, just that way. I believe you've got a real knack for this." Lexy's grin spread wide as she wound a lock of hair around her finger. "I'll go down and tell him, then I'll come back up here and tell you what he has to say to that."

"This isn't high school."

"No, it's more interesting and more fun. Oh, I know you're scalded good and proper, Jo." She patted her sister's cheek. "I'd be as spitting mad as a stomped-on cat myself. But just think how satisfying it's going to be when he crawls. Don't you take him back until he does. And he comes up with at least two bouquets of flowers and a nice, expensive present. It should be jewelry."

Jo's humor made a rapid return. "Lexy, you're a manipulative and materialistic woman."

"And proud of it, honey. You listen to your baby sister and you'll end up *owning* that man. Now I figure he's been down there waiting and sweating long enough for the next slap." She rubbed her hands together. "I'll make it count for you, don't you worry."

Jo stayed leaning against the doorjamb as Lexy flounced away. "I bet you will," she murmured. "And I'll owe you big for it."

Satisfied, Jo turned back into the darkroom. She tidied her workbench, rearranged her bottles of chemicals, then put them back in their original positions. She examined her nails and wondered if she should let Lexy give her a manicure after all.

When she heard the footsteps, she turned toward the door, prepared to hear Lexy's report. When Nathan filled the doorway, his temper shot straight into hers.

"I need you to come with me." His voice was clipped and anything but apologetic.

"I believe you were informed I'm busy. And you haven't been invited into this room."

"Save it, Scarlett." He grabbed her hand and pulled. When her free one reared back, whipped forward, and cracked hard across his face, he narrowed his eyes and nodded. "Fine, we do it the hard way."

The room turned upside down so rapidly she didn't even get out the curse burning on her tongue. He was halfway out of the room with her slung over his shoulder before she got past the shock enough to fight.

"Get your goddamn belly-crawling Yankee bastard hands off me." She punched at his back, furious that she couldn't manage a full swing.

"You think you can send your sister to brush me off? In a pig's eye." He shoved open the door with his shoulder and started down the narrow stairway. "I've been traveling the whole fucking day to get here, and you'll have the courtesy to listen to what I need to say."

"Courtesy? Courtesy? What does a snake oil New York hotshot know about courtesy?" In the confines of the stairway, her struggles only resulted in her rapping her head against the wall. "I hate you." Her ears rang from both the blow and the humiliation.

"I've prepared myself for that." Grim and determined, he hauled her into the kitchen. Both Lexy and Brian froze and gaped. "Excuse me," he said shortly, and carried her outside while she left a trail of threats and curses behind them.

"Oh." Lexy sighed, long and deep, holding a hand to her heart. "Wasn't that the most romantic thing you've ever seen in all your life?"

"Shit." Brian set down the pie he'd just taken out of the oven. "She'll rip his face off first chance she gets."

"A lot you know about romance." Lexy leaned against the counter. "Twenty dollars says he's got her in bed, fully willing, within an hour."

Brian heard Jo scream out something about castrating a certain Yankee son of a bitch and nodded. "You're on, darling."

26

Jo sat in simmering silence as Nathan drove the Jeep hissing across Shell Road. She wouldn't give him the satisfaction of leaping out of a moving vehicle, or of running away once he stopped it. She would simply tear his skin into bloody shreds when they were no longer in danger of running off the road.

"This isn't the way I wanted to go about this," Nathan muttered. "I need to talk to you. It's important. A hell of a time you pick to pull some lame female cold-shoulder routine."

Ignoring her low, purring sound of warning, he dug a deeper hole for himself. "I don't mind a fight. Under any reasonable circumstances I don't mind a good kick-ass fight. Clears the air. But these aren't reasonable circumstances, and you having your nose out of joint is only complicating an already painful situation."

"So it's my fault." She sucked in her breath as he jerked the Jeep to a halt at the cottage. "This is my fault?"

"It's not a matter of fault, Jo. That's the whole—" He broke off abruptly, too busy defending himself to bother with more words.

She didn't go at him with teeth and nails and heated accusations. She waded in with balled-up fists, and the first several blew right past his guard.

"Jesus! Jesus Christ!" He wished he could laugh at them. He wished to God he could just drag her close, pin those surprisingly well-toned arms with his and just howl at the pair of them.

He tasted blood in his mouth, wasn't entirely sure his jaw wouldn't turn out to be broken, and finally managed to hold her down on the seat while both of them panted for breath.

"Would you stop it? Would you pull out some modicum of control and stop trying to beat my brains—which I'm assured are in perfect working order—to a bloody pulp?" He tightened his grip, shifting fast as she tried to bring her knee up and render him helpless. "I don't want to hurt you."

"Well, that's too bad because I want to hurt you. I want to send you off limping for treating me this way."

"I'm sorry." He lowered his brow to hers and tried to catch his breath. "I'm sorry, Jo."

She refused to soften, refused to acknowledge the little trip her heart experienced at the utter despair in his voice. "You don't even know what you're sorry for."

"For more than you know." He eased back, met her eyes. "Please come inside. I have things to tell you. Things I wish I didn't have to tell you. After I do, you can beat me black and blue and I won't lift a hand to stop you. I swear it."

Something was wrong, horribly wrong. The anger dropped away into fear. She kept her voice cool before her imagination ran wild. "That's quite an arrangement. I'll come in, and you can say what you have to say. Then we're finished, Nathan."

She shoved him away and pushed open her car door. "Because nobody walks away from me," she said in a low, vibrant voice. "Nobody ever again."

His heart sank, but he led the way inside, switched on the lights. "I'd like you to sit down."

"I don't need to sit down, and what you'd like doesn't interest me. How could you go that way?" Even as she rounded on him, she wrapped her arms around herself in defense. "How could you leave my bed and just go, without a word? And stay away when you had to know how it would make me feel. If you were tired of me, you still could have been kind."

"Tired of you? Sweet Jesus, Jo, there hasn't been a minute of the past eight days that I haven't thought of you, wanted you."

"Do you think I'm stupid enough, or needy enough, to believe that kind of lie? If you'd thought of me, wanted me, you couldn't have turned your back on me as if none of it mattered. Had ever mattered."

"If it hadn't mattered, didn't matter more than anything else in my life, I could have stayed. And we wouldn't be having this conversation."

"You hurt me, you humiliated me, you—"

"I love you."

She jerked back as if to avoid a blow. "You expect my knees to go weak now? You think you can say that and make me run into your arms?"

"No. I wouldn't love you if you couldn't stand there and spit at me after I'd said it." He walked to her, gave in to the need to touch her. Just a brush of his fingertips over her shoulders. "And I do love you, Jo Ellen. Maybe I always did. Maybe that seven-year-old girl ruined me for anyone else. I don't know. But I need you to believe me. I need to say it, and I need you to believe it before I start the rest."

She stared into his eyes, and now her knees did start to tremble. "You do mean it."

"Enough to put my past, present, and future in your hands." He took hers in his for a moment, studied them, memorized them, then let them go. "I went back to New York. There's a friend of the family, a doctor. A neurologist. I wanted him to run some tests on me."

"Tests?" Baffled, she pushed at her hair. "What kind of—Oh, my God." It struck her like a fist, hard in the heart. "You're sick. A neurologist? What is it? A tumor." Her blood shivered to ice in her veins. "But you can have treatment. You can—"

"I'm not sick, Jo. There's no tumor, there's nothing wrong with me. But I had to be sure."

"There's nothing wrong?" She folded her arms again, hugged them to her body. "I don't understand. You went back to New York to have tests run on your brain when there's nothing wrong with you?"

"I said I needed to be sure. Because I thought I might have had blackouts or been sleepwalking or had fugues. And have maybe killed Susan Peters."

She lowered herself gingerly, bracing a hand on the back of the chair as she sat on the arm. She never took her eyes off his. "Why would you think such a crazy thing?"

"Because she was strangled here on the island. Because her body was hidden. Because her husband, her family, her friends, might have gone the rest of their lives not knowing what had happened."

"Stop it." She couldn't get her breath, had to fight back the urge to clap her hands over her ears. Her heart was beating too fast, making her head spin, her skin damp. She knew the signs, the panic waiting slyly to spring. "I don't want to hear any more of this."

"I don't want to tell you any more. But neither one of us has a choice." He braced himself not only to face it but to face her. "My father killed your mother."

"That's insane, Nathan." She willed herself to get up and run, but she couldn't move. "And it's cruel."

"It's both. And it's also the truth. Twenty years ago, my father took your mother's life."

"No. Your father—Mr. David—was kind, he was a friend. This is crazy talk. My mother left." Her voice shuddered and broke, then rose. "She just left."

"She never left Desire. He . . . he put her body in the marsh. Buried her in the salt marsh."

"Why are you saying this? Why are you doing this?"

"Because it's the truth, and I've avoided it too long already." Nathan forced himself to say the rest, to finish it while she shut her eyes and shook her head fiercely. "He planned it from the minute he saw her, when we arrived that summer."

"No. No, stop this."

"I can't stop what's already happened. He kept a journal and . . . evidence in a safe-deposit box. I found it all after he and my mother died."

"You found it." Tears leaked through her lashes as she wrapped her arms tight around her body and rocked. "You came back here."

"I came back here to face it, to try to remember what that summer had been like. What he had been like ... then. And to try to decide whether to leave it all buried or to tell your family what my family had done."

The familiar flood of sick panic rushed through her, roared in her head, raced through her blood. "You knew. You knew all along, and you came back here. You took me to bed knowing." Nausea made her dizzy as she surged to her feet. "You were inside me." Rage sliced through her an instant before her hand cracked across his cheek. "I let you inside me." She slapped him again, viciously. He neither defended himself nor evaded the blows. "Do you know how that makes me feel?"

He'd known she would look at him just like this, with hate and disgust, even fear. He had no choice but to accept it. "I didn't face it. My father ... he was my father."

"He killed her, he took her away from us. And all these years ..."

"Jo, I didn't know until after he'd died. I've been trying to come to grips with it for months. I know what you're going through now—"

"You can't know." She flung the words out. She wanted to hurt him, to scar him, to make him suffer. "I can't stay here. I can't look at you. Don't!" She jerked back, hands fisted when he reached out. "Don't put your hands on me. I could kill you for ever putting them on me. You bastard, you stay away from me and my family."

When she ran, Nathan didn't try to stop her. He couldn't. But he followed her erratic dash, keeping her in sight. If he could do nothing else, he would make certain she arrived safe at Sanctuary.

But it wasn't to Sanctuary that she fled.

She couldn't go home. Couldn't bear it. She couldn't get her breath, couldn't clear her vision. Part of her wanted to simply fall to the ground, curl up, and scream until her mind and body were empty of grief. But she was terrified that she'd never find the strength to get up again.

So she ran, without thought of destination, through the trees, through the dark, with images flipping hideously through her head.

The photograph of her mother, coming to life. The eyes opening. Confusion, fear, pain. The mouth stretching wide for a scream.

Pain stabbed into Jo's side like a knife. She gripped it, whimpering, and kept running.

On the sand now, with the ocean crashing. Her breath heaved out of her lungs. She fell once, hitting hard on her hands and knees, only to scramble up and stumble back into a run. She only knew she had to get away, to run away from the pain and this horribly tearing sorrow.

She heard someone call her name, and the sound of feet pounding the sand behind her. She nearly tripped again, righted herself, then turned to fight.

"Jo, honey, what is it?" Clad in only a robe, her hair streaming wet from the shower, Kirby hurried toward her. "I was out on the deck and saw you—"

"Don't touch me!"

"All right." Instinctively, Kirby lowered her voice, gentled it. "Why don't you come up to the house? You've hurt yourself. Your hands are bleeding."

"I..." Confused, Jo looked down, saw the scrapes and the slow trickle of blood on the heels of her hands. "I fell."

"I know. I saw you. Come on up. I'll clean them for you."

"I don't need—they're all right." She couldn't even feel her hands. Then her legs began to tremble, her head began to spin. "He killed my mother. Kirby, he murdered my mother. She's dead."

Cautiously, Kirby moved closer until she could slide a supporting hand around Jo's waist. "Come with me. Come home with me now." When Jo sagged, she led her across the sand. Glancing back, she saw Nathan standing a few yards away. In the moonlight their eyes met briefly. Then he turned and walked away into the dark.

"I feel sick," Jo murmured. Sensation was creeping back, tiny needle pricks all over her skin, and with it the greasy churning in her stomach.

"It's all right. You need to lie down. Lean on me and we'll get you inside."

"He killed her. Nathan knew. He told me." It felt as if she were floating now, up the steps, in the door of the cottage. "My mother's dead."

Saying nothing, Kirby helped Jo onto the bed, put a light blanket over her. She was beginning to tremble with shock now. "Slow breaths," Kirby ordered. "Concentrate on breathing. I'm just going in the other room for a moment. I'm going to get something to help you."

"I don't need anything." Fresh panic snaked through her, and she gripped Kirby's hand hard. "No sedatives. I can get through this. I can. I have to."

"Of course you can." Kirby eased onto the bed and took Jo's wrist to check her pulse. "Are you ready to tell me about it?"

"I have to tell someone. I can't tell my family yet. I can't face that yet. I don't know what to do. I don't even know what to feel."

The pulse rate was slowing, and Jo's pupils were returning to normal. "What did Nathan say to you, Jo?"

Jo stared at the ceiling, focused on it, centered herself on it. "He told me that his father had murdered my mother."

"Dear God." Horrified, Kirby lifted Jo's hand to her cheek. "How did it happen?"

"I don't know. I don't know. I couldn't listen. I didn't want to listen. He said his father killed her, that he kept a journal. Nathan found it, and he came back here. I slept with him." Tears trickled out of her eyes, slid away. "I slept with the son of my mother's murderer."

Calm was needed now, Kirby knew. And cool logic. The wrong word, the wrong tone, and she was afraid Jo would break in her hands. "Jo, you slept with Nathan. You cared for Nathan, and he for you."

"He knew. He came back here knowing what his father had done."

"And that must have been terribly hard for him."

"How can you say that?" Furious, Jo pushed herself onto her elbows. "Hard for him?"

"And courageous," Kirby said softly. "Jo, how old would he have been when your mother died?"

"What difference does it make?"

"Nine or ten, I imagine. Just a little boy. Are you going to blame the little boy?"

"No. No. But he's not a little boy now, and his father—"

"Nathan's father. Not Nathan."

A sob choked out, then another. "He took her away from me."

"I know. I'm so sorry." Kirby gathered Jo close. "I'm so terribly sorry."

As Jo wept in her arms, Kirby knew this storm was only the beginning.

It took an hour before she could think again. She sipped the hot, sweet tea Kirby made her. The sick panic had flowed away in a wash of grief. Now, for a moment, the grief was almost as soothing as the tea.

"I knew she was dead. Part of me always knew, from the time it happened. I would dream of her. As I got older I pushed the dreams away, but they would always come back. And they only got stronger."

"You loved her. Now, as horrible as things are, you know she didn't leave you."

"I can't find comfort in that yet. I wanted to hurt Nathan. Physically, emotionally, in every possible way to cause him pain. And I did."

"Do you think that's an abnormal reaction? Jo, give yourself a break."

"I'm trying to. I nearly cracked again. I would have if you hadn't been there."

"But I was." Kirby squeezed Jo's hand. "And you're stronger than you think. Strong enough to get through this."

"I have to be." She drank more tea, then set the cup down. "I have to go back to Nathan's."

"You don't have to do anything tonight but get some rest."

"No, I never asked why or how or . . ." She shut her eyes. "I have to have the answers. I don't think I can live with this until I have the answers. When I go to my family, I have to know it all."

"You could go to them now, I'll go with you. You could ask the questions together."

"I have to do it alone. I'm at the center of this, Kirby." Jo's head throbbed nastily. When she opened her eyes they were brutally dark in a colorless face. "I'm in love with the man whose father murdered my mother."

. . .

When Kirby dropped her off at Nathan's cottage, Jo could see his silhouette through the screen door. She wondered if either of them would ever do a harder thing in their lives than facing the past and each other.

He said nothing as she climbed the steps, but opened the door, stepped back to let her in. He'd thought he would never see her again, and he wasn't sure whether that would have been harder to live with, or if seeing her like this—pale and stricken—was worse.

"I need to ask you . . . I need to know."

"I'll tell you what I can."

She rubbed her hands together so that the small pain of her scratched palms would keep her centered. "Did they—were they involved?"

"No." He wanted to turn away but forced himself to face the pain in her eyes. "There was nothing like that between them. Even in the journal, he wrote that she was devoted to her family. To her children, her husband. Jo—"

"But he wanted there to be. He wanted her." She opened her hands. "They fought? There was an accident." Her breath shuddered, and the words were a plea. "It was an accident."

"No. God." It was worse, he thought, by every second that passed it grew worse. "He knew her habits. He studied them. She used to walk, at night, around the gardens."

"She . . . she loved the flowers at night." The dream she'd had the night they'd found Susan Peters spun back into her mind. "She loved the white ones especially. She loved the smells and the quiet. She called it her alone time."

"He chose the night," Nathan continued. "He put a sleeping pill into my mother's wine so she . . . so she wouldn't know he'd been gone. Everything he did he documented step by step in his journal. He wrote that he waited for Annabelle at the edge of the forest to the west of the house." It was killing him by degrees to say it, to look into Jo's face and say it. "He knocked her unconscious and took her into the forest. He had everything set up. He'd already set up his lights, his tripod. It wasn't an accident. It was planned. It was premeditated. It was deliberate."

"But why?" She had to sit. On legs stiff and brittle as twigs, she stumbled to a chair. "I remember him. He was kind to me. And patient. Daddy took him fishing. And Mama would make him pecan pie now and then because he was fond of it." She made a helpless sound, then pressed her fingers to her lips to hold it back. "Oh, God, you want me to believe he murdered her for no reason?"

"He had a purpose." He did turn away now and strode into the kitchen to drag a bottle of Scotch from a cupboard. "You could never call it a reason."

He splashed the liquor into a glass, tossed it back quickly, and hissed through the sting. With his palms braced on the counter, he waited for his blood to settle.

"I loved him, Jo. He taught me how to ride a bike, how to field a grounder. He paid attention. Whenever he traveled, he'd call home not just to talk to my mother but to all three of us. And he listened—not just the pretense of listening some adults think a child can't see through. He cared."

He turned back to her, his eyes eloquent. "He would bring my mother flowers for no reason. I'd lie in bed at night and listen to them laughing together. We were happy, and he was the center of it. Now I have to face that there was no center, that he was capable of something monstrous."

"I feel carved out," she managed. Her head seemed to be floating somewhere above her shoulders. "Scraped out. Raw. All these years." She squeezed her eyes tight a moment. "Your lives just went on?"

"He was the only one who knew, and he was very careful. Our lives just went on. Until his ended and I went through his personal papers and found the journal and photographs."

"Photographs." The floating sensation ended with a jerk. "Photographs of my mother. After she was dead."

He had to say it all, no matter how even the thought ripped through his brain. " 'The decisive moment,' he called it."

"Oh, my God." Lectures heard, lectures given, whirled in her head. *Capturing the decisive moment, anticipating when the dynamics of a situation will reach peak, knowing when to click the shutter to preserve that most powerful image.* "It was a study, an assignment."

"It was his purpose. To manipulate, to cause, to control, and to capture death." Nausea churned violently. He downed more Scotch, pitting the liquor against the nausea. "It wasn't all, it can't be. There was something warped inside him. Something we never saw. Something no one ever saw, or suspected. He had friends, a successful career. He liked to listen to ball games on TV and read mystery novels. He liked to barbecue, he wanted grandchildren."

It was tearing him apart, every word, every memory. "There is no defense," he said. "No absolution."

She stepped forward. Every emotion inside her coalesced and focused on one point. "He took photographs of her. Of her face. Her eyes. Of her body. Nudes. He posed her, carefully. Her head tilted down toward her left shoulder, her right arm draped across her midriff."

"How do you—"

"I did see." She closed her eyes and spun away. Relief was cold, painfully cold. An icy layer over hot grief. "I'm not crazy. I was never crazy. I didn't hallucinate. It was real. All of it."

"What are you talking about?"

Impatient, she dug her cigarettes out of her back pocket. But when she struck the match, she only stared down at the flame. "My hand's steady," she muttered. "It's perfectly steady. I'm not going to break now. I can get through it. I'm never going to break again."

Worried that he had pushed her over some line, he moved toward her. "Jo Ellen."

"I'm not crazy." Her head snapped up. Calmly she touched the flame to the tip of her cigarette. "I'm not going to shatter and fall ever again. The worst is just the next thing you have to find room for and live with." She blew out smoke, watched it haze, then vanish. "Someone sent me a photograph of my mother. One of your father's photographs."

His blood chilled. "That's impossible."

"I saw it. I had it in my hands. It's what snapped me, what I couldn't find room for. Then."

"You told me someone was sending you pictures of yourself."

"They were. It was with them, in the last package I got in Charlotte. And afterward, when I was able to function a little, I couldn't find it. Whoever sent it got into my apartment and took it back. I thought I was hallucinating. But it was real. It existed. It happened."

"I'm the only one who could have sent it to you. I didn't."

"Where are the pictures? The negatives?"

"They're gone."

"Gone? How?"

"Kyle wanted to destroy them, them and the journal. I refused. I wanted time to decide what to do. We argued about it. His stand was that it had been twenty years. What good would it do to bring it all out? It could ruin both of us. He was furious that I would even consider going to the police, or to your family. The next morning he was gone. He'd taken the photographs and the journal with him. I didn't know where to find him. The next I heard he'd drowned. I have to assume he couldn't live with it. That he destroyed everything, then himself."

"The photographs weren't destroyed." Her mind was very clear and cold. "They exist, just like the ones of me exist. I look like my mother. It's not a large leap to shift an obsession with her to one with me."

"Do you think I haven't thought of that, that it hasn't terrified me? When we found Susan Peters, and I realized how she'd died, I thought . . . I'm the only one left, Jo. I buried my father."

"But did you bury your brother?"

He stared, shook his head slowly. "Kyle's dead."

"How do you know? Because the reports say he got drunk and fell off a boat? And what if he didn't, Nathan? He had the photographs, the negatives, the journal."

"But he did drown. He was drunk, stumbling drunk, depressed, moody, according to the people who were with him on the yacht. They didn't realize he was missing until well into the next morning. All of his clothes, his gear were still on the boat."

When she said nothing, he spun around her and began to pace. "I have to accept what my father did, what he was. Now you want me to believe my brother's alive, that he's capable of all this. Of stalking you, pushing you until you collapse. Of following you here and . . ." As the rest slammed into him, he turned back. "Of killing Susan Peters."

"My mother was strangled, wasn't she, Nathan?"

"Yes. Christ."

She had to stay cold, Jo warned herself, and go to the next step. "Susan Peters was raped."

Understanding the question she was asking, Nathan closed his eyes. "Yes."

"If it wasn't her husband—"

"The police haven't found any evidence to hold the husband. I checked before I came back. Jo Ellen." It scraped his heart to tell her. "They're going to be looking more closely into Ginny's disappearance now."

"Ginny?" With understanding came horror. The cold that had shielded her melted away in it. "Oh, no. Ginny."

He couldn't touch her, could offer her nothing. He left her alone, stepped out onto the porch. He put his hands on the rail and leaned out, desperate for air. When the screen door squeaked, he made himself straighten.

"What was your father's purpose, Nathan? What were the photographs to accomplish if he would never be able to show them to anyone?"

"Perfection. Control. Not simply to observe, and preserve, but to be a part of the image. To create it. The perfect woman, the perfect crime, the perfect image. He thought she was beautiful, intelligent, gracious. She was worthy."

He watched fireflies light up the dark in quick, flirtatious winks. "I should have told you, all of you, as soon as I came here. I told myself I wanted—needed—time to try to understand it. I justified keeping it to myself because you had all accepted a lie, and the truth was worse. Then I kept it to myself because I wanted you. It got easier to rationalize it. You'd been hurt, you were wounded. It could wait until you trusted me. It could wait until you were in love with me."

His fingers flexed and released on the railing as she stood silent behind him. "Rationalizations are usually self-serving. Mine were. After Susan Peters, I couldn't ignore the truth anymore, or your right to know it. There's nothing I can do to change it, to atone for what he did. Nothing I can say can heal the damage he did to you and your family."

"No, there's nothing you can do, nothing you can say. He took my mother, and left us all to think she had abandoned us. That single selfish act damaged all of our lives, left a rift in our family we've never been able to heal. He must have hurt her." Jo's voice quavered so she bit down hard on her lip until she could steady it. "She must have been so frightened, so confused. She'd done nothing to deserve it, nothing but be who she was."

She drew a long breath, tasted the sea, and released it. "I wanted to blame you for it, Nathan, because you're here. Because you had your mother all your life. Because you touched me and made me feel what I'd never felt before. I needed to blame you for it. So I did."

"I expected you to."

"You never had to tell me. You could have buried it, forgotten it. I never would have known."

"I'd have known, and every day I'd have had with you would have been a betrayal." He turned to her. "I wish I could have lived with that, spared you this and saved myself. But I couldn't."

"And what now?" Lifting her face to the sky, she searched her heart. "Am I to make you pay what can't be paid, punish you for something that was done to both of us when we were children?"

"Why shouldn't you?" Bitterness clogged his throat as he looked out into the trees, where the river flowed in secret silence. "How could you look at me and not see him, and what he did? And hate me for it."

It was exactly what she had done, Jo thought. She had looked at him, seen his father, and hated. He had taken it, the verbal and physical blows, without a word in his own defense.

Courageous, Kirby had called him. And she'd been right.

How badly he'd been damaged, she realized. She wondered why it had taken her even this long to realize that however much harm had been done to her, an equal share had been done to him. "You don't give me much credit for intelligence or compassion. Obviously you have a very low opinion of me."

He hadn't known he had the strength left to be surprised. He stared at her in disbelief. "I don't understand you."

"No, you certainly don't if you think that after I'd had time to accept it, to grieve, I would blame you, or hold you accountable."

"He was my father."

"And if he was alive, I'd kill him myself for what he did to her, to all of us. To you. I'll hate him for the rest of my life. There will never be forgiveness in me for him. Can you make room to live with that, Nathan, or are you just going to walk away? I'll tell you what I'm going to do." She rushed on before he could speak, her words fast and hot. "I'm not going to let myself be cheated. I'm not going to let the chance of real happiness be stolen from me. But if you walk away, I'll learn to hate you. I can do it if I have to. And no one will ever hate you more than I will."

She stormed back into the house, slamming the door behind her.

He stood where he was for a moment, struggling to absorb the shock, the gratitude. But it wasn't possible. He stepped back into the house and spoke quietly. "Jo Ellen, do you want me to stay?"

"Isn't that what I just said?" She dragged out another cigarette, then furious, hurled it away. "Why should I have to lose again? Why should I have to be alone again? How could you come here and make me fall in love with you, then cut yourself out of my life because you think it's best for me? Because you think it's the honorable thing to do. Well, the hell with your honor, Nathan, the hell with it if it cheats me out of having what I need. I've been cheated before, lost what I needed desperately before, and was helpless to stop it. I'm not helpless anymore."

She was vibrating with fury, her eyes fired with it, her color high and glowing. He'd never seen anything, or anyone, more magnificent. "Of all the things I imagined you'd say to me tonight, this wasn't it. I'd prepared myself to lose you. I hadn't prepared myself to keep you."

"I'm not a damn cuff link, Nathan."

The laugh came as a surprise, felt rusty in his throat. "I can't decide what I should say to you. All I can think of is that I love you."

"That might be enough, if you were holding on to me when you said it."

His eyes stayed on hers as he walked toward her. His arms were tentative at first, then tightened, tightened until he buried his face in her hair. "I love you." Emotions swamped him as he drew in the scent of her, the taste of her skin against his lips. "I love you, Jo Ellen. Every part of you."

"Then we'll make it enough. We won't let this be taken away." Her voice was low and fierce. "We won't."

He lay very still, hoping she slept.

The woman beside him, the woman he loved, was in danger, the source of which was too abhorrent to him to name. He would protect her, with his life if necessary. He would kill to keep her safe, whatever the cost.

And he would hope that what they had together survived it.

There was no avoiding it. They had stolen a moment, taken something for themselves. But what haunted them, from twenty years before and now, would have to be faced.

"Nathan, I have to tell my family." In the dark she reached for his hand. "I need to find the right time and the right way. I want you to leave that to me."

"You have to let me be there, Jo. It should be done your way, but not alone."

"All right. But there are other things that need to be handled, need to be done."

"You need protection."

"Don't try to go white knight on me, Nathan. I find it irritating." The lazy comment ended on a gasp when he hauled her up to her knees.

"Nothing happens to you." His eyes gleamed dangerously in the dark. "Whatever it takes, I'm going to see to that."

"You'd better start by calming yourself down," she said evenly. "I'm of a mind that nothing happens to either of us. So we have to start thinking, and we have to start doing."

"There are going to be rules, Jo. The first is that you don't go anywhere alone. You don't step off your own porch by yourself until this is over."

"I'm not my mother, I'm not Ginny, I'm not Susan Peters. I'm not defenseless, or stupid or naive. I will not be hunted for someone's sport."

Because a show of temper would only wound her pride and make her angry, he latched on to calm. "If necessary, I'll haul you off the island just the way I hauled you here tonight. I'll take you somewhere safe and I'll lock you in. All it'll take to avoid that unhappy event is your promise not to go anywhere alone."

"You have an inflated image of your own capabilities."

"Not in this case I don't." He caught her chin in his hand. "Look at me, Jo. Look at me. You're everything. I'll take anything else, I'll face anything else, but I won't face losing you. Not again."

She trembled once, not from anger or fear but from the swift, hard flood of emotion. "No one's ever loved me this much. I can't get used to it."

"Practice—and promise."

"I won't go anywhere by myself." She let out a sigh. "This relationship business is nothing but a maze of concessions and compromises. That's probably why I've managed to avoid it all this time." She sat back on her heels. "We're not going to stand around and just let things happen. I'm not the only woman on the island." She trembled again. "I'm not Annabelle's only daughter."

"No, we're not going to stand around and wait. I'm going to make some calls, gather any information on Kyle's accident that I might have missed before. I wasn't thorough. It wasn't an easy time, and I might have let something slip by."

"What about his friends, his finances?"

"I don't know a lot about either. We weren't as close the last few years as we used to be." Nathan rose to open the windows and let in the air. "We drifted into different places, became different people."

"What kind of a person did he become?"

"He was . . . I guess you'd call him a present-focused sort. He was interested in now—seize the moment and wring it dry. Don't worry about later, about consequences or payment. He never hurt anyone but himself."

It was vitally important that she understand that. Just as important, Nathan realized, that he understand it himself. "Kyle just preferred the easy way, and if the easy way had a shortcut, all the better. He had a lot of charm, and he had talent. Dad was always saying if Kyle would put as much effort into his work as he did his play, he'd be one of the top photographers in the world. Kyle said Dad was too critical of his work, never satisfied, jealous because he had his whole life and career ahead of him."

He paused, listened to the words replay in his head. And suffered their implication. Was it competition? A twisted need for the son to outdo the father? His head began to pound again, hard beats at the temples.

"I'll make the calls," Nathan said flatly. "If we can eliminate that possibility, we can concentrate on others. Kyle might have gotten drunk, showed the photos to a friend, an associate."

"Maybe." It wasn't an area Jo wanted to push just then. "Whoever is responsible has a solid knowledge of photography, and quite a bit of skill. It's inconsistent, occasionally lazy, but it's skill."

Nathan only nodded. She'd just described his brother perfectly.

"He would have to be doing his own developing," she continued, relieved to be able to concentrate on practical steps. "Which means access to a darkroom. He must have had one in Charlotte, and then when he came down here, he'd have needed to arrange for another. The package I got here was mailed from Savannah."

"You can rent darkroom time."

"Yeah, and that might be what he did. Or he rented an apartment, a house, brought in his own equipment. Or bought new. He would have more control, wouldn't he, if it was his own place, his own equipment?" Her eyes met Nathan's.

"That's what drives this. The control. He could go back and forth between the mainland and the island. He'd be in control."

To control the moment, to manipulate the mood, the subject, the outcome. That is the true power of art. His father's words, he remembered, neatly written on the page.

"Yes, it's about control. So we check photo supply outlets, find out if someone ordered equipment to outfit a darkroom and had it shipped to Savannah. It won't be easy, and it won't be quick."

"No, but it's a start." It was good to think, to have a tangible task. "He'd likely be alone. He needs the freedom to come and go as he pleases. He took pictures of me all over the island, so he's wandering around freely. We can keep our eye out for a man alone with a camera, though we're just as likely to jump some harmless bird-watcher."

"If it was Kyle, I'd know him. I'd recognize him."

"Would you, Nathan? If he didn't want you to? He'd know you're here. And he'd know that I've been with you. Annabelle Hathaway's daughter with David Delaney's son. There are some who might see that as coming full circle. And if that's so, I don't believe you're any safer than I am."

27

Jo slept into midday and woke alone. She couldn't remember the last time she'd slept until ten, or when she had enjoyed such a deep and dreamless sleep.

She wondered if she should have been restless, edgy, or weepy. Perhaps she'd been all of those things long enough, and there was no need to go on with them now that she knew the truth. She could grieve for her mother. And for a woman the same age as Jo was now who had faced the worst kind of horror.

But more, she could grieve for the years lost in the condemnation of a mother, a wife, a woman who had done nothing more sinful than catch the eye of a madman.

Now there could be healing.

"He loves me, Mama," she whispered. "Maybe that's fate's way of paying us all back for being cruel and heartless twenty years ago. I'm happy. No matter how crazy the world is right now, I'm happy with him."

She swung her legs over the side of the bed. Starting today, she promised herself, they were going to stand together and fight back.

In the living room, Nathan finished up yet another call, this one to the American consulate in Nice. He hadn't slept. His eyes were gritty, his soul scorched. He felt as if he were running in circles, pulling together information, searching for any hint, any whisper that he'd missed months before.

And all the while he dealt with the dark guilt that his deepest hope was to confirm that his own brother was dead.

He looked up as he heard footsteps mounting his stairs. Working up a smile when he saw Giff behind the screen, he waved him in as he completed the call.

"Didn't mean to interrupt you," Giff said.

"No problem. I'm finished, for now."

"I was heading out to do a little work on Live Oak Cottage and thought I'd drop off these plans. You said how you wouldn't mind taking a look at the design I've been working up for the solarium at Sanctuary."

"I'd love to see it." Grateful for the diversion, Nathan walked over to take the plans and unroll them on the kitchen table. "I had some ideas on that myself, then I got distracted."

"Well." Giff tucked his tongue in his cheek as Jo walked out from the bedroom. "Understandable enough. Morning, Jo Ellen."

She could only hope she didn't flush like a beet and compound the embarrassment as both men stared at her. She'd pulled on one of Nathan's T-shirts and nothing else. Though the bottom of it skimmed her thighs, she imagined it was obvious that she wore nothing under it.

This would teach her, she supposed, to follow the scent of coffee like a rat to the tune of the pipe. "Morning, Giff."

"I was just dropping something off here."

"Oh, well, I was just . . . going to get some coffee." She decided to brazen it out and walked to the counter to pour a mug. "I'll just take it with me."

Giff couldn't help himself. It was such a situation. And since he was dead sure Lexy would want all the details, he tried for more. "You might want to take a look yourself. Kate's got that bee in her bonnet about this sunroom add-on. You always had a good eye for things."

Manners or dignity. It was an impossible decision for a woman raised on Southern traditions. Jo did her best to combine both and stepped over to study the drawing. She puzzled over what appeared to be a side view of a long, graduated curve with a lot of neatly printed numbers and odd lines.

Nathan ordered himself to shift his attention from Jo's legs back to the drawing. "It's a good concept. You do the survey?"

"Yeah, me and Bill. He does survey work over to the mainland, had the equipment."

"You know, if you came out at an angle"—he used his finger to draw the line—"rather than straight, you could avoid excavating over here, and you'd gain the benefit of using the gardens as part of the structure."

"If you did that, wouldn't you cut off this corner, here? Wouldn't it make it tight and awkward coming out from the main house? Miss Kate'd go into conniptions if I started talking about moving doorways or windows."

"You don't have to move any of the existing structure." Nathan slid the side view over to reveal Giff's full view. "Nice work," he murmured. "Really nice. Jo, get me a sheet of that drawing paper over there." Nathan gestured absently. "I've got men in my firm who don't have the skill to do freehand work like this."

"No shit?" Giff forgot Jo completely and goggled at the back of Nathan's head.

"You ever decide to go back for that degree and want to apprentice, you let me know."

He picked up a pencil and began to sketch on the paper Jo had put in front of him. "See, if you hitch it over this way, not so much of an angle as a flow. It's a female house, you don't want sharp points. You keep it all in the same tone as the curve of the roof, then instead of lining out into the gardens, it pours through them."

"Yeah, I see it." He realized that his working drawing seemed stiff and amateurish beside the artist's. "I couldn't think of something like that, draw like that, in a million years."

"Sure you could. You'd already done the hard part. It's a hell of a lot easier for somebody to look at good, detailed work and shift a couple of things around to enhance it than it is to come up with the basic concept in the first place."

Nathan straightened, contemplated his quick sketch through narrowed eyes. He could see it, complete and perfect. "Your way might suit the client better. It's more cost-effective and more traditional."

"Your way's more artistic."

"It isn't always artistic that the client wants." Nathan put his pencil down. "Anyway, you think about it, or show the works to Kate and let her think about it. Whichever choice, we can do some refining before you break ground."

"You'll work with me on it?"

"Sure." Without thinking, Nathan picked up Jo's coffee mug and drank. "I'd like to."

Revved, Giff gathered up the drawings. "I think I'll just swing by and drop these off for Miss Kate now. Give her some time to mull it over. I'm really obliged, Nathan." He tugged on the brim of his cap. "See you, Jo."

Jo leaned against the counter and watched as Nathan got another sheet of drawing paper. Finishing off her coffee, he started another sketch.

"You don't even know what you just did," she murmured.

"Hmm. How far is that perennial bed with the tall blue flowers, the spiky ones? How far is that from the corner here?"

"Nope." She got herself another mug. "You don't have a clue what you've done."

"About what? Oh." He looked down at the mug. "Sorry. I drank your coffee."

"Besides that—which I found both annoying and endearing." She slid her arms around his waist. "You're a good man, Nathan. A really good man."

"Thanks." Normality, he promised himself. Just for an hour, they would take normality. "Is that because I didn't give you a little swat on the bottom when you strolled out here in my shirt—even though I wanted to?"

"No, that just makes you a smart man. But you're a good one. You didn't see his face." She lifted her hands to his cheeks. "You didn't even notice."

At sea, he shook his head. "Apparently I didn't. Are you talking about Giff?"

"I don't know anyone who doesn't like Giff, and I don't know many who think of him as anything more than an affable and reliable handyman. Nathan—" She touched her lips to his. "You just told him he was more, and could be more yet. And you did it so casually, so matter-of-factly, he can't help but believe you."

She rose up on her toes to press her cheek to his. "I really like you right now, Nathan. I really like who you are."

"I like you, too." He closed his arms around her and swayed. "And I'm really starting to like who we are."

Kirby had a firm grip on her pride as she walked into Sanctuary. If Jo was there, she would find a way to speak to her privately. Her strict code of ethics wouldn't permit her to tell any of the Hathaways what she'd learned the night before. If Jo had come home after speaking with Nathan again, Kirby imagined the house would be in an uproar.

If nothing else, she could stand as family doctor.

But that wasn't why she'd been summoned.

She had planned her visit to avoid Brian, using that window of time between breakfast and the midday meal. And she'd used the visitors' front door rather than the friends' entrance through the kitchen.

Since they had managed to avoid each other for a week, she thought, they could do so for another day. She wouldn't have come at all if Kate hadn't hailed her with an SOS after one of the guests slipped on the stairs. Even as she turned toward them, Kate came hurrying down.

"Kirby, I can't tell you how much I appreciate this. It's a turned ankle, no more than that, I swear. But the woman is setting up such a to-do you'd think she'd broken every bone in her body in six places at once."

One glance at Kate's distracted face and Kirby knew that Jo had yet to speak of Annabelle. "It's all right, Kate."

"I know it's your afternoon off, and I hated to drag you over here, but she won't budge out of bed."

"It's no problem, really." Kirby followed her up the stairs. "It's better to have a look. If I think it's more than a strain, we'll x-ray and ship her off to the mainland."

"One way to get her out of my hair," Kate muttered. She knocked briskly on a door. "Mrs. Tores, the doctor's here to see you. Bill the inn," Kate added to Kirby in an undertone, "and add whatever you like for a nuisance fee."

Thirty minutes later, and more than a little frazzled, Kirby closed the bedroom door behind her. Her head was aching from the litany of complaints Mrs. Tores had regaled her with. As she paused to rub her temples, Kate peeked around the corner.

"Safe?"

"I was tempted to sedate her, but I resisted. She's perfectly fine, Kate. Believe me, I know. I had to give her what amounts to a complete physical before she was satisfied. Her ankle is barely strained, her heart is as strong as a team of oxen, her lungs even stronger. For your sake, I hope she's planning on a very short stay."

"She leaves day after tomorrow, thank the Lord. Come on down. Let me get you a nice glass of lemonade, a piece of that cherry pie Brian made yesterday."

"I really need to get back. I've got stacks of paperwork to wade through."

"I'm not sending you back without a cold drink. This heat's enough to fell a horse."

"I like the heat," she began, then came to a dead halt as Brian walked in the front door.

His arms were full of flowers. They should have made him look foolish. She wanted him to look foolish. Instead he looked all the more male, all the more attractive, with his tanned, well-muscled arms loaded down with freshly cut blossoms.

"Oh, Brian, I'm so glad you got to that." Kate hurried down with her mind racing at light-speed. "I was going to cut for the fresh arrangements myself this morning, but this crisis with Mrs. Tores threw me off my stride."

She chattered on as she transferred flowers from his arms to hers. "I'll just take it from here. You don't have any sense at all about how to arrange them. I swear, Kirby, the man just stuffs them into a vase and thinks that's all there is to it. Brian, you go fix Kirby a lemonade, make her eat a piece of pie. She's come all the way out here just to do me a favor, and I won't have her going off until she's been paid back. Run along now, while I take this upstairs."

She headed up the steps, willing the two of them not to behave like fools.

"I don't need anything," Kirby said stiffly. "I was just on my way out."

"I imagine you can spare five minutes to have a cold drink and avoid hurting Kate's feelings."

"Fine. It's a quicker trip home through the back anyway." She turned and started down the hall at a brisk pace. She wanted to be away from him. When he found out about his mother, she would do what she could for him. But for now she had her own pain to cope with.

"How's the patient?"

"She could dance a jig if she wanted to. There's not a thing wrong with her." She pushed through the door and stood stubbornly while he got out a pitcher of golden-yellow lemonade swimming with mint and pulp. When her mouth watered, she swallowed resolutely. "How's your hand?"

"It's all right. I don't really notice it."

"I might as well look at it while I'm here." She set her bag down on the breakfast table. "The sutures should have been removed a couple of days ago."

"You were leaving."

"It'll save you a trip out to see me."

He stopped pouring her lemonade and looked at her. The sun was streaming through the window at her back, licking light over her hair. Her eyes were a dark, stormy green that made his loins tighten.

"All right." He carried her glass to the table and sat down.

Despite the heat, her hands were cool. Despite her anger, they were gentle. She saw no swelling or puffiness, no sign of infection. The edges of the wound had fused neatly. He would barely have a scar, she decided, and opened her bag for her suture scissors.

"This won't take long."

"Just don't put any new holes in me."

She clipped the first suture, tugged it free with tweezers. "Since we both live on this island, and it's likely we'll be running into each other on a regular basis for the rest of our lives, perhaps you'd do me the courtesy of clearing the air."

"It's clear enough, Kirby."

"For you, apparently. But not for me." She clipped, tugged. "I want to know why you turned away from me. Why you decided to end things between us the way you did."

"Because they'd gone farther than I'd intended them to. Neither one of us thought it would work. I just decided to back off first, that's all."

"Oh, I see. You dumped me before I could dump you."

"More or less." He wished he couldn't smell her. He wished she'd had the decency not to rub that damned peach-scented lotion all over her skin to torment him. "I'd see it more as just a matter of simplifying."

"And you like things simple, don't you? You like things your way, in your time and at your pace."

Her voice was mild, and though he wasn't sure he could trust it, particularly when she had a sharp implement in her hand, he nodded. "That's true enough. You're the same, but your way, your time, and your pace are different from mine."

"I can't argue with that. You prefer a malleable woman, a delicate woman. One who sits patiently and waits for your move and your whim. That certainly doesn't describe me."

"No, it doesn't. And the fact is I wasn't looking for a woman—or a relationship, whatever you choose to call it. You came after me, and you're beautiful. I got tired of pretending I didn't want you."

"That's fair. And the sex was good for both of us, so there shouldn't be any complaints." She removed the last suture. "All done." She lifted her eyes to his. "All done, Brian. The scar will fade. Before long, you won't even remember you were hurt. Now that the air's all clear, I'll be on my way."

He remained where he was when she rose. "I appreciate it."

"Don't give it a thought," she said with a voice like frosted roses. "I won't." She left by the back, quietly and deliberately closing the screen behind her.

She didn't start to run until she was into the shelter of the trees.

"Well, that was fun." Brian picked up Kirby's untouched lemonade and downed it in several long gulps. It hit his tortured stomach like acid.

He'd done the right thing, hadn't he? For himself and probably for her. He'd kept things from stringing out, getting too deep and complicated. All he'd done was nick her pride, and she had plenty of it to spare. Pride and class and brains and a tidy little body with the energy of a nuclear warhead.

Christ, she was a hell of a woman.

No, he'd done the right thing, he assured himself, and ran the cold glass over his forehead because he suddenly felt viciously hot inside and out. She would have set him aside eventually and left him slack-jawed and shot in the knees.

Women like Kirby Fitzsimmons didn't stay. Not that he wanted any woman to stay, but if a man was going to start fantasizing, if he was going to start believing in marriage and family, she was just the type to draw him in, then leave him twisting in the wind.

She had too much fuel, too much nerve to stay on Desire. The right offer from the right hospital or medical institute or whatever, and she'd be gone before the sand settled back in her footprints.

God, he'd never seen anything like the way she'd handled Susan Peters's body. The way she'd turned from woman to rock, clipping out orders in that cool, steady voice, her eyes flat, her hands without the slightest tremor.

It had been an eye-opener for him, all right. This wasn't some fragile little flower who would be content to treat poison ivy and sunburn on a nowhere dot in the ocean for long. Hook herself up with an innkeeper who made the best part of his living whipping up soufflés and frying chicken? Not in this lifetime, he told himself.

So it was done, and over, and his life would settle back quietly into the routine he preferred.

Fucking rut, he thought on a sudden surge of fury. He nearly hurled the glass into the sink when he spotted her medical bag on the table. She'd left her bag, he mused, opening it and idly poking through the contents.

She could just come back and get it herself, he decided. He had things to do. He couldn't be chasing after her just because she'd been in a snit and left it behind.

Of course, she might need it. You couldn't be sure when some medical emergency would come along. It would be his fault, wouldn't it, if she didn't have her needles and prodding things. Someone could up and die, couldn't they?

He didn't want that on his conscience. With a shrug, he picked the bag up, found it heavier than he'd imagined. He thought he'd just run it over to her, drop it off, and that would be that.

He decided to take the car rather than cut through the forest. It was too damn hot to walk. And besides, if she'd dawdled at all he might beat her there. He could just leave the bag inside her door and drive off before she even got home.

When he pulled up in her drive, he thought he had accomplished just that and was disgusted with himself for being disappointed. He didn't want to see her again. That was the whole point.

But when he was halfway up the steps, he realized she'd beaten him back after all. He could hear her crying.

It stopped him in his tracks, the sound of it. Hard, passionate sobs, raw gulps of air. It shook him right to the bone, left him dry-mouthed and loose at the knees. He wondered if there was anything more fearful a man could face than a weeping woman.

He opened the door quietly, eased it shut. His nerves were shot as he started back to her bedroom, shifting her bag from hand to hand.

She was curled up on the bed, a tight ball of misery with her hair curtaining her face. He'd dealt with wild female tears before. A man couldn't live with Lexy half his life and avoid that. But he'd never expected such unrestrained weeping from Kirby. Not the woman who had challenged him to resist her, not the woman who had faced the result of murder without a quiver. Not the woman who had just walked out of his kitchen with her head high and her eyes cold as the North Atlantic.

With Lexy it was either get the hell out and bar the door or gather her up close and hold on until the storm passed. He decided to hold on and, sitting on the side of the bed, he reached out to bundle her to him.

She shot up straight as an arrow, slapping out sharply at the hands that reached for her. Patiently, he persisted—and found himself holding on to a hundred pounds of furious woman.

"Get out of here! Don't you touch me." The humiliation on top of the hurt was more than she could stand. She kicked, shoved, then scrambled off the far side of the bed. Standing there, she glared at him through puffy eyes even as fresh sobs choked her.

"How dare you come in here? Get the hell out!"

"You left your doctor's bag." Because he felt foolish half sprawled over her bed, he straightened up and faced her across it. "I heard you crying. I didn't mean to make you cry. I didn't know I could."

She pulled tissues out of the box on the bedside table and mopped at her face. "What makes you think I'm crying over you?"

"Since I don't expect you ran into anyone else in the last five minutes who would set you off like this, it's a reasonable assumption."

"And you're so reasonable, aren't you, Brian?" She yanked out more tissues, littering the floor with them. "I was indulging myself. I'm entitled to that. Now I'd like you to leave me alone."

"If I hurt you—"

"*If* you hurt me?" Out of desperation she grabbed the box of tissues and threw it at him. "If you hurt me, you son of a bitch. What am I, rubber, that you can slap at me and it bounces off? You say you're falling in love with me, then you turn around and calmly tell me that it's over."

"I said I thought I was falling in love with you." It was vital, he thought with a little squirm of panic, to make that distinction. "I stopped it."

"You—" Rage really did make you see red, she realized. Her vision was lurid with it as she grabbed the closest thing at hand and heaved it.

"Jesus, woman!" Brian jerked as the small crystal vase whizzed by his head like a glittering bullet. "You break open my face, you're just going to have to stitch it up again."

"The hell I will." She grabbed a favorite perfume atomizer from her dresser and let it fly. "You can bleed to death and I won't lift a finger. To fucking death, you bastard."

He ducked, dodged, and was just fast enough to tackle her before she cracked him over the head with a silver-backed mirror. "I can hold you down as long as it takes," he panted out as he used his weight to press her into the mattress. "Damned if I'm going to let you take a chunk out of me because I bruised your pride."

"My pride?" She stopped struggling and her eyes went from hot to overflowing. "You broke my heart." She turned her head, closed her eyes, and let the tears slide free. "Now I don't have any pride to bruise."

Staggered, he leaned back. She simply turned on her side and curled up again. She didn't sob now but lay silent with tears wet on her cheeks.

"Leave me alone, Brian."

"I thought I could. I thought you'd want me to do just that sooner or later. So why not sooner? You won't stay." He spoke quietly, trailing a finger through her hair. "Not here, not with me. And if I don't step back, it'll kill me when you leave."

She was too tired even to cry now. She slipped a hand under her cheek for comfort and opened her eyes. "Why won't I stay?"

"Why would you? You can go anywhere you want. New York, Chicago, Los Angeles. You're young, you're beautiful, you're smart. A doctor in any of those places is going to make piles of money, go to the country club every week, have a fancy office in some big, shiny building."

"If I'd wanted those things, I would already have them. If I wanted to be in New York or Chicago or L.A., I'd be there."

"Why aren't you?"

"Because I love it here. I always have. Because I'm practicing the kind of medicine here that I want to practice and living my life the way I want to live it."

"You come from a different place," he insisted. "A different lifestyle. Your daddy's rich—"

"And my ma is good-looking." She sniffled and didn't see the quick, involuntary quiver of his mouth.

"What I mean is—"

"I know what you mean." Her head felt like an overblown balloon ready to burst. Idly, she told herself she'd take something for it. In just a minute. "I don't care much for country clubs. They're usually stuffy and burdened with rules. Why would I want that when I can sit on my deck and see the ocean every day of my life? I can walk in the forest and spot a deer, watch the mists rise off the river."

She shifted just a little so she could see his face. "Tell me, Brian, why do you stay here? You could go to any of those places you named, run the kitchen in a fine hotel, or own your own restaurant. Why don't you?"

"It's not what I want. I have what I want here."

"So do I." She turned her cheek back against the bedspread. "Now go away and leave me alone."

He got up and stood looking down at her. He felt big and awkward and out of his depth. Hooking his thumbs in his front pockets, he paced away, paced back, turned to stare out the window, to stare back at her. She didn't move, didn't speak. He cursed under his breath, hissed out a breath, and started for the door. Turned back.

"I wasn't truthful with you before. I didn't stop it, Kirby. I wanted to, but I couldn't. And it wasn't just thinking, it was . . . being. I'd rather not be, I'll tell you that straight out. I'd rather not be, because it's bound to be a mess somewhere along the line. But there it is."

She brushed a hand over her cheek and sat up. No, he did not have the look of a happy man, she decided. There was resentment in his eyes, stubbornness in his mouth, and annoyance in his stance. "Is this your charming way of telling me you're in love with me?"

"That's what I said. It so happens I'm not feeling very charming at the moment."

"You boot me out of your life, you humiliate me by catching me at a weak moment, you insult me by denying my feelings and my character, then you tell me you love me." She shook her head, pushed her damp hair back from her face. "Well, this is certainly the romantic moment every woman dreams of."

"I'm just telling you the way it is, the way I feel."

She let loose a sigh. If in a corner of her heart joy was blooming, she decided to hold it in check, just for a while. "Since for some reason that I can't quite remember I seem to be in love with you too, I'm going to make a suggestion."

"I'm listening."

"Why don't we take a walk on the beach, a nice long walk? The air might clear your brain enough for you to find a few drops of charm. Then you can try to tell me again, the way it is, and the way you feel."

He considered her, discovered his head was already clearing. "I wouldn't mind a walk," he said and held out a hand for hers.

28

Something bad was in the air. Sam could sense it. It was more than the thick heat, more than the hard look to the sky. He had some worries about Hurricane Carla, which was currently kicking the stuffing out of the Bahamas. The forecasters claimed she was primed to dance her way out to sea, but Sam knew hurricanes were essentially female. And females were essentially unpredictable.

Odds were she'd give Desire a miss and take out her temper on Florida. But he didn't like the feel to the air. It was too damn tight, he thought. Like it was ready to squeeze over your skin.

He was going to go in and check the little weather station Kate had gotten him last Christmas, do a run on the shortwave. There was a storm coming, all right. He wished he knew when it was coming.

As he crested the hill he saw the couple at the edge of the east garden. The sun was slanting over them, turning Jo's hair into glittering flame. Her body was angled forward, balanced against the man's with a kind of yearning it was impossible not to recognize.

The Delaney boy, Sam thought, grown up to a man. And the man had his hands on Sam's daughter's butt. Sam blew out a breath, wondered just how he was supposed to feel about that.

Their eyes were full of each other, and with a fluid shift of bodies their mouths tangled. It was the kind of hotly intimate kiss that made it obvious they'd been spending time doing a lot more to each other.

And how was he supposed to feel about that?

Time was, young people wouldn't neck right out in the open that way. He remembered when he'd been courting Annabelle, the way they'd snuck off like thieves. They'd done their groping in private. Why, if Belle's daddy had ever come across them this way, there'd have been hell to pay.

He walked on, making sure his footsteps were loud enough to wake the dead and the dreaming. Didn't even have the courtesy to jerk apart and look guilty, Sam thought. They just eased apart, linked hands, and turned toward him.

"There's guests inside the house, Jo Ellen, and they ain't paying for a floor show."

Surprised, she blinked at him. "Yes, Daddy."

"You want to be free with your affections, do it someplace that won't set tongues wagging from here to Savannah."

Wisely, she swallowed the chuckle, lowered her eyes before he caught the gleam of laughter in them, and nodded. "Yes, sir."

Sam shifted his feet, planted them, and looked at Nathan. "Seems to me you're old enough to strap down your glands in a public place."

Following Jo's lead and warned by the quick squeeze of her hand, Nathan kept his tone sober and respectful. "Yes, sir."

Satisfied, if not completely fooled, by their responses, Sam frowned up at the sky. "Storm coming," he muttered. "Going to give us a knock no matter what the weatherman says."

He was making conversation, Jo realized, and shoved her shock aside to fall in. "Carla's category two, and on dead aim for Cuba. They're saying it's likely she'll head out to sea."

"She doesn't care what they say. She'll do as she pleases." He turned his gaze on Nathan again, measuring. "Don't get knocked by hurricanes much in New York City, I expect."

Was that a challenge? Nathan wondered. A subtle swing at his manhood?

"No. I was in Cozumel when Gilbert pummeled it, though." He nearly mentioned the tornado he'd watched sweep like vengeance across Oklahoma and the avalanche that had thundered down the mountain pass near his chalet when he'd been working in Switzerland.

"Well, then, you know," Sam said simply. "I hear that you and Giff got a mind to do that sunroom Kate's been pining for."

"It's Giff's project. I'm just tossing in some ideas."

"Guess you got ideas enough. Why don't you show me then what y'all have in mind to do to my house?"

"Sure, I can give you the general layout."

"Fine. Jo Ellen, I suspect your young man figures on finagling dinner. Go tell Brian he's got another mouth to feed."

Jo opened her mouth, but her father was already walking away. She could do no more than shrug at Nathan and turn to the house.

When she stepped into the kitchen, Brian was busy at the counter de-heading shrimp. And singing, she realized with a jolt. Under his breath and off-key, but singing.

"What's come over this place?" she demanded. "Daddy's holding full conversations and asking to see solarium plans, you're singing in the kitchen."

"I wasn't singing."

"You were too singing. It was a really lousy rendition of 'I Love Rock and Roll,' but it could be loosely described as singing."

"So what? It's my kitchen."

"That's more like it." She went to the fridge for a beer. "Want one of these?"

"I guess I wouldn't turn it down. I'm losing weight just standing here." He swiped the back of his hand over his sweaty forehead and took the bottle she'd opened for him. He took a long swallow, then tucked his tongue in his cheek. "So, is Nathan able to walk without a limp today?"

"Yeah, but I bloodied his lip." She reached into the white ceramic cookie jar and dug out a chocolate-chip. "A brother with any sense of decency would have bloodied it for me."

"You always said you preferred fighting your own battles. How in God's name can you chase cookies with beer? It's revolting."

"I'm enjoying it. You want any help in here?"

It was his turn to experience shock. "Define 'help.' "

"Assistance," she snapped. "Chopping something, stirring something."

He took another pull on his beer as he considered her. "I could use some carrots, peeled and grated."

"How many?"

"Twenty dollars' worth. That's what you cost me."

"Excuse me?"

"Just a little wager with Lexy. A dozen," he said and turned back to his shrimp.

She got the carrots out, began to remove the peels in slow, precise strips.

"Brian, if there was something you believed all your life, something you'd learned to live with, but that something wasn't true, would you be better off going on the way you'd always gone on, or finding out it was something different? Something worse."

"You can let a sleeping dog lie, but it's hard to rest easy. You never know when it's going to wake up and go for your throat." He slid the shrimp into a boiling mixture of water, beer, and spices. "Then again, you let the dog lie long enough, it gets old and feeble and its teeth fall out."

"That's not a lot of help."

"That wasn't much of a question. You're getting peelings all over the floor."

"So, I'll sweep them up." She wanted to sweep the words up with them, under the first handy rug. But she would always know they were there. "Do you think a man, a perfectly normal man, with a family, a job, a house in the suburbs, a man who plays catch with his son on a Sunday afternoon and brings his wife roses on a Wednesday evening, could have another side? A cold, dark side that no one sees, a side that's capable of doing something unspeakable, then folding back into itself so he can root at the Little League game on Saturday and take the family out for ice cream sodas afterward?"

Brian got the colander out for the shrimp and set it in the sink. "You're full of odd questions this evening, Jo Ellen. You writing a book or something?"

"Can't you just tell me what you think? Can't you just have an opinion on a subject and say what it is?"

"All right." Baffled, he tipped the lid to the pot to give the shrimp a quick stir. "If you want to be philosophical, the Jekyll and Hyde theme has always fascinated people. Good and evil existing side by side in the same personality. There's none of us without shadows."

"I'm not talking about shadows. About a man who gives in to temptation and cheats on his wife one afternoon at the local motel, or who skims the till at work. I'm talking about real evil, the kind that doesn't carry a breath of guilt or conscience with it. Yet it doesn't show, not even to the people closest to it."

"Seems to me the easiest evil to hide is one with no conscience tagged to it. If you don't feel remorse or responsibility, there's no mirror reflecting back."

"No mirror reflecting back," she repeated. "It would be like black glass, wouldn't it? Opaque."

"Do you have any other cheerful remarks or suppositions to discuss?"

"How's this? Can the apple fall far from the tree?"

With a half laugh, Brian hefted the pot and poured shrimp and steaming water into the colander. "I'd say that depended entirely on the apple. A firm, healthy one might take a few good bounces and roll. You had one going rotten, it'd just plop straight down at the trunk."

He turned, mopping his brow again and reaching for his beer when he caught her eye. "What?" he demanded as she stared at him, her eyes dark and wide, her face pale.

"That's exactly right," she said quietly. "That's so exactly right."

"I'm hell on parables."

"I'm going to hold you to that one, Brian." She turned back to her grating. "After dinner, we need to talk. All of us. I'll tell the others. We'll use the family parlor."

"All of us, in one place? Who do you want to punish?"

"It's important, Brian. It's important to all of us."

"I don't see why I have to twiddle my thumbs around here when I've got a date." Looking at her image in the mirror behind the bar, Lexy fussed with her hair. "It's nearly eleven o'clock already. Giff's liable to just give up waiting and go to bed."

"Jo said it was important," Kate reminded her. She fought to make her knitting needles click rhythmically rather than bash together. She'd been working on the same afghan for ten years and was bound and determined to conquer it before another decade passed.

"Then where is she?" Lexy demanded, whirling around. "I don't see anybody here but you and me. Brian's probably snuck off to Kirby's, Daddy's holed up with his shortwave tracking that damned hurricane—and it isn't even coming around here."

"They'll be along. Why don't you fix us all a nice glass of wine, honey?" It was one of Kate's little dreams, having her family all gathered together, cooling off after a hot day, sharing the events of it.

"Seems like I'm always waiting on somebody. I swear, the last thing I'll do to keep the wolf away from the door when I go back to New York is wait tables."

Sam ducked his head and stepped in. He glanced at Kate with amusement. That blanket never seemed to grow by much, he thought, but somehow or other it got uglier every time she dragged it out. "You know what the girl's got on her mind?"

"No, I don't," Kate said placidly. "But sit down. Lexy's getting us some wine."

"Sooner have a beer, if it's all the same."

"Well, place your orders," Lexy said testily. "I live to serve."

"I can fetch my own."

"Oh, sit down." She waved a hand at him. "I'll get it."

Feeling chastised, he lowered himself to the couch beside Kate, drummed his fingers on his knee. He looked up when Lexy held out a brimming pilsner. "Guess you want a tip now." When she arched a brow, he nodded soberly. "Recycle. The world is your backyard."

Kate's needles stilled, Lexy stared. As color crept up his throat, Sam stared into his beer.

"My God, Sam, you made a joke. Lexy, you be sure to remind me to mark this down on my Year-at-a-Glance calendar."

"Sarcastic woman's the reason I keep my mouth shut in the first place," he muttered, and Kate's laugh tinkled out.

She patted Sam's knee affectionately while Lexy grinned down at them.

That's what Jo saw when she came in. Her father, her cousin, and her sister sharing a moment together while Kate's laughter rang out.

Her heart sank. It was an image she'd never expected to see, one she hadn't known could be so precious to her. Now she, and the man who stood behind her, could destroy it.

"There she is." Kate continued to beam, and when she spotted Nathan, her idea of what Jo had wanted the family to hear took on the hint of orange blossoms and bridal lace. Fluttering, she set her knitting aside. "We were just having some wine. Maybe we should make it champagne instead, just for fun."

"No, wine's fine." Her nerves screaming, Jo hurried in. "Don't get up, Kate, I'll get it."

"I hope this won't take long, Jo. I've got plans."

"I'm sorry, Lexy." Jo clinked glasses together in her hurry to have it done.

"Sit down," Kate hissed, rolling her eyes, wiggling her brows to try to give Lexy a hint. "Make yourself comfortable, Nathan. I'm sure Brian will be right along. Oh, here he is now. Brian, turn up the fan a little, will you? This heat's just wilting. Must be cooler at your place by the river, Nathan."

"Some." He sat, knowing he had to let Jo set the pace. But he looked at Sam. They'd spend twenty minutes together that evening, outlining plans, discussing structure and form. And all the while Nathan had tasted the bitter tang of deceit.

It was time to open it up, spread it out, and accept the consequences. "I'm sorry?" he said, realizing abruptly that Kate was speaking to him.

"I was just asking if you're finding it as easy to work here as you do in New York."

"It's a nice change." His eyes met Jo's as she brought him a glass of wine. Get it done, he asked her silently. Get it finished.

"Would you sit down, Brian?" she murmured.

"Hmm." She'd interrupted his daydream about wandering over to Kirby's shortly and waking her up in a very specific and interesting manner. "Sure."

He settled into a chair and decided he'd never been more relaxed or content in his life. He even gave Lexy a quick wink when she sat on the arm beside him.

"I don't know how to begin, how to tell you." Jo took a bracing breath. "I wish I could take the chance and let sleeping dogs lie." She caught Brian's eye, saw the flicker of confusion in his. "But I can't. Whether it's the best thing or not, I have to believe it's the right thing. Daddy." She walked over, sat on the coffee table so that her eyes were on a level with Sam's. "It's about Mama."

She saw his mouth harden and, though he didn't move, felt him pull back from her. "There's no point in stirring up old waters, Jo Ellen. Your mother's been gone long enough for you to deal with her going."

"She's dead, Daddy. She's been dead for twenty years." As if to anchor them both, she closed a hand over his. "She didn't leave you, or us. She didn't walk away from Sanctuary. She was murdered."

"How can you say such a thing?" Lexy surged to her feet. "How can you say that, Jo?"

"Alexa." Sam kept his eyes on Jo's. "Hush." He had to give himself a moment to stand up to the blow she'd delivered. He wanted to dismiss it, slide over or around it. But there was no evading that steady and sorrowful look in her eyes. "You've got a reason for saying that. For believing it."

"Yes."

She told him calmly, clearly, about the photograph that had been sent to her. The shock of recognition, the undeniable certainty that it was Annabelle.

"I worked it out a hundred different ways in my head," she continued. "That it had been taken years later, that it was just a trick of the camera, just a horrible joke. That I'd imagined it altogether. But none of those were true, Daddy. It was Mama, and it was taken right here on the island on the night we thought she left."

"Where's the picture?" he demanded. "Where is it?"

"It's gone. Whoever sent it came back and took it while I was in the hospital. But it was there, I swear it. It was Mama."

"How do you know? How can you be sure of that?"

She opened her mouth, but Nathan stepped forward. "Because I've seen the photograph. Because my father took it, after he killed her."

With a storm raging in his head, Sam got slowly to his feet. "You're going to stand there and tell me your father killed Belle. Killed a woman who'd done him no harm, and then took pictures of it. He took pictures of her when he'd done with her, and showed them to you."

"Nathan didn't know, Daddy." Jo clung to Sam's arm. "He was just a boy. He didn't know."

"I'm not looking at a boy now."

"I found the photographs and a journal after my father died. Everything Jo told is true. My father killed your wife. He wrote it all down, locked the journal and the prints, the negatives in a safe-deposit box. I found them after he and my mother died."

When the words trailed away there was no sound but the whisk of the blades from the ceiling fan, Lexy's weeping, and the harsh breaths Sam pushed in and out of his lungs.

He could see her now, shimmering at the front of his mind, the wife he'd loved, the woman he'd cursed. All the lights and shadows of her shifted together to form rage. To form grief.

"Twenty years he kept it to himself." Sam clenched his fists, but there was nothing to strike. "You find out and you come back here and put your hands on my daughter. And you let him." He burned Jo with a look. "You know, and you let him."

"I felt the same way when he told me. Just the same. But when I had time to think it through, to understand . . . Nathan wasn't responsible."

"His blood was."

"You're right." Nathan moved so that Jo no longer stood between him and Sam. "I came back here to try to find a way through it, or around it, or to just bury it. And I fell in love where I had no right to."

Brian set Lexy aside so that she could weep into her hands instead of on his shoulder. "Why?" His voice was as raw as his soul. "Why did he do it?"

"There's no reason that can justify it," Nathan said wearily. "Nothing she'd done. He . . . selected her. It was a project to him, a study. He didn't act out of anger, or even out of passion. I can't explain it to myself."

"It's best if you go now, Nathan." Kate spoke quietly as she rose. "Leave us alone with this for a while."

"I can't, until it's all said."

"I don't want you in my house." Sam's voice was dangerously low. "I don't want you on my land."

"I'm not going until I know Jo's safe. Because whoever killed Susan Peters and Ginny Pendleton wants her."

"Ginny." To steady herself, Kate gripped Sam's arm.

"I don't have any proof of Ginny, but I know. If you'll listen to the rest of it, hear me out, I'll leave."

"Let him finish it." Lexy sniffed back her tears and spoke in a voice that was surprisingly strong. "Ginny didn't just run off. I've known that in my heart all along. It was just like Mama, wasn't it, Nathan? And the Peters woman, too."

She folded her hands in her lap to compose herself and turned to Jo. "You were sent photos here, to the house, pictures taken here, on the island. It's all happening again."

"You're handy with a camera, Nathan." Brian's eyes were hot blue slits.

It stung, coming from a man who had been friend in both the past and the present. "You don't have any reason to trust me, but you have plenty of reason to listen."

"Let me try to explain it, Nathan." Jo picked up her wine to cool her throat.

She left nothing out, picking her way from detail to detail, question to question, and leading into the steps she and Nathan had agreed upon taking to find the answers.

"So his dead father's responsible for killing our mother," Brian cut in bitterly. "Now his dead brother's responsible for the rest. Convenient."

"We don't know who's responsible for the rest. But if it is Nathan's brother, it doesn't make Nathan culpable." Jo stepped up to Brian. "There's a parable about apples falling from the tree someone told me recently. And how some are strong enough to roll clear and stay whole, and others aren't."

"Don't throw my own words back at me," he said furiously. "His father killed our mother, destroyed our lives. Now another woman's dead, maybe two. And you expect us to pat him on the back and say all's forgiven? Well, the hell with that. The hell with all of you."

He strode out, leaving the air vibrating in his wake.

"I'll go after him." Lexy paused in front of Nathan, studied him out of red-rimmed eyes. "He's the oldest, and maybe he loved her best, the way boys do their mamas. But he's wrong, Nathan. There's nothing to forgive you for. You're a victim, just like the rest of us."

When she slipped out, Kate said in surprised admiration, "You never expect her to be the sensible one." Then she sighed. "We need some time here, Nathan. Some wounds need private tending."

"I'm going with you," Jo began, but Nathan shook his head.

"No, you stay with your family. We all need time." He turned to face Sam. "If you have more to say to me—"

"I'll find you right enough."

With a nod, Nathan left them alone.

"Daddy—"

"I don't have anything to say to you now, Jo Ellen. You're a grown woman, but you're living under my roof for the time being. I'm asking you to go to your room for now and let me be."

"All right. I know what you're feeling, and just how it hurts. You need time to deal with it." She kept her eyes level with his. "But after you've had that time, if you still hold to this stand, you'll make me ashamed. Ashamed that you would blame the son for the father's deed."

Saying nothing, he strode past her.

"Go ahead to your room, Jo." Kate laid a hand on Jo's knotted shoulder. "Let me see what I can do."

"Do you blame him, Kate? Do you?"

"I can't get my mind clear on what I think or feel. I know the boy's suffering, Jo, but so is Sam. My first loyalty is to him. Go on now, don't pester me for answers until I can sort things through."

Kate found Sam on the front porch, standing at the rail, staring out into the night. Clouds had rolled in, covering moon and stars. She left the porch light off and stepped quietly up beside him.

"I have to grieve again." He ran his hands back and forth over the railing. "It isn't right that I should have to grieve for her again."

"No, it's not."

"Do I take comfort that she never meant to leave me and the children? That she didn't run off and forget us? And how do I take back all the hard thoughts of her I had over the years, all the nights I cursed her for being selfish and careless and heartless?"

"You can't be faulted for the hard thoughts, Sam. You believed what was set in front of you. Believing a lie doesn't make you wrong. It's the lie that's wrong."

He tightened up. "If you came out here to defend that boy to me, you can turn right around and go back inside."

"That's not why I came out, but the fact is that you're no more at fault for believing what you did about Belle than Nathan was for believing in his father. Now you've both found out you were wrong in that belief, but he's the one who has to accept that his father was the selfish and heartless one."

"I said you could go on back inside."

"All right, then, you stubborn, stiff-necked mule. You just stand out here alone and wallow in your misery and think your black thoughts." She spun around, shocked when his hand shot out and took hers.

"Don't leave." The words burned his throat like tears. "Don't."

"When have I ever?" she said with a sigh. "Sam, I don't know what to do for you, for any of you. I hate seeing the people I love hurt this way and not knowing how to give them ease."

"I can't mourn for her the way I should, Kate. Twenty years is a long stretch. I'm not the same as I was when I lost her."

"You loved her."

"I always loved her, even when I thought the worst of her, I loved her. You remember how she was, Kate, so bright."

"I always envied her the way she would light up everything and everyone around her."

"A soft light's got its own appeal." He stared down at their joined hands and missed the shock that bolted into her eyes. "You always kept that light steady," he said carefully. "She'd have been grateful for the way you mothered the children, looked after things. I should have told you before that I'm grateful."

"I started out doing it for her, and stayed for myself. And Sam, I don't think Belle would have wanted you to grieve all over again. I never knew her to nurse a hurt or cling to a grudge. She wouldn't have blamed a ten-year-old boy for what his father was."

"I'm cut in two on this, Kate. I'm remembering that when Belle went missing, David Delaney joined in the search for her." He had to close his eyes as the rage rose up black again. "The son of a bitch walked this island with me. And all the while he'd done that to her. His wife came and got the children, took them back with her to mind all that day. I was grateful to him, God forgive me for that. I was grateful to him."

"He deceived you," she said quietly. "He deceived his own family."

"He never missed a step. I can't go back to that day, knowing what I know now, and make him pay for it."

"Will you make the son pay instead?"

"I don't know."

"Sam, what if they're right? What if someone wants to do to Jo what was done to Annabelle? We need to protect what we have left, to use whatever we have to protect what we have left. If I'm any judge, Nathan Delaney would step in front of a moving train to keep her safe."

"I can see to my own this time. I'm prepared this time."

The edge of the woods on a moonless night was an excellent vantage point. But he hadn't been able to resist creeping a little closer, using the dark to conceal his movements.

It was so exciting to be this close to the house, to hear the old man's words so clearly. It was all out now, and that was just another arousal. They thought they knew it all, understood it all. They probably believed they'd be safe in that foreknowledge.

And they couldn't be more wrong.

He tapped the gun he'd tucked, combat-style, in his boot. He could use it now if he wanted, take both of them out. Like shooting ducks in a barrel. That would leave the two women alone in the house, since Brian had driven off in a stone-spitting fit of temper.

He could have both of Annabelle's daughters, one after the other, both at once. A delicious ménage à trois.

Still, that would be a detour from the master plan. And the plan was serving him so well. Sticking to it would prove his discipline, his ability to conceive and execute. And if he wanted to duplicate the Annabelle experience, he would have to be patient just a little longer.

But that didn't mean he couldn't stir things up a bit in the meantime. Scared rabbits, he mused, were so much easier to trap.

He melted back into the trees and spent a pleasant hour contemplating the light in Jo's window.

29

Kirby jogged along the beach, hugging her solitude. The sky to the east was wildly red, gloriously, violently vivid with sunrise. She supposed that if the old adage were true, sailors better take warning, but she could only think how beautiful the morning was with its furious sky and high, wild winds.

Maybe they were in for a backslap from Carla after all, she thought, as her feet pounded the hard-packed sand. It might be exciting, and it would take Brian's mind off his troubles for a little while.

She wished she knew what to say to him, how to help him. All she'd been able to do when he'd roared into her cottage the night before was listen, as she had listened to Jo. But when she'd tried to comfort him, as she had comforted Jo, it hadn't been the soft, soothing words she'd offered that he wanted. So she'd given him the heat instead and had held on for dear life as he pounded out his misery in sex.

She hadn't been able to convince him to stay and sleep past dawn. He was up and gone before the sun peeked over the horizon. But at least he gathered her close, at least he pulled her to him. And she knew she'd steadied him for the return to Sanctuary.

Now she wanted to clear her head. If the man she loved was in trouble, if he was in distress, then so was she. She would gear herself up to stand by him, to see him through this, and she hoped, to guide him toward some peace.

Then she saw Nathan standing near where the booming breakers hammered the shoreline. Loyalty warred against reason as she slowed her pace. But in the end her need to help, to heal, overrode everything else. She simply couldn't turn her back on pain.

"Some morning." She had to lift her voice over the thunder of surf and wind. Puffing only a little, she stopped beside him. "So, is your vacation living up to your expectations?"

He laughed. He couldn't help it. "Oh, yeah. It's the trip of a lifetime."

"You need coffee. As a doctor, I'm supposed to tell you that caffeine isn't good for you, but I happen to know it often does the trick."

"You offering?"

"I am."

"I appreciate it, Kirby, but we both know I'm persona non grata. Brian wouldn't appreciate you sharing a morning cup with me. I can't blame him for it."

"I do my own thinking, form my own impressions. That's why he's crazy about me." She laid a hand on his arm. No, she couldn't turn her back on pain. Even the air around Nathan was hurting. "Come on up to the house. Think of me as your kindly island doctor. Bare your soul." She smiled at him. "I'll even bill you for an office visit if you want."

"Such a deal." He took a long breath. "Christ, I could use a cup of coffee. I could use the ear too."

"And I've got both. Come on." She tucked her arm in his and walked away from the shore. "So, the Hathaways gave you a rough time."

"Oh, I don't know, they were fairly gracious all in all. That Southern hospitality. My father raped and murdered your mother, I tell them. Hell, nobody even tried to lynch me."

"Nathan." She paused at the base of her steps. "It's a hell of a mess, and a terrible tragedy all around. But none of them will blame you once they're able to think it through."

"Jo doesn't. Of all of them, she's the most vulnerable because of it, but she doesn't."

"She loves you."

"She may yet get over that. Lexy didn't," he murmured. "She looked me straight in the eye, her cheeks still wet from crying, and told me none of it was my responsibility."

"Lexy uses pretenses and masks and foolishness and uses them expertly. So she can see through them and cut to the bone faster than most." She opened her door, turned back to him. "And Nathan, none of it is, or was, your responsibility."

"I know that intellectually, and I'd almost convinced myself of it emotionally—I wanted to because I wanted Jo. But it's not over, Kirby. It's not finished. At least one other woman is dead now, so it's not over."

She nodded and held the door open for him. "We'll talk about that too."

Carla teased the southeast coast of Florida, giving Key Biscayne a quick and violent kiss before shimmying north. In her capricious way, she did a tango with Fort Lauderdale, scattered trailers and tourists and took a few lives. But she didn't seem inclined to stay.

Her eye was cold and wide, her breath fast and eager. She'd grown stronger, wilder since her birth in the warm waters of the West Indies.

Like a vengeful whore, she spun back out to sea, stomping her sharp heels over the narrow barrier islands in her path.

Lexy hurried into the guest room where Jo was just smoothing the spread on the walnut sleigh bed. The sun beamed hot and brilliant through the open balcony doors, highlighting the shadows under Jo's eyes that spoke of a restless night.

"Carla just hit St. Simons," Lexy said, a little breathless from her rush up two flights of stairs.

"St. Simons? I thought she was tracking west."

"She changed her mind. She's heading north, Jo. The last report said if she keeps to course and velocity, her leading edge will hit here before nightfall."

"How bad is she?"

"She's clawed her way up to category three."

"Winds of over a hundred miles an hour. We'll need to batten down."

"We're going to evacuate the tourists before the seas get too rough for ferry crossings. Kate wants you to help down at checkout. I'm going out with Giff. We'll start boarding up."

"All right, I'll be down. Let's hope she heads out to sea and gives us a pass."

"Daddy's on the radio getting updates. Brian went down to see that the boat's fueled and supplied in case we have to leave."

"Daddy won't leave. He'll ride it out if he has to tie himself to a tree."

"But you will." Lexy stepped closer. "I went by your room earlier, saw your suitcases open and nearly packed."

"There's more reason for me to go than to stay."

"You're wrong, Jo. There's more for staying, at least until we find the way to settle this for everyone. And we need to bury Mama."

"Oh, God, Lexy." Jo covered her face, then stood there with her fingers pressed to her eyes.

"Not her body. But we need to put a marker up in the cemetery, and we need to say good-bye. She loved us. All my life I thought she didn't, and that maybe it was because of me."

When Lexy's voice broke, Jo dropped her hands. "Why would you think something like that?"

"I was the youngest. I thought she hadn't wanted another child, hadn't wanted me. So I spent most of my life trying so hard to make people love me, people want me. I'd be whatever I thought they'd like best. I'd be stupid or I'd be smart. I'd be helpless or I'd be clever. And I'd always make sure I left first."

She walked over, carefully shut the balcony doors. "I've done a lot of hateful things," she continued. "And it's likely I'll do plenty more. But knowing the truth's changed something inside me. I have to say good-bye to her. We all do."

"I'm ashamed I didn't think of it," Jo murmured. "If I go before it can all be arranged, I'll come back. I promise." She bent down to gather up the linens she'd stripped from the bed. "Despite everything, I'm glad I came back this time. I'm glad things have changed between us."

"So am I." Lexy aimed a sidelong smile. "So, now maybe you'll fancy up some of the pictures you took that I'm in, and take a few more. I could use them for my portfolio. Casting directors ought to be pretty impressed with glossies taken by one of the top photographers in the country."

"If we shake loose of Carla, you and I will have a photo shoot that'll knock every casting director in New York on his ass."

"Really? Great." She scowled out at the sky. "Goddamn hurricane. Something's always coming along to postpone the good stuff. Maybe we can do it in Savannah. You know, rent a real studio for a couple of days, and—"

"Lexy."

"Oh, all right." Lexy waved her hands. "But thinking about that's a lot more fun than thinking about nailing up sheets of plywood. Of course, maybe Giff'll think I'm plain useless at it, and I can whisk back inside and check through my wardrobe for the right outfits. I want sexy shots, sexy and moody. We could get us a little wind machine for—"

"Lexy," Jo said again on an exasperated laugh.

"I'm going, I'm going. I've got this terrific evening gown I got wholesale in the garment district." She started toward the door. "Now, if I can just talk Kate into letting me borrow Grandma Pendleton's pearls."

Jo laughed again as Lexy's voice carried down the hallway. Things shouldn't change too quickly, she decided, or too much. Bundling the linens more securely, she carted them out to the laundry chute. Through an open door she could see the couple who had come in for the week from Toronto packing, and making quick work of it. She imagined most of the other guests were doing the same.

Checkout, usually a breezy and relaxed process, was going to be frantic.

The minute she came downstairs, she saw she hadn't exaggerated. Luggage was already piled by the front door. In the parlor, half a dozen guests were milling around or standing by the windows staring at the sky as if they expected it to crack open at any moment.

Kate was at the desk, surrounded by a sea of paperwork and urgent demands. Her hospitable smile was frayed around the edges when she looked up and spotted Jo.

"Now don't you worry. We'll get everyone safely to the ferry. We have two running all day, and one leaves for the mainland every hour." At the flood of voices, questions, demands, she lifted her hand. "I'm going to take the first group down right now. My niece will take over checkout."

She sent Jo an apologetic, slightly desperate look. "Mr. and Mrs. Littleton, if you and your family would go out to the shuttle. Mr. and Mrs. Parker. Miss Houston. I'll be right there. Now if the rest of you will be patient, my niece will be right with you."

Having no choice, she waded through the bodies and voices and gripped Jo's arm. "Out here for a minute. I swear, you'd think we were about to be under nuclear attack."

"Most of them probably haven't dealt with a hurricane before."

"Which is why I'm glad to help them on their way. For heaven's sake, this island and everything on it have stood up to hurricanes before, and will again."

Since privacy was needed, Kate took it where she could get it, in the powder room off the foyer. With a little grunt of satisfaction, she flipped the lock. "There. That ought to hold for two damn minutes. I'm sorry to leave you surrounded this way."

"It's okay. I can run the next group down in the Jeep."

"No." Kate spoke sharply, then blowing out a breath, she turned to the sink to splash cold water on her face. "You're not to leave this house, Jo Ellen, unless one of us is with you. I don't need another thing to worry about."

"For heaven's sake. I can lock the doors to the Jeep."

"No, and I won't stand here and argue about it. I just don't have the luxury of time for it. You'll help most right here, keeping these people calm. I have to swing around and pick up some of the cottage people. Brian was going by the campground. We'll have another flood of them in shortly."

"All right, Kate. Whatever you want."

"Your father brought the radio down to the kitchen." She took Jo by the arms. "He's well within hailing distance. You take no chances, you understand me?"

"I don't intend to. I need to call Nathan."

"I've already done that. He didn't answer. I'll go by before I bring the next group. I'd feel better if he was here, too."

"Thanks."

"Don't thank me, honey pie. I'm about to leave you with the world's biggest headache." Kate sucked in a breath, braced her shoulders, and opened the door.

Jo winced at the din of voices from the parlor. "Hurry back," she said and mustered a weak smile as she walked straight into the line of fire.

Outside, Giff muscled a sheet of plywood over the first panel of the wide dining room bay. Lexy crouched at his feet, hammered a nail quickly and with easy skill into the lower corner. She was chattering away, but Giff heard only about every third word. The wind had died, and the light was beginning to take on a brutish yellow hue.

It was coming, he thought, and faster than they'd anticipated. His family had their home secure and would likely ride it out there. He'd delegated one of his cousins and two friends to begin boarding up the cottages, starting on the southeast and moving north.

They needed more hands.

"Has anyone called Nathan?"

"I don't know." Lexy plucked another nail from her pouch. "Daddy wouldn't let him help anyway."

"Mr. Hathaway's a sensible man, Lexy. He wants what's his secured. And he's had a night to think things through."

"He's as stubborn as six constipated mules, and him and Brian together are worse than that. Why it's like blaming that bastard Sherman's great-grandchildren for burning Atlanta."

"Some do, I imagine." Giff hefted another sheet.

"Those who haven't a nickel's worth of brains, I imagine." Her teeth set, Lexy whacked the hammer onto a nailhead. "And it's going to be mighty lowering for me if I have to admit my own daddy and brother got shortchanged in the brain department. And that they're half blind to boot. Why, an eighty-year-old granny without her cheaters could see how much that man loves Jo Ellen. It's sinful to make the two of them feel guilty over it."

She straightened, blowing the hair out of her eyes. Then frowned at him. "Why are you grinning at me that way? Is my face all sweaty and grimy already?"

"You're the most beautiful thing I've ever seen in my lifetime, Alexa Hathaway. And you always surprise me. Even knowing you inside out, you surprise me."

"Well, honey..." She tilted her head, batted her lashes. "I mean to."

Giff slid his hand into his pocket, fingered the small box he'd tucked there. "I had different plans for doing this. But I don't think I've ever loved you more than I do right this second."

He tugged the box out of his pocket, watching her eyes go huge and wide as he flipped open the lid with his thumb. The little diamond centered on the thin gold band winked out points of fire in the sun.

"Marry me, Alexa."

Her heart swelled and butted against her ribs. Her eyes misted so that the light shooting from the diamond refracted and blinded her. Her hand trembled as she pressed it to her mouth.

"Oh, how could you! How could you spoil it all this way?" Spinning around, she thumped the hammer against the edge of the wood.

"Like I said," he murmured, "you're always a surprise to me. You want me to put it away until we have candlelight and moonbeams?"

"No, no, no." With a little sob, she struck the wood with the hammer again. "Put it away. Take it back. You know I can't marry you."

He shifted his feet, planted them. "I don't know any such thing. Why don't you explain it to me?"

Furious and heartsick, she whirled back to him. "You know I will if you keep asking. You know I'll give in because I love you so much. Then I'll have given up everything else. I'll stay on this damn island, I won't go back to New York, and I won't try to make it in the theater again. Then I'll start to hate you as the years pass and I start to think, if only. If only. I'll just shrivel up here wondering if I could ever have been something."

"What makes you think I'd expect you to give up on New York and the theater, that I'd expect you to give up everything you want? I'd hate to think you'd marry a man who wants less for you than you want for yourself. Whatever you want for Lexy, I want twice that much."

She wiped a hand over her cheeks. "I don't understand you. I don't know what you're saying."

"I'm saying I've got plans of my own, wants of my own. I don't plan on swinging a hammer on Desire my whole life."

Mildly irritated, he took off his cap to wipe the sweat off his forehead, then shoved it back on again. "Things need to get built in New York, don't they? Things need fixing there just like anywhere else."

She lowered her hands slowly, staring into his eyes, wishing she could read them. "You're saying you'd go to New York. You'd live in New York? For me."

"No, that's not what I'm saying." Impatient, he snapped the lid closed and shoved the box back into his pocket. "If I was to do that, I'd just end up resenting you, and we'd be right back where we started. I'm saying I'd go for both of us. And that even with the money I've been putting by, we'd live pretty tight for a while. I'd probably have to take some classes if I wanted Nathan to give me a chance at a job in his firm."

"A job with Nathan? You want to work in New York?"

"I've had a hankering to see it. And to see you, onstage, in the spotlight."

"I might not ever get there."

"Hell you won't." His dimples winked down, and his eyes went from sulky brown to golden. "I've never seen anybody who can play more roles. You'll get there, Lexy. I believe in you."

Tears gushed out even as she laughed and threw herself at him. "Oh, Giff, how'd you get to be so perfect? How'd you get to be so right?" She leaned back, catching his face in her hands. "So absolutely right for me."

"I've been studying on it most of my life."

"We'll have a time, we will. And I'll wait damn tables until you're out of school or I get my break. Whatever it takes. Oh, hurry up, hurry up and put it on." She jumped down, held out her hand. "I can't hardly stand to wait."

"I'll buy you a bigger one someday."

"No, you won't." She thrilled as he slipped the ring onto her finger, as he lowered his head and kissed her. "You can buy me all the other bright, shiny baubles you want when we're rich. Because I want to be good and rich, Giff, and I'm not ashamed to say so. But this . . ." She held up her hand, turning it so the little stone winked and danced with light. "This is just perfect."

After two hours, Jo's head throbbed and her eyes were all but crossed. Kate had come and gone twice, hauling guests to and from, swinging by various cottages. Brian had dropped off a dozen campers, then headed back to make another sweep in case there were any lingering. Her only news of Nathan was that he was helping board up cottages along the beachfront.

Except for the monotonous *thwack* of hammers, the house was finally quiet. She imagined Kate would be back shortly with the last of the cottagers. The windows on the south and east sides were boarded, casting the house into gloom.

When she opened the front door, the wind rushed in. The cool slap of it was a shock after the thick heat of the closed house. To the south, the sky was bruised and dark. She saw the flicker of lightning but heard no answering thunder.

Still far enough away, she decided. She would check shortly and see what track they were predicting Carla to take. And as a precaution, she would get all of her prints and negatives out of her darkroom and into the safe in Kate's office.

Because she wanted to avoid her father for a while yet, she took the main stairs, checking rooms automatically to see that nothing had been left behind by a harried guest. She flicked off lights, moving briskly toward the family wing. The sound of hammering was louder now, and she found it comforting. Tucking us in, she thought. If Carla lashed out at Sanctuary, it would hold, as it had held before.

She caught the sound of voices as she went by Kate's office. Plywood slipped over the window, blanking it as she passed. Either Brian was back or her father had gone out to help Giff, she decided.

She snapped on the lights in her darkroom, then turned on the radio.

"Hurricane Carla has been upgraded to category three and is expected to make landfall on the barrier island of Little Desire off the coast of Georgia by seven P.M. Tourists have been evacuated from this privately owned island in the Sea Islands chain, and residents are being advised to leave as soon as possible. Winds of up to one hundred and twenty miles an hour are expected, with the leading edge striking the narrow island near high tide."

Her earlier confidence shaken, Jo dragged her hands through her hair. It didn't get much worse than this, she knew. Cottages would be lost, by wind or water. Homes flattened, the beach battered, the forest ripped to pieces.

And their safety net was shrinking, she thought, with a glance at her watch.

She was going to get Nathan, and Kirby, and if she had to knock her father unconscious, she was going to get him and her family off the island.

She yanked open a drawer. She could leave the prints, but damned if she'd risk losing all her negatives. But as she started to reach for them, her hand froze.

On top of her neatly organized files was a stack of prints. Her head went light, her skin clammy as she stared down into her mother's face. She'd seen this print before, in another darkroom, in what almost seemed like another life. Over the roaring in her head, she could hear her own low moan as she reached out for it.

It was real. She could feel the slick edge of the print between her fingers. Breathing shallowly, she turned it over, read the carefully written title.

DEATH OF AN ANGEL

She bit back a whimper and forced herself to look at the next print. Grief swarmed over her, stinging like wasps. The pose was nearly identical, as though the photographer had sought to reproduce one from the other. But this was Ginny, her lively, friendly face dull and lax, her eyes empty.

"I'm sorry," Jo whispered, pressing the print to her heart. "I'm sorry. I'm so sorry."

The third print was certainly Susan Peters.

Jo shut her eyes, willed the sickness away, and gently set the third print aside. And her knees went to water.

The last print was of herself. Her eyes were serenely closed, her body pale and naked. Sounds strangled in her throat as she dropped the photo, backed away from it.

She groped behind her for the door, the adrenaline pumping through her, priming her to run. She backed sharply into the table, knocked the radio onto its side. Music jangled out, making her want to scream.

"No." She fisted her hands, digging her nails into her palms until the pain cut through the shock. "I'm not going to let it happen. I'm not going to believe it. I won't let it be true."

She rocked herself, counting breaths until the faintness passed, then grim and determined, she picked up the photo again.

Her face, yes. It was her face. Taken before Lexy had cut her hair for the bonfire. Several weeks, then. The bonfire had been at the very start of summer. She carried the photo closer to the light, ordered herself to study it with an objective and trained eye.

It took her only seconds of clear vision to realize that while the face was hers, the body wasn't. The breasts were too full, the hips too round. She set the photo of Annabelle beside it. Was it more horrifying, she wondered dully, to realize her face had been imposed on her mother's body? Making them one, she thought.

That's what he'd wanted all along.

. . .

Brian steered the Jeep down the maintenance road of the campground. Several of the sites had been left in disarray. With the way the storm was rolling in, he figured that wasn't going to matter much. The wind was already ripping like razors through the trees. A gust shook the Jeep around him, had him gripping the wheel tighter. He calculated they had perhaps an hour to finish preparations.

He had to fight not to hurry this check run. He wanted to get to Kirby, lock her safely inside Sanctuary. He'd have preferred shipping her off to the mainland, but knew better than to waste his breath or his energy arguing with her. If one resident stayed put to ride it out, she would stay put to treat any injuries.

Sanctuary had stood for more than a hundred years, Brian thought. It would stand through this.

There were dozens of other worries. They would undoubtedly be cut off from the mainland. The radio would help, but there would be no phone, no power, and no transportation once they were hit. He'd fueled the generator to provide emergency power, and he knew Kate kept an ample supply of bottled water.

They had food, they had shelter, they had several strong backs. And after Carla did her worst, strong backs were going to be a necessity.

He continued to tick off tasks and options in his mind, growing calmer as he assured himself there were no stragglers in the camping areas. He only hoped there weren't any idiots hiding out in the trees, or staking in near the beach, thinking a hurricane was a vacation adventure.

He cursed and stomped on the brakes as a figure stepped out on the road in front of the Jeep.

"Jesus Christ, you idiot." Disgusted, Brian slammed out of the vehicle. "I damn near ran you over. Haven't you got the sense to stay out of the middle of the road, much less the path of an oncoming hurricane?"

"I heard about that." His grin spread wide. "Amazing timing."

"Yeah, amazing." Resenting every second wasted, Brian jerked a thumb at the Jeep. "Get in, I might be able to get you down for the last ferry, but there isn't much time."

"Oh, I don't know about that." Still smiling, he lifted the hand he'd held behind his back and fired the gun.

Brian jerked back as pain exploded in his chest. He staggered, fought to keep the world from revolving. And as he fell, he saw the eyes of a childhood friend laughing.

"One down." Using his boot, he nudged Brian's limp body over. "I appreciate the opportunity to fix the odds a bit, old pal. And the loan of the Jeep."

As he hopped in, he gave Brian one last glance. "Don't worry. I'll see it gets back to Sanctuary. Eventually."

Rain began to lash at the windows as Kirby gathered medical supplies. She was dead calm as she tried to anticipate every possible need. If she was forced into triage, it would work best at Sanctuary. She'd already faced the very real possibility that the cottage might not survive the night.

She understood that most of the islanders would be too stubborn to leave their homes. By morning, there could be broken bones, concussions, gashes. The house trembled under a hard gust, and she set her jaw. She would be there to treat any and all injuries.

She was hefting a box, heading out to load it in her car, when her front door swung open. It took her a moment to recognize the figure in the yellow slicker and hood as Giff.

"Here." She shoved the box into his arms. "Take this out, I'll get the next one."

"Figured you'd be putting this kind of thing together. Make it fast. The bitch is coming in."

"I've nearly got everything packed." She pulled on her own slicker. "Where's Brian?"

"He was checking the campground. Isn't back yet."

"Well, he should have been," she snapped. Worry dogged her heels as she ran in for the rest of her supplies. The wind shoved her backward when she tried to step out on her porch. It whistled past her ears as she bent low and fought her way forward.

"You all secure here?" Giff shouted over the pounding of the surf. He grabbed the box from her and shoved it into the Jeep.

"As much as possible. Nathan helped me with it this morning. Is he back at the house?"

"No. Haven't seen him either."

"For God's sake." She pushed back her already streaming hair. "What in hell could they be doing? We're going by the campground, Giff."

"We don't have a lot of time here, Kirby."

"We're going by. Brian could be in trouble. This wind could have taken some trees down. If he wasn't at Sanctuary when you left, and you didn't pass him along the way here, he could still be over there. I'm not going in until I make sure."

He yanked open the Jeep door and bundled her inside. "You're the doctor," he shouted.

"Goddamn son of a bitch." Nathan beat the heel of his hand against the steering wheel. He'd loaded the most precious of his work and equipment into the Jeep, and now it wouldn't start. It didn't even have the decency to cough and sputter.

Furious, he climbed out, hissing as the rising wind slapped hard pricks of rain into his face. He hauled up the hood, cursed again. He didn't have time for the pretense of fixing whatever was wrong.

He needed to get to Jo and he needed to get to her now. He'd done everything else he could.

He slammed the hood down and, abandoning his equipment, began to trudge toward the river. He'd have to go a quarter of a mile upstream before he could cross, and the hike over to Sanctuary through the woods promised to be miserable.

He heard the ominous creak of trees being shoved and tortured by the wind, felt the hard hands of it playfully pushing him back as he lurched forward. Lightning snapped overhead, turning the sky to an eerie orange.

The wind stung his eyes, blurred his vision. He didn't see the figure step out from behind a tree until he was almost upon it.

"Christ, what the hell are you doing out here?" It took him nearly ten baffled seconds to see past the changes and recognize the face. "Kyle." Horror tripped over shock. "My God, what have you done?"

"Hello, bro'." As if they were meeting on a sunny street, Kyle offered a hand. And as Nathan shifted his gaze for a blink to stare at it, Kyle smashed the butt of the gun into his temple.

"Two down." This time, he threw back his head and roared. The storm empowered him. The violence of it aroused him. "I didn't feel quite right about shooting my own brother, irritating bastard though he is, in what some would call cold blood." He crouched down, whispering as if Nathan could hear. "The river's going to rise, you know, trees are going to go down. Whatever happens, bro', we'll just figure it's fate."

He straightened and, leaving his brother lying on ground soaked with rain and blood, started off to claim the woman he'd decided belonged to him.

30

Rain gushed over the windshield of the Jeep, overpowering the wipers. The road was turning to mush under the wheels, so Giff had to fight for every yard of progress.

"We're heading in," he told Kirby. "Brian's got more sense than to be out in this, and so do I."

"Just take the west route back." She prayed it was the storm making her heart thump and freezing her bones. "That's the way he'd have gone. Then we'll be sure."

"South road's quicker."

"Please."

Abandoning his better judgment, Giff muscled the Jeep to the left. "If we get back in one piece, he's going to skin me for keeping you out here five minutes longer than necessary."

"That's all it'll be, five extra minutes." She leaned forward, struggling to see through the waterfall streaming down the windshield. "What is that? Something on the side of the road up ahead."

"Probably some gear that fell out of somebody's camper. People were scrambling to get the hell off before—"

"Stop!" Shouting, she grabbed the wheel herself and sent them into a skid.

"Jesus Christ, you aiming to send us into a ditch? Hey—" Though he reached out to stop her, he only caught the tip of her slicker as she bolted out into the torrent of rain. "Goddamn women." He shoved open the door. "Kirby, get back in here, this wind's liable to blow you clean to Savannah."

"Help me, for God's sake, Giff! It's Brian!" Her frigid hands were already tearing open the bloody shirt. "He's been shot."

"Where could they be?" While the wind pounded the walls, Lexy paced the main parlor. "Where could they be? Giff's been gone nearly an hour, and Brian twice that long."

"Maybe they took shelter." Kate huddled in a chair and vowed not to panic. "They might have decided not to try to get back and took shelter."

"Giff said he'd be back. He promised."

"Then he will be." Kate folded her hands to keep from wringing them. "They'll be here in a minute. And they'll be tired and wet and cold. Lexy, let's go in and get coffee into thermoses before we lose power."

"How can you think about coffee when—" She cut herself off, squeezed her eyes shut. "All right. It's better than just standing here. Windows all boarded, you can't even look out for them."

"We'll get hot food, hot coffee, dry clothes." Kate reeled off the practicalities, picking up a flashlight as a precaution as she took Lexy with her.

When they were gone, Jo rose. Her father stood across the room, his back to her, staring at the boarded-up window as if he could will himself to see through the plywood.

"Daddy, he's been in the house."

"What?"

"He's been in the house." She kept her voice calm as he turned. "I didn't want to say anything to Lexy and Kate yet. They're both frightened enough. I'd hoped they'd get on the last ferry, but with Brian still out..."

Sam's stomach began to burn. "You're sure of this."

"Yes. He left—he's been in my darkroom, sometime in the last two days. I can't be sure when."

"Nathan Delaney's been in this house."

"It's not Nathan."

Sam kept his gaze hard and steady. "I'm not willing to take a chance on that. You go in the kitchen with Kate and Lexy, and you stay with them. I'll go through the house."

"I'm going with you."

"You're going to do what I tell you and go in the kitchen. Not one of you takes a step without the other two."

"It's me he wants. If they're with me, they're only in more danger."

"No one's going to touch anyone of mine in this house." He took her arm, prepared to drag her into the kitchen if necessary. The front door burst open, letting in wild wind and flooding rain.

"Upstairs, Giff, get him upstairs." Breathing fast, Kirby side-stepped to keep the pressure firm on Brian's chest as Giff staggered under his weight. "I need my supplies out of the Jeep. Now," she ordered as Sam and Jo raced forward. "I need sheets, towels, I need light. Hurry. He's lost so much blood."

Kate dashed down the hall. "God, sweet God, what happened?"

"He's been shot." Kirby kept deliberate pace with Giff, never taking her eyes off Brian's face. "Radio the mainland, find out how long it'll take to get a helicopter in. We need to get him to a hospital, and we need the police. Hurry with the supplies. I've already lost too much time."

Without bothering with rain gear, Sam ran out into the storm. He was blind before he'd reached the Jeep, deaf but for the roar of blood in his head and the scream of the wind. He dragged the first box free, then found Jo shoving past him for the next.

They shouldered the weight and fought their way back into the house together.

"She's putting him in the Garden Suite. It's the closest bed." Lexy put her back into it and managed to shut the door behind them. "She won't say how bad it is. She won't say anything. Kate's on the radio."

Jo gripped the box until her knuckles were white as they hurried up the steps.

Kirby had stripped off her blood-smeared slicker, tossed it aside. She didn't hear the rain pound or the wind scream. She had only one goal now: to keep Brian alive.

"I need more pillows. We need to keep his trunk and legs higher than his head, keep the site of the bleeding elevated. He's in shock. He needs more blankets. It went through. I found the exit wound."

She pressed padding high on the back of his right shoulder. Her ungloved hand was covered with blood. "I can't tell what the internal damage might be. But the blood loss is the first concern. His BP is very low, pulse is thready. What's his blood type?"

"It's A negative," Sam told her. "Same as mine."

"Then we'll take some of yours for him. I need someone to draw it, I'll talk you through, but I don't have enough hands."

"I'll do it." Kate hurried in. "They can't tell us on the helicopter. Nothing can get on or off the island until Carla's done with us. Everything's grounded."

Oh, God. She wasn't a surgeon. For the first time in her life, Kirby cursed herself for not heeding her father's wishes. The entrance wound was small, easily dealt with, but the exit wound had ripped a hole in Brian's back nearly as big as her fist. She felt the panic scraping at her nerves and shut her eyes.

"Okay, all right. We need to get him stabilized. Giff, for now keep pressure here, right here, and keep it firm. If it bleeds through don't remove the padding. Add more. Use your other hand to hold this arterial pressure point. Keep your fingers flat and firm. Kate, get my bag. You'll see the rubber tube. You're going to make a tourniquet."

As she readied a syringe, her voice went cool. She'd chosen to heal, and by God, she would heal. She took one long look at Brian's waxy face. "I'm keeping you with me, you hear?"

As she slid the needle under his skin, the house went black.

Nathan struggled toward the surface of a red mist, slid back. It seemed vital that he break through it, though the pain whenever he got close to the thin, shimmery skin was monstrous. He was chilled to the bone, felt as though he was being pulled down into a vat of icy water. He clung to the edge again, felt those mists close in and thicken and with a vicious leap, cut through.

He found himself in a nightmare, dark and violent. The wind screamed like a thousand demons set loose, and water gushed over him, choking him when he tried to gulp in air. With his head reeling, he rolled over, got on his hands and knees. The water from the rising river beside him was up over his wrists. He tried to gain his feet, slid toward unconsciousness. The cold slap of water as his face hit the ground jerked him back.

Kyle. It had been Kyle. Back from the dead. This Kyle had streaming blond hair rather than brown, an almost brutal tan rather than city-pale skin. And lively madness in his eyes.

"Jo Ellen." He choked it out as he began to crawl away from the sucking water of the river. Murmured it like a prayer as he dug his fingers into the streaming bark of a tree to fight his way to his feet. And as he began a stumbling, wind-whipped run to Sanctuary, he screamed it.

"I'm not going to lose him." Kirby spoke matter-of-factly as she worked by the light of a lantern. Her mind was rigidly calm, forcing out the screaming fears and doubts. "Stay with me, Brian."

"You'll need more light." Giff stroked a hand over Lexy's hair. "If you can spare me here, I'll go down and get the generator started."

"Whoever did this . . ." Lexy gripped his hand. "They could be anywhere."

"You stay right here." He lifted her hand to kiss it. "Kirby may need some help." He moved to the bed, bending low as if to study Brian, and spoke softly to Sam. "You got a gun in the house?"

Sam continued to stare at the tubing that was transferring his blood to his son. "My room, top of the closet. There's a metal box. Got a thirty-eight, and ammo." His gaze shifted briefly, measured the man. "I'll trust you to use it if you have to."

Giff nodded, turned to give Lexy a quick smile. "I'll be back."

"Is there another lantern, more candles?" Kirby lifted Brian's eyelid. His pupils were fully dilated with shock. "If I don't close this exit wound, he's going to lose more blood than I can get into him."

Kate rushed over with a flashlight, beamed it onto the ripped flesh. "Don't let him go." She fought to blink back the tears. "Don't let my boy go."

"We're keeping him here."

"We won't lose him, Kate." Sam reached out, took the hand she had balled up at her side.

"Giff may have trouble with the generator." Jo spoke quietly, laying a hand on Lexy's shoulder. "I'm going to go down and get more emergency lights."

"I'll go with you."

"No, stay here. Kirby may need another pair of hands. Daddy can't help, and Kate's not going to hold up much longer. I'll be quick." She gave Lexy's shoulder a squeeze.

She took a flashlight and slipped out quietly. She had to do something, anything to help hold back the fear for Brian, for Nathan. For all of them.

What if Nathan was shot too, lying out there bleeding, dying? There was nothing she could do to stop it. And how could she live if she only stood by?

He's taken shelter, she promised herself, as she hurried down the stairs. He'd taken shelter, and when the worst of the storm had passed, she'd find him. They'd get Brian to the mainland, to a hospital.

She jolted at the loud crack, the crashing of glass. Her mind froze, envisioning another bullet, more flesh ripped by steel. Then she saw the splintered plywood in the parlor window, the flood of rain that poured in where the tree limb had snapped through it.

She grabbed a lantern, lighting it and holding it high. She would have to find Giff. As soon as she took the light to Kirby, they would have to get more wood, block the damage before it was irreparable.

When she whirled back, he was there.

"This is nice." Kyle stepped forward into the light. "I was just coming up to get you. No, don't scream." He lifted the gun so she could see it clearly. "I'll kill whoever comes down to see what was wrong." He smiled widely. "So, how's your brother doing?"

"He's holding on." She lowered the lantern so the shadows deepened. Beside her, the storm blasted through the splintered wood and spit rain into her face. "It's been a long time, Kyle."

"Not all that long, in the grand scheme of things. And I've been in close touch, so to speak, for months. How did you like my work?"

"It's . . . competent."

"Bitch." The word was quick and vicious, then he shrugged. "Come on, be honest, that last print. You have to admit the creativity of the image, the blending of old and new. It's one of my best studies."

"Clichéd at best. Where's Nathan, Kyle?"

"Oh, I imagine he's just where I left him." He darted a hand out, quick as a snake, and gripped her by the hair. "For once, I'm not going to worry about taking my big brother's leftovers. The way I look at it, he was just . . . tenderizing you. I'm much better than he is, at everything. Always have been."

"Where is he?"

"Maybe I'll show you. We're going for a little ride."

"Out in this?" She feigned resistance as he pulled her to the door. She wanted him out, away from Sanctuary, whatever it took. "You have to be crazy to go out in a category three."

"What I am, darling, darling Jo, is strong." He skimmed his lips over her temple. "Powerful. Don't worry, I won't let anything happen to you until everything is perfect. I've planned it out. Open the door."

The lights flashed on. Using the split second of diversion, she swung back with the flashlight, aiming for the groin, but bouncing hard off his thigh. Still, he grunted in pained surprise and loosened his grip. Ripping away, Jo tore open the front door and rushed out into the teeth of the storm. "You want me, you son of a bitch, you come get me."

The minute he barreled through the door, she was pitting her will against the gale, and fighting to lead him away from Sanctuary.

The rain-lashed darkness swallowed them.

It was less than a minute later when Giff climbed the steps from the basement. He felt the wild gust of wind the instant he turned into the hall. The front door was open wide to the driving rain. With his blood cold, he pulled out the gun he'd tucked in the waistband of his jeans, flicked off the safety, and moved forward. His finger wrapped around the trigger, trembled a breath away from full pressure when Nathan fell through the door.

"Jo Ellen. Where is she?"

"What happened to you?" Hating himself, but unwilling to risk, Giff kept the gun aimed as he walked forward.

"I was coming, my brother . . ." He swayed to his feet, brushed a hand over the raw wound on his temple as his vision doubled. "It was my brother."

"I thought you said he was dead."

"He's not." Shaking his head clear, Nathan focused on the gun. "He's not," he repeated. "Where's Jo?"

"She's fine and safe and going to stay that way. Brian was shot."

"God. Oh, God. Is he dead?"

"Kirby's working on him. Step away from the door, Nathan. Close it behind you. Keep your hands where I can see them."

"Goddamn it." He bit off the words as he heard the scream. The blood that had risen to his head to throb blindingly drained. "That's Jo. She's out there."

"You move, I'll have to shoot you."

"He's going to kill her. I'm not going to let that happen to her. I'm not letting it happen again. For God's sake, Giff, help me find her before he does."

It was a choice between instinct and caution. Giff prayed the choice was the right one and held the gun butt out. "We'll find her. He's your brother. You do what you have to do."

Jo bit back another scream as a limb as thick as a man's torso crashed inches from her feet. It was all swirling dark, roaring sound and wild, tearing wind. Tattered hunks of moss bulleted past her face. Saw palmettos rattled like sabers. Stumbling, she fought for another inch, another foot while the wind raked at her.

Finally, she dropped to her knees, wrapped her arms around the base of a tree, afraid she would simply be ripped apart.

She'd led him away, she prayed she'd led him away, but now she was lost. The forest was shuddering with greedy violence. Rain came at her like knives, stabbing her flesh. She couldn't hear her own breathing now, though she knew it must be harsh and fast because her lungs were on fire.

She had to get back, she had to get back home before he gave up his search. If he got back before she did, he would kill them all. As he'd surely killed Nathan. Sobbing, she began to crawl, digging her hands into the mud to pull her body along inch by straining inch.

Inside, Kirby clamped off the tube that was transferring Sam's blood to Brian. She couldn't risk taking any more until Sam had rested. "Sam needs fluids, and some protein. This has sapped his strength. Juice," she began, wearily stretching her back before she lowered her hand to take Brian's pulse. When his fingers bumped hers, her eyes flew to his face. She caught the faint flutter of his lashes.

"He's coming around. Brian, open your eyes, Brian. Come back now. Concentrate on opening your eyes."

"Is he all right? Is he going to be all right?" Lexy crowded closer, her shoulder bumping Kirby's.

"His pulse is a little stronger. Get me the BP cuff. Brian, open your eyes now. That's the way." Her throat burned as she watched his eyes open, struggle to focus. "Take it easy, take it slow. I don't want you to move. Just try to bring my face into focus. Can you see me?"

"Yeah." The pain was outrageous, an inferno in his chest. Dimly he thought he heard someone weeping, but Kirby's eyes were dry and clear.

"Good." Her hand trembled a little, but she steadied it to shine a light in his eyes. "Just lie still, let me check you over."

"What happened?"

"You were hurt, baby." Weeping helplessly, Kate took his hand and lowered her cheek to it. "Kirby's fixing you up."

"Fuzzy," he managed, turning his head restlessly. He saw his father's face, pale and exhausted, then the tube that connected them. "Hurts like a bitch," he said, then watched in amazement as Sam covered his face with his hands and shook with sobs. "What the hell's going on. What?" He sank back, weak as a baby under Kirby's firm hands.

"I said lie still. I'm not having you undo all my work here. I'll give you something for the pain in just a minute. Blood pressure's coming back up. He's stabilizing."

"Can I get some water or something? I feel like I've been . . ." He trailed off as it snapped back to his mind. The figure on the road, the dull glint of a gun, the explosion in his chest. "Shot. He shot me."

"Kirby and Giff found you," Lexy told him, struggling to reach around and take his other hand. "They brought you home. She saved your life."

"It was Kyle. Kyle Delaney." The pain was coming in waves now, making his breath short. "I recognized him. His eyes. He had sunglasses on before. He was . . . the day I cut my hand. It was Kyle in there with you. He was with you."

"The artist?" Kirby lowered the hypo she'd prepared. "The beach bum?"

"It was Kyle Delaney. He's been here all along."

"Hold still. Hold him still, Lexy. Damn it, Brian." Frightened by his struggles to get up, Kirby plunged the needle into him with more haste than finesse. "You'll start the bleeding up again, damn it. Help me here, Kate, he'll hurt himself before the drug can take effect."

Kate pressed her hand on Brian's shoulder and looked with frightened eyes around the room. "Where's Jo? Where is Jo Ellen?"

Lost, lost in the dark and the cold. She wondered if the wind was dying down or if she was just so used to its nasty buffeting that she no longer felt it trying to kill her. She tried to imagine herself springing to her feet and running, she wanted to will herself to try it, but was too weak, too tired to do more than belly along the ground.

She'd lost all sense of direction, and was afraid she would end up crawling blindly into the river to drown. But she wouldn't stop, couldn't stop, as long as there was a chance of reaching home.

And if she was lost, he might be lost as well. Another tree crashed somewhere behind her, falling with a force that shook the ground. She thought she heard someone call her name, but the wind ripped the sound away. He would call her, she thought, as her teeth began to chatter. He would call her hoping she'd give herself away so that he could kill her as he had the others. As his father had killed her mother.

She was nearly tired enough to let him. But she wanted him dead more.

For her mother, she thought, pulling herself along another foot. For Ginny, for Susan Peters. She gritted her teeth and dragged herself. And for Nathan.

She saw the light, just the narrow beam of it, and curled herself into a ball behind a tree. But the light held steady, didn't waver as a flashlight or a lantern held in the hand of a man would.

Sanctuary, she realized, pressing her muddy hands to her mouth to hold back a sob. That narrow beam of light, from the parlor, breaking through the broken window. Gathering her strength, she forced herself to her feet. She had to brace a hand on the tree until her head stopped spinning. But she concentrated on the light and put one foot in front of the other.

When she reached the edge of the trees, she began to run.

"I knew you'd come back." Kyle stepped into her path, pressed the barrel of the gun against her throat. "I've been studying you long enough to know how you think."

She couldn't stop the tears this time. "Why are you doing this? Isn't what your father did enough?"

"He never thought I was good enough, you know. Not as good as him, certainly not as good as Golden Boy. All I needed was the right inspiration." He smiled as rain streamed down his face and his hair blew madly. "We're going to have to clean you up quite a bit. No problem. I've got plenty of supplies back at the campground. Men's showers, remember?"

"Yes, I remember."

"I love practical jokes. I've been playing them on Nathan all our lives. He never knew. Oh, did Mister Kitty-Cat run away? No, indeed, Mr. Kitty took a little dip in the river. Inside a plastic bag. Why, Nathan, how could you be so careless as to cover all the holes in the lightning bug jar with your classic boy's novel?" With a laugh, Kyle shook his head. "I used to drive him crazy doing stuff like that—making him wonder how the hell it had happened."

He gestured with the gun. "Jeep's at the base of the road. What's left of the road. We'll have to walk that far."

"You hated him."

"Oh, definitely." He gave her a playful nudge to get her going. "My father always favored him. But then, my father wasn't the man we always thought he was. That was a real eye-opener. David Delaney's little secret. He was good, but I'm better. And you're my masterpiece, Jo Ellen, the way Annabelle was his. They'll blame Nathan for it, too. That's so wonderfully satisfying. If he survives, they'll lock him away."

She stumbled, righted herself. "He's alive?"

"It's possible. He'll start screaming about his dead brother. Then sooner or later, they'll look in his cottage. I took the time to drop some photographs off there. All the angles. Too bad I won't be able to slip one of yours in with them."

He could be alive, she thought. And she was going to fight to stay alive. Turning, she pushed her sopping hair back. She'd been right, she realized, the sharpest edge of the storm was dulling. She could stand up to it. And to him.

"The trouble is, Kyle, your father was a first-rate photographer. His style was, perhaps, a bit conservative and in some cases pedestrian. But you're third-rate at best. Your composition is poor, your discipline spotty. You have no knack for lighting whatsoever."

When his hand swung out, she was ready. She ducked under it and, leading with her head, rammed his body. His feet slid out from under him, sent him skidding down on his knees. She grabbed his wrist, inching her hand up toward the gun, but he swept an arm under her legs and took her down.

"You bitch. Do you think I'm going to take your insults? Do you think I'm going to let you spoil this after all the trouble I've gone to?"

He grabbed for her hair, but his hand closed on nothing but rain as she twisted her body around and used her feet to knock him back. Shells bit into her hands as she crab-walked back, fought for purchase.

She saw him lift the gun.

"Kyle."

Kyle's attention bolted to the right, and so did his aim. "Nathan." His grin spread, the lip Jo Ellen had split leaked blood onto his chin. "Well, this is interesting. You won't use that." He nodded at the gun Nathan had leveled at him. "You don't have the spine for killing. You never did."

"Put the gun down, Kyle. It's over."

"Wrong again. Our father started it, but I'll finish it." He got slowly to his feet. "I'll finish it, Nathan, in ways even he couldn't have imagined. My decisive moment, my triumph. He only planted the seeds. I'm reaping them."

He took a careful step forward, the grin never wavering. "I'm reaping them, Nathan. I'm making them my own. Think of how proud he'd be of what I've accomplished, not just following in his footsteps. Enlarging them."

"Yeah." Despite the cold on his skin, a hot sickness churned in Nathan's gut. "You've outdone him, Kyle."

"It's about time you admitted it." Kyle cocked his head. "This is what we call a Mexican standoff. Do you shoot me, or do I shoot you?" He gave a quick, brittle laugh that raked along Nathan's brain. "Since I know you're gutless, I already know the answer to that. How about if I change the game, shift the rules like I used to do when we were kids. And shoot her first."

As he swung the gun toward Jo, Nathan squeezed the trigger. Kyle jerked back, his mouth dropping open as he pressed a hand to his chest and it came away wet with blood. "You killed me. You killed me for a woman."

Nathan lowered the gun as Kyle crumpled. "You were already dead," he murmured. He walked toward Jo, watching as she got to her feet. Then his arms were around her. "He was already dead."

"We're all right." She pressed her face to his shoulder, hanging on. "We're all right now."

Giff came skidding down the pitted road. His eyes hardened when he saw the figure crumpled on the ground. He lifted his gaze to Nathan. "Get her inside. You need to get her inside."

Nathan shifted Jo to his side and walked through the weakening storm toward Sanctuary.

Epilogue

"Helicopters are on their way. One's bringing the police. They'll med-evac you to the mainland."

"I don't want to go to the hospital."

Kirby walked to the bed, lifted Brian's wrist to check his pulse yet again. "Too bad. You're not in any position to argue with your doctor."

"What are they going to do there that you haven't already done?"

"A great deal more than my emergency patch job." She checked his bandages, pleased that there was no fresh bleeding. "You'll have a couple of pretty nurses, some dandy drugs, and in a few days you'll be on your feet and back home."

He considered. "How pretty are the nurses?"

"I'm sure they're—" Her voice broke, and though she turned away quickly, he saw the tears spring to her eyes.

"Hey, I was only kidding." He fumbled for her hand. "I won't even look at them."

"I'm sorry. I thought I had it under control." She turned back, sliding to her knees to drop her head on the side of the bed. "I was so scared. So scared. You were bleeding so badly. Your pulse was just slipping away under my hands."

"But you didn't let it." He stroked her hair. "You brought me back, stayed with me. And look at you." He nudged until she lifted her face. "You haven't had any sleep."

"I'll sleep later." She pressed her lips to his hand over and over. "I'll sleep for days."

"You could pull some strings, share my hospital room."

"Maybe."

"Then you could come back here, share my room while I'm recuperating."

"I suppose I could."

"Then when I'm recovered, you could just share the rest of my life."

She knuckled a tear away. "If that's a proposal, you're supposed to be the one on your knees."

"But you're such an aggressive woman."

"You're right." She turned her cheek into his hand. "And since I feel at least somewhat responsible that you have a rest of your life, it seems only right that I share it with you."

"The gardens are ruined." Jo looked down at the sodden, beaten blooms drowning in mud. "It'll take weeks to clean them out, save what can be saved and start again."

"Is that what you want to do?" Nathan asked her. "Save what can be saved and start again?"

She glanced over. The bandage Kirby had applied to his temple was shockingly white against his skin. His eyes were deeply shadowed, still exhausted.

She wrapped her arms around herself, turned in a slow circle. The sun was radiant, the air stunningly fresh. She could see the wreckage—the toppled trees, the broken pottery that had been the little fountain, the now roofless smokehouse. Branches and leaves and glass littered the patio.

Above them, Giff and Lexy worked on prying off the protective plywood, and opening the windows to the light. She saw her father and Kate at the edge of the trees, then with wonder and amazed joy, saw him drape an arm around Kate's shoulders.

"Yes, I'd like that. I'd like to stay a while longer, help them put things back. It won't be exactly as it was. But it might be better."

She shielded her eyes with the flat of her hand to block the sun and see him clearly. "Brian asked to see you."

"I went in to see him before I came out. We put things back. They might not be the same." He smiled a little. "But they might be better."

"And you spoke with my father."

"Yeah. He's very glad his children are safe." He slid his hands into his pockets. He hadn't touched her since the night before, when Kate had whisked her off for a hot bath, whiskey-soaked tea, and bed. "He thinks it took courage for me to kill my brother."

"It took courage for you to save my life."

"It had nothing to do with courage." He walked away from her, down the muddy path. "I didn't feel anything when I pulled the trigger. He was already gone for me. It was nothing but a relief to end it."

"Don't tell me it didn't take courage. You were hurt, in every way it's possible to be hurt. And you fought your way through it, and through that storm for me. You faced what no one should ever have to face and did what no one should ever have to do. When the police get here, I'm going to tell them you're a hero."

She laid a hand on his arm. "I owe you my life, the lives of my family, and the memory of my mother."

"He was still my father. He was still my brother." His eyes were dark with the truth of that as he looked down at her. "I can't change that."

"No, you can't. And now they're gone." She glanced up, hearing the distant *whirr* of the helicopter. She wanted it said and settled before the ugliness came back. Before the police got there, with their questions, their investigations. "You said you loved me."

"I do, more than anything."

"Isn't that what you'd call a foundation? I'd think a man with your talents would be good at seeing what needs to be dug under, what can be rebuilt, what has to be reinforced to make it stand. Do you want to save what can be saved, Nathan, and start over?"

"I do." He took a step toward her. "More than anything."

She looked back at him, held out a hand. "Then why don't we get started on the rest of our lives?"